DENNIS WHEATLEY
WHEATLEY DENNIS WH
DENNIS WHEATLEY
WHEATLEY DENNIS WH
DENNIS WHEATLEY
WHEATLEY DENNIS WH
DENNIS WHEATLEY
WHEATLEY DENNIS WH
DENNIS WHEATLEY
WHEATLEY DENNIS WH
DENNIS WHEATLEY
WHEATLEY DENNIS WH
DENNIS WHEATLEY
WHEATLEY DENNIS WH
DENNIS WHEATLEY
WHEATLEY DENNIS WH
DENNIS WHEATLEY
WHEATLEY DENNIS W

Dennis Wheatley

Dennis Wheatley

The Devil Rides Out

The Haunting of Toby Jugg

Gateway to Hell

To the Devil -a Daughter

Heinemann/Octopus

The Devil Rides Out first published in Great Britain in 1935 by
Hutchinson & Co (Publishers) Ltd
The Haunting of Toby Jugg first published in Great Britain in 1948 by
Hutchinson & Co (Publishers) Ltd
Gateway to Hell first published in Great Britain in 1970 by
Hutchinson & Co (Publishers) Ltd
To the Devil—a Daughter first published in Great Britain in 1953 by
Hutchinson & Co (Publishers) Ltd

This edition first published in 1977
jointly by

William Heinemann Limited
15–16 Queen Street
London W1

Secker & Warburg Limited
14 Carlisle Street
London W1

and

Octopus Books Limited
59 Grosvenor Street
London W1

ISBN 0 905712 18 8

Printed in Great Britain by
Jarrold & Sons Ltd, Norwich

ACKNOWLEDGEMENTS

Jacket photography by John Moss (left) and Alan Frank (right)
Inside photographs by John Moss
Back jacket portrait Mark Aerson

Contents

AUTHOR'S NOTE

I desire to state that I, personally, have never assisted
at, or participated in, any ceremony connected with
Magic–Black or White.
Should any of my readers incline to a serious study of
the subject, and thus come into contact with a man or
woman of Power, I feel that it is only right to urge
them, most strongly, to refrain from being drawn into
the practice of the Secret Art in any way. My own
observations have led me to an absolute conviction that
to do so would bring them into dangers of a very real
and concrete nature.

DENNIS WHEATLEY

The Devil Rides Out

THE DEVIL RIDES OUT

To my old friend
Mervyn Baron
of whom, in these days, I see far too little but
whose companionship, both in good times and in
bad, has been to me a never-failing joy.

DW

I

THE INCOMPLETE REUNION

The Duke de Richleau and Rex Van had gone in to dinner at eight o'clock, but coffee was not served till after ten.

An appetite in keeping with his mighty frame had enabled Van Ryn to do ample justice to each well-chosen course and, as was his custom each time the young American arrived in England, the Duke had produced his finest wines for this, their reunion dinner at his flat.

A casual observer might well have considered it a strange friendship, but despite their difference in age and race, appearance and tradition, a real devotion existed between the two.

Some few years earlier Rex's foolhardiness had landed him in a Soviet prison, and the elderly French exile had put aside his peaceful existence as art connoisseur and dilettante to search for him in Russia. Together they had learned the dangerous secret of 'The Forbidden Territory' and travelled many thousand verts pursued by the merciless agents of the Ogpu.

There had been others too in that strange adventure; young Richard Eaton, and the little Princess Marie Lou whom he had brought out of Russia as his bride; but as Rex accepted a long Hoyo de Monterrey from the cedar cabinet which the Duke's man presented to him his thoughts were not of the Eatons, living now so happily with their little daughter Fleur in their lovely old country home near Kidderminster. He was thinking of that third companion whose subtle brain and shy, nervous courage had proved so great an aid when they were hunted like hares through the length and breadth of Russia, the frail narrow-shouldered English Jew–Simon Aron.

'What could possibly have kept Simon from being with them tonight,' Rex was wondering. He had never failed before to make a third at these reunion dinners, and why had the Duke brushed aside his inquiries about him in such an offhand manner. There was something queer behind De Richleau's reticence, and Rex had a feeling that for all his host's easy charm and bland, witty conversation something had gone seriously wrong.

He slowly revolved some of the Duke's wonderful old brandy in a bowl-shaped glass, while he watched the servant preparing to leave the room. Then, as the door closed, he set it down and addressed De Richleau almost abruptly.

'Well, I'm thinking it's about time for you to spill the beans.'

The Duke inhaled the first cloud of fragrant smoke from another of those long Hoyos which were his especial pride, and answered guardedly. 'Had you not better tell me Rex, to what particular beans you refer?'

'Simon of course! For years now the three of us have dined together on my first night, each time I've come across, and you were too mighty casual to be natural when I asked about him before dinner. Why isn't he here?'

'Why, indeed, my friend?' the Duke repeated, running the tips of his fingers down his lean handsome face. 'I asked him, and told him that your ship docked this morning, but he declined to honour us tonight.'

'Is he ill then?'

'No, as far as I know he's perfectly well—at all events he was at his office today.'

'He must have had a date then that he couldn't scrap, or some mighty urgent work. Nothing less could induce him to let us down on one of these occasions. They've become—well, in a way, almost sacred to our friendship.'

'On the contrary he is at home alone tonight. He made his apologies of course, something about resting for a Bridge Tournament that starts . . .'

'Bridge Tournament my foot!' exclaimed Rex angrily. 'He'd never let that interfere between us three—it sounds mighty fishy to me. When did you see him last?'

'About three months ago.'

'What! But that's incredible. Now look here!' Rex thrust the onyx ash-tray from in front of him, and leaned across the table. 'You haven't quarrelled—have you?'

De Richleau shook his head. 'If you were my age, Rex, and had no children, then met two younger men who gave you their affection, and had all the attributes you could wish for in your sons, how would it be possible for you to quarrel with either of them?'

'That's so, but three months is a whale of a while for friends who are accustomed to meet two or three times a week. I just don't get this thing at all, and you're being a sight too reticent about it. Come on now—what do you know?'

The grey eyes of almost piercing brilliance which gave such character to De Richleau's face, lit up. 'That,' he said suddenly, 'is just the trouble. I don't *know* anything.'

'But you fear that, to use his own phrase, Simon's "in a muddle—a really nasty muddle" eh? And you're a little hurt that he hasn't brought his worry to you.'

'To whom else should he turn if not to one of us—and you were in the States.'

'Richard maybe, he's an even older friend of Simon's than we are.'

'No. I spent last week-end at Cardinals Folly and neither Richard nor Marie Lou could tell me anything. They haven't seen him since he went down to stay last Christmas and arrived with a dozen crates of toys for Fleur.'

'How like him!' Rex's gargantuan laugh rang suddenly through the room. 'I might have known the trunkful I brought over would be small fry if you and Simon have been busy on that child.'

'Well I can only conclude that poor Simon is "in a muddle" as you say, or he would never treat us all like this.'

'But what sort of a muddle?' Rex brought his leg-of-mutton fist crashing down on the table angrily. 'I can't think of a thing where he wouldn't turn to us.'

'Money,' suggested the Duke, 'is the one thing that with his queer sensitive nature he might not care to discuss with even his closest friends.'

'I doubt it being that. My old man has a wonderful opinion of Simon's financial ability and he handles a big portion of our interests on this side. I'm pretty sure we'd be wise to it if he'd burned his fingers on the market. It sounds as if he'd gone bats about some woman to me.'

De Richleau's face was lit by his faintly cynical smile for a moment. 'No,' he said slowly. 'A man in love turns naturally to his friends for congratulation or sympathy as his fortune with a woman proves good or ill. It can't be that.'

For a little the two friends sat staring at each other in silence across the low jade bowl with its trailing sprays of orchids: Rex, giant shouldered, virile and powerful, his ugly, attractive, humorous young face clouded with anxiety, the Duke, a slim, delicate-looking man, somewhat about middle height, with slender, fragile hands and greying hair, but with no trace of weakness in his fine, distinguished face. His aquiline nose, broad forehead and grey 'devil's' eyebrows might well have replaced those of the cavalier in the Van Dyck that gazed down from the opposite wall. Instead of the conventional black, he wore a claret-coloured vicuna smoking suit, with silk lapels and braided fastenings; this touch of colour increased his likeness to the portrait. He broke the silence suddenly.

'Have you by any chance ever heard of a Mr Mocata, Rex?'

'Nope. Who is he anyway?'

'A new friend of Simon's who has been staying with him these last few months.'

'What—at his Club?'

'No—no, Simon no longer lives at his Club. I thought you knew. He bought a house last February, a big, rambling old place tucked away at the end of a cul-de-sac off one of those quiet residential streets in St John's Wood.'

'Why, that's right out past Regent's Park—isn't it? What's he want with a place out there when there are any number of nice little houses to let in Mayfair?'

'Another mystery, my friend.' The Duke's thin lips creased into a smile. 'He *said* he wanted a garden, that's all I can tell you.'

'Simon! A garden!' Rex chuckled. 'That's a good story I'll say. Simon doesn't know a geranium from a fuchsia. His botany is limited to an outsized florist's bill for bunching his women friends from shops, and why should a bachelor like Simon start running a big house at all?'

'Perhaps Mr Mocata could tell you,' murmured De Richleau mildly, 'or the queer servant that he has imported.'

'Have you ever seen this bird—Mocata I mean?'

'Yes, I called one evening about six weeks ago. Simon was out so Mocata received me.'

'And what did you make of him?'

'I disliked him intensely. He's a pot-bellied, bald-headed person of about sixty, with large, protuberant, fishy eyes, limp hands, and a most unattractive lisp. He reminded me of a large white slug.'

'What about this servant that you mention?'

'I only saw him for a moment when he crossed the hall, but he reminded me in a most unpleasant way of the Bogey Man with whom I used to be threatened in my infancy.'

'Why, is he a black?'

'Yes. A Malagasy I should think.'

Rex frowned. 'Now what in heck is that?'

'A native of Madagascar. They are a curious people, half-Negro and half-Polynesian. This great brute stands about six foot eight, and the one glimpse

I had of his eyes made me want to shoot him on sight. He's a "bad black" if ever I saw one, and I've travelled, as you know, in my time.'

'Do you know any more about these people?' asked Rex grimly.

'Not a thing.'

'Well, I'm not given to worry, but I've heard quite enough to get me scared for Simon. He's in some jam or he'd never be housing people like that.'

The Duke gently laid the long, blue-grey ash of his cigar in the onyx ash-tray. 'There is not a doubt,' he said slowly, 'that Simon is involved in some very queer business, but I have been stifling my anxiety until your arrival. You see I wanted to hear your views before taking the very exceptional step of–yes *butting in*–is the expression, on the private affairs of even so intimate a friend. The question is now–what are we to do?'

'Do!' Rex thrust back his chair and drew himself up to his full magnificent height. 'We're going up to that house to have a little heart-to-heart talk with Simon–right now!'

'I'm glad,' said De Richleau quietly, 'you feel like that, because I ordered the car for half past ten. Shall we go?'

2

THE CURIOUS GUESTS OF MR SIMON ARON

As De Richleau's Hispano drew up at the dead end of the dark cul-de-sac in St John's Wood, Rex slipped out of the car and looked about him. They were shut in by the high walls of neighbouring gardens and, above a blank expanse of brick in which a single, narrow door was visible, the upper stories of Simon's house showed vague and mysterious among whispering trees.

'Ugh!' he exclaimed with a little shudder as a few drops splashed upon his face from the dark branches overhead. 'What a dismal hole–we might be in a graveyard.'

The Duke pressed the bell, and turning up the sable collar of his coat against a slight drizzle which made the April night seem chill and friend-less, stepped back to get a better view of the premises. 'Hello! Simon's got an observatory here,' he remarked. 'I didn't notice that on my previous visit.'

'So he has.' Rex followed De Richleau's glance to a dome that crowned the house, but at that moment an electric globe suddenly flared into life about their heads, and the door in the wall swung open disclosing a sallow-faced manservant in dark livery.

'Mr Simon Aron?' inquired De Richleau, but the man was already motioning them to enter, so they followed him up a short covered path and the door in the wall clanged to behind them.

The vestibule of the house was dimly lit, but Rex, who never wore a coat or hat in the evening, noticed that two sets of outdoor apparel lay, neatly folded, on a long console table as the silent footman relieved De Richleau of his wraps. Evidently friend Simon had other visitors.

'Maybe Mr Aron's in conference and won't want to be disturbed,' he said to the sallow-faced servant with a sudden feeling of guilt at their intrusion.

Perhaps, after all, their fears for Simon were quite groundless and his neglect only due to a prolonged period of intense activity on the markets, but the man only bowed and led them across the hall.

'The fellow's a mute,' whispered the Duke. 'Deaf and dumb I'm certain.' As he spoke the servant flung open a couple of large double doors and stood waiting for them to enter.

A long, narrow room, opening into a wide *salon*, stretched before them. Both were decorated in the lavish magnificence of the Louis Seize period, but for the moment the dazzling brilliance of the lighting prevented them taking in the details of the parquet floors, the crystal mirrors, the gilded furniture and beautifully wrought tapestries.

Rex was the first to recover and with a quick intake of breath he clutched De Richleau's arm. 'By Jove she's here!' he muttered almost inaudibly, his eyes riveted on a tall, graceful girl who stood some yards away at the entrance of the *salon* talking to Simon.

Three times in the last eighteen months he had chanced upon that strange, wise, beautiful face, with the deep eyes beneath heavy lids that seemed so full of secrets and gave the lovely face a curiously ageless look—so that despite her apparent youth she was as old as—'Yes, as old as sin,' Rex caught himself thinking.

He had seen her first in a restaurant in Budapest; months later again, in a traffic jam when his car was wedged beside hers in New York, and then, strangely enough, riding along a road with three men, in the country ten miles outside Buenos Aires. How extraordinary that he should find her here—and what luck. He smiled quickly at the thought that Simon could not fail to introduce him.

De Richleau's glance was riveted upon their friend. With an abrupt movement Simon turned towards them. For a second he seemed completely at a loss, his full, sensual mouth hung open to twice its normal extent and his receding jaw almost disappeared behind his white tie, while his dark eyes were filled with amazement and something suspiciously like fear, but he recovered almost instantly and his old smile flashed out as he came forward to greet them.

'My dear Simon,' the Duke's voice was a silken purr. 'How can we apolgise for breaking in on you like this?'

'Sure, we hadn't a notion you were throwing a party,' boomed Rex, his glance following the girl who had moved off to join another woman and three men who were talking together in the inner room.

'But I'm delighted,' murmured Simon genially. 'Delighted to see you both—only got a few friends—meeting of a little society I belong to—that's all.'

'Then we couldn't dream of interrupting you, could we Rex?' De Richleau demurred with well-assumed innocence.

'Why, certainly not, we wouldn't even have come in if that servant of yours hadn't taken us for some other folks you're expecting.' But despite their apparent unwillingness to intrude, neither of the two made any gesture of withdrawal and, mentally, De Richleau gave Simon full marks for the way in which he accepted their obviously unwelcome presence.

'I'm most terribly sorry about dinner tonight,' he was proclaiming earnestly. 'Meant to rest for my bridge, I simply have to these days, to be any good—even forgot till six o'clock that I had these people coming.'

'How fortunate for you Simon that your larder is so well stocked.' The Duke could not resist the gentle dig as his glance fell on a long buffet spread with a collation which would have rivalled the cold table in any great hotel.

'I 'phoned Ferraro,' parried Simon glibly. 'The Berkeley never lets me down. Would have asked you to drop in, but er–with this meeting on I felt you'd be bored.'

'Bored! Not a bit, but we are keeping you from your other guests.' With an airy gesture De Richleau waved his hand in the direction of the inner room.

'Sure,' agreed Rex heartily, as he laid a large hand on Simon's arm and gently propelled him towards the *salon*. 'Don't you worry about us, we'll just take a glass of wine off you and fade away.' His eyes were fixed again on the pale oval face of the girl.

Simon's glance flickered swiftly towards the Duke, who ignored, with a guileless smile, his obvious reluctance for them to meet his other friends, and noted with amusement that he avoided any proper introduction.

'Er–er–two very old friends of mine,' he said, with his little nervous cough as he interchanged a swift look with a fleshy, moon-faced man whom De Richleau knew to be Mocata.

'Well, well, how nice,' the bald man lisped with unsmiling eyes. 'It is a pleasure always to welcome any friends of Simon's.'

De Richleau gave him a frigid bow and thought of reminding him coldly that Simon's welcome was sufficient in his own house, but for the moment it was policy to hide his antagonism so he replied politely that Mocata was most kind, then, with the ease which characterised all his movements, he turned his attention to an elderly lady who was seated near by.

She was a woman of advanced age but fine presence, richly dressed and almost weighed down with heavy jewellery. Between her fingers she held the stub of a fat cigar at which she was puffing vigorously.

'Madame.' The Duke drew a case containing the long Hoyos from his pocket and bent towards her. 'Your cigar is almost finished, permit me to offer you one of mine.'

She regarded him for a moment with piercingly bright eyes, then stretched out a fat, beringed hand. 'Sank you, Monsieur, I see you are a connoisseur.' With her beaked, parrot nose she sniffed at the cigar appreciatively. 'But I 'ave not seen you at our other meetings, what ees your name?'

'De Richleau, Madame, and yours?'

'De Richleau! a *maestro* indeed.' She nodded heavily. '*Je suis* Madame D'Urfé, you will 'ave heard of me.'

'But certainly.' The Duke bowed again. 'Do you think we shall have a good meeting tonight?'

'If the sky clears we should learn much,' answered the old lady cryptically.

'Ho! Ho!' thought the Duke. 'We are about to make use of Simon's observatory it seems. Good, let us learn more.' But before he could pump the elderly Frenchwoman further, Simon deftly interrupted the conversation and drew him away.

'So you have taken up the study of the stars, my friend,' remarked the Duke as his host led him to the buffet.

'Oh, er–yes. Find astronomy very interesting, you know. Have some caviare?' Simon's eyes flickered anxiously towards Rex, who was deep in conversation with the girl.

As he admired her burnished hair and slumbrous eyes, for a moment the Duke was reminded of a Boticelli painting. She had, he thought, that angel look with nothing Christian in it peculiar to women born out of their time, the golden virgin to the outward eye whose veins were filled with unlit fire. A rare *cinquecento* type who should have lived in the Italy of the Borgias. Then he turned again to Simon. 'It was because of the observatory then that you acquired this house, I suppose?'

'Yes. You must come up one night and we'll watch a few stars together.' Something of the old warmth had crept into Simon's tone and he was obviously in earnest as he offered the invitation, but the Duke was not deceived into believing that he was welcome on the present occasion.

'Thank you, I should enjoy that,' he said promptly, while over Simon's shoulder he studied the other two men who made up the party. One, a tall, fair fellow, stood talking to Mocata. His thin, flaxen hair brushed flatly back, and whose queer, light eyes proclaimed him an Albino; the other, a stout man dressed in a green plaid and ginger kilt, was walking softly up and down with his hands clasped behind his back, muttering to himself inaudibly. His wild, flowing white hair and curious costume suggested an Irish bard.

'Altogether a most unprepossessing lot,' thought the Duke and his opinion was not improved by three new arrivals. A grave-faced Chinaman wearing the robes of a Mandarin, whose slit eyes betrayed a cold, merciless nature: a Eurasian with only one arm, the left, and a tall, thin woman with a scraggy throat and beetling eyebrows which met across the bridge of her nose.

Mocata received them as though he were the host, but as the tall woman bore down on Simon he promptly left the Duke, who guessed that the move was to get out of earshot. However, the lady's greeting in a high-pitched Middle Western accent came clearly to him.

'Waal, Simon, all excitement about what we'll learn tonight? It should help a heap, this being your natal conjunction.'

'Ha! Ha!' said De Richleau to himself. 'Now I begin to understand a little and I like this party even less.' Then, with the idea of trying to verify his surmise, he turned towards the one-armed Eurasian, but Simon—apparently guessing his intention—quickly excused himself to the American woman, and cut off the Duke's advance.

'So, my young friend,' thought De Richleau, 'you mean to prevent me from obtaining any further information about this strange gathering, do you? All right! I'll twist your tail a little,' and he remarked sweetly:

'Did you say that you were interested in Astronomy or Astrology, Simon? There is a distinct difference you know.'

'Oh, Astronomy, of course,' Simon ran a finger down his long, beak-like nose. 'It *is* nice to see you again—have some more champagne?'

'Thank you, no, later perhaps.' The Duke smothered a smile as he caught Mocata, who had overheard him, exchange a quick look with Simon.

'Wish this were an ordinary meeting,' Simon said, a moment later, with an uneasy frown. 'Then I'd ask you to stay, but we're going through the Society's annual balance-sheet tonight—and you and Rex not being members you know . . .'

'Quite, quite, my dear fellow, of course,' De Richleau agreed amicably, while to himself he thought. 'That's a nasty fence young sly-boots has put up for me, but I'll be damned if I go before I find out for certain what I came for'. Then he added in a cheerful whisper: 'I should have gone before but Rex seems so interested in the young woman in green, I want to give him as long as possible.'

'My dear chap,' Simon protested, 'I feel horribly embarrassed at having to ask you to go at all.'

A fat, oily-looking Babu in a salmon-pink turban and gown had just arrived and was shaking hands with Mocata; behind him came a red-faced Teuton, who suffered the deformity of a hare lip.

Simon stepped quickly forward again as the two advanced, but De Richleau once more caught the first words which were snuffled out by the hare-lipped man.

'Well, Abraham, *wie geht es?*' then there came the fulsome chuckle of the fleshy Indian. 'You must not call him that, it is unlucky to do so before the great night.'

'The devil it is!' muttered the Duke to himself, but Simon had left the other two with almost indecent haste in order to rejoin him, so he said with a smile: 'I gather you are about to execute Deed Poll, my friend?'

'Eh!' Simon exclaimed with a slight start.

'To change your name,' De Richleau supplemented.

'Ner.' He shook his head rapidly as he uttered the curious negative that he often used. It came of his saying 'No' without troubling to close the lips of his full mouth. 'Ner–that's only a sort of joke we have between us–a sort of initiation ceremony–I'm not a full member yet.'

'I see, then you have ceremonies in your Astronomical Society–how interesting!'

As he spoke De Richleau, out of the corner of his eye, saw Mocata make a quick sign to Simon and then glance at the ormolu clock on the mantelpiece; so to save his host the awkwardness of having actually to request his departure, he exclaimed: 'Dear me! Twenty past eleven, I had no idea it was so late. I must drag Rex away from that lovely lady after all, I fear.'

'Well, if you must go.' Simon looked embarrassed and worried, but catching Mocata's eye again, he promptly led the way over to his other unwelcome guest.

Rex gave a happy grin as they came up. 'This is marvellous Simon. I've been getting glimpses of this lady in different continents these two years past, and she seems to recall having seen me too. It's just great that we should become acquainted at last through you.' Then he smiled quickly at the girl: 'May I present my friend De Richleau? Duke, this is Miss Tanith.'

De Richleau bent over her long, almost transparent hand and raised it to his lips. 'How unfortunate I am,' he said with old-fashioned gallantry, 'to be presented to you only in time to say good-bye, and perhaps gain your displeasure by taking your new friend with me as well.'

'But,' she regarded him steadily out of large, clear, amber eyes. Surely you do not depart before the ceremony?'

'I fear we must. We are not members of your er–Circle you see, only old friends of Simon's.'

A strange look of annoyance and uncertainty crept into her glance, and the Duke guessed that she was searching her mind for any indiscretions she might have committed in her conversation with Rex. Then she shrugged lightly and, with a brief inclination of the head which dismissed them both, turned coldly away.

The Duke took Simon's arm affectionately, as the three friends left the *salon*. 'I wonder,' he said persuasively, 'if you could spare me just two minutes before we go–no more I promise you.'

'Rather, of course.' Simon seemed now to have regained his old joviality. 'I'll never forgive myself for missing your dinner tonight–this wretched meeting–and I've seen nothing of you for weeks. Now Rex is over we must throw a party together.'

'We will, we will,' De Richleau agreed heartily, 'but listen; is not Mars in conjunction with Venus tonight?'

'Ner,' Simon replied promptly. 'With Saturn, that's what they've all come to see.'

'Ah, Saturn! My Astronomy is so rusty, but I saw some mention of it in the paper yesterday, and at one time I was a keen student of the Stars. Would it be asking too much my dear fellow, to have just one peep at it through your telescope? We should hardly delay your meeting for five minutes.'

Simon's hesitation was barely perceptible before he nodded his bird-like head with vigorous assent. 'Um, that's all right–they haven't all arrived yet–let's go up.' Then, with his hands thrust deep in the trouser pockets of his exceedingly well-cut dress suit, he led them hurriedly through the hall and up three flights of stairs.'

De Richleau followed more slowly. Stairs were the one thing which ruffled his otherwise equable temper and he had no desire to lose it now. By the time he arrived in the lofty chamber, with Rex behind him, Simon had all the lights switched on.

'Well you've certainly gone in for it properly,' Rex remarked as he surveyed the powerful telescope slanting to the roof and a whole arsenal of sextants, spheres and other astrological impedimenta ranged about the room.

'It's rather an exact science you see,' Simon volunteered.

'Quite,' agreed the Duke briefly. 'But I wonder, a little, that you should consider charts of the Macrocosm necessary to your studies.

'Oh, those!' Simon shrugged his narrow shoulders as he glanced around the walls. 'They're only for fun–relics of the Alchemistic nonsense in the Middle Ages, but quite suitable for decoration.'

'How clever of you to carry out your scheme of decoration on the floor as well.' The Duke was thoughtfully regarding a five-pointed star enclosed within two circles between which numerous mystic characters in Greek and Hebrew had been carefully drawn.

'Yes, good idea, wasn't it?' Simon tittered into his hand. It was the familiar gesture which both his friends knew so well, yet somehow his chuckle had not quite its usual ring.

The silence that followed was a little awkward and in it, all three plainly heard a muffled scratching noise that seemed to come from a large wicker basket placed against the wall.

'You've got mice here, Simon,' said Rex casually, but De Richleau had stiffened where he stood. Then, before Simon could bar his way, he leapt towards the hamper and ripped open the lid.

'Stop that!' cried Simon angrily, and dashing forward he forced it shut again, but too late, for within the basket the Duke had seen two living pinioned fowls–a black cock and a white hen.

With a sudden access of bitter fury he turned on Simon, and seizing him by his silk lapels, shook him as a terrier shakes a rat. 'You fool,' he thundered. 'I'd rather see you dead than monkeying with Black Magic.'

3

THE ESOTERIC DOCTRINE

'Take–take your hands off me,' Simon gasped.

His dark eyes blazed in a face that had gone deathly white and only a superhuman effort enabled him to keep his clenched fists pressed to his sides.

In another second he would have hit the Duke, but Rex, a head taller than either of them, laid a mighty hand on the shoulder of each and forced them apart.

'Have a heart now, just what is all this?' His quiet, familiar voice, with its faint American intonation, sobered the others immediately and De Richleau, swinging on his heel, strode to the other side of the observatory, where he stood for a moment, with his back towards them, regaining control of his emotions.

Simon, panting a little, gave a quick, nervous wriggle of his bird-like head and smoothed out the lapels of his evening coat.

'Now–I'll tell you,' he said jerkily, 'I never asked either of you to come here tonight, and even my oldest friends have no right to butt in on my private affairs. I think you'd better go.'

The Duke turned, passing one hand over his greying hair. All trace of his astonishing outburst had disappeared and he was once more the handsome, distinguished figure that they knew so well.

'I'm sorry, Simon,' he said gravely. 'But I felt as a father might who sees his child trying to pick live coals out of the fire.'

'I'm not a child,' muttered Simon, sullenly.

'No, but I could not have more affection for you if you were actually my son, and it is useless now to deny that you are playing the most dangerous game which has ever been known to mankind throughout the ages.'

'Oh, come,' a quick smile spread over Rex's ugly, attractive face. 'That's a gross exaggeration. What's the harm if Simon wants to try out a few old parlour games?'

'Parlour games!' De Richleau took him up sharply. 'My dear Rex, I fear your prowess in aeroplanes and racing cars hardly qualifies you to judge the soul destroying powers of these ancient cults.'

'Thanks. I'm not quite a half-wit, and plenty of spiritualistic séances take place in the States, but I've never heard of anyone as sane as Simon going bats because of them yet.'

Simon nodded his narrow head slowly up and down. 'Of course–Rex is right, and you're only making a mountain out of a molehill.'

'As you like,' De Richleau shrugged. 'In that case will you permit us to stay and participate in your operations tonight?'

'Ner–I'm sorry, but you're not a member of our Circle.'

'No matter. We have already met most of your friends downstairs, surely they will not object to our presence on just this one occasion?'

'Ner.' Simon shook his head again. 'Our number is made up.'

'I see, you are already thirteen, is that it? Now listen, Simon.' The Duke laid his hands gently on the young Jew's shoulders. 'One of the reasons why my friendship with Rex and yourself has developed into such a splendid intimacy, is because I have always refrained from stressing my age and greater experience, but tonight I break the rule. My conscious life, since we both left our schools, has been nearly three times as long as yours and, in addition, although I have never told you of it, I made a deep study of these esoteric doctrines years ago when I lived in the East. I beg of you, as I have never begged for anything in my life before, that you should give up whatever quest you are engaged upon and leave this house with us immediately.'

For a moment Simon seemed to waver. All his faith in De Richleau's judgment, knowledge, and love for him, urged him to agree, but at that moment Mocata's musical lisping voice cut in upon the silence, calling from the landing just below:

'Simon, the others have come. It is time.'

'Coming,' called Simon, then he looked at the two friends with whom he had risked his life in the 'Forbidden Territory.' 'I can't,' he said with an effort, 'You heard–it's too late to back out now.'

'Then let us remain–please,' begged the Duke.

'No, I'm sorry.' A new firmness had crept into Simon's tone, 'but I must ask you to go now.'

'Very well.'

De Richleau stepped forward as though to shake hands then, with almost incredible swiftness, his arm flew back and next second his fist caught Simon a smashing blow full beneath the jaw.

The action was so sudden, so unexpected, that Simon was caught completely off his guard. For a fraction of time he was lifted from his feet, then he crashed senseless on his back and slid spread-eagled across the polished floor.

'Have you gone crazy?' ejaculated Rex.

'No–we've got to get him out of here–save him from himself–don't argue! Quick!' Already De Richleau was kneeling by the crumpled body of his friend.

Rex needed no further urging. He had been in too many tight corners with the Duke to doubt the wisdom of his decisions however strange his actions might appear. In one quick heave he dragged Simon's limp form across his shoulders and started for the stairs.

'Steady!' ordered the Duke. 'I'll go first and tackle anyone who tries to stop us. You get him to the car–Understood?'

'What if they raise the house? You'll never be able to tackle the whole bunch on your own?'

'In that case drop him. I'll get him out somehow, while you protect my rear. Come on!'

With De Richleau leading they crept down the first flight of stairs. On the landing he paused and peered cautiously over the banisters. No sound came from below. 'Rex,' he whispered.

'Yep.'

'If that black servant I told you of appears, for God's sake don't look at his eyes. Watch his hands and hit him in the belly.'

'O.K.'

A moment later they were down the second flight. The hall was empty and only a vague murmur of conversation came to them from behind the double doors that led to the *salon*.

'Quick!' urged the Duke. 'Mocata may come out to look for him any moment.'

'Right,' Rex, bent double beneath his burden, plunged down the last stairs, and De Richleau was already halfway across the hall when the dumb servant suddenly appeared from the vestibule.

For a second he stood there, his sallow face a mask of blank surprise then, side-stepping the Duke with the agility of a rugby forward, he lowered his bullet head and charged Rex with silent animal ferocity.

'Got you,' snapped De Richleau, for although the man had dodged with lightning speed he had caught his wrist in passing. Then flinging his whole weight upon it as he turned, he jerked the fellow clean off his feet and sent him spinning head foremost against the wall.

As his head hit the panelling the mute gave an uncouth grunt, and rolled over on the floor, but he staggered up again and dashed towards the *salon*. Rex and the Duke were already pounding down the tiled path and in another second they had flung themselves into the lane through the entrance in the garden wall.

'Thank God,' gasped the Duke as he wrenched open the door of the Hispano. 'I believe that hellish crew would have killed us rather than let us get Simon out of there alive.'

'Well, I suppose you do know what you're at,' Rex muttered as he propped Simon up on the back seat of the car. 'But I'm not certain you're safe to be with.'

'Home,' ordered De Richleau curtly to the footman, who was hiding his astonishment at their sudden exit by hastily tucking the rug over their knees. Then he smiled at Rex a trifle grimly. 'I suppose I do seem a little mad to you, but you can't possibly be expected to appreciate what a horribly serious business this is. I'll explain later.'

In a few moments they had left the gloom of the quiet streets behind and were once more running through well-lit ways towards Mayfair, but Simon was still unconscious when they pulled up in Curzon Street before Errol House.

'I'll take him,' volunteered Rex. 'The less the servants have to do with this the better,' and picking up Simon in his strong arms as though he had been a baby, he carried him straight upstairs to the first floor where De Richleau's flat was situated.

'Put him in the library,' said the Duke, who had paused to murmur something about a sudden illness to the porter, when he arrived on the landing a moment later. 'I'll get something to bring him round from the bathroom.'

Rex nodded obediently, and carried Simon into that room in the Curzon Street flat which was so memorable for those who had been privileged to visit it, not so much on account of its size and decorations, but for the unique collection of rare and beautiful objects which it contained. A Tibetan Buddha seated upon the Lotus; bronze figurines from ancient Greece; beautifully chased rapiers of Toledo steel, and Moorish pistols inlaid with turquoise and gold; ikons from Holy Russia set with semi-precious stones and curiously carved ivories from the East.

As Rex laid Simon upon the wide sofa he glanced round him with an interest unappeased by a hundred visits, at the walls lined shoulder high with beautifully bound books, and at the lovely old colour prints, interspersed with priceless historical documents and maps, which hung above them.

De Richleau, when he joined him, produced a small crystal bottle which he held beneath Simon's beak-like nose. 'No good trying to talk to him tonight,' he remarked, 'but I want to bring him round sufficiently to put him to sleep again.

Rex grunted. 'That sounds like double-dutch to me.'

'No. I mean to fight these devils with their own weapons, as you will see.'

Simon groaned a little, and as his eyes flickered open the Duke took a small round mirror from his pocket. 'Simon,' he said softly, moving the lamp a little nearer, 'look upward at my hand.'

As he spoke De Richleau held the mirror about eighteen inches from Simon's forehead and a little above the level of his eyes, so that it caught and reflected the light of the lamp on to his lids.

'Hold it lower,' suggested Rex. 'He'll strain his eyes turning them upwards like that.'

'Quiet,' said the Duke sharply. 'Simon, look up and listen to me. You have been hurt and have a troubled mind, but your friends are with you and you have no need to worry any more.'

Simon opened his eyes again and turned them upwards to the mirror, where they remained fixed.

'I am going to send you to sleep, Simon,' De Richleau went on softly. 'You need rest and you will awake free from pain. In a moment your eyes will close and then your head will feel better.'

For another half-minute he held the mirror steadily reflecting the light upon Simon's retina, then he placed the first and second fingers of his free hand upon the glass with his palm turned outward and made a slow pass from it towards the staring eyes, which closed at once before he touched them.

'You will sleep now,' he continued quietly, 'and you will not wake until ten o'clock tomorrow morning. Directly you awake you will come straight to me either here or in my bedroom and you will speak to no one, nor will you open any letter or message which may be brought to you, until you have seen me.'

De Richleau paused for a moment, put down the mirror and lifted one of Simon's arms until it stood straight above his head. When he released it the arm did not drop but remained stiff and rigid in the air.

'Most satisfactory,' he murmured cheerfully to Rex. 'He is in the second stage of hypnosis already and will do exactly what he is told. The induction was amazingly easy, but of course, his half-conscious state simplified it a lot.'

Rex shook his head in disapproval. 'I don't like to see you monkey with him like this. I wouldn't allow it if it was anyone but you.'

'A prejudice based upon lack of understanding, my friend. Hypnotism in proper hands is the greatest healing power in the world.' With a quick shrug the Duke moved over to his desk and, unlocking one of the lower drawers, took something from it, then he returned to Simon and addressed him in the same low voice.

'Open your eyes now and sit up.'

Simon obeyed at once and Rex was surprised to see that he looked quite wide awake and normal. Only a certain blankness about the face betrayed his abnormal state, and he displayed no aversion as De Richleau extended the thing he had taken from the drawer. It was a small golden swastika set with precious stones and threaded on a silken ribbon.

'Simon Aron,' the Duke spoke again. 'With this symbol I am about to place you under the protection of the power of Light. No being or force of Earth, or Air, of Fire, or Water can harm you while you wear it.'

With quick fingers he knotted the talisman round Simon's neck and went on evenly: 'Now you will go to the spare bedroom. Ring for my man Max and tell him that you are staying here tonight. He will provide you with everything you need and, if your throat is parched from your recent coma, ask him for any soft drink you wish, but no alcohol remember. Peace be upon you and about you. Now go.'

Simon stood up at once and looked from one to the other of them. 'Good night,' he said cheerfully, with his quick natural smile. 'See you both in the morning,' then he promptly walked out of the room.

'He—he's not really asleep is he?' asked Rex, looking a little scared.

'Certainly, but he will remember everything that has taken place tomorrow because he is not in the deep somnambulistic state where I could order him to forget. To achieve that usually takes a little practice with a new subject.'

'Then he'll be pretty livid I'll promise you. Fancy hanging a Nazi swastika round the neck of a professing Jew.'

'My dear Rex! Do please try and broaden your outlook a little. The swastika is the oldest symbol of wisdom and right thinking in the world. It has been used by every race and in every country at some time or other. You might just as well regard the Cross as purely Christian, when we all know it was venerated in early Egypt, thousands of years before the birth of Christ. The Nazis have only adopted the swastika because it is supposed to be of Aryan origin and part of their programme aims at welding together a large section of the Aryan race. The vast majority of them have no conception of its esoteric significance and even if they bring discredit upon it, as the Spanish Inquisition did upon the Cross, that could have no effect upon its true meaning.'

'Yes, I get that, though I doubt if it'll make any difference to Simon's resentment when he finds it round his neck tomorrow. Still, that's a minor point. What worries me is this whole box of tricks this evening. I've got a feeling you ought to be locked up as downright insane, unless it's me.'

De Richleau smiled. 'A strange business to be happening in modern London, isn't it? But let's mix a drink and talk it over quietly.'

'Strange! Why, if it were true it would be utterly fantastic, but it's not. All this hooha about Black Magic and talking hocus-pocus while you hang silly charms round Simon's neck is utter bunk.'

'It is?' The Duke smiled again as he tipped a lump of ice into Rex's glass and handed it to him. 'Well, let's hear *your* explanation of Simon's queer behaviour. I suppose you do consider that it is queer by the way?'

'Of course, but nothing like as queer as you're trying to make out. As I see it Simon's taken up spiritualism or something of the kind and plenty of normal earnest people believe in that, but you know what he is when he gets keen on a thing, everything else goes to the wall and that's why he has neglected you a bit.

'Then this evening he was probably sick as mud to miss our dinner, but had a séance all fixed that he couldn't shelve at the last moment. We butt in on his party, and naturally he doesn't care to admit what he's up to entertaining all those queer, odd-looking women and men, so he spins a yarn about it being an astronomical society. So you—who've read a sight too many books—and seem to have stored up all the old wives' tales your nurse told you in your cradle—get a bee in your bonnet and slog the poor mut under the jaw.'

De Richleau nodded. 'I can hardly expect you to see it any other way at the moment, but let's start at the beginning. Do you agree that after knocking him out I called into play a supernormal power in order to send him cheerfully off to bed without a single protest?'

'Yes, even the doctors admit hypnotic influence now, and Simon would never have stood for you tying that swastika under his chin if he'd been conscious.'

'Good. Then at least we are at one on the fact that certain forces can be called into play which the average person does not understand. Now, if instead of practising that comparatively simple exercise in front of you, I had done it before ignorant natives, who had never heard of hypnotism, they would term it magic, would they not?'

'Sure.'

'Then to go a step further. If, by a greater exertion of the same power, I levitated, that is to say, lifted myself to a height of several inches from this floor, you might not use the word *magic* but you would class that feat in the same category as the ignorant native would place the easier one, because it is something which you have always thought impossible.'

'That's true.'

'Well, I am not sufficient of an adept to perform the feat, but will you accept my assurances that I've seen it done, not once, but a number of times?'

'If you say so, but from all I've heard about such things, the fellows you saw didn't leave the ground at all. It is just mass hypnotism exercised upon the whole audience—like the rope trick.'

'As you wish, but that explanation does not rob me of my point. If you admit that I can tap an unknown power to make Simon obey my will, and that an Eastern mystic can tap that power to the far greater extent of making a hundred people's eyes deceive them into believing that he is standing on thin air, you admit that there *is* a power and that it can be tapped in greater degrees according to the knowledge and proficiency of the man who uses it.'

'Yes, within limits.'

'Why within limits? You apparently consider levitation impossible, but wouldn't you have considered wireless impossible if you had been living fifty years ago and somebody had endeavoured to convince you of it?'

'Maybe.' Rex sat forward suddenly. 'But I don't get what you're driving at. Hypnotism is only a demonstration of the power of the human will.'

'Ah! There you have it. The *will to good* and the *will to evil*. That is the whole matter in a nutshell. The human will is like a wireless set and properly adjusted–trained that is–it can tune in with the invisible influence which is all about us.'

'The *Invisible Influence.* I've certainly heard that phrase somewhere before.'

'No doubt. A very eminent mental specialist who holds a high position in our asylums wrote a book with that title and I have not yet asked you to believe one tenth of what he vouches for.'

'Then I wonder they haven't locked him up.'

'Rex! Rex!' De Richleau smiled a little sadly. 'Try and open your mind, my friend. Do you believe in the miracles performed by Jesus Christ?'

'Yes.'

'And of His Disciples and certain of the Saints?'

'Sure, but they had some special power granted to them from on high.'

'Exactly! *Some Special Power.* But I suppose you would deny that Gautama Buddha and his disciples performed miracles of a similar nature?'

'Not at all. Most people agree now that Buddha was a sort of Indian Christ, a Holy Man, and no doubt he had some sort of power granted to him too.'

The Duke sat back with a heavy sigh. 'At last my friend we seem to be getting somewhere. If you admit that miracles, as you call them although you object to the word magic, have been performed by two men living in different countries hundreds of years apart, and that even their disciples were able to tap a similar power through their holiness, you cannot reasonably deny that other mystics have also performed similar acts in many portions of the globe–and therefore, that there is a power existing outside us which is not *peculiar to any religion,* but can be utilised if one can get into communication with it.'

Rex laughed. 'That's so, I can't deny it.'

'Thank God! Let's mix ourselves another drink shall we, I need it?'

'Don't move, I'll fix it.' Rex good-naturedly scrambled to his feet. 'All the same,' he added slowly, 'it doesn't follow that because a number of good men have been granted supernatural powers that there is anything in Black Magic.'

'Then you do not believe in Witchcraft?'

'Of course not, nobody does in these days.'

'Really! How long do you think it is since the last trial for Witchcraft took place?'

'I'll say it was all of a hundred and fifty years ago.'

'No, it was in January, 1926, at Melun near Paris.'

'Oh! You're fooling!' Rex exclaimed angrily.

'I'm not,' De Richleau assured him solemnly. 'The records of the court will prove my statement, so you see you are hardly accurate when you say that *nobody* believes in Witchcraft in these days, and many many thousands still believe in a personal devil.'

'Yes, simple folk maybe, but not educated people.'

'Possibly not, yet every thinking man must admit that there is still such a thing as the power of Evil.'

'Why?'

'My dear fellow, all qualities have their opposites, like love and hate, pleasure and pain, generosity and avarice. How could we recognise the goodness of Jesus Christ, Lao Tze, Ashoka, Marcus Aurelius, Francis of

Assisi, Florence Nightingale and a thousand others if it were not for the evil
lives of Herod, Caesar Borgia, Rasputin, Landru, Ivan Kreuger and the
rest?'

'That's true,' Rex admitted slowly.

'Then if an intensive cultivation of good can beget strange powers is there
any reason why an intensive cultivation of evil should not beget them also?'

'I think I begin to get what you're driving at.'

'Good! Now listen, Rex.' The Duke leaned forward earnestly. 'And I will
try and expound what little I know of the Esoteric Doctrine which has come
down to us through the ages. You will have heard of the Persian myth of
Ozamund and Ahriman, the eternal powers of Light and Darkness, said to
be co-equal and warring without cessation for the good or ill of mankind. All
ancient sun and nature worship—festivals of spring and so on, were only an
outward expression of that myth, for Light typifies Health and Wisdom,
Growth and Life; while Darkness means Disease and Ignorance, Decay and
Death.

'In its highest sense Light symbolises the growth of the Spirit towards
that perfection in which it can throw off the body and become light itself; but
the road to perfection is long and arduous, too much to hope for in one short
human life, hence the widespread belief in re-incarnation; that we are born
again and again until we begin to despise the pleasures of the flesh. This
doctrine is so old that no man can trace its origin, yet it is the inner core of
truth common to all religions at their inception. Consider the teaching of
Jesus Christ with that in mind and you will be amazed that you have not
realised before the true purport of His message. Did He not say that the
'Kingdom of God was within us,' and, when He walked upon the waters
declared: 'These things that I do ye shall do also; and greater things than
these shall ye do, for I go unto my Father which is in Heaven,' meaning most
certainly that He had achieved perfection but that others had the same
power within each one of them to do likewise.'

De Richleau paused for a moment and then went on more slowly.
'Unfortunately the hours of the night are still equal to the hours of the day,
and so the power of Darkness is no less active than when the world was
young, and no sooner does a fresh Master appear to reveal the light than
ignorance, greed, and lust for power cloud the minds of his followers. The
message becomes distorted and the simplicity of the truth submerged and
forgotten in the pomp of ceremonies and the meticulous performance of
rituals which have lost their meaning. Yet the real truth is never entirely lost,
and through the centuries new Masters are continually arising either to
proclaim it or, if the time is not propitious, to pass it on in secret to the
chosen few.

'Apollonius of Tyana learned it in the East. The so-called Heretics whom
we know as the Albigenses preached it in the twelfth century through
Southern France until they were exterminated. Christian Rosenkreutz had
it in the Middle Ages. It was the innermost secret of the Order of the
Templars who were suppressed because of it by the Church of Rome. The
Alchemists, too, searched for and practised it. Only the ignorant take
literally their struggle to find the Elixir of Life. Behind such phrases,
designed to protect them from the persecution of their enemies, they sought
Eternal Life, and their efforts to transmute base metals into gold were only
symbolical of their transfusion of matter into light. And still today while the

night life of London goes on about us there are mystics and adepts who are seeking the Eightfold Way to perfection in many corners of the Earth.'

'You really believe that?' asked Rex seriously.

'I do.' De Richleau's answer held no trace of doubt. 'I give you my word Rex, that I have talked with men whose sanity you would never question, an Englishman, an Italian, and a Hindu, all three of whom have been taken by guides sent to fetch them to the hidden valley in the uplands of Tibet, where some of the Lamas have reached such a high degree of enlightenment that they can prolong their lives at will, and perform today all the miracles which you have read of in the Bible. It is there that the sacred fire of truth has been preserved for centuries, safe from the brutal mercenary folly of our modern world.'

'That sounds a pretty tall story to me, but granted there are mystics who have achieved such amazing powers through their holiness I still don't see where your Black Magic comes in?'

'Let's not talk of Black Magic, which is associated with the preposterous in our day, but of the order of the Left Hand Path. That, too, has its adepts and, just as the Yoga of Tibet are the preservers of the Way of Light, the Way of Darkness is exemplified in the horrible Voodoo cult which had its origin in Madagascar and has held Africa in its grip for centuries, spreading even with the slave trade to the West Indies and your own country.'

'Yes, I know quite a piece about that, the Negroes monkey with it still back home in the Southern States, despite their apparent Christianity. Still I can't think that an educated man like Simon would take serious notice of that Mumbo Jumbo stuff.'

'Not in its crude form perhaps, but others have cultivated the power of Evil, and among whites it is generally the wealthy and intellectual, who are avaricious for greater riches or power, to whom it appeals. In the Paris of Louis XIV, long after the Middle Ages were forgotten, it was still particularly rampant. The poisoner, La Voisin, was proved to have procured over fifteen hundred children for the infamous Abbé Guibourg to sacrifice at Black Masses. He used to cut their throats, drain the blood into a chalice, and then pour it over the naked body of the inquirer who lay stretched upon the altar. I speak of actual history, Rex, and you can read the records of the trial that followed in which two hundred and forty-six men and women were indicted for these hellish practices.'

'Maybe. It sounds ghastly enough but that's a mighty long time ago.'

'Then, if you need more modern evidence of its continuance hidden in our midst there is the well authenticated case of Prince Borghese. He let his Venetian Palazzo on a long lease, expiring as late as 1895. The tenants had not realised that the lease had run out until he notified them of his intention to resume possession. They protested, but Borghese's agents forced an entry. What do you think they found?'

'Lord knows.' Rex shook his head.

'That the principal *salon* had been redecorated at enormous cost and converted into a Satanic Temple. The walls were hung from ceiling to floor with heavy curtains of silk damask, scarlet and black to exclude the light; at the farther end there stretched a large tapestry upon which was woven a colossal figure of Lucifer dominating the whole. Beneath, an altar had been built and amply furnished with the whole liturgy of Hell; black candles, vessels, rituals, nothing was lacking. Cushioned priedieus and luxurious chairs, crimson and gold, were set in order for the assistants, and the chamber lit with electricity fantastically arranged so that it should glare through an enormous human eye.'

De Richleau hammered the desk with his clenched fist. 'These are facts I'm giving you Rex—facts, d'you hear, things I can prove by eye-witnesses still living. Despite our electricity, our aeroplanes, our modern scepticism, the power of Darkness is still a living force, worshipped by depraved human beings for their unholy ends in the great cities of Europe and America to this very day.'

Rex's face had suddenly paled under its tan. 'And you really think poor Simon has got mixed up in this beastliness?'

'I know it man! Could you have been so intrigued with the girl that you did not notice the rest of that foul crew? The Albino, the man with the hare-lip, the Eurasian who only possessed a *left* arm. They're Devil Worshippers all of them.'

'Not the girl! Not Tanith!' cried Rex, springing to his feet. 'She must have been drawn into it like Simon.'

'Perhaps, but the final proof lay in that basket. They were about to practise the age-old sacrifice to their infernal master just as your Voodoo-ridden Negroes do. The slaughter of a black cock and a white hen—Yes. What is it?' De Richleau swung round as a soft knock came on the door.

'Excellency.' His man Max stood bowing in the doorway. 'I thought I had better bring this to you.' In his open palm he displayed the jewelled swastika.

With one panther-like spring the Duke thrust him aside and bounded from the room. 'Simon,' he shouted as he dashed down the corridor. 'Simon! I command you to stay still.' But when he reached the bedroom the only signs that Simon had ever occupied it were the tumbled bed and his underclothes left scattered on the floor.

4

THE SILENT HOUSE

De Richleau strode back into the sitting-room. His grey eyes glittered dangerously but his voice was gentle as he picked the jewelled swastika from his servant's palm. 'How did you come by this, Max?'

'I removed it from Mr Aron's neck, Excellency.'

'What!'

'He rang for me, Excellency, and said that he would like a cup of bouillon and when I returned with it he was sleeping, but so strangely that I was alarmed. His tongue was protruding from between his teeth and his face was nearly black; then I saw that his neck was terribly swollen and that a ribbon was cutting deeply into his flesh. I cut the ribbon, fearing that he would choke—the jewel dropped off, so I brought it straight to you.'

'All right! you may go—and it is unnecessary to wait up—I may be late.' As the door closed the Duke swung round towards Rex. 'Simon must have woken the moment Max's back was turned, pulled on a few clothes, then slipped out of the window and down the fire-escape.'

'Sure,' Rex agreed. 'He's well on his way back to St John's Wood by now.'

'Come on—we'll follow. We've got to save him from those devils somehow. I don't know what they're after but there must be something pretty big and very nasty behind all this. It can't have been easy to involve a man like Simon to the extent they obviously have, and they would never have gone to all that trouble to recruit an ordinary dabbler in the occult. They are after really big stakes of some kind, and they need him as a pawn in their devilish game.'

'Think we can beat him to it?' Rex asked as they ran down the staircase of the block and out into Curzon Street.

'I doubt it—Hi, taxi!' De Richleau waved an arm.

'He can't have more than five minutes' start.'

'Too much in a fifteen minutes' run.' The Duke's voice was grim as they climbed into the cab.

'What d'you figure went amiss?'

'I don't know for certain, but there is no doubt that our poor friend is completely under Mocata's influence—has been for months I expect. In such a case Mocata's power over him would be far stronger than my own which was only exercised, in the hope of protecting him, for the first time tonight. It was because I feared that Mocata might countermand my orders, even from a distance, and compel Simon to return that I placed the symbol of Light round his neck.'

'And when Max took it off Mocata got busy on him eh?'

'I think Mocata was at work before that. He probably witnessed everything that took place in a crystal or through a medium and exerted all his powers to cause Simon's neck to swell the moment he got into bed, hoping to break the ribbon that held the charm.'

Rex had not yet quite recovered from the shock of learning that so sane a man as De Richleau could seriously believe in all this gibberish about the occult. He was very far from being convinced himself, but he refrained from airing his scepticism and instead, as the taxi rattled north through Baker Street, he began to consider the practical side of their expedition. There had been eight men at least in Simon's house when they left it. He glanced towards the Duke. 'Are you carrying a gun?'

'No, and if I were it would be useless.'

'Holy Smoke! You are bats or else I am.' Rex shrugged his broad shoulders and began to wonder if he was not living through some particularly vivid and horrible dream. Soon he would wake perhaps; sweating a little from the nightmare picture which De Richleau had drawn for him of age-old evil, tireless and vigilant, cloaked from the masses by modern scepticism yet still a potent force stalking the dark ways of the night, conjured into new life by strange delvers into ancient secrets for their unhallowed ends; but wake he must, to the bright, clear day and Simon's chuckle—over a tankard of Pim's cup at luncheon—that such fantastic nonsense should centre about him even in a dream. Yet there was Tanith, so strange and wise and beautiful, looking as though she had just stepped out of a painting by some great master of the Italian Renaissance. It was no dream that he had at last actually met and spoken with her that evening at Simon's house, among all those queer people whom the Duke declared so positively to be Satan worshippers; and if she was flesh and blood they must be too.

On the north side of Lord's cricket ground, De Richleau stopped the taxi.

'Better walk the rest of the way,' he murmured as he paid off the man. 'Simon's arrived by now and it would be foolish to warn them of our coming.'

'Thought you said Mocata was overlooking us with the evil eye?' Rex replied as they hurried along Circus Road.

'He may be. I can't say, but possibly he thinks we would never dare risk a second visit to the house tonight. If we exercise every precaution we may catch him off his guard. He's just as vulnerable as any other human being except when he is actually employing his special powers.'

Side by side they passed through two streets where the low roofs of the old-fashioned houses were only faintly visible above the walls that kept them immune from the eyes of the curious, each set, silent and vaguely mysterious, among its whispering trees; then they entered the narrow, unlit cul-de-sac.

Treading carefully now, they covered the two hundred yards to its end and halted, gazing up at the darkened mass of the upper stories which loomed above the high wall. Not a chink of light betrayed that the house was tenanted, although they knew that, apart from the servants, thirteen people had congregated there to perform some strange midnight ceremony little over an hour before.

'Think they've cleared out?' Rex whispered.

'I doubt it.' The Duke stepped forward and tried the narrow door. It was fast locked.

'Can't we call the police in to raid the place?'

De Richleau shrugged impatiently. 'What could we charge them with that a modern station-sergeant would understand?'

'Kidnapping!' Rex urged below his breath. 'If I were back home I'd have the strong-arm squad here in under half an hour. Get the whole bunch pinched and gaoled pending trial. They'd be out of the way then for a bit, even if I had to pay up heavy damages afterwards—and meantime we'd pop Simon in a mental home till he got his wits back.'

'Rex! Rex!' The Duke gave a low, delighted chuckle. 'It's an enchanting idea, and if we *were* in the States I really believe we might pull it off—but here it's impossible.'

'What do you figure to do then?'

'Go in and see if Simon has returned.'

'I'm game, but the odds are pretty heavy.'

'If we're caught we must run for it.'

'O.K., but if we fail to make our get-away they'll call the police and have *us* gaoled for housebreaking.'

'No—no,' De Richleau muttered. 'They won't want to draw the attention of the police to their activities, and the one thing that matters is to get Simon out of here.'

'All right.' Rex placed his hands on his knees, and stooping his great shoulders, leaned his head against the wall. 'Up you go.'

The Duke bent towards him. 'Listen!' he whispered. 'Once we're inside we've got to stick together whatever happens. God knows what they've used this house of Simon's for, but the whole place reeks of evil.'

'Oh shucks!' Rex muttered contemptuously.

'I mean it,' De Richleau insisted. 'If you take that attitude I'd rather go in alone. This is the most dangerous business I've ever been up against, and if it wasn't for the thought of Simon nothing on earth would tempt me to go over this wall in the middle of the night.'

'Oh–all right. Have it your own way.'

'You'll obey me implicitly–every word I say?'

'Yes, don't fret yourself . . .'

'Good, and remember you are to bolt for it the instant I give the word, because the little knowledge that I possess may only protect us for a very fleeting space of time.' The Duke clambered on to Rex's shoulders and heaved himself up on to the coping. Rex stepped back a few yards and took a flying leap; next second he had scrambled up beside De Richleau. For a moment they both sat astride the wall peering down into the shadows of the garden, then they dropped silently into a flower-border on the other side.

'The first thing is to find a good line of retreat in case we have to get out in a hurry,' breathed the Duke.

'What about this?' Rex whispered back, slapping the trunk of a well-grown laburnum tree.

De Richleau nodded silently. One glance assured him that with the aid of the lower branches two springs would bring them to the top of the wall. Then he moved at a quick, stealthy run across a small open space of lawn to the shelter of some bushes that ran round the side of the house.

From their new cover Rex surveyed the side windows. No glimmer of light broke the expanse of the rambling old mansion. As the Duke moved on, he followed, until the bushes ended at the entrance of a back yard, evidently giving on to the kitchen quarters.

'Have a care,' he whispered, jerking De Richleau's sleeve. 'They may have a dog.'

'They couldn't,' replied the Duke positively. 'Dogs are simple, friendly creatures but highly psychic. The vibrations in a place where Black Magic was practised would cause any dog to bolt for a certainty.' With light, quick, padding steps he crossed the yard and came out into the garden on the far side of the house.

Here too every window was shrouded in darkness and an uncanny stillness brooded over the place.

'I don't like it,' whispered De Richleau. 'Simon can't have been back more than a quarter of an hour at the outside–so there ought still to be lights in the upper rooms. Anyhow, it looks as if the others have gone home, which is something–we must chance an ambush.'

He pointed to a narrow, ground floor window. 'That's probably the lavatory, and most people forget to close their lavatory windows–come on!'

Silently Rex followed him across the grass, then gripping him by the knees, heaved him up until he was well above the level of the sill.

The sash creaked, the upper half of the window slid down, and the Duke's head and shoulders disappeared inside.

For a moment Rex watched his wriggling legs, heard a bump, followed by a muffled oath, and then clambered up on to the sill.

'Hurt yourself?' he whispered, as De Richleau's face appeared, a pale blot in the darkness.

'Not much–though this sort of thing is not amusing for a man of my age. The door here is unlocked, thank goodness.'

Immediately Rex was inside, the Duke squatted down on the floor. 'Take off your shoes,' he ordered. 'And your socks.'

'Shoes if you like, though we'll hurt our feet if we have to run–but why the socks?'

'Don't argue–we waste time.'

'Well–what now?' Rex muttered after a moment.

'Put your shoes on again and the socks over them–then you can run as fast as you like.' As Rex obeyed the Duke went on in a low voice. 'Not a sound now. I really believe the others have gone, and if Mocata is not lying in wait for us, we may be able to get hold of Simon. If we come up against that black servant, for God's sake remember not to look at his eyes.'

With infinite care he opened the door and peered out into the darkened hall. A faint light from an upper window showed the double doors that led to the *salon* standing wide open. He listened intently for a moment, then slipping out stood aside for Rex to follow, and gently closed the door behind them.

Their footsteps, now muffled by the socks, were barely audible as they stole across the stretch of parquet. When they reached the *salon* De Richleau carefully drew aside a blind. The dim starlight was just sufficient to show the outlines of the gilded furniture, and they could make out plates and glasses left scattered upon the buhl and marquetry tables.

Rex picked up a goblet two-thirds full of champagne and held it so that the Duke could see the wine still in it.

De Richleau nodded. The Irish Bard, the Albino, the one-armed Eurasian, the hare-lipped man and the rest of that devilish company must have taken fright when he and Rex had forcibly abducted Simon, and fled, abandoning their unholy operations for the night. He gently replaced the blind and they crept back into the hall.

One other door opened off it besides those to the servants' quarters and the vestibule. De Richleau slowly turned the knob and pressed. The room was a small library, and at the far end a pair of uncurtained french-windows showed the garden, ghostly and mysterious in the starlight. Leaving Rex by the door, the Duke tiptoed across the room, drew the bolts, opened the windows and propped them wide. From where he stood he could just make out the laburnum by the wall. A clear retreat was open to them now. He turned, then halted with a sharp intake of breath. Rex had disappeared.

'Rex!' he hissed in a loud whisper, gripped by a sudden nameless fear. 'Rex!' But there was no reply.

5

EMBODIED EVIL

De Richleau had been involved in so many strange adventures in his long and chequered career, that instinctively his hand flew to the pocket where he kept his automatic at such times, but it was flat–and in a fraction of time it had come back to him that this was no affair of shootings and escapes, but a grim struggle against the Power of Darkness–in which their only protection must be an utter faith in the ultimate triumph of good, and the use of such little power as he possessed to bring into play the great forces of the Power of Light.

In two strides he had reached the door, grabbed the electric switch, and pressed it as he cried in ringing tones: '*Fundamenta ejus in montibus sanctis!*'

'What the hell!' exclaimed Rex as the light flashed on. He was at the far side of the hall, carefully constructing a booby trap of chairs and china in front of the door that led to the servants' quarters.

'You've done it now,' he added, with his eyes riveted upon the upper landing, but nothing stirred and the pall of silence descended upon the place again until they could hear each other's quickened breathing.

'The house is empty,' Rex declared after a moment. 'If there were anyone here they'd have been bound to hear you about. It echoed from the cellars to the attics.'

De Richleau was regarding him with an angry stare. 'You madman,' he snapped. 'Don't you understand what we're up against? We must not separate for an instant in this unholy place—even now that the lights are on.'

Rex smiled. He had always considered the Duke as the most fearless man he knew, and to see him in such a state of nerves was a revelation. 'I'm not scared of bogeys, but I am of being shot up from behind,' he said simply. 'I was fixing this so we'd hear the servants if there was trouble upstairs and they came up to help Mocata.'

'Yes, but honestly, Rex, it is imperative that we should keep as near each other as possible every second we remain in this ghastly house. It may sound childish, but I ought to have told you before that if anything queer does happen we must actually hold hands. That will quadruple our resistance to evil by attuning our vibrations towards good. Now let's go upstairs and see if they have really gone—though I can hardly doubt it.'

Rex followed marvelling. This man who was frightened of shadows and talked of holding hands at a time of danger was so utterly different to the De Richleau that he knew. Yet as he watched the Duke mounting the stairs in swift, panther-like, noiseless strides he felt that since he was so scared this midnight visitation was a fresh demonstration of his courage.

On the floor above they made a quick examination of the bedrooms, but all of them were unoccupied and none of the beds had been slept in.

'Mocata must have sent the rest of them away and been waiting here with a car to whisk Simon off immediately he got back,' De Richleau declared as they came out of the last room.

'That's about it, so we may as well clear out.' Rex shivered slightly as he added: 'It's beastly cold up here.'

'I was wondering whether you'd notice that, but we're not going home yet. This is a God-given opportunity to search the house at our leisure. We may discover all sorts of interesting things. Leave all the lights on here, the more the better, and come downstairs.'

In the *salon* the great buffet table still lay spread with the excellent collation which they had seen there on their first visit. The Duke walked over to it and poured himself a glass of wine. 'I see Simon has taken to Cliquot again,' he observed. 'He alternates between that and Bollinger with remarkable consistency, though in certain years I prefer Pol Roger to either when it has a little age on it.'

As Rex spooned a slab of Duck *à la Montmorency* on to a plate, helping himself liberally to the *foie gras mousse* and cherries, he wondered if De Richleau had really recovered from the extraordinary agitation that he had displayed a quarter of an hour before, or if he was talking so casually to cover his secret apprehensions. He hated to admit it even to himself, but there *was* something queer about the house, a chill seemed to be spreading up his legs from beneath the heavily-laden table, and the silence was strangely oppressive. Anxious to get on with the business and out of the place now, he said quickly. 'I don't give two hoots what he drinks, but where has Mocata gone–and why?'

'The last question is simple.' De Richleau set down his glass and drew out the case containing the famous Hoyo de Monterrey's. 'There are virtually no laws against the practice of Black Magic in this country now. Only that of 1842, called the Rogues and Vagabonds Act, under which a person may be prosecuted for "pretending or professing to tell Fortunes, by using any subtle Craft, Means or Device!" But since the practitioners of it are universally evil, the Drug Traffic, Blackmail, Criminal Assault and even Murder are often mixed up with it, and for one of those reasons Mocata, having learnt that we were on our way here through his occult powers, feared a brawl might attract the attention of the police to his activities. Evidently he considered discretion the better part of valour on this occasion and temporarily abandoned the place to us–taking Simon with him.'

'Not very logical–are you?' Rex commented. 'One moment it's you who're scared that he may do all sorts of strange things to us, and the next you tell me that he's bolted for fear of being slogged under the jaw.'

'My dear fellow, I can only theorise. I'm completely in the dark myself. Some of these followers of the Left Hand Path are mere neophytes who can do little more than *wish* evil in minor matters on people they dislike. Others are adepts and can set in motion the most violent destructive forces which are not yet even suspected by our modern scientists.

'If Mocata only occupies a low place in the hierarchy we can deal with him as we would any other crook with little risk of any serious danger to ourselves, but if he is a Master he may be able to strike us blind or dead. Unfortunately I know little enough of this horrible business, only the minor rituals of the Right Hand Path, or White Magic as people call it, which may protect us in an emergency. If only I knew more I might be able to find out where he has taken Simon.'

'Cheer up–we'll find him.' Rex laughed as he set down his plate, but the sound echoed eerily through the deserted house, causing him to glance swiftly over his shoulder in the direction of the still darkened inner room. 'What's the next move?' he asked more soberly.

'We've got to try and find Simon's papers. If we can, we may be able to get the real names and addresses of some of those people who were here tonight. Let's try the Library first–bring the bottle with you. I'll take the glasses.'

'What d'you mean–real names?' Rex questioned as he followed De Richleau across the hall.

'Why, you don't suppose that incredible old woman with the parrot beak was really called Madame D'Urfé–do you? That's only a nom-du-Diable, taken when she was re-baptised, and adopted from the Countess of that name, who was a notorious witch in Louis XV's time. All the others are the same. Didn't you realise the meaning of the name your lovely lady calls herself by–Tanith?'

'No.' Rex hesitated. 'I thought she was just a foreigner–that's all.'

'Dear me. Well, Tanith was the Moon Goddess of the Carthaginians. Thousands of years earlier the Egyptians called her Isis, and in the intervening stage she was known to the Phœnicians as the Lady Astoroth. They worshipped her in sacred groves where doves were sacrificed and unmentionable scenes of licentiousness took place. The God Adonis was her lover, and the people wept for his mythical death each year, believing upon him as a Redeemer of Mankind. As they went in processions to her shrines they wrought themselves into the wildest frenzy, and to slake the thwarted passion of the widowed goddess, gashed themselves with knives. Sir George Frazer's *Golden Bough* will tell you all about it, but the blood that was shed still lives, Rex, and she has been thirsty through these Christian centuries for more. Eleven words of power, each having eleven letters, twice pronounced in a fitting time and place after due preparation, and she would stand before you, terrible in her beauty, demanding a new sacrifice.'

Even Rex's gay modernity was not proof against that sinister declaration. De Richleau's voice held no trace of the gentle cynicism which was so characteristic of him, but seemed to ring with the positiveness of some horrible secret truth. He shuddered slightly as the Duke began to pull open the drawers of Simon's desk.

All except one, which was locked, held letter files, and a brief examination of these showed that they contained nothing but accounts, receipts, and correspondence of a normal nature. Rex forced the remaining drawer with a heavy steel paper knife, but it only held cheque book counterfoils and bundles of dividend warrants, so they turned their attention to the long shelves of books. It was possible that Simon might have concealed certain private papers behind his treasured collection of modern first editions, but after ten minutes' careful search they assured themselves that nothing of interest was hidden at the back of the neat rows of volumes.

Having drawn a blank in the library, they proceeded to the other downstairs rooms, going systematically through every drawer and cabinet, but without result. Then they moved upstairs and tried the bedrooms, yet here again they could discover nothing which might not have been found in any normal house, nor was there any safe in which important documents might have been placed.

During the search De Richleau kept Rex constantly beside him, and Rex was not altogether sorry. Little by little the atmosphere of the place was getting him down, and more than once he had the unpleasant sensation that somebody was watching him covertly from behind, although he told himself that it was pure imagination, due entirely to De Richleau's evident belief in the supernatural, of which they had been talking all the evening.

'These people must have left traces of their doings in this house somewhere,' declared the Duke angrily as they came out of the last bedroom on to the landing, 'and I'm determined to find them.'

'We haven't done the Observatory yet, and I'd say that's the most likely spot of all,' Rex suggested.

'Yes—let's do that next.' De Richleau turned towards the upper flight of stairs.

The great domed room was just as they had left it a few hours before. The big telescope pointing in the same direction, the astrolabes and sextants still in the same places. The five-pointed pentacle enclosed in the double circle with its Cabalistic figures stood out white and clear on the polished floor in the glare of the electric lights. Evidently no ceremony had taken place after their departure. To verify his impression the Duke threw up the lid of the wicker hamper that stood beside the wall.

A scraping sound came from the basket, and he nodded. 'See Rex! The Black Cock and the White Hen destined for sacrifice, but we spoilt their game for tonight at all events. We'll take them down and free them in the garden when we go.'

'What did they really mean to do—d'you think?' Rex asked gravely.

'Utilise the conjunction of certain stars which occurred at Simon's birth, and again tonight, to work some invocation through him. To raise some dark familiar perhaps, an elemental or an earthbound spirit—or even some terrible intelligence from what we know as Hell, in order to obtain certain information they require from it.'

'Oh, nuts!' Rex exclaimed impatiently. 'I don't believe such things. Simon's been got hold of by a gang of blackmailing kidnappers and hypnotised if you like. They've probably used this Black Magic stuff to impose on him just as it imposes on you—but in every other way it's sheer, preposterous nonsense.'

'I only hope that you may continue to think so, Rex, but I fear you may have reason to alter your views before we're through. Let's continue our search—shall we?'

'Fine—though I've a hunch it's a pity we didn't call in the cops at the beginning.'

They examined the instruments, but all of them were beyond suspicion of any secret purpose, and then a square revolving bookcase, but it held only trigonometry tables and charts of the heavens.

'Damn it, there must be something in this place!' De Richleau muttered. 'Swords or cups or devils' bibles. They couldn't perform their rituals without them.'

'Maybe they took their impedimenta with them when they quit.'

'Perhaps, but I'd like even to see the place in which they kept it. You never know what they may have left behind. Try tapping all round the walls, Rex, and I'll do the floor. There's almost certain to be a secret cache somewhere.'

For some minutes they pursued their search in silence, only their repeated knockings breaking the stillness of the empty house. Then Rex gave a sudden joyful shout.

'Here, quick—it's hollow under here!'

Together they pulled aside an early seventeenth-century chart of the Macrocosm by Robert Fludd, and after fumbling for a moment found the secret spring. The panel slid back with a click.

In the recess some four feet deep reposed a strange collection of articles: a wand of hazelwood, a crystal set in gold, a torch with a pointed end so that it could be stuck upright in the ground, candle-sticks, a short sword, two great books, a dagger with a blade curved like a sickle moon, a ring, a chalice and an old bronze lamp, formed out of twisted human figures, which had nine wicks. All had pentacles, planetary signs, and other strange symbols engraved upon them, and each had the polish which is a sign of great age coupled with frequent usage.

'Got them!' snapped the Duke. 'By Jove, I'm glad we stayed, Rex! These things are incredibly rare, and each a power in itself through association with past mysteries. It is a thousand to one against their having others, and without them their claws will be clipped from working any serious evil against us.'

As he spoke De Richleau lifted out the two ancient volumes. One had a binding of worked copper on which were chased designs and characters. Its leaves, which were made from the bark of young trees, were covered with very clear writing done with iron point. The text of the other was painted on vellum yellowed by time, and its binding supported by great scrolled silver clasps.

'Wonderful copies,' the Duke murmured, with all the enthusiasm of a bibliophile. 'The Clavicule of Solomon and The Grimoire of Pope Honorius. They are not the muddled recast versions of the seventeenth century either, but far, far older. This Clavicule on cork may be of almost any age, and is to the Black Art what the Codex Sinaiticus and such early versions are to Christianity.'

'Well, maybe Mocata didn't figure we'd stay to search this place when we found Simon wasn't here, but it doesn't say much for all his clairvoyant powers you make such a song about for him to let us get away with his whole magician's box of tricks. Say! where's that draught coming from?' Rex suddenly clapped a hand on the back of his neck.

The Duke thrust the two books back and swung round as if he had been stung. He had felt it at the same instant—a sudden chill wind which increased to a rushing icy blast, so cold that it stung his hands and face like burning fire. The electric lights flickered and went dim, so that only the faint red glow of the wires showed in the globes. The great room was plunged in shadow and a violent mist began to rise out of the middle of the pentacle, swirling with incredible rapidity like some dust devil of the desert. It gathered height and bulk, spread and took form.

The lights flickered again and then went out, but the violet mist had a queer phosphorescent glow of its own. By it they could see the cabalistic bookcase, like a dark shadow beyond it, through the luminous mist. An awful stench of decay, which yet had something sweet and cloying about it, filled their nostrils as they gazed, sick and almost retching with repulsion, at a grey face that was taking shape about seven feet from the floor. The eyes were fixed upon them, malicious and intent. The eyeballs whitened but the face went dark. Under it the mist was gathering into shoulders, torso, hips.

Before they could choke for breath the materialisation had completed. Clad in flowing robes of white, Mocata's black servant towered above them. His astral body was just as the Duke had seen it in the flesh, from tip to toe a full six foot eight, and the eyes, slanting inward, burned upon them like live coals of fire.

6

THE SECRET ART

Rex was not frightened in the ordinary meaning of the word. He was past the state in which he could have ducked, or screamed, or run. He stood there rigid, numbed by the icy chill that radiated from the figure in the pentagram, a tiny pulse throbbed in his forehead, and his knees seemed to grow weak beneath him. A clear, silvery voice beat in his ears: 'Do not look at his eyes!—do not look at his eyes!—do not look at his eyes!'—an urgent repetition of De Richleau's warning to him, but try as he would, he could not drag his gaze from the malignant yellow pupils which burned in the black face.

Unable to stir hand or foot, he watched the ab-human figure grow in breadth and height, its white draperies billowing with a strange silent motion as they rose from the violet mist that obscured the feet, until it overflowed the circles that ringed the pentagram and seemed to fill the lofty chamber like a veritable Djin. The room reeked with the sickly, cloying stench which he had heard of but never thought to know—the abominable affluvium of embodied evil.

Suddenly red rays began to glint from the baleful slanting eyes, and Rex found himself quivering from head to foot. He tried desperately to pray: 'Our Father which art in Heaven—hallowed—hallowed—hallowed . . .' but the words which he had not used for so long would not come; the vibrations, surging through his body, as though he were holding the terminals of a powerful electric battery, seemed to cut them off. His left knee began to jerk. His foot lifted. He strove to raise his arms to cover his face, but they remained fixed to his sides as though held by invisible steel bands. He tried to cry out, to throw himself backwards, but, despite every atom of will which he could muster, a relentless force was drawing him towards the silent, menacing figure. Almost before he realised it he had taken a pace forward.

Through that timeless interval of seconds, days or weeks, after the violet mist first appeared, De Richleau stood within a foot of Rex, his eyes riveted upon the ground. He would not even allow himself to ascertain in what form the apparition had taken shape. The sudden deathly cold, the flicker of the lights as the room was plunged in darkness, the noisome odour, were enough to tell him that an entity of supreme evil was abroad.

With racing thoughts, he cursed his foolhardiness in ever entering the accursed house without doing all things proper for their protection. It was so many years since he had had any dealings with the occult that his acute anxiety for Simon had caused him to minimise the appalling risk they would run. What folly could have possessed him, he wondered miserably, to allow Rex, whose ignorance and scepticism would make him doubly vulnerable, to accompany him. Despite his advancing age, the Duke would have given five precious years of his life for an assurance that Rex was staring at the parquet floor, momentarily riveted by fear perhaps, yet still free from the malevolent influence which was streaming in pulsing waves from the circle; but Rex was not—instinctively De Richleau knew that his eyes were fixed on the Thing—and a ghastly dread caused little beads of icy perspiration to break out on his forehead.

Then he felt, rather than saw, Rex move. Next second he heard his footfall and *knew* that he was walking towards the pentagram. With trembling lips he began to mutter strange sentences of Persian, Greek and Hebrew, dimly remembered from his studies of the past—calling—calling—urgently—imperatively, upon the Power of Light for guidance and protection. Almost instantly the memory that he had slipped the jewelled swastika into his waistcoat pocket when Max returned it, flashed into his mind—and he knew that his prayer was answered. His fingers closed on the jewel. His arms shot out. It glittered for a second in the violet light, then came to rest in the centre of the circle.

A piercing scream, desperate with anger, fear, and pain, like that of a beast seared with a white-hot iron, blasted the silence. The lights flickered again so that the wires showed red—came on—went out—and flickered once more, as though two mighty forces were struggling for possession of the current.

The chill wind died so suddenly that it seemed as if a blanket of warm air had descended on their faces—but even while that hideous screech was still ringing through the chamber De Richleau grabbed Rex by the arm and dragged him towards the door. Next second the control of both had snapped and they were plunging down the stairs with an utter recklessness born of sheer terror.

Rex slipped on the lower landing and sprawled down the last flight on his back. The Duke came bounding after, six stairs at a time, and fell beside him. Together they scrambled to their feet—dashed through the library—out of the french-windows—and across the lawn.

With the agility of lemurs they swung up the branches of the laburnum—on to the wall—and dropped to the far side. Then they pelted down the lane as fast as their legs could carry them, and on until a full street away they paused, breathless and panting, to face each other under the friendly glow of a street lamp.

De Richleau's breath came in choking gasps. It was years since he had subjected himself to such physical exertion, and his face was grey from the strain which it had put upon him. Rex found his evening collar limp from the sweat which had streamed from him in his terror, but his lungs were easing rapidly, and he was the first to recover.

'God! we're mighty lucky to be out of that!'

The Duke nodded, still unable to speak.

'I take back every word I said,' Rex went on hurriedly. 'I don't think I've ever been real scared of anything in my life before—but that was hellish!'

'I panicked too—towards the end—couldn't help it, but I should never have taken you into that place—never,' De Richleau muttered repentantly as they set off down the street.

'Since we've got out safe it's all to the good. I've a real idea what we're up against now.'

The Duke drew Rex's arm through his own with a friendly gesture. Far from desiring to say 'I told you so!' he was regretting that he had been so impatient with Rex's previous unbelief. Most people he knew regarded devil worship and the cultivation of mystic powers as sheer superstitions due to the ignorance of the Middle Ages. It had been too much to expect Rex to accept his contention that their sane and sober friend Simon was mixed up in such practices, but now he had actually witnessed a true instance of Saiitii De Richleau felt that his co-operation would be ten times as valuable as before.

In the St John's Wood Road they picked up a belated taxi, and on the way back to Curzon Street he questioned Rex carefully as to the form the Thing had taken. When he had heard the description he nodded. 'It was Mocata's black servant, undoubtedly.'

'What did you say he was?'

'A Malagasy. They are a strange people. Half Negro and half Polynesian. A great migration took place many centuries ago from the South Seas to the East African Coast by way of the Malay Peninsula and Ceylon. Incredible though it may seem, they covered fifteen thousand miles of open ocean in their canoes, and most of them settled in Madagascar, where they intermarried with the aborigines and produced this half-breed type, which often has the worst characteristics of both races.'

'And Madagascar is the home of Voodoo–isn't it?'

'Yes. Perhaps he is a Witch doctor himself . . . and yet I wonder . . .' The Duke broke off as the taxi drew up before Errol House.

As they entered the big library Rex glanced at the clock and saw that it was a little after three. Not a particularly late hour for him, since he often danced until the night clubs emptied, nor for De Richleau, who believed that the one time when men opened their minds and conversation became really interesting was in the quiet hours before the dawn. Yet both were so exhausted by their ordeal that they felt as though a month had passed since they sat down to dinner.

Rex remade the remnants of the fire while the Duke mixed the drinks and uncovered the sandwiches which Max always left for him. Then they both sank into armchairs and renewed the discussion, for despite their weariness, neither had any thought of bed. The peril in which Simon stood was far too urgent.

'You were postulating that he might be a Madagascar Witch doctor,' Rex began. 'But I've a hunch I've read some place that such fellows have no power over whites, and surely that is so, else how could settlers in Africa and places keep the blacks under?'

'Broadly speaking, you are right, and the explanation is simple. What we call Magic–Black or White–is *the Science and Art of Causing Change to occur in conformity with Will*. Any required Change may be effected by the application of the proper kind and degree of Force in the proper manner and through the proper medium. Naturally for causing any Change it is requisite to have the practical ability to set the necessary Forces in right motion, but it is even more important to have a thorough qualitative and quantitative understanding of the conditions. Very few white men can really get inside a Negro's mind and know exactly what he is thinking–and even fewer blacks can appreciate a white's mentality. In consequence, it is infinitely harder for the Wills of either to work on the other than on men of their own kind.

'Another factor which adds to the difficulty of a Negroid or Mongolian Sorcerer working his spells upon a European is the question of vibrations. Their variation in human beings is governed largely by the part of the earth's surface in which birth took place. To use a simple analogy, some races have long wave lengths and others short–and the greater the variation the more difficult it is for a malignant will to influence that of an intended victim. Were it otherwise, you may be certain that the white races, who have neglected spiritual growth for material achievement, would never have come to dominate the world as they do today.'

'Yet that devil of Mocata's got me down all right. Ugh!' Rex shuddered slightly at the recollection.

'True–but I was only speaking generally. There are exceptions, and in the highest grades–the Ipsissimus, the Magus and the Magister Templi–those who have passed the Abyss, colour and race no longer remain a bar, so such Masters can work their will upon any lesser human unless he is protected by a power of equal strength. This associate of Mocata's may be one of the great Adepts of the Left Hand Path. However, what I was really wondering was–is he a human being at all?'

'But you said you saw him yourself—when you paid a call on Simon weeks back.'

'I *thought* I saw him—so at first I assumed that the Thing you saw tonight was his astral body, sent by Mocata to prevent our removing his collection of Devil's baubles; but perhaps what we both saw was a disembodied entity, an actual Satanic power which is not governed by Mocata, but has gained entry to our world from the other side through his evil practices.'

'Oh Lord!' Rex groaned. 'All this stuff is so new, so fantastic, so utterly impossible to me—I just can't grasp it; though don't think I'm doubting now. Whether it was an astral body or what you say, I saw it all right, and it wasn't a case of any stupid parlour tricks—I'll swear to that. It was so evil that my bones just turned to water on me in sheer blue funk—and there's poor Simon all mixed up in this. Say, now—what the hell are we to do?'

De Richleau sat forward suddenly. 'I wish to God I knew what was at the bottom of this business. I am certain that it is something pretty foul for them to have gone to the lengths of getting hold of a normal man like Simon but, if it is the last thing we ever do, we've got to find him and get him away from these people.'

'But how?' Rex flung wide his arms. 'Where can we even start in on the hope of picking up the trail? Simon's a lone wolf—always has been. He's got no father; his mother lives abroad; unlike so many Jews, he hasn't even got a heap of relatives who we can dig out and question?'

'Yes, that is the trouble. Of course he is almost certain to be with Mocata, but I don't see how we are to set about finding somebody who knows Mocata either. If only we had the address of any of those people who were there this evening we might . . .'

'I've got it!' cried Rex, leaping to his feet. 'We'll trace him through Tanith.'

7

DE RICHLEAU PLANS A CAMPAIGN

'Tanith,' the Duke repeated; 'but you don't know where she is, do you?'

'Sure.' Rex laughed, for the first time in several hours. 'Having got acquainted with her after all this while, I wouldn't be such a fool as to quit that party without nailing her address.'

'I must confess that I'm surprised she gave it to you.'

'She hadn't fallen to it that I wasn't one of their bunch—then! She's staying at Claridges.'

'Do you think you can get hold of her?'

'Don't you worry—I meant to, anyhow.'

'You must be careful, Rex. This woman is very lovely, I know—but she's probably damnably dangerous.'

'I've never been scared of a female yet, and surely these people can't do me much harm in broad daylight?'

'No, except for ordinary human trickery they are almost powerless between sunrise and sunset.'

'Fine. Then I'll go right round to Claridges as soon as she is likely to be awake tomorrow–today, rather.'

'You don't know her real name though, do you?'

'I should worry. There aren't two girls like her staying at Claridges–there aren't two like her in all London.'

De Richleau stood up and began to pace the floor like some huge cat. 'What do you intend to say to her?' he asked at length.

'Why, that we're just worried stiff about Simon–and that its absolutely imperative that she should help us out. I'll give her a frank undertaking not to do anything against Mocata or any of her pals if she'll come clean with me–though Heaven knows I can't think she's got any real friends in a crowd like that.'

'Rex! Rex!' The Duke smiled affectionately down into the honest attractive, ugly face of the young giant stretched in the armchair. 'And what, may I ask, do you intend to do should this lovely lady refuse to tell you anything?'

'I can threaten to call in the cops, I suppose, though I'd just hate to do anything like that on her.'

De Richleau gave his eloquent expressive shrug. 'My dear fellow, unless we can get some actual evidence of ordinary criminal activities against Mocata and his friends, the police are absolutely ruled out of this affair–and she would know it.'

'I don't see why,' Rex protested stubbornly. 'These people have kidnapped Simon, that's what it boils down to, and that's as much a crime as running a dope joint or white slaving.'

'Perhaps, and if they had hit him on the head our problem would be easy. The difficulty is that to all outward appearances he has joined them willingly and in his right mind. Only *we* know that he is acting under some powerful and evil influence which has been brought to bear on him, and how in the world are you going to charge anyone with raising the devil–or its equivalent–in a modern police court?'

'Well, what do you suggest?'

'Listen.' The Duke perched himself on the arm of Rex's chair. 'Even if this girl is an innocent party like Simon, she will not tell you anything willingly–she will be too frightened. As a matter of fact, now that she knows you are not a member of their infernal circle it is doubtful if she will even see you, but if she does–well, you've got to get hold of her somehow.'

'I'll certainly have a try–but it's not all that easy to kidnap people in a city like London.'

'I don't mean that exactly, but rather that you should induce her, by fair means or foul, to accompany you to some place where I can talk to her at my leisure. If she is only a neophyte I know enough of this dangerous business to frighten her out of her wits. If she is something more there will be a mental tussle, and I may learn something from the cards which she is forced to throw on the table.'

'O.K. I'll pull every gun I know to persuade her into coming here with me for a cocktail.'

De Richleau shook his head. 'No, I'm afraid that won't do. Immediately she realised the reason she had been brought here she would insist on leaving, and we couldn't stop her. If we tried she would break a window and yell Murder! We have got to get her to a place where she will see at once the futility of trying to call for outside help. I have it! Do you think you could get her down to Pangbourne?'

'What? To that river place of yours?'

'Yes; I haven't been down there yet this year, but I can send Max down first thing in the morning to open it up and give it an airing.'

'You talk as though I were falling off a log to get a girl to come boating on the Thames at what's practically a first meeting–can't you weigh in and lend a hand yourself?'

'No. I shall be at the British Museum most of the day. It is so many years since I studied the occult that there are a thousand things I have forgotten. It is absolutely imperative that I should immerse myself in some of the old key works for a few hours and rub up my knowledge of protective measures. I must leave you to handle the girl, Rex, and remember, Simon's safety will depend almost wholly on your success. Get her there somehow, and I'll join you in the late afternoon--say about six.'

Rex grinned. 'It's about as stiff a proposition as sending me in your place to study the Cabbala, but I'll do my best.'

'Of course you will.' The Duke began to pace hurriedly up and down again. 'But go gently with her–I beg you. Avoid any questions about this horrible business as you would the plague. Play the lover. Be just the nice young man who has fallen in love with a beautiful girl. If she asks you about our having abducted Simon from the party, say you were completely in the dark about it. That you have known me for years–and that I sprung some story on you about his having fallen into the hands of a gang of blackmailers, so you just blindly followed my lead without a second thought. Not a word to her about the supernatural–you know nothing of that. You must be as incredulous as you were with me when I first talked to you of it. And, above all, if you can get her to Pangbourne, don't let her know that I am coming down.'

'Surely–I get the line you want me to play all right.'

'Good. You see, if I can only squeeze some information out of her which will enable us to find out where Mocata is living, we will go down and keep the place under observation for a day or two. He is almost certain to have Simon with him. We will note the times that Mocata leaves the house and plan our raid accordingly. If we can get Simon into our hands again I swear Mocata shan't get him back a second time.'

'That's certainly the idea.'

'There is only one thing I am really frightened of.'

'What's that?'

De Richleau paused opposite Rex's chair. 'What I heard this evening of Simon's approaching change of name–to Abraham, you remember. That, of course, would be after Abraham the Jew, a very famous and learned mystic of the early centuries. He wrote a book which is said to be the most informative ever compiled concerning the Great Work. It was lost sight of for several hundred years, but early in the fifteenth century came into the possession of a Parisian bookseller named Nicolas Flamel who, by its aid, performed many curious rites. Flamel was buried in some magnificence, and a few years later certain persons who were anxious to obtain his secrets opened his grave to find the book which was supposed to have been buried with him. Neither Flamel nor the book was there, and there is even some evidence to show that he was still living a hundred years later in Turkey, which is by no means unbelievable to those who have any real knowledge of the strange powers acquired by the true initiate such as those in the higher orders of the Yoga sects. That is the last we know of the Book of Abraham the Jew, but it seems that Simon is about to take his name in the service of the Invisible.'

'Well—what'll happen then?'

'That he will be given over entirely to the Power of Evil, because he will renounce his early teaching and receive his re-baptism at the hands of a high adept of the Left Hand Path. Until that is done we can still save him, because all the invisible powers of God will be fighting on our side, but after—they will withdraw, and what we call the Soul of Simon Aron will be dragged down into the Pit.'

'Are you sure of that? Baptism into the Christian Faith doesn't ensure one going to Heaven, why should this other sprinkling be a guarantee of anyone going to Hell?'

'It's such a big question, Rex, but briefly it is like this. Heaven and Hell are only symbolical of growth to Light or disintegration to Darkness. By Christian—or any other *true* religious baptism, we renounce the Devil and all his Works, thereby erecting a barrier which it is difficult for Evil forces to surmount, but anyone who accepts Satanic baptism does exactly the reverse. They wilfully destroy the barrier of astral Light which is our natural protection and offer themselves as a medium through which the powers of Darkness may operate on mankind.

'They are tempted to it, of course, by the belief that it will give them supernatural powers over their fellow-men, but few of them realise the appalling danger. There is no such person as the Devil, but there are vast numbers of Earthbound spirits, Elementals, and Evil Intelligences of the Outer Circle floating in our midst. Nobody who has even the most elementary knowledge of the occult can doubt that. They are blind and ignorant, and except for the last, under comparatively rare circumstances, not in the least dangerous to any normal man or woman who leads a reasonably upright life, but they never cease to search in a fumbling way for some gateway back into existence as we know it. The surrender of one's own volition gives it to them, and, if you need an example, you only have to think of the many terrible crimes which are perpetrated when reason and will are entirely absent owing to excess of alcohol. An Elemental seizes upon the unresisting intelligence of the human and forces them to some appalling deed which is utterly against their natural instincts.

'That, then, is the danger. While apparently only passing through an ancient barbarous and disgusting ritual, the Satanist, by accepting baptism, surrenders his will to the domination of powers which he believes he will be able to to use for his own ends, but in actual fact he becomes the spiritual slave of an Elemental, and for ever after is nothing but the instrument of its evil purposes.'

'When do you figure they'll try to do this thing?'

'Not for a week or so, I trust. It is essential that it should take place at a real Sabbat, when at least one Coven of thirteen is present, and after our having broken up their gathering tonight I hardly think they will risk meeting again for some little time, unless there is some extraordinary reason why they should.'

'That gives us a breathing space then; but what's worrying me is that it's so early in the year to ask a young woman to go picnicking on the river.'

'Why? The sunshine for the last few days has been magnificent.'

'Still, it's only April 29th–the 30th, I mean.'

'What!' De Richleau stood there with a new and terrible anxiety burning in his eyes. 'Good God! I never realised!'

'What's the trouble?'

'Why, that was only one Coven we saw tonight, and there are probably a dozen scattered over England. The whole pack are probably on their way by now to the great annual gathering. It's a certainty they will take Simon with them. They'd never miss the chance of giving him his Devil's Christening at the Grand Sabbat of the year.'

'What in the world are you talking about?' Rex hoisted himself swiftly out of his chair.

'Don't you understand, man?' De Richleau gripped him by the shoulder. 'On the last night of April every peasant in Europe still double-locks his doors. Every latent force for Evil in the world is abroad. We've got to get hold of Simon in the next twenty hours. This coming night–April 30th–is Saint Walburga's Eve.'

8

REX VAN RYN OPENS THE ATTACK

Six hours later, Rex, still drowsy with sleep, lowered himself into the Duke's sunken bath. It was a very handsome bathroom some fifteen feet by twelve; black glass, crystal mirrors, and chromium-plated fittings made up the scheme of decoration.

Some people might have considered it a little too striking to be in perfect taste, but De Richleau did not subscribe to the canon which has branded ostentation as vulgarity in the last few generations, and robbed nobility of any glamour which it may have possessed in more spacious days.

His forbears had ridden with thirty-two footmen before them, and it caused him considerable regret that modern conditions made it impossible for him to drive in his Hispano with no more than one seated beside his chauffeur on the box. Fortunately his resources were considerable and his brain sufficiently astute to make good, in most years, the inroads which the tax gatherers made upon them. 'After him,' of course 'the Deluge' as he very fully recognised, but with reasonable good fortune he considered that private ownership would last out his time, at least in England where he had made his home; and so he continued to do all things on a scale suitable to a De Richleau, with the additional lavishness of one who had had a Russian mother, as far as the restrictions of twentieth-century democracy would allow.

Rex, however, had used the Duke's £1,000 bathroom a number of times before, and his only concern at the moment was to wonder vaguely what he was doing there on this occasion and why he had such an appalling hangover. Never, since he had been given two glasses of bad liquor in the old days when his country laboured under prohibition, had he felt so desperately ill.

A giant sponge placed on the top of his curly head brought him temporary relief and full consciousness of the events which had taken place the night before. Of course it was that ghastly experience he had been through in Simon's empty house that had sapped him of his vitality and left him in this wretched state. He remembered that he had kept up all right until they got back to Curzon Street, and even after, during a long conversation with the Duke; then, he supposed, he must have petered out from sheer nervous exhaustion.

He lay back in the warm, faintly scented water, and gave himself a mental shaking. The thought that he must have fainted shocked him profoundly. He had driven racing cars at 200 miles an hour, had his colours for the Cresta run, had flown a plane 1,500 miles, right out of the Forbidden Territory down to Kiev in one hop. He had shot men and been shot at in return both in Russia and in Cuba, where he had found himself mixed up with the Revolution, but never before had he been in a real funk about anything, much less collapsed like a spineless fool.

He recalled with sickening vividness, that loathsome, striking manifestation of embodied evil that had come upon them—and his thoughts flew to Simon. How could their shy, nervous, charming friend have got himself mixed up in all this devilry? For Rex had no doubts now that, incredible as it might seem, the Duke was right, and Satan worship still a living force in modern cities, just as the infernal Voodoo cult was still secretly practised by the Negroes in the Southern States of his own country. He thought again of their first visit to Simon's house as unwelcome guests at that strange party. Of the Albino, the old Countess D'Urfé, the sinister Chinaman, and then of Tanith, except for Simon the only normal person present, and felt convinced that, but for the intervention of De Richleau some abominable ceremony would certainly have taken place, although he had laughed at the suggestion at the time.

Sitting up he began to soap himself vigorously while he restated the situation briefly in his mind. One: Mocata was an adept of what De Richleau called the Left Hand Path, and for some reason unknown he had gained control over Simon. Two: owing to their intervention the Satanists had abandoned Simon's house—taking him with them. Three: Simon was shortly to be baptised into the Black Brotherhood, after which, according to the Duke, he would be past all help. Four: today was May Day Eve when, according to the Duke, the Grand Sabbat of the year took place. Five: following from four, it was almost a certainty that Mocata would seize this opportunity of the Walpurgis Nacht celebrations to have Simon rechristened. Six: in the next twelve hours therefore, Mocata had to be traced and Simon taken from him. Seven: the only possibility of getting on Mocata's trail lay in obtaining information by prayers, cajolery, or threats from Tanith.

Rex stopped soaping and groaned aloud at the thought that the one woman he had been wanting to meet for years should be mixed up in this revolting business. He loathed deception in any form and resented intensely the necessity for practising it on her, but De Richleau's last instructions to him were still clear in his mind, and the one thing which stood out above all others, was the fact of his old and dear friend being in some intangible but terrible peril.

Feeling slightly better by the time he had shaved and dressed, he noted from the windows of the flat that at least they had been blessed with a glorious day. Summer was in the air and there seemed a promise of that lovely fortnight which sometimes graces England in early May.

To his surprise he found that De Richleau, who habitually was not visible before twelve, had left the flat at half-past eight. Evidently he meant to put in a long day among the ancient manuscripts at the British Museum, rubbing up his knowledge of strange cults and protective measures against what he termed the Ab-human monsters of the Outer Circle.

Max proffered breakfast, but Rex declined it until, with a hurt expression, the servant produced his favourite omelet.

'The chef will be so disappointed, sir,' he said.

Reluctantly Rex sat down to eat while Max, busy with the coffee-pot, permitted himself a hidden smile. He had had orders from the Duke, and His Excellency was a wily man. None knew that better than his personal servitor, the faithful Max.

Noting that Rex had finished, he produced a wine-glass full of some frothy mixture on a salver. 'His Excellency said, sir,' he stated blandly, 'that he finds this uncommon good for his neuralgia. I was distressed to hear that you are sometimes a sufferer too, and if you'd try it the taste is, if I may say so, not unpleasant—somewhat resembling that of granadillas I believe.'

With a suspicious look Rex drank the quite palatable potion while Max added suavely: 'Some gentlemen prefer prairie-oysters I am told, but I've a feeling, sir, that His Excellency knows best.'

'You old humbug.' Rex grinned as he replaced the glass. 'Anyhow last night wasn't the sort of party you think—I wish to God it had been.'

'No, sir! Well, that's most regrettable I'm sure, but I had a feeling that Mr Aron was not quite in his usual form, if I may so express it—when he er—joined us after dinner.'

'Yes—of course you put Simon to bed—I'd forgotten that.'

Max quickly lowered his eyes. He was quite certain that his innocent action the night before had been connected in some way with Simon Aron's sudden disappearance from the bedroom later, and felt that for once he had done the wrong thing, so he deftly turned the conversation. 'His Excellency instructed me to tell you, sir, that the touring Rolls is entirely at your disposal and the second chauffeur if you wish to use him.'

'No—I'll drive myself; have it brought round right away—will you?'

'Very good, sir, and now if you will excuse me I must leave at once in order to get down to Pangbourne and prepare the house for your reception.'

'O.K., Max—See-yer-later—I hope.' Rex picked up a cigarette. He was feeling better already. 'A whole heap better,' he thought, as he wondered what potent corpse-reviver lay hidden in the creamy depths of De Richleau's so-called neuralgia tonic. Then he sat down to plan out his line of attack on the lady at Claridges.

If he could only talk to her he felt that he would be able to intrigue her into a friendly attitude. He could, of course, easily find out her real name from the bureau of the hotel, but the snag was that if he sent up his name and asked to see her the chances were all against her granting him an interview. After all, by kidnapping Simon, he and the Duke had wrecked the meeting of her Circle the night before, and if she was at all intimately associated with Mocata, she probably regarded him with considerable hostility. Only personal contact could overcome that, so he must not risk any rebuff through the medium of bell-hops, but accept it only if given by her after he had managed to see her face to face.

His plan, therefore, eventually boiled down to marching on Claridges, planting himself in a comfortable chair within view of the lifts and sitting there until Tanith made her appearance. He admitted to himself that his proposed campaign was conspicuously lacking in brilliance but, he argued, few women staying in a London hotel would remain in their rooms all day, so if he sat there long enough it was almost certain that an opportunity would occur for him to tackle her direct. If she did turn him down—well, De Richleau wasn't the only person in the world who had ideas—and Rex flattered himself that he would think of something.

Immediately the Rolls was reported at the door, he left the flat and drove round to Claridges in it. A short conversation with a friendly commissionaire ensured that there would be no trouble if the car was left parked outside, even for a considerable time, for Rex thought it necessary to have it close at hand since he might need it at any moment.

As he entered the hotel from the Davis Street entrance he noted with relief that it was only a little after ten. It was unlikely that Tanith would have gone out for the day so early, and he settled himself to wait for an indefinite period with cheerful optimism in the almost empty lounge. After a moment it occurred to him that somebody might come up to him and inquire his business if he was forced to stay there for any length of time, but an underporter, passing at the moment, gave him a swift smile and little bow of recognition, so he trusted that having been identified as an occasional client of the place he would not be unduly molested.

He began to consider what words he should use if, and when, Tanith did step out of the lifts, and had just decided on a formula which contained the requisite proportions of respect, subtle admiration, and gaiety when a small boy in buttons came marching with a carefree swing down the corridor.

'Mister Vine Rine—Mister Vine Rine,' he chanted in a monotonous treble.

Rex looked at the boy suspiciously. The sound had a queer resemblance to the parody of his own name as he had often heard it shrilled out by bell-hops in clubs and hotel lounges. Yet no one could possibly be aware of his presence at Claridges that morning—except, of course, the Duke. At the thought that De Richleau might be endeavouring to get in touch with him for some urgent reason he turned, and at the same moment the page sidetracked towards him.

'Mr Van Ryn, sir?' he inquired, dropping into normal speech.

'Yes.' Rex nodded.

Then to his utter astonishment the boy announced: 'The lady you've called to see sent down to say she's sorry to keep you waiting, but she'll join you in about fifteen minutes.'

With his mouth slightly open Rex stared stupidly at the page until that infant turned and strutted away. He did not doubt that the message came from Tanith—who else could have sent it, yet how the deuce did she know that he was there? Perhaps she had seen him drive up from her window—that seemed the only reasonable explanation. Anyhow that 'she was sorry to keep him waiting' sounded almost too good to be true.

Recovering a little he stood up, marched out into Brook Street and purchased a great sheaf of lilac from a florist's a few doors down. Returning with it to the hotel he suddenly realised that he still did not know Tanith's real name, but catching sight of the boy who had paged him, he beckoned him over.

'Here boy—take these up to the lady's room with Mr Van Ryn's compliments.' Then he resumed his seat near the lift with happy confidence.

Five minutes later the lift opened. An elderly woman leaning upon a tall ebony cane stepped out. At the first glance Rex recognised the parrot-peaked nose, the nut-cracker chin and the piercing black eyes of the old Countess D'Urfé. Before he had time to collect his wits she had advanced upon him and extended a plump, beringed hand.

'Monsieur Van Ryn,' she croaked. 'It is charming that you should call upon me—sank you a thousand times for those lovely flowers.'

<hr />

9

THE COUNTESS D'URFÉ TALKS OF MANY CURIOUS THINGS

'Ha! ha!—not a bit of it—it's great to see you again.'

Rex gave a weak imitation of a laugh. He had only spoken to the old crone for two minutes on the previous evening and that, when he had first arrived at Simon's party, for the purpose of detaching Tanith from her. Even if she had seen him drive up to Claridges what in the world could have made her imagine that he had come to visit *her*? If only he hadn't sent up that lilac he might have politely excused himself—but he could hardly tell her now that he had meant it for someone else.

'And how is *Monseigneur le Duc* this morning?' the old lady inquired, sinking into a chair he placed for her.

'He asked me to present his homage, Madame,' Rex lied quickly, instinctively picking a phrase which De Richleau might have used himself.

'*Ca, c'est très gentille.* 'E is a charming man—charming an' 'is cigars they are superb.' The Countess D'Urfé produced a square case from her bag and drew out a fat, dark Havana. As Rex applied a match she went on slowly: 'But it ees not right that one Circle should make interference with the operations of another. What 'ave you to say of your be'aviour lars' night my young frien'?'

'My hat,' thought Rex, 'the old beldame fancies we're an opposing faction in the same line of business—I'll have to use this if I can,' so he answered slowly: 'We were mighty sorry to have to do what we did, but we needed Simon Aron for our own purposes.'

'So!—you also make search for the Talisman then?'

'Sure—that is, the Duke's taking a big interest in it.'

'Which of us are not—and 'oo but *le petit Juif* shall lead us to it.'

'That's true.'

''Ave you yet attempted the Rite to Saturn?'

'Yes, but things didn't pan out quite as we thought they would,' Rex replied cautiously, not having the faintest idea what they were talking about.

'You 'ave satisfy yourselves that the aloes and mastic were fresh, eh?' The wicked old eyes bored into his.

'Yes, I'm certain of that,' he assured her.

'You choose a time when the planet was in the 'ouse of Capricorn, of course?'

'Oh, surely!'

'An' you 'ave not neglect to make Libation to Our Lady Babalon before'and?'

'Oh, no, we wouldn't do that!'

'Then per'aps your periods of silence were not long enough?'

'Maybe that's so,' he admitted hurriedly, hoping to close this madhatter's conversation before he completely put his foot into it.

Countess D'Urfé nodded, then after drawing thoughtfully at her cigar she looked at him intently. 'Silence,' she murmured. 'Silence, that ees always essential in the Ritual of Saturn—but you 'ave much courage to thwart Mocata—'e is powerful, that one.'

'Oh, we're not afraid of him,' Rex declared and, recalling the highest grade of operator from his conversation with De Richleau, he added: 'You see the Duke knows all about this thing—he's an Ipsissimus.'

The old lady's eyes almost popped out of their sockets at this announcement, and Rex feared that he had gone too far, but she leaned forward and placed one of her jewelled claws upon his arm. 'An Ipsissimus!—an' I 'av studied the Great Work for forty years, yet I 'ave reached only the degree of Practicus. But no, 'e cannot be, or 'ow could 'e fail with the Rite to Saturn?'

'I only said that it didn't pan out quite as we expected,' Rex hastened to remind her, 'and for the full dress business he'd need Simon Aron anyway.'

'Of course,' she nodded again and continued in an awestruck whisper, 'an' De Richleau is then a real Master. You must be far advanced for one so young—that 'e allow you to work with 'im.'

He flicked the ash off his cigarette but maintained a cautious silence.

'I am not—'ow you say—associated with Mocata long—since I 'ave arrive only recently in England, but De Richleau will cast 'im down into the Abyss—for 'ow shall 'e prevail against one who is of ten circles and a single square?'

Rex nodded gravely.

'Could I not—' her dark eyes filled with a new eagerness, 'would it not be possible for me to prostrate before your frien'? If you spoke for me also, per'aps 'e would allow that I should occupy a minor place when 'e proceeds again to the invocation?'

'Ho! Ho!' said Rex to himself, 'so the old rat wants to scuttle from the sinking ship, does she. I ought to be able to turn this to our advantage,' while aloud he said with a lordly air: 'All things are possible—but there would be certain conditions.'

'Tell me' she muttered swiftly.

'Well, there is this question of Simon Aron.'

'What question?—Now that you 'ave 'im with you—you can do with 'im as you will.'

Rex quickly averted his gaze from the piercing black eyes. Evidently Mocata had turned the whole party out after they had got away with Simon. The old witch obviously had no idea that Mocata had regained possession of him later. In another second he would have given away their whole position by demanding Simon's whereabouts. Instead—searching his mind desperately for the right bits of gibberish he said: 'When De Richleau again proceeds to the invocation it is necessary that the vibrations of all present should be attuned to those of Simon Aron.'

'No matter–willingly I will place myself in your 'ands for preparation.'

'Then I'll put it up to him, but first I must obey his order and say a word to the lady who was with you at Aron's house last night–Tanith.' Having at last manœuvred the conversation to this critical point, Rex mentally crossed his thumbs and offered up a prayer that he was right in assuming that they were staying at the hotel together.

She smiled, showing two rows of white false teeth. 'I know it, and you must pardon, I beg, that we 'ave our little joke with you.'

'Oh, don't worry about that,' he shrugged, wondering anxiously to what new mystery she was alluding, but to his relief she hurried on.

'Each morning we look into the crystal an' when she see you walk into the 'otel she exclaim, "It is for me 'e comes–the tall American," but we 'ave no knowledge that you are more than a Neophyte or a Zelator at the most, so when you send up the flowers she say to me, "You shall go down to 'im instead an' after we will laugh at the discomfiture of this would-be lover."'

The smile broadened on Rex's full mouth as he listened to the explanation of much that had been troubling him in the last hour, but it faded suddenly as he realised that, natural as it seemed compared to all this meaningless drivel which he had been exchanging with the old woman, it was in reality one more demonstration of the occult. These two women had *actually seen him* walk into the hotel lounge when they were sitting upstairs in their room peering into a piece of glass.

'In some ways I suffer the disappointment,' said the old Countess suddenly, and Rex found her studying him with a strange, disconcerting look. 'I know well that promiscuity gives a great power for all 'oo follow the Path an' that 'uman love 'inders our development, but nevair 'ave I been able to free myself from a so stupid sentimentality–an' you would, I think, 'ave made a good lover for 'er.'

Rex stared in astonished silence, then looked quickly away, as she added: 'No matter–the other ees of real importance. I will send for 'er that you may give your message.'

With a little jerk she stood up and gripping her ebony cane stumped across to the hall porter's desk while he relaxed, unutterably glad that this extraordinary interview was over.

However, he felt a glow of satisfaction in the thought that he had duped her into the belief that De Richleau and himself were even more powerful adepts than Mocata, and at having played his cards sufficiently well to secure a meeting with Tanith under such favourable circumstances. If only he could get her into his car, he was determined to inveigle her into giving him any information she possessed which might lead to the discovery of Simon's whereabouts, although, since Madame D'Urfé was ignorant of the fact that he was no longer with the Duke, it was hardly likely that Tanith would actually be able to take them to him.

With new anxiety Rex realised the gravity of the check. They had practically counted on Tanith having the knowledge, if only they could get it out of her, and even if he could persuade her to talk about Mocata the man might have a dozen haunts. If so it would be no easy task to visit all before sundown and the urgency of the Duke's instructions still rang in his ears.

Today was May Day Eve. The Great Sabbat of the year would be held tonight. It was absolutely imperative that they should trace and secure Simon before dusk or else, under the evil influence which now dominated his mentality, he would be taken to participate in those unholy rites and jeopardise for ever the flame of goodness, wisdom and right thinking which men term the soul.

After a moment Madame D'Urfé rejoined him. 'For tonight at least,' she whispered, 'things in dispute between the followers of the Path will be in abeyance—is it not?—for all must make their 'omage to the One.'

He nodded and she bent towards him, lowering her voice still further: 'If I could but see De Richleau for one moment—as Ipsissimus 'e must possess the unguent?'

'That's so,' Rex agreed, but he was horribly uncertain of his ground again as he added cryptically: 'But what of the Moon?'

'Ah, fatality,' she sighed. 'I 'ad forgotten that we are in the dark quarter.'

He blessed the providence which had guided his tongue as she went on sadly: 'I 'ave try so often but nevair yet 'ave I succeeded. I know all things necessary to its preparation, an' 'ave gathered every 'erb at the right period. I 'ave even rendered down the fat, but they must 'ave cheated me. It was from a mortuary per'aps—but not from a graveyard as it should 'ave been.'

Rex felt the hair bristle on the back of his neck and his whole body stiffened slightly as he heard this gruesome confession. Surely it was inconceivable that people still practised these medieval barbarities—yet he recalled the terrible manifestation that he had witnessed with the Duke on the previous night. After that he could no longer employ modern standards of belief or unbelief to the possibilities which might result from the strange and horrible doings of these people who had given themselves over to ancient cults.

The old Countess was regarding him again with that queer disconcerting look. 'It matters not,' she murmured. 'We shall get there just the same, Tanith and I—an' it should be interesting—for nevair before 'as she attended the Great Sabbat.'

The lift gates clicked at that moment and Tanith stepped out into the corridor. For a fleeting instant Rex caught a glimpse of her wise, beautiful face, over the old woman's shoulder, but the Countess was speaking again in a husky whisper, so he was forced to look back at her.

'Nevair before,' she repeated with unholy glee, 'and after the One 'as done that which there is to do, 'oo knows but you may be the next—if you are quick.'

Forcing himself out of his chair Rex shut his ears to the infernal implication. His general reading had been enough for him to be aware that in the old days the most incredible orgies took place as the climax to every Sabbat, and his whole body crept at the thought of Tanith being subjected to such abominations. His impulse was to seize this iniquitous old woman by the throat and choke the bestial life out of her fat body, but with a supreme effort he schooled himself to remain outwardly normal.

As Tanith approached, and taking his hand smiled into his eyes, he knew that she, as well as Simon, must be saved before nightfall from—yes, the old biblical quotation leapt to his mind—'The Power of the Dog,' that was strong upon them.

10

TANITH PROVES STUBBORN

After the muttering of the old Countess and her veiled allusions to unspeakable depravities Rex felt that even the air had grown stale and heavy, as though charged with some subtle quality of evil, but on the coming of Tanith the atmosphere seemed to lighten. The morning sunshine was lending a pale golden glow to the street outside and in her hand she held one of the sprays of lilac which he had sent up to her. She lifted it to her face as he returned her smile. 'So!' she said in a low clear voice, her eyes mocking him above the fragrant bloom: 'You insisted then that Madame should let you see me?'

'I'd have sat around this place all day if she hadn't,' Rex confessed frankly, 'because now we've met at last I'm hoping you'll let me see something of you.'

'Perhaps—but not today. I have many things to do and already I am late for the dressmaker.'

Rex thanked his stars that the old woman had unwittingly given him a lever in assuming the Duke to be an Adept of great power, and himself his envoy. 'It's mighty important that I should see you today,' he insisted. 'There are certain things we've got to talk about.'

'Got to!' A quick frown clouded Tanith's face. 'I do not understand!'

'*Ma petite*, it is you 'oo do not understan',' Madame D'Urfé broke in hastily. The she launched into a torrent of low speech in some foreign language, but Rex caught De Richleau's name and the word Ipsissimus, so he guessed that she was giving Tanith some version of the events which had taken place the night before, based on his own misleading statements, and wondered miserably how long he would be able to keep up the impersonation which had been thrust upon him.

Tanith nodded several times and studied him with a new interest as she nibbled a small piece of the lilac blossom between her teeth. Then she said with charming frankness: 'You must forgive me—I had no idea you were such an important member of the Order.'

'Forget it please,' he begged, 'but if you're free I'd be glad if you could join me for lunch.'

'That puts me in a difficulty because I am supposed to be lunching with the wife of the Roumanian Minister.'

'How about this afternoon then?'

Her eyes showed quick surprise. 'But we shall have to leave here by four o'clock if we are to get down by dusk—and I have my packing to do yet.'

He realised that she was referring to the meeting and covered his blunder swiftly. 'Of course—I'm always forgetting that these twisting English roads don't permit of the fast driving I'm used to back home. How would it be if I run you along to your dress place now and then we took a turn round the Park after?'

'Yes—if you will have lots of patience with me, because I take an almost idiotic interest in my clothes.'

'You're telling me!' he murmured to himself as he admired the slim graceful lines of her figure clad so unostentatiously and yet so suitably for the sunshine of the bright spring day. He picked up his hat and beamed at her. 'Let's go—shall we?'

To his amazement he found himself taking leave of the old Countess just as though she were a nice, normal, elderly lady who was chaperoning some young woman to whom he had been formally introduced at a highly respectable dance. And indeed, as they departed, her dark eyes had precisely the same look which had often scared him in mothers who possessed marriageable daughters. Had he not known that such thoughts were anathema to her creed he would have sworn that she was praying that they would be quick about it, so that she could book a day before the end of the season at St George's, Hanover Square, and was already listing in her mind the guests who should be asked to the reception.

'Where does the great artist hang out?' he asked as he helped Tanith into the car.

'I have two,' she told him. 'Schiaparelli just across the square, where I shall be for some twenty minutes, and after I have also to visit Artelle in Knightsbridge— Are you sure that you do not mind waiting for me?'

'Why, no! we've a whole heap of time before us.'

'And tonight as well,' she added slowly. 'I am glad that you will be there because I am just a little nervous.'

'You needn't be!' he said with a sudden tightening of his mouth, but she seemed satisfied with his assurance and had no inkling of his real meaning.

As she alighted in Upper Grosvenor Street he called gaily after her: 'Twenty minutes mind, and not one fraction over,' then he drove across the road and pulled up at the International Sportsman's Club of which he was a member.

The telephone exchange put him through to the British Museum quickly enough, but the operator there nearly drove him frantic. It seemed that it was not part of the Museum staff's duties to search for visitors in the Reading Room, but after urgent prayers about imaginary dead and dying they at last consented to have the Duke hunted out. The wait that followed seemed interminable but at last De Richleau came to the line.

'I've got the girl,' Rex told him hurriedly, 'but how long I'll be able to keep her I don't know. I've had a long talk, too, with the incredible old woman who smokes cigars—you know the one—Madame D'Urfé. They're staying at Claridges together and both of them are going to the party you spoke of tonight. Where it's to be held I don't know, but they're leaving London by car at four o'clock and hope to make the place by nightfall. I've spun 'em a yarn that you're the high and mighty Hoodoo in the you-know-what—a fat bigger bug than Mocata ever was—so the old lady's all for giving him the go-by and sitting in round about your feet, but neither of them knows where Simon is—I'm certain. In fact they've no idea that he made a getaway last night after we got him to your flat—so what's the drill now?'

'I see—well, in that case you must . . .' but Rex never learnt what De Richleau intended him to do for at that moment they were cut off. When he got through to the Museum again it was to break in on a learned conversation about South American antiques which was being conducted on another line and, realising that he had already exceeded his twenty minutes, he had no option but to hang up the receiver and dash out into the street.

Tanith was just coming down the steps of Schiaparelli's as he turned the car to meet her. 'Where now?' he asked when she had settled herself beside him.

'To Artelle. It is just opposite the barracks in Knightsbridge. I will not be more than five minutes this time, but she has a new idea for me. She is really a very clever woman, so I am anxious to hear what she has thought of.'

It was the longest speech he had so far heard her make, as their conversation the night before had been brief and frequently interrupted by Mocata. Her idiom was perfect, but the way in which she selected her words and the care with which she pronounced them made him ask suddenly. 'You're not English—are you?'

'Yes,' she smiled as they turned into Hyde Park, 'but my mother was Hungarian and I have lived abroad nearly all my life. Is my accent very noticeable?'

'Well—in a way, but it sounds just marvellous to me. Your voice has got that deep caressing note about it which reminds me of—well, if you want the truth, it's like Marlene Dietrich on the talkies.'

She threw back her head and gave a low laugh. 'If I believed that I should be tempted to keep it, and as it is I have been working so hard to get rid of it ever since I have been in England. It is absurd that I should not be able to speak my own language perfectly—yet I have talked English so little, except to foreign governesses when I was a young girl.'

'And how old are you now, or is that a piece of rudeness?'

'How old do you think?'

'From your eyes you might be any age, but I've a feeling that you're not much over twenty-two.'

'If I were to live I should be twenty-four next January.'

'Come now,' he protested, laughing, 'what a way to put it, that's only a matter of nine months and no one could say you don't look healthy.'

'I am,' she assured him gravely, 'but let us not talk of death. Look at the colour of those rhododendrons. They are so lovely.'

'Yes, they've jerked this Park up no end since I first saw it as a boy.' As the traffic opened he turned the car into Knightsbridge and two minutes later Tanith got out at the discreet door of her French dressmaker.

While she was inside Rex considered the position afresh, and endeavoured to concoct some cryptic message purporting to come from the Duke, to the effect that she was not to attend the Sabbat but to remain in his care until it was all over. Yet he felt that she would never believe him. It was quite evident that she meant to be present at this unholy Walpurgis-Nacht gathering, and from what the old woman had said all Satanists regarded it with such importance that even warring factions among them sank their differences—for this one night of the year—in order to attend.

Obviously she could have no conception of what she was letting herself in for, but the very idea of her being mishandled by that ungodly crew made his big biceps tighten with the desire to lash out at someone. He had got to keep her with him somehow, that was clear—but how?

He racked his mind in vain for a plausible story but, to his dismay, she rejoined him almost immediately and he had thought of nothing by the time they had turned into the Park again.

'Well–tell me,' she said softly.

'Tell you what?' he fenced. 'That I think you're very lovely?'

'No, no. It is nice that you should have troubled to make pretty speeches about my accent and Marlene Dietrich, but it is time for you to tell me now of the real reason that brought you to Claridges this morning.'

'Can't you guess?'

'No.'

'I wanted to take you out to lunch.'

'Oh, please! Be serious–you have a message for me?'

'Maybe, but even if I hadn't, I'd have been right on the mat at your hotel just the same.'

She frowned slightly. 'I don't understand. Neither of us is free to give our time to that sort of thing.'

'I've reached a stage where I'm the best judge of that,' he announced, with the idea of trying to recover some of the prestige which seemed to be slipping from him.

'Have you then crowned yourself with the Dispersion of Choronzon already?'

Rex suppressed a groan. Here they were off on the Mumbo Jumbo stuff again. He felt that he would never be able to keep it up, so instead of answering he turned the car with sudden determination out into the Kensington Road and headed towards Hammersmith.

'Where are you taking me?' she asked quickly.

'To lunch with De Richleau,' he lied. 'I've got no message for you but the Duke sent me to fetch you because he wants to talk to you himself.' It was the only story he could think of which just might get over.

'I see–where is he?'

'At Pangbourne.'

'Where is that?'

'Little place down the Thames–just past Reading.'

'But that is miles away!'

'Only about fifty.'

'Surely he could have seen me before he left London.'

He caught her eyes, quick with suspicion, on his face, so he answered boldly: 'I know nothing of that, but he sent me to fetch you–and what the Duke says goes.'

'I don't believe you!' she exclaimed angrily. 'Stop this car at once!–I am going to get out.'

I I

THE TRUTH WILL ALWAYS OUT

For a second Rex thought of ignoring her protest and jamming his foot on the accelerator, but the traffic in Kensington High Street was thick, and to try to abduct her in broad daylight would be sheer madness. She could signal a policeman and have him stopped before he'd gone two hundred yards.

Reluctantly he drew in to the side of the road, but he stretched his long arm in front of her and gripped the door of the car so that she could not force it open.

Tanith stared at him with angry eyes: 'You are lying to me—I will not go with you.'

'Wait a moment.' He thrust out his chin pugnaciously while he mustered all his resources to reason with her. If he once let her leave the car the chances were all against his having another opportunity to prevent her reaching the secret rendezvous where those horrible Walpurgis ceremonies would take place in the coming night. His determination to prevent her participating in those barbaric rites, of which he was certain she could not know the real nature, quickened his brain to an unusual cunning: 'You know what happened to Simon Aron?' he said.

'Yes, you kidnapped him from his own home last night.'

'That's so—but do you know why?'

'Madame D'Urfé said that it was because the Duke is also seeking for the Talisman of Set. You needed him for your own invocations.'

'Exactly.' Rex paused for a moment to wonder what the Talisman could be. This was the second time he had heard it mentioned. Then he went on slowly: 'It's him being born under certain stars makes his presence essential. We'd hunt for years before we found anyone else who's suitable to do the business and born in the same hour of the same day and year. Well, we need you too.'

'But my number is not eight!'

'That doesn't matter—you're under the Moon, aren't you?' He risked the shot on what he remembered of De Richleau's words about her name.

'Yes,' she admitted. 'But what has that to do with it?'

'A whole heap—believe you me. But naturally you'd know nothing of that. Even Mocata doesn't realise the importance of the Moon in this thing and that's why he's failed to make much headway up to date.'

'Mocata would be furious if I left his Circle—you see I am his favourite medium—so attuned to his vibrations that he would have the very greatest difficulty in replacing me. Perhaps—perhaps he would punish me in some terrible manner.' Tanith's face had gone white and her eyes were staring slightly at the thought of some nameless evil which might befall her.

'Don't worry. De Richleau will protect you—and he's an Ipsissimus remember. If you don't come right along, now he wants to see you, maybe he'll do something to you that'll be far worse.' As Rex lied and threatened he hated himself for it, but the girl had just got to be saved from herself and this form of blackmail was the only line that offered.

'How am I to know? How am I to know?' she repeated quickly. 'You may be lying. Think what might happen to me if Mocata proved the stronger.'

'You had the proof last night. We got Simon Aron away from under his very nose—didn't we?'

'Yes, but will you be able to keep him?'

'Sure,' Rex declared firmly, but he felt sick with misery as he remembered that by Mocata's power Simon had been taken from them under the hour. And where was Simon now? The day was passing, their hope of Tanith being able to put them on his track had proved a failure. How would they find him in time to save him too from the abominations of the coming night?

'Oh, what shall I do?' Tanith gave a little nervous sob. 'It is the first time I have heard of any feud in our Order. I thought that if I only followed the

Path I should acquire power and now this hideously dangerous decision is thrust on me.'

Rex saw that she was weakening so he pressed the self-starter. 'You're coming with me and you're not going to be frightened of anything. Get that now—I mean it.'

She nodded. 'All right. I will trust you then,' and the car slid into motion.

For a few moments they sat in silence, then as the car entered Hammersmith Broadway he turned and smiled at her. 'Now let's cut out all talk about this business till we see the Duke and just be normal—shall we?'

'If you wish—tell me about yourself.'

He smothered a sigh of relief at her acquiescence. At least he would be free for an hour or so from the agonising necessity of skating on thin ice of grim parables which had no meaning for him. With all his natural gaiety restored he launched into an account of his life at home in the States, his frequent journeys abroad, and his love of speed in cars and boats and planes and bobsleighs.

As they sped through Brentford and on to Slough he got her to talk a little about herself. Her English father had died when she was still a baby and the Hungarian mother had brought her up. All her childhood had been spent in an old manor house, dignified by the name of Castle, in a remote village on the southern slopes of the Carpathians, shut in so completely from the world by steep mountains on every side that even the War had passed it by almost unnoticed. After the peace and the disintegration of the Austrian-Hungarian Empire their lands had become part of the new state of Jugo-Slavia, but her life had gone on much the same for, although the War had cost them a portion of their fortune, the bulk of it had been left safe by her father in English Trustee securities. Her mother had died three years before and it was then, having no personal ties and ample money, that she had decided to travel.

'Isn't it just marvellous that I should have seen you in such different places about the world,' he laughed.

'The first time that you speak of in Budapest I do not remember,' she replied, 'but I recall the day outside Buenos Aires well. You were in a long red car and I was riding a roan mare. As you drew into the side of the track to let us pass I wondered why I knew your face, and then I remembered quite clearly that our cars had been locked side by side in a traffic jam, months before, in New York.'

'Seems as if we were just fated to meet sometime—doesn't it?'

'We both know that there is no such thing as Chance,' she said slowly. 'I believe you have a wax image of me somewhere and have worked upon it to bring today about.'

The day before he would have instantly assumed her to be joking, despite her apparent seriousness, but now, he realised with a little shock, he no longer considered it beyond the bounds of possibility that actual results might be procured by doing certain curious things to a little waxen doll, so greatly had his recent experiences altered his outlook. He hesitated, unable to confess his ignorance of such practices, and unwilling to admit that he had not done his best to bring about a meeting, but he was saved from the necessity of a reply by Tanith suddenly exclaiming:

'I had forgotten!—luncheon—I shall never be back in time.'

'Easy, put through a call and say you've suddenly been called out of

Town,' he told her, and a few miles farther on he pulled up at Skindles Hotel in Maidenhead.

While Tanith was telephoning he stood contemplating the river. Although it was early in the year a period of drought had already checked the spate of the current sufficiently to make boating pleasurable, and he noted that in the gardens of the Hungaria River Club, on the opposite bank, they were setting out their gay paraphernalia, preparatory to opening for the Season. Immediately Tanith rejoined him they set off again.

The straggling suburbs of Greater London had already been left behind them before Slough and now, after Maidenhead, the scattered clusters of red-roofed dwellings on the new building estates, which have spread so far afield, also disappeared, giving place to the real country. On certain portions of the road, the fresh green of the beech trees formed a spring canopy overhead and between their trunks, dappled with sunlight, patches of bluebells gave glory to the silent woods; at others they ran between meadows where lazy cattle nibbled the new grass, or fields where the young corn, strong with life, stretched its vivid green shoots upwards to the sun.

The sight and smell of the countryside, unmarred by man or carefully tended in his interests, windswept and clean, gave Rex fresh confidence. He banished his anxiety about Simon for the moment and, thrusting from his mind all thoughts of this gruesome business into which he had been drawn, began to talk all the gay nonsense to Tanith which he would have aired to any other girl whom he had induced to steal a day out of London in which to see the country preparing its May Day garb.

Before they reached Reading he had her laughing, and by the time they entered the little riverside village of Pangbourne, her pale face was flushed with colour and her eyes dancing with new light.

They crossed to the Whitchurch side where the Duke's house stood, some way back from the river, its lawns sloping gently to the water's edge.

Max received them, and while a maid took Tanith upstairs to wash, Rex had a chance to whisper quick instructions to him.

When she entered the low, old-fashioned lounge with its wide windows looking out over the tulip beds to the trees on the further bank she found Rex whistling gaily. He was shooting varying proportions of liquor out of different bottles into a cocktail shaker. Max stood beside him holding a bowl of ice.

'Where is the Duke?' she asked, with a new soberness in her voice.

He had been waiting for the question, and keeping his face averted answered cheerfully: 'He's not made it yet—what time are you expecting him, Max?'

'I should have told you before, sir. His Excellency telephoned that I was to present his excuses to the lady, and ask you, sir, to act as host in his stead. He has been unavoidably detained, but hopes to be able to join you for tea.'

'Well, now, if that isn't real bad luck!' Rex exclaimed feelingly. 'Never mind, we'll go right in to lunch the moment it's ready.' He tasted the concoction which he had been beating up with a large spoon and added: 'My! that's good!'

'Yes, sir—in about five minutes, sir.' Max bowed gravely and withdrew.

Rex knew that there was trouble coming but he presented a glass of the frothing liquid with a steady hand. 'Never give a girl a large cocktail,' he cried gaily, 'but plenty of 'em. Make 'em strong and drink 'em quick—come on now! It takes a fourth to make an appetite—Here's to crime!'

But Tanith set down the glass untasted. All the merriment had died out of her eyes and her voice was full of a fresh anxiety as she said urgently: 'I can't stay here till tea-time—don't you realise that I must leave London by four o'clock.'

It was on the tip of his tongue to say, 'Where is this place you're going to?' but he caught himself in time and substituted: 'Why not go from here direct?' Then he prayed silently that the secret meeting place might not be on the other side of London.

Her face lightened for a moment. 'Of course, I forgot that you were going yourself, and the journey must be so much shorter from here. If you could take me it seems stupid to go all the way back to London—but what of Madame D'Urfé—she expects me to motor down with her—and I must have my clothes.'

'Why not call her on the phone. Ask her to have your stuff packed up and say we'll meet her there. You've got to see the Duke, and whatever happens he'll turn up here because he and I are going down together.'

She nodded. 'If I am to place myself under his protection it is vital that I should see him before the meeting, for Mocata has eyes in the ether and will know that I am here by now.'

'Come on then!' He took her hand and pulled her to her feet. 'We'll get through to Claridges right away.'

Tanith allowed him to lead her out into the hall and when he had got the number he left her at the telephone. Then he returned to the lounge, poured himself another cocktail and began to do a gay little dance to celebrate his victory. He felt that he had got her now, safe for the day, until the Duke turned up. Then trust De Richleau to get something out of her which would enable them to get on Simon's track after all.

At his sixth pirouette he stopped suddenly. Tanith was standing in the doorway, her face ashen, her big eyes blazing with a mixture of anger and fear.

'You have lied to me,' she stammered out, 'Mocata is with the Countess at this moment—he got Simon Aron away from you last night. You and your precious Duke are imposters—charlatans— You haven't even the power to protect yourselves, and for this Mocata may tie me to the Wheel of Ptah—oh, I must get back!' Before he could stop her she had turned and fled out of the house.

12

THE GRIM PROPHECY

In one spring Rex was across the room, another and he had reached the garden. Against those long legs of his Tanith had no chance. Before she had covered twenty yards he caught her arm and jerked her round to face him.

'Let me go!' she panted. 'Haven't you endangered me enough with your lies and interference.'

He smiled down into her frightened face but made no motion to release her. 'I'm awfully sorry I had to tell you all those tarradiddles to get you to this place–but now you're here you're going to stay–understand?'

'It is you who don't understand,' she flashed. 'You and your friend the Duke, are like a couple of children playing with a dynamite bomb. You haven't a chance against Mocata. He will loose a power on you that will simply blot you out.'

'I wouldn't be too certain of that. Maybe I know nothing of this occult business myself and if anyone had suggested to me that there were practising Satanists wandering around London this time last week, I'd have said they had bats in the belfry. But the Duke's different–and, believe you me, he's a holy terror when he once gets his teeth into a thing. Best save your pity for Mocata–he'll need it before De Richleau's through with him.'

'Is he–is he really an Ipsissimus then?' she hesitated.

'Lord knows–I don't. That's just a word I picked out of some jargon he was talking last night that I thought might impress you.' Rex grinned broadly. All the lying and trickery which he had been forced to practise during the morning had taxed him to the utmost, but now that he was able to face the situation openly he felt at the top of his form again.

'I daren't stay then–I daren't!' She tried to wrench herself free. 'Don't you see that if he is only some sort of dabbler he will never be able to protect me.'

'Don't fret your sweet self. No one shall lay a finger on you as long as I'm around.'

'But, you great fool, you don't understand,' she waved miserably. 'The Power of Darkness cannot be turned aside by bruisers or iron bars. If I don't appear at the meeting tonight, the moment I fall asleep Mocata will set the Ab-humans on to me. In the morning I may be dead or possessed–a raving lunatic.'

Rex did not laugh. He knew that she was genuinely terrified of an appalling possibility. Instead he turned her towards the house and said gently: 'Now please don't worry so. De Richleau does understand just how dangerous monkeying with this business is. He spent half the night trying to convince me of it, and like a fool I wouldn't believe him until I saw a thing I don't care to talk about, but I'm dead certain he'd never allow you to run any risk like that.'

'Then let me go back to London!'

'No. He asked me to get you here so as he could have a word with you–and I've done it. We'll have a quiet little lunch together now and talk this thing over when the Duke turns up. He'll either guarantee to protect you or let you go.'

'He can't protect me I tell you–and in any case I *wish* to attend this meeting tonight.'

'You wish to!' he echoed with a shake of the head. 'Well, that gets me beat, but you can't even guess what you'd be letting yourself in for. Anyhow I don't mean to let you–so now you know.'

'You mean to keep me here against my will?'

'Yes!'

'What is to stop me screaming for help?'

'Nix, but since the Duke's not here the servants know I'm in charge, so they won't bat an eyelid if you start to yell the house down–and there's no one else about.'

Tanith glanced swiftly down the drive. Except at the white gates tall banks of rhododendrons, heavy with bloom, obscured the lane. No rumble of passing traffic broke the stillness that brooded upon the well-kept garden. The house lay silent in the early summer sunshine. The inhabitants of the village were busy over the midday meal.

She was caught and knew it. Only her wits could get her out of this, and her fear of Mocata was so great that she was determined to use any chance that offered to free herself from this nice, meddling fool.

'You'll not try to prevent me leaving if De Richleau says I may when he arrives?' she asked.

'No. I'll abide by his decision,' he agreed.

'Then for the time being I will do as you wish.'

'Fine—come on.' He led her back to the house and rang for Max, who appeared immediately from the doorway of the dining-room.

'We've decided to lunch on the river.' Rex told him. 'Make up a basket and have it put in the electric canoe.' He had made the prompt decision directly he sensed that Tanith meant to escape if she could. Once she was alone in a boat with him he felt that, unless she was prepared to jump out and swim for it, he could hold her without any risk of a scene just as long as he wanted to.

'Very good, sir—I'll see to it at once.' Max disappeared into the domain of which he was lord and master, while Rex shepherded Tanith back to the neglected cocktails.

He refreshed the shaker while she sat on the sofa eyeing him curiously, but he persuaded her to have one, and when he pressed her she had another. Then Max appeared to announce that his orders had been carried out.

'Let's go—shall we?' Rex held open the french-windows and together they crossed the sunlit lawn, gay with its beds of tulips, polyanthus, wallflowers and forget-me-nots. At the river's edge, upon a neat, white painted landing-stage, a boatman held the long electric canoe ready for them.

Tanith settled herself on the cushions and Rex took the small perpendicular wheel. In a few moments they were chugging out into midstream and up the river towards Goring, but he preferred not to give her the opportunity of appealing to the lock-keeper, so he turned the boat and headed it towards a small backwater below the weir.

Having tied up beneath some willows, he began passing packages and parcels out of the stern. 'Come on,' he admonished her. 'It's the girl's job to see to the commissariat. Just forget yourself a moment and see what they've given us to eat.'

She smiled a little ruefully. 'If I really thought you realised what you were doing I should look on you as the bravest man I've ever known.'

He turned suddenly, still kneeling at the end of the boat. 'Go on—say it again. I love the sound of your voice.'

'You fool!' She coloured, laughing as she unwrapped the napkins. 'There's some cheese here—and ham and tongue—and brown bread—and salad—and a lobster. We shall never be able to eat all this and—oh, look,' she held out a small wicker basket, '*fraises des bois.*'

'Marvellous. I haven't tasted a wood strawberry since I last lunched at Fontainbleau. Anyhow, it's said the British Army fights on its stomach, so I'm electing myself an honorary member of it for the day. Fling me that corkscrew—will you, and I'll deal with this bottle of Moselle.'

Soon they were seated face to face propped against the cushions, a little sticky about the mouth, but enjoying themselves just as any nice normal couple would in such circumstances; but when the meal was finished he felt that, much as he would have liked to laze away the afternoon, he ought, now the cards were upon the table, to learn what he could of this grim business without waiting for the coming of the Duke. He unwrapped another packet which he had found in the stern of the boat, and passing it over asked half humorously:

'Tell me, does a witch ever finish up her lunch with chocolates? I'd be interested to know on scientific grounds.'

'Oh, why did you bring me back–I have been enjoying myself so much,' her face was drawn and miserable as she buried it in her hands.

'I'm sorry!' He put down the chocolates and bent towards her. 'But we're both in this thing, so we've got to talk of it, haven't we, and though you don't look the part, you're just as much a witch as any old woman who ever soured the neighbour's cream–else you'd never have seen me in that crystal this morning as I sat in the lounge of your hotel.'

'Of course I am if you care to use such a stupid old-fashioned term. She drew her hands away and tossed back her fair hair as she stared at him defiantly. 'That was only child's play–just to keep my hand in–a discipline to make me fit to wield a higher power.'

'For good?' he questioned laconically.

'It is necessary to pass through many stages before having to choose whether one will take the Right or Left Hand Path.'

'So I gather. But how about this unholy business in which you've a wish to take part tonight?'

'If I submit to the ordeal I shall pass the Abyss.' The low caressing voice lifted to a higher note, and the wise eyes suddenly took on a fanatic gleam.

'You can't have a notion what they mean to do to you or you'd never even dream of it,' he insisted.

'I have, but you know nothing of these things so naturally you consider me utterly shameless or completely mad. You are used to nice English and American girls who haven't a thought in their heads except to get you to marry them–if you have any money–which apparently you have, but that sort of thing does not interest me. I have worked and studied to gain power–real power over other people's lives and destinies–and I know now that the only way to acquire it is by complete surrender of self. I don't expect you to understand my motives but that is why I mean to go tonight.'

He studied her curiously for a moment, still convinced that she could not be fully aware of the abominations that would take place at the Sabbat. Then he broke out: 'How long is it since you became involved in this sort of thing?'

'I was psychic even as a child,' she told him slowly. 'My mother encouraged me to use my gifts. Then when she died I joined a society in Budapest. I loved her. I wanted to keep in touch with her still.'

'What proof have you got it was her?' he demanded with a sudden renewal of scepticism as he recalled the many newspaper exposures of spiritualistic séances.

'I had very little then, but since, I have been convinced of it beyond all doubt.'

'And is she–your own mother, still–yes, your guide–I suppose you'd call it?'

Tanith shook her head. 'No, she has gone on, and it was not for me to seek to detain her, but others have followed, and every day my knowledge of the worlds which lie beyond this grows greater.'

'But it's extraordinary that a young girl like you should devote yourself to this sort of thing. You ought to be dancing, dining, playing golf, going places—you're so lovely you could take your pick among the men.'

She shrugged a little disdainfully. 'Such a life is dull—ordinary—after a year I tired of it, and few women can climb mountains or shoot big game, but the conquest of the unknown offers the greatest adventure of all.'

Again her voice altered suddenly, and the inscrutable eyes which gave her a strange, serious beauty, so fitting for a lady of the Italian Renaissance, gleamed as before.

'Religions and moralities are man-made, fleeting and local; a scandalous lapse from virtue in London may be a matter for the highest praise in Hong Kong, and the present Archbishop of Paris would be shocked beyond measure if it was suggested that he had anything in common, beyond his religious office, with a Medieval Cardinal. One thing and one thing only remains constant and unchanging, the secret doctrine of the way to power. That is a thing to work for, and if need be cast aside all inherent scruples for—as I shall tonight.'

'Aren't you—just a bit afraid?' He stared at her solemnly.

'No, provided I follow the path which is set, no harm can come to me.'

'But it is an evil path,' he insisted, marvelling at the change which had come over her. It almost seemed as if it were a different woman speaking or one who repeated a recitation, learned in a foreign language, with all the appropriate expression yet not understanding its true meaning, as she replied with a cynical little smile.

'Unfortunately the followers of the Right Hand Path obsess themselves only with the well-being of the Universe as a whole, whereas those of the Left exercise their power upon living humans. To bend people to your will, to cause them to fall or rise, to place unaccountable obstacles in their path at every turn or smooth their way to a glorious success—that is more than riches, more than fame—the supreme pinnacle to which any man or woman can rise, and I wish to reach it before I die.'

'Maybe—maybe.' Rex shook his head with a worried frown, 'But you're young and beautiful—just breaking in on all the fun of life—why not think it over for a year or two? It's horrible to hear you talk as though you were a disillusioned old woman.'

Her mouth tightened still further. 'In a way I am—and for me, waiting is impossible because, although in your ignorance I do not expect you to believe it, as surely as the sun will set tonight I shall be dead before the year is out.'

13

THE DEFEAT OF REX VAN RYN

For a moment they sat in silence. The river flowed gently on; the sun still dappled the lower branches of the willows and flecked the water with points of light.

Gradually the fire died out of Tanith's eyes and she sank back against the cushions of the canoe as Rex stared at her incredulously. It seemed utterly impossible that there could be any real foundation for her grim prophecy, yet her voice had held such fatal certainty.

'It isn't true!' Rex seized her hand and gripped it as though, by his own vitality, he would imbue her with continued life. 'You're good for fifty years to come. That's only some criminal nonsense this devil Mocata's got you to swallow.'

'Oh, you dear fool!' She took his other hand and pressed it while, for a moment, it seemed as if tears were starting to her eyes. 'If things were different I think I might like you enormously, but I knew the number of my days long before I ever met Mocata, and there is nothing which can be done to lengthen them by a single hour.'

'Show me your hand,' he said suddenly. It was the only thing even remotely connected with the occult of which Rex had any knowledge. The year before he had ricked an ankle, while after Grizzly in the Rockies, and had had to lie up for a week at a tiny inn where the library consisted of less than a dozen battered volumes. A book on Palmistry, which he had discovered among them, had proved a real windfall and the study of it had whiled away many hours of his enforced idleness.

As Tanith held out her hand he saw at once that it was of the unusual psychic type. Very long, narrow and fragile, the wrist small, the fingers smooth and tapering, ending in long, almond-shaped nails. The length of the first, second and third fingers exceeded that of the palm by nearly an inch, giving the whole a beautiful but useless appearance. The top phalange of the thumb, he noted, was slim and pointed, another sign of lack of desire to grapple with material things.

'You see?' she turned it over showing him the palm. 'The Arabs say that "the fate of every man is bound about his brow," and mine is written here, for all who can, to read.'

Rex's knowledge of the subject was too limited for him to do much but read character and general tendencies by the various shapes of hands, but even he was startled by the unusual markings on the narrow palm.

On the cushion of the hand the Mount of the Moon stood out firm and strong, seeming to spread over and dominate the rest, a clear sign of an exceedingly strong imagination, refinement and love of beauty; but it was tinged with that rare symbol, the Line of Intuition, giving, in connection with such a hand, great psychic powers and a leaning towards mysticism of a highly dangerous kind. A small star below the second finger, upon the Mount of Saturn, caused him additional uneasiness and he looked in vain for squares which might indicate preservation at a critical period. Yet worst of all, the Line of Life, more clearly marked than he would have expected, stopped short with a horrifying suddenness at only a little over a third of the way from its commencement, where it was tied to the Line of Head.

He stared at it in silence, not knowing what to say to such sinister portents, but she smiled lightly as she withdrew her hand. 'Don't worry please, but there is no appeal from the verdict of the Stars and you will understand now why marriage–children–a lovely home–all things connected with the future just mean nothing to me.'

'So that's the reason you let yourself get mixed up in this horrible business?'

'Yes. Since I am to die so soon no ordinary emotion can stir me any more. I look as though I were already a great way from it, and what happens to my physical body matters to me not at all. Ten months ago I began seriously to cultivate my psychic sense under real instruction, and the voyages which I can make now into the immensity of the void are the only things left to me which still have power to thrill.'

'But, why in heaven's name involve yourself with Black Magic when you might practise White?'

'Have I not told you? The adepts of the Right Hand Path concern themselves only with the Great Work; the blending of the Microcosm with the Macrocosm; a vague philosophic entity in which one can witness no tangible results. Whereas, those of the Left practise their Art upon human beings and can actually watch the working of their spells.'

'I can't get over your wanting to attend this Satanic festival tonight all the same.'

'It should be an extraordinary experience.'

'Any normal person would be terrified at what might happen.'

'Well, if you like, I will admit that I am just a little frightened but that is only because it is my first participation. By surrendering myself I shall only suffer or enjoy, as most other women do, under slightly different circumstances at some period of their life.'

'Slightly different!' he exclaimed, noting again the sudden change of eyes and voice, as though she were *possessed* by some sinister dual personality which appeared every time she spoke of these horrible mysteries, and blotted out the frank, charming individuality which was natural to her. 'This thing seems worlds apart to me from picking a man you like and taking a sporting chance about the rest.'

'No, in ancient Egypt every woman surrendered herself at the temple before she married, in order that she might acquire virtue, and sacred prostitution is still practised in many parts of the world—for that is what this amounts to. Regarded from the personal point of view, of course, it is loathsome. If I thought of it that way I should never be able to go through with it at all, but I have trained myself not to, and only think of it now as a ritual which *has* to be gone through in order to acquire fresh powers.'

'It's mighty difficult for any ordinary person to see it that way—though I suppose the human brain can shut out certain aspects of a thing.' Rex paused, frowning: 'Still I was really speaking of the hideous danger you will incur from placing yourself in the hands of—well, the Devil if you like.'

She smiled. 'The Devil is only a bogey invented by the Early Church to scare fools.'

'Let's say the Power of Darkness then.'

'You mean by receiving re-Baptism?'

'By attending this Sabbat at all. I imagined from your strange name you had received re-Baptism already.'

'No, Tanith is the name by which I was Christened. It was my mother's choice.'

Rex sat forward suddenly. 'Then you haven't—er—given yourself over completely yet?'

'No, but I shall tonight, for if De Richleau has a tenth of the knowledge which you say he has he will realise the appalling danger to which I should be exposed if he detained me here, so he will let me go immediately he arrives–and remember, you have promised not to interfere with my freedom once he has seen me.'

'But listen,' he caught her hands again. 'It was bad enough that you should have been going to take a part in this abominable business as a graduate–it's a thousand times worse that you should do it while there's still time to back out.'

'Mocata would not allow me to now, even if I had the inclination, but you are so nice it really distresses me that you should worry so. The Satanic Baptism is only an old-fashioned and rather barbarous ritual, but it will give me real status among adepts, and no possible harm can come to me as long as I do not deviate from the Path which must be followed by all members of the Order.'

'You're wrong–wrong–wrong,' Rex insisted boldly. 'De Richleau was explaining the real horror of this thing to me last night. This promise of strange powers is only a filthy trap. At your first Christening your Godparents revoked the Devil and all his Works. Once you willingly rescind that protection, as you'll have to do, something awful will take possession of you and force you into doing its will, an Earthbound Spirit or an Elemental I think he called it.'

She shrugged. 'There are ways of dealing with Elementals.'

'Aw, hell. Why can't I make you understand!' He wrung his hands together desperately. 'It's easy to see they haven't called on you to do any real devilry yet. They've just led you on by a few demonstrations and encouraging your crystal gazing, but they will–once you're a full member–and then you'll be more scared than ever to refuse, or find it's just impossible under the influence of this thing that will get hold of you.'

'I'm sorry, but I don't believe you. It is I who will make use of them–not they of me, and quite obviously you don't know what you are talking about.'

'The Duke does,' he insisted, 'and he says that you can still get free as long as you haven't been actually re-baptiscd, but after that all holy protection is taken from you. Why else d'you think we took a chance of breaking up that party last night–if not to try and save Simon from the self-same thing.'

A queer light came into Tanith's eyes. 'Yet Mocata willed him to return so he will receive his nom-du-Diable after all tonight.'

'Don't you be too certain. I've a hunch we'll save him yet.' Rex spoke with a confidence he was very far from feeling.

'And how do you propose to set about it?' she asked with a quick intuition that by some means she might utilise this factor to facilitate her own escape.

'Ah! that's just the rub,' he admitted. 'You see we thought maybe you'd know his whereabouts and I'll be frank about it. That's the reason I went round to Claridges this morning, to see if I couldn't get you down here some way so as De Richleau could question you although I should have called on you anyway for a very different reason. Still you didn't even know Mocata had taken Simon off us till you spoke to the old woman on the wire, so it's pretty obvious you don't know where he is. I believe you could give us a line on Mocata though–if you choose to.'

'I was under the impression that it was at his house that the party where we met was given.'

'No, that was Simon's place, though I gather Mocata's been living there with him for some little time. He must have a hideout of his own somewhere though and that's what we want to get at.'

'I know nothing of his ordinary life, and if I did, I do not think I should be inclined to tell you of it, but why are you so interested in this Mr Aron? That was a lie you told me about your needing him because you are also searching for the Talisman of Set.'

'He's my very greatest friend, and more than that he risked his life to come out to Soviet Russia and look for me, when I was gaoled for poking my nose into the "Forbidden Territory," a few years back. The Duke came too, and he looks on Simon almost as a son.'

'That does not give you any right to interfere if, like myself, he elects to devote himself to the occult.'

'Maybe, as long as he confines himself to the harmless side, but De Richleau says the game that you and he are playing is the most hideously dangerous that's ever been known to mankind, and after what I saw last night I certainly believe him.'

'Simon Aron did not strike me as a fool. He must be aware of the risks which he is running and prepared to face them for the attainment of his desires.'

'I doubt it–I doubt if you do either. Anyhow, for the moment, we're regarding him as a person who's not quite all there, and nothing you can name is going to stop the Duke and me from saving him from himself if we get half a chance.'

Tanith felt that now was the time to show the bait in the trap which she had been preparing. So she leant forward and said, slowly: 'If you really are so mad as to wish for a chance to pit yourselves against Mocata, I think I could give it to you.'

'Could you?' Rex jerked himself upright and the water gurgled a little at the sides of the canoe.

'Yes, I don't know if he has a house of his own anywhere, but I do know where he will be this evening–and your friend Simon will be with him.'

'You mean the Sabbat eh? And you'll give me the name of the place where it's being held?'

'Oh, no.' The sunlight gleamed golden on her hair as she shook her head. 'But I'll let you take me to it, if you agree to let me go free once we are there.'

'Nothing doing,' he said bluntly.

'I see,' she smiled, 'you are afraid of Mocata after all. Well, that doesn't surprise me because he has ample means of protecting himself against anything you could attempt against him. That is why, of course, I feel that, providing the place is not given away beforehand, he would prefer me to let you know it than detain me here–I'm quite honest you see, but evidently you are not so confident of yourself or interested in your friend as I thought.'

Rex was thinking quickly. Nothing but an actual order from the Duke, based on his assurance that Mocata might punish Tanith in some terrible manner if she failed to appear, would have induced him to let her go to the Sabbat, but on the other hand this was a real chance to reach Simon, in fact, the only one that offered. 'Do you require that I should actually hand you over to Mocata when we get there?' he asked at length.

'No. If you take me to the place that will be sufficient, but there must be no question of gagging me or tying me up.'

In an agony of indecision he pondered the problem again. Dare he risk taking Tanith within the actual sphere of Mocata's influence? Yet he would have the Duke with him, so surely between them they would be able to restrain her from taking any part in the ceremony, and it was impossible to throw away such a chance of saving Simon.

'I'm not giving any promise to let you join the party,' Rex said firmly.

'Well, I intend to do so.'

'That remains to be seen–but I'll accept your offer on those conditions.'

She nodded, confident now that once they reached their destination Mocata would exercise his powers to relieve her of restraint.

'The place must be about seventy miles from here,' she told him, 'and I should like to be there by sundown, so we ought to leave here by six.'

'Wouldn't it be possible to start later?' A worried frown clouded Rex's face. 'The truth is, that message Max gave us before lunch was phony–just a part of my plan for keeping you here. I never did count on De Richleau arriving much before the time you say we ought to start–and I'd just hate to leave without him.'

Tanith smiled to herself. This was an unexpected piece of luck. She had only met the Duke for a moment the night before, but his lean, cultured face and shrewd, grey eyes had impressed her. She felt that he would prove a far more difficult opponent than this nice, bronzed young giant, and if she could get away without having to face him after all, it would be a real relief, so she made a wry face and proceeded to elaborate her story.

'I'm sorry, but there are certain preparations which have to be made before the gathering. They begin at sunset, so I must be at–well, the place to which we are going by a quarter past eight. If I arrive later I shall not be eligible to participate–so I will not go at all.'

'In that case I guess I'm in your hands. Anyhow, now we've settled things, let's get back to the house.' Rex untied the canoe and, setting the motor in motion, steered back to the landing stage.

His first thought was to inform De Richleau of the bargain that he had made, but after pleading once more with the officials at the British Museum to have the Duke sought for, he learned that he was no longer there, and when he got through to the Curzon Street flat the servants could tell him nothing of De Richleau's whereabouts, so it was impossible to expedite his arrival.

For a time Rex strolled up and down the lawn with Tanith, then round the lovely garden, while he talked again of the places that they had both visited abroad and tried to recapture something of the gaiety which had marked their drive down from London in the morning.

Max brought them tea out onto the terrace, and afterwards they played the electric gramophone, but even that failed to relieve Rex of a steadily deepening anxiety that the Duke might not arrive in time.

The shadows of the lilacs and laburnums began to lengthen on the grass, Tanith went upstairs to tidy herself, and when she came down asked if he could find her a road map. He produced a set and for a time she studied two of them in silence, then she refolded them and said quietly: 'I know so little of the English country but I am certain now that I can find it. We must be leaving soon.'

It was already six o'clock, and he had put off shaking a cocktail until the last moment in order to delay their departure as long as possible. Now, he rang for ice as he said casually: 'Don't fuss, I'll get you there by a quarter after eight.'

'I'll give you five minutes–no more.'

'Well, listen now. Say De Richleau fails to make it. Won't you give me a break? Let me know the name of the place so as I can leave word for him to follow?'

She considered for a moment. 'I will give you the name of a village five miles from it where he can meet you on one condition.'

'Let's hear it.'

'That neither of you seek to restrain me in any way once we reach our destination.'

'No. I'll not agree to that.'

'Then I certainly will not give you any information which will enable your friend to appear on the scene and help you.'

'I'll get him there some way–don't you worry.'

'That leaves me a free hand to prevent you if I can–doesn't it?'

As he swallowed his cocktail she glanced at the clock. 'It's ten past now, so unless you prefer not to go we must start at once.'

Consoling himself with the thought that De Richleau could have got no more out of her even if he had questioned her himself, Rex led her out and settled her in the Rolls. Then, before starting up the engine, he listened intently for a moment, hoping that even yet he might catch the low, steady purr of the big Hispano which would herald the Duke's eleventh hour arrival, but the evening silence brooded unbroken over the trees and lane. Reluctantly he set the car in motion and as they ran down the gravel sweep, Tanith said quietly, 'Please drive to Newbury.'

'But that's no more than twenty miles from here!'

'Oh, I will give you further directions when we reach it,' she smiled, and for a little time they drove in silence through the quiet byways until they entered the main Bath road at Theale.

At Newbury, she gave fresh instructions. 'To Hungerford now,' and the fast, low, touring Rolls sped out of the town eating up another ten miles of the highway to the west.

'Where next?' he asked, scanning the houses of the market town for its most prosperous-looking inn and mentally registering *The Bear*. It was just seven o'clock–another few miles and they would be about half-way to the secret rendezvous. He did not dare to stop in the town in case she gave him the slip and hired another car or went on by train, but when they were well out in the country again he meant to telephone the Duke, who must have arrived at Pangbourne by this time, and urge him to follow as far as Hungerford at once–then sit tight at *The Bear* until he received further information.

Tanith was studying the map. 'There are two ways from here,' she said, 'but I think it would be best to keep to the main road as far as Marlborough.'

A few miles out of Hungerford the country became less populous with only a solitary farmhouse here and there, peaceful and placid in the evening light. Then these, too, were left behind and they entered a long stretch of darkening woodlands, the northern fringe of Savernake Forest.

Both were silent, thinking of the night to come which was now so close upon them and the struggle of wills that must soon take place. Rex brought the car down to a gentle cruising speed and watched the road-sides intently. At a deserted hair-pin bend, where a byway doubled back to the south-east, he found just what he wanted, a telephone call-box.

Turning the car off the main road he pulled up, and noted with quick appreciation that they had entered one of the most beautiful avenues he had ever seen. As far as the eye could see it cut clean through the forest, the great branches meeting overhead in the sombre gloom of the falling night, it looked like the nave of some titanic cathedral deserted by mankind; but he had no leisure to admire it to the full, and stepping out, called to Tanith over his shoulder: 'Won't be a minute—just want to put through a call.'

She smiled, but the queer look that he had seen earlier in the day came into her eyes again. 'So you mean to trick me and let De Richleau know the direction we have taken?'

'I wouldn't call it that,' he protested. 'In order to get in touch with Simon I bargained to take you to this place you're so keen to get to, but I reserved the right to stop you taking any part yourself, and I need the Duke to help me.'

'And I agreed, because it was the only way in which I could get away from Pangbourne, but I reserved the right to do all in my power to attend the meeting. However,' she shrugged lightly, 'do as you will.'

'Thanks.' Rex entered the box, spoke to the operator, and having inserted the necessary coins, secured his number. Next minute he was speaking to De Richleau. 'Hullo! Rex here. I've got the girl and she's agreed—Oh, Hell!'

He dropped the receiver and leapt out of the box. While his back was turned Tanith had moved into the driver's seat. The engine purred, the Rolls slid forward. He clutched frantically at the rear mudguard but his fingers slipped and he fell sprawling in the road. When he scrambled to his feet the long blue car was almost hidden by a trail of dust as it roared down the avenue, and while he was still cursing his stupidity, it disappeared into the shadows of the forest.

14
THE DUKE DE RICHLEAU TAKES THE FIELD

At 7.20. Rex was through again to the Duke, gabbling out the idiotic way in which he had allowed Tanith to fool him and leave him stranded in Savernake Forest.

At 7.22. De Richleau had heard all he had to tell and was ordering him to return to Hungerford as best he could, there to await instructions at *The Bear*.

At 7.25. Tanith was out of the Forest and on a good road again, some five miles south-east of Marlborough, slowing down to consult her map.

At 7.26. The Duke was through to Scotland Yard.

At 7.28. Rex was loping along at a steady trot through the gathering darkness, praying that a car would appear from which he could ask a lift.

At 7.30. De Richleau was speaking to the Assistant Commissioner at the Metropolitan Police, a personal friend of his. 'It's not the car that matters,' he said, 'but the documents which are in it. Their immediate recovery is of vital importance to me and I should consider it a great personal favour if any reports which come in may be sent at once to the Police Station at Newbury.'

At 7.32. Tanith was speeding south towards Tidworth, having decided that to go round Salisbury Plain via Amesbury would save her time on account of the better roads.

At 7.38. Scotland Yard was issuing the following *communiqué* by wireless: 'All stations. Stolen. A blue touring Rolls, 1934 model. Number OA 1217. Owner, Duke de Richleau. Last seen in Savernake Forest going south-east at 19 hours 15, but reported making for Marlborough. Driven by woman. Age twenty-three—attractive appearance—tall, slim, fair hair, pale face, large hazel eyes, wearing light green summer costume and small hat. Particulars required by Special Department. Urgent. Reports to Newbury.'

At 7.42. De Richleau received a telephone call at Pangbourne. 'Speakin' fer Mister Clutterbuck,' said the voice, 'bin tryin' ter get yer this lars' arf hour, sir. The green Daimler passed through Camberley goin' south just arter seven o'clock.'

At 7.44 Tanith was running past the military camp at Tidworth still going south.

At 7.45. Rex was buying a second-hand bicycle for cash at three times its value from a belated farm-labourer.

At 7.48. The Duke received another call. 'I have a special from Mr Clutterbuck,' said a new voice. 'The Yellow Sports Sunbeam passed Devizes going south at 7.42.'

At 7.49. Tanith reached the Andover-Amesbury road and turned west along it.

At 7.54. De Richleau climbed into his Hispano. 'My night glasses—thank you,' he said as he took a heavy pair of binoculars from Max. 'Any messages which come in for me up to 8.25 are to be relayed to the police at Newbury, after that to Mr Van Ryn at the *Bear Inn*, Hungerford, up till 8.40, and from then on to the police at Newbury again.'

At 7.55. Tanith was approaching a small cross-roads on the outskirts of Amesbury. A Police-Sergeant who had left the station ten minutes earlier spotted the number of her car, and stepping out into the road called on her to halt. She swerved violently, missing him by inches, but managed to swing the car into the by-road leading north.

At 7.56. Rex was pedalling furiously along the road to Hungerford with all the strength of his muscular legs.

At 7.58. Tanith, livid with rage that Rex should have put the police on to her as though she were a common car thief, had spotted another policeman near the bridge in Bulford village. Not daring to risk his holding her up in the narrow street, she switched up another side-road leading north-east.

At 7.59. The Amesbury Police-Sergeant dropped off a lorry beside the constable on duty at the main cross-roads of the town and warned him to watch out for a Blue Rolls, number OA 1217, recklessly driven by a young woman who was wanted by the Yard.

At 8.1. Tanith had slowed down and was wondering desperately if she dared risk another attempt to pass through Amesbury. Deciding against it she ran on, winding in and out through the narrow lanes, to the north-eastward.

At 8.2. Rex had abandoned his bicycle outside the old Almshouses at Froxfield and was begging a lift from the owner of a rickety Ford who was starting into Hungerford.

At 8.3. The Amesbury Police-Sergeant was reporting to Newbury the appearance of the 'wanted' Rolls.

At 8.4. Tanith pulled up, hopelessly lost in a tangle of twisting lanes.

At 8.6. De Richleau swung his Hispano on to the main Bath road. His cigar tip glowed red in the twilight as he sank his chin into the collar of his coat and settled down to draw every ounce out of the great powerful car.

At 8.8. Tanith had discovered her whereabouts on the map and found that she had been heading back towards the Andover road.

At 8.9. The Amesbury Police-Sergeant was warning the authorities at Andover to keep a look-out for the stolen car in case it headed back in that direction.

At 8.10. Tanith had turned up a rough track leading north through some woods in the hope that it would enable her to get past the Military Camp at Tidworth without going through it.

At 8.12. Rex was hurrying into *The Bear* inn at Hungerford.

At 8.14. Tanith was stuck again, the track having come to an abrupt end at a group of farm buildings.

At 8.17. The Duke was hurtling along the straight, about five miles east of Newbury.

At 8.19. Tanith was back at the entrance of the track and turning into a lane that led due east.

At 8.20. The Amesbury Police-Sergeant left the station again. He had completed his work of warning Salisbury, Devizes, Warminster and Winchester to watch for the stolen Rolls.

At 8.21. Tanith came out on the main Salisbury-Marlborough road and, realising that there was nothing for it but to chance being held up at Tidworth, turned north.

At 8.22. Rex had sunk his second tankard of good Berkshire ale and took up his position in the doorway of *The Bear* to watch for the Duke.

At 8.23. Tanith, possessed now, it seemed, by some inhuman glee, chortled with laughter as a Military Policeman leapt from the road to let her flash past the entrance of Tidworth Camp.

At 8.24. De Richleau entered Newbury Police Station and learned that the Blue Rolls had been sighted in Amesbury half an hour earlier.

At 8.25. Tanith had pulled up, a mile north of Tidworth, and was studying her map again. She decided that her only hope of reaching the secret rendezvous now lay in taking the by-roads across the northern end of Salisbury Plain.

At 8.26. The Duke was reading two messages which had been handed to him by the Newbury Police. One said: 'Green Daimler passed through Basingstoke going west at 7.25. Max per Clutterbuck,' and the other, 'Green Daimler passed through Andover going west at 8.0. Max per Clutterbuck.' He nodded, quickly summing up the position to himself. 'Green is heading west through Amesbury by now, and Blue was seen making in the same direction, while Yellow took the other route and is coming south from Devizes—most satisfactory so far.' He then turned to the Station Sergeant: 'I should be most grateful if you would have any further messages which may come for me relayed to Amesbury. Thank you—Good night.'

At 8.27. Tanith had reached a cross-road two miles north of Tidworth and turning west took a dreary wind-swept road which crosses one of the most desolate parts of the Plain. Dusk had come and with it an overwhelming feeling that whatever happened she must be present at the meeting. The fact that she was about seventeen miles farther from her destination than she had been at Amesbury did not depress her, for she had misled Rex as to the vital necessity of her being there by sunset, and the actual Sabbat did not begin until midnight.

At 8.32. Rex was taking a message over the telephone of *The Bear* at Hungerford.

At 8.35. Tanith was passing the Aerodrome at Upavon, and forced to slow down owing to the curving nature of the road ahead.

At 8.37. De Richleau's Hispano roared into Hungerford, and Rex, who had resumed his position in the doorway of *The Bear*, ran out to meet it. 'Any messages?' the Duke asked as he scrambled in.

'Yep–Max called me. A bird named Clutterbuck says a Yellow Sunbeam passed through Westbury heading south at five minutes past eight.'

'Good,' nodded the Duke, who already had the car in motion again.

At 8.38. Tanith was free of the twisting patch of road by Upavon and out on the straight across the naked Plain once more. If only she could keep clear of the police, she felt that she would be able to reach the meeting-place in another forty-five minutes. A wild, unnatural exaltation drove her on as the Blue Rolls ate up the miles towards the west.

At 8.39. Rex was asking: 'What is all this about a Yellow Sunbeam anyway? It was a Blue Rolls I got stung for.' And the Duke replied, with his grey eyes twinkling: 'Don't worry about the Rolls. The police saw your young friend with it in Amesbury a little after eight. They will catch her for us you may be certain.'

At 8.40. The police at Newbury were relaying a message from Max for the Duke to their colleagues at Amesbury.

At 8.41. De Richleau was saying: 'Don't be a fool, Rex. I only said that I could not call in the police unless these people committed *some definite breach of the law*. Car stealing is a crime, so I have been able to utilise them in this one instance–that's all.'

At 8.44. Two traffic policemen on a motor-cycle combination, which had set out from Devizes a quarter of an hour before, spotted the back number-plate of Blue Rolls number OA 1217 as it switched to the left at a fork road where they were stationed, but Tanith had caught sight of them, and her headlights streaked away, cutting a lane through the darkness to the south-westward.

At 8.45. The Hispano was rocking from side to side as it flew round the bends of the twisting road south-west of Hungerford. The Duke had heard Rex's account of the way Tanith had tricked him but refused to enlighten him about the Yellow Sunbeam. 'No, no,' he said impatiently. 'I want to hear every single thing you learned from the girl–I'll tell you my end later.'

At 8.46. The traffic policemen had their machine going all out and were in full cry after the recklessly driven Rolls.

At 8.47. The Police at Newbury were relaying a second message from Max for the Duke to their colleagues at Amesbury.

At 8.48. Tanith saw the lights of Easterton village looming up in the distance across the treeless grassland as she hurtled south-westward in the Rolls.

At 8.49. The traffice policeman in the side-car said: 'Steady, Bill–we'll get her in a minute.'

At 8.50. The Hispano had passed the cross-roads nine miles south-west of

Hungerford and come out on to the straight. De Richleau had now heard everything of importance which Rex had to tell and replied abruptly to his renewed questioning: 'For God's sake don't pester me now. It's no easy matter to keep this thing on the road when we're doing eighty most of the time.'

At 8.51. Tanith clutched desperately at the wheel of the Rolls as with screaming tyres it shot round the corner of the village street. The police siren in her ears shrilled insistently for her to halt. She took another bend practically on two wheels, glimpsed the darkness of the open country again for a second then, with a rending, splintering crash, the off-side mudguards tore down a length of wooden palings. The car swerved violently, dashed up a steep bank then down again, rocking and plunging, until it came to rest, with a sickening thud, against the back of a big barn.

At 9.8. The Duke, with Rex beside him, entered Amesbury Police Station and the two messages which had been 'phoned through from Newbury were handed to him. The first read: 'Green Daimler passed through Amesbury going west at 8.15,' and the second, 'Yellow Sunbeam halted Chilbury 8.22.' Both were signed 'Max per Clutterbuck.'

As De Richleau slipped them into his pocket an Inspector came out of an inner room. 'We've got your car, sir,' he said cheerfully. 'Heard the news only this minute. Two officers spotted the young woman at the roads south of Devizes and gave chase. She made a mucker of that bad bend in Easterton village. Ran it through a garden and up a steep bank.'

'Is she hurt?' asked Rex anxiously.

'No, sir–can't be. Not enough to prevent her hopping out and running for it. I reckon it was that bank that saved her and the car too–for I gather it's not damaged anything to speak of.'

'Has she been caught?' inquired the Duke.

'Not yet, sir, but I expect she will be before morning.'

As De Richleau nodded his thanks, and spread out a map to find the village of Chilbury, the desk telephone shrilled. The constable who answered it scribbled rapidly on a pad and then passed the paper over to him. 'Here's another message for you, sir.'

Rex glanced over the Duke's shoulder and read, 'Green Daimler halted Chilbury 8.30. Other cars parked in vicinity and more arriving. Will await you cross-roads half a mile south of village. Clutterbuck.'

De Richleau looked up and gave a low chuckle. 'Got them!' he exclaimed. 'Now we can talk.'

At 9.14. They were back in the car.

15

THE ROAD TO THE SABBAT

The big Hispano left the last houses of Amesbury behind and took the long, curving road across the Plain to the west. De Richleau, driving now at a moderate pace, was at last able to satisfy Rex's curiosity.

'It is quite simple, my dear fellow. Immediately I learned from you that Madame D'Urfé was leaving Claridges for the Sabbat at four o'clock, I realised that in her we had a second line of inquiry. Having promised to meet you at Pangbourne, I couldn't very well follow her myself, so I got in touch with an ex-superintendent of Scotland Yard named Clutterbuck, who runs a Private Inquiry Agency.'

'But I thought you said we must handle this business on our own,' Rex protested.

'That is so, and Clutterbuck has no idea of the devilry that we are up against. I only called him in for the purpose of tracing cars and watching people, which is his normal business. After I had explained what I wanted to him he arranged for half a dozen of his assistants to be in readiness with motor-cycles. Then I took him round to Claridges in order to point the old woman out to him. As luck would have it, I spotted the Albino that we saw at the party last night come out at half past three and drive off in the Yellow Sports Sunbeam, so that gave us a third line, and Clutterbuck sent one of his men after him. The Countess left in the Green Daimler a good bit after four, and that's why I was delayed in getting down to Pangbourne. Clutterbuck trailed her in his own car, and directly we knew that she was making for the west, sent the rest of his squad ahead in order to pick her up again if by chance he lost her. That is how the reports of the movements of the two cars came through to me.'

'How about Mocata? He was at Claridges when Tanith 'phoned the old woman, round about half past one!'

'Unfortunately, he must have left by the time I came on the scene, but it doesn't matter, because he is certain to be with the rest.'

Rex grinned. 'It was a pretty neat piece of staff work.'

The few miles across the Plain were soon eaten up, and the Duke had scarcely finished giving Rex particulars of his campaign when they reached the lonely wind-swept cross-roads half a mile south of Chilbury. A car was drawn up at the side of the road and near it a group of half a dozen men with motor-cycles stood talking in low voices. As the Hispano was brought to a standstill, a tall, thin man left the group and came over to De Richleau.

'The persons you are wanting are in the big house on the far side of the village, sir,' he said. 'You can't miss it because the place is surrounded by trees, and they are the only ones hereabouts.'

'Thank you,' De Richleau nodded. 'Have you any idea how many people have arrived for this party?'

'I should think a hundred or so at a rough guess. There are quite fifty cars parked in the grounds at the back of the house, and some of them had two or three occupants. Will you require my assistance any further?'

'Not now. I am very pleased with the way in which you have handled this little affair, and should I need your help later on, I will get in touch with you again.'

Rex nudged the Duke just as he was about to dismiss Clutterbuck. 'If there's a hundred of them, we won't stand an earthly on our own. Why not keep these people? Eight or nine of us might be able to put up a pretty good show!'

'Impossible,' De Richleau replied briefly, while the detective eyed the two of them with guarded interest, wondering what business they were engaged upon but satisfied in his own mind that, since Rex had suggested retaining him, he had not lent himself to anything illegal. 'If there's nothing else I can do then, sir,' he said, touching his hat, 'I and my men will be getting back to London.'

'Thank you,' De Richleau acknowledged the salute. 'Good night.' As the detective turned away, he let out the clutch of the Hispano.

With the engine just ticking over, they slipped through the silent village. Most of the cottages were already in darkness. The only bright light came from the tap-room of the tiny village inn, while the dull glow from curtained windows in one or two of the upper rooms of the houses showed that those inhabitants of the little hamlet who were not already in bed would very shortly be there.

To the south of the road, on the far side of the village, they came upon a thick belt of ancient trees extending for nearly a quarter of a mile and, although no house was visible behind the high stone wall that shut them in, they knew from Clutterbuck's description that this must be the secret rendezvous.

A chalky lane followed the curve of the wall where it left the main road and, having driven a hundred yards along it, they turned the car so that it might be in immediate readiness to take the road again, and parked it on a grassy slope that edged the lane.

As the Duke alighted, he pulled out a small suitcase. 'These are the results of my morning's research at the British Museum,' he said, opening it up.

Rex leaned forward curiously to survey the strange assortment of things the case contained: a bunch of white flowers, a bundle of long grass, two large ivory crucifixes, several small phials, a bottle–apparently of water–and a number of other items; but he stepped quickly back as a strong, pungent, unpleasant odour struck his nostrils.

De Richleau gave a grim chuckle. 'You don't like the smell of the Asafottida grass and the Garlic flowers, eh? But they are highly potent against evil my friend, and if we can only secure Simon they will prove a fine protection for him. Here, take this crucifix.'

'What'll I do with it?' Rex asked, admiring for a moment the beautiful carving on the sacred symbol.

'Hold it in your hand from the moment we go over this wall, and before your face if we come upon any of these devilish people.'

While De Richleau was speaking, he had taken a little plush box from the suitcase, and out of it a rosary from which dangled a small, gold cross. Reaching up, he hung it about Rex's neck, explaining as he did so: 'Should you drop the big one, or if it is knocked from your hand by some accident, this will serve as a reserve defence. In addition, I want you to set another above a horse-shoe in your aura.'

'How d'you mean?' Rex frowned, obviously puzzled.

'Just imagine if you can that you are actually wearing a horse-shoe surmounted by a crucifix on your forehead. Think of it as glowing there in the darkness an inch or so above your eyes. That is an even better protection than any ordinary material symbol, but it is difficult to concentrate sufficiently to keep it there without long practice, so we must wear the sign as well.' The Duke placed a similar rosary round his own neck and took two small phials from the open case. 'Mercury and Salt,' he added. 'Place one in each of your breast pockets!'

Rex did as he was bid. 'But why are we wearing crucifixes when you put a swastika on Simon before?' he asked.

'I was wrong. That is the symbol of Light in the East, where I learned what little I know of the Esoteric Doctrine. There, it would have proved an adequate barrier, but here, where Christian thoughts have been centred on the Cross for many centuries, the crucifix has far more potent vibrations.'

He took up the bottle and went on: 'This is holy water from Lourdes, and with it I shall seal the nine openings of your body that no evil may enter it at any one of them. Then you must do the same for me.'

With swift gestures, the Duke made the sign of the cross in holy water upon Rex's eyes, nostrils, lips, etc., and then Rex performed a similar service for him.

De Richleau picked up the other crucifix and shut the case. 'Now we can start,' he said. 'I only wish that we had a fragment of the Host apiece. That is the most powerful defence of all, and with it we might walk unafraid into hell itself. But it can only be obtained by a layman after a special dispensation, and I had no time to plead my case for that today.'

The night was fine and clear, but only a faint starlight lit the surrounding country, and they felt rather than saw the rolling slopes of the Plain which hemmed in the village and the house, where they were set in a sheltered dip. The whole length of the high stone wall was fringed, as far as they could see, by the belt of trees, and through their thick, early-summer foliage no glimpse of light penetrated to show the exact position of the house.

Since no sound broke the stillness—although a hundred people were reported to be gathered there—they judged the place to be somewhere in the depths of the wood at a good distance from the wall; yet despite that, as they walked quickly side by side down the chalky lane, they spoke only in whispers, lest they disturb the strange stillness that brooded over that night-darkened valley.

At length they found the thing that they were seeking, a place where the old wall had crumbled and broken at the top. A pile of masonry had fallen into the lane, making a natural step a couple of feet in height, and from it they found no difficulty in hoisting themselves up into the small breach from which it had tumbled.

As they slipped down the other side, they paused for a moment, peering through the great tree-trunks, but here on the inside of the wall beneath the wide-spreading branches of century-old oaks and chestnuts they were in pitch darkness, and could see nothing ahead other than the vague outline of the trees.

'*In manus tuas, domine,*' murmured the Duke, crossing himself; then holding their crucifixes before them they moved forward stealthily, their feet crackling the dry twigs with a faint snapping as they advanced.

After a few moments the darkness lightened and they came out on the edge of a wide lawn. To their left, two hundred yards away, they saw the dim, shadowy bulk of a rambling old house, and through a shrubbery which separated them from it, faint chinks of light coming from the ground floor windows. Now, too, they could hear an indistinct murmur, which betrayed the presence of many people.

Keeping well within the shadow of the trees, they moved cautiously along until they had passed the shrubbery and could get a clear view of the low, old-fashioned mansion. Only the ground-floor windows showed lights and these were practically obscured by heavy curtains. The upper stories were dark and lifeless.

Still in silence, and instinctively agreeing upon their movements, the two friends advanced again and began to make a circle of the house. On the far side they found the cars parked just as Clutterbuck had described, upon a gravel sweep, and counted up to fifty-seven of them.

'By Jove,' Rex breathed. 'This lot would rejoice an automobile salesman's heart.'

The Duke nodded. Not more than half a dozen out of the whole collection were ordinary, moderately-priced machines. The rest bore out De Richleau's statement that the practitioners of the Black Art in modern times were almost exclusively people of great wealth. A big silver Rolls stood nearest to them; beyond it a golden Bugatti. Then a supercharged Mercedes, another Rolls, an Isotta Fraschini whose bonnet alone looked as big as an Austin Seven, and so the line continued with Alfa Romeos, Daimlers, Hispanos and Bentleys, nearly every one distinctive of its kind. At a low estimate there must have been £100,000 worth of motor-cars parked in that small area.

As they paused there for a moment a mutter of voices and a sudden burst of laughter came from a ground-floor window. Rex tip-toed softly forward across the gravel. De Richleau followed and, crouching down with their heads on a level with the low sill, they were able to see through a chink in the curtains into the room.

It was a long, low billiards-room with two tables, and the usual settees ranged along the walls. Both tables were covered with white cloths upon which were piles of plates, glasses, and an abundant supply of cold food. About the room, laughing, smoking and talking, were some thirty chauffeurs who, having delivered their employers at the rendezvous, were being provided with an excellent spread to keep them busy and out of the way.

The Duke touched Rex on the shoulder, and they tiptoed quietly back to the shelter of the bushes. Then, making a circle of the drive, they passed round the other side of the house, which was dark and deserted, until they came again to the lighted windows at the back which they had first seen.

The curtains of these had been more carefully drawn than those of the billiards-room where the chauffeurs were supping, and it was only after some difficulty that they found a place at one where they were able to observe a small portion of the room. From what little they could see, the place seemed to be a large reception-room, with parquet floor, painted walls and Italian furniture.

The head of a man, who was seated with his back to the window, added to their difficulty in seeing into the room but the glimpse they could get was sufficient to show that all the occupants of it were masked and their clothes hidden under black dominoes, giving them all a strangely funereal appearance.

As the man by the window turned his head De Richleau, who was occupying their vantage point at the time, observed that his hair was grey and curly and that he had lost the top portion of his left ear, which ended in a jagged piece of flesh. The Duke felt that there was something strangely familiar in that mutilated ear, but he could not for the life of him recall exactly where he had seen it. Not at Simon's party, he was certain but, although he watched the man intently, no memory came to aid his recognition.

The others appeared to be about equal numbers of both sexes as far as the Duke could judge from the glimpses he got of them as they passed and repassed the narrow orbit of his line of vision. The masks and dominoes made it particularly difficult for him to pick out any of the Satanists whom he had seen at the previous party but, after a little, he noticed a man with a dark-skinned fleshy neck and thin black hair whom he felt certain was the Babu, and a little later a tall, lank, fair-haired figure who was undoubtedly the Albino.

After a time Rex took his place at their observation post. A short, fat man was standing now in the narrow line of sight. A black mask separated his pink, bald head from the powerful fleshy chin—it could only be Mocata. As he watched, another domino came up, the beaky nose, the bird-like head, the narrow, stooping shoulders of which must surely belong to Simon Aron.

'He's here,' whispered Rex.

'Who—Simon?'

'Yes. But how we're going to get at him in this crush is more than I can figure out.'

'That has been worrying me a lot,' De Richleau whispered back. 'You see, I have had no time to plan any attempt at rescue. My whole day has been taken up with working at the Museum and then organising the discovery of this rendezvous. I had to leave the rest to chance, trusting that an opportunity might arise where we could find Simon on his own if they had locked him up, or at least with only a few people, when there would be some hope of our getting him away. All we can do for the moment is to bide our time. Are there any signs of them starting their infernal ritual?'

'None that I can see. It's only a "conversation piece" in progress at the moment.'

De Richleau glanced at his watch. 'Just on eleven,' he murmured, 'and they won't get going until midnight, so we have ample time before we need try anything desperate. Something may happen to give us a better chance before that.'

For another ten minutes they watched the strange assembly. There was no laughter but, even from outside the window, the watchers could sense a tenseness in the atmosphere and a strange suppressed excitement. De Richleau managed to identify the Eurasian, the Chinaman and old Madame D'Urfé with her parrot beak. Then it seemed to him that the room was gradually emptying. The man with the mutilated ear, whose head had obscured their view, stood up and moved away and the low purr of a motor-car engine came to them from the far side of the house.

'It looks as if they're leaving,' muttered the Duke; 'perhaps the Sabbat is not to be held here after all. In any case, this may be the chance we're looking for. Come on.'

Stepping as lightly as possible to avoid the crunching of the gravel, they stole back to the shrubbery and round the house to the place where the cars were parked. As they arrived a big car full of people was already running down the drive. Another was in the process of being loaded up with a number of hampers and folding tables. Then that also set off with two men on the front seat.

Rex and De Richleau, crouching in the bushes, spent the best part of half an hour watching the departure of the assembly.

Every moment they hoped to see Simon. If they could only identify him among those dark shapes that moved between the cars they meant to dash in and attempt to carry him off. It would be a desperate business but there was no time left in which to make elaborate plans; under cover of darkness and the ensuing confusion there was just a chance that they might get away with it.

No chauffeurs were taken and a little less than half the number of cars utilised. Where the guests had presumably arrived in ones, twos, and threes, they now departed crowded five and six apiece in the largest of the cars.

When only a dozen or so of the Satanists were left the Duke jogged Rex's arm. 'We've missed him I'm afraid. We had better make for our own car now or we may lose track of them,' and, filled with growing concern at the difficulties which stood between them and Simon's rescue, they turned and set off at a quick pace through the trees to the broken place in the wall.

Scrambling over, they ran at a trot down the lane. Once in the car, De Richleau drove it back on to the main road and then pulled up as far as possible in the shadow of the overhanging trees. A big Delage came out of the park gates a hundred yards farther along the road and turning east sped away through the village.

'Wonder if that's the last.' Rex said softly.

'I hope not,' De Richleau replied. 'They have been going off at about two-minute intervals, so as not to crowd the road and make too much of a procession of it. If it is the last, they would be certain to see our lights and become suspicious. With any luck the people in the Delage will take us for the following car if we can slip in now, and the next to follow will believe our rear light to be that of the Delage.' He released his brake, and the Hispano slid forward.

On the far side of the village they picked up the rear light of the Delage moving at an easy pace and followed to the cross-roads where they had met Clutterbuck an hour and a half earlier. Here the car turned north along a by-road, and they followed for a few miles upward on to the higher level of the desolate rolling grassland, unbroken by house or farmstead, and treeless except for, here and there, a coppice set upon a gently sloping hillside.

Rex was watching out of the back window and had assured himself that another car was following in their rear, for upon that open road motor headlights were easily visible for miles.

They passed through the village of Chitterne St Mary, then round the steep curve to the entrance of its twin parish, Chitterne All Saints. At the latter the car which they were following switched into a track running steeply uphill to the north-east, then swiftly down again into a long valley bottom and up the other side on to a higher crest. They came to a cross-roads where four tracks met in another valley and turned east to run on for another mile, bumping and skidding on the little-used, pathlike way. After winding a little, the car ahead suddenly left the track altogether and ran on to the smooth short turf.

After following the Delage for a mile or more across the grass, De Richleau saw it pull up on the slope of the downs where the score or so of cars which had brought the Satanists to this rendezvous were parked in a ragged line. He swiftly dimmed his lights, and ran slowly forward, giving the occupants of the Delage time to leave their car before he pulled up the Hispano as far from it as he dared without arousing suspicion in the others. The car following, which seemed to be the last in the procession, passed quite close to them and halted ten yards ahead, also disgorging its passengers. Rex and the Duke waited for a moment, still seated in the darkness of the Hispano, then after a muttered conference, Rex got out to go forward and investigate.

He returned after about ten minutes to say that the Satanists had gone over the crest of the hill into the dip beyond, carrying their hampers and their gear with them.

'We had better drive on then,' said the Duke, 'and park our car with theirs. It's likely to be noticed if the moon gets up.'

'There isn't a moon,' Rex told him. 'We're in the dark quarter. But it would be best to have it handy all the same.'

They drove on until they reached the other cars, all of whose lights had been put out, then, getting out, set off at a stealthy trot in the direction the Satanists had taken.

Within a few moments, they arrived at the brow of the hill and saw that spread below them lay a natural amphitheatre. At the bottom, glistening faintly, lay a small tarn or lake, and De Richleau nodded understandingly.

'This is the place where the devilry will actually be done without a doubt. No Sabbat can be held except in a place which is near open water.' Then the two friends lay down in the grass to watch for Simon among the dark group of figures who were moving about the water's edge.

Some were busy unpacking the hampers, and erecting the small folding-tables which they had brought. The light was just sufficient for Rex to see that they were spreading upon them a lavish supper. As he watched, he saw a group of about a dozen move over to the left towards a pile of ancient stones which, in the uncertain light, seemed to form a rugged, natural throne.

De Richleau's eyes were also riveted upon the spot and, to his straining gaze, it seemed that there was a sudden stirring of movement in the shadows there. The whole body of masked black-clad figures left the lake and joined those near the stones, who seemed to be their leaders. After a moment the watchers could discern a tall, dark form materialising on the throne and, as they gazed with tense expectancy, a faint shimmer of pale violet light began to radiate from it.

Even at that distance, this solitary illumination of the dark hollow was sufficient for the two friends to realise that the thing which had appeared out of the darkness, seated upon those age-old rocks, was the same evil entity that De Richleau had once taken for Mocata's black servant, and which had manifested itself to Rex with such ghastly clarity in Simon's silent house. The Sabbat was about to commence.

16

THE SABBAT

Straining their eyes and ears for every sound and movement from the assembly in the dark shadows below, Rex and the Duke lay side by side on the rim of the saucer-shaped depression in the downland.

As far as they could judge, they were somewhere about halfway between the two hamlets of Imber and Tilshead, with Chitterne All Saints in their rear and the village of Easterton, where Tanith had crashed, about five miles to the north. The country round about was desolate and remote. Once in a while some belated Wiltshire yokel might cross the plain by night upon a special errand created by emergency; but even if such a one had chanced to pass that way on this Walpurgis-Nacht, the hidden meeting-place–guarded by its surrounding hills–was far from the nearest track, and at that midnight hour no living soul seemed to be stirring within miles of the spot which the Satanists had chosen for the worship of their Infernal Master.

In the faint starlight they could see that the tables were now heaped with an abundance of food and wine, and that the whole crowd had moved over towards the throne round which they formed a wide circle, so that the nearest came some little way up the slope and were no more than fifty yards from where the Duke and Rex lay crouched in the grass.

'How long does it last?' Rex asked, beneath his breath, a little nervously.

'Until cock-crow, which I suppose would be at about four o'clock at this time of the year. It is a very ancient belief that the crowing of a cock has power to break spells, so these ceremonies, in which the power to cast spells is given, never last longer. Keep a sharp look out for Simon.'

'I am, but what will they be doing all that time?'

First, they will make their homage to the Devil. Then they will gorge themselves on the food that they have brought and get drunk on the wine; the idea being that everything must be done contrary to the Christian ritual. They will feast to excess as opposed to the fasting which religious people undergo before their services. Look! There are the leaders before the altar now.'

Rex followed the Duke's glance, and saw that half a dozen black figures were placing tall candles–eleven of them in a circle and the twelfth inside it–at the foot of the throne.

As they were lighted the twelve candles burned steadily in the windless night with a strong blue flame, illuminating a circle of fifty feet radius including the tables where the feast was spread. Outside this ring the valley seemed darker than before, filled with pitch-black shadows so that the figures in the area of light stood out clearly as though upon a bright circular stage.

'Those things they have lighted are the special black candles made of pitch and sulphur,' muttered the Duke. 'You will be able to smell them in a minute. But look at the priests: didn't I tell you that there is little difference between this modern Satanism and Voodoo? We might almost be witnessing some heathen ceremony in an African jungle!'

While the crowd had been busy at the tables, their leaders had donned fantastic costumes. One had a huge cat mask over his head and a furry cloak, the tail of which dangled behind him on the ground; another wore the headdress of a repellent toad; the face of a third, still masked, gleamed bluish for a moment in the candle-light from between the distended jaws of a wolf, and Mocata, whom they could still recognise by his squat obesity, now had webbed wings sprouting from his shoulders which gave him the appearance of a giant bat.

Rex shivered. 'It's that infernal cold again rising up the hill,' he said half-apologetically. 'Say–look at the thing on the throne. It's changing shape.'

Until the candles had been lit, the pale violet halo which emanated from the figure had been enough to show that it was human and the face undoubtedly black. But as they watched, it changed to a greyish colour, and something was happening to the formation of the head.

'It is the Goat of Mendes, Rex!' whispered the Duke. 'My God! this is horrible!' And even as he spoke, the manifestation took on a clearer shape; the hands, held forward almost in an attitude of prayer but turned downward, became transformed into two great cloven hoofs. Above rose the monstrous bearded head of a gigantic goat, appearing to be at least three times the size of any other which they had ever seen. The two slit-eyes, slanting inwards and down, gave out a red baleful light. Long pointed ears cocked upwards from the sides of the shaggy head, and from the bald, horrible unnatural bony skull, which was caught by the light of the candles, four enormous curved horns spread out—sideways and up.

Before the apparition the priests, grotesque and terrifying beneath their beast-head masks and furry mantles, were now swinging lighted censers, and after a little a breath of the noisome incense was wafted up the slope.

Rex choked into his hand as the fumes caught his throat, then whispered: 'What is that filth they're burning?'

'Thorn, apple leaves, rue, henbane, dried nightshade, myrtle and other herbs,' De Richleau answered. 'Some are harmless apart from their stench, but others drug the brain and excite the senses to an animal fury of lust and eroticism as you will see soon enough. If only we could catch sight of Simon,' he added desperately.

'Look, there he is!' Rex exclaimed. 'Just to the left of the toad-headed brute.'

The goat rose, towering above the puny figures of its unhallowed priests, and turned its back on them; upon which one stooped slightly to give the osculam-infame as his mark of homage. The others followed suit, then the whole circle of Satanists drew in towards the throne and, in solemn silence, followed their example, each bending to salute his master in an obscene parody of the holy kiss which is given to the Bishop's ring.

Simon was among the last, and as he approached the throne, Rex grabbed De Richleau's arm. 'It's now or never,' he grunted. 'We've got to make some effort. We can't let this thing go through.'

'Hush,' De Richleau whispered back. 'This is not the baptism. That will not be until after they have feasted—just before the orgy. Our chance *must* come.'

As the two lay there in the rough grass, each knew that the time was close at hand when they must act if they meant to attempt Simon's rescue. Yet, despite the fact that neither of them lacked courage, both realised with crushing despondency how slender their chances of success would be if they ran down the slope and charged that multitude immersed in their ghoulish rites. There were at least a hundred people in that black-robed crowd and it seemed an utter impossibility to overcome such odds.

Rex leaned over towards the Duke and voiced his thoughts aloud, 'We're right up against it this time unless you can produce a brainwave. We'd be captured in ten seconds if we tried getting Simon away from this bunch of maniacs.'

'I know,' De Richleau agreed miserably. 'I did not bargain for them all being shut up together in one room in that house or coming on to this place in a solid crowd. If only they would split up a little we might isolate Simon with just two or three of them, down the rest, and get him away before the main party knew what was happening; but as things are I am worried out of my wits. If we charge in, and they catch us, I have not a single doubt but that we should never be allowed to come up out of this hollow alive. We know too much, and they would kill us for a certainty. In fact, they would probably welcome the chance on a night like this to perform a little human sacrifice in front of that ghastly thing on the stones there.'

'Surely they wouldn't go in for murder even if they do practise this filthy parody of religion?' whispered Rex incredulously.

De Richleau shook his head. 'The Bloody Sacrifice is the oldest magical rite in the world. The slaying of Osiris and Adonis, the mutilation of Attis and the cults of Mexico and Peru, were all connected with it. Even in the Old Testament you read that the sacrifice which was most acceptable to God the Father was one of blood, and St Paul tells us that "Without the shedding of blood there is no remission".'

'That was just ancient heathen cruelty.'

'Not altogether. The blood is the Life. When it is shed, energy—animal or human as the case may be—is released into the atmosphere. If it is shed within a specially prepared circle, that energy can be caught and stored or redirected in precisely the same way as electric energy is caught and utilised by our modern scientists.'

'But they wouldn't dare to sacrifice a human being?'

'It all depends upon the form of evil they wish to bring upon the world. If it is war they will seek to propitiate Mars with a virgin ram; if they desire the spread of unbridled lust—a goat, and so on. But the human sacrifice is more potent for all purposes than any other, and these wretched people are hardly human at the moment. Their brains are diseased and their mentality is that of the hags and warlocks of the Dark Ages.'

'Oh, Hell!' Rex groaned, 'we've simply got to get Simon out of this some way.'

The Goat turned round again after receiving the last kiss, holding between its hoofs a wooden cross about four feet in length. With a sudden violent motion it dashed the crucifix against the stone, breaking it into two pieces. Then the cat-headed man, who seemed to be acting the part of Chief Priest, picked them up. He threw the broken end of the shaft towards a waiting group, who pounced upon it and smashed it into matchwood with silent ferocity, while he planted the crucifix end upside down in the ground before the Goat. This apparently concluded the first portion of the ceremony.

The Satanists now hurried over to the tables where the banquet was spread out. No knives, forks, spoons or glasses were in evidence. But this strange party, governed apparently by a desire to throw themselves back into a state of bestiality, grabbed handfuls of food out of the silver dishes and, seizing the bottles, tilted them to drink from the necks, gurgling and spitting as they did so and spilling the wine down their dominoes. Not one of them spoke a word, and the whole macabre scene was carried out in a terrible unnatural silence, as though it were a picture by Goya come to life.

'Let's creep down nearer,' whispered the Duke. 'While they are gorging themselves an opportunity may come for us to get hold of Simon. If he moves a few paces away from them for a moment, don't try to argue with him, but knock him out.'

At a stealthy crawl, the two friends moved down the hillside to within twenty yards of the little lake, at the side of which the tables were set. The throne still occupied by the monstrous goat was only a further fifteen yards away from them, and by the light of the twelve black candles burning with an unnaturally steady flame even in that protected hollow among the hills, they could see the clustered figures sufficiently well to recognise those whom they knew among them despite their masks and dominoes.

Simon, like the rest, was gnawing at a chunk of food as though he had suddenly turned into an animal, and, as they watched, he snatched a bottle of wine from a masked woman standing nearby, spilling a good proportion of its contents over her and himself; then he gulped down the rest.

For a few moments Rex felt again that he *must* be suffering from a nightmare. It seemed utterly beyond understanding that any cultured man like Simon or other civilised people such as these must normally be, could behave with such appalling bestiality. But it was no nightmare. In that strange, horrid silence, the Satanists continued for more than half an hour to fight and tumble like a pack of wolfish dogs until the tables had been overthrown and the ground about the lakeside was filthy with the remaining scraps of food, gnawed bones and empty bottles.

At last Simon, apparently three parts drunk, lurched away from the crash and flung himself down on the grass a little apart from the rest, burying his head between his hands.

'Now!' whispered the Duke. 'We've got to get him.'

With Rex beside him, he half rose to his feet, but a tall figure had broken from the mass and reached Simon before they could move. It was the man with the mutilated ear, and in another second a group of two women and three more men had followed him. De Richleau gritted his teeth to suppress an oath and placed a restraining hand on Rex's shoulder.

'It's no good,' he muttered savagely. 'We must wait a bit. Another chance may come.' And they sank down again into the shadows.

The group about the tables was now reeling drunk, and the whole party in a body surged back towards the Goat upon its throne. Rex and De Richleau had been watching Simon so intently they had failed to notice until then that Mocata and the half dozen other masters of the Left Hand Path had erected a special table before the Goat, and were feeding from it. Yet they appeared strangely sober compared with the majority of the crowd who had fed beside the lake.

'So the Devil feeds, too,' Rex murmured.

'Yes,' agreed the Duke, 'or at least the heads of his priesthood, and a gruesome meal it is if I know anything about it. A little cannibalism, my friend. It may be a stillborn baby or perhaps some unfortunate child that they have stolen and murdered, but I would stake anything that it is human flesh they are eating.'

As he spoke, a big cauldron was brought forward and placed before the throne. Then Mocata and the others with him each took a portion of the food which they had been eating from the table and cast it into the great iron pot. One of them threw in a round ball which met the iron with a dull thud.

Rex shuddered as he realised that the Duke was right. The round object was a human skull.

'They're going to boil up the remains with various other things,' murmured the Duke, 'and then each of them will be given a little flask of that awful brew at the conclusion of the ceremony, together with a pile of ashes from the wood fire they are lighting under the cauldron now. They will be able to use them for their infamous purposes throughout the year until the next Great Sabbat takes place.'

'Oh, Hell!' Rex protested. 'I can't believe that they can work any harm with that human mess, however horrid it may be. It's just not reasonable.'

'Yet you believe that the Blessed Sacrament has power for good,' De Richleau whispered. 'This is the antithesis of the Body of Our Lord, and I assure you, Rex, that, while countless wonderful miracles have been performed by the aid of the Host, terrible things can be accomplished by this blasphemous decoction.'

Rex had no deep religious feeling, but he was shocked and horrified to the depths of his being by this frightful parody of the things he had been taught to hold sacred in his childhood.

'Dear God,' muttered the Duke, 'they are about to commit the most appalling sacrilege. Don't look, Rex—don't look.' He buried his face in his hands and began to pray, but Rex continued to watch despite himself, his gaze held by some terrible fascination.

A great silver chalice was being passed from hand to hand, and very soon he realised the purpose to which it was being put, but could not guess the intention until it was handed back to the cat-headed man. One of the other officiating priests at the infamy produced some round white discs which Rex recognised at once as Communion Wafers—evidently stolen from some church.

In numbed horror he watched the Devil's acolytes break these into pieces and throw them into the brimming chalice, then stir the mixture with the broken crucifix and hand the resulting compound to the Goat, who, clasping it between its great cloven hoofs, suddenly tipped it up so that the whole contents was spilled upon the ground.

Suddenly, at last, the horrid silence was rent, for the whole mob surged forward shouting and screaming as though they had gone insane, to dance and stamp the fragments of the Holy Wafers into the sodden earth.

'Phew!' Rex choked out, wiping the perspiration from his forehead. 'This is a ghastly business. I can't stand much more of it. They're mad, stark crazy, every mother's son of them.'

'Yes, temporarily.' The Duke looked up again. 'Some of them are probably epileptics, and nearly all must be abnormal. This revolting spectacle represents a release of all their pent-up emotions and suppressed complexes, engendered by brooding over imagined injustice, lust for power, bitter hatred of rivals in love or some other type of success and good fortune. That is the only explanation for this terrible exhibition of human depravity which we are witnessing.'

'Thank God, Tanith's not here. She couldn't have stood it. She'd have gone mad, I know, or tried to run away. And then they'd probably have murdered her. But what *are* we going to do about Simon?'

De Richleau groaned. 'God only knows. If I thought there were the least hope, we'd charge into this rabble and try to drag him out of it, but the second they saw us they would tear us limb from limb.'

The fire under the cauldron was burning brightly, and as the crowd moved apart Rex saw that a dozen women had now stripped themselves of their dominoes and stood stark naked in the candle-light. They formed a circle round the cauldron, and holding hands, with their backs turned to the inside of the ring, began a wild dance around it anti-clockwise towards the Devil's left.

In a few moments the whole company had stripped off their dominoes and joined in the dance, tumbling and clawing at one another before the throne, with the exception of half a dozen who sat a little on one side, each with a musical instrument, forming a small band. But the music which they made was like no other that Rex had ever heard before, and he prayed that he might never hear the like again. Instead of melody, it was a harsh, discordant jumble of notes and broken chords which beat into the head with a horrible nerve-racking intensity and set the teeth continually on edge.

To this agonising cacophony of sound the dancers, still masked, quite naked and utterly silent but for the swift movement of their feet, continued their wild, untimed gyrations, so that rather than the changing pattern of an ordered ballet the scene was one of a trampling mass of bestial animal figures.

Drunk with an inverted spiritual exaltation and excess of alcohol—wild-eyed and apparently hardly conscious of each other—the hair of the women streaming disordered as they pranced, and the panting breath of the men coming in laboured gasps—they rolled and lurched, spun and gyrated, toppled, fell, picked themselves up again, and leaped with renewed frenzy in one revolting carnival of mad disorder. Then, with a final wailing screech from the violin, the band ceased and the whole party flung themselves panting and exhausted upon the ground, while the huge Goat rattled and clacked its monstrous cloven hoofs together and gave a weird laughing neigh in a mockery of applause.

De Richleau sat up quickly. 'God help us, Rex, but we've got to do something now. When these swine have recovered their wind the next act of this horror will be the baptism of the Neophytes and after that the foulest orgy, with every perversion which the human mind is capable of conceiving. We daren't wait any longer. Once Simon is baptised, we shall have lost our last chance of saving him from permanent and literal Hell in this life and the next.'

'I suppose it's just possible we'll put it off now they've worked themselves into this state?' Rex hazarded doubtfully.

'Yes, they're looking pretty done at the moment,' the Duke agreed, striving to bolster up his waning courage for the desperate attempt.

'Shall we—shall we chance it?' Rex hesitated. He too was filled with a horrible fear as to the fate which might overtake them once they left the friendly shadows to dash into that ring of evil blue light. In an effort to steady his frayed nerves, he gave a travesty of a laugh, and added: 'The odds aren't quite so heavy against us now they've lost their trousers. No one fights his best like that.'

'It's not the pack that I'm so frightened of, but that ghastly thing sitting on the rocks.' De Richleau's voice was hoarse and desperate. 'The protections I have utilised may not prove strong enough to save us from the evil which is radiating from it.'

'If we have faith,' gasped Rex, 'won't that be enough?'

De Richleau shivered. The numbing cold which lapped up out of the hollow in icy waves seemed to sap all his strength and courage.

'It would,' he muttered. 'It would if we were both in a state of grace.'

At that pronouncement Rex's heart sank. He had no terrible secret crime with which to charge himself, but although circumstances had appeared to justify it at the time, both he and the Duke had taken human life, and who, faced with the actual doorway of the other world, can say that they are utterly without sin?

Desperately now he fought to regain his normal courage. In the dell the Satanists had recovered their wind and were forming in the great semi-circle again about the throne. The chance to rescue Simon was passing with the fleeting seconds, while his friends stood crouched and tongue-tied, their minds bemused by the reek of the noxious incense which floated up from the hollow, their bodies chained by an awful, overwhelming fear.

Three figures now moved out into the open space before the Goat. Upon the left the beast-like, cat-headed high priest of Evil; upon the right Mocata, his gruesome bat's wings fluttering a little from his hunched-up shoulders; between them, naked, trembling, almost apparently in a state of collapse, they supported Simon.

'It's now or never!' Rex choked out.

'No—I can't do it,' moaned the Duke, burying his face in his hands and sinking to the ground. 'I'm afraid, Rex. God forgive me, I'm afraid.'

17

EVIL TRIUMPHANT

As the blue Rolls, number OA 1217, came to rest with a sickening thud against the back of the big barn outside Easterton Village, Tanith was flung forward against the windscreen. Fortunately the Duke's cars were equipped with splinter-proof glass and so the windows remained intact, but for the moment she was half-stunned by the blow on her head and painfully 'winded' by the wheel, which caught her in the stomach.

For a few sickening seconds she remained dazed and gasping for breath. Then she realised that she had escaped serious injury, and that the police would be on her at any moment. Her head whirling, her breath stabbing painfully, she threw open the door of the Rolls and staggered out on to the grass.

In a last desperate effort to evade capture, she lurched at an unsteady run across the coarse tussocks and just as the torches of the police appeared over the same hillock, which had slowed down the wild career of the car, she flung herself down in a ditch, sheltered by a low hedge, some thirty yards from the scene of the accident.

She paused there only long enough to regain her breath, and then began to crawl away along the runnel until it ended on the open plain. Taking a stealthy look over the hedge, she saw her pursuers were still busy examining the car, so she took a chance and ran for it, trusting in the darkness of the night to hide her from them.

After she had covered a mile she flopped exhausted to the ground, drawing short gulping breaths into her straining lungs—her heart thudding like a hammer. When she had recovered a little, she looked back to find that the village and the searching officers were now hidden from her by a sloping crest of down-land. It seemed that she had escaped—at least for the time being—and she began to wonder what she had better do.

From what she remembered of the map, the house at Chilbury where the

Satanists were gathering preparatory to holding the Great Sabbat was at least a dozen miles away. It would be impossible for her to cover that distance on foot even if she were certain of the direction in which it lay, and the fact that she was wanted by the police debarred her from trying to seek a lift in a passing car if she were able to find the main road again. In spite of her desperate attempt to reach the rendezvous in the stolen Rolls, and the frantic excitement of her escape from the police, she found to her surprise that a sudden reaction had set in, and she no longer felt that terrible driving urge to be present at the Sabbat.

Her anger against Rex had subsided. She had tricked him over the car, and he had retaliated by putting the police on her track. She realised now that he could only have done it on account of his overwhelming anxiety to prevent her from joining Mocata, and smiled to herself in the darkness as she thought again of his anxious, worried face as he had tried so hard that afternoon on the river to dissuade her from what she had only considered, till then, to be a logical step in her progress towards gaining supernatural powers.

She began to wonder seriously for the first time if he was not right, and that during these last months which she had spent with Madame D'Urfé her brain had become clouded almost to the point of mania by this obsession to the exclusion of all natural and reasonable thoughts. She recalled those queer companions who were travelling the same path as herself, most of them far further advanced upon it, of whom she had seen so much in recent times. The man with the hare-lip, the one-armed Eurasian, the Albino and the Babu. They were not normal any one of them and, while living outwardly the ordinary life of monied people, dwelt secretly in a strange sinister world of their own, flattering themselves and each other upon their superiority to normal men and women on account of the strange powers that they possessed, yet egotistical and hard-hearted to the last degree.

This day spent with the buoyant, virile Rex among the fresh green of the countryside and the shimmering sunlight of the river's bank, had altered Tanith's view of them entirely; and now, in a great revulsion of feeling, she could only wonder that her longing for power and forgetfulness of her fore-ordained death had blinded her to their cruel way of life for so long.

She stood up and, smoothing down her crumpled green linen frock, did her best to tidy herself. But she had lost her bag in the car smash, so not only was she moneyless but had no comb with which to do her hair. However, feeling that now Rex had succeeded in preventing her reaching the meeting-place he would be certain to call off the police, she set out at a brisk pace away from Easterton towards where she believed the main Salisbury-Devizes road to lie; hoping to find a temporary shelter for the night and then make her way back to London in the morning.

Before she had gone two hundred yards, her way was blocked by a tall, barbed-wire fence shutting in some military enclosure, so she turned left along it. Two hundred yards farther on the fence ended, but she was again brought up by another fence and above it the steep embankment of a railway line. She hesitated then, not wishing to turn back in the direction of Easterton, and was wondering what it would be best to do, when a dark hunched figure seemed to form out of the shadows beside her. She started back, but recovered herself at once on realising that it was only a bent old woman.

'You've lost your way, dearie?' croaked the old crone.

'Yes.' Tanith admitted. 'Can you show me how I get on to the Devizes road?'

'Come with me, my pretty. I am going that way myself,' said the old woman in a husky voice, which seemed to Tanith in some strange way vaguely familiar.

'Thank you.' She turned and walked along the bridle-path that followed the embankment to the west, searching her mind as to where she could have heard that husky voice before.

'Give me your hand, dearie. The way is rough for my old feet,' croaked the ancient crone; and Tanith willingly offered her arm. Then, as the old woman rested a claw upon it, a sudden memory of long ago flooded her mind.

It was of the days when, as a little girl living in the foothills of the Carpathians, she had made a friend of an old gypsy-woman who used to come to the village for the fair and local Saints' Days, with her band of Ziganes. It was from her that Tanith had first learned her strange powers of clairvoyance and second sight. Many a time she had scrambled down from the rocky mount upon which her home was set to the gypsy encampment outside the village to gaze with marvelling eyes at old Mizka who knew so many wonderful things, and could tell of the past and of the future by gazing into a glass of water or consulting her grimy pack of Tarot cards.

Tanith could still see those pasteboards which had such fascinating pictures upon them. The twenty-two cards of the Major Arcana, said by some to be copies of the original *Book of Thoth*, which contained all wisdom and was given to mankind by the ancient ibis-headed Egyptian god. For thousands of years such packs had been treasured and reproduced from one end of the world to the other and were treasured still, from the boudoirs of modern Paris to the tea-houses of Shanghai, wherever people came secretly in the quiet hours to learn, from those who could read them, the secrets of the future.

As she walked on half unconscious of her strange companion, Tanith recalled them in their right and fateful order. The *Juggler* with his table—meaning mental rectitude; the *High Priestess* like a female Pope—wisdom; the *Empress*—night and darkness; the *Emperor*—support and protection; the *Pope*—reunion and society; the *Lovers*—marriage; the *Chariot*—triumph and despotism; *Justice*, a winged figure with sword and scales—the law; the *Hermit* with his lantern—a pointer towards good; the *Wheel of Fortune* carrying a cat and a demon round with it—success and wealth; *Strength*, a woman wrenching open the jaws of a lion—power and sovereignty; the *Hanged Man* lashed by his right ankle to a beam and dangling upside down while holding two money bags—warning to be prudent; *Death* with his scythe—ruin and destruction; *Temperance*, a woman pouring liquid from one vase to another—moderation; the *Devil*, batwinged, goatfaced, with a human head protruding from his belly—force and blindness; the *Lightning-struck Tower* with people falling from it—want, poverty and imprisonment; the *Star*—disinterestedness; the *Moon*—speech and lunacy; the *Sun*—light and science; the *Judgement*—typifying will; the *World*, a naked woman with goat and ram below—travel and possessions; then last but not least the card that has no number, the *Fool*, foretelling dementia, rapture and extravagance.

Old Mizka had been a willing teacher, and Tanith, the child, an eager pupil, for she had spent a lonely girlhood in that castle on the hill separated by miles of jagged valleys difficult to traverse from other children of her own position, and debarred by custom from adopting the children of the villagers as her playmates. Long before her time she had learned all the secrets of life from the old gypsy, who talked for hours in her husky voice of lovers and marriage and lovers again, and potions to bring sleep to suspicious husbands and philtres which could warm the heart of the coldest man towards a woman who desired his caresses.

'Mizka,' Tanith whispered suddenly. 'It is you—isn't it?'

'Yes, dearie. Yes—old Mizka has come a long way tonight to set her pretty one upon the road.'

'But how did you ever come to England?'

'No matter, dearie. Don't trouble your golden head about that. Old Mizka started you upon the road, and she has been sent to guide your feet tonight.'

Tanith hung back for a second in sudden alarm, but the claw upon her arm urged her forward again with gentle strength as she protested.

'But I don't want to go! Not . . . not to the . . .'

The old crone chuckled. 'What foolishness is this? It is the road that you have taken all your life, ever since Mizka told you of it as a little girl. Tonight is the night that old Mizka has seen for so many years in her dreams—the night when you shall know all things, and be granted powers which come to few. How fortunate you are to have this opportunity when you are yet so young.'

At the old woman's silken words, a new feeling crept into Tanith's heart. She had been dwelling upon Rex's face as she crossed the Plain, and all the health-giving freshness of his gay clean modernity, but now she was drawn back into another world; the one of which she had thought so long, in which a very few chosen people could perform the seemingly impossible—bend others to their will—cause them to fall or rise—place unaccountable obstacles in their path at every turn, or smooth their way to a glorious success. That was more than riches, more than fame; the supreme pinnacle to which any man or woman could rise, and all her longing to reach those heights before she died came back to her. Rex was a pleasant, stupid child; De Richleau a meddlesome fool, who did not understand the danger of the things with which he was trying to interfere. Mocata was a Prince in power and knowledge. She should be unutterably grateful that he had considered her worthy of the honour which she was about to receive.

'It is not far, dearie. Not so far as you have thought. The great Festival does not take place in the house at Chilbury. That was only a meeting place, and the Sabbat is to be held upon these downs only a few miles from here. Come with me, and you shall receive the knowledge and the power that you seek.'

A curtain of forgetfulness seemed to be falling over Tanith's mind—a feeling of intoxication—mental and physical, flooded through her. She felt her eyes closing . . . closing . . . as she muttered: 'Yes. Knowledge and Power. Hurry, Mizka! Hurry, or we shall be too late.'

All her previous hesitations had now been blotted out, and although they were walking over coarse grass, it seemed to her that they trod a smooth and even way. Her mind was obsessed again with the sole thought of reaching the Sabbat in time.

'That is my own beautiful one talking now,' crooned the old beldame in a

honeyed voice. 'But have no fear, the night is young, and we shall reach the
meeting-place of the Covens before the hour when our Master will appear.'

Tanith was holding herself stiffly as she walked. Her golden head thrown
back, her eyes dilated to an enormous size–the muscles at the sides of her
mouth twitched incessantly as the old woman's smooth babble flowed on.

They crossed the road, although Tanith was hardly conscious of it as, with
Mizka beside her, she stepped out, a new strength surging through her
despite her long and tiring day. Then as she mounted an earthy bank a dark
and furry presence brushed against her legs, and looking down she saw the
golden eyes of a great black cat.

For a moment she was startled, but the old woman chuckled in the
darkness. 'It is only Nebiros,' she muttered. 'You have played with him
often as a child, dearie, and he is so pleased to see you now.'

The cat mewed with pleasure as Tanith stooped for a moment to stroke its
furry back. Then they hastened on again.

For hours it seemed they tramped over the grassy tussocks, up gently-
sloping hills and down again into lonesome valleys unbroken by trees or
cottages or farmsteads, ever on to the secret place where the Satanists would
be gathering now, until old Mizka, walking at Tanith's left, suddenly pulled
up–clutching at her arm with her bony hand.

'Shut your eyes, dearie,' she hissed in a sharp whisper, 'Shut your eyes.
There is something here that it is not good for you to see. I will guide you.'

Tanith did as she was bid mechanically, and although she could no longer
see the rough ground over which they were passing, she did not stumble but
continued to step forward evenly at a good pace. Yet she had a feeling that
she was no longer alone with the old woman, but that a third person was now
walking with them at her right hand. Then, a low voice, bell-like and clear,
sounded in her ears.

'Tanith, my darling. Look at me, I implore you.'

At the shock of hearing that well-loved voice, the curtain lifted for a
moment and Tanith opened her eyes again. To her right, she saw the figure
of her mother dressed in white as she had last seen her before she had set out
to some great party where she had died of a sudden heart attack. Round her
neck hung a rope of pearls, and her head was adorned with a half-hoop of
diamond stars. The figure shone by some strange unnatural light in the
surrounding darkness, seeming as pure and translucent as carved crystal.

'My dear one,' the voice went on, 'my folly of encouraging your gift of
second sight has led you into terrible peril. I beg you by all that is good and
holy to draw back while there is yet time.'

Despite the urging hand which clawed upon her arm, Tanith stumbled for
the first time in the long grass and, wrenching her arm away, stood still. In a
flash of insight which seared through her drugged brain, she knew then that
old Mizka was not a living being, but a Dark Angel sent to lead her to the
Sabbat, and that her mother had come at this moment from the world
beyond as an Angel of Light to draw her back again into the safety and
protection of holy things.

Mizka was babbling and crowing upon her left, urging her onward with a
terrible force and intensity. The words 'power'–'crowning your
life'–'mastery of all' came again and again in her rapid speech, and Tanith
moved a few steps forward. But her mother's voice, imploring again, came
clearly in her ears.

'Tanith, my darling, I am only allowed to appear to you because of your great danger, and for the briefest space. I am called back already, but I beg you in the name of the love that we had for each other, not to go. There is a better influence in your life. Trust in it while there is still time, otherwise you will be dragged down into the pit and we shall never meet again.' Suddenly the voice changed, becoming cold and commanding. 'Back, Mizka—back whence you came. I order you by the names of Isis, mother of Horus, Kwan-Yin, mother of Hau-Ki, and Mary, mother of Our Lord.'

The voice ceased on a thin wall as though, all unwillingly, the spirit had been drawn back while its abjuration to the demon was only half completed. With a wild cry and arms outstretched, Tanith dashed forward to the place where that nebulous moon-white being had floated, but where the apparition of her mother had been a second before, only a little breeze ruffled the long grasses. A feeling of immense fatigue bowed her shoulders as she turned towards old Mizka and the cat. But they too had vanished.

She sank upon her knees and began to pray, feverishly at first and then less strongly, until her tongue tripped upon the words and at last she fell silent. Almost unconsciously she rose to her feet and found herself, the night wind playing gently in her hair, standing upon a hilltop gazing down into a shallow valley.

A new and terrible fear gripped at her heart, for she saw below her, by the strange unearthly light of a ring of blue candles, the Satanists gathering for their unholy ceremony, and knew that evil powers had led her feet by devious paths to the place of the Great Sabbat that she might participate after all.

She stood for a moment, the blood draining from her face, quick tremors of horror and apprehension running down her body. She wanted to turn and flee into the dark, protective shadows of the night, but she could not tear her eyes away from that terrible figure seated upon the rocky throne, before which the Satanists were making their obscene obeisance. Some terrible uncanny power kept her feet rooted to the spot, and although her mother's warning still rang in her ears, she could not drag her gaze away from that blasphemous mockery of God proceeding in a horrid silence a hundred yards down the slope from where she stood.

Time ceased to exist for Tanith then. An unearthly chill seemed to creep up out of the valley, swirling and eddying about her legs as a cold current suddenly strikes a bather in a warm patch of sea. The chill crept upward to the level of her breasts, numbing her limbs and dulling her faculties until she could have cried out with the pain. She watched the gruesome banquet with loathing and repulsion, but as she saw those ghoul-like figures tilting the bottles to their mouths she was suddenly beset by an appalling desire to drink.

Although her limbs were cold, her mouth seemed parched; her throat swollen and burning. She was seized with an unutterable longing to rush forward, down the slope, and grab one of those bottles with which to slake her all-consuming thirst. Yet she remained rooted, held back by her higher consciousness; the vision of her mother no longer before her physical eyes, but clear in her mentality just as she had seen it, tall, slender and white-clad, with a sparkling hoop of star-like diamonds glistening above the hair drawn back from the high broad forehead.

At the defamation of the Host, she was seized by a shuddering rigor in all her limbs. She tried to shut her eyes but they remained fixed and staring while silent tears welled from them and gushed down her cheeks. She endeavoured to cross herself, but her hand, numb with that awful cold, refused to do the bidding of her brain and remained hanging limp and frozen at her side. She endeavoured to pray, but her swollen tongue refused its office, and her mind seemed to have gone utterly blank so that she could not recall even the opening words of the Paternoster or Ave Maria. She knew with a sudden appalling clarity that having even been the witness of this blasphemous sacrilege was enough to damn her for all eternity, and that her own wish to attend this devilish saturnalia had been engendered only by a stark madness caught like some terrible contagious disease from her association with these other unnatural beings who were the victims of a ghastly lunacy.

In vain she attempted to cast herself upon her knees, to struggle back from this horror, but she seemed to be caught in an invisible vice and could not lift her glance for one single second from that small lighted circle which stood out so clearly in the surrounding darkness of the mysterious valley.

She saw the Satanists strip off their dominoes and shuddered afresh—almost retching—as she watched them tumbling upon each other in the disgusting nudity of their ritual dance. Old Madame D'Urfé, huge-buttocked and swollen, prancing by some satanic power with all the vigour of a young girl who had only just reached maturity; the Babu, dark-skinned, fleshy, hideous; the American woman, scraggy, lean-flanked and hag-like with empty, hanging breasts; the Eurasian, waving the severed stump of his arm in the air as he gavotted beside the unwieldy figure of the Irish bard, whose paunch stood out like the grotesque belly of a Chinese god.

'They are mad, mad, mad,' she found herself saying over and over again, as she rocked to and fro where she stood, weeping bitterly, beating her hands together and her teeth chattering in the icy wind.

The dance ceased on a high wail of those discordant instruments and then the whole of that ghastly ghoul-like crew sank down together in a tangled heap before the Satanic throne. Tanith wondered for a second what was about to happen next, even as she made a fresh effort to drag herself away. Then Simon was led out from among the rest and she knew all too soon that the time of baptism was at hand. As she realised it, a new menace came upon her. Without her own volition, her feet began to move.

In a panic of fear she found herself setting one before the other and advancing slowly down the hill. She tried to scream, but her voice would not come. She tried to throw herself backward, but her body was held rigid, and an irresistible suction dragged at each of her feet in turn, lifting it a few inches from the ground and pulling it forward, so that, despite her uttermost effort of will to resist the evil force, she was being drawn slowly but surely to receive her own baptism.

The weird unearthly music had ceased. An utter silence filled the valley. She was no more than ten yards from the nearest of those debased creatures who hovered gibbering about the throne. Suddenly she whimpered with fright for although she was still hidden by the darkness, the great horned head of the Goat turned and its fiery eyes became fixed upon her.

She knew then that there was no escape. The warnings from Rex and her mother had come too late. Those powers which she had sought to suborne now held her in their grip and she must submit to this loathsome ritual despite the shrinking of her body and her soul, with all the added horror of full knowledge that it meant final and utter condemnation to the bottomless pit.

18

THE POWER OF LIGHT

At the sight of De Richleau's breakdown Rex almost gave in too. The cold sweat of terror had broken out on his own forehead, yet he was still fighting down his fear and, after a moment, the collapse of that indomitable leader to whom he had looked so often and with such certain faith in the worst emergencies brought him a new feeling of responsibility. His generous nature was great enough to realise that the Duke's courage had only proved less than his own on this occasion because of his greater understanding of the peril they were called upon to face. Now, it was as though the elder man had been wounded and put out of action, so Rex felt that it was up to him to take command.

'We can't let this thing be,' he said with sudden firmness, stooping to place an arm round De Richleau's shaking shoulders. 'You stay here. I'm going down to face the music.'

'No—no, Rex.' The Duke grabbed at his coat. 'They'll murder you without a second thought.'

'Will they? We'll see!' Rex gave a grating laugh. 'Well, if they do you'll have something you can fix on them that the police *will* understand. It'll be some consolation to think you'll see to it that these devils swing for my murder if they do me in.'

'Wait! I won't let you go alone,' the Duke stumbled to his feet. 'Don't you realise that death is the least thing I fear. One look from the eyes of the Goat could send you mad—then where is the case to put before the police? Half the people in our asylums may be suffering from a physical lesion of the brain but the others are unaccountably insane. The real reason is demoniac possession brought about by looking upon terrible things that they were never meant to see.'

'I'll risk it.' Rex was desperate now. He held up the crucifix. 'This is going to protect me, because I've got faith that it will.'

'All right then—but even madness isn't the worst that can happen to us. This life is nothing—I'm thinking of the next. Oh, God, if only dawn would come or we had some form of Light that we could bring to bear on these worshippers of Darkness.'

Rex took a pace forward. 'If we'd known what we were going to be up against we'd have brought a searchlight on a truck. That would have given this bunch something to think about if light has the power you say. But it's no good worrying about that now. We've got to hurry.'

'No—wait!' the Duke exclaimed with sudden excitement. 'I've got it. This way—quick!' He turned and set off up the hill at a swift crouching run.

Rex followed, and when they reached the brow easily overtook him. 'What's the idea,' he cried, using his normal voice for the first time for hours.

'The car!' De Richleau panted, as he pelted over the rough grass to the place where they had left the Hispano. 'To attack them is a ghastly risk in any case, but this will give us a sporting chance.'

Rex reached it first and flung open the door. The Duke tumbled in and got the engine going. It purred on a low note as they bumped forward in the darkness to the brow of the hill.

'Out on the running-board, Rex,' snapped De Richleau as he thrust out the clutch. He seemed in those few moments to have recovered all his old steel-like indomitable purpose. 'It's a madman's chance because it's ten to one we'll get stuck going up the hill on the other side, but we must risk that. When I use the engine again, snap on the lights. As we go past, throw your crucifix straight at the thing on the throne. Then try and grab Simon by the neck.'

'Fine!' Rex laughed suddenly, all his tension gone now that he was at last going into action. 'Go to it!'

The car slid forward, silently gathering momentum as it rushed down the steep slope. Next second they were almost upon the nearest of the Satanists. The Duke let in the clutch and Rex switched on the powerful headlights of the Hispano.

With the suddenness of a thunderclap a shattering roar burst upon the silence of the valley – as though some monster plane was diving full upon that loathsome company from the cloudy sky. At the same instant, the whole scene was lit in all its ghastliness by a blinding glare which swept towards them at terrifying speed. The great car bounded forward, the dazzling beams threw into sharp relief the naked forms gathered in the hollow, De Richleau jammed his foot down on the accelerator and, calling with all his will upon the higher powers for their protection, charged straight for the Goat of Mendes upon the Satanic throne.

At the first flash of those blinding lights which struck full upon them, the Satanists rushed screaming for cover. It was as though two giant eyes of some nightmare monster leapt at them from the surrounding darkness and the effect was as that of a fire-hose turned suddenly upon an angry threatening mob.

Their maniacal exaltation died away. The false exhilaration of the alcohol, the pungent herbal incense and the drug-laden ointments which they had smeared upon their bodies, drained from them. They woke as from an intoxicated nightmare to the realisation of their nakedness and helpless-ness.

For a moment some of them thought that the end had come and that the Power of Darkness had cashed in their bond, claiming them for its own upon this last Walpurgis-Nacht. Others, less deeply imbued with the mysteries of the Evil cult, forgot the terrible entity whose powers they had come to beg in return for their homage and, reverting to their normal thoughts, saw themselves caught and ruined in some ghastly scandal, believing those blinding shafts of light from the great Hispano to herald the coming of the police.

As the grotesque nude figures scattered with shrieks of terror the car bounded from ridge to ridge heading straight for the monstrous Goat. When the lights fell upon it Rex feared for an instant that the malefic rays which streamed from its baleful eyes would overcome the headlights of the car. The lamps flickered and dimmed, but as the Duke clung to the wheel he was concentrating with all the power of his mind upon visualising the horshoe surmounted by a cross in silver light just above the centre of his forehead, setting the symbol in his aura and, at the same time, repeating the lines of the Ninety-first Psalm which is immensely powerful against all evil manifestations.

"'Whoso dwelleth under the defence of the most High: shall abide under the shadow of the Almighty.

I will say unto the Lord, Thou are my hope, and my stronghold: my God, in Him will I trust.

For He shall deliver thee from the snare of the hunter: and from the noisome pestilence.'"

From the time Rex switched on the headlights, it was only a matter of seconds before the big car hurtled forward like a living thing right on to the ground where the Sabbat was being held.

Rex, clinging to the coachwork, and also visualising that symbol which De Richleau had impressed so strongly upon him, leaned from the step of the car and, with all his force, threw the ivory crucifix straight in the terrible face of the monstrous beast.

The Duke swerved the car to avoid the throne and Simon who, alone of all the Satanists, remained standing but apparently utterly unconscious of what was happening.

The blue flames of the black candles set upon the hellish altar went out as though quenched by some invisible hand. The lights of the car regained their full brilliance, and once again they heard the terrible screaming neigh which seemed to echo over the desolate Plain for miles around as the crucifix, shining white in the glow of the headlights, passed through the face of the Goat.

A horrible stench of burning flesh mingled with the choking odour from the sulphur candles, filled the air like some poisonous gas, but there was no time to think or analyse sensations. After that piercing screech, the brute upon the rocks disappeared. At the same instant Rex grabbed Simon by the neck and hauled him bodily on to the step of the car as it charged the farther slope of the hollow.

Jolting and bouncing it breasted the rise, hesitating for the fraction of a second upon the brink as though some awful power was striving to draw it backwards. But the Duke threw the gear lever into low, and they lurched forward again on to level ground.

Rex, meanwhile, had flung open the door at the back and dragged Simon inside where he collapsed on the floor in a senseless heap. Instinctively, although De Richleau had warned him not to do so, he glanced out of the back window down into the valley where they had witnessed such terrible things, but it lay dark, silent, and seemingly deserted.

The car was travelling now at a better pace, although De Richleau did not dare to use the full power of his engine for fear that they should strike a sudden dip or turn over in some hidden gully.

For a mile they raced north-eastward while, without ceasing, the Duke muttered to himself those protective lines:

"'He shall defend thee under his wings, and thou shalt be safe under his feathers: his faithfulness and truth shall be thy shield and buckler.

*Thou shalt not be afraid for any terror by night: nor for the arrow that flieth
by day;*

*For the pestilence that walketh in darkness: nor for the sickness that
destroyeth in the noon-day.'''*

Then to his joy, they struck a track at right-angles, and he turned along it
to the north-westward, slipping into top gear. The car bounded forward and
seemed to fly as though in truth all the devils of Hell were unleashed behind
it in pursuit. Swerving, jolting, and bounding across the grassy ruts, they
covered five miles in twice as many minutes until they came upon the
Lavington-Westbury road.

Even then De Richleau would not slow down but, turning in the direction
of London, roared on, swerving from bend to bend with utter disregard for
danger in his fear of the greater danger that lay behind.

They flashed through Earlstoke, Market Lavington and then Easterton,
where, unseen by them, the Blue Rolls lay just off the road in a ditch where
Tanith had crashed it a few hours before; then Bushall, Upavon,
Ludgershall and so to Andover, having practically completed a circuit of the
Plain. Here at last, at the entrance of the town, the Duke brought the car to a
halt and turned in his seat to look at Rex.

'How is he?' he asked.

'About all-in I reckon. He is as cold as blazes, and he hasn't fluttered an
eyelid since I hauled him into the car. My God! what a ghastly business.'

'Grim, wasn't it!' De Richleau for once was looking more than his age. His
grey face was lined and heavy pouches seemed to have developed beneath his
piercing eyes. His shoulders were hunched as he leaned for a moment
apparently exhausted over the wheel. Then he pulled himself together with
a jerk and thrusting his hand in his pocket, took out a flask which he passed to
Rex.

'Give him some of this—as much as you can get him to swallow. It may
help to pull him round.'

Rex turned to where Simon lay hunched up beneath the car rugs on the
back seat beside him and forcing open his mouth poured a good portion of
the old brandy into it.

Simon choked suddenly, gasped, and jerked up his head. His eyes
flickered open and he stared at Rex, but there was no recognition in them.
Then his lids closed again and his head fell backwards on the seat.

'Well, he's alive, thank God.' murmured Rex. 'While you've been driving
like a maniac I've been scared that we had lost poor Simon for good and all.
But now we'd best get him back to London or to the nearest doctor just as
soon as we can.'

'I daren't.' De Richleau's eyes were full of a desperate anxiety. 'That
devilish mob will have recovered themselves and are probably back at the
house near Chilbury by now. They will be plotting something against us you
may be certain.'

'You mean that as Mocata knows your flat he will concentrate on it to get
Simon back—just as he did before?'

'Worse. I doubt if they'd ever let us reach it.'

'Oh, shucks!' Rex frowned impatiently. 'How're they going to stop us?'

'They can control all the meaner things—bats, snakes, rats, foxes, owls—as
well as cats and certain breeds of dog like the Wolfhound and Alstatian. If

one of those dashed beneath the wheels of the car when we were going at any speed it might turn over. Besides, within certain limits, they can control the elements, so they could ensure a dense local fog surrounding us the whole way, and every mile of it we'd be facing the risk of another car that hadn't seen our lights smashing into us head on at full speed. If they combine the whole of their strength for ill it's a certainty they'll be able to bring about some terrible accident before we can cover the seventy miles to London. Remember too, this is still Walpurgis-Nacht and every force of evil that is abroad will be leagued against us. For every moment until dawn we three remain in the direst peril.'

19

THE ANCIENT SANCTUARY

'Well, we can't stay here,' Rex protested.

'I know, and we've got to find some sanctuary where we can keep Simon safe until morning.'

'How about a church?'

'Yes, if we could find one that is open. But they will all be locked up at this hour.'

'Couldn't we get some local parson out of bed?'

'If I knew one anywhere near here I'd chance it, but how can we possibly expect a stranger to believe the story that we should have to tell? He would think us madmen, or probably that it was a plot to rob his church. But wait a moment! By Jove, I've got it! We'll take him to the oldest cathedral in Britain and one that is open to the skies.' With a sudden chuckle of relief, De Richleau set the car in motion again and began to reverse it.

'Surely you're not going back?' Rex asked anxiously.

'Only three miles to the fork-roads at Weyhill, then down to Amesbury.'

'Well, don't you call that going back?'

'Perhaps, but I mean to take him to Stonehenge. If we can reach it, we shall be in safety, even though it is no more than a dozen miles from Chilbury.'

Once more the car rocketed along the road across those grassy, barren slopes, cleaving the silent darkness of the night with its great arced headlights.

Twenty minutes later they passed again through the twisting streets of Amesbury, now silent and shuttered while its inhabitants slept, not even dreaming of the terrible battle which was being fought out that night between the Power of Light and the Power of Darkness, so near to them in actuality and yet so remote to the teeming life of everyday modern England.

A mile outside the town, they ran up the slope to the wire fence which rings in the Neolithic monument, Stonehenge. The Duke drove the car into the deserted car park beside the road and there they left it. Rex carried Simon, wrapped in De Richleau's great-coat and the car rug, while the Duke followed him through the wire with the suitcase containing his protective impedimenta.

As they staggered over the grass, the vast monoliths of the ancient place of worship stood out against the skyline–the timeless symbols of a forgotten cult that ruled Britain, before the Romans came to bring more decorative and more human gods.

They passed the outer circle of great stone uprights upon some of which the lintels forming them into a ring of arches still remain. Then De Richleau led the way between the mighty chunks of fallen masonry to where, beside the two great trilithons, the sandstone altar slab lies half buried beneath the remnants of the central arch.

At a gesture from the Duke, Rex laid Simon, still unconscious, upon it. Then he looked up doubtfully. 'I suppose you know what you're doing, but I've always heard that the Druids, who built this place, were a pretty grim lot. Didn't they sacrifice virgins on this stone and practise all sorts of pagan rites? I should have thought this place would be more sacred to the Power of Evil than the Power of Good.'

'Don't worry, Rex,' De Richleau smiled in the darkness. 'It is true that the Druids performed sacrifices, but they were sun-worshippers. At the summer solstice, the sun rises over the hilltop there, shedding its first beam of light directly through the arch on to this altar stone. This place is one of the most hallowed spots in all Europe because countless thousands of long-dead men and women have worshipped here–calling upon the Power of Light to protect them from the evil things that go in darkness–and the vibrations of their souls are about us now making a sure buttress and protection until the coming of the dawn.'

With gentle hands, they set about a more careful examination of Simon. His body was still terribly cold but they found that, except for where Rex had clawed at his neck, he had suffered no physical injury.

'What do you figure to do now?' Rex asked as the Duke opened his suitcase.

'Exorcise him in due form, in order to try and drive out any evil spirit by which he may be possessed.'

'Like the Roman Catholic priests used to do in the Middle Ages.'

'As they still do,' De Richleau answered soberly.

'What–in these days?'

'Yes. Don't your remember the case of Helene Poirier who died only in 1914. She suffered from such terrible demoniacal possession that many of the most learned priests in France, including Monseigneur Dupanloup, Bishop of Orleans, and Monsieur Mallet, Superior of the Grand Seminary, had to be called in before, with God's grace, she could be freed from the evil spirit which controlled her.'

'I didn't think the Church admitted the existence of such things as witchcraft and black magic.'

'Then you are very ignorant, my friend. I do not know the official views of others, but the Roman Church, whose authority comes unbroken over nineteen centuries from the time when Our Lord made St Peter his viceregent on earth, has ever admitted the existence of the evil power. Why else should they have issued so many ordinances against it, or at the present time so unhesitatingly condemn all spiritualistic practices which they regard as the modern counterparts of necromancy, by which Hell's emissaries seek to lure weak, foolish and trusting people into their net?'

'I can't agree to that,' Rex demurred. 'I know a number of Spiritualists, men and women of the utmost rectitude.'

'Perhaps.' De Richleau was arranging Simon's limp body. 'They are entitled to their opinion and he who thinks rightly lives rightly. No doubt their high principles act as a protective barrier between them and the more dangerous entities of the spirit world. However, for the weak-minded and mentally frail such practices hold the gravest peril. Look at that Bavarian family of eleven people, all of whom went out of their minds after a Spiritualistic séance in 1921. The case was fully reported by the Press at the time and I could give you a dozen similar examples, all attributable to Diabolic possession, of course. In fact, according to the Roman Church, there is no phenomenon of modern Spiritism which cannot be paralleled in the records of old witch trials.'

'According to them, maybe, but Simon's not a Catholic.'

'No matter, there is nothing to prevent a member of the Roman Church asking Divine aid for any man whatever his race or creed. Fortunately I was baptised a Catholic and, although I may not be a good one, I believe that with the grace of God, power will be granted to me this night to help our poor friend.

'Kneel down now and pray silently, for all prayers are good if the heart is earnest and perhaps those of the Church of England more efficacious than others since we are now in the English countryside. It is for that reason I recite certain psalms from the book of Common Prayer. But be ready to hold him if he leaps up for, if he is possessed, the Demon within him will fight like a maniac.'

De Richleau took up the holy water and sprinkled a few drops on Simon's forehead. They remained there a moment and then trickled slowly down his drawn, furrowed face. But he remained corpse-like and still.

'May the Lord be praised,' murmured the Duke.

'What is it?' breathed Rex.

'He is not actually possessed. If he were the holy water would have scalded him like boiling oil, and at its touch the Demon would have screamed like a hell cat.'

'What now then?'

'He still reeks of evil so I must employ the banishing ritual to purge the atmosphere about him and do all things possible to protect him from Mocata's influence. Then we will see if this coma shows any signs of lifting.'

The Duke produced a crutch of Rowan wood, then proceeded to certain curious and complicated rites; consisting largely in stroking Simon's limbs with a brushing motion towards the feet; the repetition of many Latin formulas with long intervals in which, led by the Duke, the two men knelt to pray beside their friend.

Simon was anointed with holy water and with holy oil. The gesture of Horus was made to the north, to the south, to the east and to the west. The palms of his hands were sprinkled and the soles of his feet. Asafœtida grass was tied round his wrists and his ankles. An orb with the cross upon it was placed in his right hand, and a phial of quicksilver between his lips. A chain of garlic flowers was hung about his neck, and the sacred oil placed in a cross upon his forehead. Each action upon him was preceded by prayer, concentration of thought, and invocation to the archangels, the high beings of Light, and to his own higher consciousness.

At last, after an hour, all had been accomplished in accordance with the ancient lore and De Richleau examined Simon again. He was warmer now and the ugly lines of distress and terror had faded from his face. He seemed to have passed out of his dead faint into a natural sleep and was breathing regularly.

'I think that with God's help we have saved him,' declared the Duke. 'He looks almost normal now, but we had best wait until he wakes of his own accord; I can do no more, so we will rest for a little.'

Rex passed his hand across his eyes as De Richleau sank down beside him. 'I'll say I need it. Would it be . . . er . . . sacrilegious or anything if I had a smoke?'

'Of course not.' De Richleau drew out his cigars. 'Have a Hoyo. It is thoughts, not formalities, which make an atmosphere of good or evil.'

For a little while the two friends sat silent, the points of their cigars glowing faintly in the darkness until a pale greyness in the eastern sky made clearer the ghostly outlines of the great oblong stones towering at varying angles to twenty feet about their heads.

'What a strange place this is,' Rex murmured. 'How old do you suppose it to be?'

'About four thousand years.'

'As old as that, eh?'

'Yes, but that is young compared with the Pyramids and, beside them, for architecture and scientific alignment, this thing is a primitive toy.'

'Those ancient Britons must have been a whole heap cleverer than we give them credit for all the same, to get these great blocks of stone set up. It would tax all the resources of our modern engineers, I reckon. Some of them must weigh a hundred tons apiece.'

De Richleau nodded. 'Only the piety of many thousand willing hands, hauling on skin ropes, and manipulating vast levers, could have accomplished it, but what is even more remarkable is that the foreign stones were transported from a quarry nearly two hundred miles from here.'

'What do you mean by "foreign stones"?'

'The stones which form the inner ring and the inner horseshoe are called so because they were brought from a great distance—a place in Pembrokeshire, I think.'

'Horseshoe,' Rex repeated with a puzzled look. 'I thought all the stones were placed in rings.'

'It is hardly discernible in the ruins now, but originally this great temple consisted of an outer ring formed of big arches, then a concentric circle of smaller uprights. Inside that, five great separate trilithons of arches, two of which you can see still standing, set in the form of a horseshoe and then another horseshoe of the smaller stones.'

'The Druids used the horseshoe, too, then?'

'Certainly. As I have told you, it is a most potent symbol indissolubly connected with the Power of Light. Hence my use of it in connection with the swastika and the cross.'

They fell silent again for some time, then Simon stirred beside them and they both stood up. He slowly turned over and looked about him with dull eyes until he recognised his friends, and asked in a stifled voice where he was.

Without answering, De Richleau drew him down between Rex and himself on to his knees, and proceeded to give thanks for his restoration. 'Repeat after me,' he said, 'the words of the fifty-first Psalm.

'"Have mercy upon me, O God, after thy great goodness: according to the multitude of thy mercies do away mine offences.
Wash me throughly from my wickedness: and cleanse me from my sin.
For I acknowledge my faults and my sin is ever before me."'

To the end of the beautiful penitent appeal the Duke read in a solemn voice from the Prayer Book by the aid of a little torch while the others repeated verse by verse after him. Then all three stood up and began at last to talk in their normal voices.

De Richleau explained what had taken place, and Simon sat upon the altar-stone weeping like a child as now, with a clear brain, he began at last to understand the terrible peril from which his friends had rescued him.

He remembered the party which had been given at his house and that the Duke had hypnotised him in Curzon Street. After that—nothing, until he found himself present in the Sabbat which had been held that night, and even then he could only see vague pictures of it, as though he had not participated in it himself, but watched the whole of the ghastly proceedings from a distance; horrified to the last degree to see a figure that seemed to be himself taking part in those abominable ceremonies, yet mentally chained and powerless to intervene or stop that body, so curiously like his own, participating in that godless scene of debauchery.

Dawn was now breaking in the eastern sky, as De Richleau placed his arm affectionately round Simon's shoulders. 'Don't take it to heart so, my friend,' he said kindly. 'For the moment at least you have been spared, and praise be to God you are still sane, which is more than I dared to hope for when we got you here.'

Simon nodded. 'I know—I've been lucky,' he said soberly. 'But am I really free—for good? I'm afraid Mocata will try and get me back somehow.'

'Now we're together again you needn't worry,' Rex grinned. 'If the three of us can't fight this horror and win out we're not the men I always thought we were.'

'Yes,' Simon agreed, a little doubtfully. 'But the trouble is that I was born at a time when certain stars were in conjunction, so in a way I'm the key to a ritual which Mocata's set his heart on performing.'

'The invocation to Saturn coupled with Mars,' the Duke put in.

'I'm scared he'll exercise every incantation in the book to drag me back to him despite myself.'

'Isn't that danger over? Surely it should have been done two nights ago, but we managed to prevent it then.'

'Ner,' Simon used his favourite negative with a little wriggle of his bird-like head. 'That would have been the most suitable time of all, but the ritual can be performed with a reasonable prospect of success any night while the two planets remain in the same house of the Zodiac.'

'Then the longer we can keep you out of Mocata's clutches, the less chance he stands of pulling it off as the two planets get farther apart,' Rex commented.

De Richleau sighed. His face looked grey and haggard in the early morning light. 'In that case,' he said slowly, 'Mocata will exert his whole strength when twilight comes again, and we shall have to fight with our backs to the wall throughout this coming night.'

20

THE FOUR HORSEMEN

Now that the sun was up Rex's resilient spirit reasserted itself. 'Time enough to worry about tonight when we are through today,' he declared cheerfully. 'What we need most just now is a good hot breakfast.'

The Duke smiled. 'I thoroughly agree, and in any case we can't stay here much longer. While we feed we'll discuss the safest place to which we can take Simon.'

'We can't take him anywhere at the moment,' Rex grinned. 'Not as he is—with only the car rug and your great-coat to cover his birthday suit.'

Simon tittered into his hand. It was the gesture which both his friends knew so well, and which it delighted them to see again. 'I must look pretty comic as I am,' he chuckled. 'And it's chilly too. One of you had better try and raise me a suit of clothes.'

'You take the car, Rex,' said the Duke, 'and drive into Amesbury. Knock up the first clothes dealer you can find and buy him an outfit. Have you enough money?'

'Plenty. I was going down to Derby yesterday for the first Spring Race Meeting if this business hadn't cropped up overnight. So I'd drawn fifty the day before.'

'Good,' the Duke nodded. 'We shan't move from here until you return.' Then, as Rex strode away across the grass to the Hispano, which was now visible where they had left it in the car-park, he turned to Simon:

'Tell me,' he said, 'while Rex is gone. How did you ever get drawn into this terrible business?'

Simon smiled. 'Well,' he said hesitantly, 'it may seem a queer thing to say, but you are partly responsible yourself.'

'I!' exclaimed the Duke. 'What the deuce to you mean?'

'I'm not blaming you, of course, in the least, but do you remember that long chat we had when we were both down at Cardinals Folly for Christmas? It started by your telling us about the old Alchemists and how they used to make gold out of base metals.'

De Richleau nodded. 'Yes, and you threw doubt upon my statement that the feat had actually been performed. I cited the case of the scientist Helvetius, I remember, who was bitterly opposed to the pretentions of the Alchemists, but who, when he was visited by one at the Hague in December, 1666, managed to secrete a little of the reddish powder which the man showed him under his finger-nail, and afterwards succeeded in transmuting a small amount of lead into gold with it. But you would not believe me, although I assured you, that no less a person than Spinoza verified the experiment at the time.'

'That's right,' said Simon. 'Well, I was sceptical but interested, so I took the trouble to check up as far as possible on all you'd said. It was Spinoza's testimony that impressed me because he was so very sane and unbiased.'

'So was Helvetius himself for that matter.'

'I know. Anyhow, I dug up the fact that Povelius, the chief tester of the Dutch Mint, assayed the metal seven times with all the leading goldsmiths at the Hague and they unanimously pronounced it to be pure gold. Of course there was a possibility that Helvetius deceived them by submitting a piece of gold obtained through the ordinary channels, but it hardly seemed likely that he practised deliberate fraud, because he had no motive. He had always declared his disbelief in alchemy and he couldn't make any more because he hadn't got the powder—so there was no question of his trying to float a bogus company on the experiment. He couldn't even claim any scientific kudos from it either because he frankly admitted that he had stolen the powder from the stranger who showed it to him. After that I went into the experiment of Berigord de Pisa and Van Helmont.'

'And what did you think of those?' asked the Duke, his lined face showing quick interest in the early morning light.

'They shook my unbelief a lot. Van Helmont was the greatest chemist of his time, and like Helvetius, he'd always said the idea of transmitting base metals into gold was sheer nonsense until a stranger gave him a little of that mysterious powder with which he, too, performed the experiment successfully; and he again had no personal axe to grind.'

'There are plenty of other cases as well,' remarked the Duke. 'Raymond Lully made gold for King Edward III of England, and George Ripley gave £100,000 of alchemical gold to the Knights of Rhodes. The Emperor Augustus of Saxony left 17,000,000 Rix dollars and Pope John XXII of Avignon 25,000,000 florins, sums which were positively gigantic for those days. Both were poor men with slender revenues which could not have accounted in a hundred years for such fortunes. But both were alchemists, and transmutation is the only possible explanation of the almost fabulous treasure which was actually found in their coffers after their deaths.'

Simon nodded. 'I know. And if one rejects the sworn evidence of men like Spinoza and Van Helmont, why should one believe the people who say they can measure the distance to the stars, or the scientists of the last century who produced electrical phenomena?'

'The difference is that the mass mind will not accept scientific truths unless they can be demonstrated freely and harnessed to the public good. Everyone accepts the miracle that sulphur can be converted into fire because they see it happen twenty times a day and we all carry a box of matches in our pockets, but if it had been kept as a jealously guarded secret by a small number of initiates, the public would still regard it as impossible. And that, you see, is precisely the position of the alchemist.

'He stands apart from the world and is indifferent to it. To succeed in the Great Work he must be absolutely pure, and to such men gold is dross. In most cases he makes only sufficient to supply his modest needs and refuses to pass on his secret to the profane; but that does not necessarily mean that he is a fraud and a liar. The theory that all matter is composed of atoms, molecules and electrons in varying states is generally accepted now. Milk can be made as hard as concrete by the new scientific process, glass into women's dresses, wood and human flesh decay into a very similar dust, iron turns to rust, and crystals are known to grow although they are a type of stone. Even diamonds can be made synthetically.'

'Of course,' Simon agreed, with his old eagerness, so absorbed now in the discussion as to be apparently oblivious of his surroundings. 'And as far as metals are concerned, they are all composed of sulphur and mercury and can be condensed or materialised by means of a salt. Only the varying proportions of those three Principals account for the difference between them. Metals are the fruits of mineral nature, and the baser ones are still unripe because the sulphur and mercury had no time to combine in the right proportions before they solidified. This powder, or the Philosophers' Stone as they call it, is a ferment that forces on the original process of Nature and ripens the base metals into gold.'

'That is so. But do you mean to tell me that you have been experimenting yourself?'

'Ner,' Simon shook his narrow head. 'I soon found out that to do so would mean a lifetime of æstheticism and then perhaps failure after all. It is hardly in my line to become a "Puffer." Besides it's obvious that transmutation in its higher sense is the supreme mystery of turning Matter into Light. Metals are like men, the baser corresponding to the once born, and both gradually become purified—metals by geological upheavals—men by successive reincarnations, and the part played by the secret agent which hurries lead to gold is the counterpart of esoteric initiation which lifts the spirit towards light.'

'Was that your aim then?'

'To some extent. You know how one thing leads to another. I discovered that the whole business is bound up with the Quabalah so, being a Jew, I began to study the esoteric doctrine of my own people.'

De Richleau nodded. 'And very interesting you found it. I don't doubt.'

'Yes, it took a bit of getting into, but after I'd tackled a certain amount of the profane literature to get a grounding, I read the *Sepher Ha Zoher*, the *Sepher Jetyirah* and some of the *Midraschim*. Then I began to see a little daylight.'

'In fact you began to believe, like most people who have really read considerably and had a wide experience of life, that our western scientists have only been advancing in one direction and that we have even lost the knowledge of many things with which the wise men of ancient times were well acquainted.'

'That's so,' Simon smiled again. 'I've always been a complete sceptic. But once I began to burrow beneath the surface I found such a mass of evidence that I could no longer doubt the existence of strange hidden forces which can be chained and utilised if one only knows the way.'

'Yes. And plenty of people still interest themselves in these questions and use the Quabalah to promote their own well-being, and the general good. But where does Mocata come into all this?'

Simon shuddered slightly at the name and drew the car rug more closely about his shoulders. 'I met him in Paris,' he said, 'at the house of a French banker with whom I've sometimes done business.'

'Castelnau!' exclaimed the Duke. 'The man with the jagged ear. I knew last night that I had seen that ear somewhere before, but for the life of me I couldn't recall where.'

Simon nodded quickly. 'That's right—Castelnau. Well, I met Mocata at his place, and I don't quite know how it started, but the conversation drifted round to the Quabalah and, as I had been soaking myself in it at the time, I was naturally interested. He said he had a lot of books upon it and suggested that I might like to visit the house where he was staying and have a look through them. Of course I did. Then he told me that he was conducting an experiment in Magic the following night, and asked if I would care to be present.'

'I see. That's how the trouble started.'

'Yes. The experiment was quite a harmless affair. He made certain ritual conjurations with the four elements, Fire, Air, Water and Earth, then told me to look into a mirror with him. It was an old Venetian piece, a bit spotted at the back but otherwise quite ordinary you know. As I watched, it clouded over with a sort of mist, then when it cleared again I could no longer see my reflection in it, but a sheet of newspaper instead. It was the financial page of *Le Temps* giving all the quotations of the Paris Bourse, which sounds pretty prosaic I suppose, but the queer part is that this issue was dated three days ahead.'

De Richleau stroked his lean face with his slender fingers. 'I saw a similar demonstration in Cairo once,' he commented gravely. 'But on that occasion it was the name of the new Commander-in-Chief, who had only been appointed by the War Office in London that afternoon, which appeared in the mirror. You took a note of some of the Bourse quotations I suppose?'

'Um. The list wasn't visible for more than ten seconds then the mirror clouded over again and went back to its normal state, but that was quite long enough for me to memorise the stocks I was interested in, and when I checked up afterwards they were right to a fraction.'

'What happened then?'

'Mocata offered to instruct me in the attainment of the knowledge and conversation of my Holy Guardian Angel as the first step on the road to obtaining similar powers myself.'

'My poor Simon!' The Duke made an unhappy grimace. 'You are not the first to be trapped by a Brother of the Left Hand Path who is recruiting for the Devil by such a promise. If you had known more of Magic you would have realised that it is proper to pass through the six stages of Probationer, Neophyte, Zelator, Practicus, Philosophus and Dominus Liminis before, as an Adeptus Inferior after many years of study and experience, you would be qualified to take the risk of attempting to pass the Abyss. Besides, there are no precise rules for attaining the knowledge and conversation of one's Holy Guardian Angel. It is a thing which each man must work out for himself and no other can help one to it. Mocata invoked your Evil Angel, of course, to act a blasphemous impersonation while your Holy Guardian wept impotent tears to see the terrible danger into which you were being drawn.'

'I suppose so, although, of course, I couldn't know that at the time. Anyhow, I had to go back to London a few days later, and I was so impressed by that time that I asked Mocata to let me know directly he arrived, because he spoke of coming over. He turned up a fortnight later and rang me up at once to urge me to unload a lot of stock that he knew I was carrying. I had faith in it myself but in view of what I'd seen in his mirror I took his tip and saved myself quite a packet, because the market broke almost immediately after.'

'Was that when you asked him to go and live with you?' inquired the Duke.

'Yes. I suggested that he should stay with me while he was in London because he had no suitable place in which to practise his evocations at his hotel. He moved over to St John's Wood then and after that we used to sit up together in the observatory pretty well every night. That's why I saw so little of you during that time. But the results were extraordinary–utterly amazing.'

'He gave you more information which governed your financial transactions, I suppose.'

'Yes, but more than that. He foretold the whole of the Stravinsky scandal. I'm not a poor man as you know, but if I hadn't been forewarned about that, it would have darn nearly broken me. As it was, I cleared every single share in the dud companies before the storm broke and got out with an immense profit.'

'By that time you had begun to dabble in Black Magic I imagine?'

Simon's dark eyes flickered away from the Duke's for a moment, then he nodded. 'Just a bit. He asked me to recite the Lord's Prayer backwards one night, and I was a bit unhappy about it but . . . well, I did. He said that since I wasn't a Christian anyhow no harm could come to me from it.'

'It is horribly potent all the same,' the Duke commented.

'Perhaps,' agreed Simon miserably. 'But Mocata is so devilish glib and according to him there is no such thing as Black Magic anyhow. The harnessing of supernatural powers to one's will is just Magic–neither black nor white, and that's all there is to it.'

'Tell me about this man.'

'Oh, he's about fifty, I suppose, bald-headed, with curious light blue eyes and a paunch that would rival Dom Gorenflot's.'

'I know,' agreed the Duke impatiently. 'I've seen him. But I meant his personality, not his appearance.'

'Of course, I forgot,' Simon apologised. 'You know for weeks now I hardly know what I've been doing. It's almost as though I had been dreaming the whole time. But about Mocata: he possesses extraordinary force of character, and he can be the most charming person when he likes. He's clever of course–amazingly so, and seems to have read pretty well every book that one can think of. It's extraordinary, too, what a fascination he can exercise over women. I know half a dozen who are simply "bats" about him.'

'What can you tell me of his history?'

'Not much, I'm afraid. His Christian name is Damien and he is a Frenchman by nationality, but his mother was Irish. He was educated for the Church. In fact, he actually took Orders, but finding the life of a priest did not suit him, he chucked it up.'

De Richleau nodded. 'I thought as much. Only an ordained priest can practise the Black Mass, and since he is so powerful an adept of the Left Hand Path, it was pretty certain that he was a renegade priest of the Roman Church. But what more can you tell me? Every scrap of information which you have may help us in our fight, because you must remember, Simon, that you have only achieved a very temporary security. The battle will begin again when he exercises his dominance over you to call you back.'

Simon shifted his position on the stones and then replied thoughtfully. 'He does the most lovely needlework, petit point and that sort of thing you know, and he's terribly fastidious about keeping his plump little hands scrupulously clean. As a companion he is delightful to be with except that he will smother himself in expensive perfumes and is as greedy as a schoolboy about sweets. He had huge boxes of fondants, crystallised fruits, and marzipan sent over from Paris twice a week when he was at St John's Wood.

'Ordinarily he was perfectly normal and his manners were charming, but now and again he used to get irritable fits. They came on about once a month and after he had been boiling up for twenty-four hours, he used to clear out for a couple of days and nights. I don't know where he used to go to at those times, but I ran into him one morning early, when he had just returned from one of these bouts, and he was in a shocking state: filthy dirty, a two days' growth of beard on his chin, his clothes all torn and absolutely stinking of drink. It looked to me as if he hadn't been to bed at all the whole time but had been wallowing in every sort of debauchery down in the slums of the East End.

'He is quite an exceptional hypnotist, of course, and keeps himself in touch with what is going on in Paris, Berlin, New York and a dozen other places by throwing various women, who used to come and visit him regularly, into a trance. One of them was a girl called Tanith, a perfectly lovely creature. You may have seen her at the party, and he says she is by far the best medium he's ever had. He can use her almost like a telephone and plug in right away to whatever he wants to know about. Whereas with the others there are very often hitches and delays.'

'You let him hypnotise you, too, of course?'

'Yes, in order to get these financial results.'

'I thought as much,' De Richleau nodded, 'And after you had allowed him to do it willingly for some little time he was able to block out your own mentality entirely and govern your every thought. That's why you've failed to realise what's been going on. It is just as though he'd been keeping you drugged the whole time.'

'Um,' Simon agreed miserably. 'It makes me positively sick to think of it, but I suppose he has been gradually preparing me for this Ritual to Saturn which he meant to perform two nights ago and . . .' He broke off suddenly as Rex appeared between two of the great monoliths.

Grinning from ear to ear, Rex displayed his purchases for their inspection. A pair of grey flannel shorts, a khaki shirt, black and white check worsted stockings, a gaudy tie of revolting magenta hue, a pair of waders, a cricket cap quartered in alternate triangular sections of orange and mauve, and a short, dark blue bicyclist's cape.

'Only things I could get,' he volunteered cheerfully. 'The people who run the local Co-op don't live on the premises, so I had to knock up a sports outfitter.'

De Richleau sat back and roared with laughter while Simon fingered the queer assortment of garments doubtfully. 'You're joking Rex,' he protested with a sheepish grin. 'I can't return to London in this get-up.'

'We're not going to London,' the Duke announced. 'But to Cardinals Folly.'

'What—to Marie Lou's?' Rex looked at him sharply. 'How did you come to get that idea . . .'

'Something that Simon said just after you left us.'

Simon shook his head jerkily. 'I don't like it—not a little bit. I'd never forgive myself if I brought danger into their home.'

'You will do as you're told my friend,' De Richleau's voice brooked no further argument. 'Richard and Marie Lou are the most mentally healthy couple that I know. The atmosphere of their sane and happy household will be the very best protection we could find for you and all of us are certain of a warm welcome. No harm will come to them if we exercise reasonable precautions, and the help of their right-thinking minds will give us the extra strength we need. Besides, they are about the only people to whom we can explain the whole situation without being taken for madmen. Now hurry up and array yourself like the champion of next year's Olympic games.'

With a shrug of his narrow shoulders Simon disappeared behind the stones while Rex added: 'That's right. I ordered ham and eggs to be got ready at the local inn and I'm mighty anxious to start in on them.'

'Eggs and fruit,' cut in the Duke, 'but no ham for any of us. It is essential that we should avoid meat for the moment. If we are to retain our astral strength our physical bodies must undergo a semi-fast at least.'

Rex groaned. 'Why, oh, why dear Simon, did you ever go hunting Talisman and let your friends in for this? When I went to Russia after the Shulimoff jewels and you came to get me out of trouble, at least it didn't prevent your feeding decently when you had the chance.'

'That reminds me,' De Richleau threw over his shoulder in the direction where Simon was struggling into his queer garments. 'What is this Talisman? Rex mentioned it last night.'

'It's the reason why Mocata is certain to make every effort to get possession of me again,' Simon's voice came back. 'It is buried somewhere, and adepts of the Left Hand Path have been seeking it for centuries. It conveys almost limitless powers upon its possessor and Mocata has discovered that its whereabouts will be revealed if he can practise the ritual to Saturn in conjunction with Mars with someone who was born in a certain year at the hour of the conjunction. There can't be many such, but for my sins I happen to be one, and even if he can find others they might not be suitable for various reasons.'

'Yes, I realise that. But what is the Talisman?'

'I don't really know. Except for conducting my business on the lines suggested by Mocata, I don't think my brain has been functioning at all in the last two months. But it's called the Talisman of Set.'

'What!' The Duke sprang to his feet as Simon appeared grotesquely attired in his incongruous new clothes, his long knees protruding beneath the shorts, the absurd cricket cap set at a rakish angle on his head, and the cycling cloak flapping about his shoulders.

Rex dissolved into tears of laughter, but the Duke's grim face quickly sobered his mirth.

'The Talisman of Set,' De Richleau repeated almost in a whisper.

'Yes, it has something to do with four horsemen I think—but what on earth's the matter?' Simon's big mouth fell open in dismay at the sight of the Duke's horror-stricken eyes.

'It has indeed! The Four Horsemen of the Apocalypse,' De Richleau grated out. 'War, Plague, Famine and Death. We all know what happened the last time those four terrible entities were unleashed to cloud the brains of statesmen and rulers.'

'You're referring to the Great War I take it.' Rex said soberly.

'Of course, and every adept knows that it started because one of the most terrible Satanists who ever lived found one of the secret gateways through which to release the four horsemen.'

'I thought the Germans got a bit above themselves,' Rex hazarded, 'although it seems that lots of other folks were pretty well as much to blame.'

'You fool!' De Richleau suddenly swung upon him. 'Germany did not make the War. It came out of Russia. It was Russia who instigated the murder at Sarajevo, Russia who backed Serbia to resist Austria's demands, Russia who mobilised first and Russia who invaded Germany. The monk Rasputin was the evil genius behind it all. He was the greatest Black Magician that the world has known for centuries. It was he who found one of the gateways through which to let forth the four horsemen that they might wallow in blood and destruction—and I know the Talisman of Set to be another. Europe is ripe now for any trouble and if they are loosened again, it will be final Armageddon. This is no longer a personal matter of protecting Simon. We've got to kill Mocata before he can secure the Talisman and prevent his plunging the world into another war.'

21

CARDINALS FOLLY

Richard Eaton read the telegram a second time:

> Eat no lunch this vitally important Simon ill Rex and I bringing him down to you this afternoon Marie Lou must stop eating too kiss Fleur love all.–De Richleau.

He passed one hand over the smooth brown hair which grew from his broad forehead in an attractive widow's peak, and handed the wire to his wife with a puzzled smile.

'This is from the Duke. Do you think he has gone crazy–or what?'

'*What*, darling,' said Marie Lou promptly. 'Definitely *what*. If he stood on his handsome head in Piccadilly and the whole world told me he was crazy I should still maintain that dear old Greyeyes was quite sane.'

'But really,' Richard protested. 'No lunch—and you told me that the shrimps from Morecambe Bay came in this morning. I was looking forward . . .'

'My sweet!' Marie Lou gave a delicious gurgle of laughter as she flung one arm round his neck and drew him down on to the sofa beside her. 'What a glutton you are. You simply live for your tummy.'

He nuzzled his head against her thick chestnut curls. 'I don't. I eat only in order to maintain sufficient strength to deal with you.'

'Liar,' she pushed him away suddenly. 'There must be some reason for this extraordinary wire, and poor Simon ill too! What can it mean?'

'God knows! Anyhow it seems that virtuous and upright wife orders preparations of rooms for guests while miserable worm husband goes down into dark, dirty cellar to select liquid sustenance for same.' Richard paused for a moment. A wicked little smile hovered round his lips as he looked at Marie Lou curled up on the sofa with her slim legs tucked under her like a very lovely Persian kitten, then he added thoughtfully: 'I think tonight perhaps we might give them a little of the Chateau Lafite '99.'

'Don't you dare,' she cried, springing to her feet. 'You know that it's my favourite.'

'Got you–got you,' chanted Richard merrily. 'Who's a glutton now?'

'You beast,' she pouted deliciously, and for the thousandth time since he had brought her out of Russia her husband felt himself go a little giddy as his eyes rested on the perfection of her heart-shaped face, the delicately flushed cheeks and the heavy-lidded blue eyes. With a sudden movement, he jerked her to him and swinging her off her feet, picked her up in his arms.

'Richard–put me down–stop.' Her slightly husky voice rose to a higher note in a breathless gasp of protest.

'Not until you kiss me.'

'All right.'

He let her slide down to her feet, and although he was not a tall man, she was so diminutive that she had to stand on tiptoe to reach her arms round his neck.

'There,' she declared, a trifle breathlessly, after he had crushed her soft lips under his. 'Now go and play with your bottles, but spare the Lafite, beloved. That's our own special wine, and you mustn't even give it to our dearest friends–unless it's for Simon and he's really ill.'

'I won't,' he promised. 'But whatever I give them, we shall all be tight if we're not to be allowed to eat anything. I wish to goodness I knew what De Richleau is driving at.'

'Something it is worth our while to take notice of, you may be certain. Greyeyes never does anything without a purpose. He's a wily old fox if ever there was one in this world.'

'Yes–wily's the word,' Richard agreed. 'But it's nearly lunchtime now, and I'm hungry. Surely we're not going to take serious notice of this absurd telegram?'

'Richard!' Marie Lou had curled herself up on the sofa again. But now she sat forward suddenly, almost closing her big eyes with their long curved lashes. 'I do think we ought to do as he says, but I was looking round the strawberry house this morning.'

'Oh were you!' He suppressed a smile. 'And picking a few just to see how they were getting on, I don't mind betting.'

'Three,' she answered gravely. 'And they are ripening beautifully. Now if we took a little cream and a little sugar, it wouldn't be cheating really to go and have another look at them instead of having lunch–would it?'

'No,' said Richard with equal gravity. 'But we have an ancient custom in England when a girl takes a man to pick the first strawberries.'

'But, darling, you have so many ancient customs and they nearly always end in kissing.'

'Do you dislike them on that account?'

'No.' She smiled, extending a small, strong hand by which he pulled her to her feet. 'I think that is one of the reasons why I enjoy so much having become an Englishwoman.'

They left Marie Lou's comfortable little sitting-room and, pausing for a moment for her to pull on a pair of gum-boots which came almost up to her knees while Richard gave orders cancelling their luncheon, went out into the garden through the great octagonal library.

The house was a rambling old mansion, parts of which dated back to the thirteenth century, and the library, being one of the oldest portions of it, was sunk into the ground so that they had to go up half a dozen steps from its french windows on to the long terrace which ran the whole length of the southern side of the house.

A grey stone balustrade patched with moss and lichens separated the terrace from the garden, and from the former two sets of steps led down to a broad, velvety lawn. An ancient cedar graced the greensward towards the east end of the mansion where the kitchen quarters lay, hiding the roofs of the glass-houses and the walled garden with its espaliered peach and nectarine trees.

At the bottom of the lawn tall yew hedges shut in the outer circle of the maze, beyond which lay the rose garden and the swimming-pool. To the right, just visible from the library windows, a gravel walk separated the lawn from a gently sloping bank, called the Botticelli Garden. It was so named because in spring it had all the beauty of the Italian master's paintings. Dwarf trees of apple, plum, and cherry, standing no more than six feet high and separated by ten yards or more from each other, stood covered with white and pink blossom while, rising from the grass up the shelving bank, clumps of polyanthus, pheasant's-eye narcissus, forget-me-nots and daffodils were planted one to the square yard.

This spring garden was in full bloom now and the effect of the bright colours against the delicate green of the young grass was almost incredibly lovely. To walk up and down that two hundred yard stretch of green starred by its many-hued clumps of flowers with Richard beside her, was, Marie Lou thought—sometimes with a little feeling of anxiety that her present happiness was too great to last—as near to Heaven as she would ever get. Yet she spent even more time in the long walk that lay beyond it, for that was her own, in which the head gardener was never allowed to interfere. It consisted of two glorious herbaceous borders rising to steep hedges on either side, and ending at an old sun-dial beyond which lay the pond garden, modelled from that at Hampton Court, sinking in rectangular stages to a pool where, later in the year, blue lotus flowers and white water-lilies floated serenely in the sunshine.

As they came out on to the terrace, there were shrieks of 'Mummy—Mummy,' and a diminutive copy of Marie Lou, dressed in a Russian peasant costume with wide puffed sleeves of lawn and a slashed vest of colourful embroidery threaded with gold, came hurtling across the grass. Her mother and father went down the steps of the terrace to meet her, and as she arrived like a small whirlwind Richard swung her up shoulder high in his arms.

'What is it Fleur d'amour?' he asked, with simulated concern calling her by the nick-name that he had invented for her. 'Have you crashed the scooter again or is it that Nanny's been a wicked girl today?'

'No—no,' the child cried, her blue eyes, seeming enormous in that tiny face, opened wide with concern. 'Jim's hurted hisself.'

'Has he?' Richard put her down. 'Poor Jim. We must see about this.

'He's hurted bad,' Fleur went on, tugging impulsively at her mother's skirt. 'He's cutted hisself on his magic sword.'

'Dear me,' Marie Lou ran her fingers through Fleur's dark curls. She knew that by 'magic sword' Fleur meant the gardener's scythe, for Richard always insisted that the lawn at Cardinals Folly was too old and too fine to be ruined by a mowing machine, and maintained the ancient practice of having it scythe-cut. 'Where is he now, my sweet?'

'Nanny binded him up and I helped a lot. Then he went wound to the kitchen.'

'And you weren't frightened of the blood?' Richard asked with interest.

Fleur shook her curly head. 'No. Fleur's not to be frightened of anyfink, Mummy says. Why would I be frightened of the blug?'

'Silly people are sometimes,' her father replied. 'But not people who know things like Mummy and you and I.'

At that moment Fleur's nurse joined them. She had heard the last part of the conversation. 'It's nothing serious, madam,' she assured Marie Lou. 'Jim was sharpening his scythe and the hone slipped, but he only cut his finger.'

'But fink if he can't work,' Fleur interjected in a high treble.

'Why?' asked her father gravely.

'He's poor,' announced the child after a solemn interval for deep thought. 'He-has-to-work-to-keep-his-children. So if he can't work, he'll be in a muddle—won't he?'

Richard and Marie Lou exchanged a smiling glance as Simon's expression for any sort of trouble came so glibly to the child's lips.

'Yes, that's a serious matter,' her father agreed gravely. 'What are we going to do about it?'

'We mus' all give him somefink,' Fleur announced breathlessly.

'Well, say I give him half-a-crown,' Richard suggested. 'How much do you think you can afford?'

'I'll give half-a-cwown too.' Fleur was nothing if not generous.

'But have you got it, Batuskha?' inquired her mother.

Fleur thought for a bit, and then said doubtfully: 'P'r'aps I haven't. So I'll give him a ha'-penny instead.'

'That's splendid, darling, and I'll contribute a shilling,' Marie Lou declared. 'That makes three shillings and sixpence halfpenny altogether, doesn't it?'

'But Nanny must give somefink,' declared Fleur suddenly turning on her nurse, who smiling said that she thought she could manage fourpence.

'There,' laughed Richard. 'Three and tenpence halfpenny! He'll be a rich man for life, won't he? Now you had better toddle in to lunch.'

This domestic crisis having been satisfactorily settled, Richard and Marie Lou strolled along beneath the balustraded terrace, past the low branches of the old cedar, and so to the hot-houses. Their butler, Malin, had just arrived with sugar and fresh cream, and for half an hour they made a merry meal of the early strawberries.

They had hardly finished when, to their surprise, since it was barely two o'clock, Malin returned to announce the arrival of their guests. So they hurried back to the house.

'There they are,' cried Marie Lou as the three friends came out from the tall windows of the drawing-room on to the terrace. 'But, darling, look at Simon—they *have* gone mad.'

Well might the Eatons think so from Simon's grotesque appearance in shorts, cycling cape and the absurd mauve and orange cricketing cap. Hurried greetings were soon exchanged and the whole party went back into the drawing-room.

'Greyeyes, darling,' Marie Lou exclaimed as she stood on tiptoe again to kiss De Richleau's lean cheek. 'We had your telegram and we are dying to know what it's all about. Have our servants conspired to poison us or what?'

'*What*,' smiled De Richleau. 'Definitely *what*, Princess. We have a very strange story to tell you, and I was most anxious you should avoid eating any meat for today at all events.'

Richard moved towards the bell. 'Well, we're not debarred from a glass of your favourite sherry, I trust.'

The Duke held up a restraining hand. 'I'm afraid we are. None of us must touch alcohol under any circumstances at present.'

'Good God!' Richard exclaimed. 'You don't mean that—you can't. You *have* gone crazy!'

'I do,' the Duke assured him with a smile. 'Quite seriously.'

'We're in a muddle—a nasty muddle,' Simon added with a twisted grin.

'So it appears,' Richard laughed, a trifle uneasily. He was quite staggered by the strange appearance of his friends, the tense electric atmosphere which they had brought into the house with them, and the unnatural way in which they stood about—speaking only in short jerky sentences.

He glanced at Rex, usually so full of gaiety, standing huge, gloomy and silent near the door, then he turned suddenly back to the Duke and demanded: 'What *is* Simon doing in that absurd get-up? If it was the right season for it I should imagine that he was competing for the fool's prize at the Three Arts' Ball.'

'I can quite understand your amazement,' the Duke replied quietly, 'but the truth is that Simon has been very seriously bewitched.'

'It is obvious that something's happened to him,' agreed Richard curtly. 'But don't you think it would be better to stop fooling and tell us just what all this nonsense *is* about?'

'I mean it,' the Duke insisted. 'He was sufficiently ill advised to start dabbling in Black Magic a few months ago, and it's only by the mercy of Providence that Rex and I were enabled to step in at a critical juncture with some hope of arresting the evil effects.'

Richard's brown eyes held the Duke's grey ones steadily. 'Look here,' he said, 'I am far too fond of you ever to be rude intentionally, but hasn't this joke gone far enough? To talk about magic in the twentieth century is absurd.'

'All right. Call it natural science then.' De Richleau leaned a little wearily against the mantelpiece. 'Magic is only a name for the sciences of causing change to occur in conformity with will.'

'Or by setting natural laws in action quite inadvertently,' added Marie Lou, to everyone's surprise.

'Certainly,' the Duke agreed after a moment, 'and Richard has practised that type of magic himself.'

'What on earth are you talking about?' Richard exclaimed.

De Richleau shrugged. 'Didn't you tell me that you got a Diviner down from London when you were so terribly short of water here last summer, and that when you took his hazel twig from him you found out quite by accident that you could locate an underground spring in the garden without his help?'

'Yes,' Richard hesitated. 'That's true, and as a matter of fact, I've been successful in finding places where people could sink wells on several estates in the neighbourhood since. But surely that has something to do with electricity? It's not magic.'

'If you were to say vibrations, you would be nearer the mark,' De Richleau replied seriously. 'It is an attunement of certain little-understood vibrations between the water under the ground and something in yourself which makes the forked hazel twig suddenly begin to jump and revolve in your hands when you walk over a hidden spring. That is undoubtedly a demonstration of the lesser kind of magic.'

'The miracle of Moses striking the rock in the desert from which the waters gushed forth is only another example of the same thing,' Simon cut in.

Marie Lou was watching the Duke's face with grave interest. 'Everyone knows there is such a thing as magic,' she declared, 'and witchcraft. During those years that I lived in a little village on the borders of the Siberian Forest I saw many strange things, and the peasants went in fear and trembling of one old woman who lived in a cottage all alone outside the village. But what do you mean by lesser magic?'

'There are two kinds,' De Richleau informed her. 'The lesser is performing certain operations which you believe will bring about a certain result without knowing why it should be so. If you chalk a line on the floor and take an ordinary hen, hold its beak down for a little time on to the line and then release it, the hen will remain there motionless with its head bent down to the floor. The assumption is that, being such a stupid creature, it believes that it has been tied down to the line and it is therefore useless to endeavour to escape. But nobody knows for certain. All we do know is that it happens. That is a fair example of an operation in minor magic. The great majority of the lesser witches and wizards in the part had no conception as to *why* their spells worked, but had learned from their predecessors that if they performed a given operation a certain result was almost sure to follow it.'

Rex looked up suddenly and spoke for the first time. 'I'd say they were pretty expert at playing on the belief of the credulous by peddling a sort of inverted Christian Science, faith healing, Coueism and all that as well.'

'Of course,' De Richleau smiled faintly. 'But they were far too clever to tell a customer straight out that if he concentrated sufficiently on his objective he would probably achieve it—even if they realised that themselves. Instead, they followed the old formulas which compelled him to develop his will power. If a man is in love with a girl and is told that he will get her if he rises from his bed at seven minutes past two every night for a month, gathers half a dozen flowers from a new-made grave in the local churchyard and places them in a spot where the girl will walk over them the following day, he does not get much chance to slacken in his desire and we all know that persistence can often work wonders.'

'Perhaps,' Richard agreed with mild cynicism. 'But would you have us believe that Simon is seeking the favour of a lady by wandering about in this lunatic get-up?'

'No, there is also the greater magic which is only practised by learned students of the Art who go through long courses of preparation and initiation, after which they understand not only that certain apparently inexplicable results are brought about by a given series of actions, but the actual reason why this should be so. Such people are powerful and dangerous in the extreme, and it is into the hands of one of these that our poor friend has fallen.'

Richard nodded, realising at last that the Duke was perfectly serious in his statement. 'This seems a most extraordinary affair,' he commented. 'I think you'd better start from the beginning and give us the whole story.'

'All right. Let's sit down. If you doubt any of the statements that I am about to make, Rex will guarantee the facts and vouch for my sanity.'

'I certainly will,' Rex agreed with a sombre smile.

De Richleau then told the Eatons all that had taken place in the last forty-eight hours, and asked quite solemnly if they were prepared to receive Simon, Rex and himself under their roof in spite of the fact that it might involve some risk to themselves.

'Of course,' Marie Lou said at once. 'We would not dream of your going away. You must stay just as long as you like and until you are quite certain that Simon is absolutely out of danger.'

Richard, sceptical still, but devoted to his friends whatever their apparent folly, nodded his agreement as he slipped an arm through his wife's. 'Certainly you must stay. And,' he added generously without the shadow of a smile, 'tell us exactly how we can help you best.'

'It's awfully decent of you,' Simon hazarded with a ghostly flicker of his old wide-mouthed grin. 'But I'll never forgive myself if any harm comes to you from it.'

'Don't let's have that all over again,' Rex begged. 'We argued it long enough in the car on the way here, and De Richleau's assured you time and again that no harm will come to Richard and Marie Lou providing we take reasonable precautions.'

'That is so,' the Duke nodded. 'And your help will be invaluable. You see, Simon's resistance is practically nil owing to his having been under Mocata's influence for so long, and Rex and I are at a pretty low ebb after last night. We need every atom of vitality which we can get to protect him, and your coming fresh into the battle should turn the scale in our favour. What we should have done if you had thrown us out I can't think, because I know of no one else who wouldn't have considered us all to be raving lunatics.'

Richard laughed. 'My dear fellow, how can you even suggest such a thing? You would still be welcome here if you'd committed murder.'

'I may have to before long,' De Richleau commented soberly. 'The risk to myself is a bagatelle compared to the horrors which may overwhelm the world if Mocata succeeds in getting possession of the Talisman–but I won't involve you in that of course.'

'This Sabbat you saw . . .' Richard hazarded after a moment 'Don't think I'm doubting your account of it, but isn't it just possible that your eyes deceived you in the darkness? I mean about the Satanic part. Everyone knows that Sabbats took place all over England in the sixteenth and seventeenth centuries. But it is generally accepted now that they were only an excuse for a bit of a blind and a sexual orgy. Country people had no motor bikes and buses to take them in to local cinemas then, and the Church frowned on all but the mildest forms of amusement, so the bad hats of the community used to sneak off to some quiet spot every now and again to give their repressed complexes an airing. Are you sure that it was not a revival of that sort of thing staged by a group of wealthy decadents?'

'Not on your life,' Rex declared with a sudden shiver. 'I've never been scared all that bad before and, believe you me, it was the real business.'

'What do you wish us to do, Greyeyes dear?' Marie Lou asked the Duke.

He hoisted himself slowly out of the chair into which he had sunk. 'I must drive to Oxford. An old Catholic priest whom I know lives there and I am going to try and persuade him to entrust me with a portion of the Blessed Host. If he will, that is the most perfect of all protections which we could have to keep with us through the night. In the meantime, I want the rest of you to look after Simon.' He smiled affectionately in Simon's direction. 'You must forgive me treating you like a child for the moment, my dear boy, but I don't want the others to let you out of their sight until I return.'

'That's all right,' Simon agreed cheerfully. 'But are you certain that I'm not—er—carrying harmful things about with me still?'

'Absolutely. The purification ceremonies which I practised on you last night have banished all traces of the evil. Our business now is to keep you free of it and get on Mocata's trail as quickly as we can.'

'Then I think I'll rest for a bit.' Simon glanced at Richard as he followed the Duke towards the door. 'The nap we had at the hotel in Amesbury after breakfast wasn't long enough to put me right—and afterwards perhaps you could lend me a decent suit of clothes?'

'Of course,' Richard smiled, 'Let's see Greyeyes off, then I'll make you comfortable upstairs.'

The whole party filed into the hall and, crowding about the low nail-studded oaken door, watched De Richleau, who promised to be back before dark, drive off. Then Richard, taking Simon by the arm, led him up the broad Jacobean stairway, while Marie Lou turned to Rex.

'What do you really think of all this?' she asked gravely, the usual merriment of her deep blue eyes clouded by a foreboding of coming trouble.

He stared down at her upturned heart-shaped face from his great height and answered soberly. 'We've struck a gateway of Hell all right, my dear, and I'm just worried out of my wits. De Richleau didn't give you the whole story. There's a girl in this that I'm—well—that I'm crazy about.'

'Rex!' Marie Lou laid her small strong hand on his arm. 'How awful for you. Come into my room and tell me everything.'

He followed her to her sitting-room and for half an hour poured into her sympathetic ears the strange tale of his three glimpses of Tanith at different times abroad, and then his unexpected meeting with her at Simon's party. Afterwards he related with more detail than the Duke had done their terrible experiences on Salisbury Plain and was just beginning his anxious speculation as to what could have happened to Tanith when Malin, the butler, softly opened the door.

'Someone is asking for you on the telephone, Mr Van Ryn, sir.'

'For me!' Rex stood up and, excusing himself to Marie Lou, hurried out, wondering who in the world it could be since no one knew his whereabouts. He was soon enlightened. A lilting voice, which had a strong resemblance to that of Marlene Dietrich, came over the wire as he placed the receiver to his ear.

'Is that you, Rex? Oh, I am so glad I have found you. I must see you at once—quickly—without a moment's delay.'

'Tanith!' he exclaimed. 'How did you tumble to it that I was here?'

'Oh, never mind that! I will tell you when I see you. But hurry, please.'

'Where are you then?'

'At the village inn, no more than a mile from you. Do come at once. It is very urgent.'

For a second Rex hesitated, but only for a second. Simon would be safe enough in the care of Richard and Marie Lou, and Tanith's voice had all the urgency and agitation of extreme fear. Anxiety for her had been gnawing at his heart ever since he had heard of her crash the previous evening. He knew that he loved her now—loved her desperately.

'All right,' he answered, his voice shaking a little. 'I'll be right over.'

Running back across the hall, he explained breathlessly to Marie Lou what had happened.

'You must go of course,' she said evenly. 'But you'll be back before nightfall won't you, Rex?'

'Sure.' All his animation seemed suddenly to have returned to him as, with a quick grin, he hurried out, snatched up his hat and, leaving the house, set off at a long easy loping trot by the short cut across the meadows to the village.

Unnoticed by him, a short figure entered the drive just as he disappeared beyond the boundary of the garden. A few moments later the newcomer was in conversation with Malin. The butler knew that his master was upstairs sitting with his friend Mr Aron while the latter rested, and had given orders that he was not to be disturbed, so leaving the visitor in the hall he crossed to Marie Lou's sitting-room.

'There is a gentleman to see you, madam,' he announced quietly. 'A Mr Mocata.'

22

THE SATANIST

For a moment Marie Lou hesitated, her eyes round with surprise, staring at the butler. In the last hour she had heard so much about this strange and terrifying visitor, but it had not occurred to her for one instant that she might be called upon to face him in the flesh so soon.

Her first impulse was to send upstairs for Richard, but like many people who possess extremely small bodies, her brain was exceptionally quick. Rex and the Duke were both absent, and, if she sent for Richard, Simon would be left alone—the one thing that De Richleau had been so insistent should not be allowed to happen. True, she and Richard would have the principal enemy under observation themselves, but he had allies. It flashed upon her that this girl Tanith was one perhaps and had purposely decoyed Rex away to the inn. Mocata might have others already waiting to lure Simon out of the house while they were busy talking to him. Almost instantly her mind was made up. Richard must not leave Simon, so she would have to interview Mocata on her own.

'Show him in,' she told the butler evenly. 'But if I ring you are to come at once—immediately, you understand?'

'Certainly, madam.' Malin softly withdrew, while Marie Lou seated herself in an armchair with her back to the light and within easy reach of the bell-push.

Mocata was shown in, and she studied him curiously. He was dressed in a suit of grey tweeds and wore a black stock tie. His head, large, bald and shiny, reminded her of an enormous egg, and the several folds of his heavy chin protruded above his stiff collar.

'I do hope you'll forgive me, Mrs Eaton,' he began in a voice that was musical and charming, 'for calling on you without any invitation. But you may perhaps have heard my name.'

She nodded slightly, carefully ignoring the hand which he half extended as she motioned him to the armchair on the opposite side of the fireplace. Marie Lou knew nothing of Esoteric Doctrines, but quite enough from the peasants' superstitions which had been rife in the little village where she had lived, an outcast of the Russian Revolution, to be aware that she must not touch this man, not offer him any form of refreshment while he was in her house.

The afternoon sunshine played full upon Mocata's pink, fleshy countenance as he went on. 'I thought perhaps that would be the case. Whether the facts have been rightly represented to you, I don't know, but Simon Aron is a very dear friend of mine, and during his recent illness I have been taking care of him.'

'I see,' she answered guardedly. 'Well, it was hardly put to me in that way, but what is the purpose of your visit?'

'I understand that Simon is with you now?'

'Yes,' she replied briefly, feeling that it was senseless to deny it, 'and his visit to us will continue for some little time.'

He smiled then, and with a little shock Marie Lou suddenly caught herself thinking that he was really quite an attractive person. His strange light-coloured eyes showed a strong intelligence and, to her surprise, a glint of the most friendly humour, which almost suggested that he was about to conspire with her in some amusing undertaking. His lisping voice, too, was strangely pleasant and restful to listen to as he spoke again in perfect English periods, only a curious intonation of the vowel sounds indicating his French extraction.

'The country air would no doubt be excellent for him, and I am certain that nothing could be more charming for him than your hospitality. Unfortunately there are certain matters, of which you naturally know nothing, but which make it quite imperative that I should take him back to London tonight.'

'I am afraid that is quite impossible.'

'I see,' Mocata looked thoughtfully for a moment at his large elastic-sided boots. 'I feared that you might take this attitude to begin with, because I imagine our friend De Richleau has been filling the heads of your husband and yourself with the most preposterous nonsense. I don't propose to go into that now or his reason for it, but I do ask you to believe me, Mrs Eaton, when I say that Simon will be in very considerable danger if you do not allow me to take him back into my care.'

'No danger will come to him as long as he is in my house,' said Marie Lou firmly.

'Ah, my dear young lady,' he sighed a little wistfully. 'I can hardly expect anyone like yourself to understand precisely what will happen to our poor Simon if he remains here, but his mental state has been unsatisfactory for some little time, and I alone can cure him of his lamentable condition. Chocolates!' he added suddenly and irrelevantly as his eyes rested upon a large box on a nearby table. 'You'll think me terribly rude, but may I?

I simply adore chocolates.'

'I'm so sorry,' Marie Lou replied without the flicker of an eyelash, 'but that box is empty. Do go on with what you were saying about Simon.'

Mocata withdrew his hand, feeling himself unable to challenge her statement by opening the box to see, and Marie Lou found it difficult to repress a smile as he made a comically rueful face like some greedy schoolboy who has been disappointed of a slice of cake.

'Really!' he exclaimed. 'What a pity. May I put it in the waste-paper basket for you then? To leave it about is such a terrible temptation for people like myself.' Before she could stop him he had reached out again and picked up the box, realising immediately by its weight that she had lied to him.

'No, please,' she put out her hand and almost snatched the box from his pudgy fingers. 'I gave it to my little girl to put her marbles in—we mustn't throw it away.' The box gave a faint rustle as she laid it down beside her, so she added swiftly: 'She puts each one in the little paper cups that the chocolates are packed in and arranges them in rows. She would be terribly distressed if they were upset.'

Mocata was not deceived by that ingenious fiction. He guessed at once her true reason for denying him the chocolates and was quick to realise that in this lovely young woman, who stood no taller than a well-grown child, he was up against a far cleverer antagonist than he had at first supposed. However, he was amply satisfied with the progress he had made so far, sensing that her first antagonism had already given way to a guarded interest. He must talk to her a little, his eyes and voice would do the rest. For a moment they stared at each other in silence. Then he opened his attack in a new direction.

'Mrs Eaton, it is quite obvious to me that you distrust me and, after what your friends have told you, I am not surprised. But your intelligence emboldens me to think that I am likely to serve my purpose better by putting my cards on the table than by beating about the bush.'

'It will make no difference what you do,' said Marie Lou quietly.

He ignored the remark and went on in his low, slightly lisping voice. 'I do not propose to discuss with you the rights or wrongs of practising the Magic Art. I will confine myself to saying that I am a practitioner of some experience and Simon, who has interested himself in these things for the past few months, shows great promise of one day achieving considerable powers. Monsieur De Richleau has probably led you to suppose that I am a most evil person. But in fairness to myself I must protest that such a view of me is quite untrue. In magic, there is neither good nor evil. It is only the science of causing change to occur by means of will. The rather sinister reputation attaching to it is easily accounted for by the fact that it had to be practised in secret for many centuries owing to the ban placed upon it by the Church. Anything which is done in secret naturally begets a reputation for mystery and, since it dare not face the light of day, the reverse of good. Few people understand anything of these mysteries, and I can hardly assume that you have more than vague impressions gathered from casual reading; but at least I imagine you will have heard that genuine adepts in the secret Art have the power to call certain entities, which are not understood or admitted by the profane, into actual being.

'Now these are perfectly harmless as long as they are under the control of the practitioner, just as a qualified electrician stands no risk in adjusting a powerful electric battery from which a child, who played foolishly with it, might receive a serious shock or even death. This analogy applies to the work Simon and I are engaged upon. We have called a certain entity into being just as workers in another sphere might have constructed an electrical machine. It needs both of us to operate this thing with skill and safety, but if I am to be left to handle it alone, the forces which we have engendered will undoubtedly escape and do the very gravest harm both to Simon and myself. Have I made the position clear?'

'Yes,' murmured Marie Lou. During that long explanatory speech he had been regarding her with a steady stare, and as she listened to his quiet, cultured voice expressing what seemed such obvious truths, she felt her whole reaction to his personality changing. It suddenly seemed to her absurd that this nice, charming gentleman in the neat grey suit could be dangerous to anyone. His face seemed to have lost its puffy appearance even while he was speaking, and now her eyes beheld it as only hairless, pink and clean like that of some elderly divine.

'I am so glad,' he went on in his even, silky tone. 'I felt quite sure that if you allowed me a few moments I could clear up this misunderstanding which has only risen through the over-eagerness of your old friend the Duke, and that charming young American, to protect Simon from some purely imaginary danger. If I had only had the opportunity to explain to them personally I am quite convinced that I should have been able to save them a great deal of worry, but I only met them for a few moments one evening at Simon's house. It is a charming little place that, and he very kindly permits me to share it with him while I am in England. If you are in London during the next few weeks, I do hope that you will come and see us there. We both know without asking that Simon would be delighted, and it would give me the very greatest pleasure to show you my collection of perfumes, which I always take with me when I travel.

'As a matter of fact, I am rather an expert in the art of blending perfumes, and quite a number of my women friends have allowed me to make a special scent for them. It is a delicate art, and interesting, because each woman should have her own perfume made to conform to her aura and personality. You have an outstanding individuality, Mrs Eaton, and it would be a very great pleasure if you would allow me some time to see if I could not compound something really distinctive in that way for you.'

'It sounds most interesting,' Marie Lou's voice was low and Mocata's eyes still held hers. Really, she felt, despite his bulk, he was a most attractive person, and she had been quite stupid to be a little frightened of him when he first entered the room. The May sunshine came in gently-moving shafts through the foliage of a tree outside the window, so that the dappled light played upon his face, and it was that, she thought, which gave her the illusion that his unblinking eyes were larger than when she had first looked into them.

'When will the Duke be back?' he asked softly. 'Unfortunately, my visit today must be a brief one, but I should so much have liked to talk this matter over quietly with him before I go.'

'I don't know,' Marie Lou found herself answering. 'But I'm afraid he won't be back before six.'

'And our American friend—the young giant,' he prompted her.

'I've no idea. He has gone down to the village.'

'I see. What a pity, but of course your husband is here entertaining Simon, is he not?'

'Yes, they are upstairs together.'

'Well, presently I should like to explain to your husband, just as I have to you, how very important it is that I should take Simon back with me tonight, but I wonder first if I might beg a glass of water. Walking from the village has given me quite a thirst.'

'Of course,' Marie Lou rose to her feet automatically and pressed the bell. 'Wouldn't you prefer a cup of tea or a glass of wine and some biscuits?' she added, completely now under the strange influence that radiated from him.

'You are most kind, but just a glass of water and a biscuit if I may.'

Malin already stood in the doorway and Marie Lou gave orders for these slender refreshments. Then she sat down again, and Mocata's talk flowed on easily and glibly, while her ears became more and more attuned to that faint musical lisping intonation.

The butler appeared with water and biscuits on a tray and set them down beside Mocata, but for the moment he took no notice of it. Instead he looked again at Marie Lou, and said: 'I do hope you'll forgive me asking, but have you recently been ill? You are looking as though you were terribly run down and very, very tired.'

'No,' said Marie Lou slowly. 'I haven't been ill.' But at that moment her limbs seemed to relax where she was sitting and her heavy eyelids weighed upon her eyes. For some unaccountable reason, she felt an intense longing to shut them altogether and fall asleep.

Mocata watched her with a faint smile curving his full mouth. He had her under his dominance now and knew it. Another moment and she would be asleep. It would be easy to carry her into the next room and leave her there, ring for the servant, ask him to find his master and when Richard arrived, say that she had gone out into the garden to find him. Then another of those quiet little talks which he knew so well how to handle, even when people were openly antagonistic to him to begin with, and the master of the house would also pass into a quiet, untroubled sleep. Then he would simply call Simon by his will and they would leave the house together.

Marie Lou's eyes flickered and shut. With a shake of her head she jerked them open again. 'I'm so sorry,' she said sleepily. 'But I am tired, most awfully tired. What was it that you were talking about?'

Mocata's eyes seemed enormous to her now, as they held her own with a solemn, dreamy look. 'We shall not talk any more,' he said. 'You will sleep, and at four o'clock on the afternoon of 7th May, you will call on me at Simon's house in St. John's Wood.'

Marie Lou's heavy lashes fell on her rounded cheeks again, but next second her eyes were wide open, for the door was flung back and Fleur came scampering into the room.

'Darling, what is it?' Marie Lou struggled wide awake and Mocata snapped his plump fingers with a little angry, disappointed gesture. The sudden entrance of the child had broken the current of delicate vibrations.

'Mummy—mummy,' Fleur panted. 'Daddy-sent-me-to-find-you. We'se playing hosses in the garden, an' Uncle Simon says he's a dwagon, an' not a hoss at all. Daddy says you're to come and tell him diffwent.'

'So this is your little daughter? What a lovely child,' Mocata said amiably, stretching out a hand to Fleur. 'Come here, my . . .'

But Marie Lou cut short his sentence as full realisation of the danger to which she had exposed herself flooded her mind. 'Don't you touch her!' she cried, snatching up the child with blazing eyes. 'Don't you dare!'

'Really, Mrs Eaton,' he raised his eyebrows in mild protest. 'Surely you cannot think that I meant to hurt the child? I thought too, that we were beginning to understand each other so well.'

'You beast,' Marie Lou cried angrily as she jabbed her finger on the bell. 'You tried to hypnotise me.'

'What nonsense,' he smiled good-humouredly. 'You were a little tired, but I fear I bored you rather with a long dissertation upon things which can hardly interest a woman so young and charming as yourself. It was most stupid of me, and I hardly wonder that you nearly fell asleep.'

As Malin arrived on the scene she thrust Fleur into the astonished butler's arms and gasped: 'Fetch Mr Eaton–he's in the garden–quickly–at once.'

The butler hurried off with Fleur and Mocata turned on her. His eyes had gone cold and steely. 'It is vital that I should at least see Simon before I leave this house.'

'You shan't,' she stormed. 'You had better go before my husband comes. D'you hear?' Then she found herself looking at him again, and quickly jerked her head away so that she should not see his eyes, yet she caught his gesture as he stooped to pick up the glass of water from the table.

Furious now at the way she had been tricked into ordering it for him, and determining that he should not drink, she sprang forward and before he could stop her, dashed the little table to the ground. The plate caught the carafe as it fell and smashed it into a dozen pieces, the biscuits scattered and the water spread in a shallow, widening lake upon the carpet. Mocata swung round with an angry snarl. This small, sensuous, catlike creature had cheated him at the last, and the placid, kindly expression of his face changed to one of hideous demoniacal fury. His eyes, muddled now with all the foulness of his true nature, stripped and flayed her, threatening a thousand unspeakable abominations in their unwinking stare as she faced him across the fallen table.

Suddenly, with a fresh access of terror, Marie Lou cowered back, bringing up her hands to shield her face from those revolting eyeballs. Then a quick voice in the doorway exclaimed: 'Hello! What is all this?'

'Richard,' she gasped. 'Richard, it's Mocata! I saw him because I thought you'd better stay with Simon, but he tried to hypnotise me. Have him thrown out. Oh, have him thrown out.'

The muscles in Richard's lean face tightened as he caught the look of terror in his wife's eyes and thrusting her aside he took a quick step towards Mocata. 'If you weren't twice my age and in my house, I'd smash your face in,' he said savagely. 'And that won't stop me either unless you get out thundering quick.'

With almost incredible swiftness Mocata had his anger under control. His face was benign and smiling once more, as he shrugged, showing no trace of panic. 'I'm afraid your wife is a little upset,' he said mildly. 'It is this spring weather, and while we were talking together, she nearly fell asleep. Having heard all sorts of extraordinary things about me from your friends, she scared herself into thinking that I tried to hypnotise her. I apologise profoundly for having caused her one moment's distress.'

'I don't believe one word of that,' replied Richard. 'Now kindly leave the house.'

Mocata shrugged again. 'You are being very unreasonable, Mr Eaton. I called this afternoon in order to take Simon Aron back to London.'

'Well, you're not going to.'

'Please,' Mocata held up his protesting hand. 'Hear me for one moment. The whole situation has been most gravely misrepresented to you, as I explained to your wife, and if she hadn't suddenly started to imagine things we should be discussing it quite amicably now. In fact, I even asked her to send for you, as she will tell you herself.'

'It was a trick,' cried Marie Lou angrily. 'Don't look at his eyes, Richard, and for God's sake turn him out!'

'You hear,' Richard's voice held a threatening note and his face was white. 'You had better go—before I lose my temper.'

'It's a pity that you are so pig-headed, my young friend,' Mocata snapped icily. 'By retaining Simon here, you are bringing extreme peril on both him and on yourself. But since you refuse to be reasonable and let me take him with me, let me at least have five minutes' conversation with him alone.'

'Not five seconds,' Richard stood aside from the door and motioned through it for Mocata to pass into the hall.

'All right! If that is your final word!' Mocata drew himself up. He seemed to grow in size and strength even as he stood there. A terrible force and energy suddenly began to shake his obese body. They felt it radiating from him as his words came low and clear like the whispering splash of death-cold drops falling from icicles upon a frozen lake.

'Then I will send the Messenger to your house tonight and he shall take Simon from you alive—or dead!'

'Get out,' gritted Richard between his teeth. 'Damn you—get out!'

Without another word Mocata left them. Marie Lou crossed herself, and with Richard's arm about her shoulder they followed him to the door.

He did not turn or once look back, but plodded heavily, a very ordinary figure now, down the long, sunlit drive.

Richard suddenly felt Marie Lou's small body tremble against him, and with a little cry of fright she buried her head on his shoulder. 'Oh, darling,' she wailed. 'I'm frightened of that man—frightened. Did you see?'

'See what, my sweet?' he asked, a little puzzled.

'Why!' sobbed Marie Lou. 'He is walking in the sunshine—but he has no shadow!'

23

THE PRIDE OF PEACOCKS

The inn which served the village near Cardinals Folly was almost as old as the house. At one period it had been a hostelry of some importance, but the changing system of highways in the eighteenth century had left it denuded of the coaching traffic and doomed from then on to cater only for the modest wants of the small local population. It had been added to and altered many times; for one long period falling almost wholly into disrepair, since its revenue was insufficient for its upkeep, and so it had remained until a few years earlier upon the retirement of Mr Jeremiah Wilkes, the ex-valet of a wealthy peer who lived not far distant.

Only the fact that Mr Wilkes suffered from chronic sciatica, which rendered it impossible for him to travel any more with his old master, had made his retirement necessary, and through those long years of packing just the right garments that his lordship might need for Cowes, Scotland or the French Riviera and exercising his incomparable facility for obtaining the most comfortable seats upon trains which were already full, he had always had it in the back of his mind that he would like to be the proprietor of a gentlemanly 'house.'

When the question of his retirement had been discussed, and Jeremiah had named the ambition of his old age, his master had most generously suggested the purchase and restoration of the old inn, but voiced his doubts of Jeremiah's ability to run it at a profit; stating that capital was very necessary to the success of any business, and adding in his innocence that he did not feel Jeremiah could have saved a sufficient sum despite the long period in his employment.

In this, of course, his lordship was entirely wrong. Jeremiah's wage might have been a modest one but, while protecting his master from many generations of minor thieves, he had gathered in the time-honoured perquisites which were his due and, since he had stoutly resisted the efforts of his fellow servants to interest him in 'the horses,' he owned investments in property which would have considerably amazed his master.

Mr Wilkes, therefore, had modestly stated that he thought he might manage providing that his lordship would be good enough to send him such friends or their retainers as could not be accommodated at the Court when shooting parties and such like were in progress. This having been arranged satisfactorily, Mr Wilkes underwent the metamorphosis from a gentleman's gentleman to host of 'The Pride of Peacocks.'

Very soon the old inn began to thrive again; quietly, of course, since it was no road-house for noisy motorists. But it became well known among a certain select few who enjoyed a peaceful weekend in lovely scenery, and Mr Wilkes' admirable attention to these, together with his wife's considerable knowledge of the culinary art, never caused them to question their Monday morning bill.

Jeremiah had further added to the attraction of the place by stocking a cellar with variety and taste from his lordship's London wine merchant on terms extremely advantageous to himself, and moreover to the added well-being of the neighbourhood. The hideous and childish tyranny of licensing hours never affected him in the least for the simple reason that all his customers were personal friends, including, of course, the magistrates upon the local bench, and had some officious policeman from the town ever questioned the fact that gentlemen were to be found there quite frequently in the middle of the afternoon taking a little modest refreshment, they would have quailed under the astonished and supercilious glance of the good Mr Wilkes, together with the freezing statement that this was no monetary transaction, but the gentlemen concerned were doing him the honour to give him their opinion upon his latest purchase in the way of port.

In short, it will be gathered that this ancient hostelry could provide all the comfort which any reasonable person might demand, and was something a little out of the ordinary for a village inn. Rex, of course, knew the place well from his previous visits to Cardinals Folly and, a little out of breath from the pace at which he had come, hurried into the low comfortably furnished lounge, the old oak beams of which almost came down to his head.

Tanith was there alone. Immediately she saw him she jumped up from her chair and ran to meet him, gripping both his hands in hers with a strength surprising for her slender fingers.

She was pale and weary. Her green linen dress was stained and mired from her terrible journey on the previous night, although obviously she had done her best to tidy herself. Her eyes were shadowed from strain and lack of sleep, seeming unnaturally large, and she trembled slightly as she clutched at him.

'Oh, thank God you've come!' she cried.

'But how did you know I was at Cardinals Folly?' he asked her quickly.

'My dear,' she sank down in the chair again, drawing her hand wearily across her eyes. 'I am terribly sorry about last night. I think I was mad when I stole your car and tried to get to the Sabbat. I crashed of course, but I expect you will have heard about that–and then I did the last five miles on foot.'

'Good God! Do you mean to say you got there after all?'

She nodded and told him of that nightmare walk from Easterton to the Satanic Festival. As she came to the part in her story where, against her will, she had been drawn down into the valley, her eyes once more expressed the hideous terror which she had felt.

'I could not help myself,' she said. 'I tried to resist with all my mind but my feet simply moved against my will. Then, for a moment, I thought that the heavens had opened and an angry God had suddenly decided to strike those blasphemous people dead. There was a noise like thunder and two giant eyes like those of some nightmare monster seemed to leap out of the darkness right at me. I screamed, I think, and jumped aside. I remember falling and springing up again. The power that had held my feet seemed to have been suddenly released and I fled up the hill in absolute panic. When I got to the top I tripped over something and then I must have fainted.'

Rex smiled. 'That was us in the car,' he said. 'But how did you know where to find me?'

'It was not very difficult,' she told him. 'When I came to, I was lying on the grass and there wasn't a sound to show that there was a living soul within miles of me. I started off at a run without the faintest idea where I was going–my only thought being to get away from that terrible valley. Then when I was absolutely exhausted I fell again, and I must have been so done in that I slept for a little in a ditch.

'When I woke up, it was morning and I found that I was quite near a main road. I limped along it not knowing what I should come to and then I saw houses and a straggling street and, after a little, I discovered that I had walked into Devizes.

'I went into the centre of the town and was about to go into an hotel when I realised that I had no money; but I had a brooch, so I found a jeweller's and sold it to them–or rather, they agreed to advance me twenty pounds, because I didn't want to part with it and it must be worth at least a hundred. An awfully nice old man there agreed to keep it as security until I could send him the money on from London. Then I did go to the hotel, took a room and tried to think things over.

'Such an extraordinary lot seemed to have happened since you took me off in your car from Claridges yesterday that at first I could not get things straight at all, but one thing stood out absolutely clearly. Whether it was you or the vision of my mother, I don't know, but my whole outlook had changed completely. How I could ever have allowed myself to listen to Madame D'Urfé and do the things I've done I just can't think. But I know now that I've been in the most awful danger, and that I must try and get free of Mocata somehow. Anyone would think me mad, and possibly I am, to come to you like this when I hardly know you, but the whole thing has been absolutely outside all ordinary experiences. I am terribly alone, Rex, and you are the only person in the world that I can turn to.'

She sank back in her chair almost exhausted with the effort of endeavouring to impress him with her feelings, but he leant forward and, taking one of her hands in his great leg-of-mutton fist, squeezed it gently.

'There, there, my sweet.' Speaking from his heart he used the endearment quite naturally and unconsciously. 'You did the right thing every time. Don't you worry any more. Nobody is going to hurt a hair of your head now you've got here safely. But how in the world did you do it?'

Her eyes opened again and she smiled faintly. 'My only hope was to throw myself on your protection, so I had to find you somehow and that part wasn't difficult. All systems of divination are merely so many methods of obscuring the outer vision, in order that the inner may become clear. Tea-leaves, crystals, melting wax, lees of wine, cards, water, entrails, birds, sieve-turning, sand and all the rest.

'I wanted sleep terribly when I got to that hotel bedroom, but I knew that I mustn't allow myself to, so I took some paper from the lounge, and borrowed a pencil. Then I drew myself into a trance with the paper before me and the pencil in my hand. When I looked at it again I had quite enough information scribbled down to enable me to follow you here.'

Rex accepted this amazing explanation quite calmly. Had he been told such a thing a few days before he would have considered it fantastic, but now it never even occurred to him that it was in any way extraordinary that a woman desiring to know his whereabouts should throw herself into a trance and employ automatic writing.

She glanced at the old grandfather clock which stood ticking away in a corner of the low-raftered room. Half an hour had sped by already and he was feeling guilty now at having left Simon. He would never be able to forgive himself if, in his absence, any harm befell his friend. Now that he knew Tanith was safe he must get back to Cardinals Folly, so he announced abruptly: 'I'm mighty sorry, but I've got Simon to look after so I can't stay here much longer.'

'Oh, Rex,' her eyes held his imploringly. 'You must not unless you take me with you. If you leave me alone, Mocata will be certain to get me.'

For a moment Rex hesitated miserably, wrestling with the quandary that faced him. If Tanith was telling the truth, he couldn't possibly leave her to be drawn back by that terrible power of evil. But was she? So far she had been Mocata's puppet. How much truth was there in this pretended change of heart? Had Mocata planted her there in order to lure him deliberately away from Simon's side?

It occurred to him that he might take her back with him to Cardinals Folly, for if she was speaking the truth she was in the same case as Simon.

They could keep the two of them together and concentrate their forces against the black magician. But he dismissed the idea almost as soon as it entered his mind. To do so would be playing Mocata's game with a vengeance. If Tanith were acting consciously or unconsciously under his influence, God alone knew what powers she might possess to aid her master once they accepted her as a friend in their midst. If he took her there it would be like introducing one of the enemy into a beleaguered fortress.

'What are you afraid might happen if I leave you?' he asked suddenly.

'You can't–you mustn't,' her eyes pleaded with him. 'Not only for my own sake, but your friends' as well. Mocata has a hundred means of knowing where Simon is and where I am too. He may arrive here at any moment. It's no good pretending Rex. I know beyond any question that I cannot resist him and he'll work through me, however much my will is set against it. He's told me a dozen times that he has never met a woman who is such a successful medium for him as myself. So you can be certain that he is on his way here now.'

'What d'you think he'll do when he turns up?'

'He will throw me into a trance and call Simon to him. Then if Simon fails to come Mocata may curse him through me.'

Rex shrugged. 'Don't worry. De Richleau's a wily old bird. He'll turn the curse aside some way.'

'But you don't seem to understand,' she sobbed. 'If a curse is sent out it must lodge somewhere, and if it fails to reach its objective because there is an equally strong influence working against it, the vibrations recoil and impinge upon the sender.'

'Steady now.' He took her hands and tried to soothe her. 'If that is so I guess we couldn't find a better way to tickle up Mocata.'

'No–no!! He never does things himself–at least I have never known him to–just in case he fails, because then he would have to pay the penalty. Instead, he uses other people–hypnotises them and makes them throw out the thought or the wish. That is what he will do to me. If he succeeds, you will no longer be able to protect Simon, and if he fails, it is I who will pay the price. That is why you've just got to stay with me and prevent him using me as his instrument.'

'Holy smoke! Then we're in a proper jam!' Rex's brain was working swiftly. If she were telling the truth, she was in real danger. If not, at least Simon still had Richard and Marie Lou to take care of him until the Duke's return.

All his chivalry and his love for her which seemed to have blossomed overnight welled up and told him that he must chance her honesty and remain there to protect her. 'All right, I'll stay,' he said after a moment.

'Oh, thank God!' she sighed. 'Thank God!'

'But tell me,' he went on, 'just why is it you're such a king-pin medium to this man? What about old Madame D'Urfé and the rest? Can't he do his stuff through them?'

Tanith looked at him through tear-dimmed eyes and shook her head. 'Not in the same way. You see there is rather an unusual link between us. My number is twenty and so is his.'

Rex frowned. 'What exactly do you mean by that?' he asked in a puzzled voice.

'I mean our astrological number,' she replied quietly. 'Give me a piece of paper, and I will show you.'

Rex handed her a few sheets from a nearby table and a pencil from his waistcoat pocket. Then she quickly drew out a list of the numerical values to the letters of the alphabet:

A = 1	K = 2	S = 3
B = 2	L = 3	T = 4
C = 3	M = 4	U = 6
D = 4	N = 5	V = 6
E = 5	O = 7	W = 6
F = 8	P = 8	X = 5
G = 3	Q = 1	Y = 1
H = 5	R = 2	Z = 7
I or J = 1		

'There!' she went on. 'By substituting numbers for letters in anyone's name and adding them up you get their occult number which indicates the planet that influences them most in all spiritual affairs. It must be the name by which they are most generally known–even if it is a pet name. Now look!'

M = 4		T = 4	
O = 7		A = 1	
C = 3		N = 5	
A = 1		I = 1	
T = 4		T = 4	
A = 1		H = 5	
20	2+0=2	20	2+0=2

'You see how closely our vibrations are attuned. Two is the value of the Moon, to which both he and I are subject, and any names having a total numerical value which reduce by progressive additions to two, such as eleven or twenty-nine or thirty-eight or forty-seven, would give us some affinity, but that they actually add up to the same *compound* number shows that we are attuned to a very remarkable degree. That is why I have proved such an exceptionally good medium for him to work through.'

'But you are utterly different from him,' Rex protested.

'Of course,' she nodded gravely. 'One's birth date gives the *material* number, which is generally that of another planet and modifies the influence of the *spiritual* number considerably. As it happens mine is May 2nd–again a two you see, so I am an almost pure type. Moon people are intensely imaginative, artistic, romantic, gentle by nature and not very strong physically. They are rather over-sensitive and lacking in self-confidence, unsettled too, and liable to be continually changing their plans, but most of them, of course, have some balancing factor. Mocata gets all his imaginative and psychic qualities from the Moon, but his birthday is April 24th which adds up to six, and six being the number of Venus, he is very strongly influenced by that planet. Venus people are extremely magnetic. They attract others easily and are usually loved and worshipped by those under them, but very often they are obstinate and unyielding. It is that in his nature which balances the weakness of the Moon and makes him so determined in carrying out his plans.'

'What do I come under?' Rex asked with sudden curiosity. 'My names are so short that I'm generally known by all three.'

Again Tanith took the paper and quickly worked out the equivalent of his name.

$$R = 2$$
$$E = 5$$
$$X = 5$$
$$\overline{} = 12$$
$$V = 6$$
$$A = 1$$
$$N = 5$$
$$\overline{} = 12$$
$$R = 2$$
$$Y = 1$$
$$N = 5$$
$$\overline{} = 8$$

$$32 \text{ and } 3 + 2 = 5$$

She looked at him sharply. 'Yes, I am not surprised. Five is a fortunate and magic number which comes under Mercury. Such people are versatile and mercurial, quick in thought and decisions, impulsive in action and detest plodding work. They make friends easily with every type and have a wonderful elasticity of character which can recover at once from any setback. Even though I do not know you well, I am certain that all this is true of you. I expect you are a born speculator as well and every type of risk attracts you.'

'That certainly is so,' Rex grinned as she went on thoughtfully: 'But I should have thought that there was a good bit of the Sun about you because you have such strong individuality and you are so definite in your views.'

'I was born on the 19th of August if that gives you a line.'

She smiled. 'Yes, 19 is 1 + 9 which equals ten and 1 + 0 equals 1, the number of the Sun. So I was right, and it is that part of you which I think attracts me so much. Sun and Moon people always get on well together.'

'I don't know anything about that,' Rex said softly. 'But I'm dead sure I could never see too much of you.'

She lifted her eyes from his quickly as though almost in fright and to break the pause that followed he asked: 'What number is Simon associated with?'

'He was born under Saturn as we know only too well, and his occult number is certain to be the Saturnian eight,' Tanith replied promptly, scribbling the name and numbers on the paper.

$$S = 3$$
$$I = 1$$
$$M = 4$$
$$O = 7$$
$$N = 5$$
$$\overline{} = 20$$

$$A = 1$$
$$R = 2$$
$$O = 7$$
$$N = 5$$
$$\overline{} = 15$$

$$35 \text{ and } 3 + 5 = 8$$

'By Jove! That's queer,' Rex murmured as he saw the name worked out quite simple to the number she had predicted.

'He is a typical number eight person too,' she went on. 'They have deep, intense natures and are often lonely at heart because they are frequently misunderstood. Sometimes they play a most important part on life's stage and nearly always a fatalistic one. They are almost fanatically loyal to persons they are fond of or causes they take up, and carry things through regardless of making enemies. It is not a fortunate number to be born under as a rule, and such people usually become great successes or great failures.'

Rex drew the paper towards him, and taking the pencil from her began to work out for himself the numerical symbols of De Richleau, Richard Eaton and Marie Lou.

$$D = 4$$
$$E = 5$$
$$\overline{} = 9$$

$$R = 2$$
$$I = 1$$
$$C = 3$$
$$H = 5$$
$$L = 3$$
$$E = 5$$
$$A = 1$$
$$U = 6$$
$$\overline{} = 26$$

$$35 = 8$$

$$R = 2$$
$$I = 1$$
$$C = 3$$
$$H = 5$$
$$A = 1$$
$$R = 2$$
$$D = 4$$
$$\overline{} = 18$$

$$E = 5$$
$$A = 1$$
$$T = 4$$
$$O = 7$$
$$N = 5$$
$$\overline{} = 22$$

$$40 = 4$$

$$M = 4$$
$$A = 1$$
$$R = 2$$
$$I = 1$$
$$E = 5$$
$$\overline{} = 13$$

$$L = 3$$
$$O = 7$$
$$U = 6$$
$$\overline{} = 16$$

$$29 = 11 = 2$$

'This is amazing,' Tanith exclaimed when he had finished. 'The Duke not only comes under the eight like Simon, but their compound number–thirty-five–is the same as well. He should have immense influence with Simon through that affinity, just as Mocata has over me, and the nine in his name gives him the additional qualities of the born leader, independence, success, courage and determination. If anyone in the world can save your friend, that extraordinary combination of strength and sympathy will enable De Richleau to do so.'

'But d'you see that the names Richleau and Ryn boil down to eight as well, linking us both with Simon. That's strange, isn't it?'

'Not altogether. Any numerologist who knew of your devotion to each other would expect to find some such affinity in your numbers. You will see, too, that your other friend, Richard Eaton, is a four person, which accounts for his sympathy towards you. The eight is formed by two halves or circles and, four being the half of eight, persons with those numbers will always incline towards each other. Then his wife, like myself, is a two which is again linked to all four of you because it is divisible into eight.'

Rex nodded. 'It's the strangest mystery I've met up with in the whale of a while. There isn't a single odd number in the whole series, but tell me, would this combination of eights be a good thing d'you reckon – or no?'

'It is very, very potent,' she said slowly. '888 is the number given to Our Lord by students of Occultism in his aspect as the Redeemer. Add them together and you get twenty-four. $2+4=6$ which is the number of Venus, the representative of Love. That is the complete opposite of 666 which Revelations give as the number of the Beast. The three sixes add to eighteen, and $1+8=9$, the symbol of Mars – De Richleau's secondary quality which makes him a great leader and fighter, but in its pure state represents Destruction, Force and War.'

At the mention of War, Rex's whole mind was jerked from the quiet, comfortable, old-fashioned inn parlour to a mental picture of De Richleau as he had stood only a few hours before with the light of dawn breaking over Stonehenge. He saw again the Duke's grey face and unnaturally bright eyes as he spoke of the Talisman of Set; that terrible gateway out of Hell through which, if Mocata found it, those dread four horsemen would come riding, invisible but all-powerful, to poison the thoughts of peace-loving people and manipulate unscrupulous statesmen, influencing them to plunge Europe into fresh calamity.

Not only had they to fight Mocata for Simon's safety and Tanith's as well but, murder though it might be to people lacking in understanding, they had to kill him even if they were forced to sacrifice themselves.

With sudden clarity Rex saw that Tanith's appeal for protection offered a golden opportunity to carry the war into the enemy's camp. She was so certain that Mocata would appear to claim her, and De Richleau had stated positively that while daylight lasted the Satanist was no more powerful than any other thug.

'Why,' Rex thought, with a quick tightening of his great muscles, 'should he not seize Mocata by force when he arrived; then send for the Duke to decide what they should do with him.'

Only one difficulty seemed to stand in the way. He could hardly attack a visitor and hold him prisoner in 'The Pride of Peacocks.' Mr Wilkes might object to that. But apparently Mocata could find Tanith with equal ease wherever she was, so she must be got out of the inn to some place where the business could be done without interference.

For a moment the thought of Cardinals Folly entered his mind again, but if he once took Tanith there, they could hardly turn her out later on, and she might become a highly dangerous focus in the coming night; besides, Mocata might not care to risk a visit to the house in daylight with the odds so heavily against him, and that would ruin the whole plan. Then he remembered the woods at the bottom of the garden behind the inn. If he took Tanith there and Mocata did turn up he would have a perfectly free hand in dealing with him. He glanced across at Tanith and suggested casually: 'What about a little stroll?'

She shook her fair head, and lay back with half-closed eyes in the arm-chair. 'I would love to, but I am so terribly tired. I had no proper sleep you know last night.'

He nodded. 'We didn't get much either. We were sitting around Stonehenge the best part of the time till dawn. After that we went into Amesbury where the Duke took a room. The people there must have thought us a queer party—one room for three people and beds being specially shifted into it at half-past seven in the morning, but he was insistent that we shouldn't leave Simon for a second. So we had about four hours' shut-eye on those three beds, all tied together by our wrists and ankles; but it's a glorious afternoon and the woods round here are just lovely now it's May.'

'If you like.' She rose sleepily. 'I dare not go to sleep in any case. You mustn't let me until tomorrow morning. After midnight it will be May 2nd, the mystic two again you see, and my birthday. So during the dark hours tonight I shall be passing into my fatal day. It may be good or evil, but in such circumstances it is almost certain to bring some crisis in my life, and I'm afraid, Rex, terribly afraid.'

He drew her arm protectively through his and led her out through the back door into the pleasant garden which boasted two large, gay archery targets, a pastime that Jeremiah Wilkes had seen fit to institute for the amusement of the local gentry, deriving considerable profit therefrom when they bet each other numerous rounds of drinks upon their prowess with the six-foot bow.

A deep border of dark wallflowers sent out their heady scent at the farther end of the lawn and beyond them the garden opened on to a natural wooded glade. A small stream marked the boundary of Mr Wilkes' domain and when they reached it, Rex passed his arm round Tanith's body, lifted her before she could protest, and with one spring of his long legs cleared the brook. She did not struggle from his grasp, but looked up at him curiously as she lay placid in his arms.

'You must be very strong,' she said. 'Most men can lift a woman, but it can't be easy to jump a five-foot brook with one.'

'I'm strong enough,' he smiled into her face, not attempting to put her down. 'Strong enough for both of us. You needn't worry.' Then, still carrying her in his arms, he walked on into the depths of the wood until the fresh, green beech trees hid them from the windows of the inn.

'You will get awfully tired,' she said lazily.

'Not me,' he declared, shaking his head. 'You may be tall, but you're only a featherweight. I could carry you a mile if I wanted, and it wouldn't hurt me any.'

'You needn't,' she smiled up at him. 'You can put me down now and we'll sit under the trees. It's lovely here. You were quite right—much nicer than the inn.'

He laid her down very gently on a sloping bank, but instead of rising, knelt above her with one arm still about her shoulders and looked down into her eyes. 'You love me,' he said suddenly. 'Don't you?'

'Yes,' she confessed with troubled shadows brooding in her golden eyes. 'I do. But you mustn't love me, Rex. You know what I told you yesterday. I'm going to die. I'm going to die soon—before the year is out.'

'You're not,' he said, almost fiercely. 'We'll break this devil Mocata—De

Richleau will, I'm certain.'

'But, my dear, it's nothing to do with him,' she protested sadly. 'It's just Fate, and you haven't known me long, so it's not too late yet for you to keep a hold on yourself. You mustn't love me, because if you do, it will make you terribly unhappy when I die.'

'You're not going to die,' he repeated, and then he laughed suddenly, boyishly, all his mercurial nature rising to dispel such gloomy thoughts. 'If we both die tomorrow,' he said suddenly, 'we've still got today, and I love you, Tanith. That's all there is to it.'

Her arms crept up about his neck and with sudden strength she kissed him on his mouth.

He grabbed her then, his lips seeking hers again and again, while he muttered little phrases of endearment, pouring out all the agony of anxiety that he had felt for her during the past night and the long run from Amesbury in the morning. She clung to him, laughing a little hysterically although she was not far from tears. This strange new happiness was overwhelming to her, flooding her whole being now with a desperate desire to live; to put behind her those nightmare dreams from which she had woken shuddering in the past months at visions of herself torn and bleeding, the victim of some horrible railway accident, or trapped upon the top storey of a blazing building with no alternative but to leap into the street below. For a moment it almost seemed to her that no real foundation existed for the dread which had haunted her since childhood. She was young, healthy and full of life. Why should she not enjoy to the full all the normal pleasures of life with this strong, merry-eyed man who had come so suddenly into her existence.

Again and again he assured her that all those thoughts of fatality being certain to overtake her were absurd. He told her that once she was out of Europe she would see things differently; the menace of the old superstition-ridden countries would drop away and that, in his lovely old home in the southern states, they would be able to laugh at Fate together.

Tanith did not really believe him. Her habit of mind had grown so strongly upon her; but she could not bring herself to argue against his happy auguries, or spoil those moments of glorious delight as they both confessed their passion for each other.

As he held her in his arms a marvellous languor began to steal through all her limbs. 'Rex,' she said softly. 'I'm utterly done in with this on top of all the rest. I haven't slept for nearly thirty-six hours. I ought not to now, but I'll never be able to stay awake tonight unless I do. No harm can come to me while you're with me, can it?'

'No,' he said huskily. 'Neither man nor devil shall harm you while I'm around. You poor sweet, you must be just about at the end of your tether. Go to sleep now—just as you are.'

With a little sigh she turned over, nestling her fair head into the crook of his arm, where he sat with his back propped up against a tree-trunk. In another moment she was sound asleep.

The afternoon drew into evening. Rex's arms and legs were cold and stiff, but he would not move for fear of waking her. A new anxiety began to trouble him. Mocata had not appeared, and what would they think had become of him at Cardinals Folly? Marie Lou knew he had gone to the inn, and they would probably have rung up by now. But, like a fool, he had neglected to leave any message for them.

The shadows fell, but still there was no sign of Mocata, and the imps of doubt once more began to fill Rex's mind with horrible speculations as to the truth of Tanith's story. Had she consciously or unconsciously lured him from Simon's side on purpose? Simon would be safe enough with Richard and Marie Lou, and De Richleau had promised to rejoin them before dusk–but perhaps Mocata was plotting some evil to prevent the Duke's return. If that were so–Rex shivered slightly at the thought–Richard knew nothing of those mysterious protective barriers with which it would be so necessary to surround Simon in the coming night–and he, who at least knew what had been done the night before–would be absent. By his desertion of his post poor Simon might fall an easy prey to the malefic influence of the Satanist.

He thought more than once of rousing Tanith, but she looked so peaceful, so happy, so lovely there, breathing gently and resting in his strong arms with all her limbs relaxed that he could not bring himself to do it. The shadows lengthened, night drew on, and at last darkness fell with Tanith still sleeping. The night of the ordeal had come and they were alone in the forest.

24

THE SCEPTICISM OF RICHARD EATON

At a quarter to six, De Richleau arrived back at Cardinals Folly and Richard, meeting him in the hall, told him of Mocata's visit.

'I am not altogether surprised,' the Duke admitted sombrely. 'He must be pretty desperate to come here in daylight on the chance of seeing Simon, but of course, he is working against time–now. Did he threaten to return?'

'Yes.' Richard launched into full particulars of the Satanist's attempt on Marie Lou and the conversation that had followed. As he talked he studied De Richleau's face, struck by his anxious harassed expression. Never before had he thought of the Duke as old, but now for the first time it was brought home to him that De Richleau must be nearly double his own age. And this evening he showed it. He seemed somehow to have shrunk in stature, but perhaps that was because he was standing with bent shoulders as though some invisible load was borne upon them. Richard was so impressed by that tired, lined face that he found himself ending quite seriously: 'Do you really think he can work some devilry tonight?'

De Richleau nodded. 'I am certain of it, and I'm worried Richard. My luck was out today. Father Brandon, whom I went to see, was unfortunately away. He has a great knowledge of this terrible "other world" that we are up against, and knowing me well, would have helped us, but the young priest I saw in his place would not entrust me with the Host, nor could I persuade him to come with it himself, and that is the only certain protection against the sort of thing Mocata may send against us.'

'We'll manage somehow,' Richard smiled, trying to cheer him.

'Yes, we've *got* to.' A note of the old determination came into De Richleau's voice. 'Since the Church cannot help us we must rely upon my knowledge of Esoteric formulas. Fortunately, I have the most important aids with me already, but I should be glad if you would send down the village blacksmith for five horseshoes. Tell whoever you send, that they must be brand new—that is essential.'

At this apparently childish request for horseshoes all Richard's scepticism welled up with renewed force, but he concealed it with his usual tact and agreed readily enough. Then, the mention of the village having reminded him of Rex, he told the Duke how their friend had been called away to the inn.

De Richleau's face fell suddenly. 'I thought Rex had more sense!' he exclaimed bitterly. 'We must telephone at once.'

Richard got on to Mr Wilkes, but the landlord could give them little information. A lady had arrived at about three, and the American gentleman had joined her shortly after. Then they had gone out into the garden and he had seen nothing of them since.

De Richleau shrugged angrily. 'The young fool! I should have thought that he would have seen enough of this horror by now to realise the danger of going off with that young woman. It's a hundred to one that she is Mocata's puppet if nothing else. I only pray to God that he turns up again before nightfall. Where is Simon now?'

'With Marie Lou. They are upstairs in the nursery I think—watching Fleur bathed and put to bed.'

'Good. Let us go up then. Fleur can help us very greatly in protecting him tonight.'

'Fleur!' exclaimed Richard in amazement.

The Duke nodded. 'The prayers of a virgin woman are amazingly powerful in such instances, and the younger she is the stronger her vibrations. You see, a little child like Fleur who is old enough to pray, but absolutely unsoiled in any way, is the nearest that any human being can get to absolute purity. You will remember the words of Our Lord: "Except ye become as little children ye shall not enter into the Kingdom of Heaven." You have no objection I take it?'

'None,' agreed Richard quickly. 'Saying a prayer for Simon cannot possibly harm the child in any way. We'll go up through the library.'

Seven sides of the great octagonal room were covered ceiling high with books and the eighth consisted of wide french windows through which half-a-dozen stone steps, leading up to the terrace, could be seen and beyond, a portion of the garden.

Richard led the way to one of the book-lined walls and pressed the gilded cardinal's hat upon a morocco binding. A low doorway, masked by dummy bookbacks, swung open disclosing a narrow spiral stairway hewn out of the solid wall. They ascended the stone steps and a moment later entered Fleur's nursery on the floor above, through a sliding panel in the wall.

When they arrived the nursery was empty, but in the bathroom beyond they found Simon, with Nanny's apron tied about his waist, quite solemnly bathing Fleur while Marie Lou sat on the edge of the bath and chortled with laughter.

It was an operation which Simon performed on every visit that he had made to Cardinals Folly so Fleur was used to the business and regarded it as a definite treat; but this tubbing of his friend's child was a privilege which De Richleau had never claimed, and as he entered Fleur suddenly exhibited signs of maidenly modesty surprising in one so young.

'Oh, Mummy,' she exclaimed. 'He mussent see me, muss he, 'cause he's a man.' On which the whole party gave way to a fit of laughter.

'Sen' him away!' yelled the excited Fleur, standing up and clutching an enormous bath sponge to her chest.

De Richleau's firm mouth twitched with his old humour, as he apologised most gravely and backed into the nursery beside Richard. A few minutes later the others joined them, and the Duke held a hurried conversation in whispers with Marie Lou.

'Of course,' she said. 'If it will help, do just what you think. I will get rid of Nanny for a few minutes.'

Walking over, he smiled down at Fleur. 'Does Mummy watch you say your prayers every night?' he asked gently.

'Oh, yes,' she lisped. 'And you shall all hear me now.'

He smiled again. 'Have you ever heard her say hers?'

Fleur thought hard for a moment. 'No,' she shook her dark head and the big blue eyes looked up at him seriously. 'Mummy says her prayers to Daddy when I'se asleep.'

He nodded quietly. 'Well, we're all going to say them together tonight.'

'Ooo,' cooed Fleur. 'Lovely. It'll be just as though we'se playing a new game, won't it?'

'Not a game, dearest,' interjected Marie Lou quietly. 'Because prayers are serious, and we mean them.'

'Yes, we mean them very much tonight, but we could all kneel down in a circle couldn't we and put Uncle Simon in the middle?'

'Jus' like kiss-in-the-ring,' added Fleur.

'That's right,' the Duke agreed, 'or Postman's Knock. And you shall be the postman. But this is very serious, and instead of touching him on the shoulder, you must hold his hand very tight.'

They all knelt down then and Fleur extended her pudgy palm to Simon, but the Duke gently laid his hand on her shoulder. 'No.' he whispered. 'Your left hand, my angel, in Uncle Simon's right. You shall say your prayers first, just as you always do, and then I shall say one for all of us afterwards.'

The first few lines of the Our Father came tumbling out from the child's lips in a little breathless spate as they knelt with bowed heads and closed eyes. Then there was a short hesitation, a prompting whisper from Marie Lou, and an equally breathless ending. After that, the little personal supplication for Mummy and Daddy and Uncle Simon and Uncle Rex and Uncle Greyeyes and dear Nanny were hurried through with considerably more gusto.

'Now,' whispered De Richleau. 'I want you to repeat everything I say word for word after me,' and in a low, clear voice he offered up an entreaty that the Father of All would forgive His servants their sins and strengthen them to resist temptation, keeping at bay by His limitless power all evil things that walked in darkness, and bringing them safely by His especial mercy to see again the glory of the morning light.

When all was done and Fleur, tucked up and kissed, left between Mr Edward Bear and Golliwog, the others filed downstairs to Marie Lou's cosy sitting-room.

De Richleau was worried about Rex, but a further 'phone call to the inn failed to elicit any later information. He had not returned, and they sat round silently, a little subdued. Richard, vaguely miserable because it was sherry time and the Duke had once again firmly prohibited the drinking of any alcohol, asked at length: 'Well, what do you wish us to do now?'

'We should have a light supper fairly early,' De Richleau announced. 'And after, I should like you to make it quite clear to Malin that none of the servants are to come into this wing of the house until tomorrow morning. Say, if you like, that I am going to conduct some all-night experiments with a new wireless or television apparatus, but in no circumstances must we be disturbed or any doors opened and shut.'

'Hadn't we ... er ... better disconnect the telephone as well?' Simon hazarded. 'In case it rings after we've settled down.'

'Yes, with Richard's permission I will attend to that myself.'

'Do, if you like, and I'll see to the servants,' Richard agreed placidly. 'But what do you call a light supper?'

'Just enough to keep up our strength. A little fish if you have it. If not eggs will do, with vegetables or a salad and some fruit, but no meat or game and, of course, no wine.'

Richard grunted. 'That sounds a jolly dinner I must say. I suppose you wouldn't like to shave my head as well, or get us all to don hair shirts if we could find them. I'm hungry as a hunter, and owing to your telegram, we had no lunch.'

The Duke smiled tolerantly. 'I am sorry, Richard, but this thing is deadly serious. I am afraid you haven't realised quite how serious yet. If you had seen what Rex and I did last night, I'm certain that you wouldn't breathe a word of protest about these small discomforts, and realise at once that I am acting for the best.'

'No,' Richard confessed. 'Quite frankly, I find it very difficult to believe that we haven't all gone bug-house with this talk of witches and wizards and magic and what-not at the present day.'

'Yet you saw Mocata yourself this afternoon.'

'I saw an unpleasant pasty-faced intruder I agree, but to credit him with all the powers that you suggest is rather more than I can stomach at the moment.'

'Oh, Richard!' Marie Lou broke in. 'Greyeyes is right. That man is horrible. And to say that people do not believe in witches at the present day is absurd. Everybody knows that there are witches just as there have always been.'

'Eh!' Richard looked at his lovely wife in quick surprise. 'Have you caught this nonsense from the others already? I've never heard you air this belief before.'

'Of course not,' she said a little sharply. 'It is unlucky to talk of such things, but one knows about them all the same. Of witches in Siberia I could tell you much—things that I have seen with my own eyes.'

'Tell us, Marie Lou,' urged the Duke. He felt that in their present situation scepticism might prove highly dangerous. If Richard did not believe in the powers that threatened them, he might relax in following out the instructions for their protection and commit some casual carelessness, bringing, possibly, a terrible danger upon them all. He knew how very highly Richard esteemed his wife's sound common sense. It was far better to let her convince him than to press arguments on Richard himself.

'There was a witch in Romanovsk,' Marie Lou proceeded. 'An old woman who lived alone in a house just outside the village. No one, not even the Red

Guards, with all their bluster about having liquidated God and the Devil, would pass her cottage alone at night. In Russia there are many such and one in nearly every village. You would call her a wise woman as well perhaps, for she could cure people of many sicknesses and I have seen her stop the flow of blood from a bad wound almost instantly. The village girls used to go to her to have their fortunes told and, when they could afford it, to buy charms of philtres to make the young men they liked fall in love with them. Often, too, they would go back again afterwards when they became pregnant and buy the drugs which would secure their release from that unhappy situation. But she was greatly feared, for everyone knew that she could also put a blight on crops and send a murrain on the cattle of those who displeased her. It was even whispered that she could cause men and women to sicken and die if any enemy paid her a high enough price to make it worth her while.'

'If that is so I wonder they didn't lynch her,' said Richard quietly.

'They did in the end. They would not have dared to do that themselves. But a farmer whom she had inflicted with a plague of lice appealed to the local commissar and he went with twenty men to her house one day. All the villagers and I among them—for I was only a little girl then and naturally curious—went with them in a frightened crowd hanging well behind. They brought the old woman out and examined her, and having proved she was a witch, the commissar had her shot against the cottage wall.'

'How did they prove it?' Richard asked sceptically.

'Why—because she had the marks of course.'

'What marks?'

'When they stripped her they found that she had a teat under her left arm, and that is a certain sign.'

De Richleau nodded. 'To feed her familiar with, of course. Was it a cat?'

Marie Lou shook her head. 'No. In this case, it was a great big fat toad that she used to keep in a little cage.'

'Oh, come!' Richard protested. 'This is fantastic. They slaughtered the poor old woman because she had some malformation and kept an unusual pet.'

'No, no,' Marie Lou assured him. 'They found the Devil's mark on her thigh and they swam her in the village pond. It was very horrible, but it was all quite conclusive.'

'The Devil's mark!' interjected Simon suddenly. 'I've never heard of that,' and the Duke answered promptly:

'It is believed that the Devil or his representative touches these people at their baptism during some Satanic orgy and that spot is for ever afterwards free from pain. In the old witch trials, they used to hunt for it by sticking pins into the suspected person because the place does not differ in appearance from any other portion of the body.'

Marie Lou nodded her curly head. 'That's right. They bandaged this old woman's eyes so that she could not see what part of her they were sticking the pin into and then they began to prick her gently in first one place and then another. Of course she cried out each time the pin went in, but after about twenty cries, the head man of the village pushed the pin into her left thigh and she didn't make a sound. He took it out then and stuck it in again, but still she did not cry out at all so he pushed it in right up to the head, and she didn't know he'd even touched her. So you see, everyone was quite satisfied then that she was a witch.'

'Well, *you* may have been,' Richard said slowly. 'It seems a horribly barbarous affair in any case. I dare say the old woman deserved all she got, but it's pretty queer evidence to shoot anyone on.'

'Er . . . Richard . . .' Simon leaned forward suddenly. 'Do you believe in curses?'

'What—the old bell and book business! Not much. Why?'

'Because the actual working of a curse is evidence of the supernatural.'

'They're mostly old wives' tales of coincidences I think.'

'How about the Mackintosh of Moy?'

'Oh, Scotland is riddled with that sort of thing. But what is supposed to have happened to the Mackintosh?'

'Well, this was in seventeen something,' Simon replied slowly. 'The story goes that he was present at a witch burning or jilted one—I forget exactly. Anyhow she put a curse on him and it went like this:

"Mackintosh, Mackintosh, Mackintosh of Moy
If you ever have a son *he shall never have a boy*."'

Richard smiled. 'And what happened then?'

'Well, whether the story's true or not I can't say, but it's a fact that the Chieftainship of the Clan has gone all over the shop ever since. Look it up in the records of the Clans if you doubt me.'

'My dear chap, you'll have to produce something far more concrete than that to convince me.'

'All right,' Marie Lou gazed at him steadily out of her large blue eyes. 'You know very little about such things, Richard, but in Russia people are much closer to nature and everyone there still accepts the supernatural and diabolic possession as part of ordinary life. Only about a year before you brought me to England they caught a were-wolf in a village less than fifty miles from where I lived.'

He moved over to the sofa and, taking her hand, patted it gently. 'Surely, darling, you don't really ask me to believe that a man can actually turn into a beast—leave his bed in the middle of the night to go out hunting—then return and go to his work in the morning as a normal man again?'

'Certainly,' Marie Lou nodded solemnly. 'Wolves, as you know, nearly always hunt in packs, but that part of the country had been troubled for months by a lone wolf which seemed possessed of far more than normal cunning. It killed sheep and dogs and two young children. Then it killed an old woman. She was found with her throat bitten out, but she had been ravished too, so that's how they knew that it must be a were-wolf. At last it attacked a woodman and he wounded it in the shoulder with his axe. Next day a wretched half-imbecile creature, a sort of village idiot, died suddenly, and when the women went to prepare his body for burial they found that he had died from loss of blood and that there was a great wound in his right shoulder just where the woodman had struck the wolf. After that there were no other cases of slaughtered sheep or people being done to death. So it was quite clear that he was the were-wolf.'

Richard looked thoughtful for a moment. 'Of course,' he remarked, 'the man may have done all that without actually changing his shape at all. If anyone is bitten by a mad dog and gets hydrophobia, they bark, howl, gnash their teeth and behave just as though they were dogs and certainly believe at the time that they are. Lycanthropy, of which this poor devil seems to have been the victim, may be some rare disease of the same kind.'

Marie Lou shrugged lightly and stood up. 'Well, if you won't believe me—there it is. I don't know enough to argue with you, only what I believe myself, so I shall go and order supper.'

As the door closed behind her the Duke said quietly: 'That may be a possible explanation, Richard, but there is an enormous mass of evidence in the jurisprudence of every country to suggest that actual shape shifting does occur at times. The form varies of course. In Greece it is often of the were-boar that one hears. In Africa of the were-hyena and were-leopard. China has the were-fox; India the were-tiger; and Egypt the were-jackal. But even as near home as Surrey I could introduce you to a friend of mine, a doctor who practices among the country people, who will vouch for it that the older cottagers are still unshakeable in their beliefs that certain people are were-hares, and have power to change their shape at particular phases of the moon.'

'If you really believe these fantastic stories,' Richard smiled a little grimly, 'perhaps you can give me some reasonable explanation as to what makes such things possible.'

'By all means.' De Richleau hoisted himself out of his chair and began to pace softly up and down the fine, silk Persian prayer rug before the fireplace while he expounded again the Esoteric doctrine just as he had to Rex two nights before.

Simon and Richard listened in silence until the Duke spoke of the eternal fight which, hidden from human eyes, has been waged from time immemorial between the Powers of Light and the Powers of Darkness. Then the latter, his serious interest really aroused for the first time, exclaimed:

'Surely you are proclaiming the Manichaean heresy? The Manichees believed in the Two Principals, Light and Darkness, and the Three Moments, Past, Present and Future. They taught that in the *Past* Light and Darkness had been separate; then that Darkness invaded Light and became mingled with it, creating the *Present* and this world in which evil is mixed with good. They preached the practice of aestheticism as the means of freeing the light imprisoned in human clay so that in some distant *Future* Light and Darkness might be completely separated again.'

The Duke's lean face lit with a quick smile. 'Exactly, my friend! The Manichees had a credo to that effect.

> "Day by day diminishes
> The number of Soul below
> As they are *distilled and mount above*."

The basis of the belief is far, far older of course, pre-Egyptian at the least, but where before it was a jealously guarded mystery the Persian Mani proclaimed it to the world.'

'It became a serious rival to Christianity at one time, didn't it?'

'Um,' Simon took up the argument. 'And it survived despite the most terrible persecution by the Christians. Mani was crucified in the third century after Christ and, by their own creed, his followers were not allowed to enlist converts. Yet somehow it spread in secret. The Albigenses followed it in Southern France in the twelfth century until they were stamped out. Then in the thirteenth, a thousand years after Mani's death, it swept Bohemia. A form of it was still practised there by certain sects as late as the 1840's and even today many thinking people scattered all over the world believe that it holds the core of the only true religion.'

'Yes, I can understand that,' Richard agreed, 'Brahminism, Budism, Taoism, all the great philosophers which have passed beyond the ordinary limited religions with a personal God are connected up with the Prana, Light, and the Universal Life Stream, but that is a very different matter to asking me to believe in were-wolves and witches.'

'They only came into the discussion because they illustrate certain manifestations of supernatural *Evil*,' De Richleau protested; 'just as the appearance of wounds similar to those of Christ upon the Cross in the flesh of exceptionally pious people may be taken as evidence for the existence of supernatural *Good*. Eminent surgeons have testified again and again that stigmata are not due to trickery. It is a changing of the material body by the holy saints in their endeavour to approximate to its highest form, that of Our Lord, so, I contend, base natures, with the assistance of the Power of Darkness, may at times succeed in altering their form to that of were-beasts. Whether they change their shape entirely it is impossible to say because at death they always revert to human form, but the belief is world-wide and the evidence so abundant that it cannot lightly be put aside. In any case what you call madness is actually a very definite form of diabolic possession which seizes upon these people and causes them to act with the same savagery as the animal they believe themselves for the time to be. Of its existence, no one who has read the immense literature upon it, can possibly doubt.'

'Perhaps,' Richard admitted grudgingly. 'But apart from Marie Lou's story, all the evidence is centuries old and mixed up with every sort of superstition and fairy story. In the depths of the Siberian forests or the Indian jungle the belief in such things may perhaps stimulate some poor benighted wretch to act the part now and again and so perpetuate the legend. But you cannot cite me a case in which a number of people have sworn to such happenings in a really civilised country in modern times!'

'Can't I?' De Richleau laughed grimly. 'What about the affair at Uttenheim near Strasbourg. The farms in the neighbourhood had been troubled by a lone wolf for weeks. The Garde-Champetre was sent out to get it. He tracked it down. It attacked him and he fired–killing it dead. Then he found himself bending over the body of a local youth. That unfortunate rural policeman was tried for murder, but he swore by all that was holy that it was a wolf at which he had shot, and the entire population of the village came forward to give evidence on his behalf–that the dead man had boasted time and again of his power to change his shape.'

'Is that a fifteenth or sixteenth century story?' murmured Richard.

'Neither. It occurred in November, 1925.'

25

THE TALISMAN OF SET

For a while longer De Richleau strode up and down, patiently answering Richard's questions and ramming home his arguments for a belief in the power of the supernatural to affect mankind until, when Marie Lou rejoined them, Richard's brown eyes no longer held the half-mocking humour which had twinkled in them an hour before.

The Duke's explanation had been so clear and lucid, his earnestness so compelling that the younger man was at least forced to suspend judgment, and even found himself toying with the idea that Simon might really be threatened by some very dangerous and potent force which it would need all their courage to resist during the dark hours that lay ahead.

It was eight o'clock now. Twilight had fallen and the trees at the bottom of the garden were already merged in shadow. Yet with the coming of darkness they were not filled with any fresh access of fear. It seemed that their long talk had elucidated the position and even strengthened the bond between them. Like men who are about to go into physical battle, they were alert and expectant but a little subdued, and realised that their strongest hope lay in putting their absolute trust in each other.

At Marie Lou's suggestion they went into the dining-room and sat down to a cold supper which had already been laid out. Having eaten so lightly during the day, their natural inclination was to make a heavy meal but, without any further caution from De Richleau, they all appreciated now that the situation was sufficiently serious to make restraint imperative. Even Richleau denied himself a second helping of his favourite Morecambe Bay shrimps which had arrived that morning.

When they had finished the Duke leant over him. 'I think the library would be the best place to conduct my experiments, and I shall require the largest jug you have full of fresh water, some glasses and it would be best to leave the fruit.'

'By all means,' Richard agreed, glancing towards his butler. 'See to that please, Malin—will you.' He then went on to give clear and definite instructions that they were not to be disturbed on any pretext until the morning, and concluded with an order that the table should be cleared right away.

With a bland, unruffled countenance the man signified his understanding and motioned to his footman to begin clearing the table. So bland in fact was the expression that it would have been difficult for them to visualise him half an hour later in the privacy of the housekeeper's room declaring with a knowing wink:

'In my opinion it's spooks they're after—the old chap's got no television set. And behaving like a lot of heathens with not a drop of drink to their dinner. Think of that with young Simon there who's so mighty particular about his hock. But spiritualists always is that way. I only hope it doesn't get 'em bad or what's going to happen to the wine bill I'd like to know?'

When Richard had very pointedly wished his henchman 'good night,' they moved into the library and De Richleau, who knew the room well, surveyed it with fresh interest.

Comfortable sofas and large arm-chairs stood about the uneven polished oak of the floor. A pair of globes occupied two angles of the book-lined walls, and a great oval mahogany writing-table of Chippendale design stood before the wide french window. Owing to its sunken position in the old wing of the house the lighting of the room was dim even on a summer's day. Yet its atmosphere was by no means gloomy. A log fire upon a twelve-inch pile of ashes was kept burning in the wide fireplace all through the year, and at night, when the curtains were drawn and the room lit with the soft radiance of the concealed ceiling lights, which Richard had installed, it was a friendly, restful place well suited for quiet work or idle conversation.

'We must strip the room—furniture, curtains, everything!' said the Duke. 'And I shall need brooms and a mop to polish the floor.'

The three men then began moving the furniture out into the hall while Marie Lou fetched a selection of implements from the house-maid's closet.

For a quarter of an hour they worked in silence until nothing remained in the big library except the serried rows of gilt-tooled books.

'My apologies for even doubting the efficiency of your staff!' the Duke smiled at Marie Lou. 'But I would like the room gone over thoroughly, particularly the floor, since evil emanations can fasten on the least trace of dust to assist their materialisation. Would you see to it, Princess, while I telephone the inn again to find out if Rex has returned.'

'Of course, Greyeyes, dear,' said Marie Lou and, with Richard's and Simon's help, she set about dusting, sweeping and polishing until when De Richleau rejoined them, the boards were so scrupulously clean that they could have eaten from them.

'No news of Rex, worse luck,' he announced with a frown. 'And I've had to disconnect the telephone now in case a call makes Malin think it necessary to disregard his instructions. We had better go upstairs and change next.'

'What into?' Richard inquired.

'Pyjamas. I hope you have a good supply. You see none of us tonight must wear any garment which has been even slightly soiled. Human impurities are bound to linger in one's clothes even if they have only been worn for a few hours, and it is just upon such things that elementals fasten most readily.'

'Shan't we be awfully cold?' hazarded Simon with an unhappy look.

'I'll fit you out with shooting stockings and an overcoat,' Richard volunteered.

'Stockings if you like, providing that they are fresh from the wash—but no overcoats, dressing-gowns or shoes,' said the Duke. 'However, there is no reason why we should not wear a couple of suits apiece of Richard's underclothes, beneath the pyjamas, to keep us warm. The essential point is that everything must be absolutely clean.'

The whole party then migrated upstairs, the men congregating in Richard's dressing-room where they ransacked his wardrobe for suitable attire. Marie Lou joined them a little later looking divinely pretty in peach silk pyjamas and silk stockings into the tops of which, above the knees, the bottoms of her pyjamas were neatly tucked.

'Now for a raid on the linen cupboard,' said De Richleau. 'Cushions, being soiled already, are useless to us, but I am dreading that hard floor so we will take down as many sheets as we can carry, clean bath towels and blankets too. Then we shall have some sort of couch to sit on.'

In the library once more, they set down their bundles and De Richleau produced his suitcase, taking from it a piece of chalk, a length of string, and a footrule. Marking a spot in the centre of the room, he asked Marie Lou to hold the end of the string to it, measuring off exactly seven feet and then, using her as a pivot, he drew a large circle in chalk upon the floor.

Next, the string was lengthened and an outer circle drawn. Then the most difficult part of the operation began. A five-rayed star had to be made with its points touching the outer circle and its valleys resting upon the inner. But, as the Duke explained, while such a defence can be highly potent if it is constructed with geometrical accuracy, should the angles vary to any marked degree or the distance of the apexes from the central point differ more than a fraction, the pentacle would prove not only useless but even dangerous.

For half an hour they measured and checked with string and rule and marking chalk; but Richard proved useful here, for all his life he had been an expert with maps and plans and was even something of amateur architect. At last the broad chalk lines were drawn to the Duke's satisfaction, forming the magical five pointed star, in which it was his intention that they should remain while darkness lasted.

He then chalked in, with careful spacing round the rim of the inner circle, the powerful exorcism:

In nomina Pa ✠ tris et Fi ✠ lii et Spiritus ✠ Sancti! ✠ El ✠ Elohym ✠ Sother ✠ Emmanuel ✠ Sabaoth ✠ Agia ✠ Tetragammaton ✠ Agyos ✠ Otheos ✠ Ischiros ✠

and, after reference to an old book which he had brought with him, drew certain curious and ancient symbols in the valleys and the mounts of the microcosmic star.

Simon, whose recent experience had taught him something of pentacles, recognised ten of them as Cabbalistic signs taken from the Sephirotic Tree; *Kether, Binah, Ceburah, Hod, Malchut* and the rest. But others, like the Eye of Horus, were of Egyptian origin, and others again in some ancient Aryan script which he did not understand.

When the skeleton of this astral fortress was completed, the clean bedding was laid out inside it for them to rest upon and De Richleau produced further impedimenta from his case.

With lengths of asafœtida grass and blue wax he sealed the windows, the door leading to the hall, and that concealed in the bookshelves which led to the nursery above, each at both sides and at the tops and at the bottoms, making the sign of the Cross in holy water over every seal as he completed it.

Then he ordered the others inside the pentacle, examined the switches by the door to assure himself that every light in the room was on, made up the fire with a great pile of logs so that it would last well through the night and there be no question of their having to leave the circle to replenish it and, joining them where they had squatted down on the thick mat of blankets, produced five little silver cups, which he proceeded to fill two-thirds full with Holy water. These he placed, one in each valley of the pentacle.

Then, taking five long white tapering candles, such as are offered by devotees to the Saints in Catholic Churches, he lit them from an old-fashioned tinder-box and set them upright, one at each apex of the five-pointed star. In their rear he placed the five brand new horseshoes which Richard had secured from the village with their horns pointing outward, and beyond each vase of holy water he set a dried mandrake, four females and one male, the male being in the valley to the north.

These complicated formulas for the erection of outward barriers being at last finished, the Duke turned his attention to the individual protection of his friends and himself. Four long wreaths of garlic flowers were strung together and each of the party placed one about his neck. Rosaries, with little golden crucifixes attached, were distributed, medals of Saint Benedict holding the Cross in his right hand and the Holy Rule in his left, and phials of salt and mercury; lengths of the asafœtida grass were again tied round Simon's wrists and ankles, and he was placed in their midst facing towards the north. The Duke then performed the final rites of sealing the nine openings of each of their bodies.

All this performance had entirely failed to impress Richard. In fact, it tended to revive his earlier scepticism. It was his private belief that a blackmailing gang were playing tricks upon Simon and the Duke so, before coming downstairs, he had tucked a loaded automatic comfortably away beneath his pyjama jacket. In deference to De Richleau's obvious concern that nothing soiled should be brought within the circle he had first, half-ashamedly, cleansed the weapon in a bath of spirit but, if Mr Mocata was so ill-advised as to break into his house that night with the intention of staging any funny business, he meant to use it. After a little pause he looked cheerfully round at the others. 'Well—here we are! What happens now?'

'We have ample room here,' replied De Richleau. 'So there is no reason why we should not lie down with our feet towards the rim of the circle and try to get some sleep, but there are certain instructions I would like to give you before we settle down.'

'I never felt less like sleep in my life,' remarked Simon.

'Nor I,' agreed Richard. 'It's early yet and if only Marie Lou weren't here I'd tell you some bawdy stories to keep you gay.'

'Don't mind me, darling,' cooed Marie Lou. 'I'm human—even if you are right about my having an angelic face.'

'No!' He shook his head quickly. 'Somehow they fail to amuse me when you're about. That's why I never tell you any. It needs men on their own sitting round a bottle of something to get the best out of a bawdy jest. My God! I wish we'd got a bottle of brandy with us now!'

'Mean pig,' she murmured amiably, snuggling up against him. 'If Greyeyes and Simon didn't know you so well they would think you nothing but an awful little drunk from the way you talk, whereas you're a nice person really.'

'Am I? Well, anyway it's fine that you should think so.' He fondled her short curly hair with his long fingers. 'My present lust for liquor is only because I've been done out of my fair ration today. But what shall we talk about? Greyeyes—this Talisman that all the bother centres on—tell us about it before you give us your final orders for the night.'

'You know the legend of Isis and Osiris?' the Duke asked.

'Yes–vaguely,' Richard replied. 'They were the King and Queen of Heaven who came to earth in human form and taught the Egyptians all they knew weren't they? The old business of a fairhaired god arriving among a dusky people and importing all sorts of new ideas about agriculture and architecture and justice–in fact–what we call civilisation.'

De Richleau nodded. 'That is so. But I mean the story of how Osiris came to die?'

'He was murdered wasn't he?' volunteered Simon. 'But I've forgotten how.'

'Well, this is the account which has been handed down to us through many thousands of years. Osiris was, apparently, as Richard says, a fair-haired, light-skinned man, alien to the Egyptian race, who became their King and, ruling them with great intelligence brought them many blessings. But he had a brother named Set–and here again you get the two principals of Good and Evil, Light and Darkness–for Set was a dark man. The legend is, of course, apocryphal up to a point but, eliminating the overlay of myth with which the priests later embroidered it, the whole story had such a genuine ring of human tragedy that it is very difficult to doubt that these two men and the woman Isis actually lived, as the progenitors of a Royal dynasty, in the Nile valley long before the Pyramids were built.

'It always amazes me, whenever I re-read the story in the Greek Classics, how Set, particularly, stands out as a definite and living figure after all these countless generations. The characters in our seventeenth century plays even are quite unreal to us now–with a very few exceptions; but Set remains, timeless and unchanging, the charming but unscrupulous rogue who might have entertained you with lavish hospitality and brilliant conversation yesterday–yet would do you down without the least compunction if he met you in the street tomorrow.

'He was tall and slim and dark and handsome; a fine athlete and a great hunter, but a cultured, amusing person too, and a boon companion who knew how to carry his wine at table. The type whose lapses men are always ready to condone on account of their delightful personality, and whose wickedness women persuade themselves is only waywardness–while they succumb almost at a glance to that dark, male virility.

'Set was younger than Osiris and jealous of his authority. Then he fell in love with Isis, his brother's wife. The old story of the human triangle you see, or rather the original, for all others in the whole literature of the world which deal with the same subject are plagiarisms. Set conspired, therefore, to slay the King and seize his wife and power for himself.

'To assassinate Osiris openly would have been a difficult matter because he was always surrounded by the older nobles, who loved him and knew that he kept the peace while the land flourished and grew prosperous. Set knew that they would defend the King's person with their lives, and he was faced with another problem too. Osiris was a god, and even if he could lure him to a place where the deed could be done in secret, he dared not spill one drop of the divine blood.

'He planned then a superlatively clever murder. You all know that the Egyptians considered this present life to be only an interlude and that almost from the age at which they could think at all their thoughts were largely focused on the life to come. Many of them spent their entire fortune upon preparing some magnificent place of burial for themselves, and at every banquet, when the slaves served the dessert, the head wine butler carried round a miniature coffin with a skeleton inside to remind the guests that death was waiting round the corner for them all.

'With diabolical cunning, Set utilised the national preoccupation with death and ceremonial burial to ensnare his brother. First, by a clever piece of trickery he secured Osiris' exact measurements. Then he had made the most beautiful sarcophagus that had ever been seen. It was a great heavy chest of fine cedar wood with the figures of the forty-two assessors of the dead, who form the jury of the gods, painted in lapis blue, and the minutest hieroglyphics in black and red; line upon line of them reciting the most effective protections against black magic, and every requisite line of ritual from the great Book of the Dead.

'As soon as this wonderful coffin was completed, Set prepared a great banquet to which he invited Osiris and seventy-two of the younger nobles, all of whom he had corrupted and drawn one by one into his conspiracy.

'Then on the night of the feast he had the beautiful sarcophagus placed in a small anteroom through which every guest had to pass on his arrival.

'You can imagine how envious they were when they saw it, and how each commented on the workmanship and the artistry of the designs—Osiris no less than the others.

'They dined, drank heavily of wine, watched the Egyptian dancing girls, saw Ethiopian contortionists, and listened to the best stringed music of the day. Then as a final hospitality to his guests, the Prince Set rose from his couch and proclaimed:

'"You have all seen the sarcophagus which stands in the little anteroom, and it is my wish that one of you should receive it as a gift. He whom it fits may take it with my blessing."

'Picture to yourselves the nobles as they scrambled up from their couches, thrusting the dancing girls aside, and elbowing their way out into the anteroom, each hoping that the princely gift might fall to him.

'One after another they got inside and lay down, but not one of them fitted it exactly. The Set led Osiris into the anteroom and, waving his hand towards the handsome chest said with a little laugh: "Why don't you try it brother. It is worthy of a King. Even of the Lord of the Two Lands, the Upper and the Lower Nile."

'With a smile Osiris lowered himself into the masterpiece. And behold, it fitted his tall, broad-shouldered body to a hair's breadth. No sooner was he inside than the principal conspirators, who were in the secret, rushed forward with the weighty lid. In frantic haste they nailed it down and poured molten lead upon it, so that Osiris may have survived an hour in agony but died at last of suffocation.

'Set thus succeeded in his treacherous design of killing his brother without spilling one drop of his blood. He and his turbulent followers then hastened to their chariots, rode forth, and seized the Kingdom. But Isis was warned in time and managed to escape.

'The coffer had been left with Osiris in it and, the Egyptian religion being so strongly bound up with the worship of the dead, it was vital to Set's newly established authority that the body should be disposed of at the earliest possible moment. Otherwise, if the priests got hold of it, they would bury it in state and erect a mighty shrine to the dead King's memory which would form a rallying point for all the best elements in the Kingdom where they would league themselves against the murderer.

'Next morning, therefore, immediately he got home, Set had the chest cast into the Nile. But Isis recovered it, and after certain magical ceremonies, succeeded in impregnating herself by means of her husband's dead body. Then she fled to the papyrus marshes of the Delta, taking Osiris' body with her in the chest since there was no time to give it proper burial.

'When Set learned what had happened, he swore that he would hunt Isis down and kill her, and that he would find Osiris' body and destroy it for ever.

'Again now, in the story, we get one of those strange glimpses of happenings many thousands of years ago which we can see more clearly than the things of yesterday.

'In a few phrases it is recounted how Set searched for months in vain, and then one night, the pregnant ex-Queen Isis, now a destitute refugee alone and unattended, is seated beneath a cluster of palm trees in the desert. Her husband's body, roughly embalmed, is in the wooden chest beside her and she is conscious of the movements of the child she bears. Suddenly her sorrowful meditations are disturbed by a distant rumble breaking the stillness of the night. The noise increases to a drumming thunder as a party of horsemen come galloping across the sand. Isis runs for cover to a nearby papyrus swamp and crouches waist high in the water watching from amidst the reeds. The dusky riders come thundering past. She sees that it is Set and his dissolute nobles hunting by the brilliant light of the Egyptian moon. One of them recognises the chest. With cries of triumph they fling themselves from their saddles, break it to pieces and drag out the body of Osiris. Hidden there, fearful and trembling, Isis watches Set's dark, proud profile as he orders the body to be torn into fourteen pieces and the parts distributed throughout the length and breadth of the Kingdom so that they might never be brought together again.

'Years later, Horus, the son of Isis, the Great God, the Hawk of Light, who restored its blessings to mankind and lifted again the veil of darkness that Set's treachery had brought to dim the world, became master of the Kingdom. Then Isis roamed the country seeking for the dismembered portions of her husband. She did not attempt to assemble them again, but wherever she found one she erected a great temple to his memory. In all, she succeeded in finding thirteen pieces of the body, but the fourteenth she never found. That Set had carefully embalmed and kept himself. It was for this reason that, although Horus defeated Set three times in battle he was never able to slay him. The portion that Set retained was the most potent of all charms—the phallus of the dead god, his brother.

'In the secret histories of esoterism it is stated that it has since been heard of many times. For long periods through the ages it has been completely lost. But whenever it is found it brings calamity upon the world, and that is the thing which we have to prevent Mocata securing at all costs today—the Talisman of Set.'

When De Richleau had ceased speaking, they sat silent for a while until Marie Lou said softly: 'I am feeling rather tired now, Greyeyes, dear, and I think I'd like to rest, even if it is impossible to sleep with all these lights.'

'All right. Then I'll say what I have to Princess. But please, all of you'—the Duke paused to look at each of them in turn—'listen carefully, because this is vitally serious.

'What may happen I have no idea. Perhaps nothing at all and the worst we'll have to face is an uncomfortable night. But Mocata threatened to get Simon away from us by hook or by crook, and I feel certain that he meant it. I cannot tell you what form his attack is likely to take, but I am sure he will literally do his damnedest to break us up and get Simon out of our care tonight.

'He may send the most terrible powers against us, but there is one thing above all others that I want you to remember. As long as we stay inside this pentacle we shall be safe, but if any of us sets one foot outside it we risk eternal damnation.

'We may be called upon to witness the sort of horrors which it is difficult for you to conceive. I mean visions such as you have read of in Gustave Flaubert's *Temptation of Saint Anthony*, or seen in pictures by the old Flemish masters such as Brueghel. But they cannot do us the least harm as long as we remain where we are.

'Again, we may see nothing, but the attack may develop in a far more subtle form. That is to say, inside ourselves. Any, or all of us, may find our reason being undermined by insidious argument so that we may start telling each other that there is nothing in the world to be frightened of and that we are utter fools to spend a miserable night sitting here when we might all be comfortably in bed upstairs. If that happens, it is a lie. Even if I appear to change my mind and tell you that I have thought of new arrangements which would be safer, you must not believe me because it will not be my true self speaking. It may be that an awful thirst will come upon us. That is why I have had this big jug of water brought in. We may be assailed by hunger, but to meet that we have the fruit. It is possible that we may be afflicted with earache or some other bodily pain which, ordinarily, would make us want to go upstairs to seek relief. If that happens we've just got to stick it till the morning.

'Poor old Simon is likely to be afflicted worst because the campaign will centre on an attempt to make him break out of the circle. But we've got to stop him—by force, if need be. There are two main defences which we can bring into play if any manifestations do take place, as I fear they may.

'One is the Blue vibration. Shut your eyes and try to think of yourselves as standing in an oval of blue light. The oval is your aura, and the colour blue exceedingly potent in all things pertaining to the spirit; the other is prayer. Do not endeavour to make up complicated prayers or your words may become muddled and you will find yourself saying something that you do not mean. Confine yourselves to saying over and over again: "Oh, Lord, protect me! Oh, Lord, protect me!" and not only say it but think it with all the power of your will, visualising, if you can, Our Lord upon the Cross with blue light streaming from His body towards yourselves; but if you think you see Him outside this pentacle beckoning you to safety while some terrible thing threatens you from the other side, *still you must remain within.*'

As De Richleau finished there was a murmer of assent. Then Richard, with an arm about Marie Lou's shoulders said quietly: 'I understand, and we'll do everything you say.'

'Thank you. Now, Simon,' the Duke went on. 'I want you to say clearly and distinctly seven times, "*Om meni padme aum.*" That is the invocation to *manathaer*—your higher self.'

Simon did as he was bid, then they knelt together and each offered a silent prayer that the Power of Light might guard and protect them from all uncleanness, and that each might be granted strength to aid the others should they be faced with any peril.

They lay down then and tried to rest despite the burning candles and the soft glow of the electric light. Sleep was utterly impossible to them in such circumstances. Yet no one there had more to say upon any point that mattered and, after a little time, no one felt that they could break the stillness by endeavouring to make ordinary conversation.

The steady ticking of a clock came faintly from somewhere in the depths of the house. Occasionally a log fell with a loud plop and hissed for a moment in the fire grate. Then the little noises of the night were hushed, and an immense silence, brooding and mysterious, seemed to have fallen upon them. In some strange way it did not seem as though the quite octagonal room was any longer a portion of the house or that outside the window lay the friendly, well-cared-for garden that they knew so well. Watchful, listening, intent, they lay silent, waiting to see what the night would bring.

26

REX LEARNS OF THE UNDEAD

Tanith slept peacefully, curled up in Rex's arms, her golden head pillowed upon his chest. For a little time anxious thoughts occupied his mind. He reproached himself for having left Simon, and the gnawing worm of doubt raised its head again to whisper that Tanith had planned to lure him away from protecting his friend, but he dismissed such thoughts almost immediately. Simon would be safe enough in the care of Richard and Marie Lou. Tanith was alone and needed him, and he soon convinced himself that in remaining there he was breaking a lance against the enemy as well, by preventing Mocata securing her again to assist him, all unwillingly, in his hostilities.

The shadows lengthened and the patches of sunlight dimmed, yet still Tanith slept on–the sleep of utter exhaustion–brought about by the terrible nervous crisis through which she had passed from hour to hour during the previous day, the past night, and that morning, in her attempt to seek safety with him.

With infinite precaution not to disturb her he looked at his watch and found that the time was nearly eight o'clock. De Richleau should be back by now and after all it was unlikely that Mocata could prevent his return before sundown. De Richleau might have lost his nerve for a few moments the night before, but he had retrieved it brilliantly in that headlong dash at the wheel of the Hispano down into the hellish valley where the Satanists practised their grim rites. Now that they had secured Simon safe and sound once more, Rex had an utter faith that De Richleau would fight to the last ditch, with all the skill and cunning of his subtle brain, and that stubborn, tenacious courage that Rex knew so well, before he would surrender their friend to the evil powers again.

It was dark now; even the afterglow had faded, leaving the trees as vague, dark sentinels in that silent wood. The undergrowth was massed in bulky shadows and the colour had faded from the grasses and wild-flowers on the green, mossy bank where he lay with Tanith breathing so evenly in his embrace.

His back and arms were aching from his strained position but he sat on while the moments fled, sleepy himself now, yet determined not to give way to the temptation, even to doze, lest silent evil should steal upon them where they lay.

Another hour crept by and then Tanith stirred slightly. Another moment, and she had raised her head, shaking the tumbled golden hair back from her face and blinking up at him a little out of sleepy eyes.

'Rex, where are we?' she murmured indistinctly. 'What has happened? I've had an awful dream.'

He smiled down at her and kissed her full on the lips.

'Together,' he said. 'That's all that matters, isn't it? But if you must know, we're in the wood behind the road-house.'

'Of course,' she gave a little gasp, and hurriedly began to tidy herself. 'But we can't stay here all night.'

The thought of taking her back to Cardinals Folly occurred to him again, but in these timeless hours he had witnessed so many things he would have thought impossible a few days before that he dismissed the idea at once. Tanith, he felt convinced, was not lying to him. She was genuinely repentant and terrified of Mocata. But who could say what strange powers that sinister man might not be able to exercise over her at a distance. He dared not risk it. However, she was certainly right in saying that they could not stay where they were all night.

'We'd best go back to the road-house,' he suggested. 'They will be able to knock us up a meal, and after, it'll be time enough to figure out what we mean to do.'

'Yes,' she sighed a little. 'I am hungry now—terribly hungry. Do let us go back and see if they can find us something to eat.'

Her arm through his, their fingers laced together, they walked back the quarter of a mile to the little stream which separated the wood from the inn garden. He lifted her over it again and when they reached the lounge of the 'Pride of Peacocks' they found that it was already half-past nine.

Knowing that his friends would be anxious about him, Rex tried to telephone immediately he got in, but the village exchange told him that the line to Cardinals Folly was out of order. Then he sent the trim maid for Mr Wilkes, and when that worthy arrived on the scene, inquired if it was too late for them to have a hot meal.

'Not at all, sir,' Mr Wilkes bent, quiet-voiced, deferential, priestlike, benign. 'My wife will be very happy to cook you a little dinner. What would you care for now? Fish is a little difficult in these parts, except when I know that I have guests staying and can order in advance, and game, of course, is unfortunately out of season. But a nice young duckling perhaps, or a chicken? My wife, if I may say so, does a very good Chicken Maryland, sir, of which our American visitors have been kind enough to express their approval from time to time.'

'Chicken Maryland,' exclaimed Rex. 'That sounds grand to me. How about you, honey?'

Tanith nodded. 'Lovely, if only it is not going to take too long.'

'Some twenty minutes, madam. Not more. Mrs Wilkes will see to it right away, and in the meantime, I've just had in a very nice piece of smoked salmon, which comes to me from a London house. I could recommend that if you would like to start your dinner fairly soon.'

Rex nodded, and the aged Wilkes went on amiably: 'And now sir–to drink? Red wine, if I might make so bold would be best with the grill, perhaps. I have a little of the Clos de Vougeot 1920 left, which Mr Richard Eaton was good enough to compliment me on when he dined here last, and his Lordship, my late master, always used to say that he found a glass of Justerini's Amontillado before a meal lent an edge to the appetite.'

For a second Rex wavered. He recalled De Richleau's prohibition against alcohol, but he had been far from satisfied by the brief rest which he had snatched that morning and was feeling all the strain now of the events which had taken place in the last forty-eight hours. Tanith, too, was looking pale and drawn, despite her sleep. A bottle of good burgundy was the very thing they needed to give them fresh strength and courage. He could have sunk half a dozen cocktails with the greatest ease and pleasure, but by denying himself spirits, he felt that he was at least carrying out the kernel of the Duke's instructions. Good wine could surely harm no one–so he acquiesced.

A quarter of an hour later, he was seated opposite to Tanith at a little corner table in the dining-room, munching fresh, warm toast and the smoked salmon with hungry relish, while the neat little maid ministered to their wants, and the pontifical Mr Wilkes hovered eagle-eyed in the background. The chicken was admirably cooked, and the wine lent an additional flavour by the fact that his palate was unusually clean and fresh from having denied himself those cocktails before the meal.

When the chicken was served, Mr Wilkes murmured something about a sweet and Rex, gazing entranced into Tanith's big eyes, nodded vaguely. Which sign of assent resulted, a little later, in the production of a flaming omelette au kirsch. Then Wilkes came forward once more, with a suggestion that the dinner should be rounded off by allowing him to decant a bottle of his Cockburn's '08. But here, Rex was firm. The burgundy had served its purpose, stimulated his brain and put fresh life into his body. To drink a vintage port after it would have been pleasant he knew, but certain to destroy the good effect and cause him to feel sleepy. So he resisted Mr Wilkes' blandishments.

After the meal Rex tried to get on to Cardinals Folly again but the line was still reported out of order, so he scribbled a note to Richard, saying that he was safe and well and would ring them in the morning, then asked Wilkes to have it sent up to the house by hand.

When the landlord had left them, they moved back into the lounge and discussed how they should pass the night. Tanith was as insistent as ever that under no circumstances should Rex leave her to herself, even if she asked him later on to do so. She felt that her only hope of safety lay in remaining with him beside her until the morning, so it was decided that they spend the night together in the empty lounge.

Tanith had already booked a room and so, to make all things orderly in the mind of the good Mr Wilkes, Rex booked another, but told the landlord that, as Tanith suffered from insomnia, they would probably remain in the lounge until very late, and so he was not to bother about them when he locked up. As a gesture he also borrowed from Wilkes a pack of cards, saying that they meant to pass an hour or two playing nap.

The fire was made up and they settled down comfortably under the shelter of the big mantel in the inglenook with a little table before them upon which they spread out the cards for appearance sake. But no sooner had the maid withdrawn than they had their arms about each other once more and blissfully oblivious of their surroundings, began that delightful first exchange of confidences about their previous lives, which is such a blissful hour for all lovers.

Rex would have been in the seventh heaven but for the thought of this terrible business in which Tanith had got herself involved and the threat of Mocata's power hanging like a sword of Damocles above her head.

Again and again, from a variety of subjects and experiences ranging the world over, and from their childhood to the present day, they found themselves continually and inexplicably caught back to that macabre subject which both were seeking to avoid. In the end, both surrendered to it and allowed the thoughts which were uppermost in their minds to enter their conversation freely.

'I'm still hopelessly at sea about this business,' Rex confessed. 'It's all so alien, so bizarre, so utterly fantastic. I know I wasn't dreaming last night or the night before. I know that if Simon hadn't got himself into trouble I wouldn't be holding your loveliness in my arms right now. Yet, every time I think of it, I feel that I must have been imagining things, and that it just simply can't be true.'

'It is, my dear,' she pressed his hand gently. 'That is just the horror of it. If it were any ordinary tangible peril, it wouldn't be quite so terrifying. It wouldn't be quite so bad even if we were living in the middle ages. Then at least, I could seek sanctuary in some convent where the nuns would understand and the priests who were learned in such matters, exert themselves to protect me. But in these days of modern scepticism there is no one I can turn to; police and clergymen and doctors would all think me insane. I only have you and after last night I'm frightened, Rex, frightened.' A sudden flush mounted to her cheeks again.

'I know, I know,' Rex soothed her gently. 'But you must try all you know not to be. I've a feeling that you're scaring yourself more than is really necessary. I'll agree that Mocata might hypnotise you if he got you on your own again, and maybe use you in some way to get poor Simon back into his net, but what could he actually do to you beyond that? He's not going to take a chance on murdering anybody, so that the police could take a hand, even if he had sufficient motive to want to try.'

'I am afraid you don't understand, dearest,' she murmured gently. 'A Satanist who is as far along the Path as Mocata does not need a motive to do murder, unless you can call malicious pleasure in the deed a motive in itself, and my having left him in the lurch at such a critical time is quite sufficient to anger him into bringing about my death.'

'I tell you, sweet, he'll never risk doing murder. In this country it is far too dangerous a game.'

'But his murders are not like ordinary murders. He can kill from a distance if he likes.'

'What—by sticking pins in a little wax figure with your name scratched on it, or letting it melt away before the fire until you pine and die?'

'That is one way, but he is more likely to use the blood of white mice.'

'How in the world do you mean?'

'I don't know very much about it except what I have picked up from Madame D'Urfé and a few other people. They say that when a very advanced adept wishes to kill someone, he feeds a white mouse on some of the holy wafers that they compel people to steal from churches for them. The sacrilegious aspect of the thing is very important, you see. Then they perform the Catholic ceremony of baptism over the mouse, christening it with the same name as that of their intended victim. That creates an affinity between the mouse and the person far stronger than carving their name on any image.'

'Then they kill the mouse, eh?'

'No, I don't think so. They draw off some of its blood, impregnate that with their malefic will, vaporise it, and call up an elemental to feed upon its essence. Then they perform a mystic transfusion in their victim's veins causing the elemental to poison them. But, Rex—'

'Yes, my sweet.'

'It is not that I am afraid to die. In any case, as I have told you, there is no hope of my living out the year, but that has not troubled me for a long time now. It is what may come after that terrifies me so.'

'Surely he can't harm anybody once they're dead,' Rex protested.

'But he can,' Tanith burst out with a little cry of distress and fear. 'If he kills me *that* way, he can make me dead to the world, but I shall live on as an *undead*, and that would be horrible.'

Rex passed his hand wearily across his eyes. 'Don't speak in riddles, treasure. What is this thing you're frightened of? Just tell me now in ordinary, plain English.'

'All right. I suppose you have heard of a vampire.'

'Why, yes. I've read of them in fiction. They're supposed to come out of their graves every night and drink the blood of human beings, aren't they? Until they're found out, then their graves are opened up for a priest to cut off their heads and drive stakes through their hearts. Is that what you call an undead?'

Tanith nodded slowly. 'Yes, that is an undead—a foul, revolting thing, a living corpse that creeps through the night like a great white slug, and a body bloated from drinking people's blood. But have you never read of them in other books beside nightmare fiction?'

'No, I wouldn't exactly say I have as far as I can remember. The Duke would know all about them for a certainty—and Richard Eaton too, I expect—because they're both great readers. But I'm just an ordinary chap who's content to take his reading from the popular novelists who can turn out a good, interesting story. Do you mean to tell me seriously that such creatures have ever existed outside the thriller writer's imagination?'

'I do. In the Carpathians, where I come from, the whole countryside is riddled with vampire stories from real life. You hear of them in Poland and Hungary and Roumania, too. All through Middle Europe and right down into the Balkan countries there have been endless cases of such revolting Satanic manifestations. Anyone there will tell you that time and again, when graves have been opened on suspicion, the corpses of vampires have been found, months after burial, without the slightest sign of decay, their flesh pink and flushed, their eyes wide-open, bright and staring. The only difference to their previous appearance is the way in which their canine teeth have grown long and pointed. Often, even, they have been found with fresh blood trickling out of the sides of their mouths.'

'Say, that sounds pretty grim,' Rex exclaimed with a little shudder. 'I reckon De Richleau would explain that by saying that the person was possessed before he died and that after, although the actual soul passed on, the evil spirit continued to make a doss-house of its borrowed body. But I can't think that anything so awful would ever happen to you.'

'It might, my dear. That is what scares me so. And if Mocata did get hold of me again he would not need to perform those ghastly rites with impregnated blood. He could just throw me into the hypnotic state and, after he had made me do all he wished, allow some terrible thing to take possession of me at once. The elemental would still remain in my body when he killed me, and I should become one of those loathsome creatures—the undead, if that happened, this very night.'

'Stop! I can't bear to think of it,' Rex drew her quickly to him again. 'But he shan't get hold of you. We'll fight him till all's blue, and I'm going to marry you tomorrow so that I can be with you constantly. We'll apply for a special licence first thing in the morning.'

She nodded, and a new light of hope came into her eyes. 'If you wish it, Rex,' she whispered, 'and I do believe that by your love and strength, you can save me. But you mustn't leave me for a single second tonight, and we mustn't sleep a wink. Listen!'

She paused a moment as the bell in the village steeple chimed the twelve strokes of midnight, which came to them clearly in the stillness of the quiet room. 'It is the second of May now—my fatal day.'

He smiled indulgently. 'Sure, I won't leave you, and we won't sleep either. One of us might drop off if we were all alone, but together we'll prod each other into keeping awake. Though I just can't think that'll be necessary, with all the million things I've got to tell you about your sweet self.'

She stood up then, raising her arms to smooth back her hair, and making a graceful, slender silhouette against the flickering flames of the heaped-up fire.

'No. The night will slip away before we know it,' she agreed more cheerfully. 'Because I've got a thousand things to tell you too. I must just slip upstairs to powder my nose now, and when I come back, we'll settle down in earnest to make a night of it together.'

A quick frown crossed his face. 'I thought you said I wasn't to let you leave me even for a second. I don't like your going upstairs alone at all.'

'But, my dear!' Tanith gave a little laugh. 'I can hardly take you with me, and I shan't be more than a few moments.'

Rex nodded, reassured as he saw her standing there, smiling down at him in the firelight so happy and normal in every way. He felt certain that he would know at once if Mocata was trying to exert his power on her from a distance, by that strange far-away look which had come into her eyes and the fanatical note that had raised the pitch of her voice each time she had spoken of the imperative necessity of her reaching the meeting-place for the Sabbat on the previous day. There was not the faintest suggestion of that other will, imposed upon her own, in her face or voice now, and obviously it would have been childish to attempt to prevent her carrying out so sensible a suggestion before settling down. The best part of six hours must elapse before daylight began to filter greyly through the old-fashioned bow window at the far end of the room.

'All right,' he laughed. 'I'll give you five minutes by that clock–but no more, remember, and if you're not down then, I'll come up and get you.'

'Dear lover!' she stooped suddenly and kissed him, then slipped out of the room closing the door softly behind her.

Rex lay back, spreading his great limbs now in the comfortable corner of the inglenook, and stretching out his long legs to the glow of the log fire. He wasn't sleepy, which amazed him when he thought how little sleep he had had since he woke in his state-room on the giant Cunarder the morning of the day that he dined with De Richleau. That seemed ages ago now, weeks, months, years. So many things had happened, so many new and staggering thoughts come to seethe and ferment in his brain, yet Simon's party had been held only a bare two nights before.

His hand moved lazily to his hip pocket to get a cigarette, but half way to it he abandoned the attempt as too much trouble, wriggling down instead more comfortably about the cushions.

He wasn't sleepy–not a bit. His brain had never been more active and his thoughts turned for a moment to his friends at Cardinals Folly. They, too, would be wide awake, braced, no doubt, under De Richleau's determined leadership, to face an attack from the powers of evil. De Richleau must be feeling pretty sleepy he thought. Neither of them had had more than three hours that morning after their exhausting night. They hadn't got to bed much before dawn the night before either, and the Duke had been up, according to Max, at seven in order to be at the British Museum directly it opened. Say six hours in sixty. That wasn't much, but De Richleau was an old campaigner and he would stick it all right, Rex had no doubt.

He glanced at the clock, thinking it almost time that Tanith should rejoin him, but saw that the slow-moving hand had only advanced two minutes. 'Amazing how time drags when one is watching it,' he thought, and his mind wandered on to the reflection that he had been mighty wise not to drink anything but that one glass of sherry and the burgundy for dinner. He would probably have been horribly drowsy by now if he had been fool enough to fall for the cocktails or the port. But he wasn't sleepy–not a bit.

His mind began to form little mental pictures of some of those strange episodes which he had lived through in the last two days–old Madame D'Urfé smoking her cigar and then Tanith; Max arranging the cushions in De Richleau's electric canoe at Pangbourne, and then Tanith again. That plausible old humbug Wilkes serving the Clos de Vougeot with meticulous care–a mighty fine thing he made out of this pub no doubt–and then Tanith once more, sitting opposite him at table, with the soft glow of the shaded electric lamp lighting her oval face and throwing strange shadows in the silken web of her golden hair.

He glanced at the clock again–another minute had crawled by, and then he pictured Tanith as he had seen her only a few moments before, bending to kiss him, her face warm and flushed by the firelight, and those strange, deep, age-old eyes of hers smiling tenderly into his beneath their heavy half-lowered lids. It must be this strange wonderful love for her, he thought, which kept him so alive and alert, for ordinarily his healthy body demanded its fair share of sleep and he would have been nodding his head off by this time. He could still see those glorious golden eyes of hers smiling into his. The face above them with indistinct and vague, but they remained clear and shining in the shadows on the far side of the fireplace. The eyes were changing now a little–losing their colour and fading from gold to grey and then to a palish blue. Yet their brightness seemed to increase and they grew bigger as he held them with his mental gaze.

He thought for a second of glancing at the clock again. It seemed that Tanith had left him ages ago now, but judging by the time it had taken for that long hand to crawl through three minutes' space he felt that it could hardly yet have covered the other two. Besides, he did not want to lose the focus of those strange, bright eyes which he could see so plainly when he half closed his own.

Rex wasn't sleepy–not a bit. But time is an illusion, and Rex never afterwards knew how long he sat awake there in the semi-darkness. Perhaps during the first portion of his watch some strange power deluded his vision and the clock had in reality moved on while he only thought that the minutes dragged so heavily. In any case, those eyes that watched him from the shadows were his last conscious thought, and next moment Rex was sound asleep.

27

WITHIN THE PENTACLE

While Rex slumbered evenly and peacefully before the dying fire in the lounge of the 'Pride of Peacocks,' Richard, Marie Lou, the Duke and Simon waited in the pentacle, on the floor of the library at Cardinals Folly, for the dreary hours of night to drag their way to morning.

They lay with their heads towards the centre of the circle and their feet towards the rim, forming a human cross, but although they did not speak for a long time after they had settled down, none of them managed to drop off to sleep.

The layer of clean sheets and blankets beneath them was pleasant enough to rest on for a while, but the hard, unyielding floorboards under it soon began to cause them discomfort. The bright flames of the burning candles and the steady glow of the electric light showed pink through their closed eyelids, making repose difficult, and they were all keyed up to varying degrees of anxious expectancy.

Marie Lou was restless and miserable. Nothing but her fondness for Simon, and the Duke's plea that the presence of Richard and herself would help enormously in his protection, would have induced her to play any part in such proceedings. Her firm belief in the supernatural filled her with grim forebodings, and she tried in vain to shut out her fears by sleep. Every little noise that broke the brooding stillness, the creaking of a beam as the old house eased itself upon its foundations, or the whisper of the breeze as it rustled the leaves of the trees in the garden, caused her to start wide awake again, her muscles taut with alarm and apprehension.

Richard did not attempt to sleep. He lay revolving a number of problems in his mind. Fleur d'amour's birthday was in a couple of weeks' time. The child was easy, but a present for Marie Lou was a different question. It must be something that she wanted and yet a surprise. A difficult matter when she already had everything with which his fine fortune could endow her, and jewellery was not only banal but absurd. The sale of the lesser stones among the Shulimoff treasure, which they had brought out of Russia, had realised enough to provide her with a handsome independent income and her retention of the finer gems alone equipped her magnificently in that direction. He toyed with the idea of buying her a two-year-old. He was not a racing man but she was fond of horses and it would be fun for her to see her own run at the lesser meetings.

After a while he turned restlessly on to his tummy, and began to ponder this wretched muddle into which Simon had got himself. The more he thought about it the less he could subscribe to the Duke's obvious beliefs. That so-called Black Magic was still practised in most of the Continental capitals and many of the great cities in America, he knew. He had even met a man, a few years before, who had told him that he had attended a celebration of the Black Mass at a house in the Earls Court district of London, yet he could not credit that it had been anything more than a flimsy excuse for a crowd of intellectual decadents to get disgustingly drunk and participate in a wholesale sexual orgy. Simon was not that sort, or a fool either, so it was certainly queer that he should have got himself mixed up with such beastliness.

Richard turned over again, yawned, glanced at his friend whom, he decided, he had never seen look more normal, and wondered if, out of courtesy to the Duke, he could possibly continue to play his part in this tedious farce until morning.

The banishing rituals which De Richleau had performed upon Simon the previous night at Stonehenge had certainly proved successful, and he had had a good sleep that afternoon. His brain was now quick and clear as it had been in the old days and, although Mocata's threats were principally directed against himself, he was by far the most cheerful of the party. Despite his recent experiences, his natural humour bubbling up very nearly caused him to laugh at the thought of them all lying on that hard floor because he had made an idiot of himself, and Richard's obvious disgust at the discomforts imposed by the Duke caused him much amusement. Nevertheless, he recognised that his desire to laugh was mainly due to nervous tension, and accepted with full understanding the necessity for these extreme precautions. To think, for only a second, of how narrow his escape had been was enough to sober instantly any tendency to mirth and send a quick shudder through his limbs. He was only anxious now, having dragged his friends into this horrible affair, to cause them as little further trouble as possible by following the Duke's leadership without question. With resolute determination he kept his thoughts away from any of his dealings with Mocata and set himself to endure his comfortless couch with philosophic patience.

To outward appearances De Richleau slept. He lay perfectly still on his back breathing evenly and almost imperceptibly, but he had always been able to do with very little sleep. Actually he was recruiting his forces in a manner that was not possible to the others. That gentle rhythmic breathing, perfectly but unconsciously timed from long practice, was the way of the Raja Yoga which he had learnt when young, and all the time he visualised himself, the others, the whole room as blue–blue–blue, the colour vibration which gives love and sympathy and spiritual attainment. Yet he was conscious of every tiny movement made by the others; the gentle sighing of the breeze outside, and the occasional plop of burning logs as they fell into the embers. For over two hours he barely moved a muscle but all his senses remained watchful and alert.

The night seemed never-ending. Outside the wind dropped and a steady rain began to fall, dripping with monotonous regularity from the eaves on to the terrace. Richard became more and more sore from the hard floor. He was tired now and bored by this apparently senseless vigil. He thought that it must be about half past one, and daylight would not come to release them from their voluntary prison before half past five or six. That meant another four hours of this acute and momentarily increasing discomfort. As he tossed and turned it grew upon him with ever-increasing force how stupid and futile this whole affair seemed to be. De Richleau was so obviously the victim of a gang of clever tricksters, and his wide reading on obscure subjects had caused his imagination to run away with him. To pander to such folly any longer simply was not good enough. With these thoughts now dominating his mind Richard suddenly sat up.

'Look here,' he said. 'I'm sick of this. A joke's a joke, but we've had no lunch and precious little dinner, and I haven't had a drink all day. Some of you have got far too lively an imagination, and we are making utter fools of ourselves. We had better go upstairs. If you're really frightened of anything happening to Simon we could easily shift four beds into one room and all sleep within a hand's reach of each other. Nobody will be able to get at him then. But frankly, at the moment, I think we're behaving like a lot of lunatics.'

De Richleau rose with a jerk and gave him a sharp look from beneath his grey slanting devil's eyebrows. 'Something's beginning to happen,' he told himself swiftly. 'They're working upon Richard, because he's the most sceptical amongst us, to try and make him break up the pentacle.' Aloud he said quietly: 'So you're still unconvinced that Simon is in real danger, Richard?'

'Yes, I am.' Richard's voice held an angry aggressive note quite foreign to his normal manner. 'I regard this Black Magic business as stupid nonsense. If you could cite me a single case where so-called magicians have actually done their stuff before sane people it would be different. But they're charlatans—every one of them. Take Cagliostro—he was supposed to make gold but nobody ever saw any of it, and when the Inquisition got hold of him they bunged him in a dungeon in Rome and he died there in abject misery. His Black Magic couldn't even procure him a hunk of bread. Look at Catherine de Medici. She was a witch on the grand scale if ever there was one—built a special tower at Vincennes for Cosimo Ruggeri, an Italian sorcerer. They used to slit up babies and practise all sorts of abominations there together night after night to ensure the death of Henry of Navarre and the birth of children to her own sons. But it didn't do her a ha'porth of good. All four died childless so that at last, despite all her bloody sacrifices, the House of Valois was extinct, and Henry, the hated Bearnais, became King of France after all. Come nearer home if you like. Take that absurd fool Elipas Levi who was supposed to be the Grand High Whatnot in Victorian times. Did you ever read his book, *The Doctrine and Ritual of Magic*? In his introduction he professes that he is going to tell you all about the game and that he's written a really practical book, by the aid of which anybody who likes can raise the devil, and perform all sorts of monkey tricks. He drools on for hundreds of pages about fiery swords and tetragrams and the terrible aqua poffana, but does he tell you anything? Not a blessed thing. Once it comes to a showdown he hedges like the crook he was and tells you that such mysteries are *far too terrible and dangerous to be entrusted to the profane.* Mysterious balderdash my friend. I'm going to have a good strong nightcap and go to bed.'

Marie Lou looked at him in amazement. Never before had she heard Richard denounce any subject with such passion and venom. Ordinarily, he possessed an extremely open mind and, if he doubted any statement, confined himself to a kindly but slightly cynical expression of disbelief. It was extraordinary that he should suddenly forget even his admirable manners and be downright rude to one of his greatest friends.

De Richleau studied his face with quiet understanding and as Richard stood up he stood up too, laying his hand upon the younger man's shoulder. 'Richard,' he said. 'You think I'm a superstitious fool, don't you?'

'No.' Richard shrugged uncomfortably. 'Only that you've been through a pretty difficult time and, quite frankly, that your imagination is a bit overstrained at the moment.'

The Duke smiled. 'All right, perhaps you are correct, but we have been friends for a long time now and this business tonight has not interfered with our friendship in any way, has it?'

'Why, of course not. You know that.'

'Then, if I begged of you to do something for my sake, just because of that friendship, you would do it, wouldn't you?'

'Certainly I would.' Richard's hesitation was hardly perceptible and the Duke cut in quickly, taking him at his word.

'Good! Then we will agree that Black Magic may be nothing but a childish superstition. Yet I happen to be frightened of it, so I ask you, my friend, who is not bothered with such stupid fears, to stay with me tonight–and not move outside this pentacle.'

Richard shrugged again, and then smiled ruefully. . . .

'You've caught me properly now so I must make the best of it; quite obviously if you say that, it is impossible for me to refuse.'

'Thank you,' De Richleau murmured as they both sat down again, and to himself he thought: 'That's the first move in the game to me.' Then as a fresh silence fell upon the party, he began to ruminate upon the strangeness of the fact that elementals and malicious spirits may be very powerful, but their nature is so low and their intelligence so limited that they can nearly always be trapped by the divine spark of reason which is the salvation of mankind. The snare was such an obvious one and yet Richard's true nature had reasserted itself so rapidly that the force, which had moved him to try and break up their circle for its benefit, had been scotched almost before it had had a chance to operate.

They settled down again but in some subtle way the atmosphere had changed. The fire glowed red on its great pile of ashes, the candles burned unflickeringly in the five points of the star, and the electric globes above the cornices still lit every corner of the room with a soft diffused radiance, yet the four friends made no further pretence of trying to sleep. Instead they sat back to back, while the moments passed, creeping with leaden feet towards the dawn.

Marie Lou was perplexed and worried by Richard's outburst, De Richleau tense with a new expectancy, now he felt that psychic forces were actually moving within the room. Stealthy—invisible—but powerful; he knew them to be feeling their way from bay to bay of the pentacle, seeking for any imperfection in the barrier he had erected, just as a strong current swirls and eddies about the jagged fissures of a reef searching for an entrance into a lagoon.

Simon sat crouched, his hands clasped round his knees, staring, apparently with unseeing eyes, at the long lines of books. It seemed that he was listening intently and the Duke watched him with special care, knowing that he was the weak spot of their defence. Presently, his voice a little hoarse, Simon spoke:

'I'm awfully thirsty. I wish we'd got a drink.'

De Richleau smiled, a little grimly. Another of the minor manifestations—the evil was working upon Simon now but only to give another instance of its brutish stupidity. It overlooked the fact that he had provided for such an emergency with that big carafe of water in the centre of the pentacle. The fact that it had caused Simon to forget its presence was of little moment. 'Here you are, my friend,' he said, pouring out a glass. 'This will quench your thirst.'

Simon sipped it and put it aside with a shake of his narrow head. 'Do you use well-water, Richard?' he asked jerkily. 'This stuff tastes beastly to me—brackish and stale.'

'Ah!' thought De Richleau. 'That's the line they are trying, is it? Well, I can defeat them there,' and taking Simon's glass he poured the contents back into the carafe. Then he picked up his bottle of Lourdes water. There was very little in it now for the bulk of it had been used to fill the five cups which stood in the vales of the pentagram—but enough—and he sprinkled a few drops into the water in the carafe.

Richard was speaking—instinctively now in a lowered voice—assuring Simon that they always used Burrows Malvern for drinking purposes, when the Duke filled the glass again and handed it back to Simon. 'Now try that.'

Simon sipped again and nodded quickly. 'Um, that seems quite different. I think it must have been my imagination before,' and he drank off the contents of the glass.

Again for a long period no one spoke. Only the scraping of a mouse behind the wainscot, sounding abnormally loud, jarred upon the stillness. That frantic insistent gnawing frayed Marie Lou's nerves to such a pitch that she wanted to scream, but after a while that, too, ceased and the heavy silence, pregnant with suspense, enveloped them once more. Even the gentle patter on the window-panes was no longer there to remind them of healthy, normal things, for the rain had stopped, and in that soundless room the only movement was the soft flicker of the logs, piled high in the wide fireplace.

It seemed that they had been crouching in that pentacle for nights on end and that their frugal dinner lay days away. Their discomfort had been dulled into a miserable apathy and they were drowsy now after these hours of strained uneventful watching. Richard lay down again to try and snatch a little sleep. The Duke alone remained alert. He knew that this long interval of inactivity on the part of the malefic powers was only a snare designed to give a false sense of security before the renewal of the attack. At length he shifted his position slightly and as he did so he chanced to glance upwards at the ceiling. Suddenly it seemed to him that the lights were not quite so bright as they had been. It might be his imagination, due to the fact that he was anticipating trouble, but somehow he felt certain that the ceiling had been brighter when he had looked at it before. In quick alarm he roused the others.

Simon nodded, realising why De Richleau had touched him on the shoulder and confirming his suspicion. Then with straining eyes, they all watched the cornice, where the concealed lights ran round the wall above the top of the bookshelves.

The action was so slow, that each of them felt their eyes must be deceiving them, and yet an inner conviction told them that it was true. Shadows had appeared where no shadows were before. Slowly but surely the current was failing and the lights dimming as they watched.

There was something strangely terrifying now about that quiet room. It was orderly and peaceful, just as Richard knew it day by day, except for the absence of the furniture. No nebulous ghost-like figure had risen up to confront them, but there, as the minutes passed, they were faced with an unaccountable phenomenon—those bright electric globes hidden from their sight were gradually but unquestionably being dimmed.

The shadows from the bookcases lengthened. The centre of the ceiling became a dusky patch. Gradually, gradually, as with caught breath they watched, the room was being plunged in darkness. Soundless and stealthy, that black shadow upon the ceiling grew in size and the binding of the books became obscure where they had before been bright until, after what seemed an eternity of time, no light remained save only the faintest line just above the rim of the top bookshelf, the five candles burning steadily in the points of the five-starred pentagram, and the dying fire.

Richard shuddered suddenly. 'My God! It's cold,' he exclaimed, drawing Marie Lou towards him. The Duke nodded, silent and watchful. He felt that sinister chill draught beginning to flow upon the back of his neck, and his scalp prickled as he swung round with a sudden jerk to face it.

There was nothing to be seen—only the vague outline of the bookcases rising high and stark towards the ceiling where the dull ribbon of light still glowed. The flames of the candles were bent now at an angle under the increasing strength of the cold invisible air current that pressed steadily upon them.

De Richleau began to intone a prayer. The wind ceased as suddenly as it had begun, but a moment later it began to play upon them again—this time from a different quarter.

The Duke resumed his prayer—the wind checked—and then came with renewed force from another angle. He swung to meet it but it was at his back again.

A faint, low moaning became perceptible as the unholy blast began to circle round the pentacle. Round and round it swirled with ever-increasing strength and violence, beating up out of the shadows in sudden wild gusts of arctic iciness, and tearing at them with chill, invisible, clutching fingers, so that it seemed as if they were standing in the very vortex of a cyclone. The candles flickered wildly—and went out.

Richard, his scepticism badly shaken, quickly pushed Marie Lou to one side and whipped out his matches. He struck one, and got the nearest candle alight again but, as he turned to the next, that cold damp evil wind came once more, chilling the perspiration that had broken out upon his forehead, snuffing the candle that he had re-lit and the half-burnt match which he still held between his fingers.

He lit another and it spluttered out almost before the wood had caught—another—and another, but they would not burn.

He glimpsed Simon's face for an instant, white, set, ghastly, the eyeballs protruding unnaturally as he knelt staring out into the shadows—then the whole centre of the room was plunged in blackness.

'We must hold hands,' whispered the Duke. 'Quick, it will strengthen our resistance,' and in the murk they fumbled for each other's fingers, all standing up now, until they formed a little ring in the very centre of the pentagram, hand clasped in hand and bodies back to back.

The whirling hurricane ceased as suddenly as it had begun. An unnatural stillness descended on the room again. Then without warning, an uncontrollable fit of trembling took possession of Marie Lou.

'Steady, my sweet,' breathed Richard, gripping her hand more tightly, 'you'll be all right in a minute.' He thought that she was suffering from the effect of that awful cold which had penetrated the thin garments of them all, but she was standing facing the grate and her knees shook under her as she stammered out:

'But look—the fire.'

Simon was behind her but the Duke and Richard, who were on either side, turned their heads and saw the thing that had caused her such excess of terror. The piled-up logs had flared into fresh life as that strange rushing wind had circled round the room, but now the flames had died down and, as their eyes rested upon it, they saw that the red hot embers were turning black. It was as though some monstrous invisible hand was dabbing at it, then almost in a second, every spark of light in the great, glowing fire was quenched.

'Pray,' urged the Duke, 'for God's sake, pray.'

After a little their eyes grew accustomed to this new darkness. The electric globes hidden behind the cornice were not quite dead. They flickered and seemed about to fail entirely every few moments, yet always the power exerted against them seemed just not quite enough, for their area of light would increase again, so that the shadows across the ceiling and below the books were driven back. The four friends waited with pound ing hearts as they watched that silent struggle between light and darkness and the swaying of the shadows backwards and forwards, that ringed them in.

For what seemed an immeasurable time they stood in silent apprehension, praying that the last gleam of light would hold out, then, shattering that eerie silence like the sound of guns there came three swift, loud knocks upon the window-pane.

'What's that?' snapped Richard.

'Stay still,' hissed the Duke.

A voice came suddenly from outside in the garden. It was clear and unmistakable. Each one of them recognised it instantly as that of Rex.

'Say, I saw your light burning. Come on and let me in.'

With a little sigh of relief at the breaking of the tension, Richard let go Marie Lou's hand and took a step forward. But the Duke grabbed his shoulder and jerked him back:

'Don't be a fool,' he rasped. 'It's a trap.'

'Come on now. What in heck is keeping you?' the voice demanded. 'It's mighty cold out here, let me in quick.'

Richard alone remained momentarily unconvinced that it was a superhuman agency at work. The others felt a shiver of horror run through their limbs at that perfect imitation of Rex's voice, which they were convinced was a manifestation of some terrible entity endeavouring to trick them into leaving their carefully constructed defence.

'Richard,' the voice came again, angrily now. 'It's Rex I tell you–Rex. Stop all this fooling and get this door undone.' But the four figures in the pentacle now remained tense, silent and unresponsive.

The voice spoke no more and once again there was a long interval of silence.

De Richleau feared that the Adversary was gathering his forces for a direct attack and it was that, above all other things, which filled him with dread. He was reasonably confident that his own intelligence would serve to sense out and avoid any fresh pitfalls which might be set, providing the others would obey his bidding and remain steadfast in their determination not to leave the pentacle, but he had failed in his attempt to secure the holy wafers of the Blessed Sacrament that afternoon, the lights were all but overcome, the sacred candles had been snuffed out. The holy water, horseshoes, garlic and the pentacle itself might only prove a partial defence if the dark entities which were about them made an open and determined assault.

'What's that!' exclaimed Simon, and they swung round to face the new danger. The shadows were massing into deeper blackness in one corner of the room. Something was moving there.

A dim phosphorescent blob began to glow in the darkness; shimmering and spreading into a great hummock, its outline gradually became clearer. It was not a man form nor yet an animal, but heaved there on the floor like some monstrous living sack. It had no eyes or face but from it there radiated a terrible malefic intelligence.

Suddenly there ceased to be anything ghostlike about it. The Thing had a whitish pimply skin, leprous and unclean, like some huge silver slug. Waves of satanic power rippled through its spineless body, causing it to throb and work continually like a great mass of new-made dough. A horrible stench of decay and corruption filled the room; for as it writhed it exuded a slimy poisonous moisture which trickled in little rivulets across the polished floor. It was solid, terribly real, a living thing. They could even see long, single, golden hairs, separated from each other by ulcerous patches of skin, quivering and waving as they rose on end from its flabby body–and suddenly it began to laugh at them, a low, horrid, chuckling laugh.

Marie Lou reeled against Richard, pressing the back of her hand against her mouth and biting into it to prevent a scream.

His eyes were staring, a cold perspiration broke out upon his face.

De Richleau knew that it was a Saiitii manifestation of the most powerful and dangerous kind. His nails bit into the palms of his hands as he watched that shapeless mass, silver white and putrescent, heave and ferment.

Suddenly it moved, with the rapidity of a cat, yet they heard the squelching sound as it leapt along the floor, leaving a wet slimy trail in its wake, that poisoned the air like foul gases given off by animal remains.

They spun round to face it, then it laughed again, mocking them with that quiet, diabolical chuckle that had the power to fill them with such utter dread.

It lay for a moment near the window pulsating with demoniac energy like some enormous livid heart. Then it leapt again back to the place where it had been before.

Shuddering at the thought of that ghastliness springing upon their backs they turned with lightning speed to meet it, but it only lay there wobbling and crepitating with unholy glee.

'Oh, God!' gapsed Richard.

The masked door which led up to the nursery was slowly opening. A line of white appeared in the gap from near the floor to about three feet in height. It broadened as the door swung back noiselessly upon its hinges, and Marie Lou gave a terrified cry.

'It's Fleur!'

The men, too, instantly recognised the little body, in the white nightgown, vaguely outlined against the blackness of the shadows, as the face with its dark aureole of curling hair became clear.

The Thing was only two yards from the child. With hideous merriment it chuckled evilly and flopping forward, decreased the distance by a half.

With one swift movement, De Richleau flung his arm about Marie Lou's neck and jerked her backwards, her chin gripped fast in the crook of his elbow. 'It's not Fleur,' he cried desperately. 'Only some awful thing which has taken her shape to deceive you.'

'Of course it's Fleur—she's walking in her sleep!' Richard started forward to spring towards the child, but De Richleau gripped his arm with his free hand and wrenched him back.

'It's not,' he insisted in an agonised whisper. 'Richard, I beg you! Have a little faith in me! Look at her face—it's blue! Oh, Lord protect us!'

At that positive suggestion, thrown out with such vital force at a moment of supreme emotional tension, it did appear to them for an instant that the child's face had a corpse-like bluish tinge then, upon the swift plea for Divine aid, the lines of the figure seemed to blur and tremble. The Thing laughed, but this time with thwarted malice, a high-pitched, angry, furious note. Then both the child and that nameless Thing became transparent and faded. The silent heavy darkness, undisturbed by sound or movement, settled all about them once again.

With a gasp of relief the straining Duke released his prisoners. 'Now do you believe me?' he muttered hoarsely, but there was not time for them to reply. The next attack developed almost instantly.

Simon was crouching in the middle of the circle. Marie Lou felt his body trembling against her thigh. She put her hand on his shoulder to steady him and found that he was shaking like an epileptic in a fit.

He began to gibber. Great shudders shook his frame from head to toe and suddenly he burst into heart-rending sobs.

'What is it, Simon,' she bent towards him quickly, but he took no notice of her and crouched there on all fours like a dog until, with a sudden jerk, he pulled himself upright and began to mutter:

'I won't—I won't I say—I won't. D'you hear— You mustn't make me—no—no— No!' Then with a reeling, drunken motion he staggered forward in the direction of the window. But Marie Lou was too quick for him and flung both arms about his neck.

'Simon darling—Simon,' she panted. 'You mustn't leave us.'

For a moment he remained still, then, his body twisted violently as though his limbs were animated by some terrible inhuman force, and he flung her from him. The mild good-natured smile had left his face and it seemed, in the faint light which still glowed from the cornice, that he had become an utterly changed personality–his mouth hung open showing the bared teeth in a snarl of ferocious rage–his eyes glinted hot and dangerous with the glare of insanity–a little dribble of saliva ran down his chin.

'Quick, Richard,' cried the Duke. 'They've got him–for God's sake pull him down!'

Richard had seen enough now to destroy his scepticism for life. He followed De Richleau's lead, grappling frantically with Simon, and all three of them crashed struggling to the floor.

'Oh, God,' sobbed Marie Lou. 'Oh, God, dear God!'

Simon's breath came in great gasps as though his chest would burst. He fought and struggled like a maniac, but Richard, desperate now, kneed him in the stomach and between them they managed to hold him down. Then De Richleau, who, fearing such an attack, had had the forethought to provide himself with cords, succeeded in tying his wrists and ankles.

Richard rose panting from the struggle, smoothed back his dark hair, and said huskily to the Duke. 'I take it all back. I'm sorry if I've been an extra nuisance to you.'

De Richleau patted him on the elbow. He could not smile for his eyes were flickering, even as Richard spoke, from corner to corner of that grim, darkened room, seeking, yet dreading, some new form in which the Adversary might attempt their undoing.

All three linked their arms together and stood, with Simon's body squirming at their feet, jerking their heads from side to side in nervous expectancy. They had not long to wait. Indistinct at first, but certain after a moment, there was a stirring in the blackness near the door. Some new horror was forming out there in the shadows beyond the pointers of the pentacle–just on a level with their heads.

Their grip upon each other tightened as they fought desperately to recruit their courage. Marie Lou stood between the others, her eyes wide and distended, as she watched this fresh manifestation gradually take shape and gain solidity.

Her scalp began to prickle beneath her chestnut curls. The Thing was forming into a long, dark, beast-like face. Two tiny points of light appeared in it just above the level of her eyes. She felt the short hairs at the back of her skull lift of their own volition like the hackles of a dog.

The points of light grew in size and intensity. They were eyes. Round, protuberant and burning with a fiery glow, they bored into hers, watching her with a horrible unwinking stare.

She wanted desperately to break away and run, but her knees sagged beneath her. The head of the Beast merged into powerful shoulders and the blackness below solidified into strong thick legs.

'It's a horse!' gasped Richard. 'A riderless horse.'

De Richleau groaned. It was a horse indeed. A great black stallion and it had no rider that was visible to them, but he knew its terrible significance. Mocata, grown desperate by his failures to wrest Simon from their keeping, had abandoned the attempt and, in savage revenge, now sent the Angel of Death himself to claim them.

A saddle of crimson leather was strapped upon the stallion's back, the pressure of invisible feet held the long stirrup leathers rigid to its flanks, and unseen hands held the reins taut a few inches above its withers. The Duke knew well enough that no human who has beheld that dread rider in all his sombre glory has ever lived to tell of it. If that dark Presence broke into the pentacle they would see him all too certainly, but at the price of death.

The sweat streaming down his face, Richard held his ground, staring with fascinated horror at the muzzle of the beast. The fleshy nose wrinkled, the lips drew back, baring two rows of yellowish teeth. It champed its silver bit. Flecks of foam, white and real, dripped from its loose mouth.

It snorted violently and its heated breath came like two clouds of steam from its quivering nostrils warm and damp on his face. He heard De Richleau praying, frantically, unceasingly, and tried to follow suit.

The stallion whinnied, tossed its head and backed into the bookcases drawn by the power of those unseen hands, its mighty hoofs ringing loud on the boards. Then, as though rowelled by knife-edged spurs, it was launched upon them.

Marie Lou screamed and tried to tear herself from De Richleau's grip, but his slim fingers were like a steel vice upon her arm. He remained there, ashen-faced but rigid, fronting the huge beast which seemed about to trample all three of them under foot.

As it plunged forward the only thought which penetrated Richard's brain was to protect Marie Lou. Instead of leaping back, he sprang in front of her with his automatic levelled and pressed the trigger.

The crash of the explosion sounded like a thunder-clap in that confined space. Again—again—again, he fired while blinding flashes lit the room as though with streaks of lightning. For a succession of seconds the whole library was as bright as day and the gilded bookbacks stood out so clearly that De Richleau could even read the titles across the empty space where, so lately, the great horse had been.

The silence that descended on them when Richard ceased fire was so intense that they could hear each other breathing, and for the moment they were plunged in utter darkness.

After that glaring succession of flashes from the shots, the little rivers of light around the cornice seemed to have shrunk to the glimmer of night lights coming beneath heavy curtains. They could no longer even see each other's figures as they crouched together in the ring.

The thought of the servants flashed for a second into Richard's mind. The shooting was bound to have fetched them out of bed. If they came down their presence might put an end to this ghastly business. But the minutes passed. No welcome sound of running feet came to break that horrid stillness that had closed in upon them once more. With damp hands he fingered his automatic and found that the magazine was empty. In his frantic terror he had loosed off every one of the eight shots.

How long they remained there, tense with horror, peering again into those awful shadows, they never knew, yet each became suddenly aware that the steed of the Dark Angel, who had been sent out from the underworld to bring about their destruction, was steadily re-forming.

The red eyes began to glow in the dark face. The body lengthened. The stallion's hoof-beats rang upon the floor as it stamped with impatience to be unleashed. The very smell of the stable was in the room. That gleaming harness stood out plain and clear. The reins rose sharply from its polished bit to bend uncannily in that invisible grip above its saddle bow. The black beast snorted, reared high in to the air, and then the crouching humans faced that terrifying charge again.

The Duke felt Marie Lou sway against him, clutch at his shoulder, and slip to the floor. The strain had proved too great and she had fainted. He could do nothing for her—the beast was actually upon them.

It baulked, upon the very edge of the pentacle, its fore hoofs slithering upon the polished floor, its back legs crashing under it as though faced with some invisible barrier.

With a neigh of fright and pain it flung up its powerful head as though its face had been brought into contact with a red-hot bar. It backed away champing and whinnying until its steaming hindquarters pressed against the book-lined wall.

Richard stooped to clasp Marie Lou's limp body. In their fear they had all unconsciously retreated from the middle to the edge of the circle. As he knelt his foot caught one of the cups of Holy Water set in the vales of the pentacle. It toppled over. The water spilled and ran to waste upon the floor.

Instantly a roar of savage triumph filled the room, coming from beneath their feet. The ab-human monster from the outer circle—that obscene sack-like Thing—appeared again. Its body vibrated with tremendous rapidity. It screamed at them with positively frantic glee. With incredible speed the stallion was swung by its invisible rider at the gap in the protective barrier. The black beast plunged, scattering the gutted candles and dried mandrake, then reared above them, its great, dark belly on a level with their heads, its enormous hoofs poised in mid-air about to batter out their brains.

For one awful second it hovered there while Richard crouched gazing upward, his arms locked tight round the unconscious Marie Lou, De Richleau stood his ground above them both, the sweat pouring in great rivulets down his lean face.

Almost, it seemed, the end had come. Then the Duke used his final resources, and did a thing *which shall never be done except in the direst emergency when the very soul is in peril of destruction.* In a clear sharp voice he pronounced the last two lines of the dread Sussamma Ritual.

A streak of light seemed to curl for a second round the stallion's body, as though it had been struck with unerring aim, caught in the toils of some gigantic whip-lash and hurled back. The Thing disintegrated instantly in sizzling atoms of opalescent light. The horse dissolved into the silent shadows.

Those mysterious and unconquerable powers, the Lord of Light, the Timeless Ones, had answered; compelled by those mystic words to leave their eternal contemplation of Supreme Beatitude for a fraction of earthly time, to intervene for the salvation of those four small flickering flames that burned in the beleaguered humans.

An utter silence descended upon the room. It was so still that De Richleau could hear Richard's heart pounding in his breast. Yet he knew that by that extreme invocation they had been carried out of their bodies on to the fifth Astral plane. His conscious brain told him that it was improbable that they would ever get back. To call upon the very essence of light requires almost superhuman courage, for Prana possesses an energy and force utterly beyond the understanding of the human mind. As it can shatter darkness in a manner beside which a million candle power searchlight becomes a pallid beam, so it can attract all lesser light to itself and carry it to realms undreamed of by infinitesimal man.

For a moment it seemed that they had been ripped right out of the room and were looking down into it. The pentacle had become a flaming star. Their bodies were dark shadows grouped in its centre. The peace and silence of death surged over them in great saturating waves. They were above the house. Cardinals Folly became a black speck in the distance. Then everything faded.

Time ceased, and it seemed that for a thousand thousand years they floated, atoms of radiant matter in an immense immeasurable void–circling for ever in the soundless stratosphere–being shut off from every feeling and sensation, as though travelling with effortless impulse five hundred fathoms deep below the current levels of some uncharted sea.

Then, after a passage of eons in human time they saw the house again, infinitely far beneath them, their bodies lying in the pentacle and that darkened room. In an utter eerie silence the dust of centuries was falling ... falling. Softly, impalpably, like infinitely tiny particles of swansdown, it seemed to cover them, the room, and all that was in it, with a fine grey powder.

De Richleau raised his head. It seemed to him that he had been on a long journey and then slept for many days. He passed his hand across his eyes and saw the familiar bookshelves in the semi-darkened library. The bulbs above the cornice flickered and the light came full on.

Marie Lou had come to and was struggling to her knees while Richard fondled her with trembling hands, and murmured: 'We're safe, darling–safe.'

Simon's eyes were free now from that terrible maniacal glare. The Duke had no memory of having unloosened his bonds but he knelt beside them looking as normal as he had when they had first entered upon that terrible weaponless battle.

'Yes, we're safe–and Mocata is finished,' De Richleau passed a hand over his eyes as if they were still clouded. 'The Angel of Death was sent against us tonight, but he failed to get us, and he will never return empty-handed to his dark Kingdom. Mocata summoned him so Mocata must pay the penalty.'

'Are–are you sure of that?' Simon's jaw dropped suddenly.

'Certain. The age-old law of retaliation cannot fail to operate. He will be dead before the morning.'

'But–but,' Simon stammered. 'Don't you realise that Mocata never does these things himself. He throws other people into a hypnotic trance and makes them do his devilish business for him. One of the poor wretches who are in his power will have to pay for this night's work.'

Even as he spoke there came the sound of running footsteps along the flagstones of the terrace. A rending crash as a heavy boot landed violently on the woodwork of the french-windows.

They burst open, and framed in them stood no vision but Rex himself. Haggard, dishevelled, hollow-eyed, his face a ghastly mask of panic, fear and fury.

He stood there for a moment staring at them as though they were ghosts. In his arms he held the body of a woman; her fair hair tumbled across his right arm, and her long silk-stockinged legs dangled limply from the other.

Suddenly two great tears welled up into his eyes and trickled slowly down his furrowed cheeks. Then as he laid the body gently on the floor they saw that it was Tanith, and knew, by her strange unnatural stillness, that she was dead.

28

NECROMANCY

'Oh, Rex!' Marie Lou dropped to her knees beside Tanith, knowing that this must be the girl of whom he had raved to her that afternoon. 'How awful for you!'

'How did this happen?' the Duke demanded. It was imperative that he should know at once every move in the enemy's game, and the urgent note in his voice helped to pull Rex together.

'I hardly know,' he gasped out. 'She got me along because she was scared stiff of that swine Mocata. I couldn't call you up this afternoon and later when I tried your line was blocked, but I had to stay with her. We were going to pass the night together in the parlour, but around midnight she left me and then—oh, God! I fell asleep.'

'How long did you sleep for?' asked Richard quickly.

'Several hours, I reckon. I was about all in after yesterday, but the second I woke I dashed up to her room and she was, dressed as she is now—lying asleep, I figured—in an armchair. I tried to wake her but I couldn't. Then I got real scared—grabbed hold of her—and beat it down those stairs six at a time. You've just no notion how frantic I was to get out of that place and next thing I knew—I saw your light and came bursting in here. She—she's not dead, is she?'

'Oh, Rex, you poor darling,' Marie Lou stammered as she chafed Tanith's cold hands. 'I–I'm afraid——'

'She isn't–she can't be!' he protested wildly. 'That fiend's only thrown her into a trance or something.'

Richard had taken a little mirror from Marie Lou's bag. He held it against Tanith's bloodless lips. No trace of moisture marred its surface. Then he pressed his hand beneath her breast.

'Her heart's stopped beating,' he said after a moment. 'I'm sorry, old chap, but—well, I'm afraid you've got to face it.'

'The old-fashioned tests of death are not conclusive,' Simon whispered to the Duke. 'Scientists say now that even arteries can be cut and fail to bleed, but life still remains in the body. They've all come round to the belief that we're animated by a sort of atomic energy—call it the soul if you like—and that the body may retain that vital spark without showing the least sign of life. Mightn't it be some form of catalepsy like that?'

'Of course,' De Richleau agreed. 'It has been proved time and again that the senses are only imperfect vessels for collecting impressions. There is something else which can see when the eyes are closed and hear while the body is being painlessly cut to ribbons under an anaesthetic. All the modern experimenters agree that there are many states in which the body is not wholly alive or wholly dead, but I fear there is little hope in this case. You see we know that Mocata used her as his catspaw, so the poor girl has been forced to pay the price of failure. I haven't a single doubt that she is dead.'

Rex caught his last words and swung upon him frantically. 'God! this is frightful. I—I tried to kid myself but I think I knew it the moment I picked her up. Her prophecy's come true then.' He passed his hands over his eyes. 'I can't quite take it in yet—this and all of you seem terribly unreal—but is she *really* dead? She was so mighty scared that if she died some awful thing might remain to animate her body.'

'She is dead as we know death,' said Richard softly. 'So what could remain?'

'I know what he means,' the Duke remarked abruptly. 'He is afraid that an elemental may have taken possession of her corpse. If so drastic measures will be necessary.'

'No!' Rex shook his head violently. 'If you're thinking of cutting off her head and driving a stake through her heart, I won't have it. She's mine, I tell you—mine!'

'Better that than the poor soul should suffer the agony of seeing its body come out of the grave at night to fatten itself on human blood,' De Richleau murmured. 'But there are certain tests, and we can soon find out. Bring her over here.'

Simon and Richard lifted the body and carried it over to the mat of sheets and blankets in the centre of the pentacle, while De Richleau fiddled for a moment among his impedimenta.

'The Undead,' he said slowly, 'have certain inhibitions. They can pass as human, but they cannot eat human food and they cannot cross running water except at sunset and sunrise. Garlic is a most fearsome thing to them, so that they scream if only touched by it, and the Cross, of course, is anathema. We will see if she reacts to them.'

As he spoke he took the wreath of garlic flowers from round his neck and placed it about Tanith's. Then he made the sign of the Cross above her and laid his little gold crucifix upon her lips.

The others stood round, watching the scene with horrified fascination. Tanith lay there, calm and still, her pale face shadowed by the golden hair, her tawny eyes now closed under the heavy, blue-veined lids, the long, curved eyelashes falling upon her cheeks. She had the look of death and yet, as De Richleau set about his grim task, it seemed to them that her eyelids might flicker open at any moment. Yet, when the garlic flowers were draped upon her, she remained there cold and immobile, and when the little crucifix was laid upon her lips she showed no consciousness of it, even by the twitching of the tiniest muscle.

'She's dead, Rex, absolutely dead,' De Richleau stood up again. 'So, my poor boy, at least your worst fears will not be realised. Her soul has left her body but no evil entity has taken possession of it. I am certain of that now.'

A new hush fell upon the room. Tanith looked, if possible, even more beautiful in death than she had in life, so that they marvelled at her loveliness. Rex crouched beside her, utterly stricken by this tragic ending to all the wonderful hopes and plans which had seethed in his mind the previous afternoon after she had told him that she loved him. He had known her by sight for so long, dreamed of her so often, yet having gained her love a merciless fate had deprived him of it after only a few hours of happiness. It was unfair—unfair. Suddenly he buried his face in his hands, his great shoulders shook, and for the first time in his life he gave way to a passion of bitter tears.

The rest stood by him in silent sympathy. There was nothing which they could say or do. Marie Lou attempted to soothe his anguish by stroking his rebellious hair, but he jerked his head away with a quick angry movement. Only a few hours before, in those sunlit woods, Tanith had run her fingers through his curls again and again during the ecstasy of the dawning of their passion for each other, and the thought that she would never do so any more filled him with the almost unbearable grief and misery.

After a while the Duke turned helplessly away and Simon, catching his eye, beckoned him over towards the open window out of earshot from the others. The seemingly endless night still lay upon the garden, and now a light mist had arisen. Wisps of it were creeping down the steps from the terrace and curling into the room. De Richleau shivered and refastened the windows to shut them out.

'What is it?' he asked quickly.

'I–er–suppose there *is* no chance of her being made animate again?' hazarded Simon.

'None. If there had been anything there it would never have been able to bear the garlic and the crucifix without giving some indication of its presence.'

'I wasn't thinking of that. The vital organs aren't injured in any way as far as we know, and *rigor mortis* has not set in yet. I felt her hand just now and the fingers are as flexible as mine.'

De Richleau shrugged. 'That makes no difference. *Rigor mortis* may have been delayed for a variety of reasons but she will be as stiff as a board in a few hours' time just the same. Of course her state does resemble that of a person who has been drowned, in a way, but only superficially; and if you are thinking that we might bring her back to life by artificial respiration I can assure you that there is not a chance. It would only be a terrible unkindness to hold out such false hopes to poor Rex.'

'Ner–you don't see what I'm driving at.' Simon's dark eyes flickered quickly from De Richleau's face to the silent group in the centre of the pentagram and then back again. 'No ordinary doctor could do anything for her, I know that well enough; but since her body is still in the intermediate stage there *are* a few people in this world who could, and I was wondering if you—'

'What!' The Duke started suddenly then went on in a whisper: 'Do you mean that *I* should try and bring her back?'

'Um,' Simon nodded his head jerkily up and down. 'If you know the drill–and you seem to know so much about the great secrets, I thought it just on the cards you might?'

De Richleau looked thoughtful for a moment. 'I know something of the ritual,' he confessed at length, 'but I have never seen it done, and in any case it's a terrible responsibility.'

At that moment there was a faint sighing as the breeze rippled the leaves of the trees out in the garden. Both men heard it and they looked at each other questioningly.

'Her soul can't be very far away yet,' whispered Simon.

'No,' the Duke agreed reluctantly. 'But I don't like it, Simon. The dead are not meant to be called back. They do not come willingly. If I attempt this and succeed it would only be by the force of incredibly powerful conjurations which the soul dare not disobey, and we are not justified in taking such steps. Besides, what good could it do? At best, I should not be able to bring her back for more than a few moments.'

'Of course I know that; but you still don't seem to get my idea,' Simon went on hurriedly. 'As far as Rex is concerned, poor chap, she's gone for good and all, but I was thinking of Mocata. You were hammering it into us last night for all you were worth that it's up to us to destroy him before he has the chance to secure the Talisman. Surely this is our opportunity. In Tanith's present physical state her spirit can't have gone far from her body. If you could bring it back for a few moments, or even get her to talk, don't you see that she'll be able to tell us how best to try and scotch Mocata. From the astral plane, where she is now, her vision and insight are limitless, so she'll be able to help us in a way that she never could have done before.'

'That's different,' De Richleau's pale face lit up with a tired smile. 'And you're right, Simon. I have been under such a strain for the past few hours that I had forgotten the thing that matters most of all. I would never consent to attempt it for any other purpose, but to prevent suffering and death coming to countless millions of people we are justified in anything. I'll speak to Rex.'

Rex nodded despondently, numb now with misery, when the Duke had explained what he meant to try to do. 'Just as you like,' he said slowly. 'It won't hurt in any way, though—I mean her soul—will it?'

'No,' De Richleau assured him. 'In the ordinary way it might. To recall the soul of a dead person is to risk interfering with their *karma*, but Tanith has virtually been murdered and, although it is not the way of the spirit to seek revenge against people for things which may have happened in this life, it is almost a certainty that she is actually wanting to come back for just long enough to tell us how to defeat Mocata, because of her love for you.'

'All right then,' Rex muttered, 'only let's get it over with as quickly as we can.'

'I'm afraid it will take some time,' De Richleau warned him, 'and even then it may not be successful, but the issues at stake are so vital, you must try and put aside your personal grief for a bit.'

He began to clear the pentacle of all the things which he had used the previous evening to form protective barriers, the holy water, the little cups, the horseshoes, placing them with the garlic and dried mandrake back in the suitcase. He then took from it seven small metal trays, a wooden platter, and a box of powdered incense; and pouring a little heap of the dark powder on the platter went up to Rex.

'I'm afraid I've got to trouble you if we're going to see this through.'

'Trouble away,' said Rex grimly, with a flash of his old spirit. 'You know I'm with you in anything which is likely to let me get my hands on that devil's throat.'

'Good.' The Duke took out his pocket knife and held the blade for a moment in the flame of a match. 'You've seen enough of this business now to know that I don't do anything without a purpose, and I want a little of your blood. I will use my own if you like but yours is far more likely to have the desired effect, since you felt so strongly for this poor girl and she, apparently, for you.'

'Go ahead.' Rex pulled up his cuff and bared his forearm, but De Richleau shook his head.

'No. Your finger will do, and it will hardly be more than a pin-prick. I only need a few drops.'

With a swift movement he took Rex's hand and, having made a slight incision in the little finger, squeezed out seven drops of blood on to the incense.

Then he walked over to Tanith and, kneeling down, took seven long golden hairs from her head. Next he proceeded to form the mixture of incense and blood into a paste out of which he made seven cones, in each of which was coiled one of Tanith's long golden hairs.

With Richard's assistance he carefully oriented the body so that her feet were pointing towards the north and drew a fresh chalk circle, just large enough to contain her and the bedding, seven feet in diameter.

'Now if you will turn your backs, please,' he told them all, 'I will proceed with the preparation.'

For a few moments they gazed obediently at the book-lined walls while he did certain curious things, and when he bade them turn again he was placing the sevon cones of incense on the seven little metal trays, each engraved with the Seal of Solomon, in various positions round the body.

'We shall remain outside the circle this time,' he explained, 'so that the spirit, if it comes, is contained within it. Should some evil entity endeavour to impersonate her soul it will thus be confined within the circle and unable to get at us.'

He lit the seven cones of incense, completed the barrier round about the body with numerous fresh signs, and then, walking over to the doorway, switched out the lights.

The fire was quite dead now, and the candles had never been re-lit, but after a moment greyness began to filter through the french-windows. The light was just sufficient for them to see each other as ghostly forms moving in the darkness, while the body, lying in the circle, was barely visible, its position being indicated by the seven tiny points of light from the cones of incense burning round it.

Simon laid an unsteady hand on the Duke's arm. 'Is it—is it—quite safe to do this? I mean, mightn't Mocata have another cut at us now we're in the dark and no longer have the protection of the pentacle?'

'No,' De Richleau answered decisively. 'He played his last card tonight when he sent the Dark Angel against us and caused Tanith's death. That stupendous operation will have exhausted his magical powers for the time at least. Come over here, all of you, and sit down on the floor in a circle.'

Leading them over to Tanith's feet he arranged them so that Rex and Marie Lou both had their backs to the body and would be spared the sight of any manifestations which might take place about it. He sat facing it himself, with Richard and Simon either side of him; all five of them clasped hands.

Then he told them that they must preserve complete quiet and under no circumstances break the circle they had formed. He warned them too, that if they felt a sudden cold they were not to be frightened by it as they had been of the horrible wind which had swirled so uncannily in that room a few hours before. It would be caused by the ectoplasm which might be drawn from Tanith's body and, he went on to add, if a voice addressed them they were not to answer. He would do any talking which was necessary and they were to remain absolutely still until he gave orders that the circle should be broken up.

They sat there, hand in hand, in silence, while it seemed that an age was passing. The square frame of the window gradually lightened but so very slowly that it was barely perceptible, and if dawn was breaking at last upon the countryside it was shut out from them by the grey, ghostly fog.

The cones of incense burned slowly, giving a strange, acrid smell, mixed with some queer and sickly eastern perfume. From their position in the circle Richard and Simon could see the faint wreaths of smoke curling up for a few inches above the tiny points of light to disappear above, lost in the darkness. Tanith's body lay still and motionless, a shadowy outline upon the thin mat of makeshift bedding.

De Richleau had closed his eyes and bowed his head upon his chest. Once more he was practising that rhythmic, inaudible Raja Yoga breathing, which has such power to recruit strength or to send it forth, and he was using it now while he concentrated on calling the spirit of Tanith to him.

Richard watched the body with curious expectancy. His experience of the last few hours had been too recent for him to collate his thoughts, and while he had so sturdily rejected the idea of Black Magic the night before he would more or less have accepted the fact of Spiritualism. It was a much more general modern belief, and this business as far as he could see, except in a few minor particulars such as the incense compounded with blood, was very similar to the spiritualistic séances of which he had often heard. The only real difference being that, in this instance, they had a newly dead body to operate on and therefore were far more likely to get results. As time wore on, however, he became doubtful, for if their vigil had lasted many hours this one, now that he was utterly weary, seemed like a succession of nights.

It was Simon who first became aware that something was happening. He was watching the seven cones of incense intently, and it seemed to him that the one which was farthest from him, set at Tanith's head, gave out a greater amount of smoke than the rest. Then he realised that he could see the cone more clearly and the eddying curls of aromatic vapour which it sent up had taken on a bluish hue which the rest had not.

He pressed De Richleau's hand and the Duke raised his head. Richard too had seen it, and as they watched, a faint blue light became definitely perceptible.

It gradually solidified into a ball about two inches in diameter and moved slowly forward from the head until it reached the centre of Tanith's body. There it remained for a while, growing in brightness and intensity until it had become a strong blue light. Then it rose a little and hovered in the air above her, so that by its glow they could clearly see the curves of her figure and her pale, beautiful face, lit by that strange radiance.

Intensely alert now, they sat still and watchful, until the ball of light began to lose colour and diffuse itself over a wider area. The smoke of the incense wreathed up towards it from the seven metal platters, and it seemed to gather this into itself, forming from it the vague outline of a head and shoulders, still cloudy and transparent but, after another few moments, definitely recognisable as an outline of the bust of the figure which lay motionless beneath it.

With pounding hearts they watched for new developments, and now it seemed that the whole process of materialisation was hurried forward in a few seconds. The bust joined itself, by throwing out a shadowy torso, to the hips of the dead body, the face and shoulders solidified until the features were distinct, and the whole became surrounded by an aureole of light.

Upon the strained silence there came the faintest whisper of a voice: 'You called me. I am here.'

'Are you in truth, Tanith?' De Richleau asked softly.

'I am.'

'Do you acknowledge our Lord Jesus Christ?'

'I do.'

A sigh of relief escaped De Richleau, for he knew that no impersonating elemental would ever dare to testify in such a manner, and he proceeded quietly:

'Do you come here of your own free will, or do you wish to depart?'

'I come because you called, but I am glad to come.'

'There is one here whose grief for your passing is very great. He does not seek to draw you back, but he wishes to know if it is your desire to help him in the protection of his friends and the destruction of evil for the well-being of the world.'

'It is my desire.'

'Will you tell us all that you can of the man Mocata which may prove of help?'

'I cannot, for I am circumscribed by the Law, but you may ask me what you will and, because you have summoned me, I am bound by your command to answer.'

'What is he doing now?'

'Plotting fresh evil against you.'

'Where is he now?'

'He is quite near you.'

'Can you not tell me where?'

'I do not know. I cannot see distinctly, for he covers himself with a cloak of darkness, but he is still in your neighbourhood.'

'In the village?'

'Perhaps.'

'Where will he be this time tomorrow?'

'In Paris.'

'What do you see him doing in Paris?'

'I see him talking with a man who has lost a portion of his left ear. It is a tall building. They are both very angry.'

'Will he stay in Paris for long?'

'No. I see him moving at great speed towards the rising sun.'

'Where do you see him next?'

'Under the earth.'

'Do you mean that he is dead—to us?'

'No. He is in a stone-flagged vault beneath a building which is very *very* old. The place radiates evil. The red vibrations are so powerful that I cannot see what he does there. The light which surrounds me now protects me from such sights.'

'What is he planning now?'

'To draw me back.'

'Do you mean that he is endeavouring to restore your soul to your body?'

'Yes. He is already bitterly regretting that in his anger against you he risked the severance of the two. He could force me to be of great service to him on your plane but he cannot do so on this.'

'But is it possible for him to bring you back—permanently?'

'Yes. If he acts at once. While the moon is still in her dark quarter.'

'Is it your wish to return?'

'No, unless I were free of him—but I have no choice. My soul is in pawn until the coming of the new moon. After that I shall pass on unless he has succeeded.'

'How will he set about this thing?'

'There is only one way. The full performance of the Black Mass.'

'You mean with sacrifice of a Christian child?'

'Yes. It is the age-old law, a soul for a soul. That is the only way and the soul of a baptised child will be accepted in exchange for mine. Then if my body remains uninjured I shall be compelled to return to it.'

'What are—'

The Duke's next question was cut short by Rex, who could stand the strain no longer. He did not know that De Richleau was only conversing with Tanith's astral body and thought that he had succeeded in restoring the corpse which lay behind him, at least to temporary life again.

'Tanith,' he cried, breaking the circle and flinging himself round. 'Tanith!'

In a fraction of time the vision disintegrated and disappeared. His eyes blazing with anger, De Richleau sprang to his feet.

'You fool!' he thundered. 'You stupid fool.' In the pale light of dawn which was now at last just filtering through the fog, he glared at Rex. Then, as they stood there, angry recriminations about to burst from their lips, the whole party were arrested in their every movement and remained transfixed.

A shrill, clear cry had cut like a knife into the heavy, incense-laden atmosphere, coming from the room above.

'That's Fleur,' gasped Marie Lou. 'My precious, what is it?'

In an instant, she was dashing across the room to the little door in the bookshelves which led to the staircase up to the nursery. Yet Richard was before her.

In two bounds he had reached the door and was fumbling for the catch. His trembling fingers found it. He gave a violent jerk. The little metal ring which served to open it came away in his hand.

Precious moments were lost as they clawed at the bookbacks. At last it swung free. Richard pushed Marie Lou through ahead of him and followed, pressing at her heels. The others stumbled up the old stone stairs in frantic haste behind them.

They reached the night nursery. Rex ran to the window. It was wide open. The grey mist blanketed the garden outside. Marie Lou dashed to the cot. The sheets were tumbled. The imprint of a little body lay there fresh and warm—but Fleur was gone.

29

SIMON ARON TAKES A VIEW

'Here's the way they went,' cried Rex. 'There's a ladder under this window.'

'Then for God's sake get after him,' Richard shouted, racing across the room. 'If that damn door hadn't stuck we'd have caught him red-handed—he can't have got far.'

Rex was already on the terrace below, Simon shinned down the ladder and Richard flung his leg over the sill of the window to follow.

Marie Lou was left alone with De Richleau in the nursery. She stared at him with round, tearless eyes, utterly overcome by this new calamity. The Duke stared back, shaken to the very depths by this appalling thing which he had brought upon his friends. He wanted most desperately to comfort and console her, but realised how hopelessly inadequate anything that he could say would be. The thought of that child having been seized by the Satanist to be offered up in some ghastly sacrifice, was utterly unbearable.

'Princess,' he managed to stammer. 'Princess.' But further words would not come, and for once in his life he found himself powerless to deal with a situation.

Marie Lou just stood there motionless and staring, held rigid by such extreme distress that she could no longer think coherently.

With a tremendous effort De Richleau pulled himself together. He knew that he had earned any opprobrium that she and Richard might choose to heap upon him for having used their house as a refuge, stated that no harm could befall them if they followed his instructions, and yet been the means of perhaps causing the death of the child whom they both idolised. But it was no time to offer himself for the whipping-post now. They must act and quickly.

'Where is nurse?' he shot out hoarsely.

'In—in her bedroom.' Marie Lou turned to a door at the end of the room which stood ajar.

'It's extraordinary that she should not have woken with all this noise,' De Richleau strode over and thrust it open.

In Fleur's nursery a greyness blurred the outlines of the furniture and shadowed the corners of the room, but in the nurse's bedroom, the curtains being drawn, it was still completely dark.

The Duke jerked on the electric light and saw at once that Fleur's nannie was lying peacefully asleep in bed. He walked over and touched her swiftly on the shoulder. 'Wake up,' he said, 'wake up!'

She did not stir, and Marie Lou, who had followed him into the room, peered at the woman's face anxiously, then cried on a louder note: 'Wake up, nannie! Wake up!'

De Richleau shook the nurse roughly now, but her head rolled helplessly upon her shoulders and her eyes remained tightly shut.

'She's been drugged, I suppose,' Marie Lou said miserably.

'I don't think so.' The Duke bent over and sniffed. 'There is no smell of chloroform or anything here. It's more likely that Mocata plunged her into a deep hypnotic sleep directly he arrived. Best leave her,' he added after a moment. 'She'll wake in due course, and obviously she cannot tell us anything if she has been in a heavy induced sleep all the time.'

They returned to the nursery and the Duke switched on the lights there to make a thorough examination. Almost at once his eye fell on a paper which lay at the foot of Fleur's empty cot. He snatched it up and quickly scanned the close, typewritten lines.

Please do not worry about the little girl. She will be returned to you tomorrow morning providing that certain conditions are complied with. These are as follows:

In this exceptional case I have been compelled to resort to unusual methods which bring me within the scope of the law. I have no doubt, therefore, that one of you will suggest calling in the police to trace the child. Any such action might embarrass my operations and therefore you are not to even consider such a proceeding. You cannot doubt by now that I have ways and means of informing myself regarding all your actions and, in the event of your disobeying my injunction in this respect, I shall immediately take steps which will ensure that you never recover the child alive.

My failure last night was regrettable, since it has caused the death of a young woman recently discovered by me as an exceptional medium, for whom I might have had some further use. Mr Van Ryn removed her body while I slept and it is now in your keeping; I am anxious that every care should be taken of it. You will leave the body just as it is in your library *until further instructions* and refrain from taking any steps towards a coroner's examination or its burial. If you disobey me in this matter, I shall command certain forces at my disposal, of which Monsieur Le Duc de Richleau may be able to inform you, to take possession of it.

All of you will confine yourselves in the library during the coming day, giving such reasons as you choose to your servants that you are not to be disturbed.

Lastly, my friend Simon Aron is to rejoin me for the continuance of those experiments in which we are engaged. He will leave the house alone at mid-day and proceed on foot to the cross-roads which lie a mile and a half to the south-west of Cardinals Folly, where I shall arrange for him to be met and, having surrendered himself to my representative, he must agree to give me his willing co-operation in the ritual to Satan tonight, which is necessary for the rediscovery of the Talisman of Set.

If any of these injunctions are disregarded in the least degree, you already know the penalty, but if they are carried out to my entire satisfaction, Simon Aron shall return to you sane and well after I have carried out my operations, and the child shall be restored as innocent and happy as she was yesterday.

Marie Lou read the document over De Richleau's shoulder. 'Oh, what are we to do?' she wailed, wringing her hands together. 'Greyeyes, this is too awful. What are we going to do?'

'God knows,' De Richleau muttered miserably. 'He has the whip hand of us now with a vengeance. The devil of it is that I don't trust his promise to return the child even if Simon is game to sacrifice himself.'

At that moment Simon's head appeared above the window sill, and he scrambled up the last rungs of the ladder into the room.

'Well!' the Duke shot at him, but Simon shook his head.

'The three of us have been round the grounds but in this filthy fog it's impossible to see any distance. He's got clean away by now.'

'I feared as much,' the Duke murmured despondently, and with a new access of miserable unhappiness, he watched Richard climb into the room.

'Not a trace,' Richard exclaimed hoarsely. 'No footmarks, even on the flower beds, to show which way he went. Where the hell is nurse? I'll sack the woman for her damned incompetence. With her door ajar, there's no excuse for her not having heard Fleur cry out.'

'It was not her fault,' said De Richleau mildly. 'Mocata threw her into a deep sleep and she is sleeping still. Until the time he has set it will be impossible to rouse her.'

Rex followed the others through the window, muttering angrily: 'This filthy mist! A dozen toughs might be racketing round the garden, but we'd never get a sight of them. Is it supposed to be daylight yet, or isn't it?'

Simon glanced at the clock on the nursery mantelpiece. 'According to this it's only ten to five. Surely it must be later than that.'

'It's stopped,' announced Richard, 'but it can't be much after half past six, or the servants would be getting up, and when I ran round the far side of the house just now, there were no lights in their windows.'

'All the better,' said the Duke abruptly. 'Mocata's left a letter, Richard, with certain instructions which he orders us to carry out if Fleur is to remain unharmed.'

'Let's see it.' Richard held out his hand.

De Richleau hesitated. 'I'd rather you read it when we are downstairs again, if you don't mind. It doesn't help us for the present and there are certain things which we should do at once—before the servants start moving about.'

'Good Lord, man! I mean to have the lot of them out of bed inside ten minutes. We shall need their help.'

'I wish, instead, that while I connect the telephone again and see if I can find out anything from the inn, you would write a brief note to Malin saying that our experiments are still in progress and that we are to be left undisturbed in this wing of the house for the whole day.'

'If you think I'm going to stay here twiddling my thumbs while Fleur's in danger—you're crazy!' cried Richard indignantly.

The Duke knew that his suggestion of continued inactivity must make his apparent negligence seem even worse, but he had never yet been known to lose his head in a crisis and he managed to keep his voice quiet and even.

'I would like you to see this letter first and talk it over with Marie Lou before you do anything reckless. In any case Tanith's body is still downstairs. It must remain there for the moment and that is quite sufficient reason for the servants to be kept away from the library. You, Rex, go along to the kitchen, take Simon with you, and between you bring us back the best cold meal that you can muster. We're half starved, and fasting has its limits of usefulness, even in an affair like this.'

Marie Lou stood there listening to the argument. She could not really believe that this awful thing had actually happened to *her*. If she had lost Fleur she would die. Even Richard would never be able to console her. It simply could not be true. The four men were phantoms—talking—, yet she could see every object in the room with a curious supernormal clarity. Strange that she had never noticed one handle on the old walnut chest of drawers to be odd before, or that one of the wires in the fireguard protruded a little. Fleur might cut herself if she fell against it. She must tell nannie to have it seen to tomorrow. Yet all the time these thoughts were drifting through her mind she was conscious of what the others were saying and of an urgent need to comfort De Richleau. Her poor 'Greyeyes' was feeling desperately unhappy, she knew, and held himself entirely responsible for the terrible thing which could not possibly be true. When he mentioned breakfast she said at once: 'I will go down and cook you some eggs or something.'

'No, no, my dear,' De Richleau looked round and then lowered his eyes quickly, his heart wrung at the sight of her dead-white face. 'Please go down to the library and read this letter of Mocata's through again quietly with Richard. Then you can talk it over together and will have made up your minds what you think best by the time the rest of us get back.'

Richard gave in to the Duke's wishes for the moment. They all descended to the ground floor again and, when the other three had gone off to the kitchen quarters, he remained with Marie Lou and read Mocata's letter quickly.

As he finished he looked up at her in miserable indecision. 'My poor sweet. This is ghastly for you.'

'It's just as bad for you,' she said softly. Then, with a little cry, she flung her arms round his neck. 'Oh, Richard, darling, what are we to do?'

'Dearest.' He hugged her to him, soothing her gently as best he could now that the storm had broken. Her small body heaved with desperate sobbing, while great tears ran down her cheeks, falling in large, damp splashes upon his hands and neck.

As he held her, murmuring little phrases of endearment and optimistic comfort, he thought her weeping would never cease. Her body trembled as it was swept with terrible emotion at the loss of her cherished Fleur.

'Marie Lou, my angel,' he whispered softly, 'try and pull yourself together, do, or else you'll have me breaking down as well in a minute. No harm can have happened to her yet, and it isn't likely to until tonight at the earliest. Even then, he'll think twice before he carries out his threat. Only a fool destroys his hostage to spite his enemy. Mocata may be every sort of rogue, but he's a civilised one at least, so he won't maltreat her in any way, you can be sure of that, and if we only play our cards properly, we'll get her back before it comes to any question of his carrying out this appalling threat.'

'But what can we do, Richard? What can we do?' she cried, looking at him wildly from large, tear-dimmed eyes.

'Get after him the second the others come back,' Richard declared promptly. 'He's human, isn't he? He had to use a ladder to get up to the nursery just like any other thug. If we act at once we'll have him under lock and key by nightfall.'

De Richleau's quiet voice broke in from behind them. 'You have decided, then, to call in the police?'

'Of course.' Richard turned to stare at him. 'This is totally different from last night's affair. It is a case of kidnapping, pure and simple, and I'm going to pull every gun I know to get the police of the whole country after him in the next half hour. If you've reconnected that line, I'll get straight through to Scotland Yard—now.'

'Yes, the telephone is all right. I've been through to the inn and had old

Wilkes out of bed. He remembers Rex and Tanith dining there last night, of course, but when I described Mocata to him, he said he hadn't seen anyone who answers to that description there at all, either yesterday or this morning. Have you written that letter for the servants?'

'Not yet. I will.' Richard left the library just as Simon and Rex came in, carrying a collection of plates and dishes on two trays, prominent upon which were a large China teapot and the half of a York ham.

'Please don't phone Scotland Yard just yet,' Marie Lou called after Richard. 'I simply must talk to you again before we burn our boats.'

The Duke gave her a sharp glance from under his grey eyebrows. 'You are not then in favour of calling in the police?'

'I don't know what to do,' she confessed miserably. 'Richard is so sane and practical that I suppose he's right, but you read the letter and I should never forgive myself if our calling in the police forced Mocata's hand. Do you—do you really think that he has the power to find out if we go against his instructions?'

De Richleau nodded. 'I'm afraid so. But Simon can tell you more of his capabilities in that direction than I can.'

Simon and Rex had put down their trays and were reading Mocata's letter together. The former looked up swiftly.

'Um. He can see things when he wants to in that mirror I told you of, and once he gets to London he'll have half-a-dozen mediums that he can throw into a trance to pick us up. It will be child's play for a man of his powers to find out if we leave this room.'

'That's my view,' the Duke agreed. 'And if we once turn to the police, we have either to go to them or else bring them here. Telephoning won't be sufficient. They will want photographs of Fleur and to question everyone concerned, so Mocata stands a pretty good chance of seeing us in conference with them, if he keeps us under psychic observation, whichever way we set to work.'

'We should be mad to even think of it,' said Simon jerkily. 'It's pretty useless for me to say I'm sorry, but I brought this whole trouble on you all and there's only one thing to do, that's obvious.'

'For us to sit here like a lot of dummies while you go off to give yourself up at twelve o'clock, I suppose?' Richard, who had just rejoined them, cut in acidly.

'I have been expecting that, knowing Simon,' the Duke observed. 'Terrible as the consquences may be for him and although the idea of surrender makes my blood boil I must confess that I think he's right, with certain modifications!'

'Oh, isn't there some other way?' Marie Lou exclaimed desperately, catching at Simon's hand. 'It's too awful that because of our own trouble we should even talk of sacrificing you.'

One of those rare smiles that made him such a lovable person lit Simon's face. 'Ner,' he said softly, 'it's been my muddle from the beginning. I'm terribly grateful to you all for trying to get me out of it, but Mocata's been too much for us, and I must throw my hand in now. It's the only thing to do.'

'It is my damned incompetence which has let us in for this,' grunted the Duke. 'I deserve to take your place, Simon, and I would—you know that—if it were the least use. The devil of it is that it's you he wants, not me.'

Rex had been cutting thin slices from the ham and pouring out the tea.

Richard took a welcome cup of his favourite Orange Pekoe from him and said firmly:

'Stop talking nonsense, for God's sake! Neither of you is to blame. After what we've all been through together in the past you did quite rightly to come here. Who should we look to for help in times of trouble if not each other? If I was in a real tight corner I shouldn't hesitate to involve either of you—and I know that Marie Lou feels the same. This blow couldn't possibly have been foreseen by anyone. It was just—well, call it an accident, and the responsibility for protecting Fleur was ours every bit as much as yours. Now let's get down to what we mean to do.'

'That's decent of you, Richard.' De Richleau tried to smile, knowing what it must have cost his friend to ease their feeling of guilt when he must be so desperately anxious about his child.

'Damned decent,' Simon echoed. 'But all the same I'm going to keep the appointment Mocata's made for me. It's the only hope we've got.'

Richard stuck out his chin. 'You're not, old chap. You placed yourself in my hands by coming to my house, and I won't have it. The business we went through last night scared me as much as anyone, I admit it; but because Greyeyes has proved right about Satanic manifestations, there is no reason for you all to lose your sense of proportion about what the evil powers can do. They have their limitations, just like anything else. Greyeyes admitted last night that they were based on natural laws, and this swine's gone outside them. He's operating now in country that is strange to him. He confesses as much in his letter. You can see he is scared of calling in the police, and that's the very way we're going to get him. You people seem to have lost your nerve.'

'No,' the Duke said sadly. 'I haven't lost my nerve, but look at it if you like on the basis which you suggest, Richard—that this is a perfectly normal kidnapping. Say Fleur were being held to ransom by a group of unscrupulous gangsters, such as operate in the States, the gang being in a position to know what is going on in your house. They have threatened to kill Fleur if you bring the police into the business. Now, would you be prepared to risk that in such circumstances?'

'No, I should pay up, as most wretched parents seem to, on the off-chance that the gang gave me a square deal and I got the child back unharmed. But this is different. I'll stake my oath that Mocata means to double-cross us anyhow. If it were only Simon that he wanted he might be prepared to let us have Fleur back in exchange. You seem to forget what Tanith told you. He doesn't know that we know his intentions, but she was absolutely definite on three points. One, he means to do his damnedest to bring her back. Two, he will fail unless he makes the attempt in the next few days. Three, *the only way that can be done is by performing a full Black Mass, including the sacrifice of a baptised child.* Kidnappings take time to plan in a civilised country unless you want the police on your track. Mocata has succeeded in one where he thinks there is a fair chance of keeping the police out of it, and no one in their senses could suggest that he's the sort of man who would run the risk of doing another just for the joy of keeping his word with us. It's as clear as daylight that he is using Fleur as bait to get hold of Simon and then he'll do us down by killing the child in the end.'

De Richleau slit open a roll and slipped a slice of ham inside it. 'Well,' he said as he began to trim the ragged edges neatly, 'it is for you and Marie Lou to decide. The prospect of sitting in this room for hours on end doing nothing is about the grimmest I've ever had to face in a pretty crowded lifetime. I would give most things I really value for a chance to have another cut at him. The only things that deters me for one moment is the risk to Fleur.'

'I know that well enough,' Richard acknowledged, 'but I am convinced our only chance of seeing her alive again is to call in the police, and trust to running him to earth before nightfall.'

'I wouldn't,' Simon shook his head, 'I wouldn't honestly, Richard. He's certain to find out if we take steps against him. We shall waste hours here being questioned by the local bigwigs, and it's a hundred to one against their being able to corner him in a single day. Fleur is safe for the moment—for God's sake don't make things worse than they are. I know the man and he's as heartless as a snake. It's signing Fleur's death warrant to try and tackle him like this.'

Marie Lou listened to these conflicting arguments in miserable indecision. She was torn violently from side to side by each in turn. Simon spoke with such absolute conviction that it seemed certain Richard's suggested intervention would precipitate her child's death, and yet she felt, too, how right Richard was in his belief that Mocata was certain to doublecross them, and having trapped them into surrendering Simon, retain Fleur for this abominable sacrifice which Tanith had told them he was so anxious to make. The horns of the dilemma seemed to join and form a vicious circle which went round and round in her aching head.

The others fell silent and Richard looked across at her. 'Well, dearest, which is it to be?'

'Oh, I don't know,' she moaned. 'Both sides seem right and yet the risk is so appalling either way.'

He laid his hand gently on her hair. 'It's beastly having to make such a decision, and if we were alone in this I wouldn't dream of asking you. I'd do what I thought best myself unless you were dead against it, but as the others disagree with me so strongly what can I do but ask you to decide?'

Wringing her hands together in agonised distress at this horrible problem with which she was faced, Marie Lou looked desperately from side to side, then her glance fell on Rex. He was sitting hunched up in a dejected attitude on the far side of Tanith's body, his eyes fixed in hopeless misery on the dead girl's face.

'Rex,' she said hoarsely, 'you haven't said what you think yet. Both these alternatives seem equally ghastly to me. What do you advise?'

'Eh?' He looked up quickly 'It's mighty difficult and I was just trying to figure it out. I hate the thought of doing nothing, waiting about when you've got a packet of trouble is just real hell to me, and I'd like to get after this bird with a gun. But Simon's so certain that if we did it would be fatal to Fleur, and I guess the Duke thinks that way too. They both know him, you must remember, and Richard doesn't, which is a point to them, but I've got a hunch that we are barking up the wrong tree, and that this is a case for what Greyeyes calls his masterly policy of inactivity. The old game of giving the enemy enough rope so he'll hang himself in the end.

'Any sort of compromise is all against my nature, but I reckon it's the only policy that offers now. If we stay put here and carry out Mocata's instructions to the letter, we'll at least be satisfied in our minds that we are not bringing any fresh danger on Fleur. But let's go that far and no farther. We all know Simon is willing enough to cash in his checks, but I don't think we ought to let him. Instead, we'll keep him here. That is going to force Mocata to scratch his head a whole heap. He'll not do Fleur in before he's had another cut at getting hold of Simon, so it will be up to him to make the next move in the game, and that may give us a fresh opening. The situation can't be worse than it is at present, and when he shows his hand again, given a spot of luck, we might be able to ring the changes on him yet.'

De Richleau smiled, for the first time in days, it seemed. 'My friend, I salute you,' he said, with real feeling in his voice. 'I am growing old, I think, or I should have thought of that myself. It is by far and away the most sensible thing that any of us have suggested yet.'

With a sigh of relief, Marie Lou moved over and, stooping down, kissed Rex on the cheek. 'Rex, darling, bless you. In our trouble we've been forgetting yours, and it is very wonderful that you should have thought of a real way out for us in the midst of your sorrow. I dreaded having to make that decision just now more than anything that I have had to do in my whole life.'

He smiled rather wanly. 'That's all right, darling. There's nothing so mighty clever about it, but it gives us time, and you must try and comfort yourself with the thought that time and the angels are on our side.'

Even Richard's frantic anxiety to set out immediately in search of his Fleur d'amour was overcome for the time being by Rex's so obviously sensible suggestion. In his agitation he had eaten nothing yet, but now he sat down to cut some sandwiches, and set about persuading Marie Lou that she must eat the first of them in order to keep up her strength. Then he looked over at the Duke.

'I left that note for Malin where he's bound to see it—slipped it under his bedroom door, so we shan't be disturbed here. Is there anything at all that we can do?'

'Nothing, I fear, only possess ourselves with such patience as we can, but we're all about the end of our tether, so we ought to try and get some sleep. If Mocata makes some fresh move this evening it's on the cards that we shall be up again all night.'

'I'll get some cushions,' Simon volunteered. 'I suppose there's no harm in bringing used articles into this room now?'

'None. You had better collect all the stuff you can and we'll make up some temporary beds on the floor.'

Simon, Richard and Rex left the room and returned a few moments later with piles of cushions and all the rugs that they could find. They placed some fresh logs on the smouldering ashes of the fire and then set about laying out five makeshift resting-places.

When they had finished, Marie Lou allowed Richard to lead her over to one of them and tuck her up, although she protested that, exhausted though she was, she would never be able to sleep. The rest lay down, and then Richard switched out the light.

Full day had come at last, but it was of little use, for the range of vision was limited to about fifteen yards. The mist outside the windows seemed, if anything, denser than before, and it swirled and eddied in curling wreaths above the damp stones of the terrace, muffling the noises of the countryside and shutting out the light.

None of them felt that the would be able to sleep. Rex's gnawing sorrow for Tanith preyed upon his mind. The others, racked with anxiety for Fleur, turned restlessly upon their cushions. Every now and then they heard Marie Lou give way to fits of sobbing as though her heart would break. But the stress of those terrible night hours and the emotions they had passed through since had exhausted them completely. Marie Lou's bursts of sobbing became quieter and then ceased. Richard fell into an uneasy doze. De Richleau and Rex breathed evenly, sunk at last in a heavy sleep.

Hours later Marie Lou was dreaming that she was seated in an ancient library reading a big, old-fashioned book, the cover of which was soft and hairy like a wolf's skin, and that as she read it a circle of iron was bound about her head. Then the scene changed. She was in the pentacle again, and that loathsome sack-like Thing was attacking Fleur. She awoke–started up with a sudden scream of fear.

Her waking was little better than the nightmare when memory flooded back into her mind. Yet that too and the present only seemed other phases of the frightful dream; the comfortable library denuded of its furniture; Tanith's dead body lying in the centre of the floor and the dimness of the room from those horrible fog banks shutting out the sunshine. They could not possibly be anything but figments of the imagination.

The men had roused at once, and crowded round her, shadowy figures in the uncertain light. De Richleau pressed the electric switch. They blinked a little, and looked at each other sleepily, then their eyes turned to the place where Simon had lain.

With one thought their glances shifted to the window and they knew that while they slept their friend had gone out, into that ghostly unnatural night, to keep his grim appointment.

<hr />

30

OUT INTO THE FOG

It was Rex who noticed the chalk marks on the floor. He stepped over and saw that Simon, lacking pencil and paper, had used these means to leave them a short message. Slowly he deciphered the scribbled words and read them out:

> Please don't fuss or try to come after me. This is my muddle, so am keeping appointment. Do as Mocata has ordered. Am certain that is only chance of saving Fleur.
>
> Love to all.   Simon

'Aw, Hell!' exclaimed Rex as he finished. 'The dear heroic little sap has gone and put paid to my big idea. Mocata has got him *and* Fleur now on top of having killed Tanith. If you ask me we're properly sunk.'

De Richleau groaned. 'It is just like him. We ought to have guessed that he would do this.'

'You're right there,' Richard agreed sadly. 'I've known him longer than any of you, and I did my damnedest to prevent him sacrificing himself for nothing, but it seems to me he's only done the very thing you said he should.'

'That's not quite fair,' the Duke protested mildly. 'I only said I thought it right that he should *with certain modifications.* I had it in my mind that we might follow him at a distance. We should have arrived at the rendezvous before Mocata could have known that we had left this place, and we might have pulled something off. As it was, I thought Rex's idea so much better that I abandoned mine.'

'I'm sorry,' Richard apologised huskily. 'But Simon's my oldest friend you know, and this on top of all the rest . . .'

'Do you—do you think the poor sweet is right, and that his having given himself up will be of any use?' whispered Marie Lou.

Richard shrugged despondently. 'Not the least, dearest. I hate to seem ungracious, and you all know how devoted I am to Simon but in his anxiety to do the right thing he's handed Mocata our only decent card. We can sit here till Doomsday, but there's no chance now of making any fresh move which might give us a new opening. We've wasted the Lord knows how many precious hours, and we're in a worse hole than we were before. I'm going to carry out my original intention and get on to the police.'

'I wouldn't do that,' Rex caught him by the arm. 'It'll only mean our wasting further time in spilling long dispositions to a bunch of cops, and you're all wrong about our not having made anything on the new deal. We've had a sleep which we needed mighty badly, and we've lulled Mocata into a false sense of security. Just because we've remained put here all morning like he said and Simon's come over with the goods, he'll think he's sitting pretty now and maybe let up on his supervision stunt. Let's cut out bothering with the police and get after him ourselves this minute.'

Marie Lou shivered slightly and then nodded. 'Rex is right, you know. Mocata has got what he wants now, so it is very unlikely that he is troubling to keep up us under observation any more, but how do you propose to try to find him?'

'We will go straight to Paris,' De Richleau announced, with a display of his old form. 'You remember Tanith told us that by tonight he would be there holding a conversation with a man who had lost the upper portion of his left ear. That is Castelnau, the banker, I am certain, so the thing for us to do is to make for Paris and hunt him out.'

'How do you figure on getting there?' asked the practical Rex.

'By plane, of course. Mocata is obviously travelling that way or he could never get there by tonight. Richard must take us in his four-seater, and if Mocata has to motor all the way to Croydon before he can make a start, we'll be there before him. Is your plane in commission, Richard?'

'Yes, the plane's all right. It's in the hangar at the bottom of the meadow, and when I took her out three days ago she was running perfectly. I don't much like the look of this fog, though, although, of course, it's probably only a ground mist.'

They all glanced out of the window again. The grey murk still hung over the terrace, shutting out the view of the Botticelli garden where, on this early May morning, the polyanthus and forget-me-nots and daffodils, shedding their green cocoons, were bursting into colourful life.

'Let's go,' said Rex, impatiently. 'De Richleau's right. 'You'd best get some clothes on, then we'll beat it for Paris the second you're fit.'

The rest followed him out into the hall and upstairs to the rooms above. The house was silent and seemingly deserted. The servants were obviously taking Richard's orders in their most literal sense and, released for once from their daily tasks, enjoying an unexpected holiday in their own quarters.

Marie Lou looked into the nursery and almost broke down again for a moment as she once more saw the empty cot, but she hurried past it to the nurse's bedroom and found the woman still sleeping soundly.

In Richard's dressing-room the men made hasty preparations. Rex was clad in the easy lounge suit which he had put on in De Richleau's flat, but Richard and the Duke were still in pyjamas. When they were dressed Richard fitted the others out as well as he could with top clothes for their journey. The Duke was easy, being only a little taller than himself, and a big double overcoat was found for Rex, into which he managed to scramble despite the breadth of his enormous shoulders. Marie Lou joined them a few moments later, clad in her breeches and leather flying coat, which she always used whenever she went up with Richard.

Downstairs again, they paused in the library to make another hurried meal. Then the door was locked, and after casting a last unhappy glance at Tanith's body, which remained unaltered in appearance, Rex led the way out on the terrace.

They walked quickly down the gravel path beside the Botticelli border, the sound of their footsteps muffled by the all-pervading mist—through Marie Lou's own garden, with its long herbaceous borders, and past the old sundial—round the quadrangles of tessellated pavement which fell in a succession of little terraces to the pond garden, with its water lilies, and so to the meadow beyond.

When they reached the hangar Richard and Rex ran out the plane and got it in order for the flight. De Richleau stood watching their operations with Marie Lou beside him, both of them fretting a little at the necessary delay, since now that the vital decision had been taken every member of the party was impatient to set out.

They settled themselves in the comfortable four-seater. Rex swung the propeller, well accustomed to the ways of aeroplanes, and the engine purred upon a low steady note. He watched it for a second, and then, as he scrambled aboard, there came the long conventional cry: '*All set.*'

The plane moved slowly forward into the dank mist. The hedges and trees on either side were shut out by banks of fog, but Richard knew the ground so well that he felt confident of judging his distance and direction. He taxied over the even grass of the long field, and turned to rise. The plane lifted, touched ground again gently twice, and they were off.

As they left the earth a new feeling came over Richard. He was passionately fond of flying, and it always filled him with exhilaration, but this was different. It was as though he had suddenly come out into the daylight after having been walking down a long, dark, smoky tunnel for many hours. At long intervals there had been brightly lit recesses in the sides of it where figures stood like tableaux at a waxworks show. The slug-like Thing and Fleur; Rex standing at the window with Tanith in her arms; Simon whispering something to the Duke; Marie Lou's face as she stood with her hand resting on the rail of Fleur's empty cot, and a dozen others. The rest of that strange journey he seemed to have made, consisted of long periods of blankness only punctuated by little cries of fear and scraps of reiterated argument, the purpose of which he could no longer remember. Now—his brain was clear again, and he settled himself with new purpose to handle the plane with all his skill.

In those few moments they had risen clear of the ground mist and were soaring upwards into the blue above. As De Richleau looked down he saw a very curious thing. Not only was the fog that had hemmed them in local, but it seemed to be concentrated entirely upon Cardinals Folly. He could just make out the chimneys of the house rising in its centre, as from a grey sea, and from the buildings it spread out in a circular formation for half a mile or so on every side, hiding the gardens from his view and obscuring the meadows between the house and the village, but beyond, all was clear in the brilliant sunshine of the early summer afternoon.

Rex was beside Richard in the cockpit. Automatically he had taken on the job of navigator, and, like Richard, his brain numbed before with misery, had started to function properly again directly he set to busying himself with the maps and scales.

The Duke, sitting in the body of the machine with Marie Lou, felt that there was nothing he could say to comfort her, but he took her hand in his and held it between his own. From his quick gesture she felt again his intense distress that he should ever have been the means of bringing her this terrible unhappiness, so, to distract his thoughts, she put her mouth right up against his ear and told him of the odd dream she had had; about reading the old book. He gave her a curious glance and began to shout back at her.

She could not catch all he said owing to the noise of the engine, but enough to tell that he was intensely interested. He seemed to think that she had been dreaming of the famous Red Book of Appin, a wonderful treatise on Magic owned by the Stewards of Invernahyle, who were now extinct. The book had been lost and not heard of for more than a hundred years, but her description of it, and the legend that it might only be read with understanding by those who wore a circlet of iron above their brow made him insistent that it must be this which she had seen in her dream. He pressed her to try and remember if she had understood any portion of it.

After some trouble she managed to convey to him that she had read one sentence on a faded vellum page, and that although the lettering was quite different from anything which she had ever seen before, she understood it at the time, but could not recall the meaning now. Then, as talking was so difficult, they fell silent.

At a hundred miles an hour the plane soared above the English counties, but they took little heed of the fields and hedges, woods and hills, which fled so swiftly from beneath them. Somehow they seemed to have stepped out of their old life altogether. Time no longer existed for them, only the will to arrive at their destination in order to be active once again. All their thoughts were concentrated now upon Paris and the man who had lost half his ear. Would he be there? Could they find him if he was? And would they arrive before Mocata?

They passed over the Northern end of the English Channel almost without noticing it; Marie Lou felt a little shock when the plane banked steeply and Richard brought it circling down.

The sun was sinking behind great banks of cloud and, as the plane tilted, she saw that a thick mist lay below them in which glowed dull patches of half-obscured light. Richard and Rex knew them, however, to be fog flares of the Le Bourget landing ground.

A few seconds more and they had seen the last of the sunset. A thin greyness closed about them. One of the flares showed bright, and the plane bounded along the earth until Richard brought it to a standstill.

Almost in a daze they answered the questions of the officers at the airport and passed the Customs, secured a fast-looking taxi and, packed inside it, were heading for the centre of Paris.

As they ran through the streets, with the familiar high-pitched note of the taxi's horn continually sounding and the subtle smell of the *epiceries* in their nostrils—the very scent of Paris—they noticed half-unconsciously that night had fallen once more.

Here and there the electric sky-signs on the tall buildings, advertising Savan Cadum or Byrrh, glowed dully through the murk, and the lights of the cafés illuminated little spaces of the boulevards through which they passed, throwing up the figures that sat sipping their aperitifs at the marble-topped tables and dappling the young green of the stunted trees that lined the pavements.

None of them spoke as the taxi swerved and rushed, seeking every opportunity to nose its way through the traffic. Only Rex leant forward once, soon after they left the aerodrome, and murmured: 'I told him the Ritz. We'll be able to hunt up this bird's address when we get there.'

They ran past the Opera, down the Boulevard de la Madeleine, and turned left into the Place Vendôme. The cab pulled up with a jerk. A liveried porter hurried forward to fling open the door, and they scrambled out.

'Pay him off, with a good tip,' Rex ordered the hotel servant. 'I'll see-yer-later, inside.' Then he led the way into the hotel.

One of the under-managers at the bureau recognised him and came forward with a welcoming smile.

'Monsieur Van Ryn, what a pleasure! You require accommodation for your party? How many rooms do you desire? I hope that you will stay with us some time.'

'Two single rooms and one double, with bathrooms, and we'd best have a sitting-room on the same floor,' replied Rex curtly. 'How long we'll be staying I can't say. I've got urgent business to attend to this trip. Do you happen to know a banker named Castelnau—elderly man, grey-haired, with a hatchet face, who's had a slice taken out of his left ear?'

'*Mais oui, monsieur*. He lunches here frequently.'

'Good. D'you know where he lives?'

'For the moment, no, but I will ascertain. You permit?' The manager moved briskly away and disappeared into the office. A few moments later he returned with a Paris telephone directory open in his hand.

'This will be it, monsieur, I think. Monsieur Laurent Castelnau, 72, Maison Rambouillet, Parc Monceau. That is a block of flats. Do you wish to telephone his apartment'

'Sure,' Rex nodded. 'Call him right away, please.' Then, as the Frenchman hurried off, he nodded quietly to the Duke: 'Best leave this to me. I've got a hunch how to fix him.'

'Go ahead,' the Duke acquiesced. He had been keeping well in the background, and now he smiled a little unhappily as he went on in a low voice:

'How I love Paris. The smell and the sight and the sound of it. I have not been back here for fifteen years. The Government have never forgiven me for the part that I played in the Royalist rising which took place in the 90's. I was young then. How long ago it all seems now. But never since have I dared to venture back to France, except a few times, secretly on the most urgent business. I believe the authorities would still put me into some miserable fortress if they discovered me on French soil.'

'Oh, Greyeyes, dear! You ought never to have come.' Marie Lou turned to him impulsively. 'With all these awful things happening I had forgotten. Somehow I always think of you really as an Englishman, not as a French exile who lives in England as the next best thing. It would be terrible if you were arrested and tried as a political offender after all these years.'

He shrugged and smiled again. 'Don't worry, Princess. The authorities have almost forgotten my existence, I expect, and the only risk I run is in knowing so many people who constantly travel through France. If someone recognised me and spoke my name too loud it is just possible that it might strike a chord in some police spy's memory, but beyond that there is very little danger.

They sat down at a little table in the lounge while Rex was telephoning. When he rejoined them he nodded cheerfully.

'We're in luck, and Lord knows we need it. I spoke to Castelnau himself, used the name of my old man's firm—The Chesapeake Banking and Trust Corporation—and spun a yarn that he had sent me over on a special mission to Europe connected with the franc. Told him the whole thing was far too hush-hush for me to make a date to see him at his office tomorrow morning, where his clerks might recognise me as the representative of an American banking house, and that I must see him tonight privately. He hedged a bit until I put it to him that I had power to deal in real big figures, and he fell for that like a sucker. He couldn't see me yet though, because he's busy putting on his party frock for some official banquet, but he figures he'll be back at the apartment round about ten o'clock, so I said I'd be along to state my business then.

'To fill in time we might go upstairs and have a bath,' remarked Richard, feeling his bristly chin. 'Then we'd better go out and dine somewhere, though God knows, I've never felt less like food in my life.'

'All right,' De Richleau agreed, 'only let us go somewhere quiet for dinner. If we go to one of the smart places it will add to the chance of my running into sombody that I know.'

'What about Le Vert Galant?' Richard suggested. 'It's on the right bank down by La Cité, old-fashioned, quiet, but excellent food, and you're unlikely to see the sort of people that we know there in the evening.'

'Is that still running?' De Richleau smiled. 'Then let us go there by all means. It's just the place.' And they moved over towards the lift.

Upstairs they bathed and tidied themselves, but almost automatically, for their uneasy sleep that morning seemed to have done little to recruit their lowered energy. As though still in a bad dream, Marie Lou undressed, and dressed again, while Richard moved about the room, for once apparently unconscious of her presence, silently and mechanically eliminating the traces of the journey. Then he submitted to the ministrations of the hotel barber with one curt order, that the man was to shave him and not to talk.

Rex finished first and wandered into their room, where he sat uncomfortably perched upon a corner of the bed, but he stared at his large feet the whole time that he sat there and did not make any effort whatever at conversation.

De Richleau joined them shortly afterwards, and Marie Lou, rousing for a moment from her abject misery, noted with a little start how spick and span he had become again, after the attentions of the barber and his bath. He had produced one of his long Hoyos, and appeared to be smoking it with quiet enjoyment. Richard and Rex, despite the removal of their incipient beards, still looked woebegone and haggard, as though they had not slept for days, and were almost contemplating suicide, but the Duke still maintained his air of the great gentleman for whose pleasure and satisfaction this whole existence is ordered.

Actually his appearance was no more than a mask with which long habit had accustomed him to disguise his emotions, and at heart he was racked by an anxiety equal to that of any of the others. He was suppressing his impatience to get hold of Castelnau only by a supreme effort; his feet itched to be on the move, and his fingers to be on the throat of the adversary; but as he came into the room he smiled round at them, kissed Marie Lou's hand with his usual gallantry, and presented a huge bunch of white violets to her.

'A few flowers, Princess, for your room.'

Marie Lou took them without a word; the tears brimming in her eyes spoke her thanks that he should have thought of such a thing at such a time, and his perfect naturalness served to steady them all a little as they went down afterwards in the lift. Rex changed some money at the *caisse*, and they went out into the night again.

'Queer—isn't it,' remarked Richard as he looked out of the taxi window at the fog-bound streets. 'I've always said what fun it is to make a surprise visit for a couple of nights to Paris—in May. It's like stealing in on summer in advance—tea in the open at Armenonville—a drive to Fontainebleau, with the forest at its very best—and all that. 'I never thought I might come to Paris one May like this.'

'I've a feeling there's something wrong about it—or us,' said Rex slowly. 'Those servants in the hotel back there didn't seem any more natural than the weather to me. It was as though I was watching them act in some kind of play.'

De Richleau nodded. 'Yes, I felt the same, and I believe Mocata is responsible. Perhaps he surrounded Cardinals Folly with a strong atmospheric force, and we have brought the vibrations of it with us, or he may be interfering with our auras in some way. I'm only guessing, of course, and can't possibly explain it.'

At the Vert Galant De Richleau ordered dinner without reference to any of them. He was a great gourmet, and knew from past experience the dishes that pleased them best, but as a meal it was one of the most dismal failures which it had ever been his misfortune to witness.

He knew and they knew that his apparent preoccupation with food and wine was nothing but a bluff; an attempt to smother their anxiety and occupy their thoughts until the time to go to Castelnau's apartment should arrive. The cooking was excellent, the service everything that one could desire, and the cellar of Le Vert Galant provided wines to which even De Richleau's critical taste gave full approval, but their hearts were not in the business.

They toyed with the Lobster Cardinal, sent away the Pauillac Lamb untasted, and drank the wines as a beverage to steady their nerves rather than with the consideration and pleasure which they deserved.

The fat *maître d'hôtel* supervised the service of each course himself, and it passed his understanding how these three men and the beautiful little lady could show so little appreciation. With hands clasped upon a large stomach, he stood before the Duke and murmured his distress that the dishes they had ordered should not appear to please them, but the Duke waved him away, even summoning up a little smile to assure him that it was no fault of the restaurant and only their unfortunate lack of appetite.

Throughout the meal De Richleau talked unceasingly. He was a born raconteur, and ordinarily, with his charm and wit, could hold any audience enthralled. Tonight, despite his own anxiety, he made a supreme attempt to lift the burden from the shoulders of his friends by exploiting every venue of memory and conversation, but never in his life had his efforts met with such a cold reception. In vain he attempted to divert their thoughts, laughing a little to himself, as he reached the denouement in each of his stories, and hoping against hope that he might raise a smile in those three anxious faces that faced him across the table.

For Marie Lou the meal was just another phase of that horrible nightmare through which she had been passing since the early hours of the morning. Mechanically she sampled the dishes which were put before her, but each one seemed to taste the same, and after a few mouthfuls she laid down her fork, submitting miserably to the frantic, gnawing thoughts which pervaded her whole being.

Richard said nothing, ate little, and drank heavily. He was in that state when he knew quite well that it was impossible for him to drink too much. Great happiness or great distress has that effect upon certain men, and he was one of them. Every other minute he glanced at the clock on the wall, as it slowly registered the passage of time until they could set forth once more on their attempt to save his daughter.

There was still half an hour to go when the fruit and brandy were placed upon the table, and then at last De Richleau surrendered.

'I've been talking utter nonsense all through dinner,' he confessed gravely; 'only to keep my thoughts off this wretched business, you understand. But now the time has come when we can speak of it again with some advantage. What do you intend to do, Rex, when you see this man?'

Marie Lou lifted her eyes from the untasted grapes which lay upon her plate. 'You've been splendid, Greyeyes, dear. I haven't been listening to you really, but a sentence here and there has been just enough to take my mind off a picture of the worst that may happen, which keeps on haunting me.'

He smiled across at her gratefully. 'I'm glad of that. It's the least that I could try to do. But come now, Rex, let's hear your plan.'

'I've hardly got one,' Rex confessed, shrugging his great shoulders. 'We know he'll see me, and that's as far as I have figured it out. I presume it'll boil down to my jumping on him after a pretty short discussion and threatening to gouge out his eyeballs with my hands unless he's prepared to come clean with everything he knows about Mocata.'

De Richleau shook his head. 'That is roughly the idea, of course, but there are certain to be servants in the flat, and we must arrange it that you have a free field for your party.'

'Can't you take us along with you?' Richard suggested. 'Say that we're privately interested in this deal you're putting up. If only the three of us can get inside that flat God help anybody who tries to stop us forcing him to talk.'

'Sure,' Rex agreed. 'I see no sort of objection to that. We can park Marie

Lou at the Ritz again, on our way, before we beat this fellow up.'

'No!' Marie Lou gave a sudden dogged shake of her head. 'I am coming with you. I'm quite capable of taking care of myself, and I will keep out of the way if there is any trouble. You cannot ask me to go back to the hotel and sit there on my own while you are trying to obtain news of Fleur. I should go mad and fling myself out of the window. I've got to come, so please don't argue about it.'

Richard took her hand and caressed it softly. 'Of course you shall, my sweet. It would be better, perhaps, for you not to be with us when we see Castelnau, but there's no reason why you shouldn't wait for us in his hall.'

De Richleau nodded. 'Yes, in the circumstances it is impossible to leave Marie Lou behind, but about these servants—did you bring that gun that you had last night with you?'

'Yes, I brought it through the Customs in my hip pocket, and it's fully loaded.'

'Right. Then if necessary you can use it to intimidate the servants while Rex and I tackle Castelnau. It is a quarter to. Shall we go?'

Rex sent for the bill and paid it, leaving a liberal tip which soothed the dignity of the injured *maître d'hôtel*, then they filed out of the restaurant.

'Maison Rambouillet, Parc Monceau,' De Richleau told the driver sharply as they climbed into the taxi, and not a word was spoken until the cab drew up before a palatial block of modern flats, facing on to the little green park where the children of the rich in Paris take their morning airing.

'Monsieur Castelnau?' the Duke inquired of the concierge.

'This way, monsieur'; the man led them through a spacious stone-faced hall to the lift.

It shot up to the fifth floor and as he opened the gates, the concierge pointed to a door upon the right.

'Number Seventy-two,' he said quietly. 'I think Monsieur Castelnau has just come in.'

The gates clanged behind them, and the lift flashed silently down again to the ground floor. De Richleau gave Rex a swift glance and, stepping towards the door of Number Seventy-two, pressed the bell.

31

THE MAN WITH THE JAGGED EAR

The tall, elaborately carved door was opened by a bald, elderly man-servant in a black alpaca coat. Rex gave his name, and the servant looked past him with dark, inquiring eyes at the others.

'These are friends of mine who're seeing Monsieur Castelnau on the same business,' Rex said abruptly, stepping into the long, narrow hall. 'Is he in?'

'Yes, monsieur, and he is expecting you. This way, if you please.'

Marie Lou perched herself on a high couch of Cordova leather, while the other three followed the back of the alpaca jacket down the corridor. Another tall, carved door was thrown open, and they entered a wide, dimly-lit *salon*, furnished in the old style of French elegance: gilt ormolu, tapestries, bric-à-brac, and a painted ceiling where cupids disported themselves among roseate flowers.

Castelnau stood, cold, thin, angular and hatchet-faced, with his back to a large porcelain stove. He was dressed in the clothes which he had worn at the banquet. The wide, watered silk ribbon with the garish colours of some foreign order cut across his shirt front and a number of decorations were pinned to the lapel of his evening coat.

'Monsieur Van Ryn.' He barely touched Rex's hand with his cold fingers and went on in his own language. 'It is a pleasure to receive you. I know your house well by reputation, and from time to time in the past my own firm has had some dealings with yours.' Then he glanced at the others sharply. 'These gentlemen are, I assume, associated with you in this business?'

'They are.' Rex introduced them briefly 'The Duke de Richleau—Mr Richard Eaton.'

Castelnau's eyebrows lifted a fraction as he studied the Duke's face with new interest. 'Of course,' he murmured. 'Monsieur le Duc must pardon me if I did not recognise him at first. It is many years since we have met, and I was under the impression that he had never found the air of Paris good for him; but perhaps I am indiscreet to make any reference to that old trouble.'

'The business which has brought me is urgent, monsieur,' De Richleau replied suavely. 'Therefore I elected to ignore the ban which a Government of bourgeois and socialists placed upon me.'

'A grave step, monsieur, since the police of France have a notoriously long memory. Particularly at the present time when the Government has cause to regard all politicals who are not of its party with suspicion. However,' the banker bowed slightly, 'that, of course, is your own affair entirely. Be seated, gentlemen. I am at your service.'

None of the three accepted the proffered invitation, and Rex said abruptly: 'The bullion deal I spoke of when I called you on the telephone was only an excuse to secure this interview. The three of us have come here tonight because we know that you are associated with Mocata.'

The Frenchman stared at him in blank surprise and was just about to burst into angry protest when Rex hurried on. 'It'll cut no ice to deny it. We know too much. The night before last we saw you at that joint in Chilbury, and afterwards with the rest of those filthy swine doing the devil's business on Salisbury Plain. You're a Satanist, and you're going to tell us all you know about your leader.'

Castelnau's dark eyes glittered dangerously in his long, white face. They shifted with a sudden furtive glance towards an open escritoire.

Before he could move, Richard's voice came quiet but steely. 'Stay where you are. I've got you covered, and I'll shoot you like a dog if you flicker an eyelid.'

De Richleau caught the banker's glance, and with his quick, cat-like step had reached the ornate desk. He pulled out a few drawers, and then found the weapon that he felt certain must be there. It was a tiny .2 pistol, but deadly enough. Having assured himself that it was loaded, he pointed it at the Satanist. 'Now,' he said, icily, 'are you prepared to talk, or must I make you?'

Castelnau shrugged, then looked down at his feet. 'You cannot make me,' he replied with a quiet confidence, 'but if you tell me what you wish to know, I may possibly give you the information you require in order to get rid of you.'

202   *The Devil Rides Out*

'First, what do you know of Mocata's history?'

'Very little, but sufficient to assure you that you are exceedingly ill-advised if, as it appears, you intend to pit yourself against him.'

'To hell with that!' Rex snapped angrily; 'get on with the story.'

'Just as you wish. It is the Canon Damien Mocata to whom you refer, of course. When he was younger he was an officiating priest at some church in Lyons, I believe. He was always a difficult person, and his intellectual gifts made a thorn in the sides of his superiors. Then there was some scandal and he left the Church; but long before that he had become an occultist of exceptional powers. I met him some years ago and became interested in his operations. Your apparent disapproval of them does not distress me in the least. I find their theory an exceptionally interesting study, and their practice of the greatest assistance in governing my business transactions. Mocata lives in Paris for a good portion of the year, and I see him from time to time socially in addition to our meetings for esoteric purposes. I think that is all that I can tell you.'

'When did you see him last?' asked the Duke.

'At Chilbury two nights ago, when we gathered again after the break-up of our meeting. I suppose you were responsible for that?' Castelnau's thin lips broke into a ghost of a smile. 'If so, believe me, you will pay for it.'

'You have not seen him then today—this evening?'

'No, I did not even know that he had returned to Paris.' There was a ring in the banker's voice which made it difficult for his questioners to doubt that he was telling them the truth.

'Where does he live when he is in Paris?' the Duke enquired.

'I do not know. I have visited him at many places. Often he stays with various friends, who are also interested in his practices, but he has no permanent address. The people with whom he was staying last left Paris some months ago for the Argentine, so I have no idea where you are likely to find him now.'

'Where do you meet him when these Satanic gatherings take place?'

'I am sorry but I can't tell you.' The Frenchman's voice was firm.

De Richleau padded softly forward and thrust the little pistol into Castelnau's ribs, just under his heart. 'I am afraid you've got to,' he purred silkily. 'The matter that we are engaged upon is urgent.'

The banker held his ground, and to outward appearances remained unruffled at the threat. 'It is no good,' he said quietly, 'I cannot do it, even if you intend to murder me. Each one of us goes into a self-induced hypnotic trance before proceeding to these meetings, and wakes upon his arrival. In my conscious state I have no idea how I get there; so this apache attitude of yours is completely useless.'

'I see.' De Richleau nodded slowly and withdrew the automatic. 'However, you are going to tell me just the same, because it happens that I am something of a hypnotist. I shall put you under now, and we shall proceed to follow all the stages of your unconscious journey.'

For the first time Castelnau's face showed a trace of fear.

'You can't,' he muttered quickly. 'I won't let you.'

De Richleau shrugged. 'Your opposition will make it slightly more difficult, but I shall do it, nevertheless. However, as it may take some time, we will make fresh arrangements in order to ensure that we are not disturbed. Press the bell, and when your servant comes, give him definite instructions that as we shall be engaged in a long conference, upon no pretext whatsoever are you to be disturbed.'

'And if I refuse?' Castelnau's dark eyes suddenly flashed rebellion.

'Then you will never live to give another order. The affair we are engaged upon is desperate, and whatever the consequences may be, I shall shoot you like the rat you are. Now ring.' De Richleau put the pistol in his pocket but still held the banker covered, and after a moment's hesitation Castelnau pressed the bell.

'You, Richard,' the Duke said in a sharp whisper, 'will leave us when the servant has taken his instructions. Wait for us with Marie Lou in the entrance hall. You have your gun. Prevent anyone leaving the apartment until we have finished. Open the door to anyone who rings yourself, and if Mocata arrives, as he may at any moment, don't argue–shoot. I take all responsibility.'

'I am only waiting for the chance,' said Richard grimly, just as the servant entered.

Castelnau gave his orders in an even voice, with one eye upon the Duke's pocket, then Richard, in his normal voice, remarked casually:

'Well, since the matter is confidential, I had better wait outside with my wife until you are through,' and followed the elderly alpaca-coated man out into the hall.

'Rex,' De Richleau lost not an instant once the door was closed. 'Take that telephone receiver off its stand so that we are not interrupted by any calls. And you,' he turned to the banker, 'sit down in that chair.'

'I won't!' exclaimed Castelnau furiously. 'This is abominable. You invade my apartment like brigands. I give you such information as I can, but what you are about to do will bring me into danger, and I refuse–I refuse, I tell you.'

'I shall neither argue with you nor kill you,' De Richleau answered frigidly. 'You are too valuable to me alive. Rex, knock him out!'

Castelnau swung round and threw up his arms in a gesture of defence, but Rex broke through his guard. The young American's mighty fist caught him on the side of the jaw and he crumpled up, a still heap on his own hearth-rug.

When the banker came to he found himself sitting in a straight chair; his hands were lashed to the back and his ankles to the legs with the curtain cords. His head ached abominably and he saw De Richleau standing opposite to him, smiling relentlessly down into his face.

'Now,' said the Duke, 'look into my eyes. The sooner we get this business over the sooner you will be able to get to bed and nurse your sore head. I am about to place you under, and you are going to tell us what you do when you go to these Satanic meetings.'

For answer Castelnau quickly closed his eyes and lowered his head on to his chest, resisting De Richleau's powerful suggestion with all the force of his will.

'This doesn't look to me as though it's going to be any too easy,' Rex muttered dubiously. 'I've always thought that it was impossible to hypnotise people if they were unwilling. You'd better let me put the half-Nelson on him until he becomes more amenable and sees reason.'

'That might make him agree verbally,' De Richleau replied, 'but it won't stop him lying to us afterwards, and it is quite possible to hypnotise people against their will. It is often done to lunatics in asylums. Get behind him now, hold back his head and lift his eyelids with your fingers so that he cannot close them. We've got to find out about this place. It is our only hope of getting on to Mocata.'

Rex did as he was bid. The Duke stood before the chair, his steel-grey eyes fastened without a flicker upon those of the unwilling Satanist.

Time passed, and every now and then De Richleau's voice broke the silence of the quiet, dimly-lit room. 'You are tired now, you will sleep. I command you.' But all his efforts were unavailing. The Satanist sat there rigid and determined not to succumb.

The ormolu clock upon the mantelpiece ticked with a steady, monotonous note, until Rex was filled with the mad desire to throw something at it. The hands crawled round the white enamelled dial; its silvery chime rang out, marking the hours eleven, twelve, one. Still the Frenchman endured De Richleau's steady gaze. He knew that they were expecting Mocata to arrive at his apartment. Mocata was immensely powerful. If only he could hold out until then the whole position might be saved. With a fixed determination not to give in, his eyelids held back by Rex's forefingers, he stared blankly at De Richleau's chin.

Outside, on the sofa of Cordova leather, Richard and Marie Lou sat side by side. It seemed to her again that she must be dreaming. The whole fantastic business of this flight to Paris and their dinner at the Vert Galant had been utterly unreal. It could not be real now that Mocata was somewhere in this city preparing to kill her darling Fleur in some ungodly rite, while she sat there with Richard in that strange, silent apartment and the night hours laboured on.

She thought that she slept a little, but she was not certain. Ever since she had fainted in the pentacle and come to with the sensation that she was above Cardinals Folly, floating in the soundless ether, all her movements had been automatic and her vision of their doings distorted, so that whole sections of time were blotted out from her mind, and only these glimpses of strange places and faces seemed to register.

The black-coated servant appeared once at the far end of the corridor, but seeing them still there, disappeared again.

Almost the whole of that long wait Richard sat with his eyes glued to the front door, his hand clasped ready on the pistol in his pocket, expecting the ring that would announce Mocata's arrival.

He too felt that somehow this person, grown desperate from an unbearable injury and lusting with the desire to kill, regardless of laws and consequences, could not possibly be himself. With every movement that he made he expected to wake and find himself safely in bed at Cardinals Folly, with Marie Lou snuggled down close against him and Fleur peacefully asleep only a few doors away.

Had he wholly believed that Fleur had been taken from him and that he was never to see her again, he could not possibly have endured those dreary hours of enforced idleness while the Duke battled with Castelnau. He would have been forced to interrupt them or at least leave his post to watch their proceedings, for his inactivity would have become unbearable.

In the richly furnished *salon*, Rex and the Duke continued their long-sustained effort without a second's intermission. The clock struck two, and as Rex stood behind the Frenchman's chair, shifting his weight from foot to foot now and then, he seemed at times to drop off into a sort of half-sleep where he stood.

At last, a little after two, he was roused to a fresh attention by a sudden sob breaking from the dry lips of the banker.

'I will not let you, I will not,' he cried hysterically, and then began to struggle violently with the curtain cords that tied him to the chair.

'You will,' De Richleau told him firmly, the pupils of his grey eyes now distended and gleaming with an unnatural light.

Castelnau suddenly ceased to struggle; a cold sweat broke out on his bony forehead, and his head sagged on his neck, but Rex held it firmly and continued to press back his eyelids so that it was impossible for him to escape the Duke's relentless stare.

He began to sob then, like a child who is being beaten, and at last De Richleau knew that he had broken the Frenchman's will. In another ten minutes Rex was able to remove his fingers from the banker's eyelids for he no longer had the power to close them, but sat there gazing at De Richleau with an imbecile glare.

In a low voice the Duke began to question him and, after one last feeble effort at resistance, it all came out. The meeting place was in a cellar below a deserted warehouse on the banks of the Seine at Asnières. They secured full directions as to the way to reach it and how to get into it when they arrived.

As Castelnau answered the last question, De Richleau glanced at the clock. 'Three and a quarter hours,' he said with a sigh of weariness. 'Still, it might well have taken longer in a case like this.'

'What'll we do with him?' Rex motioned towards the Frenchman who, with his head fallen forward on his chest, was now sound asleep.

'Leave him there,' answered the Duke abruptly. 'The servants will find him in the morning, and he's so exhausted that he will sleep until then. But stuff your handkerchief in his mouth just in case he wakes and tries to make any trouble for us. Be quick!'

Castelnau did not even blink an eyelid as Rex gagged him. They left him there and hurried out to the others.

'Come on!' cried the Duke.

'What about Mocata?' Richard asked. 'If we leave here we may miss him.'

'We must chance that.' De Richleau pulled open the door and made for the stairs.

As they dashed down the long flights he flung over his shoulder: 'Tanith may have been wrong. Messages from the astral plane are often unreliable about time. As it does not exist there, they have difficulty in judging it. She may have seen him here a week hence or in the past even. It's so late now that I doubt if he will turn up tonight. Anyhow, we got out of Castelnau the place where he's most likely to be—and God knows what he may be doing if he is there. We've got to hurry!' They fled after him out of the silent building.

Round the corner they managed to pick up a taxi and, at the promise of a big tip, the man got every ounce out of his engine as he whirled the four harassed-looking people away through the murky streets up towards the Boulevard de Clichy. Topping the hill, they descended again towards the Seine, crossed the river and entered Asnières.

In that outlying slum of Paris with its wharves and warehouses, narrow, sordid-looking streets and dimly-lit passages, there was little movement at that hour of the morning. They paid off the taxi outside a closed café which faced upon a dirty-looking square. A market wagon rumbled past with its driver huddled on the seat above the horses, his cape drawn close to protect him from the damp mist rising from the river. The bedraggled figure of a woman was huddled upon the steps of a shop with 'Tabac' in faded blue letters above it, but otherwise there was no sign of life.

Turning up the collars of their coats and shivering afresh from the damp chill of the drifting fog, they followed the Duke's lead along an evil-looking street of tumbledown dwelling houses. Then, between two high walls, along a narrow passage where the rays of a solitary lamp, struggling through grimy glass, were barely sufficient to dispel a small circle of gloom in its own area. When they had passed it the rest was darkness, foul smells, greasy mud squishing from beneath their feet, and wisps of mist curling cold about their faces.

At the end of that long dark alley-way they came out upon a deserted wharf. De Richleau turned to the left and the others followed. To one side of them the steep face of a tall brick building, from which chains and pulleys hung in slack festoons, towered up into the darkness. On the other, a few feet away, the river surged, oily, turgid, yellow and horrible as it hurried to the sea.

As if in a fresh phase of their nightmare, they stumbled forward over planks, hawsers and pieces of old iron, the neglected debris of the riverside, until fifty yards farther on De Richleau halted.

'This is it,' he announced, fumbling with a rusty padlock. 'Castelnau hadn't got a key and so we'll have to break this thing. Hunt around, and see if you can find a piece of iron that we can use as a jemmy. The longer the better. It will give us more purchase.'

They rummaged round in the semi-darkness, broken only by a riverside light some distance away along the wharf and the masthead lanterns of a few long barges anchored out on the swiftly flowing waters.

'This do?' Richard pulled a rusty lever from a winch and, grabbing it from him, the Duke thrust the narrow end into the hoop of the padlock.

'Now then,' he said, as he gripped the cold, moist iron, 'steady pressure isn't any good. It needs a violent jerk, so when I say "go!" we must all throw our weight on the bar together. Ready? Go!'

They heaved downwards. There was a sudden snap. The tongue of the padlock had been wrenched out of the lock. De Richleau removed it from the chain and in another moment they had the tall wooden door open.

Once inside, De Richleau struck a match, and while he shaded it with his hands the others looked about them. From what little they could see, the place appeared to be empty. They moved quickly forward, striking more matches as they went, in the direction where Castelnau had told them they would find a trap-door leading to the cellars.

In a far corner they halted. 'Stand back all of you,' whispered Rex, and while the Duke held up a light he pulled at the second in a row of upright iron girders, apparently built in to strengthen the wall. As Castelnau had said in his trance, it was a secret lever to operate the trap. The girder came forward and a large square of flooring lifted noiselessly on well-oiled hinges.

De Richleau blew out his match and produced the small automatic which he had taken from the banker. 'I will go first,' he said, 'and you, Rex, follow me. Richard, you have the other gun so you had better come last. You can look after Marie Lou and protect our rear. No noise now, because if we're lucky our man is here.'

Feeling about with his foot he ascertained that a flight of stairs led downwards. His shoes made no noise, and it was evident that they were covered with a thick carpet. Swiftly but cautiously he began to descend the flight and the others followed him down into the pitchy darkness.

At the bottom of the stairs they groped their way along a tunnel until the Duke was brought up sharply by a wooden partition at which it seemed to end. He fumbled for the handle, thinking that it was a door. The sides were as smooth and polished as the centre, yet it moved gently under his touch, and after a moment he found it to be a sliding panel. With the faintest click of ball bearings it slid back on its runners.

Straining their eyes they peered into the great apartment upon which it opened. A hundred feet long at least and thirty wide, it stretched out before them. Two lines of thick pillars, acting as supporters to the roof above, and rows of chairs divided in the centre by an aisle which led up to a distant altar, gave it the appearance of a big private chapel. It was lit by one solitary lamp which hung suspended before the altar, and that distant beacon did not penetrate to the shadows in which they stood.

On tiptoe and with their weapons ready they moved forward along the wall. De Richleau peered from side to side as he advanced, his pistol levelled. Rex crept along beside him, the iron winch lever which they had used to smash the padlock gripped tight in his big fist. At any moment they expected their presence to be discovered.

As they crept nearer to the hanging lamp, they saw that the place had been furnished with the utmost luxury and elegance for those unholy meetings. It was, indeed, a superbly equipped temple for the worship of the Devil. Above the altar a great and horrible representation of the Goat of Mendes, worked in the loveliest coloured silks, leered down at them; its eyes were two red stones which had been inset in the tapestry. They flickered with dull malevolence in the dim light of the solitary lamp.

On the side walls were pictures of men, women and beasts practising obscenities only possible of conception in the brain of a mad artist. Below the enormous central figure, which had hideous, distorted, human faces protruding from its elbows, knees and belly, was a great altar of glistening red stone, worked and inlaid with other coloured metals in the Italian fashion. Upon it reposed the ancient 'devil's bibles' containing all liturgies of hell; broken crucifixes and desecrated chalices stolen from churches and profaned here at the meetings of the Satanists.

Luxurious armchairs upholstered in red velvet and gold with elaborate canopies of lace above, such as High Prelates use in cathedrals when assisting at important ceremonies, flanked the altar on either side. Below the steps to the short chancel, on a level with where they stood, were arranged rows and rows of cushioned *prie-dieux* for the accommodation of the worshippers.

No sound or movement disturbed the stillness of the heavy incense-laden air and with a sinking of the heart De Richleau knew that they had lost their man. He had gambled blindly upon Tanith's message and she had proved wrong as to time. Mocata might not be in Paris for days to come; perhaps he had divined their journey and, knowing that he would be unmolested while they were abroad, returned to Simon's house where, even now, he might by foully murdering poor little Fleur. It seemed that their last hope had gone.

Then as they stepped from the side aisle they suddenly saw a thing that

had been hidden from them by the rows of chair backs—a body, clad in a long white robe with mystic signs embroidered on it in black and red, lay spreadeagled, face downwards on the floor, at the bottom of the chancel steps.

'It's Simon!' breathed the Duke.

'Oh, hell, they've killed him!' Rex ran forward and knelt beside the body of their friend. They turned him over and felt his heart. It was beating slowly but rhythmically. The Duke pulled out of his waistcoat pocket a little bottle, without which he never travelled, and held it beneath Simon's nose. He shuddered suddenly and his eyes opened, staring up at them.

'Simon, darling, Simon. It's us—we're here.' Marie Lou grasped his limp hands between her own.

He shuddered again and struggled into a sitting position. 'What—what's happened?' he murmured, but his voice was normal.

'You left us, you dear, pig-headed ass!' exclaimed Richard. 'Gave yourself up and ruined our whole plan of campaign. What's happened to *you*? That's what we want to know.'

'Well, I met him.' Simon gave the ghost of a smile. 'And he took me to Paris in his plane. Then to some place down on the riverside.' He gazed round and added quickly: 'But this is it. How did you get here?'

'Never mind that,' De Richleau urged him. 'Have you seen Fleur?'

'Yes. He sent a car for me, and when I reached the plane she was already in it. We had an argument and he swore he'd keep his word unless I went through with this.'

'The ritual to Saturn?' asked De Richleau.

'Um. He said that if I'd do it without making any fuss he'd let me take Fleur out of here immediately afterwards and back to England.'

'He's double-crossed you, as we thought he would,' Rex grunted. 'There's not a soul in this place. He's quit, and taken Fleur with him. Can't you say where he'll be likely to make for?'

'Ner.' Simon shook his head. 'Directly we started on the ritual he put me under. I let him, but of course he would have done that anyway. The last I saw of Fleur she was sound asleep in that armchair and the next thing I knew you were all staring down at me just now.'

'If you completed the ritual, Mocata knows now where the Talisman is,' De Richleau said abruptly.

'Yes,' Simon nodded.

'Then he will have gone to wherever it is—from here.'

'Of course,' Richard cut in. 'That's his main objective. He wouldn't lose a second.'

'Then Simon must know the place to which he's gone.'

'How's that? I don't quite get you.' Rex looked at the Duke with a puzzled frown.

'In his subconscious, I mean. Our only hope now is for me to put Simon under again and make him repeat every word that he said when the ritual was performed. That will give us the hiding-place of the Talisman and the place to which I'll stake my life Mocata is heading at the present moment. Are you game, Simon?'

'Yes, of course. You know that I would do anything to help.'

'Right.' The Duke took him by the arm and pushed him gently. 'Sit down in that chair to the right of the altar and we'll go ahead.'

Simon settled himself and leaned back on the comfortable cushions, his white robe with its esoteric designs in black and red settling about his feet like the long skirts of a woman. De Richleau made a few swift passes. 'Sleep, Simon,' he commanded.

Simon's eyelids trembled and closed. After a moment he began to breathe deeply and regularly. The Duke went on: 'You are in this temple with Mocata. The ritual to Saturn is about to begin. Repeat the words that he made you speak then.'

Dreamily but easily, Simon spoke the words of power which were utterly meaningless to Richard, Rex and Marie Lou, who stood, a tensely anxious audience, at the bottom of the chancel steps.

'On,' commanded De Richleau. 'Jump a quarter of an hour.' Simon spoke again, more sentences incomprehensible to the uninitiated.

'On again,' commanded De Richleau. 'Another quarter of an hour has passed.'

'—was built above the place where the Talisman is buried,' said Simon. 'It will be found in the earth beneath the right hand stone of the altar.'

'Go back one minute,' ordered De Richleau, and Simon spoke once more.

'—Attila's death the Greek secreted it and took it to his own country. In the city of Yanina, upon his return, he became possessed of devils and was handed over to the brethren at the monastery above Metsovo, which stands in the mountains twenty miles east of the city. They failed to cast out the spirits which inhabited his body and so imprisoned him in an underground cell and there, before he died, he buried the Talisman. Seven years later the dungeons were demolished and the crypt built in their place on the same site, with the great church above it. The Talisman remained undisturbed in its original hiding place. Its power gradually pervaded the whole of the Brotherhood, filling it with lechery and greed, so that it disintegrated and was finally disbanded before the invasion by the Turks. The chapel to the left in the crypt was built above the place where the Talisman is buried.'

'Stop,' ordered the Duke. 'Awake now.'

'By Jove, we've got it!' exclaimed Rex. But as he spoke a slight noise behind them made him swing upon his heel.

Four figures stood there in the shadows. The tallest suddenly stepped forward.

Richard's hand leapt to his gun but the tall man snapped: 'Stand still, *mon vieux*, I have you covered,' and they saw that he held an automatic.

The other two strangers came forward. The fourth was Castelnau.

The leader of the party turned to a little old man, who stood beside him wearing an out-of-date bowler hat that came almost down to his ears, then nodded towards the Duke.

'Is that De Richleau, Verrier? You should be able to recognise him, since he was in your time.'

'*Oui monsieur*,' declared the little old man. 'That is the famous Royalist who caused us so much trouble when I was young. I would know his face again anywhere.'

'*Bon!* All this is very interesting.' The tall, hard-eyed man glanced from the obscene pictures on the walls to the magnificent appurtenances of Satanic worship upon the altar, and went on in a silky tone: 'I have had an idea for some time that a secret society has been practising devil worship in Paris and is responsible for certain disappearances, but I could never lay my hands on them before. Now I have got five of you red-handed.'

He paused for a moment then gave a jerky little bow. '*Madame et Messieurs*, permit me to introduce myself. I am *le Chef de la Sûreté*, Daudet. *Monsieur le Duc*, I arrest you as an enemy of the Government upon the old charge. The rest of you I shall hold with him, as persons suspected of kidnapping and the murder of young children at the practice of infamous rites.'

32

THE GATEWAY OF THE PIT

For ten seconds the friends stood there staring at the detective. Castelnau's presence gave them the key to this grotesque but highly dangerous situation. Mocata must have left the warehouse at almost the same time they had left the banker's apartment. Perhaps their taxis had even passed within a few feet of each other, racing in opposite directions. Tanith had proved right after all when she had told them that she could see Mocata talking with Castelnau that night in his flat.

Mocata had found the banker there, released and revived him, and then listened to his story; realising at once that, since it was possible for De Richleau to hypnotise Castlenau against his will, it would be easy for him to do the same to Simon, learn the hiding place of the Talisman, and follow him to it.

Now that they had discovered the secret Satanic temple which was his headquarters in Paris, the place would be useless to him and only a source of danger. Unmentionable crimes had been committed there, and it would be far too great a risk for him ever to visit it again. Then the brilliant decision that, since the place had to be abandoned, he could at least use it to destroy his enemies.

The whole thing flashed through De Richleau's brain in those few seconds. Mocata's first idea that, if only he could get the police to the warehouse before they left it, he would have involved them in all the crimes associated with such a place and thrown them off his trail for good. Next, the vital question, how to get the police there in time. Would they act at once if Castelnau were sent to tell them a tale about Satanic orgies or only laugh at him? What practical crime could his enemies be charged with? Then the perfect inspiration. If the authorities were told that De Richleau, the Royalist exile, was a party to the business they would not lose a second, but seize on it as a heaven-sent opportunity to throw discredit upon their political opponents. What a magnificent scandal for the Government Press to handle. 'Secret Royalist Society practises Black Art'–'Satanic Temple raided at Asnières'–'Notorious exile arrested while performing Blasphemous Rites.' The Duke could see the scurrilous headlines and hear the newsboy's cry.

And the trick had worked. They had actually been discovered in that house of hell with Simon in the tell-tale robes, seated before the altar, while he performed what must certainly have appeared to the police as some evil ceremony and the other three had stood there, forming a small congregation.

How could they possibly hope to persuade the tall, suspicious-eyed *Monsieur le Chef de la Sûreté* Daudet of their innocence, much less get him to agree to their immediate release? Yet, as they stood there, Mocata was on his way to the place where he kept his special plane, if not already aboard it. Night flying would have no terrors for him who, if he wished, could invoke the elements to his aid. Fleur would be with him and he meant to murder her as certainly as they stood there. His determination to secure the return of Tanith made the sacrifice of a baptised child imperative, and before another twenty-four hours had gone he would be in possession of the Talisman of Set, bringing upon the world God alone knew what horrors of war, famine, disablement and death.

De Richleau knew that there was only one thing for it—even if he was shot down there and then—he sprang like a panther at the *Chef de la Sûreté's* throat.

The detective fired from his hip. Flame stabbed the semi-darkness of the vault. The crash hit their eardrums like the explosion of a slab of gelignite. The bullet seared through the Duke's left arm, but his attack hurled the Police-Chief to the ground.

Simon and Marie Lou flung themselves simultaneously upon the old detective Verrier. The thoughts which had passed through De Richleau's mind in those breathless seconds had also raced through hers. If they submitted to arrest their last hope would be gone of saving her beloved Fleur.

Richard had no chance to pull his gun. The third man had grabbed him round the body but Rex rapped the policeman on the back of the head with his iron bar. The man grunted and toppled on to the chancel steps.

Rex leapt over the body straight for Castelnau. Quick as a flash, the banker turned and ran, his long legs flicking past each other as he bounded down the empty aisle, but Rex's legs were even longer. He caught the Satanist at the entrance of the passage and grabbed him by the back of the neck. Castelnau tore himself away and stood panting for a second, half crouching with bared teeth, his back against the wall. Then for the second time that night Rex's leg-of-mutton fist took him on the chin and he slid to the ground like a pole-axed ox.

De Richleau, his wounded arm hanging limp and useless, writhed beneath the *Chef de la Sûreté* who had one hand on his throat and with the other was groping for his fallen gun.

His fingers closed upon it. He jerked it up and fired at Richard, who was dashing to De Richleau's help. The shot went thudding into the belly of the Satanic Goat above the altar. Next second the heavy *prie-dieu* which Richard had swung aloft came crashing down upon the Police-Chief's head.

Rex only paused to see that the banker was completely knocked out, then rushed back to the struggling mass of bodies below the altar steps.

Simon and Marie Lou had managed the little man between them. Almost insane with worry for her child, her thumb nails were dug into his neck and, while he screeched with pain, Simon was lashing his hands behind his back.

Richard was pulling the Duke out from beneath the unconscious *Chef de la Sûreté's* body. Rex lent a ready hand and then, panting with their exertions, they surveyed the scene of their short but desperate encounter.

'Holy smoke! That's done me a whole heap of good,' Rex grinned at Richard. 'I'm almost feeling like my normal self again.'

'The odds were with us but we owe our escape to Greyeyes' pluck.' Richard looked swiftly at the Duke. 'Let's see that wound, old chap. I hope to God the bullet didn't smash the bone.'

'I don't think so—grazed it though, and the muscle's badly torn.' De Richleau closed his eyes and his face twisted at a stab of pain as they lifted his arm to cut the coat sleeve away.

'I know what you must be feeling,' Simon sympathised. 'I'll never forget the pain of the wound I got that night we discovered the secret of the Forbidden Territory.'

'Don't fuss round me,' muttered the Duke, 'but get that damned priest's robe off. If these people don't return to the Sûreté more police will come to look for them. We've got to get out of here—quick.'

In frantic haste Marie Lou bandaged the wound while Richard made a sling and the other two wrenched off the clothes of the detective that Rex had knocked out. Simon scrambled into them and, as he snatched up the man's overcoat, the others were already hurrying towards the entrance to the passage at the far end of the temple.

Richard rushed Marie Lou along the dark corridor and they tumbled up the flight of steps. Everything seemed to fade again after those awful moments when they had been so near arrest. She felt the cold air of the wharf-side damp upon her cheeks—they were running down the narrow passage between the high brick walls—back in the gloomy square where the old woman still sat crouched upon the steps near the squalid café. Rex had taken her other arm and, her feet treading the pavements automatically, they were hastening through endless, sordid, fog-bound streets. They crossed the bridge over the Seine and, at last, under the railway arches at Courcelles, found a taxi. When next she was conscious of her surroundings they were in a little room at the airport and the four men were poring over maps. Snatches of the conversation came to her vaguely.

'Twelve hundred miles—more. Northern Greece. You cannot cross the Alps—make for Vienna, then south to Trieste—no, Vienna-Agram-Fiume. From Agram we can fly down the valley of the River Save; otherwise we should have to cross the Dolomites. That's right! Then follow the coastline of the Adriatic for five hundred miles south-east to Corfu. Yanina is about fifty miles inland from there. You can follow the course of the river Kalamans through the mountains—Shall we be able to land at Yanina, though—yes, look, the map shows that it's on a big lake. The circuit of the shore must be fifteen miles at least. It can't all be precipitous—certain to be sandy stretches along it somewhere—how far do you make it to Metsovo from there?—twenty miles as the crow flies. That means thirty at least in such a mountainous district. The monastery is a few miles beyond, on Mount Peristeri—pretty useful mountain—look. The map gives it as seven thousand five hundred feet—we must abandon the plane at Yanina. If we're lucky we'll get a car as far as Metsova—God knows what the roads will be like—after that we'll have to use horses in any case. How soon do you reckon you can make it, Richard?'

'Fourteen hundred miles. We should be in Vienna by midday. Fiume, say, half-past two. I ought to make Yanina by eight o'clock with Rex taking turn and turn about flying the plane. After that it depends on what fresh transport we can get.'

Next, they were in the plane again—lifting out of fog-bound Paris to a marvellous dawn, which gilded the edges of the clouds and streaked the sky with rose and purple and lemon.

Richard was flying the plane in a kind of trance, yet never for a moment losing sight of important landmarks or the dials by which he adjusted his controls. The others slept.

When Marie Lou roused, the plane was at rest near a long line of hangars dimly glimpsed through another ghostly fog. Someone said 'Stuttgart' and then she saw Simon standing on the ground below her, conversing in German with an airport official.

'A big, grey, private plane,' he was saying urgently. 'The pilot is a short, square-shouldered fellow; the passengers a big, fat, baldheaded man and a little girl.'

Marie Lou leaned forward eagerly but she did not catch the airport man's reply. A moment later Simon was climbing into the plane and saying to the Duke:

'He must be taking the same route, but he's an hour and a half ahead of us. I expect he had his own car in Paris. That would have saved him time while we were hunting for that wretched taxi.'

Rex had taken over the controls and they were in the air once more. Richard was sitting next to Marie Lou, sound asleep. For an endless time they seemed to soar through a cloudless sky of pale, translucent blue. She, too, must have dropped off again, for she was not conscious of their landing at Vienna, only when she woke in the early afternoon that the pilots had changed over and Richard was back at the controls.

Yet, in some curious way, although she had not actually been aware of their landing, fragments of their conversation must have penetrated her sleep at the time. She knew that there had also been fog at Vienna, and that Mocata had left the airport there only an hour before them, so in the journey from Paris they had managed to gain half an hour on him.

The engine droned on, its deep note soothing their frayed nerves. Richard hardly knew that he was flying, although he used all the skill at his command. It seemed as though some other force was driving the aeroplane on and that he was standing outside it as a spectator. All his faculties were numbed and his anxiety for Fleur deadened by an intense absorption with the question of speed—speed—speed.

At Fiume there was no trace of fog. Glorious sunshine, warm and lifegiving, flooded the aerodrome, making the hangars shimmer in the distance. The Duke crawled out from the couch of rugs and cushions that had been made up in the back of the cabin to accommodate a fifth passenger, and chosen by him as more comfortable for his wounded arm. He questioned the landing-ground officials in fluent Italian, but without success.

'From Vienna Mocata must have taken another route,' he told Richard as he climbed back. 'Perhaps a short cut over the Dinarie Alps or by way of Sarajevo. If so he will have more than made up his half hour lead again. I feared as much when I saw that there was no fog here. I can't explain it but I have an idea that he is able to surround us with it, yet only when we follow him to places where he has been quite recently himself.'

Rex took over for the long lap down the Dalmatian coast above the countless islands that fringe the Yugoslavian mainland and lay beneath them in the sparkling Adriatic Sea.

They slept again, all except Rex who, a crack pilot, was now handling the machine with superb skill.

As he flew the plane half his thoughts were centred about Tanith. He could see her there, lying cold and dead, in the library a thousand miles away at Cardinals Folly. That dream of happiness had been so brief. Never again would he see the sudden smile break out like sunshine rising over mountains on that beautiful, calm face. Never again hear the husky, melodious voice whispering terms of endearment. Never again—never again! But he was on the trail of her murderer and if he died for it he meant to make that inhuman monster pay.

The Adriatic merged into the Ionian Sea. The endless rugged coastline rushed past below them on their left; its mountains rising steeply to the interior of Albania, and its vales breaking them here and there to run down to little white fishing villages on the seashore. Villages that in Roman times had been great centres of population through the constant passage of merchandise, soldiers, scholars, travellers between Brindisi, upon the heel of Italy, and the Peninsula of Greece.

Then they were over Corfu. Banking steeply, he headed for the mainland and picked up the northern mouth of the River Kalamas. The deep blue of the sea flecked by its tiny white crests vanished behind them. Twisting and turning, the plane drove upwards above desolate valleys where the river trickled, a streak of silver in the evening light. The sun sank behind them into the distant sea. They were heading for the huge chain of mountains, which forms the backbone of Greece.

A mist was rising which obscured the long, empty patches and rare cultivated fields below. The light faded, its last rays lit a great distant snow-capped crest which crowned the water-shed.

A lake lay below them, placid and calm in the evening light but glimpsed only through the banks of fog. At its south-western end the white buildings of a town were vaguely discernible now and then as Rex circled slowly, searching for a landing-place. Suddenly, through a gap in the billowing whitish-grey, his eye caught a big plane standing in a level field.

'That's Mocata's machine,' yelled Simon who was in the cockpit beside him.

Rex banked again and, coming into the wind, brought them to earth within fifty yards of it. The others roused and scrambled out.

The mist which Rex had first perceived a quarter of an hour before, from his great altitude, now hemmed them in on every side.

A man came forward from a low, solitary hangar as the plane landed. De Richleau saw him, a vague figure, half obscured by the tenuous veils of mist; went over to him and said, when he rejoined them:

'That fellow is a French mechanic. He tells me Mocata landed only half an hour ago. He came in from Monastir but had trouble in the mountains, which delayed him; nobody but a maniac or a superman would try and get through that way at all. This fellow thinks that he can get us a car; he runs the airport, such as it is, and we're darned lucky to find any facilities here at all.'

Richard had just woken from a long sleep. Before he knew what was happening he found that they were all packed into an ancient open Ford with a tattered hood. Simon was on one side of him and Marie Lou on the other. Rex squatted on the floor of the car at their feet and De Richleau was in front beside the driver.

They could not see more than twenty yards ahead. The lamps made little impression upon the gloom before them. The road was a sandy track, fringed at the sides with coarse grass and boulders. No houses, cottages or white-walled gardens broke the monotony of the way as they rattled and bumped, mounting continuously up long, curved gradients.

De Richleau peered ahead into the murk. Occasional rifts gave him glimpses of the rocky mountains round which they climbed or, upon the other side, a cliff edge falling sheer to a mist-filled valley.

He, too, could only remember episodes from that wild journey; an unendurable weariness had pressed upon him once they had boarded the plane and left Paris. Even *his* powers of endurance had failed at last and he had slept during the greater part of their fourteen hundred mile flight. He was still sleepy now and only half awake as that unknown demon driver, who had hurried them with few words into the rickety Ford, crouched over his wheel and pressed the car, rocketing from hairpin bend to hairpin bend, onwards and upwards.

The last light had been shut out by the lower ranges of mountains behind them as they would their way through the valleys to the greater peaks which, unseen in the mist and darkness, they knew lay towering to the skies towards the east. Deep ruts in the track, where mountain torrents cut it in the winter cascading downwards to the lower levels, made the way hideously uneven. The car jolted and bounded, skidding violently from time to time, loose shale and pebbles rocketing from its back tyres as it took the dangerous bends.

In the back Richard, Marie Lou and Simon lurched, swayed, and bumped each other as they crouched in silent misery, their teeth chattering with the cold of the chill night that was now about them in those lofty regions. . . .

They were in a room, a strange, low-ceilinged, eastern room, with a great, heavy, wooden door, under which they could see the fog wreathing upwards in the light of a solitary oil lamp set upon a rough-hewn table. Bunches of onions and strips of dried meat hung from the low rafters. The earthen floor of the place was cold underfoot. On a deep window recess in a thick wall stood a crude earthenware jug, and a platter with a loaf of coarse bread upon it, which was covered by a bead-edged piece of muslin.

Marie Lou roused to find herself drinking coarse, red wine out of a thick, glass tumbler. She saw Rex sitting on a wooden bench against the wall, staring before him with unseeing eyes at the grimy window. The others stood talking round the lop-sided table. A peasant woman, with a scarf about her head, whose face she could not see, appeared to be arguing with them. Marie Lou had an idea that it was about money, since De Richleau held a small pile of notes in his hand. Then the peasant woman was gone and the others were talking together again. She caught a few words here and there.

'I thought it was a ruin . . . inhabited still . . . they beg us not to go there . . . not of an official order or anything to do with the Greek Church. They look on them as heathens here . . . associates of Mocata's?–No, more like a community of outlaws who have taken refuge there under the disguise of a religious brotherhood . . . Talisman has affected them, perhaps. Forty or fifty of them. The people here shun the place even in the daytime, and at night none of them would venture near it at any price. . . . You managed to get a driver?–Yes, of a kind–What's wrong with him?–I don't know. The woman didn't seem to trust him, but I had great difficulty in understanding her at all—Sort of bad man of the village, eh? . . . Have to trust him if no one else will take us.'

De Richleau passed his hand across his eyes. What was it that they had been talking about? He was so tired, so terribly tired. There had been a peasant woman, with whom he had talked of the ruined monastery up in the mountains. She seemed to be filled with horror of the place and had implored him again and again not to go. He began to wonder how they had conversed. He could make himself understood in most European languages, but he had very little knowledge of modern Greek; but that did not matter, they must get on—get on. . . .

The others were standing round him like a lot of ghosts in the narrow, fog-filled village street. A little hunchback with bright, sharp eyes was peering at him. The fellow wore a dark sombrero, and a black cloak, covering his malformed body, dangled to his feet; the light from the semi-circular window of the inn was just sufficient to illuminate his face. A great, old-fashioned carriage, with two lean, ill-matched horses harnessed to it, stood waiting.

They piled into it. The musty smell of the straw-filled cushions came strongly to their nostrils. The hunchback gave them one curious, cunning look from his bright eyes, and climbed upon the box. The lumbering vehicle began to rock from side to side. The one-storeyed, flat-topped houses in the village disappeared behind them and were swallowed up in the mist.

They forded a swift but shallow river outside the village, then the roadway gave place to a stony track. Ghostlike and silent, walls of rock loomed up on either side. The horses ceased trotting and fell into a steady, laboured walk, hauling the great, unwieldy barouche from bend to bend up the rock-strewn way into the fastness of the mountains.

Simon's teeth were chattering. That damp, clinging greyness seemed to enter into his very bones. He tried to remember what day it was and at what hour they had left Paris. Was it last night or the night before or the night before that? He could not remember and gave it up.

The way seemed interminable. No one spoke. The carriage jolted on, the hunchback crouched upon his seat, the lean horses pulling gallantly. The curve of the road ahead was always hidden from them and no sooner had they passed it than they lost sight of the curve behind.

At last the carriage halted. The driver climbed down off his box and pointed upwards, as they stumbled out on the track. De Richleau was thrusting money into his hand. He and his aged vehicle disappeared in the shadows. Richard looked back to catch a last glimpse of it and it suddenly struck him then how queer it was that the carriage had no lamps.

The rest were pressing on, stumbling and slithering as they followed the way which had now become no more than a footpath leading upwards between the huge rocks.

After a little, the gloom seemed to lighten and they perceived stars above their heads. Then, rounding a rugged promontory, they saw the age-old monastery standing out against the night sky upon the mountain slope above.

It was huge and dark and silent, with steep walls rising on two sides from a precipice. A great dome, like an inverted bowl, rose in its centre, but a portion of it had fallen in and the jagged edges showed plainly against the deep blue of the starlit night beyond.

With renewed courage they staggered on up the steep rise towards the great semi-circular arch of the entrance. The gates stood open wide, rotted and fallen from their hinges. No sign of life greeted their appearance as they passed through the spacious courtyard.

Instinctively they made for the main building above which curved the broken arc of the ruined Byzantine dome. That must be the Church, and the crypt would lie below it.

They crossed the broken pavements of the forecourt, the Duke leaning heavily on Rex's arm. He nodded towards a few faint lights which came from a row of outbuildings. Rex followed his glance in silence and they hurried on. That was evidently the best-preserved portion of the ruin, in which these so-called monks resided. A gross laugh, followed by the sound of smashing glass and then a hoarse voice cursing, came from that direction, confirming their thought.

All the way up from the inn half-formed fears had been troubling De Richleau that they might fall foul of this ill-omened brotherhood. He assumed them to be little less than robbers under a thin disguise, who probably eked out a miserable existence by levying toll in corn and oil and goat's milk upon the neighbouring peasantry, but this great pile upon the slopes of Mount Peristeri was so much more vast than anything that he had imagined. A matter of fifty men might easily be lost among its rambling courts and buildings.

They advanced through another great courtyard, surrounded by ruined colonnades which were visible only by the faint starlight from above. Built by some early Christian saint, when Byzantium was still an Empire and Western Europe labouring through the semi-barbarous night of the Dark Ages, the colossal ruin must once have housed thousands of earnest men, all engaged day by day in pious study, or various active tasks to provide for that great community. Now it was as dead as those African temples which have been overgrown by jungle, only a small fragment of it occupied by a small band of dissolute uncultured rogues.

In wonder and awe they passed up the broad flight of steps, through the vast portico on which the elaborate carvings, worn and disfigured by time, were just discernible, into the body of the Church.

The starlight, filtering dimly through the great rent in the dome a hundred feet above their heads, was barely sufficient to light their way as they scrambled over broken pillars and heaps of debris round the walls until they found a low door. From it, a flight of steps led down into the Stygian blackness of the volts below.

Marie Lou, stumbling along half-bemused between Simon and Richard, found herself wondering what they could be doing in this ancient ruin, then memory flooded back. It was here, below them, that the Talisman of Set was buried. There had been no fog in the courtyard outside so they must have got there before Mocata after all—but where was Fleur? She was going to die—she felt that she *was* dying—but first she *must* find Fleur.

The others had halted and Richard noticed then that De Richleau was carrying an old-fashioned lantern, which he supposed he had borrowed at the inn. The Duke lit the stump of candle that was inside it and led the way down those time-worn stairs. The others, treading instinctively on tiptoe, now followed him into the stale, musty darkness.

At the bottom of the steps they came out into a low, vaulted crypt which, by the faint light of the lantern, seemed to spread interminably under the flagstones of the Church.

De Richleau turned to the east, judging the altar of the crypt to be situated below the one in the Church above, but when he had traversed twenty yards he halted suddenly. A black, solid mass blocked their path in the centre of the vault.

'Of course,' Marie Lou heard him murmur. 'I forgot that this place was built such centuries ago. Altars were placed in the centre of churches then. This must be it.'

'We've beaten him to it, then,' Rex's voice came with a little note of triumph.

'Perhaps he couldn't get anyone to drive him up from Metsovo at this hour of night,' Richard suggested. 'Our man was supposed to be mad, or something, and they said that no one else would go.'

'Those stones are going to take some shifting.' Rex took the lantern and bent to examine the black slabs of the solid, oblong altar.

'Are you certain that this is the right one?' Richard asked. 'My brain seems to be going. I can't remember things properly any more but I thought when we got the information from Simon in his trance he said something about a side-chapel in the crypt.'

No one answered. While his words were still ringing in their ears each one of them suddenly felt that he was being overlooked from behind.

Rex dropped the lantern, De Richleau swung round, Marie Lou gave a faint cry. A dull light had appeared only ten paces in their rear. Leading to it they saw a short flight of steps. Beyond, a chapel with a smaller altar, from which the right-hand stone had been wrenched. And there, standing before it, was Mocata.

With a bellow of fury, Rex started forward, but the Satanist suddenly raised his left hand. In it he held a small black cigar-shaped thing, which was slightly curved. About it there was a phosphorescent glow, so that, despite the semi-darkness, the very blackness of the thing itself stood out clear and sharp against its surrounding aura of misty light. The rays from it seemed to impinge upon their bodies, instantly checking their advance. They found themselves transfixed–brought to a standstill in a running group–half-way between the central altar and the chapel steps.

Without uttering a word, Mocata came down the steps and slowly walked round them, carrying the thing which they now guessed to be the Talisman aloft in his left hand. A glowing phosphorescent circle appeared on the damp stone flags in his tracks and, as he completed the circuit, they felt their limbs relax.

Again they rushed at him, but were brought up with a jerk. It was impossible to break out of that magic circle in which he had confined them.

With slow steps, the Satanist returned to the chapel and proceeded to light a row of black candles upon the broken altar there. Then with a little gasp of unutterable fear, Marie Lou saw that Fleur was crouching in a dark corner near the upturned earth from which the Talisman had been recovered.

'Fleur–darling!' she cried imploringly, stretching out her arms, but the child did not seem to hear. With round eyes she knelt there near the altar, staring out towards the crypt, but apparently seeing nothing.

Mocata lit some incense in a censer and swung it rhythmically before the broken altar, murmuring strange invocations.

He moved so smoothly and silently that he might have been a phantom but for the lisping intonation of his low musical voice. Then Fleur began to cry, and the sobbing of the child had an unmistakable reality which tore at the very fibre of their hearts.

Again and again they tried to break out of the circle, but at last, forced to give up their frantic attempts, they crouched together straining against the invisible barrier, watching with fear-distended eyes as a gradual materialisation began to form in the clouds of incense above the altar stone.

At first it seemed to be the face of Mocata's black familiar that Rex had seen in Simon's house, but it changed and lengthened. A pointed beard appeared on the chin and four great curved horns sprouted from the head. Soon it became definite, clear and solid. That monstrous, shaggy beast that had held court on Salisbury Plain, the veritable Goat of Mendes, glared at them with its red, baleful, slanting eyes, and belched fœtid, deathly breaths from its cavernous nostrils.

Mocata raised the Talisman and set it upon the forehead of the Beast, laying it lengthwise upon the flat, bald, bony skull, where it blazed like some magnificent jewel which had a strange black centre. Then he stooped, seized the child and, tearing off her clothes, flung her naked body full length upon the altar beneath the raised fore-hooves of the Goat.

Sick with apprehension and frantic with distress, the prisoners in the circle heard the sorcerer begin to intone the terrible lines of the Black Mass.

Horrified but powerless, they watched the swinging of the censer, the chanting of the blasphemous prayers, and the blessing of the dagger by the Goat, knowing that at the conclusion of the awful ceremony, the perverted maniac playing the part of the devil's priest would rip the child open from throat to groin while offering her soul to Hell.

Half crazy with fear, they saw Mocata pick up the knife and raise his arm above the little body, about to strike.

33

DEATH OF A MAN UNKNOWN FROM NATURAL CAUSES

Rex stood with the sweat pouring down his face. The muscles of his arms jerked convulsively. His whole will was concentrated in an effort to fling himself forward, up the steps; yet, except for the tremors which ran through his body, the invisible power held him motionless in its grip.

De Richleau prayed. Silent but unceasing, his soundless words vibrated on the ether. He knew the futility of any attempt at physical intervention, and doubted now if his supplications could avail when pitted against such a terrible manifestation of evil as the Goat of Mendes.

Richard crouched near him, his face white and bloodless, his eyes staring. His arms were stretched out, as though to snatch Fleur away or in an appeal for mercy, but he could not move them.

Marie Lou had one hand resting on his shoulder. She was past fear for herself, past all thought of that terrible end which might come to them in a few moments, past even the horror of losing Richard should they all be blotted out in some awful final darkness.

She did not pray or strive to dash towards her child. The pulsing of her heart seemed to be temporarily suspended. Her brain was working with that strange clarity which only comes upon those rare occasions when danger appears to be so overwhelming that there is no possible escape. Into her mind there came a clear-cut picture of herself as she had been in her dream, holding what De Richleau said was the great Red Book of Appin. Her fingers could feel the very cover again with its soft hairy skin.

Simon dropped to his knees between the Duke and Rex. He made an effort to cast himself forward but rocked very slightly from side to side, stricken with an agony of misery and remorse. It was his folly which had led his friends into this terrible pass and now he did the only thing he could to make atonement. His brain no longer clouded, but with full knowledge of the enormity of the thing, he offered himself silently to the Power of Darkness if Fleur might be spared.

Mocata paused for a moment, the knife still poised above the body of the child, to turn and look at him. The thought vibration had been so strong that he had caught it, but he had already drawn all that he needed out of Simon. Slowly his pale lips crumpled in a cruel smile. He shook his head in rejection of the offer and raised the knife again.

The Duke's hand jerked up in a frantic effort to stay the blow by the sign of the cross, but it was struck down to his side by one of the rays from the Talisman, just as though some powerful physical force had hit it.

Richard's jaws opened as though about to shout but no sound issued from them.

With a supreme effort Rex lowered his head to charge, but the invisible weight of twenty men seemed to force back his shoulders.

Before the mental eyes of Marie Lou the Red Book of Appin lay open. Again she saw the stained vellum page and the faded writing in strange characters upon it. And once more as in her dream she could understand the one sentence: '*They only who Love without Desire shall have power granted to them in the Darkest Hour.*'

Then her lips opened. With no knowledge of its meaning, and a certainty that she had never seen it written or heard it pronounced before, she spoke a strange word—having five syllables.

The effect was instantaneous. The whole chamber rocked as though shaken by an earthquake. The walls receded, the floor began to spin. The crypt gyrated with such terrifying speed that the occupants of the circle clutched frantically at each other to save themselves from falling. The altar candles swayed and danced before their distended eyes. The Talisman of Set was swept from between the horns of the monstrous Goat, and bouncing down the steps of the chapel, came to rest on the stone flags at De Richleau's feet.

Mocata staggered back. The Goat reared up on its hind legs above him. A terrible neighing sound came from its nostrils and the slanting eyes swivelled in their sockets; their baleful light flashing round the chamber. The Beast seemed to grow and expand until it was towering above them all as they crouched, petrified with fear. The stench of its fœtid breath poured from between the bared teeth until they were retching with nausea. Mocata's knife clattered upon the stones as he raised his arms in frantic terror to defend himself. The awful thing which he had called up out of the Pit gave a final screaming neigh and struck with one of its great fore-hooves. He was thrown with frightful force to the floor, where he lay sprawled head downmost on the chapel steps.

There was a thunderous crash as though the heavens were opening. The crypt ceased to rock and spin. The Satanic figure dissolved in upon itself. For a fraction of time the watchers in the circle saw the black human face of the Malagasy, distorted with pain and rage, where that of the Goat had been before. Then that too disappeared behind a veil of curling smoke.

The black candles on the altar flickered and went out. The chamber remained lit only by the phosphorescent glow from the Talisman. De Richleau had snatched it from the floor and held it in his open hand. By its faint light they saw Fleur sit up. She gave a little wail and slid from the low altar stone to the ground; then she stood gaping towards her mother, yet her eyes were round and sightless like those of one who walks in her sleep.

Suddenly an utter silence beyond human understanding descended like a cloak and closed in from the shadows that were all about them.

Almost imperceptibly a faint unearthly music, coming from some immense distance, reached their ears. At first it sounded like the splashing of spring water in a rock-bound cave, but gradually it grew in volume, and swelled into a strange chant rendered by boys' voices of unimaginable purity. All fear had gone from them as, one by one, they fell upon their knees and listened entranced to the wonder and the beauty of that litany of praise. Yet all their eyes were riveted on Fleur.

The child walked very slowly forward but, as she advanced, some extraordinary change was taking place about her. The little body, naked a moment before, became clothed in a golden mist. Her shoulders broadened and she grew in height. Her features became partially obscured, then they lost their infant roundness and took on the bony structure of an adult. The diaphanous cloud of light gradually materialised into the graceful folds of a long, yellow, silken robe. The dark curls on the head disappeared leaving a high, beautifully proportioned skull.

As the chant ceased on a great note of exultation all semblance to the child had vanished. In her place a full-grown man stood before them. From his dress he had the appearance of a Tibetan Lama, but his æsthetic face was as much Aryan as Mongolian, blending the highest characteristics of the two; and just as it seemed that he had passed the barriers of race, so he also appeared to have cast off the shackles of worldly time. His countenance showed all the health and vigour of a man in the great years when he has come to full physical development, and yet it had the added beauty which is only seen in that of a frail, scholarly divine who has devoted a whole lifetime to the search for wisdom. The grave eyes which were bent upon them held Strength, Knowledge, and Power, together with an infinite tenderness and angelic compassion unknown to mortal man.

The apparition did not speak by word of mouth. Yet each one of the kneeling group heard the low, silver, bell-like voice with perfect clearness.

'I am a Lord of Light nearing perfection after many lives. It is wrong that you should draw me from my meditations in the Hidden Valley—yet I pardon you because your need was great. One here has imperilled the flame of Life by seeking to use hidden mysteries for an evil purpose; another also, who lies beyond the waters, has been stricken in her earthly body for that same reason. The love you bear each other has been a barrier and protection, yet would it have availed you nothing had it not been for She who is the Mother. The Preserver harkens ever to the prayer which goes forth innocent of all self-desire and so, for a moment, I am permitted to appear to you through the medium of this child whose thoughts know no impurity. The Adversary has been driven back to the dark Halls of Shaitan and shall trouble you no more. Live out the days of your allotted span. Peace be upon you and about you. Sleep and Return.'

For a moment it seemed that they had been ripped right out of the crypt and were looking down into it. The circle had become a flaming sun. Their bodies were dark shadows grouped in its centre. The peace and silence of death surged over them in great saturating waves. They were above the monastery. The great ruin became a black speck in the distance. Then everything faded.

Time ceased, and it seemed that for a thousand thousand years they floated, atoms of radiant matter in an immense immeasurable void–circling, for ever circling in the soundless stratosphere–beings shut off from every feeling and sensation, as though travelling with effortless impulse five hundred fathoms deep, below the current levels of some uncharted sea.

Then, after a passage of eons in human time they saw Cardinals Folly again infinitely far beneath them, their bodies lying in the pentacle–and that darkened room. In an utter eerie silence the dust of centuries was falling . . . falling. Softly, impalpably, like infinitely tiny particles of swansdown it seemed to cover them, the room, and all that was in it, with a fine grey powder.

De Richleau raised his head. It seemed to him that he had been on a long journey and then slept for many days. He passed his hand across his eyes and saw the familiar bookshelves in the semi-darkened library. The bulbs above the cornice flickered and the lights came full on.

He saw that Simon's eyes were free from that terrible maniacal glare, but that he still lay bound in the centre of the pentacle.

As he bent forward and hastily began to untie Simon's hands Marie Lou came round out of her faint. Richard was fondling her and murmuring. 'We're safe, darling–safe.'

'She–she's not dead–is she?' It was Rex's voice, and turning they saw him. Tall–haggard–distraught–a dark silhouette against the early morning light which filtered in through the french-windows–bearing Tanith's body in his arms.

Marie Lou sprang up with a little wailing cry. With Richard behind her she raced across the room and through the door in the wall which concealed the staircase to the nursery.

The Duke hurried over to Rex. Simon kicked his feet free and stood up, exclaiming: 'I've had a most extraordinary dream.'

'About all of us going to Paris?' asked De Richleau, as the three of them lowered Tanith's body to the floor, 'and then on to a ruined monastery in northern Greece?'

'That's it–but how–did you know?'

'Because I had the same myself–*if it was a dream!*'

An hysterical laugh came from the stairway and next moment Marie Lou was beside them, great tears streaming down her face, but Fleur clutched safely in her arms.

The child, freshly woken from her sleep, gazed at them with wide, blue eyes, and then she said: 'Fleur wants to go to Simon.'

The Duke was examining Tanith. Simon rose from beside him. His eyes held all the love that surged in the great heart which beat between his narrow shoulders. He covered his short-sighted eyes with his hands for a second then backed away. 'No, Fleur, darling–I've been–I'm still ill you know.'

'Nonsense–that's all over,' Richard cried quickly, 'go on–for God's sake take her–Marie Lou's going to faint.'

'Oh, Richard! Richard!' As Simon grabbed the child, Marie Lou swayed towards her husband, and leaning on him drew her fingers softly down his face. 'I will be all right in a moment–but it was a dream–wasn't it?'

'She's alive!' exclaimed the Duke suddenly, his hand pressed below Tanith's heart. 'Quick, Rex–some brandy.'

'Of course, dearest,' Richard was comforting Marie Lou. 'We've never been out of this room–look, except Rex, we are still in pyjamas.'

'Why, yes–I thought— Oh, but look at this poor girl.' She slipped from his arms and knelt beside Tanith.

Rex came crashing back with a decanter and a glass. De Richleau snatched the brandy from him. Marie Lou pillowed Tanith's head upon her knees and Richard held her chin. Between them they succeeded in getting a little of the spirit down her throat; a spasm crossed her face and then her eyes opened.

'Thank God!' breathed Rex. 'Thank God.'

She smiled and whispered his name, as the natural colour flooded back into her face.

'Never–never have I had such a terrible nightmare!' exclaimed Marie Lou. 'We were in a crypt–and that awful man was there. He . . .'

'So you dreamed it too!' Simon interrupted. 'About you finding me at that warehouse in Asnières and the Paris police?'

'That's it,' said Richard. 'It's amazing that we should all have dreamed the same thing but there's no other explanation for it. None of us can possibly have left this house since we settled down in the pentacle— Yes, last night!'

'Then I've certainly been dreaming too.' Rex lifted his eyes for a moment from Tanith's face. 'It must have started with me when I fell asleep at the inn–or earlier, for I'd have sworn De Richleau and I were out all night before careering around half of England to stop some devilry.'

'We were,' said the Duke slowly. 'Tanith's presence here proves that, but she was never dead except in our dream, and that started when you arrived here with her in your arms. The Satanists at Simon's house, our visit there afterwards, and the Sabbat were all facts. It was only last night, while our bodies slept, that our subconscious selves were drawn out of them to continue the struggle with Mocata on another plane.'

'Mocata!' Simon echoed. 'But–but if we've been dreaming he is still alive.'

'No, he is dead.' The quiet, sure statement came from Tanith as she sat up, and taking Rex's hand scrambled to her feet.

'How is it you're so certain?' he asked huskily.

'I can see him. He is not far from here–lying head downwards on some steps.'

'That's how we saw him in the dream,' said Richard, but she shook her head.

'No, I had no dream. I remember nothing after Mocata entered my room at the inn and forced me to sleep–but you will find him–somewhere quite near the house–out there.'

'The age-old law,' De Richleau murmured. 'A life for a life and a soul for a soul. Yes, since you have been restored to us I am quite certain that he will have paid the penalty.'

Simon nodded. 'Then we're really free of this nightmare at last?'

'Yes. Dream or no dream, the Lord of Light who appeared to us drove back the Power of Darkness, and promised that we should all live unmolested by it to the end of our allotted span. Come, Richard,' the Duke took his host's arm, 'let us find our coats and take a look round the garden–then we shall have done with this horrible business.'

As they moved away Tanith smiled up at Rex. 'Did you really mean what you said last night?'

'Did I mean it!' he cried, seizing both her hands. 'Just you let me show you how!'

'Simon,' said Marie Lou pointedly, 'that child will catch her death of cold in nothing but her nightie–do take her back to the nursery while I get the servants to hurry forward breakfast.' And the old familiar happy smile parted his wide mouth as Fleur took a flying leap into his arms.

Tanith's face grew a little wistful as Rex drew her to him. 'My darling,' she hesitated, 'you know that it will be only for a little time, about eight months–no more.'

'Nonsense!' he laughed. 'You were certainly dead to all of us last night, so your prophecy's been fulfilled and the evil lifted–we're both going to live together for a hundred years.'

She hid her face against his shoulder, not quite believing yet, but a new hope dawning in her heart, from his certainty that she had passed through the Valley of the Shadow and come out again upon the other side. Her happiness, and his, demanded that she accept his view and act henceforth as though the danger to her life was past.

'Then if you want them, my days are yours,' she murmured, 'whatever their number may be.'

There was no trace of fog and a fair, true dawn was breaking when, outside the library windows, De Richleau and Richard found Mocata's body. It lay on the stone steps which led up to the terrace, sprawling head downwards, in the early light of the May morning.

'The coroner will find no difficulty in bringing in a verdict,' the Duke observed after one glance at the face. 'They'll say it is heart, of course. It is best not to touch the body, presently we will telephone the police. None of us need say we have ever seen him before if you tell Malin to keep quiet about his visit yesterday afternoon. You may be certain that his friends will not come forward to mention his acquaintance with Simon or the girl.'

Richard nodded. 'Yes. "Death of a Man Unknown, from Natural Causes," will be the only epilogue to this strange story.'

'Not quite, but this must be between us, Richard. I prefer that the others should not know. Take me to you boiler-house.'

'The boiler-house–whatever for?'

'I'll tell you in a minute.'

'All right!' With a puzzled look Richard led the Duke along the terrace, round by the kitchen quarters and into a small building where a furnace gave a subdued roar.

De Richleau lifted the latch and the door swung back, disclosing the glowing coke within. Then he extended his right fist and slowly opened it.

'Good God!' exclaimed Richard. 'However did you come by that?'

In De Richleau's palm lay a shrunken, mummified phallus, measuring no more than the length of a little finger, hard, dry, and almost black with age. It was the Talisman of Set, just as they had seen it in their recent dream adorning the brow of the monstrous Goat.

'I found myself clutching it when I awoke,' he answered softly.

'But—but that thing must have come from somewhere!'

'Perhaps it is a concrete symbol of the evil that we have fought, which has been given over into our hands for destruction.'

As the Duke finished speaking he cast the Talisman into the glowing furnace where they watched it until it was utterly consumed.

'If we were only dreaming how can you possibly explain it?' Richard insisted.

'I cannot.' De Richleau shrugged a little wearily. 'Even the greatest seekers after Truth have done little more than lift the corner of the veil which hides the vast Unknown, but it is my belief that during the period of our dream journey we have been living in what the moderns call the fourth dimension—divorced from time.'

The Haunting
of Toby Jugg

THE HAUNTING OF TOBY JUGG

I dedicate this book to my friends
past and present of
The Royal Air Force

Monday, 4th May

I feel that the time has come when I must endeavour to face facts. These past few nights I have been frightened—scared stiff—really terrified. Ten months ago I was a sane, strong, healthy man; now I am weak, irresolute and, I fear, on the verge of going mad.

Perhaps I am only imagining things. But if I set down all that is happening here—or rather, that which I believe to be happening—when I look at what I have written again next day, I shall at least know that I haven't dreamed the whole horrible business overnight.

That is why I have decided to start keeping a journal. In it I intend not only to give an account of these strange experiences of which I have recently been the victim, but also make an attempt to rationalize them. If I can somehow argue matters out with myself until I reach a logical conclusion as to what lies at the bottom of my fears, I shall, perhaps, be able to face them better and save my sanity.

I used to enjoy writing essays, and the work involved in setting down my thoughts coherently should help a lot to keep my mind free from aimless, agonizing dread of the night to come. I shall not write in the evenings, though, as the accursed shadows in this big room are apt to make me jumpy near sundown, and might lead me to exaggerate the facts. I'll work on it in the mornings, or afternoons, when the good, clean daylight, streaming in through the broad windows, makes me feel more like the man I used to be.

It is not so long ago since my friends nicknamed me 'The Viking', partly, of course, on account of my appearance, but also because I was credited with having a kind of 'devil-may-care' courage with which everyone is not blessed. I wonder what they would think if they had seen me as I was last night—a gibbering nervous wreck—frantic with fear of some ghastly thing that was hidden from me only by the blackout.

Still, fear of physical danger and of this sort of thing are entirely different matters. Some of my brother officers who were hard put to it to prevent themselves showing how badly they had the jitters would probably laugh at me now; while others braver than myself, and there were plenty of them, might be every bit as scared as I am. It would depend on their individual degree of susceptibility to the supernatural.

If anyone had suggested to me a few months ago that I was a psychic type myself, I should certainly have denied it. But I must admit to being so now, as the only alternative is that I really am going nutty. Rightly or wrongly I believe that I am being haunted by some form of devil—and I don't mean the sort that comes from knocking back too much Scotch. I mean one of those forces of Evil that are said to have been let loose in the world after Satan and his host were defeated by the Archangel Michael and cast down out of Heaven.

That sounds old-fashioned stuff, I know; but either something of that kind did actually happen when the world was young, or it didn't. There is no middle way about it. And, if it did, there has been no revelation since to the effect that these age-long enemies of man have been withdrawn to another sphere, or that their infernal Master has ceased from his efforts to corrupt and destroy the seed of Adam.

Satan has become rather a figure of fun these days, or, at worst, a bogy-man with whom wicked old women sometimes frighten children; but, all the same, he still remains our ultimate expression for the most concentrated form of Evil, and everything else that is evil must in a greater or lesser degree partake of his attributes. Therefore, in endeavouring to get to grips with my own problem, it may be worth speculating on him a little, and on the reasons for the apparent decline in his powers.

In this year of Grace—save the mark; I should have said this year of world-wide death and destruction, 1942—how many people, I wonder, believe in the Devil? I mean as a definite personality with hoofs and horns and a barbed tail, waving a pitchfork and breathing brimstone over everything? I suppose a few very religious rather backward people do; lonely, timid spinsters living in remote country districts, particularly in Scotland and down here in Wales, and the older generation of peasants in Central and Southern Europe.

I can't myself. I think that all those accounts of monks and other characters coming face to face with the Devil in the Middle Ages were, as old Gibbon put it: 'The product of an empty stomach on an empty brain'; or else deliberate lying. In those days religion played such a large part in everybody's life that people thought of Heaven and Hell as only just round the corner; so the easiest way to obtain a little cheap notoriety was to come down one morning with your shirt on inside-out, and declare to a wide-eyed audience that the Devil had visited you in the middle of the night with some tempting proposition.

On the other hand one can never be certain—absolutely certain—that all such records are the ravings of unbalanced minds or pure invention. After all, why do we disbelieve them? Mainly, I think, because it seems improbable that such a V.I.P. as the Prince of Evil could be bothered to torment, or accept the homage of, quite ordinary people.

But his demons were said to be legion, and it may be that they sometimes assumed their master's form when appearing to the Godly, or attending a witches' sabbath as the guest of honour. That may be the explanation; for, while it must remain an open question whether any human being has ever seen the Devil, it seems impossible to doubt the existence of demons. Cases of demonic possession still occur from time to time, as any Roman Catholic priest will testify; and during the Middle Ages such happenings were regarded as almost everyday affairs.

The reason for their much greater frequency in the past is not far to seek. Life was so very different then, and everyone was so much more concerned with the things of the spirit. Whether they were in a state of grace or not was of vital importance to people, because they were daily reminded at morning prayers and evening Bible readings—as well as during the whole of every Sunday—that, should they meet with a sudden death, they would get no second chance, but have to give an account of their acts to date when hauled naked and trembling before their Creator.

Such constant preoccupation with thoughts of miracles and martyrs, angels and demons, must have made their minds much more open to supernatural influences than ours are today. It is, therefore, one thing to be a bit sceptical about the accounts of Old Nick putting in a personal appearance and quite another to brush aside as trash the whole vast literature dealing with Christian mysticism.

There are innumerable accounts of people who become so obsessed with the question of the Life to Come that they gave themselves up to a special devotion to their favourite Saints, and as a result of their whole-hearted fervour developed miraculous powers of their own. And of others, the bad-hats and natural rebels, who dabbled in witchcraft, Satanism and alchemy. It is certainly incontestable that there was hardly a village in Europe where someone or other was not credited with the power to cast spells and bring calamity on their enemies by ill-wishing them. The bulk of testimony to such happenings is overwhelming, and it simply is not credible that for hundreds of generations the whole population of Christendom was fooled by a succession of liars and lunatics.

Of course, in these days, there are plenty of sceptics who regard all accounts of occult phenomena as bunkum; and due either to people imagining things when in an abnormal condition, or to the machinations of rogues and charlatans who make a dubious living out of tricking the credulous.

But the opinions of such bigoted materialists do not prove anything. They are simply the outcome of the present widespread lack of Faith. It is only natural that people brought up, as I was, to believe that there are no such places as Heaven and Hell, should be strongly prejudiced against any evidence which might convince them of the existence of some fearsome Otherworld, inhabited by mysterious forces and the spirits of the dead. To accept it would compel them to abandon their comfortable philosophy–or lack of one. They would begin to get the wind up at the thought that they must have souls themselves, and the frightening question of what might happen to them when they die.

The extraordinary decline in the practice of all religions during the past thirty years no doubt accounts for the comparatively few people who now ever pause to ponder such questions seriously. Yet it would be absurd to assume that a fundamental change has taken place in the composition of human beings, and that because great numbers of them rarely think about their souls they no longer have them.

Moreover, the age of materialism has brought us no new answers to such riddles as: What took place 'in the beginning', and what is meant by 'the end of time', or, how did it come about that life started on our own small planet? Yet the more we learn of the universe the more apparent it becomes that everything in it is regulated by unchanging laws, and that chemical conditions alone are incapable of producing any form of life whatsoever.

Yet the origin of these mysteries has been questioned only in recent times. Previously, in every country and in every age since the beginning of recorded history, it has been the first article in the creed of man that the Creation was the work of a Supreme Intelligence. In addition, all religions also held in common that the souls of men were immortal, and that the unceasing struggle for them between the eternally warring forces of Good and Evil was all part of the Great Plan.

World-wide tradition asserts that these beliefs were based on a series of

Divine revelations made for man's guidance; and, all modern thought having failed to produce any other tenable theory, it seems difficult, if not impossible, to reject them.

But to accept them carries with it an awe-inspiring thought; for it then becomes unthinkable that in the past hundred years or so any part of this vast and complex system can have altered. Therefore, although the Devil may no longer appear to people—even if he ever did so in person—he cannot have become inactive, and his power for evil must remain as potent as of old.

No one has ever denied him intelligence, so it is reasonable to assume that he is clever enough to adapt his methods to suit every advance in modern thought. If wars, revolutions, the mushroom growth of the herd mentality and their resulting miseries can be attributed to a supremely evil intelligence working secretly upon the greed, fears and follies of man, he has good reason to congratulate himself on the monstrous reaping of hate and violence that his sowing has brought him in the past quarter of a century. In fact, if looked at from that point of view, it seems that the general decline of religion since the end of the Victorian era has enormously facilitated the Devil's age-long task of replacing order by chaos and, at last, entering into his Principality of this World as the Lord of Misrule.

Even to suggest that he is now taking a personal interest in myself would be atrociously conceited; but, unless I am suffering from delusions, I can only suppose that either I or this room have recently become a focus for the activities of one of his innumerable lesser satellites. How otherwise can one possibly explain the shadow; or the stark terror that has gripped me, holding me rigid in a paralysis of fear, on each of the five occasions that I have seen it—and, God forbid, may do so again tonight?

Tuesday, 5th May

I could not write anything this morning. I tried to as soon as I was alone, but my hand shook so much that it would not hold the pencil firmly. Then, at half-past-eleven, I had to go out with Deb.

It has been a lovely day and the bright sunshine in the garden restored me a little. Those sharp black eyes of Deb's don't miss much, though, and it is hardly surprising that she noticed how haggard I look.

'I haf begome quite vorried about you,' she remarked. 'I cennot t'ink vot is de metter mid you des pars' few tays. You haf develop' a nervous twitch an' you look zo peeky.'

That is an absurd exaggeration of her accent, so I shall not attempt further renderings of it. As she is quite an intelligent woman, and has been a refugee here since 1933, she actually speaks pretty good English for a German Jewess.

Naturally I don't want to put the idea into her head that I've got bats in the belfry, so I did my best to pull myself together, and simply said:

'You know quite well that I've been sleeping badly, lately. I'm only looking a bit off-colour because I had another restless night.'

What a masterpiece of understatement! With the aid of a triple bromide I got off all right; but I woke about half-past-one, and I knew instantly that the Thing was outside the window again.

I wonder if I can bring myself to describe it? Anyhow I must try. But first I must explain how it comes about that I know it to be there in spite of the blackout.

Down here in Wales people are supposed to observe the A.R.P. regulations as strictly as elsewhere, but we are over three miles from the village, and there is no one to enforce them. I don't think the Boche has ever dropped a bomb within thirty or forty miles of Llanferdrack, so when I came down here after two-and-a-half years of war I found that everyone had got pretty slack about such matters.

The room I occupy used to be the library—it still is for that matter—and I was glad that Helmuth had chosen it for me, as it makes a splendidly spacious bed-sitting-room, and as I am very fond of reading I like being surrounded with rows and rows of books. It must be close on forty feet long and has big bay windows at both ends. Those to the south have a glorious view over miles of wild country-side, and the middle one, being a glass-panelled door, gives me easy access to the garden.

All six windows of the room were originally furnished only with brocade pelmets, and hanging drapes that do not draw. On the garden side blackout curtains were added soon after the beginning of the war, but as the room was rarely used it was evidently not considered worthwhile to do anything about the north windows, because they cannot be seen from outside the building and look out on to a courtyard.

When Helmuth had the room prepared for me last March, as a glorified bed-sit, I suppose material was already getting scarce; so instead of having proper curtains fitted to each of the three windows on the courtyard side he had a big piece of brown stuff rigged up, which is drawn right across the bay at night. But it is a good six inches too short, so when there is a bright moon its light seeps in underneath and forms a broad band along the floor.

It is that damned strip of moonlight that gives me such appalling jitters. Actually it is three strips, as the mullions between the windows throw great black shadows that divide it into sections. Of course it is not the moonlight itself that unnerves me but—No! It's no good. I can't do it. I've broken out in a muck sweat at the very thought of what I see. I must think of something else. . . .

Madagascar! There was good news today on the wireless. It is cheering to know that despite all Hitler can do we still have enough punch left, and a long enough arm, to land a blow so far afield. Ever since those filthy little yellow men overran Malaya it has been quite on the cards that they would have a go at South Africa, and if the Vichy French had let them occupy the island it would have made a perfect base from which to launch an invasion of the Union.

Thank goodness it looks now as if we have put paid to that one in advance. The report says that at dawn today British naval and military forces arrived off the north-west coast of the island, landed in Courier Bay, and proceeded inland across the neck of the isthmus towards the naval base at Diego Suarez.

Well, good luck to them. How I wish I were there, instead of here! Of course, naval aircraft must have been used to cover the landing; slow, unwieldy old kites compared with the types I used to fly. Still, I'd cheerfully take up even a Gladiator against the enemy, rather than have to face this loathsome, inhuman thing that haunts the courtyard, and has recently been trying to find its way into this room.

How do I know that? I cannot say. But something inside myself tells me positively that it is so. That something can only be a supersensory apparatus which, to give it its medical name, is called man's higher consciousness; but old-fashioned people would say it was my spirit—or soul—that, knowing itself to be in danger, sends me these frantic warnings.

As I was brought up to be an atheist, the last thing I should have admitted to, up to the age of eighteen, was that I had a soul; but since then my horizons have broadened a lot; and only yesterday, on arguing matters out with myself, I reached the conclusion that, logically, one must accept the eternal verities. That too, even in these materialistic times, is still a fundamental belief held by the vast majority of educated, as well as uneducated, people.

Judging by those I met during the two-and-a-half years that I was free of Helmuth's tutelage, genuine atheists must be very rare. Most of the young men I knew were pretty hard cases—they had to be or they would have cracked under the strain—but most of them became quite offended when sometimes, for the fun of getting up an argument, I suggested that they had no souls. To have agreed with me would have been to degrade themselves to the level of animals—or rather, a bag of salts and a few buckets of water kept going only by a series of chemical reactions—and, in their heart of hearts, they were convinced that they possessed some intrinsic quality which lifts mankind above all other species of creation.

That makes it all the more curious that most people these days rarely think about their souls. But, I suppose, if they did for any length of time it would interfere with the innumerable petty interests of their daily lives.

Nearly everybody will readily admit that they believe in some form of after-life. But they take it for granted that God cannot possibly be the sort of jealous, sacrifice-loving, tyrannical potentate depicted in the Old Testament, and that the fiery-furnace version of Hell was kept going by the Churches only as a convenient means of blackmailing the laity. When they do think of such matters they visualize the Creator as a nice old gentleman with a long white beard, who invariably speaks English, and confidently anticipate that when their time is up here they will be given a pretty reasonable deal as a start off in some new existence.

As for the Devil, they never give a thought to him at all—except when it comes to discussing possible costumes for the Four Arts Ball. Neither, I confess did I, until I suddenly found myself in the situation of a rabbit who sees a ferret with red eyes and bared teeth coming after him.

One thing is certain. In these days, the vast majority of people live out their lives without bothering to propitiate the Deity, yet nothing of this kind ever catches up with them. Sooner or later, though, they have all got to die; and, maybe, when they do they will meet with a rude awakening. If so, perhaps I really ought to consider myself fortunate in being forced to thrash out these problems now.

All the same I would give anything, at the moment, to be one of those countless thousands who are entirely wrapped up in fighting Hitler, or even a charwoman scrubbing floors and queuing up for rations. But I am not. I am either going nuts or, long before my proper time, I have been brought face to face with the grim things that come and go on the borders of eternal night.

Later

I broke off to write again to Julia. I know that war charities and her billetees must keep her frightfully busy, and at the best of times she was never good about writing regularly; but I do think that she might have replied by now to the letter I wrote her early in April. That was just after the two consecutive nights upon which I first 'saw things'. I said nothing about that but asked her to come down to see me, because I wanted to talk it over with her. She is the only person I know with whom I could discuss such matters without her getting the idea that I am going mad. But after those two nights the visitations ceased, so I began to think that I must have been suffering from nightmares—until things started to happen again at the beginning of this month.

Why I didn't follow up my first letter with another, several days ago, I now cannot think; but I suppose this business has made my wits a bit woolly. Anyhow, this time I haven't minced matters. I told her bluntly that I believe this place to be haunted and that I am scared out of my wits. I asked her to keep that under her hat and to come down here as a matter of the utmost urgency. With luck she'll be here tomorrow; but I've still got to get through tonight. I must try not to think of that, though; so I had better keep my mind busy trying to prove to myself that I really am still sane.

Lwonder why it is that, apart from practising Spiritualists on the one hand and professional fortune-tellers on the other, it is rare to hear of anyone these days who can claim to have had any actual experience of the supernatural?

The falling off in the practice of religion no doubt explains it to some extent; but I am inclined to think that the general decline in psychic perception is more largely due to modern conditions, in which the daily fight for existence compels the vast majority to occupy themselves almost exclusively with material matters.

In its waking state the human brain normally picks up and registers the thoughts conveyed by any voice within its range of hearing. Experiments have shown that while in a hypnotic sleep it will also react to orders whispered in too low a tone for it to catch when awake. And mental telepathy, examples of which are known to most people, show that it is capable of picking up thoughts which have not been sent out by the human voice at all. It is therefore clear that part of the brain consists of a radio receiving set.

But a radio will pick up from the ether only the signals given out on the wavelength to which it is adjusted. And anyone can appreciate how vastly different the mentality of modern man must be from that of his counterpart of a thousand, or even a hundred, years ago.

Perforce the minds of men and women of all ages have been largely filled with their daily occupations: food, sex, family and home; but to these in modern times have been added an immense variety of anxieties and distractions.

To begin with, people are now much more generally looked up to for their money than for their real worth, so more of their time is given to endeavouring to make a good income. Moreover, in order to give the appearance of being well off, it is the rule rather than the exception for them to take advantage of the modern credit system and live on anticipated earnings, so their worry over money is all the greater.

In the past the majority never left the towns or villages in which they were born; now a great part of the population shifts to new places of abode every few years, either on account of a change in employment of fluctuation in fortune. Each move brings the anxieties attendant on finding and furnishing new living accommodation.

Clothes were formerly mainly for utility and the same garments were often worn for years at a stretch; now even the masses regard a certain smartness of appearance as a necessity, but fashions are constantly changing and the average woman spends hundreds of hours each year harassed by the question as to how she can best dress well yet continue to live within her means.

The superseding of individual craftsmanship by the manufacture of machine-made goods has robbed the working classes of their security of employment. In the old days every youngster was brought up to a trade and a good honest workman could always be sure of keeping a roof over his head; now, in peacetime, the unemployed are numbered by the million, and for them there is the crushing anxiety that if they cannot somehow manage to find the rent they will be thrown out in the street.

Even the people who have jobs never know how long they will be able to keep them; strikes, lock-outs, foreign competition, new inventions, financial crises—all matters over which they have little or no control—are an ever-present menace to the security of managements and workers alike.

Then there are the countless time-occupying distractions that our forefathers never knew: a newspaper every morning to fill the mind with fresh ideas, cheap travel bringing the seaside within easy reach of every home, games taught at school and sport developed into a vast national industry, cinemas, theatres and concert-halls in every town, radio programmes blaring forth night and day, limitless fiction and cheap magazines, crossword puzzles and football pools—and now, of course, this accursed war.

Up to Napoleonic times, at least, comparatively small professional navies and armies did all the fighting that was necessary, while the bulk of the people continued undisturbed in their normal occupations; but now war disrupts the lives of whole populations and involves everyone in countless new activities, anxieties and tribulations, so that their minds become more heavily drugged than ever with what they consider to be the imperative necessity of the moment.

I have not been endeavouring to prove to myself that in the past people, on the whole, lived happier lives, although I think a good case could be made for that, and certainly for one that they enjoyed a far greater measure of security before the industrial revolution took them from the land.

I have simply set down my reasons for believing that up to about a hundred years ago they had ample time for quiet reflection and, in consequence, thought much more about the mystery of creation, of good and evil, and of the things of the spirit generally; so that the receiving apparatus of their minds was automatically tuned in to pick up those strange vibrations that come from the other side. Whereas most moderns seldom have the leisure to contemplate the eternal, and on the rare occasions that they do their apparatus is so ill-attuned, from lack of use, that it fails to register anything. And that it is this which accounts for so few people of the present century having met with any psychic experience.

Yet there are still occasions when some people suddenly find themselves tuned in to some dark station of the Otherworld. That is entirely contrary to all that I was brought up to believe. But I have got to believe it now. Somehow I have got to convince myself of that absolutely. I must—otherwise I shall end up in a straitjacket.

The light is failing now. I had better ring for Taffy to draw the curtains. I wonder if Julia will come tomorrow? But, idiot that I am, how can she. My letter can't possibly get to her at Queensclere until Thursday morning. That means I have two more nights to face before there can be any hope of getting me away from here.

Oh, God! How can I bear it?

Wednesday, 6th May

I got quite a pleasant surprise when I looked in the mirror to shave this morning. My face was always on the thin side but it has lost that lean, drawn look it had yesterday; my grey eyes are bright again and the heavy pouches underneath them have entirely disappeared. They always say that the recuperative powers of youth are remarkable, and it is certainly wonderful what a good night's sleep has done for me.

Deb refuses to allow me to take more than one triple bromide, even when I have had a succession of bad nights; but last night I grabbed the bottle from her and swallowed a couple before she could stop me. Whether it was the effect of the double dose, or that the brute that haunts the courtyard decided to have a go at some other window, I don't know; but I slept like a log from ten o'clock right round till eight-thirty, and I am feeling a new man in consequence.

It is another lovely day, too. What fun it would be if I could go for a climb up the mountain; but that is out of the question. Helmuth used to take me climbing up in Scotland when I was a boy, and I loved it. He had promised to take me to Switzerland, and I was bitterly disappointed in 1939 when he decided that we had better go to Mull again instead, owing to the uncertainty of the European situation. As usual, he proved right, and the outbreak of war occurred while we were up there.

That last summer holiday was fun all the same, even though it differed little from its predecessors. There are grouse and quite good deer-stalking on the island, and mackerel fishing round the coast. Having our own boat always enabled us to go on exciting expeditions, and we got in some thrilling climbs on the mainland. I expect Helmuth misses his climbing too, but these days he is always so occupied with the estate, and gingering up the tenants to do better in the 'Grow More Food' campaign, that he doesn't get much time for anything else.

I don't know why I am rambling on like this, but I find it a pleasant occupation to put down my thoughts just as they come into my head. I only wish that they were all such pleasant ones. Unfortunately, I find it impossible to keep the bad ones out of my mind for long, and I am still damnably worried about myself.

What is more, I started this journal for a purpose, and I must not let the fact that nothing happened last night lull me into a false sense of security. I have still got to convince myself that I am perfectly normal, and that there really are other 'gaps in the curtain' through which people sometimes catch a glimpse of the unknown, as well as the one which has opened to disclose such a monstrous thing to me.

I think any reasonable person would agree that, while it is fair enough to question the validity of any particular supernatural manifestation, there is far too much evidence of the existence of occult forces to maintain that they are nothing but a product of man's imagination. To do so means not only the denial of a part of the Gospels and all other sacred literature, as well as countless well-authenticated records of miraculous happenings in historic times – the admission of any single one of which as fully proven automatically proves the *whole* case; it also implies a wilful disregard of modern scientific investigation into the qualities and capabilities of the brain, soul, mind, spirit – or whatever one chooses to call it – that animates every human being and gives to each a unique personality.

But before I use the words 'soul' or 'spirit' again, perhaps I had better attempt to define what I mean by them. I take them as designating not only the something extra to the physical body that all religions teach lives on after we die, but also that part of our consciousness which leaves us in no doubt whether a course is right or wrong, and, at times, enables us to become perceptive of sights, sounds and smells outside the range of our normal senses.

Although scientists have not yet obtained conclusive proof that the soul survives after death, they have gone a long way towards it. Emotions can now be registered and emanations invisible to the human eye can be photographed, showing that while alive we radiate an intangible something which disappears at death. People's hearts have stopped beating during operations; others have been drowned or asphyxiated, and they have been pronounced physically dead; yet scientific treatment has brought them to life again. For a brief space something must have gone out of them but, on its home again being rendered tenable, it returned.

That means that, quite apart from faith and wishful thinking, there is a good case for survival; and there is a far better one for the existence of supernormal powers in the living.

Thought-transference is, I suppose, the simplest form in which the non-physical manifests itself, and with some people it is almost a day-to-day occurrence. Married couples who have lived in unity for a number of years often find that anticipating one another's thoughts becomes almost a habit; and it is by no means unusual for friends who have not seen one another for a long time each to write to the other on the same day.

Death warnings are also far from unusual. I remember reading a book by the great French scientist, Camille Flammarion, in which he recorded scores of cases of people who, while employed in some quite normal occupation, suddenly broke off to explain that they felt convinced that a near relative had died, and the following day brought confirmation of their second sight.

Then there are the many instances in which for no explicable reason people wake up in the middle of the night with a feeling that something is wrong, and on going downstairs find that the house is on fire; although the sound of crackling and the smell of smoke could not possibly have been perceptible to their normal senses, even if they had been awake.

Again, there is scarcely ever a big railway disaster or liner lost at sea without someone who should have travelled on the train or ship having decided not to do so at the last moment. When questioned such people often assert that they had every intention of travelling and that having failed to do so caused them considerable inconvenience by upsetting long-standing arrangements; yet, on reaching the station or dock, they felt an imperative compulsion to postpone their journey.

Everyone must have heard of the case of that type by which the late Marquess of Dufferin and Ava escaped being dashed to death in a falling lift, while *en post* as British Ambassador in Paris. In that affair the unmistakably psychic nature of the warning was underlined by the fact of its having been conveyed to him by seeing an apparition. He vouched for that himself, and one can hardly question the veracity of such a man as the late Lord Dufferin.

From Saul's grim transactions with the Witch of Endor to the strange events preceding the death of the late Mr Justice Macarthy, history, both ancient and modern, gives innumerable instances of people seeing ghosts, many of which in recent times have been authenticated by doctors, magistrates and other trustworthy witnesses.

But why should I labour the point? It can be only because my unsettled mind craves so desperately for further support to a conviction that it has already formed. I really have no doubt that apparitions are at times seen by people who have never attempted to contact occult forces, or have even given them a thought.

It is possible that, owing to my present poor state of health, I may recently have become the victim of hallucinations. I admit that. But of one fact I am positive. I was perfectly sane and healthy when I was a boy, and at the age of eight I saw a ghost myself.

Must stop now—time for me to go out for my airing.

Afternoon

I have few dislikes in the way of food and do not take much interest in it, although my large frame calls for quite a bit of stoking up, so I have a very hearty appetite. Generally I demolish anything that is put in front of me and hardly notice what I am eating.

But I must say that I enjoyed my lunch today. Of course, down here in Wales, apart from tea and sugar, no one even pretends to accept rationing. The home farm provides us with as much meat, poultry, butter, cream and eggs as we could wish for; the lake gives us fish and the garden an abundance of fruit and vegetables. If we did not use the stuff that is brought in the outdoor staff would only sell it to the local tradesmen—so what the hell! I lunched off duck and green peas followed by the first hot-house strawberries with plenty of fresh cream.

Anyhow, I'm feeling good—better than I have at any time since the recurrence of the trouble, which was on the night of the 30th of April. In fact, I am feeling so much fitter than I did yesterday that I have decided that I am now capable of making myself describe the Thing that makes me doubt my sanity.

I have already given an account of the inadequate blackout arrangements in this room, and of how the moonlight coming through the windows of the north bay throws three broad bands of silvery radiance on the floor, this side of the curtain that cuts off the arc of the bay at night.

I should add that after the second of the two visitations early in April, I asked both Deb and Helmuth to have the curtain lengthened so that it reached the floor. Deb said with some asperity that she had neither the necessary material nor the coupons to get any, and that anyway it was not her job, so I had better get Helmuth to give instructions about it to the housekeeper. My Great-aunt Sarah has lived here most of her life and her companion, Miss Nettelfold, does the housekeeping for us. Helmuth said that he would speak to her about it; but either he is so busy that he forgot, or else it is she who has forgotten to do anything about it.

On May the 1st—that was the morning after the second bout began—I reminded Helmuth of his promise; but still nothing has been done. Perhaps I chose a bad moment to bother him, as he seemed very offhand. He said he always slept with the curtains of his room drawn back, so that when there was a moon it often shone right in on him, and he really could not believe that a little strip of moonlight on the floor could cause me any serious inconvenience.

Since then I have not liked to mention the matter to him again, as I don't see how I can press for the job to be done unless I give the real reason why I am so anxious to have those extra six inches put on the curtain; and nothing would induce me to tell him that.

I have spent hours wondering how I could lengthen it myself; but the snag is that there is nothing here I could use except some of the cushion covers, the bed linen or my underclothes, and if I started cutting any of those up it would be taken as a sign that I was crazy.

So the curtain is unaltered and the moon still throws those three damnable splodges of light across the floor. The gap between the floor and the curtain is not much more than six inches, but as the light comes in at an angle the bands it makes are very much wider, and they reach to within four feet of my bed.

Thank God they come no nearer, or I should probably lose my nerve completely and scream the house down. Even as it is, it is all I can do to prevent myself from yelling for help. I would, if I were certain that whoever came to my assistance would see the same thing as I do. But the hellish part of it is that they might not. Then I should know that what I see is only a figment of my imagination, and that I really am going mad. Perhaps that is the case, but if so I am determined not to let anyone suspect it as long as I have a will of my own.

Now for the apparently absurd and mortifying truth. I have allowed myself to be reduced to a nervous wreck simply through seeing a shadow. But what makes it? And why does it dance its devil dance on that accursed band of moonlight?

There are no trees in the courtyard, so it cannot be a waving branch that throws that animated black patch. It cannot be a person or a bird, as it is not the right shape, and its movements are unlike those that either would make. Yet something does. Something that comes out of the night and climbs up on to my window-sill, so that its dark bulk is silhouetted by the moon.

Owing to the comparative narrowness of the band of light I can never see the whole shadow at one time; but it seems to be thrown by a large ball-like body with a number of waving limbs. To be honest, I have come to the conclusion that it is an octopus.

I know it must sound as if I am a raving lunatic, to say that I believe an octopus is trying to get in at my window; but there it is. Unless I tell the truth to myself the whole point of keeping this journal is lost, and to continue it would be futile. As, too, I have never even seen the Thing itself, it must appear as if I am a pretty wet type to allow myself to be frightened by a shadow, however inexplicable its presence where no shadow should be, and however sinister its form and movements; but that is very far from being the worst part of the business.

The terrifying thing is, that the brute is not only haunting but hunting me. It moves up and down, up and down, in stealthy little runs, floundering from one window-sill to another and back again. And I *know* that in a blind, fumbling way it is trying to get in.

Yet even that is not the ultimate horror. It cannot possibly be a real octopus; a beast that one could slash at with a knife, and, if one were strong enough, blind and kill. It *must* be some intangible malefic force that has succeeded in materializing itself in hideous animal form.

Of that I am certain. For the sight of its shadow does not fill me with a normal, healthy fear; it makes my eyes start from my head and my limbs become weak as water. Its effect upon me is both different and worse than if I were brought face to face with a man-eating tiger. That is why I am positive that it can only be something unutterably Evil.

Once I wake and see that unholy weaving pattern of darkness, furtively moving to and fro across the silvery band of light, I simply cannot drag my eyes away from it. Sometimes I try to force myself to ignore it, but I never succeed for more than a moment. I long to put my head under the bedclothes; but I dare not. If I did the Thing might get in while I was not looking, and be upon me before I even had a chance to scream for help.

So I am compelled to lie there sweating with terror, my gaze riveted upon it and dreading every moment to hear one of the window-panes crack under its pressure; until at last the moon goes down and its foul shadow is blotted out. Only then can I relax. Sometimes, if I am lucky, towards morning I fall into the troubled sleep of mental exhaustion; at others my tired brain revolves round endless futile speculations, until the pale light of dawn creeps beneath the curtain.

But what is the Thing? Why does it come? Is it a Satanic entity that has battened and waxed strong upon thought-forms, thrown out at the time of some abominable crime committed long ago in the nearby ruin? If so, why is it not content to remain there haunting the scene of the crime? Why should it leave its lair and try to invade this modern house? Or can it be a monster that has been deliberately ordered up out of the Pit to attack me? If so, again why? And by whom?

Surely pretty well anyone would be more worthy of the Devil's attention than I am in my present state? Yet I *know* that it is I, and no one else, that the brute is out to get. Sometimes its shadow blurs and quivers a little, and I know then, just as surely as I know that my name is Toby Jugg, that it is trembling with a kind of repulsive lust. Some chord deep in my sub-conscious vibrates to the waves it sends out, and my flesh creeps anew from the positive knowledge that it is activated by one single, all-absorbing thought—the urge to wrap itself about my body, suck out my soul and destroy me utterly. But why? Why? Why? Why me? Why me? Why me?

Later

Half-an-hour ago I had worked myself up into such a state that I could not go on. I am feeling a bit steadier now, and in the meantime I have reconsidered a few points.

Firstly; can the brute conceivably be an honest-to-God flesh-and-muscle octopus that lives in the lake? As the lake is very deep in places, and it apparently surfaces only at night, it might have inhabited a rocky cave on the lake-bottom for years without anyone being any the wiser. The Loch Ness monster is said to lead that sort of existence and is spotted coming up for air only once in a blue moon. And this creature may not be a true octopus, but another unknown species of primitive lake-dweller.

As against that, octopi are normally ocean-dwellers, and I have never heard of one being seen in a river or lake. Llanferdrack is in Radnor, and on the eastern slope of the Cambrian mountains—over forty miles from the sea—so how could it have got here? I don't know the age to which octopi live, but such low forms of creation often survive to great ages. If octopi do, this one might have been caught generations ago and brought here by one of the old Lords Llanferdrack. But captive octopi that are kept in aquariums have to be supplied with salt-water, and the lake is fresh. Moreover, it seems highly improbable that any species of octopi is capable of coming up out of the water and crawling any distance on land.

On balance, I suppose this theory is remotely possible, but only if the brute is some form of missing link; and I regard that as most unlikely.

My original idea, that the brute is a Satanic entity and owes its origin to some dark deed that took place long ago in the ruins, seems far more plausible. This hideous modern house was built only in the 1890's and it backs on to the southern side of the original Llanferdrack Castle. Some of the rooms in the Castle are still more or less habitable. In fact they are hardly less so than those of the house, as the latter has never been modernized and lacks most of the amenities—we still have to use oil lamps, and coal or wood for cooking as well as the fires, neither electricity or gas ever having been laid on.

But the part of the Castle that is still in fair preservation overlooks the lake, and abuts on the east wing of the house, in which Great-aunt Sarah has her quarters; whereas the west wing, where I am installed, backs on to the ruined Keep. The library is separated from it only by the courtyard, so it seems a fair bet that my enemy has his lair in one of the dark, rat-infested dungeons beneath it, where in ancient times unfortunate wretches were tortured to death.

My second new theory is based on the assumption that, although the Lord of Evil is said to be intelligent, it does not necessarily follow that his lesser minions are so too. Indeed, tradition has it that they are cunning and persistent but far from clever, and have often been tricked by the wit of man.

Thus, to the lower forms of Satanic energy one soul may appear as desirable meat as any other. If so, this foulness that comes by night is probably incapable of distinguishing between myself and a country bumpkin like my servant Taffy—or, for that matter, between my very ordinary personality and the heroic spirit of Mr Churchill. Perhaps it just gropes and gropes, patiently and tirelessly seeking for a suitable victim, and my present parlous state, together with the mental loneliness that afflicts me here, renders me peculiarly vulnerable to such an attack.

For the first time in my life I have real cause to regret that I was brought up as what the Church would term a heretic. If I had not broken away from the domination of Helmuth when I did I would still know next to nothing of religious matters; but during the two-and-a-half years that I was free of his influence I read quite extensively to acquire information on what he would term 'the superstitions of the ignorant masses'.

It was a perfectly natural reaction that I should interest myself in the one and only subject which had previously been barred to me; and the fact that it was he who had inculcated in me the habit of serious reading gives a cynically humorous twist to the first use I made of my freedom to read what I wished.

Unfortunately, it is by no means easy to make up later for an almost complete lack of the type of knowledge that most children imbibe at their mother's knee, and all through a normal adolescence; so I find myself far from well-equipped to reason out these questions, the answers to which may mean for me the difference between having to admit to myself that I am going mad and finding a logical basis upon which to retain faith in my sanity. Nevertheless, I mean to stick to it; and I shall attempt to analyse the evidence supporting my belief that I saw a ghost when I was a small boy, first thing tomorrow.

Tomorrow! But first I have to get through tonight. So far this month I have had to face that ghastly ordeal four nights out of six. Last night I was blessed with a respite. Dare I hope to be granted one for two nights running?

No; I fear there is little chance of that. This month the attacks have been of much longer duration than they were on those first two nights early in April; and each time the Thing comes it seems more determined to get at me. During those early visits it came and went at intervals, so they seem to have been only in the nature of a reconnaissance. But now the attack is on in earnest. Although I cannot hear it, I know, instinctively, that it keeps throwing its weight against the window-panes with ever-increasing violence. I would to God I could believe that its failure to appear last night could be taken as a sign that it has decided to abandon its efforts; but I cannot.

Last night, too, I managed to snatch that extra triple bromide from Deb, so perhaps the brute did come, but the double dose was sufficient to prevent its malefic influence from waking me. Deb will take good care that I get no chance to trick her tonight, though, so I had better try to resign myself to another night of hell.

I wonder whether I shall be awake or asleep when it comes? On four occasions my sub-conscious has registered the malefic force that the brute radiates, causing me to wake suddenly from a sound sleep and, on starting up, to find it there. On the other two I have been awake already.

I hardly know which is the worst. In the first case there is the appalling shock of being called on to face another ordeal unexpectedly, while in the second there is the added terror of anticipation that I suffer during those awful moments before I can bring myself to look round and actually see the shadow. I think the latter is really the more horrible of the two.

At such times I suddenly become conscious that a dank, raw chill is gradually pervading the room, and it becomes very silent—as silent as the grave. Then I get a definite physical reaction—just as definite as a whiff of rotting fish making one want to vomit. I know then, for certain, that my fears are justified—that this incredibly evil thing has clambered up on to the window-sill, and is once more searching for a way to get in. Instinctively my eyes turn towards the floor, and there is the big, black undulating shadow that it causes, sprawled across the band of moonlight.

I feel my heart beating like a sledge-hammer, and I have to bite my tongue to prevent myself from letting out an hysterical scream. I would give everything I possess to be free, if only for two minutes, from the physical bonds that hold me; but I know that, short of rousing the house, there is no alternative to my continuing to lie there suffering the agonies of the damned.

If, at the first warning touch of that awful cold, I could only spring from my bed and rush from the room! If I could only sit up, press a switch, and flood the room with light! If, even, I could only reach out and turn on my radio-gramophone! But such acts are all beyond my capabilities. Even in the day-time I am unable to rise unaided from my chair, and by night I am a prisoner in my bed!

What ill have I ever done to anyone, that I should be condemned to this now that my back is broken, and partial paralysis makes me a helpless cripple?

Thursday, 7th May

Nothing happened again last night, thank God; and Julia should be here today. Even if it means upsetting Helmuth, and a certain amount of inconvenience, I am sure she will have me moved when she hears what I have to say.

I shall try to persuade her to let me go back with her to Queensclere. She'll oppose that because of the number of air-raids that they get down there in Kent; but, war or no war, it would be lovely to be living in the same house with her again.

Writing that reminds me that yesterday I had meant to go into the matter of the ghost that I saw when I was a small boy, but put off doing so because I suddenly decided that I felt up to setting down on paper a description of the Thing that is haunting me here. That affair took place not very long after I first went to live with Julia, and her knowing all about it is one of the things which will enable me to talk to her of my present plight, without giving her the idea that I've gone nuts.

I always think of this ghost as 'my burglar', because that is what I believed it to be at the time; and no doubt I should have continued to believe that up to this very day had it not been for a quite unexpected encounter several years later; but I will record that in its proper place.

At the age of eight years and four months I lost both my father and grandfather. They were killed together in October 1929, having gone up in the prototype of a new air-liner to inspect her performance for themselves; but something went wrong with the wretched kite and she crashed.

I never knew my mother, as she died in giving me birth. From her picture and all accounts she must have been very lovely, and she was a rising film star when my father first met her in Hollywood, but she gave up her career when she married him. She was an American of Norwegian extraction and I evidently take after her. My hair and moustache are a shade darker than the red-gold curl of hers that we found in a locket among father's things; but I have her large grey eyes and straight features. Like her, I am tall and strongly built, and her Norwegian blood must have come through very strongly, as my friends in the R.A.F. nicknamed me 'The Viking'.

Anyway, my father's death left me an orphan. Whether I have any living relatives on my mother's side I have no idea. I have never heard of any, so she may have been an orphan too. On my father's side, my grandmother had been dead for years and grandfather had only one sister, my Great-aunt Sarah. She never married, as her fiancé, young Llanferdrack, who owned this place, was drowned just before the happy day; and she has lived here mourning him in seclusion most of her life. But the poor old thing's romance going wrong unhinged her mind and she is a harmless half-wit, so there was never any question of my being placed in her charge.

Apart from Great-aunt Sarah my only living relative is my father's younger brother, Uncle Paul; so the Trustees decided that I should go to live with him. I have since gathered that there was quite a bit of argument about it, because Uncle Paul was regarded as the black sheep of the family, and neither my grandfather nor father approved of him at all; but, naturally, I knew nothing of that at the time, and he offered to have me. I think the thing that really decided the Trustees to accept his offer was that about a year earlier he had married and at last appeared to be settling down.

All this seems quite irrelevant to the affair I started out to write about; but having begun this journal I find it rather soothing just to ramble on, setting down any thoughts and memories that come into my head, and, after all, it is only for my own edification, so why shouldn't I write anything I damn'-well choose?

To continue, then. After the double funeral Uncle Paul took me down to his house at Kew and presented me to Julia. Of course, as his wife she was my aunt by marriage, but I never called her aunt, because she said that first evening she would rather that I didn't. She said that when I was grown up there wouldn't be much difference in our ages and tha. she felt much too young to be an aunt to anybody; so she would much prefer that I thought of her as a big sister.

I found that a bit surprising, as she seemed very grown-up to me; but it made things rather cosy, and she was quite the loveliest person I had ever seen. When she tucked me up in bed that night she kissed me, and having no female relatives I was not accustomed to that sort of thing.

Father used to go abroad a great deal on business trips and even when he was at home I didn't see much of him. I was still too young for him to have me downstairs when he was entertaining and on most days when he got back from the city he just dashed upstairs to my nursery for a few minutes, then changed and went out; so my world practically consisted of dear old Nanny Trotter and other nannies and their children that we met in the park.

Of course there was Miss Stiggins too, a dry old spinster who came to give me lessons every morning, but she never kissed me and I don't suppose that it would have registered if she had; whereas that first kiss from Julia remained an unforgettable landmark in my young life. Her lips were as soft as swansdown against my cheek and she smelled of some delicious perfume;

248 *The Haunting of Toby Jugg*

from that moment I absolutely worshipped her.

Julia was then twenty and had been married nearly a year. Uncle Paul met her in Rome, and although she was an Italian she already spoke English so well that she did not seem like a foreigner, and her faint accent made her speech only more fascinating to listen to. She was medium tall and very slim. Her eyes were black with long lashes and she had the warm, rich colouring of the south. Her face was a long oval, her lips full and very red. She wore her dark hair parted in the middle and it fell smoothly to her shoulders, curling at the ends.

That first night, I remember, she was wearing a dress of oyster satin with a long, full skirt that swayed gently as she walked; as did also her pendant diamond earrings, which were the only jewels she had on. All her movements were smooth and graceful, and when she laughed it was lazily, her red lips opening to show two rows of strong little white teeth. I was still as innocent as a new-born babe and to me she seemed like an angel—a dark angel—come to life out of a story-book.

But I must get back to the matter of my 'burglar'. I had been living with Uncle Paul and Julia for about two months when the affair occurred. Their house at Kew seemed very strange to me at first, because it was so different from those in which I had been brought up; but Julia had a flair for decoration and I found her bright, modern rooms exciting after the much bigger but rather sombre ones to which I was accustomed.

The Willows was a suburban villa of the type that was built by the thousand during Queen Victoria's reign; a square three-storied building standing in its own small garden and one of a row of similar middle-class homes. Its front door opened on to a narrow hall with two rooms on each side of it, then continued on the left as a passage to the kitchen and on the right as a staircase leading straight up to the floors above. From the hall you could see the little half-landing where the stairs made a hairpin bend, then disappeared from sight. On the first floor there were four bedrooms and a bathroom, and another flight of stairs immediately above the lower ones led up to the servants' rooms and box-room at the top of the house.

Two months is a long time when one is only eight, so to me the tragedy that had deprived me of my father and grandfather was already ancient history. As I have said, I saw very little of my father, and of my grandfather I saw even less. They were to me Olympian figures who, apart from brief routine visits, impinged upon my consciousness only when they descended from their grown-up heaven either to admonish me if I had been naughty or give me lovely presents.

Nanny Trotter told me that they had both gone to live with my beautiful mother in Jerusalem-the-Golden, which I took to be a still more remote paradise than that they had presumably enjoyed down here. She made it quite clear that they would never return and it did not take me very long to get accustomed to the idea that I should not see either of them again. Grandfather's beard had rather a nice smell, which I think was due to lavender-water, and father had a jolly laugh; but I cannot honestly say that I missed either of them very much.

Besides, there were a thousand new interests to fill my small mind—and, above all, Julia. She did not seem to have any friends in the neighbourhood—although people often came down from London to spend the evening with her and Uncle Paul—so she let me be with her for a large part of every day. Nanny Trotter had been installed at Kew to look after me, of course, but Miss Stiggins had been sacked, as it had been decided that I should go to a prep-school after Christmas and that until then I need not do any lessons.

Julia took me shopping with her—which was very exciting, as I had hardly even been in a shop before—and to the cinema, and several times up to London, where we lunched in restaurants and afterwards went to look at all sorts of lovely things in Bond Street. So with all these thrilling new experiences I had not a moment left to brood.

I record all this simply to show that when I saw the burglar I was not grieving for my father and full of morbid thoughts about death. I was a normal, healthy small boy having the time of his life and without a care in the world.

It happened about a fortnight before Christmas on one of Nanny Trotter's nights out. Julia had let me stay up a little later than usual and it was nearly seven o'clock before she packed me off to my bath with a promise that, as a treat, she would bring me up some orange jelly with my milk and biscuits.

I went up the first flight of stairs as usual, at a run, then turned the hairpin bend and took the next flight two at a time. I had the banisters on my left but was heading half right, as my room was the first on that side of the landing. As this was in December it was, of course, already dark; but the light on the landing in front of me had not yet been switched on, so it was lit only by the faint glow coming up from the hall below. I was still two steps from the top of the flight when something made me glance to my left.

As I was then only a little chap my head was not much above the level of the nearest banister rail and below the further one which served the flight of stairs running up to the second floor. What I saw stopped me dead in my tracks. For a moment I remained there, paralysed by sheer terror.

There was the figure of a man just opposite me on the upper stairs. He was crouching down as though attempting to hide; but he had one white hand on the further banister rail. That gave the impression that he was poised there ready to make an instant dash up the stairs if discovered.

The horrifying thing about it was that as he crouched there his head was below his hand and on a level with my own. He was peering at me from between the banisters and his face was less than twelve inches from mine. The light was too dim for me to see his features clearly but his face was large, round and flabby with small dark pits for eyes. He made not the slightest sound or movement but just remained there staring at me with the sort of bestial ferocity that one might have expected to see on the face of Jack the Ripper.

What broke the tension after that awful, age-long moment I have no idea. Perhaps he moved first; or it may be that my heart, having temporarily stopped, started again, so that in an automatic reaction I let out a terrified yell. As I screamed and jerked myself away I caught just a glimpse of him, still crouched almost double, gliding swiftly up the stairs.

I use the word 'gliding' because when I was questioned afterwards I could not recall having heard his footsteps, or, indeed, any noise at all. Had I been older that would certainly have struck me as queer, since the dark outline of the figure had been squat but bulky, and, even if he was wearing rubber-soled shoes, a heavy man could hardly take a flight of stairs at the run without his footfalls being audible. At the time, and for long afterwards, I simply assumed that any noise he made must have been drowned by the sounds of my own wild flight.

Scared out of my wits, I bounded towards the half-landing, swerved round the bend of the stairs and literally flung myself down the lower flight to arrive sprawling in the hall, still gasping and yelling.

Almost simultaneously, like a scene in a French farce, three of the doors opened. Julia came running from her sitting-room, Uncle Paul from his study with a friend of his who happened to be with him, and Florrie, the little housemaid, from the dining-room, where she was laying the table for dinner. To complete the party, Cook arrived a second later from the kitchen still clutching a saucepan.

As they picked me up I shouted: 'There's a man upstairs! A burglar! A burglar!'

Then, trembling with shock and excitement, I burst into tears and flung myself into Julia's arms.

The two men armed themselves with golf clubs and went upstairs. The women remained clustered about me in the hall anxiously listening for sounds of strife, but the only ones that reached us were the faint opening and shutting of doors.

Uncle Paul and his friend seemed to be away a long time, but at last they rejoined us. They said that they had searched every room, looked under all the beds and in all the cupboards, but they had not found the burglar, and as far as they could judge nothing had been taken or disturbed; so I must have imagined him.

'But I saw him!' I cried, repudiating the suggestion with indignation. 'He's a horrid, bald old man! He glared at me through the banisters and I thought he was going to spring at me. If he's not there now he must have got out on to the roof.'

Their attempts to reassure me were in vain. I flatly refused to go to bed until further search had been made. The burglar could not have come down the back stairs because there weren't any, so I feared that he must be lurking somewhere and might come creeping into my room while the grown-ups were having dinner.

To quiet my fears the attics and roof were searched; but without result. The moon had risen and in its light there was no place on the sloping tiles of that small, square house where a man could have remained hidden. As the gaps between the roof of The Willows and those of the houses on either side of it were far too wide for any man to jump, the only other possibility was that the burglar had got out of one of the second-floor windows and shinned down a drainpipe, I insisted that he must have done so and was, perhaps, hiding outside, waiting to return when we were all asleep.

Julia made the two men go out into the garden with torches. There were flower-beds all round the house and anyone coming down a drainpipe must have landed on one, but there was not a footmark to be seen on any of them.

My tears had long since dried, but I was still very excited and nothing could shake my conviction that I had seen a murderous-looking thug crouching on the stairs. However, nothing more could be done about it, so I allowed myself to be taken up to bed while Florrie got a special supper that Julia ate with me; then she read me to sleep.

Next morning, of course, the whole affair was gone into again, but no fresh light was thrown upon it, and with the approach of Christmas I ceased to think about it any more. It was not until nearly eleven years later that there came a sequel to this strange affair.

One day just as I was leaving the mess at Biggin Hill, after lunch, a trim-looking W.A.A.F. came up to me and said: 'Hello, Master Toby! Don't you remember me?'

She was rather a pert-looking blonde of about thirty, and her face was vaguely familiar, but I couldn't place her.

'I'm Florrie Meddows,' she said. 'I was housemaid at The Willows when you were a little boy. My, sir; how you've grown! But I would have known you anywhere. How's Mr and Mrs Jugg; in the pink, I hope?'

Of course, I recalled her then and we talked for a bit of old times. After a while she asked: 'Did you ever see any more spooks at The Willows?'

'Spooks!' I echoed. 'What on earth do you mean?'

'Why, ghosts, of course. Surely you remember the night when you scared us all stiff by insisting that you had seen a ghost?'

'You're mixing me up with someone else,' I laughed. 'I've never seen a ghost in my life.'

She shook her head. 'No, it was you all right. You came yelling downstairs fit to wake the dead. But I remember now, you thought it was a burglar; and I suppose your aunt, not wanting to frighten you, never told you different.'

At that the whole episode came back to my mind as clearly as though it had happened only the day before. 'I've certainly always thought it was a burglar,' I agreed in great surprise. 'Whatever makes you think it was a ghost?'

'Well, a human being couldn't have flown out of the window,' Florrie countered, 'or disappeared like that without leaving a single trace, could he? Besides, your uncle and aunt may not have let on to you about it, but they were nuts about Spiritualism. There was hardly a night when they had friends down from London that they didn't go in for table-turning, wall-rapping, and all that. It wasn't none of my business, and Cook and me just used to laugh about it, thinking them a bit cranky, till the night you gave us all such a fright. That made us think very different, knowing what we did; and we were both so scared that we gave notice first thing next morning. We'd have sacrificed our money and left there and then if it hadn't been for letting Mrs Jugg down over Christmas, and her promising not to hold any more séances while we were in the house. If it was a burglar you saw, Master Toby, then I'm a policeman and Hitler's my Aunt Fanny. No good ever comes of calling on the spirits, and it was through them doing that some horrid thing started to haunt the house.'

Friday, 8th May

Another quiet night, although rather a restless one, owing to Julia never having turned up yesterday evening, as I hoped she would. Perhaps she decided to put off her visit till today and then stay over the weekend.

Fortunately, I became so interested in writing the account of my 'burglar' that I continued at it after dinner, and that occupied my mind enough to prevent my fretting over her non-appearance until Deb settled me down for the night.

I had better finish it off now. Actually, there is little more to tell; and I find it difficult to doubt that Florrie Meddows' explanation of the vanishing without trace of the figure that I saw must be the true one.

People do not tell children ghost stories or give them books about ghouls and vampires to read. Tales of witches who turn princes into frogs and of giants who carry off princesses—yes; but anything to do with the after-life or the supernatural is taboo. Therefore, at the age of eight-and-a-half I can scarcely have known what the word 'ghost' implied, hence my immediate assumption that the thing I saw was a man.

It is this, I think, that gives the occurrence peculiar and outstanding weight as proof that astral bodies are at times visible to humans. Everyone else in that house knew what was going on there, so, if any of them had seen what I did, one might fairly argue that thinking about the séances had played Old Harry with their nerves, and that they had imagined it. But I could not possibly have done so, because before one can make a mental concept of anything it is essential to have some basic knowledge of it, and in my case this was entirely lacking.

The next time I saw Julia I tackled her about it. At first she hedged and pretended to have forgotten the whole affair; but when I told her about my meeting with Florrie she shrugged and said with her lazy smile:

'Of course it was an astral, darling. It's quite true that when you first came to us at The Willows we used to hold séances now and then. But only for fun; and after you saw your "burglar" we were much too frightened ever to hold one again. When Paul had searched the house we knew that it couldn't have been a man who had scared you, and the only possible explanation was that one of our controls must be hovering about in visual form. Naturally, as you were only a child, we concealed the truth from you and tried to make you forget the fright you'd had as quickly as we could. I don't mind admitting now that we were pretty scared ourselves, and I was thankful that we had already arranged to move from The Willows soon after Christmas.'

I tried to get her to tell me about the séances they had held, but she insisted that there was really nothing to tell, as she hadn't proved a very good medium and, apart from the totally unexpected appearance of my burglar, the results had been disappointing; so I did not press her. The important point is that she fully confirmed all that Florrie had said.

I'm glad that I took the trouble to write all this out, as recalling the affair in detail makes me as nearly certain as anyone can be that I *did* see a supernatural manifestation when I was a healthy, innocent child; and that gives real, solid support to my belief that I am not imagining things now.

However, the fact that I have good grounds for supposing that apparitions do appear to humans raises again the question of Good and Evil; and I would like to clear my mind a bit on that. It is an axiom that nothing happens without a cause; so who pulls the wires behind the scenes? Is it always the Devil, or sometimes God? What is the object of such operations? And can humans really command spirits to do their will?

If the manifestation occurs without our seeking it, is some power beyond earth attempting to influence us, or could it have been sent by some evilly disposed human? Again, if through a medium, or the exercise of our own will employed in some ancient mystery, we provoke the supernatural occurrence, is it, in the first place, really a response from some loved one who has passed over and, in the second, a minor entity compelled to obey us; or, in both cases, have the forces of Evil accepted our rash invitation to emerge from some dark and hideous cavern of the underworld?

All these questions seethe in my tired brain when I cannot sleep at night, and fear that at any moment instinct may again make my flesh begin to creep at the approach of the Thing in the courtyard.

At least, as a starting point, I feel justified in assuming that the Otherworld must be another dimension of this one, and that its denizens have the power, given suitable conditions, to impinge upon our consciousness.

There seems, too, no reason to suppose that the will of a spirit in a physical body is necessarily weaker than that of a spirit in limbo. So the former may prove equal to forcing the latter to do its bidding; and that, no doubt, is the secret of the supernormal powers with which all the great occultists have been credited. From the same premises, though, should the disembodied entity prove stronger than the will of the living person who has conjured it up, woe betide the occultist; for it would then be he who would find himself the slave of some strange, potent, and almost certainly malignant force.

By worldly and academic standards Florrie Meddows is a person of the lower orders and mean intelligence; yet surely she voiced the sound sense and clear vision so often inherited through many generations of humble folk when she said to me: 'No good ever comes of calling on the spirits.'

However cautious and intelligent a seeker after occult power may be, or one who endeavours to gain information by consulting a professional psychic, it does not seem to me that they possess any yardstick with which to measure the results that they obtain. How can they possibly tell if the entities they contact are good or evil, or be certain that they are not being deceived by malicious spirits and led on to their ultimate ruin?

In my own case, God knows, I have not deliberately tempted Providence by seeking to probe these dark secrets, but

Later

I had to stop writing this morning because Deb came in. She doesn't often do so between eleven and one on a wet day, but as it had stopped raining by a quarter to twelve she wanted me to take my daily turn round the garden before lunch; so that she would be free this afternoon to have tea with the village schoolmaster, who is a friend of hers.

Her unexpected appearance gave me furiously to think. I am most anxious that no one should learn about this journal—in case they get the idea that I've got a screw loose—and Deb, Taffy and Helmuth are all liable to barge in here without warning from time to time. I have been writing in an old exercise book, and if they notice that I've taken to scribbling as a habit one of them is bound to ask what I am writing about. Then if I said that I was trying my hand at a short story, or something like that, they would be certain to want to read it.

While I was being wheeled round the garden I decided that I would tear out the sheets that I have covered so far and hide them between the leaves of my stamp albums. In future I shall write on single sheets, using one of the albums as a writing block, and as each is finished conceal it with the others. Then, if anyone comes in while I am on the job they will think that I am making notes of the stamps I want to complete some of my sets.

This plan also provides a means of hiding the script when I am out. Nobody has any excuse for opening the albums, so it is extremely unlikely that anyone will come upon these sheets there—unless, of course, something happens to me.

That brings me to another point. I started this journal simply with the idea of putting down my recent strange experiences in black and white, so that I could consider them more objectively. At least, that is what I thought; but I believe that, all the time, I also had it in the back of my mind that since I am menaced by some intangible form of danger, should I fall victim to it I would like to leave behind a record of all that has occurred.

My stamp collection is of considerable value, so if anything did happen to me these notes are certain to be found; and the odds are that they would be found by Julia, which is what I want.

Of course it is absurd, really, even to suggest that I might be taken away from here in a straitjacket, or die in a fit one night. Still, if fate has decreed some such horror for me I would like Julia to know that I did not succumb to it tamely, but fought it with all my might.

On the face of it the simplest way of achieving my object would be to keep these papers in a packet addressed to her, but if I did that it might be tampered with, or deliberately destroyed. Why should I fear that? I'm darned if I know. Such groundless suspicions are said to be a sign of madness. Perhaps I am going mad. Oh, God, I wish I knew!

Saturday, 9th May

Still no sign of Julia! It really is extraordinary! Even if she were ill I feel sure that, on receiving my last letter, she would send some kind of message. The only possible explanation for her failure either to come here or write to me is that she must have been away from Queensclere for some days, and that my letter has not yet caught up with her—or that she is an air-raid casualty, which God forbid; but that is hardly likely as, were it so, Uncle Paul or one of the servants would have let us know of it by telegram.

If she had been coming yesterday it was a fair bet that she would have arrived in time for dinner; so when she didn't, instead of writing any more of this I wrote to her again, in the hope that if my earlier letter is still chasing her round the country this last one will catch her on her return to Queensclere. In it I did not mince matters, but spilled the whole story.

I had an untroubled night again—the fourth in succession—and I am now beginning to hope that I may remain immune from further attack until the end of the month. That proved to be the case in April, and it looks as if the Thing's activity is in some way dependent on the moon being either at, or near, full. During the dark quarter there is, naturally, no moonlight to throw the shadows; but I have never seen it while the moon was in her first or third quarters; neither have I felt the brute's presence at such times. So, now that the moon is on the wane, I am crossing thumbs that I'll be free of my accursed visitor for a bit. At present, though, the above is still only a theory, so I am certainly not going to start counting my chickens as yet.

Last night I thought a lot more about ways of ensuring that this record should reach Julia in the event of my apparently crazy forebodings taking concrete form. After all, some reason that I know nothing of may prevent her coming this week, or next; and tonight, or any night, the Thing may come again and–and succeed in forcing its way in. So I mean to keep at this journal until she does come or . . . And, in the last case, I am now convinced that using the stamp album offers a better prospect of achieving my end than any other means at my disposal.

If anything did happen to me, all my personal effects would become the property of Uncle Paul, as my next of kin; so it would be Julia who, sooner or later, would go through them, and all the odds are against anyone examining the albums before they came into her hands.

It would fall to Taffy's lot to pack up my things. He is the head gardener's son, and promoted to an indoor post as my body-servant only because of the present shortage of man-power, and the fact that his slightly deformed feet make him ineligible for National Service.

Taffy's strength lies in his muscles, not in his head; but the small, dark eyes set in his moon-like face suggest a certain slyness, and I wouldn't put it past him to pinch my cuff-links if he thought he could get away with it. But I doubt if it would ever occur to him to monkey with my stamps. He wouldn't know which ones were worth taking, and he would be frightened at the risk involved to anyone who knows nothing about such things trying to turn them into money. Even if curiosity led him to glance through the albums and he came upon these pages I very much doubt if he would bother to read them.

If he did, though, I believe he is the one person here who would really sympathize with me. The farm people round about in these Welsh hills are still pretty primitive. Taffy must have heard plenty of tales of hobgoblins, and of old women putting a murrin on their neighbour's cattle. More 'sophisticated' people might laugh at me for being frightened of a shadow, but Taffy Morgan wouldn't.

Deb would certainly laugh; or, more probably, regard my 'ravings' with cynical disdain. I have to have massage for my back every day, and Helmuth says that, with the war on, we are lucky to have got a professional nurse who is also a highly skilled masseuse to come and live down here in the back of beyond. All the same, I would gladly have put up with a little less skill from someone a bit more human and cheerful. She is a good-looking girl, or, rather, woman, but one of those thin-faced, brainy Jewesses who are not given to laughter and consider that 'Life is real, life is earnest'.

There is no race further removed from the mystic than the Jews of these days; and those whom education has lifted out of bondage to the Mammon of Unrighteousness give their minds to art or politics. Sister Deborah Kain is the latter type. She is, not unnaturally, a fanatical anti-Nazi and, I suspect, holds most advanced views on political reform.

She is so reticent by nature that I really know very little about her, except that her father was a University professor. I feel sure that she is much too respectable to be dishonest; and as she has already looked through my stamps several times with me, there could be no reason other than an impulse to steal which might cause her to open the albums after–well, after the sort of thing that I prefer not to contemplate.

As for Helmuth, it is most unlikely that he would even give a thought to my stamps. By the Grace of God he despises stamp collecting. He admitted on one occasion, with a superior air, that as a hobby for young people it has the merit of teaching them a modicum of geography without tears; but more than once when I have had my albums out he has said: 'Hello! Wasting your time again with those silly little bits of coloured paper?'

I find it strange that such an intelligent man should be so intolerant of any pursuit requiring a certain amount of knowledge, discrimination and exactitude; but Helmuth has other queer gaps in his, generally speaking, quite remarkable mentality. As it happens now, this one is particularly fortunate for me, as he is the last person whom I would wish to see these pages. In fact, I might as well be honest with myself and admit that the real reason why I am so anxious to prevent Deb or Taffy finding them is because they might tell Helmuth what I am up to.

If I were asked to explain why I am so averse to Helmuth knowing what is going on in my mind, I couldn't give a reason–other than my natural anxiety that neither he nor anyone else should have grounds for suspecting that I may be going mad. Yet several times recently it has seemed to me that he looks at me now with a queer, searching expression, as if he already knows that something is wrong, and is trying to read my thoughts.

My feeling may be a genuine instinct, or it may be due to the fact that half a lifetime in his company has bred in me a spontaneous urge to protect myself from the uncanny knack he has of ferreting out my secrets; but, whatever its cause, an inner voice insistently warns me to keep from him even an inkling of my present mental state.

Anyway, the chance of his coming upon the script–whether I am here or not–is now extremely remote; and I am inclined to think that it was his contempt for philately which led me subconsciously to choose the albums as a hiding-place for it. Even in an idle moment he would find something more congenial to him with which to occupy his mind than my stamps, so he will never glance at them casually; and he certainly would not stoop to petty pilfering.

There is nothing petty about Helmuth. His mind is extremely subtle and his motives for doing or saying things are often so elusive that it is very difficult to form an accurate estimate of his real beliefs and character. Sometimes he gives the impression of having the most lofty ideals, at others his cynicism appears positively brutal; but he always "thinks big". In all the years we have been together I have never known him do otherwise, and if he wanted to rob the family he would devise some scheme which, by comparison, would make the proceeds from stealing my stamps look like robbing the poor-box.

All this about preventing anyone here tumbling to it that I am writing a journal has put me right off my stroke again; but, on looking back, I see that I got so far as recording my youthful experience with the "burglar".

I cannot state definitely that he was an "evil" manifestation. He certainly looked horrid enough. However, I certainly did not feel what one might term "the presence of evil" at the time. My reaction was simply that of a small boy who suddenly comes face to face with a brutal criminal and, fearing physical violence, flees in panic to the protection of friendly grown-ups.

In considering the matter it is worth remembering that, because certain human beings have the misfortune to be incredibly ugly or hideously deformed, it does not in the least follow that they are evil. Again, the apparition seen by Lord Dufferin had most repulsive features, yet it saved his life; and so, to him, it played the part of a guardian angel. Therefore I think one must keep an open mind about my burglar.

There was really nothing to suggest that he was an emissary from the Devil. Yet I have good grounds for believing that forces of a definitely Satanic nature do, at times, impinge upon man's consciousness. The Thing that comes to my window arouses in me a fear and nausea of such a special kind that they alone seem enough to indicate that it can have its origin only in Hell; but I have been leading the abnormal life of a sick man for so many weary months that I am now tortured by doubts about the soundness of my judgment; and it was not the thing that makes the shadow that I had in mind. I was thinking of the only other experience of the occult with which I met while still in full health and unquestionably sane.

On that occasion I did not see anything at all. I only felt it; so the bigoted sceptic would be more inclined than ever to assert that my imagination was playing me tricks. I can only vouch for my belief that quite suddenly and inexplicably I found myself in the immediate vicinity of what I can but describe as disembodied evil.

It is a commonplace for people to speak of houses having a good or bad "atmosphere"; and every house agent knows that this intangible factor plays a very large part in determining whether empty properties are snapped up quickly or remain on his books for many months. In the majority of cases it seems reasonable to suppose that such atmospheres are created by the happiness or unhappiness of the previous tenants; and that they have left something of their healthy, cheerful mentalities or mean, base natures behind. But in exceptionally bad cases such atmospheres are openly termed "hauntings", and are attributed to suicides, murders and other evil acts which have taken place, sometimes centuries ago.

Both explanations are, of course, further evidence for the existence of the supernatural in our midst; since it is really no more inexplicable that the spirit of a murderer should haunt the scene of his crime than that a happy, carefree family of still living people should leave behind them a feeling of sunshine and laughter. Neither can be explained by any human attribute that the psychologists have yet succeeded in codifying for insertion in medical text-books; so they can be only manifestations of that something we all possess which is quite independent of the physical body.

Recalling in detail this other psychic experience of my youth will, I am sure, further strengthen my hold on the belief that I am still as sane now as I was then.

It happened soon after the beginning of the first summer term that I spent in the senior house at Weylands. That was in 1937, so I was very nearly sixteen at the time.

Later

Most people have heard of Weylands Abbey and it is only natural that opinion should be very sharply divided on the methods of education in practice there. Elderly people who have a bigoted prejudice in favour of the old Public School system, with its birchings, daily chapel and enforced games, go purple in the face at the very mention of the place. Others, with ultra-modern views, maintain that Weylands represents a new system of enlightened education which must, eventually, become universal, if future generations of children are to be brought up free of all the complexes and inhibitions that are the secret impetus behind most kinds of unhappiness and crime.

Weylands is in Cumberland, and the school take its name from the ruins of the ancient Abbey that stands nearly in the centre of its vast private park. The school itself is about a mile from the Abbey and consists of a big, ugly mansion erected in Victorian times by a wealthy Lancashire cotton-goods manufacturer; but it has since been completely modernized and considerably added to. In the stone of the pseudo-Gothic arch over its front porch are carved the words DO WHAT THOU WILT SHALL BE THE WHOLE OF THE LAW, and that gives the clue to the theory on which the system of education at Weylands was based.

There were no classes or teaching in the accepted sense, but a large part of each day was given to study hours. Every pupil could take whichever subjects he or she liked best–for of course it was co-educational–and they were given books suitable to their age to read about it, then, when they felt inclined, they discussed what they had read with the masters and mistresses.

In the recreation hours there were no organized games, as that would have entailed captains of sides and obedience to them. Instead there was tennis, golf, swimming, squash and other sports for those who liked them; those who didn't could go for a walk, laze about or even go to bed if they preferred to do so.

The only penalty for not getting up at the usual hour in the morning was that, when you did, you had to make your own bed; and the only penalty for being late for meals was that you missed them, or anyhow the first course. When newcomers got the hang of the thing they sometimes decided to live on their tuck for a bit and not get up at all; but they soon got bored with doing nothing and fell into the normal routine of their own free will.

In the junior house there were separate dormitories for girls and boys; but in the senior house the sexes were not segregated and everyone had separate cubicles. We were encouraged to express our own individualities by their furnishing and decoration, and there was no bar to a chap visiting a girl's cubicle or *vice versa*.

Whether all the parents were fully aware of the sort of thing that went on I rather doubt; but they may have been as, logically, it was simply part of the same system. We were taught that sex was a normal, healthy appetite, similar to a desire for food; and that the indulgences of it were only anti-social when jealousy entered into a sex relationship; so we must never give way to that emotion or strive to prevent those who had given us pleasure giving pleasure to others if they felt so inclined.

Even in the lower house sex had no secrets from us, and we read the books on social hygiene that were put in our way with as much, but no more, interest than we read Kipling's *Jungle Tales*. The elder girls all willingly submitted themselves to a special routine whereby Matron and the resident Doctor took steps to ensure against their getting themselves into trouble, so there was never any bother of that kind.

We were really amoral rather than immoral and cases of excess were very rare. The fact that we could have a romp for the asking at any time we felt like one reduced the thing to a matter of no more importance than going for a swim, so most of us often went quite long periods without indulging ourselves at all. Anyhow, I must admit that, at the time, I accepted everything to do with our sex-life at Weylands as perfectly normal.

Sundays there were marked by a choice of going for a picnic, or attending a private cinema show in the afternoons, and in the evenings a dance in what had been the chapel of the original house. No religious ceremony was ever held and Scripture was the one subject in which there were no facilities for learning. We were taught that all religion was a product of the Dark Ages, when the development of the individual was retarded by a multitude of absurd taboos and superstitions.

Newcomers who had already received a certain amount of religious instruction were referred to pityingly as "poor little savages" and soon laughed out of their beliefs. In order to encourage them in developing a contempt for the symbol before which the ignorant masses still bowed down all the doormats had a crucifix woven into them, so that we all trod on it every time we went in or out.

I need scarcely add that there was no prohibition on our swearing and blaspheming to our hearts' content, and the obscenities which used to issue from the mouths of some of the smaller children were, at times, remarkable; but most of them soon grew out of that, and I don't think the older pupils were any more foul-mouthed than their contemporaries at other schools.

Naturally there were no exams or end-of-term reports at Weylands, as the theory was that we were there to develop our individualities, not our brains. Nevertheless, the staff had its own methods of interesting us in all the essential subjects and it was rare for anyone to leave without having absorbed the rudiments of a fair, general education. Moreover, in those who possessed an instinctive thirst for knowledge the theory of non-compulsion and a free choice of subjects worked wonders. Many of them left equipped far in advance of their age on their special lines, and have since become noted intellectuals.

Looking back on the way we were allowed to behave—shouting, blaspheming, throwing things about, teaching the girls tricks or being taught by them, lazing away mornings in bed and taking afternoons off to go birds'-nesting—it now seems almost incredible that an English school should have been conducted on such lines. But it was; and such is the adaptability of children that, after we had been there a few weeks, none of us thought it the least strange.

On the contrary, we thanked our Stars—not God—that our parents were sufficiently enlightened to choose such a school for us. We took pride in the fact that we were not like the miserable, ignorant, backward children that we met in the holidays, but a race apart, who had sloughed off all silly superstitions, were troubled by no stupid inhibitions about sex and, while still in our teens, were the masters of our fate, like grown-up men and women.

I see now that I have rambled on over several sheets about Weylands, which was certainly not my intention. I really started out only to make it clear that at a school run on those lines there was nothing at all to prevent my spending a night out if I wished. The chaps and girls often used to go out on moonlight picnics and not return till the small hours of the morning; so I did not even think twice about it when it occurred to me that it would be rather fun to spend the night with Uncle Paul and Julia.

I see that it's later than I thought. I must leave it till tomorrow to record the damnably unnerving experience I met with on my way over to them.

Sunday, 10th May

We do not go in for Sunday services here at Llanferdrack, any more than they did at Weylands; and for the first time in my life I am inclined to wish that we did. The fact that I was brought up to despise all organized religion has never before caused me any regret; but, in view of my recent nightmares—the term will serve although I'd give a packet to be able to think they are really only that—I believe I should derive quite a lot of comfort from hearing the swell of a church organ and the murmur of voices joined in prayer.

The Church has lost nearly all her temporal power and most of her ancient wisdom, yet she still remains the only avowed champion in arms against the Devil. Probably her loss of vitality can be accounted for by the fact that comparatively few of her ministers seem to believe in the Devil these days, so they don't give their energies to fighting him any more. But the principles she represents remain unaltered, so anyone who seeks protection through her from the things that menace the spirit should be safe—at least, that is, if they have faith.

Any attempt to secure Divine protection which was made half-heartedly would obviously be futile; and I am by no means certain that I could bring myself to pronounce the Creed—or whatever it is that people do when they are confirmed—with genuine belief in what I was saying. One does not have to be educated at Weylands to have honest doubts about some bits of Christian dogma.

In any case it is a waste of time for me even to think about the matter. If I sent for the local vicar, and asked him to prepare me for confirmation, Helmuth would immediately conclude that my mind had become unhinged; and giving him that impression is the one thing I mean to avoid at all costs.

I don't think I have mentioned that Helmuth was the German master at Weylands. He is not, of course, a German himself, but a Czech, and his full name is Doctor Helmuth Lisický.

That brings us back to Weylands, and I must explain now how it was that Uncle Paul and Julia happened to be in the vicinity on the night that I was scared out of my wits.

The school is situated in one of the most desolate parts of Cumberland. It is lovely country, but there isn't an hotel, or even a comfortable inn, within twenty miles; and when the place first started that made it awkward for parents who wanted to come down in term time to see their young.

In consequence, the school authorities built a sort of bungalow village at the southern end of the park. It consists of about a dozen comfortable cottages, having from four to six rooms apiece, and a Club-house with rooms at the back for visiting chauffeurs and a permanent staff. Parents can write to the bursar and book one of the cottages for a night or two if they wish, and meals are provided for them in the Club-house during their stay.

Old boys were also accommodated there, as Weylands was very keen about keeping in touch with her ex-scholars, and some of them came down quite frequently. As a matter of fact the ramifications of Weylands resulted in a much closer community than is the case with most schools; perhaps because the new system of education practised there formed almost a cult.

Pupils were never accepted after the age of ten, in case they had already formed old-fashioned prejudices to a degree that might make them a disruptive influence; and each one had to be personally recommended by parents who had had a child at the school themselves for at least a year. So it was rather like a club; and sometimes parents who knew one another used to arrange to come down together and share one of the larger bungalows.

Anyhow, Uncle Paul and Julia had arranged to come down for a couple of nights right at the beginning of the summer term, because I had not seen them for some months owing to their having been abroad; and I knew that they had been allotted one of the smaller bungalows, where they would be alone. Naturally I had been looking forward to seeing them, but they did not expect to arrive until just in time for dinner, so in the normal course of events I should not have done so till the following day.

Actually it was not until I was just about to go to bed that I suddenly had the bright idea of paying them a surprise visit. It had been raining, but the rain had stopped, and it was warm night with the moon showing now and then between scudding clouds, so the idea of a walk seemed rather pleasant. Still, the bungalows were right at the far end of the great park, over two miles away from the school, and I didn't much relish the thought of the long tramp back after midnight, particularly as it might come on to rain again. The solution to that was easy: I could pop a pair of pyjamas and a toothbrush into my attaché-case and, after a lovely long chin-wag with my visitors, spend the rest of the night in the spare room of their bungalow.

I didn't hurry myself about setting out, as I thought that after dinner they would probably remain in the Club-house talking to some of the other visitors till about half-past-ten, so it was getting on for that when I put on my mac and let myself out of the school by one of its side doors.

Long winding drives led off from the house to the three gates of the park and the one I took passed fairly near to the ruins of the old Abbey, which was situated about half-way between the school and the bungalows. I was as fit and cheerful as any carefree youngster of nearly sixteen could be, and as I stepped out at a brisk pace I distinctly remember that I was humming jazz tunes to myself.

The drive approached the Abbey to within about four hundred yards, then curved away in a wide bend that made nearly a half-circle round it. By taking a short cut across the bend one passed within a hundred yards of the Abbey and saved quite a considerable distance. The only thing against it was that the ground was rather rough and scored every few yards with little ditches; but I had often taken the short cut in the daytime and, as the moon gave enough light to see by, I did so now.

I must have covered nearly a quarter of a mile and had the Abbey on my immediate right when I happened to glance in that direction. If I hadn't been so occupied in watching my step I should probably have noticed it before, but I suddenly saw the glow of a misty, reddish light in the middle of the ruins.

I was not so much surprised as intrigued, because it was common knowledge at Weylands that, soon after the place was started, the school authorities had converted the crypt of the Abbey into a Masonic Temple.

It was the one and only place that was out of bounds to us, and none of the masters would ever tell us anything about it, with the result that there was quite a lot of casual speculation as to what it was like inside, and what went on there.

All I had been able to gather from some of the older chaps was that it had no connection with British Masonry, but was a Lodge of the Grand Orient, as Continental Masonry is called, and that Fellowship of it gave one lots of pull in the political and financial worlds. The masters were all believed to be Fellows, and pupils who had proved satisfactory were given a special course during their last term to prepare them for initiation before they left.

These initiation ceremonies always took place the night after the end of term, so the rest of us, having already gone down, had no opportunity immediately afterwards to try to get out of the initiates what it was all about; and when they came back on visits as old boys they proved as cagey as the masters. No doubt I should have been initiated myself in due course if I hadn't run away from Weylands before the end of my last term—but that is another story.

In view of all this, the sight of the red glow in the middle of the ruins naturally aroused my curiosity, but I hesitated at the thought of trying to find out what it was on account of the risk I should be running if I went much nearer. There were no punishments of any kind at Weylands but, of course, one could be expelled, and it had been made quite clear that such a fate would overtake any of us if we were caught snooping round the Abbey. Still, the very fact that it held the one and only secret that we were 'not considered old enough to know' made it all the more tantalizing.

I knew that I could not get right into the Abbey, even if I had been prepared to expose myself to almost certain discovery, as a six-foot-high wire-mesh fence had been erected all round it; but I thought that if I went as far as the fence I should be able to get a peep at the place from which the light was coming and find out what was going on there. For a minute or two I stood there undecided, staring at the red mist. Then the moon went behind a big bank of cloud, plunging the park in darkness, and feeling that there was very little chance of my being spotted for the next minutes, I began to walk cautiously forward.

As I advanced the light waxed and waned at irregular intervals, almost disappearing for a time, then suddenly flaring up again. At first I thought that it must be caused by a bonfire; but I could not be certain, as one of the great masses of masonry which formed the roofless shell of the church stood between the centre of the glow and my line of advance.

In order to get a better view I altered my course a little, until I came opposite a big gap in the ruin, and could see through a broken archway into the body of the church. I saw then that an imposing portico had been erected in the middle of the nave, presumably over a stairway leading down to the crypt. In it were framed a big pair of wrought-iron gates. They were backed with some opaque substance which might have been frosted glass. The dull red glow was coming through them; and its intermittent flare-ups were caused by dark figures that emerged out of the shadows every frew moments, pushing one side of the gates open to pass through into the brightly lit interior of the portico.

I was still too far off to identify any of the figures, but the silhouettes of two out of the five I saw looked as if they were those of women. This intrigued me greatly, as I had once heard a rumour that the mistresses attended certain of the ceremonies, and that the pick of the girls were made associates on leaving, at the same time as eldest chaps received their initiation; so with the idea of settling the point I decided to advance as far as the wire-mesh fence. It stood only about twenty yards from the broken wall of the ruin, and on the far side of the ancient cemetery of the Abbey, which I had already entered.

The ground there was very rough, being broken with grassy mounds and, here and there, old grave-stones half-buried in the coarse grass; but having been brought up to despise all superstition it never even occurred to me that it was the sort of place in which I might meet a ghost. I was about half-way across it when I suddenly noticed that the moon looked like coming out again from behind the bank of cloud. That threw me into a bit of a flap, as I realized that if one of the people passing through the church happened to glance in my direction I was near enough now for them to spot me by its light; so I hastily looked round for cover.

Some thirty feet away I saw an old, box-like stone tomb, considerably bigger than most of the others, and I hurriedly made in that direction with the idea of crouching down behind it. Unnoticed by me my shoe-lace must have come undone, for I stepped on it just as I reached the tomb, tripped and lurched forward.

Instinctively I threw out my hands to save myself. They landed with all my weight behind them on the bevelled edge of the slab of stone that formed the flat top of the tomb. It was centuries old and may have been cracked already, or countless winters may have weakened it where there was a flaw in the centre of the stone. It gave under the sudden pressure and several large fragments collapsed inwards, leaving nearly half the tomb gaping open.

For a second my heart was in my mouth. But the bits of stone had not far to fall and their subsidence made only a faint slither, followed by a thump so gentle that it could not possibly have attracted the attention of anyone inside the Abbey. Thanking my stars that my mishap had had no worse results, I turned about and knelt down to retie my shoe-lace.

Suddenly–without rhyme or reason–I had the feeling that somebody was standing just behind me. The warning came to my brain as sharply, as unexpectedly and as imperatively, as the sudden shrilling of a telephone bell in an empty house.

In a flash I swivelled round, expecting to find myself face to face with–I don't really know who or what; certainly not a master, but someone or something that was regarding me with a fixed, hostile stare. With a gasp of relief I realized that I had been mistaken. There was nobody there; not a thing.

The moon had just come out from behind the cloud-bank, and now lit the scene with a clear, cold radiance. The shadows that it cast were sharp and black upon the ground. By it I could distinctly see the jagged edge of the broken lid of the tomb behind which I had been kneeling and, fifteen yards away, the stout wire-mesh fence that had been put up round the ruins as an additional precaution against unauthorized persons getting into them. The body of the church had become a pool of darkness splashed with irregular patches of silver light. The red glow still showed faintly from the double gates, but the figures I had seen must have been those of late-comers to the meeting, as there was now neither sight nor sound to show that there was a living thing within a mile of me.

Inclined to laugh now at the fright I had given myself, I knelt down again to do up my shoe. I had hardly twisted the ends into a bow before the same horrid feeling assailed me. I could have sworn that someone was overlooking me from behind; that a pair of eyes were boring right through my back.

A swift glance over my shoulder confirmed my previous scrutiny of the place. There was nothing there. Absolutely nothing but the gravestones glinting whitely in the moonlight.

My fumbling fingers sought to tie the knot, but they trembled so much that they could hold the laces in position. I tried to steady them, telling myself again and again that there was nothing of which to be afraid. If there was, I argued desperately, I could not possibly have failed to see it, because the full moon made the place almost as light as if it had been day.

Yet, fight as I would, I could not throw off the feeling. Instead, every second it grew worse. Shivers ran through me. The hair on the back of my neck began to prickle and rise like the hackles of a dog. A still, small voice somewhere in my mind now kept on insisting that the unseen presence behind me was something monstrous–something that meant to strike me down and do me deadly harm.

Being in such eerie surroundings within an hour or so of midnight would have been enough to lay most boys of my age open to a fit of the jitters, but the scepticism I had imbibed at Weylands had toughened me against such superstitious fears. I swore to myself that I would not give way to this childish, idiotic attack of funk, for which there was not the faintest base or cause, and that I would retie my shoe-lace before I looked round again–if it was the last thing I ever did.

How long that silent, weaponless battle lasted, I have no idea. Probably no more than a few seconds, although it seemed an age. I only know that I failed to tie the shoe-lace.

My eyes were starting from their sockets, the palms of my hands were damp, and I could feel my heart pounding against my ribs. It was suddenly borne in upon me that not for all the money in the world would I turn round again, from fear now of what I might see there. I knew, with a certainty that brooks no argument, that in another second it would be too late to escape. Something outside all human experience–something beyond belief unholy, loathsome, terrifying–was in the very act of launching itself upon me where I knelt. My will broke. I sprang to my feet and fled.

Stark fear lent wings to my feet. Lurching, bounding, tripping over old grave mounds, stumbling in ditches, I raced away from the ruins as though all the devils in Hell were after me. Somehow I got back on to the drive, but I did not pause there. I only blessed its even surface that enabled me to run the faster. Panting, gasping, sobbing for breath, I pelted along it as fast as my legs would carry me, and I did not even notice in which direction I was going until, with unutterable relief, I glimpsed the friendly lights of the bungalows shining through the trees. With a last spurt I dashed straight for the cottage where I expected to find Julia and Uncle Paul, hurled myself at its front door, which was only on the latch, and flung myself inside. There was no answer to my choking cry, and the whole place was in darkness.

I got so worked up writing this account yesterday that I forgot the time until Helmuth came in on his daily visit. He always spends an hour or two with me between tea and dinner, when we talk of this and that and discuss the war news.

Yesterday evening I took special pains to study him closely and tried to regard him as if he were someone whom I had never met before.

He is a fine-looking man and must be very nearly as tall as I am, which is six feet three in my socks. His shoulders are a good bit broader than mine and his whole frame is more powerful. I think, too, that if one were called on to describe Helmuth's outstanding quality by a single adjective, 'powerful' is the word one would choose.

He cannot be more than thirty-eight or -nine, although his hair having gone prematurely white makes him look a good bit older. It is very thick, and he wears it rather long and brushed straight back, which gives his head a massive, leonine appearance. But even if he were bald the breadth of his forehead would still give him a commanding look, and it would take a brave man to challenge those strange light-coloured eyes of his. To say that they were yellow would give a false impression of them, as that makes one think of biliousness, from which he certainly does not suffer. Actually, I suppose they are pale tawny.

His nose is a formidable hook; rather fleshy but more Roman than Jewish; although the fact that his ears are set low on his skull suggests that he may have a dash of Jewish blood acquired two or three generations back. His mouth is his only bad feature. It is too thin and in repose would be taken as a certain sign that he has a cruel nature; but his smile is so quick and friendly that it immediately cancels out any such idea.

His vitality is so great that he rarely keeps still for long, and as he strode up and down in front of the big open fireplace, shooting out ideas on all sorts of subjects, I found it exceedingly difficult to form any definite impression of what really lies behind that constantly animated, lion-like mask. The interest that he never fails to show in everything that concerns me personally, as well as the running of the estate, is perfectly natural; and, whenever he is with me, the idea that he would lend himself to anything that would cause me harm seems perfectly absurd.

Nevertheless, after he had gone I was very thankful that I have taken to writing this on loose sheets inside the cover of one of my stamp albums. The dodge worked perfectly. Although his entrance came as a surprise I was able to complete the sentence I was writing, then calmly shut the album up and put it aside; while, to my secret amusement, he remarked: 'Ha! Ha! I see you have started playing with some of your old kindergarten toys again.'

In recounting my horrible experience at Weylands, I see that I had got to the point where I burst into the cottage that Uncle Paul and Julia had been allotted, to find that they were not there and that the whole place was in darkness; so there is still quite a bit to tell about that unforgettable night.

I was still panting like a grampus and sweating like a pig; quite as much from the awful fright I had had as from the fact that I had just run a mile. Finding the place dark, silent and untenanted unnerved me afresh–although that is hardly an accurate description of what I felt, as my nerve had completely gone already.

For a moment I was near bursting into tears, but I choked them back and then a particle of sense seeped through into my fright-befuddled brain. Grabbing at the switches I snapped on the lights in the hall and sitting-room. After I had done that I began to feel a trifle less scared, but I was still very far from being my own man. I was trembling from head to foot and a succession of shudders ran through my whole body. On stumbling into the sitting-room I caught sight of myself in the mirror over the mantelpiece. The pupils of my eyes looked twice their normal size, my lips were grey, my face as white as a sheet and dripping with perspiration.

It was quite a time before I succeeded in pulling myself together. The sight of some of Julia's belongings scattered about the room showed that my visitors had arrived as arranged, earlier that evening, so I could only assume that they must still be over at the Club-house, yarning with some of the other people there, or taking part in a game of cards. The Club was only a couple of hundred yards down the road but, much as I craved human companionship, nothing would have induced me to go out into the dark again. As soon as I got a bit of a grip on myself I made up the fire and settled down by it in an armchair to await their return.

I tried not to think of the abominable thing from which I had had such a narrow escape; but the thought of it kept coming back and filling me with waves of nausea. Then, as I couldn't get it out of my mind, I endeavoured to face it squarely and see if there wasn't some possible explanation to the affair that my panic had caused me to overlook.

When I had come into the bungalow I had felt terribly cold, in spite of my long run, but as the fire warmed me up I began to feel physically better and my brain started to tick over again.

It occurred to me that the school authorities might know about whatever it was that lurked in the vicinity of the Abbey, and it was for that reason they had put the place out of bounds to us. But I dismissed the idea almost immediately. I was no longer a child, but a well-grown youth of nearly sixteen, and I felt that if entering the territory of the horror could have such an utterly devastating effect on me, its effect on a fully fledged adult could be little less shattering. Yet, as I had verified for myself less than an hour before, the masters did go to the ruins at night to attend their Masonic meetings, and so too, I now believed, did some of the mistresses. It seemed incredible that they should deliberately expose themselves to the sort of experience that I had had; so the theory that they had put the place out of bounds on that account was not tenable.

It seemed certain, too, that the unseen presence could have no connection with anything that took place at the meetings in the crypt. I mean, I have little doubt now that my having seen the 'burglar' at the Willows was the result of the séances that were held there. Of course I was not aware of that explanation when I was at Weylands, because I had not yet run into Florrie Meadows. But by the time I was sixteen I had read quite a few ghost-stories, and heard tell of séances at which spirits were said to blow trumpets and that sort of thing. So it did cross my mind for a moment that the Masonic meetings might have something to do with the occult; but only for a moment. It was so obviously absurd to think of the masters at Weylands dabbling in spiritualism.

They were all dyed-in-the-wool materialists, and if one does not believe in God one cannot believe in the Devil, or the existence of any supernatural beings; so the last thing they would have done was to meet for the purpose of calling on the spirits. They would have laughed at the very idea; and, anyhow, I had heard enough about the Fellowship to know that it was a very down-to-earth affair. It was no secret that its object was to ensure mutual co-operation in worldly matters, so that by assisting one another all its members could achieve wealth and position; and, of course, it was owing to its activities that Weylands was such an immensely rich institution.

Then, as I sat warming myself in front of the fire, a new thought struck me. I recalled that tripping on my shoe-lace had caused me to fall forward and clutch at the top of the tomb, and that under the sudden pressure it had given way. Perhaps my having opened the grave had enabled something to escape from it.

The more I thought about it, the more certain I felt that I had hit upon the right solution. A year or so earlier I had read *Dracula* and, at the time, I had taken all the stuff about vampires and the undead as pure invention; now I thought of it again in a very different light.

The gaping tomb had been behind me as I knelt; and when I swivelled round I had looked across it and all round it, but not down into it. About half the stone lid had remained intact and the open portion of the grave, into which the rest of the lid had fallen, had been obscured by deep shadow. It seemed possible that I had aroused some horrid, corpse-like thing that had been lying there in a state of suspended animation. Or perhaps, by some ancient mystery, the soul of an evil abbot had been imprisoned with his body in the grave—just as in the Arabian Nights the powerful Djinn had been sealed up in a bottle—and I had released a diabolical force that had been straining to get free for centuries, so that it could exact vengeance on humanity.

Such bizarre ideas were a world away from the atheism which we were taught to regard as enlightenment at Weylands. But human instincts and old traditions die hard; and most of us, while ready enough to sneer at religion, still retained a sneaking feeling that there might be something in the tales of ghosts and haunted houses we had heard. In any case, after what I had been through myself that night, no explanation of it sounded too fantastic. I was still vaguely speculating upon what sort of horror it could have been that had come up at me out of the grave when, mentally and physically exhausted as I was, I fell asleep.

Last night I had the horrors again. I saw the shadow, but it was mixed up with all sorts of other beastliness in a nightmare. I do not mean that I actually had another visitation of the sort that I first had early in April, and almost persuaded myself were nightmares until their recurrence at the beginning of this month. I mean a genuine bad dream.

It must have been due to the vividness of the recollections that I conjured up yesterday, while writing an account of my terrifying experience at Weylands. Anyhow I dreamed that I was there again among the graves of the long-dead monks, and that the Thing that has recently been haunting me was chasing me towards the red glow that came from the wrought-iron gates.

Although the beast was behind me as I ran, I seemed to have eyes in the back of my head, for I could see it as it leapt from mound to mound in my tracks. Its body was the big, round, multi-limbed patch of blackness that I always see, but it had the caricature of a human face—and the face was Helmuth's, with his eyes multiplied to ten times their normal size and his fleshy nose changed into a great curved beak.

Julia was there too. She was standing by the glowing gates calmly watching the brute hunt me, and she made not the slightest move to come to my assistance when I screamed to her for help.

I suppose her appearance in my dream, and then the callous attitude she displayed, are to be accounted for by a subconscious projection of the black fits of depression that I get from the thought that she seems to have abandoned me in my present plight. Why she did not arrive over the weekend, or at least answer my letter, I simply cannot think.

Of course, the only possible explanation is that she is no longer at Queensclere and has not had my letters yet. I *know* that she would come here on the very first train if she was aware of what I am up against. So it seems futile to write to her again. I can only thank God that we are now entering the dark quarter of the moon, which means I'll be safe for a bit, and pray that one of my letters catches up with her in the next few days, as it surely must.

Yesterday the village barber came to cut my hair. I am afraid I have always been a bit casual about my appearance, and I often got ticked off for letting my hair grow too long when I was in the ranks of the R.A.F., and later too, during my year's training as a Pilot-Officer. Once I became operational no one bothered me about it any more, as we Fighter boys still had a bit of a halo round our heads—even those of us who had come in only for the tail-end of the Battle of Britain—and we rather prided ourselves in going about dressed any-old-how, our caps on the backs of our heads and the top buttons of our tunics undone. It was all rather childish, I suppose, but in an inverse way it had the same sort of effect that super-smartness has on the Brigade of Guards, and added quite a bit to our morale.

Still, as my hair is unusually silky for its reddish colour and dead straight, it is apt to fall forward over my forehead and bother me when it gets too long; so every few weeks I kick myself into sending for the local clipper-wielder, and submit myself to his inartistic ministrations.

It is raining today, so as I have a clear morning in front of me I'll polish off my account of that affair at Weylands. I see that I had got to the point where I had fallen asleep in the cottage while waiting for Julia and Uncle Paul to return.

I was woken by the sound of the sitting-room door opening with a rattle, then being swiftly shut again. The lights were still on but the fire had gone out, so I must have been asleep for a considerable time. I felt very cold, and shivered as I stood up. The memory of the night's earlier events was just flooding back to me when I heard voices outside in the hall. Someone was muttering something, then Julia's voice came to me quite distinctly as she said:

'So that's why the lights were on! What on earth can Toby be doing here? Thank goodness he's asleep and didn't see me like this. Quick, pull yourself together, now! It's up to you to hold the fort, while I do something to my face.'

Instinctively I had moved towards the door, and she had scarcely finished speaking when I pulled it open. Out of the corner of my eye I caught a glimpse of her back as she hurried into her bedroom, but I found myself looking straight at Uncle Paul.

He was leaning against the wall on the other side of the narrow hallway; and it was clear that Julia's admonition, to pull himself together, had not been given without good reason. He was as drunk as an owl.

Uncle Paul must have been about thirty-seven then. He is a biggish man with red hair and a 'Guards' moustache, brushed stiffly up. He has a ruddy face and pale, rather poppy, blue eyes. Brains have never been his long suit, and he is a weak rather than a bad man. The 'Demon Drink', alas, has always been his failing, and it was the cause of most of the scrapes that he got himself into with my grandfather, when he was younger.

After he married Julia he took a pull on himself. At least, as she is the dominant partner I suppose she made him toe the line. But he continued to have lapses now and then, and it was by no means the first time that I had seen him when he had had one over the eight. Fortunately he is the friendly type of drunk; and he had always been kind to me in a casual sort of way it made no difference to the mild affection I felt for him.

Bringing himself upright with a shove of his broad shoulders, he grinned at me and said: ''Lo, old man! How—how are you?'

'I'm all right, thanks, Uncle,' I replied, 'but you're looking a bit part-worn. You seem to have been making a night of it.'

'That's it,' he hiccuped. 'Li'le party.'

'It must have been a pretty rough one,' I smiled, as I took in the details of his dishevelled appearance. There were grease-stains down one of the lapels of his dinner-jacket, his collar was a crumpled rag, his bow tie had disappeared, and there were obvious marks of lipstick all round his mouth. I had never seen him in such a state when tight before.

'Tha's it; li'le party,' he repeated. 'Was bit rough. Played khiss-in-the-ring.'

I had no idea that the parents who were up for a visit indulged in either high jinks or childish games at the Club-house in the evenings; but when one is in the middle teens one is still constantly learning unexpected things about the behaviour of grown-ups, so I made no comment.

For a moment we remained silent, just smiling inanely at one another, then he said: 'Lesh go into th' sitting-room—have a drink.'

He had obviously had far more than he could carry already, but it was not my place to tell him so. Accordingly I stood aside and he lurched through the doorway. There were whisky, glasses and a syphon on a small side-table. Swaying slightly, he walked over to it and, with a deliberation that did not prevent him spilling some of the stuff, mixed himself a stiff peg.

Having gulped half of it, he muttered: 'Tha's better,' then relapsed into another longish silence, during which he stared at the carpet.

At length he looked up and asked: 'What you doin' here thish time-o'-night? Wash game, old man?'

I had no intention of discussing the matter uppermost in my mind with Uncle Paul while he was in that condition; so I simply said: 'I knew you and Julia were arriving this evening, so I thought I would slip over and see you. While I was waiting for you to come in I fell asleep in front of the fire.'

'I she,' he nodded ponderously. 'I she. Well, here's all the' besht,' and he swallowed the rest of his drink.

A moment later Julia came hurrying in. She had changed into a dressing-gown, and evidently done her best to put her face to rights; but I was much more shocked by her appearance than I had been by that of Uncle Paul.

Her dark eyes looked bigger than I had ever seen them, and her face was dead-white, so that the patches of fresh rouge stood out on her cheeks like the dabs of paint on those of a Dutch doll. Her full red lips were swollen excessively and broken in places, as though they had been savagely bitten, and a heavy coating of powder failed to hide an ugly scratch that ran from beneath her left ear right down across her throat.

'Good Lord! What on earth has been happening to you?' I exclaimed in alarm.

She did not kiss me, but bent her head and laid her icy cheek against mine for a second; then she said:

'Toby, darling; don't be upset. I'm quite all right, but we've had a frightful time tonight. Has Paul told you about it?'

'Only that you had been hitting it up at a party,' I muttered, 'and that you played kiss-in-the-ring.'

'Paul!' she said sharply, turning to her husband. 'Get up at once and go to bed.'

My uncle had lowered himself into an armchair and closed his eyes; he was already half asleep. At the sound of her voice he blinked, lumbered to his feet, and with a vague wave of his hand by way of good night, walked unsteadily out of the room.

'I've never seen him as tight as that before,' I said, as he jerked the door to behind him.

'No, thank goodness,' Julia agreed, with a sigh. 'He doesn't often get really stinking. It's a mercy, though, that he didn't kill the two of us tonight. If I'd realized how far gone he was, I would never have let him drive the car.'

'You had a smash, then?'

'Of course! How else do you think I came to get my face in such a mess?'

'I thought you had been down at the Club all this time.'

'If Paul gave you that impression you must have misunderstood him. He is in no state to know what he is saying. We had a few drinks at the Club before we started, and by now he's probably forgotten most of what happened after that.'

'Oh, you poor darling!' I cried, taking her hand. 'Are you quite sure that you're not badly hurt?'

She shook her head. 'No, I'm all right. He drove us into a ditch, and when I was thrown sideways I hit my mouth against something. I've got a few bruises, but nothing to worry about.' Drawing me down on to the settee beside her, she went on:

'As we were coming up here, Paul thought that he would like to see some old friends of his who live about twenty miles away. We wrote and proposed ourselves for dinner. They wrote back and said they would love to have us if we didn't mind a scratch meal at the end of a children's party, as it was their eldest girl's birthday. When we arrived the party was still in full swing. There were quite a number of other grown-ups there and we must have stood about drinking cocktails for a couple of hours at least.

'It was ten o'clock by the time the children packed up, and close on eleven before we sat down to supper. Afterwards, somebody suggested that we should play the children's games. What with our steady cocktail-drinking and the champagne at supper, we were all a bit lit-up by then, and just ripe to let ourselves go at any sort of nonsense. We played kiss-in-the-ring, blind-man's-buff, postman's knock, and all the rest of it.

'You know how time flies when one is fooling like that, and I didn't notice the amount that Paul was putting away. It wasn't until we were in the car that I realized that he was carrying such a skinful, and, of course, he insisted that he was quite all right until he ran off the road and nearly turned the car over. We had a most frightful job getting it out of the ditch, and I'm feeling an absolute wreck; so be a dear and don't keep me up longer than you can help. Just tell me why you came here tonight; then I must get to bed.'

Obviously it was no time to tell her about the thing that I had released from the tomb, and, anyhow, I did not feel much like a long heart-to-heart by then, as the room seemed to have got colder than ever since they had come in. I just told her I had only come over for a lark, then we went to see if the bed in the spare room was made up.

The curtains there had not been drawn, and to my surprise I saw that it was already morning. The sun was shining and the trees were casting long shadows in the early light. By it, poor Julia looked more haggard than ever; but she smiled at me and said something about it being a perfect May Day morn, then she left me.

By the greatest of luck I had instinctively grabbed up my attaché-case when I fled—as I should have been terrified of going back for it, even in broad daylight, yet afraid to leave it there in case someone found it, and that lead to my being expelled—so I was able to put on my pyjamas and get some proper sleep.

I woke a little after ten, and on going into the sitting-room found one of the Club servants there, tidying up. There was a kitchenette in each bungalow and it was part of their job to cook breakfast on the premises for visitors; so I asked the woman to get me some. Then I telephoned the school to let them know where I was, in case they thought I had met with an accident, and had a bath.

Julia came in just as I was finishing my breakfast. She was looking slightly better, although she could not have had blacker shadows under her eyes if she had been out on the binge for a week, and it was evident that the car having run off the road had shaken her really badly. While she drank two large cups of tea in quick succession she gave me further details of the awful time they had had getting it out of the ditch. Apparently it had rained again in the middle of the night and the mud had absolutely ruined her evening clothes.

Uncle Paul was still sleeping it off, and she said that she did not mean to wake him until it was time to dress for lunch. That meant we had a good hour before us, and the sitting-room was now warm and cosy, so I launched out on an account of my own ordeal the previous night.

When I had done, Julia could offer no explanation. At first she made a half-hearted attempt to persuade me that I must have imagined it; but, in the face of my positive conviction to the contrary, she was far too sympathetic a person to insist on that; and, eventually, she agreed with me that I must have released some horrible supernatural force by breaking open the grave.

We discussed if we ought not to try to do something about it; but the idea of getting a priest to exorcize the place would have been received at Weylands about as frostily as a tart at one of Queen Victoria's tea parties; and even to mention the matter would have meant disclosing the fact that I had broken the one and only rule in the place; so we decided that we had better not say anything about it to anybody.

Unlike the affair of the burglar, there is no sequel to throw further light on the matter. Unlike that, too, it made a lasting impression on me. The first I had accepted as a natural fright, and the eager interests of childhood soon blanketed it in my mind; but that was far from being the case after my midnight fit of terror near the Abbey. For weeks afterwards I dreamed of it every few nights. I used to wake up moaning, struggling and bathed in a cold sweat. It was not till end of term came, bringing the excitements of the holidays, that those beastly dreams grew more infrequent and finally ceased altogether.

Yet I never forgot the feeling that contact with unseen evil gave me; and my reason for describing my experience at Weylands so fully is to make it quite clear that I cannot be mistaken now. In spite of the passing of the years I recognized it again instantly that first night, now just on six weeks ago, when I woke to find the full moon streaming in under the curtain and saw upon the band of light that abominable, undulating shadow.

Five times since then I have known the same awful sensation; a second time early in April, and four times early this month. Soon after the cessation of both bouts, when my nerves have had a chance to settle down again, I have debated with myself endlessly whether it can be some form of nightmare that afflicts me, or a type of periodic lunacy. If it were not for that earlier contact of mine with disembodied evil in the Abbey cemetery, I might still be hesitant about definitely rejecting both those theories. But I am now fully convinced that it can be neither. I am *not* suffering from nightmares, and I am *not* going mad. But I may yet be driven mad–if I am forced to remain here during another full moon and these Satanic attacks upon me develop again with renewed force.

Evening

Helmuth has just left me. The mystery of Julia's silence is now explained, but in a manner that fills me with new distress and apprehension. He asked me if I had heard from her lately, and on my saying that I hadn't, he said:

'I don't suppose you are likely to for a bit. I had a letter from your Uncle Paul today, in which he says that she was near having a breakdown from war-strain and her doctor has ordered her complete rest. So he got special permission from the security people for them to reside in the banned area on the west coast of Scotland, and a week ago he took her up to the house on Mull. Even if she feels up to writing, all letters coming out of the area are held up for ten days or more in the censor's office; so don't be surprised if you don't hear from her for another two or three weeks.'

Three weeks! A new moon is due on the 17th, and on the 25th she will enter the quarter in which she becomes such a menace to me. I had *counted* on Julia arranging for me to be moved from here long before that. What *am* I to do? How can I save myself? If only I could get back the full use of my legs for a single hour!

Wednesday, 13th May

I spent a restless night, worrying quite a bit about Julia; but, I'll confess, as charity begins at home, that I was worrying a darn' sight more about myself, and racking my brains for some possible means of getting away from Llanferdrack, now that there is no hope of her intervention.

I considered writing to Uncle Paul and my other Trustees, but if I don't tell them the truth they are bound to reply that while the war is on I could not possibly be better situated than I am, with Helmuth to look after me and so well out of it all, down here; whereas if I do they are certain to think that the injury to my spine has now begun to affect my brain.

Of course that isn't so; but Julia is the only person who would take my word for it. If I had had a nasty blow on the head at the time of the crash, I might be tempted to think that was the root of the trouble myself; but I didn't. I never even lost consciousness.

I had just put paid to my Jerry—I can see the whisp of smoke now that suddenly issued from his aircraft—when I got old Steve's warning that there was another of them on my tail. But it came too late. Next second I felt a frightful blow in the back, as though someone had coshed me with a rifle-butt low down on the spine. I tried to take evasive action, but for a reason that I didn't even guess then my rudder-bar refused to function. Before I could grasp that my feet were no longer responding to the orders of my brain, the aircraft had got into a spin and was hurtling earthwards.

When I found that I couldn't pull her out of it I decided that the time had come to bale out. The usual motions failed to produce the desired results, but it is not easy to co-ordinate one's actions when one is being spun round like a pea in a top; so even then I did not realize the truth, and thought that it was some of my gear having got hitched up that prevented me from heaving myself free.

The last moments, while the earth seemed to be rushing up to smash me, were pretty ghastly, and I felt certain I was for it. I remember the words of the song 'so they scraped him off the tarmac like a pound of strawberry jam' flashing grimly through my mind; but, by a miracle, the old kite plunged straight into the only big tree within a mile. Her engine broke away and crashed through the branches to the ground, but I was left up there with my lower half imprisoned in the buckled shell of her body. Some farm labourers had seen me crash and were already running to my rescue. They fetched a ladder and hauled me out from among the wreckage. I was still perfectly *compos mentis* and told them that I could climb down out of the oak on my own; but the moment they let me take my own weight my feet slithered along the branch and my legs folded up under me.

They only just managed to catch me as I fell, so that was really the nearest I came that day to breaking my neck. There are times now when I almost wish that I had, as my broken back has put an end for me to most of the things that are worth doing in life.

It was on the 10th of July that I crashed, and after that I spent eight months in various hospitals; but the doctors all reached the same conclusion in the long run. It seems that the Jerry's bullet snipped a bit out of me that it is still beyond the art of medical science to replace. In the end the specialists broke it to me as gently as they could that there was nothing else they could do for me, and that there was little hope of my ever regaining the full use of my legs.

But there has never been the least suggestion that either the injury or the shock had in any way affected my brain. Personally, I am convinced that they did not, and that I am still perfectly sane. At least, I was when they brought me here in March and, apart from the events which caused me to start this journal, there has been nothing whatever since in my quiet invalid's routine to upset my mind.

Of course I have suffered, and do still suffer, a lot of pain; but that has had no more effect on me mentally than it has on the vast majority of poor fellows who are now suffering from agonizing wounds owing to this bloody war. My hand is as steady, and my sight is as clear, as ever they were. I haven't become hesitant in my speech and I don't jump out of my skin if somebody bangs a door. My reasoning powers are unimpaired and I can justly claim that I am now far better at keeping my emotions under control that I was before the crash.

In fact, my own experience is that being a chronic invalid is about the best inducement one can have to practise self-discipline. Anyone in my position is entirely dependent on others, and therefore faced with two alternatives. Either they can allow their disability to become the centre of their thoughts, and on that account make life hell for themselves and everyone in frequent contact with them, or they can school themselves to ignore their misfortune as far as possible, and, by the exercise of endurance, patience and tact, at least secure the willing and cheerful service of those who are looking after them.

To adopt the latter course is just plain common sense, so I take no particular credit for having done so; but is needed a certain amount of will-power and is, I think, a further proof that there has been no deterioration in my mental faculties.

But what chance is there of the Trustees believing that? I mean, if I write and tell them that I want to be moved from Llanferdrack because whenever the moon is near-full an octopus tries to get in at my window? Naturally they will think I am gaga; and who could blame them?

They would send a bunch of brain specialists and psychoanalysts down here to examine me; and before I could say Jack Robinson I should find myself popped in a mental home to be kept under observation. For airing fancies far less lurid than that of being hunted over dry land by an octopus plenty of people have been carted off to those sort of places; and once in it is not so easy to get out again. No, thank you. I am not going to risk that. Not while I have a kick left in me.

(Laughter!) *Hollow* laughter—as they say in Parliamentary reports—caused by the simile I used inadvertently. Its inappropriateness must be an all-time high, in view of the fact that for the past ten months I have not been able to so much as waggle my big toe.

Later

An extraordinary thing has happened. This morning I decided that I would go fishing. It is the only sport in which I can still indulge, but I haven't had much luck so far. I have caught only a few bream and perch, and what I am after is one of the big pike; so today I thought I would try the far end of the lake, and I made Deb wheel me round there.

Deb is hardly what one would call an 'outdoor' girl, and she always looks awkward sitting on the grass reading one of her highbrow books. So, when she had settled me and wedged stones under the wheels of my chair so that it couldn't move, I said to her:

'There's no need to stay here if you don't want to. Why not walk back to the garden and sit in the summer-house? You'll be much more comfortable there, till it's time for you to come and fetch me in for lunch.'

She thought that a good idea, so off she went. The drive approaches the Castle at that end of the lake and crosses a small stone bridge from which I was fishing. Deb had been gone only about ten minutes when I spotted the postman coming up from the village. I called to the old chap and asked him if he had any letters for me. He had one, and gave it to me as he passed. It was from Julia.

It was written from Queensclere and dated the 10th of May—yet Helmuth told me only last night that Uncle Paul had taken her up to Scotland a week ago!

More extraordinary still, it said not a word about any plan for going there, or that she was feeling done in from war-strain; and it made no reference whatever to any of my recent letters to her. In fact, while acknowledging that she was hopelessly erratic about letter-writing herself and excusing her slackness on the plea that she had so much to do, she reproached me with having all the time in the world on my hands yet leaving it for so long without letting her hear from me.

For the rest, there were several pages in her firm, round hand recounting the excitements of the last local air-raid, a battle with the War Agricultural Committee owing to her refusal to have the lawns ploughed up, and an unauthorized visit to Dover, with one of the officers billeted at Queensclere, to get a peep through a telescope at the activities on the nearest bit of Hitler's Europe.

After skimming through all this light-hearted chatter I only pretended to go on fishing, and sat there with my brain revving round like a dynamo, right up till lunch-time.

It was by the merest fluke that I intercepted the postman this morning. I have never seen him before, and it is the first time since my arrival that I have been down to the far end of the lake. Had I not been there when I was I think it extremely unlikely that Julia's letter would ever have been delivered to me; and that belief is supported by the fact that in it she mentions another letter of hers, written about April the 24th, which I have never received.

One thing is now beyond dispute. Somebody has prevented all the letters that I have written to Julia in the past six weeks from being posted; and evidently whoever it is fears that if I receive one from her it might give away the fact that she is not getting mine; so in order to prevent my suspicions being aroused, my inward as well as my outward correspondence with her is being deliberately held up.

But why? And by whom?

Either Taffy or Deb take such few letters as I have for the post and bring me the few that I receive. But neither of them has any reason to interfere with my private affairs, of which they know next to nothing; and both of them have well-paid jobs with which they seem fully contented, so why should either risk the sack for a thing like monkeying with my mail?

It *must* be Helmuth's doing. That is borne out by the fact that he lied to me last night. Why, otherwise, should he have spun me that yarn about Julia having had a breakdown and Uncle Paul taking her to Scotland? It can only have been because he *knew* the contents of the letters I had written to her, and felt that the time had come when I must be provided with a reason for her failure to respond to my urgent appeals, so that I should not yet get the idea that someone was preventing them from reaching her.

In all the years that I have spent in Helmuth's charge I have never before had the least cause to suspect him of tampering with my correspondence; yet it seems impossible to doubt that he has been doing so for the past month.

It did occur to me that Julia might have used Queensclere note-paper, although actually writing from Mull, but the envelope bears the Queensclere postmark of the 11th; so it was written on Sunday and posted there on Monday. Obviously, then Julia *must* have still been there last week-end; yet Helmuth distinctly said last night: 'I had a letter from your Uncle Paul *today*', and '*a week ago* he took her (Julia) up to Mull'. The only possible explanation for such a lie is that he is double-crossing me for some purpose of his own which he wishes to keep secret.

What can that purpose be? There is only one theory which would account for his secretly sabotaging my communications with Julia. He knows from my letters to her that I have implored her to come down and make arrangements for me to be removed from Llanferdrack, and he wants to prevent that.

Yet he must also know from my letters the reason *why* I want to be moved. He *knows* that I am being haunted, or rather—as his cold, materialistic mind would assess my outpourings—that I *imagine* myself to be haunted. But his putting it down to my imagination does not detract in the least from the agony of fear that it arouses in me, and I told Julia that, in no uncertain terms. Yet, instead of taking such steps as he could for my relief, Helmuth is doing the very opposite, and deliberately preventing Julia from coming to my assistance.

Why, in God's name, should he wish to add to, and prolong, my sufferings? I can only suppose that it is because he derives some strange, sadistic pleasure from them. That would account for the queer, searching, speculative look with which I have often caught him regarding me during his evening visits, this last month or so. I can hardly believe it possible—yet what other explanation for his extraordinary conduct can there be?

These horrible suspicions about a man for whom, even if he has failed to inspire in me any deep affection, I have always thought of with respect, and regarded as a friend, are enough to make anyone think that I am suffering from persecution mania. But I am sure that I am not. Now that this business of the letters has opened my eyes, I am beginning to see clearly for the first time. There are so many little things for which I have accepted Helmuth's glib explanations, that, looked at now from the new angle, go to show that he not only knows what it is I fear, but is getting some horrible, unnatural kick out of doing all he can to deprive me of protection from it.

To start with, there is the question of the blackout curtain. It was little enough to ask that it should be lengthened by six inches, but he first postponed the issue, then vetoed it entirely.

Then there is my reading-lamp. When Deb settles me down for the night she always moves it on to the centre table. After I had the terrors on April the 30th, I asked her to leave it by my bedside, so that I could light it again and read if I felt restless; although, of course, what I really wanted it there for was to light and drown the moonlight if the Thing came again. But she refused. She said that she had had strict instructions for Helmuth that in no circumstances was the Aladdin ever to be left within my reach; because if I read late at nights I might drop asleep while reading, then if I flung out an arm in my sleep I might knock it over, the flaming oil would set the place alight, and I should probably be burnt alive in my bed before anyone could reach me.

That sounds reasonable enough, but, all the same, I tackled him about it. He said he was sorry, but while he was responsible for me he really could not allow me to run such a risk. I asked him, then, to get me an electric torch. He said he would; but next day he volunteered the information that there were none to be had in the village, as all available supplies were now being sent to London and the other big cities, where the need for them was more urgent owing to air-raids.

That sounds plausible too; but all these things add up, if one starts with the assumption that Helmuth's object is to ensure that at night I should remain a prisoner in the dark—apart from that infernal strip of light thrown by the moon—and to keep me isolated here. Which reminds me about the telephone.

The main line goes to Helmuth's office, and there are extensions to a few of the bedrooms, up to which, of course, I cannot get. The only other is here, in the library, and I thought that another point in favour of its having been turned into a bed-sit for me. But a few days before I had my first 'nightmare' it went wrong. I asked Helmuth to get it put right, and he said he would; but nothing was done about it. When I spoke to him again he said that he was awfully sorry, but he had heard from the Post-Office Engineers, and they

The Haunting of Toby Jugg

were so terribly busy installing lines to camps and airfields that they could not possibly find the time to repair extensions in private houses.

He went on to point out that in the three weeks I had been here I hadn't used it more than half a dozen times, so I should hardly miss it; and that if I did want to telephone I could always do so in the daytime by being wheeled along in my chair to his office.

That is all very well, but when Helmuth is not in his office he always keeps it locked. The tacit assumption is, of course, that I have no secrets from him, so there is nothing that I should want to telephone about which it would cause me embarrassment to mention in his presence. But with him at my elbow how can I telephone Julia, as I've wanted to a score of times in the past ten days? I mean, I couldn't possibly tell her in front of him the reason why I want her to cancel all her engagements and fag down here to Wales.

Another pointer concerns the Radiogram. Mine is a big cabinet affair, that also plays eight gramophone records off without being touched, and it lives on the far side of the fireplace. When things started to happen again at the beginning of this month I asked to have it moved up close to my bed, so that if I was subject to any more of these damnable visitations it would be within easy reach, and I could turn it on. I had small hope that the sound of martial music would scare the Thing off, but I thought it might fortify me and at least make the room seem a little less like a morgue.

Deb objected at once because the cabinet is so heavy that it takes two people to shift it, and would mean an awful performance each night and morning moving it to and from my bedside; or else it would have to remain there permanently, in which case, whichever side I had it, its bulk would prevent her from getting at me from all angles to give me my massage.

I was so set on having it by me that I appealed to Helmuth; but he supported her. He said that it was unreasonable of me to want to put people to so much bother for a sudden whim; and that, in any case, for the sake of my health I needed all the sleep I could get at nights, so he was averse to any innovation which would enable me to lie awake listening to music.

I suppose most people would consider me a pretty wet sort of type for allowing myself to be dictated to like that; but then they don't know Helmuth. He tackles every problem that arises with such cheerful briskness, and his views are always so clear-cut and logical, that it is almost impossible to argue with him. At least, I find it so; but that may be because he became the dominant influence in my life from the time I was thirteen, and years of unquestioning submission to whatever he considered best for me formed a habit of mind that I now find it almost impossible to break.

That is why I kow-towed to his decision that he could not agree to my shifting my quarters; although I am sure that it would not have made the slightest difference if I had gone off the deep end. He would have told me to 'be my age' and have walked out of the room; and he knows perfectly well that it is impossible for me to get myself moved without his consent. His attitude in this, more than in anything else, now convinces me that he is deliberately keeping me a prisoner here, because he knows it to be the focal point of my fears, and is deriving a brutal, cynical amusement from watching them develop.

After these two consecutive nights in early April I already had the wind up pretty badly, so I told him that I wasn't sleeping well, and would like to be moved to another room. There are plenty of others in this great barrack of a place, but he brushed the idea aside with reasons against which it seemed childish to argue.

Obviously, for me to be anywhere but on the ground floor would mean that all my meals would have to be brought up to me, and that I should have to be carried up and down stairs every day to go out for my airing—and that would be placing much too great a burden on our very limited staff. The rooms in the old part of the Castle have been long untenanted, and are damp and cheerless. That left only the east wing, which contained the suite of reception-rooms in which my Great-aunt Sarah vegetates, and I could not possibly turn her out after all these years. Here I have a fine big room that gets all the sun and has easy access to the garden; and if I wasn't sleeping well in it there was no reason whatever to suppose that I should sleep better elsewhere. What could I reply to that? And, as my 'nightmares' did not recur for over three weeks, it was not until the end of the month that I had cause really to worry about the matter further.

But on May the 2nd, after two more visitations, I was in a real flap, and I tackled him again. I said that I had come to the conclusion that Wales did not suit me, and I felt sure that a change of surroundings would do me good.

He dismissed that one as too silly for serious consideration; and I must admit that so long as Britain remains at death-grips with Germany we could hardly be better situated than as we are down here. It is a far cry from Whitehall to this lonely valley in the heart of the Welsh mountains, and things like rations, Home Guards, A.R.P. and Flag days, seem to belong to a different world. In fact, if it weren't for the blackout, and the odd German bomber that has got off her course passing over us at night once in a while, we might regard the war as though it was taking place on Mars.

As I did not give Helmuth my real reason for wanting to leave Llanferdrack, I thought that his refusal to consider moving me might be due in part to a feeling that if I went elsewhere he would be under a moral obligation to accompany me. It seemed only natural that he should be averse to leaving such comfortable quarters for some place where we should probably suffer all the inconveniences of the war—not to mention air-raids.

That just shows how preconceived ideas of a person's character can give one a false conception of their motives. But it is clear now that he was perfectly well aware what lay behind my anxiety to be moved. He must have been, because he had intercepted my letters to Julia. Yet, instead of seeking a good pretext to cover my departure which would also have freed him from any obligation to leave with me, he chose to allow me to continue to suffer the torture of the damned, and even took measures to aggravate my situation, so that he could gloat in secret over the signs that my experiences were turning me into a nervous wreck.

Wait, though! It goes deeper than that. Why did he *start* to intercept my mail? He has never done so in the past. I have been assuming that he could have found out about my 'nightmares' only by reading my letters, and that he then took steps to isolate me for his sadistic amusement. But that is not it. I have been putting the cart before the horse. It must be so; because some of his measures to render me vulnerable to the attacks were taken *before* I wrote about them to Julia.

Then he is *not* simply making a callous study of me in the belief that I am a victim of hallucinations. *He knows that the Thing in the courtyard exists.* Since he did not learn of it through me, he must either have seen it himself or been told about it by someone here who has done so. This is the final proof that I am *not* mad; for, if someone else has also seen the brute, it *must* be something more than a figment of my imagination.

Later

This discovery, that Helmuth must have been aware of the Thing's existence before myself, opens up the most appalling abyss of treachery, and possibilities which it is horrible to contemplate.

It infers that he put me in this room next to the courtyard, and had the blackout curtains made six inches shorter, on purpose; that in a dozen different ways he is wilfully facilitating the attacks; that he cannot be a sceptic, as I always believed, but accepts the existence of evil occult forces and is gloating over the terror that they inspire in me.

Perhaps, even, he has great knowledge of them, as he has of so many queer subjects? Perhaps he has come control over this evil entity? Perhaps—yes, perhaps it is he who has conjured it up?

This is ghastly! It has become suddenly and appallingly clear that he must be deliberately plotting my destruction.

Thursday, 14th May

In view of the mental earthquake that I sustained yesterday, it is somewhat surprising to be able to record that I had an excellent night. Perhaps that was due to my brain having become addled with fatigue from straining to find answers to so many new conundrums; but usually that kind of mental tiredness leads only to restless, unrefreshing sleep. I think it more likely that I owe my good night to subconscious relief at the knowledge that I am up against a human enemy.

Perhaps I am being a bit premature in relegating the Thing to second place; and I certainly do not mean to imply that I would rank it lower than the most evil man ever born of woman, when it is actually present.

What I am getting at is that I now know Helmuth to be at the back of this horrible business. Whether he just found out about the Thing haunting the courtyard—as it may have done for centuries—and decided to place me in its vicinity, or whether he is in some way responsible for its appearance, I have no idea. But I do know that he is deliberately detaining me here and exposing me to its attacks. Therefore it is him that I have to fight; and he is only a man like myself—except that he has the advantage of having two sound legs and a far better brain.

In a human conflict there is always a sporting chance that the weaker party may come out on top; although the fact that he has succeeded in isolating me makes me terribly aware that the odds are now pretty heavy against my being able to save myself from—well, something that even to think of makes me break out into a sweat.

Why Helmuth should wish to expose me to such a diabolical fate is entirely beyond my comprehension. I have never done him the least ill; on the contrary, his association with myself and my family has brought him comparative affluence, and he must have had the best possible reasons for believing that his position was as secure as anything could be in these uncertain times.

If I ever get a say in the matter it will be so no longer. Even if he was in complete ignorance of the Thing, he would still be guilty of the most brutal callousness in refusing my requests—to be moved to another room, to have the blackout curtain lengthened, to let me have a lamp or my Radiogram beside my bed, to get me a torch or have any telephone mended. What the Hell is he here for, anyway?

Of course, since quite early in the war he has had the job of managing the Llanferdrack estate; but from the time I was brought here his first duty was to look after me, and see that I was made as comfortable as possible.

He seems to have forgotten that he is only an employee, and still liable to be sacked. But is he? After all, he was placed in charge here by the Trustees, and it is quite certain that I could not sack him myself—or get him sacked. At least, not unless I could put up such a hell of a strong case that it would completely destroy the faith that Julia and Uncle Paul have in him—and even that might not be enough, since he managed to get appointed as one of the Trustees himself, after old Wellard died in 1939.

Why, I wonder, am I now considering him in relation to the post he fills—which is virtually that of my Guardian—and realizing for the first time since I arrived here how lamentably he has carried out its functions? It can only be because my eyes have suddenly been opened and I am thinking of him in an entirely new light.

I feel quite ashamed of myself when I think of my normal unquestioning subservience to him, and I still don't fully understand its continuance now that I am grown up. The habit of years is mainly responsible, I know, but looking back on some recent episodes, and regarding them dispassionately, I believe there is something more to it than that. The unwinking stare of those queer, tawny eyes of his, when he announces a decision, may have something to do with it. I am sure that he uses them as a vehicle for transmitting his will. Perhaps the answer is that he has secured my acquiescence to his wishes for all these years by holding me under a mild form of hypnosis.

If that is so, it is a game that two can play. Squadron-Leader Cooper, the R.A.F. doctor at Nether Wallop, told me that I had hypnotic eyes; and just for the fun of it he tried me out in the Mess one night. He had been a psychiatrist before the war, so knew the drill, and some of the successes he achieved were quite remarkable. I did not get very far, but in two instances I succeeded in putting chaps into a light sleep and got them to do simple things; and afterwards they swore that they had not known what they were up to.

This is worth thinking about. I don't suppose for a moment that I could challenge and defeat Helmuth's will; but practice might strengthen my powers of resistance; and with so much at stake I should be crazy not to try out any conceivable weapon that I may have in my sadly limited armoury.

But I have been getting off the track a bit. Whether Helmuth has performed his *in loco parentis* function as my Guardian well or ill is now entirely beside the point. For some reason that I do not pretend to understand, he has suffered a 'sea change' from my aloof and cynical mentor to my secret, implacable enemy.

I am not quite certain that I am not mad, but it seems on the cards that he may be. No one who knows him would question the brilliance of his mind, and it said that only a hair-line separates genius from madness. Perhaps two-and-a-half years of seclusion here, with no one of his own kind to talk to, have led to his indulging in the sort of long periods of morbid introspection that sometimes drive people over the edge.

Anyhow, whether he is mad or sane, I have got to get out of his clutches somehow. If I could get a letter to Uncle Paul I could make an official request that he and the other Trustees should come here to see me on business, then when they arrived have a show-down. That would be the hell of a risk to take, as I have not a shred of evidence against Helmuth, and unless I could trick him into making some stupid admission I should be laying myself open to their deciding that I ought to be put in a nut-house. Anyway, it is not worth even considering for the moment, as he would be just as certain to intercept any letter I wrote to Uncle Paul as he would another to Julia.

If only I had a doctor visiting me regularly I could try getting at him to pull a fast one over Helmuth, by ordering my removal to a local nursing home. But I haven't. Apart from the injury to my spine, my health is excellent; so there has been no occasion since I arrived here to call the local sawbones in, and I don't even know his name. The specialists in London declared that nothing further could be done for me, except to continue the massage, so Helmuth said it seemed waste of time and money to drag some country G.P. up here to look at me once a week; and, little realizing how glad I might be later to have someone like that on tap, I agreed.

Reconsidering the matter, I am inclined to wonder if the present arrangement, by which I am to be revetted by a specialist two or three times a year, really is enough; and if I ought not to have a local man keep a watching brief over my case. It looks as if the present set-up is another item in Helmuth's plan to isolate me; anyway I am certain that he would not agree to any alteration of it now.

Of course I could say that I had ear-ache, or something, and insist that the local man be called in. But if I did Helmuth would make a point of being on hand in the role of 'anxious Guardian' during the doctor's visit; so I would have no chance to talk to him in private and beg him to get me away from here.

It now seems all too damnably clear that I cannot hope to bring any influence to bear on Helmuth from outside which will force him to accept my removal; so the only remaining possibility is to take the law into my own hands and get away one night without his knowledge.

But that is utterly impossible without assistance, and the Devil of it is that there is no one here of whom I can make a confidant, or trust to help me. Both Deb and Taffy are obviously scared stiff of Helmuth, and I rarely see any of the other servants. Great-aunt Sarah's establishment is run separately from ours and she has her own dining-room, so I have scarcely exchanged a word with that gawky old stick Miss Nettelfold, who acts as her housekeeper-companion. My few friends are all up to their necks in the war, so none of them are able to come all the way down here to Wales to see me; and I know nobody locally, so I never have any visitors. Even if I could get hold of one of the servants I am sure they would not dare to aid in my escape. They would be much too scared of Helmuth and the certainty that they would lose their jobs afterwards.

Of course, if I were in a position to make it really worth somebody's while to get me into a car, or even wheel me down to the station in the small hours so that I could catch the early-morning train, that would put a very different light on my chances. If I had fifty pounds with which to tempt Taffy I'm pretty sure that I could get him to play. But Helmuth pays all my bills for me and, as he pointed out when we arranged about that soon after I arrived here, an invalid has no use for ready money; so I haven't even fifty pence.

How absurdly ironical that is, seeing that I am one of the richest men in England. At least, I shall be if I am still alive and sane on the 20th of June next—when I reach the age of twenty-one.

Saturday, 16th May

I wrote nothing yesterday, as I spent a good part of the day reading over what I have so far written. It seems an awful woffal, without any proper sequence, and practically nothing about who I am or how I came to be associated with Helmuth.

Of course, I started these notes solely with the idea of trying to get certain things clear in my own mind; but, on finding that scribbling down my thoughts just as they arose helped to keep them off the 'horror', I began to let myself ramble on about this and that. Then I began to think of this script as a sort of personal testament that I hoped would reach Julia if anything happened to me. But I see that I have covered pages and pages with stuff that she already knows about—which seems a pointless thing to have done. Still, I am not sorry about that now, as a new theory to account for what is happening here occurred to me last night; and, in view of that, this journal may yet serve a different and more practical purpose. If it does, most of what I have so far written will not, after all, have been a waste of time.

My new line of thought inclines me to believe that Helmuth is not mad, but either on his own account or in association with others has hatched a diabolical plot—the object of which is to drive me insane.

I have not a tittle of evidence to support this new theory, but it is, I believe, an axiom that the basis of all crime is motive and opportunity and both are present in my case.

It was rereading the last paragraph I wrote on Thursday that gave me this idea. There is more than a grain of truth in the old saying 'Money is the root of all Evil', and in my life and sanity are vested a great fortune.

Should anything prevent my coming into my inheritance, at the end of next month, there are quite a number of people who would benefit. Not directly, perhaps, but by continuing to enjoy the control of my grandfather's wealth, and all the opportunities that gives for amassing riches themselves. Therefore it is by no means inconceivable that one, or more, of them would like to ensure that I shall never assume the reins of power in the vast commercial Empire that old Albert Abel Jugg built up.

I do not fear murder, because scientific crime investigation has made it extremely difficult to get away with murder in these days. The sudden death of anyone so potentially rich as myself would be certain to arouse widespread comment in the press. A flock of reporters would arrive to get the story. Each of them would question everybody here in the hope of picking up some 'human interest' line that their colleagues had missed; and they are a bright lot of boys. If one of them tumbled on the least suspicious circumstance it would result in Scotland Yard being tipped off to look into matters. Besides, Julia would call the police in at once if there were the smallest thing to suggest that my death had been due to foul play. So I do not believe that any secret enemies I may have would dare to risk it.

An even stranger argument against it is that my death would result in the dissolution of the estate. Great sums would pass to the nation and to various charities; some individuals would benefit, of course, but Helmuth is not among them; and most of the other Trustees would lose on balance, because once the estate was wound up they would cease to enjoy their present lucrative and powerful stewardships.

On the other hand, should I become insane, those who are now responsible for handling the Jugg millions will firstly escape being called upon in a few weeks' time to give an account of the uses to which those millions have been put during my minority and, secondly, continue in indisputed control of them for as long as I remain a candidate for a straitjacket.

Once I was certified it would mean a life-sentence. It is said to be difficult to get a chit from the Board of Lunacy, but it must be a darn' sight more difficult to get the chit rescinded. If I am right, and there is a conspiracy to put me in a loony-bin, one can be quite certain that, in the event of its coming off, the conspirators will find it an easy wicket to prevent my getting out again.

Well, there is the motive. As for opportunity: here I am, a semi-paralysed hulk, cut off from communication with the outside world, and completely in the power of an ambitious man who has succeeded in getting himself made one of the controllers of the Jugg millions.

Perhaps my imagination really has run away with me now; but, all the same, I have decided to make this journal a very different document from anything that might have resulted from my earlier intentions. I mean to tell the whole story from the beginning; then, even if these sheets of paper never reach Julia, but fall into the hands of *any* honest person, they may yet be produced as evidence of my fundamental sanity, and perhaps assist in bringing my enemies to justice.

I shall not start on this new departure today, though. In fact I should not have made any entry at all, had I not been anxious to get down my latest ideas on what lies behind Helmuth's secret moves against me. Yesterday, after tea, I succeeded in finding a book on Hypnotism in the library, here, and I am already deep in it, so I may not have much time for writing during the next few days.

I find some of the technical stuff in the book on Hypnotism pretty heavy going, and it is no good fuddling my brain by sticking to it for too long at a time; so I shall write a page or two of this between whiles.

Here goes, then, on the facts about myself:

I am Flight-Lieutenant Sir Albert Abel Jugg, Bart., D.F.C., R.A.F.V.R. (Ret.). The title, of course, came to me from my grandfather; the Royal Air Force rank and decoration I got for myself.

My father insisted on my being christened Albert Abel after his father and himself; but my mother must have had a sense of humour, as before I was born she vowed that, whatever I might be christened, she meant to call me Toby. She died giving me birth, but my father carried out her wish, so Toby I have been to my family and friends all my life.

I know nothing at all of my forebears on my mother's side, and on my father's I can go back only two generations; although I do know that he came of Yorkshire stock and that the family were poor farm people just outside Sheffield; and that it was in the office of one of the smaller iron-founders there that my grandfather began his meteoric career.

He was a money-spinner—one of those amazing Victorians who started life an an office-boy at the age of eight and by the time they were thirty emerged as great industrialists. In those happy days British goods were the most sought-after in the world's markets, and handsome profits could be put back into a growing business to make it more prosperous still—instead of being swallowed up by the crippling demands of a fantastically high income-tax—so it is easy to understand how a clever, energetic man could soon convert a modest capital into considerable riches. But the transition from poverty to even moderate affluence is the part in such stories which always mystifies me. How did the little thirty-bob-a-week clerk without influence or backing ever manage to make his first five thousand pounds?

One thing is quite certain: no ambitious young man, however brainy and hard-working, would be able to do so now. Socialist economics have chained the masses and are relentlessly pressing them into a pattern so that in another generation they will be no more than human robots.

The Trade Unions already decree that no man must work longer hours or receive a bigger pay packet than the laziest and most incompetent of his companions employed on the same type of job—and soon they will make it illegal for him to attempt to better himself by leaving the job he is in for another. It is almost as hopeless for non-union men and black-coated workers to try to build up a little capital, or for people who already have small businesses to increase theirs; because, as soon as any of them begin to make a bit more than a living wage, the Government takes away the best part of anything they might save, in taxes largely levied to support a vast bureaucracy which is entirely non-productive.

But things were very different in Queen Victoria's day. My grandfather was only one of thousands who started from nothing and ended up a man of property. It was, I suppose, a blend of luck, thrift, scope for initiative, payment by results, and the freedom to work eighteen hours a day if they wanted to, that enabled them to make those first little sacks of golden sovereigns; then the untaxed profits on bold, imaginative business ventures did the rest.

Albert Abel Jugg was, therefore, a typical product of his times. He differed only from most of his successful contemporaries in being one of the first to realize that far greater profits could be made by operating a chain of companies, which, between them, produced a raw material and converted it to its final purpose, than from any one link in it. Thus, having started in an iron-foundry, he persuaded the partners to buy a small iron-mine; then a coal-mine so that they made a profit on the fuel they used. The firm went in for making steel plate for shipping, and his next move was to buy up a ship-building company that had got into low water.

A few years later they decided that they would sell no more ships, but run a shipping line themselves. He did not go in for luxury liners, but stout little tramps, and soon he had scores of them ploughing the seas with mixed cargoes from port to port all over the world. Later he went in for building commercial motor vehicles and, lastly, aircraft. By that time he had his own rubber plantations, timber forests, tanneries, chrome, bauxite, nickel and tungsten mines. At the time of his death he held a controlling interest in more than sixty companies, and he left over fourteen million pounds.

He had a flair for picking his subordinates and oceans of hard, sound common sense; but I never heard of him pulling off any spectacular financial coups, or, indeed, doing anything remarkable. He was blessed with excellent health, so he never retired, and remained till the end entirely wrapped up in his business. His tastes were simple and his appreciation of beauty, art, culture and grace apparently non-existent; he never went out of his way to acquire the appurtenances of great wealth; they seemed rather to collect haphazard about him.

The big mansion in Kensington Palace Gardens, where I spent most of my early childhood, was not his deliberate choice for a London home; he moved into it only because he had taken it over in settlement for a debt that a peer, who was a director of one of his companies, could not pay. Queensclere he bought, not for the lovely old house, but because the eastern part of the estate lay adjacent to the Kentish coalmines, and he was advised that some two hundred acres of it had valuable deposits beneath them.

Rather than go to the trouble of furnishing either house himself he bought the bulk of their contents with them. Queensclere had belonged for many generations to a family of moderate fortune and excellent taste, whereas the Kensington mansion had been acquired by the *nouveau riche* peer only a decade earlier; so when in the country we lived in an atmosphere of dignity and grace, and when in London surrounded by Victorian horrors; but I doubt if he noticed the difference.

Llanferdrack Castle was bought by him on account of my Great-aunt Sarah. Since the poor lady refused to leave the vicinity of the tragedy that had robbed her of her fiancé, he said that she had better have the Castle to live in. Here, too, he bought most of the contents for an all-in price; but in the library there was quite a number of rare books, and when he saw the valuation he refused to include it in the deal. In consequence the library was sold separately and the room was left bleak and denuded, with rows and rows of empty shelves. That offended his sense of the fitness of things and the way he dealt with the matter was typical of his mentality.

On Friday, when I searched the shelves for a book on Hypnotism, I already knew that they held one of the most astounding collections of junk that any room calling itself a library could ever have contained, but quite how astounding I did not realize until I started to go through them systematically. The explanation is that when my grandfather wanted to refill the shelves he contracted with a bookseller in the Charing Cross Road to do the job at a flat rate and, irrespective of size, he refused to pay more than ten shillings a foot!

Naturally, the bulk of it consists of out-of-date encylopedias, the collected sermons of long-dead divines, books of dreary personal reminiscences that their garrulous authors must have paid to have printed, fifty-year-old novels of incredible dullness, and publishers' remainders of all kinds. But, by a piece of exceptional good fortune, I found a bulky volume called *Hypnotism, its History, Practice and Theory*, by J. Milne Bramwell, which, for this array of mainly nineteenth-century trash, bears the comparatively recent date of 1903.

It could not have been out long when it was condemned to make one among the seven or eight hundred feet of books that cover the walls of this room; so no doubt its presence here is due to the fact that its title page is missing and its cover loose; but, luckily, its 470-odd pages of text are intact and they contain a wealth of information, so, thanks to Dr Bramwell, I am gradually getting a grip on the theory of this fascinating subject.

Reverting to my grandfather. It was not unnatural that a man so entirely absorbed in the great commerical structure that he had created should wish to found a dynasty, and many years before his death he laid plans to ensure that his heir should enjoy the same undisputed authority over his Empire as he had himself.

So that his heir should not be compelled to part with the controlling interest in any of the companies at his death, in order to raise the vast sum necessary to pay death duties, he devoted a considerable part of his income to insurances which would cover them; and as soon as my father showed that he had inherited his father's talent for business he was given one directorship after another, so that long before he died he was openly recognized as the heir-apparent.

That my father should have turned out to have all the makings of a worthy successor must have been a great joy to the old man; he was far from being so fortunate in his second son. Father entered the business on leaving Cambridge, and was already an important executive in it by the time the First World War broke out, so he was considered too much of a key-man to be allowed to volunteer for one of the services; but Uncle Paul was nearly ten years younger, and went straight into the war at the age of eighteen.

It may have been that which unsettled him and made him later unfitted for a business career. But I don't think he would ever have been capable of controlling a big organization. He is much too lazy and pleasure-loving, and no amount of training can give a man a first-class brain if he hasn't got the right type of grey matter to start with.

Anyway, grandfather evidently decided that he was a hopeless bet, and preferred to take a gamble on me to carry on the dynasty should anything happen to my father. As I was only a few years old when his last will was drawn up, he went to considerable pains to protect my interests in the event of both my father and himself dying while I was still a minor; and the arrangement he decided on was that a Board of seven Trustees should be formed, which would have the following powers:

(1) To appoint such of its members as it considered most suitable to directorships of the Jugg companies, for the purpose of representing the interests of the Trust.

(2) Elect new Trustees to fill any vacancies which might occur on the Board through death or retirement, and to create additional Trustees should this be considered desirable.

(3) To invest all profits accruing to the Trust during my minority, either in taking up further shares in the Jugg companies, or in acquiring holdings in other concerns which it was planned ultimately to bring within the Jugg organization.

(4) To appoint one of their number as my Guardian, who would undertake to give me the personal care of a parent, and be responsible to them that my education should be designed to fit me for taking my place as the head of the Jugg Empire in due course.

It will be seen that the old man's scheme, while sound enough in its broad principles, did give the Trustees certain opportunities to feather their own nests at my expense if, at any time, the Board included two or three dishonest members who got together and were clever enough to pull the wool over the eyes of the others. The Trustees were, no doubt, purposely given no direct remunerations, as the old man felt that they would be more than adequately paid for their trouble by the fees they would get from sharing out the sixty-odd directorships between them. That is fair enough; but the clause empowering them to invest profits in concerns which it is planned 'ultimately to bring within the Jugg organization' opens the way for all sorts of double-dealing.

The Jugg interests are now so varied that an unscrupulous Trustee might buy up the shares of pretty well any business that looked like going on the rocks, and, after nursing it for a year or two, make a very handsome profit—if he had enough backing on the Board to be sure of selling it to the Trust.

I have wondered, more than once, if that is how Harry Iswick has succeeded in making so much money during the past ten years. He owes his place on the Board to the fact that he was my grandfather's confidential secretary; and so, apart from my father, knew more than anyone else about the old man's affairs. I remember Julia telling me that, in those days, he used to live in a little semi-detached house out at Acton, but now he has a flat in Grosvenor House, a big place at Maidenhead, and just before the war he had bought himself a villa in the South of France. He has not yet been nominated by the Board as their representative director on any of the larger companies, so I should not think he collects more than two thousand five hundred a year in fees, and he certainly could not live in the way he does on that.

Of course he is a clever little devil, and his position on the Board gives him access to all sorts of information out of which he could make money more or less legitimately: so he may be reasonably honest. In any case grandfather must have thought him so, as, in selecting the original Trustees, the old man would naturally have picked only men he believed that he could trust.

The others he chose were: Lord Embleton, Sir Stanley Wellard and Mr C. J. Rootham—all men who had been closely associated with him in business for many years; two partners of the firm of Bartorship, Brown and Roberts and one partner from the firm of Smith & Co. The former were his Chartered Accountants and the latter his Solicitors. In both cases the Trusteeships were really vested in the firms rather than individuals, so as to ensure that they would retain permanent representation on the Board. The accountants nominated Mr Alec Bartorship and Mr Charles Roberts; the solicitors, Mr Angus Smith.

Since the inception of the Board there have been several changes. Mr Rootham retired in 1934, after having persuaded his colleagues to accept his son, Guy Rootham, as his successor. Mr Bartorship retired in 1935, and his firm nominated his nephew, Claud Bartorship, to take his place. Sir Stanley Wellard died suddenly in September 1939, and as, in the excitement of those first few weeks of war, the more likely candidates for this desirable vacancy appear to have been too occupied to press their claims, Helmuth succeeded in getting himself appointed; mainly, I believe, owing to the influence exerted on his behalf by Harry Iswick and Uncle Paul.

I should have mentioned that Uncle Paul was co-opted as an additional Trustee, soon after the first meeting of the Board. This was partly because everybody felt very sorry for him. The will had been drawn up four years earlier, in 1925, just after he had had to be pulled out of a most hopeless financial mess for the fourth time in six years; so the only mention of him in it was as beneficiary under a small, separate Trust, which was to administer a capital that would bring him in about fifteen hundred a year.

That really was pretty hard on the only surviving son of a multi-millionaire; and the Trustees all thought that had my grandfather made a fresh will, just before he died, he would have treated him much more generously, now that he seemed to have turned over a new leaf and looked like settling down with Julia.

Perhaps, though, their sympathy might not have gone further than to give him another chance to make good with one of the companies, had it not been for the question of myself. But it so happened that, while every member of the Board was prepared to give me a home, none of them really wanted the bother and responsibility of bringing me up.

Before Uncle Paul knew anything about the contents of the will he had announced that he considered it up to his wife and himself to take care of the orphan, and immediately after the funeral he had installed me at Kew; so he seemed to be the obvious person to act as my Guardian. As, under the will, my Guardian had to be one of the Trustees, to make him one, which would at the same time enable the Board to compensate him a little for the raw deal he had had under his father's will by giving him a few minor directorships, was clearly the solution.

At present, therefore, the Board consists of:

Lord Embledon, who is now over eighty, and rarely attends meetings; although he still retains the office of Chairman, which he has held from the beginning.

Harry Iswick, a very active, but, to my mind, not altogether trustworthy type; who, on Sir Stanley Wellard's death in 1939, got himself elected as Deputy-Chairman and, owing to Embledon's withdrawal from affairs since the war started, now more or less runs the party.

Guy Rootham, a good, sound chap; but, unfortunately for me, one with such an expert knowledge of medium-sized shipbuilding that he is now disguised as a Brigadier and on permanent loan to the United States to help them design improved types of Landing Craft.

Charles Roberts, an elderly and very staid accountant, who, on the few occasions I have met him, appeared incapable of taking an interest in anything except figures.

Claud Bartorship, of the same firm; a nice fellow, but now a Captain in the Pay Corps stationed, when I last heard of him, in Cairo.

Angus Smith, the solicitor, who, like Embledon, is now in the neighbourhood of eighty, and won't give up because he doesn't want to lose the fees his directorships bring him; but has retired to his native Scotland, and comes down only to clock-in at the minimum number of board meetings requisite to prevent his co-Trustees being able legally to demand his resignation.

Uncle Paul; who, I am sure, is very well disposed towards me, but is weak as water, and could be swayed, either by Julia in my interests, or by Helmuth against them.

Dr Helmuth Lisický, who, I am convinced, is the nigger in the wood-pile—if there is a wood-pile?

So what it boils down to is that two out of my grandfather's three remaining contemporaries, Embledon and Smith, now so rarely attend the meetings of the Board that they can know little of what goes on at it, and the third, Roberts, is so lacking in personality that he can never have exerted any great influence over its decisions; Rootham and Bartorship, the two men upon whom I could best rely to safeguard my interests, are both abroad on war-service, and Uncle Paul, who knows nothing of finance, would accept without question any proposal put up by the others. That leaves Iswick and Helmuth as the only strong men remaining in the party; and, as four out of the other six have been more or less out of the game for most of the war, they have had only old Roberts and my dull-witted uncle to deal with; so it seems pretty clear that for the past few years Messrs. I. and H. have virtually controlled the Trust between them.

Perhaps my suspicions of Iswick are entirely unfounded, but there can be no getting away from it that, if he is in collusion with Helmuth, the war has given the two of them a unique opportunity to do the Trust down. If they have, one can quite understand their now being prepared to go to pretty well any lengths rather than risk exposure by handing over the accounts.

On my coming of age, were it not for the war, I suppose there would have been gigantic celebrations; every factory and office in the combine closed for the day; beanfeasts for all the workers followed by dances and fireworks at night; a huge reception in London for all directorates and senior staffs, at which the eight Trustees would formally hand me my sceptre to the accompaniment of loud cheers and the drinking of much champagne.

As things are, all I can do is to arrange that everyone in the organization should receive a handsome bonus. There certainly won't be much celebrating so far as I am concerned; just a birthday lunch, which the Trustees will come down from London to attend before giving me an account of their stewardship; and for that the two old crocks will drag themselves out of their retirement to make a special appearance—so six out of eight of them will be here.

What an opportunity for a show-down with Helmuth! I had forgotten that, although he can prevent me from writing to ask them to come here, they will be coming anyhow on my birthday.

But June the 20th is still over a month away; and I've another full-moon period to get through before that. Somehow I've got to find a way to outwit Helmuth. Unless I can, I've a horrible conviction that by the time the big day does arrive he will have reduced me to such a state that I shall be judged incapable of taking over anything.

Monday, 18th May

I have finished Dr Bramwell's book on Hypnotism and reread some parts of it several times, so I have now got a pretty good grasp on the theory of the business. It remains to be seen whether I can apply it in practice. The fact that I succeeded with those two chaps in the Mess at Nether Wallop cannot be taken as an indication, since they lent themselves willingly to the experiment, whereas here I must attempt it without the co-operation of my subject.

Dr Bramwell says that although it is not impossible to hypnotize a person against his will, it is very difficult to do so. Unfortunately he gives no information about the relative difficulty of hypnotizing a person without their knowledge; and the two are obviously very different matters. In the first case, the subject having refused to play naturally sets up a strong mental resistance if he is seized, his eyes held open, and the experiment proceeded with; in the second, it seems to me that if the subject can be caught unawares, and proves susceptible, he might be got under with comparative ease–and provided, of course, that the operator could catch the subject's glance and hold it for long enough to do the trick without him suspecting what was being attempted.

Normally such a problem does not arise, as doctors who treat patients under hypnosis naturally never do so without first having obtained their consent, except sometimes in the case of lunatics, and then to have their eyes held open is presumably the usual method. But for me, success or failure depends entirely on whether I catch my subject napping.

As Taffy is far slower-witted than Deb I shall start on him, and I have decided that the best time to make the attempt is when he is giving me my before-dinner bath. He has to lift me in and out of it, but I am still capable of washing myself except for my lower limbs. While he is waiting to do my feet and ankles he always stands at the foot of the bath. If I say something to him he looks straight at me, but otherwise he just remains there with a vacant look on his round face; and it certainly provides the best opportunity for a prolonged attempt without risk of interruption, as no one will butt in on us and I have never known Taffy move from his habitual position until our routine is completed.

In glancing over the pages I wrote yesterday, I see that I omitted to mention what provision my grandfather had made in his will for the possibility that both my father and I might pre-decease him, or that both of us might die before I reached the age of twenty-one.

Here again, in the main, the old gentleman displayed his dominating desire that, even if there was no Jugg at the head of it, the Empire he had created should survive and prosper. As a gesture to Charity he left a million to the Benevolent Fund for his employees that he had already founded in his lifetime, and a further half-million to the Seamen's Homes; but the great bulk of his fortune was willed back to the Companies out of which it had come, to be divided amongst them in proportion to the value of the holding that he had in each and the sums concerned added to their reserves, thus enormously strengthening them against the hazards of slumps, strikes, and periods of restricted trading.

The effect of my death, therefore, would be to send up the value of the shares in all the Jugg controlled companies by several points. That would make big stockholders like Embledon, Rootham and a number of others potentially richer by several thousand pounds; but in view of their long association with the combine, it is most unlikely that they would cash in on their holdings on that account. So there is no one who would derive an immediate and really worthwhile benefit from knocking me off.

Before leaving the subject of the Will and the Trust I should like to put it on record that, up to the outbreak of the war, I never had the least reason to suppose that any of the Trustees were neglecting their duties, and that I recall with gratitude the personal interest they all showed in me.

From time to time in the holidays each of them asked me to their houses, or took me out to lunch, and put me through a friendly catechism designed to satisfy themselves that I was happy, healthy and making reasonable progress with my studies. Of course, it was part of their responsibility to make sure that I was being groomed for industrial stardom, but they did it very nicely.

As I adored Julia, regarded Uncle Paul as a good-natured stooge, and enjoyed ample opportunity for self-expression at Weylands, the only complaints I ever made were that I was seldom given the chance to be with other young people in the holidays, and was expected to continue my studies under Helmuth with as much enthusiasm as I did in term-time.

In various fashions peculiar to each they laughed that off; the gist of their refrain being that I must think of myself as a young royalty, whose duty it was to fit himself for the great power he would wield when he grew up, and that since it was necessary for me to acquire a working knowledge of a far wider range of subjects than the average boy, I must grin and bear it, if some of them had to be taken in the holidays with the result that the time I could spend just idling about with other youngsters was heavily curtailed.

As a matter of fact Julia had already sold me that one as soon as I settled down with her at Kew; and I give her full marks for the way she handled me. Her line was that the better educated I became the more enjoyment I should get out of my great wealth when I grew up; so I must not look on lessons as a bore but as a necessary preparation to the appreciation of a thousand delights to come.

She, too, encouraged me to look upon myself as different from other children, and no doubt it was in order to prevent me from realizing that I was not that she kept me away from them; but, on the other hand, she checked any tendency in me to become swollen-headed by decreeing that, until I was seventeen, I should always be known in the household as 'Master' Toby, instead of the servants addressing me by the title I had inherited, that I should never give orders to any of them without her permission, and that my pocket money should not exceed the average amount given to boys of my age.

I do not think that my brain is in any way out of the ordinary, but Julia and Helmuth between them certainly induced me to make the best of it, as I found when I went into the R.A.F. that my general knowledge far exceeded that of the great majority of the junior officers with whom I mixed. The secret of this is, I am sure, that I was never forced to continue at any subject until I got stale and tired of it.

At Weylands, of course, one was allowed a free choice of work, but the fault of the system is that, despite the cleverness of the masters in inducing the pupils to acquire at least a smattering of the subjects that attract them least, most of them do leave with some pretty thin patches in their education, and Helmuth was taken on especially to thicken up the more faulty parts of mine, during the holidays. Even so he managed to do it without arousing in me a permanent prejudice against work, by sandwiching shorts spells at the uncongenial tasks between much longer ones on such fascinating matters as early voyages of discovery, Chinese art, the transmutation of metals, the causes of revolutions, the strange fish that live at great depths, and so on.

It strikes me only now, as a point of interest, that by the time I was fifteen I was already able to talk quite intelligently with all my Trustees—except that old human calculating machine, Roberts—on their hobbies and favourite recreations. Obviously Helmuth must have found out what those were and deliberately coached me in them—although that never occurred to me at the time—but it is no wonder that they were all so well satisfied with him as a tutor for me; and no doubt it was his use of me, over a period of years, to convey to them something of his own wide knowledge and varied interests, that made it easy for Iswick and Uncle Paul to persuade the others that he would be a good man to replace Sir Stanley Wellard on the Board.

But I owe just as much to Julia as to Helmuth, since he did not become the dominant influence in my life until I was thirteen.

My sojourn at Kew lasted only a little over three months, and with it ended that happy, exciting period of exploring a new world of restaurants, cinemas and shops instead of doing lessons. The Trustees agreed that Uncle Paul must be furnished with the means to bring me up in the sort of surroundings that should have enjoyed had not father died. After he became a widower, he had returned to live in Kensington Palace Gardens, and at Queensclere, with my grandfather; so it was in these two big houses that I had spent my childhood and would, presumably, have continued to live had my father survived the accident. In consequence, soon after Christmas, the contents of the little suburban villa were packed up and we transferred ourselves to Millionaire's Row. Then, a fortnight or so later, I was sent as a day-boy to the nearby prep-school in Orme Square.

So far as I can judge, the teaching there was excellent but limited, of course, to a normal curriculum; and, as Julia remained my guiding-star, I am sure that I picked up more useful miscellaneous knowledge in my evenings, outings, week-ends and holidays with her than I did in my hours spent at lessons. But I attended the school in Orme Square only for a year. In the autumn of 1930 Julia told me about Weylands.

At the time she could not have known very much about the place herself, but some friends of hers had two boys there. After giving me a rough idea of the system, she said that it did seem to offer special opportunities for anyone who really liked learning things, as she was sure I did; so, if she sent me there, would I promise to work reasonably hard and not let her down with the Trustees by lazing about the whole time.

Like any other boy of nine-and-a-half I was most averse to the idea of leaving home; but I knew there was no escaping a move in the near future to a prep-school in the country, to get me used to being a boarder before I was sent to a public school. It seemed that my guardian angel had found a way of saving me from the worst, as she assured me that at this new-fangled place there were no prefects, no bullying and no enforced games. So I duly promised not to let her down, and off to Weylands I went in January 1931.

Looking back from my present standpoint I do not think one can possibly defend Weylands as an institution. It is a terrible thing to bring children up as atheists—just how terrible no one can fully appreciate until, like myself, they find themselves pursued by some creature of the Devil.

Then the tacit encouragement of the young to indulge in immorality must be a bad thing. Their freedom to experiment in sex without reproach may save a few of them from later developing secret complexes and abnormalities, but I believe that for every one it saves it robs a hundred—who, if subject to the usual prohibitions, would turn out quite normal—of their illusions.

It certainly did me; and that goes, too, for every other senior pupil, male or female, that I knew at all well there. We had all eaten too greedily of the tree of knowledge, and although appetite remained there was no longer any mystery surrounding the fruit. Both sexes had discovered too early that the other, like itself, had feet of clay; so when we went out into the world nothing was left to us but a cold, cynical seeking after partners in pleasure. Never could any of us hope to be carried away with the sort of mad, self-sacrificing, glorious intoxication of which we had read in books. All too late we were conscious that for us, in connection with a member of the opposite sex, three great words must for ever remain meaningless—glamour, romance, love.

Again, the whole conception of teaching people that they should develop their own ego, irrespective of every other consideration, is all wrong. It makes them hard, selfish, greedy, aggressive and incapable of co-operation in a time of crisis. When I went into the R.A.F. I knew nothing of the team-spirit, except that at Weylands it had been sneeringly defined as 'a conception typical of the human-herd mentality, as it excuses the timorous from emerging from the mass and accepting personal responsibility'. What utter tripe!

In view of the opinions I aired during my early days in uniform I must have appeared to my companions the most bumptious, self-centred young cad; and I marvel now that they were so good-natured as to do no more than laugh at me. But I was always a pretty quick learner and it did not take me long to find out the worthlessness of the Weylands definition of the 'team-spirit'. In a Fighter Squadron your life and the lives of your friends depended on it. If we had started to play for our own hands instead of for our side, when opposed to a superior enemy formation, the lot of us would have been hurtling down in flames within a matter of minutes.

Had there been no war, I would probably still believe that the Weylands creed embodied the highest achievement in logical human thinking; but I know now that much, if not all, of it is false. Nevertheless, I believe that I

acquired far more academic knowledge there than I would have at any
school where it was forced upon me, to be learned parrot fashion as an
alternative to receiving punishment; and I can look back on my school-days
as happy ones—which is more than a lot of chaps can say.

All that I owe to Julia; and I certainly do not hold her responsible for
anything I may have missed through the bad elements of the Weylands
system, for I am convinced that of those she cannot have known enough to
appreciate their possible results.

Helmuth was not at Weylands when I first went there. He did not arrive
until the summer of 1933, and during his first year I had little to do with him.
It was my backwardness in languages that brought about our special
association. Naturally, for my future it was considered important that I
should be able to speak French, German and Spanish fluently; but I was
much more interested in chemistry, engineering, history and geography, so
gave hardly any time to the uncongenial business of trying to master foreign
tongues.

My Spanish was not too bad, as it resembles Italian, and Julia had taught
me from the age of eight to speak her own soft brand of that; but she was
worried by my lack of progress in the other two, and decided that the best
way to get me on was to have someone who would talk them to me in the
holidays. In consequence it was arranged that Helmuth should spend the
August of 1934 with us at Queensclere.

Looking back, I can see now that he took great pains to make himself
agreeable to us all. He was about thirty-seven then, and his strong
personality was already fully developed. There was no trace in his manner of
the retiring diffidence often displayed by private tutors; but the ideas he
threw out were always well calculated to appeal to Uncle Paul and Julia.

My uncle's main interest has always been horses. Helmuth, as I have
learnt since, dislikes all animals and considers horses stupid brutes; but he
threw himself into helping Uncle Paul arrange the local horse show at
Queensclere that summer, as though they were his ruling passion.

With Julia he had a more congenial row to hoe, as he really likes and
understands period furniture and she was then busy planning a new *décor* for
some of the rooms at Kensington Palace Gardens. He not only helped her
find many of the pieces but got them for her much cheaper than she could
have done herself; and that was a big feather in his cap with Uncle Paul as
well as Julia, since the Trustees gave them a good allowance to keep the two
houses up, but were always a bit sticky about weighing out additional sums
for such things as antique furniture.

So far as I was concerned Helmuth played his cards most skilfully. He
announced at once that we would have no set lessons and would not bother
with books—at least, not grammars and dreary set-pieces of translation—but
he would like me to read one or two that I should find amusing, with the aid
of a dictionary.

One, I remember, was Dr Madrus's unexpurgated translation of the
Arabian Nights in French, and another an edition of Casanova's *Memoirs* in
German. Both gave vivid pictures of life in an age totally different from our
own, as well as being spiced with a wealth of bawdy stories, so they held my
interest and induced me to acquire extensive vocabularies in a very short
time. For the rest, Helmuth always talked to me when we were alone in
French or German, repeating in English any bits I didn't get, so without any

great effort on my part I was soon able to gabble my thoughts in both languages.

It is hardly surprising that he was asked to stay on through September, and to come to us again for the Christmas holidays. By the time we were due to go back to Weylands at the end of January I could speak colloquial French and German with considerable fluency, so Helmuth thought of another way in which he could make himself useful. He said he thought that, now I was rising fourteen, it would be a good thing for me to go over some of the factories that I was one day to control; so it was arranged that part of his Easter holidays should be spent taking me on a tour round the most important ones.

On our return from it, Julia broke the news to me that she and Uncle Paul were anxious to make a long tour through the United States that summer, so they had asked Helmuth to look after me. Naturally I was disappointed at first that I should not be spending my holidays with them; but the pill was gilded by the news that they had taken a little house on Mull that had excellent shooting, for Helmuth and myself; and the present of a brace of Purdys, which enabled me to have visions of doing terrific execution among the grouse.

That outlines the first of the five years that I spent with Helmuth 'as my guide, philosopher and friend'; and the others differed from it only in detail. With each year this viper, that the unsuspecting Julia has nurtured in her bosom, became more deeply entrenched in her regard and in my uncle's confidence, so that latterly they did nothing without consulting him; while I tamely accepted his authority, partly from habit and partly because he was clever enough to refrain from attempting to make me do anything he knew that I would really have hated. Nevertheless, our wills did clash eventually.

By the spring of 1939 Helmuth had established himself so firmly as the arbiter of my fate that no one even thought of contesting his opinion when he announced that, instead of my going up to Cambridge, as my father had done, at the beginning of 1940, he felt that I would derive much more benefit from being taken by a suitable mentor on a two-year tour of Europe, which would include a stay of a few weeks in the Ruhr, the Saar, Hamburg, Turin and each of the other great industrial centres.

The last point was especially calculated to appeal to the Trustees; and when it emerged that Helmuth was willing to resign his mastership at Weylands to act as my cicerone, they not only jumped at the idea but urged that the tour should be extended to two-and-a-half-years, so that the last six months of my minority might be spent visiting the industrial zones of the United States. It was even urged that we should make an earlier start, and, as my eighteenth birthday was in June, set out on our travels soon after the ending of the summer term. However, the authorities at Weylands were unwilling to release Helmuth before the end of the year, and many Weyland pupils stayed up till they were nearly nineteen, so it was agreed that we should put in a final autumn term there.

But things did not turn out according to plan. We were still up on Mull in the first week of September when the war broke out. I told Helmuth that Sunday night that in the morning I proposed to take the first train from Oban, and, on reaching London, volunteer for the R.A.F.

There was the hell of a row. Apparently it had never occurred to him that I might react to the news like that. But he soon got his bearings and, once he had recovered his temper, he began to produce all sorts of well-reasoned arguments in favour of my holding my hand for a bit.

His first line was that it would be silly to rush into the ranks when, just as in the last war, every well-educated youngster would, in due course, be needed as a junior officer. Then he said that this time the Government was better prepared, and did not need volunteers, as they had already arranged to call up such men as they required by classes. Finally he urged that so much had gone into fitting me to hold great responsibilities that my life was not my own to throw away; the least I could do was to submit the matter to my Trustees and hear what they had to say, before jeopardizing all the hopes that they had placed in me.

Thinking things over a few weeks later I came to the conclusion that none of these arguments had weighed with me in the least. I was a strong, healthy young man of eighteen and a bit, with a very fair knowledge of aircraft design and engineering. I knew perfectly well what I ought to do, and what I wanted to do. Yet I did not do it.

Helmuth's will proved stronger than mine. The battle between us went on for over a week. Again and again I tried to screw my courage up to the point of defying him and walking out. Several times I was on the verge of slipping out at night and making off in the motor-boat to the mainland. Yet I could never quite bring myself to do either.

I feel certain now that it was neither his reasoning nor my ingrained respect for his authority which was the paramount factor in keeping me there against my will. It was the silent, compelling power that at times lies behind the steady regard of his tawny eyes. He used a form of hypnotism to bind me like a spell.

I wonder what luck I'll have when I try that out on Taffy this evening. If I succeed I'll be out of here by the end of the week. I have got to be; the new moon rises on Thursday.

Tuesday, 19th May

It was no good. I have never before realized how difficult it is to catch a person's glance and hold it for any length of time. Taffy was engaged for his strength—not his brain. He is only about five feet ten, but broad and long-armed, like a gorilla. His hair is dark and curly, and his eyes are small; but his face is as round as a full moon, and he has a curiously feminine quality. He stood there, docile as usual, at the foot of the bath, for a full ten minutes while I was soaping myself, but every time I said something to him to attract his attention he just looked at me for a second, then looked quickly away again.

At last, in desperation, I said to him: 'Taffy, have you ever tried staring anyone out?'

'No, indeed, Sir Toby,' he replied. 'What would I want to be doing a thing like that?'

'For fun,' I said. 'Come on; look straight at me and let's see which of us can make the other blink first.'

'Fun it is, is it?' he repeated with a sheepish grin; and for a moment his round brown eyes peeped at me from beneath the dark, curling lashes that many a girl would envy. But almost at once he dropped his glance, gave an embarrassed laugh, and muttered: 'A strange game it is, and I no good at it.'

I felt that it might arouse the oaf's suspicions and a permanent resistance if I persisted further, at the time; so I chucked up the attempt and ate my dinner in a very bad humour. But I am hoping that I'll catch him napping some time today. A good chance is bound to present itself sooner or later; the trouble is that I have no time to waste.

After dinner last night, to take my mind off my failure with Taffy, instead of switching my radio off at the end of the nine o'clock news I listened to a broadcast on the war. I must confess that I haven't been taking very much interest in the war of late, owing to preoccupation with my own troubles; but hearing this commentator quite cheered me up, as it seems that in this past week or so things haven't been going too badly for us.

The best bit of news is that General Alexander has succeeded in extricating all that was left of our army from Burma. It must have been hell for them all these months, fighting desperate rearguard actions in that ghastly country against enormously superior forces, and it is a miracle that they were not surrounded and cut to pieces.

It was Alexander, I remember, who assumed command in the last phase at Dunkirk, after Gort had gone home, and was himself the last man to leave the beach there. I think he must be a really great General, as any fool can make a breakthrough if the odds are in his favour and he has plenty of supplies, but it requires military genius of the first order to conduct a successful retreat with war-weary troops who are short of everything. Now that he is back across the Chindwin, on the Indo-Burmese frontier, it should be easier to get supplies and reinforcements up to him; so let's hope that he will be able to hang on there and prevent those filthy little Japs from swarming down into India.

The Ruskies are still getting the worst of it in the south, and the Germans claim to have driven them from their last foothold in the Crimea; but the success of Marshal Timoshenko's counter-offensive against Kharkov more than makes up for that. Those Russian battles are on a scale that make our little set-tos in Libya look like backyard brawls, and they must be costing the Nazis tens of thousands of casualties a week. If only the Russians can keep it up they will yet bleed Hitler's Reich to death.

This morning's bulletin was cheering, too. Yesterday Coastal Command put on another good show. Our bombers caught the *Prinz Eugen* off Norway, slammed several torpedoes into her, and raked the decks of her escorting destroyers with cannon fire. God, what wouldn't I give to be able to fly again!

As must be obvious to anyone who, knowing nothing of me, comes upon this journal and has read so far, I got the better of Helmuth in the end. During those last three weeks on Mull, as he was constantly with me, his influence proved so strong that all my efforts to throw it off were in vain; and I was still in the same state when, on September the 24th, we returned to Weylands.

For the first week of the term I continued to be a bit befuddled and half-persuaded by his arguments; but about a fortnight earlier old Wellard had died, and I imagine that Helmuth was already hard at it, intriguing with

Uncle Paul and Iswick to get himself appointed to the vacant Trusteeship. Anyhow, on October 1st he was summoned to a meeting of the Trustees in London. After I had spent twenty-four hours without seeing him my mind began to clear, and the next thing I decided to make a bolt for it.

Getting away presented no difficulties. I packed into one small suitcase some spare underclothes and a few personal belongings; then, having read a book till about half past three in the morning, I quietly carried the case downstairs and strapped it on to the back of the first bicycle that I came upon in the staff bike-shed. As it was seven miles to the station I had to take an unauthorized loan of the bike; but I knew that it would be returned in due course, since I meant to leave it in the station cloak-room and post the ticket for it to the school bursar.

At the station I slipped the ticket into an envelope that I had all ready for it, and at the same time posted a note that I had written to Julia, asking her to do her best to stop Helmuth trying to find me, and telling her that she was not to worry about me, as I should be very well looked after at the place to which I was going, and that I would write to her within the course of the next few weeks. Then, twenty minutes later, the milk train came in and took me to Carlisle.

As I was still technically a schoolboy I thought it possible that when my absence was discovered a hue-and-cry would start after me, and I was uncertain what powers the authorities might have to send me back, so I had already decided to take evasive action. London was the place they would naturally expect me to head for, so, instead, I took the train from Carlisle up to Glasgow. That afternoon I went to the City Recruiting Office there and volunteered for the R.A.F.

My age was then eighteen and three months, but I could have passed for a year older had I wished, as I was both tall and well-built; also I was, as the police descriptions term it, 'A person of good address', so I had little fear of being rejected. But I did not mean to sign on in my own name, as it was quite on the cards that in another few hours the police would be looking for me, and the thought that I might be caught out in that part of the business made me go pretty hot under the collar.

I knew that I would have to show my identity card and there was no disguising the Weylands address, as it had been issued to me there the previous May; but my name had been inserted simply as JUGG, ALBERT, A., with no 'Sir' or 'Bart.' in a bracket behind it to give away my title, and the previous evening I had added the letters LER to both the block-letter surname and my scrawled signature. It was a bit of a risk to take, as the card informs one that any alteration of it is punishable by a fine or imprisonment or both; but I felt that if I could get away with it the odds would be all against anyone up in Glasgow association the missing heir to millions, Sir Toby Jugg, with Aircraftsman Albert Juggler—and get away with it I did.

I found those first few weeks in the R.A.F. extraordinarily exciting. A high proportion of my fellow recruits were Glasgow mechanics, but there were also clerks, salesmen, colonials, farmers, small tradesmen and other types, most of whom had previously been entirely outside my ken.

The life, too, was utterly different from anything I had ever known; although I did not find it as hard as I had expected, for we were excellently fed and very well looked after. No doubt the routine and restrictions inseparable from communal life under discipline would have palled after a bit, but to start with, for me, everything held the glamour of strangeness, and every new face I encountered held a thrilling real-life story of effort and achievement—or failure, which could usually be heard over a can of beer.

During the ten weeks that I was in the ranks I had no chance to get bored with any one set of companions, as in less than two months the grading system caused me to be transferred from one hutted camp to another four times. It takes a lot of people to keep an aircraft in the air, so out of the many who offered themselves comparatively few possessed the qualifications and had the luck to be graded for operational training; the others had to be content to serve as ground-crews, signallers, clerks, tradesmen and in all the scores of jobs without the conscientious performance of which the operational people could not have functioned. But my youth, health, keenness and high standard of education led to my being picked as one of the lucky ones; and it was that which resulted in the discovery of my true identity.

My one object when I volunteered had been to become a fighter-pilot, and constant application coupled with the O.K. from half-a-dozen medical boards and selection committees had got me as far as this fourth station. When I had been there about ten days it came to my turn to be summoned for a personal interview with the Station Commander.

He asked me a few questions, glanced through my papers, and said: 'I see, Juggler, that you have made a pretty good showing, so far; and that your Flight Commander considers your possibilities to be above the average. I think he is right; so I propose to recommend you for a commission. You may not get it, but at all events you will be given your chance on transfer as a Cadet to Receiving Wing.'

I suppose the good man expected me to blush, stammer my thanks, salute smartly and float out as though my elation was so great as to render me airborne already. But my surprise was only equalled by my consternation, as I knew that if I let him have his way the next step was that somebody would be demanding a copy of my birth certificate. In consequence, I blurted out, a little awkwardly, that I did not want a commission; I wanted to become a Sergeant Pilot.

He went a shade redder in the face and said a trifle huffily: 'I cannot compel you, of course; but, presumably, you joined the Royal Air Force with the object of serving your country to the best of your ability. If, in the opinion of officers such as myself, who are practised in forming judgments of this kind, you are considered to have the fundamental qualities required for commissioned rank, you must surely see that it is your duty to accept our decision and do your best to obtain it.'

Before I could reply, another officer, a Flight-Lieutenant who was sitting at a side table, stood up and said: 'D'you mind if I handle this, sir? I think I know the answer.'

The Group-Captain looked a bit puzzled, but nodded his assent, and the Flight-Lieutenant beckoned to me to follow him into the next room.

As soon as the door was closed behind us he motioned me to a chair and offered me a cigarette. He was a lean, bronzed-faced, tough-looking little man of about thirty, with very blue eyes. When we had lit up, he grinned at me and said: 'I take it the birth certificate is the snag, isn't it—Sir Toby?'

What the hell could I say? I knew I was caught out. It transpired that until the outbreak of war he had been a test-pilot at Juggernauts—the Jugg combine's biggest aircraft plant; and that he had recognized me from having met me on a visit that I paid to the factory with Helmuth in 1938.

I had watched the papers carefully, and no report of my disappearance had so far been published in them; so I took it that Julia had shown my letter to the Trustees and they thought it wiser to wait for me to reappear in my own time than to start a scandal by having me publicly hunted. But somebody on the Board must have talked, as Flight-Lieutenant Roper had heard that I had run away from school, in a letter he had had from a friend in his old firm.

He put it to me that I was in a jam. Sooner or later I was bound to be rumbled, and it might happen in circumstances where my C.O. had no alternative but to send me for court-martial on a charge of having made a false declaration to the recruiting authorities; and following that there might be a civil prosecution for having faked my identity card. He said that, as my motive had clearly been a patriotic one, he did not think either court would take a very serious view of the matter; but one could not be certain of that, as they could not afford to give the press a chance to publish the fact that anyone had been caught out breaking war-time security measures and allowed to get away with it—and, I being who I was, it was certain the press would make it a headline story. So he thought that instead of going on as I was and risking anything like that I should be much wiser to let him try to sort matters out.

I was still afraid that once the Trustees found out where I was they would endeavour to regain control of me; but Roper said that since I had managed to get into the R.A.F., and was over eighteen, it was quite certain that the Air Ministry would never agree to release me for the purpose of being sent back to school; so I accepted his very kind offer. We agreed that he should tell the Group-Captain that I had asked for a fortnight to think over the question of the commission and, in the meantime, he would put my case in confidence to an Air Marshal who was a personal friend of his.

Between them they did the trick. On the 11th of December I received orders to proceed to London and report at Adastral House. On the 12th I signed a lot of papers there, with the result that Aircraftsman Juggler was released from the service and for about five minutes I became a civilian; after which I was sworn in again under my proper name and left the building with orders to get into a civilian suit, post my uniform and kit to the R.A.F. Depot in Hallham Street, and go on leave till further notice.

Down at Queensclere Julia and Uncle Paul killed the fatted calf for me; and when Helmuth came south just before Christmas he showed not the slightest trace of ill-will at my having got the better of him. In fact he said that, while he had felt it to be his duty to keep me out of harm's way if he possibly could till I was called up, he thought the initiative I had shown did me great credit; so we quite naturally fell into our old friendly relationship.

As he had resigned his position at Weylands and there could now be no question of his taking me abroad, his co-Trustees asked him if he would like to take over the Llanferdrack estates, since it was felt that with an able man to administer them the farms, villages and forests here could make a much bigger contribution to the war. The idea of having his own small kingdom evidently appealed to him, and by a curious coincidence he left Queensclere to start his new job the same day as I left on Air Ministry orders to report at Reception Wing as one of the new intake of Cadets.

That was the beginning of months of arduous training; first at the I.T.W.; scores of lectures, hundreds of tests, then the E.F.T.S.; more lectures, more tests, solo flying, formation flying, night flying, all through the spring of the phoney war, then all through that desperate summer while Hitler smashed his way to Calais and the Loire, and on into the autumn while the Battle of Britain raged overhead.

Sometimes we saw bits of the battle fought out in the distant skies. The crowd I was training with were pretty good by then; again and again we begged to be transferred to 10 Group, or even a fighter station outside it where there might be some chance of our joining in; but the authorities were adamant.

How we raved against the old boys at the Air Ministry, with their rows of ribbons and scrambled eggs, when we learned how exhausted our first-line pilots were becoming, and were not allowed to go to their relief.

But those veterans of the last great war were right. They must have been just as worried as we were, but they knew from experience that a pilot's chance of survival in combat is in exactly relation to the perfection, or otherwise, of his training; and they had the guts to reject the temptation even at a time of crisis to reduce by a single day the schedules of training that had been laid down in peacetime. Had they allowed us to go in three-parts trained half of us would have been massacred, and it was their refusal to be panicked into doing so that gave the R.A.F. dominance over the Luftwaffe in the following year.

So we had to go on with our lessons and pretend to ignore the fact that any night the invasion might come and find us still not on the operational list.

But at last the great day came, and I was one of the lucky ones, as I was posted to Biggin Hill, right in the thick of it. My third time up I got my first Heinkel III. Her escort had been dispersed and she was trying to sneak home alone. I was on my way in, and hadn't much juice left, but just enough to turn and go after her. It was touch and go. I opened up at 300 yards and gave her two bursts, but nothing seemed to happen. As I circled and came in again some bullets from her spattered through my aircraft. I wasn't hit, but my engine began to stutter. I let her have all I'd got, but a moment later I began to lose height rapidly. I was mad with rage at the thought that I would have to make a forced landing and let her get away; but just as I was coming down in a field outside Maidstone I caught sight of her again. I had got her after all and she was a swirl of flame and smoke just about to crash among some trees half a mile away.

Then two days later I got an Me. 109. But there is no point in writing all this. It's a good thing to sit and think of, though.

Wednesday, 20th May

I have had no luck with Taffy yet; and am beginning to fear that, short of giving him a direct order to stand dead still and stare at me, I never shall. I don't want to do that, but I have got to get a letter past Helmuth somehow and can think of no way to do so other than by making Taffy act as my unconscious agent. Unfortunately I am up against the time factor, so if I fail to pull it off today I'll have to risk an all-or-nothing attempt on him tomorrow.

According to Dr Bramwell, however difficult persons are to hypnotize, once they have been got under it is always much easier to get them under a second time. So I had hoped to try Taffy out once or twice with simple tests before actually giving him a letter; but there is not now a sufficient margin of time left to take any chances. If I *can* get him under I shall have to make the most of the opportunity.

In consequence, most of the time I have spent indoors today has gone in writing a letter to have ready to give Taffy should my efforts to put him under control prove successful. I have given Julia full particulars about the haunting to which I have been subject, and have implored her to come to my rescue at once; but I have said nothing about Helmuth being at the bottom of it. She has shown such faith in his abilities and his apparent devotion to me, for such a long time past, that I feel it would be unwise to make any accusation against him in a letter.

When she recalls my 'burglar' and my horrible experience of the broken tomb at Weylands, I am sure she will not think that I am appealing to her without real cause now; and knowing Helmuth's apparent scepticism about such matters she will take that as my reason for asking *her* to arrange for my removal; but if I told her in addition that I believe he is deliberately attempting to drive me insane, I fear she would begin to wonder if I were not so already.

It will be time enough to tell her the sickening truth about him when she gets here. However, I've made it clear that I have already sounded him about my being moved, and that he is very averse to it, so she must come prepared to meet with, and overrule, his opposition. I even went so far as to suggest that she should bring with her a chit from Uncle Paul, authorizing her to take me away.

That line will prove a bit of a bombshell to her, as on no previous occasion has it ever been necessary even to consider giving Helmuth a direct order concerning me. She may put it down to my being terribly overwrought, or read into it that I have told Helmuth about my 'spooks', and since he does not (?) believe in such things, we have quarrelled violently. Whichever way she takes it will be all to the good, as in the first sense it would stress the gravity of my condition, and, in the second, prepare her for ructions between Helmuth and myself on her arrival.

I doubt very much if she will bring a chit from Uncle Paul, as it is a hundred to one that she will think it a fantastic idea, and quite unnecessary. All the same, I hope she does, as Helmuth seems determined to keep me here and may take a high-handed line with her. But Uncle Paul is still my Guardian and I believe that even Helmuth would think twice about refusing to accept his written order.

I urged it on Julia that, even if she did not bring a chit from Uncle Paul with her, she must speak to him about my letter and at least secure his verbal consent to my immediate removal, as then Helmuth would not be able to postpone the issue by saying that he must consult Uncle Paul before the matter could be finally decided.

To stress the vital importance of quashing any proposal on Helmuth's part about postponement, I pointed out to her that the full moon is due again on the 30th, so, judging by the previous bouts, I shall be in acute danger again from about the 27th on, although there is no guarantee at all that these damnable attacks may not start even earlier.

It is already the 20th, and I have yet to get this letter off; so I said that when she does get it she must act without a moment's delay, tell Uncle Paul any damn' thing she liked, and come down here with his authority to take me away, if possible before the 25th.

Thursday, 21st May

Last night proved a milestone in my silent battle against Helmuth. While I was in my bath I had another crack at Taffy, but, as on the two previous occasions, without result; until I suddenly thought of a new line of attack. I pretended that I had got something in my eye and, holding it open, asked him to fish the offending body out.

As there was nothing there he naturally could not find it, but he had to keep peering down into my eyes and I stared up at his. After we had had our glances locked like that for a few moments, with only about nine inches between our faces, I said softly:

'Taffy, you're looking very tired. You are tired, Taffy, aren't you–very tired?'

As he did not reply, I went on: 'I think you had better go to sleep, Taffy. A sleep would do you good. Go to sleep, Taffy. Close your eyes.'

Imagine my elation when his eyelids drooped and those lovely dark eyelashes of his fell like two little fans upon his cheeks. I took his hands and stroked them gently, as, according to Bramwell, a lot of hypnotists have found that touch helps the thought waves to flow into the subject.

My wheeled chair was standing beside the bath, so I made him sit down in it and relax. Then I asked him a few simple questions, such as where he had been born, if he had had a nickname when he was at school, if he would have liked to be a gardener like his father or preferred being with me, and so on; all of which he answered between half-closed lips in a toneless voice, but without hesitation.

Next, I told him to stretch his right arm straight out from the shoulder, and hold it there. In a normal state the average person can hold their arm out at right angles to their body without showing fatigue for about three minutes, then their hand begins to droop. They can keep lifting it, but each time they do so it starts to sag again almost at once; and after about five minutes the pain of keeping their arm extended becomes too much for them.

Under hypnosis the muscles hardly seem to tire at all and Bramwell's book cites instances where subjects have remained with their arms outstretched for long periods, even when heavy weights have been attached to their wrists trebling the normal strain. I sat in the bath watching Taffy while I slowly counted five hundred. That must have been a good eight minutes, and his arm was still as rigid as when he had first stretched it out in obedience to my order. I needed no further proof that I had him properly under.

Then, to my fury, I suddenly remembered that I had not got the letter to Julia with me; it was still in the top drawer of my bedside table.

Yet, having at last succeeded with Taffy, I simply could not bring myself to abandon the opportunity of using him, so long as there was the least chance of my being able to do so.

When I have had my evening bath I am not dressed again, but put to bed; Deb gives my back a quarter-of-an-hour's massage while Taffy gets me a cocktail; then my dinner is brought to me there. Sometimes Deb is ready, waiting for me, when I get back from the bathroom, but at others she is a few minutes late.

It is certain that both she and Taffy have instructions to take any letters I may give them for the post to Helmuth, so if I gave one to Taffy in front of her the odds are she would mention it to Helmuth and it would be taken from Taffy before he had a chance to get down to the village with it. Moreover, I am exceedingly anxious to keep secret the fact that I can hypnotize people, and Deb might have guessed the reason why Taffy's face was looking so wooden and expressionless if she had seen him as he was when with me in the bathroom last night.

So it came to a race against time. The second after I realized my blunder in leaving the letter behind, I saw that if I could get back to my room before Deb came in to massage me, I should still be able to pull the cat out of the bag; but if she got there first I would have to abandon my plan for the time being.

One of the most maddening things about being semi-paralysed is its effect when one wants to do something in a frantic hurry. Had I had the use of my lower limbs I would have been out of that bath in a jiffy, given myself ten seconds' rub with the towel, pulled on my dressing-gown and been back in my room under the minute. As it was I had to submit to the infuriatingly slow ministrations of Taffy; and the fact that he was still under my hypnotic control did not help matters; on the contrary, it seemed to slow him up.

At last he had me back in my chair and began to wheel me along the corridor. He was still acting like an automaton, and I did not want to wake him while there was a chance that things might be all right; because I knew that, at best, I would have only a few minutes to work in, and that might not be enough to get him under again. But I was worried stiff what construction Deb would put upon it if she saw him like that. Half-way down the passage a sudden inspiration came to me, and I said:

'If Sister Kain is in my room when we enter it, Taffy, you are to wake up. Directly you see Sister Kain you are to wake up, d'you understand; and you are to forget all that has happened in the past twenty minutes.'

'Yes, Sir Toby,' he murmured obediently, and at that moment we reached my door.

I suppose if I had been accustomed to hypnotizing people I should have said that to him earlier. Anyhow, thank goodness I did say it before we entered my room, as Deb was there.

It was a bitter disappointment. Afterwards, on glancing at the clock, I realized that it was not Deb being unusually early that had caused me to miss the boat, but our being unusually late. In the excitement of trying to beat her to it I had quite forgotten the time I had spent in putting Taffy through the tests, and including the eight or nine minutes for which I made him hold out his arm, they must have taken up the best part of a quarter of an hour.

Still, although I was stalemated last night, I am immensely heartened by this success. Now I have had Taffy under I feel confident that I can get him under again. Moreover it means a lot to know that he reacts to post-hypnotic suggestion. It was an anxious moment as he wheeled me across to my bed and I screwed my neck round to get a glimpse of his face as soon as I could. He was wide awake, and went about his duties quite normally, without indicating by a word or look that he had just passed through an unusual experience. I feel confident now that, provided no entirely unforeseen piece of misfortune upsets my plans, I shall be able to get my letter away by him tonight.

Now I will set down the little more there is to tell of my personal history, and so be finished with it.

I continued to be a fully operational G.D. officer in the R.A.F. up to July the 10th, 1941, the date on which I was shot down for good. I had, of course, been shot down several times before, as was the case with nearly everyone who flew consistently for any length of time in the early years of the war. Once a Jerry followed me in and shot me up when I was flying too low to dare to bale out, so I had to crash-land on a reservoir. That was not funny, as I darn' nearly drowned; but, if I had to make a choice, I'd rather go through that again that repeat my only experience of baling out over the North Sea. Fortunately that was in mid-May, as it was seven hours before they found me, and had it been earlier in the year I should have died of cold; I was blue when I was pulled out of the drink, and if my strength had not enabled me to go on flailing my limbs for the last hour or two, I would have died of it anyhow.

My bag was 14 Jerrys and 7 probables, more than half of them being scored during my first ten weeks as an operational pilot. After that it got more difficult, as we had given the Luftwaffe a bloody nose, and they went over to the defensive. My D.F.C. came through in May, and I was promoted to Flight-Lieutenant just before I got my packet.

As I did not hold the rank for six months I am no longer officially entitled to it. In all such cases if an officer 'goes sick'—which covers everything from appendicitis to having his eyes shot out or being burnt to a living skeleton—and is unable to perform his duties for more than three weeks, he is automatically deprived of the rank he has held and reduced by one ring.

Of course, the idea is to save money on their pensions. I am one of the fortunate ones to whom it does not matter, but by now there must be thousands of poor fellows to whom those extra few pounds a month would make an enormous difference. As the ruling applies to all three Services it is pretty obvious that it was inspired by the Treasury; and, if only I had the use of my legs again, nothing would give me greater pleasure than to have five minutes behind a haystack with the mean-minded little Whitehall rat who thought that one up.

After the excitement of flying and the fun of sing-songs in the Mess, and sometimes going with a crowd of good fellows for an evening's bust to the towns near the various airfields at which I was stationed, I got awfully browned-off in hospital; but once it had been broken to me that there was very little chance of my ever walking again I did my best to resign myself to my fate.

I was operated on five times and, within the limits they set themselves, the surgeons were successful, as they managed to repair a certain amount of the damage. In fact I owe it to them that I can sit up for two or three hours at a stretch without discomfort instead of having to be wheeled about on my back the whole time; but to get me on my feet again proved beyond them. A long-term policy of rest and massage was, in the end, all that they had left to suggest; so, after nine months of living in an atmosphere of iodoform, I was, at my own request, boarded and invalided from the Service.

The problem of what was to happen to me had already been settled. I should greatly have preferred to go to Queensclere, but Kent is constantly the scene of enemy ops; and, although I was quite prepared to stay put during air-raids, Julia and Uncle Paul would have thought it imperative to get me down to a shelter every time a siren sounded, so I could not decently make myself such a burden to them. The same applied to London. Helmuth had been running Llanferdrack for over two years then, and he had had the care of me all through my teens. One could have searched Britain and not found a place more suitable for anyone in my condition; and Helmuth as good as said he would be deeply hurt if I did not allow him to look after me.

I wonder, now, if he had already hatched this devilish plot to drive me insane once he succeeded in getting me down here?

Anyhow, on March the 14th last I arrived at Llanferdrack, and was duly installed with all the honours of a war-scarred hero. For the first fortnight I enjoyed the change of scene and the freedom from hospital routine enormously; then things began to happen. But I have already gone into that.

Perhaps I should add for the sake of anyone who, never having known me, may one day find and read this journal, that my hair and moustache—I still retain one of those fluffy affairs that many of us grew in the R.A.F.—are red. My face is freckled, my eyes are grey, my teeth are a bit uneven but white and strong. My shoulders continued to develop even while I was in hospital, and I swing a pair of Indian clubs for ten minutes every morning, so the upper part of my body is that of a minor Hercules; and if I couldn't wring a python's neck I could guarantee to give it one hell of a pain there for the rest of its life. I will eat and drink pretty well anything, but I am allergic to oysters, cauliflower, almond icing and pink gin. I was always keen on outdoor sports, but I now thank God that I have always loved reading too. My sex-life started early but, in all other respects, was, up to the time of the crash, perfectly normal—unless it can be considered abnormal that I have never been in love. I am white—inside as well as out, I hope—but I am not free, and I am not yet twenty-one.

That, then, is all about me; and also all the speculations regarding the plot of which I believe myself to be the victim, that I have to make for the present. So, for the future, the entries in this journal will consist of little more than day-to-day jottings, recording the development of the battle I am waging to retain my sanity and regain my freedom.

Later

This evening I put Taffy into a trance again without difficulty. I gave him my letter and told him after dinner he was to go down to the village on his push-bike and post it; and that he was not to mention the matter either before or afterwards to anyone.

Friday, 22nd May

I am furious. That oaf Taffy bogged it. But I suppose it was partly my fault, as I ought to have realized that the letter needed a stamp and that the village post-office would have already shut for the night when I gave Taffy my letter.

Naturally I was anxious to get confirmation as soon as possible that he had actually sent it off, so as soon as Deb had left us this morning and he started to dress me, I said: 'Look at me, Taffy,' and in a moment I had him under. It is as simple as that now, and I have only to point the two first fingers of my right hand at his eyes, then lower them slightly, for his eyes to shut.

To my amazement he immediately burst into tears. Of course, in his normal state he does not remember my having given him the letter, but directly I put him into a trance his sub-conscious again made him fully aware of that, and the fact that he had been unable to carry out my instructions.

Apparently, what happened was as follows: He had his supper with the other servants as usual, then, although he had no memory of my handing him a letter, it suddenly came into his mind that he had one, with orders to go down to the village and post it, and, when he looked in his pocket, it was there.

But it was not stamped, and realizing that he would not be able to buy a stamp in the village at that time of night, he asked the other members of the staff if any of them could lend him one. Unfortunately none of them were able to do so, but Helmuth's man, Konrad, said at once: 'There are always plenty in the office, and I am going up there now to take the Doctor his evening coffee, so I will get you one.'

A few minutes later he came downstairs again and told Taffy that the Doctor wanted to see him about something, and at the same time would give him the stamp for his letter.

Taffy went up all unsuspecting, but as soon as he reached Helmuth's room, Helmuth said: 'I hear you have a letter you wish to post. Is it one of your own or one of Sir Toby's?'

That put the wretched Taffy in a first-class fix. His sub-conscious mind reiterated the instructions I had given him, that he was to tell no one about my letter, while in his conscious mind he knew quite well that he had standing orders that he was to bring every letter I gave him to post to Helmuth.

Apparently he stood there in miserable indecision saying nothing for a few moments. Helmuth then got up from his desk, glared at poor Taffy, seized him by the shoulders, shook him violently, took my letter from his pocket, and threw him out of the room with the warning that if he was caught in any further attempt to smuggle letters out for me it would result in his instant dismissal.

Angry as I was, I could not help feeling sorry for Taffy as he stood there with the tears running down his fat face; so I told him that it was not his fault that things had gone wrong, and woke him up.

Later

I think the fates must have decided that I was due for a little something to cheer me up, after the rotten setback I suffered this morning. Anyhow, just before Deb came to fetch me in for tea I caught one of the pike. He is not a very big chap, as they go, only a ten-pounder; but I sent a message to Cook asking her to stuff and bake him for dinner, and I've told Taffy to get me up half-a-bottle of Moselle.

As a matter of fact, I darn' nearly missed him, as when he took the bait my mind was on very different matters. I had been trying to work out the implications of this Taffy business and decide on my next move.

I wish I knew for certain the role that Konrad played. Did he inadvertently arouse Helmuth's suspicions by specifically naming Taffy, instead of just saying: 'Please may I borrow stamp for one of the servants?' Or was he deliberately responsible for what followed? Perhaps, though, even the unusualness of the request would be enough to set that quick brain of Helmuth's ticking over.

I don't know what the arrangements are about the staff's out-going mail here, but presumably it goes down to the village in the carrier's cart each morning with that from upstairs, and if the servants are short of stamps they give the carrier the money to get them at the same time as they give him their letters.

Anyhow, as the servants in this part of the world live at such a slow tempo, it would be quite exceptional for any of them to have correspondence that they felt to be of such urgency that it could not wait until morning. That may have occurred to Helmuth, and caused him to ask which of them was in such a hurry to get a letter in the post overnight. Then when Konrad replied "Taffy Morgan" Helmuth guessed the rest.

On the other hand Konrad is Helmuth's man, body and soul. He looked after him for all those years at Weylands; in fact, he came over from Czechoslovakia with him in 1933 and has been in his service ever since. So it is quite probable that he is in Helmuth's confidence about what is going on here, anyhow to some extent. If so, he probably smelt a rat directly Taffy asked for the loan of a stamp; especially if Taffy gave it away—as he very likely did—that he meant to go down to the village with the letter there and then. Konrad would certainly have thought that worth reporting if he is acting as Helmuth's spy, and it was easy as winking for him to do so without Taffy suspecting his intention.

I wouldn't mind betting that is what happened; and that Helmuth is using Konrad to keep him informed of any gossip that may go on below-stairs which might jeopardize his secret intentions regarding myself. He would then be in a position to think up an excuse to sack anyone who seemed to be getting too inquisitive, before they found out enough to become dangerous to him. The way that servants get to know things is amazing, and Helmuth is too shrewd to neglect taking precautions against the truth leaking out through them.

Konrad would be just the man for such a job. He comes from Ruthenia, the eastern tip of Czechoslovakia that reaches out towards the Ukraine, and is a typical Slav; big, fair and boisterous, with a hearty laugh that deceives people, until they come to know him well and find out how cunning he is below the surface. He is cruel, too, and there has never been any love lost between him and myself since the day I caught him torturing Julia's pet monkey, at Queensclere.

Helmuth tried to laugh the matter off, and said that I was exaggerating, but Julia was so mad about it that she barred Konrad the house for the rest of that holiday, and instead of continuing to live like a fighting cock with the rest of the servants he had to do the best he could for himself in the village.

One thing emerges from this catastrophe over my letter last night; it will be useless to attempt to get Taffy to take another. Helmuth scared him out of his wits, and as that was due to his having sought to evade the censorship of my mail that Helmuth has set up, his fright will crystallize a definite centre of resistance in his mind.

A hypnotist can make his subjects perform any physical feat that their bodies are capable of enduring and many mental feats which are far beyond their normal capabilities, provided he has their full—and by full I mean their sub-conscious as well as their conscious—co-operation. He can also make them do most things to which they are indifferent—or even mildly antagonistic—according to the depth of trance state in which he is able to plunge them. But if they are strongly opposed to doing something, either on moral grounds or through fear of the consequences, that resistance remains permanently active in their sub-conscious, and it is next to impossible for the hypnotist to overcome it.

So there we are. Having got Taffy just where I wanted him, it is a sad blow that I should no longer be able to make him perform the one service that is of such paramount importance to me. I may be able to use him in some other way; but I have got to think again about a means of establishing some form of lifeline by which I might haul myself to safety from the menace that, Devil-impelled like the Gadarene swine of old, is now rushing upon me.

Saturday, 23rd May

I have had a show-down with Helmuth. Ever since I came to Llanferdrack in the middle of March he has devoted an hour or so to visiting me between tea and dinner, except on the few occasions when he has been away on business.

Now and then we see one another at other times of the day, should we chance to meet in the gardens or the hall; but I am allowed to be up and about in my wheeled chair only between ten- and twelve-thirty, and between three and five o'clock, and those are the busiest hours of his day; so, should we meet during them, we rarely exchange more than a greeting.

On his evening visits he tells me of the latest problems that have arisen regarding the estate and any news he has had from mutual friends of ours; and we discuss the progress of the war and such books as either of us happen to be reading. His mind is so active and his comments so provocative of new ideas that I have always looked forward to his visits as a mental tonic—even when I have felt at times that he was secretly trying to probe my reactions to things about which he would not ask me openly. That is, I looked forward to them up till a week ago; but since I became convinced of the hideous treachery that he is practising towards me I have found it difficult to tolerate his presence in my room.

To let him know what I know—or at least suspect him of on a basis of sound reasoning—prematurely seemed to me both pointless and stupid; so I have done my damnedest to conceal the change of my mental attitude towards him, and to continue to show the same animated interest in his sparkling discourse as I have done in the past.

But yesterday evening some devil got into me and I was seized with a sudden feeling of recklessness. He was standing in the south bay window with his back towards me, his legs apart, his broad shoulders squared and his hands thrust deep in the pockets of his plus-fours. He was wearing a suit of ginger tweed, and I don't know why but country clothes always seem to accentuate his foreignness. In evening dress he looks tremendously distinguished and might easily be taken for the 13th Earl of something, but the dash of Jewish blood that he got from somewhere always comes out when he is wearing country things, and he never looks quite right in them.

As he looked out over the vista of garden, woods and mountains, which seemed more beautiful than ever softened by the evening light, he remarked with a cynical humour which showed that he was not thinking of the view: 'From the past week's *communiqués* about the fighting on the Kerch peninsular it is quite impossible to say who holds it now, or even to form an estimate whether the Germans or the Russians are the biggest liars.'

Instead of replying I suddenly flung at him:

'Helmuth! What the blazes d'you mean by interfering with my mail?'

For a second he remained absolutely motionless, then he whipped round with a broad grin on his face. 'So Taffy told you about last night, eh.'

I had given vent to my accumulated rancour, and it had not even occurred to me that he would assume that I could have known about his stopping my letters only through Taffy having blown the gaff to me that morning. I saw now that that was all to the good, as I could have it out with him on this single issue. I need make no mention of the secret stranglehold that I knew him to have been working to secure on me for the past two months, unless it suited my book. So I snapped:

'Of course Taffy told me! He is my servant and it was his duty to do so. And you'll kindly desist from further threats to sack him, or I'll know the reason why!'

The sardonic grin remained on Helmuth's face, and his tawny eyes flickered with amusement. 'If you addressed defaulters in that tone when you were a Flight-Lieutenant you must have been the terror of your Station.'

His gibe added to my wrath, and I retorted angrily: 'I'll not have you bully my servants!'

The grin suddenly disappeared, and he said in the harsh voice that now alone makes his Czech accent perceptible: 'They are not *your* servants. Except for your Great-aunt Sarah's people, everyone here has been engaged by me. I pay them and I allocate their duties to them. If they do not give satisfaction I shall dismiss them, with or without a character, as I see fit. Also, I bully no one. I simply give my orders and take whatever steps appear necessary to ensure their being carried out.'

'The staff here are paid by the Trust,' I countered, 'and you are only its agent.'

'Why seek to split straws? At Llanferdrack, for all practical purposes, I *am* the Trust; and you know it.'

'On the contrary, you are no more than its representative,' I said firmly. 'The Board put you in charge here, but it can equally well remove you.'

He smiled again, and his glance held open mockery as he enquired: 'Are you thinking of asking them to do so?'

I knew that he had me there, for the time being anyway; so I reverted to my original attack. 'Even if you do regard yourself as answerable to no one here, that still does not give you the right to intercept my private correspondence.'

'I disagree about that.' With surprising suddenness his tone became quite reasonable. 'You have at least admitted yourself that I represent the interests of the Board. In my views it is against their interests, and yours, for them to see such letters as you have taken to writing lately.'

This was an admission that he had intercepted more than one; but I hedged a bit, hoping that he would commit himself further, and said: 'I have not written to the Board since I came here, and my letter last night was to Julia.'

He shrugged his broad shoulders. 'I know it. But what is the difference? If Julia received these letters of yours she would show them to Paul and he would tell the other Trustees about their contents. Besides, I do not wish Julia to be worried either. Your friends have quite enough anxieties these days without being burdened with additional ones concerning you.'

'For how long have you been stopping my letters?' I demanded.

'Since the beginning of April,' he admitted blandly.

'And what possible reason can you give as an excuse for ever having begun to do so?'

'My dear Toby!' He looked away from me for a moment, then an expression of hypocritical pity came over his face, and he went on: 'Surely you must realize that for the past six weeks your conduct has been, well–to say the least of it–queer.'

'In what way?' I cut in.

'It would be distressing to go into that,' he parried. 'In any case, soon after you came here it was quite apparent to me that your injury had affected your mind.'

'Such a thing was never even hinted at by the doctors.'

'Ah, but none of them knew you as intimately as I do, Toby. Besides, the symptoms were only just beginning to show when you arrived here in March. I decided at once that if you became worse the best course I could pursue was to conceal it for as long as possible. That is why I started to open your letters; and later, to account for your not getting any replies from Julia, I invented a story about her having been ill and gone up to Mull.'

I stared at him, almost taken in by his glib explanation, as he continued: 'I have been most terribly concerned for you; but, as I had accepted the responsibility of having you under my care, I felt that it would be cowardly to offshoulder that responsibility on to others so long as there seemed any chance of your getting better. And to have let your letters reach their destination would have amounted to the same thing.'

It sounded terribly plausible but I knew damn' well that he was lying. All the same I felt that there was nothing to be gained by telling him so. That he had been holding up my mail was bound to come out sooner or later; in fact he must have known that there was a good chance of Taffy's confessing to me his failure to post my letter the previous night, giving the reason, and at the same time blurting it out that for weeks past he had been under orders to take all my letters to the office; and if I had just learned about that it would have been unnatural for me to refrain from making a protest. But to let Helmuth know yet that I believe his interference with my mail to be a move in a criminal plot of the most revolting baseness would have been to give valuable information to the enemy. So, instead, I endeavoured to get him in a cleft stick by saying:

'Since you were already under the impression that I was becoming unbalanced before you read my letters to Julia, I take it that their contents fully convinced you of it?'

He nodded.

'Then why the hell didn't you do all you could to save me from suffering those terrors that I described to her?'

'What could I do?' He spread out his thick, powerful hands in a gesture of helpnessness. 'There is no way in which I can prevent your being subject to these hallucinations.'

The time was not ripe to challenge his assertion that my attacks are hallucinations; so I let that pass and cracked in on the target at which I had been aiming:

'You admit that you were fully aware of the circumstances that caused this queerness that you say you noticed in me, yet you ask what you could have done about it. You could have had me put in another room; you could have got me an electric torch; you could have had that damn' blackout curtain lengthened; you could have got me a night-nurse or stayed up with me yourself; you could have made arrangements to have me moved from here!'

Then I added, with a guile that matched his own: 'I cannot understand your refusal of my requests at all, Helmuth. If I did not know so well how devoted you are to me, I should almost be tempted to think that you have become so occupied with running the estate that you have no time left to give a thought to me once you are outside this room.'

'Toby, Toby!' He shook his leonine head and looked at me reproachfully. 'Those are just the sort of ideas which first convinced me that you are no longer your old self, and suffering from a type of persecution mania. But surely you see that my hands are tied. If I agreed to any of these things that you suggest it would mean a departure from the normal routine that we arranged when you first came here, and that would be fatal.'

'Why?' I asked.

'Because it would draw the attention of the staff to the fact that, at times, you mind becomes unhinged. Don't you understand yet what it is from which I have been endeavouring to protect you? If anyone but myself is given cause to think that you have become mental the matter will be taken out of my hands. Your own letters were positively damning, and you know how servants talk. If by any channel it leaks through to the Board that you have become abnormal, and are "seeing things", they will send brain specialists down here to examine you. In your present state that could have only one result—you would be put into a mental home. Even a short period in such a place might affect you for the rest of your life; and as it could not possibly be kept secret, it would have the most disastrous results on the confidence that all your future business associates would otherwise place in you.'

For a moment I found myself completely bewildered. Could he possibly be speaking the truth? Was I, after all, going out of my mind? Were the attacks really no more than figments of my imagination? Had he noticed the early symptoms of madness in me and ever since been loyally striving to prevent anyone else guessing my condition? Had I shamefully misjudged him?

I have not an atom of proof that he is really plotting against me. My whole theory was based on his interference with my mail and his refusal of all my requests which, in my belief, would have enabled me either to evade or lessen the effect of the attacks. And he had now explained his conduct in both matters.

A little feebly I said: 'Surely you could find an excuse to have me moved to another room without arousing Deb's suspicions that I have gone crackers?'

He passed a hand wearily over his mane of prematurely white hair. 'I'm afraid not, Toby. If only there were another room that was equally suitable I would do so gladly, but as we agreed when we talked of it before, there isn't.'

'At least you could get me a torch,' I hazarded desperately.

'There are none to be had.' His voice took on an impatient note.

'Then get the blackout curtain lengthened. Please, Helmuth, please.' All the snap had gone out of me now and I found that I was pleading with him.

'No,' he said firmly. 'Deb is a shrewd young woman. If that curtain is lengthened now she will realize that you must have insisted on it, and attribute your insistence to the moon having an upsetting effect on you. After that she would need only to pick up another hint or two from your behaviour to guess the truth. Besides, the length of the curtain makes no real difference. What you think you see is nothing but the product of your own imagination, so you would believe you saw it just the same if you occupied a bedroom at the Ritz in London or a mud hut in Timbuctoo. All I can do is to prevent others from suspecting your affliction for a time, and in that way give you a chance to recover from it before rumours of your condition reach the Board and bring about a danger of your being certified.'

So, on the face of it, he and I seemed to be dreading that the same grim fate might overtake me; and, if he was to be believed, he was doing his best to save me from it. For a minute or two he went on to reproach me, with what I felt to be commendable forbearance, for having written to Julia so fully about my fears, yet not having said one word of them to him.

I could only reply that, knowing how busy he was, I had not wanted to worry him. The discussion ended by his urging me to do my utmost to keep my imagination under control; and my promising that I would not write any more letters which would cause my friends grave anxiety and endanger my own freedom, by giving grounds for the belief that I am going mad.

Later

I am not going to keep my promise to Helmuth.

Last night, after he left me, I was fully convinced that my suspicions of him were unfounded, that I have been the victim of hallucinations, and that he was doing his best to prevent anyone knowing about my mental state so that if it proved no more than a phase I might have a chance to snap out of it without anyone being the wiser. This morning, when I wrote the last entry here, my mind was not quite clear and still partially under the strong influence that he exerts. Now, I am sure that all he said was a pack of clever lies, and am more certain than ever that he is plotting against me.

In order to excuse himself for having held up my letters, he stated his belief that my injury has affected my brain. I did not prompt him to any such theory; he produced it spontaneously, entirely off his own bat. That shows which way his mind is working. He knows from my letters that I fear I may be driven insane. He would like to see me insane. So, as a further step towards his object, he tells me that he believes me to be insane already. That, so far, is his sole contribution towards *helping* me to preserve my sanity.

Let us assume that I *have* shown signs of mental derangement. What would a true friend, who noticed this and was responsible for me, do? As soon as he was certain that I really was becoming abnormal he would call in the best doctor he could get to advise about my treatment; and, in the meantime, if he realized that any special circumstances were connected with my queerness and tended to increase it, he would at once do all he could to counteract those circumstances. Helmuth has done neither of these things, but *the exact contrary*.

If he *does* believe me mad he is guilty, not only of denying me such help as he has it in his own power to give, but also of deliberately preventing me from sending out letters which would have led to my receiving proper medical attention. If he does *not* believe me mad his stopping of my letters is inexcusable, and his suggestion that I am mad a deliberate attempt to make me think that is so. Therefore, whichever way one looks at it, there can be no doubt that he is acting in accordance with a secret design flagrantly contrary to my interests.

The amazing thing is that it has taken me the best part of twenty-four hours to throw off his influence and fully re-convince myself of his enmity. Before, I was going almost entirely on suspicion, but now that I realize the true implications of our show-down I feel that he has convicted himself out of his own mouth. It is an advance of sorts, as it stresses my danger; but, now that time is so precious, those twenty-four hours were a high price to pay merely for a clearing of the mist through which I had already seen the red light glowing.

Sunday, 24th May

A good break this morning. Quite unexpected and very cheering indeed, now that any further possibility of using Taffy to post a letter for me has been ruled out.

I settled that point quite definitely while I was having my bath last night. Without the least difficulty I put Taffy under, but a moment later he began to blubber and plead with me not to make him do anything contrary to 'the Doctor's' orders. It was just as I feared; Helmuth's treatment of him on Thursday evening has set up such a strong resistance complex in his mind that it would need powers far greater than mine to overcome it; so if I forced the issue his fears would prove stronger than my influence and send him scuttling to Helmuth the moment he was out of my sight.

If I could have got him into a really deep trance I might, perhaps, have overcome his resistance, as I could then have worked on a level of his consciousness so far down as to be still unaffected by Helmuth's prohibitions. But, for one thing, I am still only an amateur hypnotist and, for another, in some types—particularly in simple ones, I gather from Bramwell—it is often very difficult to get down to the deep levels. Anyway my efforts to get down to Taffy's failed entirely.

In such a case the only means of overcoming the resistance is to talk to the subject when he is fully conscious, explain the whole matter and endeavour to argue him round. If one succeeds, that is the end of the opposition, and, in my case, it would then be unnecessary to hypnotize Taffy further, as he would do as I wish without.

The snag is that Taffy is far too frightened of Helmuth, and the prospect of losing his job, for me to be able to persuade him to help me with his eyes open. He would, I think, take the risk if I could offer him a good fat wad of cash as a bonus if he is lucky, or compensation if he got the sack; but it would have to be the equivalent of several months' wages, and I have not even a fiver—or the means of getting one.

Still, my failure with him last night was more than compensated for by my surprising success this morning. As soon as Deb had settled me in the garden I told her that I had got a fly in my eye, and asked her to fish it out. I had intended only a tentative attempt to test her susceptibility; but the trick worked both more swiftly and more effectively than it did with Taffy. The moment I widened my eyes and projected my will through them—that her mind should empty itself and that she should become drowsy—her dark eyes became quite limpid, as though they had suddenly gone sightless, and her eyelids drooped languorously.

I have never thought of her as physically attractive before. She is certainly a handsome piece, but perhaps it was the hardness of her expression, and the intense, serious manner in which she takes everything, which have put me off. But to see her strong features softened and relaxed into a sort of dreamy, yearning look came as quite a shock to me, and I suddenly realized that if only she let herself go she could be a passionate and seductive young woman.

I doubt if my mind was occupied with that thought for more than a couple of seconds, but even that was enough for her to make a partial recovery and almost snap out of it. The change in her expression gave me an instant's warning, so I swiftly concentrated again with all the power of my will; then I had only to touch her forehead lightly with my fingers and murmur 'Sleep, Deb' to have her right under.

It was only then that I recalled a passage in Dr Bramwell's book where he states that, generally speaking, intellectual types prove much easier subjects than the less complex minds usually found among manual workers. He offers no explanation for this, but adds that he has known many cases in which people with a high standard of education have scoffed at hypnotism, yet, on agreeing to a trial, have gone into a trance almost immediately.

The relative lack of resistance in Deb compared with Taffy certainly proved his point, and I rated myself for having not taken more notice of it at the time; but Deb's surface hardness had naturally led me to assume that she would prove difficult. As it was, the unexpected success of the test caught me unprepared, as I had no letter ready to give her.

Unfortunately, too, as it is Sunday afternoon she has gone down to have tea with her friend the schoolmaster in the village. There was no chance to get a letter written, put her in a trance again after lunch and give it to her to post before she left; and I shall not see her again until she comes in to settle me down for the night. I could put her under and send her off to the village with a letter then, but I fear it is too big a risk to take, as if Helmuth spotted her going out at that late hour he would think it strange and be almost certain to question her. So, anxious as I am to get the letter off, I feel that I must curb my impatience till tomorrow morning. If I do the trick directly we get out into the garden she can hop on her bike right away with practically no risk at all of being intercepted.

All I could do this morning was to take measures which should ensure her ready submission to me in the future. While she was still under I said:

'From now on, Deb, whenever I look straight in your face you are to meet my glance and keep your eyes fixed on mine. When I raise my right hand and point my two first fingers at your eyes you will close them, and fall asleep. In your waking state you will not remember that I have hypnotized you. Now, when you wake you will remember only that you have just removed a small fly from my right eye. Wake up.'

It worked like a charm. After thirty seconds she opened her eyes; said: 'Your eye may continue to smart for a little, but don't rub it,' and she even wiped the handkerchief that she had got out to fish with for the fly, before putting it back in her pocket.

Later

I have written my letter, but this one is not to Julia. Time is getting short, and after careful thought I decided that I should do better to attempt to secure more direct action than she is really in a position to take.

If Julia were my Guardian and could give a positive order to Helmuth, I would not have hesitated for a second. But she is not, and Helmuth might take the line with her that 'in my present state' he cannot accept the responsibility for allowing her to remove me from his care.

Uncle Paul, on the other hand, *is* my legal Guardian, and if *he* says that he is going to take me away Helmuth cannot possibly refuse to let him.

The snag about this change in my plan, by which I have decided to rely on my uncle, is two-fold. Firstly, I cannot discuss the whole matter with him as I could have with Julia; secondly, he is a much weaker character than she, and so, normally, more liable to be browbeaten by Helmuth. But he *has* got the authority, and I think I know a way by which I can force him to use it.

Unfortunately, the way I mean to play it precludes me from asking him to bring Julia with him; so that I could, as it were, 'have the best of both worlds'. As he is certain to show her my letter, she may come with him anyhow, and in some ways I shall be very glad if she does; but I should find it a bit embarrassing to say in her presence what I meant to say to him, and it would be a bit awkward for him too; so with that in view I didn't feel that I could decently ask him to make it a family party.

In my letter I said nothing at all of the Horror, about my correspondence with Julia having been suppressed, of my suspicions of Helmuth, or of wanting to leave Llanferdrack. I simply told Uncle Paul that I had recently been considering certain financial arrangements that I intend to make immediately on attaining my majority, and that as time was now short I proposed to send instructions for the drafting of the necessary documents to the lawyers in the course of the next few days.

I added that I really ought to have thought the matter out much earlier, and apologized for the fact that my not having done so now compelled me to ask him to come to see me at such short notice. Lastly I said I thought it important that he should come down and let me have his comments on my proposals before I actually sent them off, as they would materially effect his own income.

If that does not bring him rattling down to Wales within twenty-four hours of receiving my letter, nothing will.

Monday, 25th May

It is 'all Sir Garnet now', as the Victorians used to say. At least, I think so; as after I had done the trick Deb went off on her mission like a lamb.

At about a quarter past ten this morning I put the 'fluence on her and gave her my letter to Uncle Paul, with instructions that she was to set off with it on her bike at once, and that if she met anyone she knew on the way she was not to stop and talk to them, but to confine herself to a friendly greeting, and push on as if she were in a hurry. That ought to ensure that she is not deflected from her purpose, even if she happens to run into Helmuth.

I also made certain that there should be no breakdown this time owing to her hunting for a stamp for the letter before she set off. That risk gave me a nasty moment when I thought about it last night, but the solution proved simple. I took an unused twopenny-halfpenny out of my own collection and stuck it on the envelope. It temporarily spoils the set, but who cares! If that little stamp gets me out of this jam I'll be able to replace it with a twopenny blue Mauritius this time next month, if I want to. How queer the old Queen's Head would look in the middle of a set of modern British! But by jove, I'll do that, even if it costs me a couple of thousand pounds, as a permanent memento of having got the better of my enemy.

Later

I am worried, and don't know what to think. Can Deb possibly have been fooling me, both today and yesterday? I should be tempted to think so if it were not for the fact that she almost entirely lacks a sense of humour.

The joke would certainly be on me if she realized yesterday that I was attempting to hypnotize her without her knowing it, and let me think that I had succeeded for the fun of quietly watching me make an idiot of myself. But Deb is not that sort of girl; she is a very serious-minded German Jewess and she simply has not got it in her. What is more, she is no actress, and I would bet my last cent that on both occasions I put her into a trance.

All the same, her behaviour is a puzzle, and I wish to goodness that I knew more about the workings of the brain of a person who has received an order while under hypnosis; but I wasn't able to gather very much from Dr Bramwell on that.

It seemed to me that all sorts of complications might arise if I had sent either Taffy or Deb down to the village while still in a trance, so, in both cases, after having given them their instructions I woke them up. Taffy said nothing, but on my waking Deb this morning she remarked: 'You won't need anything for the next hour or so, will you? as I have a job to do.'

From that I could only infer that, as a result of my order given while she was under not to tell anyone what she was about to do, her reaction on waking was that she must keep it secret even from me.

She was back by midday, as I caught a glimpse of her at her window; but I did not see her again until she came to fetch me in to wash before lunch, and I thought it a bit risky to delay our usual programme then by putting her under for a direct check on whether she had done her stuff. Naturally I was on tenterhooks to find out, but, as I was so uncertain about the drill, I thought it wiser not to ask her direct; so I said:

'Did you see anyone you knew in the village?'

'Only Mrs Evans of the Lodge,' she replied, 'but I did not stop to speak to her.'

That sounded pretty good, so I went on cautiously: 'I suppose the little post-office shop was as crowded as usual?'

'Yes,' she nodded; then she quickly contradicted herself. 'No. I'm sorry. I was thinking of something else. I really don't know, as I didn't go there.'

At that, I had to leave matters for the moment; but it is certainly very puzzling. Since I woke her out of her trance before she left here one would assume that she must have been fully conscious while in the village and that on her return she would know that she had posted a letter for me; but evidently that is not the case. Perhaps the hypnosis has the effect of isolating everything connected with certain ideas imposed on the sub-conscious, in an otherwise normally functioning brain. On the other hand, it is possible that as Deb was not in a trance while she was in the village the initial reason for her going there never emerged into her conscious mind, and she still has my letter in her pocket.

I shall soon know now, as my rest hour is nearly up, and at three o'clock Deb will be coming in to take me out to the garden again.

Evening

All is well. Deb posted the letter and, what is more, although she has seen Helmuth since, she said nothing to him about it.

I put her under directly she came to collect me this afternoon, and it now seems clear that an order given to anyone under hypnosis does create a kind of blank spot in their conscious mind. Unless circumstances over which they have no control prevent them, they carry out the order at the appropriate time without knowing why they are doing so and as soon as the thing is done they forget it. At least, that is what appears to have happened in this case.

While I had Deb under it occurred to me that it would be interesting, and perhaps useful, to find out a bit more about her. So I made her wheel me out to the summer-house, where I knew that we should be safe from interruption, then told her to sit down, relax and tell me about herself.

There ensued the most extraordinary conversation in which I have ever participated. Deb did most of the talking, while I just put in a question now and then or helped her with a few words when she seemed to find difficulty in expressing her thoughts. I told her to talk in German, as I thought that would be easier for her, and for the best part of two hours she spoke in a monotonous, toneless voice, revealing her inmost thoughts and beliefs.

I must confess that I felt rather a cad in prying into her secrets by such unscrupulous means; but this taking to pieces of a human being proved absolutely fascinating, and in my present situation I feel fully justified in taking any steps that may strengthen my hand against Helmuth.

The first thing that emerged is that she is in love with him. Apparently he made a play for her soon after she arrived here and she fell for him right away. She is thirty, and has never cared much for young men. Helmuth is forty-five and a fine specimen of manhood; besides which his outsize brain gives him an additional attraction for any woman as intellectually inclined as Deb.

She was seduced when she was seventeen by a medical student who was a lodger in her father's house, and has had a number of affairs since; she is by no means the prude that her thin-lipped, hard little face led me to believe. In fact, the glimpse that I caught of this other side to her when I asked her to fish the fly out of my eye was truly revealing. I did not go into the details of the matter, but I am sure that Helmuth met with little trouble in making her his mistress.

However, for the past few weeks the *affaire* has not been going at all well. Helmuth has been neglecting her, and it is for that reason she has been encouraging Owen Gruffydd, the village schoolmaster. It struck me as pathetic that she should attempt to make Helmuth jealous, and particularly of anyone like that.

Helmuth's sex-life is in the true Weylands tradition, and if she told him outright that she was thinking of going to bed with Gruffydd he would probably say: 'Why not, I hope you enjoy yourself.' As it is I doubt if her poor little ruse has even registered with him. If it has I can imagine him chuckling to himself at the thought of anyone attempting to set up a small-time teacher as his rival. Helmuth evidently felt like a little amusement, but is now tired of her, and nothing she can do will get him back—unless he feels the urge again, and then he is capable of taking her off a better man than Gruffydd, whether he likes it or not.

Gruffydd seems to be a respectable type, and he wants her to marry him. I can understand that, as although Deb might look pretty small game in Bond Street she must appear quite a glamour-girl to anyone who lives down here in the back of beyond. She does not love him, but they have tastes in common and the marriage would give her security; so she is toying with the idea. The trouble is that she is still in love with Helmuth and determined to get him back if she can—although she knows that the odds are all against it leading to anything permanent—but, meanwhile, Gruffydd is pressing her for an answer; and, as his 'old Mum' is fighting tooth and nail against his marrying a Jewess, Deb may lose him altogether unless she grabs him while he is all steamed up about her. So she is in a bit of a jam at the moment.

I learned quite a lot about her early life and it turns out that she is really a Russian, although she was born in Germany. Her family were Russian Jews living in Kiev until 1905. That was the year of the abortive revolution, and as many of the nihilists who staged it were Jews it was followed by an exceptionally fierce pogrom.

In those days it was quite an ordinary occurrence for a *sotnia* of Cossacks to gallop their ponies into a ghetto, apply their knouts lustily to the backs of anyone who came in their way, and loot a few of the richer houses. It was done by order and just the simple Czarist way of keeping the Children of Israel from getting above themselves. But this time the authorities had got really angry and were marching hundreds of these wretched people off to Siberia; so Deb's family decided to get out while the going was good, and the whole issue migrated to Leipzic. She was born seven years later.

In the first great war most of her uncles and cousins fought for Germany; but when the real Russian revolution came in 1917 they all deserted, or got themselves out of the army, as soon as they could, and went back to Russia to join the Bolsheviks. Deb's father seems to have been both cleverer and better educated than the rest of his clan. In the dozen years he had lived in Germany he had taken several degrees, and by the outbreak of the 1914 war he was already a junior professor at Leipzic University. So he and his wife decided to remain and bring up their children as good Germans.

Despite Germany's defeat, and the chaos and hunger that succeeded it, between 1918 and 1933 the Kain family prospered. When Hitler came to power the old boy was a leading light on his subject and much revered by his colleagues; his eldest son was a doctor, his second son reading for the law, two daughters were married, while Deb, who was then twenty-one, was getting on well with her training as a professional nurse, and engaged to a bright young journalist.

From 1930 on, while the Nazi boys were getting control of first one thing, then another, the Kains suffered a certain amount of unpleasantness, although nothing compared with what the old folks had known during their youth in Russia. But after Hitler became Chancellor things began to happen.

It was the usual sordid and horrifying story, beginning with ostracization and ending with violence. The old professor died of a heart attack, after having had his trousers pulled off and being chased ignominiously down the street by a pack of young hooligans. A Nazi truncheon smashed the nose and *pince-nez* of the doctor brother, blinding him in one eye; but all the same he was frog-marched along the gutters for a quarter of a mile before they flung him into a prison van, and he finally disappeared, presumably to a concentration camp.

Within a few months the whole family were dead, in prison or in hiding. Deb appears to have been the only lucky one, if you can call it lucky to survive seeing your fiancé caught in a *bierhalle*, hustled into a corner and used as a target for several hundred bottles, while your own arms are held behind you and you are forced to look on. Anyway, she got away to England.

I asked her how she managed it and she replied: 'The Party got me out.'

At that I was a little mystified, as we had been talking of the Germany of 1933, and in that connection, to me, 'The Party' signified the Nazis. But a brief question to her soon cleared the mystery up. Her two brothers and her fiancé were all members of the 'Communist' Party, and it was the Moscow-run Communist Underground that got her by devious means across the German frontier.

She had been provided with a letter to a Miss Smith, who runs a private nursing-home, and a nursing service for out-patients, at Hampstead. On reaching London she presented her letter and was taken on. For the first two years she worked in the home, until she had completed her training; then she was put on the regular roster for small outside jobs alternating with periods of duty in the home. Now she is one of the senior Sisters and either has charge of a floor in the home when in London or goes out to jobs such as this, where the pay and responsibility are high.

I remarked that while the pay might be good here my case was a routine one involving no danger to life, so there was little responsibility attached to it; and added that, since she had such cause to hate the Nazis, I found it surprising that she had not seized the opportunity to help in the fight against them, by volunteering for active service with one of the military organizations on the outbreak of war.

Her reply came as tonelessly as everything else she had said, but it positively made me blink. She said: 'I could not do that because if I had I should have been making a contribution to the British war-effort.'

I pondered that one for a moment, then I recalled the fact that, although she was a Jewess and an anti-Nazi, she had been brought up as a German, so I hazarded: 'I suppose you still have pleasant memories of your childhood in Germany, and so have a sentimental reluctance to see the Germans defeated?'

'No,' came the answer. 'I have long outgrown all such stupid sentimentality, and I am an Internationalist. I feel no obligation to either country.'

Again I remained silent for a bit, to think that one over. In the early years of this war I had seen enough to know that among her race her attitude could not be uncommon. The coast-resorts in south-western England and towns like Maidenhead were packed with Jews. No doubt some of them are doing valuable war-work, but how is it there is always such a high proportion of Jews in the 'safe' places where there is still good food and soft living to be had?

I met a few Jews in the R.A.F., and they weren't a bit like that; so I think there is good reason to believe that the British Jews are pulling their weight; but I am sure that does not go for the majority of the Jewish refugees to whom we have given asylum. After all, we are fighting their battle, so one would have thought that they would be only too willing to accept a full share of our dangers, privations and discomforts; but many of them are not.

I said to Deb: 'If you had remained in Germany I suppose it is a hundred to one that you would have died like your sisters from ill-treatment and starvation in a Nazi concentration camp. As it was you succeeded in getting to England, where for the best part of ten years you have had the full protection of British justice, and been free to live where you chose and earn your living in any way you like, with absolute security from any form of discrimination, oppression or persecution. Don't you really feel that you owe this country something for that; and that instead of taking cushy jobs like this you ought to have offered your services when the first call went out for nurses for the forces?'

'I could not,' she said. 'I was under orders not to do so.'

'Whose orders?'

'The orders of the Party. The Soviet Union had entered into an alliance with Germany. It was not for me to question the wisdom of Comrade Stalin and the Politbureau. The order came to us all that we must do nothing to aid

Britain in her war against Germany.'

I stared at the expressionless face in front of me. I suppose I should have realized a few minutes earlier that, if Deb's brothers and fiancé had been active Communists and 'the Party' had smuggled her out of Germany, the odds were that she was a member of it, too. But I hadn't; and, as far as I knew, I had never met a real dyed-in-the-wool Red who owned a Party ticket before.

'I see,' I said slowly. 'But how about your own feelings? I can understand your having felt a certain loyalty to the Comrades who saved you from the Nazis, but doesn't the ten years of security that we gave you mean anything to you at all?'

'I had to live somewhere,' she replied. 'I would have gone to Russia if I had been allowed to, but I was ordered to come here. The British Government is Capitalist and Imperialist; it is the keystone of resistance to world-rule by the Proletariat, and more Comrades were needed to work for its overthrow.'

At that, I began to wonder if I ought not to do something about Comrade Deborah Kain, and try to find a way to tip off our security people that she is one of the secret enemies in our midst. But on second thoughts I realized that it would be futile. The British Union, as the Fascist Party calls itself, has been banned, and its leaders live on such fat as is left in the land on the Isle of Man; but not the Communists. They are our gallant allies and are still permitted to share our dangers and ferment strikes, when and where they like. This is a free country—even if the Home Office is run by a collection of lunatics who are incapable of understanding that Fascism and Communism differ only in being two sides of the same penny—and Deb is legally just as much entitled to her opinion as I am, even if she would like to kill the King and have Churchill thrown into a concentration camp.

Still, on the offchance that some day somebody at the top may see the red light, and the information then prove useful, I asked her: 'From whom do you receive your orders?'

'From Miss Smith,' came the reply.

'Who gives her hers?'

'I don't know.'

As I expected, they are still working on the old cell system. But what a clever racket. An expensive nursing organization must get lots of calls from important people who have had operations or gone sick. Bright girls like Deb can be sent out to look after them. No one suspects a trained nurse; papers are left about and telephone calls made in their presence. The Reds must pick up quite a lot of useful information on the way the war is going, and the industrial situation, like that.

'Are all the nurses in your organization Party Comrades?' I enquired.

'Oh, no; at least I don't think so. Owing to the war there is a great shortage of private nurses, so in these days Miss Smith takes on anyone she can get.'

From that it appears that I have been honoured. No doubt Miss 'Smith' decided that as I am potentially a great industrial magnate it would be worth sending one of her ewe-lambs to look after me; but if she hopes to pick up anything worth while about the Jugg aircraft plants I fear she is going to be disappointed.

However, as a matter of interest I asked Deb if she had learned anything worth reporting since she had been in Wales.

'Only about Owen Gruffydd,' she said. 'He is Labour and wants to stand for Parliament after the war. He is very Left and has the right ideas already. If I marry him I am sure that I could make something of him. The fact that he had joined the Party would be kept secret; and it is part of the plan that we should get as many Comrades as possible elected under the Labour ticket. Besides, if he got in I should meet a lot of his fellow members. I took out naturalization papers in 1938, so I am already a British subject, and I could work on them to get me nominated by the Labour Central Office as their candidate for another constituency. I am quite as intelligent as most of the men I have met, and I am sure I could get myself elected, if only I were given a chance as the official Labour candidate in a good industrial area.'

That was the end of our conversation. I had always thought Deb to be a hard, capable, superficially intelligent little go-getter, but I was far from realizing the height of her ambitions or the depths of her perfidy. This last revelation took me so aback that I could think of nothing else to ask her, so after a few moments I told her to forget all she had said, and woke her from her trance.

Then I closed my own eyes, in order to avoid looking at her, and said I felt like a nap. But I didn't go to sleep. I sat there feeling shattered and sick—just as though I had found a toad in my bed.

Tuesday, 26th May

I had a fright last night—a very nasty fright. For the past few days the weather has been patchy, with mostly bright, sunny mornings, then getting overcast in the afternoons; and on both Sunday and Monday evenings we had showers of rain. In consequence, although there was a new moon on Saturday, cloudy skies saved me from seeing its light—until last night.

I would not have seen it then but for the fact that I had lobster for dinner. I was not, thank God, woken by my sub-conscious shrilling a warning to me that the Horror was approaching, but by an attack of indigestion, which roused me into sudden wakefulness about one o'clock.

In the old days I used to be able to eat anything with impunity, but since my crash ruled out all exercise—except the little I get from swinging a pair of Indian clubs for a quarter-of-an-hour every morning—my digestion is not what it was. I suppose I ought to be more careful what I eat, but I never seem to think about it till the damage is done. Anyhow, the lobster woke me and there was that damnable band of moonlight on the floor.

It is three weeks now since I have seen it, and it gave me a frightful shock. It has been said truly enough that 'time is the great healer', and this long immunity from attack had certainly healed, or at least dulled, the awful impression that the visitations of the Thing made on my mind. Seeing that broad strip of moonlight again, with the two sinister black bars across it made by the shadow of the piers between the windows, had the same effect upon me as if someone had suddenly ripped the bandages from a hideous wound I had received some time ago, exposing it again all raw and bleeding.

But I am glad now that lobster chanced to be the main dish last night and that I ate too much of it. In spite of my having told myself repeatedly that time was slipping away, and that I must not let myself be lulled into a false sense of security during the dark period of the moon, that is just what I have done. Not altogether, perhaps, as the fate that menaces me has never been far from my thoughts, but I feel now that I ought to have made more strenuous efforts either to secure help or to escape from Llanferdrack. What other line I could have tried that I have not yet attempted I still cannot think; but there it is. I cannot help cursing myself now for the time I have given to fruitless speculations on this and that, instead of concentrating entirely on the all-important problem of saving myself.

Last night was a blessed warning, arousing me anew to my danger as sharply as the sounding of an air-raid siren, and I am wondering now if the lobster for dinner with my resulting indigestion was, after all, pure chance. Providence is said to work in strange ways, and, although I haven't mentioned it in this journal, since early this month I have been praying for protection.

Until then I hadn't said a prayer since old Nanny Trotter left, when I went to Weylands. She taught me my prayers and always made me say them, however tired I was; but I don't think that any child prays from choice, and I was as pleased to stop praying as I was to cease from washing my neck, when other boys at Weylands told me that the first was 'not done' and the second optional.

Even when I was a fighter-pilot I never called on God to help me. In those days I was fully convinced that it was a calm head, a clear eye and a steady hand that did the trick. It was you or the Jerry and the best man won, with no darn' nonsense about Divine intervention. At least, that was how I saw it then.

But, once I had argued it out with myself to the conclusion that the Thing in the courtyard is, and can only be, a creature of the Devil, it seemed logical to fall back on God. In view of my past neglect of Him I didn't feel that I was entitled to hope for very much, but the Christian teaching is that His mercy is infinite; so night and morning, and sometimes at odd periods of the day, I began to pray.

At first I felt very self-conscious and awkward about it; particularly as I could not go down on my knees, and to pray sitting in my chair or lying on my back in bed seemed disrespectful; but after a bit I decided that if God was taking any notice of me at all He wouldn't let that make any difference, seeing how things are with me. So, although it may sound a bit far-fetched, it isn't really at all improbable that Cook may have been guided to her choice of giving us lobster for dinner last night in response to my prayers for guidance and protection.

I don't quite know why, but I am inclined to believe that God may grant us guidance and warnings but expects us to fight our own battles and protect ourselves; except, perhaps, in dire extremity when the dice are weighted too heavily against us. Anyhow, having seen the red light, whether it was a Heaven-sent one or not, I made up my mind early this morning that I must take immediate action.

My letter to Uncle Paul was posted only yesterday. It should be in London this morning, but there is no afternoon delivery at Queensclere, so even if it is now on its way down into Kent he won't get it till tomorrow. When he does get it I think he will come here as soon as he can, but Thursday is the earliest that I can reasonably expect him; and if he has engagements that he feels he cannot break he may not arrive till the weekend. Looking at the matter from his point of view, he would be quite justified in feeling that I could hardly be in such an almighty hurry to get the new financial schemes I mentioned off to the lawyers without giving him a few days' grace.

On the other side of the picture the moon will be full again on Saturday the 30th; but my danger period starts well before that. Last time the attacks occurred nightly from the 30th of April to the 4th of May, with a blank only on the 2nd, when the moon was actually full; but that was because it was a night of heavy cloud and the moon never came through. So judging by the previous bout, I'll be in danger from Thursday night on. But if the nights remain clear the attacks may start before that–perhaps on Wednesday, or even tonight.

I ought to have worked all this out before, or anyway yesterday when I was so cock-a-hoop at having got my letter off to Uncle Paul. Then, I more or less counted on his jumping into a train on Wednesday; or, anyhow, getting here on Thursday. But I feel sure now that there must be some subtle influence at work which has obscured my judgment in such matters and made me over-sanguine about the success of my plans.

My fright last night has entirely dissipated the feeling of temporary security that seems to have accumulated like fleecy clouds of cotton wool round my brain. I realize now that it would be crazy to count on Uncle Paul turning up before the trouble starts again. He may or he may not; but I am not going to stay and chance it. I am going to get out tonight, or at least have a damn' good try.

If I can hypnotize Deb to a degree at which she will post a letter for me and remember nothing about it afterwards, and send her into a trance deep enough for her to reveal her dirty little schemes against poor old Britain, I see no reason why I should not make her come and fetch me in my chair in the middle of the night and wheel me out of the house.

Once outside, Comrade Kain can damn' well keep on wheeling me along the King's highway; and if round about dawn she drops with fatigue it won't cause me any pain and grief at all. In fact I rather like the idea that this earnest little disciple of Papa Marx and Uncle Lenin should have to go to bed for a week, to recover from the effort of saving Flight-Lieutenant Sir Toby Jugg, D.F.C., R.A.F.V.R., from the Devil.

Later

This journal has been a good friend to me. When I made the first entries in an old exercise book my nerves were stretched to breaking-point, and forcing myself to make a logical analysis of my thoughts did a lot to keep me sane. Since then, writing it, besides providing what may yet prove a valuable record of events here, has whiled away many an hour of my dreary invalid existence. But I hope that this will be my last entry in it.

All is set fair for tonight. Deb has her 'Sealed Orders' (not to be opened until 00.45 hours 27.5.42). That is actually what it comes to, as my instructions, verbally issued this afternoon, are sealed up in her sub-conscious, which will not release them to her conscious mind until a quarter-to-one in the morning.

Even Helmuth keeps fairly early hours here in the country. He usually goes to bed about eleven o'clock, so by one I can count on the coast being clear. As Deb will have to get up and dress it is unlikely that she will come for me till a bit after one, and it will take another twenty minutes or so for her to get me dressed. Usually Taffy does that, but with my help Deb will manage somehow. Although I cannot stand, even for a moment, the strength of my arms is fortunately so great that I can support my dead weight by clinging to one of the posts of this big four-poster bed, and if Deb holds my chair steady I'll be able to heave myself off the bed into it. So I plan to make my break-out about half-past-one in the morning, which should give me six-and-a-half hours clear before my escape is discovered.

With my fright last night still vivid in my mind, it occurred to me that I would ordinarily have to lie here in the dark between ten o'clock and one, and that if there was a moon again the Thing might seize this last chance to attack me; so I put my blessed gift to good use again when Deb came in to settle me down. Having completed the usual ritual, she was just about to pick up my Aladdin lamp and carry it off with her, but I caught her eye, put her under, and said:

'Leave the lamp where it is, Deb. You may go now, and you will not wake until you have turned the angle of the corridor. When you wake you will have forgotten that you have left the lamp burning here.'

As she reached the door I called her back, on the sudden thought that it might be as well to do a final check-up. I made her repeat the instructions about tonight and she had the whole thing clear; so it is now only a matter of killing time until one o'clock.

That is why I am making this final entry. I am in much more of a flap than I ever was before going out on an operational sortie, and this is the best means I can think of to occupy my mind. My idea of making her leave the lamp is therefore now proving a double blessing, as I have never before been able to read or write after ten o'clock.

After Deb had gone I said prayers for the success of my venture, but one can't keep on praying for very long; at least, I can't, as I find that I start to repeat myself, which begins to make it monotonous and seems rather pointless. However, I had a new line tonight, in additional supplications that all should go well with my escape.

It suddenly struck me that it was soon after I first started to pray that I remembered Squadron-Leader Cooper telling me that I had hypnotic eyes; and it was that which led to my present prospect of getting the better of Helmuth. I think now that memory must have come to me as a direct answer to prayer, and that, seeing my utter helplessness, God has granted me the swift development of this strange power for my defence against the machinations of the Devil.

It is certainly little short of miraculous that within a few days I should have acquired such an ascendancy over Deb as to make her reveal to me her most jealously guarded secrets. She has never disguised the fact that her sympathies are with the Left, but that is a very different matter from admitting that she is a Communist agent actively working against Britain.

The idea that a foreigner like Deb is eligible to become a Member of Parliament, and actually laying long-term plans to do so, positively horrifies me. Can we do nothing to prevent such a monstrous perversion in the representation of the British people? Is Party backing, superficial intelligence and a glib tongue really all that are required, irrespective of race or creed, to gain a place in that august assembly where Walpole and Chatham, the younger Pitt, Wellington, Joe Chamberlain, and now Churchill have thundered forth the tale of Britain's defiance, courage and integrity?

I suppose it is. If Deb's husband was already a Labour member and the people who run the Labour Party Office were unaware that she was secretly a Communist, they might well agree to her nomination as a Labour candidate.

Gruffydd won't stand much chance of getting in if the country sends back the Conservatives at the next election with a large majority; but it would not surprise me at all if, after the war, there is a big landslide towards Labour. In any case, now that Liberal representation is so small, Labour is H.M.'s Opposition, and the swing of the pendulum is bound to bring them in within the next ten years; so Deb might easily get a seat by the time she is forty-five. And by then how many other Communists will there be who have infiltrated into the House on a Labour ticket?

What is the answer to that sort of thing? One cannot prevent British Communists from using the Labour Party as a stalking-horse, and we don't want to close the doors against foreigners settling here. Neither, shades of Disraeli, do we want to discriminate against our own Jews. Incidentally, his family had been resident in London for nearly a hundred years before he first went to sit at Westminster. But the laws governing the qualifications for election to Parliament were made in a different age, and I think they need bringing up to date. At least we could check this infiltration of foreigners into the House by passing a law that no man or woman whose parents were not British *born* should be eligible to become an M.P. And–perhaps even more important–to prevent their being appointed to high executive posts under the Government, make a minimum residence of twenty-five years in Great Britain an essential requirement to secure nationalization.

Is that reactionary? I don't think so. 'Reactionary' is just the parrot-cry howled at anyone these days who has the courage to think and act as did our forefathers who made the Empire.

Of course, if such a law was passed the joke would be on me, because my mother was born an American, so I should not be eligible for Parliament myself. But I would willingly surrender my present right to stand if it helped to ensure that Britain should continue to be ruled by the British.

Thank God it is just on one o'clock. Letting off all this hot air has filled in the time nicely. Deb should be here any minute now.

Later

It is two o'clock and Deb has not come. What the hell can have gone wrong? Perhaps an order given to a subject under hypnosis is not enough to rouse them from a natural sleep. I ought to have thought of that and ordered her to remain awake. She may come yet, but I doubt it. Anyhow, thank God I've got the lamp. I've turned it down a bit to economize the oil, so with luck it should last me till the moon has set.

Wednesday, 27th May

Deb never turned up, and there was a bit of a *contretemps* this morning. When she came into my room she was naturally not in a trance state and she saw the lamp still on my bedside table. I imagine Helmuth must have more or less threatened to flay her alive if he ever found out that she had failed to remove it, as she went into a frightful flap.

I managed to laugh the matter off and she thinks that she forgot it through a normal lapse of memory; but she remarked rather sinisterly: 'I can't think what came over me last night.'

Later, in the garden, I put her under, and got the low-down on why she failed to carry out my orders.

It appears that after she had tucked me up she decided that the time had come for her to have a show-down with Helmuth, so she went along to his study. With the idea of making him jealous she told him that she didn't care for him any more and was going to get engaged to Owen Gruffydd.

Helmuth's reaction to that was just what I could have told her it would be. After half-an-hour's talk over a couple of glasses of port he took her along to her room and seduced her afresh. She, poor mutt, imagines that she has pulled off her big trick and won him back to her because he could not bear the thought of losing her to another man. But I'd bet my bottom dollar that the real set-up is that Helmuth does not really give a damn for her; it simply provided him with a little cynical amusement, and flattered his sense of power, to dispose of Gruffydd with a snap of his fingers, and make her his mistress again in spite of the fact that she had told him that she now loved someone else.

It would be interesting to see what happens during the next few weeks, if I were going to remain here—but I hope to Heaven that I'm not. My forecast would be that Helmuth would derive a lot of fun from proceeding to neglect her again until she went back to Gruffydd; perhaps he would even let her get engaged, then he would seduce her once more, and so on, until the wretched woman became half crazy with misery and despair. As it is I hope to make my exit tonight, and so break up the whole party.

To continue about last night. At a quarter to one Deb's mind clicked over and she suddenly realized that she had to come and get me out of the house, so she got out of bed and started to dress. Unfortunately Helmuth was still there, and at first he could not make out what the devil had got into her, as she flatly refused either to answer his questions or obey him when he told her to come back to bed, but simply went on dressing without uttering a word. Then he jumped to the conclusion that she must have dropped off to sleep and was sleep-walking.

As far as I can make out he took her by the shoulders, imposed his will upon her and, his hypnotic powers being stronger than mine, woke her up. Luckily for me she accepted the explanation that she had been sleep-walking, although she has never known herself do such a thing before, and immediately he brought her out of her trance she naturally lost all memory of the orders I had given her. So things might have turned out worse, as it seems that neither of them suspect the real reason for her apparently strange behaviour.

Unless I am entirely wrong in my assessment of Helmuth's psychology, I don't think that he will spend the night with her again until he can get a fresh kick out of once more believing himself to have brought her to heel against her will. I don't think, either, that she is such a fool as to betray her own weakness by asking him to do so as early as tonight, and, even if she does, I can see him beginning the process of twisting her tail by making some excuse to refuse her.

So I think the odds are all against my being held up by the same sort of hitch two nights running, and while I had Deb under I laid on the operation again for 00.45 hours on the 28th May, 1942.

Thursday, 28th May

A bitter disappointment. Everything went according to plan. Deb arrived and got me dressed. With her help I struggled into my chair. She wheeled me down the passage and across the hall to the front door; then she left me sitting there for a moment while she went forward to unlock it. As the door swung open Helmuth's voice came from the stairs behind me:

'Good evening, Toby. Or should I say good morning?'

My heart missed a beat. There came the sound of his footfalls on the parquet, and he went on in a sneering tone:

'You must love the moon a great deal not to be able to resist the temptation of going out into the garden to see her. But it is not good for you to be up at this time of night. Perhaps, though I can arrange to have your blackout curtain *shortened*, so that you can see a little more moonlight from your bed.'

There was nothing to say. I sat there dumb with misery; but the threat made me break out in a slight sweat.

Meanwhile, Deb had propped open the front door and turned back towards me. It was clear from her wide eyes and blank expression that she had neither seen nor heard Helmuth, and she stepped up to my chair with the obvious intention of wheeling me out of the house.

He was beside me by that time, and I saw that his eyes were cold with fury. Suddenly he raised his open hand and struck her with it hard across the face.

'Stop that!' I yelled. 'The shock may kill her! She's in a trance!'

Deb gave a whimpering cry; her eyes seemed to start from her head and she staggered back. For a moment she stood with one hand on her heart, gasping and swaying drunkenly, then she sagged at the knees and fell full length on the floor.

Ignoring her, Helmuth swung on me. 'So that's the game you've been playing, you young fiend!'

'Never mind me!' I snapped. 'You look after your girl-friend, or you'll have a corpse on your hands.'

He continued to mouth at me furiously. 'I suspected as much last night; but I simply could not believe it. Who the hell taught you how to hypnotize people?'

'Is it likely that I'd tell you?'

'I will make you!' He grabbed my shoulder and began to shake me.

But in that he made a stupid blunder. I am much stronger in the arms than he is. I grabbed his wrist, pulled it down against my stomach and twisted, at the same time throwing my weight forward on to it. He was jerked round and forced right over sideways. His mouth fell open and there was a gleam of fear in his tawny eyes as I said:

'I'll tell you nothing.' Then I flung him from me, adding: 'Now, for God's sake, try to revive that woman.'

Almost snarling with rage, he turned, grasped Deb under the armpits, heaved her into a nearby chair, and forced her head down between her knees. After a minute or so, she began to groan. Then she gave a shudder, looked up at us, and muttered with a puzzled frown: *'Was machen wir hier?'*

'You little fool!' Helmuth rasped at her in German. 'You allowed him to hypnotize you; and with your help he nearly got away. Get along to your room. I'll come and talk to you presently.'

Deb stared at me, her black eyes distended with surprise and anger. She was about to say something, but Helmuth cut her short. Grabbing her by the arm, he pulled her to her feet and gave her a swift push in the direction of our corridor. Suddenly bursting into a passion of tears, she staggered away across the hall.

He waited until she had disappeared, then slammed the front door and turned on me. 'Now, Toby; I've had enough of your nonsense for one night. I'm going to wheel you back to your room and put you to bed.'

'Oh, no, you don't,' I said, as a vision of the Horror doing its devil-dance on the band of moonlight flashed into my mind. 'I prefer to spend the night here.'

'You can't do that,' he replied, and I felt my will weaken as his glance held mine.

With an effort I pulled my eyes away from his, concentrated on looking at my own knees and muttered: 'I'm damn' well going to. If you lay a hand on me I swear I'll strangle you.'

The threat gave him pause. For over a minute there continued an absolute and highly pregnant silence, while our wills fought without our glances meeting. Then he broke off the engagement, turned abruptly, and marched angrily away from me.

As the sound of his footsteps receded I sighed with relief. I thought I had won that round, and that he had gone off to blackguard the wretched Deb. But he hadn't. He had gone to rouse Konrad, his Ruthenian manservant.

Bitter disappointment at my failure to escape, and excitement over my scene with Helmuth, did not make me feel a bit like sleep at the moment. But he had left all the lights on in the hall, and twenty minutes or so after he had taken himself off I was vaguely wondering if I would be able to get any sleep at all in their glare, when I heard footsteps returning.

Evidently Helmuth had given his man instructions beforehand; neither of them said a word, and they ran at me simultaneously. The attack came from my immediate rear, so I could make no preparations to meet it. They seized the chair rail behind my shoulders, swung me round, and rushed me across the hall. I tried to grab, first a table, next a door-knob, then some window curtains. But they were too quick for me. Before I could get a firm grasp on anything they had raced me down the corridor back to my room.

There, a prolonged scuffle took place, while I hampered their efforts to undress me by every means in my power. But the two of them, together, were able to break every hold that I could get on them or my clothes, and at last they succeeded in getting me into bed. By then all three of us were scratched, bruised, weary and breathless with cursing. Still panting from his exertions, Helmuth picked up the lamp and, without another word, they left me.

However, my fight for time was not in vain. It had been just after half-past-one when Helmuth caught Deb and I in the hall. His angry exchanges with me, getting her out of her faint, going to find Konrad, waiting until he had pulled on some clothes and then returning with him, had occupied half-an-hour; and the struggle I put up when they undressed me had accounted for a further three-quarters. So by the time they slammed the door behind them and left me in the dark it was getting on for three in the morning; and the moon had gone down behind the ruins of the old Castle.

I was still much too excited to think of going to sleep; and, disappointed as I was at the failure of my plan, I knew worrying about that was futile, so I tried to concentrate on the future and figure out what chances remained of making any new moves.

Tonight the moon will be within two nights of full; so, unless the sky is overcast, I shall be really up against it. Think as I would I could find only three lines of thought which shed faint rays of light in the blackness of the general picture.

Firstly, Uncle Paul should have had my letter yesterday, Wednesday, morning; so it seemed a possibility that he might arrive here this afternoon. But I knew it was more likely that he would not come down until the weekend, so, fortunately, as it has turned out, I did not put too much hope in that.

Secondly, there was Deb. I realized that since she now knew I had been hypnotizing her, that was bound to set up a strong resistance in the future. But I had gained such a much greater degree of dominance over her sub-conscious than I ever did over Taffy's that I hoped I might still be able to put her into a trance and make some use of her. I counted it a certainty that Helmuth would take adequate precautions against her helping me in another attempt to escape—probably by locking my door each night and keeping the key himself—but I thought that I might get her to send off telegrams to Julia and Uncle Paul, saying that I was ill and urging them to come at once; and also to get hold of a torch for me somehow, or smuggle me in some candles, so that I could counter the moonlight tonight.

Thirdly, I decided that as a second string it would be well worth while to have another go at Taffy. I regarded it as unlikely that I should be able to overcome his resistance to taking messages, and that even if I could he would probably be subject to some form of sub-conscious reaction which would result in his giving my telegrams to Helmuth; so it would be better not to attempt that. But it seemed possible that I might succeed in using him to procure me a torch or candles.

I was still turning over such projects in my mind when I dropped off to sleep; but, alas, nearly all those hopes have since been disappointed.

Taffy called me as usual and began the morning routine, but Deb did not put in an appearance; so, after a bit, I asked him as casually as I could what had become of her.

His fat face flushed and he looked sheepishly away from me as he replied: 'She'll not be coming to you any more, Sir Toby. It is packing her trunk she is, now. For the Doctor has sacked her this very day, whatever.'

That was bad news and, in view of it, I thought I had better get to work on Taffy without delay, so I told him to look at me; but he shook his head and muttered: 'Come you, Sir Toby, don't ask me that. It is the evil eye you have, as the Doctor was telling me, himself, but ten minutes since.'

'What nonsense!' I exclaimed, and I managed to raise a laugh of sorts. 'You must have misunderstood him; or more probably he was pulling your leg.'

'No indeed, Sir Toby,' he replied resentfully. 'It is the truth he was telling; and myself has been a victim to your wickedness. It was not right in you to give me that letter and me knowing nothing of it. The look in your eyes is uncanny, right enough, and the Doctor has warned me not to look at you. I would be glad if I could now go from here to my brother Davey's in Cardiff. Indeed, go I would this very day, if I were skilled in the engineering, as he is. But the fees at the technical school are high for poor people; so it is stay here I must till I have more money put by.'

I think that was the longest speech I have ever heard Taffy make; and after I had got over my first feeling of anger I was glad that he had blown off steam, as it told me where I stood. Helmuth had sacked Deb, and aroused Taffy's superstitious fears as an impregnable barrier against my hypnotizing him. That put paid to any hope of getting telegrams despatched, or securing a light for tonight, through either of them.

Controlling my annoyance as well as I could, I told Taffy that the Doctor got queer ideas at times, and that no doubt his strange assertions about me this morning were to be attributed to the fact that we had had a disagreement the previous night. I added that he had no cause whatever to be frightened of me, and that in the long run he would find it paid much better to carry out my wishes than the Doctor's, particularly if he wanted to be an engineer, as I could easily get him free training in one of the Jugg factories.

His expression became a little less stolid at that, and he could not resist stealing a quick glance at me to see if I meant it; but he is still as nervous as a cat and it would obviously be futile to try to tempt him with any definite proposition on those lines at the moment.

Having brought me my breakfast tray, Taffy left me; and soon afterwards Helmuth came in. I gave him no greeting and throughout the interview did nothing to disguise the feelings of distrust and aversion with which I have now come to regard him. I said very little, so he did most of the talking and, somewhat to my surprise after last night, he continues to maintain the attitude of a fond Guardian who is doing his best for a troublesome ward in very difficult circumstances. How he reconciles that with his actions, and some of the remarks he made, I can't think, but that is certainly the impression he endeavoured to give.

He opened up by saying that he really could not allow me any opportunity to repeat the disgraceful scene that I had made the previous night, and had been forced to take certain precautions against my doing so.

In the first place he had sacked Deb, which was most inconvenient; but it was clear that I had 'got at her', to a degree in which she had come so much under my influence that she could no longer be trusted with the care of me in my 'unbalanced state'.

Secondly, he knew that to a lesser degree I had 'got at' Taffy, so it had been necessary that morning to put certain ideas into his head which would prevent me from 'corrupting' him further. This had resulted in his giving notice, and only with some difficulty had he been persuaded to stay on. His replacement in due course was now desirable and would be a simple matter; but with Deb gone it would have been extremely inconvenient if Taffy had insisted on walking out on us that morning.

I could not help being amused at the thought that Helmuth had nearly over-reached himself to the point of having me left on his hands without trained assistance of any kind; but I pulled my thoughts back to what he was saying.

He continued to the effect that, in spite of the *picture* he had administered to Taffy, he could not regard him as a strong enough personality to be entirely relied on. Therefore he was not prepared to let him take me out into the garden, or even to dress me and lift me into my wheeled chair. So, until arrangements can be made, I must remain in bed.

That was a nasty one; as, while Taffy had been holding the bowl for me to shave, half-an-hour earlier, it had occurred to me that when he took me outside for my airing I could send him back into the house for something, and set off down the drive on my own. I probably would not have got far before I was overtaken, but there was just a chance that I might have escaped that way; and now I cannot even attempt it.

'How long do you intend to hold me a prisoner in my bed?' I asked gruffly.

He shrugged. 'It all depends whether a suitable new nurse is available, and if so how long she takes to get here. I have already wired the Home that supplied Deb to send someone to replace her, so you may not have to remain cooped up here for more than a few days.'

His strong teeth showed in a sudden grin as he went on: 'As a matter of fact I am not altogether sorry about Deb's departure, as I was getting very bored with her. The Matron of the Home from which she came is an old friend of mine and knows my requirements. She will, I am sure, pick me out a young woman who is not only reliable but also a good-looker. In this dreary hole it will be fun to have someone fresh to sleep with.'

I said stonily that when he started his tricks I hoped she would stick a knife into him, but he only laughed and replied:

'These girls aren't that type. But I wouldn't mind if they were; it would add to my amusement to reduce anyone who tried that to abject submission afterwards,' and he walked out of the room.

So here I am, still in bed, although it is now past midday, and I am feeling far from good. Last night's catastrophe was the most damnable luck, and Helmuth's new measures this morning have deprived me of practically all my remaining chances of my escaping having to spend another night here.

In the whole pack there is now only one card left which, if it turned up, might yet save me from that ordeal. It is Uncle Paul. I dare not pin my faith on his arriving this afternoon, yet I dare not think of what awaits me if he doesn't. I must not think of that. I must not give way to morbid anticipation. I *must* keep my whole mind concentrated on seeking ways by which I may yet defeat Helmuth.

Later

Helmuth has just been in again. He flung two letters on the bed and said: 'There's your post.'

A glance was enough to show that one was an official communication from some Government department, as it has O.H.M.S. on it; and that the other envelope was in Uncle Paul's writing. The first was unopened, the second had been slit across the top.

With a sinking feeling in the pit of my stomach I picked up Uncle Paul's letter. As he writes to me only once in a blue moon I felt sure that it must be an answer to mine, and for it to have got here so quickly showed that he must have replied by return of post; but the fact that he had written could only mean that he was not coming down today, at all events; and Helmuth having brought it to me was an even more certain indication that it could not contain news I should be pleased to have.

I took the letter from its envelope, but before I had a chance to read it Helmuth said: 'From this it is clear that you hypnotized that weak-minded slut, Deborah Kain, into posting a letter for you, although you promised me last week that you would make no further attempts to get in touch with your relatives. It is most distressing that you should recently have displayed such dislike and distrust of me, Toby, but I have been appointed to look after you while you are here; and you may as well understand once and for all that I intend to continue to deal with your malady in the way I think best, whether you like it or not. And I shall not allow this proposed visit by your uncle to make the least difference to my plans.'

With an angry shake of his mane of white hair he turned and marched out of the room, leaving me a prey to the most mixed sensations.

For a moment I almost believed again that he was honestly concerned for me; that he has no hand in this devilry but really thinks me to be the victim of hallucinations and is doing his best to protect me from being publicly branded as insane. His conduct *is* explicable on those grounds. Yet my instinct flatly rejects such an explanation. I feel positive that he is developing a plot to drive me mad. And in the midst of these conflicting thoughts was that of my immense relief when Helmuth had spoken of my uncle's 'proposed visit'.

Swiftly I opened the letter out and skimmed through it. Uncle Paul said how much he appreciated my thought of wishing to consult him before I finally settled my new financial arrangements. He would be delighted to come down and discuss them with me. But lawyers always took months over the completion of such matters, anyway; so he felt sure I would agree that a day or two either way would make no material difference. He could not come down at the weekend because they had old Archie Althwaite and his wife coming to stay; and on Tuesday and Wednesday he had to attend an important sale of bloodstock, at which he was disposing of a few of his own brood mares. So the earliest he could make it was Thursday, June the 4th. Julia was down with a nasty go of summer 'flu, which had driven her to bed; but she sent her fondest love, etc.

Once more I had that empty feeling under the solar plexus. To me, next Thursday is not a week, but *a whole lifetime*, away. These next five days, while the moon glares down with her maximum intensity, may mean to me all the difference between sanity and madness; between life—as a cripple it is true, but one still able to enjoy the things of the spirit—and a living death, in which the mind is the wretched plaything of distorted emotions and terrifying visions.

What shall I do? Where can I turn for help? Yesterday, or the day before, when I was out in the garden I could have forced Deb to set off with me down the road, or to wheel me through the woods until we came to a farmhouse. But I didn't. I must have been crazy! Perhaps Helmuth *is* right, and I have softening of the brain.

Friday, 29th May

What a night! At the time I thought it the worst so far; but, viewing the whole series in retrospect this afternoon, I am sure that the attack was not as intense as that on April the 30th, or as prolonged as on at least two other occasions. Yet in some ways it was more terrifying, as there were certain new developments which now make me frightened not only for, but also of, myself.

At a few minutes to ten Taffy came in to settle me down for the night. As he has always assisted Deb to do the job in the past he knows the drill, and that I am allowed one triple bromide if my back is paining me. I had planned to snatch the bottle from him, but when I asked him for it he said in his sing-song voice:

'A sleeping-tablet, is it? See you, Sir Toby, the Doctor said you would not be needing one of those things tonight. And that naught is to be done here now without himself giving the word for it.'

I knew then that Helmuth had been at him again, and that it would be no good arguing. All the same I did, because I was so desperate at the thought of what the next few hours might bring. I even pleaded with him; but it was useless. He said he had orders not to talk to me apart from answering simple questions, and he kept his glance averted from my face the whole time, so obviously he still fears that I may ill-wish him.

An impulse came to me to cling on to him when he picked up the lamp; but had I done so the odds were that it would have upset or got smashed in the resulting struggle, and we both would have been burned to death. With an effort I checked the impulse and, in a strangled voice, answered his good-night.

The moon was already up, and the radiance from the band of it on the floor lit the room with a faint misty twilight. It was not enough to see anything distinctly, but as my eyes got accustomed to the greyness I could make out darker patches which I knew to be pieces of furniture. Having nothing else to occupy my mind, I kept staring at them, trying to make out their proper outline, but after a time, instead of solidifying, the black patches seemed to waver, grow larger and assume strange shapes.

That was simply the effect of eye-strain, and I knew that I must be imagining things, which was a bad thing to do at the very beginning of my ordeal. So I took myself to task, shut my eyes, prayed very earnestly for several minutes, then did my damnedest to get to sleep.

Of course, I couldn't. It was utterly hopeless, and how long I continued the attempt, I don't know. Anyhow, at length I gave it up, opened my eyes again and lay staring at the ceiling.

It seemed that I remained doing that for an interminable time. At first I could now and then hear distant noises, but gradually they became more infrequent until the house was very quiet. Then, I suppose because I was no longer trying to go to sleep, I dropped off; but only into a light doze.

I was roused from it by a quickening of my heart. I suddenly became conscious that it was hammering in my chest, and that the blood was pulsing more swiftly through my body. Yet my face had gone cold. It was almost as though, while I had been dozing, the temperature of the room had dropped to zero, and that the icy air was congealing into a thin rim of frost on my cheeks, nose and forehead.

Very slowly, knowing yet dreading what I should see, I turned my head and squinted at the floor below the blackout curtain. There was the shadow of the Thing, in the centre panel of the broad moonlit strip.

It was not moving but quite still, as if the beast had pressed itself up against the window and was peering in. I have never seen it still before, and was able to get a better idea of its shape that I had previously. As I see only its shadow—simply a black outline without depth—it is extremely difficult to visualize the beast itself. I have no means of telling if it has eyes, a beak, snout, or is a faceless thing like a starfish, only, instead of being flat, having a big round body from which its tentacles project.

I don't think now, though, that this evil entity can have the form of an octopus, as they have eight tentacles, whereas it has only six. Moreover, an octopus's tentacles come out from under its body, and those of the Thing seem to be joined to it about two-thirds of the way up. Then again, an octopus's tentacles are smooth, apart from the suckers on the undersides, whereas the shadow outline of these is always a little blurred, as though they might be covered with hair.

For several minutes the Thing remained as I had seen it, and might have been a gargoyle carved out of stone, except for the fact that the ball-like body undulated slightly, showing that it was really pulsing with horrid life. I, too, remained dead still, instinctively fearing that if I made the least movement it might provoke it into some form of terrifying activity.

Suddenly my heart seemed to leap up into my throat. Without a flicker of warning it had sprung to life and, with incredible fury, was flailing its limbs against the window, trying to smash its way in.

I clenched my hands until the nails dug into my palms—the red marks are still there this afternoon—and gritted my teeth. The attack must have lasted well over a quarter-of-an-hour, and every moment I feared that the window-pane would give way under the brute's weight.

At last it stopped its violent thrashing and, instead, began its devil-dance to and fro, to and fro, from one window-sill to another, blindly, persistently, seeking some crack or weakness in the barrier which might give it a better chance to break through.

In spite of the intense cold the sweat was pouring off me, and once I caught myself groaning aloud with terror. I prayed and prayed, frantically begging God to intervene and put an end to my torment, but my prayers met with no response.

I forced myself to close my eyes, first while I counted ten, then while I counted twenty; but every second while I had them shut I was terrified that when I opened them I would find that the Horror had got into the room.

Still, I kept at it, as a test of my own will-power, and I managed to get up to thirty-five. Then, when I let out my breath with a gasp and looked again, I saw that the brute had ceased its dancing and was crouching once more in the corner of the centre window. For a while nothing happened, yet I was vaguely conscious that I was becoming subject to a new form of apprehension, although I could not determine what the basis of the fresh fear could be.

Suddenly I *knew*. The Thing had a will and it was pitting it against mine. It was trying to hypnotize me.

I have never known any sound to come from it before, and it may be that I imagined this. All I can say is that it seemed to me as if it was making a faint tapping on the window–the sort of tapping that the beak of a bird might make against thick plate-glass. But the tapping was in a persistent rhythm–long, long, short, short, short–long, long, short, short, short; and those dashes and dots *translated themselves in my brain* as 'You must let-me-in. You must let-me-in.'

I shivered anew with stark horror, but there was no escaping the sounds; or rather, the refrain that trilled like a clear little silvery voice in my mind. I stuffed my fingers in my ears, but it still came through.

Then the tapping changed to a new morse rhythm, and the silvery voice said to me gently but firmly: 'Tomorrow night you will tell Taffy to leave the window open. Tomorrow night you will tell Taffy to leave the window open.'

It was exactly the same technique as I had used with Deb, when I had said to her: 'You will wake up at a quarter-to-one, dress yourself and come to me' over and over again, to impress it firmly in her subconscious.

Once more the rhythm changed, this time to 'Go to sleep. Go to sleep. Go to sleep.' And the thing that terrifies me most of all is that I *did* go to sleep.

Later

My new nurse arrived this afternoon. Her name is Cardew. She seems a pleasant, friendly sort of girl, but I shouldn't call her a real good-looker. In fact she does not seem at all the type that Helmuth was expecting his Matron friend to send him. She is a hefty wench with a freckled face, blue eyes and a broad nose that inclines to turn up a trifle.

As Helmuth was out when she got here, Taffy brought her straight in to me, without even giving her a chance to tidy herself; so she was still wearing a suit of old tweeds and the heavy brogues in which she had travelled down. Her light brown hair is naturally fluffy and had got a bit windswept; so her general turn-out put the thought into my mind that she ought to be swinging a hockey stick. I doubt if she is any older than I am, so my first impression of her is that she is a nice, healthy English hoyden, not overburdened with brains but the sort that has been brought up to believe in God and the King, and marries respectably to build bonnie babies for the Empire.

Anyhow, she shows promise of being a more cheerful companion than Deb, and I am glad that she arrived when Helmuth was out. As soon as he gets hold of her it is certain that he will put all sorts of ideas about me into her head; but, at least, she saw me for the first time without prejudice.

Later

I have been worrying myself stiff all day about this new development of the Horror attempting to hypnotize me. I don't think it can possibly have succeeded in doing so—yet, for two reasons. Firstly, I am certain that I did not go into a trance while it was urging me to tell Taffy to leave the window open; secondly, I can remember the attempt perfectly clearly, which, presumably, I should not be able to do if the brute had managed to dominate my sub-conscious. On the other hand, I *did* fall asleep at its order, and while it was still at the window—which I should not previously have believed to be even remotely possible. So, in a way, it must have succeeded in getting some sort of control over my mind.

The only precaution I can think of against my giving way to a sudden impulse to obey its order tonight is to tie a handkerchief round my wrist. The sight of that should, I trust, be enough to pull me up with a jerk if I find myself apparently talking at random. But it is damnably unnerving.

I have found out why my new nurse is not the hard-faced, good-looking type of bitch that Helmuth expected his friend to send here for his amusement. Apparently the Matron had no hand in her selection. She got his telegram yesterday afternoon and nominated a Nurse Jollef for the job, then went off for a long week-end in the country. This morning Jollef fell downstairs and sprained her ankle, so the Deputy Matron picked Cardew to come here instead.

All I hope is that Helmuth does not decide to send her back to London and ask for a substitute more to his taste, as she is young and friendly. If Helmuth does not poison her mind too much against me there seems a chance that I may be able to make her my secret ally. In any case she should be much easier to get round than Deb.

I have pulled a fast one on her already by telling her that I always take one sleeping tablet, and that the bottle is left beside my bed in case I wake in pain during the night and need another; so she put the bottle in the top drawer of my bedside table. As soon as she had left the room to get my hot-water bottle I slipped four more tablets out of it; so even if she meets Helmuth on the way back and he tells her to collect it, I'll be able to cheat the Horror tonight at all events—that is, provided that I don't suddenly get a blackout and tell Taffy to open the window.

Here they come to settle me down.

Saturday, 30th May

It is mid-afternoon, and I am still feeling like death. Five sleeping tablets proved an overdose. It did the trick all right, as within twenty minutes of my lamp being taken away I was 'out', and I remained in complete oblivion for the best part of twelve hours. This morning they had the hell of a job to get me round, and it seems that if I hadn't the constitution of an ox I should probably have kicked the bucket.

Nurse Cardew may be young, but she can be tough enough when she likes.

Naturally such an episode occurring immediately on her arrival was a bit hard on her, as it reflects on her professional competence, and she gave me a terrific raspberry.

Perhaps it was bad strategy on my part to put her in a position where, through no fault of her own, she appears to have stepped off on the wrong foot. It will certainly make it far more difficult now for me to win her sympathy and possible help. But what the devil was I to do? So long as the moon remains near-full, every night means for me a new crisis in a most hideous battle. I simply *cannot* afford to think of long-term policies; I just *have* to seize on any means that offer to escape immediate danger.

Later

At tea-time I managed to get myself partially back into Nurse Cardew's good graces. Apparently the name 'Jugg' is not quite such a bell-ringer as I have always imagined; she had never heard of it before she was sent down here, and knew nothing about me at all. She asked in what sort of accident I had broken my back, and when I told her that I had been shot down she became much more matey. Her only brother–a Lieutenant in the Fleet Air Arm–was shot down too; but that happened nearly a year ago in the Eastern Mediterranean; and as he was reported 'missing, presumed dead' it's a hundred to one against the poor girl ever seeing him again.

Like myself, she is an orphan and, now that her brother has gone, she has no close relatives. Her father was a Naval Officer. He and her mother were both drowned in a yachting fatality when she was three, and she and her brother were brought up by an aunt who lives at Dawlish, in Devonshire. I gather they have very little money, but she doesn't seem to mind that, as she says that up to the time Johnny–that is her brother–got his packet, she found life enormous fun; and she is beginning to again, now that she doesn't think quite so often about his never coming home.

I have always been distinctly allergic to this hearty attitude to life, and I still cannot believe that I should find it 'tremendous fun' to go up to London with half-a-dozen other young people on an excursion ticket, for the sake of an afternoon's shop-window gazing, a 'Club' dance of some sort at one of the lesser hotels and supper in the small hours at Lyons Corner House. Still, on the debit side I must admit that, apart from my time in the R.A.F., my own youth was extraordinarily barren of hilarity; so perhaps being surrounded by riches really has very little bearing on the amount of enjoyment that one can get, and that it depends much more on an attitude of mind.

Owing to the Naval influence in Sally's–that is, Nurse Cardew's–family, she went into the W.R.N.S. at the beginning of the war. Incidentally, she *is* older than I am, by just over a year, although I would never have thought it from either her appearance or conversation. But she was blown up by a land-mine in the Plymouth blitz and, in consequence, invalided from the Service.

She is quite all right again now, unless she hears something go off with a loud bang. Apparently a bursting motor-tyre, or even a child popping a paper bag, is enough to do it; but any noise resembling an explosion still shatters her completely. She dives for the nearest cover–which, as she told me with a loud guffaw, usually means under the table, then bursts into a flood of tears and makes a general nuisance of herself for the next two hours. That is why, since the Wrens decided that she was no longer 100 per cent reliable for any regular duty, she had herself trained as a private nurse and has been taking jobs in country areas where bombs rarely fall.

Her nursing qualifications are pretty slender; she makes no secret of that. She went in for nursing only because she felt that she could not remain idle after she was boarded out of the Wrens, and she didn't much like the idea of going into a factory.

As she cannot do shorthand she could not have got anything but a stooge-job in an office, whereas she did now a bit about massage from having been taught by a half-Swedish cousin of hers, who used to come and stay at Dawlish. So she did a course in first aid, swatted up a few books on this and that concerning the most general types of ailments, and got taken on by Miss Smith for sending to patients in the country where massage was the principal requirement. Her last case was an old Colonel with a game leg, up in Shropshire, and two days after her return to London a new throw of the dice sent her here.

It is nice to have someone fresh to talk to, however mediocre their mentality, and over tea we got on like a house on fire; but, unfortunately, later this evening I blotted it again.

Helmuth has spared me his evening visits since we had our showdown; so when Sally came in, about six o'clock, to ask if she might borrow a book from the library, I let her browse for a few moments, while concluding a paragraph of this, then opened up our conversation again.

Most regrettably, as it turned out, I chose the subject of Helmuth as a lead in. I asked her what she thought of him.

While still searching the shelves for something readable, she said: 'He's terribly distinguished-looking, isn't he?'

'The Roebuck probably thinks of the Lion that way till he takes a big jump and fixes his claws in her back,' I remarked acidly.

'Am I supposed to be the Roebuck in this analogy?' she enquired.

'You might be,' I murmured, 'and while Dr Lisický's eyes and hair give him some resemblance to the King of Beasts, you can take it from me that there is nothing kingly about his mind; it is as low as that of any reptile.'

She straightened herself a little, but continued to keep her back turned, as she replied: 'I gathered from Dr Lisický this morning that you have recently taken an acute dislike to him. That sort of twist in the mentality of a permanent invalid against the person who is looking after them does sometimes occur; but you should do your best to fight it. Personally, from what little I have so far seen of the Doctor, I think him a most intelligent and charming man; and I am not going to encourage your morbid ideas by letting you say such horrid things to me about him.'

Like an idiot, I did not see the red light, but plunged in further with a sneer: 'Since you think him "distinguished-looking, intelligent and charming" it's pretty clear that he is well on the way to getting you where he wants you already. But I warn you that he has the morals of a sewer-rat. He made your predecessor his mistress, drove her half-crazy with neglect, then, when a respectable fellow wanted to marry her, he started to sleep with her again for the fun of busting up her engagement.'

Suddenly Nurse Cardew swung round on me; her blue eyes were hard and her freckled face flushed.

'Listen to me, Toby Jugg!' she exclaimed angrily. 'At tea-time this afternoon I thought I was going to like you, and I'm still prepared to do so;

but we had better get matters straight before we go any further. When I took on this job I was not told that you were a mental case, and I don't believe that, strictly speaking, you are one. But Dr Lisický warned me last night that you've got a mind like a cess-pool, and that your letters have to be censored because of the obscenities you put in them. What you have just said of him is obviously a wicked and disgusting lie. I'm not narrow-minded but I don't like filth and I don't like slander; so for the future you will kindly refrain from both in my presence, or I'll chuck up the case and go back to London.'

'Okay!' I snapped. 'I won't sully your shell-like ears again. But if you prefer to believe Dr Helmuth Lisický rather than me, it will be your own fault if you get yourself seduced.'

At that she flounced out of the room, and a few minutes later I was regretting that I had put her back up. Personally I don't give a damn if Helmuth makes her his mistress, but it seemed only fair to warn her of the sort of man he is. Where I was stupid was in putting it so bluntly, and in losing my temper with her because she wouldn't believe me.

In normal circumstances I should have handled the business much more tactfully; but the truth is that my nerves are in absolute shreds, so that I am hardly responsible for what I am saying, and my temper is as liable to snap as the over-taut string of a violin. But how could it be otherwise, seeing what I may have to face tonight?

Sunday, 31st May

I don't think I can stand much more of this. If Helmuth's object is to drive me mad, as I am convinced it is, he is well on the way to succeeding. What is more, he is starting now to collect the evidence which will later be put before the Lunacy Board in support of an application to have me certified.

He had already had my letters to Julia, describing my 'hallucinations', and the fact that I attempted to escape from his 'loving care' in the middle of the night, with Deb; and now, after last night, he will be able to produce visual evidence that I was seen raving. I suppose that was largely my fault; but it was bound to happen sooner or later, and I expect he has been counting on an occurrence of that kind giving him a solid basis for his case.

As a matter of fact I very nearly broke down when Nurse Cardew and Taffy were about to leave me last night. I implored her not to take away my lamp; but she said that the danger of fire from my knocking it over was too great for it to be left at my bedside. So I retorted:

'All right, then, put it out of my reach if you like, but at least leave it somewhere in the room.'

She was still a bit shirty from my having rubbed her up the wrong way before dinner, but I think it was more the influence Helmuth has already gained over her that decided her to refuse me. With a shake of her head, she replied:

'If I did you couldn't put it out; and if you had to take five sleepers to get off last night you would never get off at all with a light burning in your room. Anyhow, after the way you made a fool of me over that I am certainly not going against Dr Lisický's instructions to please you.'

So that was that; and in utter misery I had to watch them go.

It was the night of the full moon and the day had been fine with hardly a cloud in the sky, so I knew that I must anticipate a maximum attack. For what seemed an age I alternatively prayed and lay there with my brain whirling round in sick apprehension, then my heart began to hammer and the cold sweat broke out on my face. I turned my head, and there was the shadow of the Thing on the band of moonlight. It was crouching on the sill in the left-hand corner of the middle window, its round body pulsing horribly. The malefic force it radiated made my flesh creep, and the back of my neck began to prickle.

I found myself counting my heartbeats, and I had got up to eighty-nine when I suddenly caught the tapping noise that I first heard the beast make two nights before. I tried to go on counting, so as to shut out from my mind the rhythm of this tapping, but I couldn't.

Again that infernal morse code translated itself in my brain into the small, clear silvery voice, and it kept on reiterating: 'You've got to give way. You've got to give way.'

Then the rhythm changed to that of the gently swinging pendulum of an old clock, which said: 'Forget. ... Remember. Forget. ... Remember. Forget. ... Remember.' And I knew as certainly as if the Brute had explained its intention that it was endeavouring to mesmerize me, so that I should accept some instruction into my subconscious, forget it, and then at a stated time remember and act upon it. I knew, too, that when the instruction came it would be on the lines that I must tell Taffy to open one of the windows looking on to the courtyard, before leaving me the following night.

In a moment of time all sorts of thoughts jostled for place in my terrified brain: Could the Horror hypnotize me against my will? Why had it left out this all-important middle stage of the process two nights before? Was it, perhaps, as much mentally blind and fumbling as it seems to be physically? How could I best attempt to thwart its evil purpose? What means could I employ to stop that sinister little silvery voice from impinging on my mind?

Of all those questions the last was that which called most urgently for an immediate answer. While the sweat trickled in icy rivulets down my face and I wrung my hands together in an agony of fear, I strove to concentrate upon it.

Suddenly, in the very midst of a groan that broke from me at my impotence, the answer came. It is difficult to catch any remark addressed to one in a room where a person is singing, and next to impossible to do so if one is singing oneself. By roaring out a song I could drown that small, insidious, evil voice that uttered its phrases over and over again in my own mind.

I suppose it was the fact that I had been praying so hard which instinctively led me to launch out with a hymn. I started with 'Rock of Ages', but the tempo seemed so slow and dirge-like that I quickly switched to 'Onward, Christian Soldiers'.

The effect was instantaneous. The voice was smothered and the Thing out in the courtyard knew. From having remained quite still it suddenly leapt into its devil-dance. Quivering with rage, hate and fury, it sprang up and down, and hurled its heavy body against the window-panes.

But my triumph was shortlived. The only Church services that I have attended since I was a child were the compulsory parades to which I was detailed during my early months in the R.A.F., so I could remember only the first verse and chorus of 'Onward, Christian Soldiers'. I sang them over three times while I frantically searched my mind for another hymn, but I could think of nothing. Then, as I began to falter, the tapping came through again.

'Stop that! Stop that! Stop that!' it commanded angrily.

In desperation, rather than fall silent, I changed from the sacred to the profane, and began to roar out 'There is a Tavern in the Town'. From that I ran through half-a-dozen old favourites that had always figured in our repertoire when, in those now far-off days, we had shouted ourselves hoarse grouped round a piano after guest-night dinners in the Mess. With one thought only in my mind–to keep on singing–I made no attempt to pick the songs, but sang them one after another as they came into my head; so it is hardly surprising that such pieces as 'Roll Out the Barrel' and 'We'll Hang Out the Washing on the Siegfried Line' became interspersed with bawdy choruses like 'A German Officer Crossed the Rhine', and 'She was Poor but She was Honest'.

I was bawling out 'The Harlot of Jerusalem' at the top of my voice, when the door was suddenly flung open. There stood Helmuth, holding a lamp aloft in his right hand, and beside him Nurse Cardew. Both of them were in their dressing-gowns.

No doubt from fear, strain and effort I was as near off my rocker as makes no difference at the time. Anyhow, the sheer impetus of the song and the paramount necessity of continuing to drown that evil voice caused me to carry on for a couple of lines. It was only when Helmuth shouted at me: 'Toby! Stop singing that filthy song–instantly!' that I realized the significance of the chorus I had been yelling.

At that second I caught Nurse Cardew's glance and, goodness knows why, but a quick flush of shame ran through me. In this day and age it takes more than a few bawdy words to shock most girls, and as a trained nurse she must have heard plenty. All the same, just for a second, I felt as though I had been caught out doing something quite frightful.

But the feeling had passed in an instant, submerged by the far more powerful causes for agitation which were still making me sweat and tremble. With my head craned up to stare at my visitors over the foot of the bed I thrust out my arm and pointed to the strip of moonlight:

'Look! Look!' I cried. 'D'you call that an hallucination?'

Then I swivelled my glance to follow my own pointing finger. With a groan I let my head fall back on my pillow. The shadow was no longer there.

Helmuth's voice came, with the false sadness of crocodile's tears in it. 'This is a tragic business, Nurse. It was lucky that I heard the poor boy and fetched you. I'm afraid he has been suffering from something worse than a bad dream, and that we have real grounds to fear for his sanity.'

At that I went off the deep end. I called him a dirty, lying, hypocritical bastard, and every other name that I could think of. For a good two minutes or more I raved and shouted at him, and their efforts to check me were in vain.

People with red hair are said to have violent tempers, and mine can be a pretty hot one if I once let myself go. When Helmuth set down the lamp and came near the bed I grabbed his arm and tried to pull him to me. If I could have got my hands on his throat I really believe I would have killed him. But

Nurse Cardew came up on my other side and gave me a sharp slap in the face.

I was so astonished that I let go of Helmuth, stopped shouting, and turned to stare at her.

'That's better,' she said quietly. 'You ought to be ashamed of yourself, making such a scene, and attacking Dr Lisický. You don't want to be put into a straitjacket, do you?'

'Oh come, Nurse! Please don't suggest such a terrible thing,' Helmuth protested. Then, after a second, he added: 'But, loath as I am to do so, I fear I shall have to call a mental specialist in if he goes on like this.'

Her remark, and his right on top of it, sobered me up completely. I cannot believe that she is a party to Helmuth's plot—as yet, at all events—so her mention of a straitjacket could only have been made spontaneously as a direct result of seeing me, as she evidently thought, behaving like a madman. It flashed on me then that Helmuth must have been waiting for something like this to happen, and had deliberately brought her along so that later he would be able to call her as an eye-witness. By letting fly at him I had played right into his hands.

With an effort I collected my scattered wits and did the little that could be done to repair the position. I said:

'I'm sorry, Nurse. I shouldn't have used such language in front of you; but, believe it or not, I have very good grounds for losing my temper with Dr Lisický. For weeks past I have been sleeping abominably badly in this room, and again and again I have asked him to move me to another. Since he flatly refuses to do so I hold him responsible for my nightmares.'

'There is nothing wrong with this room,' she replied coldly, as she began to remake my pillows. 'It's large and light and airy, and most invalids would consider themselves lucky to have such a beautiful apartment to live in. Since you suffer from nightmares you would have them just as badly anywhere else; and it is very wicked to get such horrible ideas about people who are doing their best for you. Now, if I give you two triple bromides, will you promise to behave yourself and try to get off to sleep again?'

As further argument seemed futile, I said 'Yes'; then, as soon as I had drunk the draught, Helmuth picked up the lamp and, having wished me better sleep for the rest of the night, they left me.

But the night's battle was not over. Within five minutes of their having gone, the cold came again, and I had a sudden empty feeling in the pit of my stomach. One glance at the band of moonlight was enough. There was the shadow back where it had been before, and the horrid, insistent tapping started once more.

After that I am not quite clear what really happened. I can recall praying again, sweating anew with funk, and saying choruses and nursery-rhymes over to myself in an effort to shut out the silvery voice. The struggle seemed to last for an eternity, and the frightful thing is that I have no idea how far the Horror succeeded in dominating my sub-conscious before the bromides took effect, and I drifted off into a sort of coma—or rather a nightmarish, hag-ridden sleep.

This morning I feel, and look, like a piece of chewed string. Nurse Cardew seemed quite shocked at my appearance, but she puts it down to my having over-excited myself last night; and when I started to tell her about Helmuth's refusal to have the blackout curtain lengthened, and to let me have my radio beside my bed, she wouldn't listen to me. It is clear that he has already completely won her over, and she thinks that my requests are inspired solely with a view to making trouble.

What will happen tonight, God alone knows; and I can now place my hope only in Him. If the Devil in the courtyard did succeed in hypnotizing me, the odds are that I shall become subject to a blackout sometime this evening, and ask either Taffy or Nurse Cardew to open that window after the curtain has been drawn, then come out of my trance without realizing what I have done.

If that happens I have no illusions about my fate. The Horror will slither in and across the floor, one swift spring and it will be on the bed, wrapping its filthy tentacles round me in a ghastly embrace. By the time my screams bring help it will be too late. They really will find me a raving lunatic.

Later

I believe my desperate prayers for help have been answered in the nick of time. I cannot tell for certain because, being Sunday, Taffy has the afternoon off, so I have not yet had a chance to tackle him. But an entirely unforeseen event has brought me new hope, and I have been hard put to it to conceal the intense excitement I am feeling from Nurse Cardew.

Indirectly I owe this lifeline which seems almost within my grasp to the great raid on Cologne. Last night Bomber Command went out in force–in far greater force than most people would believe possible. They sent a thousand aircraft against one objective, and at a guess I would not have thought that we could have put half that number in the sky. It makes a landmark in the war, and its effect on the city must have been too frightful to contemplate.

All the same, I would rather have been there, and taken my chance as the bombs rained down, than as I was, lying on my back here sweating with terror under the baleful influence of the Evil that is hunting me.

But that is beside the point. It was thinking about this giant R.A.F. raid that recalled to my mind the official letter Helmuth gave me when he brought me the one from Uncle Paul on Thursday. I was so put out by Uncle Paul's reply that I did not even open the other; I just pushed it into a drawer of my bedside table and forgot all about it. But this morning I remembered it, and on opening the envelope I found that it was from the Air Ministry and contained various papers, including a cheque for £147 10s. 5d.

The money is the final settlement–exclusive of pension–on my being invalided out. Most of it was due to me months ago, but as I could not account for some of the items of flying-kit which I had been issued, the usual generous procedure was followed. They hung on to the whole lot, while numerous dreary little men made quite certain that the total could not be further reduced by docking me for some other article of war-equipment graciously lent to me by the nation as an aid to fighting our enemies.

However, in this case, praises be for the dilatoriness of those chair-borne warriors whose lot is cast among ledgers. If the bulk of this cash had been paid to me last March it would long since have joined the rest of my private money in the bank, where I can't get at it without Helmuth knowing; whereas it has now arrived like manna from Heaven, providing me with the means for an attempt to bribe Taffy.

It is still a toss-up whether he will be prepared to risk Helmuth's wrath, but I think he will for close on £150. That is a lot to a young Welsh country bumpkin who, but for my arrival here, would still be doing odd jobs in the garden at about £2 a week. Besides, there is this laudable ambition of his to become an engineer, like his brother Davey in Cardiff. A wad like this would easily cover his fees at a technical school for the elementary course, which is all he is capable of mastering to begin with, and keep him while he is on it into the bargain.

The thing that I fear is most likely to put him off is the idea of taking a cheque—particularly one made out to someone else and crossed account payee. But I hope to get over that by also giving him a letter to my bank, instructing them to credit the cheque to my account and to pay the bearer out its value in cash. That would amount to giving him an open cheque in exchange for paying in the other, really; although he won't realize it. Still, it should help to allay any apprehensions he may have that when he presents the cheque the cashier will think he has stolen it and send for the police.

Of course, if only I can get to London I'll be able to see to it myself that he gets his money; but my bank being there presents another snag. Naturally, if he does his stuff and gets me out, his instinct would be to grab the cheque and make a bolt for Cardiff. But I can think of no way of enabling him to cash the cheque except by taking it to my London bank.

In one way that is an advantage as, although I could have myself put in the guard's van in my wheel-chair and make the journey on my own, it would make everything much easier, particularly at the other end, if I had him with me. But it means that I'll have the additional fence to cross of persuading him that, instead of disappearing into the blue, he must accompany me to London.

Lastly there is the question of our fares. As I have no ready he will have to ante-up for both of us. I don't doubt that he has a bit tucked away somewhere, but it may be in the Post Office; and for me it is tonight or never. If it is there he will have no time to draw it out, and God forbid that he should attempt to borrow from the other servants. Still, if the worst comes to the worst we can use whatever cash he has on tickets to carry us part of the way, and I can offer my gold cigarette-case to the collector as security for later paying the surplus on the remainder of the journey.

Taffy always gets back in time to give me my bath, and there could be no better opportunity for tackling him. He can't make any excuse to get away and leave me there, so he will have to listen to all I have to say. I shall offer him the full amount of the cheque in any case, as an assurance against failure and the loss of his job; and double the amount in addition, payable at the end of next month, in the event of his getting me safely to London.

To offer him more might make him suspicious that I mean to rat on him; but a round £500—and that's what I'll make it—won't sound to him too high a price for the successor of his family's feudal Lords to pay for freedom. On the other hand, he'll know without telling that it is only once in a lifetime that a poor gardener's son has the chance to earn such a sum for a single night's work.

If he agrees, I mean to get him to come back as soon as Nurse Cardew has gone to her room, dress me, get me into my chair and wheel me along to the bathroom. It was the old flower-room, and was specially fitted up with a bath for me so that I wouldn't have to be carried upstairs; but it has no window, only a blacked-out skylight, so I'll be safe there from the Horror while the household is settling down for the night.

I daren't leave my get-away later than midnight, in case Taffy should drop off to sleep; but by twelve o'clock everyone should be in bed, and he can come and get me.

On second thoughts, though, I think I'll keep him with me; that will eliminate the risk of his giving the game away inadvertently to any of the other servants, or anyone thinking it strange if he is seen loitering about instead of going to bed.

That is certainly an improvement in my plan, as it means that we won't have to leave the house till it is a safe bet that everyone is sound asleep.

It is four miles to the station, but downhill most of the way; so, making due allowance for Taffy's deformed foot, which has saved him from being called up, he ought to be able to push me that far in well under three hours. So if we leave at two o'clock we should reach the station by five, easily; and I doubt if the earliest train leaves much before six.

So that is what is cooking. I pray God that it comes to the boil.

Later

Taffy fell for it; and tonight's the night. I fancy my grandfather must be turning in his grave, though, as the avaricious little bounder stuck out for £1,000 and a job in the Juggernaut factory, if he succeeds in getting me to London. But who cares! I would give him the Castle and make him the Lord of Llanferdrack just for getting me out of this room until tomorrow morning.

Tuesday, 2nd June

I am still here. I could not bring myself to write anything yesterday. I was too utterly depressed and mentally exhausted. My only remaining hope is that I may manage to hang out somehow till Uncle Paul arrives on Thursday.

On Sunday night everything went according to plan, but my luck was too good to last. Taffy came for me, dressed me, took me along to the bathroom, waited there with me for nearly three hours, then got me out of the house with no more noise than a first-class burglar would have made getting in. The moon was still up and for the first time in many weeks I was glad to see it, as it lit the way for us through the grounds and for the first mile or more down the road. We reached the station by a quarter to five, and had to wait outside it for three-quarters of an hour, as it was not open; but soon after 5.30 the staff of three made their appearance and began the day's routine. Taffy is a bit suspicious of the Post Office, and he keeps his savings in an old cigarette tin concealed somewhere in his room, so we were able to buy two tickets to London, and went on to the platform.

At 5.55 a milk train came through. Why, oh why, didn't we take it? I must have been crazy not to. But everything was going so perfectly that it seemed much more sensible to wait for the 6.20, that does not dither round the loop line but goes direct to the junction.

We were the only people on the platform, and the whistling of the solitary porter was the only sound that broke the stillness of the post-dawn hour. Suddenly I caught the hum of a car engine driven all out. Next moment it roared up to the station entrance. There was a brief commotion and the noise of running footsteps, then Helmuth and Nurse Cardew shot out of the booking office and came dashing towards us.

At the sight of them I knew the game was up. The train was nearly due, but even if it had come in at that moment I could not have got Taffy to heave me into it. From fear of Helmuth, he had already taken to his heels.

All the same I meant to make a fight for it; and, anyway, it seemed a bit hard that his panic should cost him the compensation I had promised him for the loss of his job; so I shouted after him:

'Come back, Taffy! Come back, you fool! Don't go without your cheque!'

That halted him, and he came ambling back with a hang-dog look on his face, just as Helmuth and Nurse Cardew reached me.

She was in her nurse's uniform but had evidently dressed in a hurry, as her fluffy brown hair was sticking out untidily from under her cap and she had odd stockings on her long legs. Probably it was knowing about that which made her young face so flushed and angry. Without a word she grasped the back-rail of my chair, and swivelling it round made to wheel me off the station. But I was too quick for her. Stretching out a hand, I grabbed the iron railing at the back of the platform and brought her up with a jerk.

'Now Toby!' said Helmuth a bit breathlessly. 'Please don't make a scene. You've already given us an awful fright. Don't add to our distress by making an exhibition of yourself.'

'If there is any scene it will be your fault,' I retorted. 'I am about to take the train to London; and you have no right to stop me.'

Although the platform had been empty a few minutes earlier, a little crowd began to gather with mysterious suddenness. The porter, two soldiers, a land-girl, a leading aircraftsman and a little group of children had all appeared from nowhere and were eyeing us with speculative interest.

'You are in no fit state to travel,' Helmuth said sharply.

Striving to keep as calm as I could, I denied that, and a wordy battle ensued in which both of us rapidly became more heated. We were still arguing when the train came clanking in.

The little crowd had increased to over a dozen people and it was now further swollen by others getting out of the train. Seeing it there actually in the station made me desperate. If I could have only covered those few yards and heaved myself into a carriage it meant safety, freedom and sanity; whereas to let Helmuth take me back to Llanferdrack threatened imprisonment, terror and madness. He caught the gleam in my eye and endeavoured to bring matters to a swift conclusion. Grabbing my wrist, he strove to break my grasp of the railing, while Nurse Cardew pushed on my chair from behind with all her weight.

'Help! Help!' I shouted to the crowd. 'I want to get on the train to London, and these people have no right to stop me.'

An elderly Major, who had arrived on the train, stepped forward and said rather hesitantly to Helmuth: 'Look here! This is none of my business, but I really don't think you ought to use violence towards a cripple.'

Helmuth let go my wrist and turned to him; but I got in first. 'I appeal to you sir,' I cried. 'I am an ex-officer wounded in the war; but I am perfectly fit to travel, and these people are endeavouring to detain me against my will.'

'That is only partially true!' Helmuth said quickly. 'This poor young man was shot down nearly a year ago. But the injury to his spine has affected his brain. I am a Doctor and—'

'A Doctor of Philosophy!' I cut in, but he ignored the sneer, and went on:

'He is in my care, and escaped from Llanferdrack Castle last night. I assure you that he is not fit to travel, and that I am only doing my duty in restraining him from doing so. It would be dangerous both for himself and others, as he is subject to fits of insanity.'

'That's a lie!' I declared, and Taffy came unexpectedly to my assistance by adding:

'Right you. The young gentleman's as sane as myself, is it. And it is a good master he is, too.'

As the Major looked from one to another of us doubtfully, Helmuth brought up his reserves. With a gesture towards Nurse Cardew he said:

'This lady is a professional nurse. Since you appear to doubt me, she will tell you that she has seen the patient in such a violent state that she had to threaten to have him put into a strait jacket.'

She confirmed his statement at once, and added: 'Two nights ago he was screaming obscenities and attacked the Doctor.'

All these exchanges had taken place in less than a couple of minutes; but the train was overdue to leave, and the guard, who was standing on the fringe of the crowd, blew his whistle.

The Major gave me a pitying look and said: 'I'm very sorry, but I really don't think I can interfere.' Then he saluted politely and turned away.

I thrust my hand in my pocket, pulled out the cheque and the letter for my bank manager, held them out to Taffy and cried: 'Here you are! Quick, man! Jump on that train!'

As Taffy snatched them Helmuth grasped him by the arm and snapped: 'Give that to me!'

I don't know if he realized that it was a cheque or thought that it was a letter that I was trying to get off to somebody without his knowing its contents, but his act was the last straw that made me lose my temper completely.

'Damn you!' I yelled. 'Let him go. That's my money to do as I like with. He's earned it by doing his best to get me out of your filthy clutches. If you take that cheque from him I'll call the police in and have you arrested for theft.'

But Taffy had already wrenched himself away and jumped on the moving train.

To give him the papers I had had to let go the railing and Nurse Cardew seized the opportunity to start pushing me along the platform. Further resistance now that the train had gone was pointless; but, having finally lost my temper, I continued to shout abuse at Helmuth all the way to the car.

Only when they had got me into it, and were tying my wheel-chair on to the grid behind, did it suddenly dawn upon me that, by my outburst, I had provided Helmuth with invaluable fresh evidence that he could use in seeking to prove me insane, as a score of people must have heard me raving at him.

That thought, coming on top of my bitter disappointment, was more than I could bear. I broke down and wept.

Later

I had to stop writing a quarter of an hour ago, as the memory of the ignominious manner in which I was brought back here, after my attempted flight, made me start crying again.

Really it is too absurd that a grown man like myself should give way to tears, but I suppose it is because my nerves have been reduced to shreds, and the appalling strain of knowing that my situation is going from bad to worse.

The worst factor is the way in which Helmuth is steadily gaining ground towards his secret objective, of collecting enough evidence about my disturbed mental state to get me certified as a lunatic. But, in addition, there are the various changes that have resulted in the past week from my two attempts to escape.

Taffy was a great stupid oaf with a streak of low cunning and greed in his make-up; but on the whole he wasn't a bad sort, and, normally, he was willing, cheerful and friendly. His departure was admittedly my own fault, but I am paying for it now pretty heavily, as his place has been taken by Helmuth's man Konrad. There has never been any love lost between us at the best of times and, quite apart from the fact that I dislike him touching me anyhow, whenever Nurse Cardew is not with us he takes an obvious delight in handling me roughly.

Deb, too, was very far from being a gay and lovable companion and my new nurse is no better. I am sure she could be, but the trouble is that I set off on the wrong foot with her the very night she arrived, by taking that overdose of sleeping tablets; and since then she has seen little but the worst side of me. Unfortunately, I find it practically impossible to conceal any longer my hatred for Helmuth, and she has already developed a strong admiration for him; so she regards me as an ungrateful young brute, and whenever his name crops up we snap at one another.

She obviously does not like it here; which is quite understandable, seeing that she expected a quiet life looking after a simple spinal case, and now finds that she is in charge of someone whom she believes to be a dangerous lunatic. In addition, my latest escapade has made her work much more exacting, as she now has to come upstairs to me a dozen or more times every day.

When they got me back here, Helmuth again played the role of Uriah Heep and pretended to be greatly distressed about me. But his concern took the form of actually and officially making me a prisoner.

Hating him as I do, I could not help feeling a sneaking admiration for the way he did it, as in achieving his secret object he killed two birds with one stone. On the drive back he declared that some means must be derived to prevent me from escaping again, in case I did myself an injury, and devilishly led Nurse Cardew into discussing with him how best this might be done.

As I have twice succeeded in securing aid for an intended get-away and might, perhaps, corrupt another of the servants to help me in a third attempt, their problem really amounted to—what arrangements could be made so that I would need more than one person's assistance to get out of the house without their knowing?

Helmuth was driving and Nurse Cardew sitting in the back with me. By that time I had more or less recovered from my weeping fit and I cut in sarcastically:

'Why don't you take me down to one of the dungeons and chain me to the wall? That's what they used to do to the poor wretches in Bedlam, isn't it?'

That brought a shocked protest from them both, and assurances that they were only trying to protect me from the possibility of something awful happening to me as a result of my own folly.

Then Nurse Cardew said a piece of her own which left me undecided if I ought to curse or kiss her. The gist of her remarks were: (1) She thought the best thing would be for her to take away my chair at nights, as two people would be needed to carry me, and even then it would be difficult for them to get me very far without it. (2) That was, unless the Doctor would agree to moving me to an upstairs room; as in that case, even in my chair, no one person would be able to get me down the stairs. (3) In any case, it was clear that I had a phobia about my present room, and she had always understood that in mental cases the cause of phobia should never be referred to, and eliminated as far as possible. Therefore, she felt most strongly that I ought to be moved.

For the moment Helmuth did not reply, as he was just driving up to the front of the house. While they got me out of the car and into my chair, my brain was working furiously. The previous afternoon I had considered the possibility of hypnotizing Nurse Cardew if Taffy failed me, and now, quite unconsciously, she was suggesting measures which would render any success in that direction futile, as well as actively co-operating with Helmuth in seeking means to make certain that I should not get away again. On the other hand, if she managed to persuade him to move me to another room it seemed that she would be rendering me an inestimable service.

I felt sure that he would refuse, and that if he did it would cost him a lot in her estimation; even, perhaps, convince her that he was deliberately persecuting me by keeping me there; in which case I might soon be able to win her over completely. So it looked as if whichever way things went I stood to gain on the outcome.

But Helmuth wriggled out of the spot she had unconsciously put him in very neatly. When we were inside the hall he said:

'For your own protection, Toby, I shall adopt Nurse Cardew's suggestion. There is a room in the old part of the Castle on the first floor, abutting on to the chapel. It has a little terrace of its own, so if we put you there it will be unnecessary to carry you down to the garden for your airings; and tucked away in the east wing of the Castle you won't even see any of the servants, except my man Konrad, so you will not be under the temptation to try to bribe one of them.'

As he spoke I caught just the suggestion of a malicious gleam in his tawny eyes, and I knew then that to make me a real prisoner had been his aim the whole time. If he had bluntly suggested doing so that might have shocked and estranged Nurse Cardew, but he had skilfully led her into practically suggesting it herself, and had then made capital out of his willingness to pander to my phobia about being moved from my old room. So here I am.

After breakfast yesterday several of the staff were mobilized to move furniture, and by midday I was installed with all my belongings in my new quarters. It is a big square room with a vaulted ceiling, a large open fireplace and two arched doorways framing stout oak doors that have iron scrollwork and huge bolts on them. One of them leads to a spiral stone staircase, up which I was carried in my chair with considerable difficulty; the other leads to the terrace, which is about twenty-five feet across and shaped like the quarter segment of a circle. It lies in an angle of the Castle, its two straight sides being formed by the outer wall of this room and the wall of another, to which there is no entrance; the curved side is castellated, and this part of the battlements has a fine view over the lake, which lies about fifteen feet below it.

The room is not in bad condition; a little plaster has flaked off the ceiling and here and there the wainscoting that lines the walls has been stained by patches of damp, but the fire which is being lit daily to air it will soon dry them out; and now that it has been furnished with such pieces as they could get up the narrow, spiral stairs, it is quite comfortable. All the same, it gives one a somewhat eerie feeling to have been lifted out of a late-Victorian setting and dumped down in another overnight that is still redolent of the Middle Ages.

The thing about my old room that I miss most is the big south window. Here there is no window at all; at least, not in the modern sense. Instead, a large iron grating, about six feet long and three deep, let into the east wall, serves to provide the room with plenty of daylight and ample supply of fresh air. As the grill is not fitted with glass, a blind, or even curtains, the wind whistling through it must make the place an ice-house in winter; but, fortunately, we are now in high summer, so that does not worry me at the moment. No blackout is needed, as the grill is not in an outer wall, but in that beyond which lies the partially ruined chapel. If I were able to stand I could look through it down into the chapel, but as its lower ledge is about five-feet-six from the floor I can see only on an upward angle some of the groined rafters of the decaying roof, and the tops of the upright baulks of timber which have been wedged under them to prevent it falling in.

Since I have been here I have been wondering a lot what Helmuth's motive can be in agreeing to my removal from the library. At first I was tremendously elated at the thought that, at last, I had escaped from the vicinity of the courtyard and that damnable band of moonlight; but, somehow, I cannot bring myself to feel any permanent sense of security on account of my move.

The courtyard is on the far side of the chapel from the lake, but that is no great distance; and the idea has begun to prey upon my mind that the Thing, having some horrible form of intelligence, may know of my move and follow me here—or Helmuth may have some way of telling it where I am.

If it does seek me out here, and climb up the chapel wall to the grating, I shall be forced to look on it for the first time face to face—that is, if there is moonlight filtering through the broken roof of the chapel. When Nurse Cardew and Konrad left me last night I had a bad half-hour fearing that might happen; but to my great relief the weather changed, it began to rain gently and the moon could not get through the clouds.

There is another thing that has been worrying me all day. Just as I was dropping off to sleep last night, at about eleven o'clock, I heard footsteps. They were light and clear, and sounded as if someone was descending a stone staircase behind the head of my bed.

At the time I thought nothing of it. But this morning, I suddenly realized that the wall behind my bed-head is an outer wall of the Castle, and I am certain that there is no staircase there.

Can those footsteps be the first indication of some fresh manifestation of

Evil to which Helmuth is about to subject me? Is that why he put me in this room? They cannot have been made by any human agency, unless they are some curious echo. Perhaps that is the explanation. Pray God it is, for my nerves are strained to breaking-point already.

Wednesday, 3rd June

I slept badly last night, but, thank God, had no actual trouble. It was stormy again and the moonlight only showed fitfully now and then through the grating.

This morning I managed to get a look through it down into the chapel but, in doing so, I got myself into a bit of a mess, which ended with surprising and terrifically exciting results.

As I have mentioned before, my shoulders and arms are very strong. After I had had my airing on the battlements I wheeled myself up to the grating, sideways on, and stretched up my right hand as high as it would go. I was just able to get a firm grip on the ledge and, exerting all my strength, pulled myself up until I could grasp the iron grill with my left hand; then I shifted the right to a firmer hold and, hanging there, peered through.

The chapel is both long and lofty—in fact it is as big as the average country church. Its floor is a good twenty-five feet below me as, to give it additional height, the old builders sank it about twelve feet into the ground. Actually, I suppose they excavated the whole site for the Castle to that depth or more, and instead of making cellars and dungeons out of this bit, carried the walls and pillars of the chapel straight up from the foundations.

It must have been a damp and cheerless place to worship in, as its floor is well below the level of the lake, which runs parallel to its south wall and only about forty feet away, but our ancestors don't seem to have minded damp and cold as much as we do.

The roof is about fifteen feet above my head, and is not as badly damaged as I expected. There are a few big rents in it, but they are all this end. Looking down from the grill I was directly facing the altar, and the whole of the far half of the roof over the chancel and a good part of the nave is intact.

There are now no pews in the chapel, as it has not been used for many years; but there are a number of large, stone box-like graves with effigies of chaps in armour, and their ladies, on them, as the Lords of Llanferdrack were always buried here. Parts of four out of the six pillars, which were the main support of the roof, have crumbled away, and it has been shored up in places with wooden scaffolding. It looks, too, as if its distintegration has been arrested, as there is no debris littering the stone floor. In fact the whole place is as clean as if it had been swept out yesterday, which seems rather surprising. I was just wondering why anyone should bother to keep it in such good order when my chair slipped from under my feet, and I found myself stranded, like a fly on the wall, clinging to the grating.

It was a quarter of an hour before Nurse Cardew came in and found me like that. She promptly pushed my chair back and got me down into it, while scolding me for taking such a risk of injuring myself. I simply laughed at her and said that I could have hung on there for an hour or more without serious discomfort, had I wished.

She looked me straight in the eye and said: 'I don't believe it—unless you were taking some of the weight on your feet.'

I said I didn't think that I had been, not perceptibly, anyhow; upon which she told me to put my hands on her shoulders and try to stand up.

I tried, and I couldn't manage it. But she is amazingly strong for a girl, and she practically lifted me into an upright position. With one hand grasping the grating and the other round her neck we found that I could just remain erect for a moment or two.

Nurse Cardew says that is a sure sign that my back is mending; and that although we must go very carefully, if I practise standing like that for a short time every day, until I can take the whole of my own weight, there is a real chance that I may eventually be able to walk again. I gather that I should be doing well if I could walk from one room to another unaided by this time next year but, to me, even such a modest prospect is wildly exciting.

Besides, once I can manage a dozen steps they would let me have crutches. They daren't as things are, for if a crutch slipped I should go flat on my face, or on my back, and if my head struck sometime hard I might kill myself. But if I was strong enough to recover my balance there would be no danger of that, and with the aid of crutches I could get about all over the place.

This really is terrific, and Nurse Cardew seemed as pleased as I was. She has a nice smile that lights up her freckled face, and really makes her quite pretty while it lasts. But like a fool I spoilt the whole thing by asking her if she managed to keep Helmuth in his place last night; and got the tart answer to 'Mind your own business'.

I knew that she had had dinner with him because she told me she was going to yesterday afternoon. She asked me if I minded having my evening massage a little earlier than usual, so that she would have longer to change out of uniform. Naturally I agreed; I could hardly have done otherwise, and I forbore to make any comment.

However, a few minutes after having snapped me up this morning she resumed the subject of her own accord. She said:

'I do wish you would try to get these horrid ideas about Dr Lisický out of your head. It was kind of him to ask me to have dinner with him, and I hope he does again. He couldn't have been more charming, and the pre-war atmosphere of candlelight and wine made a nice change for me from the routine of having my meals served on a tray in the small library.'

There was nothing much I could say to that which would not have led to another row, so I let it pass. I wish, though, that she had been here as a fly on the wall when Helmuth was discussing the replacement of Deb, and had heard him say that it would be 'fun to have someone fresh to sleep with', as I am quite sure that he would never bother to ask her to dine with him unless he had designs on her.

As she is so young Helmuth may have decided that the best policy is not to rush his fences. On the other hand it may be a case of 'still waters run deep'. No girl can be a nurse and remain ignorant of sex, and this one looks healthy enough to have the usual urges of her age. If she had been 'educated' at Weylands she would be a veteran by this time. Still, I don't believe, somehow, that she is that kind.

Those queer footsteps came again last night, and I hard them twice; first at eleven o'clock, as before, and, as I was wakeful, again about one o'clock. The second time they were going back up the stairs. Yet there cannot be any staircase there. It hardly seems possible that the Thing could make that sort of noise–yet it gave me a slight fit of the jitters. Thank God that tomorrow is Thursday. Unless Fate plays me some scurvy trick to prevent Uncle Paul turning up, within twenty-four hours now I'll be a free man again.

Thursday, 4th June

Last night it was calm with a clear sky, so for the first time I saw the full effect of a bright moon in this room. Praises be, there is no thick bar of it on the floor, as there was downstairs, for it does not shine in direct through the grating. It comes through the holes in the chapel roof, then filters through here filling the room with a soft radiance; but it was not strong enough to throw a shadow of the criss-cross bars of the grill.

As the appearance of the Horror is so tied up in my mind with moonlight, I was naturally in a pretty nervy state; and when the footsteps came again at eleven o'clock I broke out into a sweat. But nothing happened and after a bit I managed to get off to sleep.

This morning, while I was sitting in the sunshine on my terrace, I went over in my mind what I mean to say to Uncle Paul. As he has always been very decent to me I dislike the idea of being tough with him; but I am afraid that is the only way I can make certain of getting him to stand up to Helmuth.

I have always been rather sorry for my uncle, as in the natural course of events he should have come in for his share of the Jugg millions and be a rich man in his own right. But that he did not, and will be almost entirely dependent on me after I attain my majority, is largely his own fault. His early life, before he married Julia, was really rather a shocking record of weakness and stupidity.

When he came down from Cambridge in 1917, my grandfather secured him a commission in the Welsh Guards; but early in 1919 he got tight one night at the Berkeley, and struck a waiter, who was trying to persuade him to go home. Naturally that led to a pretty nasty stink and I gather that he narrowly escaped being cashiered; but they let him off with sending in his papers. The old man sent him to South Africa for a couple of years, to be out of the way while he sowed the rest of his wild oats, then brought him home in 1921, and put him into the offices of our Newcastle shipyards.

There he got involved with a typist and his father had to pay a tidy sum to prevent an action for breach of promise being brought. He was transferred to London after that, so that an eye could be kept on him, but that didn't do much good. He was always at the races instead of the office, and in the next few years my grandfather had to pay up his racing debts on three occasions.

Then he got into the hands of a real top-line card-sharper; one of the chaps who do things on the grand scale with a nice little house in Mayfair, run a perfectly straight game for a whole season and take just one mug for a ride in a big way at the end of it. In the season of 1925 Uncle Paul was the mug selected, and in an all-night session he was stung for seven thousand pounds.

It all appeared perfectly above-board, as there were scores of other gamblers who were prepared to swear to the honesty of the crook. My grandfather paid again, but that was the end. Uncle Paul was sent abroad with a thousand a year, payable monthly, and told that in the future he could go bankrupt or go to prison, but he would not get another cent.

In 1928 he married Julia. I have no doubt that he was in love with her on account of her bewitching beauty; but, in addition, she is connected with the noble Roman house of Colona, and I think he thought that a respectable marriage would put him right with his father. But it didn't. Albert Abel I would not even receive them; and Julia has no money of her own, so they took the Willows and settled down there in the hope that the old man would relent.

That is where Uncle Paul was unlucky. Before sufficient time had elapsed for his father really to appreciate that he had turned over a new leaf the air-crash put an end to his chances. So poor Uncle Paul's own income is still no more than it was when he had the little house at Kew.

Later

Uncle Paul has been and is now on his way back to London. He arrived in time to lunch with Helmuth and immediately afterwards Helmuth brought him up here.

Perhaps it is the result of having lived for three years in an area constantly subject to air-raids, but I thought Uncle Paul was looking a lot older. He can't be much more than forty-three, but his red hair has got a lot of grey in it now and the pouches under his eyes are heavier than ever, so he might easily be taken for fifty. All the same, his ruddy face does not look unhealthy, and he greeted me with his usual hearty manner.

'Hello, old boy! It's grand to see you again. Wish I could have come down before, but this cussed war keeps me so *feahf'lly* busy. Never realized in the old days that serious farming took up so much time; still, we must all do what we can, eh?'

Helmuth was standing in the doorway, looking like a benevolent Bishop. I had feared that I might have considerable trouble getting rid of him; but not a bit of it. With a smile, he said: 'I'm sure you would like to have a talk with your uncle alone, so I will leave you now.' And off he went. I heard his footsteps echoing on the stone stairs, so I am quite sure that he did not linger to listen through the keyhole to what I had to say about him.

Meanwhile Uncle Paul was saying how Julia had sent me her fondest love, and that when he had shown her my letter she had wanted to come too; but that he hadn't let her because last week she was in bed for several days with a nasty go of summer 'flu and, although she is up again now, he didn't think she was really fit enough to make such a tiring journey.

In view of the way I meant to deal with my uncle, I was by no means sorry that she had not come; but I was a bit perturbed by the apparent indifference with which Helmuth had left us on our own, and debarred himself from the possibility of butting in on us at a critical juncture. It argued enormous self-confidence on his part, or else that he had already anticipated me and fixed Uncle Paul over lunch. So, after we had exchanged platitudes for a bit, I sought to test the situation by saying:

'I don't know if Helmuth has mentioned it to you, Uncle, but he and I haven't been on awfully good terms lately.'

'I say, old boy!' I'm *feahf'lly* sorry to hear that.' Uncle Paul looked a shade uncomfortable, but he had not answered my question, so I persisted:

'He and I hold distinctly different views as to the state of my health; and I was wondering if by any chance he had suggested to you that the injury to my spine might now be having an unfortunate effect on my brain?'

Uncle Paul looked really uncomfortable at that, and began to shuffle his large feet about, as he replied: 'To tell you the truth, old man, he did say something to that effect. Nothing definite, you know; but just that recently you seemed to be getting some rather potty ideas into your head. If I'd taken what he said seriously I'd have been damn' worried–*feahf'lly* upset. But I didn't; and anyone with half an eye can see that you're as fit as a two-year-old.'

'Thanks, Uncle,' I said quietly. 'I'm glad you feel that, because one of the reasons why I asked you to come down was to make a request which you may think rather unreasonable. I know it will sound to you like an invalid's whim, and one that is going to cause quite a lot of needless trouble; but I have given the matter very careful consideration and I am absolutely set on it. I don't like being here at Llanferdrack, and I want you to make immediate arrangements for my removal.'

Evidently Helmuth had briefed him on that one, as he produced all the arguments against it that Helmuth had used to me. I let him ramble on for a couple of minutes, then I said:

'All right, let's leave that for a minute, while I put to you another idea. You will consider this one much more startling, but I have excellent reasons for making my request. I want you to sack Helmuth.'

His pale blue eyes fairly popped out of his head. 'Sack Helmuth!' he repeated. 'My dear old boy, you can't be serious. I mean, what's he done?'

'What he's done,' I said, 'is to make himself a sort of Himmler, so far as I am concerned. He has got this bee in his bonnet that I am going nuts, so he is now treating me as if I were an escaped Borstal boy of fifteen. And I won't bloody well have it! Do you know that during the past month or more he has had the impertinence to stop all my letters to Julia?'

He nodded. 'Yes, he told me that. He was afraid it would upset us if we knew that–well, you know what I mean. Got the idea that you were going gaga, or something.'

'Look, Uncle.' I caught his glance and held it. 'I am as sane as ever I was; but if I *were* going gaga who are the first people who ought to be informed of that?'

'Myself and Julia,' he admitted a bit sheepishly.

'Right, then,' I cracked in. 'Helmuth has exceeded his duties and abused his position. I am now making a formal request to you as my Guardian that you should sack him.'

'But I can't, old man. It just isn't on, you know. With the best will in the world I couldn't do that. You seem to forget that he is a Trustee.'

'What about it?' I retorted. 'In just over a fortnight I shall attain my majority. On June the twentieth the Board of Trustees will cease to have any further function. The whole outfit has to cash in to me, then it goes up in smoke. It is you, Uncle, who seem to have forgotten that.'

He gave me an unhappy glance from beneath his red eyebrows. 'Of course, Toby old boy, I quite see what you mean. But, all the same, after all these years we can't just kick Helmuth out. It wouldn't be playing the game.'

My tone was acid as I remarked: 'After nearly a year as a helpless cripple, I am no longer interested in games. Helmuth is endeavouring to keep me here against my will, and I am not going to stand for it. I want to leave Llanferdrack, and leave at the earliest possible moment.'

'But hang it, old chap! We've just been into that and you couldn't be better situated than you are here as long as there is a war on.'

Feeling that I had now got to make him face up to the issue, I said firmly: 'That is beside the point. I want to get out, and I'm going to get out. If you're afraid to sack Helmuth leave it to me, and I'll do it myself in a fortnight's time. But either he goes, or you take me with you when you leave. Now, what about it?'

For a moment he sat in miserable silence, then he muttered: 'Toby, this isn't like you. I'm really beginning to be afraid that there is something in what Helmuth said, and that you're no longer quite all right in the upper story.'

I hadn't wanted to discuss the implications of that idea with him, as if Helmuth does succeed in getting me into a loopy-bin I may never get out; but Helmuth may have already put that possibility into his head, so on second thoughts I decided that it would be best to put all the cards on the table, and bluff for all I was worth that I was completely confident that even if I was certified I would manage to regain my freedom later. I gave him a calm, steady smile, and threw the cat among the pigeons.

'You known perfectly well, Uncle, that you have never talked to a saner man that I am at this moment. Since Helmuth has given you the idea that I am going nuts, there is something else I've got to tell you. It is my considered opinion that for criminal ends he has been deliberately trying to create that impression.'

'Oh, come, old man! That's a frightful thing to say about a chap. After all, he is one of us—even if he is a Czech. And why in the world should he?'

'Because he wants to keep his hold over me. You know as well as I do that he and Iswick are virtually running the Board of Trustees at the moment. If it could be shown that I am unfitted to take over, they would go on running it. And that's what they want. That might benefit certain innocent parties too, Uncle; such as yourself—but only for a time.'

'What the hell are you driving at?' he protested.

I shrugged, and put up my big bluff. 'Simply this. If Helmuth could get me certified you, as well as he, would continue to enjoy the directors' fees and other perks that you get from being a Trustee. But, clever as Helmuth is, he could not succeed in stalling me out of my inheritance indefinitely. Sooner or later the doctors are going to agree that I am fit to handle my affairs. Once that happens the balloon goes up. I'll be Jugg of Juggernauts and all the rest of the caboodle. For those who have stood by me nothing will be too good, but God help anyone who has lent Helmuth a hand, either actively or passively, to play his dirty game.'

I felt the time had come to be really tough; so after a moment's pause I went on: 'One way and another you've been jolly decent to me, Uncle Paul, and I'm very grateful to you; but you haven't been ill-rewarded for giving me a home. The Trustees agreed that I should be brought up in the sort of surroundings I should have enjoyed if my father had still been alive. Queensclere and Kensington Palace Gardens were kept on, and you were allowed twenty thousand a year to maintain them as a suitable background for me. I couldn't have cost you much more than a twentieth of that, and the rest was yours to play around with as you liked.

'For thirteen years you have lived like a Prince on my money. You have had your hunters, your racing-stable, your shooting, and trips to Deauville and the South of France whenever you felt that way inclined. I don't grudge you one moment of the fun you've had. All I wish to know this afternoon is if you wish it to go on?'

He stared at me, his mouth, under his brushed-up Guard's moustache, a little agape. Then he stammered: 'Is—is this what you meant when you asked me to come down to see you about—about future financial arrangements?'

'That's it, Uncle,' I said. 'Until quite recently I have always had it in mind that, when I come of age, I would make a settlement to ensure that you and Julia should have everything in reason that you wanted for the rest of your lives. I'd still like to do that; but I'm in a spot. You may think some of my present views a little eccentric, but you know darned well that I am not insane. If anyone has gone a bit haywire it is Helmuth. But you have got to side with either him or me. I am appealing to you now as my legal Guardian; and if you do as I wish you are going to be in clover; not for a few months only but for good and all.

'If you prefer to shelve your responsibility and leave me in his hands, one fine morning you are going to wake up to find yourself stark naked in the breeze. Because from the moment I *do* get control of the Jugg millions you are going to be right back where you were thirteen years ago; and, as God is my witness, you shall never see another penny of them.'

I suppose it was pretty brutal, and I could never have put it so bluntly if Julia had been with him. Afterwards, I felt an awful cad about it, but not at the time; and it had a most curious effect on him. He hunched his shoulders and almost cowered away from me, as though he was a dog that I had been giving a beating. Then, when I'd done, he gave a slight shudder, and sighed:

'You mean that, Toby, don't you? Perhaps old Albert Abel was right to leave you the Jugg Empire, lock, stock and barrel, although you were only a kid. Perhaps, even then, he sensed that you had something of himself in you and would make a go of it. I believe you will, too, if you're ever able to get about again. Anyway he was right about me. There was too much money for me to have gambled it all away; but cads like Iswick would have had the breeches off me within a couple of years. They won't off you, though. When you were speaking just now it might have been your grandfather browbeating some wretched competitor into selling out. I had no idea you could be so hard.'

'I'm not being hard,' I countered. 'I'm only being logical. I'm up against it, and I'm simply using such weapons as I possess; that's all. I know you're frightened of Helmuth; everybody is; that's why I have to go the limit to get you on my side; otherwise I would never have put it the way I did.'

He nodded. 'I see your point, old man. Lot in it, too. Mind, I don't believe for a minute that you're right about Helmuth. He honestly thinks you've gone a bit queer, and that the fewer people who get to know about it the better. As he has been stopping your letters, and you couldn't let us know how you felt about wanting to leave Llanferdrack, I suppose there's quite a case for your having tried to escape on your own. But that nice young nurse of yours tells me that you've created merry hell here more than once, and used the most *feahf'l* language.'

'True enough,' I admitted. 'And wouldn't you, if you were treated like a prisoner? I'm not even allowed in the garden now; and look at this room. Can you possibly imagine anything more like a cell in the Bastille?'

'I could get Helmuth to alter all that,' he offered, a little more cheerfully, 'but as you say yourself, he's a tough proposition. I'm afraid it would take a greater nerve than I've got to sack him. Even if that were justified, which I don't think it is. And as the Trustees placed you in his care, I don't at all like the idea of telling him that I've made other plans for you.'

'You are going to, though; aren't you?' I insisted, striving to keep the anxiety out of my voice. 'Getting him to ease up the prison routine is not enough. I am relying on you to get me out of his clutches at once, and for good.'

'Yes, old man. I quite see that.' He stood up and, thrusting his hands into his trouser pockets, began to pace agitatedly back and forth, evidently wondering how best he could set about the unpleasant task I had forced upon him. After a few turns, he stopped in his tracks and faced me:

'Look here, Toby, I can't tackle Helmuth alone. He's too fast for me. In any argument over you he'd win in a canter. You know that. You must give me a day or two to get a bit of help for the job.'

'What sort of help?' I asked suspiciously.

'Well, if I called a meeting of the Trustees, exclusive of Helmuth, and they—'

'No good,' I cut him short. 'It would take at least a week to get them together. I can't wait that long.'

'All right, old man, all right. But I could have a word with one or two of them and get their backing. Iswick and Roberts are both still in London. Besides, I simply must talk to Julia about it. She'll be *feahf'lly* upset, as she has always taken such a good view of Helmuth. But she's much cleverer than I am, and once she realizes that you're dead set on being moved she'll think of some way of doing the trick neatly.'

I saw that if I forced him to act there and then he would only make a mess of things, so with considerable reluctance I said:

'Very well then. But the best I can do is to give you forty-eight hours. I hate to put it this way, Uncle, but I really did mean all I said a little while back. So, for your own sake as well as mine, don't let Iswick, or anyone, argue you round into doing nothing. I'm pretty well at the end of my tether, and if you haven't got me away from here by the weekend I shall consider that you have deliberately let me down. Is that clear?'

'Yes, old man.' Uncle Paul nodded vigorously. 'You've made it as plain as a pike-staff. Not giving me much time to work in, though, are you? I'd meant to stay here the night; but since you're in such a desperate hurry, perhaps I'd better travel back to London this evening.'

'I think that would be an excellent idea,' I agreed. 'As a matter of fact I meant to suggest it; because as things are I think it would be a very bad thing for you to spend the evening with Helmuth. Seeing that it's a fine afternoon, he is almost certain to be out at this hour; so if you telephone for a car at once you may be able to get away without even seeing him. Anyway, I'm sure you'd be well advised to avoid a long session with him tonight. He's a persuasive devil, and drinking a couple of bottles of Cockburns '12 with him after dinner might cost you a five-figure income.'

He laughed, a little weakly. 'By gad, Toby, you've got a darned unpleasant sense of humour; but it's just like your grandfather's.'

'I wasn't being funny,' I said quietly.

After that we said goodbye, and he hurried off to order a car, and get his things repacked while waiting for it.

An hour and a half later Helmuth came in. He gave me a searching look and said: 'What's happened to your uncle? Why did he rush off like that?'

'How would I know?' I replied with a bland smile. 'He said something about not being able to stay the night because he had urgent business in London.'

A cat-like grin spread over Helmuth's face and he gave a sudden sardonic laugh. 'If you think that your Uncle Paul is capable of removing you from my care, you are making a big mistake. Kill or cure, I mean to see this matter through; and you still have a lot to learn about my powers for asserting my will.' Then he turned on his heel and marched out of the room.

In spite of what he said, there was something in his manner which told me that he was both annoyed, and a little rattled, at Uncle Paul having side-stepped him. And I am pretty confident that I have really scared my uncle into taking action. So, although I'm very far from being out of the wood, I feel tonight that I can at least see a ray of daylight.

Friday, 5th June

I have solved the mystery of the footsteps. Doing so shook me to the core. I break out into a muck sweat when I recall the terror that engulfed me as a result of my curiosity overcoming my fears.

It was the knowledge that the odds are now on my being out of here before the weekend is over that had restored my nerve and tempted me into opening this Pandora's box. When I heard those steps on the stairs again last night at the usual hour, I plucked up all my courage and rapped with my knuckles sharply on the wainscoting behind the head of my bed.

The steps halted for a moment, then went on. I rapped again. They halted again; then there came a weird creaking sound.

It is now seven nights since the moon was full, so tomorrow she will be passing into her last quarter. The light she gives is already nowhere near as bright as it was. It does no more than make the grating stand out as a luminous patch in the middle of the wall, and dilute the darkness with a faint greyness. I could barely discern the outline of my bedside table and the wall beyond it was a solid patch of blackness until, as the creaking sounded, it was split by a long, thin ribbon of light.

I held my breath and my heart began to thump. I wished to God that I had let sleeping dogs lie, but by then it was too late to do anything except curse myself for a fool.

A bony hand suddenly emerged from the strip of light. I saw it plainly. I cowered back. My teeth clenched in an instinctive effort to check the scream that rose to my throat.

It was a small hand; but the fingers were very long and the knuckles very pronounced. It seemed to claw at the nearest edge of the lighted strip. The creaking recommenced. The strip of light widened. I realized then that a panel in the wainscoting was being forced back. I wondered frantically what frightful thing I had so wantonly summoned to me. Something, I knew, was about to emerge from behind the panel into the room. Was the hand human or the limb from some ghastly, satanic entity, that has its origin in the Pit?

I was so overcome with fear as to what I might see next that I shut my eyes. The creaking ceased and was followed by a rustling sound. Then there was a faint clatter and a shuffling on the floor, only a yard from my bed. My eyes started open and I saw a vague grey figure leaning forward to peer at me. I shrunk away; thrusting out my hands to protect myself and moaning with terror.

Suddenly the figure laughed—a high-pitched, unnatural, eerie cackle. The sound seemed to turn my blood to water. Then its voice came—brittle but human, with a child-like treble note:

'Why, it's Toby Jugg. What are you doing up here?'

With a gasp of ineffable relief, I realized that this midnight visitor was only my poor, old, half-witted Great-aunt Sarah; and that the outer wall of the Castle must contain a secret stairway that she uses for some purpose of her own each night.

'God, what a fright you gave me!' I exclaimed, with a semi-hysterical laugh. Then I levered myself up in the bed with my hands, till I was sitting propped against the pillows, to get a better look at her.

She had left her candle on the steps behind the opening of the panel through which she had come. By its light I could see now that she was wrapped in a long pale-blue dressing-gown, the skirts of which trailed on the floor. Her scant hair hung in grey wisps about her thin face, and her eyes gleamed with a bright, feverish light. As I took in the macabre figure that she cut I felt that I had no reason to be ashamed of the panic with which I had been seized at the first glimpse of her. Despite the fact that she entirely lacked the aura of Evil that had made my flesh creep with the coming of the Shadow, she was infinitely nearer to the ghost of tradition, and am sure that on coming face to face with such an apparition at dead of night plenty of people far braver than I am would have lost their nerve.

Picking up her candlestick and holding the light aloft, so that she could see me better, she repeated in her shrill treble: 'What are you doing up here, Toby Jugg?'

Since my arrival at Llanferdrack I had seen her only about half-a-dozen times with her companion, in the garden; and, although I had exchanged a few words with the latter, she had never spoken to me herself, so I was surprised that she even knew who I was. Evidently the old girl was not entirely gaga, and as I wanted to find out what she was up to, I said as gently as I could:

'Dr Lisický had me moved up here a few days ago, Aunt Sarah. I'm living here now. You don't mind that, do you? But what are you doing? Why do you go down those stairs every night at eleven o'clock?'

'To dig my tunnel,' she replied at once. Then a sudden look of fear came into her eyes and she clapped a skinny hand over her mouth, like a child who realizes that it has inadvertently let out a secret.

'Why are you digging a tunnel?' I asked quietly.

'You won't tell—you won't tell! Please, Toby Jugg, please! Nettie must never know. She would stop me. He's waiting for me there. I am his only hope. You won't tell Nettie—please, please!' Her words came tumbling out in a spate of apprehension. By 'Nettie' I guessed that she meant her old sourpuss of a companion, Miss Nettelfold.

'I wouldn't dream of telling anyone,' I assured her. 'But now you've told me about the tunnel there is no reason why you shouldn't share the rest of your secret with me, is there? Where does your tunnel go to; and who is 'he'?'

'Why, he is Lancelot, of course.' Her eyes widened with surprise at my ignorance. 'Surely you know that she is keeping him a prisoner there, at the bottom of the lake?'

Bit by bit I got the whole story of the strange fancies that for many years have obsessed the poor old madwoman's brain.

The bare facts I already knew. When she was a girl of twenty she fell in love with the last Lord Llanferdrack, and he with her. She was many years younger than her only brother—my grandfather—so although he was not then the multi-millionaire that he afterwards became, he had already amassed a considerable fortune. Nevertheless, the Llanferdracks were a proud feudal family, and the young lord's mother was most averse to his marrying the sister of a jumped-up Yorkshire industrialist, so there was considerable opposition to the match.

All this happened well over forty years ago, and in Queen Victoria's time young people were kept on a pretty tight rein; so for a while the lovers had great difficulty in even meeting in secret, and every possible pressure was put on young Lancelot Llanferdrack to make him give Great-aunt Sarah up. Probably it was that opposition which made them madder than ever about one another. Anyhow, they wouldn't give in, and eventually Albert Abel took matters in hand. He came down here to see old Lady Llanferdrack and, somehow, succeeded in fixing matters for his sister. The engagement was formally announced, and little Sarah Jugg was asked down to meet her fiancé's family in the ancestral home.

She had been here only a few days when the most appalling tragedy occurred. They were out in a punt on the lake and Lancelot was fishing. He missed his footing and went in head down. It seems that he must have got caught in the weeds at the bottom of that first plunge, for he never came up. He simply disappeared before her eyes. The lake is very deep in parts and they never recovered his body.

The shock turned her brain. Against all reason she insisted that he would come up sooner or later, and that she must remain near the lake until he did. All efforts to persuade her to leave the district were in vain; and eventually Albert Abel bought the Castle from Lady Llanferdrack, so that poor Great-aunt Sarah could have her wish and live by the lake for the rest of her days.

That is where fact ends and the strange weaving of her own imagination begins. Perhaps her fiancé's name having been Lancelot is the basis of the fancies that years of brooding over her tragedy have built up in her mind; or it may be that local tradition has it that this lake in the Welsh mountains is the original one of the Arthurian legend.

In any case, she believes that the Lady of the Lake lives in it and, being jealous of her, snatched Lancelot from her arms. She is convinced that he is still alive, but a prisoner at the bottom of the lake, and that her mission is to rescue him. This apparently can be done only by digging a tunnel, over half a mile long, through the foundations of the Castle and right out to beneath the dead centre of the lake; then Lancelot will do a little digging on his own account, and having made a hole in its bottom over her tunnel, will escape through it to live with her happily ever after.

I asked her how far she still had to go, what the tunnel was like, and various other questions. It seems that it is only large enough to crawl through, and that she shores it up as she goes along with odd bits of floorboard and roofing that she collects from some of the rooms in the Castle that have been allowed to fall into ruin.

But progress is slow, and she does not get far enough to need a new roof-prop more than about once in six weeks. It was the wizard Merlin who put her on to this idea for rescuing her lover, and he told her that the whole thing would prove a flop if she used a tool of any kind, or even a bit of stick, to dig with, and that each night she must take every scrap of dirt she removes out under her clothes; so it is a kind of labour of Hercules, and the poor thing is doing the whole job with her bare hands.

Merlin also put another snag in it. He said that she must not arouse the Lady of the Lake's suspicions by digging straight towards the centre of the lake; instead the tunnel must go the whole length of the chapel, then out as far as the bridge and, only there, turn in towards its final objective. On four occasions too, while burrowing alongside the chapel, she came up against impenetrable walls of stone in the foundations, and after years of wasted work had to start again practically from the beginning.

That has worried her a lot, as she is a bit uncertain now in which direction she really is going; but she thinks it is all right, as she can hear Lancelot's voice calling to her and encouraging her more clearly than she could a few years ago. He is being very good and patient about the long delay in getting him out, and he must certainly be a knight *sans peur et sans reproche*, as he still refuses even to kiss the hand of the black-haired Circe who has made him her captive—in spite of the fact that she comes and waggles herself at him nightly. At least, that's what he tells Great-aunt Sarah, and who am I to disbelieve him?

I should have thought that after the dark enchantress had put in her first twenty years attempting, every evening, to vamp Lancelot without success, she would have gone a bit stale on the type, and started looking around for a more responsive beau; but evidently she and my great-aunt are running about neck to neck in this terrific endurance contest.

After talking to the old girl for about half-an-hour I had got the whole pathetic business out of her. By then she was obviously anxious to get along down to her digging, so I once more promised that I wouldn't give her secret away and, closing the secret panel carefully behind her, she left me.

So far, today has been one of the pleasantest that I have had for a long time. My quadrant of private terrace faces south-south-east, so it gets full sunshine till well past midday, and all the morning I sat out there with Sally. I call Nurse Cardew Sally now, as she says she prefers it.

After we had been out there a little while she asked me if I thought it would be terribly unprofessional if she sunbathed; and I said 'Of course not'; so she went in and changed into a frightfully fetching bathing dress—white satin with no back and darned little front—which she said she had bought in Antibes the summer before the war. She is a Junoesque wench, and it would take a man of my size to pick her up and spank her, but she has one hell of a good figure.

Before I had had a chance to take in this eyeful properly she started in to get my upper things off, and she stripped me to the waist, so that I could sunbathe too. Then she lay down on a rug near my chair and we spent the next two hours talking all sorts of nonsense.

But, of course, the thing that has really made such a difference to my outlook is my talk with Uncle Paul yesterday. I am certain that I scared the pants off him, and convinced him that he will practically be selling matches in the gutter unless he gets me out of this before I am a couple of days older.

Saturday, 6th June

Another lovely morning and more sunbathing with Sally on the terrace. After we had been chatting for a while I asked her if she really and truly believed that I was nuts, and would be prepared to take her oath to that effect in a court of law.

She looked up at me from where she was lying on her rug, and her nice freckled face was intensely serious as she replied:

'I'd hate to do that, but I'm afraid I'd have to, Toby. Of course, you're not out of your mind at all frequently, but very few mental people are all the time. I wouldn't have believed that you were mental at all if I hadn't seen you as you were last week, and known about your quite unreasoned hatred of Dr Lisický.'

'Surely,' I said, controlling my voice as carefully as I could, 'the riots you saw me create downstairs in the library, and after my escape, could easily be accounted for as outbursts of temper, due to the frustration felt by an invalid who believes that an undue restraint is being put upon him?'

She pulled hard on her cigarette. 'But that's just the trouble, Toby. You *imagine* that an undue restraint is being put upon you; but it isn't really so.'

'Are you absolutely convinced of that?'

'Absolutely. There is nothing whatever about the arrangements here, or Dr Lisický's treatment of you, to suggest that you are being persecuted. Yet you think you are. So I'm afraid there is no escaping the fact that you are suffering from a form of persecution mania.'

'All right, then,' I said after a moment. 'Naturally, I don't agree about that; but we'll let it pass. Do you think that my state would justify putting me in an asylum?'

'Oh, please, let's not talk about it,' she begged. 'Tell me about some of the exciting times you had when you were in the R.A.F.'

'No, Sally. I want you to answer my question,' I insisted.

'Well then,' she said in rather a small voice, 'if you must know, I think it might. That is, if these bouts of yours continue. You see, nearly all lunacy is periodic, and yours seems to take the classic form, in which the subject is affected by the moon. Dr Lisický says that you are perfectly normal during the rest of the month, but suffer from these outbreaks whenever the moon is near full. This last time you raved, used the most filthy language–which I am sure you would never do in front of me when you are your real self–wept and became violent.'

'And that,' I cut in, bitterly, 'is just what mad people do, isn't it?'

She nodded. 'I'm afraid it is. So you see, if you go on getting these attacks every month, it may become necessary to put you under restraint while they last. But that would be only for a few days each time, of course. And *please* don't worry yourself about it, because that sort of mental trouble is perfectly curable, and I'm sure that you'll be quite all right again in a few months.'

'Thanks, Sally,' I said. 'I'm very grateful to you for being honest with me. Now we'll talk of shoes and ships and sealing-wax, of cabbages and kings–or of anything else that you like'; and we did for the rest of the morning.

All the same, I am damnably disturbed by what she said. She may admire Helmuth, but I am positive that she is not under his thumb to the extent of deliberately deceiving me on his instructions. She was speaking from her own convictions, and with considerable reluctance. I am certain of that, and it has given me furiously to think.

Of course she knows nothing of the huge financial interests that are involved in this question of my sanity or madness; and she knows nothing about the Horror–which is the prime cause of my outbursts. But did I *really* see that Shadow or did I only think I did, owing to my mind having become subject to the malefic influence of the moon?

I can't help wishing now that I had never raised the matter with Sally and forced her to answer my questions.

Monday, 8th June

This journal has served an admirable purpose. Keeping it has helped to distract my thoughts from my anxieties for many hours during the past five weeks, but to continue it further is now pointless; so I am making this last entry simply to round it off neatly.

Some day, when I am quite well again–mentally I mean–I may read it through with interest and, I think, astonishment at the extraordinary thoughts that have recently agitated my poor mind; so it is worth the trouble of giving it a proper ending.

During the past forty-eight hours a lot has happened. Just before tea-time on Saturday Uncle Paul returned, as he had promised, and he brought Julia with him. They had tea with me; over it they told me that they had already had a talk with Helmuth, and that he had said that he would not raise the slightest objection to their taking me away with them. He was sorry that I wished to remove myself from his care, and considered that I should be very ill-advised to do so, but if I decided to take that course I was perfectly free to go when and where I liked.

Naturally, at the time, I thought he was putting on a hypocritical act, to cover as best he could his inability to defy the Trustees openly. But I was greatly relieved to think that the matter was already settled and that I had in the end achieved my victory with so little trouble.

After tea Uncle Paul left Julia and I together, and we settled down to a real heart-to-heart.

She was looking as lovely as ever, and it seems impossible to believe that she is thirty-three. She has hardly changed at all since she reached the height of her beauty, and I don't think a stranger would take her for more than twenty-six, or -seven. When I was a little boy I never understood why the angels in the Scripture books that Nanny Trotter used to read to me were invariably portrayed as fair; and after I first saw Julia I always used to think of her as my dark-angel.

Her big eyes and her hair—which she has always worn in her own style, smoothly curling to her shoulders—are as black as night, and her flawless skin has the matt whiteness of magnolia petals. She might well have sat as the model for a Madonna by one of the old masters, and perhaps one of her Colonna ancestresses did when the Italian school of painting was at its height. The only unsaintly thing about her is the exceptional fullness of her red lips. That makes her beauty rather startling, but even more subtly devastating, as it gives her a warm, human touch.

She began by reproaching me very gently for the way I had treated Uncle Paul. She said that I should have known that he would at once take all possible steps to safeguard my happiness, without my threatening to reduce him to penury. And that I must have known that would mean poverty for her too; so, after all we had been to one another, how could I even contemplate such a mean and ruthless act against two people who had given me their love?

I felt terribly guilty and embarrassed, but I tried to explain the dire necessity I had been under to get myself removed from Llanferdrack at all costs; and I began to tell her about the Horror.

After a bit she said: 'Please, darling, don't harass yourself further by reviving these horrid memories. I know all about it already. Helmuth gave me your letters—the ones he stopped because he didn't want me to have fits about you—before I came upstairs. I read them all, and I have them here.' Upon which she produced them from her bag.

'Then, if you know that part of the story,' I said quickly, 'you must understand how imperative I felt it to get away.'

She nodded, but a sad look came into her eyes. 'I do understand, darling. You must have been through a terrible time. But the thing that worries us all so much is that there has never been any suggestion before that this place is haunted; and we are afraid that you would have seen—or thought you saw—this terrifying apparition, during the periods of the full moon, if you had been with us at Queensclere, or anywhere else.'

'Then you don't believe that I really saw anything at all?' I challenged her.

'I wouldn't say that,' she replied thoughtfully. 'Helmuth does not believe in the Supernatural, but I do. I've never seen an apparition myself, but I am certain that the 'burglar' that you saw when we were down at Kew was one. Perhaps you are more psychic than I am, and so more receptive to such influences.'

'I've never regarded myself as a psychic type,' I admitted. 'But you remember that business of the Abbot's grave at Weylands. After that horrible experience I described my sensations to you, and I had exactly the same feelings of cold, repulsion and stark terror down in the library here.'

'That could have been caused by a recurrence in your memory of the Weylands affair.' She took out a cigarette. I lit it for her, and she went on:

'I'll tell you what makes me doubt if you really did see anything. When Helmuth and your nurse were telling us all about it, before I came up, they described the night just a week ago when you started bawling barrack-room choruses at the top of your voice, and they ran into your room. You pointed wildly to the bottom of the blackout curtain and yelled: 'Look! Look! Do you call that an hallucination?' But neither of them saw anything; and I should have thought one or other of them would have, had there been anything to see.'

'Perhaps neither of them is psychic,' I argued a little weakly.

'That might be the explanation,' she shrugged, 'but I don't think so. I have been at séances where trumpets and tambourines have floated in the air, and others where the medium has emitted large quantities of electoplasm; and it is not just one or two people who see such manifestations, but the whole audience—and sometimes some of them are convinced sceptics before the séance starts.'

For quite a time we argued round the matter. She pointed out that although Great-aunt Sarah and Miss Nettelfold had lived here for a lifetime, no complaint had ever been made by them to the Trustees that Llanferdrack had a family horror which periodically gave trouble; and that although servants were usually the first to get the wind up about such things, none of the staff here had ever given notice on the grounds that the place had a bad atmosphere.

So, eventually, I was forced to agree that such evidence as we had to go on all pointed to the Shadow having no existence outside my imagination.

About seven o'clock Julia left me to go and change; but she said that she would have her dinner sent up on a tray with mine, so that we could dine together.

I think most beautiful women look their best in evening-dress, and although Julia is a sight to gladden the heart in anything, she is certainly of the type whose proper setting is satin and pearls rather than tweeds. She looked absolutely ravishing.

We had a couple of cocktails apiece, split a bottle of Burgundy and rounded things off with some Kümmel. By the time we had finished I was feeling so good that I was almost resigned to the thought that I had gone a bit mental—provided I could get away from Llanferdrack, and there was a decent hope of my being cured pretty quickly. But I was still of the opinion that Helmuth's conduct needed a lot of explaining, and when Konrad had carried away our dinner trays I started in on the subject.

We went into the whole business piece by piece: the letters, the blackout curtains, my telephone extension; the refusal to leave me my lamp, or get me a torch, or move my radio; or let me have more than one sleeping tablet; Helmuth's arbitrary treatment of Taffy, his stopping me from getting into the train and, finally, his virtually making me a prisoner in this old part of the Castle.

Looked at in retrospect, I must honestly confess that there was really very little to it all, if one once accepts the following premiss:

(1) That shortly after my arrival here Helmuth began to suspect that my injury and eight months in hospital had, to some degree, affected the balance of my mind.

(2) That he at once began to keep me under observation and opened my mail as part of the process.

(3) That, on finding his fears confirmed, he considered it his duty to my relations to save them from worry, and his duty to myself to take all possible steps to prevent the knowledge leaking out and prejudicing my future.

(4) That he hoped the rest and a regular routine would put me right, and decided that nothing must be done which would encourage me to believe that I was suffering from anything worse than nightmares.

The above is the gist of how he had put it to Julia, and as she passed it on to me. After thrashing the matter out we fell silent for a bit; then she suddenly said:

'Besides, what possible motive could he have for adopting such an extraordinary attitude towards you? I mean, trying to make things worse for you instead of better, as you still seem to half-suspect?'

I was surprised that Uncle Paul had said nothing to her about my theory that there was a conspiracy to drive me insane; but perhaps he had thought it too far-fetched to mention. I told her my ideas on that and her eyes widened in amazement as she listened.

'But Toby!' she exclaimed at last. 'How *could* you think such base thoughts of a man who has given some of the best years of his life to developing your mind and character? This is the first time that I have ever been ashamed of you.'

'Oh, come!' I protested a bit uncomfortably. 'After all, he was damn' well paid for what he did.'

She shook her head. 'One can't pay for care and affection with money, darling. Perhaps, though, I am being a little hard on you. To talk to, you are so perfectly normal that I forget about your not being quite well in your mind. It is only when you produce ideas like that of turning Paul and myself out into the street, or this one that Helmuth wants to lock you up and rob you, that I suddenly realize how right he is about your no longer being your real self.'

'All the same,' I argued, 'you must admit that the Trustees would stand to gain if a Board of Lunacy ruled that I was unfitted to inherit.'

'Not sufficiently to provide a motive for them to enter into a criminal conspiracy,' she countered. 'You seem to forget that most of them are immensely rich already. Paul, of course, is an exception, but he knows as well as I do that if you come into your money you will make a most generous provision for him; and Smith and Roberts don't stand to lose anything, because they are professional advisers and would go on drawing their fees just the same, whatever happens.'

'That still leaves Iswick and Helmuth.'

She laughed. 'Really, Toby darling, you're being too silly. We may all look on Harry Iswick as an awful little bounder, but he is as clever as a cart-load of monkeys. In the past ten years he has made a fortune on his own account, and his interest in the Jugg combine is only a side-line with him now. I know that for a fact. As for Helmuth, surely you see that he has much more to lose than to gain from your being put in a home. Big business isn't really his line of country, so it is unlikely that he would be able to improve his position much by continuing as a Trustee. Whereas, with you in possession of your millions, he would have every right to expect you to find a suitable use for his abilities, at a handsome remuneration, in recognition of all he has done for you in the past. I give you my word, sweet, that this conspiracy idea is absolutely fantastic.'

There seemed no answer to her arguments, and reviewing them again, now that I no longer have her glowing presence before me, I still don't think there is. But accepting them brought me face to face with the question of Helmuth, and I asked her what she thought I ought to do about him.

'Sleep on it, darling,' she advised me, 'and see how you feel about it in the morning. If you find that you really cannot rid yourself of this awful prejudice that you have built up in your mind against him, I think it would be better to let sleeping dogs lie. Later, perhaps, you will feel differently; then you can let him know how sorry you are that you suspected him so unjustly. But he is terribly fond of you, and must be feeling very hurt at the moment.

'So if all that I have said has convinced you that you are in the wrong, the generous thing would be for you to let me bring him up to you tomorrow. You needn't eat humble pie, or be embarrassed about it; but just say that you realize now that you have not been quite yourself lately, and have given him a lot of unnecessary trouble. That's quite enough. He'll understand; and I am sure it would please him a lot to know that you bear him no ill-will before you leave here.'

It was late when she left me, but I lay awake thinking about it a long time after she had gone. I came to the conclusion that in many respects Helmuth had shown very poor psychology in his treatment of me, and that the arbitrary way in which he had handled matters was enough to make anyone who was slightly mental develop a persecution complex, but that my conspiracy idea was the wildest nonsense, and that there was not one atom of proof to show that he had not acted throughout in what he *believed to be* my best interests.

In consequence, on Sunday morning I told Julia that I would like to see Helmuth, and later we had a grand reconciliation on my sunny terrace.

For such entertaining as my grandfather had to do, he bought anything that was going cheap in the City, in big parcels of forty or fifty cases at a time; so the cellar he left was not distinguished for either its variety or quality. But in the past thirteen years Uncle Paul has spared no pains to make up for those deficiencies, and soon after the war broke out he had a large part of the Queensclere and London cellars moved down here as a precaution against their being blitzed. So for us to celebrate he was able to order up a magnum of Krug, Private Cuée 1926, and I don't think I have ever tasted better champagne in my life.

Everything went off remarkably easily. I said my piece and Helmuth met me more than half-way. He admitted that many of his acts must have seemed high-handed and even tyrannical, but he had been dominated by the one thought of preventing it from leaking out that I had become mental.

As he explained, it is just like a man going bankrupt; however unlucky he may have been, and even if he pays up one pound in the pound afterwards and gets an honourable discharge, it always prejudices his future commercial undertakings. So with mental trouble, the effect would be little short of disastrous to me as the head of the Jugg enterprises if it ever became known that I had once suffered from hallucinations.

He went on to say that he had moved me from downstairs only with the greatest reluctance, because he was most loth to give the servants grounds for talk; but that after my attempts to get away he had felt that to do so was the lesser evil. And that when he had decided to move me he had chosen this room because it was one of those furthest removed from the servants' quarters, so they were less likely to hear me if further attacks led to a renewal of my singing and shouting. He added, too, that he found it a considerable inconvenience to be deprived of Konrad's services, but he knew that the fellow could be trusted not to blab, so he had willingly given him up to me, rather than risk letting a new man, who might later prove untrustworthy, into our secret.

We went on then to discuss what should be done with me. Julia said that she would willingly have me at Queensclere; but the difficulty about that is that the house is occupied by the Army, and she and Uncle Paul have been allowed to retain only what amounts to a flat of half-a-dozen rooms on the first floor. So, apart from the question of air-raids, and the business of getting me down to a shelter—which they insisted would have to be done if I went there—in the event of my having further attacks it would be practically impossible to prevent the officers who are billeted in the house from learning about my condition.

Kensington Palace Gardens is out, because it has now been taken over to provide additional accommodation for the Soviet Embassy; so, of my own properties, that left only the little house on Mull. And if I were put into a nursing-home it is a certainly that the secret of my affliction would get out.

I suggested that a small house should be bought for me in Devonshire or Cornwall, but they all seemed to think that it would be practically impossible to find anything suitable at the present time, as every available property in the 'safe' areas had been taken over to house evacuees; and even if we could find one it raises the problem of who is going to run it and look after me.

Of course, the same thing applies to Mull, but eventually Helmuth offered to throw up his work here and take me up there. That was very decent of him, and it seemed a possible solution for the next few months. But it would be far from attractive as a permanency, as to have to winter there would be incredibly depressing and grim; and even during the summer we would have none of the good things, such as the garden produce, that we enjoy down here. Still, it seemed the best thing we could think of when lunch-time came, so they left me think it over.

When they joined me again about three o'clock, Julia put it to me that, since I was now reconciled to Helmuth, did I really still feel so strongly about leaving Llanferdrack? She pointed out that, so far, I had been subject to attacks only while down in the library, and that now I had been moved I might not be afflicted with them any more. The advantages of Llanferdrack over Mull needed no stressing, and my acceptance of Helmuth's offer would mean sabotaging much of the fine war-effort that he has built up here during the past two-and-a-half years. Therefore, didn't I think that I could bring myself to stay on here for a time at least—anyhow until the next full-moon period—and if it transpired that the attacks did recur, then I could always be removed at once.

Actually, while I had been eating my lunch, I had been thinking on much the same lines myself; so I agreed.

We went into the question of my birthday and it was decided that, in present circumstances, it would not be a good thing to have the Trustees down here on the 20th. If Iswick, Roberts and the rest got the least suspicion that I was not quite normal they might consider it their duty to have me examined by a committee of brain specialists before agreeing to hand over.

In consequence Uncle Paul is going to inform the others that I hope to be fit enough to make a short visit to London in the latter part of July; so I have suggested that the whole business—presents and everything—shall be put off for a month, as it will be much more convenient for them to meet me there.

It was agreed, too, that I should remain in this room; partly for the original reason that Helmuth put me here, and partly because there is no other—except the library, downstairs, which is at all suitable. Actually, this big chamber with its vaulted roof is not without its attractions. Even in summer it would ordinarily be a bit chilly, but every afternoon a fire is lit for me in the great open fireplace, and in the evenings its glow on the wainscoting and old stone makes the place rather cosy.

And I have come to love my little private terrace with its view over the lake. The only real snag is that it would require too much effort to get me to the nearest bathroom every evening; so I have to have my tub in an old-fashioned hip-bath, for which Konrad has to boil up large kettles of water on the open fire. But, after all, the types who occupied this room for hundreds of years managed quite well that way; and lots of our chaps in the Western Desert, and elsewhere, are not lucky enough to get a bath at all.

Julia and Uncle Paul returned to London this morning, and Helmuth went with them, just for the night, as he has to attend a Board Meeting of one of the Companies tomorrow. Before they left we had a final chat, and Helmuth promised that as soon as the moon begins to wax again he will come in to me every night, round about midnight, to see that I am all right. If I am not, he will make arrangements to take me up to Mull as soon as possible, and, in the meantime, he will help me to fight my trouble.

He is a tower of strength, and I have been terribly unjust to him. He was absolutely right to keep me here and showed his true fondness for me in doing so. Only here am I really safe from prying eyes and whispering tongues. Here we can keep the secret of my miserable affliction safely concealed until I am well again.

We all feel now, though, that the change of room may do the trick. Regaining confidence in Helmuth has helped me enormously to regain it in myself, and I do not believe that there is the least danger of my becoming a mental case permanently. Therefore I am able to end this journal on an optimistic note; and, now that I really do know where I stand, there is no point in continuing it further.

·

Wednesday, 10th June

Here I am again. The fact is that I have become so used to setting down my private thoughts that yesterday, during the time I usually devote to these jottings, I felt quite at a loose end. I felt the same way this morning, until it occurred to me that it was the height of stupidity to stop doing anything that helped me to while away my time pleasantly, merely because the occupation in itself had ceased to have any serious purpose. Moreover, having got that far I realized that I have something of considerable interest to record.

Helmuth did not get back from his trip to London until just before dinner last night; soon afterwards he came in to see me. He is usually rather restless when making casual conversation, but on this occasion he settled himself down in a way that showed he had something serious to say; then, after a bit, he started off more or less as follows:

'Now that we are friends again, Toby, we can talk freely together, just as we used to in the past. I have been wanting to have a heart-to-heart with you ever since you arrived here; but at first I didn't want to rush matters, and later I was afraid you might not feel like discussing your future plans with me. I am naturally deeply interested to know what they are. When you come into your inheritance, do you intend to assume control of the Companies, as far as your health permits, or will you continue to let other people handle matters for you?'

'I shall assume control,' I replied with a smile. 'At least, I hope so. After all the time and trouble you have given to educating me for the job I'd be a pretty poor specimen if I let you down to the extent of not even attempting to tackle it.'

He nodded. 'I'm glad you feel like that. I was afraid that your time in the Air Force might have altered your outlook. Since you are still prepared to take on this enormous responsibility it is doubly tragic that your health is likely to prove such a heavy handicap.'

'This new trouble may,' I agreed. 'But before that started I saw no reason why the injury to my spine should prevent me using my brain; so I had been toying with the idea of having a special motor-ambulance-caravan fitted out, in which to tour the factories. It would probably take me the best part of a year to get a real grip of things, and I had no intention of throwing my weight about to start with; but after a tour like that I should have picked up enough of the practical side to argue the pros and cons of the broader issues with my co-directors.'

Helmuth nodded his white head again. 'That sounds an admirable scheme. You will have to continue to observe your rest hours, and be careful not to overdo it until your back is a bit stronger; but if all goes well in the other matter, I see no reason why you should not start on a tour of that kind in the autumn. It would certainly prove a most popular move with all your employees, and, as you say, give much more weight to your opinions when you decide to give vent to them at Board Meetings. Yes, I congratulate you on that idea, Toby.'

'Thanks,' I said, and after a moment he went on:

'All the same, I wonder if you fully realize what you will be up against. However tactfully you set to work, most of these middle-aged and elderly industrialists who are running your Companies at the present time are not going to take at all kindly to a young man of twenty-one walking in and insisting on changes in old-established policies.'

'I hope that in most cases that will not be necessary.'

'My dear Toby; if it is not you will have put yourself to a great deal of trouble for nothing. The whole object of a new broom is to sweep clean. With your intelligence you are bound to spot all sorts of effort-wasting, obsolete practices, incompetent executives and unnecessary wastages to which the others have become blind through seeing them go on for years. If you do not initiate reforms to abolish these weaknesses you will be letting yourself down as well as your shareholders, and never become a great leader of industry.'

'I suppose you are right,' I said thoughtfully. 'If that does prove the case, I shall certainly introduce reforms and endeavour to overcome any opposition that I may meet with.'

'It will take a lot of overcoming. Most of these men have had to fight hard to attain their present positions, and they will have an instinctive prejudice against your youth and inexperience. Those who are uncertain of themselves will combine against you, from fear that you may think them not up to their jobs and get rid of them; while others, who are of stronger mettle, will do their utmost to dominate you and climb on your back to greater power.'

'You paint a gloomy picture,' I remarked. 'It looks as if instead of being able to devote most of my time to making my Companies more prosperous I shall have to spend it defending myself from the jealousy and intrigues of my co-directors.'

'I think you will—anyhow, to start with,' he said frankly. 'But, if you will let me, I can help you to overcome a great deal of such opposition.'

Naturally, I thought he was suggesting that I should make him my private adviser; and evidently he guessed what I was thinking, as he waved aside my murmur of thanks, and said quietly:

'If, later on, you find any use for my personal services I will give them gladly; but that was not what I had in mind. I expect you remember hearing about the Brotherhood when you were at Weylands?'

At that my ears fairly pricked with interest. 'Rather! It was the great mystery of the place, and we all used to speculate on what went on at those meetings in the crypt of the old Abbey. It was a Masonic Lodge of the Grand Orient, wasn't it?'

'No. A number of its members are also Freemasons who had been initiated on the Continent; so we use that Grand Orient story as cover; ours is a much older fellowship. The main reason why I tried to prevent you joining the R.A.F. was because I did not want you to miss initiation; but by running away you stymied me over that. However, it is not too late, and membership of the Brotherhood could be of immense value to you in your business life; so if you are agreeable, I propose to start preparing you for initiation now.'

'How thrilling!' I exclaimed. 'Do tell me about it. What is the object of the assocation, and what should I have to do?'

'It is a Brotherhood, based on the old principle that Union is Strength. Each member contributes to it according to his means and receives from it according to his needs.'

I laughed. 'That sounds rather like Socialism to me. As I am exceptionally rich it looks as if I should be expected to make a contribution out of all proportion to anything I was likely to get back.'

'It *is* Socialism, but on the highest plane. You need have no fears that your millions will be scattered to the masses.'

'My millions!' I echoed, raising an eyebrow at his joke.

He shrugged. 'Even if it cost you your whole fortune you would still be the gainer on balance. That may sound a tall statement, Toby; but in due course I believe you'll agree with me.'

'I'll be better able to form an opinion when I know more about it,' I said, with a grin. 'If the rumours which used to circulate at Weylands had any truth in them, the Brotherhood consists of a considerable number of people all of whom possess wealth, influence or brains; and are pledged to help one another. Is that a fact?'

As he nodded assent, I went on: 'I can fully appreciate that membership of such a fraternity must be extremely valuable; and I see now why you think it would prove a big asset to me in dealing with my fellow industrialists; but obviously there is a limit to what such secret assistance in one's dealings would be worth.'

'Why should there be?' he asked quite seriously. 'You are an immensely rich man. Your grandfather left in trust for you assets to the value of over fourteen million sterling. If that had happened half-a-century ago, by the reinvestment of the bulk of the income at cumulative interest during your minority, by now you would be worth something like thirty millions.

'But time marches on; owing to your grandfather's death not having occurred till nineteen-twenty-nine, income- and super-tax had already risen to such heights that in the past thirteen years the Trustees have been able to add only a beggarly million-and-three-quarters to your original capital. Since the war the situation of people in the top income groups has deteriorated still further. By the time it ends you will be lucky if you are allowed to keep sixpence in the pound of what your money earns. So what will your fortune be worth to you then?'

I did a quick calculation. 'In Government stocks it would bring me in only about ten thousand a year, but in my own companies it should produce at least double that. And you forget the Directors' Fees that I should draw; they would easily amount to a further twenty thousand.'

It was Helmuth's turn to grin. 'My dear Toby, Directors' Fees are taxable, and twenty thousand sixpences come to only five hundred pounds. On your own showing your net income would barely exceed twenty thousand a year, all told. You already allow your uncle that figure to keep up Queensclere and the London house, and I gather you have now promised that he shall lose nothing by your assuming control of your own money. Actually, of course, your tax-free allowances for business expenses will save you from having to give up cocktails and cigarettes; but the sooner you disabuse yourself of the idea that the possession of millions still endows their owner with almost limitless spending power, the better.'

'You have shaken me quite a bit,' I confessed. 'I have been out of touch with all this sort of thing for so long that I had no idea that the picture had become so black for the working rich. Still, however high they raise income- and super-tax, a fortune is always a fortune; and, although Grandpapa Jugg might turn in his grave, I could sell out capital to ante-up my income. Even if I live to be a hundred and spent twenty thousand a year from capital for the next eighty years, that would consume less than the million-and-three-quarters that has piled up during my minority. So I should still be able to leave my heirs the original fourteen million.'

Helmuth threw back his massive head and roared with laughter: 'Toby, Toby; did you think of nothing but Hurricanes and Heinkels while you were in the R.A.F. and in hospital? Time marches on, I tell you. If you do live to be a hundred, it is most unlikely that you will have fourteen thousand—let alone million—left to leave anybody; and if you have your heirs will be lucky if the government of the day permits them to keep more than one thousand of it.'

I smiled a little ruefully. 'Of course I know that death duties have been going up for years; and that even now they would cut the Jugg millions in half. But do you really think that in another fifty years or so there will be practically nothing left of them?'

'Indeed I do. By that time all public services and every form of industry will be State-owned: and it is highly probable that private ownership of land, houses and investments will have been abolished. But you won't have to wait that long before the bulk of your fortune is taken from you.'

I said that I thought, myself, all the odds were on the Socialists coming to power soon after the war; but that most of their leaders were sensible enough to realize the danger of throwing the nation's economy out of gear by doing anything too drastic. Helmuth shrugged and replied:

'They will be moderate to start with, but as is always the case when the Left gets into the saddle, the masses expect a Silver Age–if not a Golden one–to dawn before very long. That gives the extremists a rod with which to beat the moderates. They will never be able to raise enough money by ordinary means to propitiate the Labour electorate, by carrying out all the Socialist conceptions; but it can be taken from those who have it.

'The wiser men will realize that it is suicidal to seize a large part of the wealth, which for generations has financed the nation's commerce and industry, and fritter it away in unproductive channels; but they will be forced to it. They will introduce some form of Capital Levy. And then, my dear Toby, what of your fine fortune?'

'That would be killing the Goose that lays the Golden Eggs,' I said, 'because if they do, it is inevitable that they will skim the top off the cream. Say they introduced legislation to collect a hundred million, the great bulk of that would come from people like myself who might be paying anything up to nineteen-and-sixpence in the pound in taxes already. That means that the following year there would be the equivalent number of nineteen-and-sixpences less to go into the exchequer. And not for one year only, but for good. It is far worse than anticipating taxes; it is destroying the source from which they come. We couldn't continue to pay on what we no longer had; so they would have to introduce new taxation affecting the lower-income groups to make up the deficit. It would be a crazy policy, even from their own point of view, because sooner or later the masses themselves would be left holding the baby.'

'Of course,' Helmuth agreed. 'But political extremists are never statesmen, otherwise they would not be extremist. Such people allow their hatred of the rich to dominate every other consideration. And it would be done in gradual stages. That is the insidious part about it. As you say, they will go for the big fish first; and if you are forced to realize only half your holdings to pay up, very few people are going to think that you have been hardly done by.

'No one will squeal until some of their own savings are seized to pay the dole. You are right too about the drop in income and surtax receipts having to be made up from somewhere, but there is a limit to what can be got by normal means; so with each successive Budget the level at which the thrifty will be robbed of their savings will go down and down, until even the little man with his few hundreds tucked away in the Post Office will find himself caught.'

He paused for a moment, then went on: 'As for yourself, having paid the first time will not exonerate you from having to pay up the second, third and fourth. So, my poor friend, I fear you will find your rosy dream of being able to spend twenty thousand a year of your capital turning out to be moonshine, long before you are my age. It won't be there any longer for you to realize.'

It was a black future that he conjured up, but I had to admit to myself that his grim prognostications were based on a perfectly possible and logical sequence of events. For a bit we remained silent, then I said:

'Well, if you are right, I'll be in a pretty mess. But I suppose the State will take care of cripples?'

'Oh yes,' he smiled cynically. 'You'll get your keep in an institution and a pound a week. You might do quite a lot better, though, if you are prepared to follow my advice. All I have been endeavouring to show you is, that if you decide to play a lone hand your millions may be reduced to hundreds by the time you are forty.'

'Do you think, then, that by becoming one of the Brotherhood I could save them?'

'No, Toby; I don't think that. But I am confident that whatever loss of fortune may overtake anyone else—and even themselves, individually, as far as the possession of shares, property and bank-balances go—the members of the Brotherhood will continue to enjoy comparative affluence, and even luxury to such a degree as it is obtainable, in a world where all but a very few will live on a miserable pittance as little cogs in the machinery of a vast slave State.'

'How would they manage to do that?' I enquired.

'There must always be rulers,' he said quietly; 'and we shall be the rulers of the Britain of tomorrow. The bulk of the upper classes are bound to be submerged, because they have no unity. But we shall survive, because we are bound together by an indissoluble bond, pledged to help one another to the limit, and holding all our assets in common. We already have men in all sorts of key positions, both here and abroad. Our level of intelligence is far higher than that of any ordinary group of professional politicians, and we have resources that such people do not possess. The attainment of power in all its forms is the object of our association, and that having been our special study ever since our foundation you may rest assured that you will be shown how to attain it to—if you decide to join us.'

'I don't quite understand,' I said. 'One can study all sorts of subjects, a knowledge of which is valuable for attaining one's ends; but I shouldn't have thought that there could be any royal road to attaining power, as such.'

'Oh yes, there is,' he smiled, as he stood up, 'and at our next chat I will tell you something about it. But I must go now, as I have some letters to write. In the meantime, you might think over what I have said.'

I did think it over, and the whole thing's extremely intriguing; but I am far from certain that I would care to become involved in this Secret Society of his.

Of course, when he said that about my whole fortune not being too big a price to pay for membership, he could not have been speaking seriously. All the same it sounds as if from anyone as rich as myself they would expect the hell of a big cheque.

If Helmuth is right in his contention that when the Socialists do get in, after a time, the extremists will dominate the moderates, and introduce a series of Capital Levies which will eventually swallow up all private investments, great and small, it would certainly be worth my while to go into this thing as a form of insurance—even if they did stick me for a hundred thousand pounds. Plenty of people used to pay that much in my grandfather's day for a title, and I shouldn't miss it.

But the thing that I don't like about it is this pooling of interests business. That is all very well in its way, but they might want me to do all sorts of things that I should not care about. Helmuth more or less inferred that in exchange for their help one became subject to some form of control by them. If that is the case, I would rather stand on my own feet and keep my freedom.

As I have decided to continue this journal, I may as well record a rather revealing conversation that I had with Sally this morning.

Some reference had been made to my weekend visitors, and I asked her if she did not think Julia one of the loveliest people she had ever seen.

'I didn't think her all that,' she replied. 'I suppose when she was young she must have been rather a popper. But that's the worst of these Mediterranean types; they always age early.'

'Oh, come!' I protested. 'You talk as though she was middle-aged already.'

She shrugged. 'Well, it all depends on what you call middle-aged. I bet she'll never see thirty again.'

'She won't,' I agreed. 'But that's just the point, she doesn't look it.'

'Not to a man perhaps. Any woman who has enough money to dress a shade eccentrically, and go to a first-class beauty specialist for regular treatments, can pull the wool over a man's eyes about her age; but she can't deceive her own sex.'

I resisted the temptation to tell Sally that, however much money she had, no beauty specialist would ever succeed in turning her into a real lovely, and that I very much doubted if she would ever acquire the clothes sense to become even tolerably smart. But as I was thinking on those lines, she added with a laugh:

'Anyone could see that you think your aunt is tops. I suppose she sold you the idea that she is in the Mona Lisa class when you were in your cradle, and you have never got over it.'

I feel sure that normally Sally is not given to making catty remarks; so it was easy to guess which way the wind is blowing. Julia and Helmuth are such very old friends, that the gallantry with which he always treats her is accepted as a habit by all who know them. But Sally would not realize that, and seeing them together has made her jealous.

I knew she admired Helmuth, but evidently the handsome doctor has made a deeper impression on her than I realized. She was probably hoping that he would ask her to dine with him again over the weekend; and Julia being here put her nose completely out of joint.

Actually it is over a week now since the only occasion on which Helmuth asked her to dine. As he has not repeated the invitation it looks as if he found her too unsophisticated for his taste, and is not going to bother with her further.

On the other hand, his having turned the battery of his charm on her for just one evening and since treated her only with friendly politeness is well calculated to keep her guessing, and so predispose her to go half-way to meet him should he choose to make another move. He is up to all those tricks, and that may be the game he is playing.

I hope not, for if he does make a real set at her it is a sure thing that she will get the raw end of the deal. Of course, now that Helmuth and I are good friends again, I have nothing to lose if they do have an affair and she falls completely under his spell; but I can't help having a sort of protective feeling about her. God knows, I couldn't protect anyone from anything, as things are, but Helmuth has never made any secret to me of his attitude towards women, and I would hate to think of Sally becoming the plaything of a cynical roué.

Thursday, 11th June

I am profoundly disturbed. That is putting it mildly. I had another long talk with Helmuth yesterday evening and he told me a lot more about the Weylands Brotherhood. In view of the importance of this conversation I shall strive for the utmost accuracy in recording it.

As soon as he had settled himself comfortably in front of the fire, I said: 'Last night you were saying that there is a royal road to acquiring power. I'd be terribly interested to hear about it.'

'So you've thought things over and are inclined to regard my proposition favourably, eh?'

As I was curious to learn more, I saw no point in denying that, so I let it pass, and he went on:

'I am glad for both our sakes; and if what I said last night intrigued you, I am sure that what I have to say now will intrigue you to an infinitely greater degree. Power is the thing that men have craved more than any other, all through the ages. Now tell me, what would you say were the four most powerful forces in the world?'

I thought for a moment, then said: 'Faith, Love, Hunger and Money.'

'Wrong,' he declared. 'They are the Elements—Air, Earth, Fire and Water. If you can control those you can do anything.'

I nodded. 'I suppose Science is gradually succeeding in that. Gas and electricity are forms of fire; we harness rivers and the tides; and the Back-room boys of the R.A.F. are tackling the problem of dispersing fog.'

'Oh, Science plods along'; his tone was faintly contemptuous, 'but all those types of control require elaborate machinery to operate them. I was referring to the control of the elements by the human will.'

He saw my puzzled look, and added: 'For example, Jesus Christ *walked* upon the water.'

Never before had I heard him mention Christ's name except in connection with some sneer; and I said in surprise: 'But I thought you didn't believe in Him?'

'As a God, I don't,' came the quick reply, 'but there is no reason to doubt that he was an historic Personage, and that he had "power". However, there are innumerable other examples of the sort of thing I mean. There are well-authenticated accounts of Indian Fakirs who have mastered the art of levitation; that is, defeating gravity by remaining suspended in mid-air. The witch-doctors of the North American Indians could walk on red-hot embers without burning the soles of their feet. The juju-men of Africa can bring rain when it suits their purpose.'

'Do you seriously mean that the members of the Brotherhood can perform such extraordinary feats?'

'Some of us can. But each feat requires long and exhausting training and, after all, what point is there in devoting years to learning such tricks? They are really childish, and have no practical value except to impress the vulgar; and we are not interested in attempting to attract the multitude. Most of us prefer to devote our energies to more subtle tasks, and use the special powers that we acquire in support of our worldly activities. If you think for a moment what that means, in conjunction with brains, wealth and influence, you will be able to appreciate, far better than you could yesterday, that not only will the Brotherhood survive the general destruction of the upper classes in this country, but eventually dominate it.'

'All this is so staggering,' I murmured, 'that you must forgive me if I haven't quite gripped it yet. Accepting what you say about the Brotherhood's powers to perform miracles, I still don't see how they can be applied to further your ends in modern political and commercial life.'

'Don't you!' he laughed. 'Then I'll give you a few examples. You have already stumbled on the fringe of the matter yourself by using hypnotism to impose your will on people. You didn't get far with Taffy, but for an amateur you were amazingly successful with Deb. Properly trained you could use it with considerable effect on many of your future business associates. The trained will can also read thoughts, and confer good or bad health on the operator's friends or enemies. It can—'

'Could both my mental state and the injury to my spine be cured?' I interrupted. 'That is, if I become a member of the Brotherhood?'

He nodded. 'The first would be simple. That was what I meant when I promised that if the attacks occurred again I would help you to fight them. You need have no further worries on that score. Your spine presents a more difficult problem, because it is a physical injury. If a man has a limb shot off no power, however great, can enable him to grow another in its place. But the will can perform incredible feats of healing; and I am reasonably confident that within a few months we could enable you to walk again.'

'I would give a lot to be able to do that,' I sighed. 'I have often wondered if anything could be done for me by faith-healing.'

'This is much more than that,' he smiled, 'and far more potent, as it brings into play certain ancient laws which are entirely unknown to the ordinary faith-healer. But I was telling you of some of the feats that the human will can perform when properly directed. Quite apart from the use of hypnotism it can put thoughts and impulses into other people's heads. It can attract women and dissipate their moral scruples, so that they surrender without even realizing that they are acting entirely contrary to their original intentions. Given certain aids and great concentration of will one can foresee glimpses of the future.

'By similar means one can also see what is going on through walls or at a distance. That is how I found out that you were preparing to escape with Deb's help, and was able to come down to the hall just as you were leaving. I should have found out that you were about to escape with Taffy, too, if I had had my mental eye on you; but that night I was occupied with other matters. By projecting the will one can influence people through their dreams, and one can also ill-wish them. As a last resort one can even cause them to decline

and die. Those are only some of the weapons possessed by the members of
the Brotherhood; and it is prepared to use them all in order to overcome such
opposition as it encounters.'

I was silent for a moment; my brain whirling with the appalling thoughts
he had conjured up. At length I said:

'Hypnotism, faith-healing, thought-reading and other mental processes
where the operator imposes his will face to face with the subject, are
recognized by the medical world and explainable by the direct human
contact that takes place. But to see what is happening at a distance, to
influence people's dreams, to be able to ill-wish them and send them death,
are surely powers which can be acquired only through God or the Devil.'

He shrugged. 'That is an old-fashioned way of putting it.'

'Perhaps it is,' I muttered. But you don't deny it; although you have
always told me that you do not believe in either.'

'One may reject the teaching of the Bible, yet accept the fact that forces
outside this world govern everything in it.'

Suddenly Helmuth stood up; his tawny eyes gleamed with a strange light
and his foreign accent became more marked as he went on:

'The secret of willing down power, or, if you prefer it, setting great
supernatural forces in motion on one's own behalf, has been known to the
initiate from time immemorial. Generation by generation it has been handed
down, and today this priceless knowledge is the greatest asset of the
Brotherhood. To become an initiate one must take the oath of obedience,
subscribe to certain tenets of faith and master various complicated rituals.
Those rituals are the jealously guarded secret of the chosen few; but, once
you have become adept at them, you can operate the forces which we term
Supernatural, because they are beyond all normal experience; and, through
them, achieve your ambitions and desires. Such power is infinitely greater
than any that wealth alone can bring, and in the name of the Brotherhood I
offer it to you.'

I collected my wits as quickly as I could, and said: 'To become one of such
a gifted company would be a great honour; anybody could see that. But the
whole thing is so astonishing—so extraordinary—so,well, so utterly fantastic
by all ordinary standards, that I am still very much at sea.'

He grinned at me. 'Yes. It is hardly surprising that you should feel a bit
bowled over on first learning the magnitude of the powers that the
Brotherhood possesses. But now that you know the truth about it, if there
are any questions you want to ask, fire away.'

Controlling my voice with an effort, I replied: 'You have already answered
the one that interests me most: that about the possibilities of getting back my
health. But there is one other thing I would like to know. To put it bluntly,
what is it going to cost for me to become a member?'

'I thought I told you yesterday.' He raised the well-marked dark eyebrows
that contrast so strangely with his mane of white hair. 'In that way it is the
same as joining a Religious Order. You would make over to the Brotherhood
everything you possess. But there the resemblance ends; because the fact
that you had done so would always be kept secret, and you would not be
required to take a vow of poverty; so for all practical purposes you would
continue in the full enjoyment of your fortune.'

'Isn't that a bit too much to ask?' I protested rather meekly. 'I mean, there
can't be many new initiates who have more than a few thousand to make

over; so why should the Brotherhood require the whole of the Jugg millions to accept me?'

With a wave of his hand he brushed the question aside. 'My dear Toby! The amount that an initiate can contribute in worldly wealth does not enter into the matter. Some who have practically nothing of a cash value to offer are accepted on account of their intelligence, or the promise they show in some other direction. You cannot expect an exception to be made for you in the rules of a foundation that has existed unchanged for countless centuries. It could not be considered even if you were the King of England.'

'I see,' I said still very humbly. 'I only enquired because of my grandfather.'

'What has he to do with it?' Helmuth frowned.

I endeavoured to look as worried as I could. 'He made all this money; and he went to extraordinary lengths to leave his fortune to me intact—even to spending a considerable portion of his income during the latter part of his life in insuring against death-duties. In view of that I am wondering if I really have the right to part with the control of it.'

Helmuth took the scruple I had raised quite seriously. 'I see your point,' he said. 'But I am sure that, on consideration, you will feel that he would approve your surrendering the lesser power that his wealth can give you for the greater power that has now been placed within your grasp. Anyhow, the last thing I would wish is to influence you into doing anything against your conscience. There is no immediate hurry. Think it over, and we'll talk about it again tomorrow.'

So I succeeded in stalling him without arousing his suspicions. To fight for a little time seemed the only possible line that I could take. Had I refused point blank I would not even have gained these few hours to prepare myself to face a renewal of his hostility. But at last the naked truth is out. Helmuth *is* a Satanist.

Friday, 12th June

Yesterday was, I think, the blackest of the many black days that have fallen to my wretched lot since I arrived at Llanferdrack. After I had written out the conversation I had with Helmuth the previous night—as near word for word as I could remember it—I spent practically the whole of the rest of the day turning over in my mind the terrible implications of his admissions about the Brotherhood.

Actually, except for what little sleep I got, I had been doing that ever since hehe left me; but as the day wore on my speculations plumbed ever grimmer depths. However, to record them would be pointless, as I have since seen Helmuth again, and he has come out into the open.

He came up here soon after tea, and Sally was still with me; so for about ten minutes the conversation was general. She remarked that although there must be thousands of books in the library she could not find a thing worth reading there. Upon which he laughed, told her about how old Albert Abel I had brought them for so much the yard, then added:

'But I have plenty of good modern books in my study. You had better dine with me again one evening; we'll go through them afterwards and you can see which you would like to borrow. My evenings are rather fully occupied at present, as I am getting out some special figures in connection with the estate; but how about Sunday?'

Sally accepted with obvious pleasure. Shortly afterwards she left us, and while her high heels were still echoing on the stone stairs Helmuth grinned across at me.

'What a splendid specimen of the female *Homo sapiens*; and what an interesting contrast to Deborah Kain! Such a simple, healthy young animal is certain to possess all the normal urges, but it will be amusing to see how deeply they are overlaid by middle-class inhibitions.'

I did not reply. I've done my best to warn Sally, and if she still persists in sticking out her neck, that is her affair. I had far too much reason for acute anxiety on my own account to give it further thought at the moment; and, anyway, there was nothing I could do about it.

'Your mind is obviously on graver issues,' he remarked. 'What decision have you reached as a result of our talk yesterday?'

I took the only line I had been able to think of, and said as tactfully as I could that, while I greatly appreciated all he wished to do for me, I could not square it with my conscience to hand over my grandfather's fortune to anyone.

He stood up, thrust his hands in his pockets and began to pace up and down. Without inviting any comment from me he went on talking for a long time, and this is what he said:

'You are being very foolish, Toby; and I don't think that you can have yet fully appreciated your position.

'According to the last vetting by your doctors you are likely to remain a helpless cripple for a long time to come, if not for life. Added to which you have recently developed mental trouble, of which I will speak later. I have offered you a very good chance of being able to walk again within the next few months, and a definite cessation of what we will term your "hallucinations". Moreover, I have shown you that in ten or fifteen years at the most everything points to a Socialist Government depriving you of all but a fraction of your millions, and I have suggested a means by which, in spite of that, you may continue to enjoy all the benefits of wealth. Yet you pigheadedly refuse to accept my proposal.

'Now, I should like you to understand one thing clearly. No man can serve two masters; and I do not regard you as my master. My whole allegiance is given to the Brotherhood and all it stands for. I had hoped that while serving them I might also help you. But since you will not see reason I must proceed to carry out the project that I have in mind; even though it will result in what virtually amounts to your destruction.

'This project is no new idea conceived within the last few weeks. It was considered and approved by the Brotherhood many years ago while you were still a small boy; shortly after you came to Weylands. It was decided that, as soon as you came of age, the great fortune which is still being held in Trust for you must come under the Brotherhood's control; and I was selected to carry out the plan to secure it. That is why I have devoted so much of my life to you.

'By running away from Weylands and joining the R.A.F. you temporarily upset our calculations; because had you not done that you would have been initiated on leaving, at the end of nineteen-thirty-nine. Like all our other scholars, life at the school had prepared you to accept initiation without question. Your mind had been conditioned to do so by the elimination of all moral scruples and primitive taboos. You would have thought the ancient mysteries fascinating, the rituals exciting, and the whole conception a perfect outlet for your abilities and ambitions. Had things panned out according to our original plan you would have been a member of the Brotherhood for two-and-a-half years now; and on the twentieth of this month you would have handed over your fortune without the least hesitation or regret. But Fate decreed otherwise.

'If it had not been for your being shot down when you were we might have had some difficulty in getting you into our hands again; but, even if I had not succeeded in doing so, I think you may take it as certain that some of your old school friends would have appeared upon the scene, and sooner or later manoeuvred you into a position from which you would have found no escape but to join us.

'As things are, your crash brought you back to me with three clear months in which to work upon you before you attained your majority; so it turns out in the end that not a day will be lost in the Brotherhood assuming control of your money.

'When you arrived here, it did not take me long to see that life in the R.A.F. had undone a great part of the work that had been put in upon you during your school years. Many of the petty little ideals and outworn shibboleths of your brother officers had proved contagious. It would have taken years to argue you out of all of them, even if that had proved possible at all now that your mind has attained maturity and no longer has the plastic quality of youth. So I had to adopt other measures.

'You have no doubt heard the expression "conditioning" as applied to the Gestapo's treatment of prisoners from whom they wish to extract confessions, and so on. I am told that they plunge them into baths of ice-cold water, and tap their muscles gently for an hour or two each day with rubber truncheons. Well, during April and May, although the methods I employed were not of a violent nature, I have been conditioning you.'

'You filthy bastard!' I burst out; but he ignored me and went on:

'The object of the "conditioning" was, of course, to create a situation, and to bring you to a frame of mind, in which you would agree to sign certain papers on your birthday, and accept initiation into the Brotherhood as soon as that can be arranged.'

My temper snapped, and I shouted: 'I'll do neither! I'll be damned if I'll make my money over to a lot of Devil-worshipping crooks!'

He smiled sardonically. 'You may beg to be allowed to before I am through with you. But by then it may be too late. Your state may be such that the Brotherhood would no longer consider it desirable to have you as a member.'

'Then you'd have cut off your nose to spite your face,' I retorted, 'for in that case they wouldn't get my money.'

'Oh yes, they would!' His smile broadened to a grin. 'At least, they would be able to control the use to which it is put; and that is really all they wish to do. It is to your *mental* state that I was referring, and if it had deteriorated to that degree you would be judged unfit to inherit. The Board of Trustees would then continue to administer your affairs; and it would not take me very long so to arrange matters that the Board's future decisions were in accordance with the wishes of the Brotherhood.'

Except that Helmuth would be acting as an agent, instead of on his own account, it was the very thing I had been fearing all through the latter half of May and early June. Yet, even so, it seemed as though a trap had suddenly snapped to behind me, when I heard it actually put into words. I swore at him again; but, once more, he ignored me, and launched out on another steady spate of words.

'You must not imagine that we abandoned our project just because you had run away to the Air Force; or that I remained idle about the matter all the time you were in it. Since I managed to get myself appointed as a Trustee in the autumn of nineteen-thirty-nine I have spent thousands of hours going into your affairs, and I now know more about them than any man living. It was important that I should acquire this knowledge, because it will be my role to advise the Brotherhood on the Jugg Companies; and, if you have the sense to abandon your present attitude, give you their instructions regarding the policy they wish you to pursue. But it has also enabled me to make a personal assessment of each of my co-Trustees, and prepare the way for disposing of those we do not wish to retain, so that the Board can be re-created with all its members our willing servants.

'Rootham and Bartorship are now in the Services, so we do not have to worry about them for the moment. Embledon and Smith are almost moribund, and no longer attend meetings. That leaves your uncle, Iswick, Roberts and myself.

'Your uncle will do what I tell him. Iswick is both ambitious and unscrupulous, but he is an extremely able financier, so I wish to retain his services. At the right moment he will be offered membership of the Brotherhood. Unless I am much mistaken he will jump at it. Should he not, I know enough about his financial dealings to put him in prison, so he will be compelled to play ball with me.

'Having secured him as my ally I shall tackle Roberts. It may surprise you to hear it, but that dried-up old stick of an accountant is keeping a young woman in a flat in Maida Vale, and although he must be every day of sixty-eight, she has recently had a child by him. I feel sure he would not like his family and his fellow church-wardens at Berkhamsted to know that, and will much prefer to resign, having first put forward a resolution himself that for one member of his firm to have a seat on the Board will in future be considered sufficient. A member of the Brotherhood will be elected in his place.

'Next I shall deal with Embledon and Smith. Both will be asked to resign on account of their advanced age. If either or both refuse, appropriate steps will be taken. It is laid down in the Trust that should any Trustee fail to attend meetings for six consecutive months he thereby automatically forfeits his Trusteeship.

'At present both of them stagger up to London twice a year to fulfil this minimum requirement. However, a quite simple ritual, performed by myself, will be sufficient to ensure such a rapid deterioration in the health of these recalcitrant gentlemen that they will be compelled to exceed the limit. No excuses will be accepted, and that will be that. They will be replaced by two further members of the Brotherhood; and I shall then govern six seats out of eight.

'There remain Rootham and Bartorship. Both have been granted a special dispensation from attendance at meetings for the duration of the war; and I think the war will go on for quite a long time yet. By the time they do eventually return, my position will be impregnable; but I think, all the same, that they will both have to go. It could be arranged for Bartorship's firm to have been found negligent in some matter; and if six Trustees demand a change of Accountants to the Trust, he will have no option but to retire.

'Brigadier Rootham presents the most difficult problem, because he still has copies of all our papers sent to him, and I don't think he will like some of the transactions upon which we shall enter. He is an intelligent and determined man, so it is probable that he will come back spoiling for trouble. If he does he will be signing his own death-warrant. A Chapter of the Brotherhood will have to perform a more serious ritual, to bring about his liquidation before he has a chance to ask too many awkward questions.'

I listened to this programme of trickery, blackmail and murder with cold horror. Even in my worst imaginings of Helmuth engineering such a plot, I had counted on Tootham and Bartorship going fully into matters when they got home, and insisting on coming to see me; which would provide a chance for me to secure release from captivity. But he had evidently given the matter more thought than I had, and got the whole set-up taped.

'So you see the situation, Toby,' he went on. 'It will be easier for all concerned if only you will be sensible, and sign the papers that I intend to put before you on your birthday, without further argument. That would save me a lot of time and trouble, you a most unenviable fate, and several of your Trustees a considerable amount of pain and grief. But in the long run whether you do or don't will not make the slightest difference; because the Brotherhood will assume the direction of the Jugg enterprises, anyway. And there is nothing you can do to stop that.

'My "conditioning" of you produced exactly the results I intended. I knew that you would try to get Julia and Paul, and probably some of the other Trustees, down; but I didn't intend to let you succeed in that till I was ready for it. I stopped your letters because I wanted you to get really boiled up and desperate before there was a show-down. I *wanted* you to suspect that I was at the bottom of the trouble, and make all sorts of wild accusations against me that you could not prove. My only concern was that things should not go off at half-cock; in case you kept some card up your sleeve to play later.

'But you didn't. You gambled all out to break my hold on you, and you've gone down for a grand slam. Just as I knew I would be able to, I took every trick in the game. By priming Julia, I manoeuvred you into admitting that you had become mentally unbalanced and that your accusations against myself were groundless; then agreeing to a reconciliation with me. I got you to decide for yourself that you could not do better than to remain in my care, and stay on at Llanferdrack. I even succeeded in scotching the visit that the other Trustees would normally have made here on the twentieth, by securing your consent to your official birthday being put off for a month.

'That will not prevent your inheriting, of course, and any document you sign from the twentieth on will be legally valid. But is has the two-fold object of cutting your last possible lifeline to the outer world, and keeping the Board in being for a further period; so that, never having been dissolved, there will be no necessity to go through a complicated legal procedure to re-create it, should you continue to resist and so compel me to take steps which will result in your being certified as insane.

'If you do as I wish the Board will assemble either here or in London in five weeks' time, and formally hand over to you. If you don't, then you will simply have inherited for a short time without performing any act in connection with your properties; then the Board will learn that you have been pronounced medically unfit to handle your affairs, and automatically reassume control. So you see I've got you either way.

'You can write to Julia or Paul now to your heart's content; or if you like I will have you carried downstairs so that you can rave to them over the telephone. But they won't believe a word you say. They will only think: "Poor old Helmuth; what a time he must be having, trying to keep secret the affliction from which that unfortunate boy is suffering."

'Last weekend you burnt your boats, Toby. You are my prisoner now, as much as if I had you locked up in Brixton Jail. More so, in fact, for you are mine to do as I will with body *and* soul. There is nothing you can do about it, and if you have a grain of wisdom left you will submit with a good grace.

'The choice is still yours. But either you sign the papers that I shall produce on the twentieth, and join the Brotherhood, or I shall have to step up the conditioning process just as the Gestapo do when they have reached the conclusion that a prisoner is of no further use. If you force me to it, I will drive you mad within a month.'

He walked to the door, turned at it, and added: 'I will come for your answer tomorrow night.'

Saturday, 13th June

I have entered on my fight. Helmuth's allusion to the Gestapo was more apt than he knew. In France, Holland, Norway, and lots of other places, there are hundreds of men of the Allied Nations, and women too, who are being put through the mill by those human beasts in black uniforms. Day after day they are appallingly maltreated and made to suffer the most degrading indignities. They have no hope of rescue or reprieve, but they don't give in lightly. Some of them crack before the finish; but many of them stick it out to the bitter end, and carry with them to an unknown grave the secrets that might aid the enemy.

One likes to think that none of us are given more to bear than we can manage to sustain provided that we muster the greatest degree of fortitude of which we are capable; and that then we are overcome by a merciful oblivion. Perhaps it is like drowning, in which people usually come to the surface several times before they sink for good and all. I went under last night; but I've come up again this morning, and I still have a bit of kick left in me. Perhaps, though, that is due to Sally.

Yesterday's entry took me a long time to write; because I wanted to make it as complete and detailed as possible, in order that it may prove the more damning as an indictment of Helmuth if it ever reaches the hands of someone who is prepared to call him to account. When it was done I had not the energy left to set down my reactions, and they were too depressing to be of interest, anyhow.

It is clear beyond all doubt that he is a Satanist, and that when he spoke of 'conditioning' me he was referring to the Thing that menaced me from the courtyard. It *can* only be a manifestation of embodied Evil, that he called up with the deliberate intention of undermining my mental control. And, as he also spoke of performing mysterious rituals with the most monstrous intent, I spent most of the afternoon and evening in abject wretchedness, wondering what further horrors the future held for me.

The one thing that did bring me a ray of comfort, though, was the thought that the operation of his Satanic powers appeared to be dependent on bright moonlight; and we are still in the dark period of the month. The last full moon was on the 30th of May, so the new moon will not rise until the 20th; and, even after that, it will not reach the degree of brightness that I have come to regard as dangerous until several days later.

Alas for my hopes. Late last night they were shattered, in part at least. I had been buoying myself up with the idea that I could count on a minimum of ten clear days before Helmuth would be able to resume his ghastly 'conditioning' of me. God knows, my attempts to escape have so far ended in the most pitiful fiascos, but it is said that 'hope springs eternal in the human breast', and it did in mine, to the extent of desperately searching my mind for a way to make yet another attempt before he could get to work on me in earnest.

I am still doing that, as my belief that I shall not have to face the final crisis until towards the end of the month has been confirmed. But I am not to be given any peaceful respite to plan in; and it is now a question as to if I shall even be able to hang on to my sanity till then, let alone succeed in a last desperate bid to escape. Yesterday evening I waited for Helmuth with mixed feelings of angry defiance and nervous apprehension, but he did not come at his usual time; nor did he come after dinner. Naturally, I could settle to nothing, and those hours seemed to drag interminably. At last Sally and Konrad settled me down for the night and I was left in the dark, still wondering why he had not come for his answer.

At length I dropped into a light sleep, but a little before midnight I was roused by hearing the creak of the hinges on the heavy oak door. And there he was, framed in its entrance, the light from the lamp he was carrying glinting on his mane of white hair and powerful features.

Having closed the door and set the lamp down, he said quietly: 'Well, Toby. What have you decided?'

Gripping the sides of the bed with my hands, I heaved myself up into a sitting position, and replied: 'To put a counter-proposition to you.'

He shook his head. 'I am not interested.'

'I think you will be,' I insisted, 'when you hear what it is. I can quite understand what led you to join the Brotherhood and to work for it all these years. You love power and you are an ambitious man; but no good will come to you through seeking it this way. It is well known that the Devil always lets down his followers in the end. You would do far better to abandon the whole thing and find other channels for your energies. I can enable you to do that. If you will agree to have me sent to Queensclere, and to resign from the Board of Trustees, I will sign a document which we will have legally witnessed, promising to pay you the sum of half a million pounds within one month of my twenty-first birthday.'

With a laugh of contempt he brushed my attempt to bribe him aside. 'Really, my dear Toby, you must take me for a fool. I hold a high position in the Brotherhood, and its interests are identical with mine. Why should I be content with less than a thirtieth part of your fortune when I can have the whole of it for the taking? We need the control of your money to further the great work upon which we are engaged, and we mean to have it. The only question is, will you give it to us and thereby save yourself; or must we go to the trouble of taking it from you and, in the process, turn you from a man into a filthy, grovelling animal?'

'Get back to hell, where you belong!' I shouted at him.

He was careful to keep his distance, in case I grabbed him, pulled him to me, and attempted to strangle him; but he sat down just out of my reach on the end of the bed, and said:

'Since you insist upon it I must teach you a lesson. As you have rightly assumed, the irresistible force which we of the Brotherhood invoke is known to the vulgar as "the Devil"; but much of my personal power is derived through the agency of the moon. You will already have guessed that from your experiences down in the library on bright moonlit nights. If you remain adamant in your decision, I shall have to perform a solemn ritual to Our Lady Astoroth, when the moon is full again towards the end of the month. Once I have invoked her there will be no going back on that. All who have studied the esoteric doctrine agree that her appearance must be terrible beyond belief; for no man who has ever looked upon her face has been able afterwards even to recall his own name.

'But I still hope that extreme measure will not be necessary; and there are many other recourses of the Great Art known to me which do not require the propitiation of the Queen of the Dark Heaven.

'It may interest you to know that just as all Roman Catholics profess a special devotion to either their name-saint or some other, so all members of the Brotherhood place themselves under the protection of one of the Princes who form the entourage of the Ancient of Days. Incidentally, he is so called because he is infinitely older than any of the false gods invented since by man. He existed before Earth was created, and was given it as his Province; so he is the true Lord of This World, and everyone in it owes him allegiance. For countless thousands of years primitive man knew no other Deity, and all the cults which have developed in historic times are heresies.

'Traces of the ancient religion are still clearly to be seen in the fact that all, so called, savage races are divided into tribes, each of which regards itself as related through remote ancestry with one of the Princes of the Satanic hierarchy, and venerates his symbol in the form of a totem. The Wolf, Leopard, Scorpion, Hyena and Serpent are examples of these; and today we who perpetuate the age-old mysteries also associate ourselves with one or other of these powerful entities. My own totem is the Spider.'

I could not suppress a start, and my hands clenched spasmodically. I now knew what it was that had thrown the Shadow. That round body and the six hairy, tentacle-like legs had been those of a spider without a doubt; but a spider the like of which has never been recorded in this world. The big tarantulas of the Amazon were like flies to a bumble bee in comparison with it. Each leg must have measured at least two feet, when fully extended, and its body had been the size of a fish kettle. Leaving aside its supernatural aspect it would have proved a most formidable beast for any man to tackle.

Helmuth smiled as he saw my face whiten. 'My mention of spiders seems to call up disconcerting memories for you. If you tremble and sweat at the thought of a shadow what would you do if you were brought face to face with the Great Spider in the flesh?

'That is what he is, you know; the Great Spider. But I forgot. You would not know that as all non-human forms of life have only group-souls their collective astral is always much bigger than the species it represents. The Great Hound is as big as a horse, and the Great Rat as a panther.

'I will tell you another thing, Toby. If one has materialized an astral and wishes it to solidify, one must nurture it on rotting offal, excrement or blood. Once it has taken sufficient sustenance to form a fleshy body of its own, it can look after itself; but it still needs and seeks food. Spiders are by nature blood-sucking animals and when the Great Spider has assumed material form he would not hesitate to attack a child—or a cripple, Toby—to satiate his lust for blood. What would you do if, one night, I let him into your room?'

I was sweating in earnest now; but I tried to put a bold face on matters, by muttering: 'I'd tear the brute limb from limb with my naked hands; I'd smash it to a pulp.'

He shook his head. 'Oh no you wouldn't. You might try, but you would not succeed. The Great Spider only borrows his coat of flesh. For him it is a fluid substance to which he gives form by his will; and he is indestructible. Your grip could squeeze but not injure his body, and if you tore off one of his legs it would immediately join itself on to him again.'

After pausing to let his horrible conception sink into my mind, Helmuth took a piece of candle from his pocket. It appeared to be made of black wax and was only about two inches long. He placed it in the centre of an ashtray which was well out of my reach, and said:

'I think that one night, before I call upon Our Lady Astoroth to destroy your mind utterly, I must introduce you to the Great Spider. I would not let him kill you, of course, but his embrace might bring you to your senses, or, alternatively, render an invocation to the Moon Goddess unnecessary. But to start with I will perform a minor magic for your edification.

'You will, no doubt, recall the story of the Pied Piper of Hamelin. He piped all the rats out of the city, and then, because the citizens would not pay him the promised fee, he lured away their children. That is not fiction. It is an account of an actual happening in the remote past that has come down to us through folklore. The Piper was a Mage, and one of considerable power, since he was able to entice the children of a whole township from their parents; but what concerns us is that his totem was the Rat, and it was that which enabled him to order the rats to follow him.

'But to return to ourselves. As I have already told you, my totem is the Spider. All spiders of every kind are my little brothers, and they will do my bidding.'

He lit the piece of black candle, and went on: 'This is made out of bear's grease, sulphur, pitch and the fat of a toad. To use such ingredients in making a candle may sound to you the most childish nonsense, but, believe me, it is not. All material substances have astral qualities and when consumed by fire procure certain results owing to immutable laws which govern the relation of the natural to the supernatural. You will probably find the smell somewhat nauseating, but it will burn for some forty minutes and give you enough light to see by. I am now about to leave you. When I get back to my room I intend to send all my little brothers who inhabit the old ruin to pay you a visit. I hope the experience will prove to you that I am not to be trifled with further.'

A moment later he had picked up his lamp and gone. I was quite calm, but as I stared round the room I felt extremely uncomfortable. All he had said had seemed quite logical at the time, but a swift reaction now made me feel that much of it was the product of a distorted brain. It seemed impossible that he really had the power to summon all the spiders in the Castle to plague me; yet I had seen the shadow of the Great Spider, *and felt* the sickening, soul-shaking waves of evil that radiated from it. That vile memory was real enough, and if he could materialize a demon such as that, where lay the limit to his potency for working these hideous miracles?

The candle burned with a steady blue flame, casting long shadows on the walls that reached up to merge into the darkness that still obscured the high, vaulted ceiling. The stench that came from the melting fat was most repulsive, and after a minute or two the fumes of the sulphur made my eyes water and got into my throat, making me cough.

Anxiously, I peered from side to side, watching for the first sign of movement which would indicate that he was succeeding in carrying out his fantastic threat. I gave a swift glance at my bedside clock. The hands stood at fourteen minutes to one; it had been just on twenty to when he left me. Another minute passed; another and another; still nothing happened.

I tried to figure out how long it would take for Helmuth to get back to his room and perform the incantation, then for the spiders to reach me; but two of those three factors were imponderables; so the answer might be anything from ten minutes to half an hour. All the same, I felt that a quarter-of-an-hour should really be enough for him to set moving any spiders that were in my immediate vicinity; and when the minute hand of my clock had passed five to one I began to hope that either he had tried to hypnotize me into seeing what he wished me to see, and failed, or had attempted a ritual which had proved too much for him.

As each additional minute ticked away I grew slightly more optimistic; yet I did not relax my vigilance. Quite automatically I had dropped into the old, familiar, steady head-roll that was part of the drill for a Fighter-Pilot when searching the skies for enemy aircraft. My glance went down to the floor at my left, slowly upwards, across the opposite wall, down to the floor at my right, and back again across the bed. Now and then the beastly sulphur fumes caused me to break the rhythm in a fit of coughing, and each time that happened I looked at the clock. At one minute to one I saw the first spider.

It was a small red one; but there was no mistaking what it was, as it was actually on the clock and stood out clearly against the white clock-face.

After that things began to happen quickly. I spotted another, of the kind that have a tiny round body and very long legs, on the left-hand bottom corner of my counterpane. A third ran swiftly across my bedside table and disappeared behind my cigarette box. There came a little 'plop' on my pillow, and jerking round my head I saw that a big, hairy compact brute had fallen there from the ceiling. I made a swipe at it, and in doing so dislodged another that had just appeared over the edge of the bed. A tickling at the back of my neck caused me to slap my hand to it and at that moment a newcomer ran up the other sleeve of my pyjama jacket.

Within another minute the place was swarming with them. Minute little insects; things whose leg-span would have covered half-a-crown; round-bodied, oval-bodied, wasp-waisted, long-legged, short-legged, some hairy, some smooth, black, red, greyish, brown and mottled with nasty whitish spots; they came in scores, in hundreds, from every corner of the room, until the bed, the table and myself were spotted with them as thickly as a summer night's sky is with stars.

Frantically I beat at them to try and drive them off. Here and there my slaps caught and killed one, causing it to fold up in a little ball and roll away; but the great majority were agile enough to evade my flailing hands, or seemed to protect themselves by taking cover in the folds of the bedclothes. In a dozen places at once I could feel them crawling over me; they ran across my face and got tangled in my hair.

There was nothing supernatural about them but, all the same, it was a beastly experience, as the irritation never ceased for a second and there was something loathsome about the feel of their cold little bodies coming in contact with one's skin. Somehow, too, the longer it lasted the worse it became. For the first few minutes my mind was fully occupied by my angry attempts to fight off the little pests; but it suddenly dawned upon me that my efforts were both futile and exhausting. They were too many and too agile, and for all my wild slapping I had not succeeded in hitting more than a dozen or two. So I gave up, and endeavoured to remain still. But I found I simply couldn't for more than a few seconds at a time. It was then that my nerve began to give way.

I suppose it was pretty wet of me to allow a lot of harmless little insects to have that effect; but it was partly the impossibility of sitting still while they crawled all over me and the equal impossibility of getting rid of them; and partly, I think, the horribly disturbing knowledge of how they came to be there. Anyhow, after a quarter of an hour, that seemed to last half the night, I broke down, and began to weep with rage and distress.

Helmuth came in a few minutes later, to see how I was taking things, and he must have been extremely gratified by what he saw.

The stinking bit of black candle had burnt down to a quarter of an inch. He snuffed it, put the heel in his pocket, then went over to the terrace door and opened it wide for a few moments till the rush of cool air had driven most of the smell out of the room. Next he pronounced several sentences of what sounded like gibberish, but were, I suppose, a magical formula from some dead language. On that his legion of spiders immediately left me and scuttled away out of sight through the cracks in the wainscoting.

Holding his lamp aloft, he looked at me and said: 'Perhaps after tonight's experience I shall find you in a more reasonable frame of mind tomorrow. If not, I shall have to give you a sharper lesson. There is one family of spiders living in the ruins that I refrained from sending. They are not poisonous but their bite is painful, and if I send them to you in the dark you will find it most unpleasant. You might think that over before you go to sleep.'

When he had gone I did think it over; and I was, and am, still determined to resist. Spider bites can be most unpleasant, but I can hardly believe that they will prove more painful than would a beating with thin steel rods by a gang of Gestapo toughs. And, so long as my mind remains unimpaired, I mean to stick any pain that Helmuth may inflict on me to the limit of my will.

Nevertheless, at the time, my nerves were still in a parlous state; and, having already given way to tears, I let myself go again in a flood of self-pity. It was in that state that Sally found me.

I did not hear her come in, as my head was half buried in the pillow and my sobs drowned the sound of her footfalls. It was her voice, saying 'What is it, Toby? Whatever *is* the matter?' that made me start up and find her already leaning over me.

She was standing right beside my bed holding a torch. It dazzled me for a moment, but I could just make out that she was in a dressing-gown and had her fluffy brown hair done up in a lot of little plaits. They stuck out absurdly, like a spiky halo, but made her look very young and rather pretty.

'What is it?' she repeated gently. 'Why are you crying like this? Have you had some awful nightmare? I've just had one about you. It was horrid. You were in bed here, and there was a great black thing over your face. I couldn't see what it was, but I knew that you were suffocating. When I woke I was so worried that I felt I must come up and see if you were all right.'

'I—I had a nightmare too,' I gulped. It seemed the only thing to say. I could not possibly expect her to believe that Helmuth had done a Pied Piper of Hamelin on me with all the spiders in the place; but I snuffled out that I had *dreamed* that a hoard of them was swarming all over me.

'There, there,' she murmured. 'It's all over now, and you'll soon forget it. But I'm very glad I followed my impulse to come up, all the same.'

Then she perched herself on the edge of the bed, drew my head down on to her breast, and made comforting noises to me as though I were a small boy who had hurt himself.

By that time I had practically got control of myself again; but I must confess that I didn't hurry to show it. Perhaps Weylands made me rather a hard, self-reliant type; anyhow, circumstances have never before arisen in which I have been comforted by a girl. It was an entirely new experience and I found it remarkably pleasant.

After a bit I could no longer disguise the fact that I was feeling better; so she said she was going to send me to sleep. She has marvellous hands; strong yet slim, and very sensitive—as I already knew from her giving me my massage treatments. Having made me comfortable on my pillows, she started to stroke my forehead with a touch as light as swansdown. In no time at all I had forgotten about Helmuth and felt a gentle relaxation steal over me; a few moments later I was sleeping like a top.

Later

This morning Sally and I said nothing to one another about last night. I had half a mind to thank her for her kindness, but shyness got the better of me; and she probably refrained from mentioning the matter out of tactfulness, feeling that I wouldn't like it recalled that a girl had found me in tears.

All the same it did come up this afternoon. I was sitting in my wheel-chair looking through one of my stamp albums—I have five altogether, and two of them are now completely interleaved with these sheets, but this was one of the others—and I found I was out of cigarettes. As Sally was near my bedside table I asked her to pass me the big silver box on it, so that I could refill my case. She did so, and opened it as she handed it to me. There was a dead spider inside.

'That's funny,' she said. 'When I was making your bed with Konrad this morning I found three dead spiders in it, and there's another. I wonder how it got inside the box?'

I knew the answer to that one. The box had been open when Helmuth had come in to me at midnight. Later, while slapping at the little brutes, I had evidently hit this one as my hand caught the lid and smacked it shut.

But, without waiting for me to reply, she went on: 'It was queer finding three of them in your bed too. I've never seen any there before. Perhaps a nest of them has hatched out behind the wainscot. Anyhow I'm sure it must have been one of them running over your face that gave you that horrid dream.'

An almost overwhelming impulse urged me to tell her the truth; but I managed to fight it down. I'm very glad I did now, as a few dead spiders would not have been enough to convince her that I hadn't dreamed the whole thing, and that it was simply my old prejudice against Helmuth reasserting itself in my sleep.

All the same, I count her having found the spiders a great piece of good fortune, as it is one item of concrete evidence; and, although it may cost me pretty dear, if the next few days produce others the time may not be far off when I can spill the whole story and she will *have* to believe me. Sally is 100 per cent honest; I am sure of that; and if only I can convince her of the facts she will be 100 per cent for me. I have *got* to, for in her now lies my only hope.

As it was, I said: 'Yes, you're right. I can still feel the little devils crawling over my skin. But that doesn't explain your dream about me; how do you account for that?'

She shrugged. 'Perhaps I was worrying about you before I went to sleep. For a permanent invalid you are a wonderfully cheerful person, and in the early part of the week you were right on top of your form; but the past two days you've gone right off the boil. Naturally I've felt rather concerned about that.'

'I'm very grateful to you, Sally,' I said. 'And I'm particularly grateful to you for your kindness to me last night.'

Then an idea came to me, so I added: 'I think I can explain why I've been a bit under the weather recently. I sometimes get premonitions, and I had one about this spider dream that shook me up so. I've a feeling, too, that I'm in for another tonight. Would it be asking too much of you to sit up with a book this evening, and come in to see me round about twelve o'clock?'

She gave me a queer, half-humorous, half-annoyed look, then said a trifle sharply: 'Nothing doing, Toby Jugg. You were genuinely upset when I came in to you last night; but for a good ten minutes before I sent you to sleep you were shamming. Midnight visiting is not in the contract, and the proper relations between nurse and patient are going to be maintained. You needn't tell me that you never knew a mother's care, either; because I've heard that one before.'

I was so taken aback that I could not think what to answer. She was right, of course, but I had no idea that she had spotted my manœuvre. Evidently she thinks I was making up to her with ulterior motives; but she is quite wrong there. It was only that I have been rather starved of human affection and found comfort in the warmth of her evident concern for me. Since she assumes that by asking her to come to me again tonight I was contemplating making a pass at her, I find it distinctly humiliating that she should have shown so very plainly that she thinks me too poor a fish to bother with. Still, I suppose one can't blame her really—what healthy girl would want to start an *affaire* with a poor devil of a cripple?

Sunday, 14th June

Helmuth carried out his threat, and the result was pretty bloody. He came in to me about eleven o'clock. There was the sort of scene which it has now become redundant to record. I called him by a string of unprintable names and he retorted with variations on the theme that I was a stiff-necked little 'whatnot', whom he was determined to bring to heel.

The fun started half-an-hour after he had left me. As there was no hell-broth candle on this occasion, and the fire had practically died out, I had no immediate warning before the attack. Something suddenly scurried across the back of my neck and bit me on the ear.

I shook my head violently, clapped a hand to the place, then quickly hauled myself up into a sitting position. Nothing more happened for a while; but I don't mind admitting that as I sat there in the darkness I had no mean fit of the jitters.

I could not help visualizing swarms of the little brutes coming at me from every direction, as they had the night before, but this time every one of them having a nip like a pair of tweezers and intending to make their supper off me.

Thank God, it did not turn out to be as bad as all that, and the period of nerve-racking anticipation was really the worst part of the business. But the realization was quite bad enough. Helmuth's pet family of 'little brothers' turned out to consist of about a score of small, active and persistent horrors, as far as I could judge—although it was impossible to estimate with any certainty how many there were of them making darts at me in the darkness.

I think being in the dark made the bites seem more painful, as this morning there is not very much to show for them; but at the time each hurt like the cut of a small, sharp knife, and the shock of it coming without warning added to its intensity. It brought to my mind what I had read of a Chinese torture called 'the death of a thousand cuts' and, although of course I wasn't, I could not help believing that I must be bleeding in dozens of places from the bites on my face, arms, neck, hands and the upper part of my body.

How long the ordeal went on I don't quite know; but it must have been well over three-quarters-of-an-hour with a fresh bite about every minute. for the whole of that time I was jerking myself about and slapping at my unseen enemies; so when at last the biting ceased I was sweating like a pig and thoroughly exhausted.

For a time I remained sitting tense and vigilant, waiting for the next bite to come; but when a considerable interval had elapsed without one I gradually relaxed, and began to wonder if Helmuth would soon appear to gloat over his blood-soaked victim. But he didn't, and some time later, still propped up against my pillows, I dropped off to sleep.

One good thing, at least, has come out of this bedevilment. Sally found two more corpses in my bed this morning; and although there was no blood to show, my skin was red and slightly puffy where I had been bitten.

I twitted her, a little unfairly perhaps, on not having believed my prediction that I should be the victim of another 'nightmare'; but she took the matter seriously, and expressed contrition at having given me a raspberry instead of the benefit of the doubt.

At the moment, while I sit here writing this on the terrace, she is conducting a grand spider-hunt in my room, and is dusting insect powder into the crevices of the wainscoting behind my bed. That will not stop the spiders, if Helmuth decides to send them again, as they come from all over the place; but, now that she is so concerned about it, he may abandon this form of tormenting me from fear that she will start agitating to have me moved again.

She said this morning that proper sleep was an essential to my recovery, and that if we couldn't get rid of the spiders she would have to speak to Helmuth about it. Moreover, she volunteered of her own accord to come in late tonight to see that I was all right.

I reminded her that she was dining with Helmuth, and suggested, with what I fear must have been rather a forced laugh, that she might find his books and his conversation so interesting that she would forget all about me.

To that I got the tart reply that a few hours' relaxation had never yet made her forget her professional duties.

Let's hope that tonight does not prove an exception. It would be a great triumph for me if she came in while a spider-attack was in full progress, as I think that if I then told her the truth she might believe it. But will she come at all? She certainly won't if Helmuth gets really busy on her.

Later

I have spent a miserable afternoon. Not on account of any further threat from Helmuth, or my own situation–which, God knows, is desperate enough–but worrying about Sally.

I feel sure she has no idea what she may be letting herself in for tonight, and it would be futile to try to tell her. She would only put it down to a recurrence of the abnormal condition in which I am supposed to have sex on the brain, and I should risk disrupting to no purpose the excellent relations that now exist between us.

Sally has been here over a fortnight, and a cripple is naturally far more dependent than any other type of invalid on his nurse, so I have already spent many pleasant idle hours in her company, In fact, I have really seen much more of her than I did of any of the girls that I met casually, and ran around with for two or three months, while I was in the R.A.F.

I have come to like her enormously; and I am beginning to wonder if my intense repugnance to the thought of Helmuth getting hold of her is not partly inspired by jealousy. I have never been jealous of anyone before; the Weylands training eliminated that emotion in my make-up during my adolescence, and I thought it had done so for good; but now I am by no means certain.

Knowing Helmuth's attitude to women as I do, the thought of her spending a whole evening with him makes me squirm. I simply cannot bear the thought of his filling her up with drink, then pawing her about. Of course, she may not let him; but his personal magnetism is extraordinarily strong, and if he thinks she is likely to prove difficult he is quite capable of slipping something into her drink.

The terrible frustration that I am feeling, from being unable to protect her, can hardly be entirely attributed to a normal sense of chivalry; so I suppose there is no escaping the fact that jealousy must enter into it. If so it is a most hideous emotion; and, since jealousy of this type is a by-product of love, it brings me face to face with the question—can I possibly be in love with Sally?

As I have never been in love, I honestly don't know. I have always thought of love in this sense as an extra intense form of physical desire, and Sally has not so far had any profound effect upon my passions. She has a lovely figure, and, although she is not beautiful in the accepted sense, her face is so expressive that it gives her an attraction all her own. There is, too, a rich warmth in her voice, and she is altogether a very cuddlesome person; but I certainly would not jump off Westminster Bridge for the privilege of sleeping with her. On the other hand I think I would jump off Westminster Bridge if by so doing I could prevent what is likely to happen tonight. Which strikes me as very queer.

Monday, 15th June

I am in love with Sally. I know that now, and I wonder more than ever what ill I can have done in my short life for God to have inflicted such a series of punishments on me. To be made a cripple at the age of twenty was a life-sentence; to be left in Helmuth's clutches, with the end of the month approaching, and to date not even the germ of an idea for getting away from him, is pretty well as good as having added to the life-sentence that it shall be spent in solitary confinement; and now this!

Last night I went through purgatory. Sally gave me my massage early so that she would have plenty of time to change for dinner; then she told me that Konrad would settle me down at ten o'clock, and she hoped that I would soon get off to sleep; but she would peep in round about midnight, just in case the insect powder had not proved fully effective and some of the spiders were causing me to have another nightmare. After that she left me, and I spent five hours of unadulterated hell.

If this is love, God help every imaginative man or woman who falls into it, and ever has to remain inactive while knowing the person they love to be in the company of an unscrupulous rival. I knew both Helmuth and Sally, and the rooms in which they would pass the evening, sufficiently well to form a series of mental pictures, of their having cocktails together, dining, looking through his books, and of what might happen later.

Most of the time up till about half-past-nine my personal television set was jumping ahead, with only occasional flash-backs to what was probably happening at the moment; after that hour my imagination ran riot, and my torture was intensified a hundredfold by sickening visions of what might be taking place downstairs while I was actually thinking of it. No doubt many of the situations that I conjured up, with which to flay myself, were grossly beyond the probable, but, since Helmuth was concerned, they were never outside the bounds of the possible.

I see that I have written of Helmuth as my 'rival', which, of course, he is not, since I have never made even the suggestion of a declaration to Sally, and, if I did, I have not the least reason to suppose that she would reciprocate my feelings. On the contrary, she has already shown that, far from desiring any advance from me, she would regard it as most undesirable, on account of her professional status.

I cannot think that many young nurses allow medical etiquette to weigh much with them if they feel an inclination towards a patient; in fact, although it was officially frowned on, in the R.A.F. hospitals where I spent ten months lots of chaps had affairs with the V.A.D.s; so Sally's attitude with regard to myself must be taken as a clear indication that she has no time for me. On the other hand, she has never made any secret of her admiration for Helmuth, and she may quite well have been hoping for the past ten days or more that he would make love to her.

I don't know much about girls' reactions, but everything in such relationships must depend on the point of view. If a man of 45, like Helmuth, makes violent love to a girl of 22, like Sally, and she thinks him physically unattractive, she probably regards him as a 'beast', a 'dirty old man' and almost as a 'medical case who should have more control over himself at *his age*'; but if she *is* attracted to him she then regards his amorous assault as a compliment, and he becomes in her eyes an 'experienced lover', a 'real man of the world' and a 'connoisseur of women whom any girl of *her age* might be proud to have as a beau'.

If Sally's conception of Helmuth is on the latter lines, as well it may be, that would make the agonies I suffered last night all the more pointless and absurd. But they were none the less vivid and heartrending. And what makes things worse is that I have no idea how the party really went, or ended, as Sally is hardly on speaking terms with me this morning.

That is partly my fault, as I blotted it again, and badly; and she could hardly be expected to guess that I did so mainly out of concern for her.

Helmuth did not come in to me after tea; so there weren't even any further threats to distract my mind from Sally; and I knew that he would be too much occupied with her to come up and start an argument with me after dinner. So the spiders and myself were both given a night off.

From ten o'clock, when Konrad took my lamp away, the time dragged interminably. I thought it must be at least half-past-one, and that Sally had long since forgotten her promise to come and see that I was all right, when the sound of Great-aunt Sarah's footsteps, going down her secret staircase, told me that it was only just eleven.

She is as regular as a clock, and recently I have feared that Helmuth might hear her either coming or going on one of his late visits to me. If he did, he is quite capable of having her stopped out of pure malice, and it would be wicked shame to interfere with the only thing that makes the poor old girl's life worth living; but, fortunately, he has never been here yet at the actual time she has passed. I thought more than once on both Friday and Saturday nights of calling her in to help me against the spiders, but gave the idea up from the feeling that it would not only be useless but scare her out of the few wits she has left.

Anyhow, her passing last night told me that I had another hour or so to wait for Sally, even if she came at all, and had not forgotten me owing to Helmuth's blandishments; or because she was lying half drugged and unable to think coherently. That hour seemed to stretch into an age-long night, yet I knew that it could not be more than two hours at most, because Great-aunt Sarah always returns from her self-imposed toil at one; and she had not done so when I heard footsteps coming up the stone stairs outside my door.

It was Sally, but Helmuth was with her, and she was tight.

He held the lamp as she stumbled into the room in front of him. I had never seen her properly dressed up before. She was not wearing full evening-dress, of course, but the sort of frock that girls use to dine out informally. Her eyes were abnormally bright and her face was flushed. My heart gave an extra thump as I suddenly realized that she can look damn' pretty; but almost simultaneously I realized the state she was in, and I was filled with rage and apprehension.

Helmuth had knocked back his share of the drink. I could tell that by the slant of his tawny eyes; but he knows how to hold his liquor and, as usual when he is wearing a dinner-jacket, he looked very distinguished.

While he remained standing in the doorway, Sally came over to me with what I suppose she thought was a cheerful smile, but was actually a sick-making grin, on her face, and said:

'Well, I promised I'd come, and here I am. Any spiders?'

'No,' I said. 'You've brought the only one with you.'

Her face went stupidly blank, but Helmuth understood me and laughed. 'There you are! What did I tell you? Poor Toby's got them again. In an old place like this there are bound to be a certain number of spiders hatching out at this time of year, and because you found a few about the room he now thinks that I am one.'

'Silly boy!' She suppressed a hiccup. 'You mustn't get spiders on the brain. It's bad for you! I'm your nurse and I want you to be a credit to me. Be good now, and go to sleep.'

'It is you who need sleep at the moment,' I said sharply. 'And as you are now you are no credit to your profession or yourself. You're tight, Sally. Get to bed and sleep it off.'

I shot that line in the hope that it would pull her together, although I knew I was taking a chance that it might put her against me. It did, and came back like a boomerang on my unhappy head. She swore that she was not tight and called on the grinning Helmuth as witness to the gratuitous insult I had offered her. Then she called me an ungrateful little so-and-so for dragging her up here only to be rude, swore that she would never come near me after ten-o'clock again, and flounced a trifle unsteadily out of the room. Helmuth gave me a parting leer as he turned away to light her down the stairs; and that was that.

What happened after that I have no idea. Up to the time that I saw them, the fact that Sally was in such rollicking form showed that Helmuth could not so far have tried anything on to which she had not been a willing party. But there might have been a very good reason for that. If she told Helmuth quite early in the evening that she had promised to come up and see me at midnight, he is shrewd enough to have realized that, should she insist on keeping her promise, it would probably upset his seduction act just as he was getting going; so he might have decided to spend the first part of the evening filling her up with drink and hold the rough stuff till after their visit.

All I do know is that she is looking like the wrath of God this morning, and has one hell of a hangover.

Later

After lunch Helmuth came in to see me. He announced that he is going away this afternoon and will not be back till Friday. The surprise, relief and excitement that I felt on hearing this can well be imagined.

The length of this proposed absence is accounted for by the fact that he is going to spend two days at Weylands, and getting from central Wales to Cumberland is a most hideous cross-country journey. By road it is about three hundred miles, so could be done in a day, but wartime restrictions make going by car out of the question, and by rail there is no connection which makes the trip possible without lapping over into a second day. He is catching the afternoon train to Birmingham and spending the night there, as if he caught the night train on he would only find himself marooned at Carlisle at some godless hour of the morning; so he will travel north tomorrow, spend Tuesday night and the whole of Wednesday at Weylands, start back on Thursday after lunch and arrive here midday Friday.

He seemed to take a special delight in describing to me the object of his journey. For a long time it has been one of his ambitions to have the chapel here dedicated to his Infernal Master, and at last the Brotherhood have agreed. The ceremony is to take place on St John's Eve–that is, Midsummer-eve–Tuesday the 23rd of June. Apparently it is the second most important feat in the Satanic calendar, the first being Walpurgis, or May-day Eve–the 30th of April.

That, no doubt, explains why it was that I suffered the worst of the early attacks by the Horror in the courtyard on April the 30th. Evidently, too, it was not coincidence that it should have been on a 30th of April that I caught a glimpse of the Brotherhood gathering at Weylands, and had the fright of my young life on breaking open the old tomb. I am inclined to think now, though, that the tomb had nothing to do with it, and that I ran into some incredibly evil presence that the Satanists at Weylands had conjured up to protect their meeting from being spied upon.

Anyway, there is to be a full-scale Sabbath held here tomorrow week. Helmuth is going up to Weylands to arrange the final details and the Brotherhood is coming in force from all parts to attend it. So I know now why it was that when I looked through the grating I saw that instead of being half full of rubble the chapel had recently been cleaned out.

He asked me again if I had reconsidered matters, and on my replying in the negative, he said:

'That is a pity, as I should like to have taken north with me the news of your willingness to accept initiation. However, the Midsummer-night's ceremony will provide a perfect opportunity for that, and I still hope to induce you to see reason before then. If I fail, instead of your receiving initiation that night, we shall have to invoke the Lady Astoroth. The circumstances for such a ritual are not always propitious, but they will be on that date–and that will be the end of you. But I shall be back on Friday and able to give my entire attention to you over the weekend. By the twentieth the moon will be entering her second quarter; so if you are still recalcitrant I shall summon the Great Spider, and we will see what effect a meeting with him will have on you.'

Later

All the afternoon I have been desperately racking my wits for a way to take advantage of Helmuth's absence. It is a God-given chance to escape, and the last I will ever get. I have three clear days to work in, but even that is all too little to prepare for a break-out, and to pull it off.

The physical difficulties alone are immense. That morning when I was hauled back from the railway station, and Helmuth and Sally were discussing in the car how I could be prevented from getting away again, she was so right in pointing out that I am too heavy to be carried, so that even with help I could get very little distance without my wheel-chair. And it is such a weighty contraption that it would take more than one person to get it downstairs. Then there is the probelm of getting down after it; and the whole job would have to be done at night without arousing any of the household.

Still, I've a feeling that I would find a way to surmount such obstacles if only I were not so utterly alone and tied. If I had someone to get me from my bed into the chair, and help me out of it on to the top step of the stairs, I believe the getting down could be managed. While they supported and guided the chair from behind, I could take its weight against the back of my shoulders and lever myself down in a sitting position, taking my weight on my hands, a step at a time. But it would be utterly impossible to perform such a feat on my own, and none of the servants ever come here, except Konrad. To hope for any help from him is out of the question. So the problem really boils down to, can I or can I not win Sally over before Helmuth gets back?

Unfortunately she is sadly changed from yesterday; and goodness knows what Helmuth said or did to her, but he must now be very confident in her loyalty to him to go off like this leaving me in her charge. It was probably with his journey in view that he put off having a party with her until last night. That would be just like him. The odds are that he is not the least attracted by her, otherwise he would have done something about it long before this, but he decided that it was important to secure her allegience, and that the best way to do so was to create a strong emotional bond between them, just before his departure.

He is also, no doubt, relying to some extent on my isolated situation, up here at the top of the spiral staircase, and on Konrad keeping an eye on things for him. But Konrad, although sly and cunning, is not overburdened with brains; so it should not be difficult to outwit him. Therefore it must be principally on Sally that Helmuth is counting to keep me a prisoner here, and prevent me from obtaining any outside help, during his absence.

The fact that she is like a bear with a sore head today, and has so far treated me with frigid abruptness, is partly due to her hangover and partly to her annoyance at my having seen her tight last night. But I have an uneasy feeling that there is also something else behind it from the way she avoids my glance. Perhaps Helmuth told her about how I hypnotized Deb and warned her not to look me in the face for more than a few seconds at a time.

Since she first arrived it has occurred to me more than once to try out my hypnotic powers on her, but I felt that Helmuth would be watching for such a move on my part and be certain to nip it in the bud. Later, after Julia's visit, there was no point in attempting it–until Helmuth came out in his true colours a few days ago. That was followed almost immediately by the first spider-attack, after which Sally came and comforted me. I am sure now it was that episode which led up to my present feelings for her, and there seems to me something definitely wrong about attempting to impose one's will by such means on a girl with whom one has fallen in love.

An attempt to bribe her is equally repugnant; but my situation is so desperate that I am positively forced to try one means or the other. Of the two, to offer her a bribe seems the less unpleasant course, and the one more likely to succeed. At least she could not afterwards accuse me of having interfered with her free will, and if Helmuth has primed her against my hypnotic powers I might find it impossible to make any impression on her–except, if she guesses what I am at, to make her more prejudiced than ever against me.

Even if she did become Helmuth's mistress when she was tight last night, she may be regretting it by now. But, in any case, I can hardly believe that in an *affaire* of such short duration he could have secured such a hold over either her affections or her mind as to make her completely oblivious to her future interests.

Sally is much better born than I am. She comes of a long line of Naval people, one of whom was a Cavalier who commanded a ship in Charles I's time. She was brought up to understand and appreciate nice things, although her family has fallen on hard times and lost nearly all their money. She is quite philosophical about the fact that she would have to earn her own living even if the war did not make that compulsory; but at times I am sure she thinks it a little hard that she should have to, while all her ancestors for many generations back have enjoyed the comfort, elegance and freedom to live as they chose, which was the natural birthright of the English gentry.

I could give her all that, and with no strings attached. If only she will get me away from Llanferdrack I'll be as rich as Croesus this time next week. However right Helmuth may be in his prediction that the Socialists will reduce the whole nation to the level of beggary in a few years' time, the Jugg millions are still mine at the moment to do what I like with, if only I can get my hands on them. I'll offer to make over to her a sum which will keep her in luxury for the rest of her life. But I have no time to lose. I must tackle her tonight, after dinner. She is bound to accept; she would be mad to refuse.

Tuesday, 16th June

Last night I was stymied. When Konrad brought my dinner up he told me that Nurse Cardew had asked him to say that she felt a little indisposed, so she was going early to bed and would not to be coming up again.

Poor Sally. I love her so much that I could not help feeling sorry for her, despite the annoying set-back to my own plans. She certainly had a packet the night before, and even I don't know quite how big a one it may have been; it was very natural that she should feel that she wanted to sleep the clock round.

Perhaps, after all, so far as I am concerned, it is all to the good that I should have been compelled to postpone my offer to her of a thundering fat bribe. She is in a much better mood this morning and, although still a bit stand-offish, at least civil to me.

I have decided not to rush my fences, but to be on my best behaviour all day, so as to try to win her back to a really friendly mood; then take the plunge just after tea, when we do my second daily standing exercise.

We haven't got very far with that. I can just bear my own weight for about a minute, but I fear it will be quite a time yet before I can take even a single step, as, directly I attempt to lift one foot from the ground, the other leg crumples up. Still, Sally remains extremely persistent and quite optimistic about me; and, as she regards this business as her own special contribution towards my recovery, she is always most patient and sympathetic during our sessions at it. I shall do my very damnedest this evening to show some progress, so as to please her; then offer her a life of a luxury for the rest of her days to become my ally.

Later

I have bogged it. I don't think it was my fault. The exercise was a success. I stood erect for two minutes by Sally's watch without support, and she was delighted.

As soon as I had recovered from the effort, I put the matter to her as tactfully as I could. I did not go into a long speech about Helmuth, much less make any apparently wild statements about his possessing occult powers derived from the Devil and having deliberately wished the spiders on to me. I simply said that, mad or sane, I was thoroughly fed up with Llanferdrack, and had come to the conclusion that it was bad for my nerves to remain here.

I added that, if I could get to London, I was perfectly prepared to go straight to the Air Ministry and ask to be taken back into one of their hospitals; and that as I was one of their own types, and a D.F.C. to boot, I felt certain they would take me—provided I was willing to pay my own expenses. That seemed to me a pretty reasonable proposition.

Then I went all out, and mentally transporting Sally to the mountain top, spread all the riches of the earth before her. For several minutes I dilated on what an ample supply of money could still do in the world for a personable young woman. Freedom from work and care, the opportunity to meet an endless succession of men with charm, ability and wealth; clothes, beauty-treatments, furs, jewels, travel, horses to ride in the country and parties to go to in town, winter sports in Switzerland and sunbathing in the West Indies, but she did not let me get as far as making the actual offer.

Having listened to me with an intent expression for a bit, she suddenly got what I was driving at; and, coming to her feet with a jerk, she told me to 'Shut up'.

But I went through with it; I had to, as things I value more than my life depend on my getting away from here before Helmuth gets back.

She went red in the face, stamped her foot, and declared that nothing in the world would induce her even to consider such a proposition. Looking back on it, I realize that she presents the most adorable picture when she is flushed and angry; but I was in no mood to think of that at the time. I told her that she was crazy; and that for her to reject such a future out of loyalty to Helmuth could only mean that he had bewitched her.

She replied that Helmuth had nothing to do with it, apart from the fact that he had engaged her and she was responsible to him. Then she got on her high horse about having been left in charge of me, and her honour as a professional nurse.

Again, looking back, I really believe she meant that; and, when one considers the temptation I was holding out, one does not have to be a born cynic to believe that very few young women would have shown such splendid integrity. Whether she is still a virgin, or has been Helmuth's mistress and had a dozen lovers before him, weighs as nothing in the scales against such a flat rejection of a colossal bribe; and I know now that I am very right to love her as I do.

But, at the time, my bitter disappointment, and the awful sense of impending fate that now weighs upon me all my waking hours, overmastered all other emotions. My filthy temper got the better of me again, and I cracked at her:

'Oh, be your age; and stop talking hot air about your professional honour! You won't have any honour of any kind left if you have much more to do with Dr Helmuth Lisický.'

Her blue eyes blazed, and she retorted: 'If you were not, one—a cripple; two—my patient; and three—suffering from erotomania, I would slap your face.'

Wednesday, 17th June

I have blotted it again. Last night I decided that since there seems no possible chance of securing Sally's conscious aid, I must attempt to hypnotize her, and force her into helping me unconsciously. The idea was intensely repugnant to me, but desperate ills call for desperate remedies; and if ever a man was desperate, I am.

This morning, after we had been out on the terrace for about ten minutes, I tried the trick that had worked so well with Deb. I said that I had got a fly in my eye, and asked her to fish it out.

In an instant she rounded on me, called me an 'unscrupulous young brute' and proceeded to flay me with her tongue. I suppose that before Helmuth sacked Deb he got out of her particulars of how I had gone to work in her case. Anyhow he had told Sally about it the first night that she dined with him and warned her to be on her guard in case I attempted the same trick on her. Worse, he inferred that I had not only used the hypnotic control that I succeeded in acquiring over Deb to force her to help me to escape, but had used it before that to secure her unwilling co-operation in indulging my immoral aberrations.

Of course I hotly denied it; but that got me nowhere; and I don't wonder now that Sally takes such a dim view of me. She said that she would have thrown up the case and gone back to London days ago if she had not realized that when these fits seize me I am not responsible for my actions. So all I have succeeded in doing is to strengthen her conviction that I am an erotomaniac, and, this morning, made a most despicable attempt to make her my unwilling victim.

By this afternoon Helmuth will have been gone two days; and that is just half the period of grace that I have been granted. I have shot both my bolts with Sally, and have not another round of any kind left in the locker.

Later

It was Sally's afternoon off and she went down to the village; but there is nothing much to do there, so after tea she came up to sit with me. She was in a much more pleasant mood and, without exactly apologizing, she inferred that she was sorry about having flared out at me as she did this morning. She said that I am so normal most of the time that she is apt to forget that my mind is unbalanced, so goes off the deep end when these occasional evidences of my malady occur, instead of calmly ignoring them. So I think her early return to keep me company with partly a gesture of the *amende honourable* variety.

I accepted it as such only too willingly, and after we had talked of trivialities for a bit, she said:

'I met your ex-nurse, Deborah Kain, in the village post-office this afternoon.'

'Did you?' I exclaimed. 'I thought she had gone back to London.'

'No. I gather that she is engaged to the village schoolmaster, a man named Gruffydd, and is staying with him and his mother.'

'What did you think of her?' I asked.

Sally smiled. 'Rather a flashy type, isn't she? I mean not at all the sort of person one would expect to find in these parts; or anyhow, not dressed the way she was. Her off-smart clothes, silk stockings, high heels and hair-do might have looked all right in Oxford Street, but they were a bit startling for Llanferdrack. I had no idea who she was until she came up and introduced herself. I suppose somebody had pointed me out to her as your new nurse. She asked me how I was liking it up at the Castle.'

'And what did you say to that one?' I smiled back.

'Oh, I was very non-committal,' Sally shrugged. 'I'm quite good at minding my own business, and other people's. I said that Helmuth was charming and you were a pet—which is by no means true all of the time—and asked her why she had chucked up such a pleasant job. That shook her rather; but she took refuge in the fib that, although she had liked both you and the Doctor immensely, when she had become engaged her fiancé had insisted on her leaving so that they could be together more often.'

We laughed a lot over that, as it was so absurdly far off the facts; but it suddenly occurred to me that Sally did not know the real truth about Deb's relations with Helmuth and myself—only a small part of it, with a number of entirely false additions given her by Helmuth. I knew that it was useless to give her my own version, as she would never believe me, and only get in an ill-humour again from supposing that I was once more attempting to blacken Helmuth in her eyes. But there *was* one way which, if it did not entirely convince her of the respective parts we had played, might at least arouse doubts in her mind about Helmuth's veracity.

'Sally,' I said, 'can you keep a secret?'

She nodded.

'I mean *really* keep it,' I went on. 'To me this one is of vital importance. I want you to give me your word that in no circumstances whatsoever will you disclose it to Helmuth or anyone else without my permission.'

'I'll give you my word, then,' she agreed. 'All this sounds very mysterious.'

'No. It's very down-to-earth, really.'

While I had been speaking the idea in my mind had swiftly developed. I realized that if I was to make this final bid to convince her that Helmuth was a rogue, to give her only the part that Deb had played in the story would be like producing a single slice of a large cake. So I decided to go the whole hog, and went on:

'Ever since the beginning of May I have been keeping a journal. You must often have seen me scribbling away with one of my stamp albums open on my knees. But I was not making long notes about water-marks, perforations and freak issues, as I pretended; I was entering up my diary, which now runs to over three hundred loose sheets.

'You believe me to be mad; but you admit that for much the greater part of the time I am perfectly sane, so the great bulk of my writing must have been done when I was normal. My reason for writing the journal was because *I* believe myself to be the victim of a conspiracy to *drive* me insane. I hoped that if the conspiracy succeeded, and I was put in a lunatic asylum, some honest person might come across my papers, realize the truth, and take steps to get me out. That is why I have taken considerable pains to prevent anyone here knowing of the existence of this document. You see, they might destroy it; and I regard it as my only remaining lifeline.

'If you read what I have written you may consider much of it to be the ravings of a lunatic; but it will tell you a great deal about me that you don't know, and of which independent proof is easily available. It will tell you all about my family and my early life; of the part that Helmuth played in it and of the great financial issues that hang upon the question of my sanity or madness; of the strange school, at which Helmuth was a master, where I was educated, and of how much he has to gain by making people believe that I am mad.

'If I told you this story myself I'm afraid you would think that I was making great chunks of it up as I went along; but you won't be able to think that of this account which has been written day by day as a record of events, and of the hopes and fears which have made my life one long battle for these past two months.

'If I give you these papers will you read them through this evening, and, whatever conclusions you come to, promise faithfully to let me have them back tomorrow morning?'

'Yes, Toby,' she said. 'I promise. And whatever I think I won't give away what you have been doing. I'd like to read the biographical part especially, as it may help me to help you to get well more quickly if I know more about you. If there are over three hundred pages of it though, it is going to take a long time to read, so perhaps I had better take them downstairs and start on it now.'

I asked her to get me the albums, extracted the pages I have written in the last few days so that she should not read the entries in which I have confessed my love for her, and gave her the rest.

Looking rather sweetly serious, she took them off with her, while I settled down to make this record of our conversation.

Was I, perhaps, inspired to start this journal before I even knew of her existence, so that she should one day read it? The workings of Providence are sometimes very strange; but perhaps Sally is the 'honest person' who will see the truth through the web of lies that Helmuth has spun, and set me free.

Thursday, 18th June

Anyone can imagine the state of suppressed excitement in which I awaited Sally's verdict this morning. Her face told me nothing when she came in shortly after Konrad, to help me with my morning toilet.

As soon as we were alone together for a moment, I asked her if she had read it all, and she nodded.

'Fortunately your writing is pretty legible, except in a few parts which were evidently written when you were overwrought, so I managed to get through it; but it took me till two in the morning. Konrad will be coming up with your breakfast in a moment, though; so I think we had better wait to discuss it until we are out on the terrace.'

So I had to contain my impatience for another hour; but as soon as we were comfortably settled in our corner of the battlements, she said:

'It is an extraordinary document, Toby. I was tremendously impressed; but, honestly, I don't know what to say about it.'

'The point is,' I said a little abruptly, 'having read it, do you consider that it is the work of a man who is sane or insane?'

'Honestly, Toby, I can't answer that.' Her voice held an unhappy note. 'Whether you imagine things or whether you don't, there can be no doubt about it that you have been through absolute hell. I cried in places, I simply couldn't help it.'

I think that is the nicest thing she has ever said to me. It almost made having gone through it all worth while, to have touched her heart like that. But the third day of Helmuth's absence was nearly up; he will be back by this time tomorrow, so the paramount need for action forced me to say:

'Thanks for your sympathy, Sally. I'm very grateful for that; but as I am situated it is not enough. I'm afraid I have placed you in a rotten situation. I wouldn't have done so from choice, but I had to; because I am a prisoner here and you happen to be my goaler, and there is no one else to whom I can appeal for help.

'If I am still here when Helmuth gets back I am going to be sunk for good. You know that, from what you have read of his threats to me. If you consider that those threats are entirely the product of my imagination you will be fully justified in ignoring my plea. But if you feel that there is even a grain of truth in them you are now saddled with a very weighty responsibility. By helping to detain me here against my will you are not only aiding and abetting a criminal conspiracy, but doing something which you know to be morally indefensible.'

She took that very well, and agreed in principle that I was right; but she continued to declare that as she had nothing but my written word to go on it really was impossible for her to judge whether I had invented the more fantastic parts of my story or not. So for an hour or more we argued the matter, passing from the general to the particular, as I strove to convince her that every episode recorded was cold, hard fact.

There were two points in my favour. She had known a girl who had been at Weylands, so had some idea of the amoral principles that are inculcated there—which helped to lower Helmuth's stock—and she was not at all sceptical about ghosts or the more usually accepted supernormal occurrences. Moreover, she admitted that my whole conception of the motive for a conspiracy was built up on sound logic. But she simply could not swallow the fact that Black Magic is still practised today, and that Helmuth has been employing Satanic power with the object of reducing me to a gibbering idiot.

'All right, then,' I said at last. 'Let's leave the Brotherhood, and the Great Spider, and the question of Helmuth being a servant of the Devil out of it. If I can prove that he has told you a pack of lies, and slandered me outrageously, in connection with one particular episode, will that convince you that he has an ulterior motive in keeping me here, and induce you to help me get out of his clutches?'

After a moment she nodded. 'Yes. If you can do that, it would satisfy me that he really is plotting to get hold of your money, and whether he is using occult power to aid him, or not, becomes beside the point. Either way it would be up to me to do what I can to protect you from his criminal intentions. But I don't see how you are going to *prove* anything.'

'I may be able to,' I replied; 'but I shall need your help. Getting you to read the journal at all only arose through your running into Deborah Kain in the village yesterday, and because I wanted you to know my side of that particular story. If you will go down to the village again, and get her to come up here, I'll find a way to make her tell the truth; then you'll see if it is Helmuth or I who has been lying.'

'I can find her easily enough, because I know that she is living with the Gruffydds; but whether I can persuade her to come up here is quite another matter.'

'If you tell her that Helmuth is away until tomorrow, so there is no chance of her running into him, I think I can guarantee that she'll come back with you,' I said with a smile. 'I will write a little note for you to give to her, and when she has read it I shall be very surprised if she does not agree to play.'

'You mean to hold some threat over her?' Sally frowned suspiciously.

'I do,' I admitted. 'But only to get her up here. After that you shall see for yourself that I won't use threats on her to get the truth.'

Turning my chair, I wheeled myself back into my room, got a sheet of notepaper and wrote on it:

My Dear Deb,
    I am anxious to ask you a few questions, and it is of the utmost importance that I should put them to you at once; so would you be good enough to accompany Nurse Cardew back to the Castle.
    In view of all you told me of your early life and political persuasions I am sure you will agree that it is much better that I should have this chat with you than to have to ask Mr Gruffydd to come up to see me.

I addressed the envelope, then wheeled myself back to the terrace and showed the letter to Sally. When she had read it she said:

'I remember, now, all that business about her being a Communist, that you got out of her when you had her in a hypnotic trance. You're threatening to tell her fiancé. That is blackmail, you know.'

'My dear Sally!' I exclaimed impatiently. 'I don't care if it is theft, forgery, arson, and all the other crimes in the Newgate Calendar. I'd commit the lot to get out of here; and since you insist on my proving my words before you will help me to escape, it is you who are driving me to commit this one.'

'I'm sorry, Toby.' Her voice had become quite meek. 'You're right about me forcing you into this; but I've got to know the truth, and the sooner the better. It is nearly twelve o'clock now, and it's a good bet that she'll be at the Gruffydds' house at lunch-time. If I borrow a bicycle from one of the servants and start right away, I shall be down in the village well before one. I'll have a snack myself at the tea-shop, then if all goes well pick her up afterwards and be back here soon after two.'

So off Sally went, and at any moment now I am expecting her to return with Comrade Deborah Kain.

Later

I've won! But what a session; and what a revelation! I am writing this now only to fill in time, as, anxious as Sally and I are to get off, it would be madness to make a start until Konrad is out of the way for the night. And our interview with Deb is well worth recording.

When she arrived she was pretty sullen, which was hardly surprising; but she became almost pleasant when I apologized for having troubled her, and said that I only wanted to ask her some questions, to set Nurse Cardew's mind at rest about certain things which it was suggested had happened here. Then I said:

'I want you to tell the truth, even if it appears to be unfavourable to myself, and if you do so I give you my word that I will say nothing to Owen Gruffydd of what I know about your affairs. Now; while you were here, did I at any time make any amorous advances to you?'

She looked very surprised, gave a quick glance at Sally and said: 'No. As a matter of fact I thought you were rather stand-offish. You were always quite polite, but you hardly seemed to notice me as a person at all.'

'Right!' I said. 'When Dr Lisický discovered that on several occasions I had hypnotized you, and had an explanation with you about that which led to your leaving, did he reveal to you, or even suggest, that I had taken advantage of you while you were in a trance state?'

'No; he never said anything of the that kind.' Her eyes widened as she added: 'Did you—did you do that?'

'Certainly not,' I replied. 'But he seems to have given Nurse Cardew the impression that I did. Now, about the Doctor himself. Did he make amorous advances to you?'

'No,' she said firmly. 'He did not.'

Her denial took me by surprise, as it seemed quite pointless in view of all I knew, and the fact that Helmuth had thrown her out bag and baggage.

'Come, Deb!' I admonished her. 'I am not threatening you, and Nurse Cardew will promise not to repeat anything you may say to your detriment;

but we want the truth. Dr Lisický told me that you were his mistress, and you confirmed that to me yourself, while you were in a trance. You can't deny it.'

She stubbornly shook her head. "What I said in a trance you may have put into my mind; and if he said that of me it is because he is a vain and boastful man. He was lying.'

I saw that I was up against it, and there was only one thing to do. I said: 'All right; I will believe you, if you look me in the face and swear to that.'

She fell into the trap. The second she had her eyes fixed on mine I shot out my right hand, pointed my first and second fingers at them and gave the order: 'Sleep, Deb! At once! Go to sleep this instant!'

The old formula worked like magic. There was barely a flicker of resistance before her eyes began to glaze and the heavy eyelids drooped over them.

'Good,' I said, after a monent. 'Now we will start all over again. I am still not threatening you, but I order you to disclose the naked truth that lies in your sub-conscious. Were you telling the truth just now about me?'

'Yes.' Her voice had gone dull and toneless. 'You never laid a finger on me.'

'Were you Dr Lisický's mistress?'

'Yes.'

'I want details about that. I want Nurse Cardew to hear from your own lips the full particulars of your *affaire* with the Doctor, and how, having first taken, and then neglected you, he took you back again to spite Owen Gruffydd. You had better tell the whole story as you told it to me that day in the summer-house; with any additional details which may show how badly the Doctor treated you.'

It all came out in about twenty minutes' monotonous monologue; and when she had done Sally expressed herself as entirely satisfied that I had put no part of it into Deb's mind; her story included things that I couldn't have known, and it branded Helmuth as both a sadistic brute and outrageous liar.

I turned back to Deb and asked her, purely out of curiosity: 'Why did you seek to protect the Doctor before I put you in a trance? Why didn't you tell us the truth then?'

'Before I left he told me that I was never to mention that I had had an affair with him to anyone. And that if I was ever asked, I was to deny it.'

'But as you were leaving anyhow, he could no longer hold the threat of dismissal over you; so why should you take orders from him? Was it because you were afraid that he might tell Owen Gruffydd something about you that you did not want Gruffydd to know?'

'No. It was because I should have been severely punished if he found out that I had disobeyed him.'

'Who by?'

'By the Party.'

I drew in my breath. 'Do you mean then that Dr Lisický is also a Communist, and a member of the Party?'

'Of course, and a very high one. He is a Commissar.'

Sally and I took a swift look at one another. The reply had electrified us both. Later, I realized that I should have considered the possibility of Helmuth being a member of the Communist Party before. Deb had disclosed that Miss Smith, who ran her nursing organization, used it as cover for a Communist centre, and Helmuth had told me himself that Miss Smith was an old friend of his—hence his pull with her to send him not only good-looking, complaisant nurses, but ones who were also 'trustworthy'. The tie-up was pretty clear, and I ought to have spotted it. By 'trustworthy' it was now clear, too, that he had meant girls who were members of the Party, whom he could order around, and who would keep their mouths shut if they suspected him of the filthy game he was playing on me. What a heaven-sent blessing that Miss Smith should have gone off for the weekend and the nurse she had selected to replace Deb had injured her ankle, so that dear Sally was sent instead!

But Helmuth a Commissar! I would never have suspected that. And what a field of speculation it opened up about the real activities of the Brotherhood!

When I had had a moment to recover from the bombshell that Deb had so unwittingly thrown, I said to her:

'Did you ever hear anything about occult forces being used by members of the Party to gain their political ends?'

'We are taught to use whatever means we regard as most suitable,' she replied. 'In some cases people who are interested in the occult can be led on through it to do things which they would not like others to know; then they can easily be blackmailed into doing as we wish.'

'But have you ever known a member of the Party actually to practise Black Magic himself?' I asked. 'I mean, one who cast spells, and used incantations to call up evil entities from the other world to help him in his work?'

'Only Dr Lisický,' came the toneless answer. 'He did not tell me very much about it. But I know that the reason he would not allow your blackout curtain to be lengthened, in the room downstairs, was so that the moonlight could continue to show under it. He needed the moonlight as a path for something to come into your room.'

I looked at Sally again, and I knew that as far as she was concerned I now had Helmuth completely in the bag.

Under the hypnotic influence Deb had done her stuff, and more; so I woke her and reassured her that I would say nothing to Owen Gruffydd. Then Sally took her downstairs and got rid of her.

When Sally came back she could not have been more generous about not having believed me before; and for a little time I allowed myself the luxury of basking in her sweet sympathy about this ghastly time I have been through. But there is only tonight before Helmuth gets back, so we soon got down to brass tacks and started planning our get-away.

She was all against my idea for getting the wheel-chair down the staircase, as she says it would be much too great a strain and might do me serious injury, even if I didn't collapse before we reached the bottom. But after a bit she thought of a better idea.

The far end of the battlement along the terrace is in partial ruin already, and the rest of the stones can easily be pushed over. It is only a fifteen-foot drop to the grass verge beneath, which is about two yards wide, having the chapel on one side of it and the edge of the lake on the other. With a twenty-five-foot rope, or even that length of stout knotted cord, we could take a hitch round the nearest sound castellation of the battlement and lower the chair to the ground.

Fortunately Sally is very strong for a girl, so she is going to take me down the stairs in a semi-piggyback. I'll have my arms round her neck, and my feet dragging, but each time she takes a step down, I'll be able to take my own weight off her for a moment.

There is a side door just down a passage from the bottom of the stairs and we shall go out through that. She will be able to get me along the passage, and round the outside of the Castle to my chair, in the same way as we mean to go down the stairs. We tried it out this afternoon, and found that I could get across the room quite easily that way.

She has gone down to the village again to buy the length of stout cord, and also to order a car to meet us at the bridge at the lake end, at midnight; so she won't have far to wheel me.

I think I can hear her coming up the stairs now; so she has lost no time on the job. What a blessed, merciful relief all this is.

Friday, *19th June*

Those footsteps coming up the stairs were Helmuth's. As the door opened and I saw him the thought leapt to my mind that he must be the Fiend in person. Or, at least, that only by Satanic means could he possibly have learned of our plan to escape, and have returned eighteen hours before he was due back in order to prevent it.

Then, thunderstruck as I was by his unexpected appearance, common sense told me that, barely two hours having elapsed since Sally had agreed to help me, he could not have known of it earlier, even by a thought wave; and, if he had stuck to his schedule he would then have been in the train coming south from Carlisle. In so brief a time nothing short of a magic carpet could have whisked him from a station *en route*, back to Llanferdrack; and I put that beyond what even the Devil could do for his agents in full daylight.

I was right about that, but nevertheless it transpired that his psychic powers had hastened his return. For a moment he stood in the doorway, looking at me searchingly and almost seeming to sniff the atmosphere. Then he said abruptly:

'Well? Have you made your choice?'

Consternation, anger, hatred and fear all struggled for first place in my emotions following the shock; but, by a miracle, I managed to retain enough of my wits to realize that now Sally was on my side all was not entirely lost, and that my one hope was to play for time. So I shook my head.

'No. I've been giving my mind a holiday. The events of the week before you left put such a strain on it that I found I couldn't think coherently; so I decided not even to try to face the question till a few hours before you got back. And you said you wouldn't be back till after lunch tomorrow.'

'I know,' he said; 'but last night I felt an impulse to–er–as you would put it–consult the oracle. The stars were by no means propitious, so the portents proved unusually obscure. That does happen occasionally, even to the most gifted practitioner of the art. However, on one point I received guidance. It was to the effect that my plans might be endangered if I failed to keep you under my personal observation; so I caught the first train south this morning and hired a car to bring me from Birmingham.'

With a shrug of my shoulders I pretended an unconcern that I was far from feeling, and muttered: 'So long as I am kept in this glorified cell with Nurse Cardew and Konrad to act as my gaolers I shouldn't have thought you had much cause to worry.'

'In any case, I haven't now that I am back,' he replied. 'And now that your mind is rested you had better do a little serious thinking.'

That admonition ended his brief visit, and I was left to savour the gall and wormwood of my most promising attempt to escape having been nipped in the bud.

I was almost weeping with vexation, but my futile mental rebellion against this unforeseen blasting of my hopes was soon submerged by a specific anxiety arising out of the new situation. The question that made me sweat blood was—would Helmuth run into Sally on her return and find out that she had gone over to me in his absence? If he did he would sack her instantly, and I should never see her again. The thought was torture.

Half-an-hour after he had left me, that immediate anxiety was relieved by her reappearance. She was flushed with excitement, laughing, a little breathless, and carrying under her arm a brown-paper parcel containing the length of stout cord for lowering the chair. She had not seen Helmuth.

In a few words I told her what had happened. For a bit she was terribly upset—not frightened, but angry and disappointed. Then we discussed the possibility of carrying through our plans, but agreed that Helmuth having returned in such a suspicious mood our chances would be far better if we postponed our attempt for twenty-four hours, anyway.

Before we had time to go into matters further Konrad came in with my dinner, and Sally had to go downstairs to have hers.

While I ate I was again the prey of harrowing speculations. It suddenly struck me that Helmuth was almost certain to learn of Deb's visit. If he tackled me about it, what explanation could I invent that would not involve Sally? And when he tackled her was there one chance in a hundred that her explanation would tally with mine? That passage in our activities was obviously dynamite.

Later, Sally told me that she had been equally perturbed on the same point; but she did not dare to come up to me again till half-past-nine, in case Helmuth should suspect that we had been getting together while he was away. She had seen him and reported my attempt to bribe her. That was clever of her, and had gone with a swing, as few things could have been better calculated to convince Helmuth that she still regarded him as her boss and was capable of resisting all attempts to undermine her loyalty to him.

Fortunately he still seemed to know nothing of Deb's visit, as he had not alluded to it. We discussed that, and decided that if he asked Sally about it, she should say that she had met Deb on he bridge on her way up here; that Deb had introduced herself, spoken of her forthcoming marriage, and—as one nurse to another—disclosed the fact that she simply did not know which way to turn to raise the money for her trousseau; and had had the idea of appealing to me either to give or lend her a hundred pounds as compensation for having been the cause of her losing her job. Upon which Sally agreed to let her see me and brought her up here; but what happened at the interview she does not know.

We were rather pleased with the story we concocted, as it covered Sally's having brought Deb to the house, and is really very plausible, since nurses are notoriously ill-paid and Deb, having no family to help her, may well be up against it for cash to buy nice clothes for her wedding.

Sally and I had only just agreed on the above when Konrad came in, and, after the usual drill, they both left me for the night.

I felt terribly tired, as Helmuth's return having baulked me when I was within an ace of getting free had exasperated me almost beyond endurance; and, added to that, I had gone through some four hours of nerve-racking fear that he might find out about Sally's change of attitude and sack her. But that danger seemed over for the moment if we both kept our heads, and it was up to me to make yet another plan; so I endeavoured to shake off my mental fatigue and get to grips with the problem anew.

The results of my effort were lamentably poor. Helmuth had clearly been in a highly suspicious mood on his return, but having found everything as he had left it, and particularly Sally having told him of my attempt to bribe her, must have done a lot to reassure him. So the best I could hope for was that if nothing occurred to cause him to take special precautions, we might have a decent chance of making our escape tonight.

The devil of it is that he will come up this afternoon, or evening, for his answer. I am determined not to give in, but if I defy him there is the dreadful possibility that he may carry out his threat to employ the Great Spider.

God knows how I will ever bring myself to face that fearful Satanic beast, and the touch of it may well drive me insane. But Helmuth must know that, and such a possibility seems to be the only card that I have left. If he *does* drive me insane he will have burnt his boats as far as the short, easy way of getting control of the Jugg millions is concerned. He will get hold of them in the long run, but that will take a considerable time, and an immense amount of skilful intrigue would be required before he could oust the Trustees that might oppose his plans, and achieve absolute control of the Board. Whereas if he can get me to sign a power of attorney he will have achieved complete victory by a single stroke of the pen. So I must play on that. The Sabbath, at which I take it the Brotherhood mean to celebrate a full-scale Black Mass in the chapel here, is not to take place until Tuesday—five nights hence—so I must temporize to the utmost of my ability in the hope of winning another two or three days' grace.

If only I can get him to postpone extreme measures until Sunday or Monday, Sally may be able to get me away before then. But there is no guarantee that he will not issue an ultimatum to me this evening; and as I lay in the dark last night, realizing that in another twenty-four hours I might have to face the Great Spider, the thought alone was enough to make me sweat with terror.

It was casting frantically about in my mind for a means to defend myself that made me think of Great-aunt Sarah. What effect, if any, a bullet would have on a supernatural beast I have no idea, but I do know that I would feel considerably more courageous with a firearm in my hand if I am called on to face it.

I doubt if there is a pistol in the Castle, unless Helmuth keeps one somewhere, and, even if he does, it would be impossible to get hold of that; but there must be several shot-guns and ammunition in the gun-room, and it occurred to me that I might get Great-aunt Sarah to bring me one tonight.

In consequence, when I heard her going down the staircase in the wall behind my bed, I rapped on the panel and called her in. After making polite enquiries about the progress of her tunnel, I told her what I wanted her to do for me and, thank God, without even asking me what I meant to do with a gun up here, she readily agreed to my request.

This is a great comfort, as if I don't need the gun tonight I can hide it behind the back of my bed; then I'll have it handy and, in the last event, I'll be able to fill Helmuth full of lead.

Later

It rained this morning, so Sally and I were not able to go out on to our terrace as usual; but we had a long talk here in my room. I gave her a full account of Helmuth's conversations with me during the few days before he went away—as I did not let her have the latter pages of my journal when she read the rest of it, because they contained several passages referring to my love for her—so she is now up to date with the whole situation and, thank goodness, she no longer doubts any part of what I told her.

She was, once more, sweetly sympathetic about the hell I have been through, and when I had finished, she said:

'You must have done something pretty frightful in one of your previous lives to be landed with a packet like this; but at least you have the consolation of knowing that you are paying it off, and that whatever happens now you will go forward with a much cleaner start in the future.'

I looked at her in surprise. 'Do you honestly believe that this is what the Hindus call Karma; and that there really is something in Reincarnation?'

'Why not?' she smiled. 'It is the only creed which provides a logical explanation to any and every human experience; that is, if you believe that the power which created the world, and us, is both intelligent and just—and if you don't believe that, then the whole scheme of things does not make sense.'

'Not to believe it would be to argue that God is an inferior being to men,' I replied; 'so one must.'

'Then if He is intelligent He would not permit the destruction of His property by wars, starvation and disease, pointlessly—or allow us to be the victims of all the other ills that inflict us in this life, needlessly—but only for our own ultimate good as a part of a great pattern. And if He is just, He would not condemn anybody to suffer for all eternity because they had failed to make good in the infinitesimal fraction of a second, which by comparison is all that anyone gets in even the longest of human life-span. However much evil might have been crammed into that single life the punishment would still be out of proportion to the crime; and that is not justice.'

I nodded. 'You're certainly right there. Do go on.'

'You will remember the famous bit in the Bible about the 'sins of the fathers' and God venting His wrath on those who had displeased Him 'even unto the third and fourth generation'. Well, what could be more flagrantly unjust than punishing innocent children for the faults of their grandparents?'

'Yet it happens, in the form of syphilis,' I murmured.

'Of course it does; and lots of children are born with T.B., although there is no taint of sin about their grandparents having caught that. But it doesn't follow in the least that because a child starts life with an hereditary disease it is through God seeking to revenge Himself upon someone who may already be dead. To accept that puts God on a par with a criminal lunatic. But look at it a different way and you'll see that the disabilities with which many children are born result from a just and logical process.'

'Oh, come, Sally!' I cocked an eyebrow at her. 'You're going to find it difficult to make a case for that.'

'Not at all,' she replied quietly. 'I believe that in the course of ages the real meaning of the Bible text became obscured and was then lost altogether. I think it was originally a warning that people who led evil lives would have to pay for it "unto the third and fourth generation" of *their own personalities.* That is, if you take it that each time our spirit is reborn in a new body we *inherit* the mental and physical disabilities—and, of course, all the good things too—that are due to us as a result of the good or ill that we did in our previous lives. If, in one life, a man forces some poor girl into prostitution with the result that she contracts syphilis, and in the next he is born with it himself, you wouldn't consider such a punishment either illogical or unjust, would you?'

'You've certainly made your case,' I smiled. 'But does the punishment always fit the crime?'

'Always. It is never a fraction more or less than you deserve.'

'How about my back; what do you think I did to deserve that?'

'It may be that you were due to learn patience as a cripple; or simply that the Nazi was paying off an old score, because long ago you had broken his back with a battleaxe, or something.'

'Then will I have to break his again in some future life, to punish him in his turn? It seems a stupid game to go on playing tit for tat like that through all eternity.'

'Oh no. You will be given the chance; and if you care to take it you will be in the clear, as you are entitled to give back what you get. But not a fraction more, mind. And if you are wise you will refrain from taking your revenge. It is by suppressing one's anger, and turning the other cheek, that one achieves spiritual progress.'

'If I did that he would get off.'

Sally shook her head. 'No, he wouldn't. If you denied yourself the temporary gratification of sloshing him, he would still have to pay up for having sloshed you; but it would be through some other agency. He might have his back broken in a mine disaster, or by some scaffolding falling on him while he was walking down a street. If you *did* break his back first you are now even, on the old eye-for-an-eye and tooth-for-a-tooth principle, so he has nothing to worry about; but if this was the first round between you he has got it coming to him in some form or another.'

'How about the other thing? These hideous ordeals that Helmuth has inflicted on me?'

'I think it's pretty certain that you must have put up rather a special black to have earned those.' She smiled a little wickedly. 'Until people learn that it does not pay they are always exchanging blows of one kind and another—and a lie which does harm, or doing anyone an ill-turn of any kind, is just as much a blow as an actual slap in the face—but this is something different. I can only suppose that at some time or other you must have been a powerful Black Magician yourself, and have caused a great deal of misery and terror by your evil practices.'

'That sort of thing hardly goes with wielding a battleaxe,' I demurred.

She shrugged. 'One does not pay all the debts contracted during one life off in the next; but one may settle old ones from several lives during one short period. That is probably what you have been doing recently.'

'If you are right, where does all this lead to?'

'It fits us for a higher sphere. We all start here on a very low level, as cruel, superstitious, barbarous savages. Gradually we learn this and that—to be gentle, generous, courageous in the right way, unselfish, wise, and to exercise control over all our appetites and passions. Eventually we become really fine people; we may live our last life on earth as great religious teachers, or pass it in comparative obscurity doing a great deal of good—it is quite immaterial which—but when we have learnt all there is to learn we join the great ones who have preceded us.'

'What happens if we fail to progress, or get worse and worse with each life we lead?'

'That is impossible. If we are pig-headed, and ignore all the signposts that point the way to our becoming better people, progress will be slow; and if we give free rein to our baser instincts we slip back a bit. That is a bore, as it may mean having to go through several extra lives before the lost ground is regained. But everyone realizes their faults sooner or later and makes a determined effort to eradicate them. Even an animal has the sense not to keep on getting itself hurt in the same way over and over again.'

'What part do animals play in all this? You said just now that we all start as low types of human beings, but some religions teach us that souls have their origin in much humbler forms of life.'

'No. Mankind is a different and high form of creation than anything in the animal world. We are individuals; they are not, so they have only group-souls.'

The word 'group-souls' instantly brought to my mind what Helmuth had said when he was talking to me about totems—the Great Spider, the Great Serpent, and so on. With a quick look at Sally, I said:

'You seem very certain about all this. Where did you get it from?'

She smiled. 'I got it from a book called *Winged Pharaoh* by a woman named Joan Grant. At least that is where I got the basic principles. But somehow it rang such a bell with me that I have since been able to fill in additional little bits and pieces for myself. That is why I am so certain about it. Every other form of faith that I have ever met with has always seemed to me to demand a belief in not only a number of good things, but in all sorts of absurdities as well; whereas this is simply sound common sense.

'Hellfire apart, how could any God who was worthy of respect condemn the most wayward of His children without giving them a second chance? And how can our salvation possibly depend upon anyone but ourselves and our own actions? Going to church may be an excellent form of discipline, and a useful reminder that worldly success has no permanent value; but it is childish to think that any ceremony one attends on Sunday can cancel out meannesses, cruelties and betrayals committed during the week.

'We all know what is right and what is wrong without any telling from other people. The still small voice of our own spirit, which has lived with us through all our lives from the beginning, tells us that. We may not always be strong-minded enough to follow its counsel, but in every crisis of our lives it is an infallible guide, and we need no other.'

Sally paused for a moment, then went on, her face glowing but in a low voice, almost as though speaking to herself:

'This belief of mine also abolishes all fear of death. Naturally as long as our spirits are chained to bodies we all fear the pain that proceeds so many forms of death, but most people seem to dread death itself even more. They are frightened at the idea of being parted from the little securities of family, home and money, that they have built up round themselves during their few years on earth; they are terrified at the thought of their soul going out into the dark empty spaces as a lonely wanderer, until at last it is called on to face some dread Being who will pronounce a final and irrevocable judgment upon it.

'Such thoughts have been instilled into them by generations of ignorant priests, who have blindly followed the teachings of churches that long ago became decadent and lost the light. Death is really a release from trial and hardship. Again and again we are sent here, like children going term after term back to school. Each time in a new body with new surroundings; sometimes as men, sometimes as women, sometimes to be rich and sometimes to be poor; we are given an alloted span of days and set certain tasks to learn in them.

'We have free-will and we can cut short that span in a variety of ways. If we do we only have to make it up by going through another part-life, as an infant or child who dies while still young. But we cannot increase the span by a single instant, whatever we may do. When the term is over we may go home with a bad report or a good one, and any trials that we have shirked we shall have to face again later on. But death is a holiday; and between our lives here, while our spirits are no longer imprisoned in a dull and heavy body, we are infinitely more fully our real selves, and have a far greater capacity for understanding and enjoyment.

'Unlike a school curriculum down here, the holidays are usually longer than the terms. As we have free-will we may decide that we wish to be born again almost at once, for some special purpose; but more often it is two hundred years or so before we feel impelled to enter on another trial; so it follows that a greater number of the friends we have made in many lives are always away from earth than on it, so we have the joy of being with them. In what we call Life we are really only half alive, but constantly beset by troubles, sometimes by ill-health and often lonely; whereas what we call Death is really living to the full, without material worries or physical handicaps, and being happy in the company of those we love.'

Later

I had to break off because Helmuth came in. He mentioned Deb's visit at once, and to my great relief I learnt that Sally had already sold him our story; so I had only to add that since I had no money I had had to refuse Deb's request.

He then produced a lengthy legal document and said: 'Tomorrow is your birthday, Toby, and your signature to this document then will make it a fully valid legal instrument. Are you prepared to sign it?'

'I certainly won't until I've had a chance to study its contents,' I hedged.

He nodded, quite amiably. 'I thought you would say that; so with a view to avoiding unnecessary delays tomorrow I propose to give it to you now. You will have plenty of time to read it through this evening.'

I took it, but made no reply, as there seemed nothing to be said.

After a moment he went on: 'You have put up a good fight, Toby, and I admire you for that. It makes me all the keener to have you become one of us. You have brains and guts, so there is a great future for you in the Brotherhood. But it is both useless and dangerous for you to fight further. So don't try to back out tomorrow; because if you do I really shall have to turn on the heat—and you'll find that all you have experienced to date was only child's play compared with this next step. Instead, I want your birthday to be a happy one, marking the beginning of an entirely new treatment by which I believe we'll soon have you well again.'

As it is of the first importance that, for tonight at least, he should go happily to bed, believing that I am at the end of my resources and about to give in, I raised a smile and murmured my thanks. Then he left me.

So, without any effort on my part, I have gained the twenty-four-hour respite that I needed so desperately. It seems at last the 'Great Ones', as Sally calls them, have listened to my prayers.

Reverting to the fascinating conversation I had with her this afternoon. We talked a lot more about her beliefs, and they certainly ring a bell with me too. The more one thinks about them the sounder they seem. All the intolerable stupidities and injustices of mankind, which make so many people doubt the existence of a God, are explained by them. And if one accepts it that all the misfortunes and set-backs with which we meet are not blind, ugly chance, but obstacles to be surmounted from which lessons can be learned, and tests of our fortitude and courage, the struggle of life takes on a real meaning and becomes a great adventure.

She confirmed my own belief, too, that no one is ever given a trial that is beyond his capacity to bear; and that, in conjunction with all she said about death not really being Death at all, but a return to a fuller, happier Life, makes me feel now as if I were encased in a suit of shining armour.

Sally is a wonderful person. What would I not give for her to feel for me one-tenth of what I feel for her; but to have won her friendship is in itself a triumph and a benediction.

Before we parted she agreed that we dared wait no longer, but must make our bid for freedom tonight. She went off to bicycle down to the village and order the car to be at the bridge again. Our worst fear was that Helmuth might send the Great Spider to me, and thus wreck everything at the last moment; but we decided that we must chance that. Mercifully that fear has since been removed; so I have great hopes now that on my birthday morn Sally will give me the splendid gift of freedom.

Later

I hardly know how to write it. This afternoon I was full of a splendid new courage; now I am near to tears. Sally is to dine with Helmuth.

She met him on her return from the village, and came straight up to tell me. I implored her not to; but she said that she must, otherwise he would become suspicious that I had prejudiced her against him while he was away, and that might put all sorts of ideas into his head—especially after she had allowed Deb to see me during his absence, about which, it seems, he spoke to her rather sharply.

I have never before dared to broach the subject of her last dinner with him, from fear she would resent it. But I did this evening.

She shrugged and said: 'It wasn't particularly pleasant, and, of course, you were right about him. He played his cards skilfully enough not to be offensive, but I soon saw which may the wind was blowing. That's why I got tight. I hate getting tight, as it always makes me feel frightful the next day. But it seemed the best thing to do.'

I stared at her in amazement. 'Do you really mean that you deliberately got tight so that you shouldn't care what happened?'

'Certainly not!' she retorted with a sudden flash of anger. 'You must have a very poor opinion of me to think that. If you want to know the truth, I am still a virgin; and I have not the least intention of throwing my shoes over the moon until my own good time—and then it will be with a man that I really love. But if you had ever tried to make love to a girl who is drunk you would know that it is neither easy nor pleasant—particularly when she ends up by being sick in your immediate vicinity.'

Her outburst both confounded and cheered me; and, blushing at the awful gaffe I had made, I muttered: 'I'm sorry, Sally. That was darned clever of you; but, all the same, I'm afraid he won't let you get away with that sort of thing a second time.'

'I don't expect him to,' she agreed frankly. 'And I am not looking forward to this evening's party one little bit. But I'll get by somehow. It may make me late in coming for you, but that can't be helped; and if the man with the car has given up and gone by the time we get to the bridge, I'll have to push you a bit further, that's all.'

'Oh, Sally!' I begged. 'Please, please don't dine with him. He is capable of any dirty trick. He may put a drug in your wine or try to hypnotize you.'

She shook her head. 'He won't do either. When he warned me against your attempting to hypnotize me I told him that an expert had tried it on me once, and failed completely, showing that I'm not a good subject. And in view of what happened before, I have an excellent excuse this time for refusing to drink anything.'

'All the same,' I argued desperately, 'he is horribly clever at getting his way with women, and absolutely ruthless. I implore you to pretend you are ill, or something, and cut it out. Even at the best it will mean your going through an absolutely beastly time for several hours, and if he gets really wrought up it may end in your having actually to fight him.'

Suddenly she stooped over my bed and kissed me lightly on the forehead, then she gave me a wan smile. 'Don't worry, Toby. Try not to think about it. And remember; none of us is ever given a trial that it is beyond our capabilities to bear. So help will be sent me if I really need it.'

I think the fact that she gave that sisterly kiss makes things even worse. But Great-aunt Sarah should bring me that gun tonight. And if I learn tomorrow that Helmuth has hurt a hair of my darling Sally's head, I swear to God I'll kill him.

Saturday, 20th June

I am at my wits' end. Sally did not come last night. God alone knows what that swine did to her.

I have been awake all night, turning and twisting in the most frantic agony of anxiety that any man can ever have known. I am scribbling this by the early light, and I've got to get through another two hours yet before they come to call me. Till then I'll have no means of knowing if Sally's non-appearance was owing to an eleventh-hour decision by her that circumstances rendered any attempt to escape last night being doomed to failure, or if the poor darling was *in no state* to come to me.

Dante knew nothing about Hell.

Later

When I attempted to eat my breakfast, I was physically sick from rage, grief and impotence. It was knowing that my last surmise about Sally is correct.

Konrad came in to call me at the usual hour; but to my consternation Sally did not appear. When I asked him where she was, he said that she had been taken ill last night, and he understood that she would not be well enough to get up today.

That can mean only one thing. She must have used her wits to stall Helmuth off as long as she could, then dug her toes in. He is not used to prolonged opposition from women, and her resistance must have eventually made him see red. He has all the servants under his thumb, and whatever she said afterwards she would never be able to prove anything against him. He must have got really tough, and her being in bed today is the result of his vile brutality.

And I am tied here; unable to help or comfort her; unable even to lift a finger in her defence. I only wish I had the means to kill Helmuth. I'd like to shoot him in the stomach and watch him writhing in agony on the floor. But I haven't yet got that gun. Great-aunt Sarah passed the panel near my bed without stopping, and I had to rap hard on it to call her back. The poor old nit-wit had forgotten all about my request; but she promised to bring me a gun tonight. I only hope this second time of asking impresses it more strongly on her mind.

In the meantime I am tied here. I can do nothing against Helmuth unless he is stupid enough to come within my reach. I have no means of finding out how things are with my poor, sweet Sally. I cannot even send her a message.

Later

While I still have the sanity to do so, I wish to record that this, my twenty-first birthday, has been the most ghastly day of my whole life.

For years I have always visualized it as a day of joy, gaiety and rejoicing. Not for myself alone, but for the many thousands of people who are concerned in it. I saw it as a carnival of flowers, music, dancing, wine, and toasts to the long-continued prosperity of everyone–man, woman and child–who are connected with the Jugg enterprises. I expected many gifts, but I meant infinitely to surpass them by what I returned to my people in bonuses, special grants and unexpected pensions.

The war, and my having been rendered *hors de combat*, rendered the broad picture impossible of full realization; but it might still have been a day of smiles and happiness. Instead it has been rendered a nightmare through that fiend Helmuth.

As it was, after my long hours of full and hideous wakefulness all through the night, I dozed a little in the mid-morning. But for the rest of the day my mind has never ceased to be harrowed by thoughts of Sally.

I have had no word from her, and Konrad could, or would, tell me nothing. I dared not ask him to take a message to her from me, as he would have carried it straight to Helmuth; and I still feel that it is imperative to conceal our friendship.

Just after I had finished my dinner Helmuth came in. Again, I did not dare challenge him openly about her; but I asked him at once what had prevented her from being on duty for the whole day.

He shrugged his broad shoulders, and gave his maddeningly sphinx-like smile. 'Our evening did not go quite so smoothly as I expected. She had a fall, in which she bruised herself and hurt her ankle. That's what has kept her in bed today; but it is nothing serious, and she will soon be about again. Anyhow, we have more important things to talk of this evening.'

That told me nothing. I did not believe his story of her having had a fall, for an instant; although she might easily have been badly bruised during the sort of attack in which I had good reason to believe she had been the victim. My hands clenched spasmodically beneath the sheets, and I had to lower my eyes to prevent his seeing the blazing anger in them. To have disclosed my feelings about her might have led him to suspect that I have told her what is going on here, and that she believes me. If he thought that it would bring her into grave danger.

He shook his mane of white hair back, and went on: 'Had we not decided to postpone the celebration of your birthday till next month, I should have come up earlier to offer you my congratulations on attaining your majority. But I have been particularly busy all day making arrangements for the ceremony on the twenty-third; so I thought I would leave it till this evening to bring you my unofficial birthday greetings. You will have read the document that I brought you yesterday. It remains only for you to sign it. Then we will hold a little private celebration. I have told Konrad to bring up a bottle of Champagne that has been on the ice for a couple of hours, when he comes to take away your dinner-tray.'

On that score I was, at least, able to let myself go. Taking the document from my bedside table, I said:

'I haven't read this and I'm not going to. As for signing it, I'll see you damned first, you filthy, bloody Communist!' Then, exerting all the strength of my hands, I tore the tough paper through and through and flung the pieces at him.

He went pale with anger and snapped: 'I have another copy, and you shall sign that, yet. How did you know that I am a Communist?'

Throwing caution to the winds, I shouted: 'Your wretched cat's-paw, Deb, told me. When she was here on Thursday I put her in a trance again; and I got the whole disgusting truth out of her. You are a Commissar, acting under orders from Moscow, and you have been trying to get my money to finance a Communist revolution in Britain.'

His rock-like, leonine face broke into a fiendish grin that showed his eye-teeth gleaming ferociously, and his perfect colloquial English suddenly took on the heavy foreign accent that now reappears only when his emotions get the better of him. With all the fervour of a fanatic he flung at me:

'You miserable young fool! Since you now know so much you may as well know the rest. I am a Communist, yes; but only for a purpose. That you may the better appreciate all that you have lost by rejecting my offer to make you a member of the Brotherhood I will reveal to you the shape of things to come.

'Socialism is the easy slope which opens natural citadels to capture by Communism. The suppression of freedom which goes with all control of industry, and the nationalization of public services, is the royal road to Totalitarianism. It gags and binds all individual opposition, while placing all power in the hands of a small group of politicians and highly placed civil servants. Then, it requires only secret infiltration of Communists into those key posts for the fruit to be ripe for the picking.

'In this country, when the word is given a *coup d'état* will take place overnight. The troops, the police, the B.B.C. and every department of State will be brought under control within a few hours. And the stupid British are so law-abiding that they will never question the orders of their *legal* superiors until it is too late.

'But to provoke a situation in which this country will accept a Communist *coup d'état* without a general uprising it will be necessary first to discredit the Socialist Government. Strikes, sabotage and the skilful manipulation of money will be used to bring about industrial and financial chaos. The Jugg millions are required by us to assist in that. The deterioration in the standard of living will condition the people to accept a stronger form of Government as their only hope. The ground for the *coup d'état* will be so carefully prepared that, when it does come, the average British citizen will regard it only as a welcome break from the tyranny of an outworn semi-dictatorship by the Trades Unions, and not even suspect that by it his country has finally lost the last shadow of independence.

'Britain will become a bond slave of Moscow, and the unorganized masses will be powerless to lift a finger to prevent it. A few scattered individuals—officers, judges, politicians, professional and business men, and Trade Union leaders—may realize what is happening, and that it is the end for them. But we shall know how to deal with such reactionaries. The opening of their mouths will be the signal for us to close them for good. It will all be very quiet and orderly, as suits this country. A few hundred people will be removed from their homes by night, and the opposition will be left leaderless.

'But that is not all. That is not the end; it is only a stage in the programme of the Brotherhood. Communism is the perfect vehicle for the introduction of the return of Mankind to his original allegiance. It already denies Christianity and all other heresies. It denies the right of free-will and the expression of their individuality to all those who live under it. Communism bows down only to material things; and my real master is not Stalin but the Lord of Material Things; Satan the Great, the Deathless, the Indestructible.

'The priests of the decadent Churches, the pathetic modern intellectuals, and our little scientists who fiddle with power on the lowest plane, no longer believe in the existence of my master. Or at the most regard him as having been so idle as to become a nonentity during the past century, just because he has held his legions in check from manifesting themselves openly.

'But he has been far from idle. He saw in this movement, to give the most stupid and lazy equality with the most brilliant and active, a means to recover his sovereignty over all. He saw that if the masses could be induced to destroy their natural protectors they would be left as corn before his wind. Therefore he bent his whole energies to the fostering of Communism all over the world. He has taken the very word Communism as his new name, and he even mocks those who no longer believe in his existence by having them demonstrate in favour of rule by the Proletariat on the first of May. Have you never realized that that is *his* anniversary, and that it is born of May-day Eve—*Walpurgis Nacht*—on which *we* celebrate *his* festival?

'The true Millennium is approaching. When the war is over Hitler's Europe will fall into chaos. It will be a forcing ground for the rapid spread of Communism. Britain will be compelled to give India her so-called freedom. That will result in civil war and anarchy overwhelming a population of three-hundred-and-fifty million people; so the triumph of Communism is inevitable there. China's four-hundred-and-fifty million will be left hopeless and starving; but her great neighbour, Soviet Russia, will see to it that she is set on the right path. When Britain succumbs, her Dominions and Colonies will soon follow; and with three-fourths of the world under the red flag, the United States will not be able to stand out for long.

'So the glorious day is approaching when, through the agency of Communism, my master, the Ancient of Days, the Archangel Lucifer, the Prince of This World, will at last enter into his own again.'

After this long and horrifying revelation, Helmuth paused for a second, his yellow eyes gleaming like those of a great cat, then he added:

'You were offered what would have amounted to a Governorship in the hierarchy which will rule the new Satanic world; but you have had the folly and temerity to reject it. Tonight I shall send a Prince of the House of Satan, the Great Spider, to you. He could have been your patron and ally, and even at times your servant, to destroy others at your bidding; but he must come now as your enemy. You have brought this terrible thing upon yourself, and will have only yourself to blame if, through it, you become a poor mad creature, who for years to come screams with fear at the sight of the smallest spider or even its shadow.'

Sunday, 21st June

In the past ten hours I have been the plaything of such violent emotions that my mind is still reeling under their impact. Setting them down may help to reassure me that the thing which overwhelmed me really happened.

To get the whole picture in proper perspective I had better continue this record from where I left off.

Helmuth's fearful disclosures—*that the Devil's new disguise is Communism, and that for the past century he has devoted all his energies to wearing this dark cloak with which to blanket for ever the free-will of mankind*—kept him with me barely twenty minutes.

After his final threat he turned away to leave me, but almost collided with Konrad in the doorway. Helmuth had probably forgotten that in anticipation of his victory he had ordered up Champagne. With a cynical smile he told Konrad to leave the bottle with me, as I might 'need it in the night'. Then they both went downstairs.

To keep my thoughts off the ordeal ahead of me I spent the next hour and a half writing the last entry in my journal. At ten o'clock Konrad returned, settled me down and removed my lamp.

It was a fine night, the moon was up and threw the pattern of the grating on the floor; but only faintly, as the late summer twilight still lingered and reduced its power.

Gradually, as the last light of day disappeared outside, the big oblong with its criss-cross of black bars grew brighter. I tried not to look at it, dreading what I might see, and endeavoured to comfort myself with my last remaining hope.

I thought it unlikely that the Evil would appear much before midnight, and at eleven o'clock Great-aunt Sarah would be going down to her tunnel. I prayed, as I have never prayed before, that she would not have forgotten again her promise to bring me a gun.

At last I heard her footsteps, and I rapped sharply on the panel. It slid back and she stepped out into the room. With an awful sinking of the heart I saw that she was not carrying the weapon. Her poor old mind is evidently incapable of retaining any thought permanently, except that of rescuing her lover from the Lady of the Lake.

For a moment I thought of trying to keep her with me, but I realized that would have been a futile as well as a wicked thing to do; so I let her go off to the strange task that will end only when she becomes bed-ridden, or at her death.

My hopes of obtaining the shot-gun having been dashed, I cast about for the next best thing with which to defend myself. The reflection from the moonlight now lit the room faintly, and on glancing round my eye lit on the bottle of Champagne. Failing a fire-arm or a cutlass few things could have suited my purpose better. The tapering neck of the bottle offered a perfect handhold, and its weight made it a first-class club. As my fingers closed over the gold foil I blessed Helmuth for his cynical gesture in leaving it with me.

Between my prayers I thought a lot about Sally, and the wonderful new faith that she had given me. Without it I doubt now if I would have had the courage to defy Helmuth. Somehow, having to face the ordeal took on a new aspect, as if what I had to go through was the paying off of an old debt that I had contracted during a life when I was myself a servant of Evil, or a test of courage which, if I passed it, would give me a step up the ladder of progress. I was very far from being unafraid, but I now felt that there was a definite limit to what either man or Devil could do to me; and that those friends of the long journey, of whom Sally had spoken, who were at present untrammelled with bodies, were watching over me and would see to it that no permanent harm befell my spirit.

I tried to keep my thoughts off the Great Spider, but despite my efforts they kept reverting to it; and one thing that puzzled me greatly was the nature and consistency of my enemy. There could be no doubt that it was a Satanic entity and, since it came from another plane, it could have no *real* being here. Therefore, it seemed to follow, from what little I knew of supernatural manifestations, that it could be seen and, perhaps, heard, but not felt. If that was so, then I had little to fear, except the horror inspired by being forced to look at a terrifying and repulsive beast. And if I *knew* that it could not touch me or harm me there was really no reason to be afraid. On the other hand, Helmuth had spoken of it materializing, and having to sustain its *body* on blood and excrement; which definitely implied that at times it had the power to transform itself into a ferocious animal capable of biting and tearing at a victim with its strong, spear-pointed legs. So I did not know what to think.

Again, if it was only a form of spectre it would find no difficulty in passing through walls, or a pane of plate-glass; yet it had obviously been incapable of getting at me through the courtyard window. Alternatively, if it had a solid body, surely the same factor would prevent its getting at me up here as had prevented it from doing so downstairs. The grating through which I can look down into the chapel from my rooms has no glass in it; but the mesh of criss-cross bars make the open squares between them far too small for a brute even one-tenth of the size to squeeze itself through.

For a time I strove to draw what comfort I could from the assumptions that if it was a spirit form it could not harm me, and if it had a physical body it could not get in; then another idea came to me.

Perhaps it would come through the grating or the wall in its spirit form, and materialize a body for itself when it was inside the room. Yet Helmuth had said that it needed rotting offal, and such things, from which to form an envelope of flesh, and there was nothing of that kind here, except—yes, the thought was horrifying, but he had mentioned blood—my own blood.

With a shudder, I tried to thrust from my mind the appalling picture of myself lying there in bed, striking wildly with the Champagne bottle at an intangible form which yet seemed to smother me, and gradually became a semi-fluid substance like reddish black treacle as it sucked at a vein in my neck.

I countered that unnerving vision by arguing that if it could enter and materialize in such a manner here, it could have done so equally well down in the library. But then again, perhaps, in those early stages of my 'conditioning' Helmuth had held it in check, whereas tonight he had no such intention.

My grim speculations got no further. At that moment I heard footsteps on the stairs; the door opened and Helmuth appeared.

I could not see him very clearly, as the moonlight hardly penetrated to that corner of the room, but it shimmered faintly on the strange garment he was wearing, and as he moved forward I saw that it was a ceremonial robe of white satin with a number of large black symbols imposed upon it. The folds of the robe prevented me from making out exactly what they were, but they looked like the signs of the Zodiac. Round his neck he wore a black stole heavily embroidered in gold, and on his head a curiously shaped flattish mitre. In his hand he carried a silver wand, at one end of which there was a crescent moon.

Without a word to me, or a glance in my direction, he walked past the foot of my bed. As he did so I could see the flattish mitre more clearly; it was really a toque of dark fur with two large red jewels in front; it was fashioned to appear like a big spider and the jewels were there to represent eyes.

Holding himself very rigid and moving with slow deliberation, as though he were in a trance, he advanced to the door that gives on to my little terrace, made the sign of the Cross the wrong way round with his wand, then unlatched the door and opened it a fraction.

The question I had been asking myself was answered. He had to assist the Great Spider to materialize itself by some hideous ceremony, and once it has acquired a body it could not pass through material obstacles. He had come up to let it in.

Turning, he walked slowly back towards the door that gives on to the staircase. I did not see him go. My eyes were fixed on the terrace door. At any second I expected to see it open and disclose the beast. As the other door shut behind Helmuth I had a wild impulse to call him back and beg him to spare me; but I managed to suppress it.

If I had not actually seen him unlatch the door to the terrace I would not have known that it was open. But I did know. It was just ajar, and it needed no more than a push of a child's hand for the heavy oak postern to swing slowly inward on its well-oiled hinges.

My hands were clammy as I stared at it, imagining that I could see it moving; but for what seemed an age nothing happened.

Suddenly my heart missed a beat. The door had not moved, but I knew that the beast was approaching. It was three weeks since I had felt that awful sensation, but there was no mistaking it. The perspiration that had already broken out on my forehead now chilled it as though snowflakes were melting there; my breath was coming faster yet catching in my throat, and I had a queasy feeling in my stomach that made me want to retch.

Still the door remained as Helmuth had left it. With the saliva running hot in my mouth I kept my gaze riveted on the old oak boards. The waiting seemed unbearable, and if at that moment I had been able to pray at all, I should have prayed for something–anything–to happen, that would end my agonizing suspense.

The night was very still. It was close on twelve o'clock and I knew that all the Castle staff would normally be asleep. But even if any of them were awake and I had screamed for help, shut off as I was and at such a distance from their quarters, they could never have heard me.

All at once the eerie quiet was broken by a faint scuffling noise. The hair on the back of my head rose like the hackles of a dog. I could feel my eyes open wide with apprehension, and my ears seemed to start out from the sides of my head with the intensity of my listening.

The noise came again, louder this time. It sounded as if a boot was being scraped with quick, light jerks against rough stone. I still had my eyes fixed unswervingly upon the door; but a sudden flicker of movement just outside my line of vision caught my attention. Jerking my head round, I stared at the checkered patch of moonlight on the floor. Part of an all too familiar shadow sprawled across it. Slowly I raised my eyes; then I saw the beast itself.

It was peering through the left hand lower corner of the grating at me. I could not see the whole of it; only about three-quarters of the body, the head and parts of several legs, one of which was fully extended above it and measured more than the length of my arm. Its body was fat and furry; its legs thick, sinewy and covered with sparse stiff hairs each about two inches long. As it clung there, silhouetted against the bright moonlight that was now streaming through the grille, I could see every detail of its outline; but its face was obscured by shadow, and all I could distinguish of that were two reddish eyes, glowing luminously.

The room was now ice-cold, and filled with an appalling stench. There flashed into my mind a temporary morgue that I had once had to visit, where bomb-torn bodies were being preserved for identification on blocks of ice. The atmosphere was very similar, except that there the smell of putrefaction had been partially obscured by idioform, whereas here it came undiluted in sickening waves from the pulsing body of the beast.

After a second it shifted its position. The movement was so swift that I only glimpsed its action. One nimble sideways slither and it was still again, spreadeagled right in the middle of the grating.

I was no longer capable of any coherent thought. All I could do was to keep muttering 'This is it! This is it!' while my brain subconsciously absorbed certain physical facts about the Horror.

It was as big as a fully fledged vulture. Its skin and hair were black, but splotched here and there with patches of a leperous-looking greyish-white. It could easily have torn a cat limb from limb or made mincemeat of a hound. But there seemed no animal, short of the elephant, hippopotamus and rhino to whom the beast would not have proved a formidable opponent. Even a lion might have found himself bested by such a beast, had it sprung upon his back and, while he roared impotently, clung there, gnawing its way into his liver.

Suddenly it began its devil-dance, scampering to and fro across the grating. With chattering teeth I watched it; and slowly the fact penetrated to my mind that although it possessed immense physical activity its intelligence must be dull and sluggish. It could see the terrace door through the grille yet it made no attempt to test that way into the room; instead it kept at its frantic blind fumbling to find a means of getting through the iron bars.

For a good ten minutes it continued to leap up and down, back and forth, until I was dizzy with watching it; then, all of a sudden, it dropped from sight.

I was sitting up propped against my pillows, the champagne bottle gripped in one hand and my heavy silver cigarette box in the other. For a moment or two I remained with every muscle tensed, then I relaxed a little. The room was still very cold, and the stink of rotting offal remained strong in my nostrils; but I was beginning to have just a flicker of hope that Helmuth's plan had miscarried, and that I might yet come through unharmed—unless he had some means of communicating with, and directing, his foul emissary. I think now that must have been so.

It is impossible to estimate time with any accuracy in such circumstances. It may have been three minutes, it may have been ten, after the brute had dropped from sight, that I heard the scraping noise again. This time it came from out on the terrace.

I shuddered, swallowed hard, and tensed myself. The scraping grew louder; then there came a faint tapping, which might have been made by the brute's pointed feet. My eyes were starting from their sockets as they stared at the door. Slowly it was pushed open.

The door swung back without a sound, and there in the entrance stood the monster. Now that it was no longer between myself and the moonlight I could see it plainly. It stood a good two-foot-six from the ground and shimmered with a faint reddish radiance of its own. It appeared to have no neck and its head was sunken, like that of a hunchback, into its obese body. Under a low, vulture-like forehead the two fire-bright eyes glared at me malignantly. Instead of the beak I had expected, its mouth was a horrid cavity surrounded by fringed gills, that constantly twitched and exuded a beastly brownish saliva.

In spite of the cold the sweat was pouring off me. I knew that in another moment this awful creature—a devil out of hell in the form of a gargantuan insect—would be upon me. But Sally's assurance, that none of us are ever given a trial to bear that is beyond our capabilities, came back to me, and strengthened my determination to fight the brute to the last gasp.

Something outside myself suddenly warned me that the monster was just about to spring. With all my force I hurled the cigarette box at it.

The box caught it full and square on the body, just below its slavering mouth. Even in that moment of terror I found myself observing the curious effect of my missile with surprise and interest. It did not go through the brute, as it would have through a spectre; nor did it land with a bump and then fall to the floor, as it would have on striking a flesh-and-blood animal. It seemed to sink right into the furry mass just as though I had thrown it at a great lump of dough. And the impact had some effect, as the beast wobbled uncertainly on its spindly legs, then backed a couple of paces.

I had no other missile in reach that was heavy enough to be of any value; so gasping out a pray for help, I transferred the bottle to my right hand and grasped it firmly by the neck.

It took me only a few seconds to do so, and in that time the monster had recovered. It sidled forward again to its previous position and gathered itself to spring. At that instant my prayer was answered.

I heard the staircase door open. There came the rush of flying feet, and I saw Sally race past the end of my bed. Without a tremor of hesitation she flung herself against the terrace door and slammed it to.

The beast had been half in, half out, of the open doorway. The impact threw it back on to the terrace, but the door closed so swiftly that it caught and cut off the lower part of one of the brute's legs. Sally, her eyes distended from the awful thing she had seen, and her breath coming quickly after her valiant effort, had turned, and was standing with her back against the door staring at me.

By her feet I could see the severed leg. It seemed to have a vile life of its own, and was wriggling like a snake; but I had seen too much during the past quarter-of-an-hour to feel any surprise when it flattened itself into a ribbon and slid under the door to rejoin its monstrous owner on the terrace.

For what seemed a long time Sally and I said nothing. Both of us were rendered speechless from horror of the Thing we had just seen, and fear that it would yet manage to get at us. It must have been a good two minutes before we recovered sufficiently to feel that the stout oak door was really a strong enough barrier to keep it out.

At last Sally whispered: 'Are—are you all right?'

'Yes!' I gulped. 'But you? Oh, Sally, I love you so much! I've been in agony about you for the past twenty-four hours.'

She left the door and, coming over, stood beside my bed. 'Do you really mean that?' she asked slowly.

I nodded. 'Yes. I didn't mean to tell you that I loved you. It just slipped out in the stress of the moment. But I do–terribly. You won't mind my loving you, will you? I promise faithfully that I won't make a nuisance of myself.'

'No,' she said, and her voice seemed rather flat. 'I'm sure you won't make a nuisance of yourself; and I won't mind your loving me–not a bit.'

She was standing with her back to the moonlight, so her face was in shadow; but she turned it a little away from me, and then I saw that she was crying. The light glinted on a large tear running down her cheek.

'Sally!' I exclaimed. And I reached out and took her hand. As I did so, she openly burst into tears, crumpled up, and practically fell into my arms.

For a moment I thought that she was still frightfully overwrought from the sight of that fearsome beast; but as she clung to me she laughed a little hysterically between her sobs, and murmured:

'I won't *mind* your loving me! How could I *mind*? Oh, Toby! Haven't you guessed that I–I'm terribly in love with *you*?'

Over her shoulder I had been keeping an anxious eye on the door, but it was fast shut and no sound came from beyond it; so at those marvellous words of hers I ceased to think of the terror outside, and our mouths met in a succession of long, sweet kisses.

A little later she told me she had believed that I thought her both plain and stupid; to which I was able to reply truthfully that her dear face aroused a tenderness in me that I had never felt for any other woman, and that I *knew* her to have more real wisdom than any woman *or* man that I had ever met.

She still seemed to think it astonishing that I should have fallen in love with her, but I said that the boot was on the other foot; and that, anyhow, it was the most rotten luck on her to have developed those sort of feelings for a cripple.

'Why?' she asked. 'There is nothing wrong with you apart from the fact that you can't walk, and that does not make the slightest difference to your personality.'

'Perhaps not.' I said a little sadly. 'And I'm immensely grateful for this present blessing of your love; but I won't be able to keep it, because I can't ask you to marry me.'

She turned her head and peered at me in the moonlight. 'Does that mean that you are secretly married already and have a wife hidden away somewhere?'

'Good lord, no!' I exclaimed. 'But I couldn't ask a girl like you to tie yourself to a cripple for life. It wouldn't be fair.'

'Would you'–she squeezed my hand hard–'would you, Toby, if you were strong and well?'

I smiled up at her. 'Of course I would. I've had quite a number of affairs, but I've never before met a girl that I really loved. You've read my journal, so you know that's true. And now I have, it's only natural that I should want her to be mine for keeps.'

She nodded; then, after a moment, she said: 'I shouldn't have asked that. It was my beastly vanity that urged me to. Please try to forget it. I feel awfully touched and honoured by what you said; and I'd like you to know that your being a cripple has nothing whatever to do with it. I would marry you tomorrow if it were only that; but well or ill, if you did ask me, I'm afraid I would have to say no.'

'Why?' I asked a trifle belligerently; then I added with an attempt at lightness that I did not feel: 'Perhaps you've got a husband tucked away somewhere?'

'No, it's not that. It's just that you are far too rich.'

'Too rich!' I echoed. 'What on earth has that to do with it?'

'A lot,' she replied seriously. 'When I do marry I want it to be someone who will really stick to me. I don't mean that I'd never forgive a slip-up; in fact, human frailty being what it is, I might need forgiveness myself some time—and if I did, I expect to get it.

'But I do feel that marriage should be something much more than two people agreeing to legalize a yen for one another, and after living together for a few years accepting it as quite natural that they should take another dip in the lucky tub. That is rather like starting to build a house without bothering to select a firm piece of ground, then abandoning the job half-way because the foundations have turned out to be rotten. I think one should try to make something really fine and enduring of marriage. In fact that it should be a sort of growing together in spirit, so that the joy of it should become greater, instead of less, with the passing of the years.'

'You're right about that,' I said softly; 'just as you are about so many other things. But I still don't see why having a lot of money should prevent two people making the sort of marriage you suggest.'

'Don't you? Well, just think for a minute. Mind, I'm not advocating poverty. That is tragic and hideous, and just as bad the other way. But surely you've noticed that couples who are not very well off generally make a much better thing of marriage than the rich. It is all the little difficulties that they have to overcome in making a home and keeping it together, that act as the cement for the bare bricks of love. When one of them wants something, it is not just a matter of signing another cheque, it means that the other must forego something they would have liked to have had themselves. It is that give and take, the little willing sacrifices, the saving up out of a not very big margin to buy one's love a present, that really binds people together.

'But for the rich it is all too easy. They have their fun while it lasts and then there is nothing left. Their homes are not the centres of their lives, but only beautifully furnished settings which they occupy from time to time when they have nothing more exciting to do. They have few real friends but a legion of acquaintances, so they are always running into new people who may attract them physically, and it is an accepted thing that they should flirt just as lightly as they go to the races or play cards. And almost always one of those flirtations becomes a new craving that they feel they must satisfy at all costs. Money is no obstacle so they get expensive lawyers to arrange matters, and with very little fuss or inconvenience to anyone concerned one more divorce goes through.'

After a little pause, Sally went on: 'It is sweet of you to say that I am beautiful; but I know that I am not. I believe that I am passably good looking; and I think that I could hold my own with most girls who have had my type of upbringing, but I am not in the same class as, for instance, your Aunt Julia. I'm not being catty, either, when I say I wouldn't want to be. It's just that I'm different, and I like my own type best.

'But women like Julia Jugg make an art of beauty, and they bowl men over like ninepins. Just one slinky look from a woman like that will often do something to a man that a girl like myself can't bring off in a month of Sundays, however much she loves him. When you get better, Toby darling, as I'm sure you will, and things are normal again, you will lead the sort of life in which you'll meet dozens of women as beautiful as Julia, only younger; and because you are a millionaire they will all make a dead set at you. Well, I'm not competing. It would break my heart if I tried. That's why I wouldn't marry you, Toby.'

I was silent for a moment. I saw the sound sense of her reasoning, and admired her more than ever for her strength of character in scorning the sort of marriage that most girls would have given their eyes to make. Then I said:

'As I am still a cripple, and likely to remain one for a long time to come, the question does not arise. But if I were fit I'd never rest until I had persuaded you to think differently, as far as I am concerned. I am different, you know, from most young men who have had riches thrust upon them. I am different because my unusual upbringing disillusioned me very early. I know better than most people how utterly empty and worthless easy conquests always prove. You are the first girl that I have every really fallen for, and I think you are underrating that a bit, by suggesting that a platinum blonde, dolled up in a Schiaparelli outfit and a new shade of lipstick, is all that is needed to make me lose my head.'

'I'm sorry, Toby,' she murmured. 'I didn't mean quite that.'

I kissed her again and made a joke of it. 'Anyhow, if I do get well, there is always one way of getting over your objection. I can make all my money over to Helmuth; then we'll take a ten-bob-a-week cottage, where you can scrub the floors and do all the cooking.'

All this time she had been lying beside me on the bed, with her head pillowed on my shoulder. At my mention of Helmuth she broke from my embrace and sat up with a jerk, exclaiming:

'He mustn't find me here! I waited to come to you till I thought he was safely in bed; but as he sent that awful thing tonight he's certain to come up to find out what effect it had on you.'

As he had done so after he sent the legion of small spiders I thought the odds were on her being right, but I said quickly: 'Don't worry sweet. If he does, you can hide while he is here.'

'Where?' she asked, with an anxious glance round.

'Behind the secret panel that gives on to Great-aunt Sarah's staircase,' I replied, pointing it out to her. 'But there's another thing. He left the terrace door open slightly, and if he comes up he must find it like that, or open; otherwise, as I couldn't possibly have shut it myself, he'll know that I must have had a human visitor.'

She shuddered. 'I daren't open it again. That—that awful creature may still be out there.'

For the past twenty minutes my every thought had been of Sally, so I had not been conscious of the change in the atmosphere; but now I realized that, although the moonlight still shone brightly through the grille, the air was no longer foul with that awful stench and was once again warm with the balminess of the summer night; so I said:

'The brute has gone. I'm sure of that. It seems extraordinary that simply slamming a door on a powerful Satanic entity should have been enough to drive it off altogether. I should have thought it would have had another go at trying to get through the grating, but your presence seems to have worked a miracle.'

She shook her head. 'If it has gone, it wasn't anything that I did. It was *us*. The saying "God is Love" is true, you know. And the spiritual something we released when we discovered that we loved one another must have been terrific. It probably had the same effect on the Horror as its shadow used to have on you; and I wouldn't be surprised if it crept away somewhere to be sick in a corner.'

As far as the beast was concerned her theory sounded highly plausible, but we did not feel that we could count on it also applying to Helmuth; and if she opened the door and left me there was a chance both that it might return, and that she might run into him on her way downstairs. We decided that she had better remain and we would keep our ears open for sounds of his approach. Then, if he did come up, she could quickly open the terrace door, and get into hiding behind the panel, before he entered the room.

So that no time should be lost I suggested that she should get the panel open. She slid off the bed and, as she stepped forward, gave an 'Ouch!' of pain.

'What is it, darling?' I asked anxiously.

'My ankle,' she explained. 'I sprained it last night. That is why I wasn't able to come up to you all day.'

'So Helmuth wasn't lying about that,' I murmured. 'Last night I was half crazy with worry about you. How did you manage with him?'

She laughed, a little ruefully. 'I overplayed my hand and this is the result. Before dinner I thought out what I meant to do. If a girl has just ricked her ankle badly and is in considerable pain it is just as much out of the question to make love to her satisfactorily as if she is disgustingly drunk. He was as charming and interesting as ever over dinner, and I'm sure he thought that he had really got me going.

'Afterwards we went upstairs to look at his books. That main staircase is so highly polished that it is rather a death-trap anyway. Halfway up I slipped on purpose, pretended to clutch at him, missed and went tumbling down to the bottom. Unfortunately I was wearing high heels, the right one turned over and gave me an awful twinge. It wasn't a case of shamming any longer, and in a few minutes it had swollen to the thickness of my forearm. He put a cold compress on it, and offered to help me undress; but I said I could manage all right, and by half-past-nine I was safely in bed.'

'That was darned clever of you, darling, but the most filthy luck. Is it still giving you a lot of pain?'

'It is now, rather; as I had to put all my weight on it when I ran across the room to slam the terrace door. Of course, its swelling up like that made it impossible for him to doubt that I really had hurt myself; so I don't think he has the least suspicion that I was deliberately holding out on him; but the infuriating thing is that as long as I can hardly bear my own weight on it I can't possibly get you downstairs on my back; and now that Helmuth is taking extreme measures it is terribly urgent that you should escape.'

As she finished speaking we caught the sound of footsteps on the stairs. Limping a bit Sally ran across the room, opened the terrace door, then ran back and slipped into her hiding-place, sliding the panel too after her. Meanwhile, I quickly disarranged the bedclothes, so that it would look as if a struggle had taken place on the bed, and wriggled down flat with my head lolling over to one side. I let my right arm hang right out of bed and, under cover of a trailing corner of the sheet, I once more grasped the Champagne bottle; then I let myself go limp, as if I was unconscious.

I heard Helmuth come in, cross the room to the terrace door and shut it. Then he turned and walked over to my bed. My eyes were a fraction open and I could just see him under my lowered lids. He was still in his ceremonial robes and the moonlight glinted upon the white satin. He spoke to me. I made no reply, so he leant over and shook me.

That was my opportunity. Jerking up my arm I struck at him with the bottle. It did not, as I had hoped, smash in his nose, but caught him on the side of the face. Even so it was a fine bash and may well have cracked his cheek-bone. With a guttural cry he staggered back and fell to the floor.

For a few moments he lay moaning there, then he picked himself up. I had hoisted myself into a sitting position and, still clutching the bottle, was praying that he would come near enough for me to get another swipe at him; but he did not even look at me. With one hand held to his face, he tottered towards the door, fumbled his way out and banged it to behind him.

As soon as the sound of his uneven footsteps had died away I rapped on the panel and Sally came out. From the noises, she had guessed more or less what had happened, and I gleefully gave her details of that marvellously satisfactory come-back on our enemy.

'I can't help hoping that it is hurting him like hell,' she smiled, 'and I think in his case you must have a pretty big margin in your favour; but when you are tempted to hit people in future, don't forget that unless you owe them the blow already the time will come when they'll give it you back.'

'You give me a kiss, and I'll give you that back,' I laughed, and we were in one another's arms again.

Later we opened the Champagne and drank it; the empty bottle will still prove a useful weapon.

Sally stayed with me till the moon had gone down and the first light of dawn was coming through the grating. It was an unforgettable night and, from her arrival in my room onwards, would have been one of unalloyed happiness, had it not been that my battle with Helmuth is now rapidly approaching its final crisis, and Sally's ankle makes it impossible for us to get away for another twenty-four hours, at least.

We felt that if she rested all today, the ankle might be well enough for her to get me downstairs tonight, or anyhow tomorrow night, which is the last before the Midsummer Night's meeting of the Brotherhood; but that in the meantime we positively dared not take a chance on her being able to do so, and must take any other measures we could think of which might possibly spike Helmuth's guns.

Naturally my thoughts reverted to Julia and Uncle Paul, and I suddenly realized that now Sally had come over to my side it should not be difficult to get them down here. After our last meeting, and my reconciliation with Helmuth, they would be certain to regard anything I said in a letter to them as the outcome of a worsening of my mental state, so it was most unlikely that they would make an immediate response to an SOS from me. But there was no question about Sally's sanity, so if she got in touch with them and told them it was absolutely imperative that they should catch the first train for Llanferdrack, it was a hundred to one that they would agree to do so.

A letter would take too long, so we agreed that Sally should either telegraph or telephone to Julia as soon as she could today. The trouble is, though, that her ankle makes it out of the question for her to bicycle down to the village; and, as she is officially *hors de combat*, we could think of no reason she could give which would be even remotely plausible for asking for a car to take her there and back. So, unless she has a brain-wave, she will have to telephone from the house; and while she is supposed to be sitting in her room with her foot up, it will be far from easy for her to snoop on Helmuth until he leaves the coast clear, without his spotting her.

I very much doubt if Sally's ankle will be sufficiently better for us to make our attempt tonight, but whether it is or not she is going to come up to me a little before midnight, in case Helmuth decides to summon the Great Spider again.

It is now nearly dinner-time and he has not so far been up here today, so I still have no idea if he thinks that my attack on him was the result of his spider driving me frantic, or if he suspects that his abominable scheme broke down in some way and that I simply took the chance that came my way to slosh him.

I hope that his non-appearance can be taken as a sign that the blow I dealt him has put him temporarily out of action. Anyhow it has spared me further immediate anxieties, and as Sally has not been up here either–apart from Konrad's routine appearances–I have spent the whole day in solitude.

Thank God, once again, for this journal, as writing this long account of my twenty-first birthday night has taken me all day, and has kept me from worrying too much about the possibility of Helmuth catching Sally while she is telephoning to Julia, my own still horribly critical situation.

In the past twenty-four hours I have known the extremes of terror and happiness. Strange as it may seem I have already almost forgotten the former in the warm glow from the latter. I can still hardly believe it true that Sally loves me, but my head goes swimmy at the very thought of her sweetness, courage and wisdom. I can hardly bear to wait until she comes to me again.

Monday, 22nd June

Helmuth left me alone last night, but my sweet Sally came in to me about a quarter-to-twelve. As she had not got her outdoor clothes on I knew at once that she had decided that she was not yet up to attempting to get me out. She was using a stick to take the weight off her foot and, as I feared, sufficient time has not elapsed for her ankle to show very much improvement.

Recently Rommel seems to have been having it all his own way in Libya, and the worst news so far came in yesterday. Tobruk has fallen, without any siege at all. Sally told me about it and we talked of the campaign for a few minutes. It seems a terrible thing to have happened when it held out so long and gallantly before. We must have some rotten Generals in Africa now.

After Sally and I had kissed a lot and said many tender things to one another, she told me that she had found it impossible to telephone Julia.

In the morning, soon after the maid had brought in Sally's breakfast tray,

Helmuth came to her room. He had a glorious black eye and the rest of the left side of his face was one huge purple bruise. Having briefly explained how he came by his injuries, he asked her to bandage him up.

Thank goodness it did not occur to him to go to her right away, as he would have found the room empty and, if he had waited there, no normal excuse could have explained her absence, as she did not leave me until nearly six o'clock.

Anyhow, she sent him out while she got on a dressing-gown, then greased his hurts and swathed his head in lint. During the process he told her that the waxing moon seemed to be having a worse effect on me than ever, and he had come to the conclusion that the only thing to do was to have me put in a straitjacket. Then he went on to say that unfortunately he could give no more time to me at the moment, as the 'Ancient Society of Christian Druids' were to meet here on Tuesday, and he still had all the final arrangements to make.

About eighty people are expected and, according to Helmuth's story, a midnight service is to be held in the chapel, after which the congregation will remain to witness the rising of the sun. As the visitors will be up all night none of them will require beds, but accommodation has to be provided for them to change into their ceremonial robes and refreshments to sustain them both on their arrival and before their departure in the midsummer dawn.

No extra staff is being taken on, as they will wait upon themselves; but it is quite an undertaking to get together enough food for such a crowd, and every hire-car for twenty miles around will have to be mobilized to bring them from the station and fetch them again the following morning. So Helmuth, with a very sore jaw, was about to begin a trying day, during most of which he expected to be glued to the telephone.

The Christian Druid idea certainly provides very good cover for this sinister meeting; as Wales was the last refuge of the ancient Druids, and I believe the genuine modern ones still meet at places like Stonehenge and Avebury to watch the rising of the Midsummer-Day Sun; while the Christian touch gives a plausible reason for their first holding a service in the chapel.

Such villagers as hear about the party will undoubtedly take it to be a form of Eisteddfod, and the small permanent staff here are so completely under Helmuth's thumb that if he orders them to bed at their usual hour none of them would dare to risk staying up with the idea of spying on the proceedings. And, anyhow, if the curiosity of some bolder spirits overcomes their fear of him, they will probably meet with the same type of horrifying experience that I had near the Abbot's grave, at Weylands.

Sally knew that as it was a Sunday there was not much chance of Helmuth going out on estate work, and that had been rendered even less by the battering I had given him. The additional factor that he had all this telephoning to do had decided her that her chance of getting a trunk call through to Kent, without his finding out what she was up to, was pretty near to zero.

However, my Sally is not the type to throw her hand in; so she wrote out a long telegram to Julia, pinned a pound note on to it, and wrote a letter to the local postmaster asking him to send it off at once if he could, or, if regulations forbade sending wires on Sundays, first thing this morning. Then she put the lot in an envelope, addressed it, gave it to the maid when her lunch tray was brought up, and tipped the girl five bob to take it down to the village. As the postmaster is the grocer, and lives above his shop, there can hardly be any hitch about her delivering it to either him or his wife; so by this time Julia should have it.

Sally says her telegram ran to nearly a hundred words, so there is no possibility of Julia misunderstanding it or failing to appreciate its urgency; moreover, it suggested that to satisfy herself fully about my condition it would be a good thing if she and Uncle Paul brought a doctor with them. I feel confident that they will not ignore such an SOS from my professional nurse; so they may be here tonight, or, at all events, not later than midday tomorrow.

My darling Sally had slept all the afternoon, so she was not a bit tired, and we talked until early this morning. She lay on the bed beside me all the time and it was absolute bliss. If only I can get well I swear I'll make her marry me. She is unique, superb, adorable and I am absolutely crazy about her.

Later

All is well. Sally's telegram did the trick. Julia and Uncle Paul arrived shortly after tea. With them they brought a Dr. Arling. Helmuth was out when they arrived so they first went to see Sally, then they came up to me.

Uncle Paul looked nervous and unhappy, but Julia was as sweet, competent and sympathetic as ever. Apparently Sally had thought it better not to go into details in front of a strange doctor about Helmuth practising the Black Art; she confined herself to saying that she was convinced that I was 100 per cent sane, and that when I had told them my story she would confirm the essential parts of it.

I felt, too, that it would be asking too much of a completely strange doctor to expect him to believe in the Great Spider at a first interview, and that it would only serve to prejudice him unfavourably about the state of my mind. So I told Julia that I would like to have a private talk with her later, to put her *au courant* with what had happened here since her last visit, and suggested that to start with the Doctor should put me through a preliminary examination.

'That was what we had in mind, darling,' she agreed. 'Then if Dr Arling finds that Nurse Cardew is right about you, it may not be necessary to bother him with the sort of accusations you made against Helmuth before. We can take you away with us and sort all that out later.'

Such an arrangement suited me all right, and the Doctor went ahead. He is a tall, thin middle-aged man with a sharp nose and a big, bulging forehead that gives him the appearance of having an outsized brain. He seemed to know his stuff, too. For nearly an hour-and-a-half he questioned me about my early life, upbringing, habits and appetites; and it was no random questionnaire either, as the whole of the enquiry was aimed at ascertaining my mental reaction in scores of different circumstances.

At length he said: 'You will appreciate, Sir Toby, that most mental aberrations are periodic, so I could not give you a clean bill except after prolonged observation; but your mind does not show any signs of disturbance at the moment. If, while in your present state, you express the wish to be removed from Dr Lisický's care, I feel it that those responsible for your well-being would not be justified in refusing such a request.'

Nothing could have been more satisfactory; for, of course, Uncle Paul and Julia at once agreed, and said that they would take me away with them.

As it was getting on for my bath-time, I asked Julia to come up again when she had finished dinner, so that we could have a heart-to-heart; but she said that after the shock of Nurse Cardew's telegram, the business of having to get hold of a brain-specialist of Dr Arling's status at a moment's notice, and the long journey from Kent, she felt terribly done up. So would I mind very much if she went to bed directly after dinner and we had our chat tomorrow?

Now it is definitely settled that I should leave here with them, there is no longer any great urgency about our going into Helmuth's criminal conduct, so it was decided that she should come up about half-past-ten in the morning, and we could have a long session then.

I was simply dying to tell Sally the great news of our triumph, so I asked Julia to give her a message that, if her ankle was well enough, I should very much like her to come up and sit with me after dinner.

Helmuth will be mad with rage when he hears that Sally and I got the best of him after all. He will be still madder tomorrow night when he finds that as the owner of Llanferdrack I have the police here to take the names of all his 'Christian Druids' on arrival, as trespassers; and have forbidden the use of the chapel for their abominations.

Obviously, this is no case in which I can prosecute him for his conspiracy against me. At the moment I can do no more than give him the sack. But I do not mean to let matters rest there. I am determined to hoist his infernal Brotherhood with their own petard. They meant to use my money to foster Communism in Britain, and now I am going to use it to drive them out of the country. I am prepared to spend a million, or more if need be, on the job.

If the police can get me their names for trespassing tomorrow night that will enable me to open a dossier for each of them; and if that fails I can always start my investigation by listing the staff at Weylands. I will employ half-a-dozen detective agencies, all working independently, to watch these people in secret and uncover their private lives. Sooner or later I'll get enough evidence against a number of them to have them brought to trial for blackmail, industrial sabotage, and communicating official secrets to a foreign Power; and I'll make things so hot for the rest of them that they will be glad to take refuge with their brother thugs in Moscow.

By the time I've done my stuff I shall be quite content to leave Helmuth to the tender mercies of his Infernal Master. Unless I am much mistaken, for having started all this, the Devil is going to be very, very angry with Dr Helmuth Lisický.

Later

I hardly know how to write this. A terrible thing has happened. One that I would not have believed possible. It has shaken my faith in all humanity.

Sally has just left me and in a few minutes Konrad will be coming up to settle me down for the night. That is why I am scribbling this now. If I don't, and am not able to re-read it in my own writing tomorrow morning, I shall believe that I dreamed it—that it was part of a nightmare—or that I am beyond dispute a madman who is subject to the most ghastly hallucinations. But it happened only a quarter-of-an-hour ago. There is no shadow of doubt about it. This thing is beyond words appalling, and my mind is still numb with the shock. I cannot yet make any attempt to analyse how the fact I have discovered is likely to affect my own situation—except that in a general sense it menaces me with black disaster. I only know that I am overwhelmed with grief and misery—and that it happened. It really happened. It is true.

After dinner Sally came up to me. We made love. We talked; mainly of the visitors. After three days' rest her ankle is better, but still far from strong; and she was greatly relieved that it would not, after all, be necessary for us to take a gamble on its bearing up during an attempt to get me away tonight.

As the summer dusk deepened we suddenly noticed that artificial light was mingled with it. Sally pointed to the grating and said: 'Helmuth and Konrad must be preparing the chapel for tomorrow night; there are lights on down there.'

For a moment we sat in silence and the faint sound of voices drifted up to us, confirming her surmise. Getting up she limped quickly over to the grille. Its lower edge is over five feet from the floor, but being tall for a girl she could easily see over it and down into the chapel.

'Well?' I asked. 'What's going on?'

'Something I think you ought to see,' she replied in so low a voice that I only just caught her words.

I threw back the bedclothes and did the wriggle that throws my useless legs sideways, so that they dangle over the edge of the bed. Sally came across to me and helped me to my feet. For a few seconds I took my own weight while she turned round so that I could put my hands on her shoulders; then, step by step, I followed her over to the grating.

My first glance down into the chapel showed me that considerable activity was going on. A broad strip of red carpet had been laid down the centre of the nave, and on either side of it there were fifteen or twenty mattresses and scores of cushions, which, presumably, had been collected from all over the house. In the side aisles some men were erecting long trestle tables. The scaffolding round one of the pillars that support the roof interfered with my view, so I could not see them very plainly; but it was easy to pick out Helmuth, as one side of his face was still bandaged.

A woman in a dark cloak, who wore a red scarf tied round her head, was decorating the altar—but not with flowers. The candles on it gave ample light to see that she was making her artistic tribute in a medium that the Devil might well be expected to approve. She was arranging garlands and bunches of deadly nightshade, toadstools, hemlock, ivy, tares, pigweed and nettles.

She stepped back to admire the effect; then she turned towards me. It was Julia.

Tuesday, 23rd June

It its still very early in the morning, and I am writing this by first light. Fortunately I slept all yesterday afternoon, so although I have not slept at all during the night, I do not feel particularly tired. Anyhow, I can still get in a good couple of hours' sleep before Konrad calls me, and God alone knows what will happen tomorrow—today I mean—so this may be the last chance

I'll have to make an entry in my journal, and I wish to record the splendid courage and devotion that Sally had shown in the desperate turn of my affairs.

The sight of Julia decorating an altar to Satan—even the thought of it now stuns me afresh—left me dumbfounded, stricken to the heart, hardly able to credit what I had seen with my own eyes, yet forced to because Sally had seen it too; and I knew inside myself that it explained all sorts of little things about Julia that had vaguely puzzled me in the past. Yet, at first, I could not bring myself to accept it as a fact, and the upheaval in my mind robbed me of all initiative. So Sally took charge.

As soon as she had got me back to bed, she said that she was terribly sorry for me, but that from what we had seen there could be no doubt at all that I had been 'sold down the river' by my own people.

She had spotted Dr Arling among the men who had been helping Helmuth to erect one of the trestle tables, so he was in it too. Clearly my relatives were members of the Brotherhood, and the doctor was also a member. He had been brought down to pull the wool over my eyes and, no doubt, to remove me to a private asylum in due course. They were all actively abetting Helmuth in his criminal plot.

Sally's view was that my only chance lay in her getting me away that night. Her ankle was still paining her but she declared that she would manage somehow. It was already half-past-nine so we had very little time to plan in before Konrad came up to take away my lamp.

Her main anxiety was whether she would be able to get me around the outside of the Castle. She thought she would be able to semi-piggy-back me downstairs, but it was going to be a terribly long haul from the side door to the place under the terrace to which we meant to lower my wheel-chair, and she feared that her groggy ankle might not stand up to it.

I was still too bemused by my recent discovery to think of any possible alternative, and it was she who had the idea of using Great-aunt Sarah's secret staircase. It could lead nowhere except straight down to the chapel, and we knew that a flight of about twenty steps led up from the chapel floor to a side entrance, which gave on to the grass verge of the lake within a dozen yards of the spot where the chair would be.

That route was barely a third of the distance we should have had to cover along our old one, down the spiral stairs, along the passage and half-way round the Castle. Even allowing for the extra strain of getting me up the stone steps inside the chapel, the total effort required would be nothing like so great. I pulled my wits together sufficiently to produce the only snag I could think of—that the door at the bottom of the secret staircase might be locked, and its bolts rusted in with long disuse, so that we should not be able to get it open.

Sally countered that by saying she could get hold of some oil, a hammer, a small saw and other tools from the garage machine shop, and that she would bring with her candles as well as a torch; and that even if it took us an hour to get the door open we would still have ample time to be out of the grounds well before dawn. She also pointed out that another advantage of going by the secret staircase was that we could be certain of not running into anyone on it; so there would be much less danger of our being caught.

I had no further objections to offer, and time was getting short; so I kissed her and blessed her and, after promising to be back shortly before midnight for our eleventh-hour bid for freedom, she left me.

The entry I made in my journal took me only a few minutes, and I had hardly completed it when Konrad arrived. After he had gone the time of waiting passed with extraordinary swiftness because, I am ashamed to say, my mind was not really on the job ahead, but occupied with the most wretched speculations about Julia.

On Sally's return the first thing we decided was that she should reconnoitre the secret stairway, to make certain that there was a door at its bottom and that it would be possible to get it open. She had brought quite a large bag of tools and, taking them with her, she disappeared through the panel, closing it after her.

Going into such a place alone at dead of night must have taken more courage than most girls possess, particularly when one knew of the evil things that lurked in the vicinity; but Sally never hesitated, and somehow I did not feel afraid for her, only rather humble at the thought that I should be loved by a girl with such a valiant heart.

But as time went by and she failed to reappear I did get worried. I endeavoured to convince myself that she had found the door and was working on it; but I could not help imagining that she had met with some accident, and I began to pray frantically for her safe return.

She must have been down there over three-quarters-of-an-hour, but at last I heard her coming back and, dusty, begrimed, dishevelled, she stumbled, still panting, through the panel opening.

'It's all right,' she said with a smile. 'Luckily the bolts are on this side. I managed to get one of them back, but the other needs a stronger blow with the hammer than I can give it. The lock will have to be cut out too. I've bored the holes for that and sawed down one side, but my wrist got so tired that I thought I had better come back and get you down there to help me.'

'Thank God you did!' I murmured, pulling her to me and kissing her cheek where it was smudged with dirt.

Limping over to the staircase door she shot the bolt, so that we should not be interrupted. Then she helped me to dress and got me into my chair. Next she opened the terrace door and wheeled me out to the far end of the terrace, where the battlement is crumbling away. I helped her to push over a number of the big, loose stones until we had made a gap about four feet wide. To get out the lower ones needed all the strength of my arms and I had to lie on the ground to exert sufficient pressure, but after about twenty minutes we had the gap clear to the bottom, so that the chair needed only a push to run over.

We tied the stout cord to the backrail of the chair, took a double hitch round the nearest castellation, and I hung on while Sally wheeled the chair over the edge. She supported part of its weight for a moment, so that the jerk should not snap the cord, then I cautiously lowered away. Two minutes later the cord abruptly slackened, and we knew that we had accomplished that part of the job all right. The moon was just showing above the tree tops on the far side of the lake and on peering over the battlement we could make out the chair standing right way up fifteen feet below us.

It had been easy enough for Sally to get me out of the chair on to the ground but it proved a much harder task to get me up again. On previous occasions when she had got me to my feet I had always been sitting on the edge of the bed or in my chair, but now she had to kneel down so that I could clamber on her back, then, with a great effort, she lifted me bodily.

Once I was upright we were able to go forward slowly. She took most of my weight on her shoulders, in a semi-piggy-back, but I was able to take some of it on my feet, and with each of them dragging alternatively we made our way forward a few steps at a time. It took us ten minutes to get back to my bed. There we rested for a bit, and while we were doing so we heard Great-aunt Sarah come up the stairs behind the panel, so we knew that it was one o'clock. When her foot-steps had died away, by a further five minutes of strenuous effort Sally got me through the secret panel.

The light from her torch showed the staircase to be much broader than I had expected. It was a good six feet wide, and lofty, with a vaulting ceiling. The air inside it was warm but had none of the stuffiness that one associates with secret passages; and for that we soon saw the reason. About every five feet down the outer wall there were shallow embrasures with long arrow-slits, through which the moonlight percolated faintly.

After another short rest we essayed the descent. Before we were half-way I could feel the perspiration wet upon poor Sally's neck, and from the way she flinched each time she now put her bad foot one step further down, I knew that it must be hurting her like the devil.

I insisted that we should make longer pauses, but she said that did not really help, and that when we got to the bottom there would be plenty of time for her to rest her foot while we were getting the door open.

Between the bottom step and the door there was a short section of passage, only about eight feet in length, the floor space of which was partly encumbered by square blocks of stone. I saw that these had been removed from the left-hand wall, in which there was a big hole some four feet high and three feet across, and I knew it must be the entrance to Great-aunt Sarah's tunnel.

The blocks of stone now came in handy as they were from twelve to eighteen inches square, and were not too heavy for Sally to lift with an effort. By piling them up she made a seat for me, so that while she held the torch I could get to work on the lock.

It is no light task to cut through a three-inch-thick panel of ancient oak, and after I had been at it for a little while I marvelled that Sally had managed to get as far as she had in the time. Nearly two hours elapsed before I had completed the square round the lock, and by the time I had hammered back the remaining bolt it must have been three in the morning.

Having brushed ourselves down, we made ready for the next stage of our arduous journey. Sally put her shoulder against the door and heaved. With a loud groan of rusty hinges it gave, and reluctantly opened a couple of feet. As it did so I felt a chill draught come through from the chapel.

Instantly I knew that all our labours had been in vain; for at the same second a wave of nausea flooded through me. I was still seated on the pile of stone. As I leaned sideways to look past Sally I heard her give a sob; then I saw what she had already seen, and knew that my fears were only too well founded. The Great Spider was crouching in the middle of the aisle.

The moonlight streamed through a rent in the roof right on to the monster. Between its forefeet it held a dead cat, and it had evidently been making a meal off the cat's entrails, as they hung out from its torn stomach on to the floor; but the noise of the opening door had drawn our enemy's attention to us. Flinging aside the dead cat the black, hairy brute bounded in our direction.

Simultaneously, Sally and I grabbed the door and hauled it shut again. Then, falling on her knees beside me, she gave way to her distress in a flood of bitter tears. It was hard indeed to find our escape route barred by that hideous sentinel and, although I tried, there was little I could say to comfort her.

Afterwards, it did occur to me that if we could have gone boldly out into the chapel hand in hand the strength of our love might have created an aura that would have driven the brute back. But I could not stand alone for more than a moment, and I would not have let Sally face that incredibly evil thing with me dragging along behind her. At the time, to beat a retreat seemed the only possible course open to us.

When Sally had recovered a bit we began the ghastly business of getting back up the stairs. The eighteen or twenty steps that we had meant to go up on the far side of the chapel to its lake-shore entrance would have proved a bad enough ordeal, but here there were more than double that number. Leaning on Sally's back, I had been able to come down a step at a time, but I was much too heavy for her to carry and it was beyond my powers to take a single step upward.

We started by my clinging to her waist while she dragged me behind her, and got up about ten steps that way. But the strain on her was frightful; and when she could no longer suppress a loud moan from the pain in her ankle, I refused to let her pull me any further.

I tried pulling myself up, but as there was nothing ahead of me to grip except the smooth stones, and my knees were useless, I had to abandon the attempt. Then, turning round, I used my arms as levers to lift myself backwards from step to step. By the time I was half-way up I felt as though my arms were being wrenched from their sockets, and I could not possibly have got much further had not Sally come to my assistance. She went up backwards, too, behind me, and, stooping almost double, got her hands under my armpits so that she could heave every time I lifted. We managed that way, and at last she got me back to my room, but the final effort of supporting me to my bed proved too much for her, and as I flopped on to it she fainted.

She slipped to the floor near enough for me to sprinkle water from by bedside carafe on her face, and to my relief she soon came round sufficiently to pull herself up on to the bed beside me. We remained like that for a while, getting our strength back and wondering miserably what we should do next.

To attempt our original plan, of going down the spiral staircase, was out of the question. We were both dead-beat already, and Sally's ankle was paining her so much that she would have fainted again before we were a quarter of the way down it. So there seemed nothing for it but that I should resign myself to remaining where I was, and facing whatever was coming to me.

Suddenly I remembered that we had lowered my wheel-chair over the battlements. It was much too heavy for us to pull up again, and I could not possibly have got it down to the lake-side by myself. When that was discovered—as it must be first thing in the morning—it would be realized that someone had aided me in an abortive attempt to escape; and suspicion could point only to Sally.

When I told her my new fear she laughed a little bitterly. 'You poor sweet;

don't fret about that. Surely you realize that I have burnt my boats already. By sending that telegram to Julia I disclosed the fact that I am on your side. But she is not; and she only brought Dr Arling to hear what I had to say this afternoon to keep *me* from suspecting that they are both in this plot against you. Since we have failed to escape it is certain now that they will prevent my seeing you again, and do their best either to bribe or browbeat me into acknowledging that I was quite mistaken about your being sane.'

That gave me furiously to think. I felt convinced that Helmuth and Co. were capable of going to any lengths to ensure that Sally held her tongue. The business of the chair would give it away that her interest in me was not merely one of wanting to assure fair play for her patient; but that she was actively endeavouring to get me out of Helmuth's clutches. That presupposed that I had told her the whole story, and that she believed me. In that case they could not possibly afford to let her leave Llandferdrack, and, therefore, she was now in grave danger.

I told her that, and added: 'There is only one thing to do, darling. You can't get me out, but you can get out yourself. You must go downstairs, collect the few things that you feel you will be able to carry, and slip away before daylight.'

She shook her head. 'I'm damned if I will, Toby! What do you take me for? I love you; and I'm going to stay and fight these bloody people with you.'

For a quarter of an hour we wrangled fiercely over that. I alternately begged and ordered her to leave me; she refused to listen to my arguments and insisted on remaining. At length we agreed on a compromise. She should not return to her room, where she might find herself at their mercy, but lead them to suppose that she had got the wind up and cleared out. Actually she would retire into hiding behind the secret panel, so that she could hear all that went on in my room and render me any assistance that she could.

By the time the issue had been settled it was after four o'clock. The moon was down, so Sally lit a candle. The sweat had dried on us, caking the dirt, and we looked like a couple of sweeps. Anyone who saw me would have known at once that I must have been burrowing in some dirty hole, and the last thing we wanted was for Helmuth to start hunting for a secret passage. So Sally helped me to undress and got me properly back to bed, then brought me the basin and ewer from the washstand.

We made a cross on the water to prevent bad luck and washed our faces and hands. She threw the dirty water out on to the terrace, shut the door and unbolted the one to the spiral stairs.

Before she left me we arranged that if I gave one knock on the panel that would be the danger signal; she would know that I had heard someone coming upstairs and that she must remain quite still in case they heard her. If I gave two knocks that would be the signal that the coast was clear again, and I would knock three times if I wanted her to come out.

On my insistence she took some of the clothes from my wardrobe and a couple of cushions to make a couch to lie on; then we parted with mutual exhortations to have courage, and with great tenderness.

The grey light of dawn was already throwing the criss-cross bars of the grating into relief, so I started to scribble this; but I hope that my sweet Sally has been sleeping for the past hour or more. I am now feeling very tired myself, so I will snatch a couple of hours' sleep before Konrad comes to call me.

God alone knows what fresh ordeals the coming day will bring. I am alone in a dark world, but for the beacon of Sally's love. That must and shall sustain me.

Later

If I were not so desperately afraid of what may happen in the next twenty-four hours to Sally and myself, I should be laughing at the comedy that has just taken place.

Within a few moments of entering the room Konrad noticed the disappearance of my wheel-chair. I had only just woken, so I had not got my wits fully about me; but I think my sub-conscious must have been concerning itself with the problem during my two-hour sleep, since I replied without hesitation:

'The Archangel Gabriel appeared to me last night. He said that I no longer required it, and he took it away. I think he threw it in the lake.'

Konrad's pale blue eyes almost popped out of his head. This cunning Ruthenian peasant is terribly superstitious. He would, I am sure, have bullied me unmercifully during these past three weeks had I not taken a leaf out of Helmuth's book. H. scared Taffy by telling him that I had the evil-eye. I told that story to Konrad soon after H. made him my gaoler-bodyservant. Since then he has done his job with as little fuss as possible. He is still 100 per cent Helmuth's man, but he has been mighty careful not to give me offence.

My quiet, unemotional statement about the Archangel having visited me, threw him into a paroxysm of terror. The chair was no longer in the room and he knew perfectly well that I could not possibly have disposed of it myself, so it was not altogether surprising that he should accept the suggestion that it had been removed by a supernatural agency.

He had already dumped my breakfast tray on my bed-table; and, instead of proceeding as usual to hand me my tooth-brush and the basin, he gave me a shifty glance then sidled quickly out of the room.

I gave three knocks for Sally. A moment later she almost tumbled through the panel opening, still half asleep.

'Quick!' I said. 'Help yourself to a cup of coffee, and take some toast and fruit; then skip back to your hiding-place. Konrad has gone to fetch Helmuth and they will be up here in a few minutes.'

She poured the coffee, made a face as she gulped it down, took a handful of cherries off the plate, gave me a swift kiss on the nose, then stumbled back through the opening like a large sleepy child. I longed to call her back and put my arms round her. She is absolute heaven.

Konrad returned with Helmuth five minutes later. It is the first time I have seen him since I hit him with the bottle. He had the bandages off this morning but his eye is still black and blue.

I maintained my story about the Archangel, and for a moment I saw fear in his tawny eyes. Then his suspicions overcame his credulity. He went out on to the terrace, saw the gap in the battlement and, on looking over, the chair down by the lake-side. Striding back to me, he shouted:

'That great hoyden Sally Cardew must be responsible for this! It was she who telegraphed for Julia. And now she's tried to help you to escape; but it proved too much for her. I'll teach that young bitch to double-cross me like this!'

'Do, if you can find her,' I mocked him. 'But you won't; because she's gone back to London. And in due course she will bear witness against you in a criminal court.'

'She won't get the chance!' he snapped. 'I'll soon have her traced and stop her tongue. The Brotherhood has plenty of ways of dealing with stupid or indiscreet people. It may interest you to know that Deborah Kain will be sailing from Cardiff in the hold of a tramp steamer today. If she does not die on the voyage round Africa she will eventually reach Persia, and be sent through to Russia. She came here to see you against my orders, and in the Soviet Union they know how to punish the servants who have failed them.'

Glad as I was to know that Britain was nurturing one less viper in her bosom, I could not help feeling sorry for the wretched Deb, as it was largely my fault that such a fate had overtaken her. But Helmuth was going on:

'As for anyone bearing witness against me in a criminal court, you must be really mad if you think you will ever be in a position to prosecute me. After the dance you've led me I'm in no mood to show you further mercy. Tonight I mean to finish your business once and for all. The Brotherhood will invoke the Lady Astoroth to visit you here, and she will destroy your reason.'

Turning on his heel he flung out of the room, and I was left to contemplate anew the really desperate situation in which last night's failure to get away has placed me.

I had continued to put a bold face on matters in front of Helmuth, but I am feeling very far from bold. Sally's love, and her faith in the inevitable triumph of good over evil, alone sustained me. But I am powerless to help myself and I do not see how she can help me further. Moreover, while I now fully accept her wonderful teaching, it is a long-term policy; it may well be that in a past life I once drove someone mad, and in this one must pay the penalty by being driven mad myself.

I have only one weak straw to cling to, and that is Julia. There can be no question about her being in with Helmuth. If further proof were needed, he gave it himself by disclosing that she had told him of Sally's telegram, thus giving it away that Sally had come over to my side.

If Helmuth is with her at the moment, and mentions his disclosure, she will realize that I now know her to be in league with my enemies, and she may be ashamed to face me. But if she does not yet know that I know of her treachery she should be coming up to see me as she promised, quite soon now. If she does, there is just a chance that I may be able to save myself through her.

Later

It is afternoon. I am writing the following only because it is absolutely vital that I should do so. This time tomorrow I expect to be insane and my testimony will then be valueless.

I hereby make solemn declaration that I am now in my right mind; that the following is the truth, the whole truth, and nothing but the truth, with regard to the death of Julia Jugg.

I murdered her. Nurse Cardew was an accessory but an innocent one. She acted in defence of her crippled patient, in the belief that she could help to save him from a gang of criminals. The very fact that I shall not attempt to conceal the part she played is in itself testimony that she was innocent of the actual crime. What she did was done by my orders and the responsibility for Mrs Paul Jugg's death is entirely mine.

This is what occurred; so help me God.

A little after ten-thirty this morning, Tuesday the 23rd of June, 1942, Julia came up to see me as she had promised. Her demeanour was affectionate and unabashed. She sat down beside my bed and, after talking trivialities for a few moments, by a casual question I extracted the information from her that she had not seen Dr Helmuth Lisický since last night; as she had breakfasted in bed, only just got up, and had come straight up from her bedroom to me. I knew then that she knew nothing yet of my abortive attempt to escape last night, or that I realized that she was involved in the conspiracy against me.

I asked her when we were going to leave Llanferdrack.

'Not till tomorrow, darling,' she replied. 'Dr Arling wants to examine you again tonight in the moonlight to see if the moon really has a bad effect on you. But whether it has or not Paul and I mean to take you back with us to Queensclere tomorrow morning.'

Stretching out my hand, I took hers. Then I said quietly:

'You are lying, Julia. You have been plotting with Helmuth to drive me mad tonight, so that Dr Arling can take me away to some private asylum tomorrow.'

Her great eyes suddenly showed fear and consternation. She shook her head and struggled violently to drag her hand from my grasp; but I had a firm grip of it, and I went on:

'It is useless to deny it, Julia. I saw you last night arranging those poisonous herbs and stinging nettles on the Devil's altar. That was the most awful thing that has ever happened to me. It was like losing a limb. It was worse than when I was told that my back was broken and the odds were against my ever walking again.'

I paused and added in a husky voice: 'Even now, terribly as you have hurt me, I hate having to hurt and bully you. But I've got to; because only you can save me from Helmuth, and only by regaining my freedom can I save you from the ghastly web in which you have enmeshed yourself. I suppose you were blackmailed into becoming a Satanist. I want to know the truth about that. Then we'll make a plan to trick Helmuth at the last moment. Once I am free I mean to smash up this evil Brotherhood; but whatever you have done I'll find a way to save you from them. You see, I want to help you to become clean and free again. So you must tell me the whole truth.'

'I won't!' she moaned. 'I won't! Let me go! Let me go!'

'Oh yes, you will,' I said. 'If you won't talk freely I shall have to make you.' Then I caught her glance and held it.

'Let me go! Let me go!' her voice grew louder, and tearing her glance from mine she wailed: 'You beast! You're trying to hypnotize me!'

I knew then that even at the price of giving Sally's–Nurse Cardew's–hiding-place away I must have help, otherwise my forlorn hope was doomed to failure. Stretching across Julia I rapped thrice sharply with my free hand on the secret panel.

In leaning over I had momentarily to loosen my grip on Julia's hand. As the panel slid back and Sally came out Julia wrenched her hand from my grasp. Turning, she ran towards the door.

'Quick, Sally!' I cried. 'For God's sake catch her, and bring her back. I've got to hypnotize her by force. It's our only hope.'

Sally darted after her and caught her in the middle of the room.

For a few moments there ensued a horrid scuffle. The two women fought like tiger-cats. Julia's long nails tore three furrows in Sally's grimy cheek; then she got hold of a handful of Sally's fuzzy hair and wrenched it out, while kicking violently at her shins. But Sally was much the stronger of the two. She hit Julia hard in the face, grabbed one of her arms and twisted it behind her back, then hurtled her across the room and forced her face down on to the bed.

I seized Julia by the shoulders, but by that time she had begun to scream for help; so I transferred my grip to her throat and, much as I hated having to do it, choked her into silence.

She was now sprawled over sideways on to the bed and face upwards across my middle. Stooping over her, I stared down into her eyes and ordered her to sleep.

But she shut her eyes firmly, so I had to get Sally to turn the lids back and hold them open.

Even then, Julia put up a terrific resistance, and after we had held her like that for a quarter of an hour she still had not given in. I had always heard that it is terribly difficult to hypnotize anyone against their will, but I was determined to go through with it.

I had been holding her down by the throat the whole time, and I began to choke her again, with the idea that if I reduced her to semi-consciousness that way she would no longer be able to exert her will, and her resistance would give way. Her lovely magnolia skin began to go red in patches and her black eyes bulged from her head. Sally warned me to be careful, but I disregarded her advice. I eased the pressure a little, now and then, but kept my thumbs digging into Julia's neck each side of her windpipe. It was horrible; but it worked.

Her eyes took on that curious look of the somnambulist and I knew that she had passed into an hypnotic sleep. I released my grip at once and Sally got her into the chair beside my bed. We gave her a glass of water and a few minutes to recover; then I started on her.

'Now Julia,' I said, 'I want the truth. When did you become a Satanist?'

'When I was seventeen,' she replied hoarsely.

Her answer staggered me; but details of my reactions to her story are irrelevant now.

'How did it happen?' I asked.

'An old peasant woman in our village took me to a Witches' Sabbath in the Alban hills.'

'Did you go willingly?'

'Yes.'

'Why?'

'I wanted all the things which were mine by right, but of which I had been cheated. She promised me that if I became a witch I should make a rich marriage.'

'But you had great beauty and you were a daughter of the noble Roman house of Colona, so why shouldn't you have made a rich marriage anyhow?'

'No, My father was a Colona, but he was not married to my mother; that is why I felt myself to have been cheated. She was a peasant girl on his estate outside Rome, and I was brought up by her in a cottage that was almost a hovel.'

'What happened after the Sabbath?'

'My father rarely left the big house when he visited his estate, but one day soon after the Sabbath he came down to the village. He saw me washing clothes in the stream, and struck by my beauty he enquired who I was. When he found that I was his own daughter he expressed a wish to do something for me. He sent me to school for two years, but after that I suffered a bitter disappointment. I had expected to become one of the family, but all he did was to make me his wife's lady's-maid.'

'Was that what you were when you met Uncle Paul?'

'Yes; and he was the rich husband I had been promised. He was not rich then, but he was a gentleman, so he could lift me by marriage to the status that was mine by right of blood; and while he was courting me he told me all about the Jugg millions. I realized that he must be the husband that had been sent for me by the Old One, and I felt certain that once I was married to him I would be able to get hold of a share of those millions.'

'What happened after you came to England?'

'I thought that if I could cure Paul of his bad habits, your grandfather would forgive him and make him a handsome allowance. That was the object of the séances at Kew. By means of them I was able to frighten Paul out of drinking so much. When he got tight I used to send a ghoul to give him the horrors. Sometimes it used to get out of control for a while and appear in the house unbidden. That is how you came to see it the night you thought you had run into a burglar on the stairs.'

'Soon after that we moved to Kensington Palace Gardens and Queensclere, and you had everything you could wish for. Why did you continue to be a Satanist after that?'

'I didn't. And your coming made a lot of difference, Toby. I was very happy looking after you, and I became very fond of you. I didn't want you to be mixed up in that sort of thing; so after we left Kew I had nothing more to do with it.'

'Why did you take it up again then? And why did you send me to Weylands?'

Julia's big dark eyes were suddenly suffused with tears, and they began to run down her cheeks; but she made no motion to brush them away and, in her trance state, she probably did not know that she was crying. She made a pitiful spectacle, as she went on tonelessly:

'I had to. One of the Brotherhood came to me a little over a year later. How he found out about me I've no idea; but he knew all about my past. He told me that the time had come when I must pay for my riches or lose them; and that you were the price. I was too weak to refuse. I simply could not bring myself to face poverty again, so I agreed to send you to Weylands. But I hoped that later on I would find a way to prevent them making you one of us.'

'But Helmuth got the better of you, eh?'

'Yes. He did not arrive on the scene until you were about thirteen; but within a week of his coming to stay at Queensclere as your tutor, he became my lover. I had had others—ever since I was seventeen. Paul was never anything to me, except the vehicle for my ambitions; and he soon became the complacent husband, content to show me off and let me manage his affairs. But Helmuth was a landmark in my life. I became as wax in his hands, and have been so ever since.'

'That time at Weylands when you and Uncle Paul came up to see me, and I had that horrible experience. I take it that you had not been to a friend's house, or run off the road in the car, at all. When you found me at the bungalow had you just returned from a Black Mass in the crypt of the ruined Abbey?'

'Yes. Paul had been initiated that night as a lay-brother. He is not a type out of which a potent Satanist could be made; but as you were growing up, it was considered advisable to bind him to the Brotherhood, so as to ensure his taking his future orders from Helmuth without question, and working to get him the next vacant seat on your Board of Trustees.'

'You knew all about the conspiracy to drive me insane, in order that the Brotherhood could get control of my fortune?'

The tears welled from her eyes again. 'I knew their intention, Toby, but not the details. Helmuth knows how fond I am of you, and he did not altogether trust me. He feared that if I learned too much about the methods he meant to employ I might rebel, and try to save you. That is why he intercepted all your letters to me, and would not let me come down to see you until he gave the word.'

'Yet you came at once in response to Nurse Cardew's telegram?'

'Paul and I were coming anyway for the Black Mass tonight. When I got the telegram I telephoned Helmuth and asked him what I was to do. Directly he realized that he could no longer trust Nurse Cardew he feared that she might help you in another attempt to escape, last night. So to make you believe such an attempt unnecessary he said that Paul and I must come down at once to reassure you, and that we were to bring Dr Arling with us.'

That was the whole awful story of how her ambition for riches and luxury had led her to betray a child that she had brought up with loving care as a younger brother. There seemed nothing further left to ask her, so I said:

'Now Julia, I freely forgive you for all you have done, and intended to allow to be done, against me. It is never too late to mend. Somehow, I will get you out of the clutches of these vile people, and we will forget the whole terrible business. I still want to repay you for all the love and happiness with which you surrounded me when I came to you as a little orphan, and so long as it lies with me you shall never lack for money. But you have got to do as I tell you.

'I am going to write a letter to the district Inspector of Police. I shall tell him about the meeting that is to be held here tonight; but I shall say nothing about Satanism, or a Black Mass. I shall simply say that these people are meeting in the chapel without my consent and I have good grounds for believing that they intend to use it for sacrilegious and immoral purposes. As the owner of this property I have the right to invoke the protection of the law against this unwarranted and scandalous trespass. I shall ask that a squad of police be mustered in the grounds at ten o'clock, in readiness to take the names of the trespassers and expel them at the signal of the Inspector; and that he should come to me here at that hour in order to see for himself through the grating all that takes place in the chapel.

'I shall also draw a little sketch plan of the Castle, showing the position of the side-door which is at the end of the passage at the bottom of the spiral staircase, and enclose it with the letter.

'When I have written the letter I shall give it to you. Then you will go downstairs, beg, borrow or steal a car, make any excuse you like, and drive into the village. There you will go to the Police Sergeant and he will tell you where the nearest Inspector is stationed. You will drive on to the Inspector and give him the letter with your own hand, remain there while he reads it, make certain that he fully understands the urgency of the matter, and intends to do as I wish; then return here and come up to report to me. Lastly you will be at the side-door I have marked on the plan, yourself at ten o'clock tonight, to let the Inspector in and bring him up to me here. Is that all clear?'

She said that it was. Sally got me my pen and paper. I wrote the letter, drew the plan, put them both in an envelope and gave it to Julia. Then I gave her my instructions a second time and made her repeat them after me.

When she had done so I told her that she was to say nothing of what had passed between us to anyone except the Inspector, and woke her from her trance.

As her full consciousness came back she stared at me wide-eyed, stood up, turned to look at Sally, then clutched at her heart. Suddenly she let out a piercing scream, pitched forward and fell flat on the floor.

The echo of her scream had hardly died away when I caught the sound of footsteps on the stairs. Almost instantaneously they broke into a run. Too late I remember that I had neglected to tell Sally to bolt the door, so as to secure us from interruption. After one look at Julia she had hurried over to my washstand to get water. As she picked up the jug Helmuth and Dr Arling burst into the room.

There is little point in giving a detailed account of what happened after that. The secret panel was closed, so Helmuth still does not know how Sally came to be in my room when he thought she had gone to London; but she could not get back into her hiding-place without revealing it. As cold water failed to revive Julia, Helmuth and Dr Arling carried her out on to the terrace, hoping that the fresh air might do so. A few moments later Helmuth came back and announced that she was dead–that she had died of heart failure.

There was no disguising the fact that the two women had had a fight. The bloody scratches on Sally's face showed that, and the doctor had found some strands of her hair still adhering to Julia's fingernails. They had also come on my letter addressed to the Inspector of Police.

Helmuth took Sally's arm with one hand and waved the letter at me with the other, as he said:

'Your writing to the Inspector of Police seems to have been prompted by a forecast of events. I will save you a stamp, as I mean to telephone him now. It will be my unpleasant duty to hand Nurse Cardew over to him on a charge of murder.'

In vain I cursed him and swore that it was my doing. He took Sally downstairs to lock her up. A few minutes later he returned with a sheet; then he and Dr Arling carried Julia's dead body, draped in its awful final whiteness, in from the terrace and through my room.

The above is the truth. By Almighty God I swear it. How, I cannot think, but I hope to get these papers to Sally for her defence. Should I fail, I implore anyone who may come across them to take them to the nearest J.P.

Blessed be the person who does. Cursed for all eternity be anyone who reads this and fails to act upon it.

It is the truth, the real truth. I swear it by all I hold holy. Sally did no more than catch Julia for me. It was I who choked her and threw so terrible a strain upon her body and mind that it proved too much for her heart.

Oh, Sally! Sally! That your love for me should have brought you to such a pass is terrible beyond belief. Had I the power to save you by dying at this minute I would do it; and gladly, rather than they should harm one hair of your sweet head.

Later

At three-twenty this afternoon I signed away my fortune.

Helmuth came to me with a duplicate copy of the deed that he showed me some days ago. He said that there was a clear case against Sally for wilful murder. That, bedridden as I am, I could not have killed Julia, and that there was ample evidence that she had died as a result of Sally's assault.

He went on to say that the Brotherhood were above the petty laws and shibboleths of this world, and was not the least interested in bringing offenders to the so-called justice of the British courts. Their only interest was the immediate furtherance of their own concerns, of which obtaining control of the Jugg millions was one. By signing the document he produced I could spare them much trouble and delay in achieving this particular item in their plans. If I would do so, Dr Arling was prepared to sign a certificate that Julia had died a natural death, and there would then be no occasion to call in the police.

I attempted to make some other stipulations, but he would not listen to me. He insisted that it should be a plain one-clause bargain. Either I signed or Sally went to the rope.

He had me in a corner. There was no option. I signed.

Later

This is the end. Sally was telling me the other day what she believes to be the true interpretation of the conception that 'the unforgivable sin is to blaspheme against the Holy Ghost'. She said that it is not a matter of mere words, but the act of suicide; because we all carry a particle of the Holy Ghost within us, and to drive our spirit out of our body before the time ordained for it to go is not unforgivable–nothing is unforgivable–but it is the most heinous crime which it is possible to commit.

Yet had I the means I would be sorely tempted to take my own life tonight.

It is after nine and I am writing this by the failing light. My lamp has not been lit, nor will it be, as Konrad will not be coming up to me again. Helmuth has just paid me a final visit and he told me that before he left.

He came to gloat, and render my last sane hours unendurably hideous by disclosing the way in which he had tricked me; and, infinitely worse, tricked my beloved Sally.

Julia is not dead. It was only a heart attack she had, and she is now little the worse for her seizure. The inspiration to *say* that she was dead came to Helmuth when he and Dr Arling had her limp body out on the terrace. He realized that Sally and I were in love, and saw that by causing us to believe that we had killed Julia he could bend us both to his will.

He led me to believe that, as Julia and Sally had clearly had a fight, it was Sally who would be charged with the murder, unless I signed away my fortune as the price of Dr Arling giving a certificate that Julia had died a natural death.

He led Sally to believe that he knew the fight to have been only incidental, and that the marks on Julia's throat showed that she had really died from strangulation—and that it was I who had strangled her. He threatened to hand me over to the police unless she would do as he wished; and, believing it to be the only way to save me from hanging, she agreed.

He told me that having signed the document would not now save me from mental destruction tonight, because I had not signed it with resignation—only under extreme pressure. He said that my prolonged and bitter opposition showed that I could never be made a useful member of the Brotherhood, and would always be liable to make trouble.

Therefore, at a quarter-past-one in the morning, when the moon is at its highest, they will invoke the Lady Astoroth. She will appear here in my room, and tomorrow I shall be found a raving lunatic. Dr Arling will remove me to his private asylum, and after I have spent some time there the official Board of Lunacy will examine and certify me.

I only pray that a merciful God will allow my mind to be blotted out entirely. If I were certain of that I think I could resign myself to this miserable fate. But nothing could make me resigned to what is in store for Sally.

Helmuth stood well out of reach at the end of my bed. Leonine, rock-faced, sardonic, he grinned at me with unutterably evil malice as he told me about that.

He says that Sally knows too much to be allowed to depart in peace, and that steps have to be taken to stop her tongue once and for all. That could be done by making her a lay-sister of the Brotherhood, as, after even the lowest degree of initiation, she would never dare to risk the appalling fate reserved for a member who betrays them—there is no recorded case of anyone ever having done so yet. And she has agreed to accept initiation, believing that only by doing so can she save my life.

Helmuth said that the initiation will take place at midnight, and that although I shall not be able to see it I shall hear enough of it through the grating to imagine what is going on. Sally does not yet know what they mean to do to her, but Helmuth took fiendish delight in describing to me what will happen, in order that I could better imagine the scene when it takes place.

He is to act as the officiating priest. Sally will be spreadeagled naked on a bed of nettles before the Devil's altar. He will then do to her what he has failed to do so far. The excited cries of the congregation will inform me when the ritual is being accomplished, and the completion of the act will be the signal for a general orgy.

I do not think that when the Lady Astoroth appears to me at a quarter-past-one I shall know much about it. I shall have gone mad by midnight. may God have mercy upon dear Sally, and upon my soul.

Wednesday, 24th June

This old Castle must have seen many strange and terrible events, but it can have seen none stranger or more terrible than those which occurred here last night. It is now the scene of catastrophe and death; yet, despite everything, I am still sane.

That I am so after what I endured between nine o'clock and midnight last night is in itself a miracle.

No sound came to distract my agonizing thoughts until a little after ten; then I heard people moving in the chapel. Gradually the noise increased. I heard the clatter of plates and the clink of glasses; so I knew that the Satanists had begun to feast at the tables set up in the side-aisles.

The voices grew louder and more distinct. There came the drinking of healths and raucous laughter. That went on for well over an hour, so it must have been about half-past-eleven when the service started.

There was music, but music the like of which I have never heard before and hope never to hear again. It had no tune and or any kind of beauty, but was a series of hideous discords, rising at times to a wild cacophony of sound interspersed by catcalls, shouts and animal noises.

I knew that those beasts in human form were working themselves up into a frenzy of abandon, the better to satiate their vile lusts when the time came.

The night was stiflingly hot, and the fumes of strange and horrible things that were burning down there came up to me throught the grating. The chapel was brightly lit, and the grating stood out sharply; a great rectangle of light criss-crossed with its black bars, which illuminated the whole room almost as brightly as though it were day.

I had thrown off the bedclothes, and swung myself round so that my useless legs were dangling over the side of the bed. From time to time, as midnight approached, I tried to stand, but I could not do so for more than a minute without having to grasp the head of the bed for support.

I prayed as I have never prayed before—violently, unceasingly—supplicating God to spare Sally, or at least grant her oblivion, so that she might be spared the knowledge of the abominable things those beasts meant to do to her. I prayed aloud, and I was raving. I called on God and the Virgin Mary; on all the Powers of Good and Light and Love that there had ever been in the world.

The sweat was pouring off me. It ran into my eyes and they grew misty. I could no longer see even the brightly lit grating clearly. My effort was so intense that I was shaking all over. I tried to throw my spirit forward out of my body, and down into the chapel to protect Sally. I cried aloud my defiance of Satan and all his works.

It was then the miracle happened. God had heard my prayer. I found that I was standing up, and that I was walking towards the panel.

I seemed to be buoyed up and supported by unseen hands. Without any
effort I climbed through the panel opening on to the secret stairs. They were
faintly lit by the moonlight coming through the arrow-slits. I walked slowly
but surely down them till I reached the door at the bottom. I thrust it open
and entered the chapel.

The scene was one which will remain stamped on my memory until my
dying day. There were about eighty people present, all wearing fantastic
costumes. Many of them were women, some nude to the waist, others
dressed in eccentric arrangements of veiling through which their bodies
could be seen, or which left their sexual parts exposed. The men were in
gorgeous satins and velvets, and each wore a head-dress in the likeness of
some wild animal or poisonous reptile.

Like a reredos, behind the altar, there spread a vast web which seemed to
have been spun from liquid silver. It extended to both sides of the chapel and
right up to its roof. In the centre of the web, about twenty feet up, sat the
Great Spider.

In front of the altar stood Helmuth. He was wearing his white satin robe
with the black signs of the Zodiac on it, but the robe was now hitched up so
that he was naked from the waist down. Two women, one of whom was Julia,
knelt at either side of him in attitudes of adoration. In front of him two
assistant priests were standing, and between them they held Sally by the
arms. She was dressed in the fashion of a nun, except that her single garment
was of magenta veiling, through which one could see her white body.

Konrad was stationed quite near me, with five other men. They were all
clad alike, in red with long hose and horned head-dresses, in imitation of the
Devil; and evidently formed a Satanic guard, as they stood in a line in front
of the main door of the chapel and each of them was holding at rest long
tridents with barbed points.

It was Konrad who first saw me. He must have thought that I was an
avenging spirit. Pointing at me, he let out a howl of terror, then fell to the
ground and lay grovelling there a dozen paces from my feet.

At his shout the whole congregation turned in my direction. Sally alone
could have known how I had got into the chapel, and that by some
extraordinary means I had managed to get down the stairs. She gave a loud
cry, broke from the men who were holding her, and came running towards
me.

Helmuth and the rest must also have thought that I was a spirit sent to
disperse their diabolical gathering, as they either remained rooted where
they stood, their faces aghast with fear, or cowered away from me. The
Great Spider had begun to run frantically up and down its huge silver web.
Then, just as Sally reached me, I found myself with my right arm
outstretched again, hurling defiance at the Devil.

As I did so I could feel the power streaming into me and out through my
pointing arm like an electric current. Suddenly the Great Spider stopped its
dance, quivered violently as though struck by lightning, and began to
disintegrate. In a matter of seconds it had dissolved into a cloud of evil-
smelling black smoke.

Consternation seized the Satanists. They began to run senselessly in all
directions, covering their heads and screaming with fear. I waited no longer,
but grasped the edge of the door behind me and made to pull it open.

I had it about a foot open when it stuck. At that moment something must have clicked over in Helmuth's quick brain. He had not seen me come through the door and was probably unaware that it even existed until he saw it partly open. He must have guessed then that behind it lay a secret staircase up to my room: and that what he had thought to be an apparition was really myself in the flesh.

Above the din, I heard him bellow: 'There's nothing to be afraid of! He is only a man! Stop them! Stop them! Catch them before they get away!'

A sudden hush, all the more marked from the previous clamour, fell on that weird assembly. For a moment they hesitated, and in that moment I got the door wide open. It gave unexpectedly, and swung right back.

'Stop them, damn you! Stop them!' Helmuth yelled again; and as I thrust Sally through the doorway, the brief hush was succeeded by a new pandemonium. With howls of rage and hate the Satanists came charging towards us.

We were up about four steps when the first of our enemies reached the door. Helmuth was among them, and from the maniacal glare in their eyes I knew that if they got us they would tear us limb from limb. It was an awful moment—perhaps the worst that night—for we had so nearly got away, and I knew that only God's help could save us from being dragged down before we were half-way up the stairs. But He extended His merciful protection to us once again.

It was then that there came the second miracle of that unforgettable night. I heard a rumbling sound. It increased in volume to the noise of thunder before we were up another couple of steps, drowning the fierce cries of the mob that pursued us.

Suddenly a great torrent of water burst from the entrance to Great-aunt Sarah's tunnel. It hit the opposite wall of the passage like the tidal wave, drenching us to the skin; then turned and roared into the chapel. A second later I glimpsed the old lady's frail body as it was whirled out of the tunnel and through the open door.

Night after night for over forty years she had laboured for love's sake, and an inscrutable Providence had decreed that the culmination of her efforts should exactly coincide with the desperate need of two other lovers who were in dire peril. Her own ordeal, too, was over. At long last she had burrowed her way to the lake bottom, and in so doing had rejoined her Lancelot in a better way than she could ever have done in life.

As the first violent spate of water receded we saw that it had swept the advancing Satanists below us from their feet. They were now a flailing mass of legs and arms struggling in the torrent. Helmuth alone was still standing framed in the doorway, breasting the tide as it raced past on either side of him. For a moment he stood there hurling imprecations at us, then a screaming, half-drowned woman was thrown against him by the rushing water. He lost his balance and plunged beneath it, to be swept away with the rest.

Thousands of gallons were pouring down from the lake to the lower level of the chapel in a steady flood. But for that unholy congregation worse was yet to come. Within a few minutes of the first inrush the water took hold of the half-ruined pillar bases and the temporary structures that were shoring the building up. Beams cracked and snapped. Above the roar of the water we could hear the louder roar of great chunks of masonry giving way. The Satanists were trapped there, owing to the main door on the chapel floor level being held fast shut by the weight of water pressing against it.

After Helmuth had been swept away, Sally and I continued to stand on the stairs watching the horrific spectacle through the open doorway. It was as though Samson had come again to pull down the pillars of the temple upon another host of Philistines. We saw one forty-foot column collapse upon the screaming crowd that struggled waist-deep in water. Then big sections of the roof began to fall in, burying them beneath water-logged debris.

We were cut off from the chapel by the flood, so there was nothing that we could do to help; no act of mercy that we could perform. The chapel was soon full of water to the height of the top of the tunnel, but it still continued to rise, as I knew it must until its level reached that of the lake outside. Step by step we retreated up the stairs, until the swirling waters, now quiet, had reached the top of the door, and our last glimpse of the débâcle within was cut off. Then we turned and went slowly up to my room.

There, side by side, we gave thanks to God for our merciful deliverance from Evil, and vowed to devote our lives to fighting Evil in all its forms. Nor did we forget to pray for the happiness of that spirit which for a little time lived in the body of Sarah Jugg—who yesterday was old and mad, but today is young and sane again.

Monday, 3rd July, 1945

It was now over three years since that terrible night when God overwhelmed the Satanists at Llanferdrack.

The following morning Sally found the document I had signed for Helmuth in his study and destroyed it. That afternoon we left for London in an ambulance, and this is the first time since that we have visited the Castle.

My back caved in soon after I got back to my room, and for a time the specialists thought that my miraculous walk had placed so severe a strain upon the healing ligaments prematurely that there was little hope of my ever setting foot to the ground again.

It was then that Sally insisted on marrying me; because, as she said, with all the money in the world, I would have to be good and could not be got at by designing hussies, as long as I remained a permanent invalid.

All the same, she always maintained, against the opinions of the doctors, that I would get well in the end; and I owe it to her loving care that by the end of the year I was able to walk a few steps, and can now walk a mile without crutches.

But no designing hussy has got at me yet, or is ever likely to. Sally and I are gloriously happy and eighteen months ago she had two of the loveliest babies in the world. I mean, of course, that she had twins. They are girls and alike as two peas. They've got Sally's eyes but they are red-heads like me, and delightfully naughty.

These past three years I have been far too busy with my Companies even to think of my stamps. But on coming back here yesterday I went straight to my albums and extracted the scores of closely written pages that I had hidden in them. Sally and I read them through last night, and they recalled the time we spent here as though it had only ended yesterday.

I am going to have them bound up for her; and now that the war is over she wants me to have them published. We shall not mind if some people cannot bring themselves to believe the terrible and wonderful things that they reveal. We shall only be sorry that such people are still bound in Darkness and shut out from a realization of the Eternal Verities. We know it all to be true, and it is our testament that Evil can never triumph over the power of Love.

Gateway to Hell

GATEWAY TO HELL

For those to whom my wife and I owed many years of
happiness and comfort at
Grove Place, Lymington
Our housekeeper Betty Pigache, her
husband Captain George, and young George
My secretary Kay Turi
Mrs Shaw and Mrs Colby
and in the garden
Bob Smith and Joy Ibbetson

I

NO CAUSE FOR CELEBRATION

It was New Year's Eve, 1953. Normally the Duke de Richleau would have been occupying a suite at the *Reserve* at Beaulieu; for it was his custom to leave England shortly after Christmas and spend a month or so in the South of France. But this year he had other plans that had temporarily delayed his departure.

Usually, too, Richard Eaton would have been playing host to a carefree party of neighbours down at his ancient and gracious home in Worcestershire, Cardinals Folly. But his wife—that enchanting pocket Venus, the Princess Marie-Lou, whom he and his friends had brought out of Russia* some years before the war—had had to have an hysterectomy. So, after the Christmas festivities, they had come to London, and Marie-Lou was in King Edward VII Nursing Home, having had the operation four days earlier. Their daughter, Fleur, was about to enter London University, so had been installed in a flat she was to share with two other girl students, and Richard was staying with his friend, Simon Aron.

It was at a pleasant little Georgian house in Pond Street, Hampstead, which Simon had bought shortly after the war, that the three of them had dined that night, and they were still sitting round the table.

Simon and de Richleau delighted in producing for each other epicurean meals and fine wines. The dinner had consisted of smoked cods' roe, beaten up with cream and served hot on toast, after being put under the grill, followed by a *Bisque d'Homard* fortified with sherry, a partridge apiece, stuffed with *foie-gras*, and an iced orange salad laced with crème de menthe. With the roes they had had a glass of very old Madeira, with the soup a Marco-brunner Kabinet '33, with the partridge a Château Latour '28, and with the orange salad a small cup of cold China tea. Now, having cleared their palates with the tea, and as they lit up the eight-inch-long Hoyo de Monterreys which were the Duke's favourite cigars, Simon was giving them an Imperial Tokay of 1908.

Sitting there, they made a very diverse trio who, to a casual observer, would have appeared to have little in common.

De Richleau was in his seventies: a Frenchman who had long since made his home in England and acquired British nationality.† He was of medium height and spare figure. The exercises he did each morning, learned from a Japanese, had kept him in excellent trim and, for his age, his muscles still concealed surprising strength. His lean features were those of a born aristocrat: a broad forehead beneath neatly brushed white hair; a haughty, aquiline nose; firm mouth and chin; grey eyes flecked with yellow which, at times, could flash with piercing brilliance and, above them, upward-

---

* *The Forbidden Territory.*
† *The Prisoner in the Mask; Vendetta; The Second Seal.*

Gateway to Hell

slanting 'devil's' eyebrows.

Simon was also slim, with a frailer body and narrow shoulders. His sloping forehead, great beak of a nose and slightly receding chin would have called to mind the head of a bird of prey had it not been for his gentle and often smiling expression. When young he had been afflicted with adenoids, and his parents had neglected to have them removed until his early teens. By then the growth had caused him to keep his full-lipped mouth always a little open, and it was a habit he had never lost. His hair was black, his eyes dark and short-sighted, so that he tended to peer at people, unless he was wearing his spectacles. He was descended from Spanish Jews; but his family had lived in England for many generations and had a high reputation as merchant bankers.

Richard was a typical English country gentleman. In recent years he had put on weight; but hunting and shooting saved him from a middle-aged spread, and the worst weather never shook his nerve when flying his private aircraft. His eyes were brown, as was his hair which came down to his forehead in a 'widow's peak' with attractive wings of grey above the ears. He had a good, straight nose, a mouth with laughter lines on either side of it, and a chin that suggested that, on occasion, he could be very aggressive.

It was de Richleau who picked up the Tokay bottle, looked at the label and raised an eyebrow. 'By Jove! 1908 *Essence*; the last vintage that old Franz-Joseph thought good enough to have bottled at the Hofberg. What a treat you are giving us, Simon.'

'Must have cost you a packet,' added Richard. 'Where did you get it?'

'Justerini's,' Simon replied in his jerky fashion. 'You're right about the stuff costing a packet these days. Still, what's the good of "mun", except for what it'll buy you? Like to give you a toast. Here's luck to all of us in 1953 and—er—specially to old Rex. 'Fraid he needs it.'

His words carried the thoughts of the others to Rex Van Ryn, the great, hulking American with the enormous sense of fun. Before the war he had been the most popular playboy between Paradise Beach in the Bahamas and Juan les Pins, and a record-breaking airman. During the war he had been one of the pilots who, in 1939, had volunteered to fight for Britain, formed the Eagle Squadron and had covered themselves with glory. He was the fourth of that gallant little company, christened by him 'we Modern Musketeers'. In Russia, Spain, the Balkans, the West Indies and many other places, they had adventured together and survived many perils.*

As Simon sipped the thick, richly-scented, honey-coloured wine, his companions followed suit; but his reference to Rex had taken their minds off the wine. De Richleau was recalling Rex's gay dictum about cocktails, 'Never give a guy a large one; make 'em small and drink 'em quick. It takes a fourth to get an appetite.' He looked a question at his host. Richard anxiously voiced it.

'What's this, Simon? You imply that Rex is in trouble. Have you just heard from him?'

'Ner.' Simon shook his bird-like head as he used the negative peculiar to him owing to his failing to close his mouth. 'Not from, but about. Old Rex must be in a muddle—a really nasty muddle. He's embezzled a million dollars.'

* *The Golden Spaniard; Strange Conflict; Codeword—Golden fleece.*

'What!' exclaimed Richard. 'I don't believe it. This is some absurd rumour you've picked up in the City. It's the most utter nonsense.'

De Richleau had raised his 'devil's' eyebrows in amazement, and said more slowly, 'It is almost impossible to credit. As we all know, apart from the *nouveau riche* Texan oil kings, the Van Ryns are one of the richest families in the United States. Rex inherited several million from his father, and is one of the biggest stockholders in the Chesapeake Banking and Trust Corporation. What possible reason could he have had for doing such a thing?'

'Don't know,' Simon shrugged. 'Could have gone haywire and tried to beat the market.'

'No,' de Richleau declared firmly. 'Rex has risked his neck a score of times in making long-distance flights, in battle, and in private ventures when he has been with us. But he has never been a gambler where money is concerned.'

Simon nodded vigorously. 'You're right there. Can only tell you what I've heard. Family is keeping it dark, of course. They'd never prosecute. But we bankers have our special sources—better very often than those of the "cloak and dagger" boys in M.I.6. A fortnight or so ago Rex disappeared, and he made off with a million.'

'He's been in Buenos Aires for the past year or so, hasn't he?' Richard asked. 'Was it from there that he absconded?'

'Umm. The Chesapeake have big interests in South America. You'll recall that, when the old man died, Rex's cousin, Nelson Van Ryn, became President. It was after the war that Rex decided to cease being a playboy and take an active part in the family business. In the autumn of '49, Nelson asked him to take over their South American interests. Good man for the job, Rex. Gets on with everybody. The Latin tycoons were soon eating out of his hand. He made his H.Q. in Buenos Aires, but did a round of Brazil, Chile, Bolivia and the rest. Made excellent connections. Now this. But why? God alone knows.'

Richard took another sip of the Tokay, then said with a worried frown, 'It's past belief. Simply incredible. But I know your intelligence on this sort of thing can be graded A1. And one thing sticks out like a sore thumb. To have chucked everything and made off into the blue with a wad of his bank's funds, Rex must be in very serious trouble.'

'There can be no doubt of that,' de Richleau agreed. 'And I won't be happy until I know that he is out of it.'

Simon's dark eyes flickered from one to the other. Covering his mouth with the hand that held the long cigar, he gave a little titter. 'Yes, Rex must be in a muddle—a really nasty muddle. Felt sure that when I told you about it, you'd agree that it's up to us to get him out. We'll have to take a little trip to South America.'

2

THE SEARCH BEGINS

On January 2nd, Simon and Richard left for New York. Changing aircraft there, they flew down to Rio, changed again and arrived in Buenos Aires on the morning of the 4th. Richard had been reluctant to leave Marie-Lou, but she was sufficiently recovered from her operation to be out of all danger, and had insisted that he should accompany Simon, because it would have seriously upset de Richleau's plans to do so. Now that he was ageing, he found the winter months in England trying, even with a break on the Riviera after Christmas; so he was thinking of making his future home on the sunny island of Corfu. He had been invited out there to stay in the lovely villa of an old friend of his, with a view to buying it, and was loath to forgo this opportunity. He had told the others that he would be back in London by the beginning of February and that, should they by then still have failed to solve the mystery about Rex, he would fly out to help them.

Simon had met Rex's cousin, Nelson Van Ryn, on several occasions and, before leaving England, had had a long conversation with him over the transatlantic telephone. As soon as the President of the Chesapeake Banking and Trust Corporation was made aware that news of Rex's disappearance had reached his English friends, he spoke of that most worrying matter fully, but in guarded terms.

Apart from the mammoth embezzlement, Rex's affairs appeared to be in perfect order. He was, as Simon had believed, very rich and, in recent months, had made no inroads into his fortune. While living in Buenos Aires, his life had been the normal one of a wealthy man moving in the highest circles of American and Argentine society. His health was as robust as ever, and everyone questioned had declared that he had shown no indication that he was a prey to any kind of worry. The loss to the bank had promptly been made good from the family's private funds and, in no circumstances, were the Press to be allowed to know what had occurred. But Nelson had instructed the Pinkerton Agency that, while preserving the strictest secrecy, they were to do everything possible to trace his cousin. So far, half a dozen of that famous firm's 'private eyes' had failed to produce a single clue to Rex's disappearance.

When Simon said that he and Richard were so worried about their old friend that they had decided to fly out to Buenos Aires, on the chance that they might be able to help in the search, Nelson willingly agreed to inform his top man there—a Mr Harold B. Haag—of their intention, and tell him that he was to withhold nothing from them.

The friends' long, two-day flight was without incident and the last lap ended by landing them at Buenos Aires airport, at a little after ten o'clock on the morning of the 4th. When they left the Customs hall, they were approached by a tall, fair-haired young man who introduced himself as Silas Wingfield, and said he had been sent by his chief, Mr Haag, to meet them.

He dealt efficiently with the shouting porters and drove his charges away in a huge car, the chromium radiator of which bore a resemblance to the mouth of a grinning Japanese General.

Although not yet mid-morning, it was already very hot and, to the east, a blazing sun was mounting rapidly in a brassy sky. On either side of the broad motorway spread what appeared to be an endless park of undulating grassland, planted here and there with groups of specimen trees. When Richard commented that the city had an unusually beautiful approach, Wingfield replied, 'The quickest route from the airport to the city is real tatty, mainly through slums and shanty towns. This is a few miles longer, but a sight more pleasant.'

After a twenty-minute drive, the park-like land merged into a real park, with palm-lined avenues, playgrounds for children, flower-beds, fountains and benches. At the far end, the park was overlooked by big blocks of luxury flats, behind which was massed the city.

By that time the three occupants of the car were perspiring freely, but they had to endure another twenty minutes' grilling, while being driven right through the great metropolis. At length they reached the far side, where the broad, park-like Plaza San Martin led down to the waterfront. At the landward end, among gnarled, ancient trees, stood the statue of José San Martin, the liberator of the Argentine and, opposite it, the Plaza Hotel. The car drove into a covered courtyard and, gasping with relief, its occupants got out.

The Plaza had the atmosphere of an ancient Ritz. Upon the floor above the street level, a broad, immensely long corridor stretched away from the reception area and, opening off it, there was a whole series of lounges and banqueting rooms of varying sizes. It was strangely silent and almost deserted. Having made certain that their booking was in order, young Wingfield left Richard and Simon to be taken up in a slow but spacious lift to their suite on the sixth floor.

As the comfortable first-class seats in the several aircraft in which they had travelled had enabled them to doze for a good part of their long journey, they were not particularly tired; so they decided that, after refreshing themselves with a bath and changing into lighter clothes, they would lose no time in calling on Mr Haag.

Shortly before midday, having learned that the bank was only a few blocks away, they decided to walk there; but, before they had covered a hundred yards, regretted it. Not only was it high summer in Buenos Aires but, as they were shortly informed, for some days the city had been afflicted with a heat wave. The sun blazed down with such intensity that, each time they had to step out from the narrow band of shelter on the shady side of the street to let someone pass, or cross the road, the heat hit them like a blast from a furnace.

The marble-pillared hall of the bank was impressive, and beyond it the better part of forty people were working behind a long counter. Although the ceiling was lofty and had slowly-revolving fans, all the men were in shirtsleeves, the women in thin cotton blouses, and the garments of all of them were stained with perspiration.

After a short wait they were taken through to Mr Harold B. Haag's office. He was a middle-aged, semi-bald, paunchy man and, as his surname implied, of Dutch descent. While shaking hands he said he had received instructions from his President to render them all possible assistance, which he would willingly do. But, when it came to the point, he did little more than shake his head and murmur at frequent intervals, 'A sad business. A very sad business.'

From him they secured only the following basic information. On the morning of Saturday, 16th December, Rex had told Haag that he was negotiating to buy a small ranch from a once-wealthy man who had been nearly ruined by Dictator Peron's taxation, and was collecting as much cash as he could before leaving the country clandestinely. The price he asked for the ranch was seventy thousand dollars. Rex had said that he was going up-country for the week-end, as he had an appointment to meet this man and conclude the deal on Sunday. That morning he had brought a suitcase with him to the bank. Having cashed a cheque for the seventy thousand, he had opened the suitcase in front of Haag, and put the money into it with his week-end things. He had then said that it would be foolish to risk losing such a considerable sum by leaving the suitcase in the cloakroom of the restaurant where he was lunching, so he would put it in the bank vault and call for it later.

Although overlord of all the Corporation's branches in South America, Rex did not hold the keys to the vaults of any individual bank. They were in the custody of managers and chief cashiers; but it had not even occurred to Haag to refuse the loan of his keys to his chief, who had promised to put them in an envelope, then into the wall safe in his office, to which both of them had the combination.

No irregularity had been suspected until the Monday morning when the vault was opened. Inside, the contents of Rex's week-end suitcase has been found in a heap on the floor. When questioned, the watchman stated that Rex had returned to the bank a little after four o'clock on the Saturday afternoon, spent about twenty minutes in the vault, then relocked it, come upstairs and calmly handed the suitcase to the man to carry out to his Jaguar for him. As Rex was exceptionally large and strong, while he was holding the suitcase it had not appeared to be particularly heavy; but, as the watchman took it from him, its weight had almost wrenched out the poor man's arm. The reason was not far to seek. It must have been packed solidly with banknotes in several currencies. Apart from the seventy thousand for which Rex had given his cheque, it emerged that he had practically cleared out the bank, and had made off with the equivalent of one million one hundred and fifty-two thousand dollars.

To that Haag had nothing to add, and he could suggest no line of enquiry. Moreover, he did not seek to disguise the fact that, as the matter had been put into the hands of professionals, he considered it most unlikely that amateurs would succeed where they had failed; and that Richard and Simon were not only wasting their time but, by poking about, would increase the likelihood of this unsavoury scandal concerning a member of the Van Ryn family becoming common knowledge.

Haag went on to say that he would have liked to offer them lunch; but, unfortunately, was already committed to entertain an important client. However, he hoped that they would give him the pleasure of their company one evening during their stay. While thanking that solid but uninspiring citizen for his invitation, they made mental reservations that only in some unforeseen circumstance would they accept his hospitality. They then secured the address of the apartment Rex had occupied, cashed a considerable sum in travellers' cheques, and took their departure.

Out in the blinding glare of the street, Richard murmured, 'Not a propitious start. D'you think the feller's holding out on us?'

'Ner.' Simon shook his head. 'Typical Dutch-American middle-class mentality. No imagination and puts everyone into categories. You are an effete English "cheque-writer", as they call people with money and no obvious occupation. I'm a Jew. Both of us got an axe to grind. Trying in some way to cash in on old Rex's disappearance.'

Sweating profusely, they returned to the Plaza and found their way to a not very attractive downstairs bar. A surly barman could produce no list of drinks and refused to make up Planter's Punches to Richard's specification; so they settled for Rum and fresh limejuice on the rocks. With their drinks there was brought a dish containing a dozen, spoon-shaped pieces of Cheddar cheese, evidently dug out as one does with a Stilton. The flavour of the cheese was delicious, and they soon found that to serve it with all aperitifs was an Argentinian custom.

As they carried their drinks to a leather-covered settee, Simon said in a low voice, 'British not popular here—anyhow, not with the lower classes. During the war they made a packet by supplying us with their meat, but since Lease-Lend ceased, we've been in a spot financially, and had to limit our purchases very strictly. Peron is squeezing the rich so unmercifully, too, that the big cattle-raisers can no longer afford to maintain herds of the size they used to; so the beef is not on the hoof for other people to buy it, even if we can't. But as for generations we were their best customer, they put the blame for the slump on us.'

'Peron is a disaster,' Richard agreed, having given a cautious look round the nearly empty bar, to make certain no one was close enough to overhear their conversation. 'Before his time, the Argentine was wonderfully prosperous. She was in a fair way to becoming a minor United States, and her chances of doing so were immensely strengthened by Britain having to sell all her assets here during the early years of the war, in order to buy arms from the U.S. Instead, Peron's greed and extravagance is ruining the country. Do you know, I was told by an Argentinian friend of mine that in a basement cold store under his palace Peron keeps over a thousand fur coats, available as hand-outs to any young woman he may fancy. And that was before Eva's death last year.'

Simon tittered. 'Wonder that she stood for that.'

'Oh, come! That type of woman feels no resentment at her husband indulging himself with others. She was interested only in power and endeavouring to raise the masses from the abject poverty which she herself once endured. For that she has my admiration. The tragedy is that she pushed Peron into going the wrong way about it.'

'She was quite a girl,' Simon conceded. 'Even got votes for women, and that can't have been easy in a Latin country. Always thought our people blotted it pretty badly when the Perons were on a visit to London, and the Foreign Office advised against their being received at Buckingham Palace. That slap in the face was one of the high spots in setting the Argentine against us. Whole population resented it intensely.'

By this time it was two o'clock, but South Americans keep Spanish hours, so people were only beginning to filter into the grillroom that was adjacent to the bar. When Richard and Simon went in to lunch, they found the head-waiter much more polite and helpful than the barman; and, advised by him, they enjoyed a very pleasant meal.

Afterwards they began to feel the strain of their two-day journey, so they went up to their rooms, undressed and spent several hours dozing on their beds. At six o'clock they went out again. It was still very hot, but they were relieved to find that a light evening breeze was blowing from the river. A taxi took them to Rex's apartment, which was on the eighth floor of one of the luxury blocks overlooking the park.

The door was opened by a short, thick-set manservant with a swarthy complexion. Simon, who spoke passable Spanish, told him that they were friends of Rex's, and had come to make some inquiries about him.

The man gave him a sullen look and said, '*Señor*, I am tired of answering questions about my master. I have nothing to say that I have not already said to officials from the bank and the American detectives they sent here.'

Simon took out his pocket book, extracted a fifty-*escudo* note and said with a smile, 'Perhaps this will compensate you for your time in repeating to my friend and me what you have said to others.'

Unsmiling, but with a polite little bow, the man took the note and showed them into a large, well-furnished dining room, with a fine view over the park. As they sat down, he closed the door behind him, remained standing near it, and began in a toneless voice to recite what, by this time, must have become a familiar piece to him:

'On the morning of December 16th, my master told me that he was going up-country for the week-end. Contrary to custom, he packed several suitcases. He had me take only one of them down to the car, and drove off to the bank as usual. At about one o'clock he returned. I made for him as usual his Martinis, which he drank out on the balcony while reading *Time* magazine. He then had lunch, eating, as was his custom, a substantial meal. At about half past three he left the apartment. In a little over an hour he returned and collected his other suitcases. I have not seen him since.'

'Thanks,' said Simon. 'Had your master recently been in good health, and his usual cheerful self.'

'Yes, *Señor*. I have never known him ill; and he showed no sign of worry.'

'Had he many visitors during the weeks before his departure?'

'Not more than usual, *Señor*. Once or twice a week he had friends to drinks or dinner. Most evenings he was out being entertained by other people.'

Simon produced another fifty-*escudo* note and laid it on a small table beside him. 'No doubt you could give me the names of your master's closest friends who came here regularly?' The man nodded and, pausing now and then, mentioned a dozen people. Most of them were Americans and only three were women, all of whom had come with their husbands. Simon had taken a slender note pad from his pocket and took down the names. 'Now,' he went on, 'during the first fortnight in December, did any stranger call upon your master?'

'No, *Señor*. No-one.'

'Can you recall any unusual happening whatever, which might account for his disappearance?'

'*Señor*, there is positively nothing more than I can tell you.'

'What staff are there here besides yourself?'

'My wife, who is cook-housekeeper, and a woman who comes in the morning to do the cleaning.'

'Did your master make arrangements for you to receive your wages during his absence?'

'I do not know, *Señor*. They have since been paid by the *Señorita* Miranda.'

Simon's dark eyes gave a sudden flicker of interest, as he repeated, 'The *Señorita* Miranda. Who is she? *Señor* Van Ryn's secretary?'

'No, no, *Señor*. She is his niece, and has been staying here with him since early in November.'

After a moment's silence, Simon remarked, 'I assume that the *Señorita* is not at home, or you would have mentioned it when I told you that we were friends of your master's.'

'She is at home, *Señor*; but she is an invalid and I did not wish her to be bothered unnecessarily.'

Taking a visiting card from his wallet, Simon gave it and the second fifty-*escudo* note to the man and said, 'Please give my card to the *Señorita* and tell her that I am very anxious to see her. I will telephone tomorrow morning to ask if she will receive me.'

There being no more to be said, the two friends left the apartment and went down to the taxi they had hired to take them out there.

As they were driving back to the hotel, Simon gave Richard the gist of the conversation with the servant. When he had done, the latter asked, 'D'you think he was telling the truth?'

'Umm,' Simon nodded. 'I gave him a good sight of the wad of notes I was carrying. If he had had anything really worthwhile to tell, odds are he would have attempted to barter it for money. And it's very unlikely that his wife or the woman who comes in to clean knows anything he doesn't. That's why I didn't bother to ask him to produce his wife. This niece business is puzzling, though. Didn't know Rex had one, did you?'

'I've never heard him speak of one, although I've a vague idea that Nelson has children. On the other hand, it may be a euphemism. It wouldn't be the first time that a well-heeled widower has passed a young mistress off as his niece.'

Simon put his hand to his mouth as he tittered. 'Maybe you're right. Old Rex has always enjoyed his fun and games. Queer, though, for him to pick on an invalid for his mistress. But my Spanish isn't all that good. It's possible the word I took for invalid really meant ill, or laid up. Woman might be, if she was very fond of Rex, and he's taken a run-out powder on her.'

'Anyhow, he made a jolly neat job of flitting, I must say,'

'He certainly did. And how typical of his sense of humour suddenly to hand the watchman that suitcase stuffed with half a hundredweight of notes, to carry out to his car for him.'

Back at the hotel, Simon telephoned Pinkerton's office in Buenos Aires. He made no mention of Rex, and had no intention of raising the matter of his disappearance with them, since he felt sure they would tell him nothing. He simply gave his name, then read off the list that he had taken of Rex's most frequent guests, and asked that dossiers on them should be furnished him as soon as possible.

Reluctant to have drinks in the uncongenial bar again, they enquired if there was another. The reception clerk told them that, adjacent to it, there was the ladies' bar, which was much frequented by Buenos Aires society, and that they could also have drinks sent up to the roof garden.

Electing for the latter, they went up to the eighth floor in the lift, then walked up two flights of stairs, to emerge on what was euphemistically called the roof garden. It consisted only of three small roofs connected by narrow walkways, a few tubs of sadly-wilted flowering shrubs, a large, ugly water tank which partially blocked the view, and eight or ten garden chairs—a strange adjunct to such a palatial hotel.

Only one couple was sitting on the most distant square of roof, and no waiter was in attendance; but, on the wall in which was the door by which they had come out, there was a telephone and a small service lift. Optimistically, Simon telephoned down for two rums and limejuice, and they sat down to take stock of their surroundings.

On either side of the big water tank, over lower roofs, they could see a number of ships berthed along the docks, and lying off. Beyond them spread the estuary of the mighty River Plate; but it was so broad there that they could not see the further shore and, instead of offering a pleasant seascape, the water was an ugly, muddy yellow.

After a while the lift rattled and the two drinks appeared. A waiter then emerged from the door, to serve them. The great heat of the day was long past, and a gentle breeze from the river now made it pleasant there; so they lingered until the sun began to go down. Then, tired after their active day, they decided to dine in the grillroom and go early to bed.

Before they drifted off to sleep, both of them pondered the mystery they had set out to solve, and both felt a sense of disappointment. They had been confident that, either through Rex's bank or his servants, they would at least learn the reason for his disappearance, if not secure a possible clue to his whereabouts. But they had drawn a complete blank. There was not a single thing to indicate why a rich, sane, healthy banker should suddenly have disappeared with a million dollars.

3

ENTER THE CROOKED BARON

Next morning, when they met in the sitting room of their suite for breakfast, Simon said, 'Can't expect Pinkerton's report on Rex's friends for a while yet, and it's very much on the cards that when it does come in it will tell us nothing. In any case, Rex must have had acquaintances other than the socialites he entertained at his apartment. So we must explore other avenues. Some place where gossip can be picked up would be our best bet; but where such a place would be, I don't know.'

'His club,' suggested Richard. 'It's certain that a man like Rex would belong to the most exclusive club here, and I can find out what that is from a friend of mine. He is an Argentinian diplomat named Carlos Escalente and was for some time *en poste* in London. Of course, he may have been posted elsewhere since his recall; but I think that's unlikely, because he sent me a Christmas card from here. Anyhow, I'll make enquiries at the Foreign Office. If Escalente is still in Buenos Aires, I feel sure he'll help us, should his club be the one to which Rex belonged, by getting me made a temporary member.'

'Good. You do that, then, while I go out and call on the *Señorita* Miranda–that is, if she'll see me. Close on ten o'clock now, so I'll ring up.' As he spoke, Simon went over to the telephone and put through a call. After a brief conversation, he hung up and grinned across at Richard. 'It's O.K. That was the chap we talked to yesterday. The *Señorita* will receive me at twelve o'clock.'

Soon after half past eleven, clad as lightly as decency permitted, Simon again had himself driven in the sizzling heat out to Rex's apartment. The manservant showed him straight into a spacious drawing room, in which the blinds were drawn, shutting out the sun. As his eyes adjusted themselves to the dim light, he found himself facing two women who were sitting side by side on a sofa.

Simon judged one of them to be in her fifties. She was plain, grey-haired, flat-chested and his idea of a typical spinster. The other was at least twenty years younger. She had lustrous, short, dark, curly hair and an excellent figure, but it was obvious that at some time her face had been very badly burned. In spite of plastic surgery, it was a pale mask with the skin drawn tight, and the features slightly distorted in several places. Her eyes were large and blue, but they had a fixed stare that was disconcerting.

It was the younger woman who stood up as Simon entered the room. Taking a couple of paces forward, she extended her hand rather uncertainly and said, 'You must forgive me, Mr Aron. My sight is so poor that I can hardly see you. But please come in and sit down.'

As Simon took her hand she went on in a low, musical voice, 'I have often heard Uncle Rex speak of you and Mr Eaton, and if only Pedro had let me know yesterday evening that you were both here, I should have been delighted to see you then.'

'It wasn't exactly his fault,' Simon smiled, 'because, not knowing that you had been staying with Rex, we didn't ask for you. And when that did emerge, we got the impression you were–er–not very well, so could not be disturbed.'

She returned his smile. 'I'm not ill, only rather badly handicapped as a result of a fire several years ago, in which I nearly lost my life; and everyone insists that I must be protected from tiring myself.' Turning her head towards the older woman, she added, 'Dear Pinney, here, is a treasure as a companion, but a positive dragon when she thinks I'm about to overdo things.'

Simon gave a jerky bow to Miss Pinney, to which she responded with a curt nod. Then Miranda said to her, 'Pinney dear, I'm sure you have lots to do, so you can leave me to entertain Mr Aron.'

With ill-concealed reluctance, the companion left the room. As the door closed behind her, Miranda said, 'You have come, of course, to talk about Uncle Rex's disappearance. How much of the story do you know?'

'Nelson–that's your father, I presume?' She nodded, and Simon went on. 'Nelson instructed the bank manager, Mr Haag, to keep nothing back from Richard Eaton and me. We saw him yesterday morning and he told us all he could.'

'You do know about the money then?'

'Umm. As a matter of fact, being a banker myself, I learned of it through confidential channels in London. That's why Richard and I came out here. Obvious that Rex had got himself into some sort of nasty muddle, and we hoped we might be able to help.'

Miranda's blue eyes remained expressionless, but she smiled. 'That was good of you; yet, after all I've heard from Uncle Rex of his great friendship with you both and the Duke de Richleau, I'm not surprised.'

'Greyeyes, as we all call him, is in Corfu at the moment. He has some rather important business to settle there, otherwise he'd have come with us.'

'I see. Anyway, you do know about the embezzlement. I thought you might. That's why I sent Pinney out of the room. She and the servants know only that Uncle Rex has gone away without leaving an address. I was told by Mr Haag on my father's instructions, in case I could throw any light on the affair. Unfortunately, I couldn't. But naturally we're anxious that as few people as possible should get to know that Uncle Rex has robbed his own bank.'

'Of course. It's disappointing, though, that you can't put us on to some new line of inquiry. Is there nothing you can think of to do with your uncle's private life that might give us a lead?'

'Not a thing. I arrived here early in November. I suffer from the cold and Uncle Rex suggested that I should spend the winter months with him here, where it is summer. Since I have been here, he's been his perfectly normal, cheerful self. The whole business is an extraordinary mystery. He has masses of money. For him to have become a thief and made off with a suitcase full of notes just does not make sense. At first I refused to believe it; but there's no denying now that that is what he did.'

'Er . . .' Simon hesitated. 'Forgive my asking, but do you know if he was having a love affair, or—er—had a mistress?'

Miranda laughed, 'I don't know for certain, but I'd take a bet that he had. I don't sleep well and on the evenings that he went out I often heard him come in at three or four o'clock in the morning.'

'From his behaviour towards the women who came here to parties and so on, did you suspect that any one of those might be the lady in question?'

'No, I didn't have the opportunity. You see, owing to my—my disability, I'm not allowed to go to parties. Exposing my eyes to bright light could rob me of the little sight I have left. The small library here has been turned into a sitting room for me and, when Uncle Rex entertained, Pinney and I had our dinner served there.'

'What awful luck you've had. Life must be terribly dull for you.'

She shrugged. 'Things might be worse. At least I have every comfort and distraction that money can buy for me. The first few months were the hardest to bear. There was not only the pain after many operations to make my face a little less revolting . . .'

'It's not revolting,' Simon broke in quickly. 'You're jolly good-looking. Nothing wrong at all, except that the skin is stretched a bit tight here and there. And your eyes are lovely.'

'Thank you. You're very kind. As I was saying, apart from the pain, there were so many things I missed dreadfully. I'd loved dancing, and ski-ing and, of course, I'd had lots of boy-friends. But, after a time, I gradually became resigned. Classical music had been a closed book to me before, but I've come to enjoy it enormously and I have a splendid collection of records for my hi-fi. I can write without effort by touch-typing, and I've become very good at making lace without using my eyes. Pinney reads the newspaper to me every morning, and a lot of books. I thoroughly enjoy my food, too, and fine wine.

But that reminds me. I'm being most remiss as a hostess. After the heat outside, you must be dying of thirst. What would you like to drink?'

'Oh, many thanks. Pretty well anything.'

'I know!' Miranda exclaimed. 'I so seldom have a visitor. We must celebrate. We'll have a bottle of champagne.'

'Suits me,' said Simon with a grin. 'Nothing to beat it at this time of day.'

When the wine was brought, they sat over it for the best part of an hour, talking, laughing and telling each other about their lives. As Simon was about to take his leave, she asked hesitantly, 'Have you an engagement for this evening?'

'Ner,' he shook his head. 'Why?'

'I–I was wondering if you would come and dine with me. I mean, if you wouldn't find it too depressing having to eat in semi-darkness.'

'But I'd love to,' he said quickly. 'It's awfully kind of you to ask me.'

She smiled, 'On the contrary. It's you who will be doing me a favour. Eight o'clock then, and we'll share one or two of Uncle Rex's best bottles.'

When Simon got back to the Plaza, Richard said to him cheerfully, 'Our luck is in. I succeeded in getting hold of Don Carlos Escalente. As I thought might be the case, he is doing a spell at the Foreign Office. The top club here is the Jockey. He is a member, of course, and so is Rex. They are only nodding acquaintances, and he didn't even know that Rex has left Buenos Aires. But he is going to put me up as a temporary member, and introduce me to several men he's seen Rex lunching with. I'm afraid I'll have to desert you tonight, though, because I'm dining at the Jockey with him.'

Simon tittered behind his hand. 'Glad of that, old chap. Otherwise I would be deserting you.' He then told Richard about his visit to Miranda Van Ryn.

After a late lunch and an hour's siesta they decided, as there was nothing more they could do for the time being, to take a stroll and see something of the city. The hall porter told them that the street with the best shops was the *Floredor*, and that it lay only just round the corner.

It proved to be as long and narrow as Bond Street. By a wise decree, no traffic was allowed down it, which was just as well, as the pavements were uneven and wide enough to take only two people abreast. Apart from a few good jewellers', the shops were unimpressive and, in view of the Latin ladies' love of sweet things, it was surprising to find only one good *pâtisserie*. They went into Harrods, which in the old days was said to be famous, but found it to be a very ordinary store in the middle of one of the blocks, and bearing no resemblance to its great parent in London.

On two occasions they turned down side streets, to find, almost immediately, that these nearby narrow ways were shoddy almost to the point of being slums. The shops offered only poor quality goods behind dusty windows, and were interspersed every hundred yards or so by open stalls, carrying piles of fly-blown fruit, cheap *pâtisserie* and glass containers holding highly-coloured, dangerous-looking drinks. Lounging about these stalls, or sitting on the broken pavements, were silent, ill-clad men and bedraggled women, watching with lack-lustre eyes the half-naked children playing in the gutters.

As they made their way back to the hotel, Richard remarked, 'What a tragedy. Old Greyeyes was here for a while round about 1908. I've heard him speak of it as wonderfully prosperous, and the Paris of South America.

But now, it's plain to see that, apart from the very rich, the people have barely enough money to support themselves. That greedy devil, Peron, has a lot to answer for.'

That evening he saw the other side of the picture in the luxuriously-furnished Jockey Club. When he arrived, it was already half-full of men whose clothes suggested Savile Row, and elegant women. None of them was in evening dress, but the jewels of the women proclaimed their wealth.

Don Carlos was a jovial, middle-aged man. He came of a long line of aristocrats. One of his ancestors had been sent out by the King of Spain to govern a vast, newly-discovered territory in the Americas. Over drinks he was soon asking Richard a score of questions about their mutual acquaintances in London.

When he enquired the reason for Richard's visit to Buenos Aires and why he was anxious to get in touch with Rex Van Ryn, Richard replied, 'I came on this jaunt partly for pleasure, but also on business. I am travelling with a friend of mine named Simon Aron. He is a banker and had a proposition to put up to Van Ryn, which might have proved most profitable to them both; and, if they do come to an agreement, I'm to be cut in on the deal.'

With a nod, Don Carlos said, 'As I told you over the telephone this morning, Van Ryn is a member here, but only a casual acquaintance of mine, and I have not seen him for some time.'

'That is not surprising. His people tell me that he left Buenos Aires in mid-December, but gave no indication where he was going, and neglected to leave an address to which letters could be forwarded. Presumably he did not want to be troubled with business. It occurred to me, though, that he would be sure to have friends here, and might have mentioned his plans to one of them.'

'It will be a pleasure to help you in any way I can,' Don Carlos smiled. 'For how long do you wish to be a temporary member here?'

'A few days should be ample. If, by the end of that time, I have drawn a blank and Van Ryn has not returned, Aron and I will have to shelve our proposition, as it needs to be acted on with some urgency.'

Don Carlos stood up. 'Come along then. Five days is the usual period for which temporary membership is granted, but it can be extended. I will take you to our Secretary, and we'll go through the formalities.'

These were soon completed, after which they dined. The largest and most delicious Avocados Richard had ever eaten were followed by the famous Argentine 'baby' beef, then cheese balls of a fairy-like lightness. When they had finished dinner, Don Carlos took his guests up to see the club library. It filled five large rooms on an upper floor, and was said to be the finest in South America.

It was while they were admiring the serried row of ancient calf-bound volumes that Richard made the acquaintance of Don Salvador Marino. He was a tall, strikingly-handsome man, who appeared to be in his middle thirties. His hair was dead black and slightly wavy. He wore it full at the sides and, below his ears, it tapered off in close-cut curved whiskers that stood out against his dead-white skin. His eyes, below a pair of haughtily-arched eyebrows, were large and luminous; his nose prominent but delicately shaped, and his mouth must have been envied by many a woman, for the lips were firmly moulded, an almost startlingly natural red and, when open, disclosed two rows of gleaming, white teeth.

As he came into the room, Don Carlos exclaimed, 'Ah! Here is a man I have seen frequently with Van Ryn. Perhaps he can tell us something.'

Introductions followed, and the handsome Don Salvador could not have behaved with greater charm. After hesitating only a second, he readily agreed that he knew Rex well, and expressed his liking for him; but he had not seen him for the best part of a month and could tell Richard nothing about his recent movements.

The three of them went down together in the lift. Over coffee and liqueurs they speculated on why Rex should have left without leaving a forwarding address, and where he might have gone; but none of them could produce a plausible suggestion.

As they were about to part, Don Salvador said to Richard, 'It has just occurred to me that I know one man who might be able to help you locate Van Ryn. He is the Baron von Thumm. During the war he was a high-up Nazi–a *Gruppenführer* in the S.S. I believe–and one of those who succeeded in escaping to South America. Now, of course, he protests that he was always averse to Hitler's policies, and only narrowly escaped arrest for complicity in the Generals' abortive conspiracy to assassinate the Führer. Evidently Van Ryn believed him. In any case, they see a lot of each other, so Van Ryn may well have told him where he intended to go for a holiday.'

'Could you put me in touch with the Baron?' Richard asked.

'Why, yes.' Don Salvador gave his charming smile. 'As you no doubt know, the Jockey has its Country Club a few miles outside Buenos Aires. The Baron is a very keen golfer. As it is Sunday tomorrow, it is almost certain that he will be out there, playing a round or two. I should be delighted if you will both lunch there with me and, with luck, the Baron will be able to give you the information you are seeking.'

Don Carlos had a previous engagement, but Richard eagerly accepted.

Next morning, over breakfast, Simon and Richard gave each other accounts of their previous evenings. Simon had had a most enjoyable dinner with Miranda, and afterwards had spent the best part of two hours listening to recordings of Brahms, Liszt and Beethoven. When Richard told Simon about the Baron von Thumm, his dark eyes showed swift suspicion.

'Queer friend for Rex to make,' he said. 'He's too old a bird to fall for stories about Nazis who at heart were all the time little white lambs and hated Hitler's guts. We may be on to something here.'

A little before midday Richard set off for the Country Club. The drive proved no light ordeal. Thousands of cars were streaming out of the city to the wonderful bathing beaches at Tigre, or inland to shady glades suitable for picnics. For the first few miles the procession moved at a snail's pace. Meanwhile the sun struck down unmercifully on the roof of the car, so that all its metalwork became red-hot to the touch. Fuming with impatience, Richard sweltered in the traffic blocks. At length, the congestion lessened; although not the heat. Dripping with sweat, he was eventually set down in front of the three-block, timbered building of the Jockey Country Club.

Don Salvador gave him a smiling welcome and, apparently impervious to the heat, took him for a short tour of the grounds which far outdid those of similar clubs in Europe. There were four swimming pools, one of which, some way apart from the others, was for the use of the servants. As it was a Sunday, the whole great playground was sprinkled with family parties seated under a sea of gaily-coloured umbrellas, while the children of Buenos

Aires' richest citizens chased one another, gave vent to shrill laughter and splashed in the pools.

To Richard's relief, the tour soon ended at the back of the clubhouse, on a shady verandah and, shortly afterwards, he was enjoying a long, cool drink. The verandah gave immediately on to the golf course, and it would have been difficult to find a more beautiful vista. The greensward, undulating away into the distance, had been planted here and there with a wonderful variety of now well-grown specimen trees.

Richard soon found that his host was not only strikingly handsome, but highly intelligent. He had travelled widely, particularly in the United States, having, at one time or another, stayed in every principal city there. He was also well acquainted with every country in Central and South America. Frequently showing his splendid teeth in a flashing smile, he talked with great fluency. Yet, despite his charm, there was something Richard did not like about him. What this something was he found hard to determine, but he decided that it might be the man's arrogance and a certain, undefinable aura of ruthless power.

They were on their second round of drinks when Don Salvador spotted the Baron coming in from his morning round, and called to him to come over.

Von Thumm made a far from attractive figure, owing to serious injuries he had sustained as a result of an aircraft in which he was travelling, towards the end of the war, having been shot down. He was short, broad, ungainly and walked with a limp which caused his left shoulder to stand up permanently higher than his right. In addition, his face was twisted as though he had been the victim of an attack of apoplexy. His right eye and the corner of his mouth below it were both drawn down.

Nevertheless, his misfortune had not lessened his amiability, although he greeted them in a deep, harsh voice. As soon as a drink had been ordered for him, Don Salvador asked if he knew of Rex's whereabouts.

The Baron gave a crooked smile, and replied in very heavily accented English. 'No. Our good friend Van Ryn left Buenos Aires about three weeks ago. For me his departure quite unexpected was. Also for me this causes annoyance. For a good time now, many weeks, he has been a member of the Saturday evening school of poker that I haf. That he fail to turn up leave us one short.'

Don Salvador then explained that Rex's English friends were particularly anxious to get in touch with him about an urgent financial matter, and asked the Baron if he could suggest anyone who might know of Rex's whereabouts.

After a moment, von Thumm said, 'One person only I know that for certain Van Ryn would where he was going haf told. That is Silvia Sinegiest. But she is no longer in Buenos Aires. If to question her you wish, you will haf to make a journey to the end of the world.'

4

WHERE THERE'S A WILL THERE'S A WAY

'Silvia Sinegiest?' Richard repeated. 'Wasn't she a film star in the thirties?'

'In two big films she starred, then found it less hard work to marry her producer,' von Thumm gave his crooked smile. 'That was three marriages ago. The name under which she starred she still uses. Since then she makes two marriages and is much talked about. Her last two husbands haf been millionaires. If she married yet again, I think it all odds it would not be a man who had less than a million. Those of only modest fortune–well-known actors, authors and big-game hunters–haf to be content with being her lovers.'

'From what you said, I gather that Van Ryn is a close friend of this woman's?'

With a twisted grin, the Baron nodded. 'Most close. He was crazy about her, and judging by her past record I should be much surprised if his mistress she had not become.'

'In that case, there is certainly a good chance that she knows where he is to be found. But what on earth do you mean by saying that to see her I'll have to go down to the end of the world?'

Don Salvador smiled. 'Von Thumm means Punta Arenas. It is known here as the End of the World, because it is at the extreme tip of Chile, and further south than any other large town. Beautiful women who are free to go where they will, rarely remain in Buenos Aires during December and January. They find the heat-waves such as we are now experiencing too great a tax on their vitality and looks; so they can go down to one of the watering places in the south.'

Richard looked across at the Baron. 'Are you certain that Madame Sinegiest is in Punta Arenas?'

'I make a big bet on it. She is fond of gardening. At present season the flowers there are beautiful. A few years ago she lease a house just outside the town. Since then she spend about six week down there every winter.'

'I thought that part of the world was quite god-forsaken–perpetual ice and snow.'

'So it is during our winter,' said Don Salvador, 'but at this time of the year it can be quite pleasant. Personally I would prefer Rio Gallegos, which is on the Atlantic coast, or Puerto Montt, just over the border in Chile. Those places are somewhat warmer, and there is much more to do in them.'

The Baron nodded agreement. 'Truly so; but, as I haf told you, Silvia Sinegiest has the lease of this house at Punta Arenas. Down to it she went a few days after from Buenos Aires Van Ryn disappeared.'

'Could you give me an introduction to Madame Sinegiest?' Richard enquired.

'With much pleasure. Where do you stay?'

'The Plaza.'

'Very good.' The Baron stood up. 'Tomorrow morning I will send a line round to your hotel. Now you excuse please. I lunch with a friend.'

When he had clicked his heels in the approved German fashion and bowed himself away, Richard thanked Don Salvador for the introduction, then he added, 'I find it surprising that Van Ryn should have made such a close friend of von Thumm. Ever since the war he has displayed a rooted dislike of all Germans.'

'I, too, am surprised that they became intimates,' Don Salvador agreed. 'But they must have had some interest in common. Perhaps it was the Baron's poker school, or Silvia Sinegiest may have acted as a bridge between them.'

After a pleasant lunch, Richard returned to the Plaza, stripped and—an unusual thing for him as he infinitely preferred a proper bath—had a cold shower. He then lay naked on his bed for the siesta hour. When he roused, Simon was still absent and did not appear until close on six o'clock. When he did, Richard asked:

'Where have you been? I was getting quite worried about you.'

Simon replied airily. 'Oh, out to Rex's place. After last night, thought I ought to take his niece a few flowers. She asked me to stay to lunch; so, with you off on your own, I naturally accepted.'

'Visiting the sick, eh?' Richard commented. 'Jolly decent of you. And you didn't run out on the girl after the meal either, or was it that you didn't reach the coffee stage until five o'clock?'

'Owing to her near blindness and poor, scarred face, Miranda leads a lousy life,' Simon countered. 'But I didn't spend the afternoon with her out of charity. Stayed on because I was enjoying myself. She's a fine person. Brave, intelligent and fun to be with. You don't deserve it, but I'm taking you to lunch with her tomorrow. She doesn't normally entertain at all, but she wants to meet you because you're such an old friend of her uncle's.'

'I'll be delighted to meet her,' Richard replied. 'That is, if we are still in Buenos Aires. But if transport is available, we'll be on our way to Punta Arenas.' He then told Simon about the lead he had been given by von Thumm.

Simon agreed that no time must be lost in their endeavours to trace Rex; so they went down to make enquiries about travel facilities to the far south. It soon emerged that they were minimal. Punta Arenas was fourteen hundred miles from Buenos Aires and the railway ran only a quarter of that distance. The last thousand miles had to be covered on horseback, as in many places the tracks through the mountains were too dangerous for cars. The alternative, adopted by the majority of people going there, was a three-day voyage by ship down to the Straits of Magellan. However, it transpired that, during the past year, an intermittent air service had been started, and a small 'plane left each Wednesday, if enough passengers to justify it had booked seats.

Time being important, Simon asked the hall porter to get on to Argentine Airways, book seats for Richard and himself, and say that he would also pay for any seats that might be left vacant, in order to ensure that the 'plane would fly on Wednesday next, the 9th.

That evening they dined at a restaurant where there was a cabaret show. The dancing proved excellent, and there was an amusing mock bull-fight, where two men played the part of the bull and, as a finale, a pretty girl dressed as a matador leapt on the dying bull's back, jabbed it into new life and rode it off the stage. But the show was strictly decorous, owing to Eva Peron's ordinances aimed at eliminating vice spots.

On the Monday morning, as Punta Arenas was just over the Chilean border, they went to the Chilean Consulate to get their passports visaed. On returning to the hotel, they found both von Thumm's promised letter of introduction to Silvia Sinegiest, and Pinkerton's report on Rex's friends. As Simon had feared, the latter proved of no value. All the people Rex had entertained with any frequency were highly respectable, and had no known idiosyncrasies. They then drove out to lunch with Miranda.

On the two previous occasions when Simon had had a meal with her, they had enjoyed it *tête-à-tête*; but that day Miss Pinney was present, to make a fourth, so they kept off the subject of Rex's disappearance. Apart from Miranda's beautiful blank eyes, Richard thought her scarred face worse than the description Simon had given of it; but he formed an immediate liking for her, and was filled with admiration at the way she made light of her disability.

As they were leaving, she said to Simon, 'Your coming to Buenos Aires has proved a wonderful tonic for me, and I do want to see as much as I can of you before you fly down to Punta Arenas on Wednesday. Will you come to dinner with me again tonight?'

He shook his head. 'Ner, I'm terribly sorry. I'd love to but I've accepted an invitation to meet Richard's friend, Don Carlos Escalente, and dine with him.'

'Lunch tomorrow then?' she suggested.

He hesitated a moment, then smiled. 'Yes; but on one condition. That in the evening you let me take you out to dinner.'

'That is quite impossible,' Miss Pinney broke in. 'It would be most distressing for Miranda to show herself in a restaurant. Besides, the light would be very harmful to her eyes.'

'Nothing's impossible,' Simon retorted firmly, 'and I give my solemn word that she shall neither be embarrassed nor her sight harmed. I've thought of a way to overcome that. Miranda, what do you say?'

She smiled at him. 'How can I not trust you? Yes, I will if you like.'

The party that evening, for which they changed into dinner jackets, proved most enjoyable. It was given by Don Carlos in his own apartment. Like that of Rex, it overlooked the park and was even more luxurious. Being situated on a corner of another of the great blocks, it had two balconies, and it contained a fine collection of paintings. *Donna* Escalente was a dark, lovely woman; well read, amusing and vivacious. Richard had known her in London and she showed great delight in seeing him again. The party consisted mainly of diplomats and their wives. A dozen of them sat down to dinner at a table sparkling with crystal glasses and gay with a great centre-piece of tropical flowers. Each delectable course was washed down with wines from the best European vineyards and, out of consideration for Richard, mainly English was spoken throughout the meal.

Afterwards, tactful enquiries by him revealed that several of those present knew Rex, but none of them showed any inkling that there was anything unusual about his absence from Buenos Aires, and supposed that he had gone off on a holiday.

On the Tuesday morning, the two friends woke to the sound of teeming rain. The weather had at last broken, and it was pouring in torrents. Soon after breakfast, Simon said that, in spite of the rain, he must go out, as he had to make certain preparations which would ensure Miranda's having a happy evening. Half an hour later, Richard finished the paperback he was reading; and, although he could have bought another down in the hotel lobby, it occurred to him that he had so far seen very little of South America's largest city, and he might never have another opportunity of exploring it. So he too donned his mackintosh and went out.

A map provided by the hall porter showed him that Buenos Aires consisted of several hundred blocks, divided by parallel streets, so a stranger could not get lost. Two great boulevards, each the best part of a mile in length and about two hundred yards in width, formed a cross in the centre of the city. One was the *Avenida del Mayo* and the other the *Avenida 9th de Julio.*

As the former ran right down to the waterfront, Richard first made his way there, to find, at its end, the handsome Presidential Palace, which was Peron's residence and, on one side of the Plaza on which it faced, a cathedral that looked like a great temple.

Turning about, Richard splashed his way up the wide, tree-lined thoroughfare until he reached the other great boulevard that crossed it. Between the belts of trees lining a huge square, there reared up the tall Radio Tower, and a lofty obelisk. Having made the round of the vast open space along the sides of which there were many cafés and passable shops, he entered the upper section of the *Avenida del Mayo.* At the far end stood the imposing Congress building. From there he walked down several side streets to the *Palais de Justice*, on the corner of the *Plaza Lavalle*: a square made particularly attractive by its great palm trees and huge magnolias. From there he found no difficulty in threading his way back to the Plaza.

He reckoned that he must have walked a good seven miles, and all the time the downpour had never ceased; but the atmosphere was so warm that the rain was almost tepid and he felt no discomfort from it. Having made this tour of the principal streets and squares, he had no desire to stay longer in Buenos Aires, or to return there. Apart from the few fine buildings and blocks of luxury flats that overlooked the park, he had found the city to be shoddy and populated by gloomy-looking, down-at-heel people, which made it depressing.

On his return it occurred to him to make some enquiries about Silvia Sinegiest, so he telephoned Pinkerton's office and got on to the man there who had sent Simon the report about Rex's friends. She was so well known in Buenos Aires that the following information was sent round in less than an hour.

Her age was uncertain; but, as she had made her two films in the mid-nineteen-thirties, it could be assumed that she was at least forty. She had been born an American but was of Swedish extraction. Hers was no case of 'Poor girl makes good'. Her father had been an engineer, and sufficiently well-off to send her to a college of good standing. She had then gone to New York and swiftly became the top model in a leading fashion house. This had given her the entrée to wealthy 'Café Society'. She had not gone to Hollywood; it had come to her, in the person of Gabriele Carriano, the film producer. He had met her in New York, decided that she was star material, taken her back to California with him and groomed her for her new role. For the trouble he had taken he had been well rewarded by her success and, after her second film, he had married her. But evidently life in Hollywood had not appealed to Silvia, as she had parted from her husband a year later, and left the 'Coast', never to return.

Her second husband had been Sir Walter Willersley, the millionaire chairman of one of Britain's largest shipping lines. She had travelled extensively with him and, as his wife, been accepted into English society. The war had put an end to that, presumably pleasant, period of her life. During the greater part of the war she had remained in London, and had been decorated for bravery while driving an ambulance in the blitz. In 1943 she had had an affaire with a Swedish diplomat, which led to her being divorced by Sir Walter.

For some years after the war she had led an unsettled life in Europe, the United States, Mexico and the Caribbean. Contemptuous of public opinion she had, during that time, lived more or less openly with the pianist Ladoloski, the author Brian Stores and the playwright François Debré. In 1948 she had married again. This time it was the Argentine meat-packing king, Edouardo Varodero. But the marriage had been dissolved eighteen months later and, while remaining based on Buenos Aires, she had resumed her restless existence.

When Simon returned from his lunch with Miranda, Richard told him all this, upon which Simon grinned and remarked. 'This Silvia must be quite a girl.'

'Hardly a girl,' responded Richard. 'She cannot now be far off fifty, but she is undoubtedly a personality. Her wartime record shows that she has guts, and the fact that she does not seek to hide her illicit amours, moral courage. Moreover, while millionaires quite frequently fall for women whose only assets are their looks, for her to have captured men like Stores, Debré and Rex required a considerable degree of intelligence.'

'You're right there,' Simon nodded. 'Rex is certainly not the sort of chap to get all steamed up about a glamour-puss. Wonder if he's making a bid to marry her? Seems her price for getting hitched up is seven figures plus; d'you think he could have pinched that million as part of a campaign to make her Mrs Van Ryn?'

'No, Simon. That doesn't make sense. The money Rex made off with is stolen. Unless he takes a new identity he would be called to account for it, and a woman like Silvia Sinegiest would never be willing to live in secret under a false name. What use would a million be in such circumstances? To enjoy it, they'd have to come out into the open; and that would be impossible as long as Rex is wanted for embezzlement.'

'He's not. Not by the police, anyway. If he does reappear, what could his family do, except grin and bear it? They'd never prosecute.'

'But Rex must have much more than a million dollars of his own.'

'Maybe he has some reason for not wanting to draw on it for the time being, and the lady was impatient. She may have demanded that he settle a million on her before she agreed to become hitched up. If Rex was really bats about her, he could have taken this way to clinch matters, while intending to repay the bank later.'

'That seems a bit far-fetched. Still, I agree that it is a possibility. Anyhow, it looks as though Madame Sinegiest holds the key to our riddle. With luck, we'll get it out of her in a few days' time.'

When Simon was driven out to Rex's apartment that evening, he took with him a jeweller's leather case which, at one time, had contained a necklace supporting a large central pendant. Assuming that Miranda would have no evening dresses, he had not put on a black tie, but he found her in a black cocktail frock, trimmed with beautiful lace that she told him she had made herself. Miss Pinney was with her, radiating intense disapproval; but it was clear that she had failed to persuade Miranda to alter her decision to dine out.

Simon opened the leather case he had brought, and showed them the result of his efforts during the day. He had first gone to a costumier's which stocked every kind of item for hire during the annual carnival, and had bought there a black satin mask with a heavy fringe, and ornamented with diamanté. Next, he had gone to an optician's and bought two glass eyes with blue irises. Taking his purchases to a jeweller, he had asked for the eyes to be cut in half, so that their backs would be flat; that they should then be fitted behind the slits in the mask, and the backs covered with soft material. The result was a blindfold, with eyes in it that no-one would suspect were false, except on close inspection, and with a fringe that would hide the worst of Miranda's scars.

She could see Simon's ingenious present only through the perpetual mist in which she lived; but, when it was explained to her, she was delighted. Not only would her eyes be fully protected and her disfigurement not be apparent, but she would have the fun of knowing that everyone in the restaurant would be wondering who the mysterious masked lady was.

They dined at the *Avenida*. Simon was careful to suggest dishes for her that did not need cutting up, and long practice had made her adept at feeding and drinking without using her eyes. When they finished dinner, he insisted that she should dance with him and, as he was a good dancer, she found no difficulty in following him.

It was close on two in the morning before he saw Miranda home. As he said good night to her in the hall of the apartment, she exclaimed, 'It's been a wonderful evening, absolutely wonderful! I can never thank you enough.'

Smiling, he said, 'For me, too.' Then he put a hand behind her back, drew her quickly to him and kissed her on the lips. She made no effort to resist him, so he pressed his mouth to hers more firmly, and gave her a real lovers' kiss.

Suddenly she broke away, gave a little gulp and burst into a passion of tears.

For a moment he stared at her blind blue eyes from which the tears were running down her scarred cheeks, then he stammered:

'I . . . I'm terribly sorry. It was rotten of me to take advantage of you.'

'You haven't,' she sobbed. 'Oh, Simon, dear Simon! It's such . . . such a very long time since I've been kissed like that.'

5

THE LADY IN THE CASE

Soon after eight o'clock next morning, Richard and Simon drove out to the airport and, at nine o'clock, took off for Punta Arenas. It was an eight-seater, and all but two of the seats were occupied. For most of the journey they flew at about two thousand feet. The first lap down to Bahia Blanca was across the great cattle country: flattish land of an almost uniform colour, on which they occasionally saw a great herd grazing far below. After refuelling, they flew down the coast, at times over it, at others over the sea, with land to be seen only in the distance. When they passed within a few miles of the port of Trelew, they saw that inland from it mountains rose steeply with, in the distance, lofty, snow-covered peaks. Further south they crossed the great Golfo San Jorge, then came down for the second time at Deseado. From there on they flew overland again and, even at the height at which they were flying, they could see that it was wild, hostile country. But, as they approached Punta Arenas, instead of the grandeur of great, rugged mountains falling precipitately to deep green fiords—as they had expected would be the case—the landscape flattened out into barren, undulating plains which stretched as far as the eye could see. Beyond them lay the grey Straits of Magellan, a few miles in width, and the equally unimpressive coast of the great island of Tierra del Fuego.

The airport, like those at which they had come down to refuel, consisted of a few low hangars, grouped round a watch tower and waiting room, manned only when an aircraft was expected. Two aged hire cars carried the passengers and crew along a coast road to the town, which proved to be as disappointing as the landscape. The majority of the buildings had been erected at the turn of the century and were only two storeys high. The long main street, leading to a central square, boasted only the sort of shops to be found in a suburb in which the population was far from wealthy; and the place had the unnatural appearance of a Scandinavian town inhabited by Spaniards. Simon had telegraphed for rooms at the best hotel. It was called the *Cabo de Hornos*, and lay on the seaward side of the square.

To their surprise, they found it, in contrast to the town, not only modern and cheerful, but with a restaurant that was really excellent. Their flight had taken a little over nine hours; so, after freshening themselves up, they had a cocktail, then went in to dinner. As their main course, they selected freshly-caught *bonito* and found it delicious. Now, too, that they were across the border into Chile, they were able to wash it down with a wine greatly superior to those grown in any other South American country.

After they had dined, Richard had the telephone operator put him through to Silvia Sinegiest's house. Having got on to her, he said that he had a letter of introduction from Baron von Thumm, and asked when he might present it.

'If you have made no plans, why not drive out here tomorrow morning?'

she replied. 'Say about midday. You will find me in my garden, a much more pleasant place to be in than that dreary town.'

Next morning they learned that her house was some way along the coast, so they hired a car to take them there. As they went out to the car, a blustering wind made them grab their hats. The previous evening it had been blowing hard, but they had thought that to be the after-effects of a storm.

The road ran eastward within sight of the cliff, through bare, inhospitable country unfit for growing crops. Dotted about there were a few small factories and, here and there, barns which were the winter quarters for the flocks of sheep that are almost the only means of support available to the inhabitants of Patagonia.

Although it was high summer, the sky was only a pale blue and the green waters of the Straits were made choppy by the strong, gusty wind. When Simon remarked on it, their driver laughed and said:

'You should come here in winter, *Señor*. A tempest rages almost constantly, for here the currents of both water and air from the Atlantic and the Pacific meet and clash. Even in our best months, the sea is rarely calm, and the wind is always with us.'

After a few miles the car turned up a side road towards a belt of trees on the edge of the cliff. They were not tall, and no roof of a house stood out above them; but, having passed through a gate in an iron fence that enclosed this patch of woodland, a drive descended steeply, revealing an utterly different scene. On the landward side, the trees protected a cove between two headlands that sheltered it from east and west. In the centre stood the house. It was entirely surrounded by a succession of terraces that ran down to the beach, and the whole area was a kaleidoscopic mass of flowers.

As the car pulled up in front of a wooden porch, a woman emerged from a path on its far side, carrying a gardening basket. She was tall, broad-shouldered and carried herself very upright, walking towards them with unstudied grace. Her hair, above a broad forehead, came down in a 'widow's peak', from which it rose in a strawberry-blonde halo several inches deep. She had a regal air and was beautiful in an unusual way. Her mouth was perfectly modelled; her cheeks full, below high cheek bones; her eyebrows well-marked and her eyes bright with the joy of life. She gave them a ravishing smile, that displayed two rows of even teeth, and said in a lilting voice with only a slight American accent:

'Hello! I'm Silvia.'

As she spoke, a small shaggy dog that was pattering along beside her suddenly began a furious barking. 'Be quiet, Booboo!' she chid him. 'Stop it now! D'you hear me?' But evidently inured to such mild reproofs he ignored her and continued his excited yapping.

When, at last, his barks subsided Richard took the hand his mistress extended, bent over it with an old-world courtesy that would have done credit to the Duke, and murmured, 'Madame, my congratulations on having created in this bleak land a small paradise that forms a perfect setting for yourself.'

She gave a ready laugh. 'How nice of you to say that. But I cannot really take the credit for the garden. I only lease this house. It belongs to one of the Grau-Miraflores, whose family practically own Punta Arenas. But I enjoy keeping it in good order.'

As she shook hands with Simon, he said, 'Never seen such lupins. What a riot of colour. Pleasant change, too, to find all the old English flowers here, instead of the exotics one sees everywhere in Buenos Aires.'

Again she gave her dazzling smile as she replied. 'It's that which attracts me to the place. One of my husbands was an Englishman, and I became very fond of England. We had a house in the Cotswolds and, before the war, I had a lovely garden there.'

Her words came as a sharp reminder of the fact that she must be nearly fifty; yet neither of her visitors could believe that. With her bright hair, not even the suggestion of a wrinkle, and tall, sylph-like figure, no-one would have taken her for a day over thirty.

She went on, 'I love people and adore parties, but one can have too much of anything. After burning the candle at both ends during the winter season, I enjoy coming here to vegetate for a few weeks: sleeping a great deal, reading quite a lot and, during the daytime, pottering in the garden.'

Richard smiled. 'Few women are so sensible. They want to be the centre of attraction all the time. But I think you have discovered the secret of perpetual youth.'

Throwing back her head, with its crown of strawberry-blonde hair, she gave a happy laugh. 'Nonsense. I'm an old woman, or at least getting on that way. Anyhow, I'm old enough to have grown-up children. But you must need a drink, so come into the house.'

It was not a large place and far from pretentious. The furniture was mostly good, solid oak, of the type favoured by people of moderate fortune in late Victorian times. As a background for Silvia, it struck Simon as incongruous. Even in the simple clothes she was wearing, she had an air of great elegance, and her height gave her a commanding presence. He felt sure whenever she entered a strange restaurant, the head-waiter would at once single her out for special attention.

They followed her through a dining room to another, larger room which had a big bay window overlooking the cove. Over her shoulder she said, 'I am going to make myself a dry Martini. Would you care to join me?'

Richard shook his head. 'You must forgive me if I refuse. Martinis always give me indigestion.'

'Champagne then?' she suggested, as she opened a corner cupboard that contained a fine array of glasses and assorted drinks. 'I always keep a bottle on the ice.'

'You are very kind. I should enjoy that.'

Simon nodded. 'Me, too, if I may.'

She pressed a bell and a Spanish manservant appeared, to whom she gave the order. While the wine was being brought, she mixed herself an outsize cocktail with professional efficiency. Watching her long, slender hands move with swift precision, Simon grinned and said, 'In the unlikely circumstance of your ever needing a job, you'd make good money as a bartender.'

Her spontaneous laugh came again. 'I was one once for a few weeks, and in a luxury joint that was a very shady spot. But I made it clear that the couch was not in the contract. I've never got into the sack with anyone I didn't care about.'

Richard found her frankness refreshing, and said with a smile, 'Were I not happily married, I should endeavour to make myself one of the men you did care about.'

She gave him a steady, appraising look. 'So, Mr Eaton, you are the faithful kind. That is rather a waste of good material in a man who is so good-looking. We must go into that some time. But not for now. How long do you intend to stay in Punta Arenas, and what do you plan to do?'

'We don't expect to be here for long, as our only purpose in coming to Punta Arenas was to talk to you.' As he spoke, Richard handed her the Baron's letter.

Raising her well-marked eyebrows, she took it. While her man poured the champagne, she glanced at the few lines of writing, then said: 'This is only a formal introduction. Why has Kurt von Thumm sent you to me?'

'Because you are the only person he could think of who might be able to help us.' Richard gestured towards Simon. 'Mr Aron and I are very anxious to get in touch with an old friend of ours. It seems that he has gone off on a holiday, and he's left no address. Von Thumm told us that, before our friend left Buenos Aires, he was seeing a lot of you, so we thought you might be able to tell us where he has gone. His name is Rex Van Ryn.'

'I see.' Silvia's voice had taken on a sharp note. 'And I suppose that ugly little gossip led you to believe that I am Rex's mistress?'

'Were that so,' replied Richard smoothly, 'I should count Rex an extremely lucky fellow, and you a lucky woman.'

She smiled then. 'You are right on both counts. And I am—or, rather, was. I've never seen any reason why a woman should conceal the fact that she has taken a lover—unless it is going to harm the man. To be open about it makes things far easier, and the only people who show disapproval are women who, through circumstances or lack of attraction, are prevented from taking a lover themselves. If they don't want to know me, I couldn't care less. In fact, I'm rather sorry for the poor things. About Rex, though, I don't know what to say. He had a very good reason for going off on his own, and I'm certain that he does not want his whereabouts known.'

'Thought as much,' Simon put in quickly. 'But he told you where he was going?'

'I did not say so.'

'But you implied it. And we've got to find him.'

'I'm sure he would rather that you didn't.'

'Don't want to seem rude, but you're wrong about that. Richard Eaton and I are Rex's best friends. Rex is in a muddle. We're certain of it, and we've come all the way from England to help him out. Now, please tell us where he's got to.'

She shook her head. 'What proof have I that you are his friends? Even if I were sure of that, and did know where Rex is, I wouldn't tell you, because you might lead others to him. And, as you are right about his being in trouble, I could not risk making his situation worse than it is.'

'Do you know what sort of trouble Rex is in?' asked Richard.

She looked away from him, and lit a cigarette. 'Yes, I know. But I'm not prepared to discuss it.'

'It's clear that Rex has gone into hiding, and one of the things that worries us is that he may have had to leave in a hurry. If so, it is possible that he is leading a grim life somewhere up-country and is desperately short of money.'

This subtle approach by Richard proved abortive. Either she was unaware that Rex had absconded with a million, or, if she knew it, did not mean to give away the fact. With a shrug of her shoulders, she replied: 'I don't think you need worry about that. Rex is a rich man, and he would not have been such a fool as to take off without having cashed a fat cheque.'

'Perhaps,' Richard hazarded, 'you will at least tell us when you last saw him?'

'On the night before he left Buenos Aires. As a matter of fact, we had quarrelled. He was very upset by what had happened, and so anxious to make it up before leaving that he came to see me at three in the morning. Of course, my servants were used to his coming and going at all hours, so they thought nothing of it. He stayed for only twenty minutes. I forgave him for . . . well, that is no concern of yours . . . and that's the last I saw of him.'

She had been sitting in a low chair, with one knee crossed over the other, and the thought drifted through Simon's mind that he had never seen a more perfect pair of legs. His glance was inoffensive, but she evidently became aware of it, for she pulled down her skirt and came to her feet. Picking up the bottle of champagne, she refilled their glasses and said:

'I do understand how worried you must be about your friend. But I really don't feel that I would be justified in telling you any more than I have. At least, not until I've thought it over very carefully.'

'It's good of you to go that far.' Richard said quickly. 'When may we hope to learn your decision?'

For a moment she remained thoughtful, then she replied, 'There's not a thing for you to do in Punta Arenas, so come and dine with me tonight. When I'm down here I rarely entertain. It's an opportunity for me to slim and catch up on my sleep; but it would be a pleasant change to have a little dinner party. Presently I'll ring up a few people I know. But don't order your car to pick you up until half past eleven. By then the others will have gone and, if I decide to talk, we'll be on our own.'

Her two visitors gladly accepted. When they had finished their wine, she took them for a walk round the upper part of the garden. Only Alpine flowers were growing there, but there was an amazing variety of sub-Arctic shrubs and trees. Then she gaily waved them away in their car.

As it carried them towards the town, Richard said, 'I wouldn't mind betting that she knows about Rex's having robbed his bank, what led him to do so and where he is at the moment.'

'Don't wonder he fell for her,' Simon remarked.

'Yes; she's a quite exceptional woman and, on the face of it, a very nice one. I had expected her to be completely different: vain, spoilt from having too much money, and hard as nails.'

After a late lunch, they put on their overcoats and went for a walk round the town. Having driven through the eastern side, they turned west and, at the end of the roughly-paved streets that led seaward, they caught glimpses of the dock. It was no more than a wharf, with piers projecting from it and lying off there were a few rusty steamers. The wind had never ceased blowing hard enough to make the skirts of their overcoats flap and force their trousers hard against their legs; so they gave up and hurried back to the warm comfort of the hotel.

So far south it was still broad daylight when they drove out again to Silvia Sinegiest's retreat. Booboo was with her and again barked furiously, but evidently without animosity. His small black eyes gleaming between the hair of his long fringe, he ran round them in circles to work off his excitement.

Besides themselves, the party consisted only of the American Consul and his wife, and a member of the Grau-Miraflores' family. They were not surprised to find that, in such a distant outpost, where commercial activities were limited, the Consul was no ball of fire, and that his wife's conversation consisted largely of nostalgic references to the much pleasanter life she had led in her own small home town. But *Señor* Pepe Grau-Miraflores proved interesting.

His family was a large one. For several generations they had owned a good part of Punta Arenas and vast sheep farms in Patagonia. They had also developed many other interests in the Argentine and Chile. He was a cheerful man and showed no pessimism about the future prospects of his own family, who were in a position to increase their wealth from industry; but he spoke with deep concern of the smaller sheep farmers, for whom he foresaw a time when, although few of them yet realised it, the new synthetic fabrics, such as nylon, would make wool a drug on the market.

Silvia proved an admirable hostess. She drew her American compatriots out to talk about their children and hopes of a more congenial post, surprised Simon by showing a shrewd knowledge of stocks and shares, reminisced with Richard about Ascot and Goodwood, exchanged witticisms with Grau-Miraflores, laughed a lot and saw to it that their glasses were never empty.

At about a quarter to eleven, the party began to break up and Grau-Miraflores offered Richard and Simon a lift back into Punta Arenas; but they told him that they had a car coming for them.

When the others had gone, Silvia ordered her houseman to bring another bottle of champagne. While he was fetching it, she said, 'I hope you weren't too bored with the Consul and his dreary wife; but I've deliberately discouraged the advances of the majority of the locals and they were the best I could produce at such short notice.'

Her guests politely murmured their understanding, while both of them waited with concealed impatience to learn whether she had decided to tell them about Rex. She had been chain-smoking all the evening. As the houseman left the room, she lit another cigarette and said:

'Well, I've thought things over, and it has occurred to me that if I don't tell you why Rex left Buenos Aires, you will continue your efforts to find him; and that could bring him into grave danger. In a way I am responsible for the trouble he is in, so I feel badly about it; although, of course, I had no idea that our quarrel would have the results it did.'

She paused and sat staring down into her glass for so long that Richard decided to prompt her, and asked gently, 'What was the cause of your quarrel?'

Still looking down she replied, 'I found out that he was having an affair with another woman. I wouldn't have minded in the ordinary way, provided I remained first in his affections. After all, men are made like that. It's quite natural that they should want to get in the sack with any pretty girl who shows willing and, thank God, I've never been cursed with jealousy. But this woman was a Negress, and the idea of having him in my bed after he had been in hers revolted me. I told him that either he must give her up, or I'd have no more to do with him.'

'How did he react to that?'

'He swore he loved only me, and promised not to see her again. But he didn't keep his promise. She must have had some hold over him. What it was, I have no idea, but he freed himself of it in the most terrible fashion.'

'In what way terrible?' Richard enquired anxiously.

'He murdered her.'

Simon's eyes widened, and he clapped a hand over his mouth to suppress an exclamation of horror. Richard caught his breath; then, with an effort, keeping his voice to the same low tone, he asked: 'Are you sure?'

'Yes. He told me so on that Friday night, the last time I saw him. He said he could not bear to give me up, so he had gone to see her and told her that he had finished with her. She threatened him. They had a most ghastly row. He hit her. You know how strong he is. His fist caught her beneath the chin and jerked her head back so violently that it broke her neck.'

'So that is why he left Buenos Aires. Are the police after him? Did they come and question you?'

'No. But they may. I have reason to believe that I am being watched. It is quite possible that they are hoping that I will lead them to him.'

'I see. And that is why you are anxious that Aron and I should not try to find him?'

'Yes. Since you have been making enquiries about him in B.A., they may have learned of that. If so, they will have put a tail on you too.'

'If they know that he killed this woman, or suspect him of having done so, it's strange that they've not set on foot a public enquiry, published his photograph in the papers and that sort of thing.'

'Their line may be to lure him into a false sense of security, hoping that he will return and they they can then pounce on him.'

'That's possible. Do you think anyone other than you knows that he committed this crime—members of the woman's family, for instance?'

'I have no idea.'

'If they do, that could account for Rex's having taken such a huge sum from his bank. He could dole instalments to them, to buy their continued silence.'

'Before he left me, I asked him if he had any money, and offered him my jewels. He said he could get all the money he needed; but I did not know that he meant to take a specially large sum. Perhaps he felt that his only chance of remaining free permanently would be to change his identity. If he did that to live in any comfort he would need capital.'

'I hope that is the explanation, and not that he expected to have to pay blackmailers.'

As Richard was speaking, a telephone began to shrill somewhere in the house. After a moment he said to Silvia, 'We can only pray that by this time Rex is out of the country. Is it really true that you have no idea where he meant to head for?'

She nodded. 'Our talk on that awful night was very hurried, and he told me only that he must get out as soon as he had collected some money.'

At that moment there came a quick knock at the door, and it was opened by the manservant, who said, 'I am sorry to disturb you, *Señora*. You are wanted on the telephone. It is the Baron von Thumm calling you from Buenos Aires.'

Coming to her feet, Silvia stubbed out her cigarette, looked first at Richard then at Simon and said, 'I'm sorry. This is a private call. Please excuse me if I take it up in my bedroom.'

As the door closed behind her, Simon said in a low voice, 'Don't believe it.

Don't believe a word of it. Never known Rex to lose his head. He's well aware of his great strength. If he did hit that Negress, he'd never have bashed her with a pile-driver like that. Not in his character either to go off the deep end and commit unpremeditated murder.'

Richard nodded. 'I agree. Of course, like us, he has killed before, when it has been a matter of necessity. But even if he was berserk about our charming hostess he would not have done in the other woman. However big her price, he could have afforded to buy her off. And there is more to it than that. Rex's family come from the deep South. In the old days his ancestors would have taken Negresses as their concubines; but not in these days. Like most Southern whites, he'd have a prejudice against coloured women.'

These exchanges had taken no more than a minute. Smiling at Richard, Simon said, 'Now going to behave like a cad. But where helping one's friends is concerned, end justifies the means.' Walking over to the telephone, he picked up the receiver.

Silvia and the Baron had just greeted each other, and the Baron asked her, 'How go things with you down there?'

'Couldn't be better,' she replied. 'But I wish you hadn't called me until tomorrow. Both of them are still here. They came this morning before lunch. I led them to suppose that I knew where Van Ryn was, but refused to tell, then invited them to dinner with the bait that I might be persuaded to change my mind.' She gave a quick laugh and went on, 'I had no trouble selling them our story, that Van Ryn was on the run because he committed murder. I made it very clear, too, that, if they continued to try to find him and succeeded, it was likely they would lead the police to him, and so put him on the spot. They'll not dare risk doing that, so we've no need to fear they will give us any further trouble.'

'Well done,' the Baron chuckled. 'Well done. The Prince, he will be most pleased with you.'

'Will he attend the barbecue at Santiago?' she asked.

'I think not,' came the reply. 'If not, for him I shall deputise. I look forward to see you there, this night next week.'

They said good-bye, then Silvia rang off. Simon replaced his receiver, looked across at Richard and said earnestly:

'Whole affair now stinks of conspiracy. Our charming hostess lied in her lovely teeth. Von Thumm concocted with her a pretty little plot. Could have pulled the wool over our eyes. But now we've found them out, advantage lies with us. They know where Rex is. Bet my shirt on that. And she's going to lead us to him.'

6

THE SEARCH FOR THE BARBECUE

When Silvia returned to the room, she again apologised for leaving them. 'I'm so sorry. That was von Thumm. He was ringing up to know whether you had been here and if I had been able to tell you anything about Rex; because, apparently, he too would like to get in touch with him. I could quite well have taken the call here, but I just didn't think. I'm so used to nattering over the 'phone up in my bedroom.'

Richard and Simon had both stood up as she came in. The former said, 'Oh, don't mention it. But while you were on the telephone, I heard our car drive up; so I think we ought to be going.'

Her perfect teeth flashed in a smile, and she held out her hand. 'It was a pleasure to have you both. You must come again.'

'We should love to, if we were held up for a few days before we can get a flight back to Buenos Aires. But you were our last chance of tracing Rex. After what you've told us, it seems that there is no alternative to abandoning our quest. Apart from your delightful retreat here, I can't say I find this part of the world attractive. Such times as Aron and I can continue to live away from England I feel we should devote to visiting some of the Argentine's real beauty spots.'

'Then don't miss the Iguazu Falls,' she advised them. 'They are the biggest in the world, and in the middle of a jungle that abounds in wild life, orchids and birds with the most lovely plumage.'

Having thanked her for a most pleasant evening, they took their leave. While their car drove off, they turned to wave to her as she stood framed in the lighted doorway of the house, a tall, elegant figure, crowned by a mass of bright hair.

On the way back, as their driver understood a little English, they refrained from discussing what had transpired. Shortly before midnight they reached the *Cabo de Hornos*, to find that, in keeping with Spanish hours, a number of people were still sitting about the lounge, chatting and drinking. Ordering brandies and soda, they sat down in a quiet corner.

'Now,' said Richard, 'I can't wait to hear what you found out about the tie-up between Silvia and the Baron.'

Simon told him what they had said to each other over the telephone, and added, 'What a break, eh? Knew she was lying; but what a lovely liar. Don't wonder old Rex fell for her.'

'Nor I,' Richard agreed. 'Apart from that marvellous figure, she's not a beauty; but she has tremendous personality and no-one would credit that she is a day over thirty. It would be difficult to imagine a more delightful companion to spend carefree hours with.'

'She's on the other side, though, and covering up for someone. What d'you make of it?'

'Your guess is as good as mine. This story that Rex has disappeared because he was afraid that he might be arrested for murder is no more real than a red herring designed to induce us to give up the search for him.'

'Ummm. It's clear that they're anxious to put an end to our snooping. But not so certain that Rex hasn't done someone in. Story about his having an affaire with a Negress is a phoney. I'd take a big gamble on that. Couldn't have a better reason for quitting B.A. in a hurry than having committed murder, though.'

'True. And if there are people who could fix it on him, that would account for his having absconded with so much money.'

'Doesn't quite add up,' Simon remarked thoughtfully. 'As he was rich enough to silence blackmailers, why shouldn't he have stayed put in Buenos Aires?'

'He might not have been able to buy off the police if they were after him, and he may have believed they were.'

'D'you believe that?'

'No, I don't. If they were, it's certain that Pinkerton's people would have known. They would have reported it to that bank manager feller, Haag; and he had received orders to conceal nothing from us. So, cagey as he was, he would not have dared keep us in the dark about Rex's being suspected of murder.'

'Exactly.' Simon gave a quick nod. 'So there's no fear of our leading the police to him.'

'To my mind, not the least. So in the morning I think we should make enquiries about an aircraft to get us up to Santiago. God knows what sort of service, if any, there is from this benighted spot. But, fortunately, Silvia's date with the Baron is not for another seven days. So, if the worst comes to the worst, there should still be time for us to fly back to B.A., then across the Andes to Santiago. There must be a regular service between the two capitals.'

On the Wednesday morning, Simon made enquiries at the hotel desk. He learned that, as was the case between Buenos Aires and Punta Arenas, there was, given sufficient bookings, a weekly service up to Santiago, but it flew only on Mondays. The information perturbed him considerably, since it not only meant that they would have to kick their heels in bleak Punta Arenas for another five days, but it would give them only a single day in Santiago to try to find out where the barbecue was that Silvia and the Baron were to attend. He was just wondering if it would be possible to hire a private aircraft to take them up, when a voice behind him said:

'Good morning, Mr Aron. I gather you are going up to Santiago. Have you urgent business there?'

Turning, Simon found Pepe Grau-Miraflores at his elbow. Giving a mock shiver, he replied, 'Ner, constant wind here makes this a place to stay in no longer than one has to, though. Richard Eaton and I want to leave for the north as soon as we can, to get some sunshine.'

Grau-Miraflores smiled. 'Then, may I suggest that you fly up with me in my private aircraft? It would take a couple of days, as I have an engagement in Puerto Montt tomorrow, and intend to spend the following night at my *fonda* on the River Laja. But at least I'll get you to Santiago by Friday; three days before you could get there by the weekly service.'

Simon eagerly accepted this kind offer and agreed to be ready to leave the hotel by eleven o'clock. But when he told Richard of the arrangement, his friend said with a slight frown:

'I wonder if this is altogether wise? Grau-Miraflores is a close friend of the Sinegiest woman, and she is an enemy. Our going with him could keep her informed of our movements. There is also just a chance that if we spend a night at this *fonda* of his, he might stage an "accident" that would put us out of the game for good.'

'Ummm. You're right. Hadn't thought of that. Best perhaps to back out.'

'No. I don't think we'll do that. Such situations cut both ways, and he can't know that we are wise to the lady's having attempted to double-cross us. If he is in cahoots with her, we may be able to jolly him into unwittingly giving us some useful information. In any case, we're going to have our work cut out to learn whereabouts in Santiago this barbecue is to be held. We'll need more than a day to do that; so we'd better risk it.'

Simon then endeavoured to telephone Miranda; but, on learning that there would be a delay of at least three hours in getting through to Buenos Aires, he sent her a telegram, letting her know that he and Richard were going to Santiago, where they would be staying at the new Carrera Hilton Hotel. He sent another telegram to the Hilton, booking a suite as from the coming Friday.

On their drive out to the airstrip, they learned considerably more about their host. His family was one of the richest in southern South America. Not only were they the potentates of Punta Arenas, but they owned great estates on both coasts, and the interior of the peninsular, which they had acquired before the boundary between Argentina and Chile had been settled.

The aircraft, an ex-fighter bomber from the war, had been converted into a comfortable four-seater, and its German pilot was an ex-officer of the Luftwaffe. At midday they started on their flight up the lower part of Chile, a country made unique by its geographical situation and isolation from the rest of the world.

Chile is as long as from northern Norway to southern Spain. Yet, in one place it is only twenty miles in breadth. The Andes–that vast range of eternally snow-crowned mountains with, apart from the Himalayas, some of the loftiest peaks in the world–cut the country off from its neighbours to the east. Trackless, and still largely unexplored, few men and no commerce could possibly cross the barrier and reach Chile from Europe or Africa until the coming of the recent age of air travel. For many centuries, Chile's ports on the Pacific formed almost her sole contact with civilisation.

Yet Chile, alone of all the countries of the world, has everything that is both bad and good. In the far south the land is broken up into innumerable islands, snow-covered for the greater part of the year: barren, inhospitable, a prey to terrible storms and a thousand swift, dangerous currents. In the far north, there are vast areas of uninhabitable desert, bitterly cold at night and scorched by unbearable heat during the day. But the greater part of central Chile provides everything men could wish for. From the mild climate and green fields of an English spring, it progresses through warmer regions with Mediterranean beaches and sunny vineyards to a land of palms and tropical fruit, and abundance of flowers and trees garlanded with orchids. The many lakes and rivers abound in fish, fine herds of cattle graze on the undulating downs, birds with gorgeous plumage flit through the twilit forests and, from every township, the mountains with their snow-covered slopes offering the pleasures of winter sports could be seen in the distance against a bright blue sky.

That day they flew for several hours at only a few miles' distance from the great chain of lofty, forest-covered mountains that ran down to an archipelago consisting of many hundred islands great and small. Only the larger ones showed any sign of habitation: little clusters of primitive buildings nestling beneath the lee of cliffs that sheltered a few fishing smacks. In many places where the channels were narrow, conflicting currents churned the sea into a mass of boiling foam, and great waves broke furiously on the jagged rocks, tossing the white spray high into the air. From time to time, Grau-Miraflores pointed out to his passengers places, the names of which indicated the almost incredible grimness of this stretch of coast: Gulf of Sorrows, Ice-water Valley, Hill of Anguish, Last Hope Sound.

Well on in the afternoon they landed at Puerto Montt and, on driving into the town, found it very different from Punta Arenas. Here, six hundred miles further north, the air had the balminess of spring, and the strolling crowds on the esplanade showed it to be a popular holiday resort. Actually, it was some distance from the Pacific, but it gave the impression of looking out on an ocean, dotted in the distance with islands.

The hotel to which Grau-Miraflores had telephoned for rooms had a gay, modern décor and, in the evening, the dance floor was crowded with young people. For dinner their host gave them *Cazuela de Ave*, a delicious soup, conger-eel and, as a savoury, cheese pies. They washed down the meal with an excellent white wine called *Savereo*.

Over the meal, Grau-Miraflores talked to them about Chile and how, owing to its isolation, it differed greatly from all other South American countries. Its earliest inhabitants had been the Araucanian Indians, the most fierce and brave of all the races in the southern continent. Even the splendidly-trained armies of the mighty Inca Empire had proved no match for them, and penetrated only the northern part of the country. Then, early in the sixteenth century, had come the Spanish Conquistadores. But, as the land had no gold or silver, they had scorned it. Pizzaro, the brutal conqueror of Peru, had given Chile as a sop to his partner, Diego de Almagro, whom he had consistently cheated.

For many years Spanish settlements had been few and far between; so, although Spain's law and language had been generally accepted by the white and half-caste population, a very high proportion of the Europeans who had colonised Chile in the eighteenth and nineteenth centuries had been Italians, Irish, Germans, Scots, English, French and Dutch, with the result that inter-marriage had produced a people more broad-minded, vigorous and business-like than in the countries shackled more closely to Spain.

Next morning, while Grau-Miraflores went about his business, Richard and Simon strolled round the town. At the eastern end of the waterfront there was a large street market with, below it on the beach, a fish market the like of which they had never seen. The stalls were actually in the sea. Rowing boats brought their catch right up to them. The fishermen unloaded the still-flapping fish and wriggling squids directly on to the counters, behind which the colourfully-dressed fishwives stood up to their knees in water. There could be no better guarantee that the fish they sold were fresh. Some customers waded out in gum boots to take their pick of the best, while others waited ashore until the tide went down sufficiently for them to make their purchases dryshod.

Simon eyed the fresh-caught lobsters with a gourmet's delight, hoping that he might enjoy one for lunch. He was not disappointed, although he did not eat it in Puerto Montt. At midday, after they had rejoined Grau-Miraflores, the latter took them in a car to the airport. As they boarded his 'plane, he said:

'I am taking you for lunch to the island of Chiloe. You can see it over there to the south-west. It is Chile's largest island, over a hundred miles long, and the best lobsters in the world are caught off its shores.'

A quarter of an hour later, they landed at the little town of Castro and, after a most succulent feast, flew north once more, heading for their host's *fonda* on the River Laja.

This second stage of their journey was even more fascinating than the first, as they flew low over Chile's two largest lakes, Villarrica and

Llanquihue. The mountains on their right, many of which retained their snow caps all the year round, made the scene reminiscent of Switzerland, and here the country broadened out, with many rivers running towards the now distant sea. As they progressed, villages and towns became more frequent, and the land green with crops between easily discernible roads. They were entering Chile's fertile seven-hundred-mile-long central valley, in which grazed herds of cattle; and, at five o'clock, put down on their host's private landing strip.

They were met by the manager of the *fonda*, a young Australian, who took them to the house in a jeep. The country, with its fields, flourishing vegetation and mild climate, might have been England, but the *fonda* itself bore no resemblance to an English country house. The garden was gay with daisies, geraniums, cannas and roses, partially shaded by magnolia and chestnut trees; but it had not been laid out to any plan. The house stood a hundred yards or so from the picturesque, rock-strewn river, but had no view of it or the country on the landward side. It was not a large building, and was sparsely furnished, but there was an air of cheerful activity about the place, and they all enjoyed a plain, well-cooked dinner.

Soon after they had gone up to bed, Simon went to Richard's room, sat himself down and asked, 'What do you make of Grau-Miraflores?'

'A charming and intelligent man,' replied Richard.

'I mean, d'you think he's mixed up in this muddle about Rex?'

'No. I asked him casually whether he knew a club in Santiago called the "Barbecue", and he said he'd never heard of it.'

'That doesn't mean a thing. If there's anything fishy about the place, he wouldn't admit to knowing it anyway.'

'Not if he was in this racket and had been given the job of bear-leading us. But I don't believe that to be the case.'

'It was your idea that he'd suggested taking us in his aircraft in order to keep tabs on us.'

'I agree I thought that a possibility. But on closer acquaintance, I think I was wrong. I've laid little traps for him several times and he's not fallen into one of them. I'm convinced now that the beautiful Silvia is no more than an acquaintance of his, and that he knows nothing about Rex. He is simply a cultured and generous South American who delights in showing visitors the beauties of his part of the world.'

Simon nodded. 'Hope you're right. Still worries me that we've so little to go on in our hunt for Rex. Wonder if we're correct in assuming that our lady friend's mention of a barbecue did refer to a club?'

'You told me she said "The" barbecue, and that sounds like a club. But quite possibly it is a meeting in a private house.'

'Damn' difficult to locate if that is the case.'

'True. Remember, though, that our glamorous strawberry-blonde is coming to Santiago for the party. She did not strike me as a lady given to hiding her light under a bushel. With a little luck we should be able to find out where she is staying, and have her kept under observation.'

'Or make her talk,' Simon said thoughtfully. 'Never been much good at that sort of thing myself. But you and old Greyeyes didn't give a second thought to sticking a knife into anyone's ribs until he decides that if he wants to live he'd better do what you tell him.'

Richard laughed. 'Simon, Simon; what ogres you make de Richleau and

me out to be. Personally I've always found it most distasteful to inflict
physical suffering on people. But, if the interests of one's country or a
friend's safety are at stake, one can't afford to be squeamish.'

Their host spent the greater part of the next day riding round the estate
with his manager. Richard accompanied them; but Simon never mounted a
horse unless he positively had to, so he stayed behind and, with an Indian to
pole him some way up stream in a punt, spent several hours fishing. In
consequence, it was late in the afternoon when they again boarded the
aircraft.

The evening light gave a new beauty to the landscape as the shadows
lengthened and, twice during their flight, their pilot made detours to fly
them down to within a hundred feet of and right round the craters of active
volcanoes. Dusk was falling by the time they were over Santiago airport, so
on coming in to land, they saw the myriad lights of the city. Half an hour's
drive took them into it and Grau-Miraflores set them down at the Carrera
Hilton.

He refused their invitation to dine with them, because he already had a
dinner engagement with one of his brothers, in whose house he was staying
the night. He was then flying on to Buenos Aires the following afternoon.
With hopes that they would meet again, they thanked him warmly for
having enabled them to see so much of Chile; then, smiling and waving, he
was driven away.

They had been given a suite on the tenth floor of the hotel and, on a table in
the sitting room, stood a big bowl of tuber-roses.

'Very generous of the management, I must say,' Richard remarked; but
Simon had spotted an envelope attached to the stem of one of the flowers. It
was addressed to himself. On opening it he found it contained a note from
Miranda. She said that, on receiving his telegram, she had decided to join
him in Santiago and, accompanied by Pinney, she had flown in that day. The
few lines ended, *Only the blindfold mask you gave me has made this possible. It
has opened a new life for me. Bless you, dear Simon.* It then gave the number of
her suite.

Simon's dark eyes flickered towards Richard, and he came as near to
blushing as his sallow skin would permit, as he said awkwardly, 'They're
from Miranda. Er—jolly decent of her, isn't it? She's here. Flown across
from B.A.'

'Well! Well!' Richard roared with laughter. 'When girls start sending men
flowers, wonders will never cease.' But Simon had already picked up the
telephone and was asking for Miranda's number. She and Pinney were just
about to go down to dinner, so she said they would wait in the cocktail lounge
until Simon and Richard had freshened themselves up, then they could all
dine together.

At this hour they found the Elizabethan cocktail lounge on the ground
floor of the Hilton crowded; but the intriguing appearance of the masked
lady had led to a waiter securing a table for Miranda and her companion.
They had ordered the drink of the country, Pisco sour, a weak spirit made
from grapes, and fresh limejuice. When the men joined them, they followed
suit and declared the drink made a delicious aperitif.

Although the prim Miss Pinney was unaware that Rex had made off with a
million dollars, she knew that he had disappeared without warning and that
his friends were anxious to find him; so Simon was at once able to give

Miranda an edited account of what had occurred in Punta Arenas, and their hopes of tracing Rex in Santiago.

When Simon thanked her for the flowers, Miranda said, 'It was nothing. Only a tiny gesture to show my appreciation of what you have done for me. Before, I had to live the life of a recluse. Now I need do so no longer. I can go anywhere, wearing my blindfold mask. Pinney tells me that everyone stares at me; but it is not with repulsion or pity, only curiosity; and that is rather fun.'

After half an hour, they went up to the restaurant and, over dinner, talked of the respective flights they had made. Even Pinney thawed out and said how fascinating it had been to fly over the Andes—that strange, primitive world of hundreds of miles of mountains alternating with deep, lifeless valleys through which rushed foaming rivers. There was now a daily service between Buenos Aires and Santiago, and the aircraft had been much larger than the one in which Richard and Simon had flown down to Punta Arenas.

When Simon and Richard awoke next morning, they found that their rooms looked out on to the *Plaza Constitucion*, the principal square of the city, and that the view from their windows was positively breathtaking.

Santiago lies in a bowl which is almost entirely surrounded by mountains. To the west, behind the hotel, ran the coastal range; to the east the far higher, massed peaks of the Andes, their white caps standing out sharply against a bright blue sky. In the foreground, the irregular roofs of the city were broken in one place by a four-hundred-foot-high wooded hill, crowned by a ruined castle. Further off, to the north-east, the buildings gave way to a great expanse of tree-covered slopes rising to a thousand feet, and surmounted by several buildings, above which towered an enormous statue of the Virgin.

As a waiter wheeled a breakfast trolley into the friends' sitting room, they caught the sounds of martial music, and went to the window again. From a lower and much older, domed building on the right hand side of the plaza, a band, followed by a company of troops, was emerging to form up in the square. The waiter told them that the building, *La Monada*, had once been the Mint of Chile, but was now the President's Palace, and that the guard was changed in the square at that hour every morning.

Over breakfast they discussed what their next move should be. It had been on Tuesday the 10th that von Thumm had said he would see Silvia 'this night next week', at the barbecue. This being Saturday morning, they still had four days to go before the meeting. That Rex was mixed up with these people there could be no doubt at all; so it was possible that he might attend this party they were holding, and already be in Santiago. If so, owing to his build and character, assuming that he was still a free man, it was just possible that enquiries might enable them to find out where he was staying. But his having made off with a million dollars put it beyond question that he was in some very serious trouble; so all the odds were that he was in hiding.

On the other hand, Silvia, the Baron, or both, might arrive at any time in the Chilean capital and, if either of them could be located, a watch could be kept on him or her. There was the possibility that they might stay in private houses, but an equal chance that they might go to an hotel; so it was agreed that Simon should make the round of all the best hotels in the city and give their hall porters handsome bribes to let him know if Silvia or von Thumm booked in.

However, the meeting at 'the barbecue' was the only firm line they had to follow. That it was not a recognised club Richard had already satisfied himself, by enquiries of the head porter on their arrival at the Hilton the previous evening. But it might be a small, private club that a limited number of people would know about. Having considered the matter, he said to Simon:

'The best informed people in any city are the reporters on the largest newspapers. I know a chap who frequently comes to England and stays with neighbours of mine. His name is Don Caesar Albert, and he is probably the wealthiest man in Chile. The family are immensely rich, and among their many interests they own one of the leading dailies.'

'Ummm.' Simon lit a cigarette. 'I've heard of the Alberts. They got in early on nitrate, when it was first discovered here. The Germans gave it a nasty knock when their supplies were cut off during the First World War. Their chemists invented a substitute. But by then the Alberts had become incredibly rich, and they are very highly respected.'

Richard nodded. 'Anyhow, I feel that Don Caesar might be able to help us.' Going over to the telephone, he asked the operator to get him Don Caesar's number. He was duly put through and, after he had had a few words with a secretary, Don Caesar came on the line. He at once recalled Richard, welcomed him warmly to Chile, and asked him to lunch.

Simon rang Miranda and arranged to give her and Pinney lunch, then the two friends went out to see something of the city. Santiago being on nearly the same latitude as Buenos Aires, it was very hot; but not with the scorching heat they had experienced in the Argentinian capital, and the people in the streets displayed much more vitality. Like the majority of comparatively modern cities, its centre consists of scores of square blocks and long, straight vistas with, in this case, the snow-capped mountains in the distance. The goods in the shops were, as in Buenos Aires, of second-rate quality, but the streets were cleaner and there was much less evidence of poverty.

Don Caesar asked Richard to meet him at the Crillon; so at one o'clock Simon left him in Augustines Street. On entering the hotel, Richard immediately appreciated its atmosphere. It was a building of the last century, with all the spacious elegance and décor that is found in hotels of that period in France. In the lounge there were a few Americans, but it was clearly a resort of the Chilean aristocracy. The clothes of many of the men in the lounge suggested Anderson and Sheppard and those of the women Dior or Fath.

As Richard walked in, Don Caesar, a tall, dark-haired man of about thirty, rose from a chair and smilingly extended his hand. In an ice bucket beside his table there was already a bottle of French champagne. When their glasses had been filled, they talked of mutual friends in England, and good days' hunting in the Shires. It transpired that the Chilean millionaire had never met Rex Van Ryn, but knew of him through mutual banking interests.

Richard used the same story as he had with Don Carlos Escalente and Don Salvador Marino in Buenos Aires: that he and his friend Simon Aron were anxious to discuss an interesting business proposition with Rex but, on arriving in Buenos Aires, they had learned that he had gone off on a holiday, without leaving an address. He added that there seemed just a possibility that Rex had come to Santiago. But Don Caesar said that he had heard nothing of Van Ryn's being on holiday in Chile.

In hot weather the restaurant at the Crillon was little used, and they lunched in a delightful courtyard that ran alongside it. An awning protected them from the sun, flowering shrubs in big pots stood among the tables, and the trellised walls were covered with bougainvillaea. As a pleasant change from still wine, they drank, with an excellent meal, a really good peach *bola*.

It emerged that Don Caesar knew the Escalentes and several members of the Grau-Miraflores family. He had never heard of the Baron von Thumm, but had met Silvia Sinegiest twice at parties. If she had recently arrived at Santiago, he felt certain that a mention of her would have appeared in the social column of his paper, unless she was staying with friends and, for some reason of her own, not appearing in public.

Richard then asked if his host knew of a club called the 'Barbecue'. Don Caesar shook his dark head. 'No. Are you certain that there is such a club in Santiago?'

'I have reason to suppose so, because Van Ryn mentioned it to me once,' Richard prevaricated. 'And, if he is here, I hoped I might trace thim through it.'

'It may be a new place, or quite a small one. Anyway, my people are used to making every sort of enquiry, so I'll get them to find out and let you know.' After a moment, Don Caesar added, 'Have you made any plans for tomorrow? If not, my wife and I are driving down to Viña del Mar, and you and your friend might like to come with us.'

Anxious as Richard was to get on with his quest, there was nothing more that he could do for the time being, so he accepted for himself, and said he would pass on the invitation to Simon.

Having walked the few blocks back down the shady side of the street to the Hilton, he lay down for a siesta. Simon did not reappear in their suite until six o'clock. He had given Miranda and Pinney lunch in the roof restaurant on the seventeenth storey of the hotel. Outside it there was a sun-bathing terrace and a swimming pool and, before lunch, he had gone in for a swim. But, to his surprise and annoyance, when he came out he had been told that drinks could be served to people in bathing wraps only at four umbrella-shaded tables on the far side of the pool. At the tables on the other sides, gentlemen must wear coats and trousers, and in the restaurant itself, ties were insisted on.

After lunching, he had gone out and made the rounds of the best hotels. None of their reception clerks could give him any news of Rex, Silvia or von Thumm, but the hall porters had eagerly accepted the *escudo* notes he offered them, taken down his address and promised to let him know should any of his friends book in at their hotels.

During his tour of the city he had two pleasant surprises. He found that the taxi drivers all refused tips, and outside one of the hotels there had been a man with a barrow piled high with the largest nectarines he had ever seen. He had bought a dozen and had eaten four of these luscious fruit on the way back to the Hilton. As he offered the bag containing the others to Richard, his friend shook his head, and said uneasily:

'Really, Simon. You should know better than to eat rindless fruit in a tropical country, without first washing it in disinfectant.'

'Why?' Simon rubbed his arc of nose with his forefinger. 'They look perfectly clean.'

'Perhaps. But God alone knows by what filthy fingers they have been handled. You had better take several Enterovioform pills right away.'

That evening Richard took them all out to dine at the *Jacaranda*, a restaurant that Don Caesar had recommended to him as one of the best in the city. The night air was delightfully warm and softly-lit tables were set outside the restaurant in a broad alley that was closed to traffic. Their thoughts were never far from Rex and, although they could not mention the missing million dollars, as Pinney was present, they again speculated fruitlessly on what had become of him.

On their way back to the Hilton, Simon fell silent. Then, breaking out into a sweat, he confessed that he felt very ill. Richard's foreboding about the unwashed nectarines had proved only too well founded. Miranda was greatly perturbed and wanted to call in a doctor, but Pinney briskly declared that all he needed was dosing, and shortly after they got back, she came to their suite with appropriate medicine.

On the Sunday morning Simon still had an upset stomach and, in any case, he had already refused Don Caesar's invitation, in order to spend the day with Miranda; so, when the Alberts arrived at ten o'clock to pick Richard up, he set off alone with them to Viña del Mar.

Richard had already met *Donna* Albert in England. She was young, gay and spoke English as well as her husband, so they made a merry party. The large, comfortable car took the road to Valparaiso, and was soon running through a valley, the lower slopes of which were sparsely wooded, mainly with a silvery blue gum, above which towered holly oaks and firs of various species.

Fifteen miles outside Santiago, they began to cross a lofty region known as the 'Mountains of the Coast'. There were many hairpin bends, but the road was exceptionally wide for a highway through such terrain. In most places it had, on either side, sandy verges of ten feet or more; so, even in a collision, there was little danger of a car going over a precipice.

On the far side of the ridge there were more broad valleys and, as they approached the coast, the scenery became very picturesque. Areas of forest, consisting mainly of acacias and mimosa, were broken here and there by lakes, or fields in which grew water melons, pumpkins, wheat and, occasionally, sunflowers.

After crossing a last deep valley, they mounted to high downland; then, quite suddenly, saw the Pacific several hundred feet below them. Speeding down, they completed their ninety-mile run to the coast by entering Valparaiso, Chile's largest port: a dreary, dirty city, retaining no trace of the romance associated with it in the days of Spain's glory, when many a treasure galleon had called to revictual and take on water there.

Turning north, they ran round the huge bay and into Viña del Mar, a lovely watering place, with numerous fine hotels and a splendid Casino, of which the Chileans are justly proud. Continuing along the coast for some miles, they passed through several villages set in rocky bays, and fine beaches with white sand on which hundreds of holiday-makers were enjoying themselves. The last of these was called Concon. A little way beyond it, Don Caesar pulled up and, leaving the car, they walked out along a rocky promontory, perched on the end of which was a rustic restaurant. He told Richard that he had brought him there because the place was famous for its crabs; and, later, Richard agreed that he had never eaten better.

Afterwards, on the way back, they stopped in Viña del Mar, to spend twenty minutes strolling round the lovely park; then took the road to Santiago. On arriving at the Hilton, Richard asked the Alberts to come in and have a drink with him. To his surprise and pleasure he found that Simon was not in their suite, so he must obviously have felt much better before he would have left it.

Half an hour later Simon came in and was introduced to the Alberts. They were just about to leave, and had already asked Richard to dine with them the following night. Now, they included Simon in the invitation and when he asked, a little hesitantly, if he might bring Miranda with him, explaining about her blindness and saying that it would be a treat for her, they agreed at once. When they had gone, he told Richard that he had stayed in bed for the morning, had a light lunch, then spent the afternoon up beside the swimming pool with Miranda.

On Monday morning, at about half past ten, Don Caesar telephoned. He said that one of his reporters had picked up some information that might interest them. He was lunching at the Union Club with a friend with whom he had to discuss business; but he suggested that they might join him there at midday for a drink.

When they arrived at the Union Club, they found that Don Caesar had with him a tall, youngish man with hooded eyes and an exceptionally long nose, whom he introduced as Philo McTavish. He added, 'Mr McTavish is a Chilean, and he was born here; but his mother was Greek and his father a Scot, and they sent him to Scotland to be educated, so he speaks good English. That's why I chose him to try to find out about this barbecue place. You see, my wife and I are leaving for England on Wednesday morning, and McTavish will be able to report to you in your own language.'

They were soon settled in a quiet corner of the club smoking room, with drinks before them. Don Caesar nodded to McTavish. 'Now let's hear what you have to tell us so far.'

The tall Greco-Scot-Chilean leaned forward and, looking at Richard and Simon, spoke in fluent English, but with a strong Glasgow accent, 'There's not a club called the "Barbecue" here in Santiago, *Señor*. Of that I'm now certain. But many barbecues are given by folk here. In our summer the climate lends itself to that form of entertaining. Most folk who're wealthy enough to own a house wi' a garden of any size have one in it. Ye'll see then the only line o' investigation I could pursue was to enquire for any barbecue parties that were held regular an' might have some special feature.

''Tis customary fer the hostess's cook to buy the food an' prepare the dishes; but, in cases where the party be a large one, caterers or hotels are called on to supply the victuals. I drew a number o' blanks, then visited the *Danubio Azul*, a restaurant renowned for its Chinese food. There I got on to it that once a month the proprietor receives an order for food enough for a hundred people, everything to be of the very best, an' no expense barred. Aboot this order there are several unusual circumstances. Fer such large parties, 'tis common practice fer waiters to be provided by the restaurateur. In this case they're not; although, as far as I ken, the staff of the house consists only of an elderly couple. Also, in spite o' that, the restaurateur's delivery men are not permitted ter carry anything into the house. The food, dishes, linen an' all are received by the two servants at the gate of quite a long drive, an' the dirty things collected from there the following morning.'

'Whereabouts is this house?' enquired Don Caesar.

''Tis on the south-east outskirts o' the city, beyond the best residential district, *Señor*. You could reach it by going on past the far end of the *Avenida Amerigo Vespucci*, where you live. The property is a very extensive one, two or more hectares maybe; an' the house is screened from observation on all sides by belts o' trees.'

'Can you tell us anything more about it?'

'Nay, very little, *Señor*. I went out there an' tried to get the servants talkin', but it were not possible. Believe it or not, they were both dumb, or pretendin' to be. I then tried some of the servants at properties nearby. They could tell me nowt, except that these parties usually go on till sunup, an' are real rowdy affairs. There's drummin' goes on and, faint from the distance, strange cries: the like of animals or persons gone mad wi' excitement. Folks round about are of the opinion that these monthly barbecues are orgies. Aye, for a' that, those who attend them come an' go quiet as can be. They cause noo inconvenience, so gi' noo ground for complaints to the police. An' there's noo law against men making merry wi' lasses in private, provided the lasses be willing.'

'Who is the owner of this property?'

''Tis a rich Negro, *Señor*; by name Lincoln B. Glasshill.'

'A Negro!' Richard repeated. 'There aren't many in Chile are there? I mean, there were no great sugar plantations here for which they would have been brought in to labour as slaves during the Spanish occupation.'

'No,' Don Caesar replied. 'We have very few. However, I know of this man. He is not a Chilean, but a distinguished American lawyer. He settled here some six or eight years ago. He is reputed to be a very able man, and has built up a fine connection.'

McTavish nodded, 'Aye, *Señor*. The couple he employs are also Negroes, an' act mainly as caretakers. They keep the place habitable for him. During the week, he lives in an apartment near the Law Courts. He goes out to his place only fer weekends an' fer these monthly parties.'

'Does he always give them on the same day of the month?' Richard enquired.

'Nay, *Señor*. I asked one o' the men at the restaurant tha' does the catering aboot that. He told me these skeedoos are always held at the full o' the moon.'

7

THE BARBECUE

At the words 'full o' the moon', Simon's eyes flickered towards Richard, who raised an eyebrow then asked, 'Is there anything else you can tell us, Mr McTavish?'

The tall Chilean shook his sandy, close-cropped head. 'Naught else, *Señor*; except that I have it from the restaurateur that a barbecue is to be held there tomorrow night.'

Again Simon and Richard's eyes met, now conveying their excitement.

Don Caesar glanced at his watch and said, 'You'll forgive me if I now break up this little party, but my luncheon guest should be arriving in a few minutes.'

The others stood up and Richard smiled. 'Of course. Very good of you to let *Señor* McTavish spend his time helping us to trace our friend. I think this monthly barbecue given by the Negro lawyer must be what Van Ryn referred to. Anyhow, Aron and I will go out there and see what we can discover. In the meantime, we'll see you this evening.' He then thanked McTavish for the work he had put in, and the party broke up.

As Simon and Richard walked back to the Hilton, the former asked, 'What d'you make of it?' This full of the moon business sounds like a Witches' Sabbat to me.'

'Could be. I find it difficult to believe, though, that Rex would have got himself mixed up in that sort of thing, knowing as he does, from your clash with Satanism★ way back in the thirties, how damnably dangerous it can be.'

Up in the roof restaurant of the Hilton, they found Miranda and Miss Pinney waiting to lunch with them. Eagerly, Miranda asked if the meeting had thrown any light on the possible whereabouts of her uncle. Simon told her about the barbecue regularly held by the American Negro lawyer, and ended, 'All this secrecy and the rest of it sound pretty fishy. Could well be Satanism.'

'Oh, come, Simon!' Miranda laughed. 'What nonsense. Uncle Rex has his feet on the ground as firmly as any man I know. He is the very last person to start dabbling in devil-worship.'

Miss Pinney gave a disapproving sniff and added, 'The practice of Black Magic went out with the Dark Ages. Of course, natives in Africa and some other places still perform revolting rites; but that an American gentleman like Mr Van Ryn should do so is unthinkable.'

Simon did not pursue the matter. After they had lunched, they all went down to a car that he had hired for the afternoon. Going for drives, while wearing a heavy veil, had been one of the few pleasures that Miranda had been able to enjoy before Simon had enabled her to go about in public free from embarrassment and without harming her eyes.

They drove out to the Carro San Cristobal, the wooded mountain to the north-east of the city, and up the winding road to the wide terrace from which rose the huge statue of the Virgin. The whole area, several miles in extent, was one vast park. On a lower slope there was a Zoo, on the higher ones large public swimming baths, tennis courts, cafés and restaurants. There was ample room for thousands of people to picnic there on Sundays and national holidays; for innumerable glades, hollows and rambling paths provided so many secluded spots that no part of this fine retreat for dwellers in the close, hot streets of the city would have been crowded.

Although, unlike her companions, Miranda could not see the magnificent view, she enjoyed the cool, clean air as they sat at a table on the top terrace, eating *casata* ices.

That evening she accompanied Simon and Richard out to Don Caesar's home. As Simon gave the driver of the car the address, she asked, 'Do you know about the man after whom the *Avenida Amerigo Vespucci* was named?'

Both of them murmured that they did not, so she went on, 'As we all know, Christopher Columbus was the first discoverer actually to land in the

★ *The Devil Rides Out.*

new world, but Amerigo Vespucci was the first to write a book about it. That's why it became known as America.'

The Alberts' house proved to be a spacious, airy building, furnished with many beautiful objects, and set in a three-acre garden. Ten people sat down to dinner, and it proved a jolly party. Afterwards they went out into the garden, which a nearly full moon made as light as day. It was redolent with the scent of moonflowers, and they drank their coffee and liqueurs at the side of an artistically-designed swimming pool. After a while, Richard got Don Caesar to take him for a stroll round the garden, and when they were out of earshot of the others, he asked, 'Does much black magic go on in Chile?'

Don Caesar shook his head. 'Not as far as I know. You see, Chile is rather different from the other South American countries. Of course, in the interior the native Indians still practise their magic, but it is of a very primitive kind, and you certainly could not call it Satanism. It was the Negroes who brought voodoo to South America; but, as Chile was not particularly suitable for sugar plantations and, apparently, lacking in natural wealth, comparatively few Spaniards settled here, so only a very small part of our population consists of the descendants of Negro slaves.'

'That's interesting, as from what I have heard most of the other Latin-American countries are riddled with diabolic cults.'

'You're right. That's particularly true of Brazil. Naturally, Brazil differs from the rest of South America, because it was colonised by the Portuguese. There has never been any colour bar there, and a high proportion of the Portuguese settlers not only took Negresses for mistresses, but married them. Such women made a show of accepting Christianity, but they were too strongly imbued with a belief in their own dark gods to give up worshipping them. As wives, they acquired a much greater influence over their husbands than mistresses would have had; and, on the principle that it is better to be safe than sorry, many of the husbands were persuaded by their wives to placate the African gods by attending midnight blood sacrifices. The wives' influence over the children of such marriages was, obviously, even greater, so although they were baptised as Christians and regularly attended Mass, they in fact became devotees of voodoo, or *Macumba*, as it is called in Brazil. Even today, in spite of modern education, a large part of the upper classes pay only lip service to Christianity, and pin their faith on attending pagan rites.'

'It's your opinion, though, that this Negro lawyer's parties are not that sort of thing?'

'I doubt it. Much more likely to be sexual jamborees. But as you and Aron are going out there tomorrow night, you ought to be able to satisfy yourselves about what actually does go on. As you might have difficulty in finding the place, I've already told Philo McTavish to take you out there in his car. You had better telephone him at the office in the morning and let him know what time you want him to pick you up. As I'm off to Europe the day after tomorrow, I've also told him that he is to place himself at your disposal as long as you remain in Santiago, and that, whatever you may find out about Lincoln B. Glasshill, in no circumstances is anything to be printed in the paper.'

'That's awfully good of you, and I couldn't be more grateful,' Richard said. They then rejoined the others by the swimming pool.

The following morning Simon, Richard, Miranda and Pinney went for another drive; this time round the centre of the city and up its broadest boulevard—named after Bernardo O'Higgins—the Chilean hero who had led the war against the Spanish, which had gained Chile her independence—then along the River Mapocho, the banks of which were carefully tended lawns, gay with beds of flowers and flowering shrubs.

On the way back, Richard asked to be dropped off at the Carro Santa Lucia. It was a four-hundred-foot-high hill, which had once been the citadel of Santiago, but was now a most picturesque public park. Innumerable winding paths led up to the ancient ruin that crowned it, and Richard was interested to see that, on the benches in the many shady nooks along the paths, there were quite a number of teenage couples who were obviously courting; but all of them were behaving most decorously, just sitting silently, and holding hands.

He got back to the Hilton in time for a swim in the roof-top pool, then he and his friends lunched together and afterwards spent a good part of the afternoon dozing on their beds. In due course, they all dined together; but the meal was rather a silent one, as Richard and Simon were secretly speculating on what they might find out within the next few hours.

At half past ten, Philo McTavish picked them up. Neither Richard nor Simon had taken a very good view of McTavish. No doubt, his long nose was excellent for sniffing out news; but the sandy hair he had inherited from his father's side of his family seemed the only thing Scottish about him. His black eyes had a slightly shifty look, and his handshake was clammy. Nevertheless, they were grateful to Don Caesar for having placed him and his car at their disposal; as, to get a sight of the barbecue, they might have to leave the car for some time; and to do that from a hired car out in the country in the middle of the night would have been difficult to explain to the driver.

As the journalist drove them through the streets of the city, Richard asked him:

'While doing your job, have you ever come across any evidence that there are Satanist gatherings in Santiago?'

The Scottish-educated Chilean laughed. 'Good gracious, no, Mr Eaton. As in every city, there are a few old crones who are credited with practising witchcraft, but I've never heard of their getting together to hold a Sabbat. What with their radios, motor-cycles and self-service stores, most of the people who live in Santiago are much too modern-minded to believe in that sort of thing.'

'That applies to most other countries now,' Richard replied. 'But the fact remains that Satanism is still practised in them.'

'If you say so, *Señor*, I will take your word for it. But any educated person would now look on believing in the Devil as nonsense.'

'Of course they would, if they think of the Devil as people did in the Middle Ages: a terrifying apparition with horns, hooves and a spiked tail. But that was only a form his emissaries took as suitable to the beliefs of the period. Now that people have so many things, other than religion, to occupy their minds, they naturally gave little thought to the powers of good and evil. That is because they are not tuned in to such influences. But it does not mean that the Devil no longer exists.'

To Richard's surprise McTavish replied, 'If not by nationality, by heredity and education I'm a down-to-earth Scot. I can accept that the Devil is still stooging round tempting people with this an' that in exchange for their immortal souls.'

'May I ask if you are a Christian?'

'Aye, I'm certainly that.'

'Then, if you believe in God, you cannot logically disbelieve in the Devil, because he was part of the original Creation. What is more, when Lucifer was cast out of Heaven, God gave him this world as his province. That is made abundantly clear in the New Testament, in the passage where Satan took Jesus Christ up into a high place, showed him all the cities and the fertile valleys and said, "All this will I give to Thee if Thou wilt bow down to me." He couldn't have offered something that wasn't his to give.'

'I suppose that is so.'

'It certainly is. And it's a great mistake to imagine that the Devil went out of business with the coming of the scientific age. He simply went underground, and adapted his methods to modern conditions. One of his names is "Lord of Misrule", and his object is to destroy all law and order among mankind. What could do that more effectively than the creation of wars, in which countless thousands of people legally murder one another, and there follows widespread arson, pillage, rape and anarchy? In the present century, the Devil has brought about two world wars and a score of minor ones, by bemusing the minds of statesmen and about the best interests of their peoples; so it seems to me that he has surpassed himself.'

'Am I right, *Señor*, in thinking you have formed the idea that these parties given by Glasshill are some form of Sabbat?'

Suddenly it struck Richard that, should that prove the case, it would be just as well to keep McTavish in ignorance of the fact. Although Don Caesar had banned any account of what they found out being published, McTavish might, if the story had the making of a juicy scandal, sell it to a friend for publication in another paper. After a moment, he replied, 'It's just possible; but I doubt it. Otherwise, surely you or one of your colleagues would have picked up some rumour about Satanic rites being practised in Santiago.'

At a little before eleven o'clock, the car was running over a country road that led towards the lower slopes of the Andes. McTavish pointed to a group of trees a few hundred yards ahead on the right, and said, 'That is the place, *Señor*. Just before we reach it there is a track leading off. Would you have me take it so that I dinna' have to wait for you in the main road an' perhaps be noticed by people in other cars driving up to the entrance?'

'Yes,' Richard agreed. 'But pull up somewhere wide enough to reverse the car so that, if necessary, we can make a quick getaway.'

Two hundred yards down a curving lane, that followed the belt of trees surrounding the grounds of the house, McTavish halted the car. As Richard got out, he said, 'I'm afraid you may have a long wait: an hour at least, perhaps a bit more.'

McTavish shrugged. 'Don't worry, *Señor*. Wi' me I've a book to read, an' a flask wi' a drop in it.'

Simon followed Richard out of the car. He was carrying an attaché case which contained certain items he had procured earlier in the day, and which they might need in an emergency. The moonlight enabled them to see their way without trouble between the trees and patches of undergrowth. After they had penetrated the screen for some twenty feet, they came upon the tall wire fence that McTavish had said surrounded the property, when he had described it at the Union Club. Against the possibility that it might be electrified, Simon had brought rubber gloves. Getting them out, he put them on and held two of the strands wide apart, so that Richard could get through without touching them. Then Richard took the gloves and held the wires apart so that Simon could follow him. Cautiously they advanced through the belt of trees. On the far side of the fence it was some sixty feet in depth. When they reached its further edge, they were able to look out across a wide expanse of lawn to the house, which was about two hundred yards distant. It was a long, low building, with turrets at each corner, suggesting that it had been built in Victorian times. All the ground-floor windows were lit, and a few in the upper storey. Only light curtains had been drawn across them, and through these moving shadows could be seen here and there, showing that considerable activity was going on inside the rooms. Outside the back of the house trestle tables had been erected below a long verandah. On the far side was an ornamental lake. In the centre of the row of tables, two had been put side by side to form a broader platform, and upon it were two large elbow chairs.

As Simon surveyed the scene, he said in a low voice, 'Queer sort of dinner party, for two people to sit on top of the table.'

'They may be thrones,' Richard whispered back. 'Anyhow, if it is to be a Sabbat, the setting is right. That lake serves the purpose of the traditional pond near which such ceremonies must be held.'

After about ten minutes, four men came out of the house. They wore sombreros and the breeches and jack-boots of herdsmen; but each of them carried a Sten gun. Separating, they walked off in different directions towards the screen of trees.

'Come on,' said Richard quickly. 'They're about to search the grounds in case some curious neighbour is snooping, to find out what goes on here. We must hide, or we'll be for it.'

Here and there among the trees there were groups of bushes and tangled undergrowth. Simon had already turned and was tiptoeing his way back towards the fence. Just inside it they chose two patches of thick bramble-covered saplings, and wriggled down behind them. Presently they caught the sound of heavy footfalls snapping fallen twigs and rustling dry leaves. Slowly the footsteps grew nearer. Now and again they stopped. Evidently the man was halting every ten yards or so, to peer from side to side as he advanced.

Simon could hear his own heart pounding. Neither he nor Richard was armed. If they were caught they would be at the gunman's mercy. Anything could happen to them then. South America was not like Europe. Many people habitually went about armed, and nearly everyone kept a pistol in his car as a precaution against a hold-up in a sparsely-populated district. Shootings were everyday occurrences, and the police took scant notice of them, unless someone important was involved.

Holding their breath, they lay absolutely still. Fortunately, the clumps of undergrowth were so numerous that the searcher could not make a close examination of them all, and the trees prevented the moonlight from coming through except here and there in irregular patches.

After what seemed an age, the guard passed their hiding places and his footsteps faded into the distance. With sighs of relief they came gingerly to their feet. Having listened intently for a long moment, they crept back to the place from which they had retreated; but now they lay down there, in case their silhouettes should be spotted among the trees.

While they had been crouching behind their cover, they had caught the intermittent beat of drums. As they looked towards the house again, they saw that eight Negroes had emerged from it and were seated in a group on the verandah. It was difficult to see them clearly, as they were partially in the shadow cast by the verandah roof, but they appeared to be a band, mainly of dummers and some with other instruments, who were tuning up. The sounds they made gradually merged into a steady rhythm.

Other figures began to come out from the house; but at first sight they did not appear to be human beings. All of them were wearing costumes that made them look like animals, reptiles or enormous insects. There were leopards, wolves, jackals, pigs, cats, dogs of various kinds, a bull, a frog, a ram, several huge blue-bottles and mosquitoes. Many of them were wearing head-dresses in keeping with their costumes, all the others were masked. They came out of the house carrying dishes piled high with food, and dozens of bottles of wine, with which they proceeded to furnish the long tables.

'Going to be a Sabbat,' Simon whispered. 'Give you a hundred to one on that.'

'Not taking you,' Richard replied promptly. 'But how Rex got himself mixed up in this devilish business beats me. It's not as though he were ignorant of such matters. He was with us on that awful night, years ago, when, as near as damn it, Satan broke through the pentacle in which we were all cowering in the library of Cardinal's Folly.'

'Ummm. We've no proof yet, though, that Rex is involved.'

'Can you doubt it? He was the Sinegiest woman's lover. She must be up to the neck in this. It's a sure thing now that this must be the "barbecue" at which she and von Thumm are to meet tonight. It's clear, too, that when we asked him if he knew what had happened to Rex, he took alarm, sent us down to the Sinegiest, then concocted a yarn for her to spin that would cause us to call off our search for Rex. Somehow they've got hold of him. It's quite on the cards that he is here tonight, and one of that crowd of creatures laying the tables.'

'What do we do if we spot him? We just might, as he's a head and shoulders taller than most people.'

Richard gave a heavy sigh. 'What the hell can we do? Unarmed, we wouldn't stand an earthly if we went in against that mob. If we could get McTavish's car through the fence, we might charge them in it, as Greyeyes did when we pulled you out of that Sabbat on Salisbury Plain. But there's no possible way of getting the car in here. Even if we could, the odds are that those boys with the Sten guns would riddle us with bullets before we could get away.'

As Richard finished speaking, he turned, crawled back a few yards into the trees, then stood up. Glancing over his shoulder, Simon whispered, 'Where are you off to?'

'Speaking of those gunmen brought to my mind that one of them may come on us unexpectedly, so it would be as well to have to hand something with which we could at least defend ourselves.'

After some minutes he returned, carrying two pieces of fallen branch that would serve as rough clubs, and gave one to Simon. By then the drums were being beaten with a steady rhythm that was gradually increasing in tempo.

Also, a glow that they had noticed on the far side of the house had increased to a lurid glare, and it could be assumed that food was being cooked there. Meanwhile, the men and women in fantastic disguises had taken their places round the table.

With a final crash of drums, the band suddenly ceased playing. Complete silence fell. There was a stir on the verandah. Two figures emerged from it and walked down the steps. One was evidently a man clad as a goat, with a head-dress from which rose four instead of two, great, curved horns. The other was a tall, fair-haired woman stark naked.

Simultaneously Richard and Simon recognised the woman as Silvia Sinegiest. Nude, her broad shoulders and superb figure were displayed to the best possible advantage.

'My God, she's beautiful!' Richard muttered. 'She must be pretty chilly, though, in spite of the warm night.'

'She doesn't need clothes for this,' Simon murmured back. 'Surely you remember? The Devil's people can create a warm atmosphere or a mist that will envelop them whenever they wish. Look at the man playing the Goat of Mendes. From his height and lopsided walk, one would know him anywhere as von Thumm.'

The two figures, holding hands, advanced to the centre table and mounted by some concealed steps on to it. When they reached the two big elbow chairs, they halted in front of them and a great shout of salutation went up from the assembled company. Silvia remained standing there, but the goat turned about and bent down to rest his forelegs on the seat of the chair, revealing that the back of his costume had been cut away to expose his posterior. The other participants then filed past, in turn performing the revolting *Osculum inflâme* by kissing the man-goat's fundamental orifice.

Meanwhile, Simon had been fumbling in his attaché case, and took from it two necklaces made of small roots strung together. Passing one to Richard, he said, 'Now we're certain what we're in for, we'd better put these on.' The roots were garlic, and Richard loathed both its taste and smell; but he knew that it was a most powerful protection against evil forces, so he slipped the necklace over his head without protest.

When the procession past the goat was over and all the beast-clad men and women were back in their original places at the tables, the band started up again. But this time the drums were only subsidiary to a weird, tuneless cacophony of notes from a lyre, a trumpet and Pan pipes. It was the signal for the feast to begin. There were already many cold dishes on the table. To these there were now added steaming tureens of hot food brought from round the far corner of the house. No knives, forks, spoons or plates were used, and the company fell upon the edibles as though they were starving: grabbing up handfuls of food and cramming it into the mouths of themselves or their neighbours, then seizing the bottles and drinking from them.

This disgusting exhibition of gluttony continued for the best part of half an hour; then, at a signal from the goat, the band stopped playing. A tall man clad as a black panther rose from one end of the long table, drew a basket from beneath it and held it aloft. A great shout went up, then complete silence fell. At the same moment a hugely fat woman, wearing a cloak of feathers and the mask of a vulture, came to her feet at the other end of the table, and held on high a silver vessel shaped like a phallus. From opposite ends of the table the two advanced, until they met in front of the naked

Silvia, and the goatskin-clad von Thumm, who both rose from their thrones. The vulture-woman handed up to Silvia the big silver vessel modelled on a male organ, and the panther-man handed up to her companion something which he took from the basket. For a moment Richard and Simon could not see what it was that the panther-man had presented. Then, as he bowed and moved aside, they saw that it was a black infant.

'Oh God!' gasped Simon. 'They're going to sacrifice it! We've got to stop them! We must!' He started to scramble to his feet.

Richard grabbed him by the arm and pulled him back. 'Stay where you are, you bloody fool!' he hissed into Simon's ear. 'We haven't a hope in hell of saving the child. We'd only be murdered ourselves, and to no purpose. Those gunmen are lurking somewhere among these trees. They'd shoot us down before we were halfway across the lawn.'

With a groan, Simon sank back and shut his eyes.

The baby made no sound. Evidently it had been doped before the party started, and had since lain in a drugged sleep in the basket under the table. Von Thumm held the offering to Satan aloft. Before he did so it had been difficult to see it clearly. Now, Richard suddenly realised that it was not a piccaninny, but a young ape.

Von Thumm began a long incantation in Latin. At intervals the evil congregation shouted a loud response. These shouts roused the ape, and it began to chatter. His incantation finished, the Baron lowered the ape into the crook of his right fore-leg. At one side of the silver phallus there hung a glittering, curved black-hilted knife. He took it in his hoof-covered left hand. Silvia held the phallus out by its two great testicles. Von Thumm drew the knife sharply across the ape's throat. Its one wailing cry was cut short, and its blood poured into the vessel that Silvia was holding ready to receive it.

A great cry went up from the congregation. When all but a few drops of the ape's blood had drained from its body, the Priest of Evil threw it from him. The nearest members of the congregation seized upon it and tore it limb from limb. Meanwhile, the Baron had transferred the knife to his right hand, and plunged his hoof-covered left hand into the hollow phallus. Withdrawing it, dripping with blood, he made the sign of the Left-Hand Swastika on Silvia's stomach. Again the members of this unholy crew formed a procession and filed past the throne. As they did so, the goat sprinkled each of them with a few drops of the sacrificial blood.

All this time, Simon had been lying with his face buried in his hands, praying fervently for the Lords of Light to destroy these gruesome followers of the Left-Hand Path. Richard had witnessed everything, because he had been half hoping, half fearing, to identify Rex among the assembled Satanists. But none of the grotesque, animal-like figures was tall enough to be his friend. When the last in the procession had been anointed with the ape's blood, he said gently:

'It wasn't a child but an ape, Simon. And even though we've failed to find Rex, we can thank God he is not among that awful crew.'

As Simon looked up, the Satanic anointing with blood had just finished, but the procession did not break up. Instead, with the black panther-man heading them, the others, each clutching the one before him, entered on a strange, follow-my-leader dance, copying the leader's lewd gestures and contortions and winding about like a huge centipede. The drums had begun to beat again. As the tempo increased into a throbbing, compulsive rhythm, the procession broke up and the people began to dance singly or in couples: a big, spotted dog with a hyena, a jaguar with a baboon, a wolf with a bear, and many other unnatural combinations. For a few minutes they jigged about, then merged into circles, each of thirteen, on the broad lawn, facing outward and back to back as they pranced round and round, some of them staggering drunkenly.

Another ten minutes passed; then the circles dissolved. Most of the assembly appeared to have already selected partners for this new phase of the Sabbat. Avidly they seized upon one another, ripping down the zip fasteners that held their animal costumes in place in front. Beneath the costumes most of them were naked. Their arms were clasped round their partners, who either subsided willingly or were thrown to the ground. A babel of shouts, grunts and cries ensued as two score of fiercely-embraced couples began to copulate. From the positions that several of them took up, with one man discarding his garment altogether, it could be seen that a number of them were sodomites; in other cases the form of lust displayed was obviously lesbian.

After a while, Richard said, 'There's no point in our staying longer. We now know what we came to find out, and Rex isn't here. But now we can have Silvia and von Thumm kept under observation and I'm sure one of them will lead us to him.'

'Yes,' Simon agreed. 'Sight of all this makes me want to vomit. Let's get back to the car.'

It was at that moment that a woman dressed as a black cat, who had just staggered to her feet after being bestrode by a man dressed as a bull, was seized upon by another wearing a cobra head-dress. But she broke away from him and ran, screaming, towards the place where Richard and Simon were hiding.

Von Thumm and Sylvia had not participated in the orgy. For the past ten minutes, while it had been in progress, they had remained seated on their thrones, the living representatives of Satanic power, calling out to applaud acts of special obscenity and encouraging to new efforts those whose lechery seemed to be weakening.

On seeing the cat-woman detach herself from the writhing mob and go racing across the open lawn, the Baron jumped to his cloven-hoof-covered feet and yelled in Spanish, 'Guards! Guards! Stop that cat! She must not be allowed to get away.'

8

THE VICTIM

Richard and Simon had come to their feet just inside the screen of trees. The cat-woman could not see them. Her head-dress had fallen back, revealing her face. It was that of a girl in her twenties, and disordered by terror. Her eyes were bulging, her mouth gaped open and her dark hair streamed out behind her. With all the speed she could muster, she was blindly heading for the nearest cover.

That happened to be within fifteen feet of where Simon was standing. Swiftly he moved sideways towards the spot where she would enter the trees. Richard followed him. As he did so, he glanced over his shoulder. In all but a few cases the violent writhing among the tangle of bodies had ceased. Most of them had released their partners, or broken away from the lascivious groups of which they had formed members. More than half of them now nude, they were staring in consternation at the running woman. Their animal cries and screams provoked by sadistic acts no longer made the night hideous. A tense, stunned silence was broken only by von Thumm's continuing to shout for the guards.

They had been slow to answer his summons. Richard saw that two of them had emerged from the trees on the far side of the lawn. With their Sten guns at the ready, they were giving chase.

As the cat-woman dashed in among the trees, Simon grabbed her arm, intending to guide her to the place in the wire fence beyond which the car was waiting. Scratching at his face with her free hand, she resisted furiously, and gasped in English:

'No more! Let . . . let me go! I won't submit again. I won't. I won't!'

Simon gave her a quick shake. As her teeth snapped together, he said hurriedly, 'For God's sake don't struggle. Trust me! We'll help you to escape.'

Doubtless it was because he had spoken to her in English that she relaxed, and allowed him to pull her, still panting for breath, in the direction of the spot from which he and Richard had been watching the orgy. Seeing that Simon had the girl, Richard ran on ahead, pulled on the rubber gloves and held the strands of wire apart, so that they could get her through the fence. The two gunmen had just reached the place where their quarry had entered the belt of trees, a third could be heard crashing through the trees to the right. They were not far off. Richard feared that, at any moment, they would hear the sounds made by himself and his companions. To hold the wires apart, he had to drop his cudgel, so he had not even that with which to attempt to defend himself.

The thought of the gunmen made the hairs on the back of his neck prickle. They were somewhere behind him. The Sten guns they were carrying would not be only to scare people. He had not a doubt that their orders were to shoot at anyone they found spying on the doings of their employer and his guests. They certainly would at anyone helping an unwilling participant to escape. Simon, too, was seized by the awful fear that, at any moment, bullets would come smashing into his back and that, choking up blood, he would die there.

Somehow they got the girl through the fence. As Simon followed her, she slumped to the ground and lay there inert. She had fainted. Richard swore under his breath. The odds against their getting away were now a hundred to one, unless they abandoned the woman. Before they could carry her, unconscious, to the car, it seemed certain that the gunmen would be upon them.

In desperate haste Richard tore off the rubber gloves and thrust them at Simon. It took only a moment for him to pull them on, grab two wires and hold them wide apart so that his friend could get through, but every second was precious. The sound of trampling feet was now loud. One of the gunmen, if not two, must be within a dozen yards of them; and they were screened from sight only by the trunks of the trees and the tall patches of undergrowth.

Stooping over the woman, Richard saw that the cat costume she was wearing zipped down the front. The two sides had fallen open. Beneath it she had on only underclothes that were torn and bloodstained. It was imperative to bring her out of her faint, so that she could take at least part of her weight on her own feet. Without compunction he slapped her hard across the face. She moaned and opened her eyes. Between them, they dragged her to her feet. To their utter consternation, not yet having fully regained consciousness, she failed to realise that they were trying to save her. Desperately she endeavoured to break away and again began to shout: 'Let me go! Let me go! I won't let you! I won't! I won't!'

Answering shouts came through the trees. The woman's pursuers were no longer in doubt about the direction she had taken. To silence her, Richard jabbed his elbow hard in her ribs. Grasping her arms, they thrust her forward. Another minute and the three of them were out in the lane. But they had misjudged the place where the car had put them down. In the bright moonlight they could see it clearly; it was a good fifty yards away in the direction of the main road. Puzzled by the shouts, Philo McTavish had just got out of the car and was standing beside it.

The girl had now realised that they were helping her to get away. She no longer resisted, nor used her weight to hamper them. Fear of capture lent her new strength. With the two men still holding her arms, she began to run with them towards the car.

Richard threw a glance over his shoulder. The sound of their feet pounding on the earth could not fail to be heard by their pursuers. It needed only one of the two, or perhaps by now any of the four they had seen earlier, to reach the road, and the game would be up. The fence would prove no obstacle to them, because it would cause them no concern if they set alarm bells ringing.

Simon was not used to exerting himself. He had broken out into a sweat and was gasping for breath. As he ran he shut his eyes in an agony of apprehension. He felt certain that before they were halfway to the car they would all be riddled with bullets.

They would have been, had not the Lords of Light intervened to save them. Unnoticed by them during the past few minutes of intense activity and excitement, a dense black cloud had been approaching the moon. Almost as suddenly as though an electric light switch had been pressed down, the cloud blotted out the moon. At one minute the light was so bright that one could easily have read by it. The next they were plunged in stygian blackness.

Philo had switched out the lights of the car, to save the batteries. Now he switched them on again. The glow of the rear lights made two red spots ahead in the all-pervading gloom. It was at once a beacon of hope and a new danger: a perfect target for the gunmen to aim at. Richard yelled:

'Put out those lights! For God's sake, switch your lights off!'

It was at that moment there came a blinding flash behind them. It was followed by a scream of agony. The wires of the fence had been electrified, but not, as they had thought, only to operate an alarm bell if they were cut. They were fully charged, to inflict grievous injury on anyone who, without being insulated, touched them. In the darkness, one of the gunmen had blundered into the fence; and, as he would have been holding his Sten gun in front of him, the metal coming into contact with the wire must have caused the explosion.

Their lungs nearly bursting from the strain put upon them, the three fugitives reached the car. Philo had ignored Richard's shout, but opened all four doors. As he slipped into the driver's seat, the other two men pushed the girl into the back of the car, and Simon scrambled in after her. Richard ran round to the front. The second he slammed the door, Philo pressed the starter of the engine. He let it rev up for a moment, then threw in the clutch. The car moved forward along the bumpy track. At that moment, one of the gunmen opened fire.

All other sounds were drowned by the furious clatter of his Sten gun. Then came the thud and clang of bullets as they smashed into the metal of the boot. The rear lights were shot out. But again the Lords of Light gave their protection. No bullet hit a tyre, and the car was within yards of a bend in the lane. Only seconds later, they were round it and out of danger.

As they turned into the main road, Philo asked angrily, 'What the heck has been going on? I didna' bargain to get meself shot at.'

It was Richard, having got his breath back quicker than Simon, who answered him. 'As we thought possible, it was a wild party. So wild that Lincoln B. Glasshill thinks it worth while to employ gunmen as a protection against snoopers. We were darned lucky to get away.'

'You certainly were. How come the dame?'

'She wasn't enjoying the party. I suppose it was wilder than she had expected. Anyhow, she broke away and made a bolt for it. We could hardly sit tight in the bushes and watch her being dragged back to be raped again.'

Simon spoke from behind him. 'What are we going to do with her?'

'We'll drop her off wherever she is living,' Philo volunteered.

'No, we can't do that,' said Richard promptly. 'Those people would get hold of her again. God alone knows what they might do to stop her talking.'

'Take her to some small hotel, then.'

'How can we, dressed in this fur cat's thing?' Simon protested. 'And if she takes it off, she's next to naked.'

'Yes,' Richard agreed. 'Somehow we've got to get her some clothes.' After a moment, he added. 'There's only one thing for it. We must take her to Don Caesar's.'

'The boss *will* be pleased,' Philo observed sarcastically. 'I'd not like to haul him an' his lady oot o' bed at gettin' on fer one in the morning. Aye, and them off to Europe first thing tomorrow.'

'It can't be helped. That is, unless you've got a wife or mother who would lend the young woman some clothes.'

Philo shook his head. 'Nay, *Señor*. Taking Don Caesar's orders is ma bread an' butter. But I don't like the smell of this party at all, at all. The less I ha' to do with it, the better I'll be pleased.'

Ten minutes later, he pulled the car up before the front door of the house in the *Avenida Amerigo Vespucci*. It was in darkness. Richard said to Simon, 'We don't want any of the servants to see her. You'd better get out and take her into the shrubbery until I've had a talk with Don Caesar.'

'Ummm,' Simon agreed. 'Tell you what. If you remember, there's a summer house behind the shrubbery. We'll wait in it till you join us.'

The girl, evidently exhausted after her ordeal, had not spoken since they had got her into the car, but had lain back with closed eyes. Now she took the hand Simon extended to help her out, and obediently accompanied him along a path leading to the back garden.

Philo had also got out, and was ruefully regarding the line of holes made by the bullets from the Sten gun in the boot of his car.

'Don't worry,' Richard told him. 'I'll pay for the damage, and the hire of a car for you while yours is being repaired.'

Then, Simon and the girl now being out of sight along the path through the shrubbery, he walked up to the front door of the house and rang the bell. He had to ring a second time, and some minutes elapsed before a sleepy manservant in a dressing gown answered the door. Recognising Richard from having seen him the night before at the dinner party, he went up to get Don Caesar.

Meanwhile, Simon had escorted his charge to the summer house and settled her on the verandah, in a wicker chair with comfortable cushions. Some while back the moon had come out again from behind the big, black cloud and for the first time he had a chance to take a really good look at her. Being short-sighted, he had not before realised that she was a Jewess. Patting her on the arm, he said kindly:

'Now listen. You've nothing to be afraid of. We want to help you. To do that, we must know a bit about you. What's your name?'

'Nella Nathan,' she replied in a low voice.

'D'you live here in Santiago?'

'No. I'm here . . . here on a holiday.'

'Umm. Where do you live, then? You're an American, aren't you?'

'Yes. I come from Beaufort, South Carolina. But it's four months since I left there. I've been living up on the Sala de Uyuni.'

'Where in the world's that?'

'It's a vast plateau high up in the Andes, just over the border from Chile, in Bolivia.'

'And what were you doing there?'

'Working . . . working for . . . for the Cause.'

Simon stared at her, then said angrily, 'For the Devil's cause. Then you weren't drawn into this hellish business through some stupidity of your own. You willingly became a Satanist.'

'No!' she protested quickly. 'No. I mean the cause of Equal Rights.'

'Equal rights for whom?'

'Why, coloured people, of course.' To explain herself, she suddenly burst into a torrent of words. 'I'm a school-teacher. At least I was. I became a Freedom Marcher. The suffering that white people have inflicted on their coloured brothers is terrible—just terrible. You are a Jew, aren't you? The sufferings of our people were simply nothing to theirs. When they were brought over to America as slaves, they were treated worse than cattle. They died in agony by the tens of thousands, from thirst, disease and the most brutal flogging. It should be on the conscience of every white person to do what he can to make it up to them. Although technically they've been free for a long time now, they're still despised and rejected. Not one per cent of them are given the chance of a good education. Not one in ten thousand succeeds in fighting the prejudice which bars them from getting top jobs. The vast majority still live in squalor and misery, deprived of everything that makes life worth living. They're just made use of to do all the dirtiest, meanest jobs for a bare subsistence. Even justice is denied them if their case is opposed in the courts by a white man.'

'I know, I know,' said Simon soothingly. 'But all this is beside the point.'

'It's not,' she retorted furiously. 'It is the reason why I'm here. As I've told you, I became a Freedom Marcher campaigning for Equal Rights. I wrote articles, but the paper in my rotten little home town refused to publish them. I went on protest marches and spoke on street corners. I got the pay-off I might have expected. The School Board decided that I was a bad influence on children, so I lost my job. My parents are dead, and I lived alone. After I'd been sacked, I was hard put to earn a living. In the South no-one wanted to employ a girl who was pro-Negro. I suppose I could have become a whore, but I was a virgin and wanted to remain that way until I met a man whom I liked enough to marry. To get enough to eat I had to take dimes they could ill afford from my Negro friends, for giving private tuition to their children.'

Nella paused a moment to get her breath, then hurried on. 'A month or two after I'd been jeered out of my school by rotten little white children, I was approached by one of the leaders in the campaign for Equal Rights. He told me that they were determined to win through, but could hope to do so only if their efforts were properly co-ordinated. To have established a headquarters in the States was out of the question. The F.B.I. would have got wind of it and, on some filthy excuse, had the police raid the place, beat up everybody there and throw them into prison. So they had established a bureau in South America, at a place where there wasn't a Federal agent within five hundred miles and there they were planning a world-wide campaign aimed at achieving Black Power.'

'Black Power,' Simon repeated. 'That's a new one on me.'

'It was on me, too. But for them to secure a real say in how the countries they lived in are run seemed to me a very worthwhile project. This man told me that, at their secret headquarters, they were terribly short of people who were competent to draft manifestos, or knew anything about India, Pakistan and North Africa, as well as the problems we were faced with in the States. He offered me a job there. I took it and was flown out to La Paz, then down to Sala de Uyuni.'

'What did you find there?' Simon interjected.

'A town of hutments, where two or three hundred people were all working for the same end. They were of many races, but there were comparatively few whites. To begin with, I enjoyed it enormously. It was wonderful to meet people from so many countries and discuss with them how the white tyranny could be overthrown, so that everyone in the world had the same chances, rights and share in God's blessings. Of course, we all knew that it was a long-term project. We could not hope for big results until the sixties, or perhaps even the seventies. But in every continent we were building up cells and chains of command; so that, when the time was ripe, Black Power would be really formidable.'

'You say that, to begin with, you enjoyed it enormously. What went wrong later?'

'It was the man I was working under. His name is El Aziz and he is a Moroccan. He persistently endeavoured to seduce me, and I wouldn't play.'

'So you do draw the line about colour when it comes to going to bed with a man?'

'No. Oh no; it wasn't that. For a husband I'd prefer a coloured man. They're nearly always kinder to their wives. It was . . . well, although I'm twenty-seven, as I told you I was still a virgin. The fact is I . . . I suppose I'm just naturally frigid. I've always found the thought of sex repulsive.'

Simon nodded understandingly. 'I see. Ummm. Some women seem to be born that way. What happened then?'

'It is far from healthy up on the Sala. There are many marshes and swamps that breed fevers. That is why even the Andean Indians shun the place, and it was such a good choice to carry on secret activities. Most of the coloured folk seem to be immune. But whites and Eurasians need regular medication and, every few months, they are sent away for a change of air.

'My turn came soon after Christmas, and a party of us were flown down to Viña del Mar. We spent ten days there, having a lovely time, then we were brought up to Santiago so that we could see something of the capital before returning to our jobs. A Jamaican mulatto named Harry Benito was in charge of us. He made all the arrangements and paid the bills. Yesterday afternoon he told me he was going to give me a special treat and take me to a party. The other women were quite jealous, because he had singled me out. He had told me it was to be a late party; so I wasn't surprised that we didn't leave the little hotel where we were staying until after ten o'clock.

'He drove me out to that big house. When we got there I was told it was to be a fancy-dress affair, and taken to a room where there were a lot of animal costumes, and other women changing into them. I've always loved cats, so I chose this one. Then we joined the men and had a few drinks. I'm sure Benito put something in mine, because for some while afterwards I didn't properly take in what was going on. It wasn't until I was out in the garden that my mind began to clear. Everyone was gathered round a long table, and to my amazement a lovely woman who hadn't got a stitch of clothing on came out of the house, accompanied by a man dressed as a goat. The two of them mounted the table and sat down on sort of thrones. But, if you were watching from among those trees, you must have seen them, and what went on.'

'Ummm,' murmured Simon. 'My friend and I were there from the beginning.'

'Well, the next thing I realised was that I had Benito on one side of me and El Aziz on the other. It wasn't until much later that it struck me that the two of them must have hatched a plot to get me there. I was still terribly muzzy when they all formed a long line. Automatically I moved forward between the two men; then I found myself staring at the naked bottom of the man who was dressed as a goat. Before I could stop him, El Aziz suddenly put a hand behind my head and pushed it down, so that my face was pressed for a moment against the warm flesh. I was utterly revolted and almost sick. As I gave a gasp and jerked my face away, El Aziz whispered in my ear, "If you make a scene, we'll cut your throat."

'From that moment I was petrified with fear. I would have given anything, anything, to get away; but I simply didn't dare attempt to. The drumming began to make my heart beat faster, and my head began to ache. When the feast started, they tried to make me eat, stuffing food into my mouth. But I couldn't swallow anything solid, and spat it out. I did gulp down some wine, though. I thought it might give the courage to try to escape. There must have been something in the wine, because I felt a queer sensation and became . . . well, you know what happened, so I may as well say it . . . all moist and itching between the thighs. I've no doubt that El Aziz had given me an aphrodisiac. If it hadn't been for that, I'm sure that when the orgy started I should have resisted, whatever they had threatened to do to me. I did resist to some extent. Yet, in a way, I felt an urge to let it happen and be for good free of my inhibition. Then, when I did, I suffered absolute hell. The pain was simply terrible.'

At that point, Nella burst into a flood of tears. Patting her shoulder, Simon endeavoured to comfort her. 'There, there, my dear. Must have been ghastly for you. Don't wonder you went berserk when this chap El Aziz pushed you into the arms of a second man. But don't worry. You've nothing more to fear. We'll look after you. I promise we will.'

For all the good his words did, they might have fallen on deaf ears. Ignoring them, Nella continued to sob as though she would never stop. She was still crying bitterly when Richard appeared. He was carrying a small suitcase and over his other arm had a blue cloak. To Simon he said:

'At first, Don Caesar practically refused to believe my account of tonight's doings, and he was anything but pleased about our having brought the woman here. But I offered to take him out and show him the bullet holes in the boot of Philo's car. After that he agreed that, in the circumstances, as we are strangers in Santiago, the only course open to us was to come here and ask his help. He went upstairs then, and come down with his old suitcase. It's got some of his wife's things in, including a nightie, a toothbrush, comb and so on. Anyway, all that's needed to make our renegade witch respectable enough for us to get a room for her at an hotel.'

The three of them were on the verandah outside the summer house. Taking a pace forward, Richard thrust the suitcase at the still weeping Nella with one hand and, grasping her shoulder with the other, gave her a quick shake.

'Now then, young woman. You brought this on yourself, and no good will come of snivelling over it. Take this inside and get yourself dressed. We can't hang about here all night.'

Coming unsteadily to her feet, Nella took the case and obediently walked through the door into the semi-darkness, while the two men turned their backs.

During the few minutes she took to change, Simon gave Richard a condensed account of what she had told him, and ended by saying, 'So you see, the poor girl isn't really to blame for getting mixed up with this unholy crew; and we must be gentle with her.'

'I've not suggested that we should actually apply the thumbscrews,' Richard replied testily. 'But you're a sight too soft-hearted, Simon. The silly bitch has brought this on herself. From what you tell me, she is a typical do-gooder, and it's those people who run round carrying torches for this and that who stir up half the trouble in the world. It's interesting about this Black Power thing, though. Such a movement might cause endless trouble. We must get out of her everything she knows about it.'

Nella rejoined them, wearing the blue cloak over a dark dress and carrying the suitcase and the cat costume. Richard took the latter from her, and said, 'We'll jettison this on the way to the city. Then we'll get our driver to drop you at a small hotel where you can spend the rest of the night.'

'Ner,' countered Simon. 'We'll take her to the Hilton. Promised to look after her. Mean to see she's all right.'

'As you wish,' Richard shrugged, then turned to Nella. 'Our driver knows nothing about what went on in the grounds of that place, and I don't want him to; so please refrain from talking until we get to the hotel.'

Walking round to the front of the house, they got into the car. When it had covered half a mile, Richard threw the cat robe out of the window. Ten minutes later, Philo set them down outside the Hilton and, with evident relief, drove away.

With the calm assurance natural to him, Richard asked the night clerk for a room for the lady. While she filled in the usual form, he took a few paces back from the desk and said in a low voice to Simon, 'We'll take her up to our suite first, and get what we can out of her.'

'Why not wait till the morning?' Simon demurred. It's after two o'clock. Poor child needs some sleep.'

'Poor child, my foot,' retorted Richard. 'I'm not wasting a moment until I find out if she can tell us anything about Rex.'

'O.K. then.' Simon was already carrying Nella's case. Walking up to the desk, he collected the key to the room she had been given, and the three of them went up in the lift.

As soon as they were in their sitting room, Richard went over to the drinks table and mixed for them all badly-needed brandies and soda. Handing one to Nella, he said:

'Now, young lady. Mr Aron has passed on to me what you told him about yourself. You've been through a very bad time tonight and, naturally, we are sorry for you. But we were not lurking among those trees out of idle curiosity or for the good of our health. We have reason to believe that through your–er–friends, we may be able to trace a friend of ours who has been missing for some weeks. While you were up at this place Sala-something, did you happen to meet, or hear anything of, a compatriot of yours named Rex Van Ryn?'

Nella hesitated for a moment, then she replied, 'The name rings a bell. Yes, I remember now, Isn't he a very big man with an ugly, attractive face?'

Simon gave a jerky nod. 'That's Rex. What d'you know about him?'

She shook her head. 'Nothing really. I saw him only once; he was with a man they call "The Prince", who is the head of the movement. I asked the person I was standing beside your friend's name, only out of curiosity, because he was such a splendid specimen of manhood.'

'So Rex *is* up there!' Richard's brown eyes lit up. 'And hob-nobbing with the top brass. How extraordinary. It's almost unbelievable. What could possibly have led him to get himself mixed up in this?'

'Maybe he's not there of his own free will,' Simon suggested. 'This place sounds so isolated that escape from it may be next to impossible. If so, he could be a prisoner, but allowed to walk about.'

'That must be it.' Richard turned again to Nella. 'Tell us now what you know about this movement.'

Her face took on a sullen look. 'Why should I? What has it got to do with you? I can see you're not in sympathy with it.'

'By God, I'm not! It sounds about as dangerous as anything could be.'

'I don't agree,' Nella protested angrily. 'Its aim is to bring equality to all the coloured people in the world, to secure for them a fair share of all the good things of which they have been deprived all too long.'

With difficulty Richard retained his temper. After a moment he said,

'Now listen, my girl. You're talking through your hat. You can't possibly have grasped the significance of this thing you've got yourself involved in. I've nothing against coloured people, any more than I have against poor whites. We'll all like to see the slums abolished, every child given a decent education and a fair chance to lead a prosperous, happy life. But this Black Power idea, which woolly-minded Liberals like you have fallen for, and are abetting, is something utterly different. Surely you can see that, after what happened to you tonight?'

'No, I can't. The two things have nothing to do with one another. El Aziz and Harry Benito happened to belong to this awful sect—Devil-worshippers, I suppose you'd call them. And they tricked me into going to that house. But none of the others in the party I was with was present. They could have had no idea what would take place, otherwise they wouldn't have said how lucky I was to be chosen by Benito as his guest. They are all decent, respectable people. So are those up at Sala de Uyuni. Nothing of that kind takes place up there.'

'Maybe it doesn't; that is, as far as you know.'

'If it did, El Aziz would have fixed it for me to be taken to a meeting of that kind, weeks ago. I tell you, the people I have been working with are some of the finest I've ever met. Many of them have given up good positions to travel to the Sala and serve the cause for nothing but their keep. We're dedicated to securing equal rights for coloured people, and I'm not going to give you any information about the movement that might enable you to sabotage it.'

Richard shook his head wearily. 'I don't doubt that you're right about most of these people, but I'm convinced that you're not about the leaders. They are obviously trading on the sympathies of idealists and making use of them. The fact is that you have fallen into the hands of the enemy. By that I do not mean coloured people. They have the same sort of bodies and urges to kindness or cruelty as whites. In both cases, the majority are good and only the minority bad. And surely you can see that the men who started this Black Power idea must be evil?

'Just think what will happen if they succeed in their plans. In a few years' time this organisation you are helping to build will be given the word to begin operating. There will be increased agitation everywhere. That will lead to riots and clashes with the police. No city with a coloured population will be immune. By the sixties, there will develop a sort of sporadic civil war in the United States, and by the seventies it will have spread to Europe. There will be bloody street battles, rape, arson, murder, the lot. Nothing could be better calculated to destroy civilisation. Law and order will go by the board, and your coloured people are going to suffer even worse than the whites; because you can be sure that the whites will fight back. They won't pull any punches, either. When their shops are looted, their houses burned and their women raped, they'll take the law into their own hands and go out to kill. And, believe you me, white men are tougher than blacks. Thousands of innocent people whose lot you are trying to better will be massacred. That is the situation that you and your friends are working to bring about.'

Nella's eyes distended with horror at the picture Richard had painted. She stared at him and murmured, 'Do . . . do you really believe that?'

'I do,' he replied firmly. 'I'm certain of it. Without realising it, you have been fighting on the Devil's side. His one object ever since the Creation has been to bring about disruption. One of his names is "The Lord of Misrule". And what could possibly be better calculated to bring about disruption than this Black Power movement? It is Satan's most powerful weapon in his remorseless fight to dominate mankind. Now, you really must tell us all you have learned about it.'

'Ner,' Simon intervened. 'Nella's been through a terrible time, and she's about all in. Tomorrow, or rather in a few hours' time, when we've all had a bit of shut-eye.'

'Tomorrow,' she repeated miserably. 'Oh, what am I going to do? I can't go back to the Sala now, even if I wanted to. I've no money, not even clothes, and nowhere to go.'

'Don't worry, my dear,' said Simon. 'We'll look after you. Have you no family at all?'

'I've an aunt and uncle who live up in Connecticut.'

'Couldn't you go to them?'

'Yes, I suppose I could. Up there in New England, there is not the prejudice against sympathisers with the Equal Rights movement that there is in the South. I've got quite good qualifications, so up there I could probably get another job as a teacher.'

Simon nodded vigorously. 'That's the idea then. When we've had some shut-eye, we'll go shopping and get you an outfit, then buy you a seat on an aircraft to take you north. You needn't worry about mun, either. I've plenty in New York. I'll give you a draft on my bank there for five hundred dollars. That should keep you going until you get a job.'

Tears came into her eyes. 'You're very, very kind.'

'Not really.' He looked a little embarrassed. 'Enjoy helping people out, that's all.'

'May I take it that you'll tell us all you can?' Richard asked.

As she stood up, she nodded. 'Yes. I'm only just beginning to realise how stupid I've been. And thank you both. Thank you for everything.'

Picking up the suitcase, Simon said, 'You're on the fourth floor, aren't you? I'll see you down to your room.'

Ten minutes later, when he returned, Richard had already gone into his bedroom. Calling out 'Good night', Simon put out the light and went into his. He now felt terribly tired and, contrary to his custom, simply got out of his clothes and flung them higgledy-piggledy on the armchair. Crawling into bed, he stretched out luxuriously, gave a great yawn, switched off the light and, within five minutes, was sound asleep.

But he was not destined to sleep as long as he would have wished. A little over three hours later he was twisting, turning and moaning, in the grip of a nightmare. He was standing naked on the edge of a smoking pit. Nella was with him, and with his right hand he was grasping her wrist. Beyond her, rearing up from the depths of the pit, there was a great serpent. Its head lay pressed against Nella's terrified face, its upper part was twisted round her neck and body. It was striving to drag her from him, down into the unseen depths of the pit.

Simon awoke, his body drenched in sweat. For a moment he lay weak and spellbound. With an effort he sat up and switched on the light. He saw from his bedside clock that it was just on six o'clock. Picking up the telephone he dialled the number of Nella's room 421. He could hear the 'phone ringing, but there was no reply. Thinking it possible that he might have fumbled the dial and rung the wrong number, he put the receiver down, then dialled again. There was still no answer.

Slipping out of bed, he pulled on his dressing gown and shuffled into his slippers, then hurried through the sitting room to Richard's bedroom. Richard was lying on his side, snoring gently. Simon put a hand on his shoulder and shook him awake. Richard raised himself on one elbow, stared with sleepy eyes at his friend, and muttered:

'What the hell? Not time to get up yet, is it? I haven't overslept, have I?'

'Ner, but you've got to get up and come with me,' Simon said in an urgent voice. 'Nella's in danger.'

'Nella? Oh, the little schoolmarm do-gooder who got herself taken for a ride.'

'Yes. The girl we rescued last night. Just had a dream about her. In colour. It was a true dream, I'm sure. I must have been up on the astral. She's threatened in some way. I rang her room, but could get no reply. Only pray to God she was in too deep a sleep for it to rouse her. But we've got to find out.'

Still half asleep, Richard slid from his bed and wriggled into the dressing gown that Simon held out for him. Together they left the suite and hurried along the corridor to the lift. When they reached the fourth floor, Simon led the way to the room at the door of which he had left Nella some three hours earlier. He knocked, but there was no reply. He knocked much louder: still no response. Grasping the handle of the door, he tried it. The door was not locked, and opened easily. He switched on the light, and Richard followed him into the room.

Nella lay on the bed. She had on the nightdress she had been lent, but the bedclothes had been pulled halfway down. Her head was twisted back grotesquely. There was blood all over her, and one glance showed that she was dead. Black marks on her throat showed that she had been strangled. Her mouth gaped open and her tongue had been cut out. It had been carefully placed in the valley between her naked breasts.

9

THE GREAT GAMBLE

'Oh God, how awful!' His birdlike head thrust forward, Simon peered at the figure on the blood-soaked bed.

'Poor little devil,' murmured Richard. 'But we are partly to blame. We should have foreseen this.'

'How could we?'

'You should know well enough, after your past experience of the occult. People with power have no difficulty in overlooking others, by means of a crystal or dark glass. After we got Nella away, the first thing von Thumm and Co. would have done would be to find out where we took her. Then, an hour or two later, one or more of them got into her room somehow and did her in. Look at that bootlace laid across her neck. She wasn't strangled with it. Greyeyes told me once that Satanists always leave that symbol when they've bumped off someone who's betrayed them.'

'That's about it. Ought to have kept her with us.' As Simon spoke, he took a step towards the bed.

Richard's hand shot out and caught his arm. 'Stay where you are! You mustn't touch her!'

'Why not? Can't bear the sight of the poor girl's face. Only going to cover it with the bedclothes.'

'You bloody fool! Don't you realise that murder has been done? Within a few hours the police will be here. They mustn't find our fingerprints.'

'Suppose you're right. But oughtn't we to tell the management and ask them to send for the police?'

For a moment Richard did not reply, then he said, 'I don't think so. Heaven knows, the fact that we brought this woman here is going to be difficult enough to explain. If they know it was us who discovered her body, we'll be in it right up to our necks. The sooner we get out of here, the better.'

As he moved towards the door, he lifted the skirt of his silk dressing gown and put it over the light switch, as he turned out the light. When they were both out in the corridor, he again used the silk to shut the door, then gave the handle a good rub to remove the fingerprints Simon had left there when he opened it.

Side by side, they walked quietly along the passage. As they turned the corner into the broad main corridor, both of them halted, and drew back. They had seen a cleaner, a woman carrying a bucket, walking towards the lift. Although she had been facing their way, they did not think she had caught sight of them; but they could not be certain. Tense and silent, they waited for a good two minutes, then Richard took a quick look round the corner.

'She's gone,' he whispered, 'Come on. But we'd better take the stairs. Less likely to run into anyone than coming out of the lift.'

It was a long haul from the fourth floor up to their suite. They reached it without incident, but very short of breath. As Simon closed the door behind him, he burst out:

'The bastards! How can men perpetrate such horrifying deeds? God knows, murder is bad enough. But to have mutilated the poor girl like that after she was dead, by cutting out her tongue.'

Richard was at the drink table, pouring neat brandy into a glass. Over his shoulder, he said, 'The reason they did that is clear enough. They'd know that even if we didn't see what they'd done, we were certain to be told about it. Nella's tongue was a message to us. "If you want to stay alive, you'd better not talk."'

'Damned if I'll let them get away with this. Best not to let anyone know we found Nella's body. I agree about that. But when someone else finds it, we're certain to be questioned. Nothing to stop us giving the police a full account of what happened tonight, and why we brought Nella here.'

'No good, old chap. They'd never believe us. You can bet your bottom dollar that, within minutes of Nella's getting away, those filthy swine would have scrapped all thought of further fun and games. They would have been frantically clearing up, getting into their ordinary clothes and disappearing. If the police went out to Glasshill's place, even at this moment, I doubt if they'd find a scrap of evidence to show that a Sabbat had been held there. No. Later we may find some way of getting back at them. At the moment, our first concern is to think of some plausible reason to explain why we brought Nella here.'

'It's important if we're going to let ourselves be questioned by the police; but if we're not going to come clean with them, hadn't we better try to get out?'

'That would start a hue and cry after us.'

'Doesn't follow that they'd catch us. Not if we acted quickly.'

'There's something in the idea,' Richard said thoughtfully. After taking a second swig of brandy, he went on, 'Having brought Nella here in the middle of the night has got us in damn' deep. It's pretty certain that it will mean our being detained here for questioning, perhaps for weeks.'

'Ummm. And put a stopper on our hunt for Rex.'

'Yes. I'm afraid recent events had made me forget that for the moment. But the one good thing that has come out of this night's work is that we now know where he is. Or, at least, where he was a fortnight or so ago, before Nella left the Sala. In the normal course of events, today would see us on our way up there.'

'Then why shouldn't we skip while the going is good? Don't suppose a chambermaid will get sufficiently impatient to do Nella's room to barge in there before eleven o'clock. By that time we could be on an aircraft. Nella said the Sala is just over the border in Bolivia. With luck, there may be a 'plane flying up to the capital, La Paz.'

Richard nodded. 'If only there is, we'd be out of trouble. It's hardly likely that the Chilean Government could secure an extradition order just to get us back and ask us what we knew about Nella. Even if they could, by the time the Bolivian police started to look for us, we'd have left La Paz days before. There's one thing, though. We ought to make our leaving look as natural as possible. We could say we've been invited to stay up-country for a few days, so we're keeping on the suite; and leave most of our baggage here.'

'We'll need to do a bit of play-acting then. Carry on as usual till we actually leave the hotel.' Simon glanced at the clock. 'It's getting on for seven. Bit early for breakfast, but if we were catching a 'plane the odds are we'd be getting up by now. Shall I ring down for breakfast?'

'Yes. But don't order our usual Continental. People who are about to travel generally fortify themselves with something more solid. I'll have ham and eggs with mushrooms, and a "fruit plate" to follow.'

'Feel too sick to eat anything, but I'll try to manage an omelette,' Simon muttered unhappily.

Breakfast having been ordered, they went to their respective rooms and began to sort out the things they could cram into overnight bags. Richard had just switched on the radio when the floorwaiter wheeled in the trolley. Raising a cheerful grin, he told the man that they were leaving that morning, but would be returning in a few days, then gave him an extra large tip. Their attempts at conversation during the meal lapsed into silence. Neither could keep his mind off Nella's blood-soaked body in the bedroom down on the fourth floor, and wondering how soon it would be discovered. When they had finished, Richard rang the reception desk, asked for their bill to be ready by nine o'clock, and told an under-manager that, although they would be leaving that morning, he wished to keep on the suite.

After they had bathed, shaved and dressed, Richard said, 'It's a quarter to nine. L.A.N., the Chilean Airlines office, is only just round the corner. I expect it opens at nine o'clock. I'll go there now and see if there's any chance of getting up to La Paz.'

'While you're out, I'll go along and see Miranda.' Simon paused, then added, 'How much d'you think I ought to tell her?'

'As little as possible. The less she knows, the better, as there is a chance that the hotel people will tell the police that they've seen her up in the restaurant with us; then they'd question her. You told her only that we thought the party we were going to investigate last night might be a Sabbat, so there is no need to admit that it was.'

'True. And she brushed the idea of Satanism aside. The odds are she'll accept that it was simply a wild party, and be hoping that it gave us a line on Rex.'

'Good. Then you can tell her that it did, and we're losing no time in following it up. It would only worry her to know that her uncle is mixed up with a bunch of Satanists.'

Although Miranda could not see the sights or scenery, she enjoyed the fresh air when being driven in a car, and Simon had promised to take her for a drive that morning. When he told her that he couldn't, after all, she was very disappointed and, when he went on to say that he and Richard were leaving Santiago within an hour or two, she did not seek to hide her distress. But she cheered up when she learned that they now had a clue to Rex's whereabouts, and resigned herself to Simon's leaving her.

During the past few days they had had little chance to be alone together, because Pinney was nearly always with her. But they had made the most of the few occasions when Pinney had not been present; and now Miranda temporarily got rid of her by sending her down to the lobby to buy a magazine.

No sooner had the door closed behind the companion, than Simon moved over to the sofa on which Miranda was sitting, and took her in his arms. For some minutes they kissed passionately. Simon could not tell her that it would be impossible for him to return to Santiago in the foreseeable future, or give her an address where she could get in touch with him; so he told her that, as soon as he possibly could, he would write to her and they would then make arrangements that would bring them together again. On Pinney's return, they parted with great reluctance.

Back in his own room, Simon finished his packing, then waited with as much patience as he could muster for Richard's return. When Richard did get back, he was looking far from cheerful. There was a flight up to La Paz only once a week, leaving on Saturday, and no other aircraft by which they could leave the country until the following day.

To have remained in Santiago overnight meant that, for certain, they would be questioned by the police; and the possibility of being detained for a considerable time as material witnesses. In consequence, he had booked two seats on the flight to Valparaiso, which left daily at midday. That, at least, would get them out of the capital and, with luck, before the police caught up with them, they might find, in the big harbour, a ship about to sail for Callao, or some other port further north.

'Might be worse,' Simon commented. 'Must drive out to the airport. Can't prevent the police from learning we've gone there, and the name of the place for which we've taken off. If it was La Paz, they'd tumble to it at once that we were skipping. Perhaps they'd even have the aircraft radioed to return. As it's Valparaiso, they'll probably think that we've only gone off to spend a few nights at Viña del Mar, and not burst their guts coming after us.'

'That's true. It will certainly look less as though we had something to hide. As you say, it will need only a 'phone call to the airport for them to find out where we are heading; so we might give our departure an even greater air of innocence by telling the hotel people that we're going to get a breath of sea air at Viña del Mar. We'll do that when we pay the bill.'

For the next twenty minutes they hung about uneasily, fearful of appearing to be in too great a hurry to get to the airport; but it was a forty-minute drive so, at half past ten, they had their overnight bags taken down. While Simon was settling the account, the hall porter came up to Richard and asked him for a forwarding address for letters. Momentarily taken aback, Richard stared at the man and then said, 'We'll be back here on Friday, so there's no point in forwarding anything.'

At last they were in the car. When it had reached the outskirts of the city, Simon glanced at his watch. It was exactly eleven o'clock, the deadline after which they could expect a chambermaid to enter Nella's room at any moment, and come upon her dead body.

With luck, at the horrid sight of that gaping, tongueless mouth, the woman might faint, gaining them ten minutes before she revived or, in turn, was found and the management informed. Another ten minutes, or perhaps twenty, would elapse before the police arrived on the scene. Porters, floor waiters and other employees would be questioned. Of these the night clerk was the key man, because it was he who had seen Nella arrive with Richard and Simon, and go up with them in the lift. But the odds were that he was now in bed, and asleep. If so and, better still, he did not live in the hotel, well over an hour might pass between the discovery of Nella's body and a connection between her and them established. But those delays would bring their zero hour to midday, and none of them could be counted on.

It was eleven-twenty-five when they checked in at the airport. They spent half an hour of almost unbearable suspense, walking up and down the hall. Then, when they joined the little queue at the exit gate, a loudspeaker blared in Spanish. Simon swallowed hard, then said to Richard, 'Something wrong with the bloody 'plane. That announcement. Slight delay before take-off.'

Richard gave a sigh. 'I'm afraid it's not the 'plane. More likely that the police had just telephoned from the Hilton, ordering it to be held until they come out and pick us up.'

Grimly, they continued waiting in the queue, their eyes anxiously roving about the hall. Whenever they spotted a policeman in the crowd, coming in their direction, they felt certain that he was looking for them. But the minutes ticked by. At ten past twelve the flight was called again. They went out to the 'plane. The next five minutes seemed to them an eternity. Every moment they expected an official to come aboard and call out their names. But the brief routine of the captain's announcement and fastening safety belts passed without interruption. At twelve-fifteen the aircraft took off for Valparaiso.

Yet their ordeal was far from over. The flight would take the best part of half an hour. By this time it seemed certain that Nella's body would have been found, and the police have begun their enquiries. At any moment they might telephone the Santiago airport, to ask the destination of the 'plane by which Richard and Simon had left, then they would only have to telephone Valparaiso for them to be arrested on landing.

In an agony of apprehension they sat through the brief journey, refusing the coffee and biscuits that the air hostess offered them, but accepting American magazines and toying with, but not reading, them.

At what seemed a dangerously low altitude the little aircraft skimmed over the Mountains of the Coast, then came down out of a cloudless sky, to make a smooth landing. Tense and alert, they left the 'plane and walked across the tarmac to the airport building. As they had come in on an internal flight, there were no passport or Customs formalities, and no dreaded policeman was waiting there to accost them. Carrying their grips, they walked straight through to the taxi rank. Simon asked the driver of a cab to take them to a travel agency near the docks. The man drove them into the city and set them down outside an office in the window of which there were a number of fly-blown posters; but, by then, it was past one o'clock and the place had been closed for the siesta.

Paying off the cab, they crossed the street to a café. It was a gloomy place, with a solitary, surly waiter. They did not feel like eating anything, so ordered only pisco sours and, when they had drunk them, they repeated the order at intervals until they had whiled away the next two hours. Eventually the travel agency was reopened by a short, plump young woman whose blonde hair was obviously dyed. Simon told her that they wanted to make their way to the United States by easy stages, and asked her what ships carrying passengers were about to sail for the north. After much shuffling through papers, and two telephone calls, she told them that she could get them accommodation on a Dutch cargo ship that was sailing the next day. The ship had cabins for twelve passengers, and was bound for Curaçao in the West Indies, which was her home port; but on the way there would call at Callao in Peru, Guayaquil in Ecuador and at Panama on going through the Canal.

Simon never ventured abroad without taking a considerable sum in U.S. dollars, to supplement the travel allowance to which he was entitled as a business man. So he had ample funds to pay the fare for the two of them up to Callao, the port of Lima. The Peruvian capital being much nearer La Paz than Santiago, there was a good hope that they would reach it perhaps as soon as the Saturday 'plane would have got them there.

Outside the agency, they debated where to spend the night. Richard's view was that if the police made up their minds that it was worth going after them, at whatever hotel they stayed they would be picked up, so they might as well go to a good one in Viña del Mar. Simon disagreed, on the grounds that, if the police believed the story that they had gone to the coast only for a couple of nights, they would naturally make enquiries for them at the best places first. Whereas it would take many hours for them to check up at the scores of hotels in both the big watering place and the great port; so they would evade a police search for a few hours longer if they took a room at a small hostelry down near the docks.

Richard felt there was something to be said for that; and, after a quarter of an hour spent hunting for a suitable place, they found an inn that looked as though it might be patronised by the officers of merchant ships. There they were given adjacent rooms and, having unpacked their few belongings, went out to while away the rest of the day as best they could. By evening they were so tired of wandering aimlessly about and sitting over drinks in cafés, that they took a taxi into Viña del Mar, dined at the Casino and afterwards played roulette. Richard won the equivalent of three pounds and Simon over twenty, which cheered them up considerably as it seemed an omen that their lucky stars were in the ascendant.

Next morning Simon rang up the ship on which they had booked passages and was told that she was not sailing until the evening, but they could come aboard at any time. Having nothing else to do, they walked along to the dock at ten-thirty. A solitary Customs man lowered a newspaper he was reading, glanced at their bags and nodded to them to go through. Getting out their passports, they walked over to the Immigration desk. A policeman was lolling against it, smoking a cheroot and carrying on a desultory conversation with the Immigration official. Richard put his passport on the desk. The official opened it, laid it down and said to the policeman:

'These are the two you want.'

The policeman suddenly became alert. Putting his right hand on the holster of the revolver at his side, he said politely, '*Señors*, I regret the necessity of preventing you from going on board a ship; but police headquarters in Santiago have issued an order that, wherever found, you are to be sent there for questioning. Be pleased to walk in front of me to the exit.'

They had no option but to obey. Their careful planning, the periods of acute anxiety and dreary boredom they had suffered during the past twenty-four hours, had all been for nothing. After making a futile protest, seething with suppressed bitterness while endeavouring to appear no more than annoyed that their lawful intentions had been interfered with, they made their way back through the Customs hall, and through an archway to the street.

There, their captor spoke to another policeman, who then went into a telephone box. For the best part of a quarter of an hour they stood on the pavement, pretending to take their arrest light-heartedly, but in fact now filled with gloomy apprehension. A police car then arrived and took them to the airport. There a police inspector took charge of them and locked them in a small, bare room. For the first time they were able to talk, in low voices, of their unhappy situation. But they were not left there for long. The daily service between Santiago and Valparaiso consisted of flights each way, both of which left at twelve noon. The prisoners were put aboard with an escort and, after the short flight, taken in another police car into the city. At a little before half past one, they arrived at police headquarters.

A sergeant took charge of their bags and, when they had been searched, the contents of their pockets. Again Simon protested. He pointed out indignantly that they were not criminals, but law-abiding citizens who had every intention of aiding the police in their inquiries, to the best of their ability. It was of no avail. They were marched off to separate cells and locked in.

Had they been treated in such a way in Britain, they would have taken a very pessimistic view of their prospects; but, as they sat on the wooden benches in their cells, both of them tried to cheer themselves up with the thought that police procedure in most Latin American countries was very elastic, and on lines which differed considerably between rich and poor.

Therefore, as wealthy tourists, it seemed unlikely that, after having been questioned, they would be permanently detained.

It was not until four o'clock that they were taken from their cells to a large room on the first floor of the building. There, behind an impressive desk, a much-beribboned police officer was sitting. Just behind him stood a short, plump, dark civilian; and, at a smaller desk to one side of the room, sat a uniformed man with pens and paper.

The officer did not invite them to sit down, but stared at them for a full minute; then he asked, 'Does either of you speak Spanish?'

'I do,' replied Simon.

'That is good. But if there are any questions I ask that you do not understand, I have here an interpreter who will make them clear to you.' He jerked his thumb over his shoulder towards the short, dark man, and went on, 'What was the name of the woman you took to the Carrera Hilton, the night before last?'

Simon pretended to rack his memory. 'Nathan, I think. Yes, that's it, the *Señorita* Nathan.'

'How well did you know her?'

'Hardly at all. We met her only that night.'

'She was, then, a prostitute, and you picked her up?'

'Oh, no; she was not a prostitute; at least, not as far as I know. But I suppose you could say we picked her up.'

'Anyway, you took her back to the hotel with you for immoral purposes.'

'We did nothing of the kind,' Simon declared firmly.

'Why, then, did you take her to the hotel?'

Soon after arriving in Valparaiso, Richard and Simon had agreed on the account they would give if they were caught and questioned. Now, Simon gave it:

'My friend and I are fond of exercise, but we find it too hot here to take much in the daytime; so, after a late dinner that night, we decided to go for a long walk. I don't know how far we walked, but it was right out past the suburbs, and must have been five or six miles. On our way back, when we reached that wooded hill–the St Lucia Park I think it's called–we decided to go up to the top. Our idea was that, from the ruin up there, we'd get a wonderful view of the city in the moonlight. But we never got to the top. A little way up we came upon this woman. She was sitting on a bench, crying. I asked her what was the matter. She said she had had a terrible quarrel with her husband and had walked out on him. To calm herself down, before looking for a small hotel in which to spend the night, she had sat for a while in a café and had a couple of drinks. Five minutes after leaving it, she found that she had left her handbag behind. When she went back, it wasn't on the chair where she had left it. In her absence the waiter, or one of the other customers, must have stolen it. The bag had all her money and a few pieces of jewellery in it. Having lost it, she was penniless; she couldn't pay for a room and had nowhere to spend the night.'

'So you fell for her story that she was a respectable woman? It did not even occur to you that she might be a prostitute, hoping that you would offer to take her to your own bed?'

'I had no reason to disbelieve her. She was quietly dressed and had a small suitcase with her. That supported what she had said about having left her home.'

'Did you try to persuade her to go back to her husband?'

'Yes. But she wouldn't hear of doing that. She said she would rather starve.'

'Was there nowhere else she could have gone?'

'Apparently not, or we wouldn't have found her sitting weeping on a park bench.'

'What was her nationality?'

This was a question that had not occurred to Richard or Simon they might be asked. After hesitating a moment, thinking it hardly likely that they would have come upon a foreigner in such a situation, Simon replied, 'Chilean.'

'In that case it seems very strange that, in a great city like Santiago, she had not a single relative or friend whom she could have asked to give her shelter for the night.'

Simon shrugged. 'She may be a stranger here. Perhaps she had come up from the country with her husband and had the row with him in an hotel.'

'Did she ask you for money?'

'No.'

'Did you offer her any?'

'No.'

'I see,' commented the officer sarcastically. 'So, instead of giving her the price of a room for the night in a modest pension, you took her off to the most luxurious hotel in the capital.'

'By then, Mr Eaton and I were tired, so . . .'

'Really! Yet a few minutes earlier you had decided that, before returning to your hotel, you would walk another kilometre up steep paths, for no better reason than to see the city in moonlight.'

Simon swallowed hard. 'I meant we were anxious to get the matter settled and, as we had ample money, it seemed simplest to take the poor woman with us to the Hilton.'

'And when you got there you asked for a room for her, and she went straight up to it.'

Simon had been ready for that one. 'Not right away. She was about all in; so first we took her up to our suite and gave her a brandy and soda.'

'How long did she remain there with you?'

'Ten minutes, perhaps a quarter of an hour.'

'What then?'

'I took her down to the room she had been given on the fourth floor.'

'How long did you stay there?'

'I didn't. I didn't even go in. I gave her her case and left her at the door. Then I went back upstairs and Mr Eaton and I went to bed.'

'How long was it before one or both of you went down to her room again?'

'Neither of us did. We had already planned to go down to Viña del Mar for a couple of nights; so next morning we paid our bill and hers, and left for the airport.'

'Without even seeing her?'

'Yes. She wasn't our responsibility. We felt that, after a night's sleep, she should be able to sort out her own problems.'

'Then you did not know that she had been murdered?'

Simon had known that, sooner or later, he would be confronted with that fact. Letting his mouth gape, he exclaimed:

'What d'you say? Murdered?'

'Yes. That is what I said.'

Turning to Richard, Simon said in English, 'That poor woman. She's been murdered!'

Richard pretended equal astonishment and swiftly came out with, 'Good God! How terrible!'

Simon's dark eyes flickered back to the officer and, reverting to Spanish, he asked, 'When was this? And who murdered her?'

'The crime was committed between three and six in the morning. By whom, we have yet to find out. Tell me now. When you and your friend reached Valparaiso, instead of going to an hotel in Viña del Mar, as you say you had intended to, you booked passage in a ship that was leaving for Callao the following day. Why did you do that?'

'Just an idea,' Simon shrugged. 'Mr Eaton and I are travelling in South America for pleasure, and we've plenty of money. We have already visited Buenos Aires, Punta Arenas and Santiago. When we got down to Valparaiso, it suddenly occurred to us that a few days at sea would make a pleasant change from air travel, and the obvious place to go was Callao, as then we'd be able to see something of the nearby Peruvian capital.'

'Indeed? It had occurred to me that your sudden change of plan was due to an urgent desire to leave this country for good.'

'Why should we want to do that?' Simon asked, with an air of innocence. 'We hadn't the least intention of doing so. If you ask the people at the Hilton, you'll find that we left most of our belongings there, and arranged to retain our suite.'

'That I already know. But there are occasions when it is well worth while to abandon even valuable property. For instance, if one had reason to fear arrest.' Picking up a gold-braided cap from his desk, the officer put it on, stood up and said, 'For today, *Señors*, that will be all. I am detaining you for further questioning.'

'One moment!' Simon said quickly. 'With what are we charged?'

'Nothing, as yet. I am holding you as material witnesses in a case of murder.'

'I see, but I imagine we shall not be refused bail?'

'Perhaps bail will be granted. It all depends on how the matter develops.'

'In any case, we shall require the services of a lawyer. I formally request that the British Ambassador be informed of our situation and asked to arrange for us to have suitable legal aid.'

The officer nodded. 'That shall be done.' Then he signed to the escort, and the prisoners were marched back to their separate cells.

Later, it transpired that as they were able to pay for a dinner of their choice and bottles of wine, they were allowed to send out for them. On hard beds both of them spent a far from happy night. But they felt that, although the police obviously suspected them of not having told the whole truth about their relations with Nella. Simon's story was quite plausible and had been received reasonably well.

At a little after ten o'clock on the Friday morning, they were taken from their cells to a bleak room furnished only with a table and a few chairs. Standing there was a tall, fair-haired, youngish man. He introduced himself as Ernest Phillips, one of the secretaries at the British Embassy.

Sitting down at the table, Simon and Richard gave him their own account of their brief association with Nella, then discussed the situation. When the question of bail arose, they had reason to regret Don Caesar's departure for Europe, as they knew no other solid citizen in Santiago. Neither of them made any mention of Philo McTavish, as they would have been most reluctant to bring him into the affair. Moreover, they felt that, even had he been willing, it was unlikely that he would be able, at short notice, to produce the considerable sum required.

However, Richard stoutly maintained that, as they had not been charged with any crime, the police had no right to confine them in separate cells. Phillips agreed to do what he could to have that matter rectified, said he would arrange for the Embassy lawyer, a *Señor* Fidel Cunliffe, to come to see them that afternoon, and took his departure.

His representations proved effective. Twenty minutes after he had left them, they were taken from their cells and put together in a larger one. So, for the first time since their arrest, they were able to talk over their prospects.

Richard was inclined to be pessimistic, because of their having been arrested when about to go aboard a ship at Valparaiso. That they should have attempted to leave the country within a few hours of Nella's murder could have been a coincidence; but nothing could have suggested more strongly that either they were her murderers or in some way involved in the crime. He now felt that it had been a cardinal mistake to try to escape being questioned by the police. But he did not press the point, because it had been Simon's idea.

However, Simon argued that, although the police would continue to believe that Nella was a prostitute, and that they had brought her to the hotel for immoral purposes, it could not possibly be proved that they had had anything to do with her death. So, with the aid of a capable lawyer, they would soon be released.

Señor Fidel Cunliffe did not arrive until eight o'clock. He was a bulky, red-faced man, with grey hair, prominent blue eyes and a forceful manner. It transpired that he had lived in Chile all his life, but his father had been English and he spoke that language perfectly. Between them they gave him the same account of their brief association with Nella as Simon had given the police. Having made some notes, he then asked them a series of very searching questions. As by then they had their story pat, they did not falter in their replies, and he appeared satisfied. Before he left, Simon tactfully assured him that they had ample funds to pay for the best advice, so he need not be worried about money for expenses. The lawyer replied that, in that case, it would be worth while to instruct a private detective agency to endeavour to find out who, in fact, had murdered the *Señorita* Nathan.

Although Simon had small hope of such an enquiry proving successful, he readily agreed. *Señor* Cunliffe then said that his relations with the police were excellent, so he was confident that he could find out if they knew anything about the murder that his clients did not, and that he would come to see them again the next day.

On Saturday, the hours seemed to them to crawl by. The warders in charge of them proved well disposed. In addition to bringing them good meals and drinks, one of them went out and bought Richard some American magazines, and Simon two packs of patience cards. But, even with these aids for killing time, every few minutes their minds reverted to the promised visit from their lawyer and learning what he had found out from the police.

They had practically given him up when, at half past ten that night, they were taken from their cell to the interviewing room. Cunliffe was standing beside the table, looking very grave. When they had all sat down, he said:

'I fear you have not fully confided in me. For your own sakes I must advise you very earnestly to do so. Now, what else have you to tell me about Miss Nathan?'

It seemed to Richard that it was a question of telling all, or nothing. Although both he and Simon were convinced that Nella had been murdered by Satanists, to prevent her revealing what she knew about the Black Power movement, he could not believe for one moment that, if they gave an account of the Sabbat and of how they had carried Nella off from it, they would be believed; so he replied:

'I am sorry you distrust us, *Señor*; but we have already told you everything we know about this terrible affair.'

Simon backed him up by nodding vigorously.

Cunliffe stuck out his jaw aggressively. 'I cannot accept that. When interrogated, Mr Aron lied to the police. You do not appear to have noticed that when, just now, I referred to the murdered woman, I did not use the prefix "*Señorita*", but "Miss". Mr Aron said she was a Chilean; but she was not. She was an American.'

'What leads them to think that?'

'The shoes she was wearing had inside them the address of a shop in Beaufort, South Carolina. Her dress carried the label of an expensive Paris couturier. Her blue cloak, that of Sax, Fifth Avenue. The little suitcase also came from New York. Such items may occasionally be imported, or find their way into Chile; but, for all four of them to be the property of a Chilean woman of the middle-classes, is most unlikely. There is then the matter of your deciding to go on a short sea trip which, incidentally, would take you out of the country. In Mr Aron's disposition, it is stated that this idea did not occur to you until *after* you arrived in Valparaiso. Is that correct?'

Simon nodded.

'In that case why, earlier that morning, did you, Mr Eaton, go to the office of L.A.N., make enquiries for flights leaving that day for La Paz, Lima and places further north; and, only when you learned that there was none, take tickets for Valparaiso?'

As Richard did not answer, Cunliffe went on. 'The police suggested to you that you took the woman to your hotel for immoral purposes. You denied that. But medical examination of the body disclosed that she had been raped by a man, or men, within a few hours of her death. Her vagina was terribly lacerated and semen found in it.'

'We had nothing to do with that,' Richard declared swiftly. 'I swear to you that neither of us touched her.'

'Then what were you doing for the best part of three hours in the room to which you took her?'

'Three hours? What nonsense. After we had given her a drink up in our suite. Mr Aron took her down to her room. He rejoined me within ten minutes, then we both went to bed.'

'That you gave her a drink in your suite is accepted. There were three used tumblers there. Then you took her down to her room and remained there with her. At about six o'clock, a cleaning woman saw you both coming out of it.'

'She couldn't have!' Simon burst out. 'She was in the main corridor and Nella's . . .' He had been going to add, 'room was round the corner in a side passage'. Too late, he realised that he had given himself away.

The lawyer gave a grim little smile. 'You see? I was right. Both of you have been lying to me. And, *Señors*, I must warn you that your situation is now extremely grave. You are both about to be charged with murder.'

IO

A DESPERATE SITUATION

The eyes of Richard and Simon met. Without words, those of each told the other how fully they realised the desperateness of their situation. It was Richard who spoke first. Turning to Fidel Cunliffe, he said:

'It's useless to deny that we have not told you the truth–at least, not the whole of it. The devil of it is that if we did I greatly doubt if you, or anyone else, would believe us. The police are right about Nella–that was the woman's name–Nella Nathan's having been an American. They are right, too, that it was because we knew of her death and feared that we would become involved in it, that we attempted to leave the country. The reason we have given for bringing her to the Hilton in the middle of the night is a complete fabrication. None the less, neither of us was in any way responsible for her murder. Upon that I give you my solemn word.'

Simon nodded. 'That's the truth. Ready to swear to that on the Torah.'

The lawyer looked from one to the other. His expression had softened, and no longer held a veiled dislike. After a moment he said in a more gentle voice, '*Señors*, I find your earnestness convincing. I will now admit that only my obligations to the British Embassy would have overcome my reluctance to defend men I believed guilty of such a heinous crime. But, if you are truly innocent, I will do my utmost for you. For your part, though, however improbable-sounding it may be, you must withhold nothing from me.'

During the next quarter of an hour, the two friends gave him a full account of all that had occurred on the night of the previous Tuesday, withholding only Rex's name as that of the friend they had hoped to trace through the Satanists.

When they had done, Cunliffe said, 'No-one is ever going to believe that, by the use of spells, these Satanists had the power to conjure up an evil force capable of committing a physical act such as this murder. But that a clairvoyant could have overlooked the woman and located her at the Hilton would be regarded as plausible. Given that, one or more people could have been despatched to the hotel to kill her. There cannot have been many arrivals at the hotel in the middle hours of the night; so it should be possible to trace those who did, and an investigation into their backgrounds might provide us with valuable material for the defence.'

'Ner,' Simon murmured unhappily. ''Fraid we'll get nowhere along those lines. Hotel people have been got at. Just a chance that cleaning woman did spot us as we were about to come round the corner into the main corridor. But I doubt it. Anyhow, she definitely could not have seen us come out of Nella's room. It's clear now that those clever swine had a double motive for killing Nella. First, to silence her. Second, to pin her murder on Eaton and me, to get us out of the way. They must have either terrified or bribed the cleaning woman into saying she saw us; and I think you'll find the night clerk very unhelpful. Besides, Nella's killers may not have actually booked in at the hotel, but got in through one of the service entrances.'

'I fear you are right, Mr Aron. However, there is the house at which the "barbecue" was held. If we can produce evidence that it was actually a Sabbat, we shall have gone a long way to shake the prosecution.'

It was now Richard who struck a pessimistic note. 'It will surprise me if you succeed in that. Of course, the owner of the place, the American Negro lawyer Lincoln B. Glasshill, will not deny that he gave a party there last Tuesday night. We could produce the caterers who delivered the food, and there was so much noise that some of the nearest neighbours must have heard it. But that was four nights ago. They have had more than enough time to remove every trace that Satanic rites are practised out there.'

'That still leaves us Philo McTavish.'

'You may find him a little difficult. After we had rescued Nella, he showed great reluctance to becoming involved further in the affair. And we deliberately refrained from letting him in on the fact that the "barbecue" was actually a witches' Sabbat.'

'As things have turned out, that was a pity,' Cunliffe commented. 'But, no matter. We shall, of course, subpoena him, and he will have no option other than to give an account of what occurred during the time he was acting as your driver. That, at least, will establish the fact that you did go out to Glasshill's estate and brought back Nella Nathan from there, wearing the costume of a cat and in a state bordering on collapse. Besides, there are the bullet holes in the boot of his car. Your having been fired on will provide ample proof that those people were, even then, prepared to murder the woman and yourselves, who were protecting her. That will make it illogical for the prosecution to maintain that it was you who killed her an hour or so later. Provided we can shake the cleaning woman and other false witnesses they may produce, I feel there is a very good chance of my securing your acquittal.'

The prisoners were greatly cheered by this, and Richard asked, 'When are we to be brought before a magistrate?'

'As the police completed their investigation today, you would normally be charged tomorrow. But, as tomorrow is Sunday, you will not appear in court until Monday. That is just as well. It gives me an additional day in which to work. I will instruct the detective agency to find out all they can about Glasshill and his house, and I will see McTavish myself.'

When they had thanked him, Simon said, 'Be grateful if you'd do me a favour. This case is certain to make an awful stink in the papers. To learn of it that way would be a terrible shock to a friend of mine. She's staying at the Hilton. I'd like to let her know in advance that Eaton and I are being charged with murder, and beg her not to worry too much. If I wrote a note, would you drop it in at the hotel for me?'

'By all means. I pass the Hilton on my way home. I'll get the warder to bring you a pen and paper.'

When these had been produced, Simon wrote a brief letter to Miranda. He told her only that he and Richard had fallen foul of a group of Satanists who were attempting to fix a murder on them; but that the British Embassy had sent them an excellent lawyer, whom they hoped would secure their release on Monday.

The following morning, shortly before midday, a warder again beckoned them out of the cell, and took them to the interviewing room. They naturally expected to find Cunliffe there, having come back either to ask more questions or to bring them some piece of special news. But their visitor was Miranda, accompanied by Miss Pinney.

As soon as Miranda realised that Simon was in the room, she cried, 'I had to come! I simply had to come. I couldn't bear not knowing everything about this terrible trouble you are in.'

Simon beamed at her, 'But it's lovely to see you. Sweet of you to think of coming here to cheer us up. 'Fraid we're in a muddle, a really nasty muddle. But I think our lawyer chap will get us out of it.'

'Oh, I pray to God he does.' Sitting down at the table, Miranda added quickly, 'Now please tell me what has been happening to you. Right from the beginning, when you left the Hilton, after letting me know that you had learned something that might lead us to Uncle Rex.'

Between them Simon and Richard put her fully in the picture; then, with Pinney a silent listener, they discussed with her the pros and cons of their case. Miranda showed a very clear grasp of the situation, and suggested that the only certain way out for them was to produce an alibi, but there seemed no way in which they could do that. A warder then looked in to say that, in another two minutes, the visitors' time would be up.

For a moment Miranda was silent; then she caught her breath and said quickly, 'There's something . . . something I must tell you. I had to play a trick to be allowed to come here. When I telephoned the authorities, at first they refused me permission to visit you. They were quite adamant about it, and I felt absolutely desperate. So . . . so I went to the British Embassy. A nice young man named Phillips fixed it for me.'

Simon looked puzzled. 'Good idea. But I don't see where playing a trick comes in by your having done that.'

'No . . . no.' Below Miranda's mask, her cheeks had become pink with blushing. Suddenly she burst out, 'But I lied to him. I told him I was your fiancée.'

At her confession, Simon's mouth dropped open. Quickly grasping her hand, he gulped, 'I only wish . . . oh, I wish you were.'

Taking off her blindfold mask, she peered up into his face. 'Do you mean that, Simon? Do you really mean that?'

'My dear, of course I do. I've loved you since that first day in Buenos Aires.'

'But . . . but loving's one thing, and marrying is another. I'm so useless. I'd be a terrible handicap to you as a wife.'

'Nonsense!' He cast a glance at the other two, gave a little giggle, and put his hand up to his mouth. 'Extraordinary place to propose to a girl in, isn't it? Before other people, too. Still . . .'

Easing off the antique gold ring he always wore on his left finger, he put it on the third finger of her left hand, laughed again and said, 'Now you're committed. You're mine, and I'll never let you go.'

She came to her feet and kissed him. At that moment the warder returned. Good-byes had to be said. Dazed with happiness, Simon accompanied Richard back to their cell.

On Monday morning, a most unpleasant surprise awaited them. They had only just finished breakfast when they were taken to the interviewing room. Cunliffe was standing there. As soon as the door was shut, he glowered at them and snapped, 'I accepted the story you told me on Saturday night; but you lied to me again.'

'We did nothing of the kind,' Richard retorted hotly. 'Every word we told you was the truth.'

'Up to a point, perhaps,' the lawyer said angrily. 'But not the whole truth. You said that between approximately three a.m. and six a.m. on the day of the crime you were both in your own beds, asleep.'

'That is perfectly true.'

Cunliffe swung round on Simon. 'Of course, I understand your wish to protect the good name of your fiancée; but one can't afford to make such chivalrous gestures when one is being tried for murder. Yesterday afternoon Miss Van Ryn got my address through the British Embassy, and came to see me with her companion. She made a statement. After you had got rid of the Nathan woman, you went up to Miss Van Ryn's suite and went to bed with her.'

Simon's eyes flickered wildly, while Richard asked, 'And what was I supposed to be doing?'

'You know well enough. You were down in your own suite, playing six-pack bezique with Miss Pinney. She, of course, is entirely dependent on Miss Van Ryn, so reluctantly had to submit to her wishes. Apparently this party was arranged before the two of you went out. It was not expected that it would be so late before you returned. But Miss Van Ryn refused to forgo the–er–pleasure that she expected to enjoy in Mr Aron's company. It seems that Miss Pinney had proved squeamish about remaining in the suite while her young mistress was conducting herself in a manner of which she highly disapproved; so you had stepped into the breach and offered to keep her mind occupied with a game of cards down in your suite, while Mr Aron entertained his fiancée in hers.'

Richard and Simon exchanged a glance. They both realised that this alibi that Miranda had provided for them at the expense of her reputation would enormously strengthen their chances of obtaining a favourable verdict. Philo McTavish's evidence would show that, far from wanting to murder Nella, they had protected her. That of Miranda would show that they had not even had the opportunity. To deny it would only confuse the issue, and seriously jeopardise the credibility of such other statements as they made.

Simon swallowed hard, and muttered, 'All right. I'm sorry I didn't come clean with you about my having been with Miss Van Ryn, but my reason sticks out a mile. Everything else we told you was the truth.'

The lawyer accepted their apology somewhat coldly, then he said, 'It's just as well that Miss Van Ryn has had the courage to come to your assistance in this way, because I'm far from happy about the evidence McTavish will give.'

'I feared he might prove a bit sticky,' Richard remarked.

Cunliffe scratched his red nose. 'He is prepared to say only that he drove you out to Glasshill's, where you remained for some time; that you then emerged from the trees with a woman, upon which he drove the three of you back to the Hilton. You see, although you told him that the ''barbecue'' was only an ordinary wild party, from what he heard going on there, the woman you rescued being clad like a cat, then learning about her murder and mutilation, he has tumbled to it that she was the victim of Satanists.'

'Do you think that they have warned him not to talk?'

'They may have. I think it more likely that he is concerned to keep his job. He feels that if, in any way, he allowed Don Caesar Albert's name to be connected with this scandal, he would be out on his ear. He told me that, perjury or no perjury, he'll deny taking you to Don Caesar's house and that it was Don Caesar's wife who supplied the Nathan woman with clothes. He stubbornly refuses to confirm that, when he first saw her, she was dressed as a cat. He will say that the clothes that were found with her are, to the best of his belief, those she was wearing when you bundled her into the car.'

'We could prove that, on the way back, we went to Don Caesar's house. The servant who opened the door to me could be called.'

'He could, but would that get us anywhere, unless he actually saw the girl in her cat get-up, and his mistress's clothes being brought out for her?'

'No; unfortunately he saw neither. It is even more unfortunate that McTavish has dug in his toes. If he would give a full account of the cries and weird sounds he must have heard while the Sabbat was in progress, that would have helped a lot. Anyhow, he can't deny that we were shot at and the boot of his car riddled with holes.'

'Yes, he can. The car cannot be found. He says that it has been stolen. That may be true, or it may be that he has hidden it somewhere, owing to his anxiety to make everyone believe that nothing much out of the ordinary occurred during this trip on which he acted as your driver.'

'I can't understand why he should be so unhelpful.'

The lawyer shrugged. 'I can. Firstly, as I've told you, he believes that he'll get good marks if he can prevent his boss from being connected in any way with black magic, and very bad ones if he fails to do so. Secondly and more important, he can have very little doubt that Nella Nathan was killed by Satanists to keep her from giving them away; and he is scared that if he opens his mouth too wide they will have a crack at him.'

'If we could get Don Caesar back, I feel sure he would give evidence in our favour. He is not the sort of man to stand by and see two friends condemned unjustly, just because a few stupid people might get the wrong end of the stick and think he had some connection with Satanists. After all, he helped us when we were getting the girl away from them.'

'Do you know where he is?'

'No. He was going first to London I think; then on to Switzerland to get some ski-ing. But his office must know.'

'I will get on to it and find out. Then, if matters go badly, we could cable him. That is, if you really feel we should be justified in asking him to abandon his holiday and return. You see, he could only repeat what you told him about having witnessed a Sabbat, and that is not evidence. His giving you some of his wife's clothes proves nothing, and I gather he did not even see the woman. In any case, he knows nothing about what happened later at the Hilton; and that is the crux of the matter.'

'You're right,' Richard admitted gloomily. 'Still, we have our alibis. May

God bless Miss Van Ryn.'

An hour later, the two friends were taken into Court. Phillips from the British Embassy was present and with him an interpreter who, for Richard's benefit, translated every stage of the proceedings into English.

The prosecutor made an opening statement, then called a doctor who had carried out an autopsy on Nella's body. He deposed the cause of her death, described her mutilation and affirmed that she had been violently raped a short while before her death.

Next came the cleaning woman who had been in the main passage. She was middle-aged, with a workworn face and humble manner. She gave her evidence clearly, but in a sing-song tone that suggested she was reciting lines she had been taught. Simon thought it probable that she was being controlled from some distance by a powerful hypnotist, but there was no way of testing that. She stated firmly that it was Richard and Simon whom she had seen come out of Nella's room at about six a.m., and that she could not be mistaken.

The desk clerk related how Richard and Simon had brought Nella to the hotel, booked a room for her and taken her up in the lift. No-one else had come in and booked a room that night after they had done so.

A floor waiter testified that, when taking away the breakfast tray from the sitting room of the accused's suite, he had also collected three used glasses.

A policeman from Valparaiso described how he had detained the accused as they were about to board a steamer bound for Callao.

A woman clerk from the office of L.A.N. related how Richard had enquired there, within a few minutes of the office opening on Wednesday the 18th, about flights that day to La Paz and Lima.

Finally, the senior police officer who had interrogated them after they had been brought back to Santiago, read a long statement, showing how the replies to the questions he had asked the accused conflicted with evidence already given.

Cunliffe then made a statement on behalf of his clients. At his first mention of Satanism, a rustle of excited interest ran round the Court, and the pencils of the reporters at the Press table began to fly. As this was not a trial, but only a preliminary hearing before a magistrate to determine whether there was a case against the accused. Cunliffe's statement was no more than a brief résumé of events as described by Richard and Simon, after they had withdrawn the statement they had made to the police.

McTavish was then called. He ran true to the form Cunliffe had predicted he would show. He said that his Chief had ordered him to investigate the house of *Señor* Lincoln B. Glasshill and the nature of the parties held there. He had done so, but had no reason to suppose that they had any connection with Satanism. On Tuesday, the 17th, his Chief had ordered him to drive *Señors* Eaton and Aron out to the house late at night. He had done so. They had told him to pull up in a lane behind the house, then had left the car and disappeared into a screen of trees that bordered the estate. They had been absent for the best part of two hours. When they reappeared they were running and, with them, had a young woman. Pushing her into the car, they had ordered him to take them back to the city. When he had asked them what had been going on, they had replied to the effect that a wild party was being held in the garden of the house, and that it had proved too wild for the young lady. They had said nothing about witchcraft or black magic. During the drive the woman had not spoken. He had dropped the three of them at the Hilton Hotel shortly after two o'clock in the morning.

Cunliffe made no attempt to trap McTavish into contradicting himself, neither did the prosecutor cross-examine him. Such questioning to test the veracity of witnesses would be carried out by Counsel if the case was sent to trial.

When Miranda was led to the stand there was a new stir of interest. She gave her evidence in a low, firm voice, frankly stating that Simon was not only her fiancé, but also her lover and that, on the night in question, he had spent the hours between about three o'clock and seven in bed with her. As she stood down, a hush ensued that, in a subtle way, conveyed the sympathy of those present for the blind girl who had publicly declared her frailty to protect the man she loved.

Miss Pinney followed her. Unlike McTavish and Miranda who, although they intended to perjure themselves, had both taken the oath without hesitation, the companion held the Bible by a corner and well away from her, as though she almost expected it to burst into flames. Cunliffe took her through her evidence as quickly as possible; but she faltered several times in her replies, and spoke in such a low voice that twice the magistrate had to ask her, through the interpreter, to speak up.

It was clear to Richard and Simon that her Nonconformist conscience was giving her a very bad time. The latter wondered how Miranda had ever succeeded in persuading her to participate in this deception, and it occurred to him that Pinney had perhaps consented only because, being a Van Ryn, Miranda was very rich and had promised to settle a large enough sum of money on her to ensure her a comfortable old age.

But the fact remained that she had made a far from good impression, and the two accused were not surprised when the magistrate ruled that they should be sent for trial.

Greatly depressed, they were taken back to their cell. Shortly afterwards, Cunliffe came to see them. Angrily, he said, 'After Miss Van Ryn's evidence, I thought we were going to get away with it; but that sanctimonious companion of hers bitched everything up. When she had faltered through her piece, anyone could see they had both been lying, and it must have been obvious to the magistrate that Mr Aron's fiancée had courageously hatched this little plot in the hope of clearing you both.'

Neither Simon nor Richard sought to disabuse him of his belief, and he then proceeded to cheer them up by going on, 'But you must not be despondent. We have plenty of shots in our locker yet. I'll see to it that the Pinney woman makes a much better showing when she next gives evidence; and Counsel will take McTavish to pieces. Now that Lincoln B. Glasshill has been brought into it, we can subpoena him and the couple who look after his house. He'll have to give an account of those parties he holds. Plenty of people can be brought to testify that they take place, so something may come out of that. I'll have that cleaning woman investigated too. If it is found that she's spending much more money than she normally would, we'll insist on knowing where she got it, and may be able to show that she was bribed to give false evidence.'

When Cunliffe had left them, they held an inquest on the morning's proceedings, and the conclusions they reached were less optimistic than his. Richard summed up the situation by saying:

'What he fails to realise is that the people we are up against have occult power. I'll swear that cleaning woman was under hypnotic control from a distance, and they're much too clever to allow her to be trapped. Counsel won't shake Philo either. They've got him where they want him, and they'll keep him there. Our side can subpoena Lincoln B. Glasshill, but you can be certain we'll get nothing out of him; and Pinney is a hopelessly weak reed. Since her mind is in such a state of doubt and distress, it must be open to the Satanists. They will work on her while she is sleeping, and it would not surprise me if, at our trial, she suddenly breaks down and confesses that she has been lying.'

'Ummm,' Simon agreed. 'How I wish we had Greyeyes with us. I don't mean involved in our muddle, but on hand to help us. By pitting his occult powers against von Thumm and Co., I'm sure he'd turn the tables on them and, somehow, get us off.'

'Yes. The big mistake we made was not cabling him to come out the moment we realised that Rex had become involved in a black magic set-up.'

'I did think of it. But we had no chance. We didn't know for certain that Glasshill's parties were Sabbats until Tuesday night. Everything happened so quickly after that. Wednesday morning we were on the run.'

'D'you think it's too late to send him an S.O.S.?'

''Fraid so. Cunliffe's just told us that our trial should come on in a week. Our dear Duke will still be in Corfu, staying with those people whose villa he's thinking of buying. Could send a cable, but it would take the best part of a day to reach him. Shouldn't think for a moment that there's an air service yet to an out-of-the-way place like Corfu. He'd have to go by ship and rail to Rome; and from there it's a three or four day flight out to Santiago.'

Richard sighed. 'No, I'm afraid it's not on. The odds are that even if our trial were not over by the time he got here, at best he'd have very little time to work in.'

During the next few days, both Miranda and Cunliffe paid them several visits. The lawyer reported that he had secured a Court order to search Glasshill's house; but, when it was executed, nothing incriminating was found there. As McTavish reported earlier, the couple who lived there were either deaf and dumb, or acting the part of deaf-mutes. From the descriptions given to them it now occurred to Simon that they might be Zombies. In any case, they were completely useless to the defence. Still worse, the day after the magistrate's hearing, Lincoln B. Glasshill, evidently deciding that whatever course the trial might take, it would do his reputation no good to be interrogated as a witness, had left Santiago for an unknown destination.

Miranda brought the prisoners luxuries to eat and drink and spent every walking hour cudgelling her wits for new ways in which to help them. She had Pinney take her to Philo's lodging, upbraided him furiously for having borne false witness, then offered him a huge bribe to give a true account of what he knew. But he had told her frankly that he believed it to be more than his life was worth to accept it. She had then spent a thousand dollars inserting large advertisements in all the papers, offering ten thousand dollars' reward to anyone who could give information leading to the whereabouts of Philo's bullet-riddled car.

On the morning of Friday the 27th, the prisoners were taken, as so often before, to the interviewing room. They expected to find either Miranda and Pinney or Cunliffe waiting for them there. Instead, to their amazement, it was de Richleau who stood behind the bare table.

With fervour and delight, the three old friends embraced. To the eager questioning of the prisoners about how he came to be in Santiago, the Duke replied:

'I learned that you were in serious trouble through a dream or, rather, when I was up on the third level of the astral plane. Naturally, I left Corfu immediately for Rome, and had myself flown out. I arrived yesterday afternoon, got particulars of the trouble you are in and your lawyer's address from the British Embassy, then went to see him. He gave me all the facts as far as they are known.'

'What do you think of our chances?' Richard asked quickly.

De Richleau frowned. 'Not very good at the moment, I'm afraid. But I may be able to help. I told Cunliffe that I was gifted with clairvoyant powers and that, if he could arrange for me to go into a trance in the room in which this woman was murdered, I might be able to visualise the crime as it took place. If I could succeed in doing that, I would be able to give a description of her murderers, and that could lead to their being traced.'

He broke off for a moment then, a smile lighting up his grey, yellow-flecked eyes, went on, 'It has been arranged with the hotel people and the police that I should make the attempt this afternoon.'

For half an hour he remained with them, while they told him of their endeavours in Buenos Aires, Punta Arenas and Santiago, to trace Rex. Then he left them, infinitely more cheerful than they had been for many days.

That evening Cunliffe came to see them. He said that the Duke had telephoned to say that his session at the hotel had produced results which would justify another hearing by a magistrate, before the case came up for trial. In view of the sensation the case was causing, consent had been given to this new evidence being heard in court the following morning.

On the Saturday, at ten o'clock, the prisoners were again in the dock. Shortly afterwards de Richleau, a calm, impressive figure, took the witness stand. After the formalities were completed he gave an account of the arrangements made with the management of the hotel, and continued:

'I succeeded in establishing contact with the spirit of the dead woman. She described to me how she had been murdered by two men, one of whom was a Negro and the other, she thought, an Arab. I then asked her about her relations with Mr Aron and Mr Eaton. She related how they had helped her to escape from the Sabbat, spoke of her gratitude to them and directed my attention to the Bible in the drawer of the bedside table. Coming out of my trance, I telephoned down to the manager and he came up with two police officers. They are here, and will inform you of what followed.'

A police lieutenant replaced de Richleau on the stand. He testified to having joined the Duke in the bedroom and having taken the Bible from the drawer. Producing it, he opened the book and held it up, to show some writing in pencil on the inside of the cover, then handed it to the interpreter, who translated into Spanish what had been written there. It read:

> I am terrified. I'll never forget the horror I went through tonight. I would probably have been killed at that ghastly party if the Englishman and the kind little Jew had not got me away. He has promised to pay for me to get back to the States. But I've an awful premonition that I'm fated to die here. Those fiends will come after me, and kill me if they can, to stop me from telling what I know about them. Oh, God help me! Have mercy on me!

As the interpreter lowered the book there fell a brief, tense silence; then the magistrate dismissed the case.

Half an hour later, Simon, Richard, Miranda and Pinney were with the Duke in the suite he had taken at the Hilton. Unutterably relieved, carefree and laughing, they were toasting one another in champagne. As Simon set down his glass, he grinned at de Richleau and said:

'Lucky it didn't occur to anyone that, as you were left alone in Nella's room, you might have written that piece in the Bible. Don't see how you could have proved you hadn't.'

The Duke threw back his head and laughed. 'With your subtle mind you'd make an excellent detective, Simon. As a matter of fact, you are right. I did succeed in contacting Nella on the astral; but the poor woman was still hopelessly confused and quite unhelpful. As no-one could have produced a specimen of her handwriting; I was able to write that piece in the Bible for her. To risk you and Richard being found guilty was unthinkable.'

His statement was greeted with cries of surprise, admiration and gratitude.

Waving them aside, his face again became grave as he said. 'But now you two are out of the wood, we have other things to think of. Since it has emerged that we are up against Satanists, it has become more urgent than ever to find our dear friend, Rex.'

I I

A PERILOUS JOURNEY

That night, after dinner, the three friends held a conference. While still in prison Simon and Richard had given the Duke the main facts about their hunt for Rex. Now they filled in the details. When they had done, he said:

'Since Nella Nathan actually saw Rex up at this headquarters on the Sala de Uyuni, the obvious course is for us to go there. As the best part of a month has elapsed since she saw him, he may now be somewhere else; but, even should that be so, it is there lies our only chance of picking up his trail.'

'To go there is what Simon and I intended to do, if we had not been arrested when about to leave Valparaiso,' Richard said. 'I can't help wondering, though, whether it really was Rex the Nathan woman saw. It seemed so extraordinary that he should have been up in that place as a free man and, apparently, on excellent terms with the big-shot there.'

Simon turned on him. 'Nella more or less described Rex. On asking the name of the man she was looking at, she was told it was him. That couldn't be coincidence. And we agreed, you remember, that this place Sala being right off the map, it might be possible to detain someone there without locking him up.'

'It was that I had in mind when I said that Rex may now be somewhere else,' put in the Duke. 'They may have thought he couldn't escape; but if he had the free use of those big limbs of his, I'd back him to get away from any place other than a locked cell.'

'How shall we go?' Richard enquired. 'Rail or road? The Sala is well over a thousand miles from here as the crow flies and, of course, very much further by either rail or road. I spent half an hour before dinner going into alternatives. By rail we must go up the coast to Arica, inland for two hundred and fifty miles across the Andes to La Paz, then south. The only town of any size within a hundred miles of the Sala is Ouoro. After that the railway runs on the eastern side of Lago de Poopo. It's the hell of a long lake and the northern end of the Sala is on its western side; so it might be better to stick to the railway for another eighty miles and get off at a small place called Sevaruyo. By road, we'd have to make an immense detour through the Andes valleys, via Mendoza and Villa Maria to Cordoba; but from there we'd have the Pan-American highway, which runs almost due north, and it would take us within about seventy-five miles of the southern end of the Sala.'

De Richleau smiled. 'I had other ideas. But I shall not be the least surprised if you veto them. It occurred to me that we might hire a private aircraft, if you are willing to fly us up.'

Richard smiled back. 'I wonder if you realise what you would be letting yourself in for? The air currents among those mountains must be about as bad as one could encounter anywhere short of the Himalayas. But if you are both willing to risk your necks, I'll risk mine.'

Simon's eyes flickered wildly. 'Sounds stark crazy. No aspersions on you as a pilot, old chap, but to fly an aircraft between those scores of mountains sounds like juggling with death to me. Crossing the Andes by car, bad enough. On primitive roads subject to frequent blockages by landslides, good chance of ending up over a precipice. Train would be safer. Between Arica and La Paz we'd be reduced to grease spots, but at least we'd arrive.'

'You are right, my son,' the Duke agreed. 'My own enquiries before dinner lead me to suppose that both roads and trains in Central South America are little better than they were when I was in those parts in 1908. But it is not really a question of whether we spend many hours slowly roasting in a stinking, insanitary train, or take the very risky flight. The nub of the matter is how to penetrate the Sala de Uyuni when we arrive in the neighbourhood.'

He took a long pull on his cigar, then went on, 'The Sala is approximately one hundred and fifty miles in length and one hundred miles in breadth—roughly the area of Wales. Whether we make the greater part of the journey by road or rail, we can assume that we shall arrive on the edge of this vast, roadless plateau of salt marshes and near-impenetrable low jungle, in a car. What do we do then?'

'You're right, of course,' Richard nodded. 'Even if there were tracks along which we could drive a car—and it's very doubtful if there are—we wouldn't stand a hope in hell of finding the newly-built town in which Nella worked. The only possibility of doing that would be to fly to and fro across the area until we spot it.'

'Hadn't thought of that,' Simon conceded. 'But I get Greyeyes' point now. Got to have an aircraft to locate the place, and one might as well expect to find a Dodo bird up there. As one's got to be flown up, might as well go in it. O.K. then. I'll swallow a handful of sleepers and you can take me along as baggage.'

'Splendid,' the Duke smiled. 'Then, when we arrive, having had your sleep Richard and I can take a nap, while you prepare and cook a meal for us.'

'Ummm. We'll be landing in a wilderness; so we'll need supplies. Looks as though this is going to be a bit like going on safari.'

'Except that once we leave the aircraft we'll have to be our own porters,' Richard added, making a grimace.

De Richleau shrugged. 'We should be able to find somewhere to land far enough from the town for the people in it not to realise that we have come down, yet not so far off for it to be an easy trek to the place. We shall have to take precautions against being spotted when we enter it, though. Dressed in our usual clothes, we would stand out like sore thumbs, and immediately draw attention to ourselves as strangers. But the Nathan woman told you there are people of all races there, so we should be able to pass unnoticed in that sort of crowd if we wore sombreros and the kind of clothes most commonly seen in Andean towns.'

In consequence, it was decided that on the Monday Richard should go out to the airport and make enquiries for a suitable aircraft that could be hired, and that Simon should purchase both a good stock of supplies and the sort of garments that would make them inconspicuous.

They were well content to spend Sunday in its traditional role as a day of rest. Richard and Simon were still recovering from the awful anxiety to which they had been subjected during their nine days in prison. Miranda, too, had been under a great strain, and had lost both weight and sleep. When they all met for lunch and later in the day by mutual consent they avoided speaking of Rex and Satanism. Nevertheless, the now double mystery of why Rex should have absconded with a million dollars and fallen into the hands of the followers of the Left-Hand Path was never far from their minds.

Pinney alone was not gravely troubled by those unsolved problems, nor greatly concerned about the dangers the three men would soon have to face. De Richleau amused himself by drawing her out, and she fell completely under the spell of his charm; for once, in her somewhat acid way, enlivening the subdued atmosphere by becoming quite amusing.

On the Monday morning, Simon and Richard set off on their respective ploys. De Richleau, as befitted his age, was taking things easy and did not intend to get up until it was time to dress for lunch. At half past ten his bedside telephone rang. It was Miranda. She said she wanted to talk to him privately, and asked if she could come down to his suite.

'By all means,' he told her. 'But I'm still in bed. Give me half an hour to have my bath.'

Normally he always travelled with his manservant, Max; but, on their arrival in Rome, there had been only one seat available on the aircraft, and he had felt it to be of such urgency to join his friends that he had left Max behind. While washing and shaving himself, he ran a bath, poured a generous ration of scent into it and luxuriated there for ten minutes. Another ten went in doing his exercises, then he put the final touch to his toilette by brushing up his white 'devil's' eyebrows. A few minutes before eleven, clad in one of his beautiful silk dressing gowns—of which at home he had a large collection—he was in his sitting room ready to receive Miranda.

Pinney was with her, but had evidently been told that her presence would not be required; as, having said a polite good morning to the Duke, she at once withdrew. As soon as Miranda was comfortably settled in an armchair, the Duke said lightly:

'Now, tell me, dear, what is it you wanted to talk to me about? If it was to ask my opinion of Simon's suitability as a husband, I can assure you at once that I have never known a kinder and more sweet-natured man.'

'Oh, how right you are about him,' she agreed quickly. 'And you can have no idea what his coming into my life has meant to me. I was virtually a prisoner of my disability. For over two years, after the fire in which I so narrowly escaped death, a long series of operations to patch me up rendered me incapable of doing anything. By the time I was able to get about, doing next to nothing had become a habit and everyone treated me as a permanent invalid. Then Simon came and, like a knight in an old romance, rescued me from my prison. He has made me the happiest woman in the world.'

De Richleau smiled. 'I am delighted for you, truly delighted. And for him, too. I'm sure you will both be very, very happy. I suppose, though, it is about him that you wanted to talk?'

'Yes. Greatly as I love him, I wouldn't seek to dissuade him from continuing to take his part in the search for Uncle Rex. But I'm sure you'll understand how worried I am about him—and Richard and you—going up to the Sala. I don't think I'd be quite so scared if you were about to pit yourselves against a gang of ordinary bad men. It's the unknown that frightens me. You see, until a few days ago, I had no idea that there were still people who worshipped the Devil. Can he really give them powers to do serious harm to their enemies?'

'He can. Naturally, I should like to allay your fears; but I would not be honest if I told you the contrary. I'm speaking now of the real thing. Since the war there have been increasingly frequent reports in our newspapers of people desecrating churches, black magic circles and that sort of thing. In ninety-nine cases out of a hundred, I believe that the occult plays no part in them. They are either attributable to unscrupulous men interesting girls in this fascinating subject, with the object of getting them to participate in pseudo rituals at which they can easily be seduced; or run by clever crooks who promise their credulous victims communication with a departed loved one, or foreknowledge by which big money can be made, then photograph them committing some obscene act, and afterwards blackmail them. But there are men and women who have acquired genuine Satanic powers, and they can be very dangerous indeed.'

'Are there many of them?'

'Throughout the world there must be a considerable number, particularly in South America, Africa and the West Indies. Voodoo, of course, developed from the witch-craft practised by primitive African tribes. Haiti is its greatest stronghold, but Brazil bids fair to rival it. The lives of a good eighty per cent of the people in those countries are dominated by witch-doctors, male and female, and several times each year they make sacrifices to the Powers of Darkness. In Europe and the English-speaking world such activities are, naturally, conducted under cover, and comparatively rare. As I have said, most mentions of them in the newspapers refer to the vicious and the criminal cashing in by exploiting people who are superstitious. Nevertheless, in every great city in the States, Europe and Australia there are a limited number of Satan worshippers, vowed to use every means in their power to incite violence against law and order, sow discord between nations and bring about the disruption of civilisation.'

'How do you come to know so much about these things?' Miranda asked.

'As a young officer, I became a thorn in the flesh of the French

Government; so my superiors virtually exiled me to garrison duty in Madagascar. I found the boredom of living in that great island unbearable so, after a few months, I made friends with a powerful witch-doctor and, under his guidance, trained to fit myself to acquire occult power. One is initiated into the Mysteries by degrees, of which there are eleven. Having reached the fifth degree and become a Philosopher, one must then decide whether to follow the Right- or Left-Hand Path.'

'Does that mean to use your power for Good or Evil?'

'Yes. Those who follow the Right-Hand Path practise only white magic. That is the use of occult power for unselfish ends, such as curing warts, taking pain from others and so on. It may interest you to know that recently the British Medical Council carried out an investigation, which disclosed that white magic is still practised in every county in the British Isles. The majority of people who practise white magic are, I think, simple souls who do not realise that such powers are given from beyond. But many of the Saints must obviously have believed that their ability to perform miracles was due to a force which they regarded as being bestowed upon them by their god. The followers of the Left-Hand Path are black magicians. Their object is to gratify their own desires with regard to women, money and influence over the lives of others. For this they must pay by worshipping Satan, and carrying on the evil work of the Power of Darkness.

'In every community, whether primitive or civilised, both black and white magic are practised; but, unfortunately, there is far more black than white in the world today. Both in the East and the West the great Faiths have decayed. Few priests, whether Buddhist, Mohammedan or Christian, are any longer aware of the Great Truths and have knowledge of the Logos. They still perform their rituals and pay lip-service to their respective Gods, but during the past half-century more and more people have come to see through them as the empty vessels that they are.

'Even though their Faiths have long become distortions of the Eternal Verities from which all of them originally sprang, they were still forces for good, and those who subscribed to their doctrines were armoured against evil by the discipline they imposed. But we have now entered the age of doubt and rebellion against all controls. All over the world the new generations are rejecting the old Faiths, and have come to despise adherence to convention. It is termed "The New Freedom", but it leaves them rudderless. When in trouble they have nothing to turn to. And, with the taboos abolished, there is no restraint upon them from taking refuge in drugs, drink and promiscuity. Under the influence of these, they become the unconscious pawns of Satan, and an easy prey for recruitment as active participants in a Satanic Circle.'

'You think, then, that comparatively few people in our world have occult power? How does one acquire it?'

'By long periods of contemplation, fasting and undergoing a series of increasingly severe ordeals. After a while, one's spirit is able to leave one's body at will, and travel first on the lower astral planes when we sleep. Our dreams are memories of our experiences on them; but the untrained mind brings back only fragments of dreams, so that these telescoped events are meaningless. The Adept can recall, whether awake or sleeping, everything his ego has seen or done during its absence from his body. While on an astral plane he will meet and talk with other spirits, some whose bodies are thousands of miles away, and others whom you would term dead, but in fact are for the time being out of incarnation.'

'You are a believer in reincarnation, then?'

'I am indeed. It is the original belief held universally when the world was young, and the only logical one. If you believe in survival, it is the only possible explanation for our being here and undergoing the trials we have to face in life. Otherwise that would be pointless. We are sent here to travel the long road from being entirely self-centred, lustful, gluttonous savages, to wise, controlled, benign personalities, ever thinking of the happiness of others, until we are fitted to become one ourselves with the Lords of Light. How could one possibly achieve that tremendous transition in one life on earth? What chance would you have if you were born seriously deformed, or the child of criminal parents? It is that which makes so absurd the Christian heresy of a Last Judgement. To reward one person with unending bliss in Heaven and condemn another to eternal torment in Hell solely on the evidence of a single life on earth would be the greatest conceivable travesty of justice. It makes the present conception of the Christian God a mockery.

'But, of course, that was not the original Christian teaching. The doctrine preached by Jesus Christ was sadly perverted by that ignorant fool, Paul, and others, in the early centuries of our era. Christ knew the truth. There can be no doubt of that. You will recall His words, "The sins of the Fathers shall be visited upon the children even unto the third and fourth generation." Is it conceivable that so enlightened and gentle a man, who showed His love for children, should have threatened infants not yet born with dire punishment because their grandfather had been a murderer or sodomite? To initiates, His meaning has always been transparently clear. He was saying that every man is the father of the person he becomes in his next incarnation, and if he does evil in his present life, he will suffer for it in his future lives, until he has made good the evil that he did.'

Before Miranda had entered the room, de Richleau had pulled down the blinds, so that she would not need to wear her mask. While he was speaking, her big, blue eyes had remained fixed upon him in fascinated wonder at this, to her, new presentation of the meaning of life. As he paused, she said:

'What a tragedy that the Christian Church should for so many centuries have misled Christ's followers. Is there no way in which a new Reformation could be brought about, so that in future people would be taught the truth?'

De Richleau shook his head. 'I fear not. It is decreed by the Lords of Light that the way to enlightenment is for ever open. Those who seek shall find, and to those who are ready to receive it, it shall be given. You, my dear, I now know to be such a one, and I am overjoyed that I should have been chosen to unveil your spiritual eyes, so that henceforth you will never have any fear of death, and realise that leaving your present body is only the casting away of an outworn garment. Each life down here is like a term at school. During it we must learn some new lesson. Each time we leave an earthly body, we go on holiday. Free of the flesh, we are no longer subject to pain, and are infinitely more perceptive. Waiting to make us welcome we find beloved friends who have left their bodies before us and others whom we have loved in previous incarnations. The state of those who are out of incarnation is beautifully expressed in the Koran, by the words, "For them there are gardens beneath which rivers flow."

'But it is useless to endeavour to win converts to these beliefs. Fear and ignorance are the two states by which the Devil befuddles the wits of mankind. The Mau-Mau initiate their young warriors by hideous ceremonies in which the youth couples with a sow. The act has the effect of causing the initiate to commit himself absolutely. He feels that, after that, should he waver in his fanatic devotion to Mau-Mau, the dark gods will seize upon and destroy him utterly.

'At the other end of the scale you have the Christian clergy. They are civilised and kindly men; and they do much good among the poor and afflicted. But spiritually they are empty vessels, bound by centuries of tradition to their way of life. The great majority of them continue to gabble their rituals, although they no longer believe in them. Ask them how the eternal war between Light and Darkness is going, and they would think you a little mad. For them the Devil is a myth of the Middle Ages, and to suggest that he is still active would greatly embarrass them.'

Sadly, Miranda shook her head. Then, after a moment, she asked:

'This expedition on . . . on which you are going. Do you think you will be able to protect yourself and the others?'

'I can only pray that it will be so,' the Duke replied seriously. 'It depends upon the degree of power that can be called down by the Satanist who heads this Black Power movement. I have achieved the ninth degree, and am a Magister Templar, represented in occultism by eight circles and three squares. If my opponent is a Magus or an Ipsissimus, he could prove too much for me. But I beg you not to worry. Instead, every time you tend to do so, pray for us. Prayers often appear to be ignored, but they never go unheeded. At times they conflict with the fate decreed for the person on whose behalf they are offered up; but as others they can be of great help to those we love.'

By lunchtime Richard was able to report that he was in negotiation to buy an aircraft from the executors of a rich Chilean who had recently died. He meant to spend the afternoon going over it with mechanics. If the examination proved satisfactory, he would take it up for a trial next day.

Simon had spent the morning buying stores and, as far as tinned food could make a gourmet's mouth water, the list he produced would certainly have done so.

For that evening they had arranged a dinner party, to which they had asked Fidel Cunliffe and young Mr Phillips from the British Embassy, in order to show their appreciation of the help the lawyer and diplomat had given Richard and Simon during their ordeal.

On the Tuesday, Richard took the aircraft up, first for a few minutes, then for over an hour's flight down to Valparaiso and back. Having satisfied himself that the 'plane was reliably airworthy, he reported to Simon, who arranged for its purchase through the bankers with whom he was associated in New York.

That evening Simon produced the costumes he had selected for them to take with them, and a lighter note was brought into their preparations as, assembled in de Richleau's suite, they tried on gaudy shirts, leather breeches and other items of Andean attire which normally they would have worn only to a fancy-dress dance. The Duke had also been shopping that day, and he added a sober note to the proceedings by producing three automatic pistols, with a good supply of ammunition, remarking as he did so:

'We cannot hope to win our battle with "down here" weapons, but they may come in handy if we find ourselves up against lesser fry.'

After an early breakfast on the Wednesday morning, Miranda put on a brave face to say good-bye to them, and they were driven, with all their paraphernalia, out to the airport. The 'plane had been filled to her maximum capacity, the stores and baggage were loaded, and at ten o'clock they took off.

Heading west, they flew over the Mountains of the Coast, which presented no difficulties. On their far side, Richard turned the aircraft north and, for nine hundred miles, followed the coastline up to the port of Iquique. There they came down on the landing strip, to refuel and have a meal. On taking off again, Richard set a course due east. For a short while they flew over flat, arid land, on which small patches of cultivation struggled for existence. Ahead of them, clear in the afternoon sunshine, rose the formidable rampart of the Andes. On either side it stretched as far as the eye could see. Immediately in front, it mounted in a succession of ever-loftier highlands to a veritable forest of peaks that appeared to continue indefinitely into the distance. At this point the range was, in fact, nearly four hundred miles in depth.

The great plateau of Sala de Uyuni was situated on the far side of the Cordillero Occidenta and a little to the west of the centre of the main chain. Its nearest edge was only about a hundred and twenty miles from the coast, but the last hundred could be covered only by a continuous succession of twists and turns through valley after valley, many of which were a thousand feet deep.

Had Richard's passengers not been so acutely aware of their peril, they would have marvelled at the grandeur of the scene. The sun glared down on a desolate wilderness of rock, barren slopes and precipices, but the clarity of the atmosphere made them appear terrifyingly near and dangerous. Seeming infinitely far beneath them, turgid rivers foamed over rocky beds as they wound through the gorges towards the sea. Here and there they broadened out into placid lakes that looked as though they were bottomless. Occasionally, the dead-black shadow of a cloud blotted out the colour of an irregular patch of land, moving slowly until it slid from view. One small shadow kept pace with them, that of their aircraft, and the sun now being in the west it was always ahead, as though leading them on through the precipitous, trackless waste, in which there were neither roads nor human habitation.

As Richard had anticipated, flying through the mountains proved extremely hazardous. Although he had seen to it that they had oxygen masks, it was not possible to fly the 'plane over the high crests. He had to steer between them, and the aircraft was constantly subjected to the force of strong air currents. At times it was unexpectedly swept fifty feet higher or, on striking a pocket, dropped like a plummet for a hundred feet.

It was impossible to keep the machine on an even keel for more than a few minutes at a time. Being unheated, it was bitterly cold at that altitude; yet, although the temperature was near zero, Richard was sweating as he battled with the controls. As an adept in Yoga, de Richleau was able both to keep his body warm and render his stomach impervious to the constant bumps and lurches. But poor Simon was terribly airsick. Again and again, as the 'plane slid sideways, his heart seemed to come up into his mouth with fear that the aircraft would be smashed to fragments on the nearest cliff.

At last they passed between two lofty, snow-capped peaks and, ahead of them, they saw a vast expanse of level ground. Another few minutes and their hour-long ordeal was over. The western edge of the Sala de Uyuni lay below them.

Coming down to five hundred feet, they surveyed the uninviting prospect. As far as the eye could see the almost level plateau stretched away, with no sign of either human or animal life. The greater part of it consisted of marshes so white with crystallised salt that they looked like irregular patches of snow. Here and there they were broken by patches of stagnant water, on which the sun glinted. Where there was slightly higher land, it was a reddish colour, and covered with pampas and occasional groups of stunted trees.

Their next concern was to locate the secret headquarters of the Black Power movement. To increase their area of vision, Richard went up to two thousand feet and flew a zigzag course, while de Richleau and Simon scanned the land on either side through binoculars. After a while they realised that to spot a settlement in an area covering over ten thousand square miles was like looking for a needle in a haystack.

But the Duke solved the problem by leaving his body. Mounting to a great height, so that the whole of the Sala de Uyuni was spread below him, he was able, by his spiritual eyes, to identify their goal; then, returning to his body, he directed Richard to it.

The settlement lay some thirty miles inside the south-eastern edge of the Sala. It took a further twenty minutes before they were close enough to see it clearly. It's layout consisted of thirty or more long, low buildings, divided by parallel streets, and one solitary square building upon a piece of higher ground, some distance from the others. Between it and them there stretched an airstrip, upon which were five aircraft and several hangars. There were no roads leading from it in any direction; so, except by air, it was entirely cut off from the outer world, and no more perfect site could have been found for a secret headquarters.

Anxious that no-one down there should suspect that they were being spied upon, but assume that the 'plane was in the neighbourhood only because the pilot had lost direction, Richard flew straight on until the settlement was out of sight. He then banked and began to circle it, low down, at a gradually decreasing distance, as he searched for a place that offered a good chance of making a safe landing.

He chose a spot about four miles from the settlement, where it seemed almost certain that the ground was firm because it was well above the average level and, on three sides, bordered by an irregular screen of trees. The aircraft touched down and he brought it to a halt on the edge of a small coppice. Greatly relieved, they climbed out and set about unloading some of their stores, in preparation for a picnic meal.

By the time they had eaten, the sun was setting and the air had become chilly. Anxious to lose no time in finding out what they could about the settlement, they changed into their picturesque costumes, equipped themselves with their pistols, flasks and torches and set out on foot.

To cross the intervening piece of land in darkness would have proved impossible, as more than half of it consisted of salt marsh and treacherous stretches of muddy ground that, when trodden on, sucked evilly at their boots. But, shortly after the sun had disappeared behind the great range of now distant peaks in the west, the stars came out. In that crystal-clear, rarefied atmosphere, myriads of them could be seen sparkling in the great dome of blue-black sky, and they gave ample light by which to distinguish firm from dangerous ground.

Nevertheless, it took them well over an hour and a half to cover the four miles. Outside the settlement nothing was stirring, but there were lights in most of the windows and there was a loud murmur of activity. In view of the complete isolation of the place, the possibility of sentries being posted round it could be ruled out; so the three friends went boldly forward and entered the end of the nearest street. The buildings were all of one storey, of uniform design and apparently constructed from standard parts which had been flown in. This side street, or rather passage-way, for it had no road surface or pavements and was no more than a hard-trodden earth path between the lines of hutments, was almost deserted, and the few people they encountered took no notice of them.

As they advanced, they saw through the lighted windows that some of the buildings were long dormitories for either men or women, and others were divided into sections for couples. One was a bath house and another a communal laundry. The lighting was electric, inclined to be dim and, at times to flicker slightly.

Having walked some two hundred yards, they entered the main street. It was much broader than the others, but also unpaved. In it there were many more people. There was no traffic of any kind, and no street lighting, but all the buildings were lit up. Many of them were offices in which a few people were still working; one contained a printing press, another was a library, a third a clothes store. Further along, they caught the sound of drumming and a band. On both sides in the centre of the long street there were two mess rooms, crowded with people eating their evening meal, and between them a large kitchen. Beyond these were recreation rooms, with billiard and ping-pong tables, a cinema, a card room and a gymnasium. The sound of the band had been coming from one in which couples were dancing, but with no sign of abandon.

The men and women inside these rooms could be seen clearly. They were mainly blacks and half-breeds, with only a sprinkling of whites. Some were sitting quietly by themselves, but the majority were talking and laughing. There did not appear to be anything abnormal about any of them. The features of those outside in the street were more difficult to see, for not only was it semi-dark there, but a mist was rising from the not-far-distant marshes, having the effect of a light fog. It slightly muted all sound, and gave the people moving in it a curiously mysterious quality. But, singly or in chatting couples, they passed up and down, intent on their own business.

On reaching the far end of the main street, the Duke said, 'There is nothing for us here. Things are as Nella Nathan told you. This is a colony of innocent do-gooders who are being made use of. Like citizens of any town run on communal lines, they work in the offices or do other jobs during the day and amuse themselves according to their fancy in the evenings. There is not even the faintest suggestion that the Black Art is practised here. On the contrary, as you may have noticed, two of the huts we passed held rows of chairs and had altars at one end with crosses on. They are probably Baptist and Methodist chapels. Anyway, those who follow the Christian religion are catered for and another hutment contained a lectern carved with Moslem symbols, so was obviously a mosque. No doubt there are also a synagogue and a Hindu temple; although I didn't notice them. They were probably in darkness or, perhaps, in one of the side streets.'

'Where do we go from here?' asked Richard.

'To the building on the rise, just outside the town. The odds are that it contains the quarters of the people who run the place. We may learn something there.'

They retraced their steps for some distance, again mingling with the passing crowd, then turned down a side street that led in the direction of the rise. On the way they crossed the landing strip, and Richard was able to get a close-up look at the aircraft on it. They were one medium large and two small passenger 'planes, and two transports.

As they approached the building on the rise, they went forward cautiously, peering through the mist before and on either side of them, as they thought it possible that a look-out might be patrolling somewhere in the vicinity, to prevent anyone from the town, impelled by curiosity, sneaking up to see what was going on in what seemed probable was the administration centre of the settlement.

The place was constructed in the same way as the others, but was larger. Light came from only two windows and, like those in the town, neither of them was screened by blinds or curtains. To avoid making more noise than was necessary, the Duke sent Richard forward on his own. He tiptoed up to first one then the other lighted window and, crouching down, peered in over the sills.

The first room was a kitchen in which two Negro women were working; the second was a dining room. Seated eating at a large table were four men; one was a very tall Negro who had a fine forehead and was dressed in expensive clothes. Richard thought he was the man who, at the barbecue, had offered up the ape to the goat; but, having seen him only from the distance, could not be certain. It occurred to him that, should that be so, the man was probably Lincoln B. Glasshill. Opposite him was a round-faced man in a turban. The third had his back to the window but, from his lank, black hair, was possibly an Andean Indian. The fourth man was von Thumm.

Richard crept back. Having rejoined the others, he told them what he had seen. He then went on excitedly, 'As there are no guards, we've got them where we want them. We are armed, they don't appear to be. Anyway, we can take them by surprise. A couple of shots through that window, then we'll hold the swine up and threaten to shoot them unless they tell us what they've done with Rex.'

'No good,' de Richleau murmured. 'You forget that they are Adepts. Of what degree I do not yet know, but if von Thumm acted as Grand Master at a combined Sabbat, he would certainly have enough power to deflect bullets. He would defy us and, with the others all merging their wills with his, probably overcome us.'

It had become very cold, and Simon asked with a shiver, 'What can we do, then?'

'We shall have to wait until they go to sleep. Then I will try my strength against von Thumm on the astral.'

'It will be hours yet before they go to bed. We'll freeze to death.'

The Duke took him by the arm and turned him towards the airstrip. 'Don't worry. I will attend to that. We will wait in one of the hangars.'

Through the mist they made their way down the slight slope to the

Gateway to Hell

deserted airfield. Entering one of the hangars, Richard flashed his torch round. It lit up a small pile of empty packing cases. Rearranging the cases, they sat down and took a pull at their flasks. After a moment, de Richleau said:

'Our enemies are not yet aware we are here, and the cold we are feeling is not that of evil. It is the altitude and this accursed mist. If you each give me one of your hands I can overcome it.' Soon after they had obeyed him, the cold seemed to become less intense as he threw an aura of warm air round them. After a while they both fell into an uneasy sleep.

Three hours later, de Richleau roused them by saying, 'The time has come, and I have made a plan. If von Thumm is now asleep and I can overcome him on the astral, I will compel him to return to his body and leave the house. We will then kidnap him, hold him to ransom and compel him to have Rex delivered up to us as the price of his life.'

The others agreed this to be an excellent scheme. Having stretched their stiff limbs, they left the hangar and started to make their way back to the house. When they had first crossed the airstrip, the lights of the settlement could be seen behind them through the mist, as a rosy glow. Now all was dark in that direction; but the murk was a ground mist and, as they breasted the slight rise, they could again see the myriad of stars twinkling in the sky. There was no moon, as it was now in the dark quarter, but enough light by which to see their way.

The house was in darkness. De Richleau led the way round to the left side of it, halted opposite a window and said, 'This is von Thumm's room. Give me your hands again and concentrate with all your might on sending your spiritual energy into me. I am about to leave my body and challenge him. I need all the support I can get.'

Standing between them, he gradually became rigid so that they had to lean against and support him. For what seemed a long time nothing happened, then he gave a shudder and relaxed. Drawing in a deep breath, he murmured, 'That was very unpleasant, but I got the better of him. He is coming.'

A few minutes later an ungainly figure which Richard and Simon immediately recognised as that of the Baron, appeared round the corner of the house. As he limped up to them, the Duke said to him harshly:

'You have surrendered your soul to the demon Abaddon, but he has raised you only to an Adaptus Major with six circles and four squares. So I am your master. Do you acknowledge that?'

'*Jawohl, Sohn vom Heiligen Michael*,' muttered the Baron in his native German.

'Then you will come with us. Should you attempt to escape, we will deprive you of your present body by shooting you down. Should you call on your associates with Dark Power to come to your assistance, I will blast you on the astral.'

'*Zu Befehl, Meister*,' came the cowed reply.

The party then moved down the slope, de Richleau leading and von Thumm between Simon and Richard, the latter holding his pistol ready in his hand.

The trek back to the coppice close to which they had left their aircraft put a great strain upon them. Had it not been for the Duke's supernatural powers, they would have become hopelessly lost and ended up in one of the many quagmires. He could at least lead them in the right direction. But even so and given the aid of their torches, it was very difficult to find their way through the salt marshes and between clumps of five-foot-high pampas grass. Several times they had to turn back and search in the gently-moving mist that limited their range of vision, for another causeway of firm ground on which they could advance for a few hundred yards.

It was past two o'clock in the morning before they at last reached the slightly higher ground with its semi-circle of trees. After their long day and the ordeal of flying through the mountains, they were almost dead on their feet with exhaustion. Shining their torches before them they stumbled up the slope to the aircraft. As they reached it, there was a sudden movement near both the head and tail. From both sides a group of dimly-seen figures came rushing out to converge upon them.

De Richleau was still leading. He barely had time to raise his torch to defend his face from one attacker before another had struck him on the head with a cudgel and felled him to the ground. Richard swung round on the Baron and squeezed the trigger of his automatic; but von Thumm had thrown himself backward. As he fell, the bullets passed over him. There was a gasping grunt as one of the men behind him was hit. Next moment both Richard and Simon were seized and disarmed. Panting, they ceased their struggles and stood with their arms held behind them.

Von Thumm picked himself up, gave a guttural laugh and sneered: 'You poor fools! With the trial for murder you get away, *ja*. But haf you not sense to anticipate that we you overlooked from then? We haf expect you here to come, and make preparation. When you land, we know it. For you to come spying in our town we wait. Then send our men to make ambush for your return. Interfering *englische Schweine*! For you very soon now it is curtains, and a death very painful.'

I 2

AT THE MERCY OF A FIEND

There was nothing Richard or Simon could do, or the Duke either, when he came to a few minutes later. To have brought occult power to bear on von Thumm would have required concentration and, at the moment, his head seemed to be splitting.

The ambush had consisted of eight men. One was a powerful Arab and another a yellow-faced mulatto with a crop of tight curls. The others were all big Negroes. One of the latter had been shot by Richard in the fleshy part of the arm; but the seven uninjured men were more than sufficient to keep the captives under control. None of them had uttered a word. The Baron was now holding one of the torches, and as its beam swept over the faces of two of the Negroes, de Richleau caught sight of their gaping mouths and lacklustre, fixed stare. It confirmed the impression he had already formed from the jerky movement of their limbs as two of them had pulled him to his feet. Turning his head, he said to von Thumm:

'Do not be too certain that you have triumphed. Had you sent men with all their faculties to ambush us, they would have reacted promptly to any unexpected situation. But Zombies are incapable of doing so. When the pain in my head has lessened, I may spring an unexpected surprise on you. Then these poor wretches will only gape and look on while I again force you into submission.'

As the Duke spoke, he was well aware that several hours must elapse before he again became capable of using his occult powers; so his only object had been to undermine von Thumm's confidence in himself. The Baron replied harshly:

'Should you anything attempt, with you on the "down here" level I will deal as you threatened to do to me. A bullet in the guts you will get. But the Undead haf their uses. No tales can they tell. As you will haf guessed, we of the hierarchy take much precaution against those morons in the settlement our secret activities getting to know. Times are when one of them too inquisitive becomes. For such situation, these six Undead at headquarters we keep. No talk, no packdrill, as you English haf saying. *Ach*, I haf good new thought. To cheat me try and I will shoot only to wound. Then into the marsh I will haf you thrown, to choke out your lives in mud.'

After a moment he added, 'Also with aid I now haf, on the Astral I am also your master.' Then he jerked his head in the direction of the Arab and the mulatto. 'El Aziz is son to Baal, and Benito to Baron Samedi. United we haf power to your astral bind. March now, all of you.'

As they moved off, both Simon and Richard glanced at the two men with quick interest, as it was Benito who had brought Nella to the Sabbat and El Aziz who had raped her.

For what seemed an endless time, mud became a nightmare to the prisoners. As they were forced on by their captors, they staggered from one piece of solid ground to another, through intervening stretches of spongy, oozing soil that threatened to suck their shoes from their feet. The march back to the settlement proved incredibly laborious, and the fear grew on all of them that they would never make it. With incredible fortitude, the elderly Duke trudged on, and Richard, the fittest of the three, managed to keep going, in spite of the laboured breathing that racked his lungs. But, on the final mile, poor Simon's legs gave way with increasing frequency and he slid to his knees in the mire. Silently the two Zombies who were holding his arms dragged him to his feet and, eventually, had practically to carry him.

At long last they reached the building outside the settlement. Von Thumm led the way in. The prisoners were taken down a flight of concrete steps to the basement and pushed into an unfurnished room. A steel door clanged to behind them. The key was turned in the lock, and the light was switched off. Utterly exhausted and caring no more what happened to them, they lowered themselves to the bare floor and, very soon, fell asleep.

When they woke, still in darkness, they had no idea for how long they had been unconscious. De Richleau was convinced that they had slept the clock round nearly twice, as they had flown up to the Sala on February 1st and the 2nd was Candlemas, one of the four great Satanic feasts of the year; the others being Walpurgis Night, St John's Eve and Hallowe'en. It was certain that von Thumm, El Aziz and Harry Benito, together with the other Satanists who lived in the house, would all have flown off to a Sabbat; and that would account for their being left to have their sleep out, instead of being roughly awakened a few hours after being pushed into the cell.

Miserably they exchanged a few words on the events leading up to their capture. The Duke exhorted his companions to have faith that the Lords of Light would come to their assistance. His friends endeavoured to believe that, but were so unutterably depressed that they responded only half-heartedly. Then, for a period of several hours, they remained almost silent.

Suddenly the light was switched on. They were still blinking when the steel door of the room was unlocked and swung open. Framed in it was the big negro Richard had seen at dinner with the Baron. Without bothering to close the door behind him, he advanced into the room, glared down at Richard and said:

'I am Lincoln B. Glasshill. I've a score to settle with you and your little friend. By instigating police inquiries, you have rendered it no longer safe for us to hold Sabbats at my house in Santiago, and forced me to abandon my practice there. Stand up.'

Richard got to his feet. The big Negro's fist shot out, caught him on the jaw and hurled him back against the wall. Before he could recover and get his fists into a position to defend himself, Glasshill struck again, this time at Richard's stomach. The savage blow drove the breath from his body. He lurched forward, endeavouring to cover his face. But in vain. With cold malice, his attacker smashed down his guard and slammed his clenched fists again and again into Richard's eyes, nose, mouth and chin. Dazed and bleeding, Richard sank to the floor.

Turning to Simon, who had got up with the futile thought of coming to Richard's assistance, Glasshill seized him by the collar, shook him as a terrier shakes a rat and, towering over him, cried:

'You miserable little whitey. You are not worthy of being chastised by a proper man. I'll not stoop to skin my knuckles on your face. Instead, I'll send the fire-imps to you.'

With a great heave, he sent Simon sprawling in a corner, turned on his heel and marched from the room, slamming the door behind him.

De Richleau's immediate concern had been to get as much sleep as possible, in order to recharge with energy his physical body; so, some while before Glasshill had entered the cell, he had induced sleep to come to him again. At the sound of the shouts and scuffle as the Negro beat Richard up the Duke's ego returned down the silver cord that attached it to his body during unconsciousness; but his physical senses were too freshly aroused for him to be capable of any attempt to protect his friend.

Now he stood up, laid his hands gently on Richard's battered face, drew out the pain and soothed him. But soon afterwards he had to turn his attention to Simon. He was still lying in the corner where Glasshill had thrown him, and tiny lights had begun to flicker up and down his body. A smell of burning cloth drifted across the room, then Simon started to cry out in distress as the fire-imps settled on his face and hands, inflicting burns on him that were more painful than mosquito bites. Frantically he endeavoured to destroy the imps by smacking at them; but, with incredible swiftness, they evaded his attempts and settled on him in other places.

'Be patient for a few minutes, Simon,' de Richleau urged him swiftly. 'I have now regained enough power to deal with this at least.' Sitting down cross-legged on the floor, he bowed his head and extended his arms as high as they would go above his shoulders. Simon could not stop himself from continuing to swot about and exclaim in pain and anger; but gradually the little flames that were tormenting him went out with a faint, hissing noise, as though they were being doused with invisible water.

There followed another long period, during which they sat or lay in the darkness, changing their positions every few minutes, to ease the soreness of their flesh from pressure on the hard floor. They reckoned that they had been put in the cell at about five o'clock in the morning, and from their wrist-watches they knew that Glasshill's visit had taken place at about three o'clock, so they reckoned that they had been in the cell for at least thirty-four hours; and, as no food or drink had been brought to them, they were all now both hungry and very thirsty.

Shortly before five o'clock, the light came on again, the door opened and von Thumm limped into the room. Behind him stood a little group of his Zombies. For a moment he regarded his prisoners with his crooked smile, then his face took on a discontented look, as he snarled:

'English swine! *Ach*, to haf had you in my hands in the old days, how goot it would haf been. I was then *Gruppenführer S.S.* For English spy-swine, dirty Jews and such, we haf the ice-water bath, the steel rod to beat and the electric apparatus for attaching to genitals. These we haf not here. I haf ideas, though. *Ja*, plenty to make you for mercy scream. But for the present, no. Orders haf come that I to another place take you. *So!* Perhaps I am fortunate and you returned to me for disposal are. If not make no merriment. Others will with you deal and you curse the day when into our business your big noses you stick.'

De Richleau made no attempt to subdue the Baron mentally, because he thought it certain that he would be able to call on help to resist, and felt that, in any case, wherever they were being sent, they would not fare worse than they would in the hands of this Nazi sadist.

The Zombies hustled them up the stairs to a wash-room, where they were allowed to relieve themselves; then out on to the airstrip. Von Thumm led the way over to one of the smaller aircraft. It was already ticking over. They climbed into it and saw that the long-haired man, whose back view Richard had seen through the dining room window two evenings before, was sitting in the back seat. He had the hook nose of an Andean Indian and the thick lips of a Negro. In his right hand he held a two-foot-long blade, with a very sharp point; a more practical weapon for keeping prisoners under control in an aircraft than a pistol, a bullet from which might have damaged the structure. The Baron awkwardly levered himself up into the pilot's seat, and tested the controls; then they took off.

From the direction of the sinking sun the prisoners knew that they were flying slightly east of north. For about fifty miles the dreary Sala, with its endless marshes and stretches of reddish earth passed smoothly beneath them, then they entered mountainous country and the going became very rough. The 'plane bucked, swerved and dropped alarmingly as it struck air pockets; but von Thumm was a good pilot and evidently knew well the route he was taking. Their discomfort lasted only twenty minutes, then they came round a high peak to see, melting into the misty distance ahead, the fifty-mile long Lago de Poopo. The blueness of its waters was in startling contrast with the yellow of the heights surrounding it. But they had little time to take in the full grandeur of the scene, for the Baron had put the aircraft into a steep dive to bring it down.

Another few minutes, and it became clear that he was heading for an island about ten miles from the southern edge of the great lake. As they approached, it could be seen that to have landed on it from the water would have been next to impossible, as sheer cliffs dropped to the beaches. The southern two-thirds of it was flat, and largely covered with forest, but towards its northern end there were hills, mounting to a lofty eminence of rock, crowning which there stood an irregular building of grey stone, that looked like a ruined fortress.

The foothills at the far end of the island were broken by a half-mile-long, oval plateau. It had been developed into a landing strip, and had two small aircraft parked in bays clear of the runway. Von Thumm brought the 'plane down with practised ease. It was met by two men, both short, but of formidable appearance. They had the hook noses and lank, black hair of Andeans, and were wearing gaudy clothes, with bandoliers across their chests, pistol holsters on their hips and knives thrust through their waistbands.

The Baron signed to the prisoners to get out of the 'plane, but did not follow. With no more than a gesture, he handed them over to the two Andeans and, having thrown a malevolent glance at them, slammed shut the door of his aircraft. Two minutes later it was again in the air, and heading back towards the Sala de Uyuni. Meanwhile, one of the Indians had signed to the prisoners to follow him and the other took up the rear.

For twenty minutes they made their way laboriously up a series of steep stairways cut in the rock, until they reached the partially-ruined stronghold. Its towering walls were composed of great blocks of stone which had been cunningly dovetailed together. How man could possibly have constructed such a building without cranes and modern engineering machinery posed a fascinating problem, as do the similar pre-Hellenic palaces at Mycene and Tirens in Greece. From many photographs the prisoners had seen, they knew this one to have been built by the Incas, probably in the fifteenth century A.D., which would have made it nearly three thousand years later than those the pre-Hellenes had built with similar huge blocks of stone.

Their escort led them through a flat-topped arch, the transom of which was a monolith twelve feet in length and four in depth, into a courtyard, then through a much lower arch and down a long, narrow passage. At the far end there was a modern door of heavy wood. One of the men pressed a bell-push. They waited for a while and the door was opened by another Andean Indian, dressed in a green, scalloped jerkin and trunks that were reminiscent of the clothes worn by Robin Hood's men. Behind him stood a Negro with a wall eye, who beckoned them in.

Incongruously, after the courtyard of great stones, there was a carpeted stairway, with walls of pale, natural wood, and lit by electric light. Mounting the stairs, they reached a wide landing which might have been that of a large private house. It was furnished with a Louis XV settee and chairs of the same period. On the walls there were prints after Bouchard and Fragonard. Two passages led off it. They were taken along the one leading to the right. To one side, some way down it, there was an open arch. Through it the prisoners could see a bar, in front of which several men were sitting drinking. Among them there was an immensely fat Babu, together with a Negro with a face like a skull, an almost white Caribbean octoroon and an apparently Spanish half-cast.

The wall-eyed Negro who had met the captives signed to the green-liveried servitor and gestured for him to take them on down the corridor;

then walked through the archway to join his companions in the bar. The servitor led them along the passage for another eighty feet, then halted and knocked on a door. A voice bade him enter. He opened the door and signed to the prisoners to go into the room.

It was a boudoir, again furnished in the style of Louis XV, with a beautiful Aubusson carpet. Seated near the window was Silvia Sinegiest. She had been reading a book. As she laid it down, her little shaggy-haired dog jumped from her lap, barking furiously and bounded towards her visitors, racing round their legs giving them an excited welcome. Standing up, Sylvia cried, 'Down, Booboo, down! You bad boy! Stop it!' But she was smiling and, turning her smile on Richard, she said in her low, musical voice:

'Hello! How nice to see you again, and Mr Aron. Your friend, of course, must be the Duke de Richleau.'

The Duke made an inclination of his head. 'You are right, Madame. By hearsay you are equally well known to me, and I recall with pleasure seeing two films that you made some years ago. I only regret that we should meet under such far from happy circumstances.'

Her bright glance ran swiftly over them. Their clothing was creased and mud-stained, their hair awry, and they all had bristly stubble on their chins.

She sighed and shook her head, with its aureole of strawberry blonde hair. 'We owe you an apology. Unfortunately, so many Germans are still barbarians at heart, and von Thumm is one of them. But I suppose one must allow for the malice he feels at the destruction of his Nazi ideals and the humiliation of his country.'

'One could forgive him a lot,' Richard burst out, his speech now thick from the thirst that had been tormenting them for several hours past. 'But not for denying us water ever since we were caught.'

'Oh, you poor things!' she exclaimed; then, in a few swift steps she crossed to a drinks table and asked, 'What will you have—whisky, gin, brandy?'

'For me, water please,' replied de Richleau. 'Later we may accept your invitation to partake of something more potent.' The others nodded agreement. Quickly she poured three glasses from a carafe, popped a lump of ice into each and carried them over.

'As the Baron refused you drink, I suppose he denied you food, too,' Silvia remarked. 'If you are very hungry, I'll send for something at once, but we shall be dining in about an hour, and I can promise you a very good dinner.'

Their enforced fast had given them all excellent appetites, but they were not afflicted by hunger to the same degree as they had been by thirst; so they thanked her for her offer to send for food, but refused it.

Looking at Richard, she said, 'Your face is in a shocking state. Is that the result of your having gotten into a fight, or did von Thumm beat you up?'

'No, it was not the Baron,' he replied tartly, 'but another of your friends: that great brute of a Negro, Lincoln Glasshill.'

'They are not my friends, only my associates,' she told him with a quick lift of her chin. 'I will do my best to make amends by patching you up.'

Turning away, she tinkled a glass bell that stood on an ornate, buhl writing table. In under a minute her summons was answered by Pedro, the Spanish manservant who had been with her down in Punta Arenas. She said to him, 'Take these gentlemen to their rooms. See to it that they have everything they want.' Glancing at Richard, she added, 'When you have shaved and had a bath, say in half an hour, I'll come to you and do what

I can to your face.'

Pedro led them away down the long corridor to the landing, then down the other corridor to three rooms near its end. Their original stone ceilings and floors had been left untouched, but the walls had been plastered and painted with evidently modern murals of Inca scenes, and there were colourful handwoven mats on the floors. The beds looked comfortable, and there were fitted cupboards. Adjacent to each room was a small, well-equipped bathroom, with all they would need to make themselves presentable.

Wearily they struggled out of their filthy clothes, shaved and luxuriated for a while in hot baths. When, considerably revived, they returned to the bedrooms, they found that Pedro had removed the gaudy garments they had been wearing and, instead, laid out for them the type of suit that up-country white men wore in that part of the world. Richard had just put his on, and found that it fitted not too badly, when there came a knock at his door. He called 'Come in', and Silvia entered, carrying a tray on which were numerous items for first aid.

His lips were swollen, his chin and cheek cut, but his worst injury was to his left eye. It was already half closed, and promised to become a glorious 'shiner'. Having remarked it, Silvia had brought with her a piece of raw meat which she proceeded to lay on it and securely bandage in place. She smeared a healing salve on his mouth and the cuts, then lightly powdered over the latter.

Standing back, she said with a laugh, 'Poor Mr Eaton, you do look a guy. How very distressing for such a handsome fellow. But, never mind. In a day or two you will again be an Adonis.'

Regarding her coldly with his remaining eye, he said sullenly, 'Not if your so-called "associates" get at me again. And why you should think me good-looking, I've no idea. Apart from my wife, no-one else tells me so.'

'But you are,' she insisted. 'You're the perfect type of the well-born English gentleman, whom I have always admired. How old is your wife?'

'I should say she is the best part of ten years younger than you.'

Silvia laughed again. 'But a man is as old as he feels, and a woman as old as she looks; so if she is forty or so I'll bet she couldn't compete with me. It is part of my reward for doing what I do that I keep my face and figure so that I look not more than thirty.'

'I see. So you really are a witch?'

'Indeed I am. I can raise a wind, cast spells and make love potions.'

'I'll bet you couldn't make one that would affect me,' remarked Richard aggressively.

'I could, given the right ingredients. I'd need a lapwing, bull's gall, the fat of a white hen, ants' eggs, the eyes of a black cat, musk, myrrh, frankincense, red storax, mastic, olibanum, saffron, benzoin and valerian.'

'God, what a brew! It would stink to high heaven. No man in his senses could be persuaded to swallow it.'

'A horrid mess, I agree,' she laughed, 'and I've never resorted to it. You'd be surprised, though, what I could do with a few of your nail-parings, let alone a neat little clipping of your pubic hair. But, in my case, such aids are not really necessary. I've never failed to get a man I wanted with my own resources.'

Richard gave her a half-admiring, half-surly look. 'I've rarely seen a woman better equipped with what it takes. But, if you have designs on me, you'd better indent for the cat's eyes and bull's gall.'

'Don't worry, darling,' she laughed again. 'I just couldn't bear to wake up in the morning and see your face on my pillow, as it looks at present. But in a few days you will be your handsome self once more. Then we'll see.'

'I don't think we will. But, while we are on the subject, I'd like you to tell me something. As you know, Aron and I were onlookers at that so-called "barbecue" which took place out at Glasshill's house. After the feast, everyone let themselves go with a vengeance. But you remained sitting up on the table. As you are so keen on that sort of thing, why didn't you join in?'

'Because I am the "Maiden".'

'Oh come! With two or three marriages and what all behind you, you can hardly claim to be a virgin.'

'The Maiden does not have to be. It is a rank in the hierarchy of the true priesthood. Joan of Arc held that rank and openly acknowledged it.'

Richard frowned. 'I know that we English burnt Joan of Arc as a witch, but all the world knows that she was a saint.'

'She was a prisoner of the English, but it was not they who condemned her to be burned at the stake. It was a tribunal of the Christian Inquisition, presided over by the Bishop of Beauvais. From the account of her trial, it emerges quite clearly that she was not a Christian. Her religious instruction was given to her by her godmother, who was known to consort with the "little people". They were, of course, the descendants of a race older than the Franks, who had never wavered in the True Faith, and were steeped in the lore of magic. The wife of her first protector, the Sieur de Bourlemont, was one of them.

'In those days, early in the fifteenth century, the Christian heresy had a hold only on the upper strata of society. The great majority of the ordinary people still believed in the True God. That is why the soldiers were willing and even eager to give their lives for Joan in battle. They looked on her as a minor deity. She herself stated that she could not be killed, but would be of value to the Dauphin for one year only. That was because she had made a pact with Satan for twelve months of power. Even in prison, when there was no longer any practical point in it, she insisted on wearing men's clothes, so there could hardly be a less suitable title to give her than "The Maid", unless a special reason lay behind it. And there did. All the Grand Covens have their Queen Witch, known as "The Maiden", and she ranks next in power to the Grand Master. When Joan was first put forward by her sponsors and accepted by the Dauphin, she ranked only as "The Maid of Orleans". But later she was elevated to the highest honours as "*La Pucelle de France*".'

Richard shrugged. 'I don't know enough about the matter to argue with you; but the fact remains that millions of people venerate Joan of Arc as a saint today.'

'Of course,' Silvia showed her lovely teeth in a smile. 'The Christian priesthood is not quite so stupid as to let people continue to make a heroine of someone they condemned as a pagan. They are experts at applying whitewash to their own victims, when it suits their purpose, and in persuading people to accept new explanations for the origins of ancient festivals. As, for example, converting the Roman Saturnalia into Christmas; in spite of the fact that Jesus Christ was actually born in March. But I must go and tidy myself for dinner.'

A few minutes later Pedro came to collect the three prisoners, and led them down a flight of stairs to a long room divided by partly-drawn, heavy curtains. The part the door led into was a lounge, furnished with armchairs, tables beside them and, on one side, a cocktail bar. Through the gap between the curtains, they could see a dining table. Silvia was standing near the bar; as they came she asked them, 'What can I make you? I seem to remember, though, that you like champagne. It's here if you prefer it.'

Simon nodded. Richard said he would like a Planter's Punch if that was not too much trouble. To the surprise of his friends, de Richleau declared himself to be a tee-totaller, and said he would have only a glass of water.

Deftly Silvia produced the drinks, then she said: 'I've been given a rough idea of your recent doings, and you must all be rather tired; so perhaps it would be better if we put off talking of why you have been brought here and all that sort of thing, until you've had a chance to relax and fortify yourselves with a meal.'

De Richleau inclined his white head. 'As we are in your hands, Madame, that is considerate of you. We arrived here in very poor shape, but our baths have freshened us up and, as we slept for twenty-four hours between the time of our capture and this morning, none of us is in urgent need of sleep. Naturally we are anxious to know the intentions of your . . . your associates towards us. But that can quite well wait until after we have dined.'

Silvia smiled. 'How wise of you not to press for an immediate explanation. But, of course, we have found out a great deal about you and, as an Adept, you will have trained yourself to patience.'

A quarter of an hour later they were enjoying an excellent dinner and Silvia succeeded in temporarily banishing from their minds the fact that they were prisoners. As they were waiting for the second course to be served, she asked the Duke, 'How did you enjoy your stay in Chile?'

He replied that he had been there only long enough to see the capital, which he had found very pleasant, but Simon and Richard held forth on the extraordinary variety of the climate and the scenery and how enjoyable they had found Santiago until they had been thrown into prison. De Richleau then asked their hostess if she knew anything about the history of the fortress.

She shook her head, 'Nothing, except that it formed part of the defence complex centred on the Inca city of Potosi, which lay just across the lake and was the southernmost centre of their civilisation. But I have recently read quite a lot about them and found it fascinating. The extraordinary thing is that they should not only have created their vast Empire but brought the whole of it under complete control in so short a time. Although they are known to have been established in the Cuzco valley as early as about 1100, theirs was quite a small territory until they began their conquests in 1350. In little over a hundred years, the Lord Inca wielded absolute authority from Quito in Ecuador right down to Maule in central Chile: a territory of over three thousand, two hundred and fifty miles.'

'The secret of their power was road building,' remarked the Duke. 'Until the recent creation of the Pan-American highway, their trunk road down the Andes was the longest in the world. They had another nearly as long down the coast and shorter, lateral ones running down every valley. And, although they were mountain roads, their standard width was twenty-four feet. By means of them they could, by forced marches, rush troops in a matter of days to any part of their Empire that was threatened.'

'I know, and the Lord Inca was always warned of trouble with incredible swiftness. Their relay runners could transmit messages at the rate of two hundred and forty miles in twenty-four hours. What they achieved was fantastic when one remembers that they had no wheeled vehicles and no horses. Llamas were their only means of transport, and the blocks of stone in all their great fortresses had to be carried many miles up those steep mountains by men. But what I admire most about them is the orderly way in which they administered their Empire. Records were kept of the numbers of each age group in every village; what crops could be expected from it, and the amount of work on roads and bridges of which its people were capable; and the land was shared out among the villagers afresh each year, according to how many men there were in each family able to cultivate it.'

'I remember reading Thornton Wilder's book, *The Bridge of San Luis Rey*,' put in Richard. 'It was an incredible feat to have made a bridge a hundred and fifty feet long, with only twisted rope, and to have got it up across a deep gorge between two precipitous mountains. It was no gimcrack affair, either. It was still in use up to 1890, after five hundred and forty years.'

'The only people comparable to them were the Romans,' said the Duke, 'both as road builders and administrators. Moreover, the Romans had the enormous advantage of being able to read and write, whereas the Incas could do neither. They had to send their messages and keep their records by means of bunches of coloured strings, in which they tied knots at varying intervals.'

Silvia stubbed out her cigarette and lit another, then she asked, 'Did you know that more than half the foods the world eats today were first developed by the Inca agriculturalists? They irrigated great areas which had previously been desert, and grew an amazing variety of vegetables. They had two hundred and forty varieties of potatoes and twenty of maize. We owe to them many kinds of beans, tapioca, peanuts, squash, cashews, pineapples, chocolate, avocados, tomatoes and paw-paws. And, may I remind you, this wonderful civilisation was utterly destroyed by the zealots of the Christian Church.'

When they had done full justice to a meal ending with a savoury of flamingo tongues, Silvia asked them to make themselves comfortable in the lounge end of the room, and left them for ten minutes. On her return, she settled herself in a low armchair, crossed her peerless legs so that they were displayed to the best advantage, and said:

'You must be aware that your investigation into Rex's disappearance has aroused against you a most powerful enemy, and brought you into great danger. About the reason for Rex's leaving Buenos Aires I, of course, lied to you. I was ordered to, as it was hoped that, believing my story that he had committed murder, you would call off your hunt for fear that you might lead the police to him. However, I now give you my word that he is well, cheerful and has no regrets about what he has done. More than that, for the time being I am forbidden to tell you. Most unfortunately, I failed to stall you off, with the result that you have found out many things that we regard as most important to keep secret. In consequence, you now have only one way in which you can escape paying for that with your lives.'

They had all been mellowed by an excellent dinner. Only the Duke had refused all alcohol, but he had special resources upon which he could draw to restore his vitality and, with the dessert, Silvia had served to Richard and

Simon as a liqueur an elixir that had counteracted the fatigue they would normally have felt after such a very tiring day. So Richard asked quite amiably:

'Tell us what it is.'

'You must reassess your spiritual values.'

'How d'you mean?'

'By accepting and worshipping the True God.'

'Meaning the Devil,' Simon put in, and gave a slight shudder. 'No, thank you. Few years ago I got in pretty deep with a Master of the Left-Hand Path. But de Richleau saved me, thank God. Never again.'

She smiled at him. 'Then your friend did you a great dis-service. And you are wrong to refer to the True God as "the Devil". That is only the name bestowed upon him in hatred and fear by his enemies, the Christians who denied him. It was invented by them as late as the Middle Ages.' Glancing at the Duke, she added, 'Am I not right?'

He nodded. 'Yes, there are many mentions of demons and evil spirits from the earliest times, but none of the Devil until the Christian Church began to get the upper hand in its war against paganism in the fifteenth and sixteenth centuries.'

Richard gave him a doubting look. 'Oh come! Nearly all the monarchs in Europe were Christians the best part of a thousand years before that.'

'It is true that many kings, queens and nobles were converted by missionaries sent from Rome during what we term the Dark Ages. But it is reasonable to believe that they accepted the new faith only on the old principle that it was bad policy to refuse to acknowledge any god, in case he took offence and did you a mischief. That belief was prevalent in the Roman world, and they had inherited it. Christianity did not secure a serious hold in Britain until well after the Norman conquest. There were, of course, many priests and priestesses of the old religion, and everybody knew who they were, but very few were brought to trial as witches until early Stuart times. In fact, the first witch trial ever to be held in England did not occur until the reign of King John, and then it was brought against a Jew who, in spite of the wave of anti-Jewish feeling at that time, was found not guilty.'

'Thank you, Duke,' Silvia said. 'And one can add that, even during Norman and Plantagenet times, Christians were in the minority. Only the upper classes endowed monasteries and were in favour of the Crusades. The great majority of the people still followed the true religion. That was recognised by those who tried to put an end to it. And, even when its votaries were driven to hold their ceremonies in secret, they were still a great power in the land. One has only to recall the origin of the Order of the Garter.'

'What has that to do with it?' Richard asked.

'The account of how it happened is well known. At a ball, the Countess of Salisbury's jewelled garter fell off. She was the mistress of King Edward III, and was dancing with him. He snatched it up and founded a new Order of twenty-six knights, including himself and the Prince of Wales. Covens always consist of thirteen members, so he had created two new covens, with himself and the Prince as their Grand Masters.'

'I don't see why you believe them to be covens, or what seizing the lady's garter has to do with paganism.'

'From the earliest times the insignia of the Chief of a coven has always been a string worn round the left leg, below the knee. There is a prehistoric painting in the caves at Cogul, showing a dance in which a figure is wearing one. The Countess was the "Maiden" or, as you would put it, the Queen Witch of England, and the King knew it. By securing her garter, he supplanted her. It gave him power over the many thousands of people in his kingdom who still followed the Old Faith. And he did not look on them as evil people, because he held the garter aloft and cried "*Honi soit qui mal y pense*"—"Evil be to him who evil thinks"—and took that for the motto of the new Order. What I tell you is confirmed by the regalia worn by the Sovereign. It embodies one hundred and sixty-eight garters, and the one round the leg makes the one hundred and sixty-ninth—that is thirteen thirteens, symbolising an all-powerful combination of thirteen covens.'

Richard remarked with a slight sneer, 'You'll be telling us next that, just because Jesus Christ and His disciples numbered thirteen, they, too, were a coven.'

'They were,' she retorted swiftly. 'Jesus spent many years in the wilderness, training Himself to become a Magister Templar, the highest of all grades of occultists. That is why He was able to draw down the power to perform many miracles, and they were all what you would term white magic—for the benefit, not of Himself, but others. It was only later that the message He brought was distorted. When He spoke of God the Father, He was referring to the True God—the God of Love.'

'Ner,' Simon shook his head stubbornly. 'He was speaking of Jehovah. Plenty of evidence of that.'

'Only from people who were writing many years after Christ's death, the men who, for their own evil ends, perverted His teachings. Jehovah was the God of Hate; the terrible primitive entity whose jealousy had to be appeased by burnt offerings—and this horror still, today, remains the supreme deity of the Christian religion.'

'Nobody really believes that any more.'

Silvia gave a little laugh. 'Of course they don't. But that does not alter the fact that, through St Paul and other masochistic fanatics, Jehovah succeeded in inflicting incalculable frustration and suffering on many millions of people. His priests—the priests of the Christian Church—made a virtue of suffering. They preached self-denial; that all enjoyment was wicked. They urged the people to fast and scourge themselves, and live in dirt and squalor. They coerced them into confessing their so-called sins and, as a penalty for having succumbed to pleasure, ordered them to wear hair shirts. They stigmatised the divinely-given urge of men and women to give physical expression to their lives, as lust. Contrary to nature, they decreed that a man and woman could choose only one partner for life and, even then, cohabit only for the purpose of begetting children. These were "God the Father's" servants. But what a Father! Can you wonder that, right up to Tudor times and even later, a great part of the people doggedly refused to submit to this horrible tyranny and, in secret, continued to worship the True God? It was He who had created them in the beginning and given them their instinct to crave for all the pleasant things in life that He had provided for them. To eat, drink and be merry and to make love without fear.'

Silvia paused to light a cigarette, then went on. 'In ancient times, the True God was accepted and revered in all the great civilisations. Often, a special devotion was shown by sects to various aspects of His power and personified in the many minor gods that made up the Pantheons of Chaldea, Egypt,

India, Greece and Rome; but all acknowledged the supreme entity. It is only in recent centuries that the evil heresies of the Dark Power have gained a formidable foothold in many nations.

'That is why I am urging you to readjust your spiritual values. Because, in a great part of the world those who realised the truth have been forced to conduct their ceremonies in secret, you have been brought up to believe that they worship the powers of Darkness. But that is not so. It is they who continue to carry the torch that they know in their hearts to have been ignited from the source of Eternal Light.'

De Richleau smiled. 'Madame, I congratulate you on having presented an excellent case. I grant you that the early Christians perverted the teachings of Christ, and that the priests of His Church have inflicted untold misery on millions of people. But you have neglected to mention that the Old religion has also been perverted by its priests. Time was when they served the True God well. They were the doctors who healed the sick, the confidants who advised people wisely when in trouble, and they presided over those ceremonies at which the masses could forget the drudgery of every-day life, in feasting, revelry and in giving full licence to their sexual urges. Such Saturnalia were an admirable outlet for the frustrations of mankind. Were they permitted today, addiction to drugs would be almost unknown and one in every seven of the population of the United States would not have to go into homes for the cure of alcoholism or mental instability. But times have changed.

'The power of a faith increases or wanes in accordance with the number of people who believe in it. As the Old religion was gradually suppressed, the number of its true priests dwindled. At length they lost their authority, and by the Middle Ages, had been supplanted by evil persons who promised their followers gratifications they had not earned. That is contrary to the Logos. The cult became one of Darkness, instead of Light.

'It was used by the unscrupulous to inflict pain and loss on their enemies. To gain their ends, people trafficked with demons: the emissaries of Satan the Destroyer who, from the beginning, has waged war against the Powers of Light.

'They served him in a thousand ways to sow dissension and substitute chaos for law and order. In many cases their activities brought about wide-spread misery. To give you one example. It is known to initiates that, on the night before Worcester fight, Cromwell made a pact with the Devil. He bartered his soul for victory and seven years of power. He triumphed and seven years after to the day, the Devil's emissary came to fetch his soul. He died in the midst of the most terrible thunderstorm that had been known in England for a generation. And during his seven years the Devil ruled through him. Never have the people of Britain and Ireland lived through such periods of misery. The proof of that is the frenzied, unalloyed rejoicing with which the whole nation welcomed the return from exile of King Charles. So, you see, misguided as the clergy of the Christian Churches may have been in many matters, they were right in stigmatising this evil power by naming it the Devil.'

For a moment Silvia was silent, then she replied, 'Yet today your Christian clergy are so abysmally ignorant of spiritual matters that they do not even recognise when they see them the signs their predecessors created to represent Good and Evil. You will recall that during the war the whole centre of your city of Coventry in the English Midlands was destroyed by a great German air-raid, and that the ancient cathedral was reduced to a heap of rubble. It is now being rebuilt but on a revolutionary plan. Church architecture always decreed that the high altar should face the East, towards Jerusalem. In the new cathedral, the high altar faces very nearly south. The windows in its sides, instead of throwing light upon the body of the building, are in bays, and so slanted that they leave the altar in darkness. In the great tapestry over the altar, the figure of Jesus Christ has round it, not, as you might suppose, figures of the four Evangelists or Christian Saints, but those of four demons. Upon the spire there is a witches' broomstick and, believe it or not, upon the high altar reposes Satan's crooked cross.'

De Richleau shook his head. 'I have been told so. It seems incredible that such sacrilege should ever have been permitted by the Committee of Bishops, or whoever are responsible for passing such plans; but I have not sought to deny the decadence of the Christian Church.' On a lighter note, he added, 'Supposing that the Devil, as we term the Principle of Evil, really was a person, it would be insulting to assume that so high an intelligence has no sense of humour; so how he would be laughing at Christians bowing down before his cross.'

Giving a little laugh, Silvia said, 'You're right about that. But what is being done at Coventry is only symbolic of the Age of Unbelief. As you have admitted, Christianity is a heresy; and the True God is indestructible. He has withdrawn His countenance from mankind only because of the abuses committed in His name. If His votaries were purged of the evil priests among them, a new and happier era would dawn.'

'It could,' the Duke agreed, 'but such a hope is to build castles in Spain. Everything goes to show that, since the coming of the so-called Age of Reason, the power of Satan had steadily increased. And now the greatest blow of all against peace, prosperity and happiness is being prepared, here in this very place. It is planned to divide the world into two warring camps, so that in every country and city there will be strife and bloodshed between men and women, solely because they have different coloured skins. That must be the inevitable result of inciting the underprivileged races to attempt to impose Black Power.'

'It is clear to me that you need further instruction,' said a firm, male voice.

Amazed that anyone could have entered the room in complete silence, the three friends automatically turned their heads to look over their shoulders. Yet there was no-one there, and the voice seemed to have come from behind Silvia's chair. Swivelling their heads back, they stared at her.

As they did so, a bright light appeared above and beyond her crown of hair. A mauve mist began to swirl round the light as though it was the vortex of a miniature cyclone. The mist thickened and took form, coalescing so that it had the outline of a man. Another moment and it had solidified, so that they found themselves gaping at a tall, slim, handsome human, as much flesh and blood as themselves.

Richard instantly recognised this apparition which had so startlingly materialised. It was the man who, in Buenos Aires had introduced him to von Thumm–Don Salvador Marino.

13

BLACK POWER

Silvia had come to her feet, swung round and made a low curtsy. Don Salvador touched her on the shoulder and, as she rose, said: 'My dear, you did well. Your arguments were cogent and, of course, based on the truth. But the understanding of our friends is still obscured by the beliefs of a lifetime. That they should hold them so stubbornly is regrettable. But I do not despair of bringing them to see reason.'

The three friends had all instantly stood up. Richard, hardly able to believe that he was not dreaming, gasped, 'We met you in Buenos Aires. You . . . you are . . .'

'Yes.' The tall man gave his enchanting smile. 'You knew me there as Don Salvador Marino. But I take precautions against it becoming suspected that I am in any way associated with what goes on here. It was clear to me that you, and your friend Aron, would prove not only persistent in your enquiries about Van Ryn, but were also highly intelligent; so you might possibly have got on his trail. That was why I used von Thumm as an intermediary and had him send you to my charming associate, the "Maiden". Here I am known as the "Prince".'

'Prince of Evil,' Simon burst out, belligerently for him.

'You are mistaken,' came the quiet reply. 'A Prince in the hierarchy of the Outer Circle, yes; but not of evil. Of that I hope to convince you, and . . .' he made a slight bow '. . . your knowledgeable and partially enlightened friend, *Monseigneur le Duc.*'

De Richleau returned the bow and said, 'It would be discourteous to refuse to listen to your argument, Prince. But my own beliefs are based on the Eternal Verities; so are unshakable.'

'About that we shall see. But you have had a long day and, to my regret, suffered severely at the hands of my over-zealous associate, von Thumm. That you must attribute to his "down here" personality, in which he cherishes an abiding hatred for the English. Now it is my will that you enjoy sweet repose. Be good enough to go to your rooms. We will talk of shaping the future of the world tomorrow.'

As he finished speaking, his figure began to shimmer, then dissolved into mauve mist, leaving only the bright light. Then that, too, went out.

Awed into silence by this miraculous spectacle, they said good night to Silvia and went quietly to their rooms. During the day, making so many calls on his fortitude had drained the Duke of energy, and the effect of the vitalising elixir that Silvia had given Simon and Richard had now worn off. Too weary to hold an inquest on the situation in which they found themselves, they undressed, flopped into their beds and were asleep almost immediately.

When they awoke in the morning, they found that it was past ten o'clock. It seemed probable that, from time to time, the green-clad servitors had looked in on them; as, shortly after they had roused, they were brought trays of coffee, cream, hot rolls, butter, honey and fresh fruit. When Richard and Simon had finished eating, they joined de Richleau in his room, and Simon said jerkily:

'Seems we're in a muddle. What are we going to do?'

'Nothing,' replied the Duke quietly. 'You may be sure that we stand no chance of escaping from this place and, even if we could, that would mean abandoning our search for Rex. I have a very strong feeling that he is about here somewhere. All we can do for the time being is to play along with the Prince. Incidentally, his ability to materialise and dematerialise at will is proof that he has a right to his title. His exact rank in the hierarchy I do not yet know. But it must be higher than mine; and that makes me very far from optimistic about our chances of rescuing Rex from his clutches.'

Unhurriedly they shaved, bathed and dressed; then, at midday, walked down the long corridor to the room in which they had spent the previous evening with Silvia. She was sitting there on a sofa, with her little dog Booboo beside her. As they entered, he jumped down, began to bark furiously and raced round them. Ignoring her smiling admonishments, he continued to spring about like a Jack-in-the-box for some minutes. Then, when order was restored, they saw that she had been working on a piece of tapestry. Knowing what he now did about her, it struck Richard as incongruous that she should be employing her leisure in the same way as did many ladies of his acquaintance who lived normal lives; and, after they had all exchanged greetings, he asked to see her work.

She spread it out for him on a nearby stool. It was a large piece, nearing completion. The stitches were fine and even, and she told him it was to cover the back of a sofa at her house in Buenos Aires. The subject was a forest scene, with a blue sky above. In the foreground there was a large figure wearing an ass's head, with many small figures dancing round it, so it was obviously a portrayal of Bottom and the fairies in Shakespeare's *A Midsummer Night's Dream*. But there was one curious thing about it. The fairies had no wings. When he remarked on this anomaly, she looked up at him and laughed:

'That is because fairies never did have wings and, to be strictly accurate, I should have had them drawn very much larger. They were not really "little people", but only somewhat smaller than other races. I mentioned them to you yesterday when we were talking of Joan of Arc. It was her proved connection with the fairies—or "little people" as they were called—that sent her to the stake. The legend that they were minute beings who drank from acorn cups and flew about astride butterflies had its origin in Shakespeare's play.'

He smiled down at her. 'Are you seriously suggesting that there ever were such things as fairies.'

'Indeed I am. They inhabited the British Isles and many areas on the Continent in very early times. When England was conquered by the Romans, those who had lived there migrated to Wales, but many of them came back when the Romans withdrew. They were a race of pigmies with brown skins. That is why they were sometimes called "Brownies". Small communities of them lived in big, round huts, the floors of which were several feet below the level of the earth, and which were roofed with boughs. Their settlements were always on desolate moorland, and they were very secretive and cunning. It was so that they could easily conceal themselves when strangers were about that they always wore green. The ordinary people in the villages went in fear of them, because they could be very malicious and they were deeply steeped in primitive magic. At times they used their powers for good. But for the most part they were hated and dreaded. When the great witch-hunts of early Stuart times were taking place, it was enough for a woman to have been seen begging a favour of the fairies for her to be condemned as a witch, and burned.'

'Presumably they bred like other races, so what became of them?'

'No-one knows for certain. Each group lived only on a few cattle and odds and ends of food that they could steal or blackmail the villagers into giving them. Perhaps their cattle were stricken with some disease and, not being numerous enough to raid the villages for supplies, they died out.'

Putting aside her work, Silvia got drinks for them. As she handed the Duke a glass of water, he said, 'Tell me, what led you to become one of the people whose headquarters this is? I accept that you now believe in all that you said last night, but it does not square with your normal personality. I see no aura of evil about you; yet you are obviously collaborating with others who are evil.'

'You only think them evil because you have not yet seen the Light,' she replied.' But I am a witch, as you would call it, and a very potent one. If you must know, it was the Prince who first intrigued me with the mysteries of the occult. By then I had played every game worth playing, and found life unutterably boring; so I took up the study of the supernatural. That was the real reason why I leased that house in Punta Arenas. There, if I wanted to, I could remain undisturbed for days on end, and I spent many hours in contemplation, learning how to leave my body at will. I practised minor magics, and endured long fasts.' She gave a little laugh. 'That was excellent for my figure, so I killed two birds with one stone.'

'And then you met Rex?' asked the Duke softly.

'Yes, but that was comparatively recently.'

'Now that we are your prisoners will you not tell us what has become of him?'

She shook her head. 'No. That is not my secret. But I can assure you that he had a good reason for disappearing as he did.'

'Perhaps; but why did he make off with all that money from his bank?'

'He needed it to carry out his plans. That is all I mean to tell you, so now let us talk of something else.'

In due course they moved to the far end of the big room, where the table was set for lunch. It had been dark when they had sat round it the previous evening, and the curtains of the big bay window had been drawn. Now they could see the magnificent vista spread below them.

The Inca stronghold was three hundred feet above the lake and, from the window, there was a sheer drop to it. The view was to the north, and the great lake stretched away into the distance, the placid blue waters unruffled by wind or the passage of any craft. On either side rose the lofty mountains, equally innocent of any sign of human activity. The sun glared down, bringing out the stark colours of the earth and water, but within the big room the temperature was no more than pleasantly warm.

After the meal they again talked for a while over coffee and liqueurs, then Silvia said, 'If you wish to stay here, you are welcome; but it is possible that it may be very late tonight before we get to bed, so I am going to rest, and it might be as well if you do, too.'

Accepting her advice, they walked to the end of the long corridor but, instead of separating, they all went into the Duke's room.

As soon as the door was shut behind them, Richard asked, 'What are we going to do? Do you think there is any chance of our escaping from this place?'

'Ner. Not an earthly,' Simon volunteered.

'I agree,' de Richleau concurred. 'And, even if we could, would we want to? It is here that lies the answer to the riddle of Rex's disappearance. I don't think any of us would be willing to throw in his hand until we have solved it. If we do succeed in that, it will then be time enough to plan our next move.'

Simon gave him an uneasy glance. ''Fraid we're in a muddle, whether we learn what's become of Rex or not. Don Salvador—or the Prince, as he calls himself—struck me as a pretty high-powered performer. Think you could get the better of him if it comes to a showdown?'

The Duke spread out his long-fingered, beautifully-shaped hands. 'How can one say? I certainly would not invite a confrontation. The fact that he can materialise shows that his powers are greater than mine. I could only hope that the Lords of Light would come to my assistance. But it may be that, in their wisdom, they have decreed that this evil man should be permitted to continue in his course unchecked for a while yet, until the time appointed for his destruction.'

Separating, they lay down on their beds. De Richleau slept, recharging his body with the electricity without which it would inevitably break down. The others dozed, their minds going back and forth like squirrels in a cage; at one moment conscious that they were actually in an ancient Inca fortress and the prisoners of Satanists; at others believing the whole series of events into which they had been drawn no more than a nerve-racking dream.

By six o'clock they were fully awake. They refreshed themselves with a wash and dressed ready to face whatever the evening might bring. Shortly afterwards Pedro came to summon them; but he did not take them to the room in which they had talked and eaten two meals with Silvia. Instead, he led them down a flight of stairs and ushered them into a room that was evidently the Prince's sanctum.

As in the other rooms, the ceiling consisted of irregular, perfectly dovetailed blocks of stone. But it had a carpet so thick that the feet sank into it. All four walls were lined with books, mostly in old, calf bindings. There was a fireplace, in which logs were burning, and several big arm-chairs. Although there was no ceiling light, wall brackets or standard lamps, the room was pervaded by a warm, soft glow.

The room was empty. While the others sat down and helped themselves to cigarettes from a low table of highly-polished malachite, de Richleau browsed among the books. There were several copies of the *Mallus Maleficarum* and of comparatively modern works, such as Aleister Crowley's *Magick* and *The Doctrine and Ritual of Magic* by Eliphas Levi. But the Duke was much more interested to see books traditionally famous, yet no copies of which were believed still to exist. There were a *Clavicule of Solomon*, a *Sword of Moses* by Abraham the Jew, *The Red Book of Appin*, a *Safer YeSua*—the oldest known Kabalistic work, an *Almagest of Ptolemy*, and a *Grimoire of Pope Honorius*.

He was still studying them when the door opened and the Prince, followed by Silvia, came in. He was carrying a beautiful blue Persian cat. Silvia, as usual, had Booboo under her arm and, sitting down with him in her lap, she lit a cigarette. The Prince, with a gesture that was in part courteous, but had just a suspicion of haughty command, signed to de Richleau to settle himself in another of the armchairs; then, putting down the cat, he took up a position in front of the fire, with his hands clasped behind his back.

Anyone entering the room without knowledge of the place and its occupants, would have taken it for a cheerful domestic scene—perhaps in a French château, or a modernised English castle.

As Richard looked at the Prince, he again thought how extraordinarily handsome he was. His thin, bronzed face, under the slightly wavy black hair, portrayed health and purpose. His large, dark eyes radiated vitality. His beautifully-modelled mouth, with its very red lips, would have made most women long for his kisses. The tilt of his head, his prominent nose and high, arched eyebrows conveyed his arrogance and assumption that any command he issued would be instantly obeyed.

Having looked steadily at each of them in turn, he said: 'The Maiden put the case for worshipping the True God to you very ably last night. That Mr Eaton and Mr Aron should have rejected it does not particularly surprise me, because they have no long-time memory and their knowledge of the great truths is elementary. But you, my dear Duke, are in a very different category. You have only to elevate your ego to the astral and, from your Vase of Memory, you can recall your past lives. Among them was that during which you were a priest of Ra in Egypt, another in which as a Roman Pro-Consul you were initiated into the mysteries, and many others in which you never questioned the true faith. Last night you even admitted to Silvia that, in so-called pagan times, the people were very much happier and mentally healthier before they fell under the domination of the Christian Church. Why, then, do you now reject the beliefs you held through so many centuries?'

'I thought I made that plain,' de Richleau replied quietly. 'It is because, just as the teachings of Jesus Christ were distorted and used by ambitious, ignorant men as a vehicle to acquire worldly power, so the old faith was distorted and used by evil men as a vehicle to acquire worldly power.'

The Prince shrugged. 'With regard to the Old Faith you are wrong. Of that I hope to convince you. About the future of your companions I am indifferent; but you have acquired both power and wisdom, so would prove a great asset to the cause I serve. However, for the moment I will do no more than point out to you the obvious. In every priesthood, there have always been good and bad men. Many hundred witches were sent to the stake unjustly, but some abused their power to do harm. That does not affect the fact that those of high rank have always adhered to the fundamental principle of serving the best interests of mankind.

'My present purpose is to disabuse you of the belief that the movement to achieve Black Power has for its object the permanent destruction of law and order. The world is sick, and every year becoming sicker. You have only to look into the future, as I have done, to become aware that, unless some drastic measure is taken to prevent it, in the sixties and the seventies civilisation will begin to disintegrate. Money will lose its value. Famine will come to India, Africa and South America. The young—discontented, rudderless and fearing that, at any moment, their lives will be cut short by the use of nuclear bombs—will rise in despair and wrath against the older generation whom it holds responsible for having brought about a state of things in which they can see no security or hope of lasting happiness. Ultimately they will rise in rebellion and overturn the feeble, fumbling Governments. But they will prove incapable of replacing them, so chaos will ensue.

'The age-old remedy for discontent among a people is for their rulers to pick a quarrel with a neighbour and start a war. Personal frustrations are then forgotten in a surge of patriotism that unites all classes in a country. But the whole world is sick, so nothing short of another world war could have the desired effect. And a third world war we dare not risk. The danger of the whole earth becoming uninhabitable owing to nuclear missiles is too great.

'Our problem can be solved, though. Raising the flag for Black Power will do it. You are, of course, quite right in that it will mean street-fighting, murder, arson and looting in every city. But the resulting death, destruction and suffering caused will be incomparably less than would result from another world war. Even one in which only conventional weapons were used.

'"Out of Evil cometh Good". I repeat "Out of Evil cometh Good". We must inflict the ills of bloodshed, terror and loss upon the people, in order to arrest the decline of civilisation and bring them back to a healthy, progressive way of life. You may liken this operation to an inoculation for yellow fever. For a day or two it makes one wretchedly ill, but it can save one from a terrible death.

'One of your fears, no doubt, is that the movement will succeed so completely that the white races will be overwhelmed and those members of them who survive will be made slaves by the black races, in revenge for what they themselves have suffered in the past. Dismiss that thought. There is not the least danger of such a situation developing. It is, of course, the hope of those poor, deluded wretches of whom we are making use down in the settlement. But they are fanatics who cherish an idle dream. It is certain that the whites, with their machine-guns, tear gas and tanks, will triumph everywhere. The actual fighting will be very brief; very extensive damage and loss of property is bound to take place, but the loss of life will be no greater than would occur in a minor war, and that is acceptable in view of the final outcome at which we aim.

'That final outcome is Equal Rights. Not Equal Rights as mouthed by hypocritical politicians to win votes, but a genuine equality in which men of all colours will regard one another with respect and with open-hearted friendship. As I have said, the riots will soon be put down. It is through the events to follow that we shall reach our goal. Black Power will have organised world-wide underground. There will be secret sabotage squads in every city. Fires will be started to burn down many of the finest buildings; bombs will be placed in air-liners and oil-tankers; leading statesmen will be assassinated; trains will be wrecked; the wives and daughters of important people kidnapped. No-one will be safe, and everyone will walk in fear during this reign of terror.

'The white governments will take reprisals. Hostages will be taken and later shot in batches. They will set up huge concentration camps to confine hundreds of suspects. In desperation they may wipe out whole Negro communities. But they cannot possibly imprison all the millions of people who have coloured skins.

'The acts of violence will continue. Every day the situation will deteriorate. People will no longer dare to travel. Communications will have been cut, trade will have been brought to a standstill, factories will lie idle, cities will be threatened with starvation. In the end the white governments will be forced to capitulate. In the meantime, as in a war, the younger generation will have been purged of its degenerate tendencies. Wise leaders will emerge and insist that the only way to save civilisation is to agree to the just demands of the coloured races. Thus we shall bring about a new era, and the real Brotherhood of Man.'

All the time the Prince had been speaking, his dark eyes had never left the Duke's face; but de Richleau knew that the eyes of such a man could send out most powerful hypnotic suggestion; so, to avoid the danger of falling under it, he had kept his own eyes cast down. He lifted them only when the Prince put the question to him:

'Now do you see the error into which you have fallen, in believing that we, who serve the Old God, have entered into a conspiracy for evil? The explanation I have given will, I trust, cause you to re-orient your beliefs, and join us.'

For a full moment there was silence, then de Richleau replied, 'I have been fascinated by your dissertation, Prince, and there is much truth in what you have said. Two world wars within a quarter of a century have destroyed the foundations of society. Those who returned from them have acquired a new, and not altogether desirable freedom. Instead of pursuing a normal course of marrying and rearing a family, a high proportion of girls and men had become promiscuous. Although great numbers of them were scarcely out of their teens, they refused to submit again to parental control, or take advice from people older than themselves. They had become used to danger and excitement, and continued to crave the latter. But their new independence gets them nowhere. Owing to their frustration, crime has increased to a degree never before known; addiction to drugs, almost unheard of before the first world war has, in both Europe and the United States, become a menace; a gap is developing between the generations which, in the future, could bring about violence.

'Yes, the world is sick. But many a patient has been killed by a bad doctor. Sometimes it is better to let nature run its course, and the body works the poison out of the system. The medicine you propose would, in my view, eat away the tissues to a degree that would give the patient no hope of recovery.'

For a moment the Prince's handsome face was contorted by a spasm of anger. Then he regained control of himself and said, 'Then you persist in your blindness? You refuse to give us your aid?'

The Duke nodded. 'I do so because, all else apart, there is a great fallacy in your predictions. Even given that dozens of acts of sabotage, carried out day after day, would eventually force the white governments to accept the terms of the coloured leaders, that could bring about no genuine rapprochement. Their cities half-ruined, their trade destroyed, innumerable cases in which loved ones had been killed or injured through the activities of your saboteurs, would leave the white populations harbouring an unquenchable bitterness against the coloured. The coloureds, too, having for year after year to see the bravest among them become victims of the whites' furious reprisals, would be equally unlikely to forgive and forget.

'There would ensue no Brotherhood of Man. But you would have done the work of your master, Satan, well. Yes, I said Satan the Lord of Misrule. The Destroyer, whose objective it has always been to bring about disruption to such a degree that mankind will be plunged into darkness and misery.'

Again the Prince revealed his seething rage. His hands trembled and his mouth worked, until he rasped out:

'I can use your help, and I mean to have it. Since you refuse to give it willingly, I must make you. I have already said that I am indifferent to the fate of your friends. Either you will agree to serve me, or I will send them back to von Thumm, to vent his sadistic hate on.'

Simon drew in a sharp breath. Richard's hands were clasped and he clenched them until the knuckles stood out white, while waiting for the Duke's answer. It seemed an age in coming, then he said:

'I dearly love my friends. If you carry out your threat, thinking of them in that man's hands will cause me greater mental torture than they will suffer physically. But this issue is far too great to allow the fate of individuals to weigh in the scale. And, if it is decreed that they should forfeit their present lives, both they and I will be fortified by the knowledge that their martyrdom will be rewarded in lives to come.'

The Prince's dark eyes narrowed as he stared at the Duke. A silence ensued, so tense that it could be felt. At length he said, 'Where I have failed, perhaps another may succeed.' Then, raising his left hand aloft, he snapped his first finger and thumb together.

For perhaps three minutes none of them moved or uttered a word. Then the door opened, and framed in it stood Rex Van Ryn.

14

THE HORRORS THAT CAME BY NIGHT

Rex's friends had expected that, if they did find him at the Sala de Uyuni, it would have been as a prisoner, held there against his will for some reason they could not guess, by the Satanists into whose hands he had fallen; a prey to great distress and, perhaps, dreadful thought, even mentally deranged after being exposed to the horrors that his captors could bring from the Outer Circle.

But here he was, a splendid figure of a man, wearing the easy but expensive clothes that rich Americans favour when they are at leisure, his slightly curly hair neatly brushed, exuding as ever abundant health and bonhomie. He gave them a delighted smile and said:

'Well now, it's certainly good to see you folks again.'

They had all come to their feet. Simon's jaw had dropped and his short-sighted eyes were open to their maximum extent. Richard stared at his old friend with a puzzled frown. De Richleau said:

'We have spent quite some time and considerable exertion in endeavouring to find you, Rex. Now that we have, I am much relieved to see you do not appear to have suffered from your recent experiences.'

Rex beamed at him. 'No, I'm as fit as they make 'em, and haven't a worry in the world. I'm only sorry that you three should have been so concerned about me, and have come all this way to satisfy yourselves that I hadn't got out of orbit without good reason.'

'That we have yet to see,' the Duke returned sharply.

The Prince smiled and said, 'Rex will soon set your minds at rest about that. Since you would not accept the truth from me whom, I admit, you have no reason to trust, I felt that you might alter your views when you had talked with Rex, knowing as you must his complete integrity.'

'If he can tell us that he has freely subscribed to your views, I shall be amazed.'

'I take it you are referring to the Black Power movement?' Rex said, sitting down in an armchair and stretching out his long legs.

'Yes,' the Prince told him. 'I have explained to your friends how important it is to cure the people of the sickness that has resulted from two world wars and in that, they . . . or at least the Duke who, I assume, speaks for them . . . agrees with me. Where we are still at issue is whether Black Power would prove a remedy which would not only stop the rot but, ultimately, bring about the Brotherhood of Man.'

Rex turned to the Duke. 'I know that on many questions you're a real old-fashioned die-hard. You'd like to see Britishers still running a third of the world, and playing polo in their off-time, with a Two-Power Navy to back them up. But you've liberal views where human relations are concerned. Surely, if it lay with you, you'd not deny coloured folk equal rights?'

'My dear Rex,' de Richleau gave a sad little smile, 'amazed as I am to find you here, being used as a cat's paw by our, er, host, I have no objection to discussing these matters with you. As you say, my views in many ways are old-fashioned. With regard to the colour question, they were well expressed by a character in Maurice Edelman's excellent book: "I welcome the black man as my brother, but not as my brother-in-law". In other words, I am against mixed marriages, because the children resulting from them are saddled with a terrible handicap; but I do not regard coloured people as inferior to whites, and would like to see them enjoy a true equality with us.'

'It's not for you or me to adjudicate on mixed marriages. That's for the individuals concerned. But you've admitted my point in principle.'

'I have, but I am unshakably opposed to the Prince's plan for bringing it about.'

'Why?'

'Because it would cause immense suffering to millions of people and, in the end, fail to achieve its object.'

'Sure it will entail suffering. Riots, street-fighting, arson, murder, the lot. But you can't make omelettes without breaking eggs and, when our omelette's cooked, it'll be a better world.'

'I disagree. After your movement has brought about the deaths of thousands of people and ruined the lives of countless others, no permanent reconciliation between whites and blacks will be possible. Only a world in ruins will be left, with its inhabitants scraping a bare existence; each side blaming the other for its fate and obsessed with bitterness and hatred.'

'Oh come!' Rex gave a laugh. 'You can think that only because you haven't gotten the full picture. For a time the whites will naturally show resentment. That's to be expected. But they'll come round when the coloureds get going with their stuff.'

'Stuff? What do you mean by "stuff"?'

'Why, making good the damage that they've done. The white governments will be stunned, nearly bankrupt and incapable of clearing up the mess. But the coloureds will have both money and organised labour. They'll move in, rebuild the gutted buildings, erect refugee camps for the homeless, and become the source from which all blessings flow. Once the whites realise that and that the coloureds are really on the level, prejudice will disappear. They'll let bygones be bygones, and genuine friendship all over will result.'

'You are talking through your hat,' said Richard sharply. 'Even if you could succeed in organising hundreds of thousands of blacks into labour corps to restore the *status quo*, where is the money coming from to feed them, let alone purchase the materials needed for a world-wide rebuilding programme?'

Rex laughed again. 'We'll have it, old chap. Not a doubt about that. Remember, we don't intend to blow the works for fifteen or maybe twenty years. We have already started our fund and have over a hundred thousand contributors who are each anti-ing up a few dimes a week. Nearly half the workers down on the Sala are employed in increasing the number of subscribers. In a few years' time, we'll number them by the million.'

'Was it to support this fund that you stole a million from your bank?' asked the Duke.

'Well . . .' Rex hesitated a second. 'Yes. But we're not relying only on contributions. Maybe you know how the Bolsheviks raised the money to organise the Russian Revolution? They made armed raids on the banks. Stalin began his career as one of the bank robbers for the Party. We've started that already in a small way. But our big time for that will come after the blow-up, when our sabotage campaign is in full swing. With law and order gone for six, there'll be any number of opportunities to lift cash from the banks and hold up vans carrying pay-rolls for big factories. Don't you worry. We'll have plenty of money to replace everything we have destroyed, and lots over to distribute to white people who have been reduced homeless by the upheaval.'

De Richleau shook his head. 'Rex, my dear friend, I can only suppose that you have fallen completely under the influence of these evil people. Not consciously, of course, but by their exerting their dark power to distort your mind. They are using you as their mouthpiece. Otherwise you would never countenance this terrible plot to bring wholesale anarchy into the world. It is totally against your nature and everything you have ever stood for.'

Suddenly the Prince spoke. His handsome face had become contorted with rage. In a spate of berserk fury, he stormed at de Richleau:

'So you refuse to be persuaded! You have the impudence to defy me! To thwart my will! I have been patient with you. Given you an opportunity to play an important role in our great crusade. To use the powers you have to further the intentions of the Old God—the True God. And you have spurned it. Very well, then. I will show you who is master here. I will break your stubborn spirit and force you to obey me. You shall spend a night that you will never forget, and in the morning you will be chastened.'

Rex had come to his feet. 'No, Prince,' he pleaded. 'Have a heart. These are old friends of mine. What you have in mind might send them off their rockers. Let them have a night's sleep and, maybe, tomorrow they'll see how wrong they are.'

'Silence!' stormed the Prince. 'They need a lesson. If they survive it, they will be eager to do my bidding for fear of the power I wield. If they have gone mad by morning, no matter. I can do without them.' As he spoke he raised his hand and snapped his fingers twice.

In less than a minute the door was opened by an immensely fat Babu. Behind him stood two of the silent, green-clad servitors. With a sweeping gesture, the Prince indicated the Duke, Richard and Simon, as he snapped:

'Kaputa, take these people down to the Hall of Divination and leave them to face what I shall send them there.'

De Richleau knew it would be futile to resist. Without a glance at the Prince or Rex, he walked towards the door, Simon and Richard followed. The Babu squeezed past them and led the way along several corridors, down two flights of stone stairs and into a dimly lit, empty, circular room some forty feet in diameter.

The ceiling was low, not more than eight feet high, and the floor was an elaborate mosaic of an eight-pointed star within two circles that contained many strange hieroglyphics. The walls were of smooth, dead-black stone, undecorated except at the four corners. At these, standing out boldly in white were the reversed swastika which Hitler had taken for his emblem, the Star of David upside down, the Mohammedan Crescent with its horns pointing at the floor, and the crooked Cross. The place was dimly lit. As soon as they were inside it, Kaputa closed the door behind them.

The Duke gave a heavy sigh. 'My friends, I am afraid we are in for a very bad time. All we can do is to pray for fortitude and hope that we may survive.' Standing between them, he put his arms about their shoulders and drew them to him, then he went on:

'We shall not kneel. Only slaves make supplication in that attitude of humility. In each of us resides a tiny spark of the Eternal Light, which makes us the little brothers of the Lords of Light; so we address them as children who hope one day to become their equals. After me, repeat in silence the words I am about to say.'

For the next few minutes he spoke quietly and clearly, sending his winged words out into the silent night.

When he had finished his appeal for succour, he said, 'We must now prepare to face the evil entities the Prince will send against us. I would give half my remaining years to have here the holy water, horse-shoes, candles and other things that I collected while in Santiago and which we had to leave in the aircraft on the Sala. Then we could have made a pentacle. But at least the mosaics on which we are standing do not make a Satanic diagram. It is an Inca calendar and the two circles, together with what I have here, will at least protect us from lesser horrors endowed with little intelligence.'

As he spoke, he took from his pocket a handkerchief in which were wrapped two cone-shaped objects, an inch and a half thick and three inches in height. 'These,' he said, 'are salt-containers. Fearing that we might have to face some such ordeal as this. I managed to get away unobserved with one at dinner last night and another off my breakfast tray. Salt being essential to the well-being of man, is anathema to all entities sent by Satan to do men harm. We shall have to use it very sparingly; but I think there is just enough to sprinkle round the inner of the two circles on the floor here. A circle in itself is some protection, and this inner one must be about nine or ten feet in diameter, so there will be ample room for the three of us inside it.'

Exercising great care, he spread very thinly the grains of salt along the line that formed the circle; then, although he had nothing with which to write the letters, he traced just inside the circle, with the forefinger of his right hand, the words: IESUS + NAZARENUS + REX + IUDAEORUM + .

He had hardly completed this preparation when the dim light became still dimmer, until it had faded completely and they were plunged into total darkness. Drawing the two others to him, the Duke sat down with them in the centre of the circle and said:

'Now, there is nothing we can do but wait. I need hardly remind you that, in no circumstances, should you allow yourselves to be lured out of the circle, or even move more than a foot or so in any direction, in case, inadvertently, your foot makes a breach in the ring of salt.'

For a while they sat in silence, back to back, their legs stretched out in front of them. The stone floor was very hard and uncomfortable. Every now and then they shifted their position to ease one buttock or the other. All of them were conscious that it was gradually getting colder. From previous experience they knew that it was not a natural drop in the temperature, but that the place was becoming pervaded with the chill of evil which always precedes a Satanic manifestation.

The cold increased until their teeth began to chatter. A faint glow appeared near the place on the wall where they had seen the upside-down crescent. Its radiance increased until it lit the room with a reddish light. Their hearts began to beat faster as they watched it, expecting that it would take the form of a demon conjured up from Hell. Instead, black bars appeared across it. The light coalesced into flickering flames above them, and they saw that it was a glowing brazier heaped with red-hot coals. But no heat from it penetrated to the ice-cold circle.

As they stared at it, they yearned to warm their hands and limbs at its tempting glow, but they knew it to be a device to lure them outside their frail defences. Rigidly they kept their places and the fire in the iron brazier began to burn down until the big room was again in semi-darkness.

They still had their eyes on the brazier when, behind them, there came a slithering sound. Swivelling their heads, they peered in that direction. A creature was squatting outside the circle. It was as large as a medium-sized turtle, and had a body of that shape; but, instead of a shell, its humped back was covered with rough, pink skin which gave out a pale light. The thing was sitting still, but the skin on its back slowly pulsated so that little ridges rippled along it. Low down in front, it had a long slit that was obviously a mouth; from it there drooled a yellow liquid. Above the mouth there rose what, at first glance, appeared to be two nine-inch-long horns; but, when looked at again, could be seen to have beady eyes at the extremities. Slowly they swayed from side to side, obviously examining the inmates of the circle.

Suddenly the creature hunched itself and jumped. It came down with a plop, leaving at the place where it had been a horrid oval of phosphorescent slime. Slowly it began to advance towards the circle, with the undulating movement of a worm. As the pendulant underlip of its mouth came in contact with the salt, it gave a loud hiss, began rapidly to expand until it was twice its former size, then burst into a thousand writhing fragments, leaving behind a stench like that of a charnel house.

For a time, nothing happened. The three friends continued to shiver in the pentacle, now and again glancing apprehensively from side to side. The brazier still glowed, giving them just sufficient light to make out vaguely the perverted symbols of Christianity, Islam, Judaism and the Oldest Faith painted on the walls.

It was Richard who was the first to see a thickening of the shadows under the swastika. Quickly he drew the attention of the others to it. Straining their eyes, they saw a long patch, stretching a good twelve feet along the floor. Slowly, it materialised into a great snake. Suddenly it began to move, circling the pentacle. Every few yards it jerked to a halt, swerved its head inwards and darted out its long, forked tongue.

Instinctively the three friends came to their feet. Shuffling round they faced each attempt by the serpent to penetrate their defence. Seven times it made the circle. They were no longer conscious of the cold. Fear had caused the sweat to break out on their foreheads. Shifting round and round to keep the great beast in full view had begun to make them giddy. Simon tripped and fell to his knees. At that moment the snake reared up on its tail, so that its head was a foot above them. Its jaws were wide open, its poison fangs glinted in the light from the brazier. Richard dragged Simon back on to his feet. As he did so, de Richleau cried in a loud voice, 'Avaunt thee, Satan!' The head of the snake recoiled as though it had been smashed by a giant, unseen hand. It fell writhing to the floor, and dissolved into a cloud of evil-smelling smoke.

After that they were not troubled for a long time. In spite of the cold they began to feel drowsy. At length, a slight snore from Simon told the others that he had fallen asleep. De Richleau gave him a quick shake and said:

'Simon, you should know better than to let yourself drop off. Unless we remain alert, you may be certain that they will make some new move that will take us by surprise and we shall fall into a trap.'

'Sorry,' Simon muttered. 'Seems as though we've been here for hours. What's the time?'

The Duke glared at the luminous dial of his watch. 'It is only half past eleven, so there is still a long time to go until dawn. And, as it is eternal night down here, they may not cease their attacks on us even then.'

'Half past eleven,' muttered Richard. 'And we've had no dinner. Although we had a good lunch, I'm so hungry I could eat a horse.'

As he spoke, the door of the room opened and a table loaded with food rolled in. On it there were smoked salmon and lobsters, jellied eggs, a tongue, a York ham, trays of hors-d'œuvres, avocados, globe artichokes, snipe, pheasants, a duck, a baron of beef, steak and kidney and chicken pies, and a fine variety of puddings.

At this sight, the hunger they felt far exceeded anything that could normally have resulted from the fact that they had not eaten for ten hours. As they craned forward, eagerly eyeing these good things, the saliva ran hot in their mouths. Beside the table there materialised a tall, thin figure clad in impeccable evening clothes. All three of them recognised him instantly as a friend of many years. It was Vachelli, who had looked after them in the twenties at the Berkely, and long since moved to become the maître d'hôtel at the Savoy Grill. Smiling at them he said:

'Good-evening, gentlemen. What can I order for you? Paté, or *melone con prosciutto* perhaps, to start with. Then, for His Grace, *Canard Montmorencey*, for Mr Eaton two *beccasine* flown lightly through the flames, and for Mr Aron his favourite *Omelette Arnold Bennett*. To follow, some wood strawberries brought in by air from France this morning, with marraschino ice.'

Richard had risen unsteadily to his feet. Simon was about to follow. De Richleau said sharply, 'You fools! Do you not realise that all this is illusion? And in this they have overreached themselves. To tempt us with real food would have been possible; but not to produce Vachelli. That is no more than a likeness of him. He is ten thousand miles away in London.'

Almost sobbing with frustration, the others covered their eyes with their hands and sank back on to the hard floor.

Again, for what seemed a long time, they sat back to back, staring into the semi-darkness, wondering with trepidation what new horror or temptation they would next be called on to face. It came in the form of a multitude of small spiders. To the alarm of the inmates of the circle, the insects did not attempt to cross the thin barrier of salt, but fell inside it from the roof. Within a few minutes they were crawling with them, and the little brutes had a most powerful bite.

Jumping up they slapped at their hands and faces, ran their fingers through their hair and brushed down arms and legs, in an endeavour to kill or throw off their small tormentors. The floor inside the pentacle was soon swarming with them. They ran across their victims' shoes, up their socks and bit into their calves. Cursing, Richard stamped about, trying to shake them down. Inadvertently, he put one foot outside the pentacle.

With incredible swiftness, a monster materialised beside him. It had claws and wings like a dragon. Where its head should have been there sprouted tentacles like those of an octopus. One of them whipped round Richard's ankle. He gave a shout of terror.

The Duke swung round. In case the circle became breached, he had kept handy the handkerchief in which he had wrapped the salt containers. It still had in it a little salt which had spilled. Pulling this handkerchief from his pocket, he threw it at the tentacles of the beast. They flared up in a sheet of blue flame. It scorched Richard's face, but his leg was free. Simon pulled him back to safety. Almost weeping with relief, he slid to his knees, while the monster continued to burn, the smoke from it giving off the filthy smell of a cesspit. Meanwhile, the little spiders, having performed the task for which they had been sent, had vanished.

From this crisis it took them some while to recover. They were now very tired and knew that their resistance was being worn down. Now and again de Richleau looked up at the roof, fearing that some evil entity far more dangerous than the spiders might emerge from it. But the next visitation to which they were subjected was a very different one. The light increased until they could see the whole big room quite clearly. Then the door swung open and framed in it stood Miranda.

She was dressed in the black lace dress she had worn on the night that Simon had taken her out to dinner in Buenos Aires. But there was something different about her blue eyes. They no longer had the fixed, unseeing stare due to near-blindness. Instead they were clear, bright and beamed with happiness. In one hand she held a tray with three glasses, in the other she was carrying a large jug that was full of what looked like a delicious wine cup.

De Richleau drew a sharp breath. Richard gaped, and Simon cried, 'Miranda! Your eyes! You're no longer blind. You can see.'

She smiled. 'Yes, darling. They flew me up here from Santiago yesterday and the Prince has restored my sight. Isn't it wonderful? He has sent me to tell you that, as you have resisted all the horrors of the past few hours, he won't torment you any more, but give you another chance to think things over. And I know how thirsty you must be, so I've brought you a lovely drink.'

During the past hour thirst had plagued them even more than hunger. Their throats were parched. Their thickened tongues felt like lumps of leather in their mouths. Beaming with delight, Simon took a step forward. The Duke grabbed him by the arm and pulled him back, gasping hoarsely:

'No, Simon. No! That is not Miranda. It is a fiend who has taken her form. This is another trap. One step outside the pentacle and you will perish.'

Tears started to Simon's eyes. Overcome with bitter disappointment, he collapsed. At the sight of him crouching with bowed head on the floor, Miranda's lovely face became transformed with hate and rage. Slowly her figure faded, and once more the room dimmed to semi-darkness.

Hungry, thirsty and again shivering with cold, they huddled together in the circle, now feeling that this night of terror would never end. Filled with dread that, long before morning they must succumb, they waited for their next ordeal.

They were roused from their semi-torpor by a distant scream. It came again, this time louder. The screams continued. Suddenly the door flew open. A woman hurled herself through it. Although the light was still dim, all three of them recognised her immediately. No-one who had seen Richard's wife, that pocket Venus, Marie-Lou, could easily forget her small but perfect figure and lovely, heart-shaped face. It now portrayed stark fear, and the reason was at once apparent. A huge, naked Negro was in swift pursuit of her. Him, too, they recognised. It was Lincoln B. Glasshill.

The shock of his wife's sudden appearance and the peril she was in caused Richard to forget time, place and the danger of his own situation. Giving a loud cry, he sprang forward to intercept the Negro. Simon was still crouching on the floor; but, at the sound of the screams, he had raised his head. His mind still filled with the vision of Miranda and the snare into which he had so nearly fallen, he threw his arms round Richard's legs and brought him crashing to the ground.

By then Glasshill had caught up with Marie-Lou. Seizing her, he swung her round and began to tear the clothes from her body. As she strove to fight him off, she began to scream again:

'Richard! Richard! Save me! Save me!'

Still struggling with Simon, Richard gasped, 'Let me go! Damn you, let me go!' Kicking himself free, he staggered to his feet. But now the Duke came into action. Drawing back his fist, he hit Richard hard beneath the jaw. Richard gave a gulp, sagged at the knees and rolled over, unconscious. An instant later, the figures of Marie-Lou and the powerful Negro had vanished.

After a few minutes Richard began to moan, then came to. Once more the three friends huddled together, their nerves taut almost to breaking point, and all but exhausted. The big room was again silent, except for the sound of their heavy breathing. Many minutes passed while they knelt there, looking constantly from side to side, in grim anticipation of the next attack.

At length, the door swung open. This time they did not stir, but gazed with fear in their eyes at the tall figure that stepped through into the room. It was Rex Van Ryn.

Putting his finger to his lips, he said in a low voice, 'Not a word. Come on. Follow me, and I'll get you out of here.'

The Duke managed a laugh that held a sneer. 'Is it likely? Surely your Prince must realise by now the stupidity of repeating this game since we have shown so clearly that we are not to be trapped by it.'

Rex frowned. 'I don't know what he's been up to. Looks like you've been given a mighty bad time. But not to worry. It's over now. Come on.'

'You filth, get out!' Richard shouted. 'Get back to Hell where you belong.'

Rex swiftly raised a hand. 'Quiet, for God's sake, or you'll wake some of those bloody Satanists. Then I'll never be able to get you away.'

Simon's words came thickly from his dried-up mouth. 'Get us out of this circle, you mean, so your Infernal Master can set his ghouls upon us. No thanks.'

The light was just strong enough for the white, thinly-spaced grains of salt which made a trail round the inner circle of the Inca calendar to be seen. Looking down, Rex grasped their significance, and said, 'If this wasn't so darn serious, it 'ud be a laugh. I guess he's been sending ab-humans to lure you out of your fortress, and you think I'm one.'

'You are,' croaked the Duke, making the sign of the Cross, 'Avaunt thee, Satan.'

To the amazement of the three, instead of wilting and disappearing under the anathema, Rex burst out, 'You bloody fools! Can't you tell a live man from an apparition?' Then he stepped over the barrier of salt into the circle.

15

THE RAISING OF THE WHIRLWIND

Simon and Richard cowered back. Nearly exhausted from the horrors they had faced earlier in the night, they now felt that the end had come. It could only be that the Prince had exerted his powers to the utmost to enable this manifestation in the form of their friend to cross the barrier. They expected that, within a moment, the smiling face would become distorted with malevolence and hatred, that the form would suddenly turn into some monstrous creature that would seize upon and destroy them. Sweating with fear, they shrank away, their arms extended to fend off this menace that the Prince had called up from Hell.

But de Richleau stood his ground. The figure before them had not only ignored the sign of the Cross and his abjuration. It had actually stepped on the line of salt spread round the circle. For him that could mean only one thing.

With a gasp he thrust out his hand, grasped Rex by the arm and cried. 'Then it's really you!'

Next moment he laughed and hurried on, 'After the apparitions we've seen tonight, I just couldn't believe it. Oh, thank God, you've come to us! We couldn't have held out much longer. But from the way you behaved this evening, I thought . . .'

'No time to talk of that now,' Rex cut in. 'We're not out of the wood yet, by a long sight. And we've not a moment to lose. If anyone is awake and challenges us, leave everything to me. Come on now.'

Hardly able to take in the fact that they had survived the night's terrible ordeal, and now stood a good chance of escaping, they followed Rex as quietly as they could out of the circular room and along a succession of corridors until they came through a doorway to a courtyard. Eagerly they breathed in the fresh, cold air and looked upwards to see the myriad of stars above.

On the further side of the courtyard a flight of over a hundred steps led downward. They were very steep, broken in places, and had no handrail alongside them. One false step and anyone could have hurtled head over heels to the bottom. With Rex still leading and the others, each with a hand on the shoulder of the one preceding him, they made the perilous descent in safety.

A walk of two hundred yards brought them to the airstrip. It was in darkness, and no-one was about. Telling the others to wait where they were, Rex boarded one of the two smaller passenger 'planes and flashed a torch on the instrument board in the cockpit. A moment later, he was back on the ground and said in a low voice:

'No good. She's practically out of gas. And we daren't refuel her. The noise would rouse those lousy Andeans. Several of them sleep in that hut near the pump. I'll take a look at the other. If she's dry too, we're scuppered.'

Anxious moments passed while he clambered into the other aircraft and made a swift survey of her fitness for flight. Then he leaned out and beckoned to them. When they had scrambled aboard, and settled themselves in the bucket seats, he said:

'She's nearly full, thank God. Ample gas to take us to the coast. But I dare not attempt a night flight through the mountains. We'd sure end up as deaders. But I can fly us across to Potosi, the old Inca city south-east of the lake. I went over there out of curiosity not long ago. It's now an area of ruins, with only a handful of peasants squatting in some of the courtyards, where they've put up shacks and lean-tos. Plenty of places there where we can lie up for the rest of the night. Then, come dawn, we'll fly down to Iquique.'

The others caught his last words only indistinctly, as he was already revving up the engine. It vibrated for two minutes, then the aircraft took off smoothly. The moon was now in its first quarter. Its light silvered the placid water of the lake and, as they flew over the land on the far bank, was sufficient to throw up groups of trees here and there in a flattish landscape. They had been in the air for barely a quarter of an hour when Rex brought the 'plane down with the expertise of long practice. For a couple of hundred yards it tore through low scrub, then came to a halt.

As they were about to climb out, Richard said huskily, 'My throat's like a lime-kiln. I'd give fifty quid for a drink—even a glass of water.'

'Me, too,' agreed Simon. 'So dry I can hardly swallow.'

'Soon put that right,' Rex replied cheerfully. 'These aircraft are always furnished with supplies for several days, in case they have to make a forced landing in this bloody wilderness. Look in the tail, and you'll find lots of liquor.'

Without losing a moment, Richard and Simon opened up the several small hampers containing emergency stores of tinned food and drink.

Hastily pushing aside bottles of Pisco and Brandy, they seized on some Coca-Cola and, together with the Duke, avidly quenched their thirst.

Rex had left the aircraft. When they joined him on the ground, he pointed to a low rise about half a mile away. On it there was a patch of black, one end of which made a sharp angle which stood out against the sky line. As they looked in that direction, he said:

'We're in luck. I doubted whether at night I'd be able to locate that place so as to land fairly near it. But it's sure the building I had in mind for us to lie low in. Let's get going to it.'

Richard turned back to the 'plane. 'O.K. But I'm still as hungry as a hunter. We'll take some of those emergency stores with us, so that we can have a meal when we get there.' Simon followed him back to the aircraft, and together they repacked one of the hampers with their choice of things to eat and drink.

When they emerged, carrying the hamper between them, the four friends set off through the low scrub. It proved hard going; but, twenty minutes later, they reached the rise, and saw that the ruined building on it had been a church.

'There must have been an Inca temple here once,' the Duke remarked. 'Wherever the Spaniards found pagan temples, both here and in Mexico, they pulled them down and built a church on the ruins.'

'So I've heard,' Rex nodded. 'There was probably an Inca village here, too, once. This place is two miles or more from the ruins of the city. That's why I chose it. The Andean peons are harmless enough, but we don't want them nosing around.'

As they entered the roofless church, they saw by the moonlight that the greater part of the floor was covered with rubble; but the altar was intact and, carved in the stone above it, there was a tall cross. Beckoning to the others to follow him, the Duke scrambled over the debris to the altar and, for some minutes, they stood silently before it, rendering thanks for their preservation.

Simon and Richard then opened up some of the tins of food they had brought, sliced up chicken and ham on to cardboard plates and poured drinks into the cups. As Rex watched them, he said with a grin, 'Guess the eyes of you boys are going to prove larger than your tummies.'

Richard laughed. 'Maybe we've overdone it, but what we don't eat we can take back to the aircraft when it's daylight.'

As soon as they had satisfied their first hunger, de Richleau said, 'Now, Rex, we're all anxious to know what you've been up to. I confess that you fooled me last night. I simply could not believe that you were really in favour of this Black Power movement. I could only conclude that you were yourself no longer, and that these Satanists had caused a devil to take possession of your mind. But the fact that we owe our escape from that hellish place to you shows that I was right off the mark. What is the explanation of this mystery?'

Rex shrugged his great shoulders. 'It's simple enough. As Silvia's told you, she was my girl-friend. A couple of years before I met her, Don Salvador—or the Prince, as he calls himself in these parts, had interested her in the occult. She told me about it, and tried to get me to play, too. With the memories I have about Simon, Tanith and that devil Mocata, I naturally declined and did my best to make her understand what a hellishly dangerous game she was playing.

'Mark you, she'd not let on that Don Salvador was an Adept following the Left-Hand Path, so I wasn't particularly worried when she persisted in continuing to attend his "seances", as she called them. Then one night, when I was waiting for her in her apartment, she returned a bit potted. She talked a lot of what I took at the time to be nonsense, about how in fifteen or twenty years' time, there would be world-wide revolution, out of which would arise a new state of things. There would be one supreme government, that would control everything and, if I liked, she felt sure she could get me made a member of it.

'Naturally, I laughed and said that would be O.K. by me. At that point she seemed to sober up, and refused to say any more for the time being. I assumed that she'd gotten this pipe dream at one of Don Salvador's occult sessions, so I thought no more about it. But the next night we spent together she brought up the subject again. Evidently, in the meantime, she'd had a talk with Don Salvador and he'd O.K.d her approaching me seriously. She said they needed someone like me, with wide experience of banking, to take charge of their financial interests. Then she swore me to secrecy and told me about their Black Power movement. According to her it was simply a means to an end, a way to bring about Peace on Earth, and a good time for all.

'By then, the penny had dropped. I'd tumbled to it that Don Salvador was a real topline Black, and that he aimed to serve his Infernal Master by letting loose all hell. The idea of his pulling off this ghastly coup properly scared the pants off me. But I realised that it was up to me to get in on this thing, and somehow scotch it. I played hard to get for a bit, putting up various snags to the scheme that I knew she could find answers to. Then, when she spoke about the power I would have, I agreed to play.

'The next time I saw her, she was a bit worried. It emerged that Don Salvador was not altogether happy about taking me on. He needed a guarantee that I wouldn't rat on them. They could only be sure I wouldn't if I agreed to cut myself off entirely from the life I was then leading, and perform some act that would prevent my returning to it.'

'I see,' murmured the Duke. 'That is why you stole a million from your bank.'

'You've hit it, Greyeyes. Of course the thing they didn't realise, when they put up the idea, was that I'd not become a wanted criminal. I knew that my family would move heaven and earth to keep quiet what I had done, and anti-up the million I'd made off with from their private funds. All I have to do when I reappear is to repay the bank by selling a big block of my own shares, and everyone I know will be glad to see me back. But the fact that I did commit the crime and was apparently willing to throw up everything for the cause, convinced Don Salvador that I was on the level.'

'Have you now got the low-down on the whole organisation?' Richard enquired.

'Yes, more or less. The Prince is the Chief of a Coven, probably the most powerful in the world, as each of its twelve members are in turn the Chiefs of other Covens which dominate the whole Satanic set-up in great areas.

'Von Thumm is his number two, and responsible for the settlement down at the Sala. Under him it's run by the Moor El Aliz, Harry Benito, a Jamaican, and an Andean Indian whose name is Pucara. They have a batch of Zombies who act as their servants and, if need be, could be called on to help keep order. But, so far, that hasn't proved necessary. All the workers down there are sweet innocents. They haven't an idea that they're being used as the tools of Satanism. Their heads are in the clouds, with visions of securing for the coloureds real and permanent equality with whites.

'Lincoln B. Glasshill is number three in the hierarchy but, like von Thumm, he comes up here only occasionally, to take his orders from the Prince. The others, too, all have quarters in one city or another where they spend a part of their time. There are two other Negroes: a tall, wall-eyed fellow called Ebolite, and Mazambi, who's head was like a skull.

'Pierre Dubecq is a white. He is the Prince's top pilot, and with the assistance of a Spanish half-caste, Miguel Cervantes, runs the aircraft. The men who service them are Andeans. They are quite good mechanics, but in other ways are ignorant types and they are not allowed inside the fortress. The green-clad chaps who fetch and carry inside are Andeans, too. But they know nothing of what goes on behind the scenes, because they are always kept under light hypnosis.

'Kaputa, a fat Babu, is in charge of them. He is an ace-high hypnotist, and the only one who lives up here permanently. Singra, a Pakistani, and Ben Yussuf, an Egyptian, make up this diabolical thirteen.

'For most of the time since mid-December, I've been up here. Radio brings me quotations for all currencies on the principal markets daily, and I have a transmitter by which I can send code messages to the Prince's agents in Geneva, New York, London, Paris and the rest, instructing them to buy or sell. Before I arrived, the Babu used to handle their foreign exchange, but now he's become more or less my assistant.

'Down at the Sala, half a dozen of the innocents are employed as accountants and clerks. They keep the ledgers, showing all expenses connected with the settlement, and revenue from outside sources. Once a week I go down there and check up on the increase in the subscription lists, and transfer the surpluses from the collecting centres in scores of cities to the central funds. After that, no-one except the Babu and myself knows what happens to the money. But, having taken on this job as their foreign exchange expert has enabled me to secure particulars of all their own agents and collecting centres. So, when it comes to a show-down, we'll be in a position, by fair means or foul, to close in on the lot.'

De Richleau smiled. 'You've done a fine job, Rex.'

Rex grinned back. 'Not too bad, though it's been a tough assignment living with this hellish crew and pretending to go along with them. I'd have liked a few weeks longer before I blew the gaff. But you boys arriving on the scene with the best intentions have put paid to that: and I've got enough dope now to kill this Black Power movement in its cradle.'

Simon swallowed the last chunk of pineapple from his plate and asked, 'How d'you plan to do that?'

'No problem there,' Rex smiled. 'Way back home I know plenty of folks who're near the President. I'll get a private interview and lay out the deck. The old man's no fool. He'll jump to it that this is real dynamite. The settlement on the Sala de Uyuni and the Inca fortress being so remote from the outside world cuts two ways. It enabled the Satanists to keep their operations secret, but C.I.A. or Marines could be flown in with equal secrecy. The Bolivian Government would never hear a word of it. I'll take it on myself to see to it that the fortress and everyone in it are blown to hell. All the papers at the settlement would be seized, and that would enable us to deal with the stooges there. They'd be given a choice. Either to face a charge of conspiracy and inciting to riot, which would land them in the cooler for a term of years, or to sign a confession and receive a thousand dollars each, to tide them over until they could start a new life. Three hundred thousand dollars, or say half a million for the whole job, is only peanuts to Uncle Sam; and we'd have put paid to the most dangerous conspiracy the Devil has hatched since he made use of Hitler to wreck ten million lives.'

Rex broke off to light a cigarette, then asked, 'Now tell me your end of the story. The Prince put me wise to it that you boys had started a hunt for me, and mighty good of you it was. But he told me only the bare facts, then that you'd been caught and were being flown up here. I want to hear the details.'

Between them, Richard and Simon gave an account of their doings in Buenos Aires, Punta Arenas and Santiago, of the barbecue, Nella's murder, their imprisonment and Simon's engagement to Miranda. When Rex heard this last piece of news, he slapped his thigh and cried:

'Oh boy! Isn't that just great. I'm crazy with delight. That poor kid has had one hell of a life. And she's a real sweetie. Just think, too, of old Simon being hooked at last. But you won't regret it, Simon. Blind or not, Miranda's a girl in a million. Come now. We must have a drink on this.' And, taking a bottle of Three Star Brandy from the hamper, he filled four of the paper cups to the brim.

It was very cold there, although not with the cold of evil; and the neat brandy was welcome as a means of warming them up. As they sipped it, the Duke took over, recounted how he fooled the police by forging the statement by Nella that had got his friends off, then how they had flown up to the Sala and been captured by von Thumm.

'That Nazi swine!' Rex exclaimed. 'What wouldn't I give to get my hands round his throat. When I'd agreed to join Don Salvador's outfit, he turned me over to the Baron for instruction. We were supposed to be running a poker school on Saturday nights, but the thought of what we actually did makes me want to vomit. It was all I could do to take it; but it was that or throwing in my hand, so I just had to grin and pretend I was enjoying the fun.'

They had made their escape shortly after one o'clock. It had taken them half an hour to reach the ruined church, and they had been talking for over an hour; so it was now close on a quarter to three, and Rex said, 'Guess we'd better get a few hours' shut-eye, as I'd like to take off soon after dawn.'

'Ner, not all of us,' Simon shook his head. 'Best take turns, so that one of us is always awake. At any time the Prince may find out that we got away. He can overlook us, so he'll know where we are. He might start something, and we mustn't be caught napping.'

'You would be right, Simon, if we were in most places,' said the Duke. 'But not here. We are now under the protection of the Cross. So all of us can sleep without fear.'

They stood up and faced the altar, praying silently for continued protection, then lay down and huddled together for warmth. Soon they were all sound asleep.

Shortly after first light they were woken by a whistling and rising and falling keening sound. Inside the ruin it was perfectly still; but when they got up and went over to the broken-down doorway, they realised the reason for this eerie noise. Outside, it was blowing a hurricane.

'Hell's bells!' exclaimed Rex. 'He's raised the wind against us.'

'You are right,' agreed de Richleau grimly. 'This is no ordinary storm. The wind would be rushing through this ruin at a hundred miles an hour; but it's as still as a mill-pond. Look at the way those trees are bent over almost double. There! One of them has been uprooted and is being carried away like a matchstick.'

Incautiously, Richard stepped out through the open doorway. A fierce gust caught him and would have swept him off his feet had not Rex grabbed his arm and yanked him back to safety.

Gloomily they stumbled back over the rubble to the clear space near the centre of the nave, where they had slept.

'We're stymied,' said Simon bitterly. 'Not a hope of our flying down to the coast while this lasts.'

'He won't be able to keep it up indefinitely,' the Duke sought to comfort them. 'With luck we may be able to get away this afternoon.'

Rex grunted. 'I doubt it. The odds are that the aircraft will have been caught up and smashed to fragments.'

'I don't think so. It is half a mile away. And look at those two women.' De Richleau pointed at two distant figures with bundles strapped to their backs, and wearing the bowler-like hats favoured by the Andean peasants. They were trudging along unaffected by the wind.

'I'm certain that this is purely local. The wind is not blowing in one direction, but surging round and round the building. It is as though we were in the centre of a cyclone. Until it drops, we are as much prisoners as though we were in a big, circular cage; but there is at least one consolation.' De Richleau turned and glanced at the hamper. 'We have plenty of food and drink left to see us through the day.'

Unhappily, they set about opening two more tins and sat down to breakfast. For a while they speculated on what the Prince's next move would be, but it was impossible to do more than make guesses. They endeavoured to cheer themselves with the knowledge that, as long as they remained in the church under the protection of the Cross, they would be safe. But they could not remain there indefinitely.

During the morning they tried to forget their anxiety about the future by talking of the past: the desperate situations they had won their way out of, and the happy days of idleness and laughter they had spent together.

While they talked, the wind never ceased to howl and whine round the building. Neither did it stop as they ate a meagre lunch, nor during the long hours of the afternoon. When evening came, its force had not lessened, and it was clear that there was no longer any hope of their getting away that day.

At about eight o'clock, they ate what remained of the food they had brought from the aircraft and, an hour later, with the sound of the hurricane still at full blast, settled down to get what sleep they could.

In the early hours of the morning they had been captured, they had all been so tired out that, in spite of the fact that they were lying on cold, hard stone, they had dropped off almost at once. But now they twisted and turned for a long time, until, one by one, they fell into an uneasy sleep.

Rex was the first to wake. The pale light of dawn lit the ruin. Suddenly he was struck by the complete silence. The wind had stopped blowing. With a cry of excitement, he grasped the Duke by the shoulder and shook him. De Richleau opened his eyes and stared up at Rex for a moment, as though he did not see him, then he slowly sat up. Rex's cry had roused the others. Like him, they realised that the hurricane had ceased, and were exclaiming joyfully that they were now free to fly down to the coast.

But the Duke showed no sign of sharing their relief and excitement. His eyes were fixed on Simon and his gaze was filled with sorrow. In a low voice, he said:

'My dear son. I have bad news for you. How to break it to you I hardly know. But I have just returned from the astral. What I am about to tell you is no figment of the imagination induced by sorcery, such as we saw down in that dungeon the night before last. When I was on the Astral I was confronted by the Prince. He said that we must return to him, or pay a forfeit. He is holding someone to ransom. Yesterday, while he kept us captive here, they kidnapped a young woman in Santiago, and flew her up to the fortress. She is now there, a prisoner at their mercy. Need I . . . need I name her?'

The blood had drained from Simon's face. His mouth hung open, and his eyes were staring.

De Richleau nodded. 'Yes; Miranda.'

16

THE AGONY OF SIMON ARON

'It can't be true!' Simon's voice was almost a wail.

The Duke stood up and laid a hand on his shoulder. 'Alas, it is, my son. In this my heart bleeds for you, but there is no escaping the truth. On the Astral personalities never lie. They may like or dislike one another, but they are incapable of disguising their true feelings. It is the Law, and cannot be evaded. The Prince made the situation clear to me beyond all misunderstanding. It proved very easy to trick Miranda. Within an hour of learning of our escape, he had a wax image made, cut upon it the name Pinney, performed his conjuration, then stuck a thorn into the leg of the puppet.

'Yesterday morning, when Pinney went to have her bath, she slipped, fell heavily and broke her leg. The next move took place a few hours later. A young Frenchman, who is one of the Prince's pilots, arrived at the Hilton. He told Miranda that you had sent him to fetch her. When asked why, he said that he had no idea; that he had received his orders through a third party, but it had been impressed upon him that you needed her urgently.

'Naturally, Miranda was torn between two loyalties. Should she remain with the unfortunate Pinney, or respond to your appeal? As anyone could have foreseen, love won. Fearing that you were ill or in serious trouble, she agreed to be flown up here. She is in no immediate danger, and believes herself to be among friends. Silvia Sinegiest is looking after her, and she has been told that we are on our way to the fortress; that we shall be there for lunch.'

Simon groaned. 'What . . . what does that fiend mean to do with her?'

'Nothing, provided we surrender to him.'

'And if we don't?'

De Richleau did not reply, but looked away.

'I know! I know!' Simon almost screamed. 'You don't have to tell me. When she was trapped in that fire on her cousin's ranch, she was only nineteen and a virgin. She's still a virgin. They'll use her in their unholy rites. They'll rape and murder her. They'll offer her up as a sacrifice at a Black Mass.'

There were tears in the Duke's eyes as he gave a slight nod. 'That is what the Prince threatened unless we agree his terms. But they are not unreasonably harsh. His anxiety now is to keep secret his Black Power movement. I made it plain that, in no circumstances, would I use such powers as I have to further his plans, and he accepts that. He would, though, require all of us and, of course, Miranda, to remain up here indefinitely. We should be given one of the hutments in the settlement at Sala, and be free to enjoy such amenities as there are there.'

'Good God, what a prospect!' Richard burst out.

Simon turned to him. 'It'd mean you'd never see Marie-Lou again. I couldn't ask it of you.'

'We might persuade him to agree to a compromise,' the Duke suggested. 'I've had a wonderful life and I cannot expect to live for many years longer. If I remained here as a hostage for you keeping your word, he might accept your oath that you would never mention what is going on here, and let you go.'

'Greyeyes, be yourself,' Rex cut in abruptly. 'I'd go a long way to save Miranda, so would we all. But not that far. What is the martyrdom of one woman and ourselves when set against the appalling suffering that Black Power will inflict on the world? As long as we have the slightest chance of killing this thing, we've just got to keep on trying. And you know it.'

'Ummm,' Simon nodded. 'You're right, Rex, Greyeyes made that offer without considering its implications. Not like him; but he was thinking only of me. Tell you what, though, I'll chuck in my hand. Go on my own to the Prince. Have to . . . have to take a chance on what happens to Miranda and me. Pretend that I've been sent to try to negotiate a new deal. Keep him busy for a few hours while you three get away.'

'No dice,' said Rex. 'He's much too wily a bird to fall for that. But he might if I went, because I'm the only one of you who knows the whole set-up and it's more important to him to keep his claws on me than all three of you together.'

'I won't allow that.' De Richleau's voice was sharp. 'His resentment against you for having betrayed him will be far stronger than against any of us. His power is greater than mine when we are pitted against each other; but he must have many things beside ourselves to occupy his mind. If he takes it off us for even a short time I could subdue any of his lieutenants, protect you and, with luck, we might get away. So I shall go with you.'

'I must go,' said Simon. 'Couldn't clear out as long as they've got Miranda.'

Richard gave a little laugh. 'That settles it then. You can't possibly think I'm going to quit and leave the rest of you up to your necks in this?' "One for all and all for one", as the great Dumas put it. We'll see this hellish business through together.'

'If we do, it is certain that our chances will be better,' de Richleau told them. 'Everyone has in him a divine spark and, united in purpose, a number of ignorant but good people can defeat a warlock who has considerable power for evil. For example, powerful as he is, the Prince could not overcome the congregation of a small Christian parish church if they had faith and the will to resist him. All of us are well advanced on the path of understanding, so together, we are a force to be reckoned with. Unfortunately, we are not pitted against the Prince alone. He will have the support of his lieutenants: but, if the opportunity to confront them separately occurs—as I did the Baron down at the Sala—we may win through.'

Simon picked up the carving knife with which they had cut up the tinned meat, and thrust its point through the bottom of the pocket inside his jacket, then buttoned the jacket so that the knife could not be seen. Casting a gloomy glance at the others, he said, 'Taking no chances. If that bastard is planning to sacrifice Miranda at a Black Mass, I'll kill her first and myself afterwards.'

'How dare you contemplate suicide?' de Richleau rebuked him sharply. 'In certain circumstances one is justified in taking the life of another. When one's country is at war, for example, or to put someone one loves out of pain. But never must one take one's own life. The length of each of our incarnations is decreed to the split second and by no possible means can we lengthen it. As you all know, during these incarnations we are set certain lessons to learn and given certain trials to bear, so that we may increase our knowledge and fortitude. To cut short an incarnation is to turn back the page, and results in having to face an even greater affliction in the next. Few Christians realise it, but to commit suicide is the Sin against the Holy Ghost, for the Holy Ghost is our own spirit.'

For a moment there was silence, then Richard said, 'Come on, chaps, let's get going.'

Gathering up their few belongings, they scrambled over the rubble and out of the ruin, then crossed the intervening low scrub to the aircraft. As the Duke had felt certain, it had been outside the area of the hurricane and was just as they had left it, anchored only by two light ropes.

They had not eaten since their meagre meal the previous evening, so they opened up some more tins of meat and fruit. Then they settled in their places and, with Rex at the controls, the little 'plane took off. A half of an hour later he brought her down on the island airstrip.

Ebolite, the wall-eyed Negro and the Babu, Kaputa, had come down from the fortress to meet them. Neither uttered any sneering remarks about their Master having forced his prisoners to return. On the contrary, they might have been two officials receiving V.I.P.s. After greeting the four friends courteously, they escorted them up the steep stairway and between the towering massive walls of stone blocks, into the modernised part of the stronghold. There the Duke, Simon and Richard were shown into the rooms they had previously occupied, and Kaputa accompanied Rex to his own quarters.

Clean clothes had been laid out for them and, when they had shaved, bathed and changed, Richard and Simon joined de Richleau in his room. Less than three hours had elapsed since they had left the ruined church, so it was still only mid-morning. Simon could not contain his impatience to see Miranda and, thinking she might be in the big room at the end of the passage, he opened the door with the intention of going along there. But he found his way barred by one of the servitors, who abruptly signed to him to go back. It was a sharp reminder that, in spite of their friendly reception, they were still prisoners.

For the best part of two hours they sat in the Duke's room, talking in a desultory fashion while endeavouring to forget their equivocal situation. At length the servitor opened the door and beckoned them to follow him. He led them to the big room and ushered them in.

Miranda was sitting there alone. As Simon came through the door, she jumped to her feet and, without a second's hesitation, ran to him with outstretched arms. Previously, at the distance she had been from the door, she could have made him out only as a blur; but, as he moved to meet her, he saw how her eyes had changed. They were now clear, bright and shining.

For a moment he was utterly aghast, believing that the Prince had tricked them—that this was the same figment of his imagination conjured up from Hell as that which had tempted him with a drink two nights before, and that the real Miranda was still in Santiago. But, before he could check his forward movement, her arms were round him. They were warm flesh and blood, and she was crying:

'Oh, darling! Isn't it wonderful that you should have found this marvellous Prince and had me flown up to him? Bless you and bless him a thousand times. I can hardly believe it yet. But it's true. He's restored my sight.'

Her joy was so infectious, for the moment, they did not even wonder what their enemy's object could be in having performed this miracle. Sharing her happiness, they crowded round kissing and congratulating her.

When the first excitement had subsided and they had sat down in the easy chairs, she said, 'By now, like me you must have realised that we were all wrong about the people up here. Silvia Sinegiest explained everything to me last night. They are not Satanists at all, and they had nothing to do with the murder of Nella Nathan. It is simply that they don't believe in Christianity, as it is taught in our churches. They hold that the Church taboos make people miserable and frustrated, whereas the Old God wanted everyone to be carefree and happy. Of course, parties like that barbecue you told me about are going a bit far. But some people like that sort of thing, and one doesn't have to take part in it if one doesn't want to. As Silvia said, the only commandment they have is, "*Do what thou wilt is the whole of the Law*".'

De Richleau shook his head, 'My child, you have been grievously misled. That one and only Satanist commandment, "*Do what thou wilt shall be the whole of the Law*" frees those who subscribe to it from all responsibility. In effect, it is a decree that everyone should give way to every temptation and use any means he can think of to secure for himself anything he desires without the least consideration of the unhappiness it would bring upon others. Just consider the sort of thing that would lead to. I will give you a few examples:

'Let us say that two pretty girls are in love with the same man. One does what she wills. She slashes her rival's face to pieces with a razor, in order to put her out of the running.

'A young man has just become aware of the joys of sex. One night he picks up a street girl and contracts from her a venereal disease. His sex urge is not lessened by it. Instead of waiting until he is cured, he light-heartedly goes with other girls, passing the disease on to them.

'There are two brothers. The elder is his father's heir, but a weak character. The younger deliberately leads him into evil ways: drink, dope, laziness and theft, until the father is so disgusted that he disinherits him in favour of the younger son.

'A woman is ambitious to achieve a high position. A man stands in her way. She invites him to her flat to discuss matters, then attempts to seduce him. Whether she succeeds or not, she raises the house and accuses him of raping her. The scandal ruins both his public life and his marriage, while she achieves her object.

'A convict, anxious to have his sentence reduced, initiates a plan to escape with several others. At the eleventh hour he betrays them to the Governor. They are severely punished, while he has earned remission.

'A man desires a beautiful young girl. His attempts to seduce her fail. He succeeds in getting her alone, rapes her and makes her pregnant.

'A woman is tired of her husband and has a lover whom she wishes to marry. So she either poisons her husband or arranges some accident that will cause his death.

'A head of State is inordinately ambitious. Solely to make himself a greater figure in the world and with no thought for his people, he picks a quarrel with a smaller State and plunges his country into war.'

The Duke paused for a moment, then went on, 'Surely you see, my child, how the acceptance of this terrible doctrine "*Do what thou wilt shall be the whole of the Law*" would bring unbelievable misery on the world? No. There is only one way by which universal happiness can be achieved. That is by everyone practising the way of life urged on His followers by Jesus Christ; and that, at least, the Christian churches have continued to preach: "*Do unto thy neighbour as thou wouldst be done by*".'

Miranda stared at him, wide-eyed with consternation at the thought that she had failed to realise the universal duplicity, fear and grief that would result if a great number of people became Satanists. She was just about to express her feelings when the Prince and Silvia came in, both carrying their familiars.

In spite of the recent conversation, Miranda had developed such a liking for Silvia, that she jumped up, ran to her and kissed her as though she was a much-loved sister. As Simon saw them embrace, he gave an inward shudder. Apart from deceiving them down at Punta Arenas, Silvia had done them no ill; but she held the high office of 'The Maiden', so was steeped to her beautiful eyebrows in the Satanic faith.

Meanwhile, with his warmest smile, the Prince was saying to de Richleau:

'My dear Duke, I am so happy that you and your friends have decided to stay on with us. When that wicked fellow Rex took you off in one of my aircraft, without even letting me know his intentions, I was really quite worried. I gather now that you only wished to see those interesting ruins at Potosi. But I am annoyed with him, very annoyed.'

There was nothing to be gained at the moment by forcing a show-down and, for Miranda's sake, de Richleau even returned the smile. 'I am sorry that you were concerned about us, Prince. And it was good of you to provide such a pleasant surprise for us on our return. We are naturally delighted that you should have restored Miss Van Ryn's sight.'

The Prince shrugged. 'It was nothing. Just a minor magic, and an expression of goodwill. I felt it would compensate the three of you, particularly Mr Aron, for the discomfort you suffered while guests of von Thumm.'

'How is the Herr Baron?' asked the Duke smoothly.

'In excellent health. You will see him this evening. He is flying up from the Sala. Glasshill, El Aziz and Harry Benito are coming with him, as I have bidden them to a party.'

Richard's eyes narrowed, and his chin stuck out aggressively. Noticing his expression, the Prince laughed and chided him, 'Now, now, Mr Eaton. You must remember that Lincoln had good cause for resentment because you made it necessary for him to abandon his profitable practice in Santiago. Now that we are all to be friends, you must let bygones be bygones.'

At that moment luncheon was announced and they all walked between the curtains to the table in the window that had such a superb view. During the meal the Prince exercised his magnetism to make them feel as though they were enjoying a normal social occasion. He kept the conversation going on a variety of subjects, none of which had any bearing on the occult. De Richleau, knowing the nervous tension that his friends must be feeling, ably seconded him.

When they had finished luncheon, the Prince said, 'And now I have an unpleasant duty to perform. I trust that you, especially, Miss Van Ryn, will not be too upset, as it concerns your uncle. I maintain a strict discipline here and, by taking one of my aircraft without permission, he has deliberately broken a rule of which he was well aware. For that he must be punished.'

Taking up a dessert knife, he tapped an empty glass with it, so that it gave out a little ping. Rising from the table, he added, 'That will bring him to us.' Then he led the way to the far end of the room.

Now acutely anxious about what form the unfortunate Rex's punishment was to take, the others sat down, but the Prince remained standing. After a few minutes Rex came in and the Prince addressed him:

'I have been greatly shocked by your conduct. For a moment it even occurred to me that you intended to play the traitor. Be that as it may, you used one of my aircraft to take my guests away without my consent. I have been considering what form your punishment should take. There came to my mind the truth about the events which occurred in the Garden of Eden at the time of the Fall.

'The second chapter of the book of Genesis has been misinterpreted. There was not one enchanted tree, but two. The Tree of Knowledge of Good and Evil *and* the Tree of Life, which is mentioned both in verse nine and in chapter three, verse twenty-two. God the Creator, the One indivisible and eternal, having created Man in His own image, was so pleased with His work that he decided to make him immortal. He therefore sent His messenger, the Serpent who, at that time, was an angel with wings and limbs, to tell Man that he should eat the fruit of the Tree of Life.

'But the Serpent was vain, ambitious and had Evil in his heart. He perverted the message, beguiled Eve into eating the fruit of the Tree of Knowledge of Good and Evil, and himself ate the fruit of the Tree of Life.

'As a result, symbolically, the Serpent sheds its skin, but never dies; whilst Adam and Eve and all their descendents unto this present generation were condemned to age and die, to strife, sorrow and the pains of childbirth, then driven out of Eden. But the Serpent did not escape without punishment. The Lord God said to him:

'"Because thou hast done this, thou art cursed above all cattle and above every beast of the field; upon thy belly shalt thou go and dust shalt thou eat all the days of thy life."'

The Prince paused to glance at his gold wrist-watch, then went on, his large, limpid eyes beneath half-closed eyelids, riveted on Rex, 'This morning I cast a spell on you. In three minutes' time it will take effect.'

Rex had listened to him, pale but defiant. He made no reply and continued to stand there. The others watched him, a prey to the most awful apprehension. They felt as though they had been made rigid by being encased in invisible armour. None of them moved a hand or foot, and they were terribly aware that there was nothing they could do. Even the beautiful cat and the bouncy little dog remained completely still. An utter silence had fallen. The three minutes seemed interminable.

Suddenly Rex's legs gave beneath him. With a loud cry he fell to the floor.

For a moment the Prince's handsome features were transformed into a mask portraying sadism and hatred. In a loud voice he said: 'Even as the Lord God struck down the treacherous Serpent, I have struck you down. You shall crawl on your knees and feed on the floor like a dog until it is my pleasure to release you.'

His words broke the spell that had held them rigid. Cursing him, Richard jumped forward and grasped Rex's arm to help him to his feet. Seconds later, Simon was at his other side. But Rex was sixteen stone of splendid manhood. It was all they could do to drag him up between them, and that only for a moment. His weight proved too much for them. He sagged back on to his knees.

With an imperious gesture, the Prince waved them aside and said harshly to Rex, 'You may go now. Crawl to your quarters and remain there until I summon you again.'

Silvia had remained pale but self-contained throughout this frightful scene. Miranda had sat frozen with horror, her big, blue eyes starting from her head. Now, with a despairing cry of 'Oh, God, Uncle Rex!' she sprang out of her chair, cast herself down beside him and kissed him on the cheek. But Rex, his eyes moist with unshed tears, put her gently from him and, obeying the command he had been given, crawled out of the room.

Miranda burst into tears, rounded on the Prince and cried:

'How could you? Oh, how could you?'

He shrugged, shook his head and gave her his most charming smile. 'Please spare me your reproaches. I warned you that I must punish your uncle. But, just as I gave you back your sight, I can restore the use of his legs to him whenever I wish. For how long or how short a time he will have to suffer depends, to some extent, on the behaviour of you and your friends. I might even relent soon enough to enable him to stand up and give you away when you are married.'

'Married!' she repeated. 'But . . .'

With a sharp gesture he silenced her and went on. 'Yes. I can hardly suppose that either you or Mr Aron wish for a long engagement. So why should you deny yourselves longer than necessary the joy of being united? I have arranged for you to be married tonight.'

'But . . .' she stammered. 'But, how can we be married here?'

He smiled again. 'We have a temple, and the ceremony will take place there. The rites will be performed as they were in the beginning and you will receive the blessing of the True God.'

'No!' de Richleau came to his feet. 'I forbid it! I forbid it!'

The Prince turned and gave him a mildly contemptuous look. 'In my presence you have not the power to forbid anything. And you know it. If you and your friends prove troublesome, I will deal with you as I have dealt with Van Ryn. Then all of you shall witness the ceremony, *and* the consummation of the marriage on your knees.'

'The consummation!' cried Simon. 'Ner, ner! Damned if . . .'

Miranda's cheeks had gone scarlet and she gasped, 'You don't mean . . .? You can't!'

The Prince's voice was silky. 'My dear young lady. True marriage does not consist only of exchanging oaths and, perhaps, the giving to the woman of some symbol, such as a ring. As it is said that justice should not only be done, but be seen to be done, so with marriage. The two principals, the Yang and the Yin, must be brought together before witnesses. Then the offspring of this mating, should the woman be so blessed as to conceive, is vowed to the service of the True God.'

'What! Sold to Satan before it is even born?' Richard snapped. 'You bastard!'

'Mr Eaton, you are still comparatively young in time, or you would know that the word Satan, which you regard as a designation of Evil, is only a name used by the ignorant for the Deity from whom all blessings flow. As for your abuse of myself. I will let it pass. But it distresses me that a man of your breeding should permit himself to display such ill manners.'

Since the Prince had silenced de Richleau, the latter had stood with bowed shoulders and downcast eyes. Now, making a gesture towards Miranda who, with Simon's arm about her, was weeping hysterically, he looked up again and said:

'You tell us that the God of the Christian churches demands that His followers should deny themselves the joys of life; whereas your god is ever anxious to foster people's happiness. How can you possibly maintain that assertion when your proposals have brought such shock, distress and horror to these two?'

'Their reaction is due only to the false beliefs in which they have been reared. It is understandable that Miss Van Ryn should shrink from exposing herself naked and being possessed by others in addition to her husband. But you will find that she will swiftly overcome this reluctance. There has never yet been born a woman endowed with a good figure who, however prudishly brought up, in her secret heart would not delight in displaying her beauty.

'But that is not all. I am, of course, aware that she is a virgin. That being so, her bridegroom is unfortunate, for a first penetration rarely brings much pleasure to the man and, for the woman, is usually painful. The result in Christian marriages very often is a most unhappy period, during which the woman is unwilling to repeat the act, and the man suffers an infuriating frustration. Indeed, not infrequently, it leads to the couple never developing a satisfactory sex life.

'In his wisdom, the True God devised a means by which this sad state of affairs would be overcome. He decreed that, on her wedding night, the bride should be possessed by seven men. After the second or third has had her, she feels no more pain; with those who do so later, she experiences an ecstasy of passion. Tomorrow, when Miss Van Ryn has recovered from her exhaustion, she will be beseeching her husband to embrace her.'

So horrified had those about the Prince been by his revelation of the procedure at a Satanic wedding that they had heard him out in silence. As he ceased speaking, they gave vent to a chorus of protest.

Miranda had fainted. Simon lowered her to a chair and stood trembling, his mouth agape. Richard, his eyes glaring, was half crouched, his fists clenched and about to launch himself on their tormentor. Just in time the Duke grabbed his arm, held him back and said hoarsely:

'Young women indoctrinated into your evil cult might accept the ceremony willingly and, perhaps, enjoy it. But that could not possibly be the case with one brought up to be chaste and who, above all, is not only physically attracted to one man but has also given him her spiritual love. To be defiled by a succession of men would so revolt her that it might well drive her out of her mind. This marriage must not take place. I know well that we are in your power. But is there not some alternative, some inducement we can offer you to refrain from forcing Miss Van Ryn to submit to this hideous ordeal?'

The red lips of the Prince's beautifully-modelled mouth parted in a smile, revealing his gleaming white teeth. 'Ah, now we are talking. Yes. Since you are so bigoted and anxious to deny this charming couple entering in the true joy of life, there is an alternative. You have only to agree, as I urged you to when you first arrived here, to acknowledge the True God as your Master, and give me your aid in my undertakings.'

'No,' the Duke replied at once. 'That I cannot do. And my friends would not ask it of me.'

The Prince shrugged. 'Then there is no more to be said. Silvia will take charge of Miss Van Ryn and later prepare her for her wedding. You others will now go to your rooms. You will not communicate with one another, as I have no intention of giving you the chance to hatch some plot which might cause a temporary hitch in my arrangements. In due course, you will be sent for.'

Fixing his large dark eyes for a few moments on each of them in turn, he pointed to the door. Dominated by his will their urge to resist crumbled. Silently, with bowed heads, they filed out of the room.

Simon spent the greater part of the hours that followed alternately sitting on the edge of his bed hunched in despair and imploring the help of the God of his fathers. Richard, as an old soldier, knew how important it was to get as much sleep as possible before a battle. Feeling certain that the Duke would put up a fight, he was anxious to be in a state to give him as much support as he could. It took him a long time to clear his mind of the heart-rending scene in which he had participated, but eventually he dropped off. De Richleau deliberately left his body for the Astral. There he sought out as many of his long-time friends who were out of incarnation as he could, and asked them to spend the coming night thinking of him and supplicating the Lords of Light to come to his assistance.

In due course a meal on a tray was brought by the servitors to each of them. The Duke neither ate or drank anything. Simon, feeling that he ought to recruit his strength, attempted to eat a wing of chicken *chaud-froid*, but he was in so grievous a state that, after having swallowed a few mouthfuls with difficulty, he was sick. Richard, true to form, made a good meal and drank three-quarters of the bottle of champagne that had been brought him with the food.

In vain he had searched his bedroom early in the afternoon for something he could use as a weapon. The bottle, he decided, was the answer. It made the perfect club. But it would be missed when the servant came to collect the tray. Moreover, it was too big to be easily concealed about his person. Emptying the remaining contents on the floor, he took the empty bottle into the bathroom and smashed it on one of the bath taps. The punt fell off and several other pieces, leaving in his hand the neck of the bottle and, projecting from it, a six-inch-long sliver of glass.

Folding a light hand-towel into a narrow strip, he tied the centre twice round the lip of the bottle, thus making a handle for this improvised dagger, then wrapped the ends round the blade, so that he should not cut himself on it but, being loose, the ends would fly apart when he pulled the dagger from the side of his trousers belt where he intended to hide it. Collecting the other pieces of shattered bottle, he took them into the bedroom and threw them into the wastepaper basket.

When the silent servitor came for the tray, Richard pointed first to the wet patch where the wine had stained the carpet, then to the pieces of glass in the basket and made a grimace to indicate that he had had an accident, dropped the bottle and it had broken. The servant only shrugged and took the tray away.

Quite a long time later, he came back again, carrying a white robe with gold cabalistic signs on it, and laid it on the bed for Richard to change into. Richard ignored it as, in due course, he found had the Duke and Simon, who had had similar robes brought to them.

It was half an hour before midnight when, having been summoned by Pedro, they met Kaputa in the corridor. The grossly-fat Babu signed to them to follow him down the stairs to the basement.

They did so, knowing that the vital hour had come.

17

THE SATANIC MARRIAGE

The three friends were taken to the big, circular, underground room where, protected only by a circle of salt, they had faced the horrors that the Prince had sent against them. It was no longer cold down there, but there was a strange smell of burning herbs.

Waiting for them were von Thumm and the long-haired Andean Indian. Both of them were wearing wizard's robes of different colours, embroidered with various designs in gold and silver. The Duke recognised those on the Baron's robe as the symbols of Earth, those on the Indian's as symbols of Fire, and those on the robe the Babu was wearing as symbols of Air.

As the door of the chamber closed, leaving the two servitors outside, von Thumm limped forward to meet the prisoners. Having eyed them for a few moments with grim satisfaction, he said in his guttural voice:

'*Mein Führer*, the Prince, of your submission haf told me. After the ceremony with me to the Sala you will all come, there under me to live. My

orders you take; *ja*, and no questions ask. Do so and it will be no worse for
you than prison camp. But make for me trouble and much pleasure I haf in
teaching you good lesson. So! It is understood?'

They made no reply to this, so he went on, 'Now, for what we make
tonight. As you people Christians are, we hold service appropriate. For
Muslims, Buddhists and others we haf different ritual. All amended are, so
as to the True God to be acceptable. Tonight then we haf wedding Mass.
Follow me now. Attempt interference and you are struck blind. Stay silent.
One word and you are struck dumb.'

Walking to the wall that had the crooked Cross on it, he pressed a hidden
spring and a large panel slid smoothly back, revealing a Satanic temple. The
source of the smell was now evident. The atmosphere in the temple was
slightly misty and two young boys, both naked, one white with golden hair
and the other a coal-black Negro, were swinging censers.

There were no pews or *prie-dieux* in the temple. The furniture consisted
only of an altar raised up on a step, and so forming two stages; but the walls
glowed with the colour of several beautiful mosaics. They portrayed the
Seven Deadly Sins and under each in large lettering was the Satanic creed,
'*Do what thou wilt shall be the whole of the Law*'.

The broad upper stage of the altar consisted of a single sheet of rough-
hewn stone and had clearly been designed for sacrifices. About a foot from
the left end of it, a groove had been cut, on the step below which reposed an
onyx bowl, to catch the blood of the victim so that none of it should be lost.
But now, upon the stone of this lower shelf, there had been laid out a shallow
mattress about three inches thick, of quilted satin, the reason for which was
obvious.

Upon the upper shelf were two seven-branched, gold candelabra, in
which black candles were burning. Between them rose a hideous, bearded
figure, which de Richleau at once recognised as Baphomet, the idol before
which, in the Middle Ages, the heretical Knights Templar had been
initiated into revolting rites.

The idol had the head of a goat with two great horns between which stood
a black candle that burned with a steady blue flame, and gave off a stench of
sulphur. On its forehead there glittered a pentagon, one angle of which
pointed downwards towards its beaked nose that had monstrous, gaping
nostrils. It had human hands, held up so that they pointed to two white
crescents, above and below them were two black crescents. Its sexual organs
were those of a hermaphrodite. Its belly was green and covered with scales
like those of a fish or reptile. Its naked breasts were blue, and as full as those
of a pregnant woman's. Its lower limbs were covered in shaggy hair and
ended in cloven hooves. It was seated on a cube, the symbol of four, the
square and foundation of all things. Its hooves rested on a sphere,
representing the world. Its eyes were large, oblong and yellow. They
gleamed with a malevolence which gave the impression that, utterly still
though the creature was, it was conscious of what it saw, and was endowed
with life.

As de Richleau recognised the figure of Baphomet, he recalled the fate that
had overtaken the Knights Templar. Their Order had originally been
founded to protect the Holy Sepulchre. They had been a cosmopolitan
body, each of their companies being termed a 'Tongue', according to the
Christian nation from which its members had been recruited. Their

principal bases had been Rhodes and Malta. In both, and in many other places, they had built huge castles. They had become rich and powerful and, during the centuries of the Crusades, had protected pilgrims to the Holy Land by keeping at bay the Barbary pirates.

But their contact with the Saracens had led to their becoming Gnostic heretics. It was said that they uttered terrible blasphemies and conducted revolting rites in front of a Satanic idol. These rumours reached the Pope, who drew the attention of Philippe le Bel, King of France, to them. Philippe was in financial difficulties. He coveted the great wealth of the Templars, a considerable part of which they kept in their Paris headquarters, a fortress called the Temple.

At that time, early in the fourteenth century, Jacques de Morlay was the Grand Master of the Templars. The King invited him and his principal lieutenants to a banquet at the Louvre. There he had them arrested. They were thrown into prison terribly tortured, then burned at the stake.

Nevertheless, the Templars had the last word. As the funeral pyre that was to burn them alive was ignited, Jacques de Morlay put a solemn curse on the Royal House of France. He called on his Infernal Master to bring about its ruin and nearly five hundred years later, the monarchy was brought to an end by the imprisonment of King Louis XVI and Queen Mary Antoinette in the tower of the Temple.

This recollection of the power of Satan, exerted in support of the cult of Baphomet, ran through the Duke's mind in less than a minute, while he and his friends followed von Thumm until he halted in front of the altar, and made obeisance to the figure of Baphomet. The other two Satanic priests, who had brought up the rear, also bowed themselves down until their heads nearly touched the floor.

A silence of several minutes ensued, then came the sound of footsteps. Turning, they saw that the bride had entered the Temple. Her hand rested lightly on Rex's arm, so it was evident that the Prince had given him back the use of his legs in order that he could stand while giving her away. Behind them came Silvia and Glasshill. She was wearing the pleated white linen dress trimmed with gold of an Egyptian priestess; he had on a wizard's robe embroidered with the symbols of the fourth element–Water.

Miranda was wearing a bridal costume, but it was very different from the conventional white dress, tulle veil and wreath of orange blossom. Anyone who had seen illustrated books portraying ancient civilisations would have identified it at once. It had a very full skirt that came right down to the ground, a tight waist and was almost topless, so that the whole of her beautiful round breasts were revealed. The priestess of ancient Crete, who had worn such costumes, are always shown holding a serpent in each hand. Instead, Miranda's mauve satin skirt was embroidered with gold snakes, and a gold snake was entwined in her dark hair.

To the great surprise of Simon and his friends her expression was serene and she displayed no reluctance to approach the altar. They were even more surprised that she showed neither fear nor revulsion when von Thumm announced the form the ceremony would take. With an air of relish, he said:

'The Prince, our *Führer*, has been called away on a matter important. His place as celebrant I take. First we make prayer to our Father, the True and Only God. Next we perform Mass and urinate on Holy wafer taken from La Paz Cathedral. Bride and bridegroom then clothes remove and copulate on altar. Virgin blood most potent is. With it I anoint you all. Last, six of us in turn complete the work of in the bride passion arousing. The Lord God will determine the semen of which of us her pregnant makes. We are here eight males. After the bridegroom, our three other guests will possess her. Myself next and of my assistant priests two. There is, though, possibility that age has the Duke impotent made. If so, my third priest will his place take.'

Simon, Rex and Richard were all staring at Miranda. They were astounded that, on hearing this account of the ordeal before her, not a muscle of her face had changed. She was looking intently at the crooked Baron, and her lips were parted in a slight smile. The only possible explanation occurred to all three of them, that she must have been doped to prevent her from putting up any resistance or understanding what was going on.

The Duke's thoughts were not on Miranda. His heart had leapt at the announcement that the Prince had been called away, because some other evil business required his immediate attention. De Richleau knew himself to be a more advanced adept than von Thumm, and had, down at the Sala, used his power to overcome him temporarily. It was just possible that he might be able to do so again. But it had been the united strength of Glasshill, El Aziz, and Benito, added to that of the Baron, which had reversed the position when the prisoners were in the cellar.

Here the Baron had three Satanists to support him and all of them Adepts, whereas Richard, Rex and Simon were not. The odds were, therefore, against the Duke, but there was one possibility, the thought of which gave him a gleam of hope. His friends on the Astral were aware of his situation, and their intercession with the Lords of Light might yet lead to his winning the uneven battle. But he was far from sanguine, for he knew that, as a general principle, those on earth were expected to fight their own battles, and that their Mightiness of Eternity rarely allowed themselves to be distracted from their own great work and brought from the remote Seventh Astral Plane, which they alone occupied, to intervene in matters on earth.

While he was ruminating on these hopes and fears, von Thumm, his head—as was frequently the case—tilted towards his left shoulder, began to intone. He now spoke in Latin and recited the Lord's Prayer backwards. The Mass proceeded in that language, the assistant priests uttering the responses. In due course, the Baron produced a Holy wafer from a gold, jewel-studded casket on the altar. Crying out, 'This is the body of the impostor, Jesus Christ,' he spat upon it, threw it down, then urinated on it. His assistants followed suit. Crushing it under his heel, he said to Simon and Miranda:

'Now we consummation of your marriage make. Take off your clothes.'

Simon swung round towards Miranda. Before anyone could lay a hand on him he had whipped out the carving knife with which they had cut up the tinned food in the ruined church. At his movement, Miranda turned to face him. His arm flew up to bring the blade slashing down between her breasts.

De Richleau, having impressed on Simon how great a sin it would be to kill himself, had thought no more of the matter. But he had also said that, given certain circumstances, the killing of another could be justified and, evidently, Simon had decided that, rather than allow Miranda to be defiled, he would kill her.

She was within an ace of death when the Duke acted. It was as though those long-time friends of his on the Astral had shouted in one great chorus:

'Now! Now is your chance! If you can kill von Thumm, you will be the master down there.'

His right arm shot out from the shoulder. The first and second finger of his hand pointed at Simon. The Duke spoke no word. Simon was so placed that he did not even see the gesture. But, as though struck a violent blow from behind, his body turned in a quarter-circle. Caught by the light of the candle on the goat's head, the steel blade flashed for a second, then it streaked down and half its length was buried in von Thumm's chest.

The assistant priests uttered wild cries of rage. Glasshill had been the nearest of them to von Thumm. As the Baron, his eyes glaring, his mouth agape, collapsed on to the altar steps, the big Negro sprang forward. He raised his fist to strike Simon to the ground. That gave Richard the chance for which he had been waiting. Jerking his home-made knife from beneath his coat, he drove the big sliver of glass with all his force into Glasshill's liver. The Negro gave one awful scream and pitched forward on to the dying Baron.

The shouts and cries had brought Miranda out of her trance. She cast one horrified look at the figure of Baphomet and the two men choking out their life blood on the altar step below it, then let out a terrified cry. Next moment she realised that she was half naked, made as if to put her hands up to cover her breasts, and fainted.

The two young, naked acolytes dropped the censers they had been swinging and made a dash for the door. Silvia had turned and was also heading for it as fast as her long legs would carry her.

The Duke did not even glance in her direction. There still remained to be dealt with the two fat priests of Satan; the long-haired Andean and the grossly-fat Babu. The Duke was praying desperately that, together, they would not rank in circles and squares a magical degree higher than his own. The Babu had already raised his left hand and opened his mouth to pronounce a conjuration. Instantly, de Richleau lifted his right hand, so that it pointed at him, and shouted:

'Be silent!'

The Babu's thick lips wobbled uncertainly for a few seconds, then closed, and his arm fell to his side.

Richard had turned his glass dagger in the fatal wound he had inflicted on Glasshill, and drawn it out. As he straightened himself, he could see over the Duke's shoulder. The Andean was behind him. He had drawn a knife and was just about to stab de Richleau in the back. Richard gave a cry of warning. It came too late. The Duke heard it in time to make a sideways movement that saved his life, but the point of the knife pierced his left shoulder with such force that he was thrown forward on his face.

The fat Babu's face suddenly broke into a smile of triumph. He lifted his left arm again and opened his mouth to hurl a binding spell on the Duke's companions. But Rex was within a yard of him. Raising his 'leg of mutton' fist, he struck the Babu a terrific blow on the side of his flabby jaw. His head snapped back and he went down like a pole-axed ox.

With the agility of a panther, the Andean had gone down on one knee and raised his knife again, to finish off de Richleau. Richard flung himself forward bodily. His chest thudded into the kneeling man's shoulder, deflecting the blow and sending him over sideways. Richard came sprawling on top of him. Like an eel, the Andean wriggled from beneath the body of his attacker, and came to his knees. Again his knife went up, this time to slash at Richard.

Simon had caught Miranda as she fainted and lowered her to the altar steps a few feet from where von Thumm was gasping out his life in agony. With one arm round Miranda's shoulders, Simon was stroking her cheek and kissing her forehead, in an endeavour to bring her out of her faint. On hearing Richard's cry, he looked up. A second later he heard de Richleau crash to the floor behind him. Swinging round he pulled himself away from Miranda to go to the Duke's assistance. By then Richard had acted and the Duke was out of danger, but he himself was in imminent peril.

Jumping across de Richleau's prone body, Simon landed a kick on the side of the Andean's cheek. He dropped his knife and heeled over. A second kick from Simon and the Andean fell sideways, his head hitting the floor. With a ferocity utterly alien to his nature, Simon continued to kick and kick and kick until the evil priest's face was reduced to a mass of blood and pulp.

For a few minutes nothing was to be heard in the temple but the sound of their panting, as they strove to get back their breath. Rex was kneeling by the unconscious Duke, anxiously examining his wound. As soon as he could speak, he gasped:

'Thank God! . . . It's only a flesh wound . . . and not deep. The point of the knife struck his . . . shoulder blade. It was either hitting his head when he fell, or loss of blood that caused him to faint.'

'All the same, I don't like it,' Richard said anxiously. 'He's bleeding badly, and at his age he can't afford to lose a lot of blood.' As he spoke, he ripped off his jacket, then began to unbutton his shirt. Pulling it off he handed it to Rex, and added, 'Here, take this. Staunch the blood with it and we'll bind the wound up.'

Rex already had the Duke's coat off. As he began to tear the coat-tail of Richard's shirt into strips, Miranda gave a moan and opened her eyes. Simon bent over her again, took her hands in his and, sobbing with relief, murmured, 'Oh, my darling! Are you all right? Can you see me and hear me? Before, you acted so strangely. As though your mind wasn't working.'

'It wasn't,' she murmured. 'But I'm all right now. I . . . I only became fully conscious of what was going on round me when you stabbed that awful priest. Oh, Simon darling! How can I thank you for saving me from these beasts?'

Smiling down at her, he confessed, 'Nearly killed you instead, my precious. Had made up my mind to, rather than . . . well, seen you driven out of your mind. But we're not out of the wood yet. That hell-cat Silvia got away. May be other priests up above. If so, she'll be raising them against us by now.'

Miranda shook her head. 'Silvia's not a hell-cat. It was she who hypnotised me, so that I wouldn't know what was being done to me. Even if she is a witch, I'm sure she's not deliberately evil. She's in this thing for kicks.'

As she was speaking, Miranda had got to her feet. Slipping out of his jacket, Simon helped her into it so that she could cover her breasts. Then he turned to look down at the Duke.

There was a lot of blood on the floor that had run from the wound in his shoulder, and some of it had stained red the white hair on one side of his head. But Rex had managed to staunch the flow and, with Richard's help, got a tight bandage round his shoulder and under his armpit. As they sat him up to get him back into his torn jacket, he came to. His grey eyes were still half-closed as he looked about him, and his head wobbled unsteadily. After a minute or so, he said in a husky whisper:

'So help was sent us. Praise be, and . . . and we got the better of them. But . . . but I'm out of the game for the moment. I feel as weak as a kitten.'

'Your wound's not too bad,' Richard told him, 'but you've lost a lot of blood. Silvia disappeared while we were all fighting. By now she's probably got some of the retainers together, so we mustn't lose a moment in getting away. Think you can manage to walk with the help of Rex and me?'

Between them they got de Richleau on his feet, and with his arms round the shoulders of both of them. Resolutely he began to walk forward, but they had to bear most of his weight. Simon and Miranda, their arms round each other, followed them out of the temple, across the circular ante-room beyond it and into the dimly-lit passage.

They were reluctant to go upstairs, as to do so meant that they would be taking a big risk of running into Silvia and some of the Prince's minions. But they knew that there were several ways out of the ancient fortress. To find one was far from easy, as the stone-walled passages formed a veritable maze, with many chambers on either side evidently once doorless storerooms, opening off them. Several times they entered cul-de-sacs, that ended in a barrier of roughly-cut rock. At last they found a door which, when wrenched open, brought in a sudden cold draught and gave them a view of the star-spangled sky.

Outside was a small stone terrace, from which a flight of worn steps led down. As they went towards them they could see the airstrip below, because it was lit up. That it should be lit in the middle of the night alarmed them, for it suggested that the Prince had left in an aircraft and was shortly expected back.

The stairs were too narrow for three people abreast, so Richard led the way down, while Rex picked up the Duke in his strong arms and carried him. As they descended, they saw that there was now only one aircraft on the strip, which confirmed their supposition that the Prince had flown off in the other.

They were about halfway between the bottom of the staircase and the 'plane when a figure emerged from a nearby hut. In the glare of the arc lights they could be seen as clearly as though they were upon a brightly-lit stage. The squat figure was a man in Andean costume. He halted abruptly and gave a loud shout. His words were Chiquito, the language of the Bolivian Indian, so they did not understand them; but, obviously, he was calling on them to halt. His voice had barely ceased to echo in the still night air before he had pulled a pistol from its holster and was pointing it at them.

Simon still had the carving knife with which he had killed von Thumm, and, Richard his glass dagger. But the man who was holding them up was a good twenty paces away—much too far off for them to attempt to rush him. Inwardly they groaned. In two minutes they could have been in the 'plane, and in another five, in the air. To have come so near to escaping and now to be marched back and locked up until the Prince returned was a most bitter pill to have to swallow.

Through their minds raced sickening thoughts of what now lay before them. When he learned that four of his principal henchmen had been slain, the Prince's fury and malice would know no bounds. They would pray in vain for an easy death, but they knew him to be merciless. He would extract the last quiver of agony from their mutilated bodies before they slid into the peace of death.

It was only a matter of seconds after the challenge rang out when de Richleau cried, 'Rex! Put me down.'

Rex did as he was bidden, but kept a hold on the Duke, in order to support him. For the second time that night de Richleau extended his right arm, with the first and little fingers of his hand thrust out; but this time the movement was slower and cost him a big effort.

The effect of his gesture made them catch their breath. Invisible power streaked from his pointing hand at the man who was holding them up. There came a burst of flame, followed by a loud report. De Richleau had exploded the bullets in the magazine of the pistol. What remained of the weapon dropped from the man's shattered hand. With a shriek, he reeled away, blinded and bleeding, to fall backward on the ground.

But the effort had taken the Duke's last remnant of will power and physical strength. He suddenly sagged in Rex's arms. His bloodstained head fell forward, and he again became unconscious.

Now fearful that the sound of the explosion would bring other retainers of the Prince on the scene, Rex, carrying the Duke, ran towards the little aircraft. Richard raced him to it and yanked the door open. Between them they got de Richleau into it and sat him on one of the rear seats. Miranda and Simon scrambled after them and the latter closed the door.

Rex switched on the light and looked down at the instrument panel. With a curse, he announced, 'Nothing like enough gas to get us to the coast. What'll we do?'

'Couldn't fly through the mountains during the night, anyhow,' Simon said quickly. 'Take us down to that church near Potosi. We'll be safe there.'

'What then?' Rex snapped. 'No gas to be got there. We'll be stranded, and at any time that bloody Prince will be after us.'

'Fly us to the Sala,' Richard suggested swiftly. 'Von Thumm and his chums came up here for the wedding; so it's unlikely we shall meet with any opposition. We can refuel on the airstrip and take off again at first light.'

'Good for you,' Rex threw back, and switched on the engine.

'Get her off! Get her off quickly!' Simon shouted. Glancing through the window he had seen three men who had just come out of the hut, running across the tarmac towards the 'plane, and one of them had a Sten gun. 'They're after us!' he cried. 'Get her off, or we'll all be riddled with bullets.'

Rex revved up the engine for a moment, then the 'plane ran forward. As it lifted there came a burst of fire. A spate of bullets ripped into the tail of the aircraft. It shuddered, dipped steeply, then lifted again. They were off.

The flight down to the settlement in the Sala entailed an agonisingly anxious twenty minutes' flight through the moonlit mountains; but, in all, took only three-quarters of an hour. During this time de Richleau came round, but he was very weak, and his friends were very anxious about him. At the Sala airstrip the lights were on and, as usual, Rex brought the 'plane down in a perfect landing. Four aircraft were parked on the strip, but no-one was about. Richard and Simon climbed out and lowered de Richleau to them. Two minutes later, all five of them were on the ground.

Suddenly they caught sight of a solitary figure walking towards them. 'Not to worry,' Richard said in a low voice. 'We'll tell him that the Prince sent us down here, and take a meal off them in the house. That will kill time till we can fly off again.'

He had hardly finished speaking when the face of the man who was approaching was lit up by a beam from one of the pylon lights. The hearts of all of them jumped, then sank. It was the Prince.

His voice was sharp with anger, he cried, 'So you thought you would cheat me, eh?' Then he raised both his hands above his head. 'Down on your knees, all of you. Get down!'

For an agonising moment the muscles of their calves were seized with cramp, then the strength drained from them, and they sank to their knees.

18

CAUGHT IN THE TOILS

Unprotesting, humiliated, despairing, they knelt in a little group beside the aircraft. The Prince had halted ten feet away from them. Through Simon's quick mind, then through Richard's slower one, there drifted the thought that they had weapons. As had been clearly demonstrated less than an hour ago by de Richleau, when he had caused the gunman's pistol to blow up in his face, anyone possessing enough occult power could protect himself from physical harm if he knew he was going to be attacked. But taken by surprise, as von Thumm and Glasshill had been, they were just as vulnerable as other people. If then the Prince came close enough, there was a possibility that he could be knifed before he had a chance to defend himself.

Alas for their embryo hopes. The Prince caught the vibration made by their thoughts and said sharply, 'Mr Aron, Mr Eaton. You are armed. Throw your weapons at my feet.'

Reluctantly they took out their knives and threw them on to the tarmac within a yard of him. He looked down at them and frowned. 'A carving knife and a spearhead of glass partly wrapped in a bloodstained towel. What is the meaning of this blood?'

No-one answered him, so he snapped, 'Come! Tell me everything, and quickly. I was too occupied to overlook you earlier tonight. It was not until a quarter of an hour ago that my sixth sense suddenly told me that you were on your way here. What happened? The wedding! The girl, Miranda, is with you; so it could not have taken place. How did you escape? Whom have you killed? Van Ryn, I make you spokesman for your party. Speak now! A full account! Attempt to hide nothing, or I will send fire to consume your testicles.'

The horrible threat was redundant. Rex needed no telling that they were at the Prince's mercy and that by no means could he be prevented from learning very shortly all that had taken place that night in the Satanic temple. As briefly as he could, he related the events which had led up to their escape.

The Prince heard him out in silence, but even in the artificial light they could see that his face was going livid. When silence fell again, he glared at them for a moment, then screamed, 'Von Thumm, Glasshill, Kaputa and Pucara. All dead! Four of my best lieutenants. By Lucifer, you shall pay for this. By Ashtaroth, Memon, Theutus and Nebiros, oh! how you shall pay.'

His fury was such that he was shaking and had clearly lost control of himself. De Richleau watched him with lack-lustre eyes, sadly registering the fact that this was a moment when, had he been his normal self, he could have overcome their enemy. But the wound in his shoulder was throbbing madly, and that made it impossible for him to concentrate.

They heard the sound of swift footsteps, then caught sight of a figure pounding down the slope from the headquarters house. A minute later the curly-headed Benito came to a halt beside the Prince. He made a swift obeisance, then panted:

'My Prince. I hears yo' shout; so I come runnin'.'

The Prince ran his tongue over his now pale lips, then replied hoarsely, 'These heretics have taken advantage of my absence from the fortress to strike us a savage blow. But the Lord of Eternity is not mocked. He has cast them back into my hands. For their crime they shall spend an hour in torment for every hair on their heads. I have subdued them. They are now powerless. Take them to the house and put them in the cellar with those others.'

With a sudden gesture he removed the spell that he had put on the group. The calves of their legs began to tingle, the muscles flexed and they came slowly to their feet. Benito beckoned to them and, with the Duke again supported by Rex and Richard, they followed him up the slope.

On entering the house they were met by two of the Zombies, to whom Benito handed them over. Realising that resistance would be hopeless, they allowed themselves to be led down to the cellar. It was in darkness but, as the door was opened, the light in the passage outside showed them that two men were already there. One was a full-blooded Negro, the other a quadroon with a pale skin, thick lips and crinkly hair.

The first concern of the newcomers was the Duke. Before the door was shut on them, while there was still light enough to see, Miranda sat down in a corner and de Richleau was then lowered to the floor so that his head rested in her lap. With a sigh, he murmured:

'Thank you. Now that I am lying still, I will be able to help myself. My Yoga breathing will counteract the pain so that I can sleep. Please don't wake me until you have to.'

By then the door had been slammed and locked, and it was pitch dark. One of the other prisoners who they thought was probably the Negro, asked, 'Say, folks, what you bin thrown in de can for?'

'Getting up against the big-shot,' Rex replied succinctly.

'Same wid us, man. Leastways, that Jamaican sod didn't approve none of a talk we give the folks this evenin', an' he sent fer his boss.'

'What was the talk about?' asked Richard.

'Well, man, my buddy here an' me, we's bin doin' a lot of thinkin' dese pas' few weeks. Dis bid to bring de world under Black Power seemed jus' fine to us when we was indoctrinated. But we's bin gettin' doubts. You whites got all der guns, tear gas an' that. Reckon we don' stan' no chance. You'll sure come out on top. Slaughter'll be bad as a first-class war; an' we poor bastards'll end up wors' off than we was before.'

The other man added in a thin, piping voice, 'It's not only that. It's against the teachin' of Our Lord. He preached Peace an' Goodwill. Turn the other cheek, He said. Well, we coloured folk have done that for generations. But things are better than they were. I figure Dr Luther King has the right of it. Patience an' peaceful protest is the answer. Plenty decent white folk are on our side. It'll take a bit o' time; but given a few more years an' the good Lord Jesus will lead His coloured children out of darkness.'

'I'm sure you're right,' Richard agreed. 'But what exactly did you do?'

'First we talked o' makin' a break an' tryin' to get away from heah. But reckon that's near impossible. Fer hundreds o' miles round there's nought but marsh, scrub and them awful mountains. Guess we couldn't make it. Seemed to us then we'd best let on to some of the others 'bout our feelin's. Quite a few agreed that up heah we wasn't doin' the Lord's work arter all. No, sir; far from it. We planned ter stir up real trouble fer the badmen who run this outfit. What we were arter was to grab the aircraft, so as we could get away in them. Only chance o' that was a mass defiance of the bosses. Tonight we laid on a meetin'. Where we slipped up was to hold it arter usual time fer lights out. The bosses got on to us. They didn't interfere. Just waited till the folk had dispersed, then picked up the speakers. That was me and Malli heah. The Jamaican, the Moor and a couple o' those dumb bastards who do the chores fer the bosses come fetch us wiv' guns. That's how it happen we're thrown in the can.'

To his listeners this explained why the Prince had left the fortress at such short notice. Evidently when the threat of a revolt had been reported to him by Benito, he had thought it so grave a menace to his plans that he had decided to fly down and deal with the matter himself. To the man who had been speaking Rex said:

'That certainly was hard luck. But you're one hundred per cent right. This Black Power movement is inspired by the Devil. It could lead to bloodshed in hundreds of cities, and there's not a hope of coloured people bettering their lot through it.'

'What you think they'll do wiv' us?' the man asked anxiously.

Neither Rex nor Richard could bring himself to make a truthful reply. It was a certainty that the Prince would never let the two men return to the outer world, where they would tell others of the settlement in the Sala and about what was going on there. Neither would he allow them to go back among their fellow workers and risk their causing others to question the wisdom of the movement. And he was not the man to keep and feed two useless prisoners indefinitely; so the odds were that, within a few hours, he would have them quietly done away with.

Simon was of that opinion, too. But he could not bring himself to refrain from trying to comfort the two poor wretches. So he said, 'Can't do more than guess. Still, they wouldn't want to keep workers who're unwilling. Expect they'll have you flown back to the States, or wherever you come from.'

'Oh, man! I does hope you'se right,' the Negro said miserably. 'I's mighty scared. May the good Lord ha' mercy on His lil' chillen.'

Silence fell. De Richleau slept. The others lay or sat in great discomfort and dozed uneasily through the remaining hours of the night.

It was about six o'clock in the morning when the Zombies opened the door. Covering the Negro and the quadroon with their pistols, they stared at them with glazed eyes then, with jerky gestures, signed to them to get up and leave the cell-like room. Cowed, the two men offered no resistance and disappeared up the stairs. The door was shut on the others and they were again in darkness.

The Duke was in such a deep sleep that he had not woken. Time drifted on. The rest of them were not actually suffering from hunger and thirst, but they would have welcomed a good breakfast, or even a cup of water and some biscuits. But nothing was brought to them. They could only sit there in misery, wondering what form the Prince's vengeance would take for their having killed four of his henchmen.

At a little after eleven o'clock, Benito came to them. He had them wake de Richleau; then, with two patient Zombies as escort, they were taken upstairs and led into the washroom. The Duke's sleep had greatly improved his condition. He told them that, although he was still weak from loss of blood, he now felt only a dull ache in his shoulder.

When they had freshened themselves up, they were taken out to the airstrip. The Prince was at the controls of his 'plane, and the engine was already revving over. In a back seat sat the Moor, El Aziz. Across his knees lay a long, slender sword, the blade of which was only slightly curved.

As soon as they had settled themselves, the Prince said to Benito, 'If there is any more trouble, deal with it promptly, then report to me.' The door was shut and they took off. Three-quarters of an hour later they landed on the island in the Lago de Poopo. During the journey the Prince had not addressed a word to them. When they had all disembarked, he threw a haughty, contemptuous look at them and said to El Aziz:

'As we have no cells here, take them down to the swimming pool. In any case, to lock them up would be unnecessary, as I shall put a spell on them which will prevent them from leaving the fortress.'

Evidently having some further urgent business, he turned away and ran up the hundred and more steps to the fortress with a swiftness which put into the minds of the onlookers that he must be supported by invisible wings.

As de Richleau looked about him, he saw several of the airstrip men glaring balefully at his party. Their attitude showed that they must be aware that he or one of his friends had killed their companion during the previous night. It meant that if, in spite of the Prince, they could get down to the airfield again, the Andeans would probably open fire on them at sight. With Rex's assistance he slowly climbed the long flight of steps and they entered the stronghold.

El Aziz took them down to the big, circular Hall of Divination that served as an ante-room to the temple. As before, it was lit by a rosy glow and was empty. Crossing to the segment of the circular wall that had the panel bearing the reversed crescent upon it, El Aziz pressed a spring and a section slid smoothly back, revealing a long, low chamber.

It was dimly lit and they could see that the walls and ceiling were formed of the big, stone blocks used by the Incas; but an oblong pool filled the centre, and round it was a broad walk-way of modern tiles. At the far end the tiled space was wider and there they could make out some low tables and several lounge chairs.

Halting by the entrance, El Aziz signed for them to go ahead. Rex ignored the gesture and asked that a bed should be provided for the wounded Duke. From the expression on the Moor's face it was clear that it delighted him to refuse this request, but he did not even bother to reply. Turning his back, he left them, crossed the Hall of Divination and closed behind him the section of wall leading to the passage.

Rex then led the way along one side of the pool and said, 'In the old days this was the Incas' Treasure chamber. Occasionally the Prince enjoys a swim, so he had it converted to hold water and fitted with all the gadgets that go with a luxury pool. I've swum down here with Silvia and some of the others several times. Lord alone knows what His Satanic Highness means to do with us, but at least we'll be better off here than in that cellar down at the Sala.'

At the far end of the pool there was a bar, holding a good selection of bottles, and several tins of cocktail biscuits and nuts. As Rex went behind the bar, for the first time in days he laughed. Picking up the shaker, he said, 'Sorry there's no ice, but never mind,' and started to pour gin into it. Then he uttered his old crack, 'Come on, folks. Make 'em small but drink 'em quick. It takes a fourth to make an appetite.'

Regretfully de Richleau doused their temporary elation by saying, 'Nothing for me, Rex. I have denied myself alcohol for over a week now. That is important for an Adept who wishes to exert his powers to the full. For you others it does not matter so much, because you are not initiates. All the same, I think you should limit yourselves to two drinks each, because it could be dangerous to slow up your reactions in an emergency.'

Accordingly the Duke drank limejuice and water, and the others had only one snifter to brace them up, followed by a long drink to quench their thirst. As they had had no food that day they made swift inroads into the biscuits, except for the Duke who was determined to continue the semi-fast he had maintained ever since their arrival and, when they had made him as comfortable as possible on one of the lounge chairs, he refused all but a few small handfuls of nuts.

After the grim hours they had been through, this interlude greatly lightened their spirits; but they had had little sleep during the past night, so they soon fell silent and dozed for the greater part of the afternoon.

When they roused, their minds were again filled with thoughts of the dire peril they were in, and they began to speculate gloomily on what horrors the Prince might send against them during the coming night. Richard remarked despondently on there being nothing available with which they might form a pentacle to give them some protection, upon which the Duke said:

'The Prince must have had his mind on other things when he ordered us to be brought down here. The pool will serve us as well, if not better, than a makeshift pentacle. If an attack does come, we can take to the water.'

Looking down at the calm, unruffled sheet, Miranda asked, 'How will that help us?'

'Water, far more than bread, is the staff of life,' the Duke replied. 'One can exist without food for forty days and more; but not without liquid. For that reason most evil manifestations are highly allergic to water. For example, it is one of the few things that hamper the activities of vampires. No vampire can cross running water, not even a little stream.'

Simon asked, 'What do we do then? Stand in the shallow end fully clad, or strip and swim round in circles?'

'It would be best for us to stand in a ring, holding hands. Our vibrations are so well attuned that, when united, there is still a chance that we may be able to fight off anything that is sent against us.'

'Any idea what form the attack will take?' Richard enquired.

'None. He won't try to send us out of our minds by producing thought-forms of people we love in heart-rending situations. Having tried that, he knows it won't work. But he may send more of those revolting elementals. They are terrifying to look at, but a very low form of occult entity; so, if you all keep your nerve, we should be able to resist them. My real fear is that he may summon up one of the mighty forces from the Outer Circle. If he does that, we can only pray that the Lords of Light will take pity on us. Should that happen, though, we'll be saved only at the price of our lives. The whole fortress will be destroyed by an eruption and our present bodies with it.'

After a moment, Rex said, 'Say we do pull through. What then? It's impossible for us to escape because the Prince has put a spell on us.'

'Not through our own efforts,' the Duke agreed. 'The spell will nullify any attempt we might make to break out. But if, by a miracle, someone here took pity on us, he could get us away as though we were so many Zombies.'

'What a hope!' Richard exclaimed bitterly.

'I don't know.' Miranda said hesitantly. 'Remember Silvia put me under hypnosis last night before that awful ceremony. If she hadn't, I think I'd have died of horror and disgust. But she did, and that was quite contrary to the delight in sadism that everyone else here displays. They would have enjoyed seeing me suffer the most frightful agonies of apprehension. She saved me from that, so she can't be altogether bad.'

De Richleau smiled. 'You're right, my dear. As the Maiden of the Grand Coven of South America, she must be a powerful witch and fully approve the object that her companions are working for. Yet, unless I am much mistaken, a spark of light remains within her.'

Turning to Rex, he went on, 'Would you mind telling us exactly what your relations with Silvia are—or rather were? That might prove helpful.'

Rex spread out his hands. 'From you folks I've nothing to hide about my affair with her. If we hadn't been either too much up against it, or so tired out these past few days, I'd have given you the full story before now.

'It was this way. I met her in B.A. about eighteen months ago. I fell for her, and she didn't hide the fact that she took a good view of me. That is one of her attractions. She never seeks to disguise her feelings and calls a spade a spade. You can either like her or do the other thing, and she doesn't play hard to get. Anyhow, we made a date and, after we'd dined, she gave me that dazzling smile of hers and said, "You know, one of us may fall under a bus tomorrow, so why should we wait? Let's go back to my apartment."

'There was nothing of the whirlwind courtship about it. We were just two sophisticated people who, during our lives, had had quite a lot of fun with the opposite sex, and we liked each other. It was as simple as that. In the circumstances, it would have been a pretty queer thing if we hadn't enjoyed our roll in the hay. And you bet we did. That's how Silvia became my mistress.

'You know her record. She's slept around more than most women, and she doesn't give a cuss what people think of her. But she's got at least one good principle. I know she did her best to lead you up the garden path down at Punta Arenas; but, in the ordinary way, she never tells a lie. In view of her past, during our first few months I more or less took it for granted that when I had to go off on business to other capitals in South America, she would amuse herself with other guys. That didn't worry me over-much, because I've never really been in love with her. We had some wonderful times and were always happy when we were together, but I wasn't in love to the extent that I would have chucked everything and followed her to the other end of the world.

'I've a hunch that she felt the same way about me, but liked me enough not to tangle with anyone else when, now and then, I had to leave her for a week or so. That was the conclusion I came to after a while, because she was always so frank about everything—except in one particular. I used to spend two or three nights a week with her. Other nights we'd entertain or go out independently, and after such occasions she would always tell me how she had spent her evening. But once a month she would keep some date and clam up tight on what she'd been up to.

'Being fairly regular but so far apart, it didn't seem plausible that these dates were with some other guy. But naturally I was curious, so one night about six months ago I went to her apartment and waited for her to return. When she did get back, in the early hours of the morning, she was pretty potted. It was then that she spilled the beans to me that on these dates she attended seances.

'I've told you how things developed from there on, how she induced me to take an interest in the game, and how, when I learned about this Black Power movement, I felt that it was up to me to play along with them so that I could find out enough about this god-awful conspiracy to take steps which would bust it wide open.

'As you know, after I quit B.A., Silvia put in her annual few weeks at Punta Arenas, then came up to Santiago and on here. When she arrived we enjoyed the happy sort of reunion that we used to have after one of my trips to Rio or Lima. Since then, up till the day before yesterday, we've carried on just as we used to. Now you know how things stand between us.'

'Ner.' Simon shook his bird-like head. 'Since then situation's changed. She knows now that you ratted on them. Never even made a protest when the Prince deprived you of the use of your legs.'

'For her to have done so would have been useless. And she knew it.'

'Do you think,' asked the Duke, 'that, in spite of your having betrayed them, she still has tender feelings for you?'

'I wouldn't know. After all we've been to each other, she'd not be natural if she wasn't sorry to see me in the jam I'm in now. But it could be that she's too far committed to Satan to do more than stand on the side-lines and let matters take their course. Your guess is as good as mine.'

'I appreciate that. But you're probably right that her attitude depends on how deep she has got herself in. She is a witch, of course, but there are witches and witches. The majority of the poor old women who were burnt at the stake after the great persecution that started in the time of James I were innocent, and seized upon only because they lived alone, were ugly and kept a white mouse in a cage, or some other pet. Most of the others were capable of no more than blighting the crops of neighbours who had behaved badly towards them, or putting a murrain on their cattle, or causing their wives to miscarry. But there were a number who acted as midwives. They stole foetuses, resulting from premature births and unbaptised infants, then ate parts of them and used others as ingredients in revolting brews that could have a most potent effect on those who partook of them. They aided gangs of wreckers by raising hurricanes that drove ships on to the rocks, could influence people at a distance and brought death to their victims by melting wax images before a slow fire. How far do you suppose that Silvia has gone, in her desire for excitement, along this path of evil?'

Rex sighed. 'It's hard to say. Maybe she didn't take me into her full confidence because she has cast spells she knew I wouldn't approve of. But I've known her perform magics that you could class as bringing punishment on those who deserved it.

'One time a young maid of hers was driven out into the country and raped. Silvia managed to get hold of a pair of the man's socks and did her stuff on them. A few days later he contracted galloping syphilis and, within six weeks, his genitals rotted away.

'Another time a woman friend came to her and told her in tears how her husband used to whip her every night, and showed her her bottom, which was criss-crossed with bloody weals. Silvia had the girl bring her the whip, then returned it to her with instructions that next time she was in for a beating, she should complain to her husband that it still had dried blood on it and that he must wash it before he used it again. He took it into the bathroom and put it under the tap. What Silvia had done to it Heaven alone knows, but I imagine she had somehow charged it with electricity. Anyway, when this guy held it under the water, it earthed. The shock darn' near killed him and he got a most ghastly burn across the palm of his hand. It's clenched now, like a claw, and he'll never again be able to use it.'

'Those are certainly not the type of enchantments one would expect from a woman associated with the Prince and the Baron,' de Richleau commented. 'Either would have regarded the raping of the maid and the whipping of the wife as deeds inspired by an elemental, and approved of them. I think we can take it as proof that Silvia has not yet crossed the Abyss and become fully committed to the Left-Hand Path.'

'She has always said that she went into the game because it offered a new form of interest and excitement. She has much too happy a nature to be evil, and I doubt if she has ever seriously considered what the Black Power movement may ultimately lead to. But she enjoys the power that being a witch gives her.'

'"Power corrupts and absolute power corrupts absolutely",' de Richleau quoted. 'It seems to me that she is now standing on the brink. Since she enjoys power, they will give it to her—at a price. It is always so with those who dabble in the Black Art. It can be only a matter of time before she becomes corrupted, and as evil as the rest of them. In my opinion it is only because they have found her very useful in other ways that they have not so far lured her into taking the fatal step.'

'I guess you're right. Same as with myself. They thought me to be too valuable to them as a foreign exchange expert to press me to do things they knew I wouldn't do willingly.'

'How far have your own studies of the occult brought you?'

'Oh, I'm still only a neophyte, just coming up for the second grade. I'm capable of only small-time stuff. In secret, I concentrated on a friend of mine and succeeded in curing him of arthritis. For fun, one day I caused that old stick-in-the-mud, Harold Haag, the manager of our bank in Buenos Aires, to make a hopeless mess of his accounts. I can make cold water become tepid, but not to boil as yet. I'm getting on well as a clairvoyant, and I've made a beginning at thought transference with Silvia.'

'Ah!' exclaimed the Duke. 'There we have something. Could you manage to get into touch with her, and find out how she is disposed towards us?'

'No, I don't think I could do that. I can send thoughts out, but not receive them. At least, only now and then in a garbled version, and sometimes I have put quite a wrong interpretation on them.'

'To send her a message is the more important. Let her know that we have great cause to fear what may become of us. Ask her to aid us if she possibly can. Tell her that if she knows of any way in which we might escape we should be forever grateful if she would give us guidance to it.'

'O.K. I'll do that.' Rex got down on the floor and arranged himself in the traditional cross-legged position, then bowed his head. The Duke looked round at the others and said:

'There is no need to leave your seats, but all of you must remain silent and pray for Rex's success.'

For the best part of an hour they sat there. Rex appeared to have gone to sleep, but at last he raised his head and shook it. 'Maybe she got the message, maybe not. There was no response at all, so it's impossible to say.'

Soon afterwards two of the green-clad servitors appeared and brought them a meal, but it consisted only of a peasant fare, coarse bread and a basin each of maize mush, which made it clear that the Prince did not intend them to derive any enjoyment from their nourishment.

By the time they had finished the evening was well advanced, so they began to make preparations for the night. After they had visited the washrooms, the Duke had them arrange all the cushions from the easy chairs in one group on the pavement near the edge of the pool. The five of them then sat down on the cushions back to back, and he said:

'None of us must leave the others in any circumstance. Not only is union strength, but anyone who failed to remain in physical contact with the rest would be overcome much more easily. If an attack develops, whatever form it takes we must get up, form a line with clasped hands as quickly as we can; then, when I give the word, scramble into the shallow end of the pool here.'

Suddenly, to their consternation, the radiance that lit the swimming pool was switched off. The only light now came through the open panel of the Hall of Divination. They watched it anxiously, fearing that it, too, would go out. It remained on, but as it was over eighty feet away, it was no more than a bright patch faintly illuminating the gloom between it and them.

Looking uneasily about them, they began to imagine that the shadows thrown by pillars and buttresses were solidifying into strange forms and gruesome shapes that menaced them. The eerie half-light played havoc with their nerves and strung them up nearly to breaking point.

For a long while they hoped that Silvia would come to them, but at length they reconciled themselves to the belief that either she had not received Rex's message, or was in the enemy camp and had no intention of aiding them even if it was possible for her to do so.

At about eleven o'clock, they all jerked erect. They had caught the sound of footsteps on stone. Anxiously they peered in the direction of the ante-room, hoping that, after all, Silvia was coming to them. Holding their breath, they craned forward, only to release it in bitter disappointment a moment later. It was Singra, the Pakistani. He did not even glance through the opening into the almost dark swimming pool, but turned in the opposite direction and went into the temple. Having presumably performed some duty there after some ten minutes he came out again, recrossed the circular ante-chamber and disappeared.

Utter silence fell again. Another hour dragged by. Nothing happened. Suddenly Richard burst out, 'I can't stand this much longer. Let's have a sing-song.'

'Excellent idea,' agreed the Duke. 'I ought to have thought of that myself.' Spontaneously Rex started 'Rock of Ages', and they all joined in. 'Onward, Christian Soldiers' followed; but none of them was sure of the words of even these best-known hymns, so they fell back on old popular numbers: 'Roll out the Barrel', 'If you were the only girl in the world'. 'Keep the home fires burning', 'Land of Hope and Glory', and so on.

As they sang, they never ceased to keep an uneasy watch for some evil thing to materialise out of the shadows. But still the attack they expected failed to develop. After singing for two hours, they were so hoarse that the sound of their voices made a travesty of the tunes. At about two o'clock in the morning they fell silent. All of them felt utterly played out. By then they had ceased, except occasionally, even to throw apprehensive glances into the shadows. Still leaning back to back, their heads dropped on their chests. All of them except de Richleau fell asleep.

Without warning the dim lights of the swimming pool went on. As they roused, the Duke glanced at his watch and saw that it was morning. He told the others that while they had slept there had been no disturbances, and they felt that, for the time being, the danger was past.

They breakfasted off the remaining biscuits and nuts, then settled themselves again in the lounge chairs. De Richleau dropped off into a doze, while the others again speculated fruitlessly on what the Prince intended to do with them. As they had killed four of his principal lieutenants, they had no illusions that he would show them mercy, and could only suppose that his having left them in peace during the night meant that he intended to play a cat and mouse game with them.

Soon after they had eaten, the white pilot Dubecq and the half-caste Cervantes, both of whom they had glimpsed in the bar on their first arrival at the fortress, came down for a swim. Neither of them took any notice of the prisoners, so it could be assumed that the Prince had given orders that they were not to be interfered with.

After that nothing happened until about half past ten. Their attention was then caught by a new sound: that of high heels tapping on the stone floor of the ante-room. A moment later Silvia appeared. She was wearing a white Grecian robe, with gold embroidery at the neck and wrists. They all sat forward eagerly but, without giving them a glance, she let the robe fall to her feet, kicked off her mules and, naked, dived into the pool.

'By Jove! She's a dish, isn't she?' Richard murmured. 'I've never seen a girl with such splendid shoulders and so slim a waist.'

'Woman,' the Duke corrected him. 'We know her to be close on fifty. Obviously she's taken great care of herself; but latterly, I don't doubt, she has used her occult powers to renew her youth. The old beldames of whom we were talking last night were not in a class that knew the spells needed to make themselves physically attractive. But really potent witches always appear young and beautiful.'

Meanwhile Rex had stood up and was stripping off his clothes. It had been his custom to swim nude with Silvia, and he did not want her to think that he had suddenly become prudish; so, ignoring Miranda's presence, he dived in without a stitch on.

The onlookers watched them eagerly, but Rex and Silvia did not greet each other. At times they crossed each other's path, but anyone observing them would have taken them for complete strangers. After about ten minutes Silvia climbed out of the pool, dried herself on a towel she had brought with her and, without any indication that she was aware of the presence of the prisoners, walked away through the ante-room.

Standing in the shallow end of the pool, Rex said to his friends in a low voice, 'The Prince may be overlooking us, so we didn't dare exchange more than a few sentences, and those only because were were in the water. I did get through to her last night. She had no excuse to come down here then; but nearly every morning when she's here she has a swim, and the Prince hasn't said that while we are being kept prisoner she is not to.

'He is so furious about our having killed von Thumm and the others that he can't make up his mind what would be the most painful death to inflict on us. As we hoped might be the case, she would help us to get away if she could. You see, she's got it on her conscience that it is her fault that we have all been drawn into this. But there's nix that she can do. If the Prince even suspected that she had qualms about us, he'd blast her where she stood. So she can only play along with him.'

Their hope that Silvia would be able to aid them had been a very slender one, so they were not unduly cast down to learn that she was powerless to do so. But they were pleased, particularly Rex, to know that her mind was not entirely dominated by the Prince.

Later in the morning the skull-headed Negro, Mazambi, came down to bathe. Then, at midday, the prisoners were brought the same unappetising meal that they had been given the previous evening.

During the afternoon they dozed for a while; then, to keep their minds free from thinking of the most unpleasant forms of death and wondering which the Prince would decide on for them, they told stories, held a spelling bee and reminisced about their past adventures. Somehow they got through the dragging hours until, late in the evening, another ration of bread and mush was brought to them. Afterwards they held another sing-song; then, no longer fearful now that the Prince would send occult forces to attack them, settled down for the night.

Early next morning they all refreshed themselves by going in for a swim. In due course, Dubecq, Cervantes, and the Egyptian, Ben Yussuf, came down and swam. Then Silvia again arrived, so Rex went in to exchange a few words with her each time they passed one another in the water.

When she had gone he had the most exciting news for his friends. With a wide grin he said, 'There's more trouble down at the settlement. Seems those two poor guys who were in the cellar with us started something. The speeches they made at the meeting they called met with pretty wide agreement. Everyone down there is now debating whether this Black Power movement would pay off in the long run, and there is to be another meeting tonight. It's quite on the cards that a lot of them will decide to down tools unless they are sent back to their home towns.'

'By Jove! That really is something,' Richard exclaimed. 'It might wreck the whole movement.'

Rex nodded. 'There's still better to come. It seems there's a limit to even the Prince's powers. Silvia says that the binding spell he has put on us to keep us here is not operative at a distance. If he goes down to the settlement to quell this meeting tonight, as she thinks he means to, she should be able to get us out.'

'Oh, how wonderful!' Miranda cried. 'I knew she was good at heart. But when he comes back and finds out what she's done, won't he punish her most terribly?'

'I thought of that, and you're right. She told me she wouldn't dare remain here. If she did, it would cost her her life; so she will come with us.'

'Surely the Prince would not go off leaving her in charge here?' remarked the Duke. 'What about Mazambie, Dubecq, Singra and the rest? How would she deal with them?'

'She said that if von Thumm or Glasshill were still alive, that would have stymied her, because they were capable of reading her thoughts. But the rest of the bunch are not; so she'll offer to make them a *bouillabaisse* for dinner from the fish and what-have-you from the lake. It's quite a thing of hers, and very strongly flavoured, so they won't notice the drug she means to put in it, and that will knock them all for six. About the retainers she says we don't need to worry. Mentally they're pretty low material, and it just wouldn't occur to them to question anything she does.'

'May the Lords of Light be praised for having brought her back on to the Right-Hand Path,' murmured the Duke. But a moment later, he said anxiously, 'We shall still have one big hurdle to get over, though. As far as we know there are still two 'planes on the airstrip. The Prince will take one to fly himself down to the Sala; but how are we to get hold of the other? The Andean mechanics down there will jump at the chance of avenging their comrade, and I can subdue only one of them at a time. Unless Silvia has some way of dealing with them, the odds are that several of us may be shot down before we can reach the aircraft.'

Rex made a grimace. 'I hadn't thought of that, and it's a nasty one. Maybe Silvia could get us weapons. If so, and we could take them by surprise, we'd be able to put them out of the game before they had a chance to shoot us up.'

The best part of two nights and a day had passed since they had been caught. During those long hours they had slept little and had been in constant fear of the unguessable, but certainly agonising, death the Prince would inflict upon them. In consequence, this sudden prospect that Silvia might save them dispelled their utter despair and cheered them all enormously. Compared with the unknown horror that had filled them with such awful foreboding, they were inclined to take lightly the physical hazard of dealing with the Andean mechanics.

Now, buoyed up with optimism, they passed the rest of the morning in an almost happy frame of mind. With midday there arrived another unappetising meal, then in the afternoon they dozed. When, in the evening, food was brought to them again, as soon as the servitors had gone Richard said:

'Unless everything goes wrong, as soon as we get in that 'plane, we'll break open its stores and enjoy some decent food, so I'm not eating any more of this muck.'

De Richleau's spells of Yoga-induced sleep had done wonders for him. His wound was healing well and his voice was perceptibly more vigorous, as he said, 'Let's not count our chickens yet. You may need all your strength before morning. Think of yourself as back in the nursery and eat up your porridge like a good little boy.'

In due course the lights went out and the big chamber was plunged in darkness except at the far end, where the faint glow from the ante-room of the temple still showed.

Despite their new-found optimism, at the back of all their minds there nagged the disturbing thought that the Prince might decide to begin the torment with which he had threatened them before he flew down to the Sala; so, in order to offer the maximum resistance, they again arranged themselves sitting back to back on the cushions.

Knowing that Silvia would not be free to act until her associates had fallen into a heavy, drug-induced sleep, they thought it very unlikely that she would come to them before midnight, so they whiled away the late evening hours with such patience as they could muster.

At last midnight came and they all roused to a new alertness, listening eagerly for the least sound that might break the stillness. As time drifted by, their tension grew, but nothing occurred to relieve it. At ever more frequent intervals Rex gave a quick, nervous glance at the luminous dial of his wrist watch. One o'clock came, then two o'clock. Their suspense became almost unbearable. At last, a little before three o'clock de Richleau broke a long silence to voice the thought that, for an hour or more, had been tormenting them all and renewing their fears about their future.

'My friends,' he said softly, 'I fear we must face it. Something has gone wrong, or Silvia would have come to us by now.'

With heavy sighs they agreed, but sat on, still hoping desperately, through what seemed the never-ending hours until, at last, morning came and the light went on.

Weary and miserable, they got up and helped themselves to drinks at the bar. Now sleepy from their long vigil, they settled down in the lounge chairs where, still half awake, they mused with fresh apprehension on what fate might hold in store for them, and what might have happened to Silvia.

Her failure to appear might be owing to the Prince's having decided not to go down to the Sala after all. On the other hand it might be because the drug she had intended to give his lieutenants had failed to work on one or more of them. Still worse, her intention to help them escape might have been found out and she was now a prisoner who would share with them her Master's vengeance.

At about half past eight Dubecq and Cervantes came down to swim. As they splashed about and shouted to each other in the water, they showed no sign at all of having just come out of a heavy sleep, which seemed to indicate that they had not partaken of Silvia's drugged *bouillabaisse*.

Then, no more than five minutes after they had left, to the immense relief of Rex and his friends Silvia emerged from the ante-room, threw off her robe and, without a glance in their direction, dived into the water.

Within a couple of minutes Rex had pulled off his clothes and was swimming towards her. For nearly a quarter of an hour they passed and repassed each other without, apparently, exchanging a word; then Silvia climbed out at the far end. While she was drying herself, Rex stood only waist deep in the water and, in a low voice, said to his friends:

'She was stymied last night by the Prince's not going down to the Sala after all. Seems the trouble there has reached such proportions that he, with a few of his lieutenants and half a dozen Zombies, would be incapable of controlling such numbers by ordinary means; so he's taken a new decision. He means to turn the people there from volunteers into slaves.'

'How does he propose to do that?' Richard asked.

'By occult means. I gather that there's an exceptional source of power that they term "The Pit". He plans to open it, call up a host of elementals and send them down to the settlement.'

'The Pit!' exclaimed de Richleau in horror. 'Heavens alive! Can he really mean to open the gates of Hell?'

Rex nodded. 'That's what Silvia said. The elementals he conjures up from it will scare those poor do-gooders out of their wits for a few nights. Then they will be placed at the disposal of Benito and his pals, and anybody who refuses to do his job will wake up to find a demon sitting on his chest. It is going to be a horrible business, but it will give us a break. The Pit is somewhere in the rain forests of Brazil, and the Prince means to fly down to it tomorrow evening. With luck, while he's absent Silvia will be able to get us away.'

'Provided we're still alive to be got away,' Simon remarked gloomily.

'You've gotten a point there. It's still on the cards that he'll give us ours before he goes down to this hell-spot. But, at the moment, he's too concerned about the rebellion down at the settlement to think of much else. I gather that a good half of the stooges would have quit the place by now if they'd had transport; but it's so utterly cut off that they're scared of dying in the salt marshes or the arid mountains. Anyhow, Silvia says the Prince has hardly mentioned us since he sent us down here. This "opening of the Pit" business is going to be an all-time high Satanic jamboree. He is summoning the whole of the thirteen senior covens that operate in South America to attend it, and it's making the arrangements that is keeping him so fully occupied now.'

'What are elementals?' Miranda asked the Duke.

'They are quasi-intelligent thought creations,' he replied. 'Every thought we have produces an invisible form, and beautiful thoughts beget auras of good about the thinker. But evil thoughts are the product of evil habits and, if persisted in, they build up an elemental. Unless called up by a Black magician for some malevolent purpose, they are rarely seen. But alcoholics see them as green rats and other horrors. There are, of course, far worse ones created by murder, brutality, rape and all the vices. Drug addicts are sometimes driven to suicide by being haunted by them. The forms they take are hideous. Perhaps you have seen paintings by Breugel the Elder? In some of the most famous ones elementals are admirably portrayed.'

Miranda shuddered. 'Yes, when I was "finishing" in Paris, before I lost my sight. I was taken to the Louvre and saw some Breugels there. How awful for those poor people whom they are being sent to terrify. Are they only evil spirits or have they some sort of life?'

'They certainly have life of a kind, because to keep in being they have to feed. They batten on every sort of unpleasant substance: offal, faeces, urine, sexual secretions, menstrual blood, the pus from sores, drunkard's vomit and corpses. Some of them are termed Incubi and Succubi. The former visit women and the latter men in their beds at night. Except when deliberately summoned up by witches and wizards, they remain invisible, but copulate with their victims, drawing the vitality out of them. Their need for sustenance keeps them constantly on the prowl, seeking out vicious men and women who will provide them with regular nourishment.'

'Why, then, should they be down in the Pit?' asked Richard.

'Those would be elementals whose original creators are dead, so at the moment they are only the lowest sort of spirit. They are eagerly waiting to be despatched to someone whose vices would re-create them, or upon some mission that would gratify their Infernal Creator.'

During this second day that the friends had spent beside the swimming pool, their routine had not varied. The meals brought them continued to be prison fare. They twice went in for a swim and passed the time playing games which needed neither cards nor dice. As evening came, apprehension grew in them that the Prince would come to, or send for them that night, and despatch them, most painfully, to eternity. But somehow they managed to get through the long hours until morning came again and Silvia came down for her daily bathe.

After talking with her Rex reported that the Prince was still fully engaged on the preparations for the great occult ceremony that was to take place that night. He had been in communication with Adepts of the Left-Hand Path far and near; and appointed new Chiefs to the covens previously led by von Thumm, Glasshill, Kaputa and Pucara. He also intended to take with him the majority of his remaining lieutenants, of whom he had six there in the fortress and two down at the settlement.

In spite of the turmoil and partial stoppage of work there, he was confident that, for some time to come, his dupes would make no attempt to march out in a body. Any bid to cross the hundreds of miles of wilderness that separated the Sala from civilisation needed organisation and, as was to be expected, so far no-one among those woolly-minded people had emerged as a leader.

Moreover, the intelligence of elementals was very low; so, when they were launched against the do-gooders they could not be expected to discriminate. The Prince's lieutenants, although capable of driving them off, would be seriously plagued by them, and the Zombies would be scared out of what wits they had left.

In consequence, the Prince had decided to withdraw his own people from the settlement for three days, thus enabling them to attend the ceremony. Meanwhile, the dupes down there would be subjected to a reign of terror. After the three days their Satanic overlords would return. Using the threat of causing further terrifying manifestations, they would restore order and get the people back to work.

Silvia had not dared ask the Prince's intentions towards the prisoners, as it might have proved fatal to draw his attention to them. But the previous evening he had volunteered the information that he meant to continue to keep them on ice; so that when he returned from having opened the Pit, he could relish inflicting a long and painful death on them. It was his intention to leave El Aziz in charge of the fortress, and with him he would have the Zombies who were to be brought up from the settlement.

That had not given Silvia grounds for worry, since she felt confident that, with the aid of de Richleau, who was rapidly recovering from his wound, she could overcome El Aziz. What had worried her was the Prince's having made it clear that he took it for granted that she would accompany him to the ceremony. For her to do so would lay all their plans in ruins. But she had thought of a valid excuse to remain behind. When she went up from her swim, she intended to tell him that she had been called to the Astral and go into a trance. It was certain that he would be furious, but such a summons from a powerful Master temporarily out of incarnation could not be ignored.

On the previous day Rex had put to her the hazard they would have to face from the enmity of the Andean mechanics, before they could get hold of an aircraft. But about that she had now reassured him. The odds were that all the aircraft would be used, so she was not counting on one being left behind. But below the almost sheer cliff on the far side of the stronghold there was a small harbour, which could be reached by steps cut in the rock, and in it there was a powerful motor boat. It would easily carry then the thirty miles to the north-east corner of the lake. There lay the little town of Poopo, which gave the lake its name and, only a mile or so beyond it, ran one of the greatest arterial roads in the world: the Pan-American Highway.

Learning of her plan cheered them immensely. Instead of the risks entailed by a flight through the mountains, or having to march, ill-equipped and with scant provisions, for several days through uninhabited areas, it meant that within a couple of hours of leaving the fortress they would be in direct touch with civilisation. Cars and long-distance lorries were constantly passing along the broad highway; so there should be little difficulty in getting a lift which would carry them right out of the area in which, during the past twelve days, they had miraculously survived so much suffering and danger.

But all of them needed no telling that 'there is many a slip 'twixt the cup and the lip'. Would the Prince sense that Silvia was deceiving him? Would she succeed in evading El Aziz or, failing that, would they be able to overcome him? De Richleau had assessed the Moor's psychic powers as only a little less than those von Thumm had possessed. Silvia, not having passed the Abyss, certainly could not contend with him, and the Duke had lost so much blood from his wound that his powers were far from fully restored. Worst hazard of all, would the Prince, while flying across to Brazil, spare a moment to overlook them, learn that they were escaping and promptly take measures to stop them?

As the day wore on, the elation they had felt on learning of Silvia's plan to get them speedily to the Pan-American Highway gradually evaporated. Fears that some hitch would occur, or that the Prince would again alter his arrangements at the last moment, took its place. Should their attempt to escape fail, they realised only too well what the consequences would be for them. The Duke had forbidden them the possibility of endeavouring to abbreviate their sufferings by suicide. With flayed nerves they would have to stick out their torment until unconsciousness brought them merciful oblivion.

All through the morning they sat nearly silent, exchanging a remark only now and again. Their midday meal of maize gruel and coarse bread was brought to them. This fare, unappetising at any time, now made them feel sick at the sight of it. Somehow they got most of it down. They then endeavoured to settle to their afternoon doze, but found it impossible to put out of their minds the alternative possibilities of freedom or death that the night would bring.

At about three o'clock they were roused by the sound of footsteps in the ante-chamber. Looking swiftly across the pool, they saw that it was El Aziz, accompanied by two Zombies. Purposefully the powerful Moor strode along the side of the pool towards them. Coming to a halt, he said tersely:

'His Highness the Prince desires speech with you. Follow me.'

Getting up from their chairs, they obeyed. Without a glance behind him, he led them through the Hall of Divination, along the stone-walled passages and up to the library. The Prince was alone in the room, except for his familiar, the beautiful Blue Persian cat, and standing in front of a blazing log fire. Having surveyed them for a moment, he smiled and said:

'The stubble on your chins does not improve your appearance, and the lady's hair looks like a bird's nest. But no matter. These physical imperfections will shortly be burned away. For a purpose which is no concern of yours, tonight I intend to open the Pit. Apart from a comparatively small circle of Adepts, only the entities on the higher planes know of its existence; but, deep in the rain forests of Brazil, there are the ruins of an ancient temple–probably the oldest in the world. It is one of the few gateways by which man can physically contact that part of the Great God's domain which is termed the Underworld. I have decided that there could be no more fitting end for you than to enter it while still alive. So I am taking you to Brazil with me.'

19

THE OPENING OF THE PIT

The Prince's words came as a most shattering blow. Frequently as their hopes of escape had been eroded by fears that, for a dozen reasons, they would be prevented from getting away, hope *does* 'spring eternal in the human breast'. After seven days of terrible uncertainty they had, that morning, felt incredibly keyed up but confident that, before dawn came again, they would be safe and free. Now, at the eleventh hour, they were to be dragged off to die in a manner the horror of which they could not even imagine.

Like invisible armour, the aura of power round the evil Prince protected him from attack. To argue or plead they knew to be equally futile. When he summoned El Aziz and two of his Zombies to take them away, there was no alternative but to submit and allow themselves to be escorted out of the stronghold, down to the airstrip.

The only aircraft there was a twenty-seater passenger 'plane. Pierre Dubecq already sat at the controls. Near it stood Benito, the Pakistani, the Egyptian and the two Negroes. Presumably the Spanish half-caste, Miguel Cervantes, had flown off one of the other 'planes as, now that the prisoners were to be taken down to the rendezvous, it was no longer necessary to leave anyone in the fortress other than the hypnotised servitors. The Prince came down the steps, followed by the remaining Zombies that Benito had brought up from the settlement, and took his seat beside the pilot. All the others followed him into the 'plane. The prisoners were seated together about halfway along the aircraft. De Richleau glanced round and gave a sigh. Against such a formidable array of black vibrations, even had the Prince not been present it would not have been possible for him to do anything at all.

The door was slammed shut, the engine revved up. Suddenly there was a shout from near the front of the 'plane, an arm pointed upwards. Rex and Richard, who were sitting on the same side of the aircraft, looked in that direction. They saw a woman descending the steps. One glance at her halo of strawberry blonde hair was enough to tell them that it was Silvia. She was coming down the steep steps two and three at a time. They marvelled that she succeeded in keeping her balance. Had she stumbled, she would have pitched forward, bounced down the rest of the flight and ended up a crumpled heap of broken bones and blood at the bottom.

By a miracle she reached the tarmac safely and, her long legs flying, came racing towards the aircraft. The Prince had put his hand on the arm of the pilot. The engine died. Someone opened the door of the 'plane. White-faced and panting Silvia was hauled into it. While watching her make her dash to join them, everyone had fallen silent, so the friends heard her gasp out to the Prince:

'I persuaded the Master to allow me to leave the Astral. I . . . I couldn't miss this.'

He gave her a smile of approbation and she collapsed into a vacant seat a few rows behind him. The engine revved up again. The 'plane made a smooth take-off.

The route the aircraft took was north-east across the lake. It had been in the air only a few minutes when the friends saw below them the small, straggling town of Poopo, where they had hoped to land in freedom that night. Twenty minutes later they had crossed the eastern Andes, leaving La Paz on their left. The pilot found the Rio Beni and followed its course up to its junction with the Memora River. From that point he took a more easterly course, keeping in sight the mighty Madeira River for about a hundred miles, then he turned north towards the upper waters of the Amazon. Another hundred or more miles, and he began to come down.

They had been in the air for the best part of four hours and, after leaving the mountains behind, had been flying all the time over dense areas of jungle, broken here and there by patches of waste land. The only villages were situated many miles apart along the rivers. Otherwise there was no sign of human habitation.

Twilight had fallen, but as they descended they approached two clearings in the forest, both lit by a number of bonfires. On the larger, for which they were heading, they could make out a dozen or more aircraft of varying sizes, which had evidently brought the senior covens of witches and wizards from other parts of South America to this Grand Sabbat.

Slowly the 'plane sank to earth, bumped three times on the uneven ground, then slowed to a halt. A crowd of some hundred and fifty people ran towards it. As the Prince emerged from the cockpit, he was greeted with a great ovation. Men and women of every shade of colour pressed forward to kiss his hands.

After a while the greater part of the multitude withdrew, leaving in the Prince's company only his lieutenants, several men, who were evidently the chiefs of other covens he had summoned, and Silvia. As she had alighted from the 'plane, Rex had heard the Prince say to her, 'I am so pleased that you managed to return to earth and accompany me. I have quite enough on my hands tonight without having to choose another woman to take the role of the "Maiden".'

The prisoners stood a little apart, with El Aziz keeping an eye on them, and his armed Zombies close at hand. De Richleau assumed that the Prince and the group about him were discussing the form the ceremonial should take, or it might be that they were killing time while waiting for the completion of the assembly for, nearly half an hour after they had landed, another belated aircraft came in.

The conference seemed to go on interminably, and this period of waiting put a great strain on the prisoners. They had now accepted that there was no escape, and that before morning they would certainly be dead. Having keyed themselves up to face whatever fate might be inflicted on them, their one thought was now to get it over.

Simon stood with his arm about Miranda's waist. Her head rested on his shoulder. From time to time he murmured endearments and strove to comfort her. The Duke had been with his three friends in too many tight corners to feel the need to urge them to have fortitude. But he did for a while speak of the fact that no-one is ever subjected to more pain than he can bear—to ensure that is one of the duties of each person's Guardian Angel—and that, although they were about to leave their physical bodies, they would not be separated. They would ascend together to the Astral, and there would be many long-time friends there to welcome them.

At last the conference ended, torches were lit from the bonfires and a procession was formed. Half a dozen torch-bearers led the way, followed by the Prince and Silvia. After them came the chiefs of nine covens and deputies for the other four of which von Thumm, Glasshill, Kaputa and Pucara had been the chiefs representing in all the one hundred and sixty-nine witches and warlocks who had assembled to take part in this Grand thirteen-coven Sabbat. Behind the chiefs came the rank and file. The prisoners brought up the rear, escorted by the Zombies.

Leaving the big, open space where the aircraft had landed, they entered what amounted to a tunnel that had been cut through the dark forest. In the light of the torches the boles of gigantic trees, some of them as much as thirty feet in circumference, loomed upon either side. Above, only occasionally could a few stars be seen; for, in most places, the topmost branches met overhead. They were an immense height. From them trailed the green ropes of lianas and other creepers, making the sides of this long lane so dense that they could not be penetrated except at a dozen feet an hour by the arduous use of a machete.

The only sounds that broke the stillness of the night were the steady padding of the many marching feet and an occasional swift rustle in the undergrowth. Although little of it was visible, the forest teemed with life. Occasionally they glimpsed a boa-constrictor hanging head down from a low branch and, along others, a jaguar or wild cat crouched, its yellow eyes fixed and glowing as they caught the light from the torches.

The tunnel was over a mile in length, then it debouched into the other clearing lit by bonfires they had seen from the aircraft. In the centre stood the ruin of what had evidently once been a large temple. Broad flights of steps led up to a pillared portico that was cracked and broken. The roof was gone, but there was no debris on the floor, and urns holding masses of orchids lined the walls.

It had no resemblance to an Inca building and, indeed, it was several hundred miles outside the territory the Incas had occupied even when their Empire was at its maximum extent; but there was a definite suggestion of Egyptian architecture about it, and the Duke thought that it had probably been built by Atlanteans who had survived the deluge that had submerged their great island about 9600 B.C.

The Prince and the chiefs of covens entered the temple while the mass of the people remained outside. At its far end there were two low doorways. Passing through one of them, the Prince and his entourage disappeared, except for El Aziz, who waited until the prisoners were brought forward then led them in and lined them up at right angles to one side of what had been the altar. In front of it lay a strange phenomenon. Instead of ancient stone covering the whole floor, there was an area about twelve feet square, formed of some other substance. It looked like a thick, leprous skin, with some form of life beneath it, for it slowly pulsed and undulated.

While the prisoners were still looking at it with repulsion and dread, the multitude had been taking off their clothes outside the temple. Now they began to trickle in: tall and short, fat and thin, their naked bodies forming a motley mass ranging in colour from pink to coal black. There was no wind, and the humid atmosphere was so hot that many of them were still sweating from the march.

When they had all assembled in the body of the temple, a trumpet sounded. It was the signal for the Prince, and those who had accompanied him to the rooms behind the altar, to return and take their places. He was now clad in flowing robes of white satin, on which were embroidered in black the signs of the Zodiac. Upon his proud head he wore a triple crown that resembled the tiara of a Pope. The other Satanic dignitaries had robes of varying colours, emblazoned with dragons, serpents, toads and other beasts associated with the Satanic cult. The Prince took up a central position in front of the altar, his assistants lined up on the far side from the prisoners of the square of crepitating skin. Silvia, now sheathed in skin-tight gold and wearing a black crown on her strawberry-blonde hair, placed herself facing the Prince, on the nave side of the sinister square.

Silence fell. Suddenly the Prince lifted both his arms. A tremendous shout went up from the congregation. When its echoes had subsided, in a loud, clear voice he proceeded to intone a litany in Latin. The responses from a hundred and sixty-nine throats rolled through the ruin like thunder.

The service went on and on. The prisoners thought it would never end. But, as it proceeded, the square of leprous skin became more and more agitated. It began to heave. Big, oily bubbles appeared on the surface. As they burst, a horrid stench filled the air. Gradually the repulsive crust broke up into scores of smaller pieces. From between them steam began to rise. Soon even the pieces were obscured by it. The whole square had become a Pit from which clouds of smoke were billowing upward.

The Prince shrieked a last conjuration. *Zazas, Zazas, Nasatanada, Zazas!* The congregation repeated it three times. Then silence fell. Now, in the smoky-mist, forms were perceptible. They were not solid, but transparent, yet their appearance was terrifying. Among them were human faces supported by bats' wings, snakes with arms and claws, rats with eyes on stalks and two tails, toads with eyes as large as the rest of their bodies, mosquitoes as big as pheasants, winged swine that had only hind legs, grossly fat, undulating slugs that were armed with claws, three-foot-long phalli, women's genitals in proportion on four legs, a griffin with webbed feet and a spiked tail, a lynx with two heads and a curved horn between them.

These horrors, the prisoners knew, were the demons and demiurges that the Prince was raising out of Hell, to batten on all that was unclean down in the settlement, and drive the people there half crazy with fear.

As they surged upward through the smoke and out through the open roof, an awed silence had grasped the whole community. Rex swung round on the Duke and cried:

'Can we do nothing? Is there no way to stop it?'

The Duke's reply came clearly. 'Only one way. The Pit could be closed by a voluntary sacrifice. Someone who does not fear Satan must throw himself down into Hell.' Drawing a quick breath, he added, 'That could also save all of you.' Next moment he had taken a quick step forward.

'No!' cried Richard. 'No!' and grasped one of his arms to pull him back, while Rex grabbed the other.

Silvia was standing only a few feet away and had heard de Richleau's words. Her face chalk white, she gave one swift glance at the prisoners, and shouted, 'I brought you into this. I renounce Satan and all his works.' Throwing up her arms, she hurled herself forward and through the smoke into the Pit.

Instantly, there came an ear-splitting crash of thunder. Forked lightning streaked down from the sky. The walls of the temple began to rock. Simon grasped Miranda. He pulled her to him, so that her face should be buried in his chest and she should be spared the sight of the terrible things that were happening about them. Screams and curses rent the air. The scores of naked black, white and brown bodies of the congregation now formed a writhing mass. The lightning played among them, causing terrible havoc. Struck down or reeling about with terrible burns, they endeavoured in vain to escape. Some were crushed under falling masonry, others fell fainting to the floor. The twelve chiefs of covens on the far side of the Pit from the prisoners fared no better. Their robes on fire, their faces scorched, they fled screaming, only to trip and crash into the heaps of dead and dying that now filled the body of the temple.

The Duke's eyes were on the Prince. His features were handsome no longer. In seconds he had aged fifty years. His cheeks had sunk, teeth fell from his gaping mouth, his hair had become white and sparse. The Papal diadem tilted and slid from his head. It crashed on the altar stones, rolled forward and into the Pit. Next moment, as though suddenly pushed by an unseen hand the Prince staggered, lurched forward and followed it.

A terrible storm had arisen. Thunder continued to boom and lightning to strike, but now the scene was obscured by torrents of water gushing down from the heavens. Drenched to the skin, the friends huddled together, their minds still bemused by the holocaust that was taking place round them.

After ten minutes the tempest ceased as suddenly as it had begun. When the steamy atmosphere caused by the downpour had cleared, the friends could see that they were the only survivors. The body of the church was a mass of tangled corpses. Arms, legs, heads, were twisted into grotesque positions; but not a muscle was moving.

Rex gazed gloomily at the Pit. Too late, he was wondering whether he could not have endeavoured to prevent Silvia from sacrificing herself. Wisps of mist were still rising from it. One larger than the others began to take form. His eyes starting from his head, he seized de Richleau's arm and cried:

'Look! Look!'

They all stared in the direction he was pointing. The misty form was the figure of a woman. It began to give out a bright radiance. As it drifted upward, the features became clear. They were those of Silvia, serene and smiling. There came a great peal of trumpets, and her spirit was lost to sight above their heads.

'Bless her!' exclaimed Rex fervently. 'Bless her for her courage. And God be thanked that she cannot have suffered for long.'

The Duke nodded. 'The Lords of Light are far away; but they miss nothing, and they could not ignore such an act as hers.'

Richard had not grudged the time he had given to the search for his good friend Rex, and had accepted with fortitude the perils into which it had brought them. But, during these many weeks, he had frequently thought with longing of his beloved Marie-Lou.

Turning, he pointed in the direction of the tunnel through the forest, and said, 'Not much more than a mile away there are a score of aircraft for us to choose from. Come on, chaps. Time to go home.'

To the Devil -a Daughter

TO THE DEVIL
–A DAUGHTER

For our good friends
Diane and Pierre Hammerel
With my most grateful thanks for their boundless
hospitality and innumerable kindnesses to
Joan and myself during our recent visit to Nice;
not the least vivid memory of which remains our
fatiguing but intriguing expedition
(by daylight) to the Cave of the Bats.

I

STRANGE CONDUCT OF A GIRL UNKNOWN

Molly Fountain was now convinced that a more intriguing mystery than the one she was writing surrounded the solitary occupant of the house next door. For the third morning she could not settle to her work. The sentences refused to come, because every few minutes her eyes wandered from the paper, and her mind abandoned its search for the appropriate word, as her glance strayed through the open window down to the little terrace at the bottom of the garden that adjoined her own.

Both gardens sloped steeply towards the road. Beyond it, and a two-hundred-feet fall of jagged cliff, the Mediterranean stretched blue, calm and sparkling in the sunshine, to meet on the horizon a cloudless sky that was only a slightly paler shade of blue. The road was known as the 'Golden Corniche' owing to the outcrop of red porphyry rocks that gave the coast on this part of the Riviera such brilliant colour. To the right it ran down to St Raphael; to the left a drive of twenty-odd miles would bring one to Cannes. Behind it lay the mountains of the Esterel, sheltering it snugly from the cold winds, while behind them again to north and east rose the great chain of snow-tipped Alps, protecting the whole coast and making it a winter paradise.

Although it was only the last week in February, the sun was as hot as on a good day in June in England. That was nothing out of the ordinary for the time of year, but Mrs Fountain had long since schooled herself to resist the temptation to spend her mornings basking in it. Her writing of good, if not actually best-seller, thrillers meant the difference between living in very reasonable comfort and a near-precarious existence on the pension of the widow of a Lieutenant-Colonel. As a professional of some years' standing she knew that work must be done at set hours and in suitable surroundings. Kind friends at home had often suggested that in the summer she should come to stay and could write on the beach or in their gardens; but that would have meant frequent interruptions, distractions by buzzing insects, and gusts of wind blowing away her papers. It was for that reason she always wrote indoors, although in the upstairs front of her little villa, so that she could enjoy the lovely view. All the same, to-day she was conscious of a twinge of envy as she looked down on the girl who was lazing away the morning on the terrace in the next garden.

With an effort she pulled her mind back to her work. Johnny, her only son, was arriving to stay at the end of the week, and during his visits she put everything aside to be with him. She really must get up to the end of chapter eight before she abandoned her book for a fortnight. It was the trickiest part of the story, and if she had not got over that it would nag at her all through his stay. And she saw so little of him.

Despite herself her thoughts now drifted towards her son. He was not a bit like his father, except in his open, sunny nature that so readily charmed everyone he met. Archie had been typical of the Army officer coming from good landed-gentry stock. After herself, hunting, shooting and fishing had been his passions, and on any polo ground he had been a joy to watch. Johnny cared for none of those things. He took after her family, in nearly all of whom a streak of art had manifested itself. In Johnny's case it had come out as a flair for line and colour, and at twenty-three his gifts had already opened fine prospects for him with a good firm of interior decorators. But that meant his living in London. He could only come out to her once a year, and she could not afford to take long holidays in England.

She had often contemplated selling the villa and making a home for him in London; but somehow she could not bring herself to do that. When she and Archie married in 1927 they had spent their honeymoon at St Raphael, and fallen nearly as much in love with that gold-and-blue coast of the Esterel as they were with each other. That was why, when his father had died in the following year, they had decided to buy a villa there. As a second son his inheritance amounted to only a few thousand, but they had sunk nearly all of it in this little property and never regretted it. During the greater part of each year they had had to let it, but that brought them in quite a useful income, and for all their long leaves, while Johnny was a baby and later a growing boy, they had been able to occupy it themselves; so every corner of the house and every flowering shrub in the garden was intimately bound up with happy memories of her young married life.

The coming of the war had substituted long months of anxious separation for that joyful existence, and in 1942 all hope of its resumption had been finally shattered by an 8-mm. shell fired from one of Rommel's tanks in the Western Desert. Johnny had then been at school in Scotland, and his mother, her heart numb with misery, had striven to drown her grief by giving her every waking thought to the job she had been doing since 1940 in one of the Intelligence Departments of the War Office.

The end of the war had left her in a mental vacuum. Three years had elapsed since Archie's death, so she had come to accept it and was no longer subject to bouts of harrowing despair. But her job was finished and Johnny had just gone up to Cambridge; so she was now adrift without any absorbing interest to occupy the endless empty days that stretched ahead. Nearly six years of indifferent meals, taken at odd hours while working, often till after midnight, on Top-Secret projects that demanded secretarial duties of the most conscientious type, had left her both physically and mentally exhausted; so when it was learned that the villa had not been damaged or looted of its furniture, her friends had insisted that she should go south to recuperate.

She went reluctantly, dreading that seeing it again would renew the intolerable ache she had felt during the first months after her loss. To her surprise the contrary had proved the case. If Archie's ghost still lingered there, it smiled a welcome in the gently moving sunlight that dappled the garden paths, and in the murmur of the sea creaming on the rocks there seemed to be a faint echo of his laughter. It was the only permanent home they had ever had, and in these peaceful surroundings they had shared she found a new contentment.

For a few months her time had been amply filled in putting the house to rights, getting the neglected garden back into order and renewing her acquaintance with neighbours who had survived the war; but with her restoration to health her mind began to crave some intellectual occupation. Before the war she had occasionally written short stories for amusement and had had a few of them accepted; so it was natural that she should turn to fiction as an outlet. Besides, she had already realized that Archie's pension would be insufficient to support her at the villa permanently, and by then she had again become so enamoured of the place that she could not bear the thought of having to part with it. So, under the double spur, she set to work in earnest.

Very soon she found that her war-time experiences had immensely improved her abilities as a writer. Thousands of hours spent typing staff papers had imbued her with a sense of how best to present a series of factors logically, clearly and with the utmost brevity. Moreover, in her job she had learned how the secret services really operated; so, without giving away any official secrets, she could give her stories an atmosphere of plausibility which no amount of imagination could quite achieve. These assets, grafted on to a good general education and a lively romantic mind, had enabled her agent to place her first novel without difficulty. She had since followed it up with two a year and had now made quite a name for herself as a competent and reliable author.

Molly Fountain's books were set in a great variety of countries, but they were always mystery thrillers with a background of secret service. No one knew better than she that truth really was stranger than fiction; yet she never deliberately based a plot upon actual happenings to which she had been privy during the war. On the other hand, while taking considerable care to avoid any risk of an action for libel, she had no scruples about using as characters in her stories the exotic types frequently to be met with on that cosmopolitan coast, or incorporating such of their more lurid doings as the tittle-tattle of her bridge club in Cannes brought her, if these episodes could be profitably fitted in to add zest to the tale. That, subconsciously at least, was one of the reasons for her interest in the girl next door. Everything about this new neighbour suggested that she was the centre of a mystery.

Four days earlier Molly had just sat down to tea on her own little terrace when a taxi drew up in the road below and the girl had stepped out of it. She came from the direction of Cannes. In the taxi with her was a middle-aged man and some hand luggage. From the time and circumstances of her arrival it could be inferred that she had not come south on the Blue Train, but had landed from a 'plane at Nice airport. The man who accompanied her was strongly built, stocky and aggressive-looking, yet with something vaguely furtive about him. His clothes had struck a slightly incongruous note as he stood for a moment in the sunshine, looking up at the villa. It was not that there was anything really odd about them, and they were of quite good quality; but they were much more suited to a city office than either holidaying on the Riviera or travelling to it. He had helped the driver carry the suitcases up to the house, but remained there only about ten minutes, then returned to the waiting taxi and was driven off in it. That was the first and only time that Molly had seen him, and it now seemed evident that, having gone, he had gone for good.

There was nothing particularly strange in that. He might have been a house agent who had arranged to meet the girl and take her out to the villa that she had rented on a postal description through his firm; but in spite of his office clothes he had looked much too forceful a personality to be employed on such comparatively unimportant tasks. It seemed more probable that he was a relative or friend giving valuable time to performing a similar service. Anyhow, whoever he was, he had not bothered to come near the place again.

The strange thing was that no one else had either; nor, as far as Molly knew, had the girl ever gone out—at least in the daytime—and there was certainly something out of the ordinary about a young woman who was content to remain without any form of companionship for three whole days.

Stranger still, she made not the least effort to amuse herself. She never brought out any needlework or a sketching block, and was never seen to write a letter. Even when she carried a book as far as the terrace she rarely read it for more than a few minutes. Every morning, and a good part of each afternoon, she simply sat there gazing blankly out to sea. The theory that she was the victim of a profound sorrow suggested itself, yet she wore no sign of mourning and her healthy young face showed no trace of grief.

Molly had never encouraged her servants to bring her the local gossip, but in this case so intrigued had she become that she had made an exception. Like most women with a profession, she was too occupied to be either fussy or demanding about her household, provided she was reasonably well served; so she still had with her a couple named Botin whom she had engaged on her return to France in 1946. They had their faults, but would allow no one to cheat her except themselves, and that only in moderation. They were middle-aged, of cheerful disposition and had become much attached to her. Louis looked after the garden and did the heavy work, while Angèle did the marketing, the cooking and all those other innumerable tasks which a French *bonne à tout faire* so willingly undertakes. On the previous day Molly had, with apparent casualness, pumped them both.

Louis produced only two crumbs of information, gleaned from his colleague, old André, who for many years had tended the adjoining garden. The mademoiselle was English and the villa had been taken for only a month. Angèle had proved an even poorer source, as she reported that the *bonne* who was looking after the young lady next door was a stranger to the district; she had been engaged through an agency in Marseilles and was a Catalan, a woman of sour disposition who had rejected all overtures of friendship and was uncommunicative to the point of rudeness.

Negative as Angèle's contribution appeared to be, it had given Molly further food for speculation. Why should an English visitor engage a semi-foreigner from a city a hundred miles away to do for her, when there were plenty of good *bonnes* to be had on the spot? It would have saved a railway fare, and quite a sum on the weekly household books, to secure one who was well in with the local shopkeepers and knew the best stalls in the St Raphael market at which to buy good food economically. The answer that sprang to mind was that a stranger was much less likely to gossip, and therefore something was going on next door that the tenant desired to hide.

Then, last night the mystery had deepened still further. Molly was a light sleeper. A little after one o'clock she had been roused by the sound of a loose stone rattling down the steep slope of a garden path. Getting out of bed she went to the window. The moon was up, its silvery light gleaming in big patches on the cactus between the pine-trees, and there was the girl just going down the short flight of steps that led from her little terrace to the road.

Fully awake now, Molly turned on her bedside light and settled down to read a new William Mole thriller that she had just had sent from England; but while reading, her curiosity about her neighbour now still further titillated, she kept an ear cocked for sounds of the girl's return. As a writer she could not help being envious of the way in which Mr Mole used his fine command of English to create striking imagery, and her sense of humour was greatly tickled by his skilful interpolation of the comic between his more exciting scenes; so the next hour and a half sped by very quickly. Then in the still night she heard the click of the next-door garden gate, and, getting up again, saw the girl re-enter the house.

Why, Molly wondered, when she never went out in the daytime, should she go out at night? It could hardly be that she was in hiding, because she spent the greater part of each day on the terrace, where she could easily be seen from the road by anyone passing in a car. The obvious answer seemed to be that she had gone out to meet someone in secret; but she had been neither fetched in a car nor returned in one, and she had not been absent quite long enough to have walked into St Raphael and back. Of course, she could have been picked up by a car that had been waiting for her round the next bend of the road, or perhaps she had had an assignation at one of the neighbouring villas. In any case, this midnight sortie added still further to the fascinating conundrum of what lay behind this solitary young woman having taken a villa on the *Corniche d'Or*.

For the twentieth time that morning Molly's grey-green eyes wandered from her typewriter to the open window. Just beneath it a mimosa tree was in full bloom and its heavenly scent came in great wafts to her. Beyond it and a little to the left a group of cypresses rose like dark candle-flames, their points just touching the blue horizon. Further away to the right two umbrella pines stood out in stark beauty against the azure sky. Below them on her small, square, balustraded terrace the girl still sat motionless, her hands folded in her lap, gazing out to sea. About the pose of the slim, dark-haired figure there was something infinitely lonely and pathetic.

Molly Fountain knew that she had no right whatever to poke her nose into someone else's business, but she could bear it no longer. Her new neighbour, although unconscious of it, was playing the very devil with her work, and, worse, she would know no peace of mind until she had at least made an effort to find out if the girl were in trouble. That it was not the sort of trouble which sometimes causes young women to seek seclusion for a while in order to protect their reputations was evident, as the villa had been leased for only a month and the girl showed not the slightest sign of pregnancy. Yet there must be some cause for her abnormal conduct and obvious melancholy. Molly was far from being a motherly soul, but she had her fair share of maternal instinct and, quite apart from her desire to satisfy her curiosity, she now felt an urge that would not be denied to offer her help if it was needed, or at least endeavour to animate this woebegone young creature with something of her own cheerful vitality.

There was only one thing for it. On the Riviera it was not customary to call upon temporary neighbours, but the fact that they were both English would be excuse enough for that. With Molly, to make up her mind was to act. Pushing back her chair from the typing table, she stood up. For once a real-life mystery had been thrust beneath her nose. There and then she decided to go out and attempt to solve it.

2

COLONEL CRACKENTHORP'S TECHNIQUE

Going through into her bedroom, Molly Fountain pulled her linen working smock up over her head. Anyone seeing her at that moment would never have guessed that she was forty-five. Her upstretched arms emphasized the lines of her good figure; her hips had broadened comparatively little since she had reached maturity and her legs were straight and shapely. Only as she jerked off the smock and threw it on a chair did the fact that her youth was past become apparent, from a slight thickening of the muscles in her neck and her grey hair.

From her wardrobe she selected a white, hand-embroidered blouse and a grey coat and skirt. The cut of these, together with her medium-weight nylons and practical, lowish-heeled shoes, did nothing to detract from her real age, since the one thought Molly could not bear was that anyone should have cause to regard her as 'mutton dressed as lamb'. For that reason, too, except when going out at night to a party, she used very little make-up. Yet, even so, the face that looked back at her from the mirror as she quickly tidied her hair would have been judged by most people to be that of a woman still under forty. There were laughter-lines round the mouth and the beginnings of crow's-feet round the eyes, but not a hint of sagging in the still firm flesh, and it was moulded on that fine bone formation that preserves the basis of youthful good looks right into old age.

Reaching up on tip-toe she pulled a battered hat-box from off the top of the wardrobe and took from it a three-year-old straw hat bedecked with cornflowers. Molly hated hats and never wore one if she could possibly avoid it, but she felt that on this occasion a hat should be worn in support of her pretence that she was making a formal call. Securing it on her head at what she believed to be a *chic* angle, she collected a pair of gloves and her bag, then set off on her self-appointed mission.

It was a little before mid-day and the sun was strong enough now to tan anyone who was not used to it. As she made her way down the garden path that zig-zagged among spiky cactus and strange-shaped succulents she saw a little green lizard run up the trunk of a tall palm-tree, and on reaching the terrace at the bottom she made a mental note that enough roses were in bloom in the bed behind it to furnish her with another bowl. Out in the road she walked along under the tall retaining wall of rough-hewn rock that supported both her garden and those of several medium-sized villas situated on the same slope. At intervals along it hung festoons of large-flowered yellow jasmin and purple bougainvillaea. The scent of flowers, mingled with that of the primaeval pine-wood among which the villas had been built, was delicious. For the ten-thousandth time the thought crossed her mind that never could she bring herself to leave it and face another English winter.

By then she had reached the gate to the next garden. Opening it, she went up the steep stone steps set in a narrow cleft of the stonework. As her head emerged above ground level she turned it towards the terrace. The girl had heard her approach and was looking in her direction. Slowly she stood up, but she did not move forward and gave no sign of welcome. Her face had a guarded look and Molly thought she detected just a trace of fear in her dark eyes.

Stepping up on the the terrace, Molly said, 'I'm Molly Fountain, your nearest neighbour. As we're both English I thought—'

The girl's eyes widened and her broad face suddenly became animated as she exclaimed, 'Not *the* Molly Fountain?'

Molly smiled. Her name was by no means universally known, but during the past two years it had become sufficiently so for quite a high proportion of English people to whom, for one reason or another, she had to give it to ask if she was the author; yet the question still never failed to arouse in her a slightly bashful pleasure, and she replied with becoming modesty:

'I don't know of any other, and if you are thinking of the writer of secret service yarns, that would be me.'

'Of course!' said the girl. 'I've read several of them, and they're awfully thrilling.'

'That makes things easier, doesn't it?' Molly quickly took advantage of the bridge unexpectedly offered by her literary activities. 'Having read some of my stories will, I hope, make you look on me as a little less like a total stranger. You must forgive me making my first call on you in the morning, but social customs are more elastic here than at home, and I thought you might prefer it to cards left formally on you in the afternoon.'

It was the first time Molly had seen the girl face to face, and while she was speaking she was taking quiet stock of her. Tall above the average, so slim as to be almost gawky, and a slight awkwardness in the control of her long limbs gave her somewhat the appearance of an overgrown schoolgirl. Seen from the distance Molly had put her down as about twenty-three, but now she revised her estimate and decided that nineteen would be nearer the mark. Her forehead was broad and surmounted by thick, wavy, dark-brown hair parted in the middle; her mouth was wide, full and generous. A snub nose robbed her of all pretence to classical beauty, and her complexion was a trifle sallow; but she possessed two excellent features. When her teeth flashed in a smile they were dazzlingly white: more striking still, her brown eyes were huge and extraordinarily luminous.

Molly's reference to formal calls caused her to remember the duties of hospitality, and with only a fraction of hesitation she said. 'Won't you . . . come up to the house?'

'Thank you; I should love to,' Molly replied promptly. Then, as they turned towards it, she added, 'But, you know, you haven't told me your name yet.'

'Oh!' Again there was a slight hesitation before the answer. 'It's Christina Mordant.'

The path between the prickly-pears and oleanders snaked from side to side round a succession of hairpin bends, yet despite that it was still steep enough to require all their breath as they mounted it; so they spoke no more until they reached a small lawn on the level of the villa.

Molly had never been up there before and the lemon-washed house was partly concealed both from her windows and the road by umbrella-pines and palm-trees. She saw now that it was somewhat smaller than her own and probably contained only six or seven rooms including the servants' quarters. As they crossed the lawn she asked:

'Is this your first visit to the Riviera?'

'Yes,' Christina nodded, leading her guest through a pair of french windows into the sitting-room. 'But I've lived in France for quite a while. I was at a finishing school in Paris until just before Christmas.'

'I first came to this part of the world in 1927, and have made my home here for the past five years; so you must let me show you something of this lovely coast,' Molly volunteered.

Christina's hesitation was much more marked this time. Her underlip trembled slightly, then she stammered, 'Thank you . . . awfully; but . . . but I don't care much for going out.'

A moment's awkward pause ensued, then she pulled herself together and added in a rather breathless attempt to atone for what might be taken as rudeness, 'Do please sit down. Let me get you a drink. I'm afraid we don't run to cocktails, but Maria could soon make some coffee, or we have delicious orange-juice.'

Molly did not really want a drink, but realized that acceptance would give her an excuse to prolong her call, and the longer they talked the better her chance of winning the girl's confidence; so she said, 'I'd love some orange-juice if it's not too much trouble.'

'Oh, none at all,' Christina cried, hurrying to the window. 'There are masses of oranges in the garden. I'll pick some. It won't take me a moment. We've lemons, grape-fruit and tangerines, too. Would you like it straight, or prefer a mixture?'

'I always think orange and grape-fruit half and half is the nicest out here, where there's no shortage of sugar,' Molly replied; and as the girl left the room she began to take detailed stock of it.

The villa belonged to a café proprietor in Cannes who had never occupied it himself, but bought it as an investment and made a good thing out of it by letting it furnished for short periods to a succession of holiday-makers. In consequence it contained only the barest necessities, and its furniture was of that positively hideous variety favoured by the French bourgeoisie. In vain Molly's glance roved over the monstrosities in cheap wood and chromium for some indication of Christina's personality, until her eye lit on a manicure-set which lay open on a rickety spindle-legged table half concealed by the chair in which she was sitting. Picking it up she saw that it was comparatively new, bore the mark of a Paris manufacturer, and that its morocco leather cover was stamped with the initials E. B.

When Christina returned she came in by the door from the hallway carrying a tray with a jug of fruit-juice, two glasses and sugar. As she poured out, she asked, 'Do you live here all the year, Mrs Fountain?'

'Most of it. I usually spend June in London and have a fortnight in Paris in the autumn; but the cost of living has become so high both in France and England that I can't afford to live for more than about six weeks in hotels.'

Christina raised her dark eyebrows. 'Really! I should have thought you were terribly rich. Your books must bring you in thousands.'

'That's a popular illusion that the public have about all authors,' Molly smiled. 'Except for a handful of best-sellers, writing is one of the worst-paid jobs in the world; and even in France, these days, a big part of one's earnings is taken away by taxation.'

For ten minutes or so she went on talking about books and authors, as Christina was obviously interested, and it seemed a good line for tuning in on the girl's mind without arousing her suspicions. Then, having learnt that she had a liking for historical novels, Molly said:

'In that case it surprises me all the more that you don't make some excursions. This coast is full of history right back to Phœnician times. Fréjus was a Roman town. The streets of the old quarter in Nice are absolutely fascinating, and both Marshal Massena and Garibaldi were born there. Napoleon landed from Elba at Cap d'Antibes and at Haute Cagnes there is a fine old castle that belonged to the Counts Grimaldi. When I was your age I would have given anything for the chance to visit all these places.'

Christina gave her an uncomfortable look, then averted her eyes and muttered, 'I'm quite happy lazing in the garden.'

'How long are you here for?'

'About another three weeks. The villa is taken for a month.'

'Are you quite on your own?'

'Yes.'

'Surely you find it very lonely? Have you no friends you could go to visit, or who could come to see you?'

'No. I don't know anyone at all down here. But . . . but I like being on my own.'

'In that you are lucky,' Molly commented quietly. 'It is a great blessing to be content with one's own company and not be driven constantly to seek some new distraction from one's own thoughts. But all the same I should have thought you would have sometimes liked a change of scene. Don't you ever go out at all?'

Christina shook her head.

'An exciting book kept me reading very late last night, and when I got out of bed to get one of my sleeping pills I thought I saw you coming in through the garden.'

For a moment the girl's face remained closed and secretive, then she replied, 'Yes. I had been for a walk. I sleep most of the afternoon and go for a walk every night. I don't know why, but I've always felt listless after mid-day; then, as darkness falls, I seem to wake up and want to do things.'

'Some people are like that. The astrologers say that we are influenced all our lives by the hour of our birth, and that people born in the evening are always at their best at night.'

'Really! That seems to fit my case. I was born at nine forty-five in the evening.' After a second Christina volunteered the additional information, 'My birthday is March the sixth, and I'll be twenty-one next month.'

'You will be here for it, then. It seems an awful shame that you should be deprived of the chance to celebrate. But perhaps you have relatives or friends who will be joining you before that?'

'No; I expect still to be quite alone.'

There fell a pause while Molly considered this new evidence of the girl's complete isolation. A twenty-first birthday is such a landmark in any young person's life that it seemed quite extraordinary that she had not a single person in the world who wished to make it a happy day for her. Then, after a moment, Molly realized that so far she had got nowhere; she had not succeeded in getting the faintest clue to this mystery.

Swiftly she began to consider what line the favourite hero of her own creation, Colonel Crackenthorp, would take on having reached such an impasse. She knew this fiction character of hers as well as she knew herself; so the answer came automatically. The debonair and resourceful 'Crack' would employ shock tactics. Shock tactics it should be then. Looking the girl straight in the eye, she said suddenly:

'Christina Mordant is not your real name, is it?'

Caught off her guard, the girl winced as if she had been struck, and gasped, 'How . . . how did you know?'

Then she recovered herself. Her face had gone white, but she slowly rose to her feet. As she did so her big brown eyes narrowed and filled with an angry light. Her whole body was trembling as she burst out:

'What has it to do with you? I didn't ask you to come here! What right have you to pry into my affairs? How dare you spy upon me and come here to catechize me? Get out! D'you hear me? Get out at once!'

This was not at all the sort of response that the shock tactics of the gallant 'Crack' would have met with in one of Molly's books. The girl would have broken down, wept upon his broad shoulder and confessed all. But then 'Crack' was a handsome fellow who had the devil of a way with women, whereas his creator was only a middle-aged lady novelist. No doubt, thought Molly, that explained why his technique had failed so lamentably in this real-life try-out. Anyhow, it was clear that she had botched the whole business beyond repair; so she stood up and said:

'I *do* apologize. My inquisitiveness was quite unjustified and I'm afraid I was very rude. I'm not either usually, and in the ordinary way I'd never dream of forcing myself on anyone. My work keeps me far too busy to waste time calling on strangers. But I couldn't help being worried by seeing you sitting on your terrace hour after hour doing absolutely nothing. And you looked so terribly unhappy that I felt sure you must be in some sort of trouble. Had other people come to see you I would never have come here; but you're very young and seemed to have no one you could turn to. I'm old enough to be your mother, and I was hoping that you might care to confide in me, because I would willingly have helped you if I could. As it is I can only ask you to forgive my unwarranted intrusion.'

Mustering the remnants of her shattered dignity, Molly squared her shoulders then, with a brief inclination of her head, walked past the tall, now stony-faced, girl, through the french windows and out on to the lawn. She was only half-way across it when she was halted by a despairing cry behind her.

'Oh, Mrs Fountain! Come back! Come back! I didn't mean what I said. You're nice! You're kind: I'm sure I can trust you. I can't tell you why I'm here, because I don't know myself. But I'm worried out of my wits. Oh, please let me talk to you.'

Molly turned, and next moment the slim girlish figure was weeping in her arms. Without elation, but in faint surprise, she was conscious of the thought that good old 'Crack's' technique had worked after all.

3

THE MYSTERIOUS RECLUSE

A good ten minutes elapsed before Christina—as she called herself—became fully coherent. During that time the only concrete fact that Molly had got out of her was that the purposeful-looking middle-aged man who had arrived in the taxi with her four days before was her father.

They were now back in the house and sitting together on the cheap, velvet-covered settee. Molly had one arm round the girl's shoulders and was gently wiping the tears from her cheeks with a totally inadequate handkerchief. When her sobbing at last began to ease, Molly said:

'My dear, do you really mean to tell me that your father brought you here and left you without giving any reason at all for doing so?'

'The . . . the only reason he gave was that I . . . I have enemies who are hunting for me.'

'What sort of enemies?'

The girl gave a loud sniff, then fished out her own handkerchief and blew her snub nose. When she had done, she said in a firmer voice, 'I don't know. I haven't an idea. That's just what makes the whole thing so puzzling.'

Molly poured some more of the fruit-juice into a glass and handed it to her. She drank a little, said 'Thanks,' and went on, 'He simply said that I was threatened by a very great danger, but that I had nothing at all to worry about providing I obeyed his instructions implicitly. When I pressed him to tell me what the danger was, he said it was far better that I should know nothing about it, because if I knew I might start imagining things and do something silly. All I had to do was to lie low here for a few weeks and I should be quite safe.'

'You poor child! I don't wonder now that you've been unable to give your thoughts to any form of amusement, with a thing like this on your mind. But have you no idea at all what this threat might be, or who these enemies are from whom your father is hiding you?'

'No. I've cudgelled my wits for hours about it, but I haven't a clue. I've never done any grave harm to anyone. Honestly I haven't. And I can't think why anyone should want to harm me.'

After considering the matter for a moment, Molly asked, 'Are you by chance a very rich girl?'

'Oh no. Father left me ample money to pay for my stay here, and he gives me a generous dress allowance; but that's all I've got.'

'I really meant, are you an heiress? Has anyone left you a big sum of money into which you come when you are twenty-one?'

'No: no one has ever left me anything. I don't think any of my relatives ever had much to leave, anyway.'

'How about your father? Is he very well off?'

'I suppose so. Yes, he must be. We live very quietly at home, but all the same he must make a lot of money out of the factory, and all the other businesses in which he is mixed up. But why do you ask?'

'I was wondering if there could be a plot to kidnap you and hold you to ransom.'

The big brown eyes showed a mild scepticism. 'Surely that sort of thing happens only in America? Besides, my father is no richer than scores of other British industrialists; so I can't see any reason why kidnappers should single him out for their attention.'

'What does he make at his factory?'

'Motor engines.'

The reply instantly aroused Molly's instinct for good thriller plots, and she exclaimed, 'Then he may be one of the key men in the rearmament drive. Perhaps he holds the secret of some new type of aircraft. It may be the Russians who are after you, in the hope that he will betray the secret as the price of getting you back.'

With a shake of the head, the girl swiftly damped Molly's ardour. 'No, Mrs Fountain, it can't be that. He only makes dull things like agricultural tractors.'

Again Molly pondered the problem, then she asked a little diffidently, 'Before you left England, did you go into a private nursing home to have a minor operation?'

'Yes.' The brown eyes grew round with surprise. 'However did you guess?'

'I didn't. It was just a shot in the dark. But since you admit it, that may explain everything. The probability is that your father brought you out here to hide you from the police.'

'I can't think what you're talking about. Having an operation isn't a crime.'

'It can be, in certain circumstances,' Molly replied drily.

'Well, I'm sure they don't apply to me.'

'They might. Is your mother still alive?'

'No; she died when I was six.'

'Have you any elder sisters?'

'No, I am an only child.'

Molly nodded and said gently, 'That makes what I have in mind all the more likely. Even in these days quite a number of girls, particularly motherless ones, reach the age of nineteen or twenty without knowing enough about life to take care of themselves. When you found you were going to have a baby and your father put you in the nursing home to have it removed, he evidently decided that you had quite enough to worry about already without his telling you that such operations are illegal. But they are, and if the police have got on to that nursing home they are probably investigating all the operations that took place in it. Everyone concerned would be liable to be sent to prison. As you were an innocent party I don't think you need fear that for yourself; but, for having authorized the operation, your father might get quite a heavy sentence. So it's hardly to be wondered at that he wants to keep you out of the way until the police have got their evidence from other cases and the danger of your being drawn into it is past.'

The girl had listened in silence, but as Molly ceased speaking she began to titter; then, with her white teeth flashing, she burst into a loud laugh. But, catching sight of Molly's rather aggrieved expression, she checked her laughter and said quickly:

'I'm so sorry, Mrs Fountain, I didn't mean to be rude, and I'm awfully grateful for the way you are trying to help me get my bearings. But I couldn't prevent myself from seeing the funny side of your last theory; and you would, too, if you knew the way I had been brought up. I learnt all about sex from other girls, ages ago, but up to last December I've spent nearly the whole of my life in schools—including the holidays. And in all the schools I've been to we were as carefully guarded from everything in trousers as if we had been nuns; so I haven't even ever had a boy friend yet, let alone an illegal.'

Molly felt slightly foolish; but, hiding her discomfiture, she smiled. 'I'm glad to hear that, but what sort of operation did you have?'

'I had my tonsils out. During January I had rather a nasty sore throat, and although the local doctor said he didn't think it really necessary, Father insisted that it should be done. He put me in a private nursing home at Brighton for the job and made me stay there for three weeks afterwards to convalesce. He collected me from there to bring me straight out here.'

'It rather looks, then, as if he has been attempting to hide you for some time, and used the excuse of your tonsils to get you out of the way as early as the end of January.'

'Perhaps. At the time I was rather touched, as I thought he was showing an unusual solicitude about me. You see, to tell the truth, although it sounds rather beastly to say so, he has never before seemed to care very much what happened to me; and I am quite certain that he would not risk going to prison on my account, as you suggested just now. In view of what has happened since, I think you must be right; but the thing that absolutely stumps me is why he should be taking so much trouble to keep me away from everyone I've ever known.'

Her heart going out more warmly than ever to this motherless and friendless girl, Molly said, 'Don't worry, my dear. We'll get to the bottom of it somehow; but I'll have to know more about you before I can suggest any further possibilities. As you have had such a secluded life, there can't be much to tell me about that. Still, it's possible that I might hit on a pointer if you cared to give me particulars of your family and your home. To start with, what is your real name?'

'I'm sorry. I'll tell you anything else you wish, but that is the one thing I can't tell you. Father made me swear that I wouldn't divulge my name to anyone while I was down here. I chose Christina for myself, because I like it. Would you very much mind calling me that?'

'Of course not, my dear. Start by telling me about your father, then, and his reasons for always keeping you at school. We might get some clue to his present treatment of you from the past.'

Christina fetched a packet of cigarettes from the hideous mock-Empire sideboard, offered them to Molly and took one herself. When they had lit up, she began:

'I can't say for certain, but I think the reason that Father has never shown me much affection is because he didn't want me when I arrived. He was then only a working-class man—a chauffeur who had married the housemaid—but he was always very ambitious, and I think he regarded me as another burden that would prevent him from getting on.

'I was born in Essex, in the chauffeur's flat over the garage of a house owned by a rich old lady. You must forgive me for not giving you the name of the house and the village. It's not that I don't trust you, but we live in the house now ourselves, and everybody in those parts knows my father; so it would practically amount to breaking my promise about not telling anyone down here my real name. Anyhow, the house had no bearing on my childhood, because when I was only a few weeks old my father chucked up his job and bought a share in a small business in a nearby town.

'We lived in a little house in a back street, and it was not a happy household. I don't remember it very clearly, but enough to know that poor Mother had a rotten time. It wasn't that Father was actively unkind to her—at least not until towards the end—but he cared for nothing except his work. He never took her for an outing or to the pictures, and he was just as hard on himself. When he wasn't in his office or the warehouse he was always tinkering in a little workshop that he had knocked up in the backyard of the house, even on Sundays and often far into the night.

'Within a year or two of his going into business one of his partners died and he bought the other out. But that did not content him. As soon as he had the business to himself he started a small factory to make a little motor, many of the parts of which he had invented, and it sold like hot cakes. When I was five we moved to a bigger house in a somewhat better neighbourhood, but that did not make things any better for Mother. He had less time to give her than ever, and he would never buy her any pretty clothes because he said he needed every penny he was making for expansion.

'There doesn't seem any reason to believe that Mother was particularly religious as a young girl, and she was only twenty-eight when she died; so I suppose it was being debarred from participating in all normal amusements that led her to seek distraction in the social life of the chapel. My memory about it is a little vague, but I know that she spent more and more of her time there during the last two years of her life, and that for some reason it annoyed Father intensely that she should do so. I was too young to understand their arguments, but I have an idea that she got religion and used to preach at him. Naturally, he would have resented that, as he is an agnostic himself, and does not believe in any of the Christian teachings.

'Eventually he became so angry that he forbade her to go to chapel any more. But she did, and on my sixth birthday she took me with her. That proved an unhappy experience for both of us, as I was sick before I even got inside the place, and had to be taken home again. She made a second attempt a few Sundays later, when Father was out of the way seeing some friend of his on business, but again I was sick in the porch. Undaunted, she seized on the next occasion that he was absent from home on a Sunday morning, and for the third time I let her down by being as sick as a puppy that has eaten bad fish, up against the chapel doorway.

'Why chapels and churches have that effect on me I have no idea. I think it must be something to do with the smell that is peculiar to them; a sort of mixture of old unwashed bodies, disinfectant and stale cabbages. No doctor at any of the schools I've been to has ever been able to explain it, or produce a cure; so I've always had to be let off attending services. I suppose it has become a case of association now, but I am still unable to look inside a church without wanting to vomit.

'Anyway, after my mother's third attempt to take me to chapel, the connection between chapel-going and being sick must have been quite firmly established in my mind. No child could be expected to like what must have appeared to be a series of outings undertaken with the deliberate intention of making it sick; and, of course, I was still too young to realize what I was doing when I spilled the beans to Father.

'I let the cat out of the bag at tea-time, and he went absolutely berserk. He threw his plate at Mother, then jumped up and chased her round the table. I fled screaming to my room upstairs, but for what seemed an age I could hear him bashing her about and cursing her. She was in bed for a week, and afterwards she was never the same woman again; so I think he may have done her some serious injury. It is too long ago for me to recall the details of her illness, but I seem to remember her complaining of pains in her inside, and finding the housework heavier and heavier, although it is probable that her decline was due to acute melancholia as much as to any physical cause. By mid-summer she could no longer raise the energy to go out, and became a semi-invalid. Naturally her chapel friends were very distressed and used to come in from time to time to try to cheer her up. The pastor used to visit us too, once or twice a week, when it was certain that Father was well out of the way, and sit with her reading the Bible.

'It was one of his visits that precipitated her death. Father came home unexpectedly one afternoon and found him there. I was out at kindergarten, so I only heard about it afterwards. By all accounts Father took the pastor by the shoulders and kicked him from the front door into the gutter.

'Most people take a pretty dim view about anyone laying violent hands on a man of God, and the episode might have resulted in a great deal of unpleasantness for Father, but on balance he got off very lightly. For one thing he was popular, at any rate with his work-people and their families, whereas the pastor was not. For another, a story went round that the pastor had been Mother's lover, or that, anyway, Father had caught him making a pass at her. I don't believe that for one moment. I haven't a doubt that it was put about by Father himself in an attempt to justify his act, and that the real truth was that finding the pastor there had sent him into another of his blind rages against the chapel and everything connected with it.

'The affair cost him the goodwill of a certain number of his more staid acquaintances, and it stymied his standing for the town council, as he had planned to do, that winter. But it didn't prove as serious a set-back to his upward progress as it might have done; and although the pastor had talked of starting an action for assault, he didn't, because in view of what happened afterwards he decided that it would have been un-Christian to do so. He was thinking, of course, of the fact that when Father woke up next morning he found Mother dead in bed beside him.

'It was generally accepted that she had died as the result of delayed shock. There can be no doubt that such a scene must have struck at the very roots of her being. When I was older, friends who had known her told me that she had regarded her pastor as inspired by God; so for her to have seen him set upon must have been like witnessing the most appalling sacrilege. At that moment, in her morbid state of mind, I dare say my father must have appeared to her to be the Devil in person, and the thought that she was married to him may have proved too much for her. She fainted and was put to bed by a neighbour. It was she who told me most of what I know about it, some years later. The doctor was called in and he was a bit worried because Mother would not answer his questions or speak to anybody; but he thought she would be all right when she got over the shock.

'It may be true that she didn't get over it, and her heart suddenly failed, or something; but she had been taking pills to make her sleep for some time, and when our neighbour came in next morning she found the bottle empty. She said nothing about it, but it was her opinion that Mother had taken an overdose to escape having to go on living with Father. Perhaps he knows the truth about what happened, but if so he is the only person who does.'

Christina paused to light another cigarette, then she went on, 'For a time our neighbour looked after me. Then, in the autumn, Father brought a woman named Annie to the house. She was a big blonde creature, lazy but kind-hearted, and he gave out that he had been married to her in London; but of course that wasn't true, and I am sure now that she was just a tart that he had picked up somewhere. Mother had been much too weepy and religious to inspire a passionate devotion in any child; so I had soon got over her loss, and I grew to love Annie. She said she had always wanted a little daughter just like me, and my life with her was one long succession of lovely surprises and jolly treats. No doubt she was common, rather silly and the sort who is too lazy to earn her own living except by haunting dance-halls and shady clubs; but the nine months she was with us were far and away the happiest of my childhood, in fact the only really happy ones I ever had, and I was inconsolable for weeks after she went away.

'The affair broke up because Father was getting on so fast. He felt it was bad for business for his to continue living in the sort of house more suited to one of his own foremen; so he bought another out in the town's best residential district. To me, at the time, it seemed huge, but actually it was just an eight-roomed house with a garage and an acre or so of garden. Still, as far as we were concerned it was a great step up in the world; and although Father may not have been quite as keen on Annie as he had been at first, it was mainly because she did not fit into the new picture that he ditched her.

'It was a few days before we were due to move that I found her in tears. She told me then that they had never been married and that he didn't consider her good enough for him any longer. But she didn't make a scene. She had more natural dignity than many better-bred women whom I've met, and I'll always remember her walking out, dry-eyed and smiling, to the taxi that was to take her to the station. I never saw her again.

'For me, her going robbed the new house of all its glamour, and very soon I came to hate the place. Father never again made the mistake of getting married, or pretending that he had divorced Annie and acquired a new wife. Instead, he replaced Annie with a girl who had been one of his secretaries. They never bothered to conceal the fact from me that they slept together, but to preserve the proprieties she was given the status of governess-housekeeper. Her name was Delia Weddel, and she had been brought up in quite a good home, but if ever there was a bitch she was one.

'She was another blonde, but the thin kind, and strikingly good-looking, until one came to realize the hardness of her eyes and the meanness of her mouth. Why she should have taken a hate against me I have no idea, but she made my life hell, and she was so cunning and deceitful that neither Father nor the daily woman we used to have in to do the housework guessed what was going on.

'As a child I was subject to sleep-walking. That meant if sounds were heard in the night someone had to get up and put me to bed again. Annie used to do that so gently that I hardly realized it had happened, but Delia used to put me outside the back door until the cold woke me up. While I was there she would go upstairs, strip my bed and throw the clothes on the floor; so that when she let me in, shivering with cold, I had to make it again myself before I could get to sleep. Next day, too, she always gave me some punishment for having disturbed her, and, of course, that only made me worse.

'Then there was the agony of lessons. As she was officially my governess she had at least to make a pretence of teaching me. But all she ever did was to point out a passage in a history or geography book and order me to learn it by heart, while she read a novel or went shopping. It was torture, because I wasn't old enough to master things like that. I had got to the stage of reading only fairy stories and books about animals; yet if I couldn't say my piece at the end of the hour I knew that I was going to get my knuckles rapped. I would have given anything in the world to be back at kindergarten with the common little children, singing songs and playing games with bricks. But at that age a child is absolutely at the mercy of grown-ups; so there was nothing I could do about it.

'A breakdown in my health saved me from Delia. Perhaps the doctor suspected what had led up to it. Anyhow, he advised that I needed sea air to build me up, and that as I was getting on for eight I should be sent to a boarding-school at the seaside after Christmas. Delia was only too glad to be rid of me; so in January 1939 I was packed off to a school at Felixstowe.

'It wasn't a very good school. They fed us shockingly and cheesepared on the central heating, although it was quite an expensive place and supposed to be rather smart. I had a thin time to start with, too, because most of the other girls where awful snobs. When they found out that I had been at a National Kindergarten and spent my childhood in a back street, they christened me 'the little alley cat' and were generally pretty beastly. Still, anything was better than Delia, and from then on going back to her for the holidays was the only thing I really had to dread.

'Soon after war broke out the school was moved to Wales, and when I came home the following Christmas I found to my joy that Delia had gone the way of Annie. The house was being run for Father by a middle-aged couple named Jutson. Their status was simply that of servants: she was cook-housekeeper and he did the odd jobs and the garden. They have been with us ever since. Later I learned by chance that from 1940 Father was well off enough to have a flat in London. Or, rather, that he kept a succession of popsies in flats that were nominally theirs and used to stay with them whenever he went up; so I know very little about his later mistresses.

'The Jutsons are a respectable, hard-working couple, but she is rather a sour woman. During the holidays and the Easter ones that followed she did what she had to do for me, but no more. I was fed at regular hours and seen to bed at night, otherwise I was left to amuse myself as well as I could. I think Father has always paid them well to keep their mouths shut about his affairs, because when I asked either of them why he was often absent from home, or where he had gone to and when he was coming back, they always used to say 'Ask no questions and you get no lies!' And that has been their attitude ever since.

'That April the real war began and Father decided it would be best for me to remain at school for the summer holidays. Many of the other parents felt the same way about their daughters, so more than half of us stayed on in Wales, and while the Battle of Britain was being fought we had quite a jolly time. We couldn't foresee it then, but for most of us that was only the first of many holidays spent at school. In my case I didn't see my home again for the next five years.

'As part of the drill at school I wrote to Father every week, and occasionally he sent me a typed letter in reply. It was always to the effect that producing war supplies kept him desperately busy, but he hoped to find time to come down to see me soon. He did, about two or three times a year, but I would just as soon that he hadn't, as we had absolutely nothing to say to one another, and I could almost hear his sigh of relief when the time came for him to catch his train back to London. I must say, though, he always treated me very generously. He allowed me to take any extras that I wished, and I had only to ask for anything I wanted in one of my letters and his secretary would have it sent down.

'The summer that the war ended I was fifteen and I came home at last, but not for long. Apart from a few of Mother's old friends I didn't know a soul, and I hope I haven't become a snob myself, but I seemed to have moved right out of their class. I no longer talked the same language as their children, and although I tried to get over that, Father said he did not wish me to have those sort of people in the house. Within a fortnight I was at a dead end and hopelessly bored.

'One day Father suddenly realized how isolated I was and took the matter in hand with his usual efficiency. He explained that his own social life was in London, but for various reasons he could not have me with him there; so some other step must be taken to provide me with suitable companions of my own age. He had found a place in Somerset that ran courses in domestic science and was open all the year round. His suggestion was that I should go there for the rest of the summer holidays.

'Anything seemed better than staying at home doing nothing; so I agreed. And I was glad I had. It was a lovely old house and most of the pupils were older than myself; so we were treated much more like grown-ups than are the girls at an ordinary school. I liked it so much that I asked Father to let me go back there for good after one last term in Wales. That suited him; so I spent nearly the whole of the next two and a half years in Somerset. Occasionally, just for a change, I spent a week at home, and seven or eight times I was invited to stay at the homes of girls with whom I had become friends. My best friend lived in Bath; another one lived in Kensington, and with her I saw something of London; but such visits were only short ones and at fairly long intervals.

'I was perfectly content for things to go on that way indefinitely, but just before my eighteenth birthday the principal wrote to Father to say that as I had taken all the courses they ran and passed all the exams it did not seem right to keep me on there any longer. Faced with the same old problem of what to do with me, he decided to send me to a finishing school in Paris, and I was there until last December.'

Christina lit another cigarette, and added, 'I forgot to tell you than in 1949 old Mrs Durnsford died and Father bought The Grange. . . .'

She paused and a look of consternation came over her face. 'Oh damn, now I've given away the one thing I didn't mean to tell you.'

Molly smiled. 'Don't worry, my dear. I won't try to ferret out your name from that, and a little slip of that kind can't really be considered as breaking your promise to your father.'

'No, I suppose not,' Christina agreed. 'Anyhow, the fact of his going back there made very little difference as far as I was concerned. The Jutsons now live in the flat over the garage where I was born; but we have no other servants living in, and Father never does any entertaining. On balance, I prefer it out there in the country to living in a suburb of the town, although there are no shops and cinemas handy. When I get back I hope to interest myself in the village, but until this winter I've never lived there for more than a few days at a time; so I've had no chance yet to get to know any of our neighbours—except old Canon Copely-Syle, and I've known him as long as I can remember.'

Again Christina paused, before ending a little lamely, 'Well, there it is. I really don't think there is anything more to tell you.'

'You poor child.' Molly took her hand and pressed it. 'I think your father has been terribly selfish in not providing you with a proper home life. You seem to have missed all the jolly times that most young people have on seaside holidays and at Christmas parties.'

'Oh, I don't know. People never miss what they haven't been used to, do they? Except when I first went to school, I've always got on well with the other girls, and most of the mistresses were awfully kind to me.'

'Perhaps; but that isn't the same thing. What about your grandparents? And had you no aunts and uncles to take an interest in you?'

'I know nothing about Father's family. I have an idea that he was illegitimate; but if he ever had one he must have broken with it as soon as he began to get on, so that it should not prove a drag upon him. Mother was an only child and her parents both died when I was quite young; so I have no relatives on that side either.'

'Tell me about your father's friends. Although you have been at home so little, you must have met some of them. Recalling the sort of people they were might give you a line on what this present trouble is about.'

Christina shook her head. 'For the past ten years Father has spent a great deal of his time in London, and the only social life he has is there. He subscribes quite generously to local charities, but after he had to withdraw his candidature for the town council he would never mix himself up with public activities in the district. The only people he has ever asked home as far as I know were senior members of his office staff, and then it would only be to discuss confidential business with them over a drink in the evening.'

'Just now you mentioned a Canon somebody?'

'Oh, old Copely-Syle is an exception. He lives only a mile or so from us, on the way to the village, at the Priory. Although, even when he lived in . . . in the town, he used to drop in occasionally.'

'In view of your father's bias against religion it seems rather strange that he should have made a life-long friend of a canon.'

'He is not a practising clergyman, and I think he helped Father to make his first start in business. Anyhow, they knew one another when Father was chauffeur to Mrs Dunsford, and it may be partly on my account that the Canon has always called whenever I've spent a few days at home. You see, he is my godfather.'

'Have you any idea what your father's plans for you are when your month's tenancy of this villa is up?'

'Yes and no. That is one of the things that worries me so much. He said that if everything went all right he would come back and collect me. If he didn't, I was to return to England and go to the head office of the National Provincial Bank in London. If I made myself known at the Trustee Department and asked for a Mr Smithson he would give me a packet of papers. When I had read them I could make up my own mind about my future; and I need have no anxiety about money, as he had made ample provision for me to receive an income which would enable me to live quite comfortably without taking a job.'

'Good gracious!' Molly exclaimed. 'From that one can only infer that the danger threatens both of you, and that it is something much more serious than blackmail, or even being sent to prison.'

Christina nodded. 'Yes, it's pretty frightful, isn't it, to think that he may already be dead, and that if they find me I may be dead too before the month is up?'

'My dear child!' Molly quickly sought to reassure her. 'You mustn't think such things. He may only have meant that he might have to leave you for a much longer period, and that during it you would have to make arrangements for yourself. I must confess, though, that in spite of all you've told me, I haven't yet got an inkling who this mysterious "They" can be.'

For a further quarter of an hour they speculated on the problem in vain; then, as Molly stood up to leave, Christina said, 'You have been terribly kind, Mrs Fountain; and just being able to talk about this wretched business has made me feel much less miserable already.'

Molly went on tip-toe to give her a quick kiss. 'I'm so glad; and you do understand, don't you, that you can come in to me at any time. If I don't see you before I shall expect you to-morrow for lunch; but if you have the least reason to be frightened by anything don't hesitate to come over at once.'

Together they walked out into the sunshine and began the descent of the steep garden path. They were about half-way down it when there came a rustling in the undergrowth and a joyful barking.

'That's Fido, my cocker spaniel,' Molly remarked. 'The wicked fellow must have seen me and broken through the pittosporum hedge.'

Skilfully avoiding the prickly cactus, the dog came bounding towards his mistress. On reaching her he barked louder than ever and jumped up affectionately.

'Down, Fido! Down!' she cried in mock severity. 'How dare you invade someone else's garden without being invited to call. You are as bad as I am.'

Like the well-trained animal he was, he ceased his transports, but ran towards Christina, expecting to find in her a new friend.

Suddenly he halted in his tracks. His body seemed to become rigid; the hackles rose on his neck, his jaws began to drool saliva, and through them came a low whimper of fear.

'Whatever can be the matter with him?' Molly exclaimed in astonishment. 'I've never known him behave like that before.'

Christina's face had become half sullen and half miserable as she said in a low voice, 'It's not my fault! I can't help it. But animals always take a dislike to me on sight.'

4

ENTER THE WICKED MARQUIS

It was March 1st and John Fountain had arrived that morning. He and his mother had just finished lunch, and with a sigh of satisfaction he smiled across at her.

'What a meal! How good it is to eat in France again. I bet there were six eggs in the omelette. And that fillet of beef—as tender as *foie gras* and as big as a month's ration! Real butter instead of National grease, and the pineapple *au Kirsch* topped with lashings of cream. Most of our wretched people at home have forgotten that such food still exists.'

Molly nodded. 'It is years now since there has been a shortage of anything down here. Food is expensive, of course, but the markets are always overflowing with it. The rich alone could not consume one-twentieth of the perishable stuff that is offered for sale every day, and even the poorest classes show no signs of being hungry. It's simply that the French people always have spent most of their earnings on food and they still insist on the right to do so. I can't think why our people continue to allow themselves to be half starved by their Government. I'm sure it isn't necessary.'

'I can answer that one.' John's voice was bitter. 'It's due to the Socialists and their insistence on continued bulk buying by the nation. That may have been necessary during the war, but by forcing it on us for six years afterwards they destroyed the whole organization that had been built up over centuries of private firms importing our food from the best markets at the best prices. It will be years before the incredible muddle they made can be unsorted. But tell me more about this girl next door.'

'I don't think there's much more to tell, Johnny. During the past three days I've seen quite a bit of her. She is still nervous of going out in the day-time but, quite illogically, she doesn't seem to mind at night. On Sunday I always dine out for a change, so yesterday afternoon I suggested that she should come with me to the Reserve at St Raphael. She said she would rather not, but about half-past six she turned up here and asked if she might change her mind. Of course I said "Yes", and I'm sure she thoroughly enjoyed herself.'

'Do you really believe her story?'

'Yes. She has the naturally frank expression and well-spaced eyes that can nearly always be taken as a sign of honesty; and I don't see what she could possibly hope to gain by deceiving me. After all, it wasn't a case of her approaching me and attempting to win my sympathy, perhaps in the hope of a loan; but I who invited her confidence. Then the way she inadvertently let out the name of her home and its previous occupant shows that she is not an accomplished enough liar to have made the whole thing up.'

'With a pre-1949 telephone directory of Essex those two items of information should be sufficient for us to trace the village she comes from, and the initials on the manicure-set make it pretty certain that her real name begins with B; so it shouldn't be very difficult to find out who she is.'

'I don't think it would be quite playing the game for us to do that.'

'It may be necessary if these people who are after her suddenly appear on the scene.'

'Let's not meet trouble half-way, Johnny. I'm hoping, though, that while you are here you'll give some of your time to her. With a man she would probably be less scared of going out during the day, and it would do her a world of good to be taken about a bit.'

His rather thin face broke into a slightly cynical grin. 'No doubt. But what about me? I'm on holiday remember. Do you think she is my cup of tea?'

Mrs Fountain did not reply immediately, but smiled a little dubiously at her attractive son. He was of medium height, well-made, although not powerful. His principal charm lay in his lively, intelligent eyes and humorous mouth. He had dark hair and his nose was slightly aquiline. Although only twenty-three the responsible position he had secured in a good firm had matured him early; so he was very much a man now, and she was wise enough to seek no longer to control him.

She was thinking of his previous holidays. Last year he had run around with that little Italian countess, who was certainly no better than she should be. The previous year he had given her even more serious cause for secret alarm by attaching himself to an American widow of glamorous appearance, but uncertain age and most dubious antecedents. Johnny's taste certainly did not run in the direction of *jeunes filles*. That was natural enough for a young man in his early twenties, and it would do him no harm as long as he did not get himself seriously entangled. Knowing that the Riviera swarmed with harpies, she dreaded the sort of designing female that he might so easily pick up, and during the past few days she had been rather hoping that this year Christina might prove a sufficient attraction to keep him out of mischief. She thought the chances of that were very slender, but she was clever enough not to spoil the market by boosting the goods, and after a moment she said:

'To be honest, Johnny, this girl is not up to your weight. She is practically a new-born lamb, and after a couple of days you may find yourself hopelessly bored with her. But she seems to have had so little fun in her life and she is so desperately lonely, it really would be a generous act to spare her an hour or two now and then.'

He smiled at her. 'You horrible woman! I can scent the maternal match-making instinct a mile away in this.'

'Good gracious, no!' she protested. 'We don't really know anything about her, and her father sounds a most undesirable type.'

'One doesn't marry their fathers, dearest—except in the tale of the chap who killed the dragon, who when offered his choice said he'd rather marry the king than any of the three princesses.'

'What *are* you talking about?'

Putting his head on one side, he wriggled his shoulders, smirked, and replied in an effeminate voice, 'It's a fairy story.'

'Johnny, you are awful,' she laughed.

'On the contrary, I am nobly defending myself against a conspiracy to make me break my plighted word, given freely long ago, that when I grew up I would marry you.'

'Idiot! I tell you, the idea of your entering on a serious affair with this young woman never entered my mind. It is simply that she has been starved of youthful companionship and—'

'I know. That she could be a sweet little sister to me. Really, Mumsie! How you can sit there looking so innocent while you tell such tarradiddles, I cannot think.'

'But you will do as I ask?'

'Knowing that you will starve and probably beat me if I refuse, it seems I have no option.'

'Splendid. I expect you would like to sleep off your lunch now; then I thought that about tea-time I would take you over and introduce you.'

'O.K., honoured parent.' John stood up, but before turning away he screwed his face into a leery expression and gave a slow, sardonic wink. 'Before retiring to my slumbers I'd like to know just where I stand. I take it that there will be no kick coming from you if I seduce her?'

Molly knew perfectly well that he was only pulling her leg, but all the same she replied with a hint of seriousness, 'I've already told you, she's as inexperienced as if she had just come out of a convent; so you'll jolly well behave yourself.'

'Oh, I'll be as good as gold,' he assured her blandly. 'But I know these innocent types. The odds are that she'll seduce *me*. Then what? I'll get the blame, of course, and have to pay the seven-and-six maintenance for the baby. Or has it gone up to a quid now? I think that the least you can do is to guarantee me against that.'

'You're a horrid boy, with a horrid, low mind, and I dislike you intensely,' said his mother, giving him a light kiss on the cheek. 'Now, run along and get your nap. It's past three al . . .

Her last words trailed away into silence as she caught a quick step on the gravel outside the french window of the dining-room. Next moment a tall shadow was thrown by the sunlight on the parquet, and turning she saw Christina standing on the threshold.

'Oh, Mrs Fountain,' the girl began rather breathlessly, 'I hope I'm not interrupting you. I knew your son was arriving to-day, and I waited until I thought you would have finished lunch; but I wanted to talk to you rather . . . rather urgently.'

'Of course not, my dear. Come in.' Molly waved a vague hand. 'This is John—Johnny, our new neighbour, Christina Mordant.'

The two young people nodded and smiled politely at one another. Neither made any move to shake hands. John was thinking, 'God, what a nose! But her eyes really are remarkable'; while Christina thought, 'He's really quite nice-looking: what a pity he has such a prominent Adam's apple.'

'Do sit down.' Molly offered the cigarettes and Christina took one. As she lit it, John hurried forward. 'What about a liqueur? A Béné, or a spot of Sticky Green?'

'No thanks,' Christina replied quickly. 'I only go in for soft drinks, and I don't want anything now.'

'I expect you would rather John left us,' Molly said after a moment. 'He has so gorged himself with food that he can hardly keep awake, anyhow.'

John sighed. 'See how my own mother derides and dismisses me. But take no notice. I am hardened now to the feminist streak in her, which has ever thwarted my ambition to emulate St George.'

'What! And marry the king like your friend in the fairy story?' Molly said with a twinkle.

'That's one up to you, Mumsie,' he replied with a grin.

After a puzzled look from one to the other of them, Christina's glance came to rest on Molly. 'Over dinner last night you suggested telling John about me, because, if the sort of thing I have to fear happened, a man's help might prove invaluable; and I agreed. If you have told him, and he cares to stay, it would be just as well for him to hear about this new development.'

'Yes. Mother has given me an account of the extraordinary situation in which you find yourself,' John said, his voice now low and serious. 'You must forgive our fooling; and please believe that I am just as anxious as she is to help you in any way I can.'

She gave him a faint smile. 'Thanks; you're both most awfully kind. Well, just before lunch I had a visitor.'

Molly's face showed her dismay. 'Then the enemy has run you to earth already?'

'No; this was a friend—or, at least, an old acquaintance. But I was so surprised to see him coming through the gate that for a moment I thought I must have got a touch of the sun, and be imagining things. It was Canon Copely-Syle.'

'As he is an intimate friend of your father's, your father might quite well have confided to him the place where he had hidden you.'

'No. That's the strange part about it. His finding me here was pure chance. He hasn't seen my father for some weeks and had no idea I was in the South of France. He has been staying at Cannes for a few days, and this morning he was motoring in to St Raphael for lunch. He just happened to catch sight of me sitting on the terrace; so he made his friend who was driving the car stop, and came in to see me.'

'There doesn't seem to be anything particularly perturbing about that,' John remarked.

'Oh, but there is!' Christina protested. 'His first words to me were, "My dear child, whatever are you doing here? Why aren't you in England with your father?" I replied, "Why should I be?" At that he looked quite staggered, and said, "But surely you've heard the bad news about him? Has no one informed you that he was seriously injured in a car smash? I had it yesterday in a letter from a mutual friend. I would never dream of upsetting you without good reason, but I gather there are grave fears for his life."'

'Perhaps this is just the sort of thing your father feared might happen to him,' Molly said, her thriller-writer's mind having gone swiftly into action. 'I mean, it wouldn't be the first time that unscrupulous people had deliberately engineered a car smash, in order to get out of the way somebody against whom they had a grudge.'

'Yes; I suppose such things do happen. Anyhow, the Canon said that he is returning to England to-morrow, and he offered to take me with him.'

'You will be leaving us then?'

Christina shook her head. 'No. Father told me that no matter what messages I might receive, even if they were said to come from him, in no circumstances was I to leave the villa until he returned to fetch me; or, failing that, before the twentieth of next month.'

'It is quite natural that he should have said something of the kind as a reasonable precaution against your falling into a trap set by your enemies;

but when he said it he cannot possibly have had the Canon in mind. Didn't you tell me at our first talk that the Canon is your godfather?'

'Yes; but the fact that he is my godfather doesn't mean very much. He has always sent me a small present on my birthday, and I've written to thank him; but we have never got any closer than that. I have seen him perhaps thirty or forty times in my life, but never for any length of time, and father has always been present, except at two accidental meetings; so I've never got beyond exchanging polite platitudes with him.'

'Still, he is a life-long friend of your father's; so I'm afraid, my dear, there cannot be very much doubt about this shocking news he has brought you. It is hardly credible that he would cause you such anxiety had he not been certain of his facts.'

'Yes, I suppose so.' Christina sighed. 'I think, though, I may have unconsciously misled you a little about his relationship to Father. I have always had the impression that their association is based more on some common interest than on genuine friendship. One of the occasions when I ran into him by chance was soon after we had moved into our present home, and when I told Father about it he said that should the Canon ever ask me to the Priory I was to make some excuse for not accepting. At the time I put that down to a revival of his anti-Christian bias, and a fear that I might get religion, like Mother. But quite apart from that I'm pretty certain that Father does not really like him, and for some reason that I can't explain I don't either.'

'Apart from this personal prejudice, do you know anything against him?'

'No, nothing at all. In the village he is highly respected.'

'Then it doesn't seem as if he is the sort of person who would be mixed up in anything shady, or lend himself to practising such a brutal deception on you.'

'It doesn't, does it? Yet, all the same, I feel I ought to stick to Father's orders and remain where I am.'

'What did the Canon say when you refused his offer to take you back to England to-morrow?' John enquired.

'He spent quite a time trying to persuade me to change my mind, and, when I wouldn't, seemed to think me very callous.'

'What excuse did you make for digging your toes in?'

'I said I thought the friend who had written to him must have exaggerated Father's danger, and that his office would have been certain to let me know if my presence was really required in England; so I meant to remain here until I heard something more definite. I took the precaution, too, of telling him that I was living under the assumed name of Christina Mordant, and asking him not to divulge my real identity to anyone down here. Naturally he looked very surprised, but he did not ask me for a reason, and gave me his promise.'

'Clever girl,' John smiled. 'There is one way one could find out about your father for certain though. Why not telephone your home or his works?'

'No, I can't do that. He said that whatever happened I was not to attempt to get him on the telephone; because, if the call was traced back, it would give away my hiding-place.'

For a while longer they discussed matters without getting any further, then Molly said, 'Johnny and I are going to dine in Cannes to-night, and we'd like you to come with us. We thought of going to the Carlton, but if you haven't got an evening dress with you we could go to some quieter place.'

'It's terribly kind of you,' Christina hesitated a second, 'but I don't think I ought to. It doesn't seem right somehow, as there is a possibility that Father may be dying.'

'Just as you like, my dear; but I think it is a great mistake ever to anticipate the worst, and that you would be much wiser to let us take you out and try to cheer you up, rather than stay at home brooding about unhappy possibilities. I won't press you, but should you change your mind, as you did last night, we shall be leaving about half-past seven.'

Christina did change her mind, and returned at twenty-past seven dressed to accompany them to the Carlton. As she stepped from the half-darkness of the garden into the lighted room, both Molly and John had difficulty in hiding their astonishment. She was wearing a long frock of oyster satin. It was backless, strapless and low cut, to display her good neck and shoulders to the best advantage, but at the moment she had draped over them a short cape of dark skunk. Neither of them had seen her before in anything but very ordinary and rather girlish day clothes; so the difference in her appearance was quite striking. It made her look several years older and entirely sophisticated—a change that was further stressed by a new expression in her face and a much brisker manner.

Molly was thinking, 'I wonder where she learned to dress like this? It can only have been at her finishing school in Paris. That must be quite a place! I'll swear the scent she has got on is by Dior. Too old for her—pity she didn't choose something a little less exotic. Her father may have neglected her, but he certainly isn't mean with her about money. The little number she's got on must have cost a packet.'

John's mind was running on the lines, 'Gee whizz! Call that nothing! And after lunch I thought she looked like Skinny Lizzy, the sixth form's tallest girl. All the same she must be darn near as tall as I am. If the mind under that brown hair fits this evening's turnout she won't prove as dumb as I feared. Anyhow, if we see anyone I know I shan't be accused of cradle-snatching.'

At the moment he was shaking a cocktail, and producing a third glass he said, 'Can't I tempt you?'

'Why not?' she replied lightly. 'When the drinks were offered round at our social evenings in Paris, we girls were only allowed to take sherry; but I suppose one must make a start on the hard liquor some time. You must warn me, though, if you think I am getting tight.'

He laughed. 'As a confirmed drunk myself I should certainly lead you astray if I got the chance, but you can rely on my Mama to provide a restraining influence.'

Soon after eight they were in Cannes. As it was the height of the winter season the big restaurant at the Carlton was quite crowded. Everyone was in evening dress and at the many tables one could hear spoken every language outside the Iron Curtain. French and Americans predominated, but there were Indians and Egyptians, as well as Swiss, Belgians and Scandinavians. The only major nation ill-represented for its size was Britain, but as an acid commentary on mismanagement after victory the richer citizens of the defeated nations, Germany and Italy, were back again in force, enjoying themselves once more. The fact that champagne cost £4 a bottle did not prevent its flowing freely. The scene was glittering, the service excellent and the menu a triumph in gastronomic art. Nothing more could have been desired to ensure a gay and happy evening.

Yet, before they were half-way through dinner, Molly was conscious that her little party was a flop. Johnny and Christina seemed to have nothing in common except an unhappy inability to do full justice to the good things set before them. Neither had anything but a vague recollection of the time when food had not been rationed in England, and so many years of meagre feeding had reduced the capacity of their stomachs to a point where they were incapable of containing more than would sustain life. Johnny was the worst affected, as he had eaten an exceptionally large lunch and, although he was not particularly greedy by nature, it irritated him not to be able to enjoy all the rich dishes which would normally have been such a treat; while Christina, who had also found herself defeated after the second course, was obviously worried that she might give offence to her hostess, as she kept on apologizing for only toying with the rest of her dinner.

In addition to this unsatisfactory state of things, Molly found herself quite unable to get a spark going between them. They had no mutual friends, had been brought up in totally different surroundings, and seemed to have no tastes in common. Johnny, she could see, was suffering from indigestion, and although the girl had drunk two glasses of champagne, her tongue showed no signs of being loosened by the wine.

When the time came for them to have coffee, she was commiserating with herself on the failure of this expensive evening, and thinking how much simpler it would have been to draw them out had she had either of them alone. It was only then the thought struck her that the barrier between them was almost certainly herself. All men, she knew, loved to talk about themselves, but Johnny would not do so in front of her for obvious reasons; and if they were alone the girl, no doubt, would trot out her little stock of airs and graces, but not with his mama looking on.

At a table not far off there were an American couple whom Molly had known for some years. They were elderly people, and did not dance or gamble; so it was certain they would be going home fairly early, and their villa was situated not much more than a mile from hers. Before coming out she had given Johnny ample francs to pay for their evening; so with commendable guile she concealed her disappointment and said to the young couple:

'I'm sure you two will want to dance, and I'm not feeling like sitting up very late to-night. I've been overworking a bit lately and I am paying for it now with a headache; so you must forgive me if I desert you. My friends, the Pilkingtons, are over there and they are sure to be going home soon. I can easily get a lift from them, so as to leave the car for you.'

Her reward was to see Johnny's quick concern, and hear his protest that she would be ruining the first evening of his holiday, which they always spent together; but Molly Fountain was not given to changing her mind once she had made it up, and, blowing a kiss from her finger-tips to Christina, she left them to join the Americans.

When John was staying with his mother on the Riviera he often got home at unconscionable hours, and like most young people he required a lot of sleep; so it was an accepted thing that he should never be called, but should ring when he woke for Angèle to bring him coffee and croissants.

On the following morning he did not wake till nearly eleven. Then, having breakfasted in bed, he dawdled for another hour over his bath and dressing; so it was half-past twelve before he came downstairs and joined his mother.

'Well,' she asked, as soon as he had kissed her good morning, 'how did things go last night after I left you? I do hope you weren't too terribly bored by my little protégé?'

'Bored!' His eyebrows shot up in a comical grimace. 'Believe me, Mumsie, you're jolly lucky to get me back all in one piece.'

Molly smiled and patted her grey hair. 'Making due allowances for your usual exaggerations, I'm rather pleased to learn that she has something that ticks inside her.'

'Something that ticks! Why, the girl's a human bomb. Honestly, this new-born lamb of yours—this little sister of Saint So-and-so straight out of a convent—is a positive danger to the public.'

'Oh come, Johnny! Mix yourself a Vermouth-Cassis, and one for me too. Then put reins upon your imagination, tie it up to the fence, and tell me what happened.'

He walked over to the side table and while mixing the drinks spoke over his shoulder. 'Well, to start with, we danced. The fact that she seems to have had very little practical experience of dancing with a man is the one piece of evidence we have in support of your theory that she has only just come out of the egg. Otherwise, hold me up, Uncle! Her sense of timing is not at all bad, so I think she'd be pretty good if she had some practice. But that's not the point. She clung to me as if I was her favourite woolly bear. I got really scared she meant to rape me on the dance-floor. And that scent of hers! It played old Harry with my libido.'

'Johnny, don't be disgusting.'

'Don't you pretend to be a little innocent, Mumsie. You know as well as most people what goes on in the world, and how that sort of thing can affect a chap. Anyhow, after we had danced for a bit she said she'd like to try a liqueur brandy. In the next hour she knocked back three doubles and she didn't blink an eyelid.'

'She must have a remarkably good head.'

'I'll say she has.' John brought the drink over to his mother, and went on, 'About half an hour after midnight she suggested that I should take her to the Casino to do a spot of gambling. I hedged a bit at first; as on the one hand I would have liked an excuse not to dance with her any more for the time being, while on the other I didn't particularly want to go to the rooms, because you know how it has always been with me. I can make money if I work for it, but I never seem to have any luck at the tables.'

'You had a perfectly good excuse for refusing, as they wouldn't have let you in without your passports; and as she is still under twenty-one they wouldn't have let her in anyway.'

He shook his head sadly at her. 'Darling, how you do under-rate the resourcefulness of your offspring. I'm ten times as good as your pet 'Crack', if you only knew it. I've known that chap Fleury, the under-manager, for years. All I had to do was to ask for him and say we'd forgotten to bring our passports. It was a safe bet that he would pass me in, and anyone else who was with me. So, on the basis that if "Paris was worth a Mass" my chastity must be worth a couple of thousand francs, I agreed. By a quarter to one we were in the Casino. And what do you think happened then?'

'How in the world should I know, silly?'

'Well, for the next hour and a half, while I piddled around dropping six *milles*, little orphan Annie played baccarat with a poker face that could hardly have been equalled had she been born inside the Sporting Club; and at the end of it she walked off with half a million francs.'

'Johnny, she didn't?'

'She did, Mumsie. If I hadn't been so well brought up, I'd have had it off her in the car on the way home. Just think of it! Five hundred quid, and free of Income Tax.'

Molly nodded. 'How lovely for her. One hears a lot about beginner's luck, but I must say I've never heard a better example of it.'

'It must have been mainly that; although the old Canon stood behind her chair all the time, and was tipping her off what to do now and then.'

'What! Her godfather, Canon Copely-Syle?' Molly sat up in surprise. 'This is the first you've said of him.'

'Sorry. I'm afraid I telescoped the story a bit to give you the exciting *dénouement* about her big win. The Canon was there when we entered the rooms, and came over to us.'

'What did you make of him?'

'I thought he was rather a nice old boy. He's certainly a picturesque one. All black satin front, pink face, and long silvery locks curling down behind his ears—like a parson in a Restoration play. He couldn't have made himself pleasanter.'

'I'm glad he didn't spoil her evening. His attitude towards her might have been pretty frigid on meeting her in such a place, after having told her only that morning that he believed her father to be dying.'

'I think he was a bit shocked at first. I happened to catch sight of his face before she saw him, and he was staring at us with a rather worried, annoyed sort of look. But as soon as we got chatting butter wouldn't melt in his mouth, and he never even mentioned her father until just before we were leaving.'

'Was there anything fresh in what he said then?'

'No; he only introduced us to a friend of his who had been playing at another table, for the purpose of telling her that should she change her mind about going home, and want an air passage at short notice, this chap would be able to fix it for her. He was another distinguished-looking old boy with grey hair, only the tall and thin type. With a nice red ribbon across his shirt front he could have walked on to any stage in the rôle of the French Ambassador, and he wouldn't even have had to change his name for the part. It was the Marquis de Grasse.'

Molly nearly dropped her glass, and her mouth fell open. Then she gave a cry of consternation. 'Oh, Johnny! What can be at the bottom of all this? De Grasse is one of the most evil men in France.'

5

BATTLE OF FLOWERS AND BATTLE OF WITS

John knew about his mother's work in the war–at least he thought he did. All she had ever told him was that her fluent French had secured her an interesting job as a secretary, and that later she had acted as P.A. to one of the senior officers of a department of the War Office situated in Baker Street. Since the war he had run across several people who had been connected with the same office, and from odd scraps of information they had dropped he had formed a pretty shrewd idea of the activities in which they had been engaged. Those who knew his mother spoke most highly of her, and the association had led him to believe that she too had actively participated in all sorts of cloak and dagger business designed to bring alarm and despondency to the enemy.

The belief was strengthened by the fact that she still kept a private armoury, consisting of two pistols and a number of other lethal weapons. She had often assured him that her 'museum', as she called it, had been acquired only because such things had always fascinated her and, in addition, helped her to describe accurately the use to which they could be put when writing of scenes of violence in her books. In this she was speaking the entire truth. Much as she would have liked to try some of them out, she had never used any of them. Neither had she ever been in the least danger, except during air-raids, as her work had lain inside the office, helping to direct the activities of others. Nevertheless, it had given her an exceedingly wide knowledge of the French Resistance, secret agents, collaborators and the crooks who were mixed up with them.

After a moment he said, 'I suppose you ran up against the Marquis when you were doing your stuff as Molly Polloffski, the beautiful spy?'

'No, Johnny. I've told you hundreds of times that there was nothing the least glamorous about my job; and I've never met de Grasse. But I know plenty about him.'

'There was a chap of that name up at Cambridge when I was there. I knew him slightly, but he went down at the end of my first year.'

She nodded. 'That would have been the son, Count Jules de Grasse. His father is as slippery as they make 'em. In the war he was far-sighted enough to back both sides; and his having sent his boy to school in England in 1940 went a long way towards saving him from a heavy sentence of imprisonment when the French began to catch up with collaborators after the liberation. He had been in it up to the neck with the Germans, but was able to produce that card as evidence that he had always thought and hoped that the Allies would win; then plead that he had done no more to help the Germans than thousands of other patriotic Frenchmen had been compelled to do as the only alternative to having their businesses taken from them. Of course, we knew that wasn't true, but he is immensely rich and money talks in France with a louder tongue than in most countries. His story about his son proved a good enough peg on which to hang a pardon, so he was able to bribe his way out, and he got off scot-free.'

'What was his business?'

'He is ostensibly a respectable shipping magnate; but that covers a multitude of sins. We had plenty of proof on our files that he used his ships for running every sort of contraband. Before the war he used to specialize in dope and white slaving; but more recently, I understand, he has concentrated on smuggling Jews out to Palestine, and arms to anyone in the Near East who wants to make trouble for us.'

'How do you know that, Mumsie?'

Molly coloured slightly. 'Oh, sometimes friends who worked with me in the old firm come out here, and we talk of this and that.'

He laughed. 'Boys and girls who are still in it, eh? I've always suspected that they kept you on unofficially to tip them off about anything you might tumble to in their line that was going on down here.'

'Johnny, you do get the silliest ideas. The department I worked for was wound up soon after the war ended.'

'Maybe; but there are others: for example, your old friend Conky Bill's outfit. I know he pretends to be only a sort of policeman whose job it is to hunt out Communists; but like this shipping racket I bet it covers his poking that big nose of his into a multitude of other dubious goings on.'

'And if you don't keep *your* nose out of other people's business you may one day get it chopped off,' retorted Molly aptly.

'*Touché!*' he grinned. 'Let's get back to the wicked Marquis, then. What else do you know about him?'

'His headquarters used to be at St Tropez. The choice was appropriate, as before the war it had the most evil reputation of any town west of Suez. Every vice racket flourished there. At night, down by the port, it was dangerous for decent people; and your father would not allow me to leave him to do even ten minutes' shopping on my own there in the middle of the day.'

'Really! On the few occasions I've been there I've never noticed anything peculiar about it.'

'You wouldn't, now. The Germans, and later the French, have cleaned it up a lot since then. But I am told that de Grasse still spends quite a lot of his time there.'

'He is living there at present. He told Christina so. He and his wife have a permanent private suite at the Capricorn. You know, that big modern hotel that overlooks the bay from the high ground to the right of the road, just before you enter the town. On learning that Christina had never been to St Tropez, he said that his wife loved entertaining young people, and offered to send a car to fetch her if she could lunch with them there to-day.'

Molly set down her glass with a bang. 'I hope to goodness she refused?'

'No: she accepted. It is only in the day-time that she seems to shy off any suggestion that she should go out; but of course she may have changed her mind this morning.'

'I'm afraid not. I had to go into St Raphael earlier to do some shopping, and I got back only just before you came down. I remember now noticing that she was not on her terrace when I drove past it, and she always is at that hour. If you were very late getting in she may still have been sleeping, but . . . Oh, Johnny, run round next door and make certain.'

Seven or eight minutes elapsed before John returned, panting slightly. He spread out his hands. 'No dice, dearest. She was called for around twelve by a chap a few years older than myself. From the rather sketchy description which was all I could get out of her old Catalan woman, it might have been Jules de Grasse. Evidently she had changed her mind about going, though, and did not mean to, as she wasn't dressed ready to go out. It seems that they had quite an argument before she went upstairs and changed her clothes. It was close on half-past when they left; so you must have passed them on your way back.'

Standing up, Molly helped herself to a cigarette. When John had lit it for her she drew hard on it for a moment, before she said, 'I do hope she will be all right. I don't like this new development a little bit. I wish to goodness there was something we could do to ensure her getting safely out of the clutches of those people.'

John shrugged. 'We certainly can't arm ourselves from your museum, give chase, and do a 'stand and deliver' on the de Grasses to get her back—if that is the sort of move your agile mind is beginning to toy with. They are not the Germans and there's no longer a war on; so snap out of it, Mumsie. She went off in broad daylight of her own free will, and judging by the form last night she is perfectly capable of taking care of herself.'

'You did make a pass at her, then?'

'Well, not exactly. She made it quite clear that she expected me to say good-night to her in the orthodox manner. And, although she said afterwards that it was the first time she had been kissed by a man, she took to it like a duck to water. If it hadn't been that she didn't seem to know the opening moves of the game I certainly wouldn't have believed her, and I still have my doubts about it. But it wasn't of that sort of thing that I was thinking. I meant in her general behaviour; and particularly at the Casino, she undoubtedly had all her wits about her.'

Lunch was announced at that moment. They dealt with the *hors-d'œuvres* in thoughtful silence; then when Angèle had put the sweetbreads on the table and gone out again, Molly said, 'You know, I believe she is a schizophrenic.'

'What, dual personality?'

'Yes. It is the only way one can account for the quite extraordinary changes which we have both seen in her. By day she is still an affectionate, overgrown child who is scared stiff that something awful is going to happen to her, and obsessed with the thought that she must remain in hiding; while by night she becomes a rather hard-boiled, sophisticated young woman, who is perfectly prepared to take the risk of being recognized for the sake of having a good time. It goes even further than that, because I am sure that during the day-time she is both innocent in mind and instinctively modest; whereas, from what you tell me, by night she is only too eager to have a necking party with the first man she sets eyes on.'

'Hi! Have a heart!' John protested, swiftly swallowing a piece of fried courgette. 'That is not very complimentary to your only begotten.'

'Do you seriously suggest that she would have preserved a virginal aloofness had she been out with any other personable young man than yourself?'

'Thank you, Mumsie. The word "personable" salves my wounded pride. No, to be honest, I don't. And I think you've hit the nail on the head with this theory of yours that she is a schizo'. All the same, that does not get us any further in solving the mystery of who is after her blood, and why.'

'At least we now have good reason to suppose that the Canon is not to be trusted. No clergyman who had a proper respect for his cloth would show himself in the gambling-rooms of a Casino—anyhow after midnight—and he being a friend of de Grasse makes him suspect in the highest degree. I wouldn't mind betting the serial rights of my next book that the story he told Christina about an accident to her father was a pack of lies, and designed solely to lure her away from her villa. Then, this invitation of de Grasse's: he and his wife are not the sort of people to spend their time showing young girls the beauties of the Riviera. It is all Lombard Street to a china orange that the Canon put him up to asking her to St Tropez for some nefarious purpose of his own.'

John nodded; his voice was serious now. 'I'm afraid you're right, dearest. But there is nothing we can do about it for the moment. We can only wait to see if she gets back all right and, if not, call in the police.'

That afternoon there was to be a Battle of Flowers at St Maxime. As they had planned to go to it, they set off there immediately after lunch. The little town was only about fifteen miles away; so by half-past two John had parked the car and they were installed in the seats for which Molly had already secured tickets. Their chairs were in the front row facing the sea, with only a temporary barrier of chestnut-pale fence railing them off from the promenade down which the procession would come; and while they waited for it they could scarcely prevent their gaze from frequently coming to rest on the white houses of St Tropez, which lay in the shelter of the headland just across the bay. Both of them were wondering how Christina was faring there, and although John endeavoured to engage his mother's attention, he did not succeed in doing so until the sounds of the town band in the distance heralded the beginning of the fête.

The battle was not on the grand scale of those held at Nice, Cannes and Monte Carlo; but there were nearly thirty carriages, and a lovely sight they made. The wheels, body and shafts of them all were entirely hidden by massed flowers, each seeking to outdo the others in colour, variety or originality. In most cases stocks, violets and carnations of many hues provided the ground work; while towers, trumpets, sheaves and fountains, on which were wired hundreds of roses, hyacinths, arum lilies and gladioli, surmounted the backs of the carriages. In each rode two or more young women, specially selected for their good looks. Some were displaying their charms in *décolletée* evening frocks, or in ballet skirts below which they wore black, large-mesh, fish-net stockings, while others were wearing light summer dresses and big floppy hats; but in every case their toilettes had been chosen to carry out the main colour motive of their floral chariots.

In every carriage the girls had big baskets of surplus flowers, with which to pelt the onlookers, and everyone in the crowd had a supply of similar ammunition bought from the gaily-dressed flower vendors. At a slow walk the colourful procession passed along between the barriers, while to and from both sides hundreds of little bunches of mimosa, stock, short-stemmed narcissi and carnation heads sailed up into the bright sunlight, thrown by the laughing girls and applauding people. To give the audience ample opportunity to enjoy the spectacle to the full, at intervals of about a quarter of an hour the procession passed and re-passed three times; so it was half-past four before the battle was finally concluded.

After it was over, remembering his mother's fondness for hot chocolate, John proposed that they should adjourn to a *pâtissière*. While they were there she again became distrait. Then, after a time, she suggested that they should go on to St Tropez in case Christina was still with the de Grasses at the Capricorn; as if she were they could pretend to have run into her by chance and by offering her a lift ensure her returning safely with them.

John considered the idea for a moment, then pointed out that as she had been asked over only to lunch the probability was that she would have left a couple of hours ago, so be home by now; while if the de Grasses had persuaded her to remain with them for the afternoon it would pretty certainly have been on the excuse of taking her for a drive, or to see the town; so the odds were all against her still being at the hotel, and it seemed going a bit too far to add twenty miles to their return journey for such a slender chance of finding her.

Molly thought his reasoning sound, so she did not press her suggestion. In consequence, having collected the car, instead of heading west, they headed east for home, arriving there just before six. Leaving John to put the car away, Molly went straight up to Christina's villa, hoping to find her there, and learn as soon as possible what had transpired at the lunch. But Christina was still absent.

More perturbed than ever for the girl's safety, Molly mounted the steep path to her own house, to be met in the hall by Angèle, who told her that at about half-past three the English mademoiselle who lived next door had telephoned, but had left no message. When John came in they discussed the situation again, but there seemed nothing they could do, as to have appealed to the police on the bare facts that a girl had gone out to lunch with friends and failed to return home by six o'clock would have been laughable.

They had fallen into an unhappy silence when, a quarter of an hour later, the telephone rang. John answered the call, and it was Christina. A little breathlessly she said, 'I tried to get you earlier this afternoon. I lunched with the de Grasses and am still with them. We've just got back to the hotel, and I'm telephoning from the call-box in the ladies' cloakroom; but we shall be going up to their private suite again in a minute. They have made me promise to stay and dine with them on their yacht. But I don't want to. Can you . . . can you possibly think of some excuse to come over here and . . . and get me away from them? Please, oh please!'

'O.K.," replied John promptly. 'Was it Count Jules who collected you this morning?'

'Yes; and it was he who took me round the town this afternoon.'

'Right! We'll be with you in three-quarters of an hour. All you have to do is to sit tight until we turn up, and in no circumstances fall for any pretext they may trot out with the idea of getting you to leave the hotel. Keep your chin up, and don't worry that pretty head of yours. We'll have you home in time for dinner.'

He had spoken with calm assurance, in order to quiet her evident fears; but as he replaced the receiver he felt far from confident about the outcome of the next few hours; and, while he repeated to his mother what she had said, it became even more clear to him that to get her away from the de Grasses was going to prove an extremely tricky business.

'If they once get her on their yacht it will be long odds against our ever seeing her again,' said Molly, now giving free rein to her anxiety.

He nodded glumly. 'It looks as if the Marquis is at his old white-slaving game again. Unless we can pull a fast one on him that poor kid may end up in Port Said or Buenos Aires.'

'Perhaps. She might, if they simply want to get rid of her. But I'm sure the Canon is behind this, and it may be that he wants to force her into doing something for some purpose of his own.'

'Anyhow, I'll be damned if I'm going to let him.'

John had spoken with sudden fierceness, and his mother shot him an appraising look as she asked, 'You do rather like her, then?'

He shrugged, gave a quick grin, and reverted to his usual gaily inconsequent manner. 'Don't be silly, Mumsie. It is solely that my sense of chivalry has been aroused. I feel like the knight who was riding through a forest and came upon a beauteous damosel tied to a tree. She cried out to him, "Frugal me, frugal me!" So he frugalled her.'

'Stop talking nonsense,' Molly admonished him, turning away. 'We've got to hurry. While you get the car out, I must just run upstairs. I won't be a moment.'

'You had better not,' he called after her, as he ran towards the door, 'otherwise I shall start without you.'

Five minutes later she rejoined him in the road, carrying a crocodile-skin bag that she generally used only when travelling. As she got into the car he gave it a suspicious glance, and said, 'You haven't brought the armaments, have you?'

She had never lied to him, and, after a second, she admitted, 'I've brought my small automatic—but it's only a very little one.'

Instead of letting in the clutch, he sat back and folded his arms. 'Now look, dearest. Things may be done that way in your thrillers, but they are not in real life. It's too damn' dangerous. For one thing the de Grasses would make mincemeat of us, and for another, if we survived the first five minutes they are clever enough to ensure that it is we who would find outselves in prison afterwards. Before I drive you a yard, you have got to give me your solemn promise that you won't start anything.'

'All right, I promise,' she said with a sigh. 'But it is a bit hard. This might have been a real chance to find out what it feels like to hold somebody up with a pistol.'

'Try it sometimes when I am elsewhere on my lawful occasions,' he advised. 'Then I'll at least remain free myself to come and bail you out.'

As he spoke the car shot forward. He was feeling guilty now at having scotched his mother's suggestion that they should drive on to St Tropez from St Maxime, as the sun was already going down beyond the hills ahead of them, and had he not opposed her they would by this time have been with Christina. In consequence, while exercising a fair degree of caution going round the sharp bends of the Corniche, he drove much faster than was his custom.

It was a good twenty-five miles from the villa to St Tropez; but, after St Raphael, for about half that distance the road was nearly flat and moderately straight, as it followed the shallow curve of the great bay in the centre of which lay St Maxime; so until they reached Beauvallon he was able to make good going. There, the road made a hairpin bend round the deep narrow gulf, then wound its way along the peninsula that had St Tropez as its seaward end. When they pulled up in front of the great modern building of concrete and glass, that looked more like a block of flats than an hotel, it was just after seven and twilight was falling.

While on their way they had made their plan of campaign, and on entering the hotel, instead of enquiring for the Marquis at the desk, they walked straight to the lift and asked the lift-man to take them up to de Grasse's suite. The lift shot up to the top floor, and as they stepped from it the man pointed out to them a door at the end of the corridor. Their footfalls making no sound on the heavy pile carpet, they advanced towards it; then John rang the bell.

After a moment the door was opened by Count Jules. He was a shortish but athletic-looking young man in his middle twenties, with slim hips, broad shoulders and a plump round face. His eyes were very dark and his lips a trifle thick, but the corners of his mouth turned up slightly, giving him an expression of humorous good nature.

For a few seconds he stared blankly at his visitors, then recognition dawned in his eyes, and he exclaimed in English that had no more than a faint trace of accent:

'Why! Surely it is John Fountain?'

'Of course,' John smiled. 'I thought you were expecting us.'

Count Jules looked his astonishment. 'Forgive me, but I did not know, even, that you were in this part of the world.'

John made a gesture of annoyance. 'I'm so sorry. They must have made a muddle downstairs. I asked for you at the desk, and after telephoning the chap said we were to come up. But there was a woman beside us asking for somebody else, and in making the calls he must have got his lines crossed.'

A slight narrowing of the Frenchman's eyes suggested either suspicion or that he was not used to such inefficient service and meant to give the unfortunate receptionist a sharp reprimand; but before he had time to make any comment John hurried on:

'I happened to meet your father last night in the Casino at Cannes. That's how I learned you were here. My mother and I have been visiting friends in St Tropez this afternoon. On the spur of the moment I thought I would look you up, before we drive back to our little villa for dinner.'

'But how nice! I am delighted, delighted.' There was no trace now in the Count's voice of anything but genuine pleasure.

'I don't think you've ever met my mother,' John said.

'*Enchanté, madame.*' Count Jules took Molly's hand as though it were a fragile piece of porcelain, and went through the motion of kissing the back of it, although he did not actually touch it with his lips. Then he murmured, 'Forgive me for keeping you standing like this in the hall. Please to come in. We are so happy to see you.'

The small hallway of the suite had four doors leading from it. That on the immediate right stood partly open. Issuing from it John had heard the murmur of voices, and he guessed that Christina was with someone there. He had spoken to Jules rather loudly in the hope that she might hear what he said, and so not sabotage his story by giving any indication that they had really come to collect her. As their host pushed the door back and bowed Molly through it, John saw over her shoulder that Christina was looking in their direction with anxious expectation. But Molly forestalled any gaffe she might have made by exclaiming:

'Why, Christina! John told me you were lunching with these friends of his, but I never expected to find you still here.'

Jules' glance switched swiftly from the girl to the newcomers, and he said in a surprised voice, 'You know one another, then?'

'Oh yes,' Molly replied lightly. 'We are next-door neighbours and quite old friends.'

When they entered the room a woman, who at first sight looked quite young, had been curled up in one corner of a big settee. As she uncurled herself and sat up Jules turned and addressed her in rapid French:

'*Belle mère*, may I present Mrs Fountain and her son John, who was up with me during my last year at Cambridge.' Then he added in English, 'My stepmother, the Marquise de Grasse.'

The sitting-room of this luxury suite was unusually spacious for an hotel, and from floor to ceiling one of its sides was composed entirely of sliding glass windows. But as the light was already fading and the Marquise was sitting with her back to them, it was difficult to tell her age. She was slim, extremely *soignée*, and, in the latest fashion, she had had several curls of her elaborately-dressed dark hair dyed gold. Her eyes were round and blue, her mouth a little sulky-looking. She was wearing a silk blouse, grey slacks with knife-like creases, and over her shoulders a chinchilla fur. Extending a limp hand she said:

'I am ver pleas to meet you. But my English, et ess not much good. You forgive? Perhaps you spik French?'

Molly's French being excellent, and that of both John and Christina adequate, most of the conversation which followed was carried on in that language. But the Marquise took little part in it; except to inform Molly a little later, while John and Jules were talking over old times, that although her husband owned houses in several parts of France, she much preferred to live for most of the year in hotels, as it was far less trouble.

They were already drinking cocktails, and while Jules made a fresh mix for the new arrivals, Christina said, 'Madame la Marquise and Count Jules have been most kind. They insisted on my spending the afternoon here. He took me up to the old fort, then all round the harbour; and now they want me to stay and dine with them on their yacht.'

'I wish I were as young as you are and could still keep such hours,' Molly replied with a smile. 'If I had been up till near dawn this morning I should be dropping asleep by now.'

Christina took the ball quickly. 'That's just the trouble. I'm not used to late nights, and I really don't feel up to it.'

'Nonsense!' said Jules. 'After a few glasses of champagne you will forget there is such a place as bed.'

'Unfortunately champagne does not agree with me. And as I told you some time ago, I already have quite a headache. Please don't think me rude, but I'd really rather go home.'

'If you are feeling like that it's lucky we turned up,' John put in casually. 'We can give you a lift back, and save Jules from being late for his dinner.'

'No, no!' Jules protested. 'A couple of aspirins will soon put your headache right, and we are not dining till nine; so if you wish you can lie down for an hour before we start. How about lying down for a while now? *Belle mère* will make you comfortable in our spare room.'

'No thank you. I'd rather not.'

He shrugged. 'Well, our friends will not be going yet. See how you feel a little later on.' Turning to John, he added, 'There are fireworks at Le Lavendou to-night and we are taking the yacht round the cape to witness them. It would be a pity for her to miss that. I wish that I could ask you and your mother to accompany us, but unfortunately the dining space on the yacht is limited, and my father has already made up his party.'

Dismissing the matter, he then went on to talk about mutual friends they had known at Cambridge.

Outside darkness was falling rapidly, and during the quarter of an hour that followed Molly noticed a perceptible change in Christina. She had become much more lively as she described with enthusiasm the things she had seen with Count Jules that afternoon. When he switched on the lights and drew the curtains, she was laughing gaily about her big win at the tables the previous night, and saying that she could hardly wait to get back to them to try her luck again.

Scenting danger in her change of mood, Molly said to her, 'John was going to suggest taking you in to Cannes again to-morrow night. But you won't feel much like it if you don't get a good sleep to-night; so from that point of view your decision to come home with us is a wise one. It is a great pity that you are feeling so rotten this evening and have to disappoint Count Jules, but I'm sure he will forgive you and ask you to go out on the yacht again some other time. And, talking of time, I really think it's time that we were going.'

'Oh, not yet!' cried Jules. 'You have been here hardly twenty minutes, and Christina is looking better already. I feel sure she will keep her promise and come with us after all.'

'How late should we be?' Christina asked.

'We need not be late at all. We shall sit down to dinner as the yacht leaves harbour. The fireworks start at ten. They last only half an hour. The yacht will be back in her berth again by half-past eleven. Normally we should then dance for a while; but if you wish I could run you straight home, and you would be in bed not long after midnight.'

'In that case ...' Christina hesitated, then said with, for her, unusual brazenness, 'Give me another cocktail, and while I am drinking it I will make up my mind.'

'But certainly!' As Jules jumped to his feet, to John's surprise his mother called out, 'And me, too, if you please.' Then, with sudden apprehension, he saw her pick up and open her crocodile-skin bag. But, to his considerable relief, she only took out her compact and powdered her nose.

When Jules had replenished their glasses, Molly drew John's attention to a rather novel arrangement of bookcases at the far end of the room, and suggested that they might be a good idea for incorporation in some of his designs. He had not previously mentioned the fact to the de Grasses that he had taken up interior decorating as a profession, but did so now, while they were all looking at the bookcases.

The Marquise showed a sudden interest, and asked his opinion of the room, which she had had redecorated to her own specification. It displayed considerable taste, so he was able truthfully to compliment her upon it, before making a few tactful suggestions on quite minor points.

For a few minutes they discussed them. Then John happened to glance at Christina. Her face had gone deadly white. With quick concern he asked:

'I say; you're looking awfully pale. Are you feeling all right?'

She shook her head. 'No ... I ... I feel awfully queer.'

The Marquise uncoiled her long legs in the beautifully tailored grey slacks, and said, 'Poor little one. Would you like to go to the bathroom? Come with me. I will take you there.'

'No,' murmured Christina. 'I don't want to be sick. I ... just feel muzzy.' She pointed to her glass, which was nearly empty, and added, 'That ... that last cocktail must have been too much for me.'

'Drinking a spot too much when one is overtired often has that effect,' John remarked. 'But this settles it. She must come home with us; and the sooner the better.'

'No!' A sharp note had crept into Jules' voice. 'She shall stay here until she recovers. *Belle mère*, oblige me, please, by taking her to your room and looking after her.'

'I'm afraid that is not a very good idea,' John countered smoothly. 'She'll only fall asleep, and wake up in a few hours' time feeling like hell. Then you would have the unenviable task of driving her home.'

John's contention was amply supported by the fact that, although Christina was trying to keep her head up, it now kept falling forward on to her chest. But Jules replied coldly:

'I should not in the least mind putting myself out a little for a young guest of mine who has been taken ill.'

'Perhaps; but has it occurred to you that someone will have to stay with her, and that if your stepmother does so it would mean depriving her of the party and your father's other guests of their hostess?'

'That can be overcome. My stepmother's maid is most competent.'

'But,' Molly put in, 'it would be bad for the girl when she wakes, to be taken for a twenty-five mile drive.'

Jules' black eyes had gone as hard as pebbles as he turned them on her. 'She can stay here for the night. What is to prevent her?'

'I am,' replied Molly firmly. 'As an older woman I know better than you how to deal with a case like this. She will feel miserable and ashamed if, after having allowed herself to drink too much, she wakes up among comparative strangers and in a strange bed. I intend to take her back to her own villa.'

Jules could barely conceal his anger any longer. 'Madame!' he snapped, 'I will not be dictated to in this manner. She is in no condition to be driven anywhere. A doctor should see her, and I mean to send for one. I insist that she stays here.'

'Sorry, old chap!' John's voice was still quite good-humoured and level. 'But my mother has known her for some time and is more or less responsible for her. So what she says goes.'

As he spoke he advanced towards Christina, took her firmly by the arm, and pulled her to her feet. Then he added quietly, 'Give me a hand to get her to the lift, will you?'

Quite suddenly Jules' determination to keep her there seemed to collapse. With a tight smile he stepped forward, took Christina's other arm, and helped John support her to the door. The Marquise asked Molly to telephone them next morning to let them know if Christina was all right, then the two older women exchanged polite adieus, and Molly followed the others out into the corridor.

There, at Jules' suggestion, she went down ahead of them in to the lift, to bring the car round to a side door of the hotel, so that they should not have to take the half-conscious girl right across the big lounge. By making a great effort, Christina could manage to walk a few steps at a time, as long as she was supported on both sides. Ten minutes later, with few people having seen them, they had her safely in the back seat of the car. Just as it was about to drive off, Jules leaned forward and said smoothly through the window to John:

'My father will be so sorry to have missed you; but you must come over and see us again.'

'Thanks,' John replied, with the appearance of equal cordiality, 'I should love to.'

Molly had overheard the exchange, and as the car ran down the drive she murmured, 'I thought at one moment he was going to prove really troublesome. I wonder what caused him suddenly to change his mind.'

'I've no idea.' John shrugged. 'Anyhow, we pulled it off. But what a bit of luck that she asked for that last cocktail. God alone knows how we should have got her away if it hadn't been for that.'

'Yes. That, and what I put in it.'

'Mumsie!' He turned to stare at her for a second. 'What the devil do you mean?'

'I gave her a Micky Finn, darling.'

'You didn't!'

'Well, to be accurate, only about a quarter of one, because I didn't want to knock her right out.' Molly's voice was just a trifle smug. 'I'm really rather pleased with myself. I've had some of those little tablets in my museum for years. I souvenired them during the war, and I've always wanted to try them on someone, but a suitable opportunity has never arisen before. The way it worked was most gratifying.'

'How on earth did you manage to put it in her drink without anyone seeing you?'

Molly tittered with pleasure at the thought of her skilful coup. 'I didn't. I put it in my own, and used the cherry-stick to help dissolve it quickly. Then, when I had made you all look away from the table to the bookcases, I exchanged her glass for mine.'

'Well, played, Mumsie!' John spoke with genuine admiration. 'But you've let the cat out of the bag, you know. This night's work dispels my last lingering doubts about your having been Molly Polloffski, the beautiful spy.'

'No, Johnny. Really, I assure you I never did anything but work in an office.'

'Tell that one to the Marines!' he replied, closing the conversation.

As Christina had been given only a small dose of the powerful drug, she recovered fairly quickly from its worst effects, and when they got back to Molly's villa she was able to walk up the path to it unassisted. As soon as they reached the sitting-room Molly sat her down in an armchair, then went upstairs and fetched her a bromo-seltzer.

She was now fully conscious again, but in a curious mood, half tearful and half defiant. Several times she apologized for having made a fool of herself, and for having given them so much trouble. But she did not seem to realize that they had saved her from some very grave danger. Every now and then she harped back to the de Grasses' party and said how sorry she was to have missed it. In fact it soon became clear that she now resented their having prevented her remaining at the Capricorn until she recovered, so that there might still have been a chance of her being able to go on the yacht.

At length Molly said, 'I'm afraid, my dear, that this business has been getting on your nerves, and that you are no longer in a quite normal state. If you were, you would recall that it was at your own request, made earlier this evening, that we got you out of the clutches of the de Grasses.' Pausing for a moment she fished something out of her bag and concealed it in her hand; then she went on, 'Our only wish is to get to the root of your trouble, and see you out of it. Here is something which may help us to do that, and help you, too.'

As she finished speaking she threw the thing she was holding towards Christina's lap, and cried, 'Catch!'

Christina cupped her hands and caught the spinning object. It was a small gold crucifix. The second it fell into her palms she gave a scream of pain. Then, as though seared by white-hot metal, she thrust it from her.

'I feared as much!' Molly said grimly. 'And now we know the worst! Every night when darkness falls, you become possessed by the Devil.'

6

THE CHRISTINA OF THE DARK HOURS

With her eyes glaring, Christina sprang up from the armchair. Then, as though suddenly stricken by a fit, her long limbs grew rigid, she fell back into it, and little flecks of froth began to appear at the corners of her mouth.

Molly went quickly over to the side-table on which stood the drinks, filled a tumbler half full of Perrier water and, turning about, sloshed its contents into the girl's face. She whimpered, the rigor passed, and she sat up, the water dripping from her brown hair and running down her pale cheeks. laying a hand on her shoulder, Molly said kindly:

'God help you, child; but I am right, aren't I? You are only your real self in the day-time, and at night you become possessed.'

With a moan, Christina buried her face in her hands, and burst into a flood of tears.

Turning to John, Molly said, 'She had better stay here to-night. Before we left I told Angèle that we might be late for dinner, so we would have something cold. Slip out to the kitchen and tell her that we shan't be ready for it for another half-hour, and that she is to go up at once and make the spare room ready.'

John was standing with his mouth a little open, staring at Christina. He could still hardly believe that he had not been the victim of a sudden amnesia and imagined the happenings of the last few moments. But he pulled himself together, nodded, and left the room.

For a few minutes Molly remained silently beside Christina, then when the girl's weeping ceased she said, 'My dear, you must be quite exhausted, and are in no state to talk further about this to-night. I'm going to put you to bed here, and to-morrow when you are feeling better we will decide what it is best for us to do.'

'There is nothing that you can do,' murmured Christina a little sullenly.

'Oh yes, there is,' countered Molly, in her most determined voice. 'And we're going to do it; but it is not the time to go into that now.'

At that moment John returned; so his mother said to him, 'You had better stay with her, while I go over to her villa and get her a few things for the night.'

Christina was now sitting staring at the floor. After another swift glance at her, John mixed himself a drink and, feeling extremely awkward, sat down some way from her on the edge of the sofa. For once he was completely out of his depth. The very idea of anyone in this modern world being possessed by the Devil struck him as utterly fantastic. Yet Christina had reacted to the touch of the crucifix as though she had been stung by a hornet, and there seemed no normal explanation for that. Moreover, she had made no attempt to explain it herself, or deny his mother's diagnosis of her case. In such extraordinary circumstances he could think of nothing whatever to say to her; but fortunately she did not seem to expect him to start a conversation; so they both remained sitting there in silence until Molly returned.

Much to his relief, no further scene ensued. Molly's attitude to the girl was now the same as she would have adopted to any young guest who had suddenly been taken ill in her house. With brisk efficiency, she hurried her off to bed; and Christina went without a word of protest.

Shortly afterwards Angèle came in to say that she had laid supper, and when Molly came down she found John in the dining-room pulling the cork of a bottle of *vin rosé*. As she took her seat at the table she said:

'For a moment I feared that poor child was going to run screaming from the house. It was a great relief that after her fit she became so docile, and allowed me to put her to bed, where I can keep an eye on her. She is fairly comfortable now, but as a result of that Mickey Finn she naturally does not feel like eating any dinner. I have told Angèle to take her up a cup of *bouillon*, and later I shall give her a good dose of some stuff I have.'

'I suppose,' John remarked, 'that if we made her drink a noggin of Holy water she would start to fizz, then blow up; so no doubt you're right to play for safety and stick to your panacea for all childish ills—a grey powder disguised in a spoonful of raspberry jam.'

His rather poor attempt at humour brought the quick reproof, 'I was referring to some stuff which will make her sleep. And, Johnny, this is nothing to joke about.'

'Sorry; but I haven't yet got my bearings. What was the big idea in putting a fast one over on Christina while she was still too doped to fully understand what was going on?'

'If you mean my throwing her that little crucifix, I should have thought my reason for doing so immediately became obvious.'

'No, I didn't mean that. While she was in that state, throwing anything at her might have made her scream. I meant putting the idea that she was possessed into the poor girl's head at a time when she was too goofy to repudiate it?'

'She didn't repudiate it because she knows—or at least suspects—that it is true.'

'Oh come, Mumsie! You can't really believe that people become possessed. That is now just a form of speech for a particular kind of religious lunacy.'

'It is not, and *she is*,' Molly announced with decision. 'I have been wondering all day if that could be at the bottom of her extraordinary behaviour, and now I am certain of it. The acid test is to touch anyone who is suspected of possession with a crucifix. If they react as though they have been burnt, that is a sure sign that they have a devil inside them.'

John helped himself to another chunk of *paté maison*, spread it lavishly on a *brioche*, and asked sceptically, 'How do you know? Is it just that you have read about it in some old book, or have you actually seen it happen on a previous occasion?'

'I was told about it by a Roman Catholic priest whom I knew years ago. He specialized in exorcism, and had witnessed many strange happenings. One experience that he told me of I shall never forget. It was in Ireland and he was endeavouring to drive a devil out of a poor cottager. The place was deep in the country, so the wife had prepared a meal. In honour of the priest she had bought a leg of mutton, but as the time when he could get out there was uncertain she cooked it in advance and placed it cold on the table of the living-room, all ready for when he had fulfilled his mission. The case proved a very stubborn one. The possessed man became violent, struggling and blaspheming, and had to be tied down. For over two hours the priest wrestled with the fiend, conjuring him to come forth without success; but at last he triumphed. A wisp of evil-smelling black smoke issued from the cottager's foaming mouth, sped across the room, apparently passing through the leg of mutton, then disappeared through the wall. When the exhausted victim had been put to bed the priest and the rest of the family sat down to supper. But they were unable to eat the mutton. When it was touched it fell from the bones, absolutely rotten and alive with maggots.'

'Did the chap who told you this story produce any supporting evidence to substantiate that he was telling the truth?'

'No, and I did not need it. He was a most saintly old man. I am sure he would have allowed himself to be torn in pieces rather than lie about any matter connected with his faith.'

'Have you any other sources for believing that such things still happen?'

'Not direct ones, but occasionally one sees cases reported in the French papers.'

'Why the French papers, particularly?'

'Cases are probably also reported in the Spanish and Italian press, and those of other Catholic countries; but I don't see them.'

'The inference is, then, that these occurrences are confined to Catholic countries?'

'No, I don't think that is so. I think that the profound knowledge of demonology that has been handed down by the Roman Catholic Church enables certain of her priests to recognize possession and deal with it; whereas when a case occurs in a Protestant country hardly anyone is capable of distinguishing it from ordinary lunacy, so the sufferer is simply certified and put in an asylum.'

John could not help being impressed, and after remaining silent for a moment he said, 'If you are really right about all this, Mumsie, it looks as if we ought to call a Catholic priest in to cope with Christina.'

'That is easier said than done, darling. You see, although all Roman Catholic priests are qualified by their office to perform ceremonies of exorcism, very few of them ever do so. Experience has shown it to be a job for experts who have made a special study of that sort of thing; much in the same way as only a very limited number of doctors are capable of prescribing the most efficient treatment for a rare disease. As we are not Catholics ourselves and Christina isn't one either, I'm afraid it would prove difficult to interest the local man in her case sufficiently to induce him to send for a first-class exorcist, perhaps from some distant part of France.'

'How do you propose to handle this extraordinary business, then? She is quite sane most of the time, and we can't let her be popped into a loony bin.'

Molly looked down at her plate. 'When we've finished supper I thought I would ring up London, and try to get hold of Colonel Verney.'

'What, Conky Bill!' John exclaimed in astonishment.

'Yes. He usually dines at his club in the middle of the week and never goes home much before eleven, so there is quite a good chance of my catching him. If he is not too desperately busy I might be able to persuade him to fly down to-morrow and stay with us for a few days.'

'But hang it all, Mumsie, what's the idea? Of course, I know you've always had a bit of a yen for C.B., so one can't blame you for seizing on any excuse . . .'

'Johnny, I've told you often enough that I had to act as liaison between my chief and C.B. during the war, and that after your father died he was extremely kind to me. That's all there is to it.'

'Dearest, you know jolly well that the two of you flirt like mad whenever you are together. I think he's a grand chap, and nothing would please me better than to get tight at your wedding, but that is beside the point at the moment. The thing I don't get is why you should regard him as a suitable substitute for a Catholic priest who has trained as an expert exorcist.'

'If I tell you, you must promise never to repeat it.'

'Go ahead. I can give as good an imitation of a bearded oyster as you can about things that really matter.'

'Well, you are quite right in assuming that for the past few years C.B. has given most of his time to checking up on the activities of Communists and fellow travellers. But that is only because they have now become the principal source of danger to our right to choose whom we want to rule us at free elections. Before the war he spent just as much of his time keeping his eye on the Fascists. Actually he is responsible for keeping his chief informed about all groups that may be engaged in subversive activities. That, of course, covers every type of secret society, including circles that practise Black Magic.'

John raised his dark eyebrows. 'Such circles do really exist, then? I remember reading an article some months ago in the *Sunday Empire News* by ex-Superintendent Robert Fabian, giving a most lurid account of how young girls were lured into lending themselves to all sorts of obscene rites in secret Satanic Temples. He even went so far as to state that he knew there to be such places in Kensington, Paddington and Bloomsbury. But I thought it was all poppycock, and that now Fabian is retired he was just making himself a bit of easy money.'

'No; Fabian was telling the truth. And when he was an officer of the Special Branch he worked in close collaboration with C.B. You have no idea of the horrors they uncovered.'

'Why are there never any prosecutions , then?'

'Because the Satanists who run these circles are too clever. They recruit their disciples from among the people who attend quite respectable spiritualist and theosophical societies, many of whom can easily be intrigued by a promise of revealing to them the real secrets of the occult at some small private gathering. The obtaining of power is, of course, the lure, and they start them off with Yoga exercises; then prescribe a special diet for them, including a course of pills which are actually aphrodisiacs to increase their sexual appetite. After that there is usually not much difficulty in involving them with some more advanced Satanist of the opposite sex. For them that starts as just as a rather intriguing affair, but it is the thin end of the wedge. Their instructor promises the revelation of higher mysteries if they will consent to be hypnotized, and they nearly always do. Once they have been fully dominated they no longer have a mind of their own and become willing subjects for every kind of abomination. A few of the stronger-minded ones survive to achieve the rank of real Satanists themselves, but most of them are used only for obscenities and soon degenerate into physical and moral wrecks. Many of them end up as suicides, and those who are rescued by their friends always prove useless from the police point of view. Either they have not gone far enough to be able to give evidence of any actually criminal activities, or, if they have, they have been hypnotized into a state in which their minds are blank about the Satanists they have been mixed up with and the places where the rituals in which they participated took place. That is why there are never any prosecutions.'

'It sounds a ghastly business,' John said, pushing his plate away; 'but I don't quite see where Conky Bill comes into it. From Fabian's article and what you say, it seems that the Satanists' only interest is to get hold of young people upon whom to practise sexual perversions at their orgies. Beastly as that may be, it is a form of private fun and has no connection with subversive activities against the State.'

'You are quite wrong about that, Johnny. The people who direct these circles really are the henchmen of the Devil. The sexual excesses that take place under their auspices are only a means to an end—a focus for concentrating evil forces which they can use for the furtherance of their own wicked designs. You must have read at some time that in the old days the Devil was often referred to as the Lord of Misrule. The object of these high-up Satanists is to deliver the world up to him, and the only way they can do that is to cause the breakdown of good rule so that misrule may take its place. With that as their goal they do everything they can to foment wars, class-hatred, strikes and famine; and to foster perversions, moral laxity and the taking of drugs. There is even reason to believe that they have been behind many of the political assassinations that have robbed the world of good rulers and honest statesmen, and naturally Communism has now become their most potent weapon. So you can see that breaking up these Black Magic circles, wherever they can be found, is very much in C. B.'s province.'

'Oh come, Mumsie! I agree that they may exert their influence for political evil, but by suggesting that they are working to a plan and have supernatural backing, aren't you letting your imagination run away with you a bit? After all, no one really believes in the Devil any more.'

'My dear, he was part of the original creation, and no amount of popular education can destroy that. It is simply that in modern times he has gone underground, and judging by the amount of havoc and misery there has been in the world during the present century he must be very pleased with the success of his latest stratagem. It was his own apparent abolition, resulting from the decay of religion, that gave him his big chance, and he is using it with a greater skill than he has ever displayed before in his attempts to ensnare mankind.'

'You honestly believe that?'

'I do. Now that more than half the people in the world have become godless, they have also become rudderless. Once they have put away from themselves the idea of a hereafter they think only of their own selfish ends of the moment. That leaves them an easy prey to unscrupulous politicians. Before they know where they are, they find themselves robbed of all personal freedom; their family life, which is their last tie with their better instincts, is broken up, and their children are taken from them, to be educated into robots lacking all individuality. That is what nearly happened in Nazi Germany and what has happened in Russia; and if that is not the state of things that Satan would like to see everywhere, tell me what is?'

John did not reply. Instead, after a moment's thought, he asked, 'Have you any idea where Christina fits into all this?'

'No. I have heard that now and then one of those Paris finishing places is discovered to be no better than a high-class brothel. When girls who are just becoming women are cooped up together they corrupt one another very easily, you know; and in the type of place that caters for those whose parents want to be rid of them for two or three years at a stretch, an unscrupulous principal with a clever man behind her might get away with a vice racket of that kind for quite a long time without being found out. As sexual promiscuity is the first step towards greater evils, if Christina was at such a place she may have got herself involved in something there. But somehow I don't think so. She does not give me the impression of a girl who has gone very far down the slope of her own free will. I am more inclined to think that she is the victim of a spell, and has been bewitched.'

'If we can get hold of C.B., do you think he will be able to free her from the . . . er . . . sort of trouble you have in mind?'

'I don't know, Johnny. We can only hope so. All I do know is that in the course of his job he must have picked up a lot about the principles on which Satanists work, and he is the only person I know of who may be able to advise us what to do. Even if he is busy I feel sure he will come if he possibly can, as, quite apart from any wish to help the girl, there is the de Grasse angle, and that should prove an additional justification for him to leave his office.'

Three-quarters of an hour later Molly succeeded in getting Lieutenant-Colonel William Verney on the telephone. They then talked for a few minutes in the curious jargon that such people had used in the war, even when their conversations were protected from listeners-in by a scrambler. It consisted of short phrases, interspersed with apparently irrelevant allusions to mutal friends, places, books and past happenings, which could mean little to any third person, but rang bells in the minds of both. She proved right in her belief that he would respond to her appeal; and it was agreed that, unless he telegraphed her that he had been unable to get a seat on the plane, she should meet him at Nice airport on the following day.

In consequence, in spite of the concern she was feeling about Christina, Molly went to bed in a happy frame of mind; while the girl fell into a heavy slumber as a result of the draught she had been given. But John lay long awake, turning over and over all that his mother had said about Satanism, veering between belief and disbelief, and quite unable to decide whether it was only her vivid imagination that caused her to credit the Devil with being active in the modern world, or if in sober truth the unfortunate Christina was, during certain hours, possessed by some evil force that had been conjured up from the traditional Pit, said to be inhabited by Satan's legions.

At length he dropped off, but only to become the victim of a nightmare, in which he was chained to a rock and an angel and a devil were fighting over him. Both of them had Christina's face, and while that of the angel glowed with beauty, that of the devil was rendered peculiarly horrifying by the fact that luminous smoke was curling up from its flared nostrils.

In the morning, contrary to custom, his mother had him called and his breakfast brought to him at eight-thirty; so he was dressed and downstairs well before ten. From her he learned that Christina had had a good night, was none the worse for her experiences of the previous evening, and had gone over to her own villa to change her clothes, but had promised to return as soon as she had done so.

A quarter of an hour later she came in through the sitting-room window, looking a little subdued but otherwise perfectly normal, and very pretty in a square-necked frock made gay with broad bands of red and yellow peasant embroidery. In the morning sunshine it seemed difficult to believe that she was the same girl whose eyes had glared hatred during a fit as a result of having a crucifix pitched to her, in that very room, little more than twelve hours before. But all three of them were uncomfortably aware that no good purpose could be served by refraining from going into the matter, and Molly set about it with commendable briskness.

'Tell me, my dear,' she said as they sat down, 'how much do you remember about what happened last night?'

Christina turned her big, frank brown eyes upon her questioner. 'A certain amount, but not everything. There are some quite big gaps. I remember you arrival at the Capricorn and how relieved I was, because I felt sure you would get me away from those people. Then I have a vague recollection of your disputing with them about me, and that I became increasingly annoyed with you for wanting to take me home. What occurred after this is completely gone, until I woke up feeling dreadfully ill and found myself in the back of your car. We came in here and I was trying to figure out a way of getting back to the Capricorn without your knowing. Then . . . then I had a sort of fit, and from that point on my mind is a blank again until I woke up in bed here this morning.'

'Is it usual for you to have those sort of lapses of memory about much of what has been happening to you the night before?'

'Yes. Somehow at night I seem to be quite a different person. I often get up and roam about, and at such times I get all sorts of nasty impulses of a kind that I rarely have during the day. As far as I know I don't often give way to them, but I can't be quite certain of that, because afterwards I nearly always get these blackouts. The thought of what I may have done during them distresses and frightens me next morning. But to the best of my belief I do remember if I have actually done anything wicked, because I have had numerous instances of that. Any really definite action seems to register permanently in my mind.'

'Can you give us any examples?'

'Well, for one thing, I'm afraid I'm a thief.' Christina lowered her eyes and went on unhappily, 'Honestly, I don't mean to be; but several times in

Paris I stole trinkets and scent and money from the other girls at night. When I remembered what I had done the following morning I was terribly ashamed. Fortunately I was able to put the things back before my thefts were noticed; and no others were reported. It is that which makes me believe that when I do give way to these awful impulses I know what I have done when I wake up.'

'Was the impulse to steal the only one that came to you?'

'No. I seem to become horribly malicious. My best friend was engaged to be married. One night I stole the love-letters that her fiancé had written to her, and burnt them down in the furnace. Several times I used a steel crochet hook to make ladders in other girls' stockings and spilt ink on their clothes, but I was so cunning that they never found out who had done it. Then I became subject to a special feeling about anything connected with religion. It is a sort of mixture of hatred and fear. I can't bring myself to touch any sacred object, but . . . but I've defiled them. Three times I did that with little lockets containing holy symbols belonging to different girls. There was a frightful row afterwards, but no one had the least suspicion that I was the culprit.'

'Is there anything else you can tell us about your state during these midnight forays?' Molly asked after a moment.

Christina flushed, and her voice was very low. 'Yes. I realize that if you are going to help me I ought not to keep anything back. Sometimes I feel the most awful urge towards immorality—but I'd rather not talk about that.'

'Let's go back to last night,' said Molly, promptly changing the line of the conversation. 'Do you remember my throwing a crucifix to you, and what happened then?'

'Yes,' Christina replied in a whisper. 'As it touched me it felt like a live coal. I sprang up and screamed. Then you said that I was possessed by the Devil.'

'I know it was a terrible thing to say, my dear; but do you think you are?'

'I don't know. At times I've wondered if I am, myself. But why should I be? What can I possibly have done to deserve such an awful fate?'

So far John had not spoken; but seeing that the girl was now very near to tears, he stretched out his hand, took one of hers, and pressed it. 'We are sure it's not your fault. Even if it's true—even if you have done something to bring it on yourself—Mother and I wouldn't stop wanting to help you. And we wouldn't like you any the less.'

'Thanks.' She gave him a faint smile and let her hand remain in his, as Molly added, 'John is quite right about that; and my own belief is that it is nothing you have done, but that somebody has bewitched you. Have you ever known anybody who was interested in witchcraft, magic or sorcery?'

'I don't think so. In Paris one of the girls used to tell fortunes with a pack of cards; but one couldn't really call that witchcraft, could one? And she wasn't very good at it. As a matter of fact I could do it far better myself, but I didn't; not when I was there. I gave it up several years ago, because it frightened me. Twice when I was at that school in Somerset I predicted serious accidents; and in one case I saw death in the cards, although I didn't say so, and the person died a month later.'

Molly nodded. 'Such an uncanny gift is additional proof that you have some special link with occult powers; and evidently it is not a recent one.

How long is it since you took to prowling about at night, and feeling these distressing impulses?'

'Ever since I can remember; but, as I told you the other day, when I was young it took the form of sleep-walking. It may have been because I did naughty things at such times that Delia was so unkind to me. I didn't even begin to be aware of what I was doing until I was thirteen, and even then it came as a gradual transition. I must have been over seventeen before I was fully conscious when I got out of bed at nights. But the occasions on which I did so were fairly few and far between, and the impulses I felt were neither as strong nor as wicked. It is only during the past year that I have been getting so much worse. That is what frightens me so much.'

'Have you ever been to a séance, or gone in for table-turning and just for a lark called on the Devil to aid your enquiries?'

'No, never.'

'And there is no special episode in your childhood, or anything else you can remember, that might have a bearing on your present state?'

'No. I have already told you everything about my life that I can think of.'

There fell a pause, then John asked, 'How about Canon Copely-Syle? I wouldn't mind betting that he didn't turn up here by chance, and that the story he told you about your father having had a serious accident was a fake, designed to get you away from your villa. I didn't know it when we met the Marquis de Grasse at Cannes, but Mother has since told me that he is a crook. The fact that the Canon introduced you to him, and his son afterwards tried to get you on to their yacht, makes the case against the Canon pretty black. In fact, it is ten to one that he is at the bottom of the whole business.'

'Yes. I came to that conclusion yesterday; although I then had little more than my instinct to go on. It was that which made me refuse to go on the yacht yesterday afternoon, when Count Jules took me down to the harbour and pressed me to. It was only after I had made an excuse not to, and dug my toes in, that he invited me to dine on board instead; and as he had first made certain that I had no engagement for the evening, I could think of no way to wriggle out of accepting. But I'm afraid I can't help much about the Canon. I told you all I know about him on the morning of his visit.'

'There are two things you can tell us,' Molly said, 'although I hesitate to ask you, and I wouldn't if I didn't think it important that we should know them. They are your real name, and your father's address.'

Christina shook her head. 'I'd rather not break my promise to him.'

'Just as you like, my dear. But when he asked you for it, neither of you could possibly foresee the sort of thing that has happened since; and if he knew how you were situated at present I feel sure he would release you from it. You see, now that the Canon has discovered your hiding-place, and it looks as if he is employing crooks to get hold of you, we have to face the fact that however carefully John and I endeavour to guard against it, you might be taken from us. If that happened our best hope of getting you back would be to call in the police; and it might be a great help to them in tracing you if we could give them your proper name and enable them to communicate with your father.'

For a moment Christina considered the matter, then she said with sudden decision, 'All right. My name is Ellen Beddows, and we live at The Grange, Little Bentford, near Colchester. My father is Henry Beddows of Beddows Agricultural Tractors.'

'Thank you, my dear. Of course we shall continue to call you Christina, and you may be sure we will not abuse your confidence. Now, there is just one other thing. Your father must hold the key to both your own peculiar state and the mystery of why the Canon is so anxious to get hold of you. Don't you really think the time has come when we should try to get in touch with him?'

'No!' Christina's voice was firm. 'He told me that it was unlikely that his office would know where to find him, and even if they did I must not ring him up. I have already broken one promise that I gave him, and there is some reason to believe that he may be in danger himself; so I will do nothing which might bring him here and perhaps place him in greater danger still.'

'Very well then.' Molly stood up. 'I must leave you now, because I have to drive to Nice to meet a friend of mine at the airport. He is coming to stay for a few days, and I do hope you will like him, as it is really you who he is flying out from England to see.'

'Me!' exclaimed Christina with a surprised look.

'Yes. He is not a psycho-analyst or anything of that kind; so you have no cause to be frightened that he will try to delve into your sub-conscious and drag out the sort of little personal secrets we all prefer to keep to ourselves. But he has had considerable experience of the way in which occultists get young people into their clutches; so I am hoping very much that he may know of a method of countering the evil influence that is being exerted on you. The plane doesn't get in till one; so I shan't be back much before tea-time. But John will look after you while I am away, and I thought you might like to take a picnic lunch out together.'

John and Christina agreed that a picnic was a good idea; so as soon as they had seen Molly off they set about their preparations. An inspection of the larder revealed a fine choice of good things. Angèle prepared a salad for them, while Christina stuffed some crisp rolls with ham and gruyère cheese, and John collected fruit, a bottle of wine and glasses. When they had finished packing the things into a basket, Christina said:

'As we are going to walk, I think I will put on a pair of thicker shoes. You don't mind waiting while I slip over to my villa, do you?'

'Of course not,' John replied. 'It has not yet gone half-past eleven; so we have tons of time. In fact it might not be a bad idea if we didn't start till twelve. That would give you a chance to pack a suitcase with some other things you may want, as Mother was saying this morning that she thought it would be best if you stayed on with us here—for the time being anyhow. I'll come across and collect it later.'

'Will there . . . ?' she hesitated. 'Are you quite sure there will be room for me, now that this friend of your mother's is coming?'

'Oh yes. You needn't worry about that. This villa is slightly larger than yours, I think. Anyhow, I'm giving up my room to Conky Bill—Colonel Verney, that is—and Angèle will move my things into the little slip-room at the back, next to the one you occupied last night.'

'All right, then. It really means that you'll be giving up your room for me, though. I'll never be able to repay you and your mother for all your kindness.'

As she turned away, he called after her, 'You had better put in a frock for this evening. Not a "knock 'em in the Old Kent Road" effect like you wore the other night; but something simple. Conky Bill is an old-fashioned type and likes changing for dinner; so black tie and sea-boots will be the order of the day.'

When she had disappeared he went upstairs and carried most of his smaller belongings through to the slip-room, then came down and asked Angèle to move the rest while he was out. Picking up the basket with the lunch in it, he walked through the sitting-room to the french windows, but halted there with a slight frown on his face. Count Jules de Grasse was coming up the garden path.

The Count saw him at the same moment and called out gaily, 'Good morning! You see how prompt I am to repay your call.'

Putting down the basket, John advanced to meet him, a smile now disguising the faint uneasiness he felt. 'How nice of you. I am so sorry we had to drag Christina away from you last night; but she really was not fit to stay.'

'Oh, we quite understood. How is she this morning?'

'I'm glad to say she is fully recovered,' John replied, as they turned back towards the house. Then, to forestall any further invitation Count Jules might have brought for her, he added, 'As a matter of fact you only just caught me. I am about to take her out for the day.'

'Dear me! Then I fear I have timed my visit badly.'

Feeling that it would be wisest to continue this pretence of friendship, and at least hear what the Count had come to say, John waved a hand towards the french windows. 'No. Do come in. We shan't be starting for a little while yet. Can I offer you a drink?'

'Thanks. If you happen to have any *pastis* I should like one.'

'I expect there is some here. There is usually.' Having found the bottle among the drinks on the side-table, John poured from it two good portions of the clear spirit into tumblers, added the water that turned it a cloudy opal, and handed one to his stocky, round-faced visitor.

The Frenchman raised his glass, and, having drunk, gestured with it towards the view. 'You have a charming place here; and I envy you having a mimosa tree just outside your windows. Now that it is in blossom the smell is heavenly.'

'My father bought this villa some years before the war, and my mother has lived here almost continuously since.'

'Indeed! Then you must have been here many times yourself. I wish I had known before this that we were neighbours. There is little I do not know about the towns of the Riviera, so I could have provided you with a lot of fun.'

'It's a kind thought,' John smiled, 'but I have managed pretty well on my own.'

Jules took another swig of the absinthe and remarked, 'This is really excellent. Where did you find it?'

'It is a private brew made by the barman at the Negresco. I think my father was rather a favourite customer of his. Anyhow, when my mother goes in to Nice, he still lets her have a bottle now and then.'

'My congratulations on it. Also, since madame, your mother, is not here, be kind enough to give her my compliments, please.'

'Thanks. I will.'

A short silence fell, then Jules passed a hand over his dark, slightly crinkly hair, and said:

'I would like to have a word with you strictly in private, *mon ami*. Might we, perhaps, take our drinks down to your little terrace?'

'By all means, if you wish,' John replied, much intrigued by the implication of this request.

Side by side, they walked in silence down the path between the clementine and lemon trees. When they had settled themselves on two of the white-painted, comfortably-sprung iron chairs that are peculiar to French gardens, Jules asked:

'How do you find life in England these days? I mean this decorating business of yours, and making from it a decent income?'

John shrugged. 'I've no complaints about business, but money is quite another matter. The trouble is to keep a little when you've made it. We are almost taxed out of existence.'

'So I gather; and it is getting to be the same way here. The illusion still persists that French people do not pay their taxes; but that is no longer true. The Government now assesses us arbitrarily and forces us to meet its demands in anticipation of our incomes. Since in both our countries the Government has become only another name for the People, it really amounts to the idle and stupid stealing from those who work hard and show initiative. But now, alas, they have come to consider it as a right; and I see little prospect of any change in this iniquitous system.'

Wondering what all this could be leading up to, John nodded, and replied, 'I fear you are right; and the great danger is that before any change is likely to occur they will have killed off all the geese that lay the golden eggs.'

'In France that has happened already—at least, as far as those families who were the mainstay of the country up to the early years of this century are concerned. In 1914 the franc had stood for many generations at 25 to the £. It has since been devalued again and again so that it now stands at round 1,000 to the £. In one half a normal life-time it has been reduced to one-fortieth of its former value. Think what that has meant to the great property owners and others who depend mainly on fixed incomes.'

Again John nodded. 'Its effect must have been devastating; in fact, as destructive as a series of capital levies.'

Jules lit a Gitane cigarette and let it remain dangling from his full lips. 'You have said it, *mon ami*; and it is just that point I wished to make with you. Less than half a century ago my family owned great estates. They administered them well and took from them what they wanted, but in reason. Now, my father and I have only our intelligence left; so even to live in reasonable comfort we must take what we can get anywhere we can get it.'

'I thought your father was a wealthy ship-owner,' John remarked.

Shrugging his shoulders, Jules crossed one leg over the other, sat back and stuffed his hands in his trouser pockets. 'It is true that we own a few ships, but these thieves of tax collectors always have their noses in our books and steal most of the profits. Therefore we have been compelled to develop as a side-line the acceptance of commissions for cash, which is not taxable.'

'Really? I suppose you mean carrying certain cargoes without declaring them?'

'Exactly. And there is one commission we accepted recently, of which, as an old friend, I feel it is only fair to inform you.' Jules paused for a moment, then went on, 'It is to transport the young woman you know as Christina Mordant to England before March the 6th. On the completion of that transaction we are to receive the sum of one thousand pounds.'

'I see,' said John quietly.

'Now!' Jules' smile broadened. 'It appears that you are interested in Christina. Why, is a question that I am still asking myself; for she is as yet no more than a hoydenish young girl, and still lacking in all the attributes which go to make women intriguing to men of our intelligence. Should you care to stand aside entirely, and not seek to prevent my collecting Christina from her villa at any time I may choose, I will willingly give you introductions to a dozen ladies, all more charming and sophisticated than she is, who live within easy reach; and you can take your pick of them to console you for your loss. Do you agree?'

'No,' said John firmly. 'I do not.'

Jules shrugged. 'I feared that might prove the case. Therefore I will put up to you an alternative proposition. As I took some pains to point out to you just now, the age of chivalry is past, and most regrettably its passing has compelled my father and me to become business men. We cannot afford to forgo a thousand pounds, but as no contract has been signed we are not strictly bound to carry out our undertaking. In view of your evident desire to continue enjoying Christina's innocent prattle, how would it appeal to you to pay us twelve hundred pounds to leave her alone?'

Such a bare-faced attempt at blackmail caused John's eyes to open wide with astonishment. For a second he felt inclined to laugh, but he knew that it was no laughing matter, and, getting to his feet, he said angrily:

'What the hell do you take me for?'

'Should you refuse both my offers, I shall take you for a fool.' Jules also had come to his feet, but his voice remained level. If, as your attitude now leads me to suppose, you wish to marry the girl, why not approach your mother? She must make a great deal from her books, so could easily find the money.'

'That is beside the point,' John snapped. 'I will neither let you take Christina away, nor pay you one brass farthing to refrain from attempting to. And now, get out!'

Jules' eyes had gone very dark, but his tone was still mild. 'I am sorry that you should prove so unreasonable. I came here hoping that we might arrange matters on a friendly basis, and I am still sufficiently well-disposed towards you to give you a warning. Do not think that because you came out on top last night you will be lucky enough to do so a second time. I let you get away with it only because my father and I will never permit any situation to arise which might cause trouble in the hotel at which we live. If you attempt to interfere in my business again you must not blame me if you get seriously hurt.'

7

NIGHT MUST FALL

John watched Count Jules drive off in a big blue Citroën, then he turned about and looked up at Christina's villa. It was now about a quarter-past twelve, but there was no sign of her in the garden or at those windows of the house that he could glimpse between the umbrella-pines; so it looked as if she had not yet finished her packing. Picking up the empty glasses, he stumped up the path with them, and collected the lunch basket. Then, as he left the house, he saw that she had come out just ahead of him and was now half-way down to her terrace; so they met in the road.

Assuming that she had not seen Count Jules, John decided that to make any mention of his visit would be to give her needless cause for anxiety; so he greeted her with a smile and said, 'I think we'll go towards Agay, then turn inland. If you don't mind an hour's trudge uphill, there is a lovely view from the lowest spur of the ridge.'

She nodded. 'We will go wherever you like. But tell me about your visitor. I was ready to start at twelve o'clock, as we arranged, but I saw him with you on the terrace; so I thought it wiser to remain under cover till he had gone. What did he want?'

'He said it was just a friendly call; and he enquired most tenderly about your health.'

'I bet he didn't come all the way from St Tropez only for that. Please be honest with me, John. Now that I have told you everything I can about myself, it wouldn't be fair of you to keep me in the dark. I would much rather know about it if you have reason to believe that they are plotting anything fresh against me.'

On reconsideration, he decided that she was right, and, if warned, would be additionally careful in watching her every step. So, as they walked at an easy pace along the broad, curving road, flanked with occasional stone balustrades surmounted by urns gay with geraniums and small yellow-striped cactus, he gave her the full story of his recent interview. When he had done she said with a shrug:

'He really must be crazy to have thought that you might pay him twelve hundred pounds to leave me alone.'

'Oh, I don't know. Most people have the idea that popular authors make enormous sums. It isn't true, of course: few of them earn as much as most Harley Street specialists—let alone a leading barrister. Still, he probably believes that my Mama could lay her hand on a thousand or so without batting an eyelid.'

'But even if she could, what can possibly lead him to suppose that she would be willing to part with a sum like that on my account?'

'You must remember that although Jules was educated in England he is very much a Frenchman, and has the typical Frenchman's outlook on women,' John told her. 'Custom and lack of inclination combine to prevent them from developing the sort of friendships that English people like ourselves enjoy in the normal course of events. They regard women solely from the point of view of sex, and divide them into two categories—those whose circumstances readily invite an amusing love-affair, and those who are in no position to offer such an attraction. To anyone of Jules' nationality and class it is unthinkable that a chap like myself might have an affair with a young unmarried girl; because she falls into category number two. It is not entirely a matter of principle that restrains them from entering on such affairs, but also because they would be bored to tears. They regard it as essential that their mistresses should be sexually experienced and take the matter as lightly as they do themselves, so that they run no danger of becoming permanently entangled. Therefore, Jules would argue that, since

I should get little fun out of seducing you, and landing myself with a packet of trouble afterwards, the only reason for my interest in you must be that I want to marry you.'

'Surely he can't think that? We . . . of course it seems much longer, but we have known one another only a few days.'

'He is probably not aware that I arrived here only on Monday; and for all he knows we might have already met before you left England.'

'But even if you were keen on me, it is unlikely that your mother would be willing to fork out twelve hundred pounds. Anyhow, until something had been definitely settled and we had become engaged.'

'I don't know so much about that. From the French point of view such a payment might be regarded as a lever to clinch the deal, and more or less part of a contract by which you agreed to marry me.'

'I have always thought that in France it was the other way about, and that in a marriage contract it was the girl's parents who had to put up the money.'

'Ah, but you've forgotten that you are an heiress. If your old man owns a controlling interest in Beddows Agricultural Tractors he must be worth a packet; and you are an only child. As Jules would see it, for my mother to put up twelve hundred to get you for me as a wife would be a jolly good bet.'

Christina laughed. 'It is one I wouldn't care to make. As I've told you, I really know awfully little about my father's private life. I don't think he has married again, but he might have. Anyhow, by his mistresses he may have had children of whom he is much fonder than he is of me. It is quite on the cards that when he dies the bulk of his money will go to people I have never heard of, and that he will leave me only a few hundreds a year to keep me from actual want.'

While they were talking they had reached the little village of Dramont, and after walking over to look at the memorial, which commemorated the landing of the Americans there on August the 15th, 1944, they took the by-road that led up into the Esterel.

Their way now lay through the pine forest, which here and there had clearings in it of a few acres devoted to intensive cultivation. In most of them stood a lemon-washed farmhouse, and the land was occupied by crops of fruit, vegetables and flowers, all growing on series of terraces which had been laboriously constructed out of the hillside and were kept in place by walls of rough-hewn stone. On some there were rows of orange, lemon and tangerine trees, or short bare-stalked vines, on others globe artichokes, young beans and *primeurs* of all sorts for the Paris markets; while many were small fields of carnations, grown in a four-feet-high wooden trellis-work which enabled long mats of split canes to be rolled over them at night to protect them from the frost.

The going was stiff; so they did not talk very much, and then only of trivial things, such as the thrifty care with which the peasants cultivated every available inch of their soil, and of how utterly different the scene was from any that could be found in England at that time of year. In an hour they had covered barely three miles, but they then came out on the summit of the lowest foothill of the range, and paused there to admire the view. Dramont was now hidden from them by the tops of the trees, but beyond it, no great distance from the shore, they could see the little Golden Isle with its pseudo-feudal tower, and to either side of the twin capes of Agay the Mediterranean stretched away in an infinity of blue.

To one side of the road lay an orchard of ancient olive-trees, their gnarled trunks and grey-green leaves standing out in charming contrast to the yellower green of the short grass in which they had been planted a century or more ago. In the hush of mid-day, with sunlight dappling the grass through leaves unstirred by a breath of wind, it was a truly sylvan spot, having that spell-like quality which made them almost expect that a nymph or faun would peep out at them from behind one of the trees at any moment. Instinctively feeling that they could find no more delightful place in which to picnic, they turned into the orchard without exchanging a word, and, sitting down under one of the trees a little way from the road, unpacked their lunch.

When they had satisfied their first hunger, John asked Christina what sort of a time she had had at her finishing school in Paris, and after describing the life there she summed it up as more interesting but not so much fun as that she had had in Somerset. In Paris the only lessons had been French grammar and the study of the Arts; the girls had been taken to the opera, the *Salon*, concerts, classical plays, the best films, special dress shows for *jeunes filles*, the museums and all the places of historical interest. She had enjoyed all that; but the mistresses had been much stricter and the girls less friendly than at the school of domestic science, and she had greatly missed the fine old mansion that housed it, with its park, swimming-pool and lovely garden; the paper-chases and cricket in the summer, and in winter the bicycle rides on Saturdays into the local town for tea and shopping.

John had never been in Somerset, but he knew Paris well, particularly the intellectual side of life there; so they talked for a while of painting, ballet and books. The extent of her knowledge, and especially the wideness of her reading, rather surprised him; but she explained that never having been home for the holidays she had had much more time than most girls in which to devour her favourite authors and dip into all sorts of unusual subjects.

In turn she asked him about his work, and he told her that on the whole he thoroughly enjoyed it; but that like every other business it had its irritating moments. As was natural, he lamented the passing of the great house, which had given such marvellous scope to the interior decorators of the Georgian age and been so hideously abused by those working a hundred years later. In the previous year his directors had given him a real plum—a Canadian millionaire who wanted a permanent home in London, fully equipped regardless of expense, but did not wish to be bothered with any of the details, or even be informed of the colours of the rooms, until he walked into it; but that sort of thing did not happen often. Most of his clients were people compelled by taxation to move from country houses that their families had occupied for generations into medium-sized West End flats. The majority of them had taste; so they were usually not difficult to deal with, and the major trouble in such cases was generally that the furniture they wished to retain was much too big for the rooms; so it often spoiled the final *décor*. The real headaches were the black marketeers and other *nouveaux riches*, who went round on their own, buying ghastly suites or fake antiques, guaranteed to make any interior look garish or pretentious. Yet he declared that he would not for the world be in any other business, as every day brought its new problem that kept his mind alert, and now and then an achievement which gave him real artistic satisfaction.

'Do you ever have to do kitchens?' Christina enquired.

'Yes, sometimes.'

'How many sinks do you put in a new scullery?'

'Why, one of course,' he replied promptly. 'In these days of small staffs no one would want more.'

'Then if I ever need a kitchen designed I shan't employ you,' she laughed. 'It makes the work infinitely lighter if one has two sinks side by side; and they should both be on a much higher level than most architects place them, to save backache from bending unnecessarily far over.'

'It is certainly a thought,' he admitted in a slightly chastened tone. 'I suppose you got the idea from that domestic place you were at?'

'Yes: our kitchen expert had learned her stuff in America, where most wives have to do their own housework. It is scandalous how far behind we are in Britain; and in France things are even worse, in spite of the good cooking. For years past all housework has continued to be far more laborious than it need be. If I ever have a home of my own I shall install all the new labour-saving devices. I'll have toe hollows instead of protruding bases along the floor level of the cupboards, so that the paint is not knocked off, compo-rubber sinks and draining-boards to save breakage, laundry chutes, a mix-and-whip, an electric dish-washer, and one of those lovely things to throw the garbage into that chews up even bones.'

'And the Queen Anne teaspoons too, when some careless woman-in fails to notice them among the debris,' John added with a smile, pleased at this opportunity to get in a return shot for hers about the sinks. All the same, he was impressed with her grasp of the subject, and went on jokingly, 'We had better go into partnership. You could do all the expensive gadgets on the domestic side, while I crib ideas like the arrangement of those bookcases we saw at the de Grasses last night.'

Her expression immediately became serious, and she asked, 'Do you think there is any risk that they may try to get hold of me by force?'

'I doubt it,' he replied with a confidence he was far from feeling. 'In any case, you may be sure that we shall do our utmost to protect you. Still, it is a possibility that they might lure you away by some trick, and, as a matter of fact, while we were trudging up the hill, an hour back, I had an idea about that.'

'Did you? Tell me what it was.'

He hesitated a second. 'Well, if by chance they did manage to entice you away, we shouldn't be on a very good wicket. I mean, if we had to go to the police and ask them to trace you, they would naturally want to know what authority we had for making such a request, particularly if things pointed to your having gone off of your own free will. They would get down to the job quickly enough if we were relatives of yours, but they might refuse to act at all if they took the view that, as we were only acquaintances, we had no right to stick our noses into your business.'

'I see what you mean; but I don't see how that can be got over.'

'It can be. I think the germ of the idea came into my mind when we were nattering about marriage. Mama and I could raise Cain, and get them running round in circles, if I could say that you were my fiancée.'

Christina's big brown eyes were round with astonishment as she turned them on him. 'You ... you aren't making me a proposal of marriage, are you?'

He had been lying full length on the grass, but now he sat up and looked at her with a grin. 'Sorry, but I'm afraid I'm not. Although I suppose it is presumptuous of me even to infer that I might have raised false hopes in your maidenly breast. I only had in mind that stupid old saying "marriages are made in heaven and engagements to be broken". Ours, if you thought the idea worth pursuing, would be only for the "duration of the conflict", and afterwards we should go our own separate ways, seeking more suitable partners to dig our hooks into in earnest. What do you say?'

'It is a bit shattering to have all one's girlish dreams about first proposals rendered farcical like this,' she said, half seriously. 'But I do see your point about an engagement giving you the right to get a hue and cry going, should I disappear. I'd feel bound to make it a condition, though, that we should tell your mother that there is nothing serious between us.'

'Of course. And Conky Bill, too. I wouldn't like either of them to think later that I had bilked you. But we ought to put up a bit of a show to establish our state of bliss in the minds of the retainers.'

She gave him a rather dubious look. 'What exactly do you mean by that?'

'Why, the usual concrete evidence that you are about to be made into an honest woman.' As he spoke, he drew a gold signet ring from the little finger of his left hand and held it up. 'Here! Let me slip this on your engagement finger. It was my father's, and I regard it as one of my few treasures. So for God's sake don't lose it. You can flash it in front of that old Catalan woman of yours and Angèle. Tell them that I mean to buy you something more spectacular when we get home, but that in the meantime it is the symbol of my undying love.'

'All right then,' she laughed, and held out her left hand. It was shapely, but large, and he had considerable difficulty in working the ring over her knuckle. At length he succeeded, and as it slipped down to the waist of the finger he muttered:

'That's done it; but you have got big hands for a girl, haven't you?'

She flushed to the roots of her hair and retorted angrily, 'Yes! And large feet, and a snub nose; so you're jolly lucky not to have got me for keeps.'

His eyes showed surprise and immediate contrition. 'Damn it all, Christina!' he exclaimed. Then, putting out both hands, he took her by the shoulders and looked straight in her face. 'I didn't mean to be rude. I swear I didn't! You've got the loveliest eyes I've ever seen, and if you only knew it, that funny nose of yours is one of your best features. It gives you an individuality that awfully few girls have got.'

'You don't mean that. You are just trying to be nice to me now, to make up for having been unintentionally nasty.'

'I do mean it. And your lips are as soft as any I have ever kissed.' He smiled suddenly. 'You know, when one gets engaged to a girl it is usual to kiss her. That's always done, even in boy-and-girl affairs that are not intended to come to anything.' Next second, before she had a chance to resist, he slipped his arms round her, pulled her to him, and kissed her firmly on the mouth.

For a long moment she lay passive in his embrace, then he withdrew his lips, smiled down at her and said, 'You are not doing your best, darling. That's not a patch on the kisses you gave me the other night.'

Instantly she pulled away from him. Tears sprang to her eyes, and she cried, 'How horrid of you to remind me of that!'

'Why?' he asked, momentarily at a loss. 'You are the same girl, and there is nothing to be ashamed of in what you did.'

'I was not myself then, and you know it.'

He gave a little shrug. 'If you take my advice, then, should a chap ever make love to you seriously and you want him for a husband, you will let him kiss you only when you are, as you put it, not yourself.'

Christina's cheeks were scarlet as she murmured unhappily, 'But it isn't normal. It's not decent. No girl could do that sort of thing and not be ashamed of it afterwards—at least not until she was married.'

Smiling slightly, John shook his head. 'My dear, I'm sure you really believe that, but you are talking the most utter rot. I give you my word of honour that grown-up people who are going places together nearly always kiss that way—even when they haven't the faintest intention of getting married. There is no harm in it, and it's part of the fun of life. You might just as well say that, because as children we have no urge to smoke or drink, it is wicked of us to take to it when we get older. Learning to kiss properly, and enjoying it, is just one of the normal processes of becoming a man or woman. You did enjoy being kissed by me the other night, didn't you?'

'Yes,' Christina whispered. 'I . . . I . . . of course I did.'

'Then stop being a baby, and let me kiss you again.' As he spoke, he drew her gently into his arms and this time kissed her parted lips.

From the distance came the faint clink of metal against small stones as a peasant hoed one of his terrace plots, and once a seagull circled overhead; but no one came to disturb them. John sat with his back against the bole of the tree, his right arm round Christina, and her head lay on his shoulder. Few places could have been nearer the ideal for a first lesson in kissing, and once Christina let herself go she proved an apt pupil; but John was careful to keep matters on the level of a game not to be taken seriously. He had set out to take the girl's mind off the grim anxieties which he knew must lie at the back of it. That he had succeeded was clear, and he was thoroughly enjoying the process, but he said nothing which she could take as an indication that he was falling in love with her, as he feared that being so inexperienced she might think him in earnest and later, perhaps, suffer from disappointment.

As the sunny afternoon wore on they became drowsy and, still embraced, fell asleep. John was the first to wake and, glancing at his watch, saw that it was after five o'clock. With a gentle kiss he aroused Christina, and said:

'Wake up, my pretty. It's time for us to be going. We ought to have started before, really.'

As she disentangled herself and began to tidy her hair she shivered and replied, 'Yes, I suppose we ought. Although the sun is still shining, it has turned quite cold.'

'At this time of the year it always does at this hour. The sun loses its power and the wind changes, bringing the icy currents down from the snow on top of the mountains. More elderly people die of pneumonia on this coast than anywhere else in the world. They only have to once forget to take an overcoat with them if they are going to be out after five o'clock, and they've had it. I don't wonder you're chilly in that light frock. Come on now! We'll step out and get your circulation going.'

She stood up and brushed down her skirt, while he crammed the empty bottle and glasses back into the basket. Two minutes later they were on their way down the hill, but its steepness prevented their pace from being much faster than that at which they had come up; so it was well past six when they arrived back at Christina's villa to collect the things she had packed that morning.

John carried the suitcase across, and in Molly's sitting-room they found her with Colonel Verney. He was a tall, rather thin, man, and, as he stood up to be introduced to Christina, would have appeared even taller but for a slight stoop that was habitual to him. His hair was going grey, parted in the centre, and brushed smoothly back. His face was longish, with a firm mouth and determined chin; but the other features were dominated by the big aggressive nose that had earned him the nickname of Conky Bill—or, as most of his friends called him for short, C. B. His eyebrows were thick and prawn-like. Below them his grey eyes had the curious quality of seeming to look right through one. He usually spoke very quietly, in an almost confidential tone, and gave the pleasing impression that there were very few things out of which he did not derive a certain amount of amusement.

To Christina he said, 'Well, young lady, I hear you are being pursued by bad men, but I usually eat a couple for breakfast; so you must lead me to them. Perhaps we can have a little talk after dinner, then I'll have a better idea how to set my traps.'

Christina smiled in reply. 'I don't think there is much I can tell you that I haven't already told Mrs Fountain, but I'll answer any questions you like.'

Taking her by the arm, Molly said, 'Come along, my dear. Last night we had to pop you into bed just anyhow; so I'll come up with you to your room and see that you have everything you want.'

C. B. and John had already smiled a greeting at one another; so the latter followed the two women out of the room with Christina's bag. When he returned two minutes later, the tall Colonel said:

'Well, young feller! How's the world been treating you?'

'I've no complaints, sir, thanks,' John replied cheerfully. 'And it's nice to have you with us again.'

'To tell the truth, I was delighted when your mother rang up. I was due to spend the next few days getting out a lot of tiresome statistics, and it gave me just the excuse I needed to unload the job on to one of my stooges.'

'I'm very glad you could come, sir. This seems a most extraordinary business, and I can't make head or tail of it.'

'You mean the Black Magic slant to it, eh? Well, I don't suppose you would. Those boys are experts at keeping their lights under bushels; so the general public rarely hears anything about them—except from an occasional article appearing in the press, and they generally write that off as nonsense.'

'May I give you another drink, sir? Then perhaps you would tell me something about it.'

'Do, John.' C. B. began to refill a very clean, long-stemmed pipe. 'Mine's a gin-and-French. But why so much of the 'sir' all of a sudden? I know I'm an old fogey, but you've known me long enough to call me C. B. You always used to when you were a little chap.'

John grinned. 'Ah! But I've done my military service since then, and we were taught that we should always call the Colonel 'sir' at least three times before slapping him on the back.'

'Not a bad precept either. Come and sit down, and tell me what you make of this girl Christina, and the set-up next door.'

'I don't think there is much to tell about her villa.' John handed the Colonel his drink, then perched himself on the sofa. 'The old gardener who looks after the place and caretakes when it is empty has been there for years. Maria, the Catalan *bonne*, is a rather surly type, but as she was engaged by Christina's father there doesn't seem any reason to suppose that there is anything fishy about her. We know definitely now that the de Grasses are simply acting as the Canon's agents, but—'

'How do you know?' put in C. B. quietly.

'Because Jules de Grasse told me so himself,' John replied, and went on to give an account of the visit he had received that morning.

'Sounds good enough—on the face of it,' commented the Colonel. 'All right. Carry on.'

'I was only going to add that, while we haven't the ghost of an idea why the Canon wants to get hold of Christina, I believe we would be more than half-way to solving the whole problem if we could find out what is wrong with the girl herself.'

'Good reasoning, John. Your mother is convinced that it is a case of possession: but what do you think?'

'I'm damned if I know. There can be no question about these changes in her personality. I've seen them for myself. During the day-time she is a nice kid—straightforward, good-natured, and as far as worldliness goes you wouldn't put her age as much over seventeen. But at night she becomes utterly different—bold, sensual as a cat and, according to her own account, evil-minded and malicious. If we were still living in mediæval times I suppose one would regard possession by the Devil as a perfectly reasonable explanation; but it is a bit much to swallow in these days, isn't it?'

'For you, perhaps; but not for me. I've seen scores of such cases, John; and at this very moment there are hundreds of people in our asylums whose apparent lunacy is really due to an evil spirit—or, to call it by its right name, which I prefer, a demon—having got into their bodies.'

'Well,' John gave a faint smile, 'as you and Mother are both so positive that such things still happen I suppose I must accept it that they do. But if what you say about the asylums is correct, why is no attempt ever made to get the devils out of all these poor wretches?'

'Because the modern medicos refuse to recognize the facts. Even if they did they wouldn't know how to set about it; and for that matter very few other people would either.'

'When Mother and I were talking about it last night, she seemed to think you would.'

'Lord bless you, no! I'm no exorcist. I've never dabbled in Magic—Black or White—in my life. I regard it as much too dangerous.'

'Does that mean you won't be able to do anything for Christina?'

'That depends.' Conky Bill's voice became low and slightly conspiratorial. 'If I can get a half-Nelson on the Black who has bewitched her, I could. Even a few facts about minor breaches of the law might enable me to pull a fast one. There is nothing that these birds dislike so much as the police taking an interest in their affairs, and given something to go on there would be a good chance for me to exert enough pressure on them to get the spell taken off.'

'You think Mother's right, then, about her having been bewitched?'

'I am accepting that theory for the moment.'

'But why in the world should they pick on a girl like Christina? She has never been mixed up in spiritualism, or anything of that kind.'

'Ask me another, young feller. But I expect we shall find that there is a tie-up of some sort. On the other hand, any girl who has so few intimate relationships is always particularly vulnerable. Nine times out of ten they are the ones who disappear; because they have no friends and relatives to start a hue and cry about them. If those people at the place where she was at in Paris had been crooks, she might have been shipped off to Buenos Aires, and her father would have been none the wiser for months afterwards.'

'It looks to me as if he got in first; and it is the very fact that he got wise to it that something pretty nasty was being planned against her that accounts for her present situation.'

C.B. nodded. 'Yes, you've got something there.'

'Do you think their object is to White Slave her?'

'No; although if they did get hold of her she would be a darn' sight better off in a brothel.'

'What exactly is their game, then?'

'They are always on the hunt for neophytes. Satan is a greedy master, and to retain his favour they need a constant supply of new bodies to defile and souls to corrupt. The more victims they can offer up, the greater becomes their power.'

'Apart from that, is Mother right in what she told me last night, about their being a menace to all established Governments that stand for freedom and decency?'

'Yes, if she was speaking of the high-direction of the show, she was. Of course, there are lots of little outer circles, or covens, as they are called. They are generally run by ordinary crooks who have muscled-in on the game. Most of the time their object is blackmail. They get hold of paederasts, lesbians and over-sexed people of all ages, and provide them with the chance to indulge their secret vices. Then in due course they put on the squeeze and make quite a bit of money by it. Pedalling dope is another of their activities and generally proves a pretty useful side-line.'

C.B. paused to fiddle with his pipe, then went on, 'But the big shots are right up and away above that sort of thing. In most cases I doubt if they even know the chiefs of the little covens. Anyhow, they leave it to their subordinates to supervise them and pick likely lads to form new ones. Their job is to use occult forces to destroy good influences. Their usual line is to cause the illness or death at a time of crisis of the key man who might be able to tide it over; or, alternatively, to produce conditions which will favour some unscrupulous individual getting control of the situation. The best example I can give you of an ace-high Black Magician in modern times is the monk Rasputin. He did more than all the Bolsheviks put together to bring about the Russian revolution; and I don't need to tell you the extent of the evil that has brought to Russia, and may yet bring to the rest of the world.'

Molly rejoined them at that moment, and as John got up to get her a drink she enquired how he had enjoyed his day.

'Oh, all right,' he replied casually. 'We found a nice place to picnic but as a matter of fact we slept for most of the afternoon.'

'Dear me, you must have been bored then.' With a smile she turned to C.B. 'This business really is rather hard luck on Johnny. Three days of his holiday have gone already, and he hasn't had a moment yet to look up his old friends or hit any of the high spots along the coast. I think he is being very sweet to devote all his time to this poor girl.'

'Perhaps he doesn't find her as boring as you think,' C.B. smiled back; and, standing up, he carefully removed a long brown hair from the open collar of John's pale blue sweat shirt.

'Well played, Sherlock,' John laughed. 'But don't let that little souvenir give either of you any wrong ideas. It signifies only the sealing of the sort of deal that Hitler used to call 'A Pact of Eternal Friendship' when it suited his book to enter into a political understanding with someone for a few weeks.' He told them then about his phony engagement to Christina, and the reason that had prompted him to suggest it.

'Now I'm here, I'll be able to get the French police moving, should we need them,' C.B. commented, 'but all the same it was quite a sound idea.'

Then Molly added, 'Christina showed me your father's ring and explained why she was wearing it directly we got upstairs. She told me, too, about Count Jules' visit after I left this morning.'

'John has just given me particulars of that.' C.B. stretched out his long legs, and went on thoughtfully, "In view of young de Grasse's threat, I think we ought to set a watch to-night, just in case they attempt a snatch. We could put an armchair on the landing outside her room. I need very little sleep, so I can easily sit up reading until two. Then if John relieved me until five, I'd come on again then. By seven your *bonne* will be about, so I could get another couple of hours shut-eye before breakfast. How about it, John; are you game to do the three hours before dawn?'

'Sure. Longer if you like. After all, now she is my fiancée I don't have to stay outside her door, do I?'

'Any nonsense of that kind, and I'll pack you off back to England,' his mother said severely.

He gave a mock sigh and shot an injured look at the Colonel. 'You see, sir, how old-fashioned she is in her ideas about the latitude that should be allowed to engaged couples. I do wish you would try your hand at educating her up a bit for me.'

Both of them picked up the innuendo. C.B. let his gaze fall to his big feet. Molly flushed and said quickly, 'I really came down to say that if you want to change to-night, it is time we went up.'

The Colonel levered himself out of his chair. 'It is just as you like, my dear. As I always have a tub before dinner, I find it no more trouble, and considerably more enlivening to the mind, to get into *le smoking*, as they call it out here.'

'I know you do,' she smiled, 'so while you are with us I have put dinner back to eight-thirty. But you and John will have to share the guests' bathroom, and it is nearly half-past seven now.'

Finishing up their drinks, they followed her out. An hour later they reassembled.

John was first down, and having switched on the lights he mixed another round of cocktails. When his mother joined him he noted with secret amusement that she was considerably more made-up than usual, and was wearing a very pretty frock that he had not seen before. C.B. came in a moment later, gave her one appraising glance, and said:

'Molly, my dear, you're looking positively stunning. If it wasn't for John, here, I'd stake my oath that you couldn't be a day over thirty.'

She gave a happy laugh. 'Well, they say a woman is as old as she looks and a man is as old as he feels, so perhaps we had better leave it at that. But you're not looking so bad yourself. I don't wonder you like to change in the evenings. Dark, well-cut clothes instead of those baggy things you wear in the day-time take at least ten years off you.'

'You sweet children,' purred John, as he handed them their cocktails, 'How I wish I were your age; then I should have so many new experiences to look forward to.'

'You insolent pup!' C.B. made a pretence of cuffing him; and they continued laughing together until the gong went.

'Christina has been an awfully long time dressing,' Molly remarked, 'but we will give her a few minutes' grace.'

They shared out the remaining contents of the shaker, but still Christina had not appeared; so Molly said to John, 'I think you had better slip up and find out how much longer your fiancée is going to spend titivating herself for your benefit.'

'Right-oh!' he nodded, and, leaving the room, ran upstairs. A minute later he came pounding down again, shouting as he came, 'She isn't there! Her room's empty! She's gone!'

8

KIDNAPPED?

As John burst into the room, C.B. gave him a rueful smile. 'Seems we've been caught on the hop. Any sign of a struggle?'

'I don't think so: I didn't notice any.'

'We should have heard it if there had been,' said Molly.

'I doubt if we would have taken any notice, while we were up there dressing, unless she had let out a shout; and we might not even have heard that during the past ten minutes while we've been joking together down here.'

'She must have been gone longer than that. Her evening frock is still on the bed. Come up and see.' Turning, John hurried from the room.

'After you, my dear.' C.B. politely stood aside for Molly. He had not so far raised his voice, and his movements, although actually as quick as those of the others, appeared quite leisurely.

Upstairs they halted together in the doorway of the big room at the back of the house that Christina had been given. At first glance there was nothing to suggest that she had been forcibly removed; neither was there any paper prominently displayed, which might have been a note left by her, giving a reason for her having left of her own accord.

'I suppose she *has* gone?' C.B. murmured. 'Better look in the bathroom, though. I've known young women faint in hot baths before now.'

Swinging round, Molly ran to a door on the opposite side of the passage and thrust it open. The bathroom was empty. Hastily she tried the W.C. next door, but that was empty too. Her face showed her distress as she cried:

'This is entirely my fault! It has been dark for well over an hour. It was criminal of me to forget the way her personality changes at nightfall, and that she might take it into her head to go off somewhere. I should never have left her on her own. I could so easily have arranged for her to have changed in my room with me.'

'I'm just as much to blame, Mumsie,' John said miserably. 'I promised her this afternoon that I'd take care of her; and now I've let her down the very first time that I ought to have been on the look-out for Jules.'

'If anyone is to blame, it is the old professional,' C.B. put in quietly.

'Nonsense!' Molly protested. 'You had only just come on the scene.'

'For God's sake don't let's stand here arguing.' John's voice was sharp with anxiety. 'We must get after her. Come on! Hurry?'

'Half a mo', young feller. So far there is nothing to point to the de Grasses having snatched her, and it doesn't always pay to jump to conclusions. Your mother may be right. Knowing we are on the side of the angels she may have taken a sudden dislike to us after sundown, and gone back to her own villa. Just step over and see, will you?'

'Right-oh!' John ran down the stairs and the others followed more slowly. When they reached the hall, C.B. said:

'Got a telephone directory, Molly? There is a number I want to look up. John may find her at her villa, but I doubt it. My own bet is that the de Grasses have got her. Young Count Jules told John this morning that they had undertaken to get her to England before the 6th and to-day is the 3rd; so they haven't much of a time margin.'

Molly found him the directory and he began to flick through it, but went on talking: 'That is why I felt pretty certain they would try something to-night, and suggested keeping watch. It was stupid of me, though, not to anticipate that they might get to work immediately darkness made the girl vulnerable to suggestion.'

'No, Bill; you are being unfair to yourself. No one would expect kidnappers to stage a raid while all of us were moving about the house. They would wait till we were asleep.'

'You are wrong there, Molly my love. The changing hour is a very favourite one with cat burglars. They shin up a drain-pipe, cling on there, and take an occasional peep through the window of the room which they intend to burgle. Then, when its occupant goes along to the bathroom, or has finished dressing and goes downstairs, they nip in and do their stuff. If they have to make a certain amount of noise, it doesn't matter, because if the servants hear it they think it is being made by their employers, or one of the guests who is still upstairs changing.'

'Do you think, then, that they got Christina out by way of the window?'

'No. The dressing-table had not been pushed back out of place, and the blind was still down. It isn't easy to pull a blind down from outside; and, anyway, why should they bother?'

'Perhaps they got her out by the window in the passage. Surely we should have heard them if they had carried her downstairs?'

'Not necessarily, provided they were fairly careful about it. As I've just said, with a servant getting dinner, and people bathing and banging cupboards all over the place, no one takes any notice of noises at that hour. Besides, it is possible that she went because she wanted to, and walked quietly out one her own.'

C.B. broke off for a second. 'Ah, here we are—Malouet, Alphonse. Do you remember him?'

'By name, yes. Wasn't he the Inspector of Police who put up such a good show in Nice during the Resistance?'

'That's him. The old boy retired a couple of years ago. Apparently he is now living out a Cimiez. The address looks like that of a flat in one of the big hotels there that they have converted into apartments since the war. Although he is no longer on the active list, he will be able to pull more guns for me than some bird I don't know, if we have to call in the police."

Flicking over the leaves again, he added, 'In case we can't get hold of him to-night, I had better look up the number of the Prefecture at Nice. That is the top police H.Q. in this part of the world, and in a case like this it is a waste of time going to the small fry.' He had just found the second number when John came rushing in. Still breathless from having run up the steep garden path, he panted:

'I was right! The de Grasses have got her. Jules carried her off from her own villa about an hour ago. Come on! I'll get out the car!'

'Steady on!' C.B. admonished him. 'Let's have such details as you can give us first.'

Between gasps to get his breath back, John reported, 'Old Maria says Christina came in at about a quarter to eight. She ran upstairs and came down again two minutes later. She was carrying a small suitcase and immediately went out with it. But she returned almost at once. Maria didn't see her come back, but saw the lights go on in the sitting-room. From her kitchen she can see the glow they throw from . . . from the side window of the sitting-room on to the trees in the garden; so . . . so she looked in to see who was there. It was Christina and a chap who answers the description of Jules. They were arguing about something. She must have given him a drink and had one with him. Their glasses are still on the table. Maria didn't hear them leave. But she doesn't think they could have remained there much more than ten minutes. She happened to glance at her clock just before the sitting-room lights were switched off again, and it had not yet gone eight.'

'Good! Now we at least have a line of enquiry we can pursue.' C.B. picked up the telephone.

'What are you going to do?' John asked impatiently.

'Ring up the police—or rather an old friend of mine who is an ex-police officer of exceptional ability.'

'Then for God's sake hurry! They must be nearly at St Tropez by now. If we don't start at once we may not arrive in time to prevent him from putting off to sea with her in that damn yacht.'

C.B. gave the number of Inspector Malouet's apartment, then covered the receiver with his hand. 'Listen, partner. I'm not going to let you run your head into a hornet's nest, or land up in a cell at a French police station either, if I can prevent it. We are by no means certain yet that Jules is taking her to the yacht, and—'

'Where the hell else would he take her?'

'Maybe to some hide-out anywhere between Nice and Toulon. There must be plenty of places along the coast where he has pals who would keep her locked up for the night. Remember, he has got to get her back to England by the 6th, and he couldn't possibly do that by sea. Getting her on to the yacht could be only a temporary measure anyhow. He probably means to drug her, than have her flown home.'

'Still, the fact that he tried to get her on the yacht last night is the only line we have to go on.'

'Agreed; and we'll draw that covert as soon as I've made this call.'

'Can't you telephone your police friend later—if we fail to find her on the yacht?'

'No, we must get this chap moving as soon as we possibly can. You don't seem to realize what we are up against. That yacht is private property, just as much as if it were a house. You can't go busting your way aboard like a bandit. If you did, de Grasse's boys would be fully entitled to slog you on the head, then hand you over to the police. You have to be able to show justification for any act of that sort.'

'C.B., you make me tired! What better justification could we have than knowing that poor kid has been carried off by thugs?'

Molly had never known her son display such rudeness to an older man. It crossed her mind that, *blasé* about girls as he like to think himself, Christina, by striking an entirely new note, might have bowled him over. That could explain both the extreme agitation he was showing and his lapse of manners. Nevertheless, she spoke with unusual sharpness:

'That will do, John. Colonel Verney has not wasted an unnecessary moment; and he is the best judge of what should be done.'

'Sorry!' he muttered. 'But I'm damned if I'll let Jules get away with this. I'm damned if I will.'

At that moment the telephone began to make shrill whistling sounds. C.B. jangled the receiver, said, ''Allo! 'Allo!' and repeated the number, but nothing happened the other end; so he turned his smiling grey eyes on John.

'What I meant was some legal, or at least moral, justification. Strictly speaking, we are not entitled to take any action ourselves, and should turn the whole job over to the police. If there had been signs of a struggle in her bedroom, or old Maria had seen her hauled from her villa by a couple of woolly-headed negroes, we'd have some excuse for taking a hand ourselves; but as it is . . .'

Again the telephone made odd noises, but again no satisfactory result followed; so he went on, 'As it is, she walked out of this house of her own accord, and left her own villa a quarter of an hour later with Jules. He is, for all practical purposes, a respectable citizen, and as far as we know she went with him perfectly willingly; so if you butted in, from the legal point of view you wouldn't have a leg to stand on.'

'I'm her fiancé, aren't I?' John demanded truculently.

'Yes. And I give you full marks now for your foresight in thinking up that bright idea. In France, as marriage is so mixed up with cash and property, people take a much more serious view of a fiancé's rights than they do in England. But even that would not condone your breaking into what amounts to a private dwelling, without obvious cause. It will be a help, though, in getting a search warrant if we can bring evidence to the effect that she was definitely taken on to the yacht.'

Once more noises came from the telephone, and this time it proved to be the number that C.B. had called. With a nod to the others, he said, 'Our luck is in. It is Malouet himself.' Then he spoke for several moments in his own particular brand of French. It was good French from the point of view of fluency, but it did not sound good, as he spoke very quietly, and without using any of the ejaculations or inflections of the voice which are such a feature of that language.

When he hung up, he said, 'As you may have noticed, I had to be a bit obscure; but the old boy tumbled to my meaning. He confirms my own view of the matter. In the remote chance of our happening on somebody prepared to vouch for it that they saw Christina either taken aboard by force, or carried aboard unconscious, the authorities will not hold it against us if we force our way on to the yacht and insist on being taken to her. But if such evidence as we can get is to the effect that she went aboard of her own free will, the only way in which we can insure against a nasty come-back is for John, as her fiancé, to swear an affidavit, stating that he believes her to have been lured aboard for an illegal purpose; then we will be granted a search warrant.'

'So *that* is all we have been wasting a precious ten minutes to be told,' said John sarcastically. 'Why didn't you get on to your office in Whitehall and ask them to send us a couple of hundred forms to fill up?'

'Johnny!' his mother exclaimed. 'You will apologize at once!'

'Sorry, C.B.,' he murmured a trifle sullenly. 'But for goodness' sake, let's get going and *do* something.'

C.B. gave him a good-natured pat on the shoulder. 'That's all right, John. Now you can run and get the car out.'

'I'll just slip upstairs,' said Molly.

John gave her a quick look. 'Going to collect the armaments, Mumsie? Good! I'll come with you.'

'What's that?' exclaimed C.B., as they ran across the hall. Then he called after them, 'If you are thinking of taking any of those museum pieces of yours, Molly, scrap the idea. Otherwise you can count me out.'

Both of them ignored him, and as John ran up the stairs close on his mother's heels he muttered, 'Funny he should say that, isn't it? Just the line I took with you last night; but now things are very different.'

With a sigh C.B. decided he had better check up on them. His long legs moving effortlessly, he took the stairs three at a time, and entered Molly's work-room just as they went down on their knees in front of a cupboard. She pulled it open, revealing on the bottom shelf an array of highly-dangerous objects. Among them were pistols, bowie-knives, grenades, a garotter's cord, several stilettos and coshes, a knuckle-duster and a stick of gelignite. Looking down between their shoulders, he asked:

'Has that Mills bomb still got its detonator in?'

'Of course!' Molly replied with an air of pride. 'Otherwise it would not be a perfect specimen.'

'You crazy woman! Some day a maid will have the bright idea of cleaning it, and when she pulls the pin out it will go off.'

'Oh no. I'm much too fond of my little collection to let anyone clean it except myself,' she replied lightly.

John was quickly cramming 9-mm. bullets into the spare magazine of the larger of the two automatics. C.B. stooped and with a swift, unexpected grab picked up the weapon. 'Nothing doing, partner,' he said firmly, pushing it into his own pocket. 'If you insist on risking a spell in a French prison, that is your look-out; but I dig my toes in at your taking a running jump to land on the guillotine.'

Turning an angry face up to him, John protested, 'You said yourself that if anyone saw her shanghaied we could bust the yacht open without waiting for the police. It's only common sense to take a weapon of *some* kind.'

Stooping again, C.B. selected a light cosh. It was a beautiful thing, about twelve inches long, its head egg-shaped and filled with lead, its stock a thin nine-inch steel spring, the whole being covered with dull black leather. 'Here, take this then. But don't lam anyone on the head with it; a blow on the shoulder would be quite enough to land most people in hospital for a week.'

'Thanks,' John murmured a little ungraciously; and he began to stuff it first in one pocket, then in another, in an endeavour to find a suitable place for it.

'Ram it down the front of your trousers,' C.B. advised. 'Provided you don't push it too far, the top end will keep it from slipping, and it won't prevent you from sitting down in comfort. It is easy to draw from there, and if anyone frisks you for a weapon, in that position there is quite a good chance of it being overlooked.'

As John tucked away the cosh, C.B. turned to Molly. Relieving her of the smaller automatic, which she had been just about to slip in her bag, he said in a tone of mild reproof, 'Now, ducks, I really can't allow you to go around shooting people.' But slipping out the magazine he handed it back to her and added, 'Lord forbid that I should rob you of all your fun. You can point it at anyone you like now, and it's a small beer to a magnum of champagne that it will prove every bit as effective.'

'Oh, really, Bill' she pleaded. 'Can't I have just one bullet in the chamber, in case I get a chance to fire it? I do so want to see how much light the flash gives.'

'No. I'd rather you took a pot-shot at me in the garden to-morrow night, if you must have a human target to aim at.'

'You *are* rude! You infer that I couldn't hit a haystack.'

'Come *on*!' cried John angrily, from the doorway. 'By nattering like this you two are chucking away our only chance of saving Christina.'

C.B. glanced at his watch. 'It is just twenty-two minutes since we discovered her disappearance. Not bad, considering I had to make a telephone-call to Nice. But we would have saved four minutes if you had gone to get the car out when I asked you to, instead of abetting your mother in her whimsies about weapons. Get cracking now.'

John dashed downstairs. The others followed him and collected their coats from the hall. As they walked down the garden path, C.B. said to Molly, 'I'm taking you only as a spare driver, if we have to leave the car. I'll have my hands quite full enough preventing that boy of yours from sticking out his neck. You are under orders again. Is that clear?'

'Yes, sir,' said Molly, out of ancient habit and quite meekly.

Once they were in the car John lost not a second, and the moment they were under way he jammed his foot down on the accelerator. As they rounded the second corner they met one of the big auto-buses returning from the St Raphael direction to Cannes and had to swerve violently to avoid it. Molly was thrown sideways on the back seat; C.B. stiffened his long legs and cried:

'Go easy, young feller, or you'll break all our necks!' Then he went on in his normal voice. 'Don't get the idea that I am sitting down on the job, but the fact is that five minutes either way is unlikely to make much difference now. Try to consider our prospects dispassionately. Jules has the best part of an hour's start of us. If he meant to take her to the yacht and the crew were only waiting till he got her on board to put to sea, they will have sailed long before we get there. We couldn't have caught them, even if we had set off the moment we discovered her disappearance. On the other hand, he could not have been certain that he would succeed in getting hold of her, or if he did at what hour he would be able to pull it off; so the odds are that he would not have ordered his crew to stand by from half-past eight till dawn, and will have to collect them.'

'That shouldn't take him long.'

'It all depends how many of them there are and whereabouts they live when they are on shore. But that is not my main point: it is his mental attitude of which I am thinking. Once he has got her on board I see no reason at all why he should burst a blood vessel in getting the yacht out of harbour.'

'He would hardly be such a fool as to gamble on our not learning of Christina's disappearance until to-morrow morning. She may even have told him that we were expecting her to dine with us.'

'True, but what has he to fear if we do turn up? If we go on board he can have us thrown off again—that is unless we are accompanied by the police with a search warrant.'

'How long do you reckon it would take us to get one?'

'As we have not got the ghost of a case, we should have one hell of a job in persuading the police that we had real cause for alarm. We should have to show great persistence and tell our story four or five times before we got high enough up to secure action. With waits between interviewing a series of unenthusiastic officials, that might take us anything up to three hours. Jules must know all about the slowness of police procedure when the applicant for help can produce no definite evidence that any crime has been commited; so up till about eleven o'clock he can afford to snap his fingers at us. Anyhow, that is my appreciation of the situation. Either the yacht has sailed already or we'll find when we get to St Tropez that, like Drake, we'll have plenty of time for a game of bowls before we go into action.'

'I suppose you are right,' John admitted grudgingly. 'I wish that I could take matters so calmly.' But he moderated his pace a little, and did not let the car out full again until they were through St Raphael and had entered the long flat stretch round the curve of the great bay. It was ten to ten when he jammed on the brakes and brought the car to a halt on the cobbles of St Tropez harbour.

In summer, at that hour, it would still have been thronged with people, drinking both at the scores of tables outside the cafés on the waterfront and in the cabins of dozens of craft in the port itself. But it was too early in the year to sit outside at night, and the season for the small yacht owners had not yet begun.

Like most of the ports on that coast, the harbour formed a rectangle with tall, ancient houses on three sides of it. The basin was partially filled by several groups of shipping moored beam to beam. Most of them were fishing-boats, or sailing yachts that had been dismantled for the winter; a few were larger, fully-powered craft, although not of the size that millionaires had kept for luxury cruises in those waters before the war. Apart from riding lights, it was from the cabins of these bigger vessels that the only lights showing in the harbour came, but the landward end of it was lit by the windows of several cafés, which were still open and occupied by a sprinkling of people.

Scrambling out of the car, John glanced quickly up and down. Outside the cafés the broad quay was deserted, except for a group of three loungers standing some distance away on the edge of the pavement. In the uncertain light they looked like seamen, and he began to run towards them.

'Hi!' C. B. called after him. 'Where are you off to?'

Slowing his pace, he called back over his shoulder, 'I'm going to ask those chaps which the yacht is—if she's still in the harbour.'

'No, you're not.' In a few long strides C. B. caught up with him and added in his conspiratorial voice, 'We don't want to let the whole town know our business. You go back to the car and leave this to me.'

After giving the crestfallen John's arm a friendly squeeze, he walked on to the end of the block and entered a café on the corner. He was absent for about six minutes. When he returned, he said:

'She hasn't sailed yet; but you can't see her very well from here. Her berth is up near the entry to the port on the right-hand side; and from the description I was given we can't mistake her. I'm told there is a good little fish restaurant up there that will still be open, and I'm beginning to miss my dinner; so while we are waiting for developments I think we'll have a snack at it.'

'Damn it, C. B.!' John exploded. 'How can you be so heartless while that poor girl—'

'I know! While that poor girl is at the mercy of a double-dyed villain. Try to be your age, John. Count Jules' only interest in Christina is to get her to England and collect a nice wad of banknotes. The odds are that he is feeding her on asparagus and pêche Melba at the moment and that, in her present state of mind, she is thoroughly enjoying herself.'

'But you spoke of "waiting for developments". Since the yacht's still here we mustn't waste a moment in finding out if she is on board. Why should we wait for anything?'

'Drive me to my chosen grazing ground, sonny, and I'll tell you on the way.'

With an ill grace John got the car moving, and C. B. went on in a lower tone, 'I didn't telephone old Malouet only to ask after his health. The police always have several narks on tap in all these ports. I wanted the name of the best one here. He told me to ask for Henri at the café on the corner. It is the favourite *bistrot* of the yacht stewards, and as barman there Henri picks up from them most of the dirt about what goes on. He pointed out de Grasse's yacht to me and he is going to slip out for a quarter of an hour to get us a little info'. By the time we have fortified the inner man with oysters and a glass of wine, I shall be very surprised if he is not able to let us know definitely whether Christina is on that yacht.'

In the back of the car Molly burbled her admiration for his efficiency with the same delight that a mother will display at seeing her offspring do its parlour trick, but John only asked:

'What happens if the yacht puts off in the meantime?'

'Then you've had it, chum. There is nothing you can do to stop her sailing, anyway.'

They pulled up at the fish restaurant and went inside. Two of its tables only were occupied, by people lingering over the last stages of their dinners. C. B. chose one in a corner, which was well away from the other diners, and ordered *marennes* with a bottle of Pouilly. While they ate he talked in a low monologue about butterflies, the collection of which was his hobby; but his companions appeared singularly disinterested. When they had finished the oysters, he invited them to join him in attacking a dish of sea-urchins, but they declined; so, still discoursing on the habits of the *Papilio machaon*, he set about a plate of the spiky crustaceans himself.

He was only half-way through them when the outer door opened and a short, tubby figure came in. C.B. glanced casually in the direction of the newcomer, then as though suddenly recognizing an old acquaintance cried, 'Hello, Henri! How is the world using you?'

The plump man had been advancing towards a buffet on which were displayed a selection of sea-foods, fruit and cheeses. At the greeting he turned his head, smiled, swerved from his course and, coming up to the table, bowed politely. 'Thank you, Monsieur; I cannot complain. It is a pleasure to see you here; but unexpected so early in the year. Do you stay long?'

'No, I am only down here on business for a few days this time.' C.B. added something about Henri mixing the best Angel's Kiss on the coast and introduced him to Molly and John in a mumble that made their names unintelligible. Meanwhile the patron of the place had come out from behind the buffet.

At his approach, Henri said, 'Excuse me, please,' turned, shook hands with him and asked, 'Can you let me have two dozen *rosés*? I have an American in my bar. He is a little drunk and he demands *rosés* to eat while he goes on drinking; so I said I would slip out and get him some.'

'Certainly.' The patron smiled. 'A pleasure to oblige you, Monsieur Auer.'

As he went off to get a paper bag in which to put the prawns, Henri said to C.B., in a voice hardly above a whisper, 'The crew were warned for to-night, but given no hour of sailing. The girl is on the yacht. She arrived in the car of Count Jules at about nine. His chauffeur and the boatswain, Chopin, were with them. Chopin went off on foot—I expect to let his crew know the hour at which they will be wanted. Count Jules took the girl on board. There was no suggestion of violence. They were laughing together.'

'Any idea when the yacht will sail?' murmured C.B.

'Not for a while yet, I think; otherwise the crew would have reported by now. It is possible that Count Jules is expecting a second passenger to arrive at a later hour. I fear there is no more that I can tell you.'

'Thanks; you have been most helpful.' C.B. slipped a five-*mille* note into Henri's hand, and when the patron returned with the bag of prawns they were talking of the prospects for the summer season. Having shaken hands all round, Henri bowed himself out, and C.B. looked across at John.

'Now we know where we stand, anyway; and the situation might be worse. It would be if Jules had taken her to some dive along the coast, and we hadn't the faintest idea where to look for her. But her having gone on board willingly rules out your doing the irate fiancé stuff except at the risk of being arrested if you offer him or any of his people violence.'

'I could go to the yacht and demand to see her.'

'You could, but I doubt if it would get you much further. The odds are they would let you go below, then beat you up and afterwards hand you over to the police with a cut-and-dried story about your having started it.'

'To do that they would have to call the police in. Once they came on the scene I could bring a counter charge of assault against Jules and demand a full enquiry. There would be a good hope then of the authorities preventing the yacht from sailing. To-morrow morning Christina will be herself again, and whatever may happen to me, you and Mother would be able to get her away from them.'

C.B. shook his head. 'I'm afraid it wouldn't work out like that. They are much too leery to call in the police before the yacht sails. They would probably put you ashore in a boat just as she is leaving harbour. Or they might take you along to keep you out of mischief; then swear afterwards that the row had started only after she had sailed!'

'What do you suggest then?' John asked impatiently. 'I flatly refuse to just sit here and let things take their course.'

'Since you feel that way about it,' replied C.B. thoughtfully, 'I can put up to you two alternatives. Malouet should be here round about midnight and—'

'Will he?'

'Yes. At the end of our talk on the telephone the old boy agreed to get out his car and start at once. But it is the best part of a two-and-a-half-hours' drive from Nice. He will go straight to Henri's café and I am to meet him there. The police will take his word for anything that may happen while he is with us; so when he does turn up he could accompany you on board for a show-down. In his presence they would not dare to touch you.'

John nodded. 'I must say you have done everything you possibly could in the circumstances, C.B., and I'm jolly grateful to you. But the devil of it is that the yacht may have sailed by midnight.'

'I know. The period during which Jules can reasonably count on immunity is getting short now; so my bet is that she will sail within the next half-hour.'

'Then what is your alternative to waiting for Malouet, and probably missing the boat?'

C.B. put a finger alongside his big nose, winked and whispered, 'To go with her.'

9

ILLEGAL ENTRY

John regarded C.B. with a puzzled frown. 'I don't get the idea. How could we manage to do that?'

C.B. shook his head. 'This would not be a case of "we", I'm afraid; and I'd better make my own position clear. I am a Civil Servant and have very definite responsibilities; so I have to think twice before I risk blotting my copy-book. If I had been put on this job officially I might consider it worth while to take that risk. If Jules were just off to Russia with our latest H-bomb secrets in his pocket, I certainly would. But if I got myself arrested and was unable to convince my Chief that it had happened while I was engaged on some matter of real importance to British interests, there would be the hell of a stink. Still worse, it might seriously prejudice the outcome of other work on which I am engaged.'

'I quite understand that. It seems, though, that you have changed your mind about me, and are about to suggest that I should do something illegal.'

'I am. Mind, I wouldn't but for the fact that you've just said that you refuse to sit here and let things take their course. What I am about to propose may land you in for the very things I have been trying to keep you out of—namely, a beating-up and finding yourself in the cells to-morrow. I don't like it a bit, but—'

'Since there seems to be no legal means of intervening on the yacht, I mean to take that risk anyhow.'

'It will be a certainty, instead of a risk, if you simply go on board and demand that Christina should be restored to you. My idea is that you should attempt to slip on board unobserved.'

'What then?'

'Lie doggo. If the yacht has not sailed by midnight we will come aboard with Malouet. Then you can come out of hiding and stake your claim to Christina. If the yacht sails earlier, you will sail with her as a stowaway.'

'I don't see how that would improve my chances of getting Christina out of their clutches.'

'It won't if they find you; and I've already warned you that by going on board at all, without the police, you are asking for a packet of trouble. But if you can remain hidden for eight or ten hours there is quite a good chance that you may succeed in pulling the chestnuts out of the fire.'

'How?' asked Molly, now considerably concerned for John's safety.

C.B. leaned across the table and his voice sank still lower. 'They have got to get her to England by the 6th; so they can't be taking her far. Toulon or Marseilles, perhaps. But at present we have no idea of their destination. If she sails in the yacht as things are, we lose track of her; but we won't if John is in the yacht too and has succeeded in keeping himself under cover. At the first opportunity to-morrow morning he could get ashore and let us know where the yacht has docked. By that time Christina will have, as one might say, come out from under the influence. Now, she would probably tell us all to mind our own damn' business, but by then she will be ready to scream "murder". As soon as John informs us where the yacht has got to, we'll come down with Malouet like wolves on the fold, and young Jules will be darn' lucky if he doesn't find himself in quod for kidnapping. See the idea?'

Molly nodded rather ruefully. 'As a plan, it is as good as anything we can hope for; but I'll never forgive you if they do John a serious injury.'

'At least it gives a sporting chance for him to keep out of trouble.' C.B. shrugged. 'I put this up only to prevent his butting his head right into it.'

'That's true enough, Mumsie,' John declared. 'Don't you dare blame C.B. if anything goes wrong. But it is nearly half-past ten; so if I'm to get on that yacht without being spotted we had better be moving.'

C.B. paid the bill and they went out into the darkness. The yacht lay only two hundred yards or so further seaward along the quay. Keeping in the shadow of the buildings, they walked along until they were opposite to her.

At a steep angle her fo'c'sle sloped up from the base of her single mast and bridge-structure, which were placed well forward. The two-thirds of her abaft the bridge lay much lower in the water. No trail of smoke came from her one large squat funnel, as she was diesel-engined. Her design gave the impression of rakishness and power; and C.B. judged her to be of about eight hundred tons burthen.

Some of her main cabins were lit, but as their portholes lay just under the level of the wharf edge the light from them came only as a diffused glow amidships. Except for a pool of brightness below her mast light and another on her bridge, her upper structure was plunged in deep shadow. A gangway, the slope of which was scarcely noticeable, led up from the quay to her main deck, just astern of her bridge. She might have been completely deserted, had it not been for an occasional movement in her bridge-house, which showed that someone was keeping watch up there.

After they had studied her for some moments, C.B. said to John, 'I thought you might have to borrow a small boat, approach her from the seaward side, and shin up on deck as best you could; but I don't think that is necessary. Her deck is so near level with the wharf, and she is made fast so close against it that you should be able to jump the rail near her stern and scramble over. All that is needed to give you a good chance of getting aboard unseen is for us to occupy the watchman's attention while you approach as quietly as possible.'

'Johnny,' Molly whispered anxiously, 'you are not used to this sort of thing. Do be careful, won't you?'

He gave her a swift kiss on the cheek. 'Don't worry, Mumsie; of course I will.'

Ignoring the interruption, C.B. went on, 'Let's all go back to the car now. Molly and I will get in it, and we will give you a bit of a lead before we start. Walk right on the edge of the quayside, so that you will have only to swerve and jump at the critical moment. Don't walk too fast, because I want to pass you in the car about fifty yards before you come level with her stern; but for God's sake don't give the impression of stealth, in case anyone notices you. The noise of the car engine will drown any noise you make, and when I pull up opposite the bridge of the yacht our lights will be pointing away from you; so you will have the extra benefit of the contrasting darkness behind us. Whatever you do, don't jump before we have pulled up and you have heard me hail the chap in the bridge-house; otherwise he may be looking in your direction. I shall pretend that we are trying to find another yacht that was supposed to have docked this evening, and will hold his attention for about three minutes. That should be ample for you to do your stuff.'

Still keeping in the shadow of the buildings, they walked back to the fish restaurant. While they did so C.B. made Johnny repeat their programme, to make certain there should be no slip-up. He had only just finished when they reached the car.

Knowing that C.B. disliked driving, and never did so if he could get anyone else to do it for him, Molly gave John's hand a quick squeeze, then slipped into the driver's seat.

C.B. said to him in a low voice, 'Should anything go wrong, and you have to make a bolt for it, go round a few back streets, then come to Henri's café. Your mother and I will be waiting there until Malouet turns up. Off you go, now. Good luck!'

With a nod and smile, barely glimpsed in the semi-darkness, John turned away, while C.B. got in beside Molly. He did not at all like the idea of letting the boy tackle such a dangerous business on his own, but had seen no way to prevent it. In the past he had on many occasions risked worse things than were likely to happen to John, but he was not his own master, and knew it to be unfair to his department to embroil himself in matters that had no definite connection with his job. He could only console himself with the thought that, as from the first John had shown a determination to stick his neck out, he had at least now been manœuvred into doing it in a way that might, perhaps, prove well worth while.

Molly, meanwhile, was torn by conflicting emotions—her confidence in C.B., which gave her assurance that any plan of his would combine the maximum amount of caution possible with a fair prospect of success, and her distress that her beloved Johnny must inevitably run considerable risks in carrying it out. For a few moments she watched him walking away, until he had disappeared beyond the beams thrown by the car lamps; then she started the engine and slipped in the clutch.

The timing was good, as when the car passed John, and he was momentarily thrown up in the glare of its headlights, he was still too far from the yacht to be noticed by anyone in her. He had just about halved the remaining distance when the car pulled up, and by the time he drew level with the yacht's stern C.B. already had the watchman engaged in conversation.

John's glance switched to the gulf that gaped between the quayside and yacht's rail. For a second his heart contracted. It was much wider than he had expected. Poised there on the edge, he stared down at the oily water gurgling sinisterly ten feet below. If he bungled his jump and fell into that dark crevasse it could easily prove a death-trap. Wide as the gap appeared on the wharf level, it looked much narrower further down, and the horrid thought flickered through his mind that he might find himself jammed between the ship and the wharf with his head under water. Yet he knew that every second was now precious; so, striving to suppress his qualms, he launched himself into space.

Those nervous fears lent extra strength to his muscles; so his leap would have carried him double the distance. His outstretched hands overshot the mark, and instead it was his stomach that came into violent contact with the top of the rail. The wind was driven from his body; his arms and legs flailed wildly. For a moment he was in acute danger of slipping backwards into the gulf before he could get a foot- or hand-hold. A desperate wriggle saved him. His head went down, his legs up, and he fell inboard on the deck.

Alarmed at the noise he had made, he scrambled hastily for the nearest cover. It was a hooded wooden hatchway leading down to the deck below. Crouching behind it he wondered what he had better do next. The obvious course seemed to creep down and look for a good place in which to hide; but while leaping on to the rail he had glimpsed a thing which was inconspicuous from the level of the wharf. On either side of the long after-deck there were three large sloping skylights, and the four nearest were all aglow, suggesting that the saloons below them were occupied. If he went down this after-companionway it seemed highly likely that he would run straight into somebody.

Peering round the side of the hatch, he saw that all was still quiet forward. It was darker up by the bridge; so it seemed probable that there were fewer people below decks there. Feeling certain that if he could reach the waist of the ship unobserved he would find another companionway, he left his cover, but at a crawl, so that he could instantly flatten himself out beside one of the skylights if he heard anyone approaching.

He took the starboard side of the deck, and on reaching the first skylight paused to peer down through it. Below lay the galley, bright with steel and copper fitments. In it two men were eating at a small square table. From their dress, one was obviously the chef and the other the steward. A bottle of wine stood between them, and it looked as if they were making a hearty supper from the planned surplus of a meal that had been served earlier in the dining saloon.

Wriggling on again, John peered through the next skylight. Below him now was the dining saloon. Although the light there was still on, the table had been cleared and the room was empty. He was just about to move towards the skylight further forward, from which no light showed, when he heard, faint but unmistakable, a laugh that he felt certain was Christina's. It had come from the skylight opposite, on the port side of the deck, which was open a little for ventilation.

Regardless of the fact that three minutes had already gone, so it was not to be expected that C.B. would be able to keep the watchman in conversation much longer, John could not resist the temptation to slither swiftly across the deck and peep through the skylight from which the laugh had come. It gave on to the saloon, which occupied as much space on the port side as did the dining saloon and galley together on the starboard side. By holding his head at an awkward angle, John could see both Jules and Christina.

She was sitting in a corner with her legs up on the *banquette* that ran along the ship's side. Jules was ensconced opposite her in an armchair. Between them on a small table stood two squat, tulip-shaped glasses and a bottle of Grand Marnier. No one else was present, and they were talking and laughing together like old friends.

Looking at them had a curious effect on John. He knew that he should have been pleased to find Christina safe, well and apparently happy, but he was not. Even making allowances for her change of personality after dark, it annoyed him to see her enjoying Jules' company. He now admitted to himself that, in spite of the additional danger in which it would have placed him, he would rather have come upon her in some difficult situation, from which there could have been no excuse for his not attempting her immediate rescue.

Even as it was, he began to play with the thought of endeavouring to get her away before the yacht sailed. The lights glowing through the four skylights had suggested that quite a number of people were down there in the compartments below the after-deck. But that had not proved the case. There were only the chef and steward in the galley and Jules and Christina in the saloon.

John felt that if he could surprise Jules he would have quite a good chance of overcoming him. But what then? Even if Jules were swiftly rendered incapable of giving a general alarm, the sounds of the struggle might bring the two servants from across the passage. And what of Christina? If she came willingly and at once they might gain the deck, race down it and across the gangway on to the wharf, before they could be stopped. But if she at first refused to budge—if he had to waste precious moments trying to persuade her to come with him—the steward and the chef would be upon them before they could even get up the companionway.

Reluctantly, John decided that he dare not chance it. He must stick to C.B.'s plan and stow away until the morning, when he would be certain of Christina's co-operation. Stealthily he moved again towards the darker area of deck amidships.

Suddenly a horn sounded, the arcs thrown by headlights swept across the buildings on the far side of the wharf, and a car ran past moving in the direction of the town. John knew that it must be C.B. and his mother. They had done their job, and he was supposed by this time to be under cover; but he was not, and now the watchman was again free to keep a general look-out.

It was the first time that John had ever done anything of this kind. He was not at all frightened, but felt terribly excited. His worst handicap was that, owing to lack of experience, he did not realize the importance of making swift decisions. While he was still hesitating whether to risk going forward towards the bridge, another horn sounded, lights flashed again on the quay, and a *camion* drew up opposite the gangway. Out of it piled seven or eight men, who came aboard laughing and joking.

Crouching behind the nearest skylight, John watched them vanish down the companionway in the middle of the bridge-structure that he had hoped to use himself. He reckoned that the crew of such a yacht would number somewhere around a dozen. With one on the bridge and two in the galley, the newcomers nearly made up that complement.

As they had all disappeared, the long stretch of deck to the gangway was now clear again, but he no longer dare risk going below by the midship companionway, even if he could reach it unseen from the bridge. The arrival of the crew had left him no choice but to retreat down the after-hatchway in the hope of finding a good hiding-place somewhere in the stern of the vessel.

Cautiously, he made his way back to the hatch behind which he had first hidden. After listening for a moment, he tip-toed down the stairs beneath its hood. The first flight brought him opposite a long passage, in which he knew that the galley and dining saloon were on the right and the saloon on the left; a second flight, immediately under the first, led down to a lower deck.

Feeling that the further he could get from the major activities on board the yacht the safer he would be, he crept down the second flight. Again he found himself faced by a long corridor, but in it there were double the number of doors. On each side there were six, and evidently they were those of the cabins for the passengers. Beyond them a bulkhead, with a door in it, presumably cut the after part of the ship off from the engine-room and crews' quarters.

Advancing stealthily, John peered through the partly-open door of one of the cabins. It was empty, and showed no sign of occupation; so he wondered if he dare doss down there for the night, but decided against it as too risky. Moving on, he reached the bulkhead, cautiously opened the door in it and looked through.

As he did so the hum of engines struck his ears, and only then did he realize that they had been almost imperceptibly reverberating through the ship for several minutes past. Evidently she was very shortly about to put to sea.

For a moment he stood where he was, wondering whether to step through the door in the hope of finding a good hiding-place further forward, or to return aft and look for a cubby hole right in the stern. He was still trying to decide which course offered the better possibilities when all chance of making a choice was suddenly snatched from him.

Without any sound of warning, a cabin door some ten feet beyond the bulkhead was pulled open. Through it stepped a big, ginger-haired man. His uniform, and the single band of gold braid round its cuffs, showed that he was a junior officer. His glance instantly fell upon John. Surprise dawned in his blue eyes; then, striding towards him, he exclaimed:

'Who are *you*? What do you want down here?'

IO

'ONCE ABOARD THE LUGGER . . .?'

The unexpected encounter had taken John as much by surprise as it had the ginger-haired officer. For a moment they stared at one another. John's first impulse was to turn and run, but he knew that would be fatal. This was obviously a case for bluff—if he could only think of one. He wondered what line C.B. would have taken in these circumstances, but could not, for the life of him, imagine. The big man spoke again, more sharply:

'What are you doing down here? Answer me!'

'I am looking for Count Jules,' John blurted, that being the first plausible lie that had come into his head.

'How did you get aboard?'

'By the gangway, of course.'

'And the watchman did not give you directions where to find Monsieur le Comte?'

'No, he was busy talking to someone else at the time.'

'Why did you not wait and ask?'

'I was in a hurry, and I thought that in a small yacht like this I would have no difficulty in finding him.'

John's voice gained in confidence as he developed his bluff, but his heavily-built questioner continued to stare at him suspiciously, and muttered with a scowl, 'You are a foreigner; are you not?'

There being no point in denying it, and his accent making it futile to do so, John nodded. Then, in an attempt to escape from this dangerous interrogation, he said, 'I'm sorry to have invaded the private quarters of the ship, but I must have come down a deck too far by mistake. I'll go up again and—'

Before he could finish his sentence and turn away, the man interrupted aggressively, 'What do you want with Monsieur le Comte?'

'I am an old friend of his.'

'Is he expecting you?'

For a second John hesitated, and in that second he was lost. His 'Yes' came too late to carry conviction. The blue eyes staring into his showed frank disbelief. In two strides the officer was upon him. Seizing John by the arm, he rapped out:

'Very well! I will take you to him.'

John's brain worked quickly enough now. He realized that if he once allowed himself to be taken up to Jules his goose would be cooked. He might have tackled Jules alone, had he followed his impulse of a few minutes back to take him by surprise in the saloon, but he could not hope to overcome both Jules and this strapping young man. It seemed certain now that he had let himself in for just the sort of thing C.B. had feared might happen to him if he took the law into his own hands by coming aboard the yacht. They would first beat him up, then hand him over to the police. Such a prospect was bad enough, but the thought which infuriated him beyond all else was that his attempt to protect Christina should be foiled almost before it had started. It was barely ten minutes since he had come on board, and he was now to be lugged before her as a captive. It was revolt at such a swift and ignominious end to his venture that spurred him to action.

The officer had him firmly by the left arm, but his right was free. Thrusting his hand under his coat, he whipped out the cosh, raised it, and struck sharply at his captor. He did not need to deliver a second blow. The leather-covered egg-shaped piece of lead came down on the man's uniform cap with hardly a sound; but his blue eyes suddenly bulged, his grip on John's arm relaxed, and he slumped in a heap on the deck.

For a second John held his breath; then he felt himself beginning to tremble. He had belatedly remembered what C. B. had said about using the cosh with caution. If he had killed the officer it would be a clear case of murder. Thrusting the weapon back into his trouser top, he stooped, and with frantic hands pulled the limp body towards him, so that he could thrust off the cap and examine the man's head.

The passage was lit only dimly by the small blue ceiling lights that are usually kept on permanently in ship's corridors. Anxiously John peered down at his victim's mat of short, ginger curls for signs of blood. He could see none, and his searching fingers found only a little wetness. With intense relief he realized that the man's cap and the thickness of his hair must have saved him from serious injury. Even if his skull was slightly cracked the absence of any mushy depression or copious bleeding seemed clear indications that there was no risk of his dying.

Relief at being freed from the awful thought that he might have killed a man was swiftly succeeded by a lesser, but still pressing, anxiety. If he had not got a corpse on his hands, he had something like it. The limp body at his feet showed no signs of returning animation; so he was not faced with the unhappy choice of either humanely rendering it assistance at his own peril or giving it another biff on the head to prevent its calling on anyone else to do so; but if he left it lying where it was some other member of the crew might come upon it at any moment. Should that happen, and a general alarm be raised, unless he had first found himself a safe hiding-place, he would again be caught before the yacht left harbour.

The obvious course was to carry the unconscious officer back into the cabin from which he had emerged. John knew that good old 'Crack' and others of his mother's fiction characters performed such feats without the least difficulty; but, being of slight build himself and having already felt the dead-weight of the powerfully built body, he had serious misgivings about his ability to get it there. Nonetheless, feeling that to be the only step by which he could prevent the discovery within a very short time that an act of violence had been committed aboard, he set about the job with feverish energy.

Getting his hands under his victim's arm-pits, he endeavoured to half-lift, half-drag him towards the cabin; but the best he could manage was to pull him a few inches at a time along the floor. At every tug his head jerked and rolled ludicrously on his shoulders, his arms flapped like mechanical fins, and the heels of his boots scraped noisily on the boards. While John heaved, strained, and panted from his exertions, he expected every moment that someone would appear at one or other end of the corridor and catch him red-handed; but after three minutes' gruelling struggle he had the body over the door sill. For him to have got it up on to the bunk unaided would have required further precious moments of exhausting effort; so, instead, he pushed a pillow under the injured man's head before stepping out of the cabin and closing its door behind him.

Breathless, and still trembling a little, he again considered whether his best prospects of coming upon a good hiding-place lay forward or, through the bulkhead, astern. As he hesitated a sudden thought struck him with fresh dismay. Getting the unconscious officer back into his cabin had only put off the evil hour of discovery. In a crew of only a dozen or so he would soon be missed. Someone was certain to come down to his cabin to look for him. Had John been able to lock it, there would have been a chance of them assuming that the officer had been detained ashore and missed his ship. But there was no key in the door, so whoever came to look for him would walk straight in on his body.

That would mean an immediate enquiry. Perhaps by then he would have come round sufficiently to describe how he had been attacked. In any case he would do so before many hours had passed. The yacht would then be searched from stem to stern as a precaution against the foreigner who had attacked him still being on board. An 800-ton yacht was very different from a liner, or even a tramp; it had no great air-ducts, baggage holds or mountains of cargo, which would help a stowaway to elude a search.

As these disconcerting thoughts ran through John's mind he was quick to see that wherever he concealed himself the chances were now at least ten to one on his being dragged from his hiding-place within the next hour or two. By knocking out the ginger-haired man he had burnt his boats, and could now only save himself by getting ashore again before the yacht sailed. If he failed to do so he was not only liable to be rough-handled by the crew, but would later find himself faced with a charge of having assaulted a ship's officer in the execution of his duty.

Visions of a French prison spurred him to fresh action. A few swift steps took him back through the bulkhead. Pausing only to close the door in it behind him, he hurried along the semi-dark corridor to the foot of the after-companionway. In going up it he proceeded with more caution, and, before exposing himself to view in the better-lighted corridor above, peered along it at deck level, to assure himself that it was still empty.

It was, and as his glance swept it the sight of a key, protruding from the lock of a door which he knew must be that of the galley, stirred in him a sudden impulse to rail against fate. He felt that it was ill-luck alone that had brought his venture to nought, and compelled him to abandon it so quickly; for he might have been safely hidden by now, had he not had the misfortune to run into the officer; and, even then, had that key been in the door of the man's cabin, instead of in that of the galley, the simple act of turning it would at least have spared him the mortification of having to make a bolt for it from fear that a hue and cry might start after him at any moment.

On tip-toe he ascended the upper ladder of the companionway, and from behind its curved hatch peeped out along the deck. It was still in semi-darkness, and the members of the crew whom he had seen come aboard were still below decks. He glanced towards the rail, but decided against again leaping the gulf between the ship and the quay, as the rail would make it so awkward to get a good take-off from this direction. Not much more than sixty feet of clear deck lay between him and the gangway. He had only to cross it at a run and before anyone had a chance to stop him he would be ashore. The watchman might shout after him, but that was very different from being challenged when coming aboard. Even if he were pursued he should have no great difficulty in getting away down one of the dark alleys that intersected the buildings facing the quay.

Swiftly now his thoughts flowed on. Why should he risk pursuit at all? There was still no sign of any intention shortly to take the yacht to sea. If he walked calmly along the deck and down the gangway the watchman would probably think that he was one of the crew going ashore for ten minutes on some small errand, and would not even challenge him.

Standing up, he moved out from behind the hatchway, his eyes fixed on the bridge. It was dully lit, but he could see no one up there; so it looked as if the watchman was either in the wheel-house, which faced forward, or behind the canvas screen at its starboard side, where, leaning on the rail, he could look down on the wharf. With firm, light steps John walked forward along the starboard side of the deck.

As he reached the first skylight he gave a swift glance through it. Below in the galley the steward and the chef were still at table: the latter was busily mixing a large bowl of salad. A few paces farther on John came level with the skylight through which he had seen Jules and Christina. It lay on the port side, and ten feet away, but he could not resist the temptation to cross over for a quick peep. On his way he glanced up at the bridge to assure himself that nothing had altered there; then he peered down between the brass protecting rods of the skylight into the saloon. Jules and Christina were still sitting on either side of a small table and, apparently, had hardly altered their positions since he had last seen them.

In the interval he had been subject to so many emotions that it was difficult for him to realize that not much over ten minutes could have passed; and that during them events had entirely re-orientated the impulses that governed his actions. Then they had been inspired by a determination to protect Christina; now, they were the outcome of a craven fear to get out of danger as quickly as he could.

It was looking down on them again that made him aware of the change in mentality he had undergone, and no sooner was he conscious of it than he began to feel terribly ashamed. It had been bad luck to run into that officer, but he had handled the situation promptly and, as yet, had no reason at all to suppose that anyone else suspected his presence on board. As a result of the encounter he might find himself in very hot water unless he got off the yacht before she sailed; but that was no reason why he should not attempt to take Christina with him.

His prospects of succeeding in such an attempt were considerably better than they had been when he had contemplated making it ten minutes earlier. The major part of the crew could not turn up unexpectedly just as he was hoping to get Christina away, as they had arrived and gone below already. Having now had experience in using his cosh effectively, he felt far more confident of his chances of rendering Jules *hors de combat* before he could give the alarm. The way was clear from the after-hatch to the gangway. Above all, he knew now that he had but to turn the key in the galley door to ensure that the only two people within Jules' call would be unable to come to his assistance if they heard him give a shout.

With a fresh wave of shame, it was borne in on John that he had been granted as near perfect conditions for a rescue as anyone could hope for, yet had very nearly thrown the opportunity away during a brief period of unjustifiable panic. He qualed at the thought of what C. B.'s opinion of him would have been afterwards had he done so, and that imperturbable secret agent had ever learned the facts. It needed only this last goad to his *amour-propre* to confirm John in his new resolution. Turning away from the skylight, he walked swiftly back to the after-hatch.

Losing not a second now, he ran lightly down the ladder, turned the key in the galley door, crossed the passage, opened that of the saloon, stepped inside, and closed it behind him.

Lack of experience in resorting to violence robbed him of an advantage he might otherwise have taken. Jules was sitting with his back to the door. A gangster or professional agent would have had the cosh ready in his grasp as he entered the saloon; so could have run forward and laid Jules out with it before he had time to get up and swing round. John took a couple of strides, then had to pause while he pulled the cosh out from his trouser top. Short as the delay was, it was long enough for Jules to spring to his feet, half turn, and kick the chair in which he had been sitting against John's legs.

John had the cosh only shoulder high as the chair caught him. He stumbled and fell half across it, his arms shooting forward. Instantly Jules leapt at him. With his right he struck John a glancing blow on the side of the face, with his left he seized the wrist that held the cosh and gave it a violent twist. The attack was so sudden that, still off his balance as he was, John had no chance to defend himself. A second blow from Jules landed on his left eye. Again his wrist was wrenched down and backward. With an 'Ouch' of pain, he dropped the cosh.

For a moment more they struggled with the chair between them, then Jules let go John's wrist, gave him a swift push, and stepped back. John was panting and uneasily aware that so far he had had the worst of the encounter. He too stepped back, and his glance swiftly swept the floor, seeking the cosh, in the hope that he might recover it; but it had rolled away under a settee. Jules had seen where it had gone and, now that he had disarmed his attacker, appeared fully confident of his ability to deal with the situation. He was not even breathing quickly, and an amused smile twitched his full lips as he said:

'I thought you might put in an appearance in spite of the warning I gave you. I told my father so, but he said it would not matter if you did; and, of course, he was quite right, as you cannot possibly bring any charge against us.'

'Don't you be too certain of that,' John snapped, and his eyes switched to Christina.

As he burst in she had removed her long silk-stockinged legs from the *banquette* and, with a newly-lit cigarette between her fingers, half risen; but had then sat down again. Now, she had both elbows planted on the table and was smoking calmly, while watching the two men with the detached air of one looking on at a scene in a play.

Jules laughed. 'If you are expecting my charming guest to go ashore with you and tell the police that I brought her here by force, you are much mistaken. We have been having a very pleasant time together. You, on the other hand, have come aboard clandestinely, and assaulted me. We are waiting only for my father to join up before putting to sea, I will leave it for him, when he arrives, to decide if we shall have you thrown into the harbour, or hand you over to the police.'

John had recovered his breath and, now that he had landed himself in real trouble, found his brain working with unexpected clarity. It seemed obvious that he could expect no help from Christina; but if he could get round the chair there was a chance that by hurling himself on Jules he might yet put him out of action.

Without taking his eyes from John, Jules spoke again. 'Christina! Just behind you there is a bell-push. Please ring for the steward. He is quite a gorilla; so we'll let him take charge of our uninvited guest. Then we can resume our conversation.'

'No,' replied Christina composedly. 'I am enjoying this. You can fight it out between you.'

Shaken out of his complacency, Jules shot her a surprised glance. It gave John just the opportunity for which he had been hoping. The second that Jules' eyes left his, he thrust the chair aside and sailed in.

John was much the slighter of the two, and at both school and university he had tended to despise athletics; but during his military service he had been made to take up boxing and had not done at all badly for his weight. Now, these bouts under the exacting eyes of tough Army instructors stood him in good stead. Jules put up his fists, and awkwardly fended off the first few blows, but was driven against the after-partition of the saloon. John slammed a left to his chin and his head banged back against the wooden panelling. As it jerked forward he opened his mouth to yell for help, but John drove a right into his stomach. With a gasp he half doubled up, thrusting his head out and clutching at his belly. He was now so obviously helpless that for a second John was reluctant to strike again; but he knew that to forgo this chance of finishing him off would be crazy. Stepping back a pace, he landed a blow that had all his force behind it under Jules' left ear. The Frenchman pitched over sideways, struck his head hard on the leg of a chair as he went down, and rolled over, out cold, face upward on the carpet.

'Well done! Oh, well done!' The words came from Christina more as breathless gasps than exclamations.

Sucking the broken skin of his knuckles, John turned towards her. She had stubbed out her cigarette and was standing up now, her huge brown eyes round with excitement. Pushing her way out from behind the table, she ran to him, flung her arms about his neck and, opening her mouth wide, glued it on his.

It was the sort of kiss calculated to rock any man's senses, and John was no exception. She had nothing on over her thin day frock and through it he could again feel the warmth of her body; yet it seemed an entirely different body from that which he had held in his arms during the afternoon. That had been soft and hesitantly yielding with occasional tremors due to girlish diffidence. This strained against him with a fierce virility, and every few seconds was shaken by a spasmodic trembling caused by uncontrollable passion.

Momentarily overcome as he was, his brain instantly protested that this was no time or place for love-making. Then instinct rowed in and told him that love played no part in this monstrous embrace, or even natural passion. It was night and Christina was not her true self. She was the victim of a primitive emotion which had been aroused in her by witnessing a scene of violence. She was the female who had just seen two males fighting over which of them should possess her. With shock, and almost a feeling of nausea, it suddenly came to him that had he been the senseless body on the floor and Jules the victor, it was Jules whom she would now be seeking to devour with her luscious, breathless kisses.

Lifting his arms from about her, he grasped her wrists, broke her grip round his neck, thrust her away from him, and cried:

'Christina! Pull yourself together! We've got to get out of here; and at once.'

She seemed to sober, and murmured, 'All right,' but gave him a slightly sullen look as she turned to pick up from the back of a chair a heavy Shetland tweed coat, and added, 'Now you have settled matters with Jules, what's the hurry?'

'I'll give you all the reasons later,' he said, endeavouring to humour rather than bully her, as he helped her into the coat.

'Anyhow, there is time for you to get this off me.' As she spoke she turned. He had noticed with vague surprise that she was wearing gloves, and drawing off the left one she thrust her hand out towards him.

'D'you mean my ring?' he asked in a puzzled voice. 'But why?'

'Of course, stupid!' she exclaimed, turning away her head. 'It has been hurting me all the evening. It's like a hot band round my finger, and I can't look at it. Every time I do it dazzles me.'

He stared at the signet ring and wondered if he could possibly be imagining things. To him it was not dazzling, but its gold seemed to be shining with a brighter, purer light than it had ever done during the years he had worn it himself. His father, to whom it had originally belonged, had not been a pious man, but upright and fearless, and the thought flashed into John's mind that perhaps the precious metal had mysteriously absorbed some of his father's qualities; so was now having on Christina, in a minor degree, a similar effect to that of the crucifix his mother had thrown to her the previous night. Seeing that the knuckle above the ring was red, angry and swollen, he said:

'You have been trying to get it off yourself, and failed; so I don't suppose I can.'

'That was Jules,' she replied with an impatient shrug. 'I asked him to try, and offered to kiss him if he could; but he couldn't; so I wouldn't. But you put it on; so you must get it off.'

Suddenly it occurred to him that the ring might, perhaps be acting to some extent as a charm against evil and, as long as she wore it, would reduce the strength of her nocturnal inclinations to play into the hands of her own enemies; so he shook his head.

'No. I'll take it off to-morrow morning for you if you like; but there is no time now. We've lost a couple of minutes as it is. And Jules isn't the only person I've had to lay out in order to get hold of you. Ten minutes ago I slogged an officer. Any moment—'

'Did you?' she broke in, her eyes glowing again. 'Oh, John, I think you're wonderful! Let's get away then. I'll go anywhere you wish.'

'Right; come on!' He grabbed her by the arm and hurried her to the door. 'It's not Jules I'm worried about, but the other chap. The Captain may send someone to look for him. The moment they find him the hunt will be up.

Alarm bells, lights all over the ship, and God knows what else. If that starts before we can get ashore our number will be up.'

The passage was empty. No one was battering on the door of the galley; evidently the steward and the chef had not heard the struggle in the saloon, or yet discovered that they were locked in. Still holding Christina by the arm, John drew her up the companionway after him. As his head emerged above deck level he glimpsed through the stern rail a man standing on the quay, some thirty feet away, by a bollard round which was looped the yacht's stern hawser. It looked as if he was awaiting orders to cast off, but the deck of the yacht was still in darkness.

Feeling certain that if they ran the length of the deck they would be bound to attract the watchman's attention and that, with his suspicions aroused, he would dash down the ladder from the bridge in an attempt to stop them before they reached the gangway, John whispered:

'Steady, now. We must walk off just as if we had dined aboard and I was now going to see you home. With luck the watchman may take me for Jules, as he and I are about the same height. If we could be laughing over something, that would be all to the good. My mind is a blank about funny stories at the moment, but perhaps you can think of one.'

'Yes,' replied Christina promptly, as they set off along the deck. 'Do you know the one about the five brides describing to one another what had happened on the first night of their honeymoon? The first said, "My husband was just like Roosevelt, he . . ."'

The rest of her sentence was drowned by the siren of a car. Next moment its headlights rolled back the darkness from the quay. As it ran past them it was slowing down and its driver brought it smoothly to a halt opposite the gangway.

'Hell!' exclaimed John, pulling Christina up. 'That will be the Marquis! Quick! We must hide!'

But it was too late. He had scarcely got the words out when there was movement on the bridge, a whistle shrilled, and all the lights were switched on. Momentarily dazzled by the glare, they were caught in it, standing between two of the skylights right in the middle of the deck.

The passengers were getting out of the car; two tall men and one short one. A bearded officer, who looked as if he might be the Captain, was leaning over the after-bridge rail looking down at them. Another man stood beside him. Two more sailors ran out from the bridge-house and took up positions on either side of the gangway.

Suddenly it dawned on John that of all these people not one was looking in the direction of Christina and himself. If they could get below again and find some place in which to conceal themselves Jules would believe that they had succeeded in getting ashore before his father's arrival. With luck they might remain as stowaways, undiscovered, until the yacht reached its port of destination, then slip ashore there. Swiftly he turned Christina about and pushed her towards the after-hatch at a quick walk.

They still had ten feet to go when they caught a muffled shouting from the galley; then, as they reached the hatch, a loud banging on its door. The steward and the chef had just discovered that they were locked in, and were endeavouring to draw attention to their plight.

Before John was half-way down the companionway, the banging abruptly ceased. As he neared its bottom he saw the reason, and consternation seized him. Jules had come round from being knocked out and striking his head on the chair leg much more quickly than might have been expected. Perhaps he had pushed the buzzer for help, and it was that which had led to the steward, on going to answer it, finding that the galley door was locked on the outside. In any case, Jules had staggered out into the passage and, only a moment earlier, unlocked the door. He now stood swaying, a little drunkenly, as the steward and the chef tumbled out through it.

Once more John's lack of experience in affairs of violence had let him down; but it was vain now for him to curse himself for not having had the forethought to tie Jules up and gag him while he had the chance.

A trickle of blood was running down from a cut on Jules' forehead into his left eye. With a shaky hand he brushed it away and focused his unsteady glance on John's legs as they appeared down the companionway. The second he saw his face, he flung out a pointing arm and shouted to his men:

'There he is! Get him! Get him!'

The chef was a small plump man with a mild expression, and did not look at all a type who would willingly get himself mixed up in a rough house; but the steward was a brawny specimen with a low forehead, flattened nose and bull-dog jaw. Jules' description of him earlier as 'quite a gorilla' had been an apt one.

John gave the group one glance, swung about, yelled to Christina to get back up the ladder, and scampered after her. Quick as he was, they would have been on him before he was half-way up had it not been that the chef, who was nearest, hesitated a second and the steward had to push past him.

Christina stubbed her toe and tripped over the top step. Hopping out on to the deck she let go a spate of foul language that sounded peculiarly shocking coming from her young, innocent-looking mouth; but John registered the fact only subconsciously. In tripping she had held him up for a moment. The gorilla-like steward was right on his heels and grabbing at them. He cleared the top step only just in time, but, swinging round, managed to kick his pursuer in the face.

With a howl of rage and pain, the man swayed backward. His eyes goggling and his hands clutching frantically at the empty air, he hovered for a second, then overbalanced. More yells came from below as his heavy body went crashing down on the little chef and Jules, who had been mounting the ladder behind him. Seizing the advantage this débâcle had given him, John stepped back, swung to the double doors of the hooded hatch cover, and flicked over into its staple the stout iron hook that secured them.

But his victorious retreat from below gained him no more than a breathing space. The shouting and sounds of strife had been heard up on deck. The group from the car were now half-way along it. In the lead was the tall, hatchet-faced Marquis, and beside him a man of about forty, with a large, fair, fluffed-out moustache of the style favoured by some R.A.F. pilots. Close behind them were the little man, who looked like a valet, and the two sailors who had stood by the gangway. Others were running up from amidships, and the officers on the bridge were now staring aft to see what the commotion was about.

John gave a hurried glance over his shoulder. The stern rail was only a few feet behind him. In three paces he could reach the spot where it curved in towards the wharf. To balance on it for a jump would be almost impossible; but he could scramble over, cling to the rail with one hand, then leap. The ease with which he had cleared the gap when coming aboard proved that it was nothing like as formidable as it looked.

Now, though, his situation was very different. Someone on the yacht had only to call 'Stop Thief' to the wharf-hand, who was waiting to cast the hawser off from the bollard, for the man to run forward and grab him as he landed on the quay. Then there was Christina: her legs were long enough to make the jump, but might easily become entangled in her heavy coat. To urge her to attempt it would be asking her to take an appalling risk.

These thoughts flashed through his mind within a moment of his fastening the doors to the companionway; but even in that brief span of time the dispositions of the other protagonists in the scene had changed. The approaching group and Christina had both taken a few quick steps towards one another. Barely fifteen feet now separated them. With a swift contraction of the heart John accepted it as certain that in another minute he would be attacked, and that against such odds he had no possible chance. Then all his preconceived ideas of what was about to happen were suddenly altered by the totally unexpected attitude of the Marquis.

Sweeping off his hat he made a smiling bow to Christina. 'My apologies, Mademoiselle, that a tiresome appointment should have prevented me from joining you earlier. And Mr Fountain, is it not? This is an unexpected pleasure. When we met the other night in Cannes, I did not know that you were an old friend of Jules. I trust he has been giving you both a pleasant time?'

John was so nonplussed that he could think of no immediate reply. Then it occurred to him to take the Marquis's words at their face value, in the wild hope that he meant them. Hastily he blurted out, 'Thank you, sir. Yes, it's been grand. I'm sorry you should arrive to find us on the point of leaving.'

By then the Marquis had taken Christina's hand and was going through the gallant motion of kissing it. By then, too, Jules, the chef and the steward had had time to sort themselves out at the foot of the companionway, and one of them had run up it. There came a loud hammering on the doors of the covered hatch, accompanied by muffled shouts and curses.

The Marquis glanced in that direction, shrugged, and said suavely. 'I fear some of my new crew are ill-disciplined fellows. No doubt the reason why Jules is not with you is that he remained below, endeavouring to quell a brawl among them. I am desolated that your visit should have been terminated so unpleasantly. Permit me to escort you to the gangway.'

He was still holding Christina's hand. Drawing it through his arm in a paternal manner, he turned and led her forward. John could hardly believe his ears and eyes, but followed automatically and found himself in the middle of the little group that had come aft.

As they walked forward the Marquis conveyed kind messages to Christina from his wife. It seemed that the Marquise had also intended to dine aboard, but had been prevented from doing so by a slight indisposition. Had she not been aware that young English ladies were quite accustomed to dispensing with the presence of a chaperon she would naturally have made a special effort, but as things were she felt sure Christina would forgive her.

No one said a word to John. The sailors and the little man had deferentially stepped aside, so were now behind him; the tall R.A.F. type with the fluffy moustache was walking at his side, but in silence.

The sixty feet of after-deck was soon covered. They passed round the big squat funnel. Just beyond it, to starboard, lay the gangway. Six feet farther on the bridge-structure rose up across the whole breadth of the yacht. Between it and the funnel lay a band of deep shadow. It was broken only in the middle by the glow of light coming up from the main companionway, which lay under the centre of the bridge.

The Marquis turned towards the gangway, and said to Christina, 'I see there is no car here to fetch you. But no matter; you must allow me to send you home in mine.'

Suddenly into John's brain there flashed an explanation for the Marquis's strange behaviour. The reason why he had pretended not to grasp the fact that he had come upon them endeavouring to escape, and continued to ignore the shouts and banging that still came faintly from the stern, must be because it had never been intended to take Christina to sea in the yacht. As C. B. had pointed out, their contract was to get her to England by the 6th, and they now had barely two days in which to do the job. It must be that Jules had got hold of her much earlier than he had expected; so brought her to the yacht as a temporary measure until his father had completed their other arrangements. The Marquis had arrived only to collect her, and was now in the act of doing so.

In an instant John forecast the next move. The Marquis would put Christina in the car, get in himself, then give a swift order to his men. They would seize him, so that he could not attempt to follow, while the Marquis drove off, carrying Christina to some dive where she would be doped, then put on a plane for England. There were only a matter of seconds to go and John raked his mind frantically for a means to sabotage this plan at the last moment.

There were four men round him and others within close call; so he knew that any attempt to stop the car or rescue Christina was far beyond his powers. The only thing he could do was to anticipate the order to seize him. If, the second his foot was on the wharf, he dodged between the men about him and ran for it, he might get away. Should he succeed, he could be with C. B. at Henri's bar in ten minutes; and although he would temporarily have lost Christina, they could at once set about tracing the car in which she had been kidnapped.

These swift thoughts had barely coursed through John's mind when the Marquis reached the head of the gangway. Still keeping hold of Christina's arm, he halted and looked back. Suddenly he shot out his free hand, pointed it at John and cried:

'Throw him down the hatch!'

II

THE MARQUIS CALLS THE TUNE

Before John could raise a finger, the man with the moustache and one of the sailors were upon him. His assumptions had been only partially correct. The Marquis had, in fact, assessed the true situation at a glance as soon as he had come on board; but his subtle tactics had had a different aim from the one that John had guessed. He had been quick to realize that a fight on the open, brightly-lit deck could be seen from the buildings on the quay, and that later police enquiries might elicit the fact that a woman answering Christina's description had been involved in it; so he had led his visitors into the shadow cast by the bridge and funnel before resorting to violence to prevent their escape.

The *mêlée* in front of the companionway was brief. John saw the Marquis pull Christina back from the gangway and push her towards a dark doorway that stood open in the bridge structure. After that he had only a confused impression of a violent struggle with himself as its centre. Both his arms were seized and he was forced forward. Next moment he was hurtling down the companionway ladder. He struck the middle steps, which slightly broke his fall, and slithered head-foremost to the bottom. Following him came the sound of pounding feet, and before he could rise his attackers were on him again. One kicked him in the ribs; two more grabbed him by the shoulders and lugged him to his feet. As he stood swaying there, half-dazed between them, the man with the moustache hit him hard beneath the chin. Stars and circles in vivid array danced on a background of dense blackness before his eyes: he felt his knees sag, and he passed out.

When he came to, his first sensations were the throbbing of his head, a horrid ache in his ribs, another in his right forearm, and several minor pains in various parts of his face and body. After a moment he remembered how he had come by them and realized that he was still on board the yacht.

For a while he lay unmoving, wondering vaguely how long he had been unconscious. The yacht was pitching slightly, so obviously she was now at sea, and he had the impression that it was days ago that he had been flung down the companionway, although he knew that it could not really be so.

Gradually he began to take stock of his surroundings. He was lying on a hard bunk in a narrow, dimly-lit cabin. It had no porthole, so must be below the water-level. Such light as there was filtered in through an iron grille in the door, which suggested that this was not the first time the place had been used as a prison. That, he concluded, was why his captors had not bothered to tie his feet and hands.

Getting painfully off the bunk, he verified the impression. The door was of steel and had no bolts, handle, or even a key-hole on its inner side; so even had he had some implement available he could not have attempted to pick the lock. The cabin had no furniture other than a single chair and a small, dirty wash-basin with a cracked mirror above it. There was no bulb in the solitary electric fitting in the ceiling, so he could not switch on a light. But his eyes were now getting accustomed to the little light there was, and peering at his face in the mirror he turned it first one way, then the other, in an endeavour to assess the damage it had suffered.

His dark hair was rumpled and his face streaked with dirt. The left side of his chin was swollen and very tender, where the man with the moustache had hit him. It gave his face a slightly lop-sided appearance, which was accentuated by the fact that his left eye was half closed and colouring up, as evidence that Jules had had the best of their first encounter.

Pressing the single button-tap, he ran some water into the basin and, as there was no towel, used his handkerchief to bathe his hurts. The cold water refreshed him and helped to clear his head a little, but there was nothing he could do about the injuries to his body. His forearm was scraped raw where he had slithered on it down the last few stairs of the companionway, and his side pained him every time he took anything approaching a deep breath, although on gingerly feeling his ribs he did not think that any of them were broken.

While examining himself he found that his pockets had not been rifled and, rather belatedly, it occurred to him to look at his watch. On holding it up to the light from the grille he saw that its glass had not been broken and that it was still going. To his surprise it was only twenty-five minutes past eleven, and as a single blow on the chin could hardly have rendered him unconscious for over twelve hours it now seemed clear that he must have come round quite soon after the yacht had left harbour. Seeing that it was not yet midnight made him realize that, wherever she was bound, there was small likelihood of her reaching port for some hours to come; so he lay down again on the bunk.

A little grimly he began to wonder what they would do with him when she did reach port. C.B. had warned him that if he went aboard without an authority to do so he would risk a beating-up, and he had been beaten up; but he did not now think it very likely that they would hand him over to the police, as C.B. had forecast they would should he find himself in his present circumstances. Any police doctor would attest that injuries such as he had sustained could not normally have been received simply while being prevented from attacking someone. It would be clear that it was he who had been attacked, and handled much more brutally than even being caught while committing a theft could warrant. Moreover, he could now justify his having come on board to look for Christina. Whatever might have happened earlier, he could swear that when he, as her fiancé, had been escorting her ashore, he had been set on himself and had seen the Marquis forcibly prevent her from walking down the gangway. The de Grasses would surely not willingly give him the opportunity to make a sworn deposition of that kind.

On the contrary, it was to their interest to keep him silent. But how would they do that? His close acquaintance with his mother's professional efforts immediately suggested the now unnerving phrase, 'Dead men tell no tales.' Yet he could not believe that the de Grasses would run the risk of committing murder in order to cover up the much lesser crime of kidnapping. It seemed far more probable that they would keep him a prisoner until they had got Christina safely to England and had had a chance to manufacture ample evidence that she had gone willingly. They would then have very little to fear if they released him, particularly if they first gave him a crack on the head, followed it when he came round with a shot of something to keep him muzzy, and then took him to a hospital with a story that they had found him wandering. There would not be much point in his mother and C.B. swearing that they had seen him board the yacht illegally; and any evidence he might give of recent events would be most dubiously regarded owing to his condition.

Such a prospect was very far from pleasant; but he felt that Christina's prospects were infinitely worse. He had good reason to suppose that she was still on board, but if she had been taken off after he had been thrown down the companionway, that made no difference. She was now in the clutches of these people and there was not a soul who could do anything to aid her.

At the moment, under the strange influence that night had upon her, it was probable that she was not at all apprehensive about her future; but she would wake to-morrow a young and frightened girl, knowing herself to be at the mercy of men she knew to be her enemies. It seemed unlikely that the de Grasses would do her any injury; but what would happen to her when they had delivered her in England? If C. B. was to be believed—and his word must be accepted as authoritative on all criminal matters—she would be drugged, hypnotized, bedevilled and given over to the lusts of evil men, until such time as the evil had entered into her to the exclusion of all else and, debauched in mind and body, she willingly lent herself to every filthiness that imagination could suggest.

The thought of what she would suffer during periods of lucidity, and the awful fate that must finally overtake her, made the perspiration break out on John's forehead. For a long time he sought desperately for possible ways of saving her, but each grew more far-fetched and hopelessly impractical, until at last he drifted off to sleep.

He was woken by the steel door of the cabin being swung back with a clang. Starting up, he saw two seamen standing in the doorway. Both were brawny, tough-looking fellows with hard eyes. The elder, whose hair showed grey at the sides under a rakishly-worn peaked cap, beckoned to him to come out, and said:

'Get between us; and keep your hands at your sides, or it will be the worse for you.'

The yacht's diesels had been stopped and her only movement now was a gentle rise and fall; so it seemed that she must have entered a port or have anchored in some sheltered bay. John gave a quick glance at his watch. It was a quarter-past three. That told him that she might have run between forty to fifty miles along the coast, but in which direction he had no means of guessing. Obviously this was no time to argue; so he slid off the bunk, placed himself between the two sailors, so that the three of them formed an Indian file, and in this manner allowed himself to be escorted up on deck.

He saw then that he had been right in believing the yacht might be anchored in a bay. The moon was almost down, but the stars were bright and there was sufficient light for him to make out a headland on either side, from which the land dropped away. Between them rose an outline of dark hillside, with low down on it several lighted windows which appeared to be in one large, solitary house.

A rigged gangway, slung from davits on the yacht's port-side, had been lowered. John was marched on to it, and saw that a motor-launch was rocking gently beside the square grating which formed the lowest stage of the ladder. As he walked down to it he began to play with the thought of taking a swift dive; but he was not much good at swimming under water; so he was very doubtful of his ability to get out of sight before he could be spotted and recaptured. The idea was definitely rendered stillborn when they reached the launch by the grey-haired sailor producing an ugly sheath-knife, showing it to him and saying:

'Should Monsieur show any desire to go for a swim, he will enter the water with this in his liver. Those are my orders.'

Evidently the man felt that it was not for a member of the crew to enter the launch's cabin, as he prodded John towards the bow and made him sit down on the fore-deck with his back against the cabin's forward end, then sat down beside him. A moment later John heard voices, and among them Christina's, confirming his belief that the Marquis had not taken her off in his car, but detained her on the yacht. By turning his head he caught a glimpse over the low top of the cabin of several people coming down the gangway, and she was among them. The party scrambled on to the launch and, as soon as they had settled themselves in the cabin, it cast off.

John's spirits were now on the upgrade. As long as he had been in his cabin prison he had thought it certain that he would be kept there, perhaps for several days, or anyway until Christina had been got safely away, and that it was even possible that he might never see her again. But now it looked as if they were both to be taken to the house with the lights, and that the place was to be used as a staging point in the arrangements for getting her to England. If so, it was at least conceivable that a chance might occur for him to rescue her, or to escape himself and let C.B. know where she was before she was moved on again.

Two-thirds of the way to the shore these new hopes were sadly dashed. The launch passed close to a small seaplane that lay rocking gently at its moorings. The sight of it instantly brought into John's mind the tall man with the fair fluffy moustache. He looked a typical pilot and probably this was his aircraft. If so, here were the means by which Christina was to be transported to England, and the odds were that they meant to fly her off at dawn. With so short a time to go, all chance of rescue, or bringing C.B. and Inspector Malouet on the scene, would be ruled out.

John had barely assimilated this new cause for depression when the launch pulled in at the shoreward end of a long curved mole that formed a small private harbour. The party in the cabin landed first, and he could now see that it consisted of Christina, the Marquis, Jules, the pilot-type and the little man who looked like a valet. John's escort again showed his knife, then signed to him to follow them.

With the Marquis and Christina leading, they crossed the hard, went through a gate in a low wall and entered a garden. The trees there made it darker than it had been on the water, but there was still enough light to see by. The ground sloped up, but not sufficiently to require a path with hairpin bends, and as soon as they were within a hundred yards of the house John could make out its main features.

Unlike most large properties on the Riviera, it was a flat-faced, pedimented eighteenth-century château with tall windows. It had two floors only of residential accommodation and from the first jutted out a broad terrace. Below the terrace the façade was broken only by a low central door and on either side of it a row of small, square windows protected by iron grilles. As John was aware, it was usual for the ground floor of such buildings to be used solely as cellarage, store-rooms and offices; and as no lights showed from any of the small windows it seemed that this château was no exception.

The central door opened on to a small, stone-flagged hall with a low vaulted ceiling, and a curved stairway having a wrought-iron balustrade, which led up to another much loftier hall on the main floor. When they reached it the Marquis opened one of a pair of tall, white, heavily-gilded double doors and bowed Christina through into a brightly lit *salon*. With its panelled walls, tapestries, Aubusson carpet and delicate furniture, it had all the elegance of a genuine *Louis Seize* apartment. The others followed, but as John stepped inside Jules said to the sailor who had brought up the rear of the party:

'You may go now, Chopin. Monsieur Upson and I will take care of your prisoner.'

The Marquis meanwhile was addressing the little man who on closer inspection was obviously a servant, and John heard him say:

'Frederick, see that all is in order in the du Barry room. Mademoiselle may like to rest there for a while before she sets out on her journey. Then prepare our special accommodation downstairs for Monsieur Fountain. He will be our guest for some days.'

These orders confirmed John's belief that within a few hours they intended to fly Christina off in the seaplane. It was the first chance he had had to get a proper look at her since they had been separated on the yacht, and as Jules closed the door behind him he shot a glance at her.

She was half-turned away from him, so he could not catch her eye; but he was given a swift indication of her mood. As the valet left the room by a further door, she asked the Marquis angrily:

'Where are you sending me?'

'To England, Mademoiselle.' He waved a hand towards the pilot-type, who was now leaning negligently against a large marble-topped table. 'I have already presented Mr Reg Upson to you. He was an ace airman in the last war, so you need have no fears for your safety while he flies you home.'

Jules and John were still standing within a few feet of the door to the hall. Seeing that everyone's attention was concentrated on Christina, this seemed to John as good an opportunity as he might ever get to make a bolt for it. Taking a swift step back, he seized the door handle.

Quick as his movement had been, Upson's was quicker. Out of the corner of his eye he had seen John brace himself and guessed his intention. Whipping a small automatic from a shoulder holster, he cried in English:

'Halt; or I fire!'

John had not even got the door open. Under the menace of the pointing pistol there was nothing he could do but let go of the handle and give a resigned shrug. Jules then grabbed him by the arm, pulled him into the middle of the room and pushed him into an armchair.

The airman laid his automatic down on the top of the table and said in a lazy drawl, 'It's just as well you stopped when you did, or I'd have put one through the calf of your leg.'

Riled by Jules' rough handling of him, but knowing it to be no time to start another fight, John turned and snapped at Upson, 'If you are an ex-R.A.F. officer you ought to be ashamed of yourself.'

'Got to earn a living somehow,' Upson replied indifferently. 'And I'm paid darn' well for taking care of troublesome types like you.'

Christina was still staring at the Marquis, and she suddenly burst out, 'I will not be sent home! I wish to remain out here!'

'We are not concerned with your wishes, Mademoiselle; and you will do exactly as you are told,' said the Marquis coldly.

She was standing within a few feet of Upson. Turning towards her, he said, 'And while you are with me, little lady, don't try any funny business. Can't afford to do gentle restraining acts in a small aircraft like mine. If you start anything, you'll get a backhander, hard, right on your snub-nose. Understand?'

With glaring eyes she spat at him, 'I am not coming with you! I'll scratch your eyes out if you try to make me.'

Upson shrugged, and looking across at his employer broke into French. 'Monsieur le Marquis will agree that it would be dangerous to take her up in her present state, as she might easily bring about an accident. May I suggest that she should be given a shot of dope?'

The Marquis nodded, and Jules commented, 'We thought that might be necessary. Obviously it is, and we'll see about it in good time before you start.'

Christina's lips drew back in a snarl. 'I will not let you! I will tear the face off the first one of you who touches me!' Then, after a moment, she added in a different tone, 'I will go only if you will let John Fountain come with me.'

'That,' said the Marquis firmly, 'is impossible.'

Jules turned to John and said, 'I may as well tell you now what we intend to do with you. I warned you that you would get hurt if you tried to interfere with us, and you have. I got hurt, too, although not as much, and that's all in the day's work; so I bear no malice. But that is beside the point. By butting in you have seen enough to bring a case against us for kidnapping; therefore we cannot afford to let you go. In fact, you have made it necessary for us to keep you out of the way for a considerable time. You will remain here for a few days, then you will be picked up by one of our cargo steamers on its way from Marseilles to North Africa.'

'Africa!' John exclaimed, aghast.

'Yes. You will be put ashore without money or papers in some small Libyan port, and by the time you have made your way home all this will be ancient history. Should you still bring a case, we shall be able to show that you went at your own wish, and had been suffering from mental trouble.'

John had come to his feet, but he endeavoured to keep the anger and apprehension out of his voice as he asked, 'How would you show that?'

'Because you are going to write a letter to me, saying that, owing to overwork, you have recently caught yourself imagining things and fear a nervous breakdown; so feel that a long sea trip is just what you need to put you right, and are very glad to accept my offer to send you round the Mediterranean in one of our vessels. Incidently, should it come to a case, our Captain will swear to it that you left the ship without warning him of your intention to do so; and to land without money or papers will be further evidence that you have been off your nut.'

'And what if I refuse to write such a letter?'

Jules sighed. 'I fear that we shall be unable to provide you with food or drink until you do.'

To everyone's surprise Christina cried, 'Send me to North Africa with him!'

'You are going to England,' declared the Marquis, his lean face for the first time showing irritation.

'I am not! I refuse!' cried Christina furiously. Then she pulled off her left glove and, looking away from it herself, displayed the glistening ring on her swollen finger. 'Do you not see! I am tied to him by this. I must go wherever he goes.'

Jules stared at her in astonishment. 'But . . . you told me this evening that your engagement to him was only a phoney one.'

She shuddered and violently shook her head. 'That was before the two of you had a fight. When he overcame you I knew I was his. Now I am bound to him . . . bound to him.'

Flecks of foam had appeared at the corners of her mouth, and they all thought that at any moment she was going to have a fit. The Marquis moved quickly over to a side-table on which there was an array of drinks. A siphon was among them, and squirting some soda-water into a glass he carried it over to her.

'Mademoiselle, calm yourself, I beg,' he said. 'Drink this, and sit down for a moment.'

Christina took the glass and drank most of its contents. She gasped and set it down on the marble-topped table, but she did not sit down. No one spoke for a moment, then Jules said to John:

'There is another letter which it would be advisable for you to write. This one would be just as much in your interest as in ours. It would be to your mother, to allay her anxiety about your disappearance. You could simply say that you have accepted an invitation from me to go for a cruise round the Mediterranean and expect to be back in about six weeks.'

'You want me to do that in the hope that it will stop her putting the police on to you?'

'Exactly. She will realize, of course, that the "invitation" was one which you were not allowed to refuse; but if she knows what has happened to you and believes you to be safe, there will be no point in her asking the police to trace you.'

'Again, what happens if I refuse?'

'Nothing!' Jules smiled. 'We shall have to have you kept on board the ship a few weeks longer, to counteract the possibility of a French Consul having you flown back, should your case have been put on his list by the police if your mother asked them to conduct a search for you; but that is all. The point is that once you are on board it will be quite impossible for the police to trace you until you land. And no one else will inform your mother what has become of you, unless you agree to do so yourself. Therefore, if you refuse this offer, she may be caused great distress for some time to come, believing you to be dead. It was to suggest to you that you should write this letter now, for delivery to-morrow, that we had you brought up here instead of putting you straight into a cell. Come, what do you say?'

John found himself caught in a cleft stick. The last thing he wanted to do was to protect the de Grasses from police enquiries, and by giving a reason for his disappearance he might hamper his mother in getting them to take the case further than a routine questioning of Jules—who, of course, would have a plausible story all ready for them. On the other hand, he knew how desperately worried his mother would become if she had no news of him. To allow her to remain in a state of terrible anxiety for several weeks, when he could easily reassure her, was unthinkable. So he said:

'Very well. I will write to my mother on the lines you suggest.'

It was at that instant that Christina shot the Marquis.

12

THE FIGHT IN THE CHÂTEAU

John did not see Christina grab the gun up from the table, or fire it. He was looking at Jules; and Jules, the Marquis and Upson were all looking at him, waiting to hear whether he would decide to write the letter to his mother. Christina had taken advantage of that moment. She had stretched out her hand as though to pick up the glass she had set down a few moments before and finish the drink the Marquis had given her; instead, she snatched the automatic that Upson had left lying within a few inches of his own hand, aimed it, and pressed the trigger.

Simultaneously with the crash of the pistol, the Marquis clasped his right shoulder. Reeling back, he collapsed on a *Louis Seize* settee. It was as well for him that he did, as Christina sent a second shot at him. It thudded into the Gobelin tapestry behind his head.

Upson was the first to move. The Marquis had hardly staggered under the impact of the bullet before the airman swung a blow at Christina's head. She ducked it as she fired her second shot, sprang away and turned the pistol on him. There was murder in her eyes. Seeing it, his face blanched and he made a futile gesture, throwing out his hands as though to ward off the bullet.

There was barely four feet between them; so had it not been for John he would certainly have been shot. But, as he had struck out at Christina, John had swung round on his other side, run in, and struck at him. The blow landed squarely on the side of his face. He was already slightly off balance and it sent him spinning. Christina's third shot sang harmlessly over his shoulder.

Jules was standing near the table on which was the tray of drinks. Snatching up a bottle of Dubonnet by the neck, he flung it at Christina. The cork came out as it flew through the air, and the sticky liquid splashed all over her face and neck, but the bottle missed her.

Letting out a scream of rage, she ran towards him, firing as she went. With extraordinary agility he flung himself aside, pirouetted like a ballet dancer and kicked her on the thigh. She went over with a crash and the pistol exploded for the fifth time. Her fourth shot had missed Jules, but the fifth paid an unexpected dividend. At that moment the door by which the valet had left the room opened, and he poked his head in. The bullet fired at random splintered the woodwork within an inch of his chin. His eyes popping with fright, he jerked back his head and slammed the door shut again.

As Christina measured her length on the floor Jules ran at her, but John was in the act of rushing at him. They collided. John's rush had carried him half across the room, so there was more force behind it. Jules went over backward, striking his head hard on the parquet floor. He rolled away, then struggled to his knees, but remained there grasping a chair with one hand and swaying from side to side, temporarily incapable of further action.

Christina was up again, the automatic still clutched in her hand. The Marquis had also staggered to his feet, and with his sound arm was clutching a silken bell-rope. As he jerked it up and down a bell could be heard clanging in the distance. Christina had pitched forward to within a few feet of him. No sooner was she up than she pointed her gun at his heart. Only just in time to stop her from committing murder, John knocked it aside. The bullet shattered the centre panel of a cabinet displaying a beautiful Sèvres dinner service.

The tinkle of glass and china merged into the thunder of feet charging across the parquet. As John and Christina stood together Upson was coming at them from behind with a chair raised above his head. They swung round to face him. For a second it seemed certain that it must fell one, or both, of them.

There was no time to step aside; no time even for Christina to bring up her pistol. John gave her a push that sent her reeling back on to a chaise longue. Lowering his head he went right in under the chair and butted the airman in the stomach. Upson lost his grip on the chair; it crashed to the floor behind John's back. He managed to keep his feet, but Upson went over backwards, the breath driven from his body, and lay writhing in agony.

From the time Christina had fired her first shot, not one of these violent, kaleidoscopic actions had occupied more than ten seconds; yet in this bare minute or two the crack of the shots and the clanging of the bell had roused the house. The sound of running feet could be heard pounding along a corridor somewhere beyond the door through which the valet had poked his head.

As Christina pushed herself up from the chaise longue on to which John had thrust her, he grasped her arm, turned her towards the double doors by which they had been brought in, and cried:

'Quick! The servants are coming! This way, or they'll catch us!'

Still clutching the pistol, she ran through into the hall. He darted after her, but as he slammed the door behind him he had the presence of mind to swing round and turn the big ornate key that protruded from the lock. In three strides he reached the head of the short flight of stone stairs. Christina was halfway down them. Suddenly she lurched sideways, let out a yell, and fell, sprawling the last few steps to bring-up against the terminal post at the bottom of their curved wrought-iron balustrade.

'You hurt?' he panted, helping her to her feet.

She took a couple of steps and screwed up her face with pain. 'It's my ankle. It twisted under me.'

The little automatic had been dashed from her hand, but had not exploded. John stooped, grabbed it up, put on the safety-catch and slipped it into his pocket as he cried anxiously, 'Will it bear you? Can you possibly manage to run?'

'It has got to,' she gasped, her eyes flashing with determination.

'Well done! Here, lean on my shoulder.'

She flung an arm round his neck, and together they trotted across the stone flags to the outer door. On emerging from it they could hear loud banging on the doors of the *salon*, and excited shouts. Jules was yelling for the servants—'Marcel! Henri! Frederick! Where the devil are you?'

As the fugitives ran out into the garden, by contrast with the brightly lit interior of the château it seemed pitch black. The moon had now set and the stars gave only a pale light in the open spaces between the trees. Their instinct was to take the way they had come and head down the broad central walk for the harbour. But no help was to be expected there, and, after a second, John realized that they would stand a better chance of getting away if they could find a side entrance to the grounds. Swerving to the right, he ran Christina along under the terrace till they got to the end of the building. A wall continued from it, in which there was a tall arch with a wrought-iron gate leading to a stable-yard.

By the time they reached the arch, the windows of the *salon* had been flung open and several people had run out on to the terrace. Jules was shouting to the servants, 'Get out into the garden. Quick now! Quick!'

John pushed open the iron gate. As he did so a furious barking started and a big wolfhound came bounding from a kennel towards him. Christina screamed and he swiftly pulled the gate shut. At that instant two men ran out from the main door of the house. Hearing the barking and the scream, they swerved to the right and came racing towards the stables.

The second John had the gate shut, he and Christina made a dash for a path that led down the side wall of the garden. It was screened from the château by a belt of trees and thick shrubs which hid it in almost total darkness. Fifty feet along it he came upon the thing he had been hoping so desperately to find—a postern gate. As his hand grasped the latch he prayed frantically that it would not be locked. His prayer was answered: at the first pull it flew open. With Christina still leaning on him, he stepped through it.

One glance in each direction, and his heart sank with dismay. It gave on to the road leading up from the harbour to the carriage entrance of the château, and on, inland. On its far side was a steep bank topped by another wall, which ran unbroken both ways as far as he could see. Behind them they could hear the flying feet of their pursuers nearing the stables. Christina was moaning with pain, and the tears were running down her face. The road between the two walls was like a long, curved corridor, and in it there was no scrap of cover. Once out on it, the stars would give enough light for them to be seen. However game Christina's effort, within two hundred yards they must be run down and caught.

Pulling her back, John whispered, 'We must hide: it's our only chance.'

Leaving the postern door wide open, he drew her swiftly with him down the path. Fifty feet farther on he pushed her in among the bushes and they stood there with their hearts pounding, trying to still the rasping of their breath.

It was none too soon. Jules' men had found the iron gate to the stable-yard still shut and the hound baying on its far side. Realizing that the fugitives could not have gone that way, they darted towards the dark path. Fifty feet along it they came upon the open postern. As John had hoped, they ran through it. He gave them a minute, fearing that, seeing no one up or down the road, they might come back. Then, after a mutter of voices, he heard their running steps again as they headed towards the nearest bend, which lay up the slope.

Coming out from their cover, John and Christina continued to follow the path, but now at a quick walk and making as little noise as possible. Temporarily they had escaped from the likelihood of immediate capture; but people calling to one another from the centre of the garden told them that Jules, Upson, and perhaps some of the other servants had come out to join in the hunt; and where the shrubbery was thinnest John twice caught the flash of torches.

He knew that now there was little chance of slipping unseen out of the gate down by the port, and was desperately casting about for some place where they might hope to lie concealed when the hunt moved in their direction. By this time they were nearly at the bottom of the garden and could see part of the wall that ran parallel with the shore. Above it showed the starry sky, but at the corner where the two walls met a patch of blackness reared up to double their height, its faint outline having the appearance of a square, topped by a triangle. After a second John realized what it was, and whispered:

'That's a gazebo just ahead of us. With luck they will think we got away along the road. They may not look in there. Anyhow, it's our best bet. We must chance it.'

'A what?' murmured Christina.

'A gazebo—a raised summer-house built on the corner of the wall, to give a view of the bay.'

Swiftly but cautiously, they covered the short distance to the end of the path and made their way up the curving wooden stair they found there. The door of the gazebo was not locked, but it squeaked a little and, fearful of being heard, when they had crept inside they closed it gently behind them. For a moment they could see nothing, then panels of greyness showed the position of the windows and they realized that the place was sexagonal with a window in each of its sides except that occupied by the door. By groping about they found that it held basket chairs with cushions in them, a table and a low cupboard. Lowering themselves into two of the chairs, they subconsciously stilled their breathing while listening anxiously for sounds outside.

Muffled now by the wooden walls of the garden house, they could still hear the calls of the searchers. Once they caught the quick tread of heavy feet nearby, and the reflected glow from a torch lighted one of the windows on the garden side; but after a quarter of an hour of agonizing apprehension no sound had reached them for several minutes, so it seemed that the search had been abandoned.

Till then neither of them had dared to speak from fear that one of Jules' people might be hunting about in the shrubbery beneath them; but now John thought it safe to ask in a whisper:

'How is your ankle?'

'Not too bad,' Christina whispered back. 'It gave me hell while we were running; but since I've had it up on a chair the pain has eased a lot. I don't think it's sprained—only twisted.'

'It ought to have a cold compress on, but there's no hope of that. Still, I could bind it up tightly, and that may help when we have to move again. Shall I try what I can do?'

By this time their eyes had become a little accustomed to the darkness; so he could just make out her nod. 'I wish you would; but do you think you can see enough?'

'We could use my cigarette-lighter, but I don't like to risk it. This place may be visible from the house.' As he spoke he knelt down and groped about till he found her foot. Having taken off her shoe, he felt the ankle gently with his finger-tips. It was swollen, but not very much. Getting out his silk handkerchief, he folded it on the seat of a nearby chair, as well as he could by touch, cornerwise into a long strip. Then he said:

'You had better take off your stocking.'

She undid the suspender and rolled it down for him. He peeled it off and for a moment held her bare foot in his palm. It was cool, firm and delightfully smooth. His hand closed round it easily, and on an impulse he remarked:

'You were grumbling this afternoon about the size of your feet. I can't think why. This is a lovely little foot.' The words were scarcely out when he regretted them from the sudden fear that she might take the compliment as an amorous overture. He had experienced how swiftly she could be aroused to uncontrollable passion during the dark hours, and the last thing he wished for was to have to repel advances of which she would be ashamed in the morning light.

His fears were not altogether unfounded. After a second's hesitation, she said very softly, 'If you like to kiss the place, that might make it well.'

Instead, he laid on the bandage. It was the handkerchief he had used to bathe his face in the cabin, so it was still damp and cold. As it touched her she gave a little gasp, and, to distract her mind from the thoughts on which he felt sure it was running, he told her about the use to which he had put it; then, as he drew the bandage tight and tied the pointed ends in a knot a few inches above her heel, went on to describe the hurts he had received on the yacht.

The ruse served to some extent, as she immediately became all concern. Then leaning forward she found and stroked his face, as she murmured, 'Poor John! You've had a frightful time. And all for my sake. But I'll do anything I can to make it up to you.'

He got her stocking on over the bandage, then told her to pull it up; but she gave a low laugh.

'No; you do it for me, darling. I'm glad you like my feet; although you'd find them much bigger than you think if you saw them. Of my legs, though, I have real reason to be proud. They are a lovely shape and above the knees as soft as satin. Just feel, here by my suspenders.'

Suddenly taking his hand, she pulled it forward till it touched the inner side of her thigh on a line with the top of her other stocking. The flesh there was like a cushion of swansdown under a taut-stretched skin of tissue-thin rubber; it had that indefinable quality of being cool at first touch, then instantly radiating heat. The back of his fingers were pressed for only a second against it. Jerking them away, he tore his hand from hers, and snapped:

'That's quite enough of that! Do it up yourself.'

For a moment she was silent, then she said in a voice near to tears, 'Oh, John, you are unkind. Have you been playing with me? Don't you love me at all?'

His mouth had suddenly become dry. He swallowed, but his words came huskily in the darkness. 'If you want to be seduced, ask me to fix your stockings for you to-morrow afternoon. But I'm damned if I'll make love to you now, while you are under some accursed influence.'

She sighed. 'But it's now I want you to. I'd make you if I wasn't so tired.'

He laughed a little grimly. 'You would probably succeed if I wasn't so tired myself. My ribs are still giving me gyp, and I'm one big ache all over. It must be past four o'clock, too; so it is over twenty hours since we had any sleep, except for our nap in the olive grove.'

'That was nice.' Her tone was warm at the memory. 'But I'm such a stupid little fool in the daytime. I was nervous of you then.'

'I like you better when you are like that, because you are your real self.'

'What is my real self?' she asked cynically. 'My feelings are as real by night as they are by day. I shall be the way you like me best again soon, though. The change always comes an hour or so before dawn, and I can feel it coming on. But you can't have it both ways. If they find us here and we have to try to escape again I'll probably behave like an hysterical schoolgirl, and I'll never have the pluck to fire that gun.'

'Don't worry. I have it, and I felt it over soon after we got in here. There are still two bullets left in it. They should be enough to give us a sporting chance of a break-out if we are found here, but it looks as if they have made up their minds that we got away along the road. The thing that troubles me is your ankle. I should like to give them another half-hour, then go out and reconnoitre. If no one is about it would be the perfect opportunity to slip away inland behind the château. No one would ever find us up there in the *maquis*. But there is always the chance that we might be spotted leaving the garden and have to run for it again; and, anyway, I'm sure your ankle would never stand up to a long tramp over broken ground up into the hills.'

'No, John. I'm afraid I should let you down if we tried that. Still, if they don't look for us here soon, it is very unlikely that they will to-morrow; so we could stay here in hiding all day. By the evening my ankle will be much stronger and we could slip away soon after dark.'

'We'll be jolly hungry and thirsty by then; but it would certainly be our safest plan.'

'A day's fasting won't do either of us any great harm. If you agree, let's try to get some sleep now.'

'All right,' he said, standing up. 'There is a bigger chair here with a pull-out for the legs. I'll pile some cushions on it and you had better have that.'

When he had arranged the chair, she rested one hand on his shoulder and pulled herself up beside him. Quietly, with no hint of seduction in her voice, she asked, 'Do you care about me at all, John? Tell me honestly. I want to know.'

'I can only say that in a very short time I have grown very fond of you,' he hedged. 'I've already told you that I refuse to make love to you except in the daytime.'

'You are still afraid of me,' she whispered, 'but you needn't be. The windows are lighter already, with that pale light that comes before dawn. But I still have enough shamelessness left to tell you something. I love you. You may think that is just because I've never been kissed by any other man. It's not. It's something deep inside me. I know that at night my wanton thoughts might make me easy game for anybody; but during the day, although I am shy and awkward, I long every bit as much to feel your lips on mine. I love you. I love you terribly. I'd die for you, John, if I had the chance.'

He could find no words with which to reply, and after a moment she went on, 'Even if you are only a little fond of me, do something for me, please. Let's lie down in the chair together. I want to feel your arms round me. You have been so gallant in the way you have protected me; but at any time my enemies may prove too much for you. We may never have this chance again. Although you can't tell me that you love me, let me go to sleep making believe that you do.'

Gently he lowered her on to the pile of cushions, then lay down beside her and took her in his arms. She put her cheek against his, but made no attempt to kiss him. Her limbs relaxed and she gave a sigh of contentment. On a sudden impulse that overbore all his scruples, he murmured, 'I love you, Christina. I love you,' and drew her more closely to him.

For making love the pile of cushions on the long basket chair was quite adequate, but not for a prolonged sleep. It was too narrow, and beneath the cushions its arms dug into their backs. Dozing was all that either of them could manage, and some three hours later John kissed Christina lightly on the forehead, then got up.

He did so cautiously, as it was now full daylight; and if he showed himself above the level of the window-sills of the gazebo there was a risk that he might be seen. First he peeped out on the garden side. He could see no one in it, and the iron roller blinds of the château windows were all down. A glance at his watch showed him that it was just after half-past seven, so the lack of activity was not surprising in view of the fact that its occupants could not have got to bed much before half-past four.

Still crouching, he crossed to one of the windows overlooking the shore. That, too, presented a peaceful early morning scene, but a disappointing one. John had hoped to see there at least a few fisherfolk who in an emergency—such as Jules suddenly thinking of the gazebo later in the day and ordering it to be searched—could be called on for help. There was not a soul to be seen and it was quite clear now that the little harbour was a strictly private one. The only craft in it were a twenty-foot sailing yacht, a sailing dinghy, a speed-boat and Upson's seaplane. The big yacht in which they had been brought there was still lying at anchor about a quarter of a mile beyond the point of the mole. Made fast to it were the launch in which they had come ashore and another more powerful vessel that looked like a converted submarine-chaser.

He was just wondering if they could get out of the garden unobserved, swim out to the speed-boat and make off in it, when the submarine-chaser cast off from the yacht and turned her nose in towards the harbour. In a graceful curve she rounded the point of the mole, reversed her engines, and manœuvred a little until her pilot had brought her skilfully alongside its outer end. Two sailors with lines jumped ashore and she was swiftly made fast. A moment later a gangway was put out and a group of people landed from her.

Suddenly John jerked himself erect and gave a shout. 'Christina! We're saved! There's Mumsie! I'd know that absurd hat of hers anywhere. And there's C. B.! They've got the police with them. Hurrah! They must have found out where the yacht had gone, and come to rescue us.'

Christina had still been dozing. She scrambled to her feet and joined him at the window. Both of them could make out the group clearly now, as it advanced along the mole. In addition to Molly Fountain and C. B. it consisted of a very tall old man with a drooping grey moustache, and three men in uniform.

'Come on!' cried John. 'Let's go down and meet them. But how is your ankle? Is it up to walking?'

She tried her weight on it. 'Yes, it's much better. I'll be all right if you give me your arm. Oh, John, what wonderful luck their coming and finding us here.'

As she spoke they turned to look at one another. It was the first time they had done so in daylight since the evening before. Neither realized what a sight they themselves presented, and grinned at the marks of battle on the other.

'You *are* in a mess,' Christina laughed. 'Your chin's all swollen and you have a glorious black eye.'

'You look as if you had been dragged through a hedge backwards, yourself,' he retorted cheerfully. 'The sticky liquor from that bottle Jules shied at you has collected so much dirt that you'll have to scrape it off your neck with a knife; and your hair is a veritable bird's nest.'

As he spoke he took the little automatic out of his pocket, and added, 'I'll keep this handy, just in case anyone tries to stop us between here and the gate. Come along now! Let's go!'

When he opened the door of the gazebo the garden still appeared to be deserted; so they went down the steps to the path. On their way to the gate he said, 'Now that the police have been brought into this we ought to be careful what we say. If I had had the wit and the chance to snatch this gun last night I have no doubt I should have shot someone with it myself; but such acts usually have repercussions. Mind, I don't think there is the least likelihood of the Marquis bringing an action against you. He would find it much too difficult to explain away his part in the affair. I'm only a bit worried that wounding with firearms may be what is termed a crime against the state. If so, and the French police are told about it, they would have no option but to arrest you; so I think we had better skip your grand performance with the heavy armaments.'

'Tell them what you like,' she shrugged. 'I was mad as a hatter at the time; so I suppose it's lucky I didn't kill someone; but I'm not feeling a bit like Two-gun Annie now.'

'May be,' he answered with a smile. 'But it would be pretty mean of me to let them infer that I rescued you, when it was really you who rescued me. I think I'll say—'

'Oh, don't be silly, John! I could never have got away without you. The less you say about my part in it, the better. They are much more likely to believe that you slew all the dragons and carried me away across your shoulder. Anyhow, I'll leave all the talking to you.'

On reaching the gate they found that it was not locked, so they walked straight out on to the hard; and there, now only fifty feet away, were the group from the submarine-chaser.

With exclamations of surprise, followed by shouts of delight, the rescuers joined the rescued. Molly was so overcome at seeing her boy safe and sound that she dared not kiss him from fear of bursting into tears; so, much to his surprise, she shook him vigorously by the hand. With a laugh, he picked her up and hugged her. Then, in turn, she hugged Christina. C. B. introduced the tall old man as ex-Inspector Malouet, and the senior police officer as Sergeant Bouvet. The next ten minutes passed in a gabble of questions and explanations.

It emerged that they were on the island of Port Cros, the smallest of the three main islands known as the Iles d'Hyères. The de Grasses had long owned the château and a fine estate there, but otherwise it was almost uninhabited. On arriving at St Tropez, Malouet had suggested it as the most likely place for the yacht to have taken Christina, as in any public harbour along the coast the arrival of a vessel of her size would at once have been reported. After a lengthy discussion with the local police, he had persuaded them to co-operate by getting the customs temporarily to place at his disposal one of the fast craft they used for the prevention of smuggling. On reaching the Ile de Port Cros they had boarded the yacht with a search warrant. Her Captain had refused all information, so they had spent an hour going through her; then, having drawn blank, they had just come ashore to pursue their enquiries at the château.

John gave an abbreviated version of what had happened to him and Christina, concluding with their escape to the gazebo. When he had done, Sergeant Bouvet said:

'It appears that Mademoiselle accepted an invitation to go aboard the yacht, and that Monsieur joined her there in an irregular manner. However, that could not excuse the treatment to which you allege that you were later subjected. Does either of you wish to make a charge? If so, I must take down your deposition in detail.'

'Hold yourself, my son, hold yourself,' said the elderly Malouet, patting him kindly on the shoulder. 'Your enthusiasm does you credit, but there is more in this matter than appears on the surface. If you will permit me, I should like to talk privately with these young people before they commit themselves to any legal action.'

'But of a certainty, Monsieur,' replied the sergeant, and from his tone it was clear that he regarded the ex-inspector with a sentiment akin to veneration. 'It is a privilege to have your guidance in such an affair, and you have only to make your wishes known to me.'

Malouet favoured him with a courteous little bow. 'Since you are so kind, I suggest that we should all return to our ship. For the time being I think it would be as well if we made it as difficult as possible for anyone to trace Mademoiselle's movements. I am, therefore, loath to take her back to St Tropez. Perhaps on your way there you could land us at some little-frequented place. Later, should it be decided that a charge is to be preferred, you may be sure that I shall lose no time in getting in touch with you.'

'As you will, Monsieur. Let us go back on board, then. Have you as yet decided whereabouts you would like us to land you?'

For a minute or two the old man did not reply; but when they had covered about fifty paces towards the submarine-chaser he said, 'If we take the route between the islands and the coast we must pass a little place called Cavalaire. The village is on a shallow, sandy bay, facing eastward; but it is not that I have in mind. To the south of it there is a headland, and on the headland is a small hotel called the Sur Mer. In the old days it was owned by a man named Gandini and was famous for its good food, as he was once a *maître d'hôtel* at the Negresco. He has long since sold it, but it has a private bay on which we could be landed from a boat.'

'I know it!' The sergeant waved an airy hand. 'You are as good as there already, Monsieur. A perfect spot to go ashore discreetly, observed only by a handful of people. So early in the year I doubt if even the hotel itself will be open.'

'I had rather hoped it would,' Malouet confessed, 'as I am beginning to feel the need for my *petit déjeuner*. But if it is not, we can walk down to the village, hire a car there, and drive to some other small place for a meal, before progressing further.'

Ten minutes later they were on board and the vessel had cast off. Having installed Molly, Christina, Monsieur Malouet, C. B., and John in the after-cabin, Sergeant Bouvet tactfully withdrew; so they were able to talk more freely.

Rounding the western point of the Ile de Port Cros, they left the much larger Ile de Porquerolles on their left, and headed in towards Cap Benat on the mainland. Meanwhile, John and Christina gave the old walrus-moustached ex-inspector a more detailed account of what had happened to them during the night, suppressing only Christina's hectic performance with the gun. Then Malouet asked her to tell him of her earlier meetings with the de Grasses, and anything else she could remember having a possible bearing on her case that had occurred since she had come to the South of France, and she did so while the low-throbbing craft carried them swiftly across the bay towards Le Lavendou.

Although it was still only the first week in March, no cold or boisterous wind disturbed the serenity of their short voyage. The sun was shining in an almost cloudless sky of pale blue, and its rays could already be felt, promising another day of pleasant warmth. The sea still held the greeny-blueness of early morning, but its surface was unruffled by white horses and the wave crests were hardly perceptible except where they creamed upon the rocks along the shore. Behind them lay the Iles d'Hyères, now holding the suggestion of romance that always attaches to green islands set at a distance in a sparkling sea. Ahead rose up the indented coast of the mainland, with its rocky foreshore, verdant slopes and background of snow-topped mountains.

The twenty miles was soon covered and by half-past eight the ex-submarine-chaser was nosing her way into a small bay with rugged cliffs on either hand. A dinghy was lowered, Sergeant Bouvet and the captain of the vessel were taken leave of with warm thanks for their help, and the shore party were landed on a flat shelf of rock at the foot of the right-hand promontory, from which visitors to the hotel bathed in summer.

Slowly they made their way up the rough, steep path to the hotel. It was a small two-storey building, having only a dozen bedrooms and a single *salon*, the whole length of its ground floor on the seaward side being devoted to a covered terrace which served as its restaurant. It had not yet been opened for the season, but the proprietor and his wife readily agreed to provide breakfast for their unexpected visitors. A small boy was despatched on a bicycle to buy *croissants* in the village, 'Monsieur' set about his preparations for making a big ham omelette, and 'Madame' showed her guests up to five bedrooms that had fixed basins, so that they could freshen themselves up after their night out.

John was still in his shirt-sleeves, putting the finishing touches to his hair with a borrowed comb, when there came a gentle knock on the door of the room he had been given. On his calling, 'Come in,' Christina limped in and closed the door behind her.

She held out her left hand. The middle of the engagement finger was covered with a thick lather, and she said, 'I've come for you to get your ring off. The knuckle is still a bit swollen, but I think you will be able to wriggle it over now I've made it slippery with soap.'

'Why do you want to take it off?' he asked in surprise.

'You said you would this morning. You promised to just after you had had your fight with Jules in the cabin of the yacht.'

'I wasn't speaking seriously. I said that only to pacify you at the time. You know how different you become from your real self at night.'

She coloured, looked quickly away from him, and stammered, 'I . . . I'd rather not talk about last night. I mean about . . . about what occurred between us. Although my memory of it is a bit blurred now, I know that I behaved abominably. I feel terribly ashamed.'

'You needn't be.' He smiled, cutting her short. 'You were really very sweet once we had settled down in the summer-house.'

'It was you who were sweet to me. You said you loved me, and I shall never forget that.' Her words came out in a rush now. 'I know you don't really, and that you probably said it only to comfort me, but please don't admit it, or protest that you do, out of kindness. You see, you may have really meant it just for that brief time. Anyhow, I'd like to believe so, because it will be a lovely memory to take away with me.'

'Take away!' he echoed. 'What on earth are you talking about?'

She extended her hand again. 'That is why I want you to have back your ring. I'll have no more use for it now, even for make-believe. I thought it all out while we were dozing early this morning. I have repaid your mother's kindness by causing her a night of desperate anxiety about you, and I brought you into a situation where you might have lost your life, or anyhow have been seriously injured. That isn't right. This horrible affair is a matter for myself and my father. If anyone is responsible for me, it is he; so I have decided that the time has come when I must disobey his orders. I am going back to join him in England.'

13

PRISON FOR ONE

'You can't do that,' John said quickly. 'He brought you out here to keep you out of danger.'

Christina nodded. 'I know that was his idea; but it has failed. The danger has caught up with me just the same. As soon as our secret enemies discovered my hiding-place his plan broke down; so there is no point in my staying here any longer.'

'Oh, yes there is. For some reason we can't yet guess at, they want to get you back in England. To go there would be to play into their hands.'

'You may be right about that, but there is a chance that when Father knows what has happened he may be able to think of a new plan to foil them. Anyhow, I have caused your mother and you more than enough trouble already. You've both been wonderful to me; but I can't let things go on like this. If Father is in no position to help me I'll go into hiding somewhere and face what is coming on my own.'

'No you won't! I won't let you.'

'John, I've made up my mind about this, and I am in my right senses now.

Please take off your ring.'

He shook his head. 'Nothing doing, my dear. While you were distraught last night you declared that it bound you to me. As far as you are concerned I am on the side of the angels, and if you felt that so strongly even in the dark hours, it is a symbol that you cannot yet afford to do without. So you are going to stay bound to me until we have seen this business through. Afterwards you can give it back to me if you like.'

'All right then,' she sighed. 'I'll keep your ring. But that doesn't alter what I said about going back to England.'

'We'll talk about that over breakfast,' he hedged. Then with a sudden grin he held out his arms. 'In the meantime you continue to be my fiancée; so come and give me a kiss.'

Her big brown eyes were full of tears as she put up her hands, took his face between them, and said, 'Very well then; but this is good-bye.'

'No it isn't, silly,' he smiled. 'It is only good-morning.'

As they kissed another knock came on the door, and 'Madame's' voice called, 'Breakfast will be ready in about five minutes, Monsieur.'

'*Merci, Madame,*' he called back, and they broke their embrace; but, seeing that her left hand had made the right side of his face soapy, Christina picked up a towel and began gently to wipe it. As she did so, she murmured:

'What a good thing that I didn't mess up the other side. Your poor eye still looks awfully tender.'

'If it is not too repulsive a sight, a kiss on it might help to make it well,' he suggested.

As soon as he had spoken he regretted his words. Christina went scarlet, exclaimed, 'How horrid of you to make me remember!' and throwing down the towel, ran limping from the room.

Down on the terrace he found his mother, C. B. and Malouet already assembled; but it was some time before Christina joined them, and when she did he saw that she had been crying. During the first part of the meal she was very silent; then gradually she seemed to forget the episode that had caused her such distress, and responded more readily to the questions Malouet put to her.

Although the previous afternoon now seemed days away to all of them, it was not yet twenty-four hours since C. B. had left London, and so far he had had no opportunity to hear Christina's own version of her story; so when the meal was finished he asked her, for his own benefit as well as Malouet's, to tell them all she could about her life from the beginning.

It took her the best part of an hour, and while there was nothing new to Molly and John in her account, when she had done both the old Frenchman and C. B. agreed with their view, that she was suffering from possession. As John had expected, none of the others would listen to her when she announced that she had decided to return to England; so he felt that he could leave it to their united firmness to dissuade her. They all pointed out in turn that the worst that was likely to happen to her while she remained in France was that the de Grasses might yet succeed in kidnapping her; whereas a far graver danger would threaten her once she had crossed the Channel; so it would be absurd for her to go to meet it voluntarily, when they might be able to save her from it altogether.

As she proved very stubborn, a prolonged wrangle ensued, but eventually their various arguments based on the same theme took effect and she agreed to stay on, at least until after the 6th, which appeared to be the target date for whatever was being hatched against her.

However, out of her wish not to expose her friends to further trouble and danger, one new factor of considerable importance had arisen. Previously she had been adamant in her determination that her father should not be informed of what was happening to her, in case any communication by her should jeopardize his own plans; whereas now she had conceded that he was ultimately responsible for her safety as well as his own, and had proposed to go home and tell him what had happened herself. From this it followed that she no longer had any real grounds for objecting to anyone else doing so.

At first she protested, but both Malouet and C.B. pointed out that her father alone held the key to the mystery that surrounded her, and that it was not only unreasonable, but now also illogical, for her to insist on their fighting her battle for her in the dark. C.B. proposed that he should return to England that afternoon, and on his promising to use the utmost discretion in getting in touch with her father, she was persuaded to agree.

The next question was how best to protect her from further attempts by the de Grasses to get hold of her until C.B. returned and, having found out what they were really up against, some new plan could be made.

'Couldn't we stymie the de Grasses by bringing an action against them for kidnapping and assault?' Molly asked.

Malouet shook his head. 'I would not advise it, Madame. That is why, having made use of our good friend Sergeant Bouvet, I temporized with, and got rid of, him. Mademoiselle went on board the yacht willingly and your son clandestinely. Although they were both forcibly detained later, you may be sure that none of the crew would give evidence to that effect. There is the fact, too, that your son knocked out one of the officers who was quite rightly asking what business he had on board. That renders his position most precarious, and would certainly lead to a counter prosecution if we started anything. They are very averse to having the police enquire into their affairs; so I think it most unlikely they will bring an action against him. On the other hand, I am equally strongly of the opinion that he may get into serious trouble unless we let sleeping dogs lie.'

Thinking of the Marquis with a bullet in his shoulder, John remarked, 'In view of the rough handling we managed to give them before we escaped from the château, I should have thought there was quite a good chance that they may feel they have had enough of this affair. After all, they are only acting as agents; so they may quite well decide that the game is no longer worth the candle, and throw their hand in.'

'Perhaps.' Malouet pulled thoughtfully at his long moustache. 'The sum they were offered was a thousand pounds, was it not? That would not mean very much to M. le Marquis, and you will note that he has hardly appeared in this matter himself. That the sailing of the yacht was delayed for him last night suggests that his reason for going to the Ile de Port Cros had no connection with Mademoiselle. It seems probable that from the beginning he regarded the matter as small game, and so handed it over to Count Jules. M. le Comte may, as you suggest, now feel that it has become too troublesome a way of earning the amount concerned; but I think we should be most unwise to assume that.'

'Besides,' C.B. glanced at John, 'no one likes being made a monkey of; and, the money apart, your having got the best of Jules may now have made him hopping-mad to get his own back on you. In any case it is up to us to take all the precautions we would if we were certain that he meant to have another crack.'

John admitted that his idea had been prompted by unreasoning optimism, and said that he did not mean to suggest for one moment that they should relax their vigilance in guarding Christina. They then reverted to their discussion about what to do with her.

It was obvious that her own villa and Molly's were no longer safe; and Malouet thought that if they took her to any hotel upon the Riviera there was a strong probability that the de Grasses' grape-vine would soon locate her; so there would then be an immediate renewal of the risk that they would again succeed in luring her away. To form a more accurate estimate of that risk, he asked her to tell them again in more detail how Jules had managed to do so the previous night, and exactly what her feelings had been while she was with him.

Looking at Molly, she said, 'You will remember that when John and I came in I spent only a few minutes downstairs being introduced to Colonel Verney; then I went up to my room to arrange my things. Darkness had fallen some time before I had finished and began to think of changing for dinner. It wasn't until I had had my bath that the thought of the frock I was going to wear came into my mind. I had brought over rather a quiet little thing, and I decided that I should look much nicer in a red and silver affair that I bought just before I left Paris; so I slipped on my day dress again and went over to my villa to fetch it.

'I put it with its etceteras into a small suitcase, and had just left the house when I met Jules coming up the garden path. He told me that he was on his way back from Cannes to St Tropez with a friend, and felt that he must just look in to see if I had quite recovered from my attack on the previous night. By then we had walked back to the sitting-room, and although I had only fruit-juices I felt that I ought to offer him a drink. Rather to my surprise, he accepted, and naturally I had one with him.

'Perhaps he slipped something into mine when I was not looking. I couldn't say for certain. All I know is that after I had finished my drink I felt a little muzzy; and I don't remember anything more very clearly until I found myself sitting with him in the back of a big car. A chauffeur was driving it, and with him in front there was a grey-haired man wearing a yachting cap, whom I later heard them call Chopin.

'By that time we were half-way to St Tropez; and, although no mention was actually made of it, I was subconsciously aware that I had already agreed to dine with Jules in the yacht. I had the sort of light-headed, irresponsible feeling that I get at such times, and was rather amused at the thought that you and John would wonder what had happened to me. In fact, far from having any sense of guilt at my rudeness in going off without a word, I felt that I had played quite a clever trick in slipping away; and when the car drew up alongside the yacht I went on board without any suspicion that I was running into danger.

'Temporarily, the memory of my resistance to Jules' previous attempts to get me on to the yacht was entirely obliterated. To dine on board was a novel experience for me, and I thoroughly enjoyed it—apart from one petty annoyance. That was the discomfort caused me by John's ring. It was not only physical discomfort, owing to a queer heat that it seemed to be generating, but that tied up in some way with a growing mental uneasiness, vaguely suggesting that, although I was enjoying myself, I was playing with fire.

'But it was not till John actually appeared on the scene that I was seriously disturbed. Then I suddenly found myself a prey to violently conflicting emotions. One half of me intensely resented his intrusion; the other demanded that I should do whatever he told me to. I felt like that all the time he was fighting Jules, but the moment he knocked Jules out the tension disappeared. I knew then without a shadow of doubt that John had come to save me from something terrible, and that at all costs I must get away with him.'

For a moment they were silent, then C. B. said, 'That is interesting about the ring. Don't take it off whatever you do.'

Malouet shrugged. 'It is a strange phenomenon and one of which I have never previously heard; but clearly it is not sufficient to protect her. I wonder if M. le Comte did slip anything into the fruit drink? I think he must have, as how else can we account for her sudden muzziness followed by a lapse of memory lasting some twenty minutes?'

'I don't think the point of much importance,' C. B. rejoined, giving his big nose a quick rub. 'In my view the crux of the matter lies in Christina's sudden impulse to wear a more striking frock. It was that which got her out of the house, and it was followed by another—to ask Jules into her villa, instead of threatening to shout for help unless he cleared off. Those two mental processes taken in conjunction show that she was being influenced by some occult force to her own detriment before Jules even had a chance to open his mouth let alone dope her drink.'

'I am sure you are right,' Molly agreed, 'and it is that which sets us such a problem in devising means for her protection. All I can suggest is that we should go to some small hotel, and that she should share a room with me. I should be on hand then to counter these dangerous impulses, and at least that would make it much more difficult for anyone to get at her.'

'It would certainly be a big help,' C. B. conceded. 'But I'm afraid even an arrangement of that kind would be far from watertight. You see, I consider it certain that the Satanists who are interested in Christina are having her overlooked from time to time by means of a crystal. That is how they know the right moment to send out a thought wave which gives her a certain impulse—such as that which led to her going across to her own villa last night just as Jules was due to come up the garden path. If you come into the picture they will try to work on you too.'

'Then they won't have much luck,' declared Molly truculently.

'Don't you be too certain of that. They are much too clever to try to make you do anything abnormal, but they might get at you in ways you would never suspect. You have got to sleep sometime; so they would send waves of sleep at you in the hope that you would drop off and leave them a free field with her. Even if you managed to keep awake all night, I am sure you would find it difficult to remain with Christina for every moment between dusk and dawn; and if they could succeed in separating you from her for only a few minutes that might prove enough for them to get her away altogether. Then, occult forces apart, if Jules has his dander up he may try a snatch. Remember, he came with a pal and a driver last night, which shows he was prepared to use violence if he did not find Christina open to suggestion.'

'Well, can you think of any better plan?'

'Not for the moment. I feel sure that it was Christina being overlooked that enabled the Canon to discover her first hiding-place so quickly. For that reason. I don't think it would help if you took her off to Lyons or Genoa. He would soon locate her and offer some local gang the thousand quid to do a snatch. Better the devil you know than the devil you don't, and we do know the de Grasses; so I think it would be wiser to keep her down here. I was only pointing out the sort of thing you and John may find yourselves up against while acting as her guardians.'

'How about pretending she has had a nervous breakdown and putting her temporarily into a private mental home?' John suggested. 'The nurses and porters in such places would never allow a patient to walk out in the middle of the night.'

C.B. shook his head. 'You are wrong there, John. We could not tell them that we had put her there to prevent her being kidnapped; so it would be easy to distract their attention. Our unknown enemy would have her out of a place like that in no time.'

'I could have solved the problem for you had the war still been on,' smiled Malouet. 'At times, when the pace was getting too hot for some key man in the Resistance, we used to pretend to mistake him for an habitual criminal, pick him up under the criminal's name, fake a charge against him and pop him inside. The Boches never got wise to our using the prisons as hiding-places, and as soon as the hue and cry died down we let our friend escape. If only we could put Mademoiselle behind bars for a few days, neither the de Grasses nor a score of Satanists would be able to get her out. But unfortunately for our present business, it is no longer possible to commit a person on a false charge.'

John was sitting beside Christina. He gave her a swift glance, then took Upson's pistol from his pocket and showed it to her under the table. She nodded; so he said to Malouet:

'What would happen, Monsieur, if I had shot somebody through the shoulder last night, and now surrendered myself at a police station, confessing what I had done?'

'They would take you into custody pending an enquiry.'

'And then?'

'Presumably the person you had shot would come forward and charge you with having caused him grievous bodily harm.'

'Say that for his own reasons he preferred not to bring a charge and denied that anything of the kind had happened?'

'Then you would be discharged as a harmless lunatic.'

'Say he did bring a charge? I take it that in spite of my confession I should still be entitled to plead that I shot my man in self-defence?'

'Certainly; and if you could bring a reliable witness to swear to that, or even sound circumstantial evidence in support of your plea, the probability is that a verdict would be given in your favour. That, too, would be rendered all the more likely through your having surrendered yourself in the first place.'

Again John looked at Christina, and again she nodded. He laid the pistol on the table, and said, 'Then Christina and I propose that she should give herself up for having shot the Marquis de Grasse with that soon after half-past three this morning.'

His announcement created quite a stir. At first the others would not believe that it was Christina who had used the weapon; but John gave them the true version of the fight in the château, and Christina filled in some of its more lurid details herself. Their account was so vivid that it carried conviction, and when they had done Molly exclaimed, with an envious glance at Christina:

'Oh, you lucky girl! What wouldn't I give to have had such an experience.'

'Her luck is that she didn't kill him,' commented C.B. grimly. 'If she had, she could not possibly escape being tried for murder; and as she went on the yacht willingly, even a plea of self-defence might not have saved her from a nasty sentence for manslaughter.'

'Nevertheless, I congratulate Mademoiselle on her courage,' Old Malouet made her a courtly little bow. 'And I am sure this will enable me to arrange matters. We will not, I think, make use of our friend Sergeant Bouvet at St Tropez. It will be better if I take you in to Nice, as I am more intimate with many of the officials there; so can make certain that you have every comfort that is allowed during your stay in prison.'

'Thank you,' said Christina. 'You are very kind. Going to prison is a far from pleasant prospect, but it certainly seems the best idea for my protection, and I am sure you will do your utmost to make it as little disagreeable for me as possible. How long do you think they will keep me there?'

'To-day is Thursday, the 4th. Should M. le Marquis decide to charge you, the case could not come up for a first hearing before Monday. You would then be remanded while the lawyer we should find for you prepared your defence, and we could get you out on bail—if that was thought desirable—until you had to come up for trial. But, as I have already said, I think it very unlikely that the de Grasses will wish to have their affairs gone into in open court. Should M. le Marquis say that you shot him by accident and fled in panic afterwards, as he probably will, you will be released; but again, not before Monday, as once having been taken into custody you must be formally discharged by a magistrate. So in either case you will remain in prison over the week-end. And that is the important thing, for Saturday the 6th appears to be the critical date by which your enemies wish to get you to England.'

Christina gave a rueful smile. 'My birthdays have never meant very much to me, but all the same it seems a bit hard that I should have to spend my twenty-first in prison.'

'What's that?' exclaimed C.B. 'D'you mean that you will be twenty-one on the 6th? If so, that may be very important. Why didn't you tell us so before?'

'I'm sorry,' Molly put in. 'Christina did tell me the first time I talked to her. I ought to have told you, but there has been no mention of it since, and it entirely slipped my memory when I was telling you her history last night.'

'Why may it be important?' Christina asked.

'Because it is the principal landmark in anyone's life. In addition the three sevens have a special magical property. As it is Satanists who are after you, that would explain why they are so anxious to get hold of you by that particular date. It looks now as if they are planning some special ritual at which the presence of an unmarried girl of twenty-one is required. To make use of her on her actual birthday would, of course, enormously increase the potency of the conjuration. In fact, that is probably essential to the success of the whole business.'

'If that is so, and we can protect her over Saturday, she will be out of the wood then?' John put in eagerly.

C.B. nodded. 'Yes, if we can do that I think the worst danger to her will have been averted. But we should still have to get her freed from this spell, or whatever it is, that causes her personality to become evil at night. Her father must hold the key to that; so putting her in prison will not affect my decision to go and demand his help.'

John looked at his mother. 'If Christina is to be put behind bars there will be nothing that I can do here; so, if you don't mind, Mumsie, I think I'll go with C.B. to England. Should Christina's father resent C.B.'s interference, I could justify it by telling him that I am her fiancé. That might make him more willing to co-operate.'

'Yes, that's true. Then go by all means, dear.'

'If you do, and her old man thinks you would make a good husband for her, this fake engagement of yours may land you in for a breach of promise case,' C.B. grinned.

'Not a bit of it.' John laughed, 'If she jilts me, it is I who will bring the action. You've forgotten that she is an heiress.'

Christina coloured slightly, but joined in the general laughter.

After a glance at his watch, C.B. said, 'It is half-past ten; so if John and I are to get to England to-day, we ought to be moving. I wonder which is the best bet for an aircraft, Nice or Marseilles?'

'Nice is some thirty kilometres nearer,' replied Malouet, 'and there is a plane that leaves at one o'clock for London. Even if you cannot get places on it, a lot of air traffic passes through Nice now; so you should be able to get an Air France or some other line by which you could go *via* Paris.'

'Going by Nice has the additional advantage that you could collect your things at the villa on the way,' Molly added.

'Come on, then.' C.B. stood up. 'I'll pay the bill while one of you telephone the local garage for a car.'

Malouet did the telephoning, and ten minutes later an ancient but comfortable car arrived from the village to pick them up. The sun was hot now and as they skidded down the rough track they could smell the scent of the pines and wild thyme growing in the *marquis* through which it ran. At the village they turned on to the main coast road and three-quarters of an hour's drive brought them to Molly's villa. There, Christina, John and C.B. hastily packed suitcases and said good-bye to her. Another three-quarters of an hour, with the driver urged on by the promise of a handsome *pourboire*, and the others were set down at the Nice airport.

It was twenty-five to one when they got there, and they were lucky enough to pick up two seats that had been returned that morning on the B.E.A. plane. C.B. sent a telegram to his office, asking that his car should be sent to meet him at Northolt; then, as there was still a quarter of an hour to spare, they had drinks and some delicious snacks at the airport bar.

When the time came to say good-bye, John and Christina both tried to make light of the matter; and he jokingly told her that when he met her at the prison gates on Monday he would have his pockets sewn up, as it was certain that by then she would have become a real old lag. Since they were in public he made no attempt to kiss her, but their eyes held one another's in a long glance as they parted. Malouet watched with her until the plane had taken off, then they returned to the car and did the last four miles in to the centre of Nice. By two o'clock Christina's name had been entered on the prison register, and, now a number, she was being escorted by a fat, garlic-breathing wardress to a cell.

The journey in the aircraft proved uneventful; and, having been up most of the night, John and C.B. slept through the greater part of it. The Côte d'Azur, with its sun and palms, was soon left behind. Over Avignon they ran into cloud and only occasional patches of land or sea were visible for the rest of the way. When they came down at Northolt it was raining. Everyone at the airport was polite and helpful, so the formalities of landing were over in a few minutes, and a pretty air hostess led them out to the place where C.B.'s car was waiting. He took it over from the junior who had brought it out, made John get into the driver's seat, and soon after four o'clock they set out for Essex.

North of London the earliest daffodils and almond-trees were not yet out, so there was no colour in the gardens, and the branches of the trees still displayed their winter bareness. The skies were grey, a chill wind was blowing and the rain lashed against the windows of the car; so their sixty-mile drive was a depressing contrast to the one through a smiling land of summer they had taken only that morning. It was already dark when at six o'clock they entered Colchester.

There, they engaged rooms at the Red Lion for the night, dropped their bags, and, having enquired the way to Beddows Agricultural Tractor plant, drove straight out to it.

As the factory was working night shifts, it was brilliantly lit and still a hive of activity. On asking for Mr Beddows they were told that he was not there, and had not been to his office for a week or more. They then asked to see his secretary. She had gone home for the night, but after stating that their business was personal they were shown into a garish modern waiting-room. Presently a Mr Hicks came down to see them, and he proved to be a senior member of the staff. In spite of all their pressing that they must see Mr Beddows on a matter of the utmost urgency, he assured them that his chief had gone abroad ten days before, leaving no address, and orders that all correspondence was to be dealt with in his absence as he could give no certain date for his return.

Their failure to learn Beddows' whereabouts was a bitter disappointment; so they returned to the Red Lion, had a wash, and sat there very despondently drinking Gimlets until dinner was served. The meal, and even a bottle of claret, followed by half a bottle of port, to wash it down, did little to cheer them.

There was, however, still a chance that something might be learned at Beddows' home, so at half-past eight they got out the car again and took the road leading east out of Colchester to Walton-on-the-Naze.

The country they were now entering was that north-eastern segment of Essex which has its curve upon the sea and its two sides formed by the Rivers Stour and Colne. Its only towns of any size are the pleasure resort of Clacton in the south and the naval base of Harwich in the extreme north. For many centuries the two rivers almost enclosing it shut it off from easy communication with neighbouring districts; so no great highway passes through it, and to this day it remains almost as unindustrialized as it was when Cromwell raised a company of his Roundheads from its scattered hamlets.

When they had covered a few miles the road forked, and they ran on through a series of narrow, winding lanes. Twice they took wrong turnings and had to ask their way—once at an old thatched cottage and once of a benighted cyclist from whose mackintosh-cape the rain was streaming: but at length they came to a triangular village green with half-a-dozen buildings dotted round it. One was a pub called the Weaver's Arms. On C.B. enquiring at it, they found that this was Little Bentford and that The Grange lay about two miles beyond it on the road to Tendring.

After following a sharp bend for half a mile, they passed an ancient stone church with a squat, square tower, and a little farther on a moderate-sized private house of hideous Victorian-Gothic design; they then ran through a wood and out again into the open country.

From the description C.B. had been given, they had no difficulty in finding The Grange. It stood some way from the road in a slight hollow and a curved drive led down to it. As the car approached and the headlights threw it up, they saw it was one of those inelegant, nondescript houses, not uncommon in the English countryside, which have resulted from two or more generations adding bits in the style of their own day to an original building. No light showed in any of its windows; in spite of the rain a suggestion of mist lurked round it up to the first-floor level, and it had a chill, forbidding air.

C.B. got out and rang the front door-bell. He could hear it ringing, but no one came to answer it; so, after waiting a few minutes, he rang again. Still there was no reply and there was no sound of movement within the house.

John left the car, went over to join him and said, 'I remember Christina telling us that the only servants were a couple named the Jutsons, and that they lived over the garage, in the flat where she was born. Let's go round there and see if they are about.'

At the back of the house they saw lights in two first-floor windows of the outbuildings and, locating a narrow door next to the big ones of the garage, C.B. rang the bell beside it. Footsteps sounded on the stairs and the door was opened by a thin-faced, rather sour-looking middle-aged woman. To C.B.'s enquiry she replied:

'No: Mr Beddows is away. I'm afraid I can't help you.'

C.B. clinked some silver in his pocket. 'We're very anxious to get in touch with him; perhaps you could suggest some way . . .'

A man's voice cut him short by calling, 'Who's that, Mary?'

There came more clumping of feet, then Jutson appeared and pushed past his wife. He was a small man with grey hair close-cropped at the sides; his face was careworn and tight-lipped. He was in his shirt-sleeves and wearing an unbuttoned waistcoat, but no collar. A wireless was reeling off sporting news upstairs, and evidently he was annoyed at being disturbed, as he gave his callers a most unfriendly stare while C.B. repeated his request.

'No.' He shook his bullet head. 'The guv'ner's from home. Has been for near a fortnight, an' we dunno when 'e'll be back.'

'Can't you possibly think of someone who might be able to help us?' John asked persuasively. 'We are friends of Miss Chris . . . Miss Ellen Beddows.'

'That don't make no difference. I tell you 'e ain't 'ere, an' we dunno where 'e is neither. 'Tain't none of our business; an' it's no good you fiddlin' with your note-case neither. G'night.'

With that Jutson slammed the door and they were left standing in the rain. As they walked back to the car John said miserably, 'What appalling luck! Everything depends on our getting hold of him. How else can we hope to free Christina from this beastly thing that gets into her at night? There must be some way we can trace him.'

'I'll get on to a pal of mine at Scotland Yard to-morrow. They will do more for me than for most people without asking any questions.' C.B. made the promise in the hope of cheering John up, but he was by no means optimistic of getting results, as it now seemed certain that Beddows was still abroad.

Climbing into the car again, they took the road back to Little Bentford. Half a mile before they reached it, on the corner of a lane opposite the church, there was a pillar-box, and the car lights showed a man just posting a letter in it. His back was turned to them, but they could see that he was elderly, as a rim of silvery hair caught the light between the collar of a dark cloak and the clerical hat he was wearing. As they passed him John said in an excited whisper:

'I'll swear that was Canon Copely-Syle. Christina said that he lives in the village at a house called The Priory; so it must have been.'

C.B. turned quickly in his seat and looked back. He saw that the elderly clergyman was now crossing the road diagonally towards the pseudo-Gothic house. 'Pull up, John,' he called, as they entered the long bend that led to the village green. 'I think I've got the germ of an idea.'

John brought the car to a standstill, and they sat in it for some minutes in silence, while C.B. smoke a cigarette. As he stubbed the end out he said, 'Turn round and drive back a little way, so that you can park in the shadow of that belt of trees. I'm going to pay the old boy a visit. Maybe it will come to nothing, but with a little luck I might find out a lot.'

When John had driven the car in under the trees, C.B. murmured in his most conspiratorial voice, 'Now listen, partner. This bird may be dangerous. If he catches me out all sorts of unpleasant things might happen to yours truly. I don't want you to start anything prematurely, because if matters go well I may be with him for a considerable time. But if I am not out of his house by midnight you are to go along to the village, telephone the police, then come in to get me.'

14

THE BLACK ART

The rain was still falling in a steady downpour, and now that the light was failing the little turrets surmounting the steep gables roofing the house presented only a blurred outline. As C.B. squelched his way up the garden path the coppice twenty yards away on his right was already pitch-dark, but to his left the tall, ancient yews of the churchyard still stood out, like sombre sentinels guarding the dead, against the heavy grey sky that presaged a night of inky blackness.

Under the Gothic porch there lingered enough light for him to make out a scrolled iron bell-pull beside an arched front door of solid oak and studded with massive nail heads making a curious pattern. He jerked it vigorously and heard the bell clang hollowly in a distant part of the house. No approaching footsteps told him that anyone was on the way to answer it, but after a moment the door swung silently open on well-oiled hinges.

Framed against the dim light from a Moorish lantern that hung in the centre of a small square hall stood a manservant of a type that one would hardly have expected to find in an Essex village. He wore a red fez and was robed in a white burnous. His skin was very dark, but only his thick lips suggested negro blood; and C.B. put him down at once as an Egyptian. Crossing his black hands on his chest he made a deep bow, then waited silently until C.B. asked:

'Is Canon Copely-Syle in?'

The man salaamed again and replied in excellent English, a slight lisp alone betraying his foreign origin, 'My master has just settled down to his writing, and at such times he is averse to being disturbed. But if you will give me your name, sir, I will enquire if he is willing to receive you.'

'My name is Verney; but that won't convey anything to him. Just say that I arrived from Nice this afternoon.'

As C.B. spoke he stepped into the hall and the Egyptian closed the door. His felt slippers making no sound on the tiled floor and his white robe billowing out behind him, he seemed almost to float away down the corridor. Two minutes later he returned; his white teeth flashed in a smile, he bowed and murmured, 'Allow me, sir, to take your things. Then if you will follow me . . .'

Having divested himself of his wet coat, C.B. was led to the back of the house and shown into a room that, unlike the appearance of the house itself and the Egyptian servant, had nothing even suggestive of the sinister about it. In fact it might well have been the workroom of a wealthy but unimaginative clergyman. Wealthy, because of the great array of valuable books that covered all its walls from floor to ceiling: unimaginative, because its owner was evidently content to have left unchanged its Victorian *décor* and hideous furnishings of elaborately-carved light oak. Nevertheless, it had an air of solid comfort. It was a large room, but the fact that it was not very lofty made it cosier than it would otherwise have been. The light from three standard lamps shone warmly on the gilding of the books and a big log fire blazed on an open hearth. In front of it stood the Canon.

C.B. thought John's description of him good. He was shortish and plump both in face and figure. His cheeks were rosy but tended to sag a little; the rest of his skin had such a childlike pinkness that it was difficult to visualize him ever having the need to shave. His forehead was broad and smooth; his long silver hair swept back from it to fall in curls on the nape of his neck, but gave no impression of untidiness, suggesting rather the elegance of a Georgian parson. His eyes were hazel, but very pale, and his expression benign. His features were well cut, the only thing unpleasant about them being an exceptionally thick and out-jutting lower lip. He was dressed in a black frock-coat, ribbed satin vest, clerical collar, breeches, gaiters and black shoes with silver buckles; all of which added to the impression that he was a divine of a past generation.

Stepping forward, he smiled and extended a plump hand as he said, 'I take it you have news for me, Mr—er, —Verney. It was good of you to come here in such shocking weather.'

His smile detracted from the pleasantness of his expression, as it revealed a lower row of blackened, uneven teeth. His hand was slightly damp and so soft as to seem almost boneless. C.B. found its touch so repulsive that he had to restrain himself from withdrawing his own unduly quickly, as he replied:

'Yes, it's a horrid night, isn't it? But our mutual friend, de Grasse, had an urgent message for you, and knowing that I was returning to England to-day he asked me to come here this evening.'

The Canon pushed a big horsehair-covered armchair a little nearer to the fire and murmured, 'Sit down, Mr Verney. Sit down and warm yourself.' Then he bustled over to a table on which stood an array of drinks, and added, 'A whisky-and-soda now? You must need it after your chilly journey.'

C.B. would have preferred to accept neither food nor drink while in that house, but as his object was to win Copely-Syle's confidence he accepted, and, producing his pipe, said, 'D'you mind if I smoke?'

'No, no. Please do.' The Canon carried over two whiskies, handed one to his caller, and went on, 'I trust you have not come to tell me that de Grasse has bungled this affair. It is to me of the utmost importance.'

'I gathered that.' C.B. began to fill his pipe. 'So I'm afraid you won't be very pleased to hear what I have to say. Mind, it's through no fault of de Grasse that things have gone wrong, but on account of the interference of that infernal young man, John Fountain.'

The Canon made an impatient gesture. 'Then de Grasse *has* bungled the affair! How utterly infuriating. With his resources he should never have allowed a boy like Fountain to get the best of him. That is no excuse. No excuse whatever! But tell me what happened.'

In his usual leisurely manner C.B. then related all that had taken place, from Jules de Grasse luring Ellen—as he now called her—away the previous evening, to her escape that morning; except that he refrained from making any mention of his own participation in these events. When he had done, the Canon said petulantly:

'Really! To think that a man like de Grasse should allow two children to set him at defiance. But he is not the type to lie down under such treatment. No doubt he means to teach that young man a lesson; and even if he has to use force will get the girl back again from Mrs Fountain to-night.'

'I don't somehow think he'll be able to get her to-night.' said C.B. slowly.

'Why not? His wound may incapacitate him personally, but it should not prevent his sending Jules and some of his people to carry her off.'

C.B. felt confident that next morning's post would bring the Canon an airmail letter from de Grasse with full particulars of the latest situation; so, there being no point in concealing it overnight, he replied, 'It's not quite as simple as that. The girl is no longer with Mrs Fountain. She is in prison.'

'What!' Copely-Syle's drink slopped over, and he jumped to his feet. 'What's that you say? In prison! Surely de Grasse has not been idiot enough to bring a charge against her for shooting him?'

'No, it's not that.'

'What then?'

'We don't know ourselves. At least de Grasse didn't know when I left him. All we know is that soon after she landed this morning she was taken into custody. Perhaps she thinks she killed de Grasse, so gave herself up pending enquiries. Or, as she has been living under a false name, it may be something to do with her passport.'

'But this is calamitous!' The Canon's heavy underlip trembled and his babyish face screwed up, so that for a moment C. B. thought he was about to burst into tears. An instant later it became apparent that the contortion of his features was due to rage. Abandoning all control, he began to stamp up and down the room, flinging wide his arms and reviling de Grasse in the most filthy language for his incompetence. Then, turning about, he screamed curses at C. B. for having brought him such unwelcome tidings.

C. B. watched the performance with detached interest, pulled on his pipe, and said with a suggestion of a smile, 'It's no good swearing at me; and cursing de Grasse can do your case nothing but harm.'

At his quiet words the Canon's fury subsided as swiftly as it had arisen. He took a gulp of his drink and muttered, 'You are right. This is no fault of yours, and curses should be used only with solemn intent.'

'Exactly; so if you are hoping that de Grasse may yet pull the chestnuts out of the fire for you, it's silly to hamper his efforts with even the most casual vibrations of ill-wishing.'

Copely-Syle gave him a half-furtive glance, and asked, 'What do you know of such matters?'

'Oh, quite a bit.' C. B. shrugged the question aside. Having sown the seed, and feeling that enough had now passed between them for him to begin his probe without arousing suspicion, he said, 'I can understand your being annoyed at young Fountain having thrown a spanner in the works; but surely the girl being temporarily in prison scarcely justifies your getting into such a tizzy? The odds are that she'll be out before the end of the week; then de Grasse's boys should have little trouble in collecting her for you.'

'The end of the week!' Copely-Syle threw up his plump hands and the little veins in the whites of his eyes became suffused with blood from the intensity of his annoyance. 'That's no good! No earthly good! This matter is one of the utmost urgency. Surely I cannot have failed to make that plain to de Grasse?'

C. B. felt that he was getting warm, and nodded with becoming solemnness. 'Yes, I feel sure you did. That must be why he was so upset this morning. Of course, I'm not in on this thing, except as an old friend whom he knew he could trust to bring you an account of what has happened to date. I know only the bare outline of the affair—merely that you are anxious to get this young woman back to England. But why the frantic haste?'

'Because to-day is the 4th. I must have her here by the 6th.'

'Can't you possibly rearrange your plans so that a few days' delay won't make any difference?'

'You might as well suggest that I should attempt to stop the stars in their courses,' snapped the Canon. 'The 6th of March is her birthday. At nine forty-five that evening she comes of age. If she is not under my control by then the hopes that I have cherished for years will be dashed.'

'Oh, I see; this is a family affair and a case of a young woman having kicked over the traces,' remarked C. B., deliberately misunderstanding. 'Naturally, then, you are anxious to have her back in time to bury the hatchet on her twenty-first birthday. May I ask what relationship she bears you?'

'None; but I have known her since her birth, and am, in a sense, her guardian.'

'Has she given you this sort of trouble before, or behaved like a flighty type generally?'

'On the contrary. She has lived a very retired life, and shown no inclination to do otherwise.'

The quiet indifference of C. B.'s tone when he made his next remark did much to lessen its impertinence. 'Then, as she didn't run away with a man, there's some hope of her still being a virgin?'

The Canon's pale eyes narrowed a trifle and he said quickly, 'What leads you to speculate on that?'

'The thought automatically came into my mind that a combination of three times seven years and virginity have immense mystical significance. In fact, there is no state which even approaches its tremendous potence for good or evil; and that if . . . But no, this is your affair and nothing to do with me.'

'If what?' the Canon insisted.

'Why, that if the hesitant manner in which you admit your guardianship of this young woman is due to your status being unofficial; er—like, shall we say, one who prefers to remain in shadow . . .'

Copely-Syle had slowly risen to his feet. As he did so he seemed to increase in stature. His plump face lost all trace of babyishness. It looked old now, but extraordinarily strong and menacing. Suddenly he burst out harshly:

'You have said either too much or too little. Explain yourself, or it will be the worse for you.'

C. B.'s work brought him into touch with all types of tough customers; so, although he knew that he was on exceptionally dangerous ground, he remained outwardly imperturbable, and even smiled slightly as he replied:

'Hold your horses, Canon. There's nothing to get excited about. I thought I had made it clear that I'm not one of de Grasse's thugs, and that our association is simply that of two people who have been of use to one another from time to time. You have no need to fear that he suspects the reason for your interest in the girl and may start trying to blackmail you. I shouldn't have suspected it myself but for what you've just told me—and the fact that, although you may not remember it, we've met before.'

'Have we? Where?'

'I can't remember exactly, but I know it was with Aleister Crowley.'

'That charlatan! I hardly knew him.'

With the object of passing himself off as a brother initiate in the Black Art, C. B. had risked a shot in the dark. He had felt confident that anyone of Copley-Syle's age and interests must have come into contact with the infamous Crowley at one time or another, and, although the Canon's reactions were disappointing, he could not now go back on his statement. To get on firmer ground, he began to reminisce about the dead magician.

'If you had known Aleister as well as I did, you certainly wouldn't dub him a charlatan. Of course in his later years he couldn't have harmed a rabbit; everyone knew that. The poor old boy degenerated into a rather pathetic figure, and was reduced to sponging on all and sundry in order to keep body and soul together. But when he was a young man it was a very different story. He unquestionably had power, and there were very few things of this world that he could not get with it. Even as an undergraduate he showed how far advanced he was along the Left Hand Path. You must have heard about the Master of John's refusing to let him put on a bawdy Greek play, and how he revenged himself. He made a wax image of the

Master and took it out to a meadow one night with some friends when the moon was at the full. They formed the usual circle and Crowley recited the incantation. He was holding the needle and meant to jab it into the place that was the equivalent of the image's liver, but at the critical moment one of his pals got the wind up and broke the circle. Crowley's hand was deflected and the needle pierced the image's left ankle. That was a bit of luck for the Master of John's. Instead of dying of a tumour on the liver, he only slipped and broke his left ankle when coming down the college steps next day. Up to then Crowley's friends had regarded the whole business as a joke spiced with a vague sort of wickedness; but afterwards they were scared stiff of him, and naturally they were much too impressed to keep their mouths shut; so the facts are known beyond any shadow of doubt.'

Copely-Syle shrugged slightly. 'Of course, it's perfectly possible, and I do remember hearing about it now. But the story can be no more than hearsay as far as you are concerned. You are much too young to have been up at Cambridge with Crowley.'

'Oh yes. I didn't meet him till years later, when he was in middle life and at the height of his powers.' After pausing for a moment C.B. added the glib lie, 'I was initiated by him at the Abbaye de Thelema.'

'Really? I was under the impression that Crowley did no more than use his reputation as a mystic to lure young neurotics there, and kept the place going as a private brothel for his own enjoyment.'

'Most of its inmates were young people, and as the whole of his teaching was summed up in '*Do what thou wilt shall be the whole of the Law*' a state of general promiscuity naturally followed from it. New brothers and sisters soon lost their shyness, and after that he had little difficulty in persuading them to participate in sexual orgies when the stars were propitious for the performance of special rites. But you can take it from me that he knew his stuff, and that the perversions practised under his auspices were only a means to an end. You must know as well as I do that certain types of Satanic entity feed upon the emanations given out by humans while engaged in the baser forms of eroticism. As far as Crowley was concerned the orgies were simply the bait that lured such entities to the Abbaye and enabled him to gain power over them.'

The Canon had sat down again. He now appeared deeply interested as he said, 'You are really convinced that he conducted Satanic rituals with intent, and not merely performed some mumbo-jumbo as an excuse to possess a series of young women?'

'Each of his rituals was performed with a definite intention. Of that I am certain, and I know that many of them produced the desired result. He always insisted on everyone present behaving with the greatest solemnity, and when celebrating pagan rites he was most impressive. He could even render the receiving of the *osculam infame* a gesture of some dignity, and his memory was prodigious; so he experienced no difficulty at all in reciting the lines of the Roman communion backwards.'

'In Christian countries there are few ceremonies more potent than the Black Mass; but from my memory of him I am much surprised to learn from you that he ever proved capable of celebrating that mystery.'

'I have never seen it better done,' C.B. averred seriously. 'Although, of course, he was not able to fulfil the technical requirements in their entirety.'

'You mean that among the women neophytes there was never a virgin who could be used as an altar?'

'No, I didn't mean that. It's true that on most occasions he had to make do with young women who had already been seduced, but twice while I was there he managed to get hold of a virgin. And naturally there was no difficulty about holy wafers for desecration and that sort of thing. I was simply referring to the fact that to be one hundred per cent potent the celebrant should have been a Roman Catholic priest, and Crowley had never been ordained.'

'Quite, quite. That was a pity, but would be overlooked if suitable propitiation were made to the Prince by way of blood offerings. Did Crowley—er—ever achieve the apotheosis in that direction?'

'I can't say for certain. In medieval times life was held so cheap that adepts such as Gilles de Rais could decimate a dozen parishes for the furtherance of their magical operations, and no one powerful enough to interfere felt sufficiently strongly about it to do so. But in these days matters are very different. The Italian police must have had a pretty shrewd idea of the sort of thing that went on at the Abbaye; but they were a tolerant lot and were well bribed to keep their ideas to themselves, so they never gave us any trouble. I'm sure they would have, though, had they had the least grounds to suppose that we were offering up human sacrifices. Usually Crowley used cats or goats, and once I was present when a monkey was crucified upside down. After I had left I heard rumours that one or two children had disappeared from villages round about; but I'm inclined to suppose that was simply malicious gossip put about by Crowley's enemies.'

The pale eyes of Copely-Syle had a faraway look as he murmured thoughtfully, 'Ah, for the culminating act in such rituals there is nothing so efficacious as the warm blood of an unweaned child.'

C.B. had to bite hard on the stem of his pipe to repress a shudder; but he felt that he was now well on the way to achieving his object in going there, which was to establish such an apparent community of interests with the Canon that the latter would voluntarily give himself away. For a few moments they both sat staring silently into the fire, then the Canon said:

'From all you say, Crowley must have reached at least the degree of Magus, if not Ipsissimus. What I cannot understand is how by the middle nineteen-thirties, when I met him, he should have degenerated into an impotent windbag, incapable of impressing anyone except a handful of credulous old women.'

'That is easily explained. It was that unfortunate affair in Paris towards the end of the nineteen-twenties. You are right in supporting that before that he ranked as an Ipsissimus, but that night he was cast right back across the Abyss. In fact, he was stripped of all his powers and afterwards the most callow neophyte could have bested him in an astral conflict.'

'What an awful thing to happen to an adept,' said the Canon a shade uneasily. 'Did he then recant and offer to make a full confession in exchange for being accepted back into the Church? I can imagine no other act deserving of such terrible punishment.'

'Oh no, it was nothing like that. It was simply that his ambition was so great that he over-reached himself. If he could have bent Pan to his will he would have been the most powerful being on earth. With Pan's pipes playing as he directed he could have made even governments dance to his tune. He attempted to master Pan, but he wasn't quite strong enough; so he paid the price of failure: that's all.'

'I find this most interesting,' said Copely-Syle in a low voice. 'Do you happen to know any details of what took place?'

'Yes. As a matter of fact I was still one of his disciples, so with him at the time.' C.B. was on safer ground now, as he had actually had a first-hand account of this grim affair from one of Crowley's young men, and he went on:

'The attempt took place in Paris. Crowley made up a coven, so including himself there were thirteen of us; and in this instance we were naturally all males. We were staying at an hotel on the Left Bank. The proprietor was an initiate, and it was quite a small place; so we took the whole premises for the night, and all the servants were got rid of from mid-day to mid-day. There was a big room at the top of the house which seemed just the thing for the purpose. In the afternoon we moved out every scrap of furniture and cleaned it with the utmost thoroughness. Then in the evening all of us assisted at the purifactory rites; but fortunately as it turned out, Crowley had decided that only his senior disciple, a chap who had taken the name of McAleister, should assist him at the actual evocation.

'At ten o'clock the rest of us robed them, then left them there, and Crowley locked the door behind us. He had already issued strict injunctions that whatever sounds we might hear coming from the room, even if they were cries for help, we were in no circumstances to attempt to enter it; as such cries might be a trick of Pan's made in an endeavour to evade him, and any interruption of the ritual would render the spell abortive. We had fasted all day, so our associate, the landlord, had prepared an excellent cold buffet for us downstairs in the dining-room. It wasn't a very gay meal, as all of us were aware of the magnitude of the task the Master Therion had set himself. We had great confidence in his powers, but it was probably several centuries since any adept had had the audacity to attempt to summon the Horned God in person, so we were naturally a bit nervy.

'It was just on midnight when we heard the first noises upstairs. There were thumpings and shouts, then all Hell seemed to break loose. Piercing screams were mingled with what sounded like sacks of potatoes being flung about. We had the impression that the whole building was rocking. In fact it was, as the chandelier above us began to swing, the glasses jingled on the sideboard and a picture fell from the wall with a loud crash. It was like being in the middle of an earthquake, and the room in which we were sitting had suddenly become icy cold.

'We had all been inmates of the Abbaye at one time or another and had passed pretty severe tests in standing up to Satanic manifestations, so we were by no means a chicken-hearted lot. But on this occasion we were seized by abject terror, and none of us made the least effort to hide it. We just sat there, white to the gills and paralysed by the thought that at any second the terrible Being up above might descend on us.

'After a few moments the pandemonium subsided, and we tried to pull ourselves together. With our teeth chattering from the cold, we debated whether we had not better ignore Crowley's orders and go up to find out what had happened. But the room began to get warm again and that, together with the continued silence, led us to hope that Crowley had won his battle and succeeded in binding Pan. If so, for us to have gone in then might still have ruined everything, and Crowley's rage would have been beyond all reckoning. Knowing his powers, none of us felt inclined to risk the sort of punishment he might have inflicted on us for disobeying him; so we decided to let matters be, and I for one was not sorry about that.

'We were all too scared to face the solitude of going to bed, and started to drink in an attempt to keep our spirits up; but that didn't work. Somehow we couldn't even get tight, and we sat on hour after hour, hardly speaking.

'At last that miserable night ended. Dawn came and we began to hope that Crowley would soon come down, his fat face beaming with triumph, to make our fears seem ridiculous; but he didn't. We waited till seven o'clock. There was still not a sound from the top of the house, so by then we felt that we were no longer justified in evading the issue. All the same, we didn't exactly run upstairs, as by that time we were feeling pretty apprehensive about what we might find when we got there. For a moment or two all eleven of us stood huddled on the top of the landing, listening; but with the early morning noises coming up from the street we could not definitely make out any sound coming from the room. Someone suggested that after their exhausting ordeal Crowley and McAleister might still be sleeping, and the idea gave us fresh hope for the moment; but another fellow knocked hard on the door, and there was no reply. That left us with no alternative but to break down the door.'

15

CHAMBER OF HORRORS

Like the good *raconteur* that he was, C.B. paused to knock out his pipe. Copely-Syle jerked his head forward and exclaimed in a breathless whisper, 'Go on, man! Go on! What did you find?'

C.B. looked him straight in the eyes, and, certain of his facts on this final point, said quietly, 'McAleister was dead. He was stretched out on his back with his arms flung wide, absolutely rigid, just as though he had been electrocuted, and with an appalling look of stark horror on his face such as I never wish to see again. Crowley's pontifical robes were scattered in ribbons about the floor. It looked as if they had been ripped from his body by some ferocious animal. He was crouching in a corner naked. He didn't know any of us. He had become a gibbering idiot.'

The Canon took a quick gulp at his drink and muttered, 'Horrible, horrible! Have you any idea what went wrong?'

'No; none of us had. We could only suppose that McAleister had been unable to take it, and cracked at the critical moment. Crowley was in a private asylum outside Paris for six months. He was very lucky to recover his sanity, and afterwards he would never speak of the affair. In fact, I doubt very much if he had any definite memory of what had happened. But you'll understand now why from that time on he seemed like a washed-out rag, and why when you met him he entirely failed to impress you.'

'Yes,' the Canon nodded. 'I was not introduced to him until the early 'thirties, and what you have told me explains the disappointment I felt at the time. But we have not yet recalled where it was that I met you.'

Again C.B. was on dangerous ground, but he knew that Crowley had spent much of the 'thirties in London, and that the better-off mystics preferred the privacy of houses to living in flats; so he punted for that area of the capital which then had a greater number of moderate-sized private houses than any other, and said, 'For the life of me I can't recall the occasion definitely, but I have the impression that it was at a party held out Regent's Park way, or in St John's Wood.'

'Ah!' said the Canon. 'Then it must have been at Mocata's house: at least at a house just behind Lord's that he made his headquarters for a while; although I believe it was actually owned by a wealthy young Jew who had become a disciple of his.'

This was the acid test. C.B. was acutely aware that, if Copely-Syle entertained any suspicions of his *bona fides*, in the question of where they might have met before lay the perfect opportunity to set a trap. He had only to suggest a place in which he had never been and, if his visitor accepted it, unmask him as a fraud. But C.B. felt it reasonable to hope that their talk of Aleister Crowley had gone a long way to still any early doubts about himself that the Canon might have held, and that his suggestion was free from guile. Gambling boldly on that, and using his excellent knowledge of London even to gild the lily a little, he replied:

'Of course that must have been it. And unless my memory's failing me again the house was in Medina Place.'

'That is so,' the Canon nodded. 'I went there on a number of occasions and on none of them were there less than twenty people present. That is why I failed to recall you at first sight. There was an observatory at the top of the house, and it proved most useful for the performance of certain rituals.'

'It was Crowley who took me there, but only once.' C.B. hedged cautiously to avoid being questioned on how well he knew this Mr Mocata; but his host went on reminiscently:

'Poor Mocata; he too fell by the wayside through attempting too much. That must have been shortly after we met, as the house at St John's Wood was his last address. He was engaged in a search for the Talisman of Set, but he came into conflict with a White Magician of greater power than himself, and was found dead one morning outside a house called Cardinal's Folly, in Worcestershire. The coroner's jury brought it in as heart, of course; but I've no doubt at all that it was the rebound of an unsuccessful curse sent out by himself that killed him.'

'I trust,' said C.B., 'that the work you are engaged upon is not of such a dangerous nature.'

Copely-Syle's light hazel eyes lit up again, and now held a fanatical gleam. 'There is always danger in great magical operations; but I should have no fear whatever of the outcome if only this accursed girl had not eluded me. Whatever it costs, whatever risks are run, she must be in my hands by the evening of the 6th.'

'You have less than forty-eight hours left to work in; and as long as the French authorities keep her in prison I don't see how de Grasse can get hold of her for you.'

Standing up, the Canon began to walk agitatedly up and down. 'You are right. De Grasse can no nothing now except under my direction. I must handle this myself.'

'How do you propose to set about it?'

'I shall fly out to France to-morrow. Some of de Grasse's thugs will at least be able to help from their knowledge of the prisons and the warders.'

'In so short a time it is not going to be easy to plan an escape—or rather, the even more difficult job of an abduction—as it is unlikely now that she would be willing to leave prison with any of de Grasse's people. It may take days of cautious enquiry before one or more jailers who are susceptible to bribery can be seduced, and then one would have to wait until it was their turn to go on night duty.'

'No, no!' The Canon's voice was sharp with impatience. 'This is a case for the use of occult weapons; only so can the time factor be overcome. I shall telephone de Grasse to find out the names of the jailers who will be on duty to-morrow night. Then he must get me some things belonging to them. Nail clippings or hair are too much to hope for at such short notice, but it should not be difficult to steal some of their soiled linen; unwashed pants or pyjamas would serve quite well. With those to work on I could easily bemuse their minds and make them temporarily my servants. As for the girl, after sunset she is ruled by Asmodeus, so will do as she is directed.'

Having let the Canon know that Christina was in prison, a few hours before he would otherwise have learned it, had enabled C.B. to fish very skilfully for the steps her pursuer would take in consequence. Now that he knew them he was able to make a bid to counter them in advance; and, being no mean psychologist, he put a price on the bait in the trap he was laying so that the Canon would be less likely to suspect it to be one. With a thoughtful air, he remarked:

'I came back from the South this morning only on account of some urgent personal business I had to attend to in London. I tackled that before coming down here, and I am flying out again to-morrow. I have quite enough experience to perform the minor magics you have in mind, so could save you the trip—if you cared to make it worth my while.'

The fat little Canon halted in front of him. 'That certainly is an idea, as de Grasse would give you the same co-operation as he would me. But are you absolutely certain you could do that which is necessary? Remember, should you fail there will be no second chance; for if we do not get her out of prison by to-morrow night there will be no time left to transport her to England before her birthday is over. No! I dare not risk it. Much as I dislike air travel, I must fly down to-morrow and cast these spells myself.'

'Just as you like.' C.B. shrugged with apparent indifference. 'But I performed just the type of operation you have in mind successfully several times during the war. During the latter part of it I was working in France for the Gestapo, and I managed to get several of their agents out of the clutches of the de Gaullists by such means.'

'What grade do you hold?' asked the Canon uncertainly.

'I have eight circles and three squares.'

'Really! Then you are past the Abyss.'

'Yes. I passed it on Walpurgis Night, 1946.'

'As a Magister Templi you could hardly fail. But what did you mean by "making it worth your while" to act for me? With such powers you surely cannot be short of money?'

C.B. shook his head. 'It is not that, and it will cost you nothing. What I had in mind was this. Virgins of three times seven years are never particularly easy to come by, and to procure one for use on the night of her twenty-first birthday, when nearly every girl is given a party of some sort, makes the success of such a quest a matter of extreme difficulty. That such a combination is essential to the completion of your work tells me that you must be engaged on a magical operation of quite exceptional importance. As an initiate of twenty-five years' standing I am naturally interested now only in the most advanced types of conjuration; but in those I am very interested indeed. Would it be too much to ask you to tell me the end towards which you are working and, perhaps, when we have got the girl, allow me to act as your assistant in the final transubstantiation?'

Copely-Syle thought for a moment, then he replied. 'Were you still below the Abyss I would not consider it fitting to disclose to you such formula as I must use; neither would I risk allowing you to make one in a coven for such a ceremony were I not an Ipsissimus, and free to choose my associates within certain limits. But since you are an Adept of the S.S. with only two circles to gain and two squares to lose before reaching the highest plane of the Order, I see nothing against acceding to your request. I should warn you, though, that this is a matter which it would be sheer madness for anyone of a lesser degree than Ipsissimus to attempt, for it is the greatest of all the Great Works.'

'You must refer to the achieving of Oneness with God,' said C.B., stroking back his grey hair.

'Yes. No one would deny that the transmutation of base metals into gold, or the distillation of the Elixir that will renew youth and prolong life indefinitely, are Great Works; but for many years I have devoted myself to a greater. I have now reached a point where only one thing is necessary for me to become the equal of God. On the 6th of March I, Augustus Copely-Syle, will also create Life.'

'Homunculi?' murmured C.B., suppressing a start.

The Canon bared his ugly, blackened teeth in a smile. 'Yes, homunculi; and one of them at least shall be a creature capable of thought and speech.'

C.B. was swiftly recalling all he could remember about this strange and awe-inspiring subject. There were many legends of minor deities having transformed inanimate objects into human beings, and the experts on folklore now recognized that such legends were usually race memories of priest-kings and witch-doctors who had actually lived in pre-historic times. No doubt during many generations of repetition the story-teller's art had embellished these legends to such a degree that in their final form they bore little resemblance to the original happenings; but the possibility remained that some of them at least had been based on more than entirely factless imagination.

From the earliest historical times, through all the great civilizations of antiquity, and in the classic Graeco-Roman era, the practice of magic had been not merely widespread, but accepted as the proper occupation for every priesthood, and a natural subject for study by everyone with any pretence to education. In consequence, among the clay tablets of Babylonia, the papyrus of Egypt and the esoteric writings of the great nations of the Mediterranean, ample evidence could be found of attempts to create spontaneous generation, often with claims to varying degrees of success.

The spread of Christianity had driven the old religions underground; but it had never quite succeeded in smothering the knowledge gained by countless generations of Pagan priests, who had based their teachings on their observations of natural laws rather than on blind faith. Much was lost until, after a thousand years, there came the revolt against the Church's power to fetter men's minds, and the age of reason ushered in that of scientific investigation. Even then, many secrets known to the ancients had not been recovered; yet through the centuries others had been handed down and, not infrequently, put to the test by bold men and women who were prepared to risk being burnt at the stake as the price of acquiring power, riches or wisdom.

Among those who had trafficked in these forbidden mysteries was a Count von Küffstein, and C.B. remembered reading in an old book of the experiments he had carried out in the year 1775 at his castle in the Tyrol. With the aid of an Italian Abbé named Geloni, the Count had succeeded in producing ten living creatures who resembled small men and women. They had, however, been more in the nature of fish than mammals, as they were incapable of living for long in anything so rarefied as air, and had to be kept in large strong glass jars that were filled with liquid. Once a week the jars were emptied and refilled with pure rain water, to which certain chemicals were added, and human blood on which the homunculi fed. That they had been capable of thought and emotion was instanced by perhaps the strangest of all love stories, for one of the males was said to have escaped from his jar and died from exhaustion while attempting to get into the jar that imprisoned the prettiest of the females.

The evidence for these extraordinary happenings was given unusual weight by the fact that they had not been recorded by the Count himself, but in a secret diary kept by his butler, which had not come to light until long after the events described; also, it was further stated that, among others, such reputable noblemen as Count Max Lemberg and Count Franz-Joseph von Thun had visited the castle and vouched for having examined the homunculi themselves.

C.B. also recalled that the great German scientist, Paracelus von Hohenheim, who had been the first doctor to give his lectures in the vulgar tongue at the University of Basle, had expressed himself as entirely satisfied with his experiments in imbuing inanimate matter with life.

All these thoughts raced through C.B.'s mind in a few seconds as he sat with his long legs stretched out in front of him, staring at the round, excited face of the Canon. His reading told him that this fantastic thing was just remotely possible, as there was too much evidence for it to be shrugged aside as utter nonsense; yet he considered it much more likely that this evil little man was mad.

'You don't believe me, eh?' Copely-Syle's thick underslip was thrust forth in an aggressive grin. 'Well, come with me and you shall see.'

Turning abruptly, he led the way out of the room and down the corridor connecting the new with an old part of the house, till they reached a heavy iron door built into a low stone archway that must have been many centuries old. Taking a small key attached to a long gold snake-chain from his pocket, he inserted it in a modern Chubb lock, gave a quick turn, pressed, and the weighty door swung silently open.

They were standing at the top if a flight of stone steps, and C.B. found himself looking down into as strange and eerie an apartment as it was possible to imagine. At first sight it appeared to be a chapel, but as its floor was a good six feet below ground-level it could, perhaps, be more accurately described as a crypt. A double row of slender pillars supported its roof. At its far end, fifty feet away, three broad shallow steps led up to an altar, now partially hidden by flanking curtains. On it a candle burned before a shadowy something that C.B. could not make out. This solitary candle apart, the place was lit only by the reddish glow coming from a large furnace to the right of the flight of steps, at the top of which they stood.

As the vaguely-seen furnishings of the chamber became clearer, C.B. felt as though he had been transported back to the Middle Ages, for before him were spread out all the paraphernalia of an alchemist's laboratory. To his right stood the open furnace with its scalloped canopy, funnel-shaped chimney, and iron pull-handle for working its bellows: to his left was a great astrolabe and a human skeleton with wired joints such as are used to teach medical students anatomy. In the centre of the chamber were four stout oak refectory tables. On them stood many strange-shaped bottles, balances and retorts, and beneath the nearest showed the outline of a mummy-case. Behind the pillars, in one side aisle, stood a line of what looked like huge round tea-cosies, and in the other, only dimly seen, what appeared to be a number of large hen-coops. The only items lacking to complete the traditional picture were a stuffed alligator and other fearsome reptiles hanging from the roof; yet even this type of adjunct to the wizard's art was not entirely lacking, as the scampering of little feet and a faint whimpering, coming from the coops and a row of cages beyond them, told of living things imprisoned there for the magician's use.

C.B. had hardly gathered a general impression of the place, and taken one step down, before the Canon first closed and locked the door behind them, then switched on a row of electric lights.

Now every detail of the interior could be seen, and it instantly became obvious that in addition to being a 'puffer's workshop' this ancient half-crypt was used as a Satanic Temple. On one of the curtains which partially shut off the semi circular bay containing the altar there was embroidered in rich colours the figure of a rearing goat, on the other the figure of a woman who had seven breasts and a serpent's tail. Between them the altar could now be clearly seen. Against a beautiful backcloth showing Adam and Eve in relation to the Macrocosm, a black and broken crucifix stood out. Nailed to it, head uppermost, which in this instance was the equivalent of upside down, hung a large bat. Upon the altar lay a jewelled sword, a vellum-bound book and a gold, gem-encrusted chalice. The front of the altar was covered with cloth of gold, into which were woven semi-precious stones forming the ten signs of the Cabala; but in places the fabric showed brownish stains, suggestive of dried blood. The solitary candle that burned in front of the desecrated crucifix was black.

Feeling that some remark was called for, and knowing that in no circumstances must he show surprise or disgust, C.B. said, 'You have splendid quarters here. I don't think that I've ever seen better.'

'I was lucky to find them,' replied the Canon. 'It is extremely difficult to acquire a comfortable house which has adjacent to it an altar that was consecrated for many centuries; and, of course, the use of it enormously increases the potency of my operations. I chanced to hear of it shortly after the first world war. For many years it had been lived in only by a succession of caretakers. As it was the abode of quite a number of elementals, I got it for a song.'

While he was speaking he turned to the furnace and began to make it up.

It was similar to those used by old-fashioned blacksmiths—a great open bed of coke in an iron trough nearly five feet square. By a few puffs from the bellows the lower layers of fuel could soon be made white-hot, but now they gave out only a reddish glow that shone here and there through cracks in the layers of still-black fuel above them. The Canon spread a new layer of coke on top, blotting out the glow entirely, then damped it down for the night by spraying cold water on it.

As soon as he had finished, he led the way over to one of the big tables. Pinned out upon it were what amounted to a number of blue-prints, each showing in the greatest detail the structure of various portions of the human body. Beyond them were rows of glass-stoppered jars containing pieces of skins, muscles, ligaments, arteries, kidneys, livers and other viscera pickled in spirit. The sight of them told C.B. that whatever element of magic there might be in this horrible process it must be basically, at least, scientific; and a moment later Copely-Syle confirmed his thoughts by saying:

'To you, as a Magister Templi, I need hardly refer to the fact that magic is no more than the application of natural laws as yet unrecognized by all but a very limited number of people, such as ourselves. In the initial stages of my work I do nothing of which a moderately intelligent biologist is not capable, given the necessary materials and a considerable degree of patience. Even in the more advanced stages there is little that a fully trained scientist would find difficult to follow and imitate. In fact, were I prepared to give my secrets to the world and the masses could be prevented from sabotaging such work on account of their childish prejudices, there is no reason whatever why an unlimited number of homunculi should not be manufactured.'

C.B. suppressed a shudder at the idea of a world in which even a limited proportion of the population were soulless robots, liable at any moment to behave like homicidal maniacs should they escape from the control of their creators. In an attempt to counteract the horror he felt, he remarked lightly:

'Wouldn't that lead to virgins of twenty-one soon becoming in short supply—that is, if the assistance of one is needed for the creation of each homunculus?'

Taking his observation quite seriously, the Canon replied, 'To begin with, yes; for, like mules, the early types of homunculi would prove incapable of breeding. But that is a deficiency which science could undoubtedly find a way to make good in due course. In the meantime, a government such as that of Soviet Russia, which is not hampered by the scruples and inhibitions of its people, might consider it well worth its while to segregate for several years large numbers of female children, in order to ensure their retaining their virginity until they reached an age when they could be used for the production of homunculi. You see, for any country bent on making war the process offers a new weapon of inestimable value. As suicide troops these fabricated beings would prove enormously superior to the most patriotic humans, because they would require no food other than the blood from the bodies of their enemies, and under the hypnotic direction of their masters they would carry out their allotted tasks with the same ruthless efficiency as machines.'

The hair on the back of C.B.'s neck prickled as he listened to this ghastly conception. Judged by all standards, moral or divine, he considered Copely-Syle to be criminal lunatic, who should be shot with even less scruple than a mad dog; but that did not alter the fact that he displayed none of the symptoms which made a man certifiable. On the contrary, his conscientious research and logical reasoning showed him to be possessed of an unquestionable, if perverted, sanity. All C.B. could think of to mutter was:

'The Atlanteans did as you suggest, didn't they? And to people like ourselves it is common knowledge that it was their magicians producing large numbers of homunculi which led the White Powers to destroy the whole continent of Atlantis by fire and flood.'

'True; but the human race was much younger in those days. In the past century, working through Communism, which openly denies all manifestations of God, Prince Lucifer has secured a far firmer grip upon it than he had then. With the minds of nearly half the population of the world attuned in opposition to the so-called Light, I do not think the Brethren of the Right Hand Path would now prove strong enough to bring about another deluge.'

The plump little black-clad man paused for a second, then shrugged and went on, 'However, it is for the Lord of this World himself to decide when and how we should give battle. For us, it is sufficient that we are working towards His ends, and that our reward will be great. Come now and see my contribution to our Master's business.'

As he spoke he led the way across to the row of huge, conical tea-cosies. Each of them stood about four feet high, and as he removed one at the end of the line, C.B. saw that its thick padded material had concealed a great glass jar over two feet in diameter.

Again C.B.'s hackles rose, and, in spite of all that had gone before, he could hardly believe his eyes. In the clear liquid that filled the giant bottle was a naked female monster. She was about the height of a child of eight, yet far broader, having big breasts and thick thighs; but from the crutch downwards her legs were tied, and ended in tiny tapering feet, so that she resembled a squat and hideous mermaid. Her flesh was pink. There were no hairs on any part of her body and she was entirely bald. As he stared at her she slowly opened a pair of red-rimmed lashless eyes and blinked at him.

Fighting down his disgust, C.B. uttered the sort of exclamations of astonishment and interest that he knew were expected of him, then he asked, 'Will her legs always be tied, or can you perform some operation, magical or otherwise, to separate them?'

The Canon shook his silvery head. 'No; about that there is nothing I can do. As you will see, most of the others are also imperfect. I assemble the basic ingredients for the creation of flesh, muscle, bone, blood and glands, but it is impossible to forecast how they will develop. All I can do is to improve my blends by experience, and this endeavour to control unnatural or extraneous growths. These I keep only in order to record changes in their development and to ascertain how long they will live.' Replacing the cover, he removed those of the other jars in turn.

One male had only stumps where its arms should have been; another was much smaller than the rest, but had an enormous organ of generation. Among them were an hermaphrodite, a female with two heads and another whose head rose grotesquely straight out of her shoulders without the least trace of a neck. Only one other was bald and the males all had sparse beards. The faces of all of them were hideous and their gaze held a stony malevolence. Only the last had no obvious deformity.

Like the first, she was a squat and repulsive-looking female. Unlike several of the others, she had grown both hair and nails, but the latter, which protruded from thick, stubby fingers, looked more like talons. Her mouth was very large and she kept opening and shutting it slowly in the same manner as a fish. When the cover was first removed from her jar she appeared to be asleep, but almost instantly she awoke and became imbued with horrid life, grimacing at them and clawing furiously at the glass as though she would rend and devour them if she could.

Copely-Syle stood there smiling at her, obviously immensely proud at having produced this evil travesty of a human being, and after a moment he murmured, 'Behold the child of my creation, who is to be the first of our new race. Another forty-odd hours and the final mystic rite will render her capable of breathing air as easily as we do; then she will be able to come forth into the world. Although her womb will never bear fruit, she is destined to be the forerunner of many of her kind; so is the Lord Satan's answer to Eve.'

'I count it a great privilege to have seen her still, as it were, in a state of gestation,' replied C. B. 'But if she continues in her present mood, aren't you afraid that she will give you great trouble when once she is out of her bottle?'

'No. In this stage she is still an animal, so it is quite natural that she should display an animal's resentment of confinement; but when she emerges she will be a different creature. You will recall that God blew into the nostrils of Adam to give him Life, but He did not blow into the nostrils of the animals He had made; so Life in that sense was something quite other than the capacity to move in obedience to instincts. The rite that I shall perform on the 6th is analogous to that final act of creation which differentiated man from beasts, so it will bring about a fundamental change in her. Besides, in Ellen Beddows we are fortunate in having a young woman of mild and pleasant disposition.'

'I see; you are, then, assuming that her personality will exert an influence on the formation of a personality in this creature?'

'I think it is bound to have some effect, as the homunculus will be infused with her spirit.'

C. B. swallowed hard. He had thought it certain that the Canon intended to perform a Black Mass on Christina's body, and that probably she would be subjected to certain physical obscenities afterwards. Unless she was hypnotized and rendered unconscious first, the shock would be appalling and perhaps even result in temporarily unbalancing her mind. That would have been bad enough, but what the Black Magician actually implied was infinitely worse. It was nothing less than the drawing forth of her spirit from her body, and, while it was absent, there was the awful possibility that some elemental might take possession of her permanently, by day as well as by night, turning her into a lunatic. After a moment he asked:

'How long will the ceremony take?'

'No great while,' replied the other placidly. 'I shall, of course, first celebrate Mass, with the girl's body lying on the altar. After that come the recitation of the formula of the Holy Grail, and that of the Temple of Solomon the King, for the achievement of Unity with the Cosmos and as signifying the completion of the Great Work. The jar containing the homunculus will be placed on the floor on the left of the altar, close up to it, and the young woman's body will be so arranged that her head dangles down off the end of the altar over the open top of the jar. Having uttered the Gnostic Name of the Seven Vowels to evoke the Soul of Nature, and called upon Our Lady of Babylon as my witness, it will remain only for me to slit the girl's throat with the sacrificial knife and ensure that her life-blood, which will carry her spirit with it, shall flow into the jar.'

Few men had such a wide knowledge of unorthodox crime as C. B. In the course of his work he had broken up secret societies, freed a Cabinet Minister from blackmail, supervised the execution of a spy in the Tower of London, unravelled plots involving a dozen political murders, and, on occasion, when convinced that it was in the best interests of his country to do so, taken life himself without legal warrant. But never had he come across anything so utterly heinous as this project for the cold-blooded murder of an innocent girl. For him it was a new experience to feel faint; yet he did so now as he visualised Christina with her head half severed from her body, and the blood pouring from her neck to feed this loathsome, fiendish monstrosity that, barely a yard away, was still glaring at him with a hatred beyond any of which even the most savage animal was capable.

His tongue clove to the roof of his mouth. He could no longer think of anything to say. Yet he knew that if he allowed the Canon to sense the horror he felt it would immediately expose him as an impostor. In vain he strove to get a hold over himself so that he might cope with the situation. His brain refused to work. Suitable words of understanding and approval simply would not come. Then, at the very moment that he thought his sick repulsion of the whole frightful business must become obvious, he was given an unexpected chance to conceal it.

A heavy knocking sounded on the iron door. The Canon stepped forward and quickly replaced the cover over the homunculus, turned on his heel, and hurried across to the steps. C. B. took a deep breath and, whipping out his handkerchief, swiftly wiped away the tell-tale perspiration that had broken out on his forehead. As Copely-Syle opened the door the flutter of a white robe disclosed the presence of his Egyptian servant on the far side of it. The two of them exchanged a few low-voiced sentences in Arabic, then the Canon glanced over his shoulder and said, 'Excuse me, please. I shall be back quite soon,' Stepping through the door, he locked it behind him, leaving C. B. alone in that chamber of horrors.

Within a few moments he had fully regained his composure and his mind was once more working with its accustomed lucidity. A glance at his wrist-watch showed him that it was close on half-past ten, so he had been in the house for an hour and a quarter. The time, he felt, had been remarkably well spent, as he had achieved far more than he had hoped to do when he had, on the spur of the moment, decided to make this reconnaissance. He had found out not only that even prison was no certain sanctuary for Christina, but also the steps the Canon would take to get her out, and by offering himself as their instigator had now ensured that they would not be taken. By the time Copely-Syle discovered that his visitor had been an impostor it would be too late for him to make the arrangements necessary to secure Christina's release from prison during the night of the 5th, and if she remained there until the 6th it would then be too late for him to get her back to England on her birthday. More, by his skilful winning of the Black Magician's confidence, C. B. had become privy to the foul and terrible operations in which he was engaged, and had a good prospect of being able to render them abortive.

As he looked again at the row of huge tea-cosies he was tempted to do so now, by using one of the furnace irons to smash the jars, and so end the horrid, unnatural life that squirmed and grimaced within them. But to have done so would have jeopardized his chances of saving Christina, and, by disclosing to their evil creator that he had been discovered, enable him to escape retribution. Feeling that he had the situation well in hand, and now had only to maintain his imposture a little longer in order to clean up the whole revolting business in a satisfactory manner, C.B. quickly decided against precipitate action, and once more began to glance about him.

Now that he was alone his attention was again caught by the shuffling, squeaks and low whining that came from the other side of the crypt. Walking round the big tables, he crossed to the aisle in which stood the row of coops and cages. Behind the pillars the light was dim, but when he got to within a few feet of them he could see that each contained an animal, bird or reptile. There were black cocks and white hens, bats, toads and doves, evidently for use as sacrifices. Then he suddenly became conscious of a new horror.

The birds and reptiles were free, but the animals were not. All of them were crouching or lying in unnatural positions with their limbs pinioned. There were dogs, cats, rabbits, a badger, a mongoose and four monkeys: all were alive, but all had had some operation performed upon them. Many had had their genitals removed, some had had legs amputated, others lacked eyes or had had their claws cut out. From the bandages of several of them small bottles and test tubes protruded, into which was draining the fluid from their wounds.

At this heart-rending and nauseating sight C.B. was filled with a furious rage. Again the impulse came to him to take immediate action and put these miserable little creatures out of their agony. But again he fought down his personal feelings from the realization of how much was at stake and must be forfeited if he disclosed his hand prematurely.

How many minutes he stood staring with a sick feeling at these small martyrs to Evil he could not have said, but a slight sound behind him caused him to swing round. Unheard and unseen by him, the Canon had re-entered the crypt and was standing in his rear beside the nearest pillar.

Still the picture of a benign and erudite prelate of another age, Copely-Syle was smiling as he said, 'I see that you are interested in my pets?'

In spite of his age and silver hair, C.B. itched to pound his smooth face into a jelly; but he stuffed his hands deep into his trouser pockets, and twisted his lips into a semblance of a grin, as the Canon went on blandly:

'They are indispensable to my work. Ample quantities of gland secretions are an essential in the production of homunculi. It is regrettable that I should have had to make do with animals, and it is that, of course, which accounts for the ill-proportioned lumpishness of my creations. Had I had human beings at my disposal I could have produced men and women fair of face and shapely in form. But the day will come. Oh yes, the day will come when having seen my prototype the people for whom it has been designed will readily supply me with more suitable materials.'

Carefully controlling his voice, C.B. said, 'I take it you refer to the people in the Kremlin?'

The Canon nodded. 'Who else? For is it not into their hands that the Lord Satan has placed the greatest power to serve him? I have no doubt whatever that they will be most interested when I submit my masterpiece to them.'

For a moment he stood there, his pale eyes glowing with a fanatic light. Then they dimmed a little and he said with a swift change of manner, 'But now that I have shown you my great secret we have no more to do here for the moment. It is still pouring with rain, and I do not know what arrangements you have made. If you prefer not to face the elements, I should be happy to offer you a bed here for the night.'

'Thank you.' C.B. shook his head. 'It is very kind of you, but I arranged to pick up a taxi in the village, and I've booked a room at the Red Lion in Colchester. I think I had better go back there, as I must catch the first train up to London in the morning.'

'Just as you wish.' Copely-Syle turned and took a few paces towards the door; then he halted in his tracks and exclaimed, 'Ah! There is one thing I nearly forgot. Since we are to work together, and you are to do that which there is to do on my behalf down at Nice to-morrow night, it is only fitting that before you depart we should pledge one another in the cup of Brotherhood.'

C.B. was most reluctant to participate in any such rite, quite apart from the fact that he expected it to entail his having to swallow at least a few sips of some horrid brew; but he saw no way in which he could evade the proposal without arousing belated suspicions in his host's mind; so, comforting himself with the thought that within a few minutes now he would be out of this den of iniquity, he agreed with tactful promptness.

Leading the way to the altar, the Canon took the gold chalice from it: then he went to a cabinet nearby, produced a wicker-covered bottle and poured about a wineglassful of its contents into the chalice. Returning to the altar he genuflected three times before the crucified bat, elevated the chalice, and in a sonorous voice chanted a few sentences of abracadabra in what C.B. took to be Hebrew. Putting the chalice to his lips, he tilted back his head, held it so for a moment, lowered it, and wiped the moisture from his mouth with the back of his free hand; then, with a courtly bow, he handed the vessel to C.B.

Having bowed in reply, C.B. lifted it in turn and took a small sip. To his surprise it was no Devil's potion distilled from frogs' testicles and newts' tails, but a rich wine highly flavoured with aromatic spices; so he took a small mouthful before lowering the chalice.

As Copely-Syle stretched out a hand for the vessel he saw that a good part of the wine remained in it. His eyes seemed to flash with suspicion, and he exclaimed angrily:

'You, a Magister Templi, should know better than to leave unconsumed wine that has been offered as a sacrament.'

To cover his blunder C.B. replied swiftly, 'I had not intended to leave any. I was taking my time to savour this beautiful concoction.' Then he lifted the vessel again and emptied it.

As he lowered the chalice a second time the Canon began to laugh. It was not a pleasant genial laugh, but a gloating chuckle that rose to a high-pitched malicious titter.

Suddenly C.B. was filled with a terrible fear. That evil mirth confirmed an impression of which he had become conscious only a moment earlier. As the liquid he had drunk coursed through his veins he could feel his limbs becoming paralysed. With extraordinary swiftness his body assumed an intolerable weight. Turning, he took a few faltering steps in the direction of the door; but he knew that he could never reach it. His knees sagged and the Canon gave him a sudden push. Losing his balance, he slumped into a carved ebony elbow-chair that stood to one side of the altar steps. That contemptuous push destroyed his last desperate hope that he might be the victim only of some natural seizure. He had been tricked into drinking a powerful drug, and was now at the mercy of the most unscrupulous Satanist he had ever encountered.

16

DEAD MEN TELL NO TALES

The Canon's pale face, no longer a benign mask, but displaying unconcealed the evil in his soul, leered down into C.B.'s. His thick lower lip jutted out aggressively and from between his blackened teeth he spat the words:

'You fool! You miserable fool! You would have done better to walk naked into a den of lions than to come here. That you managed to deceive me for an hour shows that you knew enough to have some idea of the risk you ran. How could you hope to pit yourself against me—an Ipsissimus? In a day or less it was certain that I should have found you out and caught up with you.'

C.B.'s sight, hearing and the faculties of his mind remained unimpaired, but all his limbs had become limp and useless. Concentrating his will, he strove desperately to struggle to his feet. The attempt was futile and resulted only in a slight stiffening of his spine. He could do no more than wriggle feebly where he sat, and by the greatest effort raise one hand a few inches. While he squirmed there helplessly, the Canon went on:

'When I left you just now it was because an authentic messenger sent by de Grasse had just arrived from France. From my description of you he identified you at once as Mrs Fountain's friend who arrived from London yesterday. I know you now, Colonel Verney, for what you are. And you may be sure that I do not mean to allow you to carry away with you the secrets you have learned to-night.'

'You damn' well let me go or . . . or it'll be the worse for you,' muttered C.B. thickly.

'There is no way which you can harm me.'

'Not at the moment, perhaps. But . . . my friends know that I came here. If . . . if I don't rejoin them they will soon be asking you some . . . very awkward questions.'

'They will ask none that I shall not be able to answer to their satisfaction. I have already decided how to deal with this situation, and what I shall tell them. You called here at a quarter-past nine and left again at about eleven o'clock. In view of the wildness of the weather we decided that you should take the short-cut through my garden to the village. My servant will say that he let you out of the back door and described the way you should go. At the bottom of the orchard there is a little gate. Beyond it lies the railway line. The last train from London passes at about eleven-five. To-morrow morning, when your dead body—'

'My body?' gasped C.B. 'You can't mean—'

'To murder you?' the Canon finished for him. 'Yes: why not? But no one will suspect me of having done so. As I was about to say—when your mangled body is found it will be assumed that you tripped in the dark, fell, and stunned yourself when crossing the rails.'

C.B.'s mind was still perfectly clear; but he was having great difficulty in keeping his chin from falling forward on his chest, and his tongue felt swollen and clumsy. He had not often been really frightened in his life, but he was frightened now. Jerking back his head, he forced out the words:

'You're mad! You can't do this!'

'Oh, but I can!' The Canon's voice had become cruelly bantering. 'It is only a little after half-past ten, so there is ample time to put you on the line before the train passes. Even should someone enquire for you during the next half-hour, if they are told that you have already left I do not believe for an instant that they would risk breaking in without some concrete reason for supposing that harm has befallen you. To do so would ruin your own success, had you managed to carry through your imposture; so before taking any action they would certainly go back to the inn to make quite sure you had not returned there. You are as much my creature now as any of the homunculi, and there is no power in the world that can prevent my doing what I like with you.'

'Perhaps. All the same . . . if you do as you say you . . . you'll swing for it.'

Copely-Syle shook his silvery head and smiled. 'Wishful thinking, my poor friend; wishful thinking. There will not be one scrap of evidence against me. Your death will so clearly be an unfortunate accident. "How sad," people who know you will say. "Colonel Verney was really no age, and such a nice man." Naturally, although you were a stranger to me, as you met your death soon after leaving my house I shall send a wreath. Have you any preference in flowers? Since it was poking your nose into other people's business while in the South of France that has brought you to this sorry pass, I think carnations and mimosa would be rather suitable.'

'You . . . you'll swing, I tell you!' C.B. croaked. 'The people who knew I was coming here knew my suspicions about you. If I'm found dead they'll pull this place to pieces. They'll find what I found. Once they've nailed your motive for getting rid of me, the rope will be as good as round your neck.'

His face suddenly distorted with rage, the Canon took a step forward and began to strike C.B. again and again in the face with his small flabby hands.

'Swine! Swine! Swine!' he cried. 'So owing to you there is now a risk that my sanctum here may be desecrated! That clods incapable of apprehending the significance of the most elementary mystery may break it; may destroy my priceless possessions; may ruin the work of a life-time. But no! Once you, who have some understanding of these things, are out of the way, I can deal with them.'

Calming down with the same suddenness as he had flown into a passion, he added, 'This is England. No one will dare force their way into the house without a search warrant. If I held you prisoner they might apply for one. But your body is certain to be found soon after it is light; so there will be nothing for which to search here. You did not know about my homunculi before I told you of them; so your friends cannot suspect the work upon which I am engaged. They can know nothing more than that I planned to have Ellen kidnapped. I shall find no difficulty in fooling anyone who may call here to make enquiries.'

'That will not save you!'

'Yes it will. You are my only danger. Once you are silenced for good I shall have nothing to fear.'

'You are wrong.' C.B.'s voice came hoarsely. It was still an effort to speak, but he knew that he was fighting for his life. 'I shall still be a danger to you when I am dead. However cleverly you may lie to my friends, they will still be suspicious at my sudden death. They will insist on a post-mortem. My body will be found full of this infernal poison. They'll get you on that.'

The Canon laughed again, his good humour quite restored. 'No, no! As with most drugs that paralyse the body while leaving the brain unimpaired, its effects are only temporary. They soon wear off. To keep you as helpless as you are at present I shall have to give you another dose before we carry you out, and yet a third when we leave you on the line. By the time your body is found all traces of the drug will have disappeared.'

This piece of information brought C.B. a glimmer of hope. Perhaps it was no more than the effect of a suggestion, but he had the impression that his feet were not quite so dead to all sensation as they had been when he had first endeavoured to struggle up from the chair. If he could keep Copely-Syle talking for a while there now seemed a chance that he might recover the use of his limbs at least enough for one violent movement. The Canon obviously lacked both muscle and stamina. If suddenly sprung upon by a much weightier man, it was certain that he would go down under the impact. Once down and grasped by hands that would be growing stronger every moment, it would be long odds against his being able to free himself. C.B.'s fears eased a little. He knew that he was very far from being out of the wood, yet all the same he began to savour the thought of getting his long fingers round that plump neck.

His hopes were short-lived. Almost as though the Canon had read his victim's thoughts, he said, 'With such a big man as yourself, Colonel Verney, the effects of the drug may be of unusually short duration, and such a hearty specimen of British manhood can hardly be expected to accept calmly the fact that death is waiting for him at the bottom of the garden. There is too much at stake for me to take any chances. Just in case you should recover sufficiently so show a belated resistance to my will, it would be best if I put any temptation to do so beyond your powers.'

As he spoke he went over to the cabinet from which he had taken the bottle containing the drugged wine. From a drawer in the lower part of it he got out a ball of string and a pair of scissors. With deft movements he cut off several pieces of string, each about a yard in length, and proceeded first to lash C.B.'s wrists to the arms of the chair, then his ankles to its front legs. C.B. was still too weak to put up anything but a feeble opposition, and, once the job was done, even had he been in possession of his full strength, he could not have moved without dragging the heavy chair with him like a snail's shell on his back, much less broken free from it.

Again C.B. felt fear closing down like a black cloud on his mind. Yet still a lingering hope sustained him. If his death was to be made to appear an accident, it was clear that they could not leave him bound hand and foot when they laid him on the railway line. Neither would they dare gag him. Although he could speak only with some difficulty, he might be able to cry out loud enough to attract the attention of a passer-by. At such an hour and in such weather that hope was an incredibly slender one. But there was another one slightly more substantial. They could not remain with him until the train was actually in sight, from fear of being seen in its headlamps. He would have at least a few minutes unbound and alone. As the effects of the drug wore off so quickly, he might regain just enough strength to squirm clear of the rails.

The thought had hardly come to him when it was shattered by another. Copely-Syle would not be such a fool as to give him that last chance, and risk finding himself facing a judge on a charge of attempted murder. He or the Egyptian would knock their victim on the head before they left him. To do so would not add in the least to any chance of his death being traced to them, as his fractured skull would be assumed to be one of the injuries received when the engine made mincemeat of him.

Once more it seemed as if the Canon read his thoughts; but he had other views for ensuring against any last-minute escape, for he said smoothly, 'No doubt you are hoping that when we leave you on the line you will manage to wriggle off it. Do not deceive yourself. I shall take precautions against that. As you are aware, homunculi must be fed on human blood. Fortunately the modern practice of people giving their blood to hospitals saves me considerable trouble in obtaining supplies. For a sufficient recompense a man in London finds no difficulty in arranging for several bottles to be stolen from the hospitals for me every week; but your visit provides me with an opportunity to save a little money.'

His meaning was clear enough, and a shudder ran through C.B. at the thought that his blood was to be used to sustain the life of those foul creatures in the jars.

'A pint is the usual quantity given by blood donors,' the Canon went on thoughtfully, 'but that hardly affects them; so I shall take from you at least a quart. Such a drain on your vitality will more than double the effect of the drug; so for a quarter of an hour or more you will be too weak to lift a finger. And to render you incapable of all movement for ten minutes will be ample for our purpose.'

C.B.'s strength was now fast returning to him. He could move his toes, clench his fingers, and flex the muscles of his arms and legs. Temporarily giving way to the fear that was upon him, he began to shout curses at the Canon and strive violently to free himself. His struggles were in vain; the string cut into his wrists and ankles, but his efforts failed even to loosen it materially.

With a contemptuous smile, the Canon watched his abortive squirming for a few moments; then he said, 'Directly I learned that you were an impostor I hurried back here, in case you took it into your head to harm the homunculi during my absence; so I have yet to hear the full report of de Grasse's messenger. It would be a great mistake to put you on the line unnecessarily early, in case someone stumbled on you. I am, therefore, about to fill in ten minutes by listening to what else the messenger has to say, and putting in a personal call to de Grasse for midnight, so that I may give him fresh instructions. When I return I shall give you your second dose of the drink you found so palatable. They say that when near death one recalls one's childhood. My having to hold your nose while you take your medicine should help you to remember similar episodes when in your nursery. We shall then perform the little operation by which you will donate your blood to such an admirable cause. That should take us up to about five minutes to eleven. In the meantime my man, Achmet, will have brought the wheelbarrow round from the gardener's shed. The margin of ten minutes I have left should be just right for me to give you your final dose, and have you transported to the scene of your execution.'

Turning on his heel he walked sedately the length of the crypt with his hands clasped behind his back. As he switched out all the lights except two and left it, locking the door after him, C.B. watched him go with a feeling of sick despair. There seemed such an air of terrible finality about the Satanist's present calmness. That he was apt to fly into rages was evident from the intense anger he had shown at the suggestion that his sanctuary might be invaded; but there was something infinitely more menacing in his general behaviour since he had discovered that C.B. was an impostor. Swiftly, yet carefully, he had made his arrangements to commit a cold-blooded murder, and had discussed it in detail with such unruffled composure that it looked as if nothing short of a miracle could prevent his going through with it.

A cold perspiration broke out on C.B.'s forehead as he thought how slender were the chances of such a miracle occurring. He had already dismissed the idea that he might be rescued by John as in the highest degree unlikely. He had told John that if he was not out of the house by midnight he was to telephone the police and come in to find him. But by midnight, if the train was punctual, he would have been dead for fifty-five minutes; and John would certainly not attempt to force his way in more than an hour before the time he had been given. For all he knew, matters were going excellently and, as the Canon was certain to recognize him as Ellen's friend, his premature entry, seeking C.B., might have thrown a spanner in the works at their most promising point. Besides, there was no earthly reason why he should ignore his instructions and risk upsetting everything, unless . . .

C.B. stiffened in his chair . . . unless John had seen the messenger arrive and recognize him as one of de Grasse's people. If that had happened he would know that the odds were on C.B. being caught out. Then, if C.B. did not appear within quite a short while, there would be grounds for assuming that he was in trouble. What would John do in such circumstances? If he enquired at the front door he would be told that C.B. had already left by the back entrance and was taking the short-cut to the village. He would not believe that, but he might decide to return to the village to make certain. In any case he would do so, to telephone the police before taking further action. Then what? John would come back and endeavour to get into the house. If he succeeded, and was discovered, he would be one against three. Even if he managed to get in undetected he would not know where to look for C.B. The windows of the crypt had all been bricked up, so there was no chance of his entering it direct from outside; and he could not possibly force its iron door. Only one slender chance remained: he might come upon the Satanists when they were carrying their victim out into the garden.

With frantic anxiety C.B. began to calculate times. De Grasse's messenger had arrived just before half-past ten. John would wait at least ten minutes to see if C.B. came out of his own accord, before taking any action. To enquire at the front door would take him from three to five minutes, and it was a good ten minutes' walk to the village. There might be a public call-box on the green, but never having been in the place before John would not know where to find it, and the odds were all against his running into it in the darkness. He would have to telephone from the pub, but that would now be closed. To knock it up and get on to Colchester would take him another ten minutes; then he would require ten more minutes to walk back to the house. There was the possibility that he would take the car both ways, but on such a short distance the best to be hoped for from that was that it would reduce the total time from forty-five to thirty-five minutes. Therefore, at the earliest reasonable moment that John could be expected to begin reconnoitring the house for the easiest place to break into it, the London train would be thundering over C.B.'s body; and even that was on the assumption that he had seen de Grasse's messenger, recognized him, and decided to take prompt action.

At the conclusion of his calculations C.B. let go a gasp rather than a sigh. It was no good. He was caught without hope of rescue. His number was up, and he must face it. He had barely a quarter of an hour of life left.

Fruitlessly, he cursed himself for his foolhardiness in having walked into such danger on an impulse, and without making provision for an adequate life-line. He felt that he, of all people, had had experience enough to know better. Yet, on consideration, had he really been so very rash? At worst there had been no reason to anticipate anything more serious than that the Canon might find him out and have him beaten up, then locked up in a cellar or attic till the morning. Had he speculated for a week on the possible outcome of such a visit, it would still not have occurred to him that by making it he might lose his life. Neither would there have been the least likelihood of his doing so, had not the success of his imposture led to his being taken into the Canon's confidence so unreservedly and shown things, the existence of which he had not even remotely suspected.

It was his having learned about the homunculi that put the rope round his neck, and it was that which made it futile to hope that Copely-Syle was seeking only to frighten him. Having given away his awful secret, no oaths or pledges that the Canon could extract from his prisoner would satisfy him that he might not now be called on to account for his hideous practices. Should he once release C.B. he would lose all power to enforce his silence, whereas in this next half-hour he had the chance to close his mouth once and for all. It was this final realization that the Canon had no option but to kill him that made C.B.'s heart contract with despair and his face sweat with terror.

Yet he was not the man to give in until in the last ditch. For several moments he succeeded in almost banishing his fears, and even reducing a little the furious pace at which his heart was beating, while he cast hither and thither for some means of escape or an argument with which he could induce the Canon to postpone his execution. By the end of that time he had thought of nothing. Again there intruded on his mental vision a picture of himself lying helpless in the dark night across the railway line, and feeling it vibrate as the train hurtled towards him.

He began to pray, but the picture would not go. It became a series of pictures. Himself, half-comatose, being wheeled through the garden, his long legs dangling from the barrow. The Canon and the Egyptian arranging his limp body on the line. The train roaring down upon him at sixty miles an hour. His mangled corpse, the head severed from the body, still lying there at dawn. Its discovery by plate-layers on their way to work.

It was then an idea came to him. He could not save himself, but he could revenge himself on the Canon. Into his mind there came the vaguely-remembered story of a British sergeant who had been taken prisoner by the Japanese and mercilessly tortured by one of their camp guards. It was to the effect that the soldier, having had his tongue cut out, had, with extraordinary fortitude, carved the name of his torturer with a penknife in the flesh of his own stomach; and he had survived long enough for that to lead to the execution of the swinish Japanese.

C.B. was in no position to emulate this act, even had he had the time and courage to do so; but by dragging at his wrists and ankles with all his might he could cause the string that bound them to cut so deeply into his flesh that the marks would remain visible long after he was dead. Next day, when his body was found, it would be obvious that his hands and feet had been tightly bound, and that would immediately suggest that he had been the victim of foul play. No accusation that John could bring would lead to a prosecution, unless some direct evidence of assault could be brought to support it, but with such evidence Copely-Syle's carefully-built-up picture of an accident would be blown sky-high, and he would find himself facing a charge of murder.

Gritting his teeth, C.B. set about screwing his wrists back and forth and jerking up his knees with all his force, so that the tight string cut into his ankles. The pain made him wince, but he kept at it till he had drawn blood at both his wrists, then he allowed himself a breather.

As he sat, slumped now in the chair, panting heavily, another thought came to him. For a second he hardly dare consider it as a real possibility; then he saw that it was perfectly logical. With the wounds he had inflicted on himself he might yet save his life. When Copely-Syle returned he would show them to him, then dare him to stage his 'accident'. The Canon was no fool; and even by the aid of magic it was hardly thinkable that in the few minutes, which were all that would be at his disposal, he would be able to cause bleeding wounds to disappear so that they left no trace. He would know that to carry through his plan would now bring him into acute danger. He might be a criminal lunatic, but he was not mad in that way. He would either devise some other plan for killing and disposing of his victim or, if he could, would perform an involved magical ceremony to heal the wounds, before having him taken out and put on the line to be run over by a night goods train. Whichever course he took it meant a postponement of the execution. And even half an hour might now bring John, and after him the police, upon the scene.

It was at that moment, tense with excitement at this new-found hope, that C.B. suddenly realized that something was happening at the far end of the crypt.

He had caught the sound of a faint 'plop'. Screwing round his head he stared towards the furnace. From it there was coming a hissing noise. The only lights the Canon had left on were near the altar, so since he had gone from the crypt the whole of its bottom end had been plunged in deep shadow. The bed of the furnace, under its big scalloped canopy, now looked like a black cavern; yet it seemed to C.B. that wisps of steam were rising from it. There came another heavier 'plop', then something began to writhe upon the furnace bed among the greyish swirls of steam.

C.B. drew a sharp breath. His heart began to hammer violently. He was seized by a new fear, and one totally different from that which had afflicted him since he had drunk the poison from the chalice. That had been straight physical fear at the realization that he was in acute danger and within twenty minutes, or less, might find himself face to face with a most painful death. This was a terror of the spirit.

The walls of this ancient stone chamber had witnessed many fearsome rites. Only God and the Devil could know to what abominations Copely-Syle had resorted in order to give his homunculi life. That life at present was only fish-like, and they were powerless to leave their glass prisons. But the whole place reeked of Evil. For his hellish acts of creation the Canon would have had to compel the aid of those strange potent Spirits that govern the behaviour of Earth, Air, Fire and Water. He would also have had to call up those brutish groping foeti from the Pit; things that lived upon a lower plane, yet were always seeking means to enter this one and, given propitious circumstances, could not only appear to human eyes, but also take hideous solid form. It was even possible that to complete his devilish work he had had to invoke some chill intelligence of the Outer Circle: an entity beside which even the terror inspired by the loathsome horrors of the Pit would pale; for such Sataii could drive men mad or strike them dead, as had proved the case with Crowley and McAleister.

Fearful of what he might see, C.B. peered with straining eyes into the shadows. Within a few seconds of his having heard the second 'plop' he knew that his senses had not deceived him. The bed of the furnace was no longer flat. It seemed to have arched itself up into a hump. Among the smoke and steam some fearsome thing was materializing from it. Swiftly the hump rose, a whitish blob appeared in its middle and it assumed an irregular outline. C.B. distinctly heard the coke crunch under it. Next moment it heaved itself outward from the furnace bed and landed with a thud upon the floor.

Now it was hidden from C.B. by the tables. His spine seemed to be dissolving into water. Shrinking back, he grasped the arms of the chair, while cold sweat broke out anew on his face. For an instant an intense bitterness surged through his mind at the thought that he should have devised a means of saving himself from the Canon, only to fall a victim to one of the dread Satanic forces that he had made his familiars. He could hear the monster scrabbling on the ground. Dreading intensely what he would see when it emerged from behind the tables, he called upon the God of Mercy, Peace and Love to help him in his dire extremity.

There came the sound of swift movement across the stone flags of the crypt; then, as a lump rose in his throat that almost choked him, his prayer was answered. Loud, clear, unmistakable, John's voice was called him by name; and, an instant later, a human hand grasped his shoulder.

As C.B. opened his eyes, John's words came tumbling out. 'Thank God I've found you. Twenty minutes ago a taxi drove up. As its passenger was paying off the driver I caught sight of his face. It was Upson, that air pilot of de Grasse's—the fellow Christina snatched the gun from. I felt certain that if he ran into you there would be trouble. I padded round the house till I found a bay window with lights showing through the chinks of the curtains. One of the windows was a few inches open. I listened at it and caught the old boy's voice. He was in a screaming passion. I gathered that you were waiting for him in the chapel, and that he was just about to pull a fast one on you. I lost ten minutes trying to find a way in here. As a last resort I climbed up on the roof to see if there was a skylight. There wasn't, but the chimney is a good three feet square inside; so I threw my mac down first, in case there was a fire going at the bottom, then let myself drop on to it.'

'Well done! Well done!' breathed C.B. 'If you hadn't found me the odds are I'd have been dead before morning. But we haven't a moment to lose.

That fiend may be back here any second. Look! There's a sword on the altar. Use it to cut me free.'

Obediently John snatched up the sword, but as he clasped it he cast a scared glance over his shoulder, and muttered, 'This place gives me cold shivers down my spine. What's been going on here?'

'Never mind that now,' C.B. said impatiently. 'For God's sake cut these strings.'

The blade of the sacrificial sword was sharp as a razor. Once John set to work the strings parted under it with as little resistance as though they were threads of cotton. Yet even for so short a time C.B. could not keep his eyes on the strokes that were liberating him. A new fear impelled him to keep darting swift glances from side to side into the shadows behind the two rows of pillars. The possibility of the Canon surprising them before they could get away had now taken second place in his mind. It seemed as if some malignant unseen force, already in the crypt, was stirring into evil life with intent to prevent their leaving it.

As the last string snapped C.B. jerked himself to his feet, and John, his thin face now chalk-white, gasped:

'Come on! For Christ's sake let's get out of here!'

Side by side, they began to run down the crypt. But their feet felt as though they were weighted with lead. The strength seemed to be ebbing from their limbs as though they had received many wounds and their life-blood was draining away with every step they took. Half-way along the tables they faltered into a walk. The air ahead of them no longer had the feeling of air. It had become intensely cold and was as though they were endeavouring to force their way through water.

In a half-strangled voice, C.B. began to recite the Lord's Prayer aloud. 'Our Father which art in Heaven . . .'

Almost instantly the pressure eased and they found themselves able to stagger forward to the furnace. When jumping from it John had pulled his mackintosh after him. Sooty and scorched, it lay on the ground nearby. As he snatched it up, C.B., still praying aloud, looked hastily round for something else to throw on the bed of coke that would protect their feet from burning. His glance lit on the robes used by the Canon when he officiated as a minister of the Black priesthood. They were of heavy scarlet satin embroidered in black with magical insignia, and hung upon a stand on the far side of the door. While John sprayed the top layer of coke with water, C.B. fetched the vestments and flung them on to the hissing furnace bed; then he cried:

'Go on, up you go!'

John hesitated a moment, glancing at C.B.'s bleeding wrists; but the older man pushed him forward, so he scrambled up into the steam-filled cavity. His head and shoulders disappeared into the wide funnel made by the chimney, and he quickly began to feel about for hand-holds inside it. Within a few seconds his searching fingers found the iron rungs that had been used by sweeps' urchins in times gone by. As he began to haul himself up, C.B. followed. Two minutes later, grimy with soot and half choked by coke fumes, they stood side by side on the roof of the chapel.

Yet so powerful was the evil radiating from the gateway to Hell below them that they did not feel safe from pursuit. Scarcely heeding the danger of slipping on the wet roof, or tripping in the darkness, they scrambled down its slope to the nearest gutter, hung by it for a moment, then dropped the eight feet to the ground. Picking themselves up from the soaking grass, by a common impulse they ran round the side of the house, across the garden to the road, and down it for nearly a quarter of a mile before the fresh night air and the rain in their faces restored their sense of security sufficiently for them to pull up.

In their terror they had passed the car; but now they walked back to it, got in and bound up C. B.'s wrists as well as they could with their handkerchiefs. Then they lit cigarettes. After a few puffs they began to feel more like themselves, and C. B. gave John an outline of the hour and a quarter he had spent with the Canon. At the description of the homunculi John was nearly sick, but his nausea turned to fury when he learnt of the fate planned for Christina, and on hearing of the cold-blooded murder which would at that moment have been taking place had he not got C. B. away, he wanted to drive off at once to fetch the police.

C. B. laid a restraining hand on his arm. 'Easy, partner! It's not quite so simple as all that. You could give evidence that you found me tied to a chair; but that's no proof of intended murder. The old warlock, his Gippy servant and the airman would probably all swear themselves blind that they had caught me breaking into the house; and it is a fact that you broke in later. If they took the line that we had gone to the police first with a cooked-up story, because we feared being caught and charged to-morrow, it would be only our word against theirs.'

'Yours would be taken. Your people in London would vouch for you.'

'Oh yes. A telephone call to the Department would bring someone down to-morrow to identify me and give me a good character. In fact had you fetched the police before coming in to get me, that's what I should have had to do. It would have been worth it, even as an alternative to remaining locked up in a cellar indefinitely, which was the worst I feared when I went in. All the same, I'm extremely glad that you managed to get me out without calling in the minions of the law.'

'From what you tell me, if I'd spent half an hour collecting them before going in your goose would have been cooked by the time we got there.'

'Yes. That's one reason; and I can never thank you enough, John, for the guts you displayed in coming in on your own when you did. Another reason is that, even when acting officially, I am no more entitled to break into people's houses without a warrant than any other citizen; and in this case I haven't got even the unofficial blessing of the Department; so if Copely-Syle had charged me with breaking and entering that would have put me in quite a nasty spot.'

'I see. All the same I think it's monstrous that this criminal lunatic should be allowed to get away with attempted murder and all the other devilry he is up to.'

'We won't let him. But we've got to play our cards carefully if we are to lay him by the heels without burning our own fingers. We've got to get some solid evidence against him before we can make our next move.'

'What about the homunculi? Surely his having those filthy creatures in the house is against the law?'

'I rather doubt it. As far as I know there is no precedent to go on; and since such matters were removed from the jurisdiction of the old ecclesiastical courts prosecution for the practice of witchcraft has dropped into abeyance. Besides, we have not an atom of proof that he intends to harm anyone or is, in fact, engaged in anything which could not be defended as a scientific experiment. All the same, I wish we had remained there long enough to smash the jars and kill the horrible things inside them.'

John shivered. 'I don't think I could have done it. I mean, stay on there for a moment longer than I positively had to. I wasn't frightened about going in—at least no more than I would have been when breaking into any other place where I might have got a sock on the jaw—but once inside I felt as if I was being watched by invisible eyes all the time. It was as though there was something indescribably evil lurking in the shadows behind me: something that had the power to rend and destroy, and that at any second might leap out on to the back of my neck. Then, just before you began to pray, I felt as if I was being suffocated; and I began to fear that I'd never get out at all.'

C.B. nodded. 'I felt the same. The explanation is that the place has become the haunt of some very nasty elementals. As the Canon's familiars they would naturally try, in their blind, fumbling way, to prevent our escape. Perhaps if we had lingered they might have materialized. Anyhow, I had the feeling that they might, and I was scared stiff. My one thought was to get away while the going was good, and I wasn't capable of thinking of anything else till we were well down the road.'

Stubbing out his cigarette, John put his foot on the self-starter. As it ceased to whirr and the engine began to fire, he said, 'Since we've had the luck to get out all right, I'm glad we went in. It enabled you to find out a tremendous lot, and at least we know what we are up against now. I wish we could have made a job of it to-night, and called in the police to haul him off to jail; but since you've ruled that out, the sooner we can grab a hot toddy, get our wet things off, and hop into bed, the better.'

'Not so fast, laddie,' C.B. replied, as the car gathered speed. 'I'll gladly dig the barman out to fix us hot toddies, whatever time we get back to Colchester, but I've no intention of returning yet. First, I mean to try to pick up a little evidence against his Satanic Reverence.'

Slowing down the car, John turned and stared at him. 'You . . . you don't mean that you're going back into that hellish place?'

'No. I'm not poking my head into that hornets' nest again till the hornets have had a chance to settle down. But we are up to our necks in this thing now, and we've got no time to lose. I hate to think what my Chief will have to say should matters go wrong, and you had better keep out of it; but I really do mean to risk finding myself in the dock this time. I intend to break, enter and, I hope, burgle private premises without the least excuse to justify my act if I'm caught.'

17

THE MYSTERY OF THE GRANGE

John let out a low whistle, then said, 'It's not for me to teach my grandmother to suck eggs, but d'you really think you ought to take such a risk, C.B.? I mean, of blotting your copy-book so badly that even your Department will feel that it must wash its hands of you?'

'Yes. I think so in a case like this, for which no provision is made by our ordinary laws. I don't want to sound stuffy, but there are times when every man must be guided by his own conscience, and this is one of them. We have learnt to-night that we are up against not just a dabbler in Black Magic who threatens the well-being of one young woman, but a Satanist of the first order, who is striving to perfect and launch upon the world one of the worst horrors that even his master, the Devil, can have conceived. To stop that I am prepared to go to any lengths.'

'Since you put it that way, you are absolutely right; but where is this place you intend to break into?'

'I mean to pay a midnight visit to The Grange.'

'What good will that do us, as Beddows isn't there?'

'Probably none. It's just a long shot; but there's a chance that we might find some useful pointers to Beddows' whereabouts and his tie-up with the Canon.'

John spoke with a touch of deference. 'I don't pretend to be psychic, but I didn't at all like the atmosphere of The Grange when we called there this evening. Perhaps that is because it is such a gloomy old place, but as these two beauties appear to be mixed up together I should think it is quite on the cards that The Grange, too, has got some pretty nasty spooks in it. Haven't you had enough of that sort of thing for one night?'

'To be honest, John, I have,' C.B. replied quietly. 'But in the late war, whenever one of the R.A.F. boys was shot down, or made a crash landing, they used to send him up again just as soon as they could. It was an excellent principle. That's the way to keep one's nerve, and if it wasn't for the fact that the Canon and his pals must be on the *qui vive* I'd make myself go back into that crypt. As such a move would mean sticking out my neck a bit too far, I'm going into the moated Grange at midnight instead.'

'Well, you're the boss.' John tried to make his voice sound flippant. The few minutes he had spent in the crypt had been more than enough for him. He could only guess what C.B. must have been through while bound hand and foot there and expecting to be murdered within the hour; but he knew that to show admiration for the elder man would only embarrass them both, so without further remark he took the car round the village green and drove back the way they had come.

As they were passing the church, C.B. said, 'All the same, John, you musn't get the idea I'm about to risk running into something very nasty, or having to appear in the dock, for no better reason than to test my own nerve. I'm going into The Grange because this matter has become too urgent for me to neglect any chance of getting a new line on these people. We left France with the object of interviewing Beddows, because we felt confident that he would be able to tell us what lay behind Copely-Syle's attempts to get hold of Christina. We have found that out from the Canon himself; but what we have learnt to-night makes it more important than ever that we should get hold of Beddows with the least possible delay. At the moment we have only half the picture. He must be able to give us the other half. We've got to know why it was Christina that the Canon selected as his potential victim, and why her father left her marooned in the South of France. I have an idea that Copely-Syle may be blackmailing him. If so, we'll get something on the enemy that way. If not, he may be able to provide us with some other line by which we can use the normal processes of the law to spike the Canon's guns. But we've got to trace him first, and it seems to me that our best chance of doing that is by raiding his house. With a little luck we may find some papers there which will give us a lead to where he has got to.'

'I hadn't thought of any of those things,' John admitted ruefully, and, angry with himself for having suggested going to bed while the night still held a chance to further elucidate the grim mystery which surrounded Christina, he pressed his foot down on the accelerator.

Two minutes later he drove the car a little way up a blind turning that he had noticed earlier, barely a hundred yards from the gates of The Grange, brought it to a standstill and switched out its lights. C.B. produced a big torch from under the seat and went round to the boot. From it he got out several implements that are not usually found in a motor repair outfit, then they walked along the road to the entrance to the drive. As they reached it, C.B. said:

'Now this time—'

'Sorry, C.B.,' John interrupted him before he had a chance to get any further, 'I'm much too cold and wet to hang about here. I'm coming in with you.'

'Then if we are caught we may both be jugged for house-breaking.'

'No. You know jolly well that doesn't follow. If we are surprised, the odds are that one of us will have time to get away. I couldn't go in with you before, because the Canon would have recognized me; but this is different. Honestly, we'll both be much safer if we stick together.'

'You won't, because you will be taking a quite unnecessary risk.' C.B. grinned at him in the darkness. 'Still, since you insist, I won't deny that I'll be glad to have you with me. Come on, then.'

In single file they walked along the grass verge of the drive until they reached the sweep in front of the house; then C.B. led the way round to its back. The rain had eased a little and in one quarter of the dark heavens the moon was now trying to break through between banks of swiftly drifting cloud. The light it gave was just enough to outline dimly the irregularities of the building, parts of which were four hundred years old, and it glinted faintly on its windows. No light showed in any of them, neither was there now any sound of a wireless; but as it was still only a little after eleven o'clock C.B. feared that the Jutson couple might not yet have gone to sleep; so he continued to move with great caution.

As John peered up at the flat over the stables in which they lived, he whispered:

'I wonder if they keep a watchdog.'

'If they do it would be a pretty definite indication that there is nothing worse here. Dogs will always run away rather than stay in a place where there are spooks.'

No growl or whine disturbed the stillness and, having been right round the house, they turned back. Drawing on a pair of rubber gloves, C.B. told John to put on his wash-leather ones; then he selected a small window in a semi-circular two-storied turret that jutted out from a main wall, and had evidently been built on at a much later date. Inserting a short jemmy opposite the catch, he pressed down on it: there was a sharp snap, and the window flew open.

Climbing inside he found, as he had expected, that the turret contained a back staircase, added no doubt when the original farm-house had been enlarged and become the property of gentry. As he turned to help John in after him he whispered:

'Never break in by a room, my lad, unless you know it to be the one room in the house you want to get into. Otherwise the odds are that you will find its door bolted and may have half-an-hour's hard work before you can get any further. On the other hand, if you come in by the hall or stairs the whole house is your oyster.'

He flashed his torch for a second. It disclosed a short passage ahead of them and a baize door. Tip-toeing forward, he reached the door and pushed it gently. Yielding to his touch, it swung silently open. They listened intently for a moment, but no sound came to them. C.B. shone his torch again and kept it on while he swept its beam slowly round, then up and down. The door gave on to the main hall of the house. It was large and lofty, with heavy oak beams. A broad staircase on one side of it led up to the landing of the first floor, and there was a small minstrels' gallery on the other. Opposite the intruders stood the front door, and to either side there were other doors, evidently giving on to the principal rooms of the house. The moving beam was suddenly brought to rest on a large oak chest under the stairs. On it stood a telephone.

Moving softly forward, C.B. shone the light down behind the chest till it showed a square, plastic box that was fixed to the skirting. Producing a pair of clippers from his pocket, he cut the main wire a little beyond the box. John, who had come up behind him, said in a low voice:

'In for a penny, in for a pound, eh? We won't be able to laugh off the breaking and entering business now by spinning a yarn that we found a window open and just came in out of the rain.'

'Worth it,' replied C.B. tersely. 'On a job like this, cutting the enemy's communications as a first move quadruples one's chances of getting away safely. If it becomes necessary to run for it they can't call out the police cars to scour the roads.'

'It's a great comfort to be in the hands of a professional.' John's voice betrayed his amusement.

'That's quite enough from you, young feller. I have to know these things; but my own visits to strangers are nearly always by way of the front door, with a search warrant.'

'I suppose that's why you carry such things as jemmies, wire-cutters and rubber gloves in your car kit, and always . . .'

John's banter was cut short by a faint noise that seemed to come from the top of the house. It sounded like the muffled clanking of some small pieces of metal. C.B.'s torch flicked out: they stood in silence for a minute; then John whispered a trifle hoarsely:

'What was that? It . . . ghosts don't really ever rattle their chains, do they?'

'Not as far as I know; but it certainly sounded like it,' C.B. whispered back. 'Keep dead quiet now, so that next time we'll hear it clearly.'

For three minutes, that seemed like thirty to John, they stood absolutely still in the darkness; but the only sound they could catch was that of one another's breathing. At last, switching on his torch again. C.B. shone it aloft and round about. There was no sign of movement up on the landing or in the minstrels' gallery, and nothing to be seen other than the black oak beams outlined against the white walls and ceiling. Lowering the light, he said:

'False alarm, I think. Just one of those noises there is no accounting for that one often hears in old houses at night. Come on! Let's explore.'

Crossing the hall, he opened the door on the right of the entrance. It gave on to a long low-ceilinged drawing-room. The place had a slightly musty smell, as though it had been shut up and no fire lit in it for a considerable time. The furniture in it was very ordinary: some of it had faded chintz covers, the rest was black, spindly-legged stuff. On the walls there were some quite awful pictures, of the 'Monarch of the Glen' and 'Souls Awakening' type, in gilt frames.

As they advanced into it John caught sight of a photograph of Christina on an occasional table, which must have been taken when she was about seventeen. Picking it up, he stared at it and said:

'How fantastic that anything so sweet should be even remotely connected with such ugly surroundings as these.'

C.B. had always preferred small, fair, vivacious women, so he saw nothing particularly attractive in Christina; and, being a realist, it was on the tip of his tongue to reply, 'I've known better lookers who were reared in the slums of Paris and Vienna', but it occurred to him that that might be unkind; so he forbore to comment and continued to flash his torch this way and that, until he had decided that the room contained nothing worth closer examination—at all events for the time being.

Leaving the drawing-room, they crossed the hall to the room opposite. It proved to be the dining-room. It also had an air of long disuse and chill dampness owing to lack of regular heating. John followed C.B. in and walked straight over to the bulky Victorian sideboard. At one end of it stood a tarnished silver tantalus containing the usual three square cut-glass decanters. Taking the stopper from one, he smelt it and said:

'Good. This is brandy. Shine your torch here a moment, C.B., and we'll have a quick one.'

'I see you are becoming quite a professional yourself.' C.B. smiled as he focused the beam.

John found some glasses in one of the sideboard cupboards, poured two stiff tots, then turned and grinned back. 'Oh no; I'm only carrying out my rôle of Christina's fiancé. If I were really Mr Beddows' prospective son-in-law, I'm sure he would expect me to play host to you in his absence.'

'You've certainly taken to the rôle like a duck to water,' C.B. twitted him. 'I believe you have become jolly keen on that girl, although you haven't yet known her a week.'

'We've seen a great deal of each other in a short time, and in quite exceptional circumstances,' John replied in a non-committal voice. 'That makes a big difference; so naturally I've a very personal interest in helping to protect her.'

'Here's to our success in that, then.'

They clinked glasses and drank. The brandy was not of very good quality, but it was nonetheless welcome at the moment. John's shoes were soaked right through from standing about in the mud and wet, while C.B. had had to leave his hat and coat in the Canon's house; so he had since had a steady wetting from the drizzling rain. Both were feeling the chill of the raw night; and, although their behaviour was now light-hearted, beneath the surface the nerves of neither of them had yet fully recovered from the shaking they had had in the crypt.

Warmed in body and fortified in mind by the fiery spirit, they put the glasses back and resumed their reconnaissance. While they were drinking,

C.B. had already surveyed the dining-room, and it contained no piece of furniture in which it seemed likely that papers would be kept; so they went out into the hall and tried a door under the stairs. It led only to a stone-flagged passage, which was obviously the way to the kitchen quarters. Closing it quietly, C.B. shot its bolt, so that should Jutson be roused and, entering the house by a back door, seek to come through it, he would find his way blocked. They then tip-toed across to the door opposite and, opening it, found themselves in a study, three walls of which were lined shoulder-high with books.

'Ah, this looks more promising,' C.B. murmured, as the torch lit up a big roll-top desk. 'You stay by the door, John, and keep your ears open, just in case the Jutsons are not asleep yet and we have disturbed them. If you hear anyone trying that door across the hall that leads to the kitchen quarters, slip in and warn me. We'll have time then to get back into the drawing-room and out through one of the front windows.'

While he was speaking he walked to the study window and drew its curtains as a precaution against the Jutsons seeing a light in the room, for it looked out on to the backyard. Then, producing a bunch of queer-looking keys from his pocket, he set to work on the desk. In less than a minute he had its roll-top open.

With swift, practised fingers he went systematically through one pigeon-hole after another. When he had done, the owner of the desk would never have guessed that the papers it contained had been examined; but the search had revealed nothing of interest. The pigeon-holes and shallow drawers held only Henry Beddows' household accounts, note-paper, cheque-books, pencils, rubbers and so on. None of the bills or receipts suggested any activity which could be considered unorthodox.

C. B. was just about to reclose the desk-top when John stepped back through the door and swiftly swung it nearly shut.

'What is it?' C. B. asked below his breath.

'The clanking of that chain again,' John whispered.

He was still holding the door a few inches open. C.B. stepped up to him and, their heads cocked slightly sideways, they listened with straining ears for some moments. As no further sound reached them, John mumbled rather shame-facedly:

'Sorry. I could have sworn I heard a chain being dragged across the floor somewhere at the top of the house; but I must have been mistaken. Nerves, I suppose.'

'The dank, unlived-in atmosphere of this place is enough to give anyone the willies,' C. B. said understandingly. 'It was probably a fall of soot in one of the chimneys brought down by the rain.'

Returning to the desk, he closed its top, and set about opening the drawers in its two pedestals, most of which were locked. The locked ones he found to contain a number of stamp albums and the impedimenta of a philatelist.

A glance showed him that the albums covered only the British Empire. Quickly he flicked through a couple of them and saw that they were a fairly valuable collection. Then he noticed a curious thing. The pages for some of the smaller Colonies had on them the remains of a number of stamp hinges but not a single stamp of any denomination. Turning to John he said:

'This is interesting. Beddows evidently started a general collection of the British Empire; then, unless I'm right off the mark, he began to specialize in

Barbados, Cyprus and perhaps a few other places. Being a rich man, he could afford to buy rarities and his special collections soon grew too valuable for him to leave them with the rest; so he removed his pet Colonies into a separate album.'

'Where does that get us?' asked John, a little mystified.

'Come, come, my dear Watson. Surely you realize that a keen philatelist would never keep the best part of his collection in his office, where he couldn't look at it in the evenings. The fact that it is not here suggests that it is in a safe somewhere in the house. If Christina's papa has a safe, it is there that he would also keep the sort of highly private papers in which we are interested.'

'That sounds logical; but if there is a safe surely it would be a bit beyond you to get it open?'

'Probably, but not necessarily. If it is an old type, patience and my skeleton keys might do the trick. Anyhow it would be worth trying.'

Returning the stamp albums to their drawers C.B. relocked them. He had already noticed a door between two sets of bookshelves that stood against the further wall. Walking over, he opened it and looked through. The room beyond was another sitting-room. From some fashion magazines, a bowl of *pot-pourri* and a work basket it looked as if it might be Christina's sanctum on the rare occasions when she was at home. After a quick glance round he left it and they returned to the hall.

Next to the passage leading to the kitchen they found a breakfast-room, and beyond it another room that was half pantry, half flower-room. Neither contained anything having the remotest resemblance to a safe; so, as they had now explored all the downstairs living-rooms without success, it seemed that if there was a safe in the house at all it must be up in Beddows' bedroom.

At the foot of the main staircase they paused, while C.B. shone his torch upward. No movement was to be seen and no sound reached them. Yet the very silence of the damp, chill house seemed to have something vaguely sinister about it; so that, instead of advancing boldly, both of them half-held their breath and trod gently as they went upstairs.

They were within two steps of the main landing, and could see across it to a dark rectangle between a pair of oak uprights, through which a narrower flight of stairs led to the top floor of the house, when the clanking came again.

This time it was distinct and unmistakable; a noise of chains being dragged across a wooden floor. The sound was so eerie, so uncanny, in that dark, deserted house that it caused their hearts to leap. The blood seemed to freeze in their veins, and momentarily they were inflicted with a semi-paralysis. Yet it was the very terror that caused their throats to close and their muscles to contract that saved C.B. from a broken neck.

He was in the act of planting his right foot on the landing. Instead of coming down firmly, it was arrested in mid-air by the same nervous shock that made his scalp prickle. For a second or so it hovered; then, by no act of will but by the residue of its own momentum, it sank gently on to the carpet.

The carpet gave as though it was a feather bed. There came a faint snap, then a swift slithering noise. A large piece of carpet suddenly flopped downwards from the topmost stair. Its loose end and sides had been secured to the main carpet of the landing only by threads. It now hung straight down between the newel post of the banisters and the wall, leaving a four foot square gulf of blackness. The square of carpet at the stairhead had been cunningly suspended to conceal the fact that the flooring beneath it had been removed. Anyone stepping firmly upon it must have been flung down into the hall fifteen feet below.

C.B. gasped, staggered, and recovered his balance. Then flashing his torch through the gaping hole that the vanished carpet had left in the nearest corner of the landing, he muttered:

'My God, that was a near one! It's a modern *oubliette.* The sort of death-trap that the French Kings used to have in their castles for troublesome nobles whom they invited to stay with intent to murder. But this one must have been made quite recently. Look at the torn edges of those boards, where some tool has been used to prise up the ones that have been removed.'

John nodded. 'Anyhow, this isn't the work of spooks. It is good solid evidence that friend Beddows keeps something up here, and is so anxious that no one should see it that he doesn't even stick at killing as a method of keeping out intruders.'

As he finished speaking there came the rattling of the chains once more.

It was a horribly unnerving sound. In spite of what had just been said the blood drained from the faces of the two men as they looked quickly at one another.

'I expect it is some mechanical gadget made to scare people,' John said a little dubiously.

'Perhaps.' C.B. hesitated. 'On the other hand, if Copely-Syle and Beddows are buddies it may be something very different. Still, if you're game to go on, I am.'

The vitality of both was now at a very low ebb, and John would have given a lot for a sound excuse to abandon their investigations there and then; but he hated the idea of losing face with C.B.; so he said in a low voice:

'All right. But as we cross the landing I think you had better recite the Lord's Prayer, as you did in the crypt, and I'll join in.'

Handing the torch to John, C.B. grasped the newel post firmly and swung himself across the gap, carefully testing the firmness of the floor beyond before letting go. John passed him back the torch and followed. Together, they began to pray aloud. Shining the light downward on to the floor and taking each step cautiously, in case there was another trap, C.B. led the way across the landing. In the archway he paused, put one foot on the lowest stair of the upper flight, tested that, then swiftly raised the beam. The thing it fell upon caused them to break off their prayer. The chain clanked loudly. Simultaneously they jumped back.

For a moment the light had swept across a crouching form and lit up two reddish eyes. A dark hunched thing, with eyeballs that glowed like live coals, was squatting half-way up the narrow flight of stairs.

In a choking voice John cried, 'For God's sake let's get out of here!' And turned to run.

C.B.'s flesh was creeping and his tongue seemed to cleave to the roof of his mouth. Yet, as he swung round to follow, he managed to shout a warning:

'Careful! Look out for the hole!'

John was already half-way across the landing. He pulled up so abruptly that C.B. cannoned into him. The torch was knocked from C.B.'s hand, fell to the floor with a crash, and went out.

Total darkness descended upon them like a pall. John had been thrown off his balance. He staggered sideways a few steps. Their collision had robbed him of his sense of direction. He was no longer certain if the gaping chasm in the floorboards was in front of him or to his left. A few steps either way and he might become a whirling mass of arms and legs, hurtling down into the hall.

The chain was now rattling violently. Other sounds mingled with it. There was an irregular thumping, as if a soft, heavy body was flopping about on the upper stairs; and a quick champing noise, like the repeated snapping together of strong teeth.

John felt a cold sweat break out all over him. He was terrified of the Thing behind him, yet was held where he stood from fear of breaking his neck. Meanwhile C.B., cursing furiously, was on his hands and knees, frantically searching for the lost torch.

Within a matter of seconds his right hand knocked against it. Snatching it up, he pressed the switch. To his infinite relief it lit. The bulb had not, as he had feared, been broken. Still on his knees, he swung the beam towards the opening through which lay the upper stairs.

It was barely thirty seconds since he had dropped the torch. He expected to see that hideous Thing framed in the opening and about to spring upon them. There was nothing there–nothing whatever. Yet the rattling of the chain and the other noises continued with unabated violence.

As the torch flashed on, John swung half-right and grabbed the newel post at the head of the main stairs. Only his sense of loyalty to C.B. restrained him from jumping the hole and dashing down them; but hearing no following footsteps he halted, looked over his shoulder, and shouted:

'Come on! What the hell are you waiting for?'

C.B. was still kneeling in the middle of the landing with his torch focused on the archway from which came the din of clanking, banging and champing. Without taking his eyes from it, he called:

'Half a minute! Don't go, John! I'm going to have another look.'

'You're crazy!' John shouted back, but he turned towards the landing again. With tightly clenched hands he watched C. B. rise and walk forward, once more reciting the Lord's Prayer. As he reached the opening he made the sign of the Cross in front of his face, then he shone the torch upwards.

Again it fell upon the hunched form and pair of burning eyes; but this time he kept it there. Round the eyes there was dark shaggy hair; below them a huge mouth, in which two rows of yellowish, gleaming teeth were gnashing. Chattering with fury, the creature began to leap up and down, its long limbs throwing grotesque shadows against the stairs behind it. C.B.'s voice came, no longer sharp from tension, but level and unhurried:

'The fact that it didn't come down and attack us made me think that this particular bogy must be chained up; and I was right. Its chain is attached to a post in the wall of the upper landing.'

John moved up beside him. For a moment they both stood staring at the creature on the stairs. It was a big ape; not as large as a baboon, but quite big enough to maul a man and do him serious injury. The chain was attached to a thick leather belt round its waist.

'The presence of this pretty pet in addition to the *oubliette* makes one thing quite certain,' said C.B. softly. 'There is something up at the top of the house that friend Beddows is extraordinarily anxious that no one shall see.'

'Yes. But how the devil are we to get up there?'

'As you know, I've got quite a way with animals; so given an hour or two I don't doubt that I could tame this chap sufficiently for him to let us pass. But we haven't got that time to spare; so we'll have to take stronger measures.'

As C.B. spoke, he turned away towards the nearest of four doors that were ranged round the landing. It opened on to a bedroom. Beside the bed hung an old-fashioned bell pull. Getting up on a chair he detached the rope from the wire spring and handed it to John, with the remark:

'This is just the thing with which to secure our furry friend. By slipping one end of the rope through the pull ring at the other you'll have a lasso that will run much more smoothly than if you knotted a loop. I want you to throw it over his head when I give the word. Get it well down to his waist, so that it pinions his arms, and tie it as tight as you can. But watch out that he doesn't claw you with his feet.'

Taking the eiderdown from the bed, C.B. led the way back to the stairs and propped his torch up on the lowest one, so that its beam shone full upon the angry, snarling animal. Holding the eiderdown in front of him by two of its corners, he went up a few steps until he was near enough to flick its lower end as a matador does his cape. The enraged ape sprang at him, but was brought up with a jerk by the chain. C.B. darted forward up two more stairs, threw the eiderdown over the brute and grasped it firmly round the body.

'Quick, John!' he called; and next moment, squeezing past him, John had the rope round the heaving bundle. The strength and fierceness of the ape made it a far from easy matter to truss him securely, but the rope was long enough to take a second turn round his thighs, and after that had been managed the rest was easy. They rolled him up in his own chain till they had him up on the top landing, and there slipped his feet through a half-hitch in it.

To secure the creature without injury to themselves had required all their attention as well as their strength, so it was not until the job was done that either of them noticed another surprise that was in store for them. The top landing was quite small and had only two doors leading from it. From under one of them came a ribbon of light.

They would not have noticed it, had it not been almost dark up there, owing to C.B. having left his torch at the bottom of the stairs. It was faint, but quite unmistakable, as its glow was enough to show the outline of the ape's water-trough and a tin tray on which were the remains of his last meal. Their attention was caught by the narrow strip of light almost at the same second, and they looked quickly at one another, wondering what this new mystery could portend.

Why should there be a light in a room at the top of the house in the middle of the night, unless the room was occupied? If it was, even if its occupant had dropped asleep with the light still on, he must have been roused by the noise made by his guardian ape and the struggle with it that had ensued. Why, knowing that intruders were in the house, and on their way up to his well-protected sanctum, had he shown no sign of life?

Stretching out a hand, C.B. grasped the door-handle firmly and turned it. But the door did not yield to his pressure: it was locked. Not a sound came from beyond it. Except for the faint scuffling of the trussed ape, the house was again utterly silent.

John slipped down the stairs, retrieved the torch and shone it on the door. The light revealed nothing to indicate the use to which the room was put.

Apart from the black oak beams in the walls and ceiling, the woodwork of this upper landing was painted cream; but it looked as if a dozen years or more had passed since it had received its last coat. About the bare boards of the floor the ape had scattered some of its food; otherwise the landing was reasonably clean, but the doors showed the slight griminess and innumerable small scratches that only time can bring. It seemed reasonable to assume that they led either to box-rooms or servants' bedrooms.

For a second it flashed into C.B.'s mind that Christina might have been wrong about the Jutson couple being her father's only servants. Perhaps he had some other private retainer; or had taken someone else on since she had left The Grange, and they had their quarters up here. But that seemed unlikely when there was such a good choice of rooms more conveniently situated at the back of the premises. Again, why should they seek to protect themselves with an *oubliette* and a ferocious ape? If they had sought refuge up in these remote attics, behind such ugly barriers, of what were they afraid? If they were huddled in terrified silence behind the door, what form of menace could it possibly be that they must be expecting to see come through it at any moment now?

C.B. knocked on the door. There was no reply. Again he rapped, louder this time. Still not a sound came from the room. Putting his shoulder to the door, he threw his weight upon it. The upper part gave slightly but the lock held. Taking a few steps back he ran at the door, lifting his right foot so that it landed flat across the key-hole with the full force of the kick behind his heel. There was a sound of tearing wood and the door flew open.

The room was much larger than they had expected, and lofty enough for the crossbeams of its roof to be only vaguely discernible by a dim blue light that radiated from the centre of its floor. It was, in fact, a huge attic which must have occupied the full breadth and nearly half the length of the house. In it there was no furniture, carpet or curtains, and its three dormer windows appeared to have been pasted over with thick brown paper. The low walls were naked; the whole place was as empty as a drum but for a single human figure and a number of strange objects in its immediate vicinity.

Of these, the thing that first sprang to the eye was a great five-pointed star. It was formed of long glass tubes, all connected together in the same manner as strip-lighting designed to show the name over a shop; and through their whole length glowed electric wires that gave off the cold blue light. Five tall white candles were placed in the points of the star; but these were unlit, so evidently there only against an emergency failure of the electric current. Behind them were placed five bright, brand-new horseshoes. In the valleys of the star were five little silver cups half full of water and some bunches of herbs. More faintly seen were two thick circles that had been drawn in chalk on the floor. The inner, which was about seven feet across, connected the valleys of the star; the outer, which was very much bigger, connected its points. Between the two were chalked a number of Cabalistic formulæ and the signs of the Zodiac.

Unmoving, in the very centre of the star sat a man. He was dressed in striped pyjamas and socks, but appeared to have on several layers of underclothes beneath the pyjamas, as their coat was stretched tightly across his chest. He was short, thick-set and looked about fifty. His hair was dark, his face broad, and his square, determined jowl so blue with bristles that it looked as if he had not shaved for a week. He was sitting cross-legged upon a thick pile of blankets, his back lightly touching a large tea-chest, and he was facing the door.

Neither of his uninvited visitors had the least doubt who he was. C. B. took a step into the room and said, 'We must apologize for breaking in on you like this, Mr Beddows; but out business is extremely urgent.'

The man neither moved nor spoke.

'You are Henry Beddows, aren't you?' C. B. asked.

Still the man stared through them as though they were not there.

'Come on!' exclaimed John impatiently. 'We've come all the way from the South of France to see you. They told us at your office that you had gone abroad; and when we called here the Jutsons lied to us. Now we've run you to earth in spite of them, for goodness' sake stop pretending to be dumb. Your daughter Ellen is in great danger.'

The man's hands began to tremble and he averted his eyes, but he did not speak.

Together John and C. B. advanced into the room. The latter said, 'What my friend has told you is quite true, sir. At the moment your daughter is in prison. We are doing our best—'

'In prison!' exclaimed the man, coming swiftly to his feet. Then his expression changed from one of surprise to disbelief. Suddenly he stretched out his hand, made the sign of the Cross and cried loudly:

'Avaunt thee, Satan!'

John stared at him and muttered, 'Good Lord! I believe he's mad.'

C. B. shook his head. 'No, he's not mad. And he is Beddows all right. His attitude explains the mystery of all we've found in this house. Somebody is after him and he is scared stiff. That is why he has gone into hiding. The *oubliette* and the ape were to prevent his enemy paying him a visit in person; but there is something which terrifies him much more than that. He is afraid that some frightful monster from one of the lower astral planes may be sent to get his spirit. That's why he has made this pentacle. He has locked himself up in what amounts to an astral fortress, and he doesn't believe that we are real people at all. He thinks we are evil entities sent to lure him from safety to destruction.'

Suddenly Beddows gave a defiant laugh, then cried, 'And so you are! Your cunning talk does not deceive me! Get back to him who sent you!'

'Don't talk like a fool!' John snapped at him. 'Surely you can tell real people when you see them? We're real and we're friends. You're the only person who can give us the truth about this whole awful business; and we've got to have it to help us in our fight to save Christina . . . to save Ellen.'

'Liar! And spawn of the Father of Lies! Get back whence you came.'

'We are real flesh and blood, I tell you!' cried John angrily. 'Since you won't believe me I'll prove it to you.'

As he moved forward to step into the pentacle, C. B. gave a warning shout. 'Stop! The shock may kill him.'

But his cry came too late. In a stride John had crossed the line of blue light, and was stretching out a hand to touch Beddows.

The wretched man's face became transfixed with terror. He threw up his arms, gave a piercing scream, and fell at John's feet as though he had been pole-axed.

18

WITHIN THE PENTACLE

Beddows had fallen flat on his face. His outflung right hand had knocked over one of the small vases that stood in each of the valleys of the pentacle; but his magical fortress had suffered no other damage and the big five-pointed star still glowed without a flicker.

C.B.'s mind was racing with visions of an inquest and all sorts of awkward questions which might have to be answered; yet within a moment he had jumped forward to give John a hand. Together they turned over the limp body and got it up into a sitting position.

In the full light of C.B.'s torch the unconscious man's face looked an ugly sight. His head now lolled back over the edge of the tea-chest, his mouth hung slackly open—a dark cavern in his heavy blue jowl—and the whites of his turned-up eyes could be seen between half-closed lids. John got his victim's pyjama jacket open and tore frantically at the buttons of the three vests beneath it. As he exposed a V of hairy chest, C.B. thrust his free hand into the opening, held it there a moment, then gave a sigh of relief.

'His heart is quite strong, and it doesn't look as if he had a stroke. I think he fainted from sheer terror. He'll probably be quite all right when he comes round.'

'Thank God!' John murmured. 'From what you said I thought I'd killed him.'

Ignoring the remark, C.B. swivelled round, set the fallen vase upright, and picking up another poured from it about half its contents into the one that had been knocked over.

'What's the point of doing that?' John asked.

'To repair the breach in this astral defence work, of course.'

'Do you really think that herbs and horseshoes and candles can protect people from evil spirits?'

'Certainly I do; if they are arranged in accordance with the proper formula. There are natural laws which govern everything. These, although scorned and ignored by modern science, are just as potent in achieving their object as a radar screen, or the use of our latest inventions for dispersing fog.'

John glanced round a little nervously. 'After the terror I felt in that crypt to-night, I'm no longer sceptical about there being all sorts of horrors lurking in such a place as this; so it's a comfort to know you think this bag of tricks will provide an effective protection for us.'

'I'm not quite so worried about ourselves, as about him,' C.B. said, and he began to slap Beddows' face in an attempt to bring him round. As his slaps had no effect, he lowered the body into a more comfortable position and went on, 'I don't think we've much to fear at the moment, but the danger to him will be acute as long as he remains unconscious.'

'Why should that be, since he is in the pentacle with us?'

'Because his spirit is temporarily out of his body. That will give his enemies the best possible chance to capture it. If they were quick off the mark when we broke the magic circle by entering it, and the vase was upset, they may have done so already. If not, I think there is a good chance of the restored pentacle protecting him. But I don't know enough about these things to be certain. All I do known is that in his present state he is ten times more vulnerable than we are; so it's obvious that if there are any evil forces in this room it is him they will attempt to destroy.'

'What . . . what will happen if they succeed?'

'When he comes round it won't be him. The personality inside him will not longer be Henry Beddows. His body will have been taken possession of by a demon.'

'Just as you say occurs with Christina every night?'

'No. Far worse than that. She still makes sense. He will be permanently demented. Off his chump for good.'

'You are really convinced that evil spirits can drive people mad?'

'I haven't the least doubt about it. Ignore the Bible if you will, and scoff at all the records of such happenings in mediaeval times as based upon ignorant superstition. That gets you nowhere, unless you can account in some other way for certain types of loss of mental control that have afflicted great numbers of people from the earliest times, and still continue to do so. Most cases of lunacy are obviously due to physical causes; but any doctor will tell you that he has met with forms of madness which cannot be explained by any theory so far accepted by science; and most of the honest ones will admit that the symptoms in such cases tally with those described by the priests of all nations who have studied these things, as indications that the victim is 'possessed of a devil'.'

John nodded. 'I suppose in these days we are far too apt to discount the Bible; and, if one believes at all, one can hardly refuse to accept the account of Christ and the Gadarene swine. Still, all that apart, it seems to me that we have good grounds for regarding this chap as a bit round the bend already. No one who wasn't would choose for a costume in which to sit up all night three suits of underclothes and pyjamas, instead of day things and an overcoat—or anyway a good warm dressing-gown.'

'On the contrary, the clothes he is wearing show that he understands what he is up against.' C.B. flashed his torch round the floor. 'Look how thoroughly the whole place has been swept and garnished before the pentacle was laid out. That shows he was aware that elementals are helped to materialize by dirt and filth. Above all they are attracted by the impurities of the human body. When he decided to fortify himself in here he evidently took every possible precaution against bringing in with him anything that might aid the enemy. Soiled clothes of any kind, or cushions and rugs that had been in use, would do so; that is why he made do with such underclothes and bedding as he could take straight from the linen-cupboard.'

'From the bristles on his chin it looks as if he has been sitting here for several days; but I suppose he must have left the pentacle now and again in the daytime.'

'Why? Were you thinking about his natural functions?'

'Yes. If you are right about human impurities, his own would form a dangerous focus within the pentacle, and he could not possibly have controlled himself long enough to grow that beard.'

'An Indian fakir could; so could he if he is an expert practitioner of

Yoga—particularly if he has eaten very little. Each time he left the pentacle he would have to remake it to restore its maximum potency, and seeing the state he was in it is most unlikely he would leave its protection even for a few minutes, unless it was absolutely unavoidable.'

'He must practise Yoga then, otherwise . . .'

'No. He got round that problem another way.' C.B. was shining his torch down into the tea-chest. More than half of it was occupied by a large metal container, and he added, 'Look, I'll bet that thing is a form of Elsan specially fitted with an air-tight lid.'

The only other things in the chest were two tins of dry biscuits and a dozen bottles, about half of which were still full of water. 'I expect you're right,' John conceded. 'Anyhow, you are about his not eating much.'

'He wouldn't dare to bring meat, game or fish into the pentacle, and after a day or two even fruit might start to go bad.'

'He must have been mighty scared to shut himself up here and go on a prison diet.'

'Yes, scared stiff,' C.B. agreed, switching out his torch to economize its battery. 'But what luck to have found him here. If only he is all right when he comes round, and we can get him to talk freely while he is so scared, we shall have solved the riddle of where Christina stands in all this.'

'We know that already. That devilish Canon is after her to feed her blood to his filthy homunculi.'

'I mean we'll get to the bottom of the whole business: we'll find out how she came under Copely-Syle's influence in the first place, and what the tie-up is between him and her father. I thought it might be blackmail, but there's more to it than that. Finding him in this pentacle shows that he, too, is an occultist of no mean order. I want to know if he is another Black who has quarrelled with the Canon, or a White who has found the odds too much for him; and if either or both of them are associated with other practitioners of the Black Art. We know that the day after to-morrow is the peak point of Christina's danger; and we have every hope now of keeping her out of their clutches till it is past; but we've got to think of her future too. Having been mixed up with these people, she is highly liable to get drawn in as a witch unless we can take steps to prevent it. Only by getting at the full truth can we hope to free her from their evil influence once and for all.'

John nodded. 'Of course, we've got to do that somehow, or the way in which they are able to dominate her mind at night will continue to make her vulnerable at any time. But what is likely to happen if, when Beddows comes to, we find that he is possessed?'

'Then we are in for something extremely unpleasant,' C.B. replied grimly. 'He will probably act like a raving maniac and attempt to kill us.'

'In that case we'll have no alternative but to knock him on the head.'

'If he becomes violent, yes. But he may resort to cunning, and by some plausible story attempt to lead us into danger.'

'What is the drill, then?'

'We'll give him his head for a bit. Fortunately the sort of elementals that get possession of humans are said to be of very low intelligence. They usually give themselves away; so we should be able to tell whether it is really Beddows who is talking to us or some horror that has got into him and is making use of his tongue. Anyhow, if we have any doubts there is one acid test we can apply.'

'What is that?'

'The little vases have Holy water in them. They would be pointless otherwise. I shall take a few drops from one and sprinkle it on him. Demons can't stand Holy water. If he is possessed, he will scream as though he had been scalded.'

Beddows still showed no sign of coming round, so they settled themselves beside him to await events. The glow from the blue ribbon that formed the star was sufficient to make large print readable inside the pentacle, or a few feet from it; but farther off the gloom thickened into almost complete darkness. Even now that they had been there for some minutes without the torch, so that their eyes had had a chance to become accustomed to the faint blue light, they could barely make out by it the dark beams and uprights in the white walls, while above them the great rafters were only vaguely discernible as strips of denser blackness in the black vault overhead.

As soon as they stopped talking they again became conscious of the uncanny silence that gripped the old house. Out on the landing the ape had ceased its scuffling attempts to free itself. C.B. was troubled for a moment by the thought that they might have suffocated the poor brute; but, tightly as its arms were pinioned, he felt sure that enough air would get up between the folds of the eiderdown for it to breathe. The odds were that its struggles had tired it out and it had dropped into a doze.

John tried to keep his thoughts on Christina, but they would slide away from her to the fact that the motionless body at his side was that of her father, and to the fantastic situation in which they had found him. It seemed unbelievable that a twentieth-century industrialist should be mixed up with witchcraft and have shut himself up for days on biscuits and water in a pentacle as the only safe refuge from evil spirits. Yet that he had done so was beyond dispute.

From that it was only a step to imagining the sort of things he had feared to see while sitting there day after day and night after night. John closed his eyes, hoping to shut out from his mind the winged and crawling monstrosities that his memory of Breughel's paintings conjured up so vividly. The darkness of closed eyelids proved less conducive to such gruesome imagery than the pale light that hardly reached the walls. Nevertheless, he found that he could not keep his eyes closed for more than a few moments at a time. The urge to open them, to make quite certain that nothing was stirring in the shadows, proved irresistible. Each time he did so his glance wavered swiftly back and forth, probing anew the darkest corners of the room, seeking reassurance that no unclean denizen from the grim world of Eternal Night was forming in any of them.

There came a moment when he could have sworn that at the far end of the room from the door, where it was darkest, a humped thing like a big turtle had taken shape, and that the curve of its back was slowly undulating as it pulsed with malevolent life. Loath as he was to risk making a fool of himself by giving a false alarm, he had just made up his mind to attract C.B.'s attention to it when Beddows gave a loud groan.

It was an eerie sound in the tense stillness that held the lofty room. John, staring into the darkness, had his back turned. His whole body jerked at the unexpectedness of it, and he swivelled round as swiftly as if a glass of cold water had been poured down his spine. C.B. switched on his torch. As he brought it round to level it on Beddow's face, the beam cut the darkness at the far end of the room with a swathe of light. Swift as its passage was, John was in time to glance over his shoulder while it swept the floor. With a gasp of relief he realized that either he must have imagined the humped thing, or the powerful light had caused it instantly to disintegrate.

As the beam came round on Beddows they saw that his eyes were open and that he was licking his dry lips. He groaned again, made a feeble gesture as though trying to push the light away from his face, then struggled into a sitting position. John helped him up and C.B. lowered the torch a little. Neither showed the acute anxiety they felt, but the thought uppermost in the minds of both was how much hung on the new few moments. If Beddows was himself and sane, their journey to England should prove a hundred times worth while, as he must know the truth about the strange relationship between his daughter and the Canon; and, with his help, the tie could be broken for good. On the other hand, he might be possessed and, instead of helpful, highly dangerous.

His opening move on regaining consciousness was by no means reassuring. Thrusting them aside, he got to his knees and cried in a harsh voice:

'Who are you? How the hell d'you get here?'

'My name is Verney,' replied C.B. quietly, 'and that of my friend is John Fountain. We mean you no harm: on the contrary—'

'Why should I believe that?' shouted Beddows.

'Anyhow, you'll admit now that we are real?' John cut in.

Beddows turned, glared at him and muttered, 'I wonder! I wonder!'

'Oh come!' John put a hand on his shoulder; but he shook it off and staggered to his feet with the evident intention of jumping out of the pentacle.

C.B. caught him round the knees in a rugby tackle. Next moment he was sprawling full length on the blankets. As he attempted to rise John joined in, and between them they held him down flat on his back.

He was a powerful man and he struggled violently, but in spite of that they managed to keep him down. The very fact that they were able to do so inclined C.B. to suppose that he was not possessed, but simply a very frightened and angry man. So when Beddows stopped cursing from lack of breath, he said:

'Now listen! You have got yourself into an unholy mess, and we are here to help you out of it.'

'I don't believe it!' Beddows panted. 'I don't believe it! How did you get up here? Jutson or his wife must have let you in, and told you about the trap and the ape. In spite of all their promises they've sold me out to Copely-Syle.'

'Oh no they haven't. We broke in.'

Beddows gave a sudden snarl. 'If that's true I'll have the law on you.'

'No you won't. Not unless you are prepared to have a full description of how we found you to-night come out in court. How would your shareholders react to that, eh? Can't you imagine the headlines in the papers: "Chairman of Directors found sealed in magic pentacle. Satanic rituals practised in Essex manor house," and so on?'

'Damn you!' Beddows gave a mighty heave, and nearly succeeded in breaking away.

'Steady!' C.B. shifted his grip and pressed down with his full weight on him again. 'Don't be a fool, Beddows. Just now you tried to hurl yourself out of the pentacle. That wouldn't be a very clever thing to do, would it? As long as you are inside it you are safe, but once you leave it all sorts of unpleasant things might succeed in getting hold of you.'

Beddows relaxed. For a moment he lay silent, then he let out something between a sigh and a moan and said, 'What the hell do you want of me?'

Sensing that his resistance was lessening, C.B. said firmly, 'We want the truth about your association with Canon Copely-Syle.'

'That has nothing to do with you.'

'Yes it has. Fountain and I came all the way from the South of France specially to talk to you about it.'

'It's none of your business.'

'It *is* our business. It is the business of every decent person to lend a hand in scotching the sort of devilry that Copely-Syle is engaged in. And you've got to help us.'

'No! No! I won't talk about him! I daren't! The danger I am in from him is bad enough as it is.'

C.B. loosened his hold a little and took a more persuasive tone. 'Come! Pull yourself together, man. You're not the only one in danger. How about your daughter Ellen?'

'Ellen!' Beddows repeated miserably. 'I . . . I thought I had managed to keep her out of this.'

'Far from it. She has been in very grave danger indeed, and is a long way from being safely out of the wood yet.'

Now that Beddows was no longer actually being held down, he struggled up into a sitting position and demanded. 'What has been happening to her?'

'The Canon is after her blood. I mean that literally, and I'll bet any money you know what he would do with her blood if he got it. That's why we came back to England to hunt you out. You've got to tell us everything you know about the Canon.'

'No! I'm not talking!'

'Damn it, man!' John cried. 'Think of your daughter! How can you possibly refuse to help us free her from the influence that devil exerts over her?'

'No!' Beddows repeated doggedly. 'I did my best for her. I can't do more. She must take her chance now. I'm not talking. It's too dangerous.'

'Yes, you are going to talk,' said C.B. quietly. 'Do you know what I mean to do if you persist in your refusal?'

'What?' faltered Beddows uneasily. 'What will you do?'

'I shall smash this pentacle to pieces; then Fountain and I will leave you here alone.'

'No! No! You can't do that.'

'I can and I will. Either you are going to answer any questions or I'll make hay of your astral defences.'

For a moment Beddows sat there panting heavily, then he muttered, 'All right. What do you want to know?'

'How long have you known Copely-Syle?'

'A bit over twenty years.'

'Where did you first meet him?'

'Here.'

C.B. raised his eyebrows. 'I thought you bought this place only in 1949?'

'That's so.' Beddows now seemed to have resigned himself to talking freely, and went on in a normal voice, 'I'd been wanting to for a long time, but the stiff-necked old bitch who owned the place wouldn't sell. Even after the war had reduced her to scraping in order to stay on here she still refused my offers; so I had to wait till she died. Her name was Durnsford—the Honourable Mrs Bertram Durnsford—and I was her chauffeur from 1927 to 1931.'

'I see; so it was while you were employed here as chauffeur that you first met the Canon?'

'That's right. When I said I had known him for twenty years, it's really nearer twenty-five; but to begin with it was only as a servant knows his mistress's visitors. He was a great chum of the old girl's, and from the time I took the place he was often here.'

'Was she a witch?'

'Yes. There's a lot of it still goes on in Essex. Parts of it are so isolated that modern influences are slower to penetrate than in most other places. She had been mistress here so long that she always thought of herself as one of the gentry; but she wasn't. She started life as daughter of the village witch and, so they say, put a spell on the young squire here to marry her. It's said, too, that as soon as she got tired of him she used a wax image to cause him to sicken and die. After that she acted the high-mightiness and ruled the village with a rod of iron. She was over eighty when she died and more or less bedridden for the last few years; so she had lost much of her occult power, and with it most of her money; but she still had enough power by such means to keep me from getting her out after she had refused my offers to buy.'

'Why were you so keen to own The Grange?' John asked.

'Sentiment,' came the unexpected reply. 'I came here as a young man of twenty-three. I—er—formed an attachment soon after I took the job, and one of the few really decent things I have got out of life are the memories of it. I wanted the place on that account. I suppose, too, the idea of owning the big house in which I had once been a servant appealed to my vanity. But it was wanting to live where *she* had lived that made me determined to have it.'

'Let's get back to Copely-Syle,' said C. B. 'How did it happen that you got to know him more intimately than as one of your mistress's visitors?'

Beddows gave a heavy sigh, then shrugged resignedly. 'Well, since you insist, I suppose I had better give you the whole story from the beginning.'

19

THE SAGA OF A SATANIST

After a moment Beddows started to talk in a flat, low monotone, more as if he were talking to himself than to them. He began:

'It can't be news to you that I'm a self-made man. I've never sought to conceal it. I was born less than a dozen miles from here as the son of a farm labourer, and I started life myself as a farmer's boy. But for all that I was born ambitious. I soon made up my mind that two-ten a week and work in all weathers wasn't good enough. Knowing about machines seemed to me the one way out; so instead of spending my pennies on the pictures and trashy novelettes, I bought the weeklies from which I could learn about the insides of motors. That way I picked up enough to get a job in a garage.

'Later they let me drive one of their hire-cars; then one of their customers, who was a doctor, took me on as his private chauffeur. I stayed with Doc for eighteen months, and while I was with him I attended evening classes at the Colchester Technical College. You see, by then I'd made up my mind to become an engineer. I got a lot out of those classes, but nothing like as much as I should have if I'd had more time for home study; and by the nature of things, a doctor's chauffeur is far harder worked than most. That's why I left him and came here. Mrs Durnsford was already over sixty and didn't go out very much. In fact, sometimes during the winter months a whole week would pass without her using the car at all; so the job offered just the easy hours I wanted to go in for correspondence courses and study for exams.

'For a year or so I did quite well in that way, then my thoughts were taken right off engineering. I don't propose to go into the details of what happened, but for a long time I never even opened one of my books. As I told you just now, I formed an attachment for a certain person, and afterwards . . . well, afterwards I simply hadn't the heart to start work again.

'It was while I was still in that state that I got involved with Hettie Weston. She was the parlourmaid here. Pretty young thing, and the flighty type. She asked for trouble and she got it. If it hadn't been me, it would have been the next feller who came along. I didn't give a cuss for her, but she set her cap at me, and if ever a chap needed a warm-blooded young woman to take him out of himself, I did. I bought it all right, and the next thing we knew was that the silly young bitch had let herself get in the family way.

'Well, plenty of them do that in these country parts long before there's been any talk of marriage. If the feller is willing they make a go of it and put up the banns. If he's not, there are usually a few tears, but no harm done. The girl picks on another likely lad to go hedging and ditching with on her evenings off, and lands him with the kid. Second or third time lucky, and she usually gets some mug to the altar. That's what would have happened in Hettie's case if it hadn't been for the old woman.

'Hettie spilt the beans to the mistress and I was put on the mat. I suppose I could have told her to go take a running kick at herself. If I had, the worst that could have happened was that I'd have lost my job and had a maintenance order made against me for seven and six a week. But I didn't. I was still in a state of not giving a damn what happened to me, and believing that I had no future worth making a struggle for. You must add to that several other factors, one of which I was certainly not aware of at the time.

'To start with, there was the hereditary angle. Youngsters of my class had allowed themselves to be dictated to for countless generations by old women in Mrs Durnsford's position, especially when it seemed that moral right was on their side. Next, as a person she was pretty formidable. When those beady black eyes of hers bored into you, it wasn't easy to say "No". Lastly, although I didn't realize it then, she knew all about me. She knew both how ambitious I had been, and what it was that had caused my ambitions temporarily to take a line that had nothing to do with engineering. It wasn't any high-falutin' motive of wanting to see the right thing done by Hettie that made her row in as she did. It was the malice that was in her. From what she knew had gone before, she got a special kick out of getting me married to a parlourmaid and saddled with the sort of liabilities that make it near impossible for a young working man to rise above his station.

'Anyhow, she bullied me into making an honest woman of Hettie and we settled down in the flat above the stables, where the Jutsons are now. It took a bit of time for me to realize what a muck I had made of my life; but in a young man ambition dies hard, and in me it started to stir again after the new experience of being married began to wear off. I somehow couldn't find the energy to take up my correspondence courses again, but I was subconsciously seeking a way out. Then, three nights before Ellen was born, it seemed as if it had been thrust right at me.

'I'd been out doing a bit of poaching, and returned late. The curtains of one of the drawing-room windows were not quite drawn, and through the chink I caught sight of a flicker that might have meant the place was on fire. I took a peep in, and what d'you think I saw? The flicker I'd seen was fire all right, as the room was lit only by a pile of logs blazing on the hearth. But all the furniture had been pushed back to the sides of the room, a lot of circles and figures had been drawn on the parquet, and in the middle of them stood my mistress and the Canon. Both of them were stark naked.

'He must have been getting on for forty then, so he was already well past his youth and had a little pot. I found him comic rather than repulsive, but there was nothing the least funny about her. She was twenty years older and the scraggy kind. Her withered shanks and flabby, hanging breasts made her a horrible caricature of what a woman should be. You can imagine how weird they looked against the firelight, and how I stared. But after a minute it was not at them I was looking; it was at the thing that stood between them. I can only describe it as a sort of blacksmith's anvil, and belly up on it they had tied a live cat.

'The cat didn't remain alive for long though. As I watched, the Canon produced a knife and slit its throat. Old Mother Durnsford caught the blood in the sort of chalice you see on the altar of a church. Of course, I know now that it must have been stolen from one; but at the time all this made no more sense than if I'd found myself at the Mad Hatter's tea-party. Still, this was clearly no tea-party, as the next thing they did was to each drink some of the cat's blood.

'The sight turned my stomach, so for a bit I missed seeing what they got up to after that. When I looked again they both had some clothes on. She was rubbing the chalk-marks off the floor and he was pushing the furniture back into place. Knowing her reputation as a witch, I suppose I ought to have put two and two together, but somehow I didn't. It was catching them naked that was uppermost in my mind. I thought then that he was a proper clergyman, and that the business with the cat was some sort of sexual perversion, or that drinking cat's blood might be a way of making old people feel young again.

'Anyhow, as far as I was concerned one thing stuck out a mile. Here was my opportunity to break out of the dead end in which I had landed myself. Setting up house with Hettie had cost me the hundred or so I had put by. Since we had been married I'd had little chance to start saving again, and I knew that once the baby arrived I'd have even less. By then I was twenty-seven. Ten years had slipped by without my getting very far—ten of the best years of my life—and I didn't want to remain a chauffeur all my natural. Here was my chance to make a brand-new start.

'We may as well call a spade a spade. My mind instantly turned to blackmail. I reckoned that the Canon and the old woman were good for five hundred smackers between them, and that they'd pay that to keep my mouth shut. For a pound a week I could park Hettie and the baby back on her parents. Then I'd go to London. Four hundred, eked out by taking night jobs in garages now and then, would see me through two years as a full-time student at a technical college. Before I was thirty I'd emerge as a qualified engineer, capable of earning good money. It didn't take me long to work that out, or how to set about it.

'They had to dispose of the body of the cat. I reckoned they wouldn't risk the stench that would fill the house if they burnt it on the drawing-room fire; so all the odds were that the Canon would take it out to the furnace. I nipped round there and hid behind the boiler. Sure enough, a few minutes later in he comes, opens the furnace door, rakes up the coke a bit and pops in the dead pussy. The moment he had gone I fished the animal out. Its fur was a little singed, which showed that an attempt had been made to burn it, and its throat was slit from ear to ear; so it provided the evidence I needed to turn the heat on him.

'Next morning I put it in an oyster-barrel filled with brine, to preserve it, and hid the barrel in the loft. Then in the evening I cycled over to The Priory to have a little talk with the Canon. But I was told that he had gone to London and was not expected back for about a week. Two days later Hettie had her baby. As it happened I didn't have to call on the Canon after all, as the day he got back he came to see the old woman. Having seen him go into the house, I lay in wait for him in the garden until he came out. As he turned a corner of the shrubbery we came face to face. Nice as pie, he congratulates me on becoming a father and asks me what I would like for the child as a christening present.

'I say, "Five hundred pounds in pound notes to be delivered before the end of the week at a place and time chosen by me."

'At that he gave a rather twisted grin, thinking it just a cheeky sort of joke. But when I told him what I knew, and how I meant to make the neighbourhood too hot to hold him unless he paid up, his grin became even more twisted.

'Of course he tried bluster, and said that no one would believe me. Even when I told him I had got the body of the cat, he still maintained that proved nothing, as anyone might have killed and partially burnt it. But I was ready for that one. I told him that I had taken the furnace-rake to a friend of mine who was a sergeant in the Colchester police, and asked him, just as a matter of interest, to see if he could get any finger-prints from it. The prints were there all right and we had photographed them. So if I had to tell my story about the goings on at The Grange and he sued me for defamation of character, he would have to explain how his finger-prints had got on the furnace-rake in somebody else's back premises on the night in question.

'I was lying about having a friend in the police; but he couldn't know that, and it sank him. He agreed to find the money in exchange for the body of the cat, and he asked me to come to his house that night to arrange when and where the exchange was to be made. I suspected a trap, but pointed out that as long as I had the cat and the furnace-rake, I had the whip hand of him; so I agreed to go.

'That night he received me in his study, and after giving me a drink, asked

me what I meant to do with the money when I had it. I saw no reason to
conceal my plans; so I told him. When he had heard me out, he said, "You
don't mind being separated from your wife and child, then?" and I replied,
"Why should I? Hettie was forced on me against my will, and the child
means nothing to me."

'He asked me, then, into what church I intended having the child
baptized. The question seemed natural enough coming from a parson, as at
that time I took him to be. I had been brought up C. of E. myself, but Hettie
was Chapel; and in spite of her flightiness as a single girl she thought a great
deal of standing well with her own Chapel folk; so we'd been married Chapel
and I took it for granted she'd want her brat christened there. I told the
Canon how matters stood and he went on to talk about religion for a bit.
Then he said:

'"You know, Mr Beddows, the little scene that you chanced to witness last
week had nothing to do with sex. It was a religious ritual—a sacrifice to a God
far older than Christ, and one who was universally worshipped when the
world was a much happier place than it is to-day. He still exists, of course,
since Gods cannot die; and he is still worshipped in secret by a few of us who
understand his mysteries."

'At that, the local gossip about old Mother Durnsford being the daughter
of a witch, and a witch herself, came back to me. It all fitted in, so I said, "I
suppose you are talking about the Devil?"

'He nodded; and as I've a first-class memory for statements made to me, I
can still recall pretty well word for word his reply, which was, "That is a
name that was bestowed upon him in fear and opprobrium by the early
ascetics, when they were still striving to win the nations over to the worship
of the Jewish tyrant God, Jehovah; but he is more fittingly called the Lord of
this World. In any case, while the God of the Christians offers nothing to His
followers but the meagre possibilities of an austere heaven in a life to come,
the God whom I serve rewards those who honour him with wealth and
happiness here and now. There may or may not be a hereafter; but
everything in this life is his to give. Even the Christian Church admits that;
and it is only superstitious fear that prevents people from returning to the
old faith. You should give it a trial, Mr Beddows, for at little cost to yourself
you could make an offering to my Master which would ensure his behaving
most generously towards you."

'Naturally I didn't get what he was driving at, *then*; neither could I make
up my mind if he was really in earnest about this old religion. His saying that
the cat had been a sacrifice certainly had the ring of truth, and he didn't
sound as if he was goofy; but all that about getting riches in this life was a bit
too much to swallow. More to see what replies he would make than anything
else, I began to question him about it. His answers seemed logical enough,
but even so I couldn't bring myself to believe him. Then he asked me if I
would like him to reveal my future.

'Well, everyone likes having their fortune told, and I saw no harm in that.
When I'd agreed, he took me through to the old part of The Priory and down
into the crypt. It had evidently been used as a chapel at some time, but he
had turned it into a sort of laboratory. There, he made me sit in front of a
mirror. It wasn't made of glass, but of some highly polished metal, and it was
pitted round the edges as though it was very old. He gave me a big brass bowl
to hold in my lap and put some cones of incense in it. When he had lit them

he said to me as follows:

'"Within certain limits all men have free will; therefore their futures are not irrevocably fixed, but depend upon the decisions they take at certain major crossroads in their lives. I am about to give you an idea what your future will be, should you decide to rely upon my guidance and become the servant of Prince Lucifer. Keep your eyes fixed on the mirror and through the smoke you will see pictures form upon it." Then he began to chant in a sing-song voice behind me, and I seemed to become a little drowsy.

'You will remember what it says in the Bible about Satan taking our . . . our . . . taking J. C. up on to the mountain and showing Him the kingdoms of the Earth. Well, me being just a chauffeur saddled with an unwanted wife and kid, it wasn't far off that. There were quite a number of pictures and afterwards they became a bit confused in my mind. The general impression was of myself, a little older, but not much, dressed in expensive clothes, wining and dining with other rich men, and having necking parties with lovely women in the luxury suites of big hotels. But a few of the scenes I saw remained clear cut. There was one of me walking through a great machine-shop where hundreds of people were working, and from the respectful way they all looked up at me as I passed it was clear that I was the boss of the whole outfit. Another confirmed that: it was the outside of my plant near Colchester pretty much as it stands to-day; and blazoned across its front in letters six feet high were the words "BEDDOWS AGRICULTURAL TRACTORS". The one that really got me, though, was myself in a check suit, standing in front of a long, low grey car. That car had something that no car in the time of which I am talking had got. Its rake was completely different. It was quite unlike anything that had so far been made and obviously an advance in design. It was something slap out of the future, and I knew that whatever else Copely-Syle might have faked up to gull me he couldn't have faked up that.

'When the show was over I told him at once that he had made a convert, and asked what I must do to become the me in the pictures I had seen. He replied, "There is nothing very difficult about it, if you are prepared to forswear the gloomy Christian God and all His works. Prepare yourself for that by reciting the Lord's Prayer backwards every night from now on, and return here at the same hour a week from to-day."

'It wasn't until he was showing me out of the front door, a few minutes later, that I remembered the reason I had come to see him; and with a sudden feeling that somehow he had made a monkey out of me, I said pretty sharply, "We haven't settled anything about that five hundred pounds."

'"No," he said, "and if you've any sense we shan't need to. When you come here next week you'd better bring that dead cat with you as a first offering. If you don't I will buy it off you later, as we arranged this morning. But don't imagine that the money will do you any good. By taking it you will decree a very different future for yourself from the one I showed you. The choice is yours."

'During the week that followed I was torn first one way, then the other. After all, the five hundred smackers was as good as a bird in the hand, and I hated the idea of giving it up; yet I couldn't get the image of that car of the future out of my mind, and as a sort of token payment towards it in advance I wrestled for half an hour each night with the tricky business of getting through the Lord's Prayer said backwards. When the week ended I still hadn't made any definite decision; but, all the same, when I called again at The Priory I took the dead cat with me.

'That night Copely-Syle took me straight to the crypt, and the first thing he did was to shove the cat into the furnace there. Then he said to me, "Now I propose to call upon Prince Lucifer in order that you may make your bargain with him."

'"What bargain?" I asked, rather taken aback.

'"Why, the usual one, of course," he replied a little sharply. "As Lord of this World he will give you every reasonable success, pleasure and gratification in it that you may desire; but for all that he naturally asks something in return. You must sign a pact making yourself over to him body and soul."

'I didn't much like the idea of doing that, and I said so.

'He laughed then, and gave me a pat on the back. "Don't worry. You must sign it, and in your own blood; but you need never honour it. In your case it will merely be similar to a Life Insurance Policy lodged at a bank as security. You are lucky in having just had a little daughter. All you have to do is to have her baptized into the old faith, and undertake that should she reach the age of twenty-one you will produce her here in this crypt on her twenty-first birthday. In that way you may redeem your bond and it will be handed back to you."'

John gave a low exclamation of horror at this frightful revelation, but C.B.—who had guessed what was coming from what had gone before—grabbed his arm and squeezed it sharply, to check him from bursting into angry words that might have put an abrupt end to Beddows' story; while Beddows, now apparently almost self-hypnotized by the recital of his confession, ignored the interruption, and went straight on:

'Although I didn't give a damn for the brat, it did not seem right somehow; but what was I to do? By letting him burn the cat I had burnt my own boats. I no longer had anything on him. It had become a choice of my going through with the business and a prospect of getting everything I'd ever wanted, or of walking out of the house worse off than I had ever been before; because in him I would have made a powerful and unscrupulous enemy, who could have got me the sack and used his influence to chivvy me out of the district.

'Well, I signed the pact, and afterwards he put me through a long ritual that I could not make head nor tail of, except that in symbolical submission to Lucifer he made me kiss his arse; but by that time I felt it was a case of in for a penny, in for a pound; so I made no bones about it. Then he gave me his instructions about the baptism of the child and sent me home.

'By that time I'd tumbled to it that the five hundred didn't mean much to him, and it wasn't either to save it or to get me as a convert that he had gone to quite a lot of trouble. It was the child he was after, and I was still in half a mind to ditch him about that. I think I would have, but for the fact that three days after I had signed the pact I learnt that I had won seven hundred and twenty-three pounds in a football pool.

'It wasn't a fortune, but it seemed to me a real earnest of Prince Lucifer's good faith. All the same, there was something a bit frightening about getting a sum like that out of the blue so soon after I had abjured the Christian God. It scared me enough to make me decide that I had better not try to wriggle out of taking the baby to be baptized.

'We had fixed on the following Saturday night for that, and I slipped some dope that he had given me into Hettie's evening cup of cocoa. No sooner was she in bed than she was sleeping like a log. I wrapped the child up well and carried her to a field about a mile away from The Grange, where the Canon had told me to meet him. There were a number of other people there, women as well as men, and among them old Mother Durnsford, although I did not know that at the time, as all of them were wearing cloaks and great animal masks that hid their identities. Later, when I was made a regular member of the coven, I got to know them all; but she would never forgive me for having tried to blackmail Copely-Syle, and nothing I could offer would persuade her to sell me this house. But to get back—I saw only the beginning of that first Sabbat I attended, as the Canon was very anxious that the child should not take a chill. The actual baptism didn't take long. It was a revolting business; but as soon as it was over he packed me off home with her.

'As you've met Ellen, you will probably have noticed that she is different from other girls. She can't go into a church without being sick, and animals won't go near her. At night, too, she seems to assume a different personality. Naturally, she has never understood why she should be affected as she is, because she knows nothing at all of what I've told you; but it is having been baptized into the Satanic faith which causes these instinctive reactions, and the fact that during the hours when the Powers of Darkness are abroad she becomes readily subject to their influences.

'For many years I had no cause to regret what I had done. Once I had taken the plunge, Copely-Syle advised me that I'd be a fool to strive for success the hard way, by going to London and spending two years studying engineering; so I used my win from the football pools to buy a share as a working partner in the business of a secondhand agricultural implement dealer in Colchester. It was only a small concern, but from the day I started there it began to flourish. I found myself imbued with enormous energy, so that I could work eighteen hours a day and enjoy it.

'All sorts of ideas came to me, too. I began to design gadgets that made tractors more efficient and took out patents for them. Soon they were bringing me more money than my regular earnings. My senior partners were an old man and his son. When I'd been with them just on two years the son had a car smash one night coming home from a dance, and died as a result of his injuries. His loss caused the old man to lose all interest in the business, and he let me buy him out for a song. That was in '33, and in '34 I started a little plant of my own to make the first Beddows All-purposes Garden Motor. It was an instantaneous success. Another invention to do with decarbonizing brought me enough capital to expand without taking in a partner. By 1936 I was employing four hundred hands. In '38 I merged all my interests as Beddows Ltd., with a capital of half a million, and in the same year work was begun on the big factory. It was completed just in time for the war. By the end of it I was rolling in money and a director of half-a-dozen big firms, in addition to being chairman of my own.

'To begin with I saw quite a lot of Copely-Syle and often assisted him in his magical rituals. That is how I learned enough to erect this pentacle myself last week: but as my own concerns began to occupy me more and more I lost interest in the higher aspects of the Great Art. Then it gradually got down to my simply paying homage to Prince Lucifer once a year, at the great Sabbat on Walpurgis Night. Apart from round about the time of those annual gatherings I never gave a thought to the real source of my money and success.

'That may sound strange, but it isn't really, because my principles were no better and no worse than those of most of the other big business men with whom I was constantly mixing, and it seemed to me that my achievements, like theirs, were the natural outcome of ability, shrewdness and hard work.

'It wasn't till after last Walpurgis Night that I began to worry a bit. Attending the great Sabbat brought it home to me with something of a shock that I had only just over ten months to go before I was due to hand over Ellen. But even then I didn't think about it much, as a hundred and one urgent business matters drove it into the back of my mind. Then, just before Christmas, Ellen came home for good, and that gave me a real jolt.

'I don't think I've mentioned it, but poor Hettie committed suicide while Ellen was still only a little girl. I've never married again, but I took several women to live with me for various periods, and that was one of the reasons why I sent Ellen away to boarding-school at the age of eight. The other was an instinctive feeling that, anyhow until she was grown-up, I ought to keep her away from Copely-Syle. Of course I could not prevent her from meeting him now and then, but she has never been at home for long enough at a time to fall under his influence. It was for that reason, too, that when she was too old to stay at boarding-schools any longer I sent her to a finishing place in Paris. Her two-and-a-half years there came to an end last December, and her return brought me face to face with the fact that my twenty-one years of having everything for nothing were darn' near up.

'Ellen has been at home so little in all this time that I hardly know her; so I'm not going to pretend that I suffered frightful pangs of remorse at having sold her to Lucifer when she was a baby. She has meant practically nothing in my life, and I imagined that all that would happen when she was twenty-one was that she would be initiated as a witch. I reckoned that by having kept her away from Copely-Syle and seeing to it that she was educated by decent people I was doing the best I could for her in the circumstances. Naturally, I disliked the idea of having to hand her over to the Canon, but that was all I had undertaken to do, and it seemed to me that at the age of twenty-one she would be perfectly capable of telling him to go to blazes if she felt that way. If she liked the idea of becoming a witch, that was her look-out. If not, they couldn't make her practise witchcraft against her will. Anyhow I'd quieted my conscience with the idea that I could honour my bond, while ensuring that when she had to take her decision she should do so with an unprejudiced mind.

'Had I been right in my belief that there was no more to it than that, I should be taking her to The Priory on the evening of her birthday; but purely by chance I found out that I had been fooling myself. Ever since I've been in business in a fairly big way I've given Copely-Syle sound financial tips from time to time, and he has quite a bit invested in my companies. A few months ago I wanted to tip him off to sell out from one of my subsidiaries. Instead of dropping him a line, as I usually did, I called in at The Priory one evening on my way home. After we had had a drink his vanity got the better of his discretion, or perhaps he thought that I know less about magical operations than I do. Anyhow, he took me to his crypt and showed me his homunculi.

'Apparently he has been working on them for years, although I was unaware of that. He has got one there now as near perfect as any magician is ever likely to produce. To enable it to leave its jar and function like a normal human being it needs only one thing—the lifeblood of a twenty-one-year-old virgin.

'Naturally he never hinted that to me; but it so happened that I knew it. In a flash I realized what he was planning to do with Ellen. It solved, too, a question that had vaguely puzzled me for a long time. He had never pressed me to give him an opportunity to get to know Ellen, and had most heartily endorsed my policy of keeping her at school until she was grown up. I saw then that he had done so to lessen the risk of her meeting some young man and being seduced, or getting married, before she was twenty-one.

'Well, I knew then that I was up against it. Although I had no special love for the girl I couldn't let that happen. After a lot of thought I decided that there was only one thing for it—both Ellen and I must go into hiding for a time and remain so till after the fateful day.

'It may sound queer to you, but it is a fact that Prince Lucifer is quite a sportsman. He has always been willing to match cunning with cunning. There are plenty of cases in which people have enjoyed his gifts and managed to cheat him in the end. Ellen was used to doing what she was told without argument; so I decided to get her out of the way. She had a nasty sore throat just after Christmas; so as a first step I fixed it for her to have her tonsils out, and whisked her off to a nursing home at Brighton. Then I made arrangements to get her quietly out of the country and park her in the South of France, under an assumed name.

'On my failure to produce her, my bond made me liable to act as forfeit in her place, and as Copely-Syle held my bond it would be up to him to enforce it. I could not hope to escape him by taking a plane to the United States or Australia; because with me he has occult links which would enable him to find and attack me on the astral, wherever I was; so I made up my mind to tell my office that I had gone abroad, then dig myself in here. Only here could I hope for the absolute privacy necessary to protect myself. The trap on the landing and the ape were designed to prevent Copely-Syle getting in to me in the flesh and using the cunning that Lucifer has given him to weedle out of me where I had hidden Ellen. The pentacle, as you evidently know, is my defence against his getting at me on the astral.

'He hasn't attempted to do either yet. That may be because he is occupied with other matters. Some while ago, you said that he was after Ellen's blood. As you know that, and why, you probably know what he has been up to this past week. I shut myself in here as soon as I returned from taking Ellen down to the Riviera; so about what has happened since you must be better informed than I am. Anyhow, I can give you no further information.'

Suddenly Beddows' voice changed, rising to an hysterical note, as he added, 'If I were a free agent I'd hand the two of you over to the police for having broken in here. As I am not, and you threatened to expose me to the most frightful peril, I've told you everything there is to tell about my awful situation. Everything, d'you understand? Everything! Now get out! And leave me unencumbered to fight my own battle.'

Silence descended on the room like a curtain of draped black velvet.

Neither C. B. nor John had dared to interrupt Beddows' long monologue. Both of them had been acutely conscious that although he was definitely not possessed, he was, all the same, in a quite abnormal state. From the toneless voice in which he had spoken for most of the time it was clear that he was using them only as a focus at which to pour out his own story; and it was reasonable to suppose that in all the twenty-one years since he had made his pact with the Devil he had never told it to anyone before. To have cut in at any point with question, or even comment, might well have checked the flow and deprived them of having the all-important latter part of the revelations.

A good half minute elapsed before C.B. said, 'We are very grateful to you for having been so frank with us; and I can only repeat that we are here as friends who want to help. We got drawn into this thing because John Fountain's mother lives in the villa next door to that which you rented for Ellen. I had better tell you what has happened since you left her there; then we shall better be able to decide between us on a plan of campaign for overcoming our mutual enemy.'

'I can give you no help in that.' Beddows' voice was sharp. 'I'll have my work cut out to protect myself as it is, without inviting further trouble.'

C.B. ignored the remark and proceeded to give him an account of the events centring round Ellen that had taken place in the South of France. When he had done, Beddows said thoughtfully:

'Copely-Syle must have smelt a rat as soon as he learned that I had gone abroad so near the date. The odds are that he came to The Grange in our absence and managed to get hold of some of the girl's personal belongings; an old hairbrush or anything she had used for her toilet would enable him to overlook her and find out where she had gone. Evidently the reason that he has so far made no move against me is because he has been too occupied with his attempts to have her kidnapped. I'm grateful to you for all you've done to keep her out of his clutches, and I quite understand now your reasons for breaking in here; but all the same I'd be glad if you would leave me.'

'Oh come!' John protested. 'Now you know the danger she is in surely you don't propose to ignore it?'

'Since you had this bright idea of having her arrested, she is no longer in danger. These crooks who are acting for the Canon will be far too scared of the police to attempt to abduct her from a French prison.'

'You are forgetting the Canon,' C.B. put in. 'By using his occult powers he may be able to get her out; and it is as good as certain, now, that he will fly out there to-morrow morning. We know that he'll stick at nothing to get hold of Ellen and he still has over forty hours to work in.'

'Well, there's nothing I can do about it.'

'Yes there is. You and he must have been mixed up in all sorts of queer business. It's a sure thing that a thoroughly unscrupulous man like Copely-Syle has committed a number of criminal acts in order to carry on his sorcery and that you know of some of them. From time to time he must either have robbed churches or instigated others to do so, in order to get hold of Holy Communion wafers for desecration. We know, too, that he is having blood donors' gifts of blood stolen from hospitals to feed his homunculi. I want you to come with us to the police and make a statement. On that we'll get a warrant for his arrest, and even if he leaves for France in the morning I can get it executed there. That is the only way we can make absolutely certain of protecting Ellen until her maximum period of danger is past.'

Beddows gave a short, harsh laugh. 'What the hell d'you take me for? A lunatic? Can't you see that now you've queered his pitch with Ellen by having her imprisoned, the odds are that he will round on me? As long as I remain in this pentacle I've good hopes of cheating Lucifer yet; but the moment I move out of it I'm liable at any time to have my soul snatched, and my body will spend the rest of its days in an asylum. No thank you!'

'You got Ellen into this!' cried John angrily. 'The very least you can do is to run some risk to get her out of it.'

'She's safe enough where she is! A darned sight safer than I am, anyway! I did my best for her by taking the risk that I'm running already, instead of handing her over in accordance with my bond; and I'll do no more. Nothing you or anyone else can say is going to get me out of this pentacle within the next forty-eight hours.'

'What is to prevent our smashing it up?'

'I can't; and if you do I'll be in hideous danger for a while. But better that than the far worse risk of going with you now and committing myself to having to face Copely-Syle in open court as a witness against him to-morrow. If you do bust the electric current, I can use candles instead, and the moment you've gone I'll make another pentacle. Besides, I've already paid your price for not interfering with this one by telling you what you came here to find out.'

For a further twenty minutes they argued and pleaded with Beddows, but in vain. Nothing would move him, and when C.B. found that they were repeating themselves over and over again he said at last:

'It's no good, John. We must do what we can on our own. Let's get out of this and back to Colchester.'

With a curt good-night to Beddows, they left him and, having eased the bonds of the ape a little, made their way downstairs. On slipping out of the window by which they had come in they found that it was no longer raining, and with heartfelt relief at leaving the dank, dark house, they gratefully breathed in the cool night air.

As they turned into the drive, John muttered, 'The callous swine! I would have liked to strangle him.'

C.B. shrugged. 'After having had the luck to run him to earth like that it was damnably disappointing that he should refuse to help us; but he's far from being a hundred per cent evil, otherwise he would not have tried to hide Ellen and be facing the music himself. Just think what an ordeal he undertook when he decided to coop himself up in that grim room for days on end and wait for some frightful thing to come and attempt to get him! It can hardly be wondered at that he is half crazy from fear already.'   .

'All the same, he might at least have given us some pointer which would help us to lay the Canon by the heels. The very idea of a father selling his child to the Devil in the beginning is almost unbelievable, and for him to refuse to utter a word that might help to save her from being murdered now is fantastic.'

'Fantastic is the word for this horrible business, partner. What could be more so than the thought of Henry Beddows, a down-to-earth inventor of motor engines, who has constantly to deal with Trade Union officials, and is a power in the commercial world of Britain, sitting up there in a magic pentacle preparing to wrestle with demons for his soul; or a man who was, apparently, once a Canon of the Church of England planning to murder a girl in order to give a semblance of human life to a monster of his own creation? Nevertheless, we know these things to be actually happening.'

'I know, I know! But what are we going to do now?'

'Get some sleep. I can do with it.'

It was getting on for three o'clock in the morning by the time they reached their hotel. By then they were too tired even to tip the night porter to get them a drink. On reaching their rooms they pulled off their clothes, flopped into bed and within a few moments were in the deep sleep of exhaustion.

Next morning they had their breakfasts sent up to C. B.'s room and while they ate them discussed the position to date. During the previous evening and night they had found out a great deal. They now knew more about Christina's past than she knew herself, and the reason for her queer behaviour. They knew why the Canon was so anxious to get hold of her, and that if he succeeded it would cost her not only her freedom, but her life. They had traced her father and learned his reason for taking her to the South of France and abandoning her there; but he had positively refused to give them the aid they had expected from him. On the other hand it had been definitely verified that the danger in which she stood would be acute for only one day; since, should the Canon fail to carry out his abominable ritual on her twenty-first birthday, there would be no point whatever in his killing her afterwards. Therefore, their immediate problem boiled down to immobilizing the Canon for the next thirty-six hours.

Their prospects of doing so seemed exceedingly slender, as it was a foregone conclusion that either he was already, or would very soon be, on his way to France. The fact that Upson had arrived at The Priory the previous night made it certain he had come by air. C.B. thought it probable that during the war Upson had served in Coastal Command and had been stationed in that area. In any case, as it had been intended that he should fly Christina home, it was evident that he was familiar with the Essex coast and had already reconnoitred some of the many lonely creeks to select a good illicit landing-place. It was, therefore, long odds that when de Grasse had decided that his latest news was of too compromising a nature to convey by telephone, and sent it instead by personal messenger, Upson had travelled in his own seaplane and made a secret landing by last light somewhere along the coast, not far from Little Bentford.

If so, the Canon had a pilot and aircraft at his disposal, and could leave at any hour he chose. Obviously his only chance of getting hold of Christina now lay in flying south himself, so that he could exercise his occult powers on her jailers. However, there was one factor which might cause him to delay his departure for a few hours—namely that the Satanic writ did not run, as far as Christina's mind was concerned, except during the hours of darkness. Only during them could he influence her voluntarily to leave prison, should the way have been opened for her to do so. Having considered this, C.B. said:

'I had pretty well made up my mind that our best plan would be to make for Northolt right away, so as to catch the 10.30 plane for Nice, then bank on our being able to head him off from getting at Christina to-night. But an afternoon plane to Paris would still enable us to get down there by Air France or K.L.M. in time for that; so I think it would be worth-while making a bid against Copley-Syle's planning to leave before mid-day, and the sporting chance that we may then be able to prevent his leaving at all.'

'I'm game to use force,' John said quickly. 'And if we manage to catch him, you have only to tell me what to do. But a charge of assault and battery would blot your official copybook really badly, so—'

'Thanks, partner,' C.B. cut him short with a smile, 'but I don't think either of us need risk being hauled up before the beak on that count. I am proposing to lay an information against him for practising cruelty to animals, and request the police to apply for a search-warrant. They have only to see those poor brutes I saw in the crypt last night to issue a summons. It is illegal to leave the country with a summons pending against one, and I have enough pull with the police to get them to keep a watch on him. If he attempts to clear out after the summons has been served he will be prevented from doing so by the coppers.'

'By Jove! That's a grand idea.'

'I hope it may prove so; but it won't do us any good if he has gone before the police get out there. And they won't be able to secure a warrant until ten o'clock at the earliest, because the magistrates' court does not open until that hour.'

'Well, if he *has* gone, I have another idea.'

'Let's hear it.'

John's dark eyes narrowed slightly. 'The Canon can't do his final job on the homunculus without Christina; and Christina is no good to him without the homunculus. That's so, isn't it?'

'Yes. Unless he can bring her back here by to-morrow night he is sunk.'

'Even if he does, it won't do him any good if his prize homunculus is no longer in a state to lap up Christina's blood. If we find that he has already left for France, I mean to go down into that crypt and destroy it.'

'Good for you, John.' C.B. laughed for the first time in many hours. 'I really am beginning to feel a bit more hopeful now. One way or the other I think we'll manage to spike his guns. As soon as we are dressed we'll go round and do our stuff with the police.'

At the station, after the usual formalities, they were shown into the office of an elderly inspector named Fuller. To him C.B. produced his card and a small trinket that he carried, after which the inspector listened to all he had to say with considerable respect. Although C.B. refrained from giving more than a general indication of what lay behind the excuse on which he desired a search-warrant to be obtained, that was quite enough to have caused most people to show incredulity; but police officers of long experience have usually come up against so many extraordinary happenings that they are prepared to consider with an open mind every conceivable aberration possible to a diseased or criminal brain. In consequence Inspector Fuller took down C.B.'s formal deposition about the maimed animals without comment, and quietly agreed to put the matter in hand at once.

However, at the magistrates' court some delay was unavoidable, as no special priority attached to an application regarding cruelty to animals, and the lists had already been made out. So it was half-past ten before the application was granted, and after a quarter to eleven by the time the formalities of drawing the search-warrant were completed.

There was no hurrying the law, and John fumed with impatience in vain; but at last Inspector Fuller and a constable came out to join C.B. and himself in the car, and they set off.

Anxious as C.B. was to learn the results of his move, he felt that any attempt on his part to accompany the police into the house might be met by the Canon, if he was still there, with legal objections, or possibly even a false accusation of having broken in the previous night, which might have seriously complicated matters. So it was decided that he and John should wait in the car just down the lane until the inspector had carried out his search of the premises.

It was twenty-past eleven when they pulled up under the trees that fringed the road some fifty yards east of The Priory, and the two police officers got out. Both C. B. and John thought it almost certain that by this time the Canon would be on his way to France; so they had lost much of the optimism that had buoyed them up earlier that morning, and they found the wait before they would know the best or worst extremely trying. In anxious silence for the most part, they sat side by side smoking cigarette after cigarette while they watched the clock on the dashboard of the car tick away the minutes.

It was close on twelve before the inspector and the constable reappeared. Without a word C. B. and John got out of the car and walked with anxious faces to meet them.

The inspector smiled rather ruefully as he addressed C. B. 'Canon Copely-Syle is there all right, sir, and he couldn't have been more helpful. But there is no one in the house answering your description of the airman. There are no animals either, or human-looking fish in big glass jars like you described. We visited the crypt and it has the appearance of being used as an ordinary laboratory; no curtains embroidered with pictures of the Devil, or anything of that sort. We went over the whole house from basement to attic, and there is nothing whatever in it on which we could ask for a summons.'

John looked at C. B. in amazement and dismay. The Canon had completely outwitted them. He was still there, but free to leave at any time he chose; for he had anticipated the raid, and there was now no legal pretext on which he could be detained. Moreover, he had removed his homunculi; so it was no longer possible to go in and destroy them.

20

THE SECRET BASE

The police constable's face remained wooden, but C. B. felt sure that he was deriving a secret satisfaction from being in on a case where a plain-clothes high-hat from London had made a fool of himself. The inspector, on the other hand, knew that men like Colonel Verney did not apply for search-warrants without good reason, and he said:

'I'm sorry, sir. It looks as if they were tipped off that you were after them.'

C. B. rubbed the side of his big nose. 'That's about it, Inspector. We won't go into the source of my information, but you can take it from me that it was red-hot last night. They have destroyed most of the goods and unloaded the prize exhibit that I was after.'

'Is there any other way in which we can help, sir?'

'Only by telephoning for a car to take you back to Colchester. I shan't be going back yet. Let's go along to the pub and have one while you are waiting for transport.'

Getting into the car, they drove along to the Weavers Arms and went into the private bar. When C.B. had ordered a round of drinks and the constable had gone to telephone, he drew the inspector aside and said, 'There is one thing you can do for me. Some time this morning a big crate or package, about four feet six high and three feet square, must have been removed from The Priory, either in a lorry or on a trailer. In such a quiet place as this it is a good bet that someone will have seen it being loaded up or passing along the road. Have a word with the landlord. The public bar is sure to be pretty full at this hour. Ask him to enquire of everyone there, and tell him there's a quid for himself and a quid for anyone who can give us any useful information.'

The enquiry being made by a police inspector naturally secured the immediate co-operation of the landlord with no questions asked. A few minutes later a lean, elderly man with a weather-beaten face was brought into the private bar. His name was Sims and he proved to be the gardener at The Vicarage. He had seen a crate of the size described and a number of smaller packages loaded on to a lorry outside The Priory about ten o'clock. The loading had been done by the coloured servant and a tall man with a fair, fluffy moustache, under the Canon's supervision. The lorry was owned by one Joe Cotton, a local character who was no better than he should be, and he had driven off in the direction of Weeley.

Having obtained as detailed a description of Cotton and his lorry as Sims could give, C.B. paid for the information and the drinks, took leave of Inspector Fuller and, accompanied by John, left the pub.

As John turned the car in the direction of Weeley he said, 'Well done, C.B. If we can catch the fellow with the lorry we'll do in that filthy homunculus yet.'

'Yes—if!' C.B. replied dubiously. 'But he's got two and a half hours' start of us, and remember Copely-Syle runs a coven in these parts. The odds are that it has been stowed away in the cellars of a house belonging to one of his brother warlocks an hour or more ago.'

At the village of Weeley they got out and made enquiries; but no one they asked had seen such a lorry, so they decided to go back to the last crossroads. On reaching them they took the road east to Thorpe-le-Soken, and there they had what they thought might turn out to be better luck. Soon after midday a woman had seen a lorry pass through and take the road north towards Great Oakley. It sounded like the one they were after, but as she was certain that there had been two men in its cabin there was a possibility that it was another. No one else they asked had noticed a lorry at all; so they drove on, now heading north.

They were still about five miles from the open sea, but approaching a great area of lakes, creeks and islands known as Hansford Water. To their left there were still occasional farms and coppices, but to their right was only an almost trackless waste of marshes. The road was straight, flat and empty; so they could see a considerable way along it, and about two miles out of Thorpe-le-Soken they sighted a lorry coming towards them. As it came nearer C.B. exclaimed:

'By Jove! I believe this is it. Pull into the centre of the road, John, and signal it to stop.'

As the two vehicles pulled up within a few yards of one another, C.B. got out. A glance showed him that the lorry was empty, but it answered the description he had been given, as did also the small ferret-faced man who was the sole occupant of its cabin. Walking up to him, C.B. said:

'Good afternoon. You are Joe Cotton, aren't you?'

'Yes, guv'nor.'

'I thought so.' C.B.'s smile was a triumph of candid innocence. 'You have done the job quicker than we expected. Canon Copely-Syle will be pleased about that, providing you've done it all right. But he is nervous as a cat on hot bricks about the safe delivery of his stuff, so he sent us after you to make certain the big crate had come to no harm.'

Cotton gave C.B. a rather doubtful stare. 'Why would 'e do that, when 'e sent the other gent wiv me so as 'e could help wiv the unloading 'isself?'

'Because that crate is very valuable. The Canon wanted confirmation that everything was O.K. as soon as possible.'

'Well, I'm giving it you, ain't I?'

'All the same, I think you'd better turn round and come with us, so that we can vouch for it to him that we have seen that everything is all right for ourselves.'

'What d'you want me to come wiv you for?' Cotton's close-set eyes showed sudden suspicion.

'He told us the road to take; but we are strangers in these parts, and we'll lose a lot of time if we miss our way across the marshes.'

'So that's the lay, is it? You don't know where I bin an' want me ter take yer there. Nothin' doin', guv'nor.' As Cotton spoke his ferrety face had become taut with something between fear and anger.

C.B. saw that his bluff had failed; but he showed no resentment. As he had nothing on the man he decided that bullying would get him nowhere; so he shrugged and said with a smile:

'You're a fly one, Cotton. It didn't take you long to see through me, did it? Still, there's no harm done, and I've private reasons for wanting to know where you delivered that crate. How about a tenner, to take us near enough to point out the house; and we won't let on afterwards that it was you who put us wise?'

'Not for ten quid, nor for twenty,' came the prompt reply. 'I ain't done nothin' wrong; but, all the same, I ain't tellin' no tales.'

Starting up his engine, Cotton swung one wheel of his lorry on to the grass verge, scraped past the car and drove off down the road.

'Blast the fellow!' exclaimed John angrily. 'That's the second trick we've lost to-day.'

'We didn't lose it altogether,' C.B. murmured more philosophically. 'When a man like that says "I ain't done nothin' wrong", you can be quite certain that he has. He wouldn't have refused a tenner without a good reason, either, and a suspicion that we might be connected with the police.'

'Even if he knew what the crate contained, there is nothing illegal in delivering it to a house.'

'No. You noticed, though, that the woman in Thorpe-le-Soken, who put us on his trail, was right about there having been two men in the cabin of the lorry when it passed her. Any guess who the other was?'

'Upson?' said John, after a second.

C.B. nodded. 'Any guess where the crate has got to?'

'Hell's bells!' John exclaimed. 'They've put it aboard that blasted seaplane.'

'Well done, Watson! You see now why friend Cotton was to scared to take a bribe to say where he had off-loaded it. Seeing Upson's aircraft moored in some quiet creek miles from anywhere would have told him that it had come down there to evade the authorities, and he would know darn' well that to help load anything into it that had not been passed by the Customs was a serious offence.'

'Of course! But let's get on. We may be able to find the seaplane and stop it before it takes off.'

'Not much hope of that, I'm afraid. This group of creeks covers an area more than twice the size of Birmingham, and Cotton was over two hours ahead of us; so he may have taken the crate to a stretch of water miles from here.'

'What filthy luck!' Exasperation made John almost spit with rage. 'Then that swinish Canon has got the best of us again! He's put it out of our power to get hold of his homunculus and destroy it, anyhow for the next twenty-four hours. What a cunning move to have Upson fly it out to the Riviera, then bring it back in time for the ceremony, with Christina if they get her. But let's pray to God they won't. The only bright spot so far to-day has been finding that he is still here, instead of having gone to France to work his filthy spells on her jailers.'

'That is one thing that has been puzzling me,' C. B. said as he got back into the car. 'the creation of fully-functioning homunculi is Copley-Syle's life-work; so you can be certain that up to the very last moment he will strive to seize this chance of pulling it off. When I told him that Christina was in prison he immediately decided that he must go out there, and he changed his mind only when I persuaded him that I could do the necessary for him. His discovery that I was an impostor ruled that out; so why hasn't he gone himself? I can't believe for one second that he's chucked his hand in.'

'No; but think of the work involved in getting that private hell of his cleared up in anticipation of a possible visit. It must have taken him all night and probably well into the morning to burn or bury all his animals and those awful deformed creatures he created. Obviously his first concern would be with that and getting his prize homunculus out of danger.'

'That's true; and it gives me a nasty thought. As he was so fully occupied himself he may have decided to get somebody else to do what I offered to do for him. Since he is head of a coven he might have got in touch with one of his pals during the night. If so, they could have gone up to London first thing this morning and caught an aircraft from Northolt to Nice.'

John groaned. 'I never thought of that. If you're right, and they caught the earliest one, they will be in Nice by now.'

'It's a possibility; so we can't ignore it, although I think it would take a pretty high-grade Black to use effectively what amounts to hypnotism at a distance on several people he has never seen, with only their soiled garments as a medium. Anyway, we still have a choice of strong cards left. Earlier on you were arguing that we could save Christina by depriving the Canon of his homunculus. That is true, of course, but not the best way of expressing the core of the matter. To put it in a nutshell, we win out on the big issue if we can prevent any one of those three factors from joining up with the other two for the next thirty-six hours. Our object in trying to get a summons against the Canon was to keep him from going to Nice. We failed to get the summons; but as it turns out he has remained here of his own accord. The homunculus will be brought back here, and possibly Christina. By keeping a watch on the Canon we should be able to cut in at the last moment and prevent their reaching him. Alternatively, by making full speed for London, we can still get on a Paris plane and be in Nice late this evening. We could then get Malouet to try to find out where Upson has brought his seaplane down, with the object of destroying the homunculus; and, should we fail in that, we might anyhow lend a hand in preventing Christina from being whisked out of prison. My own feeling is that our chances are pretty good either way; but this is really your party, John; so I'm going to leave the choice to you.'

After a moment's thought, John said, 'It will be dark before we can get to Nice; so if Copely-Syle has sent a brother wizard down there, he may get Christina out before we arrive on the scene; and Malouet's chances of finding out at short notice where Upson comes down seems pretty problematical. Of course, that is taking the worst view. All the same, a bird in the hand is worth two in the bush; so I think our best bet would be to remain here and concentrate on isolating the Canon.'

'That seems sound to me. We'll return to Colchester, then collect our bags from the Red Lion and transfer to the Weavers Arms at Little Bentford. By making that our new H.Q. we will be able to maintain a twenty-four-hour turn and turn about watch on The Priory, with only half a mile's walk to relieve one another, and between watches get food and sleep. Let's go.'

John drove on till he found a suitable place to reverse the car, then they drove through fourteen miles of twisting lanes back to Colchester. By two o'clock they had packed, paid their bill, and left. Half an hour later they took up their new quarters at Little Bentford and tossed to decide which of them should do the first two-hour spell of duty. John lost, and went out to take up a position in the coppice from which he could keep an eye on The Priory without being seen. As he did so he thanked his stars that throughout the day the weather had taken a turn for the better; so it seemed unlikely that the dreary vigils he and C.B. proposed to keep would be made additionally unpleasant by rain.

He need not have concerned himself about the weather prospects for the night. At a quarter past three he came racing back to the inn and burst into its small parlour. C. B. was just sitting down to an early tea, which he had hoped would make up a little for the lunch he had missed. He looked up to hear John shout:

'Didn't you see that car go by? It was he, driven by his black servant. They've taken the road the lorry took this morning.'

With a sigh, C.B. abandoned his untasted tea and followed John out to the yard, where they had parked the car under a lean-to. Three minutes later they were on the road to Weeley. The Canon's car was out of sight; so they had to take a chance at the crossroads and, instead of continuing south, turned off to Thorpe-le-Soken. There they took another chance and turned north towards Great Oakley. They passed the place where they had met Joe Cotton in his lorry two and a half hours earlier, and still they had not picked up the Canon's car. It was not until they had covered another three miles that C.B. spotted a low moving blob that he thought must be it, far away to their right in the midst of the apparently trackless marshes.

A quarter of a mile farther on they found a narrow track that led seaward, and took it. A few minutes later, after passing a patch of tall reeds, they caught sight of the car again, and some way beyond it the upper structure of the seaplane.

'Look!' cried John bitterly. 'I've been expecting this ever since I saw the road the Canon took out of Little Bentford. Upson didn't leave for France early this afternoon, as we thought. If only we had looked around a bit we might have caught him in his lair, and made a darn' good bid to sink his aircraft.'

'Once the horse was out of the stable, and one saw the direction it was taking, it was easy enough to guess where it would pull up,' C.B. agreed. 'But we might have hunted this wilderness for a couple of days without catching sight of Upson's plane. Given a nice straight piece of Nile it would have been easier to find Moses among the bulrushes.'

Within a few hundred yards of leaving the road, it became clear that they were not on the same track as the Canon's car had taken; but it also led towards the sheet of open water upon which the seaplane sat motionless.

'Stop, John!' C.B. cried. 'We must go back! This way we'll be cut off by the water from getting at him.'

At that moment they came out from behind another wide patch of tall reeds and could again see the Canon's car. It had halted about four hundred yards away. Near it, on the water's edge, rose the roof of a low boat-house. John had already put on the brake, but as the car continued to run forward at a slower pace they saw that the track curved round in the direction they wanted to go. Assuming that it joined the other further on, John took off the brake. Gathering speed again they covered another hundred yards, once more behind a screen of reeds. When they could next see the water, the Canon was out of his car and down by the boat-house. Beside it lay a broad duck-punt. In the punt stood a countryman holding a tall pole.

The track had now become a narrow causeway and was very bumpy. As they bucketed along they could see the Canon looking in their direction. Only two hundred yards separated them from him. Stooping down, he made the gesture of picking up something from the ground. Raising his arm he appeared to throw it at them.

John jerked his head aside. The car swerved violently.

'Look where you're going—not at him!' yelled C. B. But his shout of warning came too late. The near front wheel had gone over the edge of the low bank. The stiff reeds made a sharp rustling sound as they scraped along the coachwork of the car. Heaving on the steering-wheel, John strove to right it; but the bank was too steep. The car heeled over sideways, ran on for a dozen yards, then lurched to a stop, both its near wheels axle-deep in mud and water.

'You idiot!' snapped C. B. 'Why the hell didn't you keep your eyes on the track?'

'I couldn't help ducking when he threw that stone,' John protested angrily. 'It was instinct.'

'He made the motion of throwing, but he didn't throw anything.'

'Yes he did; a damn' great stone. It came hurtling straight at the windscreen.'

'He didn't, I tell you. He couldn't have thrown anything that distance.'

'I saw it.'

'No you didn't,' C.B. said bitterly. 'But I don't doubt you thought you did. It just shows what a powerful Black he is to have been able to cast the thought into your mind so successfully.'

While they were speaking they had scrambled out of the car and started to run down the track. It curved again round another island of reeds, then came to an abrupt ending at a rough wooden landing-stage.

With a curse John made to plunge into the water, Grabbing his coat collar, C. B. pulled him back, and cried, 'Don't be a fool! The mud in these marshes is yards deep in places, and there are under-water reeds as well. You would drown for a certainty.'

To have run all the way back to the road, then down the other track which followed the far side of the creek on which they were standing, would have taken at least twenty minutes. Impotent and furious, they could only remain where they were, watching the final scene of their enemy's triumph.

The coloured servant had already turned the Canon's car and was driving it back towards the road. The Canon was now in the punt and being poled out to the seaplane. They could see now that, although small and tubby, it was a powerful twin-engined affair. Upson came to its door and helped his passenger aboard.

As the labourer in the punt pushed off C.B. cupped his hands and yelled to him to come and pick them up, offering him treble the money he had received for ferrying out his last passenger if he would do so. He made the bid only as a forlorn hope and, as he expected, it proved futile. Either from fear of the Canon, or because he knew that he had been assisting an illegal emigration, the fellow ignored C.B.'s shouts, poled the punt back into the boat-house, then disappeared among the reeds. By that time Upson had the seaplane's engines running. Two minutes later it turned into the wind and ran forward. A double sheet of spray hissed up from beneath its stern and a quarter of a mile down the creek it sailed gracefully into the air.

Returning to the car, they spent twenty minutes trying to get it unditched; but there was no brushwood, or anything else of that kind in the vicinity that they could stuff under the wheels to give them a grip; so they were forced to abandon their efforts.

C.B. glanced at his watch and said, 'This is not so good, John. It is a quarter-past four and we are miles from anywhere. If we had the use of the car we could have reached London before dark and, perhaps, managed to hire a plane to fly us out to Nice; but that is ruled out now. It must be a good hour's tramp to the nearest village and in these little places they don't run to hire cars. By the time we've telephoned to Colchester and got a car to pick us up, then done the seventy miles to Northolt, it will be getting on for eight o'clock; and the aircraft of the private companies are not equipped for night flying.'

John looked a little puzzled as he replied, 'But we decided to stay here.'

'That was when we thought the Canon meant to stay here too, and we could keep a watch on him.'

'I know; and the fact that he will now be down on the Riviera by about nine o'clock naturally adds to the chances of his being able to get Christina out of prison. After your visit last night he is certain to have telephoned de Grasse to make all the preliminary arrangements for his attempt; and now he'll have the whole of the night to work in. But all the same, it seems to me that we still have a good hope of spiking his guns at the last moment.'

'You mean if the prison authorities do their stuff? I agree about that. From the moment the idea of putting her inside was mooted I felt that we were on a winner. And in spite of what the old so-and-so said to me last night I'd still lay three to one against his or any other Black Magician succeeding in getting her out at such short notice.'

'No, I didn't mean that, C.B. I meant in the worst event—saying that he does succeed. He has still got to bring her and the homunculus back here to-morrow. Seaplanes can't just land anywhere. At least, this one can't if it is to fulfil its purpose of putting the Canon, Christina—either unwilling or unconscious—and the heavy crate safely ashore. And I should think the odds are very much against his having another prepared base in this neighbourhood, because he could hardly have foreseen that we should discover this one. Now that we have, you can go to the police, report his unauthorized departure from the country, and have it watched for their return. We'll relieve him of Christina as he lands, and have him and Upson arrested.'

C.B. looked at John and his face was troubled. 'It's a good idea, laddie; but I'm afraid it won't work out. Now he knows we know his base he is much too crafty to return to it. And there is more to it than that. You remember what we were saying a while ago; about our being certain of winning out on the big issue only if we could prevent one of the three factors—Canon, homunculus and Christina—from joining up with the other two? Well, that is now beyond our power. In a few hours' time all three of them will be in Nice. You know the story of Mahomet when he couldn't get the mountain to come to him? In this case Christina is the mountain; and so far the Canon has failed to budge her. Since we have made things so hot for him here, and the time in which to get her back is now so short, it is my bet that he decided this morning to do the job out there. That is why he had the homunculus put on the seaplane instead of hiding it in the house of a pal. And now Mahomet has gone to the mountain.'

21

THE PACT WITH SATAN

'Oh God!' muttered John. 'So far that fiend has won every trick, and soon there will be only a few locked doors between him and Christina. Is there nothing we can do to help in preventing him from getting at her?'

'We can send a telegram warning Malouet that the Canon is on his way,' C.B. suggested. 'There is just a chance that the French police might pick him up on landing. If so, he could be arrested for illegal entry. But you can be sure that he has been in communication with de Grasse about flying out; so the seaplane will not come down at the Ile de Port Cros. De Grasse would not risk that. He will appreciate that since our visit to it yesterday morning Malouet may have got the police to keep it under observation; so he will have instructed Upson to land at one of his other haunts, where there is little chance of his being spotted. I'm afraid, John, that for tonight you'll have to pin your faith on the French prison system; and believe me, it's a pretty good one.'

'I only hope you're right. Anyhow, the sooner we send that telegram, the better.' Leaning through the window of the car, John pulled a map from the pocket next to the driver's seat. A glance at it showed that the nearest village was probably Great Oakley. They could not be certain of their exact position among the tangled creeks of Hansford Water, but judged the village to be between three and five miles distant. Having locked the car they set off there.

The sky was a uniform grey, but somewhere in the west the sun was now getting down towards the horizon, and as they began to trudge in that direction John wondered miserably how fate would deal with Christina during this last critical night before her birthday. He would have given a great deal to be with her or, that being out of the question, at least able to keep watch outside her prison; and his impotence riled him all the more from the fact that it was he who had taken the decision to remain in England to watch the Canon. C.B. had given him the choice early that afternoon, and had he chosen the alternative they could have been well on their way to Nice by now. Yet he knew that it was silly to blame himself for his blunder, as it had seemed the best course to take at the time.

It was half-past five when they reached Great Oakley and the light was fading. From the village pub they telephoned their telegram to Malouet, then put through a call to a garage in Colchester for a breakdown van with a searchlight. It picked them up at a quarter-past six and they returned to the marshes. They lost twenty minutes searching along several tracks for the point at which C.B.'s car had become ditched, but once they found it there was little difficulty in hauling the car out. Both of them now thought it unlikely that the seaplane would bring the Canon back and land again on the same stretch of water next day, but that possibility could not be ignored; so they intended asking the police to keep a watch on it. To do so meant going in to Colchester and, with the Canon gone, there no longer seemed any point in their sleeping at Little Bentford. In consequence, in the car with John at the wheel once more, they collected their bags from the Weavers Arms and drove to the market town. There John dropped C.B. off at the police station and went on to book rooms and order dinner at the Red Lion.

By then it was getting on for eight o'clock. Soon afterwards C.B. came in and they sat down to dine. While they ate, in low voices they reviewed the situation, and could not escape the fact that they had far graver grounds for depression than they had had when dining there the night before. Then, their only cause for gloom had been that their journey appeared to have been rendered futile by their failure to locate Beddows through his office. Now they had found him, but he had refused them his help. They had also found out a great deal about the Canon; above all, that he was not merely seeking to corrupt Christina but, if he could get hold of her, meant to kill her.

The thought of the night to come, and his utter helplessness during it, to which he must attempt to reconcile himself, had now been preying on John's mind for four hours. He seemed obsessed with the idea that if only they could think of it, there must be some way in which they could either foil the Canon in his bid to get at Christina, or strengthen her mind to resist his influence.

C.B. could only suggest that they should rout out a parson, beg the keys of his church and pray for her in it. John said he would willingly spend the night on his knees, but had always believed that God helped those who helped themselves; and felt sure that there must be some active measure which might bring about more definite results. Yet it was the suggestion of prayer that gave him an idea, and after a moment he said:

'I am still convinced that something could be done through Beddows.

After all, he is much more than Christina's physical father. As it was he who sold her to the Devil, he is her godfather as well—and not just in the modern sense of buying her a christening-mug and trying to remember to give her a quid on her birthdays. By inducting him as a Satanist the Canon took spiritual responsibility for him, and he in turn took spiritual responsibility for Christina. If we could only persuade *him* to pray to Jesus Christ for her to-night I believe we would achieve something really worth while.'

'I get the idea,' murmured C.B. dubiously. 'As he admitted to us that it was having her baptized into the Satanic faith which makes her subject to evil influences during the hours of darkness, your theory is that if we could get him to recant she would no longer be subject to those influences.'

'Exactly! Then, whatever success the Canon may have in casting spells on her jailers to-night, when it comes to willing her to leave her cell she would reject the thought and sit tight there.'

C.B. rubbed his big nose. 'Your reasoning seems sound enough; but I'd as soon hope to jump Becher's Brook on a donkey as get Beddows to do as you suggest. Do you realize that after all these years of battening on the fruits of evil he would have to abjure his Master? It isn't even as if he really cares very deeply what happens to Christina. And the risk! If he forswears Satan now, it wouldn't surprise me to see him struck dead by some form of seizure.'

'Well, he has had his fling; and if he lives on he will be lucky if he escapes being hounded into a madhouse by the Canon. Providing he abjures, even if he does die, we shall have achieved our object, and I wouldn't allow his life to weigh with me for one moment against Christina's. I agree that it is a thousand to one against our being able to persuade him to rely on God's mercy, but there is that one chance; and to make the attempt is a thousand times better than spending the night doing nothing.'

'O.K., partner.' C.B. finished his port. 'We'll pay him another visit.'

Soon after ten they were again approaching The Grange. Now that they knew its owner was there they were indifferent to the possibility of the Jutsons hearing them and coming on the scene; so they drove straight up to the front door. But, knowing that their ring would not be answered, on getting out they walked round to the yard. No chinks of light showed between the curtains of the windows above the stable, and with no more than a glance at them they entered the house through the staircase window, the catch of which C.B. had forced the night before.

By the light of C.B.'s torch they proceeded through the baize door, across the hall and up the stairs. The atmosphere of the house was still chill and eerie, but to-night it did not fill them with the fears that had racked their nerves during their previous visit. Swinging themselves across the gap in the floorboards of the landing, they approached the upper flight of stairs. The clanking of the ape's chain came clearly, telling that it had been freed—no doubt by Jutson when he had come up to give it fresh food and water that morning—so they expected to have to catch and bind it again. That proved unnecessary. The creature had evidently learnt its lesson, for the moment C.B. shone his torch it cowered away, chattering with fright, into the farthest corner of the upper landing. Keeping a wary eye on it, they climbed the stairs and sidled past to the door of the great attic. Its lock had not been repaired and the door opened at a touch.

Beyond it the scene was the same almost unbelievable one that would for ever remain engraved upon their memories. There sat the twentieth-century business man cross-legged on his blankets, his back propped against the tea-chest, surrounded by the paraphernalia of mediaeval witchcraft, his form dimly lit by the unflickering blue light given off from the glass tubes of the pentacle that enclosed him.

This time he showed no fear of his visitors. Their approach had roused him from a doze, and after giving himself a little shake he said, none too cordially, 'So it's you two again. What d'you want now?'

C.B. felt that this was John's party; so he waited for him to speak, and John, having decided on the way there that a tactful approach was essential to any hope of success replied quietly:

'A lot has happened since we saw you last night, Mr Beddows; so we thought we ought to come and report.'

'Why? I'm not employing you.' Beddows gave him a chilly stare.

'No; but I'm sure you are not indifferent to Chris ... to Ellen's fate; otherwise you would not have gone to such trouble to hide her in the South of France. What is more, you are vitally concerned in the outcome of this affair yourself.'

'I can't stop you talking, if you want to,' came the ungracious reply; 'but if you think you are going to wheedle me into taking any action you might as well save your breath.'

'We've come to you partly because we want your advice.'

'All right.' Beddows' voice sounded as though he was slightly reassured. 'Advice costs nothing. Go ahead.'

'Thanks.' Feeling a trifle awkward standing there, John took a step forward and sat down on the floor as near as he could get to Beddows while remaining outside the pentacle. As C.B. followed his example, he began to give an account of all that had happened that day. When he had done, he went on:

'Now! One of the things we wanted to ask you, Mr Beddows, is can the Canon perform his ritual with the homunculus and Ellen anywhere, or will he have to bring them back to do the job to-morrow night in his own crypt?'

'He needn't bring them back, but he can't do it anywhere. The ceremony must be performed on an altar that has been properly dedicated to the Lord Satan.'

'We feared as much. Are there many such altars in the South of France?'

'A certain number. There is at least one in every big city in the world. All over Europe they are scattered in the country parts too; mostly in ruined abbeys, old castles and such.'

'Do you know the whereabouts of any of those on the Riviera?'

Beddows shook his head. 'No; I've never attended a ceremony outside England.'

After a moment John asked, 'What do you really think of the Canon's prospects of getting Ellen out of prison?'

'It is difficult to say. To do so he has got to temporarily paralyse a system. That is a far more formidable undertaking than enforcing sleep on the members of an ordinary household. No one of average powers would even attempt it; but he is an Ipsissimus, and there are few things impossible to a Mage of that highest grade. There is, too, one thing in his favour. If he can succeed in bemusing the jailers into unlocking the right doors, he will have no difficulty with Ellen. He will have only to call her on the astral, and she will walk out.'

'Yes; that is just what we fear. Can you suggest any means by which we might cause her to resist his will?'

'Only a White Magician who has greater power than Copely-Syle could cause her to do that.'

'Do you know of one?'

'No. I've naturally kept clear of anyone I believed to be working on the Right Hand side.'

Again John paused, then he said, 'I take it from what you were telling us last night that Ellen's subservience to evil during the dark hours is not a part of her nature, but entirely due to the fact that you . . . you had her baptized into the Satanic faith?'

'That's so.'

'If she were re-baptized into the Christian faith, would that destroy the influence that the Dark Powers have over her?'

'No. There is no point in hiding the truth. It was I who sold her to the Devil; so only I can redeem her.'

'How would you do that?'

Beddows gave a harsh laugh. 'I wouldn't! Is it likely? It would mean my abjuring Satan.'

'But if you did? Say you abjured Satan here and now, on her behalf and on your own, would that take immediate effect? Would it result in her resisting when the Canon calls her to-night on the astral, and remaining in her cell?'

'Yes. The effect would be instantaneous. Of course, she would still be subject to hypnotic suggestion, like her jailers or anyone else, in normal circumstances in the future; but not to-night. Such an act would restore the powers of her Guardian Angel, who has been chained all these years. Once freed, he would give her everything he'd got, and throw an aura round her which would protect her from every harmful thought.'

Beddows ceased speaking for a moment, then added suddenly in an aggressive voice, 'But don't think what I've told you is going to get you anywhere. If you've come here to try to get me to abjure, you've backed the wrong horse. I've no intention of being struck dead by an apoplectic fit and frying for all Eternity.'

'Is that what it would mean for you?'

'Yes. Hell is real! Don't you believe these modern parsons who are fools enough to tell their congregations otherwise. I know, because I've seen it. Copely-Syle showed it to me the night that he initiated me as a Neophyte of the Left Hand Path. And it is gaping wide with great tongues of flame for anyone like me—should I betray the Master.'

'The mercy of God is infinite,' said John quietly.

'Maybe,' sneered Beddows. 'But not till after one has paid the price for what one has taken at Satan's hands. God would leave me to burn for a thousand years before He even had a look at me. If you think I'd give a blank cheque of that kind to save Ellen you must be crazy.'

John remained silent long enough for Beddows to cool down, then he said, 'There is another thing we wanted to ask you about. Last night you told us that for a time you gave up your engineering studies on account of a personal attachment. Would you tell us about that?'

'Why? It has nothing whatever to do with this business of Copely-Syle and Ellen.'

'I'm not so sure. I think it might have. Every major emotional experience in your life must have had some bearing on your present situation. Please tell us about it.'

Beddows shrugged. 'Very well. Since I've told you the rest of the story, I may as well fill in the gap. When I first came here as chauffeur old Mrs Durnsford had a companion. She was a girl named Isobel—a frail, gentle little thing, but very beautiful and the sort that is too good for this world. The old girl made her life hell, but she had to grin and bear it. You see, she was a poor relation, with no other relatives to go to, and neither the training nor the stamina to take any other job; so she had no alternative to staying on here.

'When I had been here for a bit Mrs Durnsford had the idea that I should teach Isobel to drive the car. She didn't want to, and I didn't want to teach her, as I thought it might result in my being given the sack; but it was an order. Things being like that, Isobel's progress was not very fast; so I had plenty of opportunity to get to know her. At first she was very shy, but gradually we got to confiding in one another. I found then that behind her timid manner lay a wonderful mind, filled with courage, unselfishness and an infallible understanding of all the things that really matter.

'She held that money, birth and position counted for nothing; that real happiness could be gained only by giving happiness to others; that God always provided for His children if they did the right thing; that one should never strive to pile up possessions, but only to make people kinder to one another; and that one should live from day to day, so that if death came unexpectedly one could face it with the certainty that one's heart would weigh no more in the scales of judgment than the feather of truth.

'I fell in love with her; and, although I have never understood why, she fell in love with me. When she had got the hang of driving the car sufficient for there to be no excuse to give her further lessons, we continued to meet, but in secret, at any odd times we could snatch. Naturally I had told her all about my engineering ambitions, but she wasn't in favour of that. Partly because it would have meant living in a town, but more, really, because I had frankly admitted that my object in taking it up was solely to make money out of it.

'She had money coming to her: not a lot, but enough. Under a trust Mrs Durnsford enjoyed the income on condition that she gave Isobel a home until she was twenty-five. It could not be touched before that, but then the capital had to be handed over with no strings attached. We had eighteen months to go, but we were content to wait. Isobel wanted to start a small school for crippled and backward children. She would have given them the indoor lessons and I was to teach them gardening, carpentry, and a bit about the inside of cars, and generally run the place. That may sound very different from what I have made of my life, but I would have been far happier doing that. With those kiddies to look after there would have been more new interests every day than I get out of all my businesses; and no man could have been unhappy with Isobel for a wife.'

Beddows sighed heavily. 'But it was not to be. Before Isobel was twenty-four she fell ill. She was so frail that I think she must always have had it in her, but she caught a chill and soon afterwards T.B. developed. After a bit they sent her to Switzerland, and I was distraught. But I managed to see her alone before she left. We swore we would love one another always and, of course, we promised to write frequently.

'We did; and for the first few weeks I received her letters quite regular.

They told me about the place, and the other patients; about the nice young doctor who was looking after her, and how she was sure she would be well enough to come home in time for Christmas. Then her letters grew more infrequent, and after two intervals of ten days they stopped altogether. If I'd been a town chap I suppose I would have telegraphed her to know what was wrong, but sending cables to foreign countries was away over the head of a young country feller like I was in those days. I put her silence down to the young doctor. You see, I'd never been able to convince myself that I was good enough for her; so I didn't even write and ask her to let me know if she had changed her mind about marrying me. I just let my misery have free reign, and decided to stop writing till I heard from her again.

'About three weeks went by like that; then one day, as Mrs Durnsford was getting into the car, she told me quite casual that Isobel was dead. It was a dirty, wicked lie—may her soul rot! But I never found that out until years later; in fact not until after she was dead herself. She had no near relatives, and when she died her executors sold off the whole contents of the house as well as the place. I had my own furniture, and I didn't want any of hers; but I thought the shelves in the study would look a bit bare without some books, so I bought those at the sale. Naturally, the executors removed her private papers, but there was one lot they overlooked. I came on them soon after I moved in. They were with a pack of Tarot cards and a collection of witch's-brew recipes in what was left of a big old family Bible that had had its middle cut out to form a box. Among them was a score of letters from Isobel to me that I had never had.

'It was quite clear then what had happened. My post had always been delivered to the house with the rest of the letters before being brought across the yard to me by one of the maids. The old bitch must have seen a letter with Swiss stamps on addressed to me in Isobel's writing, steamed it open and read it. In our letters we naturally wrote of our love for one another and of our future plans. The thought of people being happy and making life better for a lot of crippled kids would have been poison to old Mother Durnsford. I bet she got no end of a kick out of sabotaging all our hopes. It would have been easy for her to intercept Isobel's letters—a few at first, then all of them later on. That's what she had done; and when she judged that she had got me really worried she both provided an explanation why I had not received any letters from Isobel for the past few weeks and gave me the knock out; because the inference was that for some time before her death Isobel had been too ill to write. Mother Durnsford had rounded the affair off nice and neatly the other end too. The envelope of Isobel's last letter was marked 'to await collection' and I saw from it that the old woman had written her saying that I'd gone away and left no address.

'Even that was not the full measure of her malice. Naturally, after I thought Isobel was dead I went all to pieces for a bit. But I was young and healthy, and next spring I started to tumble Hettie evenings in the barn. I've told you how she got in the family way with Ellen and spilled the beans about it. That must have given Mother Durnsford a fine old laugh. I didn't know it then, but she had learned from Isobel's letters how anxious I was to educate and improve myself. Nothing could have been more likely to scotch that than to tie me up to a brainless little working-class slut who was going to have a kid, and would probably go on producing them like rabbits.

'Well, it didn't work out that way. But she succeeded in robbing me of

Isobel; and you are quite right in your idea that losing her altered my whole life. I still don't see, though, what that has to do with the Canon and Ellen.'

John had listened to Beddows' love-story with intense interest, and now he asked, 'Did you ever find out what happened to Isobel?'

'Yes. After I found those letters I had enquiries made. There had been a world war in between, but they succeeded in tracing her up. She did die, but not till nearly a year after I believed her dead; and ever since I learned that I've been tortured by the belief that she just let herself die of a broken heart.'

'Say she had lived, Mr Beddows, and you had found out sooner that she was still alive—would you have married her after your first wife died?'

'Of course I would.'

'But you couldn't possibly have married a person as fine as she was, unless you had first forsworn the Devil. To have continued secretly as a Satanist would have robbed your marriage with her of all the genuine happiness you expected to derive from it.'

'Yes; I see that,' Beddows admitted slowly. 'Still, love is the greatest protective force in existence. I think hers would have proved strong enough to shield me from all but loss of my worldly wealth. Anyhow, it's true that I should have had to abjure in order to put myself right with her; and for her sake I would have risked anything.'

'You must have loved her very deeply.'

'More than anything in this world or the next.'

'Then you will be able to understand how I feel, Mr Beddows, when I tell you that I love your daughter.'

Beddows raised his eyebrows. 'Is that so? You haven't known her very long, have you?'

'No; but in the hours we have spent together much more has happened than during an ordinary courtship. We are already engaged to be married.'

For the first time a glint of humour showed in Beddows' brown eyes as he asked, 'Am I to take it that you've come here to-night to ask my consent?'

'We should be glad to have your blessing,' John answered seriously. 'But first we need the help that only you can give. And you know how desperately we need it.'

'I'm sorry. Indeed I am. But it's no good harking back to that.'

'Mr Beddows, you have just said that you loved Isobel more than anything in this world or the next. That implies that you still love her spirit. If it were here in this room to-night—as it well may be—and could speak to you, what would it say? You know as well as I do that it would beg you to become again the person it knew and loved. It would urge you to defy Satan in order to save your daughter and make possible the happiness of another pair of lovers.'

'Yes,' Beddows muttered. 'That's what it would say.'

'Then if you still love her, do this for her sake.'

The eyes of the man in the pentacle suddenly blazed, and he shouted, 'Damn you, stop torturing me! I can't! I won't! Get to hell out of here!'

After his long and skilful guidance of their talk, John had felt that he was almost on the verge of victory; so Beddows' outburst came as a bitter disappointment. For a moment he remained silent, searching his mind for some last card that might yet win him over. To his distress he could think of nothing approaching the potency of the arguments he had already used; so he could only fall back upon what he felt to be a frail piece of reasoning, unlikely to alter a mind so evidently fixed by terror in its determination. Nevertheless he threw out the suggestion with no lessening of persistence.

'You were saying a little while ago that if Isobel had still been alive and you had abjured to put yourself right with her, you thought that her love would have protected you from all but the loss of your worldly wealth. Surely, although she is now a spirit, her love would continue to protect you?'

'No.' Beddows' voice was firm. 'For all I know, during those last months she may have believed that I had deliberately jilted her, and died hating me. I can't afford to chance that. There is one thing and one thing only that could protect me. That is to cheat Satan by getting back the Pact I signed with him.'

John's muscles tensed. 'D'you know where it is?'

'Copely-Syle has it.'

'I naturally supposed so; but he wouldn't carry it about on him. I mean, do you know where he keeps it?'

'I don't know for certain, but I can give a good guess. It is a hundred to one that after offering it up he would place a document of that kind under the Satanic altar in his crypt.'

'Then . . .' John hesitated.

Beddows flung out his hands in a violent gesture of protest. 'No, no! Don't think of it. Forget what I said! You're young and healthy! You should have many years of happiness ahead of you. There are plenty of other girls in the world besides Ellen. You would be crazy to try to raise that altar. You would be blasted where you stood. If you did survive you would be found as a gibbering idiot in the morning. I wouldn't let my worst enemy attempt to get that Pact.'

Slowly John stood up. 'If I do get it, and give it to you to destroy, will you swear to me by your love for Isobel immediately to abjure Satan?'

A shudder ran through Beddows. With eyes distended by horror he stared up at John. For a moment he was silent, then he gasped, 'All right! I swear. But I warned you: I warned you! You'll be going to your death.'

22

THE DEVIL'S ALTAR

The palms of John's hands were already sweating. His memory of the impotence and fear he had felt when in the crypt twenty-four hours earlier was still vivid in his mind; yet he had made his decision the moment Beddows had spoken of the Pact as the price on which he must insist for his co-operation.

John had come there determined to secure that co-operation somehow; not only because it could bring to nought the Canon's attempt to get Christina out of prison during the night that was already upon them, but also because on that depended her whole future. To save her from an abominable death at the hands of Copely-Syle was the overriding consideration for the moment, but even success in that could later prove a barren victory if she were to continue to be the nightly victim of evil cravings which, now she was out in the world, must soon lead her to become cynically immoral, decadent, unscrupulous and, perhaps, criminal. Only her father could save her from that by ratting on his bargain with the Devil. Since his price for that was the Pact, he must have it.

The mere idea of going into the crypt again filled John with terrifying qualms. He felt that to argue the matter further could only weaken his resolution, and that in immediate action lay his sole hope of maintaining it long enough to force himself to enter that Satanic stronghold when he got there; so he said abruptly:

'Perhaps you are right, and I'll be dead in an hour. If not, I'll be back here.' Then he turned towards the door.

'Hi!' C. B. called after him. 'If we've got to do this thing, we had better take some weapons with us.'

'You are not in this!' John's voice was made surly by fear. 'This is my show. You stay where you are.'

'Is it likely?' C. B. grunted. 'I've never liked anything less in my life; but how could I ever face your mother if I let you go alone?' Turning to Beddows, he said, 'These cups in the valleys of the pentacle have Holy water in them, haven't they? Where's the rest of it?'

Reaching behind him into the tea-chest. Beddows produced a quart bottle half full. As he handed it over, C. B. asked:

'Have you any spare horse-shoes?'

'No. I'm afraid not.'

'That's a pity.' muttered C. B. 'And I daren't deprive you of any of your defences, in case something gets at you while we are away. I suppose you haven't got a crucifix in the house?'

Beddows shook his head. 'Of course not! I could hardly bear to look at one, and it would burn me if I touched it. As it was I had to be mighty careful when I poured the Holy water out: if I had spilt any on my hands it would have scalded me.'

John was already at the door. Without another glance at Beddows, C. B. joined him and they hurried downstairs. When they reached the hall John made for the baize door, but C. B. called after him:

'Hold your horses! We've got to forge a few astral weapons before we leave here. I wish to goodness we had a little time to make proper preparations. We ought to have necklaces of garlic and asafoetida grass, not to mention purifying ourselves with the smoke of sweet herbs and putting on clean underclothes. Still, we must do the best we can.'

As he spoke he led the way through the breakfast room to the pantry, and began to pull open its rows of drawers one after another. In one he found string and scissors, in another a bundle of firewood. Handing them to John, he said:

'Here, take these. Use four of the sticks to make two crosses. Bind them together with the string and attach long loops to them so that we can hang them round our necks.'

In a corner of the room were stacked several crates. The top ones contained quart bottles of beer, but underneath he found one holding small bottles of lemonade. Taking two of them, he opened and emptied them at the sink, then refilled them with Holy water and corked them roughly with tight wads of screwed-up newspaper.

'Put this in your pocket,' he said, handing one of them to John. 'And don't use it until I tell you to.' The other he pocketed himself.

Picking up a broom that stood behind the door, he wrenched out the long handle, then laid it over a Windsor chair and snapped it in two pieces about one third of the way up. With another length of string he lashed them together, so that they formed a large cross to carry in the hand. After a quick look round, he went to the further door that led to the rear quarters of the house, opened it and said:

'I am going to hunt round for something with which to prise up the altar slab. In the meantime pull down some curtains, soak them with water and carry them out to the car. Unbolt the front door and go out by that. It will save time.'

John did as he was told, and he was still piling the sopping mess on the floor in front of the back seat when C.B. rejoined him, carrying a steel case-opener. As he held it out, he remarked, 'This is not much bigger than my own jemmy, but the best thing I could find. You take it, and I'll carry the cross.'

As they got in the car and he started up the engine, John said, 'I take it the wet things are for throwing down the furnace chimney?'

'Yes. We've been lucky here in finding that the Jutsons go to bed early; but it's only just eleven o'clock; so that coloured servant of the Canon's may still be up. I had thought of going to the front door and knocking him out as soon as he answered it. We would be almost sure of having the free run of the place then, as it is most unlikely that anyone who performs the Canon's tricks would have any other servants living in; but the door to the crypt is of iron and has a Chubb lock. As Copely-Syle keeps the key to it on him we wouldn't be able to get in that way; so I think we would do better to ignore the Egyptian and go straight in down the chimney.'

A few minutes' drive brought them to The Priory. Pulling up a hundred yards short of it, John parked the car under the trees that overhung the road, and they got out. A light wind had risen, keeping off more rain, but the sky was four-fifths scudding cloud and it was only when the moon broke through at intervals for a minute or two that there was enough light for them to see their way at all clearly.

Carrying the sopping curtains between them, they broke through the hedge into the coppice and approached the house by the route that John had taken the previous night. On reaching the crypt they dumped their burden and made a brief reconnaissance round the house and back. No light showed in any of the windows; so it looked as if the Egyptian had gone to bed. C.B., as the taller, gave John a leg up, passed him the bundle of curtains, and scrambled on to the roof after him. In single file they crossed it to the chimney.

'Now,' said C.B. in a low voice, 'I needn't stress the fact that we are going into great danger. We must kneel down and pray.'

Side by side they went down on their knees, and remained so in silence for a few minutes. As they got up, C.B. murmured, 'I wish I could remember the Twenty-third Psalm. It is said to be exceptionally potent as a protection against demons. Do you recall how it goes?'

John shook his head. 'I think it is the one that has in it "though I walk through the valley of the shadow of death, I will fear no evil"; but I can't say for certain.'

'Then we had better stick to the Lord's Prayer. Keep on repeating it to yourself; and if anything nasty comes at you cry aloud, "In the name of Jesus

Christ I defy thee, Satan.'''

John dropped the curtains down the wide chimney mouth. As they fell on the furnace at its bottom with a faint thud, he made to follow them; but C. B. pushed him firmly aside. 'No, John. I am carrying the cross; so you must let me be the leader of this party. What is more, if at any time I tell you to get out, you will *get out*, and not stop to argue about it. By doing so you will not only save yourself, but will be able to bring help, with at least some chance of saving me later. Is that clear?'

As John nodded, C. B. swung his long legs over the chimney lip, found the first rungs inside and disappeared down it. Dropping the last few feet, he landed on the wet curtains. Beneath them the coke made a crunching sound, but the fire was dull and he scarcely felt its heat as he jumped off it.

The crypt was in darkness. Holding the cross in his left hand, he pulled his torch from his pocket with his right and switched it on. The instant he could see his way, he ran up the steps that led to the iron door and brushed down all the switches beside it, flooding the central aisle of the crypt with light. Pushing the torch back in his pocket he turned, planted his back firmly against the door, and only then let his glance rove round the vaulted chamber.

There was less change in it than he had expected from what Inspector Fuller had implied. The curtains at the far end, embroidered with the Goat of Mendes and the Woman with Seven Breasts, were gone; so were the sorcerer's robes, the altar cloth, the black candle, and the broken crucifix with the bat nailed upside down on it: but the sword, the chalice and the book still reposed upon the altar slab, looking not inappropriate in the rôle of harmless ornaments. The skeleton still dangled grotesquely from its wire and the mummy-case lay undisturbed beneath the nearest table; but both were the sort of exhibits that might be found in the museum-workshop of any amateur scientist. That also applied to the astrolabe, the six out of the seven great glass jars that had contained the homunculi, and the bottles, measures, balances and retorts that loaded the four long refectory tables.

One sweeping glance was enough for C. B. to take that much in, and he had hardly had time to register it before John thumped down on the furnace, sprang off it and pulled the now steaming curtains after him. Neither had the least intention of staying there one moment longer than they had to, and both simultaneously started forward towards the altar. They had taken only two steps when a cock crowed.

The cock's raucous challenge, seeming unnaturally loud as it echoed from the stone arches overhead, sounded like the voice of doom. The two men halted in their tracks. The blood rushed to their hearts. Fearfully they jerked white faces round towards the left-hand aisle and the shadowy tier of cages behind the row of pillars, from which the crowing came.

There was nothing really terrifying about the sound itself—it was hearing it so unexpectedly in those surroundings. They had forgotten that although, according to the inspector's account, the Canon had disposed of all his maimed animals, he had not removed the chickens, doves and other fowl which he used for sacrifices. In the darkness they had all been silently sleeping, till the sudden switching on of the lights had aroused them to chirp and flutter in a false dawn.

As realization dawned upon the two intruders, that this was no demon giving tongue in the likeness of a bird, they let go their breath and breathed again; but only for a moment. Something moved swiftly behind one of the pillars. Both of them glimpsed the quick, furtive jump of a shadowy body, but neither could have said what it was. Instead of advancing further, they remained there, staring apprehensively at the base of the pillar behind which it had disappeared.

Before they could make up their minds to leave it unaccounted for in their rear, their attention was distracted to the roof. A faint squeaking sounded up in the shadows above the row of lights. There was a sudden movement up there too, then the squeaking ceased.

'Come on!' said John. 'We're wasting time.'

As he spoke the thing behind the pillar moved again. It sprang out into the open, a yard ahead of them, right in their path. Their gasps merged into sighs of relief. It was an obscene and ugly creature, but appeared to be no more than an exceptionally large toad.

John took another step forward. His foot had not reached the ground when something hurtled at his head from above, like a small dive-bomber. He gave a cry of fear and ducked, but caught a swift sight of the thing as it streaked downward between his upturned face and the nearest light. As he did so he upbraided himself for showing such funk, when the squeaking should have told him that the creatures above the lights were only bats.

Next moment he had cause for real terror. The toad had been watching him with bright, jewel-like, unwinking eyes. Suddenly its mouth opened and it laughed.

That deep unholy chuckle, coming from a reptile, sent chills rippling down both their spines. Instinctively they backed towards the steps.

'We've got to go forward.' said C. B. hoarsely. 'If we lose our nerve now, we're finished.'

In two paces they recovered their lost ground; but the toad held his. Then an extraordinary thing happened. Its outline blurred and it crepitated until it turned into a yellowish-green ball of gaseous matter. An instant later there were two toads squatting where there had been only one before.

With unbelieving eyes they stared at the twin creatures begotten so mysteriously. As they did so they heard a swish in the air above them, and this time two bats came hurtling at their heads. Both of them ducked; the two toads laughed, wobbled into whirling balls and became four.

It was at that moment that the lights went out.

For a few seconds they were blinded by the darkness; then they became conscious of a glow behind them. Swinging round they saw that the door had opened, and the Canon's coloured servant stood framed in it.

It occurred to them only then that he must have a key to the door in order to keep the furnace going and feed the birds. What had brought him on the scene they could not guess. They had been in the crypt for about two minutes. It was possible that he had heard the cock crow, or seen a line of light below the door, or simply come to stoke the furnace up for the night, or perhaps been summoned as the guardian of the place by some occult signal. They could only be certain that it was he who had turned out the lights; for, as they swung upon him, he still had his dark hand on the two lowest switches.

After the unnerving episode of the toad a human enemy held few terrors for the nocturnal intruders. The Egyptian was as tall as C. B. and the flowing white burnous which concealed his limbs gave him the appearance of being considerably more powerful; yet without a second's hesitation John tensed his muscles to spring up the steps towards him.

C.B. did likewise, then swiftly averted his gaze and shouted a warning. 'Don't look at his eyes! Don't look at his eyes!'

It came too late. John was already staring straight into the coloured man's white-rimmed eyeballs. The reason why he had switched out the lights instantly became clear. It was to prevent them dazzling him and to enable his eyes to become luminous in the semi-darkness. In his coffee-coloured face they now showed up brilliantly. They held John's gaze so that he could not draw it away, and seemed to increase in size with extraordinary swiftness. To his fury and amazement his body made a futile jerk, but he was incapable of launching himself up the stone stairway. The eyes that bored into his grew bigger and bigger, until they merged and became one great blinding circle of light. An intolerable pain shot through his head, his knees gave under him and he crumpled up on the lowest step.

The Egyptian had overcome him in a matter of seconds by catching his glance as he was about to jump. But C.B., after one glimpse of the baleful light in the coloured man's eyes, had torn his own away. Riveting his gaze on the stone flags of the floor for a moment, he concentrated both his mental and physical strength. Swiftly, he muttered a short prayer; then, without raising his glance, he hurled himself at the Egyptian's legs.

John had at that second collapsed. Having dealt successfully with one intruder, the Egyptian turned on the other. But he had time only to kick C.B. in the chest. The force of the kick would have broken C.B.'s breast-bone had the man been wearing boots, but he had on only soft leather sandals. The jolt was no worse than a punch from a pugilist wearing boxing gloves; yet that was bad enough. It shook C.B. sufficiently to make him gasp and boggle his tackle. Instead of getting the man beneath the knees, he succeeded in grasping him only by one ankle. Tightening his grip, he drew a deep breath, then threw his weight backward.

The Egyptian's foot flew from beneath him and he crashed to the ground. Without losing a second he kicked out with his other foot. It caught C.B. on the head and sent him reeling down the steps. But John, now freed for a few seconds from the paralysing effect of that hypnotic stare, was on his feet again. He still grasped in his right hand the steel case-opener that he had been holding when he came down the chimney. Rushing up the steps he beat wildly at the coloured man with it just as he was struggling back on to his feet. One blow caught him on the shoulder, and he let out a yell of pain. The second landed on his forehead. Without another sound, he went down like a pole-axed bullock.

C.B. came panting up the steps into the doorway. Seeing the look on John's face he muttered, 'Don't worry! These Arab types have heads like cannon balls. You haven't killed him. But he'll be out long enough not to bother us again. Help me to get him back into the passage.'

Grasping the unconscious man by the legs and shoulders, they pulled him from the stairhead and clear of the door; then for a second they stood in it side by side, staring down into the crypt.

It was lit now only by the glow coming from the passage behind them, and was no longer silent. From all sides of it came weird discordant noises, as though it was filled with horrible, half-human, half-animal life. A lunatic-like chuckling mingled with the bleating of a goat. The cock was crowing

again, the bats squeaked as though they were now legion, a pig grunted, and
as a background to it all there came a low rhythmical throbbing of Voodoo
drums.

'We've got to go in at the charge this time,' said C.B. urgently. 'The
longer we wait, the worse it will get. They can't harm us as long as we remain
defiant and trust in the Lord. To tackle the Gippy I had to drop my cross at
the bottom of the steps. I've got to get that; so you must give me a moment to
snatch it up. I'm going in now. As I grab it I'll give a shout. Switch on all the
lights, then come hell for leather after me.'

As he finished speaking, he ran down the steps. Stooping he seized the
broomstick cross, lifted it on high and cried, 'Oh Lord be with us!' The
lights flashed on. John leapt down beside him. Together they dashed
forward.

They had fifty feet to cover. In the brief space that the lights had been out
the huge toads had multiplied exceedingly. A company of them, dozens
strong, now barred the way between the tables and either side of them. From
the roof a cloud of bats streaked down.

The first rush carried them fifteen paces. They were halfway along the
crypt, but there they lost momentum and their footsteps faltered. The bats
thudded into their bodies and dashed themselves against their faces. The
toads spat venom which turned into clouds of greenish vapour. It had the
awful stench of rotting corpses. In a few moments it had formed a thick
barrier through which the altar could no longer be seen. The poisonous
fumes it carried stung their eyes and made their throats feel raw.

'Satan, I defy thee!' cried C.B. 'Satan, I defy thee!' And John chimed in,
'Oh God, destroy our enemies! Dear God, destroy our enemies!'

Suddenly the babble of sound subsided to a muted, angry muttering. The
clouds of poisonous vapour dissolved. The bats flopped helplessly upon the
floor, and the toads wilted into weak, flabby, grovelling creatures.

Again C.B. and John ran forward; but a new terror arose to halt them. The
lights flickered twice, then dimmed almost to extinction. Ahead of them the
floor began to glow with a dull, reddish light, and to heave like the swell of an
oily pond. It seemed to be imbued with some weird malevolent life of its
own. With the next steps they took they could feel its heat through the soles
of their shoes, and wisps of smoke curled up from the leather. The flagstones
had become red hot, and those in front of the altar were molten.

For a moment they remained half crouching, shoulder to shoulder, their
eyes nearly dazzled by the glare that came from the shimmering crucible that
threatened to engulf them if they advanced another few steps. A blast of
intense heat hit against their hands and faces; so that in another few seconds
the sweat was streaming from them.

'Have faith, John! Have faith!' whispered C.B. 'If we trust in the Lord we
can walk unharmed through this fiery furnace. We must go forward boldly.'

Simultaneously they began to recite the Lord's Prayer and walk steadily
towards the altar. Their shoes ceased to char and, although the stones about
them continued to appear white hot, they no longer felt any heat on the soles
of their feet.

As they reached the altar the glow of the stones faded. Only then did they
become aware that some awful thing was materializing on the altar itself.
The lights remained dimmed and out of the shadows immediately in front of
them emerged a monster that made them blanch with fear. It had a woman's

face set in the middle of a round, fleshy body. The face was beautiful, yet incredibly evil: the body was covered with filthy suppurating sores and from it eight writhing, octopus-like tentacles reached out to seize them.

Terror again gripped them as they sprang back to evade the groping tentacles. Then, recovering himself, C.B. pulled the small bottle of Holy water from his pocket. Holding the cross aloft in his left hand, he tore the paper stopper from the bottle with his teeth and flung its contents at the demon.

The red lips of the woman's mouth opened and emitted a piercing scream. The tentacles threshed wildly. The leprous body suddenly exploded in a great puff of magenta-coloured smoke. Its stench was so nauseating that both C.B. and John were seized with a fit of retching. When they could raise their heads again no trace of the awful thing remained upon the altar. They had just time for that one glance; then the dim lights flickered and went out, plunging that end of the crypt in total darkness.

Instantly they became aware that with the darkness had come a cessation of all sound. The Voodoo drums, the horrid laughter, the snarling pandemonium made by the denizens of the Pit had given way, as at an order, to utter silence. There was something more frightening about the eerie stillness than the hideous noises that had preceded it. Quite suddenly, too, the crypt had become as cold as the interior of an ice-house.

With every nerve alert they waited, as though a paralysis had descended on them, riveting them there unable to move hand or foot. Then out of the blackness behind them came a clear silvery voice. It said:

'I have always admired courage. You have proved yours; so I will give you that for which you came. You no longer have cause to be afraid. I have here the Pact which Henry Beddows signed with my servant Copely-Syle. Turn round and you shall receive it as a free gift from me.'

'Don't look, John!' gasped C.B. 'For God's sake don't turn round! Shut your ears to everything you hear and prise up the altar slab.'

As he spoke he lugged his torch from his pocket and shone it on the flat piece of stone. At that moment the voice came again, low and persuasive:

'You foolish men. The Pact is not there. I have it here in my hand. For those who are not prepared to serve me willingly I have no use; and no one has ever accused me of meanness. I am not one to hold a man to his word when he regrets having given it. You may take the Pact back to Beddows and tell him that I release him from his bond.'

Ignoring the honeyed words, John forced the edge of the case-opener under the slab and heaved upon it. The four-foot-long stone lifted a little. Another heave and a gap of a few inches showed below it. John dropped the heavy jemmy, got the fingers of both hands under the slab and prepared to exert all his strength in lifting it back like the lid of a great box.

Again the voice came, but its tone had changed. It now rang out like the clash of cold steel and was vibrant with menace.

'Stop!' it commanded. 'I have allowed you to trifle with me long enough. I give you two minutes to leave my temple. Remain and I will make Hell gape open to receive you.'

With the sweat pouring from him in spite of the icy cold, John strove with all his might to raise the stone. It would not budge, and C.B. could not help him as he was holding the torch with one hand and the cross in the other.

Without warning, there came an ear-splitting crash of thunder. The floor of the crypt heaved; its walls rocked. Throwing the arm with the hand that held the torch round John's shoulders, C.B. raised the cross high above both their heads and cried:

'Oh Lord, defend us!'

There was a blinding flash. A fork of light streaked down through the roof striking, not them, but the centre of the altar slab, shattering it into a hundred fragments. God had intervened. Instantly a deafening din broke out. Cries, screams, moans and groans sounded from every direction, as the minions of Hell fled back into the dark underworld.

Still dazed, C.B. shone his torch down into the cavity now gaping where the altar stone had been. Among its fragments reposed a small, brass-bound coffer. John pulled it out, snatched up his jemmy from the floor, and broke it open. It contained about twenty pieces of parchment. On all of them were several lines of writing in dried blood. Hastily John shuffled through them until he came on one signed 'Henry Beddows'; then, with a sigh of relief, he crammed the whole lot into his pocket.

In the frightful stress and excitement of the last few moments they had scarcely been conscious that all the lights had come on again, or that big drops of rain were splashing upon them. Turning now, they saw that the crypt was as peaceful and empty as when they had entered it; then, on glancing up, they noticed that a three-foot-wide hole had been torn in the roof above the alter by the thunderbolt that had smashed it.

'Let's get out this way,' C.B. suggested, and, clambering up on the altar, they wriggled through the hole.

Outside the rain was sheeting down, and by the time they reached the car their outer garments were almost soaked through with it; but for the time being they could think of nothing except their delivery from the awful perils they had so recently encountered.

The car swiftly covered the mile back to The Grange. As they got out C.B. looked at his watch and said, 'How long do you think we have been?'

'Goodness knows,' John muttered. 'Two hours—three perhaps.'

'No. It is now nineteen minutes past eleven. Allowing for going and coming back, and our reconnaissance round the house before we went in, we could not have been in the crypt much more than seven minutes.'

Two minutes later they were upstairs with Beddows. Until John showed him the Pact he could not believe that they had got it. At first he was overcome by astonishment at their success; then, as he looked at their haggard faces and realized what they had been through, his gratitude was pathetic.

C.B. took the rest of the papers from John with the remark, 'I'll turn these in to Scotland Yard. They may of use in tracing up some of the Canon's associates; although I doubt if any of them could be persuaded to give evidence against him. Still, the people who signed these other Pacts will be informed that they have now been freed.'

He then stepped into the pentacle, removed the contents of the tea-chest, turned it upside down, leant his broomstick cross upright against its back and set two of the unlit candles upon it, thus transforming it into a temporary altar. Having lit the candles, he said to Beddows:

'Now, take the Pact in your right hand and burn it; then say these words after me.'

Beddows took the Pact, lit one corner of it, and repeated sentence by sentence as C.B. pronounced the abjuration:

'By this act I, Henry Beddows, renounce Satan and all his Works, now and for evermore, both on my own behalf and on that of my daughter Ellen. I have sinned grievously; but, trusting in the Divine Mercy promised by our Lord Jesus Christ to sinners who repent, I beg to be received back into God's grace. In the name of Christ I now call upon the Archangel Michael and his Host to protect my daughter, Ellen, this night; to guard her from all harmful thoughts and to deliver her from evil. Blessed by the names of the Father, the Son and the Holy Ghost for evermore. Amen.'

John and C.B. then knelt down beside Beddows and prayed, giving thanks for the courage they had been granted and their safe delivery from the Valley of the Shadow.

When they all stood up, and Beddows stepped from the pentacle, they saw with amazement that an extraordinary change had taken place in his appearance. He seemed to have aged twenty years. His broad shoulders slumped, his hair and the bristles of his beard had turned white; and he had the look of an old man. Yet, after thanking his rescuers, he said firmly:

'I shall leave for the South of France first thing in the morning. Ellen should be safe now; but I mean to hunt Copely-Syle down, and see to it that he goes to the Hell to which he has led so many others.'

C.B. endeavoured to hide his surprise at the transformation in Beddows, which was evidently the first sign of the payment he would now have to make for the twenty-one years of favour he had secured by unholy means: then he said to John, 'The outside chance of the Canon's coming back to-morrow is taken care of by the police. They will pinch him if he lands illegally in the marshes. There is nothing more we can do here now; so we'll go South too.'

Glancing again at Beddows, he added, 'I think it would be best if you accompanied us back to Colchester, as we must make a very early start. They will find you a room at the Red Lion, then we can all drive up to London together.'

'That suits me,' Beddows agreed. 'But I'll have to get into some clothes and pack a bag. I am feeling very weak, too, from my long semi-fast. While I am getting dressed perhaps you would go down to the larder. Jutson asked me through the door this morning if I was all right, as he had seen that somebody had been up here; but he doesn't know why I locked myself in, or anything about this business. He is very well paid to ask no questions; but all the same, the less he knows, the better; so I'd rather not have him routed out. It would save time, too, if you'd open up a tin or two for me yourselves, and I'll leave a note for him before we go. You will find quite a selection of tinned stuff down there, but anything will do.'

Together they descended to the first floor. Beddows went into his bedroom and the others continued on downstairs to prepare a picnic meal. A quarter of an hour later, when he joined them in the dining-room, they had ready a spread of sardines, cold ham and tinned peaches. After their ordeal C.B. and John also felt hungry; so they sat down with him and, while he ate ravenously, kept him company.

Soon after midnight they left the table and went out to the car. As Beddows stowed his suitcase in the back he said, 'I've never done the Government down more than I've had to; but this is a case in which I have no scruples. It may need big money to finance bringing Copely-Syle to book;

so we can't afford to observe currency restrictions. Fortunately, I've always kept a tidy sum in my wall-safe against an emergency; so I was able to pack the best part of three thousand pounds in fivers into a couple of pairs of shoes.'

C.B. smiled a little wryly. 'I'd rather you hadn't told me that; but since you have, how about it if the emigration authorities search your baggage?'

Beddows smiled. 'They might if I went to and fro regular. But the odds are all on my getting away with it once.'

At twenty-five past twelve the night porter let them into the Red Lion. He booked Beddows a room on the same floor as the others, and entered an order from C.B. to call them all at a quarter to five. Before they went upstairs C.B. telephoned his office and asked the night duty officer to ring Northolt, and use all the pull he could to secure three seats on the plane leaving for Nice at 7.16. Then they went up to their rooms, got the worst of the dirt off themselves with a quick wash, and, mentally exhausted from the strain of the past few hours, fell asleep as soon as their heads touched their pillows.

When C.B.'s bedside telephone rang, he roused out of a deep sleep and picked up the receiver. It was the night porter, who said:

'Your call, sir. It's a quarter to five and about half an hour ago I took a telephone message from your office. It was to report a telegram which reads:

"Special stop Despatched from Police Headquarters Nice at nought hours twenty stop Christina removed from prison without authority twenty-three hours fifteen stop Has since disappeared without trace stop Signed Malouet."'

'Thank you,' said C.B. quietly; but as he hung up, his face was grim. In a few minutes he would have to break it to John that, although they had braved such fearful perils during the earlier part of the night they had, after all, failed to save Christina. Beddows had abjured Satan at a little after half-past eleven. By about eighteen minutes the Canon had beaten them to it again.

23

THE CAVE OF BATS

Over the cups of coffee that the night porter had made for them and on the long drive to the airport, John and his two companions spoke little. After learning the contents of Malouet's telegram they could only hope that by the time they got to Nice the police would have succeeded in tracing the vanished prisoner: in the meantime all speculation on their chances of rescuing Christina was futile.

At Northolt a young man from C.B.'s office met them to take over his car, and told them that only by luck had it been possible to get three passages for Nice by the first plane that morning. The Riviera season was still at its height and the aircraft booked to capacity; but one travel agency had rung up the previous afternoon to charter a special plane for ten; so B.E.A. had decided to put an additional Viking on the run, which would carry Colonel Verney's party. C.B. then asked him to send a telegram to Molly, to let her know that they were on the plane and ask her to meet them at Nice.

The regular plane left on scheduled time, but there was some delay in its relief getting off, as it was held for two of the party of ten who, it transpired, were motoring down from Scotland. The others all appeared to know one another and were all middle-aged or elderly people. Their clothes and hand baggage suggested that they were all very well off, which was borne out by a remark that John heard exchanged between two of the three women in the party, to the effect that they had decided to make the trip at the last moment only to attend a wedding.

While in the waiting-room he had ample time to study their fellow passengers, but his thoughts being otherwise occupied he took little notice of them, except to remark that they seemed an exceptionally ugly lot. He reminded himself then that most fellow travellers seen at airports, railway stations and boarding liners appeared unprepossessing until one got to know them; yet his impression was strengthened on the arrival of the couple who had been motoring through the night from Scotland. The man was very tall and so lean that his skin seemed stretched over the bones of his face to a degree that made it almost corpse-like, while the woman had the most disconcerting squint that he ever remembered seeing.

In spite of the delay, which held up the take-off until twenty minutes to eight, the flying conditions were so good that the aircraft made up most of the lost time, and they came down in the brilliant sunshine of Nice at ten past one. Molly and Malouet were both there to meet them and, after Beddows had been introduced, the elderly ex-inspector said:

'I regret to say I have no news for you; but one gets as good a lunch at the airport restaurant here as anywhere in Nice; so I have booked a table. While we eat I will tell you all that is known of the most extraordinary occurrence last night.'

The meal justified his recommendation, but John scarcely noticed the wonderful selection of *hors-d'œuvres*, or the point at which he passed from eating *Loup flambé* to *Escalope de Veau Milanese*—he was too intent on Malouet's report and the discussion that followed.

Apparently getting Christina out of prison had proved a much easier matter for the Canon than her friends had supposed would be the case, as he had found it necessary to exert his occult powers on only one person.

Three nights before, a murder had occurred in Nice. At a *bistrot* in the old part of the town a sailor had been mortally wounded by a knife-thrust during a brawl in which several men were concerned. There was some doubt which of two men had delivered the fatal stab, and the *patron* of the place declared that a girl called Marie Courcelle must know the truth, because the quarrel had been over her and she had been within an arm's length of the victim when the stabbing took place. The two suspects were Marie's lover and her brother, and both were under arrest, but she, evidently reluctant to give evidence against either, had promptly disappeared. However, the police had picked her up the previous morning in Marseilles, taken her into custody as a material witness, brought her back to Nice in the afternoon and lodged her in the women's prison which also held Christina.

In accordance with French police practice, the *Juge d'Instruction* had ordered a re-enactment of the affair at the scene of the crime with all the principal participants present; and that no time might be lost he had ordered it for that evening at approximately the same hour as the stabbing had taken place two evenings earlier. It was at this point that the Canon must have entered the game.

The assumption was that he had learnt of the affair when, on his arrival, he had discussed ways and means with the de Grasses and had decided to make use of the *Juge d'Instruction*. In any case, for some reason which this examining magistrate was afterwards utterly unable to explain, he had written Christina's name instead of Marie's on the form authorizing the release of prisoners under guard for questioning. A Black Maria had picked up the two men then called for Christina. The head wardress on duty knew nothing of the enquiry the magistrate was conducting and had acted on the instruction to hand over Christina, simply assuming that she was required for questioning about her own case at the *Préfecture*.

On the arrival of the Black Maria at the *bistrot* the mistake had at once become apparent. The magistrate, still presumably under the influence of the Canon, had then decided that the Black Maria should remain outside for the time being with the two men in it, while Christina was sent back to prison in a taxi and Marie brought there instead. A single *gendarme* had, quite reasonably, been considered an adequate escort for one young woman, and as a taxi driver, who had been having a drink at the *bistrot* when it was temporarily cleared by the police, was still outside among the little crowd that had collected they set off in his cab.

In the light of what had then occurred it seemed certain that the taxi driver was one of de Grasse's people, and had been deliberately planted in the *bistrot*. After driving a few hundred yards he had turned into a dark alley-way, pulled up and opened the door of his cab. He had told the *gendarme* that he had stopped only to slip into his lodgings to pick up the thermos of hot coffee his wife would have ready for him for his night's work. While he was talking, another man opened the other door of the cab and, as the *gendarme* turned, squirted a water pistol in his eyes. The driver had then hit him on the back of the head, rendering him unconscious. He had come round to find himself bound, gagged and face down among some bushes. Later he had recovered sufficiently to squirm his way on to a path near the gate of a private garden, and to attract the attention of a passer-by. He had been dumped in the grounds of a villa on the road to Villefranche and he naturally had no idea what had become of the taxi or Christina.

When Malouet had finished his report, C.B. asked, 'How about Upson's seaplane? Is it known where he landed the Canon?'

'We think so;' Malouet pulled at his grey moustache; 'but we cannot be absolutely certain. Last night there was a strange occurrence out at the great reservoir from which Nice draws her water supply. It is situated some miles inland from the city, up a broad valley in which few people live, other than scattered market-garden cultivators. Soon after dark a car drove up to the quarters of the Superintendent. The men who work there had gone for the day; so he was alone except for his wife and son and the night watchman, who has a small office in the building. Four armed men got out of the car, entered the place, herded its inmates into the boiler-room and kept them there for three-quarters of an hour. There was no attempt at robbery and no damage done, other than the disconnecting of the telephone.

'When the intruders had gone the Superintendent reported this apparently pointless hold-up to the police. They could offer no theory to account for it then; but further enquiries in the neighbourhood this morning elicited the information that a seaplane was seen to come down on the reservoir about an hour after sunset. It would not have been visible from any considerable distance, but several people saw it land, and take off again about twenty minutes later. A woman living nearby states that a covered lorry with powerful headlights had been stationary on the road alongside the reservoir for some time before the plane came down. Such a large sheet of water would, of course, be easy to pick up as long as there was any light at all; so the headlights near it were probably used not only to help guide it in, but also as a signal to the pilot that all preparations had been made for his landing. Evidently, too, the men who held up the Superintendent and night watchman did so to ensure that they should know nothing of this illegal proceeding until after it had been completed; so they would be unable to interfere or communicate with the police.'

'I take it the police have not succeeded in tracing the lorry?' C.B. asked.

Malouet made a negative gesture. 'One could hardly expect them to. Its presence there was not reported till this morning, and the description given of it was only of the vaguest.'

'Then the Canon has got away with the game again,' John commented bitterly. 'It is a hundred to one on that having been Upson's seaplane. And how darned clever of them to have planned the timing of the job so well. By delaying his departure till the afternoon, Copely-Syle was able to fly practically straight in to Nice, yet give Upson the benefit of last light for crossing the mountains. He must have worked fast, though, to have pulled that one over the *Juge d'Instruction* so soon after his arrival.'

C.B. shrugged. 'Two and a half hours should have been ample if the de Grasses had the job already planned and everything prepared for him. Then there is always the possibility that it proved unnecessary to resort to a magical operation. Not all law officers would be above taking a bribe to alter a name in an official document.'

'This man is, I think, an honourable magistrate,' Malouet said. 'But one can never be certain of such things. There is, too, the fact that Satanism is world-wide in its ramifications; so it is even possible that he is a secret associate of the Canon's, and acted as he did on a simple request.'

'Have you reason to suppose that Black Magic is widely practised down here?' C.B. enquired.

'I would not say that. Among the peasants up in the hill villages sorcery has played its part from time immemorial, and still does so. On the coast there is some sorcery, too, of a quite different type, which is resorted to by people who live here only for the gambling. Inveterate gamblers are always superstitious and easily become the dupes of occultists who promise them aid to win money at the tables. But activities which suggest the presence of genuine Satanists are no more frequent here than in Paris or Marseilles.'

'I ask because I think it very unlikely that the Canon will attempt to tackle this business to-night on his own. Even if he doesn't assemble a full coven, he will almost certainly need a few brother warlocks to assist him with the homunculus. It occurred to me that if there are certain people in these parts whom you suspect of being practitioners of the Black Art, we might trace him through them.'

'You have been thinking on the same lines as myself,' Malouet nodded. 'There is an antique dealer in Cannes, a Polish countess living here in Nice, and one or two others who may be worth investigating. I was going to suggest that this afternoon we should see if we could pick up a lead from one of them.'

'What about the de Grasses?' John demanded. 'They are up to their ears in this.'

The ex-inspector gave him a pitying look. 'Is it likely that we should have neglected them, Monsieur; or that they are such fools as to have exposed themselves? M. le Marquis is still laid up with his wound and Count Jules has an alibi covering him from seven o'clock till past midnight.'

'But they must know the whole story. Upson is their man and the Canon travelled by his seaplane.'

'There is no proof whatever, Monsieur, that the seaplane that landed on the reservoir was Upson's.'

'Who can doubt it; or that the de Grasses did all the spade work for getting Christina out of prison?'

'Let us accept that,' agreed Malouet. 'The police are endeavouring to trace the lorry which presumably drove away the Canon and the homunculus, and the taxi in which Mademoiselle Christina was carried off. But in both cases they have very little to go on, and nothing at all that links either up with the de Grasses.'

'They know the truth! We must get it out of them!' exclaimed John impatiently.

Molly laid a hand on his arm. 'Johnny dear, don't be unreasonable. Since there is nothing with which they can be charged, the police have no excuse for questioning them; and they certainly won't give anything away to us.'

'But, Mumsie, we've got to make them, somehow,' he protested. 'It is our only chance to find out what has been done with Christina.'

'There is still a chance that we may get a line through one of these occultists whom Monsieur Malouet suggests that we should investigate this afternoon,' C.B. put in quietly.

'Perhaps! But we have only this afternoon left to work in,' John argued desperately. 'So we can't possibly afford to ignore the only people we are all convinced could give us the facts if they liked. I am going to ring up Jules and make him give me an appointment.'

'Just as you like.' C.B. gave a little shrug. 'But I'm afraid you will be knocking your head up against a brick wall.'

John jumped up and left the table to telephone. When he returned a few minutes later he said, 'I got on to Jules at the Capricorn, and he has agreed to see me at four o'clock. Mumsie, you'll drive me over, won't you? And I'd like Mr Beddows to come with us. He has certain arguments which I think might induce Jules to talk.'

Beddows had taken very little part in the conversation, but he now gave a quick nod and said, 'I get the idea: it's O.K. by me.'

C.B. had also got it, and turned a serious glance on John. 'It's worth trying, though I doubt if Jules will prove willing to make any admissions, whatever you offer. Still, I can guess how you must be feeling; so good luck.'

As they left the table Malouet said, 'Colonel Verney and I will maintain contact with the police in case they pick up any information about the lorry or the cab, and will spend the afternoon ourselves making enquiries in other quarters. If you wish to get in touch with us, ring up Inspector Drouet at the *Préfecture* in Nice. I will see to it that he knows from time to time where to get hold of us.'

Outside the airport they separated, C.B. and Malouet taking a taxi into the city, while Molly took the road to St Tropez with John and Beddows as her passengers. At her villa they made a brief halt to drop their suitcases, but out of his Beddows took the bulk of his bank-notes and stuffed them in his pockets. They reached the Capricorn soon after four, and as they drove up to the hotel Molly said to John:

'I don't think I'll come in with you, Johnny. I'll just wait in the car and say a little prayer that things may go the way you want them to.'

'Thanks, Mumsie.' He leaned over and gave her a quick kiss. 'Keep on praying till we come out, please. This means an awful lot to me.'

On giving his name he was shown up at once to the de Grasses' suite. Jules let them in and John introduced Beddows to him. The young Frenchman gave Christina's father a swift, appraising look, then led them into the sitting-room. When they were settled there John said:

'I'd like to come straight to the point. A few days ago you offered to double-cross Canon Copely-Syle if I would make it worth your while to do so. Is that offer still open?'

Jules' eyebrows rose in evident amusement. 'A lot has happened since then; and things are rather different now, aren't they?'

'You mean that I caused you a lot of trouble, and that it was largely owing to my having taken a hand in the game that your father was wounded?'

To John's surprise, Jules replied, 'No; I wasn't thinking of that. You made yourself a nuisance, of course, but even if you hadn't been with us at the château that hell-cat might have got hold of Upson's pistol and run amok as she did; so I reckon that what we lost on the swings owing to your intervention we more than made up for on the roundabouts. I saw you knock the gun up when she was about to shoot my father through the heart. I am very fond of my father, and it was your having saved his life that decided me to hear anything you had to say this afternoon.'

John smiled a little awkwardly. 'I'm afraid I can't take any great credit for that, as it's a natural instinct not to want to see murder done. But of what were you thinking, when you said things are different now?'

'Simply that as we have already handed over the goods I don't think there is much that we can do.'

'You could put us on to the men who met the Canon, and those who later kidnapped Christina.'

'Perhaps; but that would mean laying certain friends of mine open to criminal proceedings; and that I am naturally not prepared to do.'

'I'm ready to ante-up handsome, Count,' Beddows put in. 'I've quite a tidy sum on me, and if more is needed I don't doubt I could fix passing it through the Tangier International Zone.'

'Thank you, sir,' said Jules, with a frigid little bow. 'But it is not in the tradition of my family to sell our servants.'

John was tempted to make a swift retort to the effect that it was even more shameful to traffic in dope, arms and women; but he checked himself in time, and said, 'May I ask you a question?'

'By all means.' Jules snapped a gold, pocket gas-lighter to the Gitane cigarette that was hanging from his lips.

'Do you know where Christina is now?'

'I haven't an idea.'

'Then do you know where the Canon plans to hold this abominable ceremony to-night?'

With a genuinely puzzled look Jules asked, 'What ceremony?'

'Surely you are aware of the reason why he has been trying to get hold of Christina?'

'No. I thought he just had a yen for her. Old boys do get that sort of thing for young girls, you know; and are often willing to part with a lot of money for a chance to gratify it.'

'This is something very different. He wants to use her in what, for the lack of a better name, we will call a Black Mass.'

'Really!' Jules' plump face showed only a cynical interest. 'That sounds very intriguing. Ellen, or Christina, or whatever you like to call her, would look pretty good stretched out naked on an altar. I think I must try to muscle in on that.'

John fought down an impulse to hit him, and said, 'If you did, as the culminating point of the ritual consists in cutting her throat, you might find yourself later being charged as an accessory to murder.'

Letting out a low whistle, Jules stood up. 'So it's not just fun and games, eh? Well, I don't wish her any harm, even if she is half off her nut; but I'm afraid there is not much I can do about it.'

'You said that you might muscle in on the ceremony. Could you do that? Or, at all events, find out where it is to take place?'

'I might, but it would not be easy. We did all that was required of us last night and were paid well for our trouble; but, to be honest, I don't think my own people could help much. What you have just told me explains a lot. You must already have a pretty shrewd idea how the two jobs were done; so there's no point in my concealing from you what happened afterwards. The Canon and the big crate he brought with him were taken to a villa on the outskirts of the town. Some three hours later Christina, doped and concealed in a large trunk, was delivered at what I imagine to have been the same place; but of that I can't be certain. You see, when the men who did these jobs reported to me this morning, none of them had anything but the vaguest idea where they had been. They couldn't even recall the district in which the villa lay.'

'Oh hell!' John groaned, at the thought that his last hope was slipping away. 'Then that swine of a Canon pulled a fast one on you too, and hypnotized your men into forgetting where they had driven.'

Jules nodded. 'That's about it. I couldn't understand what had come over my chaps this morning; but now you tell me that he is contemplating murder, the reason why he went to such lengths to cover up his tracks is obvious.'

'All the same,' Beddows put in, 'you said just now that you might be able to find out where the ceremony is going to take place.'

'I could try; but it would mean putting a lot of people on the job, and they would have to work fast. You see, by this time the Canon may have carted Christina off to anywhere between Mentone and Marseilles, to have her handy to some devil-ridden spot suitable for doing her in; so we shall have to cast a very wide net.'

'Then get to it! Money is no object.'

Giving Beddows an unfriendly stare Jules remarked, 'If I do anything at all it will be for John, because he prevented that crazy daughter of yours from killing my father.' Then, as an afterthought, he added, 'Still, we may as well look after the old firm as far as expenses are concerned. How much are you willing to pay?'

'I'll give you a thousand pounds down, and another thousand if you get results.'

'Good. I'll have my people get a line on all the queers along the coast. There is an old priest at Cagnes who has a pretty gruesome reputation, and a fortune-teller in Monte Carlo who does not stick to telling the cards. There is one man in Nice, too, who might know something—if only we can persuade him to talk. He is an elderly cabaret singer with a husky bass voice, and he does his act at a dirty little dive off the Place Massena. One of his stunts is to intone the *Paternoster* backwards. However, the telephoning I am about to do is strictly private; so I must ask you to leave me now. I may be unlucky; in any case it will be a couple of hours or more before I am likely to have anything to tell you; so you had better make yourselves as comfortable as you can in the lounge downstairs.'

Beddows produced the thousand pounds; and John, now blessing the impulse which had caused him to save the Marquis from a bullet in the heart, thanked Jules for what he was about to do. Then they went down, collected Molly from the car, and ordered tea in the lounge as a means of killing a little time, although none of the three felt like drinking it.

John never remembered a longer hour than the one that followed. From time to time one of them endeavoured to start a conversation, but it inevitably tailed off into silence after the exchange of a few sentences; and, now that he had the leisure to con the cold, hard facts, the slenderness of their chance of saving Christina became more and more apparent to him. He had pinned his faith on either bribing or bullying Jules into giving them the information that they needed so desperately; but it had turned out that he had not got it to give. He had, through a strange freak of fate, become friendly instead of hostile; but, in the event, all that he had actually done was cynically to accept a thousand pounds to institute the same sort of enquiry as Malouet was already engaged upon gratuitously.

John knew that on the Riviera there must be more people than anywhere else in the world who, having once been rich, had through wars, revolutions or gambling lost all but a pittance, and so were peculiarly susceptible to the temptation to attempt to regain something of their past affluence by trafficking with the supernatural; yet it seemed beyond all reason to hope that, in a matter of a few hours, one such could be found who was not only in the Canon's confidence, but prepared to betray him.

Outside, the sun was shining. Through the broad windows could be seen the lovely prospect of the blue, unruffled bay; with, in the foreground, two mimosa trees in blossom, a row of striped yellow cactus, and some brilliant scarlet geraniums in pots. Inside, there was the constant passing of well-dressed men and women, laughing and carefree, all intent on the enjoyment of a summer holiday snatched from the grim winter in northern lands whence most of them came.

The contrast between the scene and the thoughts of the little party at the tea-table made the long wait all the more intolerable. The minutes crawled by. For John each of them brought a new vision of Christina—as she might be now, locked in some cellar; or in an attic room with barred windows; or with her clothes removed so that she could not escape, lying in bed half drugged—as she would be to-night, carried away again, stifling in a trunk, to some secret place; fighting on her release until she was beaten into submission; stripped and cowering among a group of ghouls excited to a frenzy by unnatural lusts; screaming as the sharp sacrificial knife severed the muscles of her throat; still and dead with the blood gushing from her neck.

At half-past five John ordered a round of drinks. In the next hour he knocked back five double Martinis. As he ordered a sixth Molly laid a hand on his arm and said:

'Johnny, haven't you had enough—anyhow for the time being?'

He turned and gave her a weak semblance of his old familiar grin. 'Don't worry, Mumsie. People can't get drunk when they feel as wretched as I do.'

It was a quarter to seven when a page came to their table and said that Count Jules de Grasse would like to see them upstairs. Molly went out to the car; the two men hurried over to the lift. As soon as Jules had let them into the suite he said:

'I think I have the information you want; but there is one proviso that I must make before I go any further. I require you both to give me your word of honour that you will not inform the police, either directly, or indirectly through your friends who brought them to the Ile de Port Cros, if I enable you to make use of the tip-off I have secured.'

'Why?' asked John.

'Because you will need guides to take you to the place where the ceremony is to be performed; and the only guides with which I can provide you at such short notice are two smugglers who are wanted by the police. They are key men in our organization for exchanging goods across the Italian frontier. What is more, they trust me; so I cannot allow their safety to be jeopardized by the police being brought to the scene by other guides at round about the same time as they arrive there with you.'

'The Canon will probably have a number of people with him,' Beddows pointed out uneasily. 'Last night I . . . I was subjected to a shock that seems to have aged me greatly; so I'm afraid I wouldn't prove the man I was, in a fight. With only my help John Fountain might not be able to overcome them. In fact, instead of rescuing Ellen the two of us may be knocked on the head.'

Jules shrugged. 'You must take your chance of that. In an affair of this kind the participants are certain to be nervy. If you use your wits you should be able to succeed in breaking the meeting up. Once my friends have taken you to the place and left you, I naturally have no objection to your getting help from wherever you like; but I will not have you telephone to the police in advance any information likely to lead them to the place to which you will be taken. Now, what do you say?'

Glancing at one another, Beddows and John nodded; so the latter said, 'All right; we both promise.'

'Good! I accept your promises; but even so it is unnecessary that you should know your final destination for the next hour or two. It is enough for me to tell you that the job is to be done up in the hills behind Nice. Drive back towards the city, but do not enter it. Across the Var and about two kilometres past the airport you will come to a turning that leads inland up to the little town of St Pancrace. Outside the church there you will find two men waiting for you. The taller of the two has a red beard. They are your guides, and will take you to the spot where the Canon and his friends are meeting. But I should warn you that you have none too much time. The meeting is due to start at nine o'clock.'

'It would be,' Beddows muttered. 'Christina's birth hour is nine forty-five, and they would want to perform the . . . the actual sacrifice as near that time as possible.'

'And it is nearly seven already!' exclaimed John. 'Come on! We must not waste a second!'

Beddows threw the second thousand pounds worth of bank-notes on the table; and with brief good-byes to Jules they ran from the room. As they came hurrying out of the hotel Molly saw them and started up the car. John took the wheel, and within three minutes of leaving Jules' suite they were on their way back to Nice.

It was still light, but there was a sharp chill in the air and the end of the sunny day was fast approaching. There was quite a lot of traffic on the road—auto-buses taking work-people home and bringing less well-off holiday-makers back from day excursions, many motor-cycles, and the cars of the wealthy carrying couples and foursomes to neighbouring towns to dinner—but John snaked his way through it at high speed without taking too many risks that might have brought them to grief.

Before they had gone far he said, 'It would save a little time if we could stick to N.7 and cut across inland from Fréjus to Cannes, instead of going round by the coast road; but now we have to tackle the Canon's crowd on our own I think it's more important that we should call at the villa to collect some weapons.'

'No,' replied Molly promptly. 'I thought this afternoon that we might need the armaments before we were through; so you can go by N.7. While you were dropping your bags at the villa on our way out I picked up some things. C.B. has still got my big gun, but I have the small one in my bag, and I've two heavy truncheons, knuckle-dusters and knives in the back of the car for you. I put in a couple of extra torches and a bottle of brandy as well.'

'Good old Mumsie! You've thought of everything. I wish you'd let me have your gun, though.'

'No, darling. I'm hanging on to that. This is a chance in a life-time to see how it works.'

The streets of St Maxime and Fréjus hardly caused John a check, but he had to slow down to go through Cannes, and by then the sun was setting. When they passed Antibes the sky behind them was a rich glow of orange and salmon pink which by the time they crossed the River Var had faded to a few streaks. It was half-past eight and the light had gone as they wound their way up the hill into St Pancrace.

The sweep of their headlights picked out a man who was standing on the steps of the church. As John pulled up he came forward. He was tall and bearded. Leaning down to the car window he asked in a low voice:

'Has Monsieur come from St Tropez?'

'Yes,' replied John. 'We are the friends of Monsieur le Comte.'

'Good!' nodded the man, and went on, 'Monsieur will excuse me if I do not introduce myself. It will serve if you call me Number One and my companion, who you will meet later, Number Two. Do you know the road to Falicon?'

John shook his head.

'It is through Gairaut and no great distance; but perhaps it would be best if Madame would allow me to occupy the front seat next to Monsieur.'

The rearrangement was soon made by Molly getting out and joining Beddows in the back. As they set off along the twisting road up hill again, John asked:

'May we know where we are going?'

'Monsieur has given his word to M. le Comte not to communicate with the police until I and my friend have left him?'

'Yes; we won't let you down about that.'

'Then I am about to take you to the Cave of the Bats.'

Into John's mind there flashed a memory of the first time he had been in the crypt at The Priory, and had seen the bat nailed upside down to the broken crucifix on the altar. He suppressed a shudder as Beddows asked, in French that had an appalling accent but was just comprehensible:

'What sort of place is it?'

'A very unusual cave, Monsieur. Most caves are natural fissures in the rock and run more or less level for some distance into a mountainside; but this is not at all like that. It is entered by dropping through a hole high up on the side of a hill and was made by man, or at least has been much adapted by him, as it has several passages of uniform size and one quite large vaulted chamber. Even the archaeologists who visit it at times cannot say what race of men first used it. There is a legend that the Phoenicians offered up human sacrifices to their god, Moloch, there; but many think that long before that prehistoric man had hewed the little temple nearly a hundred metres below the surface of the hillside as a place to perform his secret rites with doves and virgins.'

John felt the palms of his hands go damp upon the wheel. He had expected that he might have to break into some little wayside chapel which was being desecrated, or stumble his way through the ruins of a long-since-abandoned monastery; but this underground warren which had been the scene of countless ritual murders through the centuries sounded infinitely more terrifying. He began to pray that they would catch up with the Satanists before the latter reached their horrible rendezvous.

After they had covered another five kilometres up the winding hill road they approached a group of houses, and Number One said, 'This is the hamlet of St Michael. It is here that we leave the car. To the left of the crossroads there is an inn. You can park your car in the open space alongside it.'

As they pulled up and got out, a figure emerged from the shadow of some trees and gave a low whistle. Number One replied to it and the figure approached. It was Number Two. In a husky voice he made his report:

'The tip-off that M. le Comte got about the meeting being here was a right one. The party arrived in five cars nearly an hour ago. There were thirteen of them; nine men and four women. Out of the cars they unloaded a packing-case, a big trunk, two stretchers to carry them on and some suitcases; then they sent all the cars away. One of the men led the way as guide and the other eight carried the loads on the stretchers. It was all very orderly with everything evidently arranged beforehand, as none of them uttered a word. They just formed a little procession and set off up the hill.'

John drew a quick breath. 'Then they are nearly an hour ahead of us! I was told that the meeting was not due to start till nine o'clock. It can't be much more than twenty-to, and they may have started already.'

'No, Monsieur.' Number One shook his head. 'They should be punctual, but not much in advance of the time set. They cannot have yet reached the cave. With burdens to carry over rough ground and uphill all the way they will find it a good hour's walk.'

Beddows swore, then apologized to Molly. Like John, he felt that the fact that they should be able to catch up a little through having nothing to carry was small consolation. He, too, had an eye on the time, but had not realized that a long, hard walk lay ahead of them; so he had believed that there was a good hope of their coming up with the Canon's party before it reached the cave. Now that hope was dashed and they would have no alternative but to go down into it.

'There are times when I become profane myself,' Molly replied a little grimly; then she added to John, 'I shan't keep you a moment, but I'm just going into the inn.'

'Would it not be as well if Madame remained there?' suggested Number One.

'Yes, Mumsie,' said John quickly, 'you must. You can't come up to this place with us.'

'Of course I'm coming,' she retorted, as she turned away.

'No, you are not,' he called after her. 'I won't let you! And, anyhow, we can't possibly wait.'

'If you don't I'll get lost trying to follow you and probably fall down a precipice,' she called back. 'I tell you I won't keep you a moment; but I've been out all day and I simply must pop in here before I start climbing that hill.'

As she disappeared through the lighted doorway of the inn, John and Beddows got the weapons and torches out of the back of the car and distributed them in various pockets. Molly was as good as her word and rejoined them after a few minutes. Then, with Number Two leading the way, they set off in Indian file up a track that curved round behind some outhouses and chicken runs.

Within a few minutes they were out on the bare hillside and began to appreciate how rough the walking was going to be. The path was barely a foot wide and in places disappeared entirely. It wound in and out among knee-high boulders between which grew myrtle, wild thyme and a low leafless shrub that had sharp prickles. Before they had covered two hundred yards they had barked their ankles half a dozen times stumbling over rocks and Molly's nylons were ruined.

'The Canon and his crew must have had the hell of a job getting up here with loaded stretchers,' John muttered.

'They were using torches, and that would have made keeping to the track much easier for them,' replied Number Two. 'But we dare not do so, in case one of them is acting as a sentry on the hilltop and spots us following them.'

The path zigzagged diagonally along the slope of the hill and on their left its crest was visible against a starlit sky. After twenty minutes' gruelling tramp they reached a sparse belt of low trees, and Molly stopped to ask breathlessly:

'How much further is it?'

'We are not half-way yet, Madame,' Number One told her. 'But higher up you will find the going a little less difficult.'

'Why not wait for us here, Mumsie?' John pleaded.

'No.' She shook her head. 'I shall manage, somehow.' Panting, they stumbled on through the trees until they came to a series of low terraces, which suggested that the hilltop had once been a Roman fort. Now they had to scramble up the rough stone walls of each terrace. Even with help Molly was sobbing for breath, and upon mounting the second she panted:

'Is . . . is the entrance to the cave . . . on the hilltop here?'

'No, Madame.' Number Two shook his head. 'We have to go up this way; but when we reach the top we have another half-mile to do along the crest of the ridge.'

Gamely she struggled on up the last terraces, where there were again some trees and the low walls of ruins that might have been the remains of a few cottages. The men were all conscious that she was delaying the pace of the party, and John was half crazy with exasperation, but had not the heart to insist on leaving her behind.

Coming out from among the scattered trees they had to scramble down a further series of terraces, which proved nearly as arduous as getting up those they had scaled five minutes earlier. As they reached the last, Number Two halted. From their elevation they could now see the moon just over the crest of a much higher ridge to the east, and its light faintly lit the scene. Pointing along the ridge on which they stood he said:

'Can you see that blob of white ahead of us and a little way down the slope to our right? That is a small pyramid of rough stone, erected no one knows when, to mark the entrance to the cave.'

They could just make it out; but Molly had sunk sobbing and exhausted on to a large flat rock.

'I'm sorry!' she gasped, as the others again moved forward. 'I can't go on yet! And I'm holding you up. You must leave me. I . . . I'll follow you when I've had a few minutes' rest.'

'Hard luck, Mumsie,' John muttered, but they did not stop to argue with her. Every moment was now vital, and having brought her with them had already cost them most of the gain they might have made on the Satanists through having nothing to carry.

Below the terrace they struck another path, which Number Two told them was a smugglers' track, centuries old, leading in a dead straight line over the mountains to a point on the Rhine only forty kilometres from Strasbourg. John asked him then if he could tell them anything about the interior of the cave, and he replied:

'Yes; I went down into it once as a boy. When one is older one has no stomach for such places, but youngsters have no fear of them. The air in it is good; so those who made it must have provided some system of ventilation, and it is always bone dry in there. As far as I recall it, from the entrance there is a sheer drop of about six metres. At the bottom one finds a flat space and a few shallow steps; then comes a steep slope downwards for some fifty metres. Where it ends there are three passages. Two of them are *culs-de-sac*, but I cannot remember which. The third is roughly ninety metres long and runs back under the hill here. At its end is what is called the sacrificial chamber.'

Still panting and stumbling, they advanced among the rocks until they were within forty feet of the pyramid. No one was on guard near it, and after the constant rustling made by their feet their coming to a halt brought a sudden eerie silence. They could see now by the moonlight that it was built with small uneven pieces of stone fitted skilfully together, and must originally have been about twenty feet in height; but its point and uppermost six feet of stones had been broken away, leaving it truncated, with its top an irregular platform. Its base was about thirty feet square and the side they were facing curved slightly inward to disappear into a black, gaping hole.

'Here, Messieurs, we will leave you,' said Number One. 'It remains only for us to wish you good fortune.'

'Come with us,' said Beddows in his atrocious French. 'I'll make it well worth your while. I'll pay you a hundred thousand francs apiece to come in with us.'

'I would not for a million, Monsieur,' replied Number One quickly; while Number Two shook his head, crossed himself and muttered, 'We have only our suspicions of what has led thirteen people to go down there together to-night; but that is enough. I wish to die shriven; not of a fit from coming face to face with the Devil.'

Seeing that it would be useless to attempt to persuade them to change their minds John said, 'Then pray for us, please.'

'We will, Monsieur! We will!' they answered readily. Then both of them swung about and hastened away, taking a much more precipitous route across rocks between which no path could be seen.

Within a few moments John and Beddows reached the pyramid. Beside it lay the two stretchers. At its base yawned the big hole, about ten feet in length, four feet across and roughly oval in shape. Dug firmly into its nearest lip were two strong steel hooks, and, suspended from them, the upper few feet of a rope ladder could be faintly discerned. Below that lay impenetrable darkness.

John shone his torch, and they could then see the bottom of the ladder trailing loose on a rough floor of stone twenty feet down. He was about to get on his knees when Beddows pushed him aside and said gruffly:

'You keep your torch on. I got the girl into this; so I'm going first. Pray God we'll be in time, and that we manage to get her out.'

All day he had walked with a stoop, and shown signs of the new feebleness that had descended on him; but he seemed to have managed the climb up the hill without suffering the exhaustion one might have expected, and now both his voice and movements gave evidence of a sudden return of rugged strength.

Swinging himself over the edge, he got his feet on one of the rungs of the ladder and began to descend. John held the torch steady and took a quick look at his watch. Having been handicapped by Molly, the two-mile climb had taken them a full three-quarters of an hour. The margin left them was now reduced to a bare thirteen minutes. His heart began to hammer wildly.

The instant Beddows reached the floor of the shaft John followed him down. Each holding his truncheon in his right hand and torch in his left they went forward. There were five shallow steps, then came the long steep slope leading into the bowels of the earth. As they slithered down it both were thinking of the countless gruesome companies of priests and victims which must have preceded them along it. For perhaps as much as ten thousand years, to mark the changing seasons, youths and maidens selected for their strength and beauty had been dragged down that slope by brutal witch-doctors and demon-ridden magicians; so that, by the infliction of a horrible death, their blood might appease Satan in the form of many monstrous, evil gods.

At the bottom of the slope they came upon the big trunk in which Christina had been brought there, and the packing-case—now empty but for the great masses of cotton-wool that had been used to protect the glass jar containing the homunculus. Beside them were several suitcases, a pile of cloaks and several soft hats. Quickly now, they ran down the nearest passage. It was only four feet wide and after about thirty paces they found that it ended in a blank wall. Hurrying back, they tried the next. Some eighty feet from its entrance it curved slightly and in the distance they suddenly saw a faint light. Beddows was still leading and again broke into a run. John tapped him sharply on the shoulder and whispered urgently:

'For God's sake go easy! Our only chance is to surprise them! Put out your torch, and make as little noise as possible.'

'You're right,' Beddows whispered back, and he dropped into a swift padding trot.

When they had covered another hundred feet, they could see part of the chamber. It was lit only by a red glow from a brazier that was burning in its centre. Grotesque shadows were thrown up by people congregated round it. The murmur of voices reached them, and a thin discordant music, like a violin string being twanged at random, helped to cover the noise of their approach. On tip-toe now, they advanced another sixty feet. As they did so they were able to make out more clearly what was going on in the temple. Only its central section, framed in the four-feet-wide and six-feet-high doorway, was visible to them; but that was enough for them to see that the ritual had already started.

The Canon was standing with his back to them, intoning Hebrew from a large book. On either side of him stood another man. One of them was making the discordant music on a stringed instrument; the other was swinging a censer to and fro, from which issued wisps of evil-smelling smoke. All three were clad in Satanic vestments in which they must have come to the cave, wearing over them the cast-off cloaks that had been left in the little chamber where the long slope ended. Facing them stood Christina.

With the Canon practically blocking the line of vision it was difficult to catch more than glimpses of her from the passage; but John and Beddows could see that her eyes were closed and that she appeared to be fully dressed still. Turned towards her on either side, two women were holding her arms, but she looked as if she was standing without their support. Her hair was tousled, an ugly bruise disfigured one of her cheeks and she had a cut lip, from which a trickle of blood was running. The other members of this evil congregation were shut off from sight by the sides of the passage, as was also the jar containing the homunculus.

Beddows now had less than forty feet to go to reach the doorway. He had taken four more swift, cautious paces when the Canon stopped intoning and closed his book. Christina opened her eyes. Over the Canon's shoulder she saw her father, his face now lit by the glow from the brazier, advancing towards the entrance to the chamber. The mingled emotions of shock and hope proved too much for her. Unable to control herself, she let out a sudden scream.

As though they had been waiting for some such signal, Beddows and John rushed in. Brandishing their cudgels, they raced down the last thirty feet of passage and fell upon the Satanists. Taken completely by surprise, the devilish crew were seized by panic and cowered into groups for mutual protection. Beddows cracked in the head of one, and John delivered a swipe which smashed the face of another. Christina broke free from the two women, and threw the smaller of them to the floor.

For a moment it looked as if the champions of Light were to be granted an easy triumph; but only for a moment. Beddows felled another man with a glancing blow, but a black-haired woman with feverish eyes threw herself upon him like a tiger cat. Burying her teeth in his chin, she flung her arms about him, rendering abortive his further attempts to strike out. John's truncheon came whizzing down on a fourth man's shoulder, causing him to reel away with a scream of pain; but next second his arm was seized and he was flung back against the wall.

In two groups the remaining Satanists then hurled themselves on the intruders and bore them kicking to the ground. By then Christina had smashed her fist into the face of the second woman who had been holding her, and made a dash for the doorway; but there she was caught and dragged back by the Canon.

After some few moments of confusion a semblance of order was restored. Two of the Devil's congregation lay senseless and three others were groaning from their injuries; but eight remained unharmed, and between them they now held John, Beddows and Christina with their arms firmly grasped behind their backs. Still panting, and slobbering with rage, the Canon addressed his evil flock:

'Brothers and Sisters in Satan! Do not for one moment allow this interruption to our ceremony to lessen your faith in the protection of our Master. That some of our number should have been injured is most regrettable; but Prince Lucifer must have willed it so. I know these men. One is the girl Ellen's father and the other her would-be lover. Take notice that they come here alone, unsupported by the slaves of the Christian Law. They have been sent here and given into our hands for a purpose. Beyond doubt it is the Proud One's intention that they should witness the sacrifice, and be made fully aware of His greatness by also witnessing the miracle which will follow from it. Afterwards they too shall know the coldness of the altar slab upon their bare backs and feel the sharpness of the sacrificial knife as it cuts through their throats. But we have not a moment to lose. Temporarily we must ignore the hurts of our brethren. The fateful hour approaches. We must allow nothing to prevent us from completing the ritual while the woman's birth star is at the zenith. The time has come to strip her.'

At this clarion call new heart entered into the Satanists. The men had nothing handy with which to bind John and Beddows; so they forced them to their knees and held them there. The women fell upon Christina like a pack of furies. She struggled wildly, until one of them hit her a savage blow under the chin, rendering her half unconscious. But, even then, instead of removing her clothes garment by garment they tore them from her body shred by shred, till she stood swaying among them stark naked except for her shoes and stockings.

Beddows was giving vent to an unending flow of curses. John ground his teeth in silent agony. He knew now that their hope of saving Christina was gone. They had made their last desperate bid and failed. He tried to pray, but the words would not come.

Christina, still struggling, was forced back against the altar and stretched out upon it. John could see her long, silk-stockinged legs dangling over the right-hand end of the altar; but he could not see the upper half of her body or her face, as they were hidden from him by one of the acolytes. The Canon again began to recite, this time in Latin, saying the Mass backwards. Parodying the motions of a priest, he bobbed and gestured to his assistants, who from time to time made hoarse responses to his muttering. A chalice was produced and Copely-Syle spat into it several times, then again he muttered feverishly and genuflected while breaking Holy wafers, stolen from some church, into it. Then he picked it up and carried it to each member of the congregation in turn, for them to sup of some of the horrid, sodden mess.

As he reached the men who were holding Beddows, they relaxed their grip on him slightly, and he strove desperately to knock the chalice from Copely-Syle's hands; but the Canon managed to protect his vile sacrament and enable Beddows' captors to partake of it. When all the members of his coven, except the two who were still unconscious, had done so, he carried it back to the altar, held it above Christina and swallowed what remained himself.

Setting the chalice down, he took from one of his assistants a small metal box that appeared to contain soot, and dipping his finger in it began to draw black symbols on each of Christina's limbs. As he did so he chanted unintelligible words in a high, excited voice. The sweat was now pouring down his flabby face and, as he proceeded with this new ritual, a frenzy seized upon his congregation, causing them to give vent to hideous animal noises and those who were free to do so pulled up their robes, exposing themselves.

With distended eyes John stared at the frightful spectacle being enacted before him. Already he had become vaguely conscious that some of the faces about him were familiar. Suddenly he realized where he had seen them before. Ten of them were those of the party who had flown out with him from Northolt that morning. Before leaving England the previous afternoon the Canon must have sent an S O S to ten of the leading Satanists of Britain to join him in Nice for the ceremony. The mention of a wedding he had overheard must have been a covert reference to the spiritual union of Christina with the homunculus. He could only guess that the two others, making up the coven of thirteen, were French Satanists who had selected the Cave of the Bats as an appropriate setting for this unholy marriage.

John's distraught glance switched to the homunculus. He had been given a description of it by C.B., but had never seen it. The big glass jar that contained it had been placed by the left-hand end of a low altar, hewn from the living rock, at the far end of the small chamber. In the jar the squat, repulsive travesty of a female figure undulated gently, its arms and legs moving with the same apparent aimlessness as the tentacles of an octopus. Slowly the red-rimmed eyes swivelled from side to side, while the mouth opened and shut with a fish-like motion. As John gazed at it his flesh began to creep, and he felt that for sheer unadulterated filthiness the reality utterly beggared the description.

Suddenly the ritual of the symbols ended. The acolytes threw themselves on Christina, hauled her, now only half conscious, from the altar and stood her upright. One of the women near her produced a sack-like robe with strange designs upon it. The garment was thrown over her and her arms were then pulled through slits in its sides. Another of the witches put a pointed fool's cap on her head and tied it there by a ribbon beneath her chin. Into John's mind came a picture of the Spanish Inquisition. The costume was evidently designed with the same intent, but had the symbols of the Devil instead of those of Christ figured upon it. A third witch tied Christina's hands in front of her with a strip from her torn dress. Next moment the three of them had flung her down again on her back along the altar. Her head now rested on the top of the jar that held the homunculus. The black-haired witch removed its big round stopper. Sick with horror, John closed his eyes and again strove to pray.

When he opened them the Canon had begun another incantation. In a frenzy of excitement he mouthed and postured, while the witches held Christina down. The congregation screamed responses. Beddows shouted and cursed, and strove to break away; but he could not get up from his knees or shake off the men who held him. The Canon drew a long curved knife from his girdle and waved it aloft. Breaking into English he shrieked in a high falsetto:

'The hour has come! The great hour has come! I, Augustus Copely-Syle, Prince of the Bats and High Priest of the Lord Satan, by this act give a soul to my creation.'

'Stop!' John's yell cut through the hideous din. 'Stop, I say, Your ceremony is useless. She is no longer a virgin! I took her virginity that night we were together on the Ile de Port Cros.'

A sudden deathly silence descended on the vaulted chamber. The Canon swung upon him, his face livid with ungovernable fury.

'It is not true!' he gasped. 'It cannot be true.'

'It is! I swear it!' cried John desperately.

Copely-Syle's eyes bulged, and he groaned. For a moment he remained silent and motionless, then he muttered, 'Oh, I feared it! I feared it from the moment I saw you with her in the Casino!'

Again, for the space of a dozen heart-beats, he stood glaring but seemingly paralysed. It was Beddows who broke the spell by suddenly emitting a harsh, unnatural laugh.

It seemed to electrify the Canon. With blazing eyes he leapt towards John, brandishing the knife on high and screaming, 'My life-work is ruined. I will cut out your heart. I will cut out your heart!'

The knife cleaved the air with a swish. It was aimed at John's neck above the collar-bone. Another second and it would have cleaved his jugular vein. Of the two men holding him on his knees one was the tall, gaunt-faced individual who had come from Scotland. At the penultimate instant he struck the blade aside and cried:

'No, Prince of the Bats, no! You cannot sully the sacred knife dedicated to the sacrifice of offerings on the altar. Do your will upon him, but not in blind anger. We are not here to witness common murder. I demand that he be sacrificed in due form, so that his blood may mingle with hers and the altar be deprived of neither.'

'Yes! Yes!' chorused the others, and the squint-eyed witch who had also come from Scotland screamed above the rest, 'But the woman first. She is ready for you, and we are waiting.'

Slowly Copely-Syle turned about. His anger seemed suddenly to have drained from him, and he muttered to himself, 'The incantation may yet work. It is her birth hour and she is twenty-one.'

Again he approached the altar, and this time raised his knife with quiet deliberation. John felt as if his heart was about to burst from impotence and distress. For a moment hope had sprung wildly in his breast, but now he knew that final defeat was rushing upon him. Only seconds of life remained to Christina.

Suddenly, on an unbidden impulse, he found himself shouting with all the power of his lungs, 'Christina, darling! I love you! I love you!'

As his voice rang through the chamber Christina's whole body tensed. With a violent jerk her wrists snapped the strip of fabric that bound them. From the impetus, her freed hands were flung out and backward. At the end of its swing her left hand struck the jar that contained the homunculus. John's ring hit it with a loud clang. The inch-thick glass shivered and broke as though it had been paper-thin crystal. As the jar fell to pieces the liquid in it gushed out. For a moment the naked and obscene homunculus stood among the falling fragments; then she leapt straight at the Canon.

With a piercing shriek he staggered back under the impact. Her taloned hands dug into his shoulders; her claw-like feet fixed themselves in his legs above the knees. For a few seconds her slimy, dripping face was pressed against his in an awful mockery of a kiss; then, her eyes goggling with her hunger for blood, she lowered it and fixed her teeth fiercely in his neck.

The rushing water from the jar swirled against the low brazier. The coals in it hissed and dulled, reducing the glow of light in the chamber to a glimmer. Pandemonium broke loose. Screaming, the Canon fell to the floor with the homunculus on top of him. Two of the men holding Beddows and John left them to run to his aid. By violent efforts both succeeded in throwing the others off. Beddows groped for his knuckle-duster and pulled it from his pocket. John whipped out his knife. Savagely and indiscriminatingly they laid about them. Shrieks and curses told how their weapons were finding their marks.

Rushing forward, Beddows kicked over the brazier. The remainder of the live coals hissed in the water and swiftly dulled. Near darkness engulfed the awful *mêlée*. Beddows shouted to John:

'Get the girl out! I'll keep these bastards busy.'

John had already reached Christina and pulled her to her feet. The squint-eyed witch barred their path. Without hesitation John knifed her in the breast. With a filthy imprecation she clutched at the wound and staggered sideways. Jumping the still-hissing coals, John and Christina dashed towards the doorway. As they did so, by the dying light they glimpsed the tall bony-faced man charging at them. Evading his clutch by inches they gained the passage and sped down it.

Before they were half-way to the foot of the slope John knew that Christina's strength was failing. With one hand he had thrust his knife into his pocket and pulled out his torch, so that he could light the way ahead of them: the other he had round her waist and, as they ran on, he could feel her flagging. From behind them came the sounds of pounding feet, telling that they were very far from being out of danger. A veritable madness had seized upon the remaining Satanists, and those not occupied in endeavouring to overcome Beddows were in full pursuit, headed by the lean man from Scotland.

Gasping and reeling, the flying couple reached the slope, but after a few steps up it Christina staggered and fell. This last effort after her terrible ordeal had proved too much for her; she had fainted. She was nearly as tall as John, yet, temporarily granted superhuman strength, he pulled her arm across the back of his neck, heaved her up in a fireman's lift across his shoulders and continued the steep ascent.

Bent nearly double, he lurched a dozen steps; then he knew that he could never make it. He had still a hundred and twenty feet of slope to mount, and at its top he would have to get her up the twenty-foot-long rope ladder. Even a Hercules could not accomplish such a feat in time to escape the fiends who were now coming up the slope behind him, howling for vengeance.

Then for a moment he was given fresh hope by hearing Beddows' voice mingled with the rest, shouting, 'Go on, John! Stick to it! I'll stop them following!'

That cheering sound told him that Beddows had either dealt with, or escaped from, the Satanists remaining in the temple, and was now attacking the others at the bottom of the slope. It meant a brief respite and he did his utmost to make the best of it. Holding his torch in one hand and grasping Christina's wrist with the other, he dragged his feet yard by yard upward. Yet he was barely half-way to the top when he fell to his knees, weighed down by Christina's limp body, and mentally crushed by the knowledge that he was at the end of his tether. In vain he tried to rise. He could not. He could only pray, and mutter over and over again:

'Oh Lord, help us! Oh Lord, help us!'

And then indeed help came. There was the sound of slithering footsteps above him, and the light of torches shone in his eyes. Echoing back from the stone walls C.B.'s voice reached him:

'John! John! Thank God we are in time!'

Willing hands lifted Christina off him. Still gasping for breath he staggered up the last half of the awful slope. At its top, C.B. and another man got Christina up the ladder. A third helped him to climb it.

Half-dazed, he stepped out into the moonlight. His mother was there and flung her arms about him. Beside C.B. stood old Malouet, and with them were several *gendarmes*. It was they who carried Christina to one of the stretchers and covered her sacking garment with warm cloaks.

John was still standing on the edge of the hole when he again caught the clamour of the surviving Satanists. They had reached the platform immediately below the opening. Molly and C.B. ran to it. The latter shone his torch downwards. It lit a group of wild upturned faces. That of Beddows was among them. It was covered with blood, but he was still striking out at the nearest of the enemy. In the darkness and confusion they had failed to identify and overcome him.

What John took to be a stone fell into their midst. Next second there came a blinding flash of light and a shattering explosion. C.B. swore and pulled Molly back. Two of the *gendarmes* came running up to ask what had happened. No one could say. It could only be assumed that one of the Satanists had been carrying a package of explosives, and a blow upon it during the *mêlée* had set it off. When C.B. shone his torch down the hole again it revealed a tangle of dead and dying men and women.

Leaving all but two of the police, who had already picked up the stretcher on which Christina lay, to perform such rescue work as might still be possible, the others set off down the hill. When John had recovered a little he asked C.B.:

'How did you manage to come on the scene like this and save us at the very last moment?'

'It was your mother, my boy,' C.B. replied. 'She is a woman in a million.'

'Nonsense!' cut in Molly, who was walking just ahead of them. 'I did no more than use my common sense. Your having promised Count Jules that you would not communicate with the police was not binding on me.'

'No,' said John slowly. 'I suppose not. But how on earth did you manage to do it?'

'I didn't go into the inn for the reason you thought I did. It was to write a brief message. I gave it with a five-hundred-franc note to the woman I found behind the bar, in exchange for a promise that she would telephone it at once to Inspector Drouet. I knew that would bring our friends to St Michael as soon as they received it. But I thought I ought to make certain of being able to find you as well; so I went up to the top of the hill with you, then threw a weak woman act as soon as the smugglers had pointed out the entrance to the cave. Immediately you were out of sight I hurried back to the inn, so that when the police arrived there I was able to lead them straight up to it.'

'Bless you, Mumsie; you really are a wonder.' John laughed. 'And if it is true that you are not still on the secret list as Molly Polloffski the beautiful spy, that's a great loss to the nation.'

The arrival of the police at the inn an hour before had resulted in the good woman who ran it keeping it open a little later than usual, and it was still not yet eleven o'clock when the stretcher party arrived there. In the public room a warm fire was glowing in the stove, and Christina, now fully conscious again, was made comfortable in borrowed wraps beside it. C. B. ordered coffee laced with cognac for them all to warm them up, and when John carried two cups over to the corner where Christina was sitting the others discreetly took theirs to the far end of the room.

When John had settled himself beside Christina, he told her how Jules had enabled him to trace her to the Cave of the Bats, and how his mother's quick wits had brought the police on the scene in time to save them; but she smilingly shook her head.

'It was clever of you to think of making use of Jules, and wonderful of your mother to think of a way of getting help to us; but your first attempt to rescue me failed, and the police would have arrived too late if it hadn't been for your eleventh-hour inspiration.'

'What do you mean by that?' he asked with a puzzled look.

'Why, that frightful lie you told about my no longer being a virgin.'

'By Jove!' he grinned. 'D'you know, I'd already forgotten about that. It was a whopper, wasn't it? What's more I swore it, and that is perjury, or something. Do you think I'll be forgiven?'

'I'm sure you will. It must have gained us the best part of five minutes, and so saved my life. But that is not all. It was your ring that really saved us both.'

'Yes. There must have been some blessed magic in it for a single tap from it to have shattered that thick glass. Would you like to keep it?'

'Do you want me to?'

He hesitated, then asked, 'Do you know that your father is dead?'

'No,' she replied calmly. 'I was absolutely staggered to see him there. How did he come to be with you?'

'That is a long story, and I'll tell it to you to-morrow. For the present it is enough to say that just after we got out of the cave there was an explosion and I saw him with his head half . . . well, so badly injured that he couldn't possibly recover.'

'Poor Father,' she sighed. 'It is sad to hear that; but he never loved me or I him; and you haven't told me yet how you induced him to come in with you.'

'Up to last night he was a Satanist himself. He sold you to the Devil when you were a baby. That was what made you so unlike your real self during the hours of darkness. But last night he repented and released you.'

'That would explain, then why I felt so different soon after I was taken out of the prison, and again this evening after sunset.'

'Yes. He abjured Satan and all his works on your behalf; then he came back here with us to help try to rescue you. But he is dead now. I am certain of it, and I have a reason for telling you so at once, instead of waiting until later. Before he died he had no chance to alter his will; so nobody can yet know how he had left his money.'

'I don't quite see what you are driving at,' she murmured.

'Simply that I would like to ask you to marry me before it is known whether you are a great heiress or a pauper.'

'Oh John,' she smiled. 'What has money got to do with it? Only one thing matters. Did you really mean it or not when, just before I snapped the stuff that bound my wrists and smashed the jar with your ring, you called out to me, "Darling, I love you! I love you!"?'

'Of course I did.'

Her big brown eyes shone with happiness as she leaned towards him and whispered, 'Then your own words are my answer.'

Inspector Drouet joined the party at the inn about half an hour later, and he confirmed that Henry Beddows was among the dead who had been recovered from the cave. As Christina was still technically under arrest he discussed her position with Malouet, then agreed to her provisional release on the ex-inspector's stating that he would go surety for her.

Very tired now, John, Christina and C.B. went out to Molly's car, and it was she who drove them home. When they arrived at the villa it was after one o'clock, and John and Christina went straight up to their rooms; but C.B. asked Molly for a night-cap.

Knowing his preference, she mixed him a whisky-and-soda; then made one for herself. He raised his glass, said, 'Chin, chin!', then added in his most conspiratorial voice:

'Can you tell me, Mrs Fountain, any good and sufficient reason why I should not hand you over to the police on a charge of having committed mass murder?'

She suppressed a start, then asked with a bland smile, 'What *are* you talking about, C.B.? I'm afraid all this excitement has proved a little too much for even you.'

'No, Molly,' he said seriously. 'You can't laugh this thing off. I saw you drop that Mills bomb on to the heads of those wretched people.'

'Did you?' She smiled archly. 'Well, I don't mind if you did. They were all horrors and menaces to everything decent in life. It is a good thing that they are dead. Perhaps it was a pity about Beddows; but I'm not even certain about that, since he had lived as a Satanist all his adult life. And it . . . er . . . did the job perfectly, didn't it?'

'Yes. I'm not questioning your act on ethical grounds or its efficiency. But the thing that troubles me is that someone else might have seen you do it. If they had you would be in prison now, and well on your way to the scaffold. Really, Molly, it's time that you had somebody to look after you.'

'Meaning you, C. B.?'

He rubbed his big nose, then looked up at her. 'Yes, dear one; meaning me.'

She came across and sat down on his knees. Suddenly she gulped. 'It was a frightful thing to do, wasn't it?' Next moment she was crying, with her cheek pressed against his, and she murmured, 'Oh, you're so right, darling! I'm a horribly irresponsible sort of woman. Please, please take care of me.'